DEADLIER

Also available from

HEAD *of* ZEUS

THE STORY

Love, Loss and the Lives of Women

100 Great Short Stories

CHOSEN BY VICTORIA HISLOP

THAT GLIMPSE OF TRUTH

100 of the Finest Short Stories Ever Written

CHOSEN BY DAVID MILLER

GHOST

100 Stories to Read with the Lights On

CHOSEN BY LOUISE WELSH

DESIRE

100 of Literature's Sexiest Stories

CHOSEN BY MARIELLA FROSTRUP

and the *Erotic Review*

DEADLIER

100 OF THE BEST
CRIME STORIES
WRITTEN BY WOMEN

CHOSEN BY
SOPHIE HANNAH

HEAD
of ZEUS

First published in the UK in 2017 by Head of Zeus Ltd.

9 7 5 3 1 2 4 6 8

A catalogue record for this book is available from the British Library.

ISBN (HB) 9781784975463
ISBN (E) 9781784975456

Typeset by PDQ, Bungay, Suffolk

Printed and bound in Germany by CPI Books GmbH

Head of Zeus Ltd
5-8 Hardwick Street
London EC1R 4RG
WWW.HEADOFZEUS.COM

*For Lucy Cavendish College, Cambridge – which,
rather like this anthology, is a wonderful place full
of brilliant women.*

CONTENTS

INTRODUCTION

I have a confession to make: I'm a mystery addict. I have been since the age of six, when I discovered Enid Blyton's The Secret Seven books. It was like magic – I couldn't get enough of the seemingly impossible scenarios that ended up not only fully explained, but also revealed as the only logical way in which events could have unfurled. Then at the age of twelve I discovered Agatha Christie, thanks to my father, who brought me home a copy of *The Body in the Library* that he'd found at a second-hand book fair. I started to read it and found myself in a new kind of heaven – this was even better than Enid Blyton, I thought, because it seemed to have been designed specifically for me at my particular point in life. It was a grown-up mystery novel, that was nevertheless totally accessible to a twelve year old. When I opened the book and found the list of all the novels Christie had written, I was even happier – this, I knew, would keep me entertained and on the edge of my seat for years.

I was not wrong. By the time I was fourteen I'd devoured, and collected, every book the Queen of Crime had ever published. I went on, some years later, to get hooked on, and also to collect, the complete works of Ruth Rendell – my mystery fiction addiction was complete! When I came to write my first crime novel, it did not occur to me that I must already have had a deeply-ingrained internal blueprint for what the ideal crime novel should be and do – a blueprint that I'd acquired as a result of my serial immersions in the works of three geniuses: Blyton, Christie and Rendell. It's thanks to them that I fell in love with, and still love to this day, the promise of a puzzle with a solution that's un-guessable but inevitable.

I started reading the genre more widely, taking in the wonderful Charles Paris novels by Simon Brett, Caroline Graham's hugely entertaining Inspector Barnaby mysteries, Sue Grafton's Kinsey Millhone (with whom I wanted to be best friends, though my envy of her lovely sounding apartment might have caused trouble between us), Colin Dexter's superb Inspector Morse and Sara Paretsky's brilliantly kick-ass V.I. Warshawski. Throughout secondary school, sixth-form college and university, I proudly neglected the work I was supposed to be doing, and instead lapped up crime fiction's puzzle plots and the dark, twisted psychological insights that came with them. This genre that I had chosen – and decided to devote my life to even before I'd written any of my own – showed me what people can become at their most extreme, and expanded my intellect and my imagination in a way that nothing anyone was teaching me in an educational establishment came close to matching.

At a certain point, I realised that my favourite authors – Agatha Christie, Ruth Rendell, Tana French – were all women. I thought nothing more of it at the time. But then I started writing crime fiction, and the gender question became one I couldn't avoid. It's probably the thing I've been asked most often in interviews – a hundred times at least, over the years: 'Why are women so good at writing crime fiction?' Another variation of the same question is 'Do you think women are better than men at writing crime novels?' Another is 'Do women write crime fiction differently from men?' I am also regularly asked whether the murder method in a crime novel is likely to be different – less brutally bludgeoning; more poisonously, subtly devious – depending on the sex of the killer, or the author, or the author and the killer.

I've always thought this to be rather an odd preoccupation – particularly when most people are aware, presumably, that the bestselling crime novelist of all time was a woman: Dame Agatha Christie, whose books have sold billions of copies worldwide and who is outsold only by the Bible and Shakespeare. Crime fiction is the best genre in the world: from the psychological to the political, from domestic to international spheres, it runs the bloodstained gamut. There's a lot to love, and a lot to talk about, in relation to the genre. So why do people want to focus on gender when it comes to mystery and suspense in fiction? Does anyone question, for example, why women, specifically, are good swimmers or garden designers? Or why so many females love their pet dogs, or, if they don't yet have pet dogs, yearn to have a pet dog at the earliest possible opportunity? Or why women love pizza, or wine?

Could it be that crime fiction – which centres around dark, criminal and violent acts – is assumed, by some, to be more naturally the province of the male writer and reader, because women are believed to be too gentle, timid or delicate for such harsh matters? In which case, the frequency with which the 'Why women?' question is asked could be seen, along with the assumption that romantic fiction is of no interest to men, as evidence that sexism is still very much at large. Usually, when people want to gather evidence of the powerful sexist forces at work in the literary world, they look at the relative numbers of male and female reviewers – or reviewees – in highbrow newspapers and journals; perhaps instead they ought to ask female crime writers how often they've been asked to explain why they like a thing, and are able to do a thing, that everyone takes for granted male writers can do and might enjoy doing.

After choosing the stories for this anthology – an anthology of crime and suspense writing by women – I am finally in a position to answer all the crime-fiction-related questions that begin 'Why are women…?' and 'Why do women…?' So, 'Why are women so good at writing crime fiction?' you may ask, and I will answer a) some aren't, and b) the ones that are – it's because women are people, and some people are good at writing crime and others aren't. Choosing the stories for *Deadlier* I have read works by women who are household names, and women who are just starting out on their writing careers; women who have won prizes, and women who have topped best-seller lists. The one thing they all have in common is that they are all excellent at crafting crime stories, which is an art in itself and worth celebrating.

Whatever mood I'm in, crime fiction will satisfy it, and I've tried to reflect that in this anthology. The variety and range of the stories here is vast, but they do all contain a central puzzle – something I believe essential to all successful crime fiction stories, be they long or short.

The puzzle element of crime fiction is something that's occasionally derided, even by crime-lovers. In connection with Agatha Christie, for example, I've taken part in panel discussions where other panellists have said, 'Oh, I don't deny that Christie was an excellent puzzle-maker, of course…' and I've silently seethed at the way this is said, as if being a brilliant maker of puzzles is somehow inessential to the business of writing crime, rather than absolutely vital and central. It's interesting that no crime writer would, in a similar tone, passively or covertly discount the importance of psychology or insight into the human condition. The puzzle component, though – the mystery and solution combination that so many crime fiction readers adore – is too often spoken of as if it's a trivial or shallow pleasure, and a component to which crime writers shouldn't pay too much attention.

I couldn't disagree more – but, at the same time, I *will* disagree more. I'll disagree, loudly, whenever and wherever I encounter this silly prejudice. It's related to, though perhaps not interchangeable with, the equally silly idea that serious crime writers should be more interested in character than plot, when in fact the two are so inextricably linked in any good novel, that it almost makes no sense to speak of them as if they are separate entities to be played off against one another.

There is nothing shallow about the pleasures offered by puzzle plots, and nothing about them that reduces both writer and reader to the status of crossword- or Sudoku-obsessed geeks who care little for feelings or deeper truths. Puzzles arise in life because of psychological depth, because people have hidden worlds in their heads that they can't admit to having. People are puzzles, and crime writers set themselves the task of trying to solve these puzzles. But then there's the even bigger puzzle of what happens when the mystery of one person clashes or enmeshes with the mystery of another – how can all these individual puzzle-people exist in the world together? This, to me, is the single most useful activity you can engage in if your aim is to arrive at a more profound understanding of the world.

I firmly believe that one reason for the enduring success of crime fiction is its use of puzzles. It is the only genre in which the key feature is a puzzle, and this mimics the experiences of our everyday lives. We're trying to piece things together all the time: after job interviews 'Did I do well?' we ask, 'Did the panel like me?'; in love 'Does he fancy me?'; and in family life 'Did my brother-in-law mean that snidely or is he just tactless?' Puzzles drive us every day. If we knew all the answers, there would be no motivation to press on with life. There would be no point. Life is full of suspense; it's full of puzzles we can't solve, so it should come as no surprise that the best genre in fiction is the same.

This anthology contains all kinds of crime and suspense stories. They are not all conventionally, or even mainly, puzzle-based, but there are certainly puzzles – human and practical – in each and every one. There are traditional whodunits, private eye stories and psychological suspense narratives; there are stories for children as well as adults; there is social realism side-by-side with outlandish escapism. Margaret Atwood brings her very dark sense of humour to 'Pretend Blood', which centres on a group of people who believe they've lived before, as royalty. Agatha Christie's Miss Marple is on form in 'Tape-Measure Murder', while Sheila Quigley's 'Black Betty' is as dark and gritty as you could hope. Several stories appear here for the first time, including the wonderfully twisted 'King Clorox of the Eastern Seaboard' by Caroline Kepnes, Anya Lipska's haunting 'Another Kind of

Man' and 'The Problem of the Kentish Ghost', a tribute to Sherlock Holmes by Sarah Perry.

It has been a pleasure to select the tales that you're about to read. I believe short stories can and should offer exactly the same amount of narrative satisfaction as novels. They may be smaller, but structure, suspense and the alchemy of plot and character remain crucial. Perhaps they are even more crucial in short stories because the smaller something is, the more clearly we see its imperfections.

One time, I heard Ruth Rendell speaking at Waterstones in Manchester, and I took her words to heart: 'You have to hook the reader with the first line, or they'll close the book.' That's true for novels, and it's all the more true for short stories, where the first line makes up a greater percentage of the whole. In short fiction, every line counts – as it should in all fiction. Not a single word of this anthology is wasted. Whether you like your crime hard or soft, gritty or cosy, domestic or political, I hope and trust that *Deadlier* contains something to delight you. My aim is to make mystery addicts of you all!

Sophie Hannah, 2017

A DOUBLE TRAGEDY: AN ACTOR'S STORY

Louisa May Alcott

Louisa May Alcott (1832–1888) is best known for the American classic *Little Women*. However, she wrote prolifically across genres for both adults and children. Her 1865 short story 'V.V., or Plots and Counterplots' is one of the earliest detective stories in English.

I.

Clotilde was in her element that night, for it was a Spanish play, requiring force and fire in its delineation, and she threw herself into her part with an *abandon* that made her seem a beautiful embodiment of power and passion. As for me I could not play ill, for when with her my acting was not art but nature, and I *was* the lover that I seemed. Before she came I made a business, not a pleasure, of my profession, and was content to fill my place, with no higher ambition than to earn my salary with as little effort as possible, to resign myself to the distasteful labor to which my poverty condemned me. She changed all that; for she saw the talent I neglected, she understood the want of motive that made me indifferent, she pitied me for the reverse of fortune that placed me where I was; by her influence and example she roused a manlier spirit in me, kindled every spark of talent I possessed, and incited me to win a success I had not cared to labor for till then.

She was the rage that season, for she came unheralded and almost unknown. Such was the power of beauty, genius, and character, that she made her way at once into public favor, and before the season was half over had become the reigning favorite. My position in the theatre threw us much together, and I had not played the lover to this beautiful woman many weeks before I found I was one in earnest. She soon knew it, and confessed that she returned my love; but when I spoke of marriage, she answered with a look and tone that haunted me long afterward.

"Not yet, Paul; something that concerns me alone must be settled first. I cannot marry till I have received the answer for which I am waiting; have faith in me till then, and be patient for my sake."

I did have faith and patience; but while I waited I wondered much and studied her carefully. Frank, generous, and deep-hearted, she won all who approached her; but I, being nearest and dearest, learned to know her best, and soon discovered that some past loss, some present anxiety or hidden care, oppressed and haunted her. A bitter spirit at times possessed her, followed by a heavy melancholy, or an almost fierce unrest, which nothing could dispel but some stormy drama, where she could vent her pent-up gloom or desperation in words and acts which seemed to have a double significance to her. I had vainly tried to find some cause or explanation of this one blemish in the nature which, to a lover's eyes, seemed almost perfect, but never had succeeded till the night of which I write.

The play was nearly over, the interest was at its height, and Clotilde's best scene was drawing to a close. She had just indignantly refused to betray a state secret which would endanger the life of her lover; and the Duke had just wrathfully vowed to denounce her to the Inquisition if she did not yield, when I her lover, disguised as a monk, saw a strange and sudden change come over her. She should have trembled at a threat so full of terror, and have made one last appeal to the stern old man before she turned to defy and dare all things for her lover. But she seemed to have forgotten time, place, and character, for she stood gazing straight before her as if turned to stone. At first I thought it was some new presentiment of fear, for she seldom played a part twice alike, and left much to the inspiration of the moment. But an instant's scrutiny convinced me that this was not acting, for her face paled visibly, her eyes dilated as they looked beyond the Duke, her lips fell apart, and she looked like one suddenly confronted by a ghost. An inquiring glance from my companion showed me that he, too, was disturbed by her appearance, and fearing that she had over-exerted herself, I struck into the dialogue as if she had made her appeal. The sound of my voice seemed to recall her; she passed her hand across her eyes, drew a long breath, and looked about her. I thought she had recovered herself and was about to resume her part, but, to my great surprise, she only clung to me, saying in a shrill whisper, so full of despair, it chilled my blood —

"The answer, Paul, the answer: it has come!"

The words were inaudible to all but myself; but the look, the gesture were eloquent with terror, grief, and love; and taking it for a fine piece of acting, the audience applauded loud and long. The accustomed sound roused Clotilde, and during that noisy moment a hurried dialogue passed between us.

"What is it? Are you ill?" I whispered.

"He is here, Paul, alive; I saw him. Heaven help us both!"

"Who is here?"

"Hush! not now; there is no time to tell you."

"You are right; compose yourself; you must speak in a moment."

"What do I say? Help me, Paul; I have forgotten every thing but that man."

She looked as if bewildered; and I saw that some sudden shock had entirely unnerved her. But actors must have neither hearts nor nerves while on the stage. The applause was subsiding, and she must speak. Fortunately I remembered enough of her part to prompt her as she struggled through the little that remained; for, seeing her condition, Denon and I cut the scene remorselessly, and brought it to a close as soon as possible. The instant the curtain fell we were assailed with questions, but Clotilde answered none; and though hidden from her sight, still seemed to see the object that had wrought such an alarming change in her. I told them she was ill, took her to her dressing-room, and gave her into the hands of her maid, for I must appear again, and delay was impossible.

How I got through my part I cannot tell, for my thoughts were with Clotilde;

but an actor learns to live a double life, so while Paul Lamar suffered torments of anxiety Don Felix fought a duel, killed his adversary, and was dragged to judgment. Involuntarily my eyes often wandered toward the spot where Clotilde's had seemed fixed. It was one of the stage-boxes, and at first I thought it empty, but presently I caught the glitter of a glass turned apparently on myself. As soon as possible I crossed the stage, and as I leaned haughtily upon my sword while the seconds adjusted the preliminaries, I searched the box with a keen glance. Nothing was visible, however, but a hand lying easily on the red cushion; a man's hand, white and shapely; on one finger shone a ring, evidently a woman's ornament, for it was a slender circlet of diamonds that flashed with every gesture.

"Some fop, doubtless; a man like that could never daunt Clotilde," I thought. And eager to discover if there was not another occupant in the box, I took a step nearer, and stared boldly into the soft gloom that filled it. A low derisive laugh came from behind the curtain as the hand gathered back as if to permit me to satisfy myself. The act showed me that a single person occupied the box, but also effectually concealed that person from my sight; and as I was recalled to my duty by a warning whisper from one of my comrades, the hand appeared to wave me a mocking adieu. Baffled and angry, I devoted myself to the affairs of Don Felix, wondering the while if Clotilde would be able to reappear, how she would bear herself, if that hidden man was the cause of her terror, and why? Even when immured in a dungeon, after my arrest, I beguiled the tedium of a long soliloquy with these questions, and executed a better stage-start than any I had ever practised, when at last she came to me, bringing liberty and love as my reward.

I had left her haggard, speechless, overwhelmed with some mysterious woe, she reappeared beautiful and brilliant, with a joy that seemed too lovely to be feigned. Never had she played so well; for some spirit, stronger than her own, seemed to possess and rule her royally. If I had ever doubted her love for me, I should have been assured of it that night, for she breathed into the fond words of her part a tenderness and grace that filled my heart to overflowing, and inspired me to play the grateful lover to the life. The last words came all too soon for me, and as she threw herself into my arms she turned her head as if to glance triumphantly at the defeated Duke, but I saw that again she looked beyond him, and with an indescribable expression of mingled pride, contempt, and defiance. A soft sound of applause from the mysterious occupant of that box answered the look, and the white hand sent a superb bouquet flying to her feet. I was about to lift and present it to her, but she checked me and crushed it under foot with an air of the haughtiest disdain. A laugh from behind the curtain greeted this demonstration, but it was scarcely observed by others; for that first bouquet seemed a signal for a rain of flowers, and these latter offerings she permitted me to gather up, receiving them with her most gracious smiles, her most graceful obeisances, as if to mark, for one observer at least, the difference of her regard for the givers. As I laid the last floral tribute in her arms I took a parting glance at the box, hoping to catch a glimpse of the unknown face. The curtains were thrown back and the door stood open, admitting a strong light from the vestibule, but the box was empty.

Then the green curtain fell, and Clotilde whispered, as she glanced from her full hands to the rejected bouquet —

"Bring that to my room; I must have it."

I obeyed, eager to be enlightened; but when we were alone she flung down her fragrant burden, snatched the stranger's gift, tore it apart, drew out a slip of paper, read it, dropped it, and walked to and fro, wringing her hands, like one in a paroxysm of despair. I seized the note and looked at it, but found no key to her distress in the enigmatical words —

"I shall be there. Come and bring your lover with you, else —"

There it abruptly ended; but the unfinished threat seemed the more menacing for its obscurity, and I indignantly demanded,

"Clotilde, who dares address you so? Where will this man be? You surely will not obey such a command? Tell me; I have a right to know."

"I cannot tell you, now; I dare not refuse him; he will be at Keen's; we *must* go. How will it end! How will it end!"

I remembered then that we were all to sup *en costume*, with a brother actor, who did not play that night. I was about to speak yet more urgently, when the entrance of her maid checked me. Clotilde composed herself by a strong effort —

"Go and prepare," she whispered; "have faith in me a little longer, and soon you shall know all."

There was something almost solemn in her tone; her eye met mine, imploringly, and her lips trembled as if her heart were full. That assured me at once; and with a reassuring word I hurried away to give a few touches to my costume, which just then was fitter for a dungeon than a feast. When I rejoined her there was no trace of past emotion; a soft color bloomed upon her cheek, her eyes were tearless and brilliant, her lips were dressed in smiles. Jewels shone on her white forehead, neck, and arms, flowers glowed in her bosom; and no charm that art or skill could lend to the rich dress or its lovely wearer, had been forgotten.

"What an actress!" I involuntarily exclaimed, as she came to meet me, looking almost as beautiful and gay as ever.

"It is well that I am one, else I should yield to my hard fate without a struggle. Paul, hitherto I have played for money, now I play for love; help me by being a calm spectator to-night, and whatever happens promise me that there shall be no violence."

I promised, for I was wax in her hands; and, more bewildered than ever, followed to the carriage, where a companion was impatiently awaiting us.

II.

We were late; and on arriving found all the other guests assembled. Three strangers appeared; and my attention was instantly fixed upon them, for the mysterious "he" was to be there. All three seemed gay, gallant, handsome men; all three turned admiring eyes upon Clotilde, all three were gloved. Therefore, as I had seen no face, my one clue, the ring, was lost. From Clotilde's face and manner I could learn nothing, for a smile seemed carved upon her lips, her drooping lashes half concealed her eyes, and her voice was too well trained to betray her by a traitorous tone. She received the greetings, compliments, and admiration of all alike, and I vainly looked and listened till supper was announced.

As I took my place beside her, I saw her shrink and shiver slightly, as if a chilly wind had blown over her, but before I could ask if she were cold a bland voice said,

"Will Mademoiselle Varian permit me to drink her health?"

It was one of the strangers; mechanically I offered her glass; but the next instant my hold tightened till the slender stem snapped, and the rosy bowl fell broken to the table, for on the handsome hand extended to fill it shone the ring.

"A bad omen, Mr. Lamar. I hope my attempt will succeed better," said St. John, as he filled another glass and handed it to Clotilde, who merely lifted it to her lips, and turned to enter into an animated conversation with the gentleman who sat on the other side. Some one addressed St. John, and I was glad of it; for now all my interest and attention was centered in him. Keenly, but covertly, I examined him, and soon felt that in spite of that foppish ornament he *was* a man to daunt a woman like Clotilde. Pride and passion, courage and indomitable will met and mingled in his face, though the obedient features wore whatever expression he imposed upon them. He was the handsomest, most elegant, but least attractive of the three, yet it was hard to say why. The others gave themselves freely to the enjoyment of a scene which evidently possessed the charm of novelty to them; but St. John unconsciously wore the half sad, half weary look that comes to those who have led lives of pleasure and found their emptiness. Although the wittiest, and most brilliant talker at the table, his gaiety seemed fitful, his manner absent at times. More than once I saw him knit his black brows as he met my eye, and more than once I caught a long look fixed on Clotilde, — a look full of the lordly admiration and pride which a master bestows upon a handsome slave. It made my blood boil, but I controlled myself, and was apparently absorbed in Miss Damareau, my neighbor.

We seemed as gay and care-free a company as ever made midnight merry; songs were sung, stories told, theatrical phrases added sparkle to the conversation, and the varied costumes gave an air of romance to the revel. The Grand Inquisitor still in his ghostly garb, and the stern old Duke were now the jolliest of the group; the page flirted violently with the princess; the rivals of the play were bosom-friends again, and the fair Donna Olivia had apparently forgotten her knightly lover, to listen to a modern gentleman.

Clotilde sat leaning back in a deep chair, eating nothing, but using her fan with the indescribable grace of a Spanish woman. She was very lovely, for the dress became her, and the black lace mantilla falling from her head to her shoulders, heightened her charms by half concealing them; and nothing could have been more genial and gracious than the air with which she listened and replied to the compliments of the youngest stranger, who sat beside her and was all devotion.

I forgot myself in observing her till something said by our opposite neighbors arrested both of us. Some one seemed to have been joking St. John about his ring, which was too brilliant an ornament to pass unobserved.

"Bad taste, I grant you," he said, laughing, "but it is a *gage d'amour*, and I wear it for a purpose."

"I fancied it was the latest Paris fashion," returned Keen. "And apropos to Paris, what is the latest gossip from the gay city?"

A slow smile rose to St. John's lips as he answered, after a moment's thought and a quick glance across the room.

"A little romance; shall I tell it to you? It is a love story, ladies, and not long."

A unanimous assent was given; and he began with a curious glitter in his eyes, a stealthy smile coming and going on his face as the words dropped slowly from his lips.

"It begins in the old way. A foolish young man fell in love with a Spanish girl much his inferior in rank, but beautiful enough to excuse his folly, for he married her. Then came a few months of bliss; but Madame grew jealous. Monsieur wearied of domestic tempests, and, after vain efforts to appease his fiery angel, he proposed a separation. Madame was obdurate, Monsieur rebelled; and in order to try the soothing effects of absence upon both, after settling her in a charming chateau, he slipped away, leaving no trace by which his route might be discovered."

"Well, how did the experiment succeed?" asked Keen. St. John shrugged his shoulders, emptied his glass, and answered tranquilly.

"Like most experiments that have women for their subjects, for the amiable creatures always devise some way of turning the tables, and defeating the best laid plans. Madame waited for her truant spouse till rumors of his death reached Paris, for he had met with mishaps, and sickness detained him long in an obscure place, so the rumors seemed confirmed by his silence, and Madame believed him dead. But instead of dutifully mourning him, this inexplicable woman shook the dust of the chateau off her feet and disappeared, leaving everything, even to her wedding ring, behind her."

"Bless me, how odd! what became of her?" exclaimed Miss Damareau, forgetting the dignity of the Princess in the curiosity of the woman.

"The very question her repentant husband asked when, returning from his long holiday, he found her gone. He searched the continent for her, but in vain; and for two years she left him to suffer the torments of suspense."

"As he had left her to suffer them while he went pleasuring. It was a light punishment for his offence."

Clotilde spoke; and the sarcastic tone for all its softness, made St. John wince, though no eye but mine observed the faint flush of shame or anger that passed across his face.

"Mademoiselle espouses the lady's cause, of course, and as a gallant man I should do likewise, but unfortunately my sympathies are strongly enlisted on the other side."

"Then you know the parties?" I said, impulsively, for my inward excitement was increasing rapidly, and I began to feel rather than to see the end of this mystery.

"I have seen them, and cannot blame the man for claiming his beautiful wife, when he found her," he answered, briefly.

"Then he did find her at last? Pray tell us how and when," cried Miss Damareau.

"She betrayed herself. It seems that Madame had returned to her old profession, and fallen in love with an actor; but being as virtuous as she was fair, she would not marry till she was assured beyond a doubt of her husband's death. Her engagements would not allow her to enquire in person, so she sent letters to various places asking for proofs of his demise; and as ill, or good fortune would have it, one of these letters fell into Monsieur's hands, giving him an excellent clue to her whereabouts, which he followed indefatigably till he found her."

"Poor little woman, I pity her! How did she receive Monsieur De Trop?" asked Keen.

"You shall know in good time. He found her in London playing at one of the great theatres, for she had talent, and had become a star. He saw her act for a night or two, made secret inquiries concerning her, and fell more in love with her than ever. Having tried almost every novelty under the sun he had a fancy to attempt something of the dramatic sort, so presented himself to Madame at a party."

"Heavens! what a scene there must have been," ejaculated Miss Damareau.

"On the contrary, there was no scene at all, for the man was not a Frenchman, and Madame was a fine actress. Much as he had admired her on the stage he was doubly charmed with her performance in private, for it was superb. They were among strangers, and she received him like one, playing her part with the utmost grace and self-control, for with a woman's quickness of perception, she divined his purpose, and knowing that her fate was in his hands, endeavored to propitiate him by complying with his caprice. Mademoiselle, allow me to send you some of these grapes, they are delicious."

As he leaned forward to present them he shot a glance at her that caused me to start up with a violence that nearly betrayed me. Fortunately the room was close, and saying something about the heat, I threw open a window, and let in a balmy gust of spring air that refreshed us all.

"How did they settle it, by duels and despair, or by repentance and reconciliation all round, in the regular French fashion?"

"I regret that I'm unable to tell you, for I left before the affair was arranged. I only know that Monsieur was more captivated than before, and quite ready to forgive and forget, and I suspect that Madame, seeing the folly of resistance, will submit with a good grace, and leave the stage to play 'The Honey Moon' for a second time in private with a husband who adores her. What is the Mademoiselle's opinion?"

She had listened, without either question or comment, her fan at rest, her hands motionless, her eyes downcast; so still it seemed as if she had hushed the breath upon her lips, so pale despite her rouge, that I wondered no one observed it, so intent and resolute that every feature seemed under control, — every look and gesture guarded. When St. John addressed her, she looked up with a smile as bland as his own, but fixed her eyes on him with an expression of undismayed defiance and supreme contempt that caused him to bite his lips with ill-concealed annoyance.

"My opinion?" she said, in her clear, cold voice, "I think that Madame, being a woman of spirit, would *not* endeavor to propitiate that man in any way except for her lover's sake, and having been once deserted would not subject herself to a second indignity of that sort while there was a law to protect her."

"Unfortunately there is no law for her, having once refused a separation. Even if there were, Monsieur is rich and powerful, she is poor and friendless; he loves her, and is a man who never permits himself to be thwarted by any obstacle; therefore, I am convinced it would be best for this adorable woman to submit without defiance or delay — and I do think she will," he added, significantly.

"They seem to forget the poor lover; what is to become of him?" asked Keen.

"*I* do not forget him;" and the hand that wore the ring closed with an ominous gesture, which I well understood. "Monsieur merely claims his own, and the other, being a man of sense and honor, will doubtless withdraw at once; and though 'desolated,' as the French say, will soon console himself with a new *inamorata*. If he is so unwise as to oppose Monsieur, who by the by is a dead shot, there is but one way in which both can receive satisfaction."

A significant emphasis on the last word pointed his meaning, and the smile that accompanied it almost goaded me to draw the sword I wore, and offer him that satisfaction on the spot. I felt the color rise to my forehead, and dared not look up, but leaning on the back of Clotilde's chair, I bent as if to speak to her.

"Bear it a little longer for my sake, Paul," she murmured, with a look of love and despair, that wrung my heart. Here some one spoke of a long rehearsal in the morning, and the lateness of the hour.

"A farewell toast before we part," said Keen. "Come, Lamar, give us a sentiment, after that whisper you ought to be inspired."

"I am. Let me give you — The love of liberty and the liberty of love."

"Good! That would suit the hero and heroine of St. John's story, for Monsieur wished much for his liberty, and, no doubt, Madame will for her love," said Denon, while the glasses were filled.

Then the toast was drunk with much merriment and the party broke up. While detained by one of the strangers, I saw St. John approach Clotilde, who stood alone by the window, and speak rapidly for several minutes. She listened with half-averted head, answered briefly, and wrapping the mantilla closely about her, swept away from him with her haughtiest mien. He watched for a moment, then followed, and before I could reach her, offered his arm to lead her to the carriage. She seemed about to refuse it, but something in the expression of his face restrained her; and accepting it, they went down together. The hall and little ante-room were dimly lighted, but as I slowly followed, I saw her snatch her hand away, when she thought they were alone; saw him draw her to him with an embrace as fond as it was irresistible; and turning her indignant face to his, kiss it ardently, as he said in a tone, both tender and imperious —

"Good night, my darling. I give you one more day, and then I claim you."

"Never!" she answered, almost fiercely, as he released her. And wishing me pleasant dreams, as he passed, went out into the night, gaily humming the burden of a song Clotilde had often sung to me.

The moment we were in the carriage all her self-control deserted her, and a tempest of despairing grief came over her. For a time, both words and caresses were unavailing, and I let her weep herself calm before I asked the hard question —

"Is all this true, Clotilde?"

"Yes, Paul, all true, except that he said nothing of the neglect, the cruelty, the insult that I bore before he left me. I was so young, so lonely, I was glad to be loved and cared for, and I believed that he would never change. I cannot tell you all I suffered, but I rejoiced when I thought death had freed me; I would keep nothing that reminded me of the bitter past, and went away to begin again, as if it had never been."

"Why delay telling me this? Why let me learn it in such a strange and sudden way?"

"Ah, forgive me! I am so proud I could not bear to tell you that any man had wearied of me and deserted me. I meant to tell you before our marriage, but the fear that St. John was alive haunted me, and till it was set at rest I would not speak. To-night there was no time, and I was forced to leave all to chance. He found pleasure in tormenting me through you, but would not speak out, because he is as proud as I, and does not wish to hear our story bandied from tongue to tongue."

"What did he say to you, Clotilde?"

"He begged me to submit and return to him, in spite of all that has passed; he warned me that if we attempted to escape it would be at the peril of your life, for he would most assuredly follow and find us, to whatever corner of the earth we might fly; and he will, for he is as relentless as death."

"What did he mean by giving you one day more?" I asked, grinding my teeth with impatient rage as I listened.

"He gave me one day to recover from my surprise, to prepare for my departure with him, and to bid you farewell."

"And will you, Clotilde?"

"No!" she replied, clenching her hands with a gesture of dogged resolution, while her eyes glittered in the darkness. "I never will submit; there must be some way of escape; I shall find it, and if I do not — I can die."

"Not yet, dearest; we will appeal to the law first; I have a friend whom I will consult to-morrow, and he may help us."

"I have no faith in law," she said, despairingly, "money and influence so often outweigh justice and mercy. I have no witnesses, no friends, no wealth to help me; he has all, and we shall only be defeated. I must devise some surer way. Let me think a little; a woman's wit is quick when her heart prompts it."

I let the poor soul flatter herself with vague hopes; but I saw no help for us except in flight, and that she would not consent to, lest it should endanger me. More than once I said savagely within myself, "I will kill him," and then shuddered at the counsels of the devil, so suddenly roused in my own breast. As if she divined my thought by instinct, Clotilde broke the heavy silence that followed her last words, by clinging to me with the imploring cry,

"Oh, Paul, shun him, else your fiery spirit will destroy you. He promised me he would not harm you unless we drove him to it. Be careful, for my sake, and if any one must suffer let it be miserable me."

I soothed her as I best could, and when our long, sad drive ended, bade her rest while I worked, for she would need all her strength on the morrow. Then I left her, to haunt the street all night long, guarding her door, and while I paced to and fro without, I watched her shadow come and go before the lighted window as she paced within, each racking our brains for some means of help till day broke.

III.

Early on the following morning I consulted my friend, but when I laid the case before him he gave me little hope of a happy issue should the attempt be made. A divorce was hardly possible, when an unscrupulous man like St. John was bent on opposing it; and though no decision could force her to remain with him, we should not be safe from his vengeance, even if we chose to dare everything and fly together. Long and earnestly we talked, but to little purpose, and I went to rehearsal with a heavy heart.

Clotilde was to have a benefit that night, and what a happy day I had fancied this would be; how carefully I had prepared for it; what delight I had anticipated in playing Romeo to her Juliet; and how eagerly I had longed for the time which now seemed to approach with such terrible rapidity, for each hour brought our parting nearer! On the stage I found Keen and his new friend amusing themselves with fencing, while waiting the arrival of some of the company. I was too miserable to be dangerous just then, and when St. John bowed to me with his most courteous air, I returned the greeting, though I could not speak to him. I think he saw my suffering, and enjoyed it with the satisfaction of a cruel nature, but he treated me with the courtesy of an equal, which new demonstration surprised me, till, through Denon, I discovered that having inquired much about me he had learned that I was a gentleman by birth and education, which fact accounted for the change in his demeanor. I roamed restlessly about the gloomy green room and stage, till Keen, dropping his foil, confessed himself outfenced and called to me.

"Come here, Lamar, and try a bout with St. John. You are the best fencer among us, so, for the honor of the company, come and do your best instead of playing Romeo before the time."

A sudden impulse prompted me to comply, and a few passes proved that I was the better swordsman of the two. This annoyed St. John, and though he complimented me with the rest, he would not own himself outdone, and we kept it up till both grew warm and excited. In the midst of an animated match between us, I observed that the button was off his foil, and a glance at his face assured me that he was aware of it, and almost at the instant he made a skilful thrust, and the point pierced my flesh. As I caught the foil from his hand and drew it out with an exclamation of pain, I saw a gleam of exultation pass across his face, and knew that his promise to Clotilde was but idle breath. My comrades surrounded me with anxious inquiries, and no one was more surprised and solicitous than St. John. The wound was trifling, for a picture of Clotilde had turned the thrust aside, else the force with which it was given might have rendered it fatal. I made light of it, but hated him with a redoubled hatred for the cold-blooded treachery that would have given to revenge the screen of accident.

The appearance of the ladies caused us to immediately ignore the mishap, and address ourselves to business. Clotilde came last, looking so pale it was not necessary for her to plead illness; but she went through her part with her usual fidelity, while her husband watched her with the masterful expression that nearly drove me wild. He haunted her like a shadow, and she listened to him with the desperate look of a hunted creature driven to bay. He might have softened her just resentment by a touch of generosity or compassion, and won a little gratitude, even though love was impossible; but he was blind, relentless, and goaded her beyond endurance, rousing in her fiery Spanish heart a dangerous spirit he could not control. The rehearsal was over at last, and I approached Clotilde with a look that mutely asked if I should leave her. St. John said something in a low voice, but she answered sternly, as she took my arm with a decided gesture.

"This day is mine; I will not be defrauded of an hour," and we went away together for our accustomed stroll in the sunny park.

A sad and memorable walk was that, for neither had any hope with which to cheer the other, and Clotilde grew gloomier as we talked. I told her of my fruitless consultation, also of the fencing match; at that her face darkened, and she said, below her breath, "I shall remember that."

We walked long together, and I proposed plan after plan, all either unsafe or impracticable. She seemed to listen, but when I paused she answered with averted eyes —

"Leave it to me; I have a project; let me perfect it before I tell you. Now I must go and rest, for I have had no sleep, and I shall need all my strength for the tragedy to-night."

All that afternoon I roamed about the city, too restless for anything but constant motion, and evening found me ill prepared for my now doubly arduous duties. It was late when I reached the theatre, and I dressed hastily. My costume was new for the occasion, and not till it was on did I remember that I had neglected to try it since the finishing touches were given. A stitch or two would remedy the defects, and, hurrying up to the wardrobe room, a skilful pair of hands soon set me right. As I came down the winding-stairs that led from the lofty chamber to a dimly-lighted gallery below, St. John's voice arrested me, and pausing I saw that Keen was doing the honors of the theatre in defiance of all rules. Just as they reached the stair-foot some one called to them, and throwing open a narrow door, he said to his companion —

"From here you get a fine view of the stage; steady yourself by the rope and look down. I'll be with you in a moment."

He ran into the dressing-room from whence the voice proceeded, and St. John stepped out upon a little platform, hastily built for the launching of an aeriel-car in some grand spectacle. Glad to escape meeting him, I was about to go on, when, from an obscure corner, a dark figure glided noiselessly to the door and leaned in. I caught a momentary glimpse of a white extended arm and the glitter of steel, then came a cry of mortal fear, a heavy fall; and flying swiftly down the gallery the figure disappeared. With one leap I reached the door, and looked in; the raft hung broken, the platform was empty. At that instant Keen rushed out, demanding what had happened, and scarcely knowing what I said, I answered hurriedly,

"The rope broke and he fell."

Keen gave me a strange look, and dashed down stairs. I followed, to find myself in a horror-stricken crowd, gathered about the piteous object which a moment ago had been a living man. There was no need to call a surgeon, for that headlong fall had dashed out life in the drawing of a breath, and nothing remained to do but to take the poor body tenderly away to such friends as the newly-arrived stranger possessed. The contrast between the gay crowd rustling before the curtain and the dreadful scene transpiring behind it, was terrible; but the house was filling fast; there was no time for the indulgence of pity or curiosity, and soon no trace of the accident remained but the broken rope above, and an ominous damp spot on the newly-washed boards below. At a word of command from our energetic manager, actors and actresses were sent away to retouch their pale faces with carmine, to restoring their startled nerves with any stimulant at hand, and to forget, if possible, the awesome sight just witnessed.

I returned to my dressing-room hoping Clotilde had heard nothing of this sad, and yet for us most fortunate accident, though all the while a vague dread haunted me, and I feared to see her. Mechanically completing my costume, I looked about me for the dagger with which poor Juliet was to stab herself, and found that it was gone. Trying to recollect where I put it, I remembered having it in my hand just before I went up to have my sword-belt altered; and fancying that I must have inadvertently taken it with me, I reluctantly retraced my steps. At the top of the stairs leading to that upper gallery a little white object caught my eye, and, taking it up, I found it to be a flower. If it had been a burning coal I should not have dropped it more hastily than I did when I recognized it was one of a cluster I had left in Clotilde's room because she loved them. They were a rare and delicate kind, no one but herself was likely to possess them in that place, nor was she likely to have given one away, for my gifts were kept with jealous care; yet how came it there? And as I asked myself the question, like an answer returned the remembrance of her face when she said, "I shall remember this." The darkly-shrouded form was a female figure, the white arm a woman's, and horrible as was the act, who but that sorely-tried and tempted creature would have committed it. For a moment my heart stood still, then I indignantly rejected the black thought, and thrusting the flower into my breast went on my way, trying to convince myself that the foreboding fear which oppressed me was caused by the agitating events of the last half hour. My weapon was not in the wardrobe-room; and as I returned, wondering what I had done with it, I saw Keen standing in the little doorway with a candle in his hand. He turned and asked what I was looking for. I told him, and explained why I was searching for it there.

"Here it is; I found it at the foot of these stairs. It is too sharp for a stage-dagger, and will do mischief unless you dull it," he said, adding, as he pointed to the broken rope, "Lamar, that was cut; I have examined it."

The light shone full in my face, and I knew that it changed, as did my voice, for I thought of Clotilde, and till that fear was at rest resolved to be dumb concerning what I had seen, but I could not repress a shudder as I said, hastily,

"Don't suspect me of any deviltry, for heaven's sake. I've got to go on in fifteen minutes, and how can I play unless you let me forget this horrible business."

"Forget it then, if you can; I'll remind you of it to-morrow." And, with a significant nod, he walked away, leaving behind him a new trial to distract me. I ran to Clotilde's room, bent on relieving myself, if possible, of the suspicion that would return with redoubled pertinacity since the discovery of the dagger, which I was sure I had not dropped where it was found. When I tapped at her door, her voice, clear and sweet as ever, answered "Come!" and entering, I found her ready, but alone. Before I could open my lips she put up her hand as if to arrest the utterance of some dreadful intelligence.

"Don't speak of it; I have heard, and cannot bear a repetition of the horror. I must forget it till to-morrow, then — ." There she stopped abruptly, for I produced the flower, asking as naturally as I could —

"Did you give this to any one?"

"No; why ask me that?" and she shrunk a little, as I bent to count the blossoms in the cluster on her breast. I gave her seven; now there were but six, and I fixed on her a look that betrayed my fear, and mutely demanded its confirmation or denial. Other eyes she might have evaded or defied, not mine; the traitorous blood dyed her face, then fading, left it colorless; her eyes wandered and fell, she clasped her hands imploringly, and threw herself at my feet, crying in a stifled voice,

"Paul, be merciful; that was our only hope, and the guilt is mine alone!"

But I started from her, exclaiming with mingled incredulity and horror —

"Was this the tragedy you meant? What devil devised and helped you execute a crime like this?"

"Hear me! I did not plan it, yet I longed to kill him, and all day the thought would haunt me. I have borne so much, I could bear no more, and he drove me to it. To-night the thought still clung to me, till I was half mad. I went to find you, hoping to escape it; you were gone, but on your table lay the dagger. As I took it in my hand I heard his voice, and forgot every thing except my wrongs and the great happiness one blow could bring us. I followed then, meaning to stab him in the dark; but when I saw him leaning where a safer stroke would destroy him, I gave it, and we are safe."

"Safe!" I echoed. "Do you know you left my dagger behind you? Keen found it; he suspects me, for I was near; and St. John has told him something of the cause I have to wish you free."

She sprung up, and seemed about to rush away to proclaim her guilt, but I restrained her desperate purpose, saying sternly —

"Control yourself and be cautious. I may be mistaken; but if either must suffer, let it be me. I can bear it best, even if it comes to the worst, for my life is worthless now."

"And I have made it so? Oh, Paul, can you never forgive me and forget my sin?"

"Never, Clotilde; it is too horrible."

I broke from her trembling hold, and covered up my face, for suddenly the woman whom I once loved had grown abhorrent to me. For many minutes neither spoke or stirred; my heart seemed dead within me, and what went on in that stormy soul I shall never know. Suddenly I was called, and as I turned to leave her, she seized both my hands in a despairing grasp, covered them with tender kisses, wet them with repentant tears, and clung to them in a paroxysm of love, remorse, and grief, till I was forced to go, leaving her alone with the memory of her sin.

That night I was like one in a terrible dream; every thing looked unreal, and like an automaton I played my part, for always before me I seemed to see that shattered body and to hear again that beloved voice confessing a black crime. Rumors of the accident had crept out, and damped the spirits of the audience, yet it was as well, perhaps, for it made them lenient to the short-comings of the actors, and lent another shadow to the mimic tragedy that slowly darkened to its close. Clotilde's unnatural composure would have been a marvel to me had I not been past surprise at any demonstration on her part. A wide gulf now lay between us, and it seemed impossible for me to cross it. The generous, tender woman whom I first loved, was still as beautiful and dear to me as ever, but as much lost as if death had parted us. The desperate, despairing creature I had learned to know within an hour, seemed like an embodiment of the murderous spirit which had haunted me that day, and though by heaven's mercy it had not conquered me, yet I now hated it with remorseful intensity. So strangely were the two images blended in my troubled mind that I could not separate them, and they exerted a mysterious influence over me. When with Clotilde she seemed all she had ever been, and I enacted the lover with a power I had never known before, feeling the while that it might be for the last time. When away from her the darker impression returned, and the wildest of the poet's words were not too strong to embody my own sorrow and despair. They told me long afterwards that never had the tragedy been better played, and I could believe it, for the hapless Italian lovers never found better representatives than in us that night.

Worn out with suffering and excitement, I longed for solitude and silence with a desperate longing, and when Romeo murmured, "With a kiss I die," I fell beside the bier, wishing that I too was done with life. Lying there, I watched Clotilde, through the little that remained, and so truly, tenderly, did she render the pathetic scene that my heart softened; all the early love returned strong, and warm as ever, and I felt that I *could* forgive. As she knelt to draw my dagger, I whispered, warningly,

"Be careful, dear, it is very sharp."

"I know it," she answered with a shudder, then cried aloud,

"Oh happy dagger! this is thy sheath; there rust, and let me die."

Again I saw the white arm raised, the flash of steel as Juliet struck the blow that was to free her, and sinking down beside her lover, seemed to breathe her life away.

"I thank God it's over," I ejaculated, a few minutes later, as the curtain slowly fell. Clotilde did not answer, and feeling how cold the cheek that touched my own had grown, I thought she had given way at last.

"She has fainted; lift her, Denon, and let me rise," I cried, as Count Paris sprang up with a joke.

"Good God, she has hurt herself with that cursed dagger!" he exclaimed, as raising her he saw a red stain on the white draperies she wore.

I staggered to my feet, and laid her on the bier she had just left, but no mortal skill could heal that hurt, and Juliet's grave-clothes were her own. Deaf to the enthusiastic clamor that demanded our re-appearance, blind to the confusion and dismay about me, I leaned over her passionately, conjuring her to give me one word of pardon and farewell. As if my voice had power to detain her, even when death called, the dark eyes, full of remorseful love, met mine again, and feebly drawing from her breast a paper, she motioned Keen to take it, murmuring in a tone that changed from solemn affirmation to the tenderest penitence,

"Lamar is innocent — I did it. This will prove it. Paul, I have tried to atone — oh, forgive me, and remember me for my love's sake."

I did forgive her; and she died, smiling on my breast. I did remember her through a long, lonely life, and never played again since the night of that DOUBLE TRAGEDY.

DOCTOR DORN'S REVENGE

Louisa May Alcott

Louisa May Alcott (1832–1888) is best known for the American classic *Little Women*. However, she wrote prolifically across genres for both adults and children. Her 1865 short story 'V.V., or Plots and Counterplots' is one of the earliest detective stories in English.

They stood together by the sea, and it was evident the old, old story was being told, for the man's face was full of pale excitement, the girl's half averted from the ardent eyes that strove to read the fateful answer in her own.

"It may be folly to speak when I have so little to offer," he said, with an accent of strong and tender emotion in his voice that went straight to the girl's heart. "It may be folly, and yet if you love as I love we can wait or work together happy in the affection which wealth cannot buy nor poverty destroy. Tell me truly, Evelyn, may I hope?"

She longed to say "yes," for in her heart she knew she loved this man, so rich in youth, comeliness, talent, and ardor, but, alas! so poor in fortune and friends, power and place. He possessed all that wins a woman's eye and heart, nothing that gratifies worldly ambition or the vanity that is satisfied with luxury regardless of love. She was young, proud, and poor, her beauty was her only gift, and she saw in it her only means of attaining the place she coveted. She had no hope but in a wealthy marriage; for this end she lived and wrought, and had almost won it, when Max Dorn appeared, and for the first time her heart rebelled. Something in the manful courage, the patient endurance with which he met and bore, and would in time conquer misfortune, woke her admiration and respect. He was different from those about her, and carried with him the unconscious but sovereign charm of integrity. The love she saw in his eloquent eyes seemed a different passion from the shallow, selfish sentimentality of other men. It seemed to ennoble by its sincerity, to bless by its tenderness, and she found it hard to put it by.

As she listened to his brief appeal, made impressive by the intensity of repressed feeling that trembled in it, she wavered, hesitated, and tried to silence conscience by a false plea of duty.

Half turning with the shy glance, the soft flush of maiden love and shame, she said slowly:

"If I answered yes I should wrong both of us, for while you work and I wait that this may be made possible, our youth and strength will be passing away, and when the end is won we shall be old and tired, and even love itself worn out."

"If it be true love it never can wear out," he cried, impetuously; but she shook her delicate head, and a shadow passed across her charming face, paling its bloom and saddening its beauty.

"I know that poets say so, but I have no faith in the belief. Hearts grow gray as well as heads, and love cannot defy time any more than youth can. I've seen it tried and it always fails."

"So young, yet so worldly-wise, so lovely, yet so doubtful of love's dominion," murmured Max, on whom her words fell with a foreboding chill.

"I have felt the bitterness of poverty, and it has made me old before my time," she answered, with the shadow deepening on her face. "I could love you, but I will not." And the red lips closed resolutely as the hard words left them.

"Because I am poor?"

"Because we are poor."

For an instant something like contempt shone in his eyes, then pity softened their dark brilliance, and a passionate pain thrilled his voice as he said, with a despairing glance:

"Then I may not hope!" She could not utter the cruel word "No" that rose to her lips; a sudden impulse ruled her; the better nature she had tried to kill prompted a truer answer, and love, half against her will, replied:

"You may hope—a little longer."

"How long?" he questioned, almost sternly, for even with the joy of hope came a vague disquiet and distrust.

"Till to-morrow."

The tell-tale color flushed into her cheeks as the words escaped her, and she could not meet the keen yet tender eyes that searched her downcast face.

"To-morrow!" he echoed; "that is a short probation, but none the less hard for its brevity if I read your face aright. John Meredith has spoken, and you find money more tempting than love."

Her head dropped on her hands, and for an instant she struggled with an almost irresistible impulse to put her hand in his and show him she was nobler than he believed. But she had been taught to control natural impulses, to bend her will, to yield her freedom to the one aim of her life, and calling it necessity, to become its slave. Something in his look and tone stung her pride and gave her strength to fight against her heart. In one thing he was mistaken; John Meredith had not spoken, but she knew a glance from her would unlock his tongue, for the prize was almost won, and nothing but this sudden secret love had withheld her from seizing the fruit of her long labor and desire. She meant to assure herself of this beyond all doubt, and then, when both fates were possible, to weigh and decide as calmly as she might. To this purpose she clung, and lifting her head with a proud gesture, she said, in the cold, hard tone that jarred upon his ear and made discord in the music of her voice:

"You need not wait until to-morrow. Will you receive your answer now?"

"No; I will be patient, for I know something of temptations like this, and I have faith in the nobility of a woman's heart. Love or leave me as you will, but, Evelyn, if you value your own peace, if you care for the reverence of one who loves you utterly, do not sell yourself, for wealth so bought is worse than the sharpest poverty. A word will put me out of pain; think of this to-day; wear these to remind you of me, as that jewel recalls Meredith; and to-night return my dead roses or give me one yourself."

He put the ruddy cluster in the hand that wore his rival's gift, looked into her face with a world of love and longing in his proud eyes, and left her there alone.

If he had seen her crush the roses on her lips and drench them in passionate tears, if he had heard her breathe his name in tones of tenderest grief and call him back to save her from temptation, he would have turned and spared himself a lifelong loss, and saved her from a sacrifice that doomed her to remorse. She crept into a shadowy nook among the rocks, and searched her self as she had never done before. The desire to be found worthy of him swayed her strongly, and almost conquered the beliefs and purposes of her whole life. An hour passed, and with an expression more beautiful than any ever seen upon her face till now, Evelyn rose to seek and tell her lover that she could not give his flowers back.

As she stood a moment smiling down upon the emblems of love, a voice marred the happiest instant of her life, a single sentence undid the work of that thoughtful hour.

"Meredith will never marry pretty Evelyn."

"And why not?" returned another voice, as careless as that sarcastic one that spoke first.

"He is too wise, and she lacks skill. My faith! with half her beauty I would have conquered a dozen such as he."

"You have a more potent charm than beauty, for wealth will buy any man . . ."

"Not all." And the girl's keen ear detected an undertone of bitterness in the light laugh that followed the words. A woman spoke, and as she listened, Dorn's words, "I know something of such temptations," returned to her with a sudden significance which the next words confirmed.

"Ah, Max will not thaw under your smiles nor be dazzled by the golden baits you offer. Well, my dear, you can find your revenge in watching Evelyn's folly and its dreary consequences, for she will marry him and ruin herself for ever."

"No doubt of that; she hasn't wit enough to see what a splendid career is open to her if she marries Meredith, and she will let a girlish romance rob her of success. That knowledge is an immense comfort to me."

The speakers passed on, leaving Evelyn pale with anger, her eyes keen and hard, her lips smiling scornfully, and her heart full of bitterness. The roses lay at her feet, and the hand that wore the ring was clinched as she watched mother and daughter stroll away, little dreaming that their worldly gossip had roused the girl's worst passions and given her temptation double force.

"She loves Max and pities me—good! I'll let her know that I refused him, and teach her to fear as well as envy me. 'A splendid career'—and she thinks I'll lose it. Wait a day and see if I have not wit enough to know it, and skill enough to secure it. 'Girlish romance' shall not ruin my future; I see its folly, and I thank that woman for showing me how to avoid it. Take comfort while you may, false friend; to-morrow your punishment will begin."

Snatching up the roses, Evelyn returned to the hotel, congratulating herself that she had not spoken hastily and pledged her word to Dorn. Everything seemed to foster the purpose that had wavered for an hour, and even trifles lent their weight to turn the scale in favor of the mercenary choice. As if conscious of the struggle going on within her, Meredith forgot the temporary jealousy of Dorn, that had held him aloof for a time, and was more devoted than before. She drove with him, and leaning in his luxurious barouche, passed Dorn walking through the dust. A momentary pang smote her as his face kindled when he saw her, but she conquered it by whispering to herself, "That woman would rejoice to see me walking there beside him; now I can eclipse her even in so small a thing as this."

As the thought came, her haughty little head rose erect, her eye wandered, well pleased, from splendid horses, liveried servants and emblazoned carnage, to the man who could make them hers, and she smiled on him with a glance that touched the cold heart which she alone had ever warmed.

Later, as she sat among a group of summer friends, listening to their gossip, she covertly watched her two lovers while she stored up the hints, opinions, and criticisms of those about her.

Max Dorn had youth, manly beauty and native dignity, but lacked that indescribable something which marks the polished man of fashion, and by dress, manner, speech and attitude betrayed that he was outside the charmed circle as plainly as if a visible barrier rose between him and his rival.

John Meredith, a cold, grave man of forty, bore the mark of patrician birth and breeding in every feature, tone, and act. Not handsome, graceful, or gifted, but simply an aristocrat in pride and position as in purse. Men envied, imitated, and feared him; women courted, flattered, and sighed for him; and whomsoever he married would be, in spite of herself, a queen of society.

As she watched him the girl's purpose strengthened, for on no one did his eye linger as on herself; every mark of his preference raised her in the estimation of her mates, and already was she beginning to feel the intoxicating power which would be wholly hers if she accepted him.

"I will!" she said, within herself. "To-night he will speak and to-morrow brilliant future shall begin." As she dressed for the ball that night an exquisite bouquet of exotics was brought her. She knew who sent them, and a glance of gratified vanity went from the flowers to the lovely head they would adorn. In a glass on her toilet bloomed the wild roses, fresh and fragrant as ever. A regretful sigh escaped her as she took them up, saying softly, "I must return them, but he'll soon forget—and so shall I."

A thorn pierced her hand as she spoke, and as if daunted by the omen, she paused an instant while tears of mental, not physical pain, filled her eyes. She wiped the tiny drop of blood from her white palm, and as she did so the flash of the diamond caught her eye. A quick change passed over her, and dashing away the tears, she hid the wound and followed her chaperon, looking blithe and beautiful as ever.

John Meredith did speak that night, and Max Dorn knew it, for his eye never left the little figure with the wild roses half hidden in the lace that stirred with the beating of the girlish heart he coveted. He saw them pass into the moonlit garden, and stood like a sentinel at the gate till a glimmer of white foretold their return. Evelyn's face he could not see, for she averted it, and turned from the crowd as if to seek her room unseen. Meredith's pale features were slightly flushed, and his cold eye shone with unwonted fire, but whether anger or joy wrought the change Dorn could not tell.

Hurrying after Evelyn, he saw her half way up the wide staircase, and softly called her name.

No one was near, and pausing, she turned to look down on him. Never had she seemed more lovely, yet never had he found it hard to watch that beloved face before. Without a word he looked up, and stretched his hands to her, as if unconscious of the distance between them. Her rich color faded, her lips trembled, but her eyes did not fall before his own, and her hand went steadily to her breast as in silence, more bitterly significant than words, she dropped the dead roses at his feet.

"Is Doctor Dorn at home?"

The servant glanced from the pale, eager speaker to the elegant carriage he had left, and, though past the hour, admitted him.

A room, perfect in the taste and fitness of its furnishing, and betraying many evidences, not only of the wealth, but the cultivation of its owner, received the new comer, who glanced hastily about him as he advanced toward its occupant, who bent over a desk writing rapidly.

"Doctor Dorn, can you spare me a few moments on a case of life and death?" said the gentleman, in an imploring tone, for the sight of a line of carriages outside, and a crowded anteroom inside, had impressed him with the skill and success of this doctor more deeply than all the tales he had heard of his marvelous powers.

Doctor Dorn glanced at his watch.

"I can give you exactly five minutes."

"Thanks. Then let me as briefly as possible tell you the case. My wife is dying with a tumor in the side. I have tried everything, every physician, and all in vain. I should have applied to you long ago, had not Evelyn positively forbid it."

As the words left his lips both men looked at one another, with the memory of that summer night ten years ago rising freshly before them. John Meredith's cold face flushed with emotion in speaking of his suffering wife to the man who had been his rival. But Max Dorn's pale, impassive countenance never changed a muscle, though a close observer might have seen a momentary gleam of something like satisfaction in his dark eye as he answered in a perfectly business-like tone: "I have heard of Mrs. Meredith's case from Doctor Savant, and know the particulars. Will you name your wish?"

He knew it already, but he would not spare this man the pang of asking his wife's life at his hands. Meredith moistened his dry lips, and answered slowly:

"They tell me an operation may save her, and she consents. Doctor Savant dares not undertake it, and says no one but you can do it. Can you? Will you?"

"But Mrs. Meredith forbids it."

"She is to be deceived; your name is not to be mentioned; and she is to think Doctor Savant is the man."

A bitter smile touched Dorn's lips, as he replied with significant emphasis:

"I decline to undertake the case at this late stage. Savant will do his best faithfully, and I hope will succeed. Good morning, sir."

Meredith turned proudly away, and Dorn bent over his writing. But at the door the husband paused, for the thought of his lovely young wife dying for want of this man's skill rent his heart and bowed his spirit. With an impulsive gesture he retraced his steps, saying brokenly:

"Doctor Dorn, I beseech you to revoke that answer. Forgive the past, save my Evelyn, and make me your debtor for life. All the honor shall be yours; she will bless you, and I—I will thank you, serve you, love you to my dying day."

Hard and cold as stone was Dorn's face as the other spoke, and for a moment no answer came.

Meredith's imploring eyes saw no relenting sign, his outstretched hands fell at his side, and grief, resentment and despair trembled in his voice as he said, solemnly:

"For her sake I humbled myself to plead with you, believing you a nobler man than you have proved yourself. She took your heart, you take her life, for no hand but yours can save her. You might have won our gratitude forever, but you refused."

"I consent." And with a look that went straight to the other's heart, Dorn held out his hand.

Meredith wrung it silently, and the first tears that had wet his eyes for years fell on the generous hand that gave him back his idol's life.

The affair was rapidly arranged, and as no time was to be lost, the following day was fixed.

Evelyn was to be kept in ignorance of Dorn's part in the matter, and Doctor Savant was to prepare everything as if he were to be the operator. Dorn was not to appear till she was unconscious, and she was not to be told to whom she owed her life till she was out of danger.

The hour came, and Dorn was shown into the chamber, where on the narrow table Evelyn lay, white and unconscious, as if dead. Savant, and two other physicians, anxious to see the great surgeon at work, stood near; and Meredith hung over the beautiful woman as if it was impossible to yield her up to them. As he entered the room Dorn snatched one hungry glance at the beloved face, and tore his eyes away, saying to the nurse who came to him, "Cover her face."

The woman began to question him, but Meredith understood, and with his own hands laid a delicate handkerchief over the pallid face. Then he withdrew to an alcove, and behind the curtain prayed with heart and soul for the salvation of the one creature whom he loved.

The examination and consultation over, Dorn turned to take up his knife. As he did so one of the physicians whispered to the other, with a sneer:

"See his hand tremble; mine is steadier than that."

"He is as pale as the sheet; it's my opinion that his success is owing to luck's accidents more than to skill or science," returned the other. In the dead silence of the room, the least whisper was audible. Dorn flushed to the forehead, he set his teeth, nerved his arm, and with a clear, calm eye, and unfaltering hand made the first incision in the white flesh, dearer to him than his own.

It was a strange, nay, an almost awful sight, that luxurious room, and in the full glow of the noonday light that beautiful white figure, with four pale men bending over it, watching with breathless interest the movements of one skillful pair of hands moving among the glittering instruments or delicately tying arteries, severing nerves, and gliding heedfully among vital organs, where a hairsbreadth slip might be death. And looking from behind the curtains, a haggard countenance full of anguish, hope and suspense.

With speechless wonder and admiration the three followed Dorn through the intricacies of this complicated operation, envying the steadiness of his hand, firm as iron, yet delicate as a breath; watching the precision of his strokes, the success of his treatment, and most of all, admiring his entire absorption in the work; his utter forgetfulness of the subject, whose youth and beauty might well unnerve the most skillful hand. No sign of what he suffered during that brief time escaped him; but when all was safely over, and Evelyn lay again in her bed, great drops stood upon his forehead, and as Meredith grasped his hand he found it cold as stone. To the praises of his rivals in science, and the fervent thanks of his rival in love, he returned scarce any answer, and with careful directions to the nurse went away to fall faint and exhausted on his bed, crying with the tearless love and longing of a man, "Oh, my darling, I have saved you only to lose you again!— only to give you up to a fate harder for me to bear than death."

Evelyn lived, and when she learned to whom she owed her life, she covered her face, saying to her hungry heart, "If he had known how utterly weary I was, how empty my life, how remorseful my conscience, he would have let me die."

She had learned long ago the folly of her choice, and pined in her splendid home for Max, and love and poverty again. He had prospered wonderfully, for the energy that was as native to him as his fidelity, led him to labor for ambition's sake when love was denied him. Devoted to his profession he lived on that alone, and in ten years won a brilliant success. Honor, wealth, position were his now, and any woman might have been proud to share his lot. But none were wooed; and in his distant home he watched over Evelyn unseen, unknown—and loved her still.

She had tasted the full bitterness of her fate, had repented and striven to atone by devoting herself to Meredith, who was unalterable in his passion for her. But his love and her devotion could not bring happiness, and when he died his parting words were, "Now you are free."

She reproached herself for the thrill of joy that came as she listened, and whispered penitently, "Forgive me, I was not worthy of such love." For a year she mourned for him sincerely; but she was young, she loved with a woman's fervor now, and hope would paint a happy future with Max.

He never wrote nor came, and wearying at last, she sent a letter to a friend in that distant city, asking news of Doctor Dorn. The answer brought small comfort, for it told her that an epidemic had broken out, and that the first to volunteer for the most dangerous post was Max Dorn.

In a moment her decision was taken. "I must be near him; I must save him—if it is not too late.

"He must not sacrifice himself; he would not be so reckless if he knew that any one cared for him."

Telling no one of her purpose, she left her solitary home and went to find her lover, regardless of danger. The city was deserted by all but the wretched poor and the busy middle class, who live by daily labor. She heard from many lips praises, blessings and prayers when she uttered Doctor Dorn's name, but it was not so easy to find him. He was never at home, but lived in hospitals, and the haunts of suffering day and night. She wrote and sent to him. No answer came. She visited his house to find it empty. She grew desperate, and went to seek for him where few dared venture, and here she learned that he had been missing for three days. Her heart stood still, for many dropped, died, and were buried hastily, leaving no name behind them.

Regardless of everything but the desire to find him, dead or living, she plunged into the most infected quarter of the town, and after hours of sights and sounds that haunted her for years, she found him.

In a poor woman's room, nursed as tenderly by her and the child he had saved as if he had been her son, lay Max, dying. He was past help now, unconscious, and out of pain, and as she sat beside him, heart-stricken and despairing, Evelyn received her punishment for the act which wrecked her own life and led his to an end like that.

As if her presence dimly impressed his failing senses, a smile broke over his pallid lips, his hand feebly groped for hers, and those magnificent eyes of his shone unclouded for a moment, as she whispered remorsefully:

"I loved you best; forgive me, Max, and tell me you remember Evelyn."

"You said I might hope a little longer; I'll be patient, dear, and wait."

And with the words he was gone, leaving her twice widowed.

PERILOUS PLAY

Louisa May Alcott

Louisa May Alcott (1832–1888) is best known for the American classic *Little Women*. However, she wrote prolifically across genres for both adults and children. Her 1865 short story 'V.V., or Plots and Counter-plots' is one of the earliest detective stories in English.

"If someone does not propose a new and interesting amusement, I shall die of ennui!" said pretty Belle Daventry, in a tone of despair. "I have read all my books, used up all my Berlin wools, and it's too warm to go to town for more. No one can go sailing yet, as the tide is out; we are all nearly tired to death of cards, croquet, and gossip, so what shall we do to while away this endless afternoon? Dr. Meredith, I command you to invent and propose a new game in five minutes."

"To hear is to obey," replied the young man, who lay in the grass at her feet, as he submissively slapped his forehead, and fell a-thinking with all his might.

Holding up her finger to preserve silence, Belle pulled out her watch and waited with an expectant smile. The rest of the young party, who were indolently scattered about under the elms, drew nearer, and brightened visibly, for Dr. Meredith's inventive powers were well-known, and something refreshingly novel might be expected from him. One gentleman did not stir, but then he lay within earshot, and merely turned his fine eyes from the sea to the group before him. His glance rested a moment on Belle's piquant figure, for she looked very pretty with her bright hair blowing in the wind, one plump white arm extended to keep order, and one little foot, in a distracting slipper, just visible below the voluminous folds of her dress. Then the glance passed to another figure, sitting somewhat apart in a cloud of white muslin, for an airy burnoose floated from head and shoulders, showing only a singularly charming face. Pale and yet brilliant, for the Southern eyes were magnificent, the clear olive cheeks contrasted well with darkest hair; lips like a pomegranate flower, and delicate, straight brows, as mobile as the lips. A cluster of crimson flowers, half falling from the loose black braids, and a golden bracelet of Arabian coins on the slender wrist were the only ornaments she wore, and became her better than the fashionable frippery of her companions. A book lay on her lap, but her eyes, full of a passionate melancholy, were fixed on the sea, which glittered around an island green and flowery as a summer paradise. Rose St. Just was as beautiful as her Spanish mother, but had inherited the pride and reserve of her English father; and this pride was the thorn which repelled lovers from the human flower. Mark Done sighed as he looked, and as if the sigh, low as it was, roused her from her reverie, Rose flashed a quick glance at him, took up her book, and went on reading the legend of "The Lotus Eaters."

"Time is up now, Doctor," cried Belle, pocketing her watch with a flourish.

"Ready to report," answered Meredith, sitting up and producing a little box of tortoiseshell and gold.

"How mysterious! What is it? Let me see, first!" And Belle removed the cover, looking like an inquisitive child. "Only bonbons; how stupid! That won't do, sir. We don't want to be fed with sugar-plums. We demand to be amused."

"Eat six of these despised bonbons, and you will be amused in a new, delicious, and wonderful manner," said the young doctor, laying half a dozen on a green leaf and offering them to her.

"Why, what are they?" she asked, looking at him askance.

"Hashish; did you never hear of it?"

"Oh, yes; it's that Indian stuff which brings one fantastic visions, isn't it? I've always wanted to see and taste it, and now I will," cried Belle, nibbling at one of the bean-shaped comfits with its green heart.

"I advise you not to try it. People do all sorts of queer things when they take it. I wouldn't for the world," said a prudent young lady warningly, as all examined the box and its contents.

"Six can do no harm, I give you my word. I take twenty before I can enjoy myself, and some people even more. I've tried many experiments, both on the sick and the well, and nothing ever happened amiss, though the demonstrations were immensely interesting," said Meredith, eating his sugar-plums with a tranquil air, which was very convincing to others.

"How shall I feel?" asked Belle, beginning on her second comfit.

"A heavenly dreaminess comes over one, in which they move as if on air. Everything is calm and lovely to them: no pain, no care, no fear of anything, and while it lasts one feels like an angel half asleep."

"But if one takes too much, how then?" said a deep voice behind the doctor.

"Hum! Well, that's not so pleasant, unless one likes phantoms, frenzies, and a touch of nightmare, which seems to last a thousand years. Ever try it, Done?" replied Meredith, turning toward the speaker, who was now leaning on his arm and looking interested.

"Never. I'm not a good subject for experiments. Too nervous a temperament to play pranks with."

"I should say ten would be about your number. Less than that seldom affects men. Ladies go off sooner, and don't need so many. Miss St. Just, may I offer you a taste of Elysium? I owe my success to you," said the doctor, approaching her deferentially.

"To me! And how?" she asked, lifting her large eyes with a slight smile.

"I was in the depths of despair when my eye caught the title of your book, and I was saved. For I remembered that I had hashish in my pocket."

"Are you a lotus-eater?" she said, permitting him to lay the six charmed bonbons on the page.

"My faith, no! I use it for my patients. It is very efficacious in nervous disorders, and is getting to be quite a pet remedy with us."

"I do not want to forget the past, but to read the future. Will hashish help me to do that?" asked Rose with an eager look, which made the young man flush, wondering if he bore any part in her hopes of that veiled future.

"Alas, no. I wish it could, for I, too, long to know my fate," he answered, very low, as he looked into the lovely face before him.

The soft glance changed to one of cool indifference and Rose gently brushed the hashish off her book, saying, with a little gesture of dismissal, "Then I have no desire to taste Elysium."

The white morsels dropped into the grass at her feet; but Dr. Meredith let them lie, and turning sharply, went back to sun himself in Belle's smiles.

"I've eaten all mine, and so has Evelyn. Mr. Norton will see goblins, I know, for he has taken quantities. I'm glad of it, for he does not believe in it, and I want to have him convinced by making a spectacle of himself for our amusement," said Belle, in great spirits at the new plan.

"When does the trance come on?" asked Evelyn, a shy girl, already rather alarmed at what she had done.

"About three hours after you take your dose, though the time varies with different people. Your pulse will rise, heart beat quickly, eyes darken and dilate, and an uplifted sensation will pervade you generally. Then these symptoms change, and the bliss begins. I've seen people sit or lie in one position for hours, rapt in a delicious dream, and wake from it as tranquil as if they had not a nerve in their bodies."

"How charming! I'll take some every time I'm worried. Let me see. It's now four, so our trances will come about seven, and we will devote the evening to manifestations," said Belle.

"Come, Done, try it. We are all going in for the fun. Here's your dose," and Meredith tossed him a dozen bonbons, twisted up in a bit of paper.

"No, thank you; I know myself too well to risk it. If you are all going to turn hashish-eaters, you'll need someone to take care of you, so I'll keep sober," tossing the little parcel back.

It fell short, and the doctor, too lazy to pick it up, let it lie, merely saying, with a laugh, "Well, I advise any bashful man to take hashish when he wants to offer his heart to any fair lady, for it will give him the courage of a hero, the eloquence of a poet, and the ardor of an Italian. Remember that, gentlemen, and come to me when the crisis approaches."

"Does it conquer the pride, rouse the pity, and soften the hard hearts of the fair sex?" asked Done.

"I dare say now is your time to settle the fact, for here are two ladies who have imbibed, and in three hours will be in such a seraphic state of mind that 'No' will be an impossibility to them."

"Oh, mercy on us; what have we done? If that's the case, I shall shut myself up till my foolish fit is over. Rose, you haven't taken any; I beg you to mount guard over me, and see that I don't disgrace myself by any nonsense. Promise me you will," cried Belle, in half-real, half-feigned alarm at the consequences of her prank.

"I promise," said Rose, and floated down the green path as noiselessly as a white cloud, with a curious smile on her lips.

"Don't tell any of the rest what we have done, but after tea let us go into the grove and compare notes," said Norton, as Done strolled away to the beach, and the voices of approaching friends broke the summer quiet.

At tea, the initiated glanced covertly at one another, and saw, or fancied they saw, the effects of the hashish, in a certain suppressed excitement of manner, and unusually brilliant eyes. Belle laughed often, a silvery ringing laugh, pleasant to hear; when complimented on her good spirits, she looked distressed and said she could not help her merriment; Meredith was quite calm, but rather dreamy; Evelyn was pale, and her next neighbor heard her heart beat; Norton talked incessantly, but as he talked uncommonly well, no one suspected anything. Done and Miss St. Just watched the others with interest, and were very quiet, especially Rose, who scarcely spoke, but smiled her sweetest, and looked very lovely.

The moon rose early, and the experimenters slipped away to the grove, leaving the outsiders on the lawn as usual. Some bold spirit asked Rose to sing, and she at once complied, pouring out Spanish airs in a voice that melted the hearts of her audience, so full of fiery sweetness or tragic pathos was it. Done seemed quite carried away, and lay with his face in the grass, to hide the tears that would come; till, afraid of openly disgracing himself, he started up and hurried down to the little wharf, where he sat alone, listening to the music with a countenance which plainly revealed to the stars the passion which possessed him. The sound of loud laughter from the grove, followed by entire silence, caused him to wonder what demonstrations were taking place, and half resolve to go and see. But that enchanting voice held him captive, even when a boat put off mysteriously from a point nearby, and sailed away like a phantom through the twilight.

Half an hour afterward, a white figure came down the path, and Rose's voice broke in on his midsummer night's dream. The moon shone clearly now, and showed him the anxiety in her face as she said hurriedly, "Where is Belle?"

"Gone sailing, I believe."

"How could you let her go? She was not fit to take care of herself!"

"I forgot that."

"So did I, but I promised to watch over her, and I must. Which way did they go?" demanded Rose, wrapping the white mantle about her, and running her eye over the little boats moored below.

"You will follow her?"

"Yes."

"I'll be your guide then. They went toward the lighthouse; it is too far to row; I am at your service. Oh, say yes," cried Done, leaping into his own skiff and offering his hand persuasively.

She hesitated an instant and looked at him. He was always pale, and the moonlight seemed to increase this pallor, but his hat brim hid his eyes, and his voice was very quiet. A loud peal of laughter floated over the water, and as if the sound decided her, she gave him her hand and entered the boat. Done smiled triumphantly as he shook out the sail, which caught the freshening wind, and sent the boat dancing along a path of light.

How lovely it was! All the indescribable allurements of a perfect summer night surrounded them: balmy airs, enchanting moonlight, distant music, and, close at hand, the delicious atmosphere of love, which made itself felt in the eloquent silences that fell between them. Rose seemed to yield to the subtle charm, and leaned back on the cushioned seat with her beautiful head uncovered, her face full of dreamy softness, and her hands lying loosely clasped before her. She seldom spoke, showed no further anxiety for Belle, and soon seemed to forget the object of her search, so absorbed was she in some delicious thought which wrapped her in its peace.

Done sat opposite, flushed now, restless, and excited, for his eyes glittered; the hand on the rudder shook, and his voice sounded intense and passionate, even in the utterance of the simplest words. He talked continually and with unusual brilliancy, for, though a man of many accomplishments, he was too indolent or too fastidious to exert himself, except among his peers. Rose seemed to look without seeing, to listen without hearing, and though she smiled blissfully, the smiles were evidently not for him.

On they sailed, scarcely heeding the bank of black cloud piled up in the horizon, the rising wind, or the silence which proved their solitude. Rose moved once or twice, and lifted her hand as if to speak, but sank back mutely, and the hand fell again as if it had not energy enough to enforce her wish. A cloud sweeping over the moon, a distant growl of thunder, and the slight gust that struck the sail seemed to rouse her. Done was singing now like one inspired, his hat at his feet, hair in disorder, and a strangely rapturous expression in his eyes, which were fixed on her. She started, shivered, and seemed to recover herself with an effort.

"Where are they?" she asked, looking vainly for the island heights and the other boat.

"They have gone to the beach, I fancy, but we will follow." As Done leaned forward to speak, she saw his face and shrank back with a sudden flush, for in it she read clearly what she had felt, yet doubted until now. He saw the telltale blush and gesture, and said impetuously, "You know it now; you cannot deceive me longer, or daunt me with your pride! Rose, I love you, and dare tell you so tonight!"

"Not now—not here—I will not listen. Turn back, and be silent, I entreat you, Mr. Done," she said hurriedly.

He laughed a defiant laugh and took her hand in his, which was burning and throbbing with the rapid heat of his pulse.

"No, I will have my answer here, and now, and never turn back till you give it; you have been a thorny Rose, and given me many wounds. I'll be paid for my heartache with sweet words, tender looks, and frank confessions of love, for proud as you are, you do love me, and dare not deny it."

Something in his tone terrified her; she snatched her hand away and drew beyond his reach, trying to speak calmly, and to meet coldly the ardent glances of the eyes which were strangely darkened and dilated with uncontrollable emotion.

"You forget yourself. I shall give no answer to an avowal made in such terms. Take me home instantly," she said in a tone of command.

"Confess you love me, Rose."

"Never!"

"Ah! I'll have a kinder answer, or—" Done half rose and put out his hand to grasp and draw her to him, but the cry she uttered seemed to arrest him with a sort of shock. He dropped into his seat, passed his hand over his eyes, and shivered nervously as he muttered in an altered tone, "I meant nothing; it's the moonlight; sit down, I'll control myself—upon my soul I will!"

"If you do not, I shall go overboard. Are you mad, sir?" cried Rose, trembling with indignation.

"Then I shall follow you, for I am mad, Rose, with love—hashish!"

His voice sank to a whisper, but the last word thrilled along her nerves, as no sound of fear had ever done before. An instant she regarded him with a look which took in every sign of unnatural excitement, then she clasped her hands with an imploring gesture, saying, in a tone of despair, "Why did I come? How will it end? Oh, Mark, take me home before it is too late!"

"Hush! Be calm; don't thwart me, or I may get wild again. My thoughts are not clear, but I understand you. There, take my knife, and if I forget myself, kill me. Don't go overboard; you are too beautiful to die, my Rose!"

He threw her the slender hunting-knife he wore, looked at her a moment with a far-off look, and trimmed the sail like one moving in a dream. Rose took the weapon, wrapped her cloak closely about her, and crouching as far away as possible, kept her eye on him, with a face in which watchful terror contended with some secret trouble and bewilderment more powerful than her fear.

The boat moved round and begin to beat up against wind and tide; spray flew from her bow; the sail bent and strained in the gusts that struck it with perilous fitfulness. The moon was nearly hidden by scudding clouds, and one half the sky was black with the gathering storm. Rose looked from threatening heavens to treacherous sea, and tried to be ready for any danger, but her calm had been sadly broken, and she could not recover it. Done sat motionless, uttering no word of encouragement, though the frequent flaws almost tore the rope from his hand, and the water often dashed over him.

"Are we in any danger?" asked Rose at last, unable to bear the silence, for he looked like a ghostly helmsman seen by the fitful light, pale now, wild-eyed, and speechless.

"Yes, great danger."

"I thought you were a skillful boatman."

"I am when I am myself; now I am rapidly losing the control of my will, and the strange quiet is coming over me. If I had been alone I should have given up sooner, but for your sake I've kept on."

"Can't you work the boat?" asked Rose, terror-struck by the changed tone of his voice, the slow, uncertain movements of his hands.

"No. I see everything through a thick cloud; your voice sounds far away, and my one desire is to lay my head down and sleep."

"Let me steer—I can, I must!" she cried, springing toward him and laying her hand on the rudder.

He smiled and kissed the little hand, saying dreamily, "You could not hold it a minute; sit by me, love; let us turn the boat again, and drift away together—anywhere, anywhere out of the world."

"Oh, heaven, what will become of us!" and Rose wrung her hands in real despair. "Mr. Done—Mark—dear Mark, rouse yourself and listen to me. Turn, as you say, for it is certain death to go on. Turn, and let us drift down to the lighthouse; they will hear and help us. Quick, take down the sail, get out the oars, and let us try to reach there before the storm breaks."

As Rose spoke, he obeyed her like a dumb animal; love for her was stronger even than the instinct of self-preservation, and for her sake he fought against the treacherous lethargy which was swiftly overpowering him. The sail was lowered, the boat brought round, and with little help from the ill-pulled oars it drifted rapidly out to sea with the ebbing tide.

As she caught her breath after this dangerous maneuver was accomplished, Rose asked, in a quiet tone she vainly tried to render natural, "How much hashish did you take?"

"All that Meredith threw me. Too much; but I was possessed to do it, so I hid the roll and tried it," he answered, peering at her with a weird laugh.

"Let us talk; our safety lies in keeping awake, and I dare not let you sleep," continued Rose, dashing water on her own hot forehead with a sort of desperation.

"Say you love me; that would wake me from my lost sleep, I think. I have hoped and feared, waited and suffered so long. Be pitiful, and answer, Rose."

"I do; but I should not own it now."

So low was the soft reply he scarcely heard it, but he felt it and made a strong effort to break from the hateful spell that bound him. Leaning forward, he tried to read her face in a ray of moonlight breaking through the clouds; he saw a new and tender warmth in it, for all the pride was gone, and no fear marred the eloquence of those soft, Southern eyes.

"Kiss me, Rose, then I shall believe it. I feel lost in a dream, and you, so changed, so kind, may be only a fair phantom. Kiss me, love, and make it real."

As if swayed by a power more potent than her will, Rose bent to meet his lips. But the ardent pressure seemed to startle her from a momentary oblivion of everything but love. She covered up her face and sank down, as if overwhelmed with shame, sobbing through passionate tears, "Oh, what am I doing? I am mad, for I, too, have taken hashish!"

What he answered she never heard, for a rattling peal of thunder drowned his voice, and then the storm broke loose. Rain fell in torrents, the wind blew fiercely, sky and sea were black as ink, and the boat tossed from wave to wave almost at their mercy. Giving herself up for lost, Rose crept to her lover's side and clung there, conscious only that they would bide together through the perils their own folly brought them. Done's excitement was quite gone now; he sat like a statue, shielding the frail creature whom he loved with a smile on his face, which looked awfully emotionless when the lightning gave her glimpses of its white immobility. Drenched, exhausted, and half senseless with danger, fear, and exposure, Rose saw at last a welcome glimmer through the gloom, and roused herself to cry for help.

"Mark, wake and help me! Shout, for God's sake—shout and call them, for we are lost if we drift by!" she cried, lifting his head from his breast, and forcing him to see the brilliant beacons streaming far across the troubled water.

He understood her, and springing up, uttered shout after shout like one demented. Fortunately, the storm had lulled a little; the lighthouse keeper heard and answered. Rose seized the helm, Done the oars, and with one frantic effort guided the boat into quieter waters, where it was met by the keeper, who towed it to the rocky nook which served as harbor.

The moment a strong, steady face met her eyes, and a gruff, cheery voice hailed her, Rose gave way, and was carried up to the house, looking more like a beautiful drowned Ophelia than a living woman.

"Here, Sally, see to the poor thing; she's had a rough time on't. I'll take care of her sweetheart—and a nice job I'll have, I reckon, for if he ain't mad or drunk, he's had a stroke of lightnin', and looks as if he wouldn't get his hearin' in a hurry," said the old man as he housed his unexpected guests and stood staring at Done, who looked about him like one dazed. "You jest turn in younder and sleep it off, mate. We'll see to the lady, and right up your boat in the morning," the old man added.

"Be kind to Rose. I frightened her. I'll not forget you. Yes, let me sleep and get over this cursed folly as soon as possible," muttered this strange visitor.

Done threw himself down on the rough couch and tried to sleep, but every nerve was overstrained, every pulse beating like a trip-hammer, and everything about him was intensified and exaggerated with awful power. The thunder-shower seemed a wild hurricane, the quaint room a wilderness peopled with tormenting phantoms, and all the events of his life passed before him in an endless procession, which nearly maddened him. The old man looked weird and gigantic, his own voice sounded shrill and discordant, and the ceaseless murmur of Rose's incoherent wanderings haunted him like parts of a grotesque but dreadful dream.

All night he lay motionless, with staring eyes, feverish lips, and a mind on the rack, for the delicate machinery which had been tampered with revenged the wrong by torturing the foolish experimenter. All night Rose wept and sang, talked and cried for help in a piteous state of nervous excitement, for with her the trance came first, and the after-agitation was increased by the events of the evening. She slept at last, lulled by the old woman's motherly care, and Done was spared one tormenting fear, for he dreaded the consequences of this folly on her, more than upon himself.

As day dawned he rose, haggard and faint, and staggered out. At the door he met the keeper, who stopped him to report that the boat was in order, and a fair day coming. Seeing doubt and perplexity in the old man's eye, Done told him the truth, and added that he was going to the beach for a plunge, hoping by that simple tonic to restore his unstrung nerves.

He came back feeling like himself again, except for a dull headache, and a heavy sense of remorse weighing on his spirits, for he distinctly recollected all the events of the night. The old woman made him eat and drink, and in an hour he felt ready for the homeward trip.

Rose slept late, and when she woke soon recovered herself, for her dose had been a small one. When she had breakfasted and made a hasty toilet, she professed herself anxious to return at once. She dreaded yet longed to see Done, and when the time came armed herself with pride, feeling all a woman's shame at what had passed, and resolving to feign forgetfulness of the incidents of the previous night. Pale and cold as a statue she met him, but the moment he began to say humbly, "Forgive me, Rose," she silenced him with an imperious gesture and the command, "Don't speak of it; I only remember that it was very horrible, and wish to forget it all as soon as possible."

"All, Rose?" he added, significantly.

"Yes, all. No one would care to recall the follies of a hashish dream," she answered, turning hastily to hide the scarlet flush that would rise, and the eyes that would fall before his own.

"I never can forget, but I will be silent if you bid me."

"I do. Let us go. What will they think at the island? Mr. Done, give me your promise to tell no one, now or ever, that I tried that dangerous experiment. I will guard your secret also." She spoke eagerly and looked up imploringly.

"I promise," and he gave her his hand, holding her own with a wistful glance, till she drew it away and begged him to take her home.

Leaving hearty thanks and a generous token of their gratitude, they sailed away with a fair wind, finding in the freshness of the morning a speedy cure for tired bodies and excited minds. They said little, but it was impossible for Rose to preserve her coldness. The memory of the past night broke down her pride, and Done's tender glances touched her heart. She half hid her face behind her hand, and tried to compose herself for the scene to come, for as she approached the island, she saw Belle and her party waiting for them on the shore.

"Oh, Mr. Done, screen me from their eyes and questions as much as you can! I'm so worn out and nervous, I shall betray myself. You will help me?" And she turned to him with a confiding look, strangely at variance with her usual calm self-possession.

"I'll shield you with my life, if you will tell me why you took the hashish," he said, bent on knowing his fate.

"I hoped it would make me soft and lovable, like other women. I'm tired of being a lonely statue," she faltered, as if the truth was wrung from her by a power stronger than her will.

"And I took it to gain courage to tell my love. Rose, we have been near death together; let us share life together, and neither of us be any more lonely or afraid?"

He stretched his hand to her with his heart in his face, and she gave him hers with a look of tender submission, as he said ardently, "Heaven bless hashish, if its dreams end like this!"

THE CASE OF THE WIDOW

Margery Allingham

Margery Allingham (1904–1966) was one of the 'crime queens' of British detective fiction's golden age. Her mysteries, including *The Crime at Black Dudley*, *More Work for the Undertaker*, and *Tiger in the Smoke*, featured the aristocratic detective Albert Campion. She also wrote under the name Maxwell March.

DATE: Feb. 1, 20, 25 and 26, 1936
VENUE: London and Norfolk coast.
OFFICIALS: Superintendent Stanislaus Oates of the Central Branch, Criminal Investigation Department, Scotland Yard.
PRIVATE NOTES: Audacity of the fellow. Curiously attractive.
   Demonstration utterly convincing.
   Remarkable brandy.
   Thistledown gave me seven bottles of Imperial Tokay.
   Probably priceless. Very handsome of him (incredible stuff).

The second prettiest girl in Mayfair was thanking Superintendent Stanislaus Oates for the recovery of her diamond bracelet and the ring with the square-cut emerald in it, and Mr Campion, who had accompanied her to the ceremony, was admiring her technique.

She was doing it very charmingly; so charmingly, in fact, that the superintendent's depressing little office had taken on an air of garden-party gaiety which it certainly did not possess in the ordinary way, while the superintendent himself had undergone an even more sensational change.

His long dyspeptic face was transformed by a blush of smug satisfaction and he quite forgot the short lecture he had prepared for his visitor on The Carelessness Which Tempts the Criminal, or its blunter version, Stupidity Which Earns Its Own Reward.

It was altogether a most gratifying scene, and Mr Campion, seated in the visitor's chair, his long thin legs crossed and his pale eyes amused behind his horn-rimmed spectacles, enjoyed it to the full.

Miss Leonie Peterhouse-Vaughn raised her remarkable eyes to the superintendent's slightly sheepish face and spoke with deep earnestness.

"I honestly think you're wonderful," she said.

Realising that too much butter can have a disastrous effect on any dish, and not being at all certain of his old friend's digestive capabilities, Mr Campion coughed.

"He has his failures too," he ventured. "He's not omnipotent, you know. Just an ordinary man."

"Really?" said Miss Peterhouse-Vaughn with gratifying surprise.

"Oh yes; well, we're only human, miss." The superintendent granted Mr Campion a reproachful look. "Sometimes we have our little disappointments. Of course on those occasions we call in Mr Campion here," he added with a flash of malice.

Leonie laughed prettily and Mr Oates's ruffled fur subsided like a wave.

"Sometimes even he can't help us," he went on, encouraged, and, inspired, no doubt, by the theory that the greater the enemy the greater the honour, launched into an explanation perhaps not altogether discreet. "Sometimes we come up against a man who slips through our fingers every time. There's a man in London today who's been responsible for more trouble than I can mention. We know him, we know where he lives, we could put our hands on him any moment of the day or night, but have we any proof against him? Could we hold him for ten minutes without getting into serious trouble for molesting a respectable citizen? Could we? Well, we couldn't."

Miss Peterhouse-Vaughn's expression of mystified interest was very flattering.

"This is incredibly exciting," she said. "Who is he?—or mustn't you tell?"

The superintendent shook his head.

"Entirely against the regulations," he said regretfully, and then, on seeing her disappointment and feeling, no doubt, that his portentous declaration had fallen a little flat, he relented and made a compromise between his conscience and a latent vanity which Mr Campion had never before suspected. "Well, I'll show you this," he conceded. "It's a very curious thing."

With Leonie's fascinated eyes upon him, he opened a drawer in his desk and took out a single sheet torn from a week-old London evening paper. A small advertisement in the Situations Vacant column was ringed with blue pencil. Miss Peterhouse-Vaughn took it eagerly and Mr Campion got up lazily to read it over her shoulder.

WANTED: *Entertainer suitable for children's party. Good money offered to right man. Apply in person any evening. Widow, 13 Blakenham Gardens, W. 1.*

Leonie read the lines three times and looked up.

"But it seems quite ordinary," she said.

The superintendent nodded. "That's what any member of the public would think," he agreed, gracefully keeping all hint of condscension out of his tone. "And it would have escaped our notice too except for one thing, and that's the name and address. You see, the man I was telling you about happens to live at 13 Blakenham Gardens."

"Is his name Widow? How queer!"

"No, miss, it's not." Oates looked uncomfortable, seeing the pitfall too late. "I ought not to be telling you this," he went on severely. "This gentleman—and we've got nothing we can pin on him, remember—is known as 'The Widow' to the criminal classes. That's why this paragraph interested us. As it stands it's an ad for a crook, and the fellow has the impudence to use his own address! Doesn't even hide it under a box number."

Mr Campion eyed his old friend. He seemed mildly interested.

"Did you send someone along to answer it?" he enquired.

"We did." The superintendent spoke heavily. "Poor young Billings was kept there singing comic songs for three quarters of an hour while W——I mean this fellow—watched him without a smile. Then he told him he'd go down better at a police concert."

Miss Peterhouse-Vaughn looked sympathetic.

"What a shame!" she said gravely, and Mr Campion never admired her more.

"We sent another man," continued the superintendent, "but when he got there the servant told him the vacancy had been filled. We kept an eye on the place, too, but it wasn't easy. The whole crescent was a seething mass of would-be child entertainers."

"So you haven't an idea what he's up to?" Mr Campion seemed amused.

"Not the faintest," Oates admitted. "We shall in the end, though; I'll lay my bottom dollar. He was the moving spirit in that cussed Featherstone case, you know, and we're pretty certain it was he who slipped through the police net in the Barking business."

Mr Campion raised his eyebrows. "Blackmail and smuggling?" he said. "He seems to be a versatile soul, doesn't he?"

"He's up to anything," Oates declared. "Absolutely anything. I'd give a packet to get my hands on him. But what he wants with a kids' entertainer—if it is an entertainer he's after—I do not know."

"Perhaps he just wants to give a children's party?" suggested Miss Peterhouse-Vaughn and while the policeman was considering this possibility, evidently the one explanation which had not crossed his mind, she took her leave.

"I must thank you once again, Mr Oates," she said. "I can't tell you how terribly, terribly clever I think you are, and how awfully grateful I am, and how frightfully careful I'll be in future not to give you any more dreadful trouble."

It was a charming little speech in spite of her catastrophic adjectives and the superintendent beamed.

"It's been a pleasure, miss," he said.

As Mr Campion handed her into her mother's Daimler he regarded her coldly.

"A pretty performance," he remarked. "Tell me, what do you say when a spark of genuine gratitude warms your nasty little heart? My poor Oates!"

Miss Peterhouse-Vaughn grinned.

"I did do it well, didn't I," she said complacently. "He's rather a dear old goat."

Mr Campion was shocked and said so.

"The superintendent is a distinguished officer. I always knew that, of course, but this afternoon I discovered a broad streak of chivalry in him. In his place I think I might have permitted myself a few comments on the type of young woman who leaves a diamond bracelet and an emerald ring in the soap dish at a public restaurant and then goes smiling to Scotland Yard to ask for it back. The wretched man had performed a miracle for you and you call him a dear old goat."

Leonie was young enough to look abashed without losing her charm.

"Oh, but I am grateful," she said. "I think he's wonderful. But not so absolutely brilliant as somebody else."

"That's very nice of you, my child," Mr Campion prepared to unbend.

"Oh, not you, darling." Leonie squeezed his arm. "I was talking about the other man—The Widow. He's got real nerve, don't you think?—using his own address and making the detective sing and all that . . . So amusing!"

Her companion looked down at her severely.

"Don't make a hero out of *him*," he said.

"Why not?"

"Because, my dear little hideous, he's a crook. It's only while he remains uncaught that he's faintly interesting. Sooner or later your elderly admirer, the superintendent, is going to clap him under lock and key and then he'll just be an ordinary convict, who is anything but romantic, believe me."

Miss Peterhouse-Vaughn shook her head.

"He won't get caught," she said. "Or if he does—forgive me, darling—it'll be by someone much cleverer than you or Mr Oates."

Mr Campion's professional pride rebelled.

"What'll you bet?"

"Anything you like," said Leonie. "Up to two pounds," she added prudently.

Campion laughed. "The girl's learning caution at last!" he said. "I may hold you to that."

The conversation changed to the charity matinee of the day before, wherein Miss Peterhouse-Vaughn had appeared as Wisdom, and continued its easy course, gravitating naturally to the most important pending event in the Peterhouse-Vaughn family, the christening of Master Brian Desmond Peterhouse-Vaughn, nephew to Leonie, son to her elder brother, Desmond Brian, and godson to Mr Albert Campion.

It was his new responsibility as a godfather which led Mr Campion to take part in yet another elegant little ceremony some few days after the christening and nearly three weeks after Leonie's sensational conquest of Superintendent Oates's susceptible heart.

Mr Campion called to see Mr Thistledown in Cheese Street, E.C., and they went reverently to the cellars together.

Mr Thistledown was a small man, elderly and dignified. His white hair was inclined to flow a little and his figure was more suited, perhaps, to his vocation than to his name. As head of the small but distinguished firm of Thistledown, Friend and Son, Wine Importers since 1798, he very seldom permitted himself a personal interview with any client under the age of sixty-five, for at that year he openly believed the genus homo sapiens, considered solely as a connoisseur of vintage wine, alone attained full maturity.

Mr Campion, however, was an exception. Mr Thistledown thought of him as a lad still, but a promising one. He took his client's errand with all the gravity he felt it to deserve.

"Twelve dozen of port to be laid down for Master Brian Desmond Peterhouse-Vaughn," he said, rolling the words round his tongue as though they, too, had their flavour. "Let me see, it is now the end of '36. It will have to be a '27 wine. Then by the time your godson is forty—he won't want to drink it before that age, surely?—there should be a very fine fifty-year-old vintage awaiting him."

A long and somewhat heated discussion, or, rather, monologue, for Mr Campion was sufficiently experienced to offer no opinion, followed. The relative merits of Croft, Taylor, Da Silva, Noval and Fonseca were considered at length, and in the end Mr Campion followed his mentor through the sacred tunnels and personally affixed his seal upon a bin of Taylor, 1927.

Mr Thistledown was in favour of a stipulation to provide that Master Peter-house-Vaughn should not attain full control over his vinous inheritance until he attained the age of thirty, whereas Mr Campion preferred the more conventional twenty-one. Finally a compromise of twenty-five was agreed upon and the two gentlemen retired to Mr Thistledown's consulting room glowing with the conscious virtue of men who had conferred a benefit upon posterity.

The consulting room was comfortable. It was really no more than an arbour of bottles constructed in the vault of the largest cellar and was furnished with a table and chairs of solid ship's timber. Mr Thistledown paused by the table and hesitated before speaking. There was clearly something on his mind and Campion, who had always considered him slightly inhuman, a sort of living port crust, was interested.

When at last the old gentleman unburdened himself it was to make a short speech.

"It takes an elderly man to judge a port or a claret," he said, "but spirits are definitely in another category. Some men may live to be a hundred without ever realising the subtle differences of the finest rums. To judge a spirit one must be born with a certain kind of palate. Mr Campion, would you taste a brandy for me?"

His visitor was startled. Always a modest soul, he made no pretensions to conoisseurship and now he said so firmly.

"I don't know." Mr Thistledown regarded him seriously. "I have watched your taste for some years now and I am inclined to put you down as one of the few really knowledgeable younger men. Wait for me a moment."

He went out, and through the arbour's doorway Campion saw him conferring with the oldest and most cobwebby of the troglodyte persons who lurked about the vaults.

Considerably flattered in spite of himself, he sat back and awaited developments. Presently one of the younger myrmidons, a mere youth of fifty or so, appeared with a tray and a small selection of balloon glasses. He was followed by an elder with two bottles, and at the rear of the procession came Mr Thistledown himself with something covered by a large silk handkerchief. Not until they were alone did he remove the veil. Then, whipping the handkerchief aside, he produced a partly full half bottle with a new cork and no label. He held it up to the light and Mr Campion saw that the liquid within was of the true dark amber.

Still with the ritualistic air, Mr Thistledown polished a glass and poured a tablespoonful of the spirit, afterwards handing it to his client.

Feeling like a man with his honour at stake, Campion warmed the glass in his hand, sniffed at it intelligently, and finally allowed a little of the stuff to touch his tongue.

Mr Thistledown watched him earnestly. Campion tasted again and inhaled once more. Finally he set down his glass and grinned.

"I may be wrong," he said, "but it tastes like the real McKay."

Mr Thistledown frowned at the vulgarism. He seemed satisfied, however, and there was a curious mixture of pleasure and discomfort on his face.

"I put it down as a Champagne Fine, 1835," he said. "It has not, perhaps, quite the superb caress of the true Napoleon—but a brave, yes, a brave, brandy! The third best I have ever tasted in my life. And that, let me tell you, Mr Campion, is a very extraordinary thing."

He paused, looking like some old white cockatoo standing at the end of the table.

"I wonder if I might take you into my confidence?" he ventured at last. "Ah— a great many people do take you into their confidence, I believe? Forgive me for putting it that way."

Campion smiled. "I'm as secret as the grave," he said, "and if there's anything I can do I shall be delighted."

Mr Thistledown sighed with relief and became almost human.

"This confounded bottle was sent to me some little time ago," he said. "With it was a letter from a man called Gervaise Papulous; I don't suppose you've ever heard of him, but he wrote a very fine monograph on brandies some years ago which was greatly appreciated by connoisseurs. I had an idea he lived a hermit's life somewhere in Scotland, but that's neither here nor there. The fact remains that when I had this note from an address in Half Moon Street I recognised the name immediately. It was a very civil letter, asking me if I'd mind, as an expert, giving my opinion of the age and quality of the sample."

He paused and smiled faintly.

"I was a little flattered, perhaps," he said. "After all, the man is a well-known authority himself. Anyway, I made the usual tests, tasted it and compared it with the oldest and finest stuff we have in stock. We have a few bottles of 1848 and one or two of the 1835. I made the most careful comparisons and at last I decided that the sample was a '35 brandy, but not the same blend as our own. I wrote him; I said I did not care to commit myself, but I gave him my opinion for what it was worth and I appended my reasons for forming it."

Mr Thistledown's precise voice ceased and his colour heightened.

"By return I received a letter thanking me for mine and asking me whether I would care to consider an arrangement whereby I could buy the identical spirit in any quantity I cared to name at a hundred and twenty shillings a dozen, excluding duty—or in other words, ten shillings per bottle."

Mr Campion sat up. "Ten shillings?" he said.

"Ten shillings," repeated Mr Thistledown. "The price of a wireless licence," he added with contempt. "Well, as you can imagine, Mr Campion, I thought there must be some mistake. Our own '35 is listed at sixty shillings a bottle and you cannot get finer value anywhere in London. The stuff is rare. In a year or two it will be priceless. I considered this sample again and reaffirmed my own first opinion. Then I reread the letter and noticed the peculiar phrase—'an arrangement whereby you will be able to purchase.' I thought about it all day and finally I put on my hat and went down to see the man."

He glanced at his visitor almost timidly. Campion was reassuring.

"If it was genuine it was not a chance to be missed," he murmured.

"Exactly." Mr Thistledown smiled. "Well, I saw him, a younger man than I had imagined but well informed, and I received quite a pleasant impression. I asked him frankly where he got the brandy and he came out with an extraordinary suggestion. He asked me first if I was satisfied with the sample, and I said I was or I should hardly have come to see him. Then he said the whole matter was a secret at the moment, but that he was asking certain well-informed persons to a private conference and something he called a scientific experiment. Finally he offered me an invitation. It is to take place next Monday evening in a little hotel on the Norfolk coast where Mr Papulous says the ideal conditions for his experiment exist."

Mr Campion's interest was thoroughly aroused.

"I should go," he said.

Mr Thistledown spread out his hands.

"I had thought of it," he admitted. "As I came out of the flat at Half Moon Street I passed a man I knew on the stairs. I won't mention his name and I won't say his firm is exactly a rival of ours, but—well, you know how it is. Two or three old firms get the reputation for supplying certain rare vintages. Their names are equally good and naturally there is a certain competition between them. If this fellow has happened on a whole cellar full of this brandy I should like to have as good a chance of buying it as the next man, especially at the price. But in my opinion and in my experience that is too much to hope for, and that is why I have ventured to mention the matter to you."

A light dawned upon his client.

"You want me to attend the conference and make certain everything's above-board?"

"I hardly dared to suggest it," he said, "but since you are such an excellent judge, and since your reputation as an investigator—if I may be forgiven the term—is so great, I admit the thought did go through my mind."

Campion picked up his glass and sniffed its fragrance.

"My dear man, I'd jump at it," he said. "Do I pass myself off as a member of the firm?"

Mr Thistledown looked owlish.

"In the circumstances I think we might connive at that little inexactitude," he murmured. "Don't you?"

"I think we'll have to," said Mr Campion.

When he saw the "little hotel on the Norfolk coast" at half-past six on the following Monday afternoon the thought came to him that it was extremely fortunate for the proprietor that it should be so suitable for Mr Papulous's experiment, for it was certainly not designed to be of much interest to any ordinary winter visitor. It was a large country public house, not old enough to be picturesque, standing by itself at the end of a lane some little distance from a cold and sleepy village. In the summer, no doubt, it provided a headquarters for a great many picnic parties, but in winter it was deserted.

Inside it was warm and comfortable enough, however, and Campion found a curious little company seated round the fire in the lounge. His host rose to greet him and he was aware at once of a considerable personality.

He saw a tall man with a shy ingratiating manner, whose clothes were elegant and whose face was remarkable. His deep-set eyes were dark and intelligent and his wide mouth could smile disarmingly, but the feature which was most distinctive was the way in which his iron-grey hair drew into a clean-cut peak in the centre of his high forehead, giving him an odd, Mephistophelean appearance.

"Mr Fellowes?" he said, using the alias Campion and Mr Thistledown had agreed upon. "I heard from your firm this morning. Of course I'm very sorry not to have Mr Thistledown here. He says in his note that I am to regard you as his second self. You handle the French side, I understand?"

"Yes. It was only by chance that I was in England yesterday when Mr Thistledown asked me to come."

"I see." Mr Papulous seemed contented with the explanation. Campion looked a mild, inoffensive young man, even a little foolish.

He was introduced to the rest of the company round the fire and was interested to see that Mr Thistledown had been right in his guess. Half a dozen of the best-known smaller and older wine firms were represented, in most cases by their senior partners.

Conversation, however, was not as general as might have been expected among men of such similar interests. On the contrary, there was a distinct atmosphere of restraint, and it occurred to Mr Campion that they were all close rivals and each man had not expected to see the others.

Mr Papulous alone seemed happily unconscious of any discomfort. He stood behind his chair at the head of the group and glanced round him with satisfaction.

"It's really very kind of you all to have come," he said in his deep musical voice. "Very kind indeed. I felt we must have experts, the finest experts in the world, to test this thing, because it's revolutionary—absolutely revolutionary."

A large old gentleman with a hint of superciliousness in his manner glanced up.

"When are we going to come to the horses, Mr Papulous?"

His host turned to him with a depreciatory smile.

"Not until after dinner, I'm afraid, Mr Jerome. I'm sorry to seem so secretive, but the whole nature of the discovery is so extraordinary that I want you to see the demonstration with your own eyes."

Mr Jerome, whose name Campion recognised as belonging to the moving spirit of Bolitho Brothers, of St Mary Axe, seemed only partly mollified. He laughed.

"Is it the salubrious air of this particular hotel that you need for your experiment, may I ask?" he enquired.

"Oh no, my dear sir. It's the stillness." Mr Papulous appeared to be completely oblivious of any suggestion of a sneer. "It's the utter quiet. At night, round about ten o'clock, there is a lack of vibration here, so complete that you can almost feel it, if I may use such a contradiction in terms. Now, Mr Fellowes, dinner's at seven-thirty. Perhaps you'd care to see your room?"

Campion was puzzled. As he changed for the meal, a gesture which seemed to be expected of him, he surveyed the situation with growing curiosity. Papulous was no ordinary customer. He managed to convey an air of conspiracy and mystery while appearing himself as open and simple as the day. Whatever he was up to he was certainly a good salesman.

The dinner was simple and well cooked and was served by Papulous's own man. There was no alcohol and the dishes were not highly seasoned, out of deference, their host explained, to the test that was to be put to their palates later on.

When it was over and the mahogany had been cleared of dessert, a glass of clear water was set before each guest and from the head of the table Mr Papulous addressed his guests. He made a very distinguished figure, leaning forward across the polished wood, the candlelight flickering on his deeply lined face and high heart-shaped forehead.

"First of all let me recapitulate," he said. "You all know my name and you have all been kind enough to say that you have read my little book. I mention this because I want you to realize that by asking you down here to witness a most extraordinary demonstration I am taking my reputation in my hands. Having made that point, let me remind you that you have each of you, with the single exception of Mr Fellowes, been kind enough to give me your considered views on a sample of brandy which I sent you. In every case, I need hardly mention, opinion was the same—a Champagne Fine of 1835."

A murmur of satisfaction not untinged with relief ran round the table and Mr Papulous smiled.

"Well," he said, "frankly that would have been my own opinion had I not known—mark you, I say 'known'—that the brandy I sent you was a raw cognac of nearly a hundred years later—to be exact, of 1932."

There was a moment of bewilderment, followed by an explosion from Mr Jerome.

"I hope you're not trying to make fools of us, sir," he said severely. "I'm not going to sit here, and——"

"One moment, one moment." Papulous spoke soothingly. "You really must forgive me. I know you all too well by repute to dare to make such a statement without following it immediately by the explanation to which you are entitled. As you're all aware, the doctoring of brandy is an old game. Such dreadful additions as vanilla and burnt sugar have all been used in their time and will, no doubt, be used again, but such crude deceptions are instantly detected by the cultured palate. This is something different."

Mr Jerome began to seethe.

"Are you trying to interest us in a fake, sir?" he demanded. "Because, if so, let me tell you I for one am not interested."

There was a chorus of hasty assent in which Mr Campion virtuously joined.

Gervaise Papulous smiled faintly.

"But of course not," he said. "We are all experts. The true expert knows that no fake can be successful, even should we so far forget ourselves as to countenance its existence. I am bringing you a discovery—not a trick, not a clever fraud, but a genuine discovery which may revolutionise the whole market. As you know, time is the principal factor in the maturing of spirits. Until now time has been the one factor which could not be artificially replaced. An old brandy, therefore, is quite a different thing from a new one."

Mr Campion blinked. A light was beginning to dawn upon him.

Mr Papulous continued. There seemed to be no stopping him. At the risk of boring his audience he displayed a great knowledge of technical detail and went through the life history of an old liqueur brandy from the time it was an unripe grapeskin on a vine outside Cognac.

When he had finished he paused dramatically, adding softly:

"What I hope to introduce to you tonight, gentlemen, is the latest discovery of science, a method of speeding up this long and wearisome process so that the whole business of maturing the spirit takes place in a few minutes instead of a hundred years. You have all examined the first fruits of this method already and have been interested enough to come down here. Shall we go on?"

The effect of his announcement was naturally considerable. Everybody began to talk at once save Mr Campion, who sat silent and thoughtful. It occurred to him that his temporary colleagues were not only interested in making a great deal of money but very much alarmed at the prospect of losing a considerable quantity also.

"If it's true it'll upset the whole damned trade," murmured his next-door neighbour, a little thin man with wispy straw-coloured hair.

Papulous rose. "In the next room the inventor, Mr. Philippe Jessant, is waiting to demonstrate," he said. "He began work on the idea during the period of pro-hibition in America and his researches were assisted there by one of the richest men in the world, but when the country was restored to sanity his patron lost interest in the work and he was left to perfect it unassisted. You will find him a simple, uneducated, unbusinesslike man, like many inventors. He came to me for help because he had read my little book and I am doing what I can for him by introducing him to you. Conditions are now ideal. The house is perfectly still. Will you come with me?"

The sceptical but excited little company filed into the large "commercial" room on the other side of the passage. The place had been stripped of fur-niture save for a half circle of chairs and a large deal table. On the table was a curious contraption, vaguely resembling two or three of those compli-cated coffee percolators which seemed to be designed solely for the wedding-present trade.

An excitable little man in a long brown overall was standing behind the table. If not an impressive figure, he was certainly an odd one, with his longish hair and gold-rimmed pince-nez.

"Quiet, please. I must beg of you quiet," he commanded, holding up his hand as they appeared. "We must have no vibration, no vibration at all, if I am to succeed."

He had a harsh voice and a curious foreign accent, which Campion could not instantly trace, but his manner was authoritative and the experts tiptoed gently to their seats.

"Now," said Mr Jessant, his small eyes flashing, "I leave all explanations to my friend here. For me, I am only interested in the demonstration. You understand?"

He glared at them and Papulous hastened to explain.

"Mr Jessant does not mean the human voice, of course," he murmured. "It is vibration, sudden movement, of which he is afraid."

"Quiet," cut in the inventor impatiently. "When a spirit matures in the ordinary way what does it have? —quiet, darkness, peace. These conditions are essential. Now we will begin, if you please."

It was a simple business. A clear-glass decanter of brandy was produced and duly smelt and sampled by each guest. Papulous himself handed round the glasses and poured the liquid. By unanimous consent it was voted a raw spirit. The years 1932 and 1934 were both mentioned.

Then the same decanter was emptied into the contraption on the table and its progress watched through a system of glass tubes and a filter into a large retort-shaped vessel at the foot of the apparatus.

M. Jessant look up.

"Now," he said softly. "You will come, one at a time, please, and examine my invention. Walk softly."

The inspection was made and the man in the brown overall covered the retort with a hood composed of something that looked like black rubber. For a while he busied himself with thermometers and a little electric battery.

"It's going on now," he explained, suppressed excitement in his voice. "Every second roughly corresponds to a year—a long, dark, dismal year. Now—we shall see."

The hood was removed, fresh glasses brought, and the retort itself carefully detached from the rest of the apparatus.

Mr Jerome was the first to examine the liquid it contained and his expression was ludicrous in its astonishment.

"It's incredible!" he said at last. "Incredible! I can't believe it. . . . There are certain tests I should like to make, of course, but I could swear this is an 1835 brandy."

The others were of the same opinion and even Mr Campion was impressed. The inventor was persuaded to do his experiment again. To do him justice he complied willingly.

"It is the only disadvantage," he said. "So little can be treated at the one time. I tell my friend I should like to make my invention foolproof and sell the machines and the instructions to the public, but he tells me no."

"No indeed!" ejaculated Mr Campion's neighbour. "Good heavens! it would knock the bottom out of half my trade . . ."

When at last the gathering broke up in excitement it was after midnight. Mr Papulous addressed his guests.

"It is late," he said. "Let us go to bed now and consider the whole matter in the morning when M. Jessant can explain the theory of his process. Meanwhile, I am sure you will agree with me that we all have something to think about."

A somewhat subdued company trooped off upstairs. There was little conversation. A man does not discuss a revolutionary discovery with his nearest rival.

Campion came down in the morning to find Mr Jerome already up. He was pacing the lounge and turned on the young man almost angrily.

"I like to get up at six," he said without preamble, "but there were no servants in the place. A woman, her husband and a maid came along at seven. It seems Papulous made them sleep out. Afraid of vibration, I suppose. Well, it's an extraordinary discovery, isn't it? If I hadn't seen it with my own eyes I should never have believed it. I suppose one's got to be prepared for progress, but I can't say I like it. Never did."

He lowered his voice and came closer.

"We shall have to get together and suppress it, you know," he said. "Only thing to do. We can't have a thing like this blurted out to the public and we can't have any single firm owning the secret. Anyway, that's my opinion."

Campion murmured that he did not care to express his own without first consulting Mr Thistledown.

"Quite, quite. There'll be a good many conferences in the City this afternoon," said Mr Jerome gloomily. "And that's another thing. D'you know there isn't a telephone in this confounded pub?"

Campion's eyes narrowed.

"Is that so?" he said softly. "That's very interesting."

Mr Jerome shot him a suspicious glance.

"In my opinion . . ." he began heavily but got no further. The door was thrust open and the small wispy-haired man, who had been Campion's neighbour at dinner, came bursting into the room.

"I say," he said, "a frightful thing! The little inventor chap has been attacked in the night. His machine is smashed and the plans and formula are stolen. Poor old Papulous is nearly off his head."

Both Campion and Jerome started for the doorway and a moment later joined the startled group on the landing. Gervaise Papulous, an impressive figure in a long black dressing gown, was standing with his back to the inventor's door.

"This is terrible, terrible!" he was saying. "I beseech you all, go downstairs and wait until I see what is best to be done. My poor friend has only just re-gained consciousness."

Jerome pushed his way through the group.

"But this is outrageous," he began.

Papulous towered over him, his eyes dark and angry.

"It is just as you say, outrageous," he said, and Mr Jerome quailed before the suppressed fury in his voice.

"Look here," he began, "you surely don't think . . . you're not insinuating . . ."

"I am only thinking of my poor friend," said Mr Papulous.

Campion went quietly downstairs.

"What on earth does this mean?" demanded the small wispy-haired gentle-man, who had remained in the lounge.

Campion grinned. "I rather fancy we shall all find that out pretty clearly in about an hour," he said.

He was right. Mr Gervaise Papulous put the whole matter to them in the bluntest possible way as they sat dejectedly looking at the remains of what had proved a very unsatisfactory breakfast.

M. Jessant, his head in bandages and his face pale with exhaustion, had told a heartbreaking story. He had awakened to find a pad of chloroform across his mouth and nose. It was dark and he could not see his assailant, who also struck him repeatedly. His efforts to give the alarm were futile and in the end the anaes-thetic had overpowered him.

When at last he had come to himself his apparatus had been smashed and his precious black pocketbook, which held his calculations and which he always kept under his pillow, had gone.

At this point he had broken down completely and had been led away by Papulous's man. Mr Gervaise Papulous then took the floor. He looked pale and nervous and there was an underlying suggestion of righteous anger and indignation in his manner which was very impressive.

"I won't waste time by telling you how appalled I am by this monstrous attack," he began, his fine voice trembling. "I can only tell you the facts. We were alone in this house last night. Even my own man slept out in the village. I arranged this to ensure ideal conditions for the experiment. The landlady reports that the doors were locked this morning and the house had not been entered from the outside. Now you see what this means? Until last night only the inventor and I knew of the existence of a secret which is of such great importance to all of you here. Last night we told you, we took you into your confidence, and now . . ." he shrugged his shoulders. "Well, we have been robbed and my friend assaulted. Need I say more?"

An excited babble of protest arose and Mr Jerome seemed in danger of apoplexy. Papulous remained calm and a little contemptuous.

"There is only one thing to do," he said, "but I hesitated before calling in the police, because, of course, only one of you can be guilty and the secret must still be in the house, whereas I know the publicity which cannot be avoided will be detrimental to you all. And not only to yourselves personally, but to the firms you represent."

He paused and frowned.

"The Press is so ignorant," he said. "I am so afraid you may all be represented as having come here to see some sort of faking process—new brandy into old. It doesn't sound convincing, does it?"

His announcement burst like a bomb in the quiet room. Mr Jerome sat very still, his mouth partly open. Somebody began to speak but thought better of it. A long unhappy silence supervened.

Gervaise Papulous cleared his throat.

"I am sorry," he said. "I must either have my friend's notebook back and full compensation, or I must send for the police. What else can I do?"

Mr Jerome pulled himself together.

"Wait," he said in a smothered voice. "Before you do anything rash we must have a conference. I've been thinking over this discovery of yours, Mr Papulous, and in my opinion it raises very serious considerations for the whole trade."

There was a murmur of agreement in the room and he went on.

"The one thing none of us can afford is publicity. In the first place, even if the thing becomes generally known it certainly won't become generally believed. The public doesn't rely on its palate; it relies on our labels, and that puts us in a very awkward position. This final development precipitates everything. We must clear up this mystery in private and then decide what is best to be done."

There was a vigorous chorus of assent, but Mr Papulous shook his head.

"I'm afraid I can't agree," he said coldly. "In the ordinary way M. Jessant and I would have been glad to meet you in any way, but this outrage alters everything. I insist on a public examination unless, of course," he added deliberately, "unless you care to take the whole matter out of our hands."

"What do you mean?" Mr Jerome's voice was faint.

The tall man with the deeply lined face regarded him steadily.

"Unless you care to club together and buy us out," said Mr Papulous. "Then you can settle the matter as you like. The sum M. Jessant had in mind was fifteen thousand pounds, a very reasonable price for such a secret."

There was silence after he had spoken.

"Blackmail," said Mr Campion under his breath and at the same moment his glance lighted on Mr Papulous's most outstanding feature. His eyebrows rose and an expression of incredulity, followed by amazement, passed over his face. Then he kicked himself gently under the breakfast table. He rose.

"I must send a wire to my principal," he said. "You'll understand I'm in an impossible position and must get in touch with Mr Thistledown at once."

Papulous regarded him.

"If you will write your message my man will despatch it from the village," he said politely and there was no mistaking the implied threat.

Campion understood he was not to be allowed to make any private communication with the outside world. He looked blank.

"Thank you," he said and took out a pencil and a loose-leaf notebook.

"Unexpected development," he wrote. "Come down immediately. Inform Charlie and George cannot lunch Tuesday. A. C. Fellowes."

Papulous took the message, read it and went out with it, leaving a horrified group behind him.

Mr Thistledown received Mr Campion's wire at eleven o'clock and read it carefully. The signature particularly interested him. Shutting himself in his private room, he rang up Scotland Yard and was fortunate in discovering Superintendent Oates at his desk. He dictated the wire carefully and added with a depreciatory cough:

"Mr Campion told me to send on to you any message from him signed with his own initials. I don't know if you can make much of this. It seems very ordinary to me."

"Leave all that to us, sir." Oates sounded cheerful. "Where is he, by the way?"

Mr Thistledown gave the address and hung up the receiver. At the other end of the wire the superintendent unlocked a drawer in his desk and took out a small red manuscript book. Each page was ruled with double columns and filled with Mr Campion's own elegant handwriting. Oates ran a forefinger down the left-hand column on the third page.

"Carrie . . . Catherine . . . Charles . . ."

His eye ran across the page

"Someone you want," he read and looked on down the list.

The legend against the word "George" was brief. "Two" it said simply.

Oates turned to the back of the book. There were several messages under the useful word "lunch." "Come to lunch" meant "Send two men." "Lunch with me" was translated "Send men armed," and "Cannot lunch" was "Come yourself."

"Tuesday" was on another page. The superintendent did not trouble to look it up. He knew its meaning. It was "hurry."

He wrote the whole message out on a pad.

"Unexpected developments. Come down immediately. Someone you want (two). Come yourself. Hurry. Campion."

He sighed. "Energetic chap," he commented and pressed a bell for Sergeant Bloom.

As it happened, it was Mr Gervaise Papulous himself who caught the first glimpse of the police car which pulled up outside the lonely little hotel. He was standing by the window in an upper room whose floor was so flimsily constructed that he could listen with ease to the discussion taking place in the lounge below. There the unfortunate experts were still arguing. The only point on which they all agreed was the absolute necessity of avoiding a scandal.

As the car stopped and the superintendent sprang out and made for the door Papulous caught a glimpse of his official, looking figure. He swung round savagely to the forlorn little figure who sat hunched up on the bed.

"You peached, damn you!" he whispered.

"Me?" The man who had been calling himself "Jessant" sat up in indignation. "Me peach?" he repeated, his foreign accent fading into honest South London. "Don't be silly. And you pay up, my lad. I'm fed up with this. First I do me stuff, then you chloroform me, then you bandage me, then you keep me shut up 'ere, and now you accuse me of splitting. What you playing at?"

"You're lying you little rat." Papulous's voice was dangerously soft and he strode swiftly across the room towards the man on the bed, who shrank back in sudden alarm.

"Here—that'll do, that'll do. What's going on here?"

It was Oates who spoke. Followed by Campion and the sergeant he strode across the room.

"Let the fellow go," he commanded. "Good heavens, man, you're choking him."

Doubling his fist, he brought it up under the other man's wrists with a blow which not only loosed their hold but sent their owner staggering back across the room.

The man on the bed let out a howl and stumbled towards the door into the waiting arms of Sergeant Bloom, but Oates did not notice him. His eyes were fixed upon the face of the tall man on the other side of the room.

"The Widow!" he ejaculated. "Well I'll be damned!"

The other smiled.

"More than probably, my dear Inspector. Or have they promoted you?" he said. "But at the moment I'm afraid you're trespassing."

The superintendent glanced enquiringly at the mild and elegant figure at his side.

"False pretences is the charge," murmured Mr Campion affably. "There are certain rather unpleasant traces of blackmail in the matter, but false pretences will do. There are six witnesses and myself."

The man whose alias was The Widow stared at his accuser.

"Who are you?" he demanded, and then, as the answer dawned upon him, he swore softly. "Campion," he said. "Albert Campion . . . I ought to have recognised you from your description."

Campion grinned. "That's where I had the advantage of you," he said.

Mr Campion and the superintendent drove back to London together, leaving a very relieved company of experts to travel home in their own ways. Oates was jubilant.

"Got him," he said. "Got him at last. And a clear case. A pretty little swindle too. Just like him. If you hadn't been there all those poor devils would have paid up something. They're the kind of people he goes for, folk whose business depends on their absolute integrity. They all represent small firms, you see, with old, conservative clients. When did you realise that he wasn't the real Gervaise Papulous?"

"As soon as I saw him I thought it unlikely." Campion grinned as he spoke. "Before I left town I rang up the publishers of the Papulous monograph. They had lost sight of him, they said, but from their publicity department I learned that Papulous was born in '72. So as soon as I saw our friend The Widow I realised that he was a good deal younger than the real man. However, like a fool I didn't get on to the swindle until this morning. It was when he was putting on that brilliant final act of his. I suddenly recognised him and of course the whole thing came to me in a flash."

"Recognised him?" Oates looked blank. "I never described him to you."

Mr Campion looked modest. "D'you remember showing off to a very pretty girl I brought up to your office, and so far forgetting yourself as to produce an advertisement from an evening paper?" he enquired.

"I remember the ad," Oates said doggedly. "The fellow advertised for a kids' entertainer. But I don't remember him including a photograph of himself."

"He printed his name," Campion persisted. "It's a funny nickname. The significance didn't occur to me until I looked at him this morning, knowing that he was a crook. I realised that he was tricking us but I couldn't see how. Then his face gave him away."

"His face?"

"My dear fellow, you haven't spotted it yet. I'm glad of that. It didn't come to me for a bit. Consider that face. How do crooks get their names? How did Beaky Doyle get his name? Why was Cauliflower Edwards so called? Think of his forehead, man. Think of his hair."

"Peak," said the superintendent suddenly. "Of course, a widow's peak! Funny I didn't think of that before. It's obvious when it comes to you. But even so," he added more seriously, "I wonder you cared to risk sending for me on that alone. Plenty of people have a widow's peak. You'd have looked silly if he'd been on the level."

"Oh, but I had the advertisement as well," Campion objected. "Taken in conjunction, the two things are obvious. That demonstration last night was masterly. Young brandy went in at one end of the apparatus and old brandy came out at the other, and we saw, or thought we saw, the spirit the whole time. There was only one type of man who could have done it—a children's party entertainer."

Oates shook his head.

"I'm only a poor demented policeman," he said derisively. "My mind doesn't work. I'll buy it."

Campion turned to him. "My good Oates, have you ever been to a children's party?"

"No."

"Well, you've been a child, I suppose?"

"I seem to remember something like it."

"Well, when you were a child what entertained you? Singing? Dancing? *The Wreck of the Hesperus?* No, my dear friend, there's only one kind of performer who goes down well with children and that is a member of the brotherhood of which Jessant is hardly an ornament. A magician, Oates. In other words, a conjurer. And a damned good trick he showed us all last night!"

He trod on the accelerator and the car rushed on again.

The superintendent sat silent for a long time. Then he glanced up.

"That *was* a pretty girl," he said. "Nice manners too."

"Leonie?" Campion nodded. "That reminds me, I must phone her when we get back to town."

"Oh?" The superintendent was interested. "Nothing I can do for you, I suppose?" he enquired archly.

Campion smiled. "Hardly," he said. "I want to tell her she owes me two pounds."

DEAD CLOSE

Lin Anderson

> **Lin Anderson** has made significant contributions to the 'Tartan Noir' genre. The creator of forensic scientist Rhoda MacLeod, her novels include *Driftnet*, *Dark Flight*, and *None But the Dead*. In 2012, she co-founded the Bloody Scotland crime writing festival.

Doug Cameron stared wide-eyed into the darkness, his heart racing, fear prickling his skin. The dream. As fresh now as it had been seventeen years ago. For a few moments Rebecca was alive, the swell of her pregnancy as clear as her terrified expression, then she was running from him as though he was the source of her fear.

A police siren wailed past in tune with his thoughts, its blue light flickering his rain-splattered window. He rose and went to watch the squad car's progress, leaning against the window frame, reminding himself that in 48 hours that sound would belong to his past. Just like the view from the bedroom window. Just like Rebecca.

When he felt steadier, he went through to the kitchen and began the process of making coffee, glancing at the photograph on the fridge door as he fetched out the milk carton. He'd taken the picture from the garden of his future home. A view of the flat-topped slopes of Duncaan on the Island of Raasay instead of Edinburgh Castle. Not a bad exchange, he decided.

Cameron settled at the kitchen table, pulled over his work box and began the intricate task of tying a new fishing fly. The only thing that helped him forget the dream, and the past.

Detective Sergeant James Boyd woke with a start. Immediately, his body reacted to its cramped position on the sofa, sending waves of pain through his knees and lower back. Boyd wasn't sure which noise had wakened him, the screaming baby or his mobile. Through the open bedroom door he could see Bev put their young son to the breast, silencing his cries. Boyd answered the duty officer in monosyllables, pulling on his trousers and shirt as he did so. He turned, sensing Bev in the doorway. She looked pointedly at him.

'I have to go to work.'

Bev said nothing, but her expression was the same as always. Tired, resentful, desperate.

'I'm sorry,' he tried.

'Will Susan be there?' she said sharply.

Boyd covered guilt with irritation. 'She's forensic. If there's a crime, she's there.'

Bev turned on her heel, Rory still attached to her breast. The last thing Boyd saw before the bedroom door banged shut was a small chubby hand clutching the air.

When his phone rang, Cameron contemplated ignoring it. The only call he would get at this time was one he didn't want.

'Glad you're up, Sir.' His Detective Sergeant's voice was suspiciously cheery. 'We've had a call out.'

'I've retired,' Cameron tried.

'Not till Tuesday,' Boyd reminded him.

Cameron listened in silence to the details. A serious incident had been reported at Greyfriars Churchyard, a stone's throw from his flat.

'I'll walk round,' he offered.

'No need, Sir. I'll be with you in five minutes.'

Cameron wondered if Boyd suspected he wouldn't come otherwise.

Boyd's car stank of stale vinegar, the door pocket stuffed with fish and chip wrappers, a sure sign he wasn't eating at home. His DS looked rough; stubble-faced and bleary-eyed.

'How's the new arrival?' Cameron asked.

'Only happy when he's attached to Bev's tit.'

'A typical male then.'

Boyd attempted a smile. Cameron thought about adding something, like 'Hang on in there. Things'll get better', but didn't know if that was true.

They were at the graveyard in minutes, sweeping past the statue of Greyfriars Bobby and through the gates of the ancient churchyard. Ahead, the pale edifice that was the church loomed out of an early morning mist.

A couple of uniforms stood aside to let the two men enter the mausoleum; one of many that lined the walls of the graveyard. Inside, the air was musty and chill. The light-headed feeling Cameron had experienced earlier returned, and he reached out to steady himself against the doorframe, bowing his head to relieve the sudden pressure between his eyes. The beam from Boyd's high-powered torch played over the interior, finally settling on a pool of fresh blood next to a stone casket.

'The caller reported seeing a figure run in through the gate. Then they heard a woman scream.'

Cameron said nothing. He wanted to make it plain that if Boyd expected to take over as DI, this was the time to start.

'We've done an initial search of the graveyard. Nothing so far. And no blood except in here.'

Cameron registered the oddity of this, but made no comment. He didn't want to be drawn in. He didn't want his brain to focus on anything other than his departure.

They emerged to find a parked forensic van and two SOCOs getting kitted up. Cameron watched as Boyd and the young woman exchanged looks. He walked out of hearing, not wanting to be party to something he couldn't prevent. Besides, what could he say? Don't piss on your wife or you could end up like me?

He had no idea what made him look up. The medieval stone tenement behind him merged with the back wall of the crypt. It was blank-faced, except for one narrow window. The young woman who watched him was in shadow but Cameron briefly made out a pale face and long dark hair, before she stepped out of sight.

It took him five minutes to circumnavigate the building and gain entry. The internal stairwell spiralled swiftly from ground level, one door on each floor. He climbed to the second landing and knocked.

When the young woman opened the door, Cameron's voice froze in his throat.

Cameron had been a detective long enough to read body language pretty accurately. Susan was on her knees on the muddy grass, Boyd trying hard not to look at her upturned buttocks. He stood to attention when he spotted Cameron. Another sign.

'I spoke to a girl living up there,' Cameron pointed at the window. 'She says she was wakened by the siren. Didn't see or hear anything before that.'

Boyd gave him an odd look. Cameron wasn't planning to say the girl looked so like Rebecca it'd almost given him a heart attack, but wondered if the shock still showed on his face.

'Well the police dog was right. It is a grave, but not a fresh one.' Susan sat back to reveal a sunken area in the muddy trampled grass. 'They buried plague victims here in medieval times. There were so many it raised the ground level by twenty feet. Heavy rain sometimes washes the top soil away, exposing the remains.'

Cameron stepped closer, his eye caught by a glint of metal.

'What's that?'

Susan fished it out and wiped off the mud. 'Looks like a brooch.' She handed it over.

Cameron felt the prick as the pin caught his thumb. Blood oozed from the wound to form a red bubble. The sight of it made him nauseous.

'The plague bacteria are way out of date,' Susan quipped, 'but I'd renew your tetanus if I were you.' She slipped the brooch into an evidence bag. 'I should have something for you on the blood in the crypt in twenty-four hours.'

'That's Boyd's department now,' Cameron told her.

He left them to it, giving the excuse of packing to cover his early departure. The truth was, in his head he was no longer a policeman. Thirty-five years of detective work had come and gone and the city was no better or safer now than when he'd begun. Worse than that, the dream this morning and the young woman he'd spoken to in the flat above the graveyard had only served to remind Cameron that the one case he should have solved, he never had.

It wasn't much for a lifetime. Cameron surveyed the meagre group of boxes. Everything had been packed except the books. There wasn't much shelf space at the cottage. He would have to be ruthless.

He started well, splitting the books into two piles, one for Cancer Research, the other destined for Raasay. There were at least half a dozen on fly fishing, all of which went on the Raasay pile. The last book on the shelf was one about Edinburgh's past. Cameron recognised it as belonging to Rebecca. Not a native to the city, she'd taken an amused interest in its medieval history, both fact and fiction. The photograph fell out as he transferred the book to the Raasay pile.

Rebecca stood by a dark expanse of water, laughing as she tried to anchor her long dark hair against the wind. On the lapel of her jacket she wore a brooch. Cameron suddenly remembered buying her the brooch from a silversmith near Glendale as a birthday present – a swirling Celtic pattern, not unlike the one they'd found in the ancient grave.

The flashback had all the power and detail of the original event. Rebecca standing next to the counter, her head bowed as she examined the selection. He could even smell her perfume as she turned to show him which one she'd chosen.

Cameron sat down heavily, his legs like water. This was how it had been when she'd first disappeared. The powerful, terrible dreams; the intensity of her presence. The fear that she was in danger and he couldn't save her.

He had no idea how long he sat there, unmoving, before he heard the buzzer.

Boyd stood awkwardly amidst the packing cases. Cameron thought again how much he liked his DS. He wanted to tell Boyd he would make a good Inspector but he shouldn't let the job take over his life. Instead, Cameron said nothing.

He'd laid the Edinburgh book on the Raasay pile. Boyd picked it up, checked out the cover and flicked through a few pages. Cameron was aware his DS was stalling for time. There was something he wanted to say, but didn't know how.

'You don't believe in all this stuff, Sir?'

'What stuff?'

'Ghosts?'

Boyd's eyes were shadowed from lack of sleep. The pregnancy, Cameron gathered, had been unplanned. The timing wasn't good for him or Bev, Boyd had said. Cameron suddenly recalled his own reaction when Rebecca had told him she was pregnant. The worry and confusion mingled with his desire to say the right thing.

'We're all haunted, one way or another, Sergeant.' Cameron handed Boyd the photograph. 'This is Rebecca, my wife, taken just before she went missing. Look at the brooch she's wearing.'

Boyd studied the picture. 'That's what I came about, Sir. We've found something I think you should see.'

On the way, Cameron had this expectant feeling. It was something he'd experienced countless times on the job, the breakthrough moment, when the pieces of the jigsaw fell into place.

An incident tent had been raised over the plague pit. A foot below the surface they'd exposed a mummified body. Cameron could make out strands of long dark hair.

'There's a lot of sandy soil in this section,' Susan was saying. 'It leeched the fluids from the body. That's why it's preserved. The brooch must have been attached to the clothes.'

Cameron's heart was in his mouth. 'How long has it been there?'

'At a guess a couple of decades,' Susan avoided his eye.

Cameron stared into the grave. Was it possible that this could be Rebecca? That all the time she'd been buried here, half a mile from her home?

He recalled with utmost clarity the morning he'd returned from work to find the flat empty, Rebecca gone. She'd been tearful when he'd been called out the previous night. The pregnancy had made her vulnerable – something he'd resented, because it made his life difficult. Cameron still felt guilty at the relief he'd experienced when the door had closed on the sound of her distress.

The months following her disappearance had been hell. He'd been in charge of missing person cases himself; interviewed husbands about their wives, known the statistics that pointed to the partner as the prime suspect. He'd had to endure the same accusations himself.

It had all ended nowhere. No Rebecca, no body. And all the time Cameron had hoped she'd simply left him. That they were both alive somewhere, Rebecca and the child. This morning when the girl opened the door, her extraordinary likeness to Rebecca, for a moment he'd hoped . . .

'The girl in the flat. Have you spoken to her?'

The look he'd seen earlier was back on Boyd's face.

'The flat's unoccupied, Sir.'

'Nonsense. I spoke to a young woman. She looked like . . .' Cameron stopped himself.

'According to the neighbours, the flat's been empty for months, Sir.'

Cameron took the stairs two at a time. He was already banging on the door when Boyd caught him up. Boyd let him go through the process three times, before he intervened.

'There's no one there, Sir.'

'I saw her, Sergeant.' Cameron was pissed off by Boyd's expression. He might be about to retire, but he wasn't senile yet. Cameron put his shoulder to the door.

The room was empty – of everything. For a terrible moment Cameron thought the dream that haunted his nights had somehow spilled over into the day. The fantasy of Rebecca being alive, of the child surviving, had fuelled his daytime imagination. But why here? Why now?

Boyd was standing silently in the doorway.

Cameron pushed past, suddenly desperate to be out of that room.

'I don't see how that's possible.' Boyd looked again at the DNA results. Anyone working with the police had their DNA taken and stored on the database. It was routine. Susan's tests on the blood traces in the crypt had come up with two types. One matched the boss, the other was an unknown.

'There must have been contamination when the samples were taken,' Boyd insisted.

Susan was adamant. 'The only way for this to happen is for him to have bled in that room.'

'He cut his finger on the brooch,' he tried in desperation.

'That was afterwards.'

Boyd was at a complete loss. He would have to bring Cameron in, ask him how the hell his blood got in that crypt. Boyd didn't relish the thought.

'What about the body?' he asked.

'Tests are ongoing. Superficially it's the same build as Rebecca, but what's left of the clothes suggest it may be older. We're checking the teeth against Rebecca's dental records. The brooch is the only real match and it's not unique.'

Boyd had pulled the file on Rebecca's disappearance and spent most of the previous night reading it. Seventeen years ago he hadn't even joined the force, so anything he'd heard about the boss's missing wife was hearsay. Boyd wished he'd read the story sooner. It would have explained a lot about the old man.

He thought about the last few weeks, the boss's odd behaviour. Boyd knew he hadn't been sleeping. The DI had made a joke of it, suggesting it was excitement at getting out at last, but Boyd suspected that wasn't the real reason.

He flicked through the well-thumbed documents in the file. There were transcripts of at least six interviews with Cameron.

'What if the boss did have something to do with his wife's disappearance?'

Susan looked unconvinced. 'Why? There was nothing wrong between them. No evidence of an affair . . .' she halted mid-sentence.

A sick feeling anchored itself in the pit of Boyd's stomach. He had a sudden image of life repeating itself. The same stupid people doing the same stupid things.

'Susan . . .'

She held up her hand to stop him. 'Don't.'

The Royal Mile hummed with life in the late summer light. Cameron passed the usual mix of street artists and musicians circled by enthusiastic tourists. Near the Mercat Cross a young woman was regaling a group with stories of Edinburgh's past. Cameron checked the nearby advertising boards for city tours.

The poster he sought had been on the wall of the flat. He'd spotted it when the girl opened the door. An advert for a ghost tour, one of several that roamed the old city, above and below ground. Like many Edinburghers, Cameron had left that sort of thing to the tourists. *Dead Close*. Had he imagined the poster in the same way he'd imagined the girl?

He spotted a board for a ghost tour of Greyfriars Churchyard with a cancelled notice stuck across it. There was nothing advertising *Dead Close*.

In the end, he found it by chance. Later, Cameron would recall the entrance, remember it as the one in his dream, yet knowing there were scores of such archways lining the Royal Mile.

A young man wearing a long black cloak was calling a group to order outside a heavy wooden door, asking who among them was willing to cross the threshold of *Dead Close*.

The passageway was narrow, low and rough underfoot, dropping steeply. Cameron knew of Underground Edinburgh, the bowels of the older city beneath its current counterpart, but had never visited it before. He was fascinated by the narrow stone passageway, the small cell-like rooms to either side. It was bare and clean now, but the squalor in medieval times must have been horrendous. No wonder plague had broken out here.

The tour guide had brought them to a halt, encouraging the group to view one of the rooms. Cameron took his place at the back. The guide was telling the story of a child, separated from its mother when plague broke out and the city authorities quarantined the Close.

Cameron wasn't shocked by the story, but by the room. Rough shelves housed a multitude of toys and sweets left by visitors who'd professed to sense the ghost-child's loneliness. Cameron turned away, irritated by the guide's tone, no longer willing to be part of this make-believe. It was then he saw the doll, wedged in the corner, three shelves up.

'We're not supposed to touch the presents.'

Cameron showed him his ID card. The guide lifted the doll down and handed it over. A ripple of excitement moved through the group. They were wondering if this was for real or just part of the tour. Cameron examined the doll. It looked just like the one he'd seen on the window seat in the flat, one eye dropped in its socket, the blue dress faded.

'I believe a young woman may have left this here. She was in her late teens, long dark hair?'

The guide looked blank. He must have taken scores of people round this place. 'Wait a minute. There was a girl, a couple of nights ago. She joined just as we came in. I wasn't sure she'd paid, but I decided to let it go.'

'Did she give a name?'

The guide shook his head.

This wasn't fucking real. Boyd shifted his feet, discomfort showing in every inch of his body. Across the table, the old man looked calm. Boyd tried to work out what he was thinking and couldn't. Had it been anyone else, the interview would have been formal.

'You've never been in there before that night?'

Cameron shook his head.

'Then how did traces of your blood get on the scene, Sir?'

'I have no idea.'

Jesus, he didn't want this to end up as an investigation into an officer contaminating a scene of crime. Boyd contemplated keeping quiet about it, at least until the boss handed in his badge.

Cameron looked impatient, as though he had no interest in the fact that his blood had been found in the crypt.

'What about the body? Is it Rebecca?'

Boyd hesitated. The tests weren't complete yet, but there was no point keeping the old man thinking they'd found his dead wife. He shook his head. 'Forensic think it's much older.'

Cameron gave a small nod as though he wasn't surprised.

'The girl I met in the flat looked like Rebecca. Our daughter would have been her age by now. Rebecca had an old-fashioned doll that was hers as a kid. It was the only thing missing from the house when she left.'

Boyd's heart was sinking fast. He didn't want the old man to go on, but couldn't bring himself to stop him.

Cameron produced a china-faced doll in a faded blue dress. One eye hung low in its socket.

Something cold crawled up Boyd's spine.

Cameron's eyes were bright with excitement. 'The girl I spoke to had this doll in the flat. There was a poster on the wall. It advertised a ghost tour called *Dead*

Close. I took that tour. There's a room dedicated to a child ghost. This doll was on the shelf.'

Cameron was staring at him, waiting for Boyd to respond.

What the hell was he supposed to say? That he'd had the flat searched again, even had Susan go over it forensically. That she'd been adamant no one had set foot in it for months. That this girl the DI kept going on about didn't exist, except in his imagination.

Pity engulfed Boyd. Thirty-five years of service, on the point of retirement, and the old man had lost it.

Cameron wandered down the Royal Mile, silent and deserted in the dark hours before dawn. It was the time he liked best. The right time to say goodbye. Without people, cars and lights, the city felt like his alone.

Boyd had humoured him. Organised a search for the mysterious girl but, apart from the tour guide, no one had professed to seeing her. The other occupants of the tenement continued to insist the flat had lain empty for months.

So he'd imagined it all; conjured up a daughter who didn't exist? Cameron could have accepted that, had it not been for the doll.

The rain had come on, beating heavily on his head and shoulders. Cameron was impervious to it, his gaze fastened on the arch leading to *Dead Close*. The Royal Mile had grown darker under the sudden downpour, the space around him airless, making it difficult to breathe. Cameron leaned against the stone wall, his legs suddenly weak.

He watched as a figure emerged from the archway opposite. The figure turned towards him, the swell of her pregnancy suddenly visible.

'Rebecca?'

The figure turned, and for a moment Cameron believed she recognised him. A sob rose in his throat. Then she was off, hurrying up the steep cobbles of the Mile, turning left towards Greyfriars.

Cameron ran like he had never run before, yet always her fleeing figure was the same distance ahead. Fear drove him forward. He knew this time he must catch her up, or else lose her for ever.

He reached the Greyfriars gate, his breath rasping in his throat, his heart crashing. Ahead, the door of the mausoleum lay open. Cameron slithered across the rain-soaked grass and stood at the crypt door.

'Rebecca?' he called.

The moon broke through the cloud, dropping a faint line of light on the stone casket. Cameron could see nothing but that line of light yet every nerve and fibre of his body told him someone was in there and that they could hear him.

He poured out his heart to the darkness and shadows. He loved her. He should never have left her alone that night. He should never have stopped searching.

He fell silent as a figure stepped from behind the casket. Cameron called out Rebecca's name, but the woman wasn't looking at him but at someone else.

The shadow of a male loomed against the wall, then took form. Words were exchanged between them. Words that Cameron did not understand. His own voice was silenced, his body frozen in time.

The woman screamed and launched herself at the man. Cameron heard a grunt of surprise then saw him crumble and fall. Blood pooled at Cameron's feet. He looked round in vain for its source, for there was no longer anyone there but him.

Boyd steeled himself and went inside the flat. Packing cases were stacked neatly in the hallway, each one with its contents detailed on the side. Two fishing rods stood upright in the corner.

He hesitated before pushing open the sitting room door. The place was empty. Boyd chose the kitchen next. He had been in this room many times. It was where the DI liked to sit. From the window, the Castle stood resolute against the sky. Cameron's tin box sat open on the table, a part-assembled fishing fly nearby.

Boyd listened outside the bedroom door. Maybe the old man was fast asleep? Praying wasn't something Boyd did, but he made an exception as he pushed open that door.

Cameron was lying fully clothed on top of the bed. For a moment, Boyd thought he was sleeping. The Edinburgh book lay open on his chest. The doll he'd pestered Boyd about sat in the crook of his arm. Blood running from his nostrils, eyes and ears had caked on his face and neck.

The book was just one of many that told the story of Edinburgh's haunted places. Most of the stories were invented. This one was no different. Boyd read the passage the boss had circled.

> *The mausoleum is haunted by the ghost of the man responsible for quarantining Dead Close. He was killed by the mother of a child he'd walled in to die. The authorities executed the woman and she was buried in a mass grave with other plague victims. Visitors have reported seeing a pool of blood on the floor of the mausoleum and hearing the woman scream.*

Boyd closed the book and slipped it in a drawer of his filing cabinet. Whatever it said, he didn't believe in ghosts.

Blood, on the other hand, was real.

They'd had no luck trying to find the person who'd bled in the crypt. As for the boss's contribution – that was the warning they'd all missed.

Boyd wondered if the boss knew his life had sat on a knife edge. Maybe that was why he'd made up the story of the girl – the daughter he'd never had. Perhaps the old man just wanted one last chance to make things right.

The pathology report had stated that the brain aneurysm that killed Cameron had been developing for some time. He would have experienced all the symptoms: light-headedness, rapid heartbeat, nose bleeds and finally a massive drop in blood pressure as it burst.

Detective Inspector Boyd sat for a minute in the darkness of his office. Everyone else had gone. He picked up the phone and called home. After a few moments Bev answered.

'What's wrong?'

'Nothing,' Boyd said, happy just to hear her voice.

*

Bev lay on her right side, her swollen breasts leaking through the T-shirt. She was sound asleep, her breath coming in small puffs. Boyd went to the cot and looked in at the other male in Bev's life, the one who had stolen those breasts. The lips were puckered from sucking, eyes moving behind blue lids.

'I know what you're dreaming about,' Boyd whispered.

The eyes flickered open, a tiny fist thrust the air. Bev stirred in response as though the two were still attached, umbilical cord unbroken.

Boyd offered his finger. At his touch, the fist fastened round him. Boyd was amazed at its strength.

He undressed and got into bed, gathering his wife in his arms. Bev pressed against him, damp, smelling of milk. Boyd kissed her hair, her eyes, her mouth.

THE LIFTED BANDAGE

Mary Raymond Shipman Andrews

Mary Raymond Shipman Andrews (1860–1936) is best known for her iconic American short story 'The Perfect Tribute'. Born in Alabama, she had a long career writing diverse stories, including 'The Lifted Bandage', which are rarely anthologised.

The man let himself into his front door and, staggering lightly, like a drunken man, as he closed it, walked to the hall table, and mechanically laid down his hat, but still wearing his overcoat turned and went into his library, and dropped on the edge of a divan and stared out through the leaded panes of glass across the room facing him. The grayish skin of his face seemed to fall in diagonal furrows, from the eyes, from the nose, from the mouth. He sat, still to his finger-tips, staring.

He was sitting so when a servant slipped in and stood motionless a minute, and went to the wide window where the west light glared through leafless branches outside, and drew the shades lower, and went to the fireplace and touched a match. Wood caught and crackled and a cheerful orange flame flew noisily up the chimney, but the man sitting on the divan did not notice. The butler waited a moment, watching, hesitating, and then:

"Have you had lunch, sir?" he asked in a tentative, gentle voice.

The staring eyes moved with an effort and rested on the servant's face. "Lunch?" he repeated, apparently trying to focus on the meaning of the word. "Lunch? I don't know, Miller. But don't bring anything."

With a great anxiety in his face Miller regarded his master. "Would you let me take your overcoat, Judge?—you'll be too warm," he said.

He spoke in a suppressed tone as if waiting for, fearing something, as if longing to show sympathy, and the man stood and let himself be cared for, and then sat down again in the same unrestful, fixed attitude, gazing out again through the glittering panes into the stormy, tawny west sky. Miller came back and stood quiet, patient; in a few minutes the man seemed to become aware of him.

"I forgot, Miller. You'll want to know," he said in a tone which went to show an old bond between the two. "You'll be sorry to hear, Miller," he said—and the dull eyes moved difficultly to the anxious ones, and his voice was uninflected—"you'll be sorry to know that the coroner's jury decided that Master Jack was a murderer."

The word came more horribly because of an air of detachment from the man's mind. It was like a soulless, evil mechanism, running unguided. Miller caught at a chair.

"I don't believe it, sir," he gasped. "No lawyer shall make me. I've known him since he was ten, Judge, and they're mistaken. It's not any mere lawyers can make me believe that awful thing, sir, of our Master Jack." The servant was shaking from head to foot with intense rejection, and the man put up his hand as if to ward off his emotion.

"I wish I could agree with you," he said quietly, and then added, "Thank you, Miller." And the old butler, walking as if struck with a sickness, was gone.

The man sat on the edge of the divan staring out of the window, minute after minute; the November wind tossed the clean, black lines of the branches backward and forward against the copper sky, as if a giant hand moved a fan of sea-weed before a fire. The man sat still and stared. The sky dulled; the delicate, wild branches melted together; the diamond lines in the window blurred; yet, unmoved, unseeing, the eyes stared through them.

The burr of an electric bell sounded; some one came in at the front door and came to the door of the library, but the fixed figure did not stir. The newcomer stood silent a minute, two minutes; a young man in clerical dress, boyish, with gray, serious eyes. At length he spoke.

"May I come in? It's Dick."

The man's head turned slowly and his look rested inquiringly on his nephew. It was a minute before he said, as if recognizing him, "Dick. Yes." And set himself as before to the persistent gazing through the window.

"I lost you at the court-house," the younger man said. "I didn't mean to let you come home alone."

"Thank you, Dick." It seemed as if neither joy nor sorrow would find a way into the quiet voice again.

The wind roared; the boughs rustled against the glass; the fire, soberly settled to work, steamed and crackled; the clock ticked indifferently; there was no other sound in the room; the two men were silent, the one staring always before him, the other sitting with a hand on the older man's hand, waiting. Minutes they sat so, and the wintry sky outside darkened and lay sullenly in bands of gray and orange against the windows; the light of the logs was stronger than the daylight; it flickered carelessly across the ashiness of the emotionless face. The young man, watching the face, bent forward and gripped his other hand on the unresponsive one in his clasp.

"Uncle," he asked, "will it make things worse if I talk to you?"

"No, Dick."

Nothing made a difference, it seemed. Silence or words must simply fall without effect on the rock bottom of despair. The young man halted, as if dismayed, before this overpowering inertia of hopelessness; he drew a quick breath.

"A coroner's jury isn't infallible. I don't believe it of Jack—a lot of people don't believe it," he said.

The older man looked at him heavily. "You'd say that. Jack's friends will. I've been trained to weigh evidence—I must believe it."

"Listen," the young man urged. "Don't shut down the gates like that. I'm not a lawyer, but I've been trained to think, too, and I believe you're not thinking squarely. There's other evidence that counts besides this. There's Jack—his personality."

"It has been taken into consideration."

"It can't be taken into consideration by strangers—it needs years of intimacy to weigh that evidence as I can weigh it—as you—You know best of all," he cried out impulsively, "if you'll let yourself know, how impossible it was. That Jack should have bought that pistol and taken it to Ben Armstrong's rooms to kill him—it was impossible—impossible!" The clinched fist came down on the black broadcloth knee with the conviction of the man behind it. The words rushed like melted metal, hot, stinging, not to be stopped. The judge quivered as if they had stung through the callousness, touched a nerve. A faint color crawled to his cheeks; for the first time he spoke quickly, as if his thoughts connected with something more than gray matter.

"You talk about my not allowing myself to believe in Jack. You seem not to realize that such a belief would—might—stand between me and madness. I've been trying to adjust myself to a possible scheme of living—getting through the years till I go into nothingness. I can't. All I can grasp is the feeling that a man might have if dropped from a balloon and forced to stay gasping in the air, with no place in it, nothing to hold to, no breath to draw, no earth to rest on, no end to hope for. There is nothing beyond."

"Everything is beyond," the young man cried triumphantly. "'The end,' as you call it, is an end to hope for—it is the beginning. The beginning of more than you have ever had—with them, with the people you care about."

The judge turned a ghastly look upon the impetuous, bright face. "If I believed that, I should be even now perfectly happy. I don't see how you Christians can ever be sorry when your friends die—it's childish; anybody ought to be able to wait a few years. But I don't believe it," he said heavily, and went on again as if an inertia of speech were carrying him as an inertia of silence had held him a few minutes before. "When my wife died a year ago it ended my personal life, but I could live Jack's life. I was glad in the success and honor of it. Now the success—" he made a gesture. "And the honor—if I had that, only the honor of Jack's life left, I think I could finish the years with dignity. I've not been a bad man—I've done my part and lived as seemed right. Before I'm old the joy is wiped out and long years left. Why? It's not reasonable—not logical. With one thing to hold to, with Jack's good name, I might live. How can I, now? What can I do? A life must have a *raison d'être.*"

"Listen," the clergyman cried again. "You are not judging Jack as fairly as you would judge a common criminal. You know better than I how often juries make mistakes—why should you trust this jury to have made none?"

"I didn't trust the jury. I watched as I have never before known how to watch a case. I felt my mind more clear and alert than common."

"Alert!" he caught at the word. "But alert on the side of terror—abnormally clear to see what you dreaded. Because you are fair-minded, because it has been the habit of your life to correct at once any conscious prejudice in your judgment, you have swayed to the side of unfairness to yourself, to Jack. Uncle," he flashed out, "would it tear your soul to have me state the case as I see it? I might, you know—I might bring out something that would make it look different."

Almost a smile touched the gray lines of his face. "If you wish."

The young man drew himself into his chair and clasped his hands around his knee. "Here it is. Mr. Newbold, on the seventh floor of the Bruzon bachelor apartments, heard a shot at one in the morning, next his bedroom, in Ben Armstrong's room. He hurried into the public hall, saw the door wide open into Ben's apartment, went in and found Ben shot dead. Trying to use the telephone to call help, he found it was out of order. So he rushed again into the hall toward the elevator with the idea of getting Dr. Avery, who lived below on the second floor. The elevator door was open also, and a man's opera-hat lay near it on the floor; he saw, just in time, that the car was at the bottom of the shaft, almost stepping inside, in his excitement, before he noticed this. Then he ran down the stairs with Jack's hat in his hand, and got Dr. Avery, and they found Jack at the foot of the elevator shaft. It was known that Ben Armstrong and Jack had quarrelled the day before; it was known that Jack was quick-tempered; it is known that he bought that evening the pistol which was found on the floor by Ben, loaded, with one empty shell. That's the story."

The steady voice stopped a moment and the young man shivered slightly; his look was strained. Steadily he went on.

"That's the story. From that the coroner's jury have found that Jack killed Ben Armstrong—that he bought the pistol to kill him, and went to his rooms with that purpose; that in his haste to escape, he missed seeing that the elevator was down, as Mr. Newbold all but missed seeing it later, and jumped into the shaft and was killed instantly himself. That's what the jury get from the facts, but it seems to me they're begging the question. There are a hundred hypotheses that would fit the case of Jack's innocence—why is it reasonable to settle on the one that means his guilt? This is my idea. Jack and Ben Armstrong had been friends since boyhood and Jack, quick-tempered as he was, was warm-hearted and loyal. It was like him to decide suddenly to go to Ben and make friends. He had been to a play in the evening which had more or less that *motif*; he was open to such influences. It was like the pair of them, after the reconciliation, to set to work looking at Jack's new toy, the pistol. It was a brand-new sort, and the two have been interested always in guns—I remember how I, as a youngster, was impressed when Ben and Jack bought their first shot-guns together. Jack had got the pistol at Mellingham's that evening, you know—he was likely to be keen about it still, and then—it went off. There are plenty of other cases where a man has shot his friend by accident—why shouldn't poor Jack be given the benefit of the doubt? The telephone wouldn't work; Jack rushed out with the same idea which struck Mr. Newbold later, of getting Dr. Avery—and fell down the shaft.

"For me there is no doubt. I never knew him to hold malice. He was violent sometimes, but that he could have gone about for hours with a pistol in his pocket and murder in his heart; that he could have planned Ben Armstrong's death and carried it out deliberately—it's a contradiction in terms. It's impossible, being Jack. You must know this—you know your son—you know human nature."

The rapid *résumé* was but an impassioned appeal. Its answer came after a minute; to the torrent of eager words, three words:

"Thank you, Dick."

The absolute lack of impression on the man's judgment was plain.

"Ah!" The clergyman sprang to his feet and stood, his eyes blazing, despairing, looking down at the bent, listless figure. How could he let a human being suffer as this one was suffering? Quickly his thoughts shifted their basis. He could not affect the mind of the lawyer; might he reach now, perhaps, the soul of the man? He knew the difficulty, for before this his belief had crossed swords with the agnosticism of his uncle, an agnosticism shared by his father, in which he had been trained, from which he had broken free only five years before. He had faced the batteries of the two older brains at that time, and come out with the brightness of his new-found faith untarnished, but without, he remembered, scratching the armor of their profound doubt in everything. One could see, looking at the slender black figure, at the visionary gaze of the gray wide eyes, at the shape of the face, broad-browed, ovalled, that this man's psychic make-up must lift him like wings into an atmosphere outside a material, outside even an intellectual world. He could breathe freely only in a spiritual air, and things hard to believe to most human beings were, perhaps, his every-day thoughts. He caught a quick breath of excitement as it flashed to his brain that now, possibly, was coming the moment when he might justify his life, might help this man whom he loved, to peace. The breath he caught was a prayer; his strong, nervous fingers trembled. He spoke in a tone whose concentration lifted the eyes below him, that brooded, stared.

"I can't bear it to stand by and see you go under, when there's help close. You said that if you could believe that they were living, that you would have them again, you would be perfectly happy no matter how many years you must wait. They are living as sure as I am here, and as sure as Jack was here, and Jack's mother. They are living still. Perhaps they're close to you now. You've bound a bandage over your eyes, you've covered the vision of your spirit, so that you can't see; but that doesn't make nothingness of God's world. It's there—here—close, maybe. A more real world than this—this little thing." With a boyish gesture he thrust behind him the universe. "What do we know about the earth, except effects upon our consciousness? It's all a matter of inference—you know that better than I. The thing we do know beyond doubt is that we are each of us a something that suffers and is happy. How is that something the same as the body—the body that gets old and dies—how can it be? You can't change thought into matter—not conceivably—everybody acknowledges that. Why should the thinking part die then, because the material part dies? When the organ is broken is the organist dead? The body is the hull, the covering, and when it has grown useless it will fall away and the live seed in it will stand free to sunlight and air—just at the beginning of life, as a plant is when it breaks through earth in the spring. It's the seed in the ground, and it's the flower in the sunlight, but it's the same thing—the same life—it is—it *is*." The boy's intensity of conviction shot like a flame across the quiet room.

"It is the same thing with us too. The same spirit-substance underlies both worlds and there is no separation in space, only in view-point. Life goes on— it's just transfigured. It's as if a bandage should be lifted from our eyes and we should suddenly see things in whose presence we had been always."

The rushing, eager voice stopped. He bent and laid his hand on the older man's and stared at his face, half hidden now in the shadows of the lowering fire. There was no response. The heavy head did not lift and the attitude was unstirred, hopeless. As if struck by a blow he sprang erect and his fingers shut hard. He spoke as if to himself, brokenly.

"He does not believe—a single word—I say. I can't help him—I *can't* help him."

Suddenly the clinched fists flung out as if of a power not their own, and his voice rang across the room.

"God!" The word shot from him as if a thunderbolt fell with it. "God! Lift the bandage!"

A log fell with a crash into the fire; great battling shadows blurred all the air; he was gone.

The man, startled, drew up his bent shoulders, and pushed back a lock of gray hair and stared about, shaking, bewildered. The ringing voice, the word that had flashed as if out of a larger atmosphere—the place was yet full of these, and the shock of it added a keenness to his misery. His figure swung sideways; he fell on the cushions of the sofa and his arms stretched across them, his gray head lying heedless; sobs that tore roots came painfully; it was the last depth. Out of it, without his volition, he spoke aloud.

"God, God, God!" his voice said, not prayerfully, but repeating the sound that had shocked his torture. The word wailed, mocked, reproached, defied—and yet it was a prayer. Out of a soul in mortal stress that word comes sometimes driven by a force of the spirit like the force of the lungs fighting for breath—and it is a prayer.

"God, God, God!" the broken voice repeated, and sobs cut the words. And again. Over and over, and again the sobbing broke it.

As suddenly as if a knife had stopped the life inside the body, all sound stopped. A movement shook the man as he lay face down, arms stretched. Then for a minute, two minutes, he was quiet, with a quiet that meant muscles stretched, nerves alert. Slowly, slowly the tightened muscles of the arms pushed the shoulders backward and upward; the head lifted; the face turned outward, and if an observer had been there he might have seen by the glow of the firelight that the features wet, distorted, wore, more than all at this moment, a look of amazement. Slowly, slowly, moving as if afraid to disturb something—a dream—a presence—the man sat erect as he had been sitting before, only that the rigidity was in some way gone. He sat alert, his eyes wide, filled with astonishment, gazing before him eagerly—a look different from the dull stare of an hour ago by the difference between hope and despair. His hands caught at the stuff of the divan on either side and clutched it.

All the time the look of his face changed; all the time, not at once, but by fast, startling degrees, the gray misery which had bound eyes and mouth and brow in iron dropped as if a cover were being torn off and a light set free. Amazement, doubting, incredulous came first, and with that eagerness, trembling and afraid. And then hope—and then the fear to hope. And hunger. He bent forward, his eyes peered into the quiet emptiness, his fingers gripped the cloth as if to anchor him to a wonder, to an unbelievable something; his body leaned—to something—and his face now was the face of a starved man, of a man dying from thirst, who sees food, water, salvation.

And his face changed; a quality incredible was coming into it—joy. He was transformed. Lines softened by magic; color came, and light in the eyes; the first unbelief, the amazement, shifted surely, swiftly, and in a flash the whole man shone, shook with rapture. He threw out before him his arms, reaching, clasping, and from his radiant look the arms might have held all happiness.

A minute he stayed so with his hands stretched out, with face glowing, then slowly, his eyes straining as if perhaps they followed a vision which faded from them—slowly his arms fell and the expectancy went from his look. Yet not the light, not the joy. His body quivered; his breath came unevenly, as of one just gone through a crisis; every sense seemed still alive to catch a faintest note of something exquisite which vanished; and with that the spell, rapidly as it had come, was gone. And the man sat there quiet, as he had sat an hour before, and the face which had been leaden was brilliant. He stirred and glanced about the room as if trying to adjust himself, and his eyes smiled as they rested on the familiar objects, as if for love of them, for pleasure in them. One might have said that this man had been given back at a blow youth and happiness. Movement seemed beyond him yet—he was yet dazed with the newness of a marvel—but he turned his head and saw the fire and at that put out his hand to it as if to a friend.

The electric bell burred softly again through the house, and the man heard it, and his eyes rested inquiringly on the door of the library. In a moment another man stood there, of his own age, iron-gray, strong-featured.

"Dick told me I might come," he said. "Shall I trouble you? May I stay with you awhile?"

The judge put out his hand friendlily, a little vaguely, much as he had put it out to the fire. "Surely," he said, and the newcomer was all at once aware of his look. He started.

"You're not well," he said. "You must take something—whiskey—Miller——"

The butler moved in the room making lights here and there, and he came quickly.

"No," the judge said. "I don't want anything—I don't need anything. It's not as you think. I'll tell you about it."

Miller was gone; Dick's father waited, his gaze fixed on the judge's face anxiously, and for moments no word was spoken. The judge gazed into the fire with the rapt, smiling look which had so startled his brother-in-law. At length:

"I don't know how to tell you," he said. "There seem no words. Something has happened, yet it's difficult to explain."

"Something happened?" the other repeated, bewildered but guarded. "I don't understand. Has some one been here? Is it about—the trial?"

"No." A slight spasm twisted the smiling lines of the man's mouth, but it was gone and the mouth smiled still.

A horror-struck expression gleamed for a second from the anxious eyes of the brother-in-law, but he controlled it quickly. He spoke gently. "Tell me about it—it will do you good to talk."

The judge turned from the fire, and at sight of his flushed cheeks and lighted eyes the other shrank back, and the judge saw it. "You needn't be alarmed," he said quietly. "Nothing is wrong with me. But something has happened, as I told you, and everything—is changed." His eyes lifted as he spoke and strayed about the room as if considering a change which had come also to the accustomed setting.

A shock of pity flashed from the other, and was mastered at once. "Can you tell me what has happened?" he urged. The judge, his face bright with a brightness that was dreadful to the man who watched him, held his hand to the fire, turning it about as if enjoying the warmth. The other shivered. There was silence for a minute. The judge broke it, speaking thoughtfully:

"Suppose you had been born blind, Ned," he began, "and no one had ever given you a hint of the sense of vision, and your imagination had never presented such a power to your mind. Can you suppose that?"

"I think so—yes," the brother-in-law answered, with careful gentleness, watching always the illumined countenance. "Yes, I can suppose it."

"Then fancy if you will that all at once sight came, and the world flashed before you. Do you think you'd be able to describe such an experience?"

The voice was normal, reflective. Many a time the two had talked together of such things in this very room, and the naturalness of the scene, and of the judge's manner, made the brother-in-law for a second forget the tragedy in which they were living.

"Why, of course," he answered. "If one had never heard of such a power one's vocabulary wouldn't take in the words to describe it."

"Exactly," the judge agreed. "That's the point I'm making. Perhaps now I may tell you what it is that has happened. Or rather, I may make you understand how a definite and concrete event has come to pass, which I can't tell you."

Alarm suddenly expressed itself beyond control in the brother-in-law's face. "John, what do you mean? Do you see that you distress me? Can't you tell clearly if some one has been here—what it is, in plain English, that has happened?"

The judge turned his dreamy, bright look toward the frightened man. "I do see—I do see," he brought out affectionately. "I'll try to tell, as you say, in plain English. But it is like the case I put—it is a question of lack of vocabulary. A remarkable experience has occurred in this room within an hour. I can no more describe it than the man born blind could describe sight. I can only call it by one name, which may startle you. A revelation."

"A revelation!" the tone expressed incredulity, scarcely veiled scorn.

The judge's brilliant gaze rested undisturbed on the speaker. "I understand—none better. A day ago, two hours ago, I should have answered in that tone. We have been trained in the same school, and have thought alike. Dick was here a while ago and said things—you know what Dick would say. You know how you and I have been sorry for the lad—been indulgent to him—with his keen, broad mind and that inspired self-forgetfulness of his—how we've been sorry to have such qualities wasted on a parson, a religion machine. We've thought he'd come around in time, that he was too large a personality to be tied to a treadmill. We've thought that all along, haven't we? Well, Dick was here, and out of the hell where I was I thought that again. When he talked I thought in a way—for I couldn't think much—that after a consistent voyage of agnosticism, I wouldn't be whipped into snivelling belief at the end, by shipwreck. I would at least go down without surrendering. In a dim way I thought that. And all that I thought then, and have thought through my life, is nothing. Reasoning doesn't weigh against experience. Dick is right."

The other man sat before him, bent forward, his hands on his knees, listening, dazed. There was a quality in the speaker's tone which made it necessary to take his words seriously. Yet—the other sighed and relaxed a bit as he waited, watched. The calm voice went on.

"The largest event of my life has happened in the last hour, in this room. It was this way. When Dick went out I—went utterly to pieces. It was the farthest depth. Out of it I called on God, not knowing what I did. And he answered. That's what happened. As if—as if a bandage had been lifted from my eyes, I was—I was in the presence of things—indescribable. There was no change, only that where I was blind before I now saw. I don't mean vision. I haven't words to explain what I mean. But a world was about me as real as this; it had perhaps always been there; in that moment I was first aware of it. I knew, as if a door had been opened, what heaven means—a condition of being. And I knew another thing more personal—that, without question, it was right with those I thought I had lost and that the horror which seemed blackest I have no need to dread. I cannot say that I saw them or heard or touched them, but I was with them. I understand, but I can't make you understand. I told Dick an hour ago that if I could believe they were living, that I should ever have them again, I should be perfectly happy. That's true now. I believe it, and I am—perfectly happy."

The listener groaned uncontrollably.

"I know your thought," the judge answered the sound, and his eyes were like lamps as he turned them toward the man. "But you're wrong—my mind is not unhinged. You'll see. After what I've gone through, after facing eternity without hope, what are mere years? I can wait. I know. I am—perfectly happy."

Then the man who listened rose from his chair and came and put a hand gently on the shoulder of the judge, looking down at him gravely. "I don't understand you very well, John," he said, "but I'm glad of anything—of anything"—his voice went suddenly. "Will you wait for me here a few minutes? I'm going home and I'll be back. I think I'll spend the night with you if you don't object."

"Object! Wait!" The judge looked up in surprise, and with that he smiled. "I see. Surely. I'd like to have you here. Yes, I'll certainly wait."

Outside in the hall one might have heard the brother-in-law say a low word or two to Miller as the man helped him on with his coat; then the front door shut softly, and he was gone, and the judge sat alone, his head thrown back against his chair, his face luminous.

The other man swung down the dark street, rushing, agitated. As he came to the corner an electric light shone full on him and a figure crossing down toward him halted.

"Father! I was coming to find you. Something extraordinary has happened. I was coming to find you."

"Yes, Dick." The older man waited.

"I've just left Charley Owen at the house—you remember Charley Owen?"

"No."

"Oh, yes, you do—he's been here with—Jack. He was in Jack's class in college—in Jack's and Ben Armstrong's. He used to go on shooting trips with them both—often."

"I remember now."

"Yes, I knew you would." The young voice rushed on. "He has been away just now—down in Florida shooting—away from civilization. He got all his mail for a month in one lump—just now—two days ago. In it was a letter from Jack and Ben Armstrong, written that night, written together. Do you see what that means?"

"What!" The word was not a question, but an exclamation. "What—Dick!"

"Yes—yes. There were newspapers, too, which gave an account of the trial— the first he'd heard of it—he was away in the Everglades. He started instantly, and came on here when he had read the papers, and realized the bearing his letter would have on the trial. He has travelled day and night. He hoped to get here in time. Jack and Ben thought he was in New York. They wrote to ask him to go duck-shooting—with them. And, father—here's the most startling point of it all." As the man waited, watching his son's face, he groaned suddenly and made a gesture of despair.

"Don't, father—don't take it that way. It's good—it's glorious—it clears Jack. My uncle will be almost happy. But I wouldn't tell him at once—I'd be careful," he warned the other.

"What was it—the startling point you spoke of?"

"Oh—surely—this. The letter to Charley Owen spoke of Jack's new pistol— that pistol. Jack said they would have target-shooting with it in camp. They were all crack shots, you know. He said he had bought it that evening, and that Ben thought well of it. Ben signed the letter after Jack, and then added a postscript. It clears Jack—it clears him. Doesn't it, father? But I wouldn't tell my uncle just yet. He's not fit to take it in for a few hours—don't you think so?"

"No, I won't tell him—just yet."

The young man's wide glance concentrated with a flash on his father's face. "What is it? You speak queerly. You've just come from there. How is he—how is my uncle?"

There was a letterbox at the corner, a foot from the older man's shoulder. He put out his hand and held to the lid a moment before he answered. His voice was harsh.

"Your uncle is—perfectly happy," he said. "He's gone mad."

PRETEND BLOOD

Margaret Atwood

Margaret Atwood is a major literary novelist and activist. Her extensive output includes *The Handmaid's Tale*, *The Blind Assassin*, and *Oryx and Crake*. Atwood holds awards, honours, and honorary doctorates from around the world, including the Booker Prize and the Order of Canada. She lives in Toronto, Canada.

Marla got into Past Lives through Sal. They were friends at work – they often had lunch together, and went shopping, and sometimes to movies, with nothing unusual being said. But one day Sal confided to Marla that in a past life she'd been Cleopatra. The reason she was telling Marla this was that she'd just got engaged – out came a hulking diamond – because she'd run into a man through an internet chat site who'd been Marc Antony, and they'd got together in real life, and needless to say they'd fallen in love, and wasn't that wonderful?

Marla nearly choked on her coffee. First of all, if Sal had been Cleopatra she herself had been the Queen of Sheba, because Sal wasn't exactly anyone's idea of Miss Sexy Ancient Egypt – she was thirty-five and tubby, with a pasty complexion and an overbite. Also, Marla had seen that play – a long time ago, granted, but not so long that she didn't remember the death of Marc Antony, and also that of Cleopatra, what with the asps in a basket.

'It didn't end very well, the first time,' she managed to croak out. It was cruel to laugh at someone else's nutty illusion, so she managed not to do that. Anyway, who was she to laugh? Nutty illusion or not, the Cleopatra thing had got results for Sal.

'That's true,' Sal said. 'It was awful at the time.' She gave a little shudder. Then she explained that the good thing about having a past life was that you got the chance to return to earth as the same person you'd once been, but this time you could make things come out better. Which was why so many of the Past Lifers were historic figures who'd had tragic finales. A lot were from the Roman Empire, for instance. And kings and queens, and dukes and duchesses – they'd been prone to trouble because of their ambition and other people's jealousy of them and so forth.

'How did you know?' asked Marla. 'That you were Cleopatra?'

'It just kind of came over me,' said Sal. 'The first time I saw a pyramid – well, not a pyramid, a photo of a pyramid – it looked so kind of familiar. And I've always had this fear of snakes.'

So has half the population, thought Marla. Better you should have a fear of

Marc Antony: you're marrying an obvious wacko. Most likely a serial killer with a bunch of former Cleopatras stacked up in the cellar like cord-wood. But her scepticism faded when she actually met Marc, whose name in this life was Bob, and he turned out to be perfectly nice, though a lot older and richer than Sal; and darned if Sal and Bob, or Marc, didn't get married after all, and take off for a new life in Scotland, where Bob lived. The climate there wasn't very Egyptian, but that didn't bother Sal: there were many sad parts about her past life she'd just as soon forget, she told Marla, and spending too much time in Egypt might be depressing for them both. Though they did intend to take a vacation there for a bit of nostalgia. Sal wanted to revisit her ancient barge trips, because those had been pretty splendid.

Before leaving for her new married life, Sal told Marla the name of the internet chat site – PLAYS, for Past Lives And Your Self – and said Marla should give it a try: she had a feeling in her bones that Marla too was an Old Soul. Anyway, said Sal, Marla had nothing to lose, meaning she wasn't getting any younger, and unlike Sal – the new Sal – she had a dead-end job and no man in sight. Marla hadn't missed that gloating subtext. It irritated her.

It took Marla a while to seek out PLAYS, and she felt like an idiot even considering it – with my luck I'll meet Jack the Ripper, she thought – but she finally went on-line. It cost fifty dollars to join, and then you had to read the rules and pledge to abide by them. No duels with former enemies, for instance, and no questioning anyone else's identity, not even if there were two or three of someone. There were several Anne Boleyns, for instance, but the claimants got around that by being Anne at different times of her life – while courted by Henry, while pregnant, while waiting in the Tower to get her head chopped off. The feelings you'd have during such phases would be very different, so each set of feelings might have come back into a different present-day person. That was the PLAYS rationale.

Once you'd swallowed the initial premise, or pretended to – which was what Marla herself did – Past Lives turned out to be surprisingly entertaining. Sort of like a virtual masquerade ball: by being someone else, you could be more truly yourself. At first Marla held back, and merely listened in while other people exchanged historical factoids and favourite recipes – syllabub, sack posset, stuffed peacock. She watched friendships form, she watched flirtations – Henry the Fourth with Eleanor of Aquitaine, Marianne Evans with George Henry Lewes. Couples went off into private cubicles where they could have one-on-ones. She longed to know what happened to such pairings. Sometimes there would be an announcement – an engagement, or a wedding, like Sal's – but not very often.

To participate more actively, as she now longed to do, she needed more than a password: she needed a past life of her own. But how to decide which one? Marla suspected by now that PLAYS might be merely a kinky dating agency; even so, it could be crucially important who she chose to be, or to have been. She didn't want to end up playing Eva Braun to some psychopath's Adolf Hitler, though this duo had in fact flitted briefly across the screen.

She surprised herself by plunging into Mary Stewart, Queen of Scots. She'd had no prior interest, she didn't have any preparation for it – she chose it because both their names began with M and she'd once had a crush on a man named

Stewart – but once she was in, she found herself getting caught up in the part. After she declared herself, she started receiving messages from several Elizabeth the Firsts. 'Were you really plotting against me?' said one. 'We could have been such good friends, we had so much in common.' 'I so much regret what happened,' said another. 'I felt terrible about the whole beheading thing. It was all a mistake.' 'The lead coffin was not my idea,' said a third. 'Well, anyway, your son inherited. And your embroidered elephant still exists. So it's not all bad.'

What lead coffin? thought Marla. What embroidered elephant? She went off to read up. You did learn a lot on PLAYS – it was an education in itself.

Marla kept up with Sal via email. At first the bulletins were short and bubbly. She and Bob/Marc had a lovely house, the garden flourished so well in that climate, Bob was so attentive, and so lavish. In return, Marla proffered her newfound Queen Maryness, though she was a little miffed when Sal didn't respond with the enthusiasm she'd expected.

Meanwhile, she got several rude messages from a John Knox, and met a David Rizzio – in the flesh, they went to a concert – who turned out to be gay but fun, and she turned down dating invitations from several Darnleys: the man had been a snot in his past life and surely wouldn't be any better now. But she accepted an Earl of Bothwell who'd looked like sort of a hunk, and had three martinis with him in a lava bar, and had almost got raped.

She felt she was beginning to understand the character of Mary from the inside. She was also leading a more interesting and varied life than she'd led in years. Still, despite that, nothing much to show.

After a silence of several months, she got a doleful email from Sal. Bob/Marc had fallen off a boat, on the Nile. He'd drowned. His arthritis, or else a crocodile, may have been involved. Sal was heartbroken: they never should have gone back there, it was bad luck for them. Would Marla like to come over on her vacation, to Edinburgh, just to be with Sal at this difficult time in her life? She, Sal, would pay for the ticket, she had lots of money now. Anyway, Sal thought Marla might like to see the ancient city where she herself had undergone such extremely crucial experiences, once upon a time.

Marla quickly accepted. Her vacation was two months away, so she had time to bone up. She bought a couple more history books of the period: she had a size-able collection by now. There was nothing about those casket letters she didn't know – forgeries, planted by spies and enemies. She remembered with anguish the murder of her Italian secretary, clever David Rizzio, though she had mixed feelings about her useless husband Darnley being found dead in the garden after they blew up his house, the poxy shit. Not that she'd known about the explosion plans in advance. Naughty Bothwell!

She was looking forward.

However, she gathered from the tone of Sal's emails that Sal wasn't as keen on Marla's visit as she'd been at first. Tough, thought Marla. I'm not turning down my chance to see the old stomping grounds once again.

Sal met her at the airport. At first Marla didn't recognise her: she was thinner, and she'd had her hair changed – she was a strawberry blonde now. She'd definitely had something done to her nose, and her chubby underchin was gone, and her teeth were whiter. Her make-up was laid on with a trowel. Marla knew the clothes were expensive, but she couldn't tell how expensive: they were well beyond Marla's range. The total effect was striking. Not what you'd call beautiful, thought Marla grudgingly, but striking. Beyond a doubt. You had to look at Sal twice, as you'd look at a parade.

Sal gave Marla a hug, teetering forward on her massively high heels, and said coolly how nice it was that Marla could visit. 'The Earl's in the car,' she said as they walked towards the exit. 'You'll like him, he's a sweetie!'

'The Earl?' said Marla.

'Of Essex,' said Sal.

Marla stopped. 'The Earl of Essex?'

'In a past life,' said Sal. 'His name's Dave, in the present. Dave McLeod.'

'What are you doing with the Earl of Essex?' she asked. 'Which Earl of Essex?' She was getting a bad feeling.

'Well, as Elizabeth the First,' said Sal, 'I feel I owe it to him. To make it turn out better this time around. After all, I did sign his death warrant, although I loved him passionately. But what choice did I have?'

'Just a minute,' said Marla. 'You're not Elizabeth the First. You're Cleopatra!'

'Oh, Marla,' said Sal. 'That was then!' She laughed. 'You can have more than one! It's a game! Anyway, we're cousins now!' She linked her arm through Marla's. 'Cousin Mary! Too bad we never met, in the old days. But carpe diem!'

Evil witch, thought Marla. I was innocent, but you had me killed for treason. Then you tried to get out of it by saying you'd been fooled. She had a vivid memory of the humiliation she'd felt when her red wig had come off as the executioner hoisted her severed head. And then her dog had run in under her skirts. What a farce.

Dave, the Earl of Essex, was a red-faced, white-haired Scotsman who'd been in the construction business. He was older than Bob/Marc had been, and Marla was willing to bet he was richer. He pried himself up and out of the car to shake Marla's hand.

'She's my little Gloriana,' he chortled, patting Sal on her designer bum, winking at Marla. 'And I take it you're our long-lost Mary!'

Watch your back, Marla wanted to tell him. Don't drink any syllabubs. Don't go on any barges.

Sal was no longer in mourning for Bob/Marc. In fact she barely mentioned him, apart from saying that this particular segment of her past had now been 'resolved'. Her main object in having Marla visit appeared to be showing off. Her house was vast, and so were the grounds around it, and so was the garage in which she kept her several Mercedes, and so were the closets in which she stored her extensive wardrobe: there was a special walk-in for her shoe collection. She had a lot of jewellery, as well. Just like Elizabeth the First, thought Marla: her clothes were always better than mine, even before she was keeping me cooped up in those draughty, damp castles, with nothing at all to spend on decent cloaks. So cheap of her. Vindictive. Jealous of my charisma. Dancing around in luxury, while I sat embroidering elephants. Neglected. Laughed at. So unfair.

The next day Essex/Dave was visiting his grandchildren in Stirling and getting together with a friend, one of the many William Wallaces; so, after her hair appointment in the morning and an argument with her crabby Scottish gardener, Sal took Marla to see Holyroodhouse.

'Don't be too disappointed,' she said. 'It's a bit of a tourist trap. It won't be what you remember.'

Marla thought the building looked vaguely familiar, but she'd seen a lot of pictures of it. So much is since my time, thought Marla. It's too clean. We never used to bother much with that. She didn't like the long gallery, with all those portraits of Stewarts – going back to Adam to show how noble they were, said Sal with a dismissive laugh – and all with the same big noses. Whoever'd done the arms hadn't been paying much attention: if extended, some of those arms would dangle down to below the knees.

Her own portrait was awful – not pretty at all. But everyone had raved about her beauty, back then. Men had strewn themselves. She remembered Bothwell, his burning eyes, his kidnapper's passion . . . it ended badly though. And he could have done with a toothbrush, thought Marla in her present mode. We all could, back then.

'There's some resemblance, don't you think?' said Sal. 'You know, you should try auburn, for your hair. That would bring it out more.'

They went through more rooms, Sal's heels clacking annoyingly. Not too sensible for sightseeing, thought Marla. Purple. Jimmy Choos, as Sal had pointed out.

They went upstairs. They saw more furniture. They looked at pictures. Marla kept waiting for a frisson of recognition – something she'd known, something that was hers – but there was nothing. It was as if she'd never lived there.

'Here's the bedchamber,' said Sal. 'And the famous supper room.' She was watching Marla, with a little smirk. 'Where Rizzio was murdered,' she added. 'Your so-called private secretary.'

'I know,' said Marla. Now she really did feel something. Panic, despair . . . she'd screamed a lot. They'd held a gun on her, while poor David . . . He'd hidden behind her, but they'd dragged him out. There were tears in her eyes now. What if it was all true, and she'd really been there somehow?

No. Surely not.

'They used to do the pretend blood with red paint,' said Sal, laughing a little. 'But people kept chipping it off, and anyway it looked so fake. It's much better now, with brown varnish. See, over here.'

Sure enough, there on the wooden floor were some realistic-looking stains. On the wall beside them was a plaque – not claiming exactly that the varnish was Rizzio's actual blood, but pointing out that this was the spot where he'd been stabbed fifty-six times and then thrown down the stairs.

And those were the very stairs. Marla was shivering now. It had been a terrible shock, and her six months pregnant. She could have lost the baby. They'd taken off David's lovely clothes, like the robbers they were. And his jewels. Stuck him naked in a hole in the ground.

'Tell me,' said Sal. 'Was it true? That you were sleeping with him? That ugly little music master?' She seemed not to notice Marla's tears.

Marla got control of herself. 'How could you even think that?' she said. 'I was the Queen!' Now she felt anger. But she kept her voice low: there were some American tourists over by the four-poster bed, examining the embroidered hangings.

'A lot of people thought it,' said Sal teasingly. 'You were really hot, back then. You didn't exactly restrain yourself. The French Dauphin, then Darnley, then Bothwell, and who knows who else? So why not Rizzio?'

'He was gay,' said Marla faintly, but Sal went right on.

'They said you were quite the slut. You should get into that mode again, have some fun for a change. If you lost a few pounds . . .'

'You put them up to it,' said Marla. Had she read that somewhere? She felt her hands clenching into fists. 'You paid them! Those conspirators! You wanted me dead, so you could have everything!' Queen bee, she thought. Her and her shoe collection, and her fucking fraudulent rich old Earl of Essex. And her fleet of Mercedes. She took a step towards Sal. Sal took a step backwards, wobbling on her high heels. Now her back was to the stairwell.

'Marla, Marla,' she said nervously. 'Don't get carried away! It's a game!'

Not a game, thought Marla. She didn't consciously mean to push so hard. Sal went over backwards, down the stairs. There was a screech, and an unpleasant crack. Tit for tat, thought Marla.

'It was the shoes,' she said afterwards. She was sobbing uncontrollably by then. 'She turned her ankle. She shouldn't have been wearing them, not for sightseeing. I told her!'

The Earl of Essex was dismayed at first, but Marla helped him through the mourning period. 'Poor Gloriana,' he said at last. 'It was vanity killed her. She was always too stuck on herself, don't you think?'

Then he confessed that, like so many men, he'd secretly fancied Mary all along. Although he'd never met her in the flesh. Until now.

ICARUS

Belinda Bauer

Belinda Bauer was raised in England and South Africa. A former journalist and screenwriter, she won a BAFTA for her screenplay, *The Locker Room*. Her first novel, *Blacklands*, won the Crime Writers Association Gold Dagger award, and the following six novels have been critically acclaimed and sold to publishers throughout the world.

The old man thinks I'm better than this and, sometimes, I think he's right. I'm watching Eddie riding a pink Barbie bike in the falling snow, with his knees around his ears, laughing that stupid laugh.

"Stop arsing about."

That's Nige. He's the brains. He keeps the records. Eddie tosses the Barbie bike in the back of the van with the others and we get in the cab and watch Nige write in the big book. 87 Capstan Road, 1x Barbie, 2x 13" BMX

It's a full load. All kids' bikes – BMXs, mountain bikes, tricycles. You name it. More than 30 just today. We drive the lot to a farm near the railway and dump them in a pit. Nige gives the farmer £20 to cover them with slurry.

It's a week before Christmas and my fingers are numb. All through November and December we're on the bikes. After Christmas we'll be back for the brand new replacements. That's where the money is.

I never had a new bike. None of us did. The old man spent his whole life guarding treasure and never had two pennies to rub together. Forty years of standing by a door, staring at people staring at Picassos and Rembrandts.

In all that time he only stirred once – and then never tired of telling anyone who would listen how he stopped a woman pushing a bronze of Icarus out of the museum in a pushchair.

"I knew something was up," he always said when he told the story, "because the baby looked nothing like her!" When I was little I laughed. Not now.

Now it makes me angry to think of him saving a million quid statue – then he gets the Big C, and no one from the museum even sends a card.

Nick and Charlie are playing Snap on the old man's legs. Nick works at a timber yard and Charlie makes small metal things in a factory. The old Nick and Charlie have gone home, so I play Patience in the dark. The nine of clubs is missing.

Something in the old man's eyes changes when he wakes to find Icarus at his bedside, watching over him.

"The museum sent it," I say. "They want you to know they appreciate what you did. What you've always done."

The old man stares at the boy with the wings and smiles.

He dies on Christmas Eve.

On Christmas morning I call the police from a phone box and leave Icarus there for them to find.

On Boxing Day, Nige calls from the van and asks why I'm not at work, so I tell him I don't feel well.

But that's not true . . .

I feel just fine.

HELL'S BELLS

M.C. Beaton

M.C. Beaton has won international acclaim for her Hamish Macbeth and Agatha Raisin mysteries, which have had multiple appearances on *The New York Times* bestseller list. The Agatha Raisin mystery series is also an eight-part television series starring Ashley Jensen, available on Acorn TV. She is also the author of 100 historical romance titles. You can learn more at www.MCBeaton.com.

Mary Bolton, a widow, who lived in the Cotswold village of Weston Magna, considered herself to be the beating, generous heart of the village. She was a great manager. She ran charity boot car sales, dances at the bowling club, read to the elderly and any other do-good thing she could think of.

Although in her late forties, she considered herself – like Miss Jean Brodie – to be in her prime. She had curly brown hair, a figure rigorously trimmed with a body stocking, and a wide mouth that always seemed to be smiling. The smile, however, did not reach her rather prominent pale grey eyes.

She was delighted when a wealthy farmer died and left money to re-hang the bells in the church. Only the tenor bell had been fit for ringing for over twenty years.

Mary threw herself into the study of campanology, dragging along with her five other villagers, to the nearby village of Ancombe for lessons in bell ringing.

Then when the bells of St. Edmund's in Weston Magna were being re-hung, they gathered in the bell tower and sent the brazen clamour of the bells sounding out over the countryside as Mary called for rehearsal after rehearsal.

Jessica Brand, a former Olympic swimmer, whose cottage lay in the shadow of the bell tower, thought she would be driven mad by the hellish sound. She was a tall, muscular woman with big hands and feet. It was believed she was about the same age as Mary.

Jessica confronted Mary in the village store one morning. "You've got to confine that bell ringing to Sundays only, d'you hear?"

"But we must practise," protested Mary with that turnip lantern smile of hers. "As soon as we have reached perfection, we will rehearse on Thursday evenings and then Sundays."

"And how long is that going to take?" demanded Jessica threateningly, looming over Mary.

"Oh, a month or two."

"A month or . . . Listen you," said Jessica. "That damned cacophony is driving me mad. Go on the way you're going and I'll throttle you and hang you from your damned bell rope."

But the noise went on. In vain did Jessica protest to the vicar and then to the parish council. Powerful woman though she was, everyone was more frightened of Mary than they were of Jessica. Mary had sneaky ways of getting her own back if anyone crossed her. Hadn't Mrs. Bryce, who had won the jam-making competition for years, been foolish enough to vote Mary off the sale of work committee? Mary put it about that Mrs. Bryce was putting in shop-bought jam. This proved to be the case. Mrs. Bryce wept and said someone had deliberately substituted the shop jam for her own, but she lost the prize for the first time in ten years. Only Jessica had been bold enough to suggest that Mary had made the substitution.

At long last, the bell ringing rehearsal was confined to Thursday evenings. Jessica once more found life bearable. The first Thursday's rehearsal, she took herself off for dinner with friends, returning late when she was sure the bell ringing was over.

She was just settling down with a nightcap when she heard it – the deep-throated boom of one of the large bells. The sound reverberated through her small sitting room.

Jessica strode out of her cottage and marched to the bell tower. She thrust opened the door, and then screamed.

For swinging towards her with a bell rope wrapped around her neck, her eyes bulging in her purple contorted face, came Mary Bolton.

Jessica seized the body and stopped its swing. Far above, the bell gave one last mocking boom and then there was silence.

Two days later, private detective Agatha Raisin, and Jessica Brand, faced each other in Agatha's office in the town of Mircester. Jessica looked doubtfully at Agatha. She saw a woman with glossy brown hair, a round face and bearlike eyes, wearing, in her opinion, too short a skirt.

"So you think you are going to be accused of murder?" said Agatha.

"I was heard threatening to strangle her," said Jessica miserably. "Evidently someone had strangled her and then strung her up."

"Do you know of anyone who hated her enough?" asked Agatha.

"She was by way of being a managing bully, but no one really stood up to her."

"Well, tell me all you know about her." While Jessica talked, Agatha took notes.

When Jessica had finished, Agatha said, "I'll do my best. Leave it with me."

After Jessica had left, Agatha sat, deep in thought. What were the usual reasons for murder? Sex and money. So who inherited? She asked one of her detectives, Patrick Mulligan, who had contacts with the police, to find out if Mary had made a will.

The next day, Patrick had the news. "It's an old will," he said. "She left everything to her husband."

"That's no good," said Agatha. "He's dead. Jessica said she was a widow."

"No, she was posing as a widow. They were divorced four years ago. He was paying alimony. His name is John Brand. He owns the Gloucester deli in Mircester."

Agatha sat outside the deli until closing time. Patrick had given her a photograph of John Brand so she recognised him when he came out. He was followed by a pretty young blonde. He was a squat florid man in his fifties. The blonde looked as if she were not long out of her teens. He looked around and gave the blonde a hurried kiss. Agatha got out of her car and set off in pursuit of the blonde.

She caught up with her in a quiet street near the abbey. "Excuse me," said Agatha. "Do you know that John Brand is shortly going to be arrested for the murder of his ex wife?" Agatha's methods were often the despair of the police.

The girl turned white. "Who are you?" demanded Agatha.

"Are you the police?"

"I am in plain clothes," said Agatha jesuitically.

"I'm Tracey Forest. I ain't had nuffink to do with it. He said the old crow was bleeding him dry. He hated her. He said he had to kill her."

"Wait there, I'm calling the police," said Agatha.

"I thought you was the police," wailed Tracey.

"Sort of," said Agatha.

"Do you have to arrest him? He was going to take me to Paris."

Agatha sat drinking coffee with Jessica a week after the arrest of John Brand. The bells pounded out for the funeral of Mary.

"Hellish noise," shouted Agatha.

Jessica grinned.

"Music to my ears, Agatha."

THE SECRET OF THE OLD MILL

Enid Blyton

Enid Blyton (1897–1968) was a leading British author for children. Her works, including *The Famous Five*, *The Magic Faraway Tree* and *Noddy*, have been in print continually since the 1940s, and have often been adapted for screen and stage.

1. Peter Has an Idea

Peter was reading a book. He was sitting under a bush, almost hidden, and he hadn't said a word for over an hour.

'Peter!' said Janet. 'Peter! Do talk to me.'

Peter took no notice of his sister at all. He just went on reading. Then Scamper, the golden spaniel, pushed himself close to Peter and licked his nose.

Peter took no notice of Scamper either. Janet got cross.

'PETER! I keep talking to you and you don't answer. You're mean.'

Peter turned over a page, and was lost in his story again. Janet wondered what he could be reading. It must be a very, very interesting book! She crawled under the bush beside him.

She looked at the title of the book, printed at the top of the left-hand page: 'The Secret Society.' Well, it sounded exciting. Janet felt as if she must read it, too! She leaned over Peter's shoulder and began to read as well. But he didn't like that.

'Don't,' he said, and pushed his sister away. 'You know I hate people reading the same thing as I am reading.'

Then a bell rang in the distance.

'Bother!' said Peter. 'Now I'll have to stop. Janet, this is a lovely book; really, it is.'

He got up, and Janet got up, too. 'Tell me about it,' said Janet, as they went up to the farmhouse for tea.

'It's about a Secret Society,' said Peter. 'There's a band of men who have a secret meeting place and a secret password they use to let one another know they're friends. And they plan all kinds of things together.'

'Oooh, how lovely!' said Janet. 'I shall like reading that book. It's the one Granny gave you, isn't it?'

'Yes,' said Peter. Then he suddenly stopped, his face glowing with excitement. 'Janet! Why shouldn't *we* have a Secret Society, too – a secret band of boys and girls – and a secret meeting-place?'

'With a secret password,' said Janet, standing still, too. 'Peter – that would be marvellous!'

'Where could we meet?' wondered Peter. 'We'd have to plan all that. Oh, I know! Up at the tumbledown Old Mill!'

The tea-bell rang again, more loudly and impatiently. 'Mother's getting cross,' said Janet. 'We'd better hurry. We can talk about it after tea. Oh, Peter – what a lovely idea!'

They went in to tea with Scamper at their heels. They were so excited that they almost forgot to go and wash their hands and brush their hair first. But Mother soon reminded them!

They hardly said a word at teatime, because they were both so busy making their plans. Mother felt quite worried.

'What's the matter with you both? You hardly say a word!' she said. 'Have you quarrelled?'

'Oh, no,' said Peter. 'Of course not. We've thought of a lovely plan, that's all.'

'Well, so long as it doesn't mean you getting too dirty, and so long as it's nothing dangerous, that's all right,' said Mother. 'What is it?'

Peter and Janet looked at one another. 'Well,' said Peter, at last, 'it's a secret really, Mother.'

'Then, of course, I won't ask any questions,' said Mother at once. That was always so nice of her – she never made the children tell her anything if they didn't want to.

'I expect we'll tell you sometime,' said Peter. 'But we don't really know enough of the secret ourselves yet. I've finished my tea, Mother. Can I go?'

He and Janet and Scamper rushed out of the old farmhouse, which was their home. It was called Old Mill Farm because of the tumbledown mill on the hill nearby, which had once belonged to the farm. It had been a famous mill in its day, and its great vanes had swung round thousands of times in the wind, to work the machinery that ground the corn for the farmer.

It stood up on the sunny hill, its vanes broken and still now. The farmer no longer ground his corn there. It was an empty, dark old place, full of mice, owls, and spiders.

'Shall we go to the mill and talk over our plan?' said Janet. 'Nobody will hear us then.'

So off they went to the mill. They went in at the crooked old door, and found themselves in darkness, except for a few thin rays that crept in at cracks in the wall. The children didn't mind the quietness and the dark – they liked the old mill very much. They sat down in a corner.

'We'll talk in a low voice, because it's very, very secret,' said Peter. 'Now – who shall we have for our band, our Secret Society, Janet? Only boys and girls we really like and trust. We mustn't have anyone who will give the password away.'

'I should have Colin – and Jack – and Pam – and George,' said Janet. 'We both like them – and we know they can keep a secret, because we've tried them before. Let's get them all here on Saturday and have our first Secret Society meeting!'

'Yes – and choose the password, and plan what we are going to do!' said Peter. 'It *will* be fun! Let's have Barbara, too. I like her – she's good fun.'

'Right,' said Janet. 'Well, that's the first thing done – we've chosen the members of our Secret Society. Oh, isn't it going to be exciting, Peter!'

*

2. The First Meeting

Colin, Pam, Jack, George, and Barbara, each had a strange message the next day. This is what they got:-

'Please come to the Old Mill at five o'clock on Saturday evening. Say nothing to anyone! VERY SECRET!'

The five children were puzzled and excited. They didn't say a word to anyone. As Janet had said, they could all be trusted to keep a secret.

Peter and Janet were at the Old Mill at half past four, waiting. At ten to five Colin came. Two minutes later George and Jack arrived together. Then Barbara and Pam came exactly at five o'clock. They crouched down in the darkness, wondering why they had been told to come.

Peter suddenly spoke from a dark corner and made them all jump, because nobody knew that he and Janet were there.

'Hello, everyone!' said Peter.

'Why – that's Peter's voice,' said Jack, and switched on a torch he had brought with him. Then they all saw one another.

'Why did you get us all here like this?' asked Jack. 'Is it a trick or something?'

'No,' said Peter. 'It's just an idea Janet and I had. We want to form a Secret Society of just a few boys and girls. With a secret meeting place and secret password, you know.'

'And we chose you five because we like you, and we know we can trust you all to keep a secret,' said Janet.

'It sounds fine,' said George. 'What shall we have for a secret password?'

'Everyone must think hard,' said Peter. 'It's a word we must always say in a very low voice when we meet one another – or if we want to send a secret message, we must put the word in the message. And when we have secret meetings no one will be allowed in unless they first say the password.'

'What about Mississippi? Or some word like that?' said Barbara.

'Yes – or pomegranate, or some other unusual word?' said George.

'We might forget an ordinary word,' said Colin. 'We wouldn't forget one like pomegranate.'

'It's too difficult,' said Peter. So they all thought again. Then Pam spoke. 'What about something out of a nursery rhyme – Handy-Spandy – or Humpty Dumpty?'

'Or a game – tiddly-winks!' said Colin. 'I always like that name.'

Everyone liked the sound of tiddly-winks, and so they chose that for their secret password.

'The secret meeting place will be easy,' said Janet. 'It can be here, in the dark old mill. Nobody ever comes here. We wouldn't be disturbed at all.'

'Couldn't we go up high in the old mill?' said Pam. 'There used to be an old stairway, or steps, or something, that led to a little room behind the middle of the vanes. I remember your father telling me about it once when I came to tea, Peter.'

'Well, the stairs are awfully broken now,' said Peter, getting up. 'But I dare say we could manage to climb up all right. It would be fun to go into that tiny room behind the vanes. If we wanted to keep things there, they would be quite safe.'

'Yes – we could bring food here – make it a proper Society Headquarters,' said Colin. 'We might even meet here once in the middle of the night!'

'Gracious! I wouldn't dare to do that,' said Pam.

Everyone felt excited. They got up and looked for the old stairway. It was a good thing Jack had a torch with him, because there really wasn't enough light to see properly.

Some of the steps were missing. Some were half broken. It was quite exciting to get up them into a dusty, cobwebby barn-like room above. This wasn't the little room Pam meant. Peter knew which that was. He took Jack's torch and shone it on to a small, narrow, spiral stairway in one corner. This led up to the tiny room behind the vanes.

This stairway wasn't as tumbledown as the one downstairs. The seven children climbed up one behind another. Peter stood still at the top barring the way.

'Secret Society Headquarters,' he said. 'Give me the password, please – in a whisper!'

'Tiddly-winks!' whispered Jack. 'Tiddly-winks,' whispered Pam, and they were let in. The others all remembered the password too, and were soon sitting down in a ring on the dirty floor.

'This is a very nice secret place,' said Jack. 'Peter, what's our society called? Have you thought of a name? What shall we be?'

'We'll be the Seven Society,' said Peter. 'There are just seven of us.'

'Yes! And Pam and Barbara and I will make tiny buttons with S.S. on,' said Janet. 'One for each of us!'

Everyone thought that was a good idea. 'You must all promise most solemnly to keep our Seven Society a dead secret,' said Peter. And one by one they took his hand and promised very solemnly and earnestly.

'Usually a Society has a plan for something,' said Janet. 'Something to work for, I mean. What shall we plan?'

'Well – I've got an idea – though I don't know if you'll think it's a good one,' said Barbara, sounding rather shy. 'You know that little lame boy called Luke in the village? Well, he's got to have something done to his bad leg – but before it's done he's got to go away and have a really good holiday to be fit for it.'

'And we'll get the money somehow for his holiday!' cried Janet. 'That's what you mean, isn't it, Pam? I heard Mother say his poor old Granny couldn't afford to send him away to the sea. I think that's a good idea for our Secret Society! I do, really!'

'Well – it would have been nice to plan something more exciting,' said Colin. 'But we can have another plan later. Are we all agreed? Yes, we are!'

3. The Secret Seven Society

And so the Seven Society was formed – with Peter for its chief, and Colin, George, Jack, Janet, Pam, and Barbara for the other members.

The girls set to work that very evening, as soon as they got home, to make the little badges. Janet begged three small buttons from her mother, and a bit of cloth. She covered each button in red, and then threaded a needle with bright green silk.

She neatly sewed S.S. on each button in green. They really looked beautiful when they were finished. Janet wondered if the other girls were making theirs as nicely as she had made hers.

She had made one for herself, one for Peter, and one for Colin. Pam was making Jack's and her own, and Barbara was making George's and her own. They had to be worn on Monday.

Peter and Janet pinned on theirs on Saturday night to see how they looked. 'You've made them beautifully,' said Peter, pleased. 'I feel very important wearing a button like this, with a secret sign on. Do you remember the password, Janet?'

'Skittles,' said Janet. Peter looked at her in horror.

'*Janet!* You've forgotten the password already. I'm ashamed of you, really I am. Skittles wasn't the word we chose. Think again.'

'Er – was it Musical Chairs?' said Janet, screwing up her face as if she was trying hard to think. Peter groaned.

'Oh, Janet – to think *you* should have forgotten it! I don't think I ought to tell you, either. You will have to confess your bad memory to the others and let them see if you can still belong.'

'Is it Hopscotch – or Tip and run?' said Janet, giggling. Peter gave her a little punch.

'You're a bad girl! You do remember really! You're only making fun. Go on – what's the password?'

'Wuff-wuff,' said Scamper suddenly. He had been listening to all this with his head on one side.

'Oh – didn't it sound exactly as if he wuffed out Tiddly-winks!' said Janet. 'Good old Scamper – you remembered the password, didn't you? Of course, I remembered it, Peter. I was just being funny.'

Peter was very relieved. He took off his button and hid it away. He would wear it on Monday, when all the others did. He stroked Scamper's smooth silky head.

'We didn't make you a member, did we?' he said. 'But you remembered the password all right, Scamper. What was it, now?'

'Wuff-wuff,' said Scamper again, and Peter and Janet laughed and laughed.

All the Society wore their S.S. buttons on Monday morning. The other children in the class were puzzled and rather jealous. They all wanted buttons, too, but they didn't know what they were for.

'Sorry,' said Peter. 'It's a secret. Can't tell anyone, I'm afraid.'

The Society met on Monday evening again, at the Old Mill. They had all quite decided this should be their meeting place. Janet and Peter were up in the tiny room before the others came. It had been arranged that as soon as the rest came, they were to stand at the bottom of the broken stairway and say the password. Then Peter would say: 'Pass, brother, and come up the stairs.'

Colin came in. He stood at the bottom of the staircase, whilst Peter, in the little room far above, put his head out and listened. He heard Colin's voice down below.

'Tiddly-winks!'

Peter grinned to himself. 'Pass, brother, and come up the stairs!' he called, and up came Colin.

Everyone arrived, said the password, and was allowed to go up into the little room. There they made more plans.

'We shall need quite a lot of money to send Luke away,' said Janet. 'I was asking Mother how much it would cost, and she said at least thirty pounds a week.'

Colin whistled. 'Thirty pounds! That's a lot of money – and even then it would only pay for one week, you say.'

'Yes. But one week is better than nothing,' said Janet. 'And if all seven of us work hard at something, surely we could earn five pounds each by the end of term.'

'I'm going to earn my five pounds helping with the haymaking,' said George.

'And I'm going cherry picking,' said Jack. 'I believe I could earn more than five pounds if I go each evening.'

They each had some kind of plan. They sat and talked eagerly up in the little dark room. It was really rather uncomfortable there, and when Janet had been sitting on the hard floor for a time, she had a good idea.

'Let's make this a *proper* headquarters,' she said. 'With a rug or two to sit on – and let's clean the place up a bit – and get a lamp or something to light it.'

'Oooh, yes – and a box for a table,' said Jack. 'And we'll bring a moneybox here and drop our earnings into it at every meeting.'

'I like all these plans,' said Pam. I'll bring a brush and a pan – I've got small ones of my own.'

'And I'll bring an old rug out of our shed at home,' said Barbara. 'Nobody uses it but me. Mother gave it to me last year.'

'Meet here on Wednesday evening,' commanded Peter, 'with anything likely to make our headquarters really comfortable. And if anyone can bring any food or drink, they can. We could have supper here one night then. It would be fun!'

'The Seven Society is *great* fun!' said Colin – and everyone agreed. But it was going to be even more exciting soon!

4. A Very Surprising Thing

The next time the Secret Society met, its members were very busy indeed! Pam brought a brush and pan. Barbara brought her old rug, and a broom to help in the cleaning. Janet brought a stool.

Jack brought a lantern that the gardener had lent him. It was filled with oil, and he had to be very careful when he lit it.

'I've got to put it in a very safe, steady place,' he said. 'The gardener said we mustn't play the fool and knock it over, or we'd go up in smoke.'

'Well, we don't behave stupidly,' said Peter. 'I'm your chief, and I chose you all because you're sensible people. I wouldn't have chosen Gordon, because he's always messing about, being silly – and he'd have knocked over the lamp at once!'

The lamp certainly made a difference to the Old Mill room. It lighted up all its dark corners, and made everything look very cheerful.

They all set to work to clean the little room. The dust was thick and made them choke as it rose into the air.

'Oh, dear – I suppose it will all settle again as soon as we've finished!' said Janet. 'Well, I've swept quite a lot into this corner, anyway!'

When they had finished their job, they put down the old rug that Barbara had brought. It made a very nice carpet in the centre of the little room. Then Janet's stool was set down, and a box that Colin had found down on the ground floor of the mill.

'That's our table,' said Peter. 'Anyone brought anything for a meal?'

'I've got some cakes that Mother gave me,' said Pam. 'And Jack's got a whole bag of cherries. He's allowed to have as many as he likes when he goes cherry picking.'

'And I've got some tarts Mother made,' said Barbara.

The things were put on the table. 'It's a pity we haven't any spoons and forks, and plates,' said Janet. 'Mother wouldn't let me bring any of those. I did ask her.'

Jack rapped on the box table. 'Spirit of the Old Mill, we want spoons and forks and cups!' he said, loudly. Everyone laughed. They began to eat the food hungrily. They wished they had thought of bringing something to drink.

'We'd better have a kind of storecupboard somewhere here,' said Jack. 'Then if any of us comes here by himself, and is terribly hungry, he can help himself.'

'Does that mean you're going to visit the Old Mill each day?' said Colin, who knew what a big appetite Jack had. 'If you are, *I'm* not leaving anything behind!'

'Has everyone finished?' asked Peter. 'Because, if so, we ought to put our earnings into the moneybox I've brought, and count it up.'

'Yes, we'll do that,' said Janet, and she put an old moneybox on the table. It belonged to Peter and was in the shape of a pig. There was a slit in his back for the money. Underneath was a little place to unlock his tummy and take out the money. Peter had the key to that.

'How much is in the pig?' asked Colin, as each of them put in his bit. Peter was counting as it all went in.

'Goodness – we've put in eighteen pounds and fifty-four pence already!' he said. 'I think that's really marvellous!'

'Have we, really?' said Janet, pleased. 'We'll soon have thirty pounds, then, and probably more by the time the term has ended. I think we're a very very good Secret Society!'

It really was fun to have a Secret Society, with a secret name and badges, and a password. Sometimes, when one of the members met another, they whispered the password just to enjoy feeling they belonged to the Society.

'Tiddly-winks!'

'Pass, brother!'

It was not long before the Seven Society had a nice little larder up in the tiny room. Into it was packed a whole lot of things – tins of condensed milk, packets of jelly cubes, jars of potted meat, biscuits, and bars of chocolate. Bottles of ginger-beer were also put away in the dark corners, ready to be brought out at a Seven Society feast.

It was difficult to eat the condensed milk without a spoon, but nobody's mother would allow knives, forks, spoons, or crockery to be taken out of the children's homes. So they had to take it in turns to dip in their fingers and lick them.

'It's really disgusting, of course, eating it like this,' said Barbara. 'I do wish we had spoons and things.'

'I can't think what the spirit of the Old Mill is doing!' said Jack, with a grin. 'I told him to provide us with spoons and forks and cups the other day – and not a thing has he produced!'

'You're an idiot, Jack,' said Janet. 'Have you all finished? If so, I'll clear away.

I'll put the things on this funny old shelf here – not on the floor. They won't get so dusty.'

She stood on tiptoe to put the things away on the high shelf. As she was pushing a tin to the back, it bumped into something. Janet got the stool and stood on it. She saw a bag at the back of the shelf, and she pulled it out.

'Who put this bag here?' she asked. She shook it, and it clinked.

Nobody seemed to have put the bag there. So Janet climbed down from the stool and opened it. She shook out the things that were in it.

Down they fell on the rug – forks and spoons by the dozen!

Everyone stared in astonishment. 'Spoons – and forks!' said Barbara, in a rather shaky voice. 'Oh, goodness, Jack – the spirit of the Old Mill must have taken you at your word – and sent you the spoons and forks you commanded!'

Well, what an extraordinary thing! But there were the spoons and forks, shining on the rug – it was all perfectly true and real!

5. Eleven O'clock at Night

Barbara and Pam were rather frightened.

It seemed such a strange thing to happen. As for Jack, he just made a joke of it.

'Thanks, old spirit of the Mill!' he said, and took up a spoon. 'Very nice of you. What about a few cups now to drink ginger beer in? I did ask for some, you know.'

'Oh, don't!' said Pam. 'I'd just hate some cups to come from nowhere.'

'I'll see if there are any put ready for us on the shelf where Janet got these from,' said Jack, and he stood on the stool and felt about at the back of the rather deep shelf.

And he felt something there! Something very heavy indeed – a sack full of things that clinked.

Jack pulled it off the shelf. It was so heavy that when it fell to the ground he was almost pulled off the stool. Everyone stared in scared amazement. What next?

'Oh – I hope it's not cups,' whispered Barbara. 'I'd hate it to be cups.'

Without saying a word, Jack undid the rope that tied the neck of the sack. He put in his hand – and brought out a silver cup! And another and another – all gleaming and shining brightly.

'Well – they *are* cups!' he said. 'Sports cups, it is true – but, still, cups. What shall we ask for next? Teapots or something?'

'You're not to talk like that,' said Janet. 'It's making me feel peculiar. Peter – what do you think is the meaning of this?'

'Well,' said Peter, 'it's nothing to do with Jack's silly commands, of course. *I* think that some thieves are using this old mill for a hidey-hole for their stolen goods.'

There was a silence. 'Do you really?' said George. 'Well, I hope they don't come whilst we're here!'

'Shouldn't let them up!' said Peter, at once. 'They wouldn't know the right password!'

'Idiot!' said Jack. 'They'd come up just the same.'

'I know what we'll do,' said Colin. 'We four boys will come along here late at night and watch to see who the thieves are. That would be a real adventure!'

'Yes!' cried Jack, George, and Peter at once. The girls were only too glad to be left out of this idea.

'We ought to tell somebody,' said Janet.

'Wait till we find out who the thieves are,' said Peter. 'Then we can go straight along to the police station and tell our great news.'

The other boys were all for going to the Old Mill at eleven o'clock that night, and hiding to watch for the thieves. They felt sure they would be along to fetch their hidden goods. Janet was certain the sacks hadn't been there when they had cleaned the tiny room. So the thieves must have been along only a little time ago and would, no doubt, come to get their goods at the first chance.

'There's no moon tonight, so it would be a good night for them to come,' said Jack. 'Well, boys – meet here at eleven. Give the password at the bottom of the stairs, and go up when you hear "Pass, brother," as usual.'

They all went home, excited. What an adventure that night for the boys!

At eleven o'clock, Peter was up in the tiny room in pitch darkness. A rat scuttled across the floor and made him jump. He waited for the others, wishing they would come.

Ah – that was somebody. It sounded like old Colin, blundering in. Peter was just about to call out to him when he stopped himself. Of course – he must wait for the password! What was he thinking of, not to wait for the password?

He waited. No password came. But somebody was coming up the broken stairs. In a panic, Peter stood up quietly in the tiny room far above. Soon whoever it was would be in the room beside him – he would be found by the thieves!

It *couldn't* be one of the Seven, because he hadn't heard any password. Silently, Peter made for a corner, and pushed himself behind a great beam he knew was there, though he couldn't see it.

A man came up the spiral stairway and into the tiny room. He switched on a torch and went to the shelf. He ran his torch over the shelf and then gave an angry grunt.

'Gone! The sacks are gone! That pest of a Lennie has been here first. I'll teach him he can't do things like that to me! Wait till I find him!'

Peter kept as still as a mouse whilst the angry voice was going on. Then his heart almost stopped beating. The light of the torch was shining steadily on the pig moneybox! The thief had seen it.

He picked it up and shook it. When he heard the money inside, he dashed the pig to the floor and trod hard on it. The pig broke. The money came rolling out.

'Now, who put that pig up there?' said the man, and stooped to pick up the money. Peter could have cried to see all their hard earned savings going into the thief's pocket. But he simply didn't dare to say a word.

At last the man went. Peter hoped the other boys wouldn't run into him! They were very late. The sounds of stumbling down the broken stairs stopped, and there was silence again in the Old Mill.

After a bit, Peter crept out of his hiding-place. He was surprised to find that his knees were shaking. He almost jumped out of his skin when a word came up the stairs to him.

'Tiddly-winks!'

'Pass, brother,' said Peter, thankfully, and up came the other three boys – and behind them came Scamper the spaniel. Oh, how pleased Peter was to see them all!

6. What an Adventure!

Peter told them all what had happened. They listened without a word, most astonished – and were very upset when they heard that their savings had been stolen from the moneybox.

'The girls *will* be miserable!' said Jack. 'I think we've made rather a mess of this, Peter. We ought to have told our parents, or the police, after all.'

'Yes. We ought,' said Peter. 'But I'll tell you what I think, boys – I think the second thief will be along soon, because I believe they were to meet here to-night and divide the stolen goods. This fellow thought Lennie, the other thief, had already been here and taken them. He didn't know we had hidden them safely away.'

'I see – and you think we might catch the second thief?' said Jack. 'Right. But I'm not risking anything now – one of us must go the police station and bring back a policeman!'

'All three of you can go,' said Peter. 'But I'll stay here and watch with Scamper. I'll be safe with him. Somebody must stay here and watch for the other thief, in case he comes before you get back.'

So the three boys set off again in the darkness, leaving Scamper cuddled against Peter's knees in the tiny room above. 'Now, you mustn't make a sound, see, Scamper?' said Peter. 'Ah – listen – what's that?'

It was a noise down below. Perhaps it was the boys coming back? Peter listened once more for the password. But it didn't come. So it must be the second thief. He tightened his hold on Scamper, who was longing to growl.

The thief came right up into the room. He, like the other man, went to the deep shelf and found nothing there. He swept his powerful torch round the room – and suddenly saw Peter's feet sticking out from behind the beam!

In a flash he pulled him out – but he let him go in a hurry when Scamper flew at him. He kicked at the dog, but Scamper wouldn't stop trying to bite him.

In the middle of all this a voice came up the stairs. The thief heard what it said in the greatest surprise. The voice said: 'Tiddly-winks,' very loudly indeed.

'*Tiddly-winks*,' said the thief, amazed. 'What does he mean, Tiddly-winks?' He went to the top of the spiral stairway and called down.

'Is that you, Jim Wilson? Have you taken the sacks? They're not here – but there's a boy and a dog here. Got to be careful of the dog!'

'Tiddly-winks!' yelled the voice again. It was Jack, anxious to know if Peter was all right.

'Pass, brother!' yelled back Peter. Look out – the other thief is here. Did you bring a policeman?'

'Two!' yelled back Jack. 'Nice big ones. Make the thief come on down. They're waiting for him.'

The thief was scared. He ran to some rickety steps in the corner of the room. They led up to a tiny attic at the very top of the mill. But Scamper was there before him, growling.

'That's right, Scamper! Send him down, send him down!' cried Peter. And Scamper obeyed. He worried at the thief's trousers, giving him nasty little nips in the leg till the man went stumbling down the spiral staircase. In the room below were the two policemen, waiting.

'All right, I'll come,' said the thief. 'Just call this dog off, will you? He's bitten my legs from ankle to knee, the little pest!'

'And what about your friend, who helped you to do the robbery?' asked one of the policemen, taking hold of the thief's arm. 'What about Jim Wilson?'

The thief had forgotten that he had called out Jim Wilson's name a few minutes before. He stared angrily at the big policeman.

'Oh, so you know about Jim Wilson, do you?' he said. 'Has he been telling tales of me? Well, I'll tell tales of *him* then!'

'Yes, go on,' said the policeman, and he took out a big black notebook to write down what the thief said.

'Jim Wilson's my mate and he lives at Laburnum Cottage,' said the thief. 'He and I did this job together, and we hid the stuff here. We meant to share it. But Jim's been here first and taken it. Yes, and hidden it somewhere safe, too, where *you'll* never find it!'

'But *we* know where it is!' cried Jack, and he swung his torch round the room where they were all standing. 'Look – do you see that loose board there? Well, we put the spoons and forks and cups there, before we left here tonight! I think they're all solid silver. They feel so heavy.'

'Yes, they're silver all right,' said one of the policemen, pulling the sacks out of the hole under the board, and taking out a few of the things.

'The other thief took all our money out of the moneybox,' said Peter, sadly. 'We'll never get that back, I suppose.'

'He'll have hidden it already, I'm afraid,' said the policeman. He snapped his black notebook shut. 'Well, come along, Lennie. We'll take you away safely and then go to Laburnum Cottage for Jim. Nice of you to tell us all about him.'

'You tricked me!' shouted Lennie. But his loud voice made Scamper growl again and fly at his trousers. 'Call this dog off!' he begged. Peter called him off. Scamper came back to him, still growling fiercely. Good old Scamper!

'What were you doing here, you boys?' said one of the policemen, as they left the Old Mill and went down the hill.

'Well – we four and three girls often come here,' said Peter. 'Sort of meeting-place, you know?'

'Oh – you've got a Secret Society, I suppose,' said the policeman. 'All children belong to one at some time or other. I did myself. Passwords and badges, and all that!'

'Yes,' said Peter, surprised that the policeman guessed so much.

'Tiddly-winks! Ho, that was a password, then?' said the first policeman, and he chuckled. 'I must say I wondered why you boys stood down there calling Tiddly-winks in the night! Well – your Secret Society did a lot of good, didn't it? It's caught us two thieves.'

'Yes. But it's lost us our precious savings,' said Peter. 'We worked hard for that money. We wanted it for Luke – to send him away on a holiday, you know.'

'Very nice idea,' said the policeman. 'I hope you get the money back – but I'm afraid you won't.'

They didn't. They were very sad about that when they met again the next day, being very careful indeed to use the password before climbing up the stairs.

The girls could hardly believe their ears when they heard about all the happenings of the night. They stared sadly at the battered, broken pig on the floor, and thought of all their hard work wasted.

But a day later something lovely happened. A letter came to Peter's house. It was addressed rather strangely:-

THE CHIEF,
    THE SECRET SOCIETY,
       OLD MILL FARM.

'Well, look at that!' said Mother. 'I suppose it's for you, Peter.'

It was, of course. Inside was a letter that made Peter and Janet squeal for joy.

'Dear Secret Society,

    I hear from the police that you helped them to catch the thieves who stole my silver, and that you hid it in safety when you found it. I am most grateful. Please accept this hundred pounds in gratitude for your Society's good work.

    Yours sincerely,
    Edward Henry White.'

'Gracious! That's the man the silver belonged to!' cried Peter. 'Mother, look! A hundred pounds! That will send Luke away for three whole weeks on a holiday!'

Well, what a surprise! The two rushed off to tell the others the good news, and then off they all went to Luke. He could hardly believe his good luck.

The Secret Society of Seven is still going strong, although they meet now in Janet and Peter's garden shed. But Tiddly-winks is no longer their password, because too many people know it now. They choose a new one for each adventure.

"MR AND MRS JANSEN" AND THE MERMAID

Sharon Bolton

Sharon Bolton is an internationally acclaimed author of mystery thrillers, including *Sacrifice*, *Little Black Lies* and the Lacey Flint series. Her work has garnered many awards including the Crime Writers' Association's Dagger in the Library. She was born in Lancashire.

Amsterdam before dawn is a place of long, stealing shadows, of street lights dancing on water and of a silence that hovers like mist. The man walking swiftly along the Herengracht could be alone in the city; he sees no one and no one sees him.

He is a little out of breath by the time he reaches the third floor of the hotel but the lifts of this old building are noisy and he doesn't want to draw attention to himself.

'Would you believe she didn't call?' He steps into a room as dark and quiet as the city outside. 'I could have stayed.' He thinks perhaps he can hear Juliette sigh in anticipation as he pulls off his clothes but, then again, it could be the floor-boards settling.

The bed creaks beneath his weight, the sheets are cool. He slides across, already erect, and stretches to kiss her shoulder. She is naked, just as he left her.

She is cold as the air outside, her flesh oddly resistant to his touch. Like congealing clay.

With the numb acceptance of someone who knows disaster is imminent and unavoidable, Ralf switches on the bedside light. The corpse he sees beside him comes as no surprise.

The previous evening

The mermaid scuttles her way along the canal-side as the water tells her how it is doing. It's not been the best of days, one of those murky brown, troubled days, when litter hangs around and ferries piss out oil. The mermaid taps her stick along the edge, negotiating her way around parked bicycles and thinks of a time when her body was young and strong and the cool water of the city's canals stroked her skin like the hands of the lover who, ultimately, never arrived.

'Buy a nice silk scarf for your lady friend?'

The man hurrying past her is rich – only the rich have that particular smell of new wool, spiced fruit and cedar wood. Rich and young, only the young move at that speed. His voice comes from inches above her head.

'I don't think so.'

Only the handsome have that arrogant tone to their voices. The mermaid catches the man's hand and at the touch of his flesh sees his urgency, his excitement. The emotions bubble inside him like the water behind a power-boat.

He pulls back. He is not used to being touched by strangers. The mermaid lets him go.

Ralf pushes at the heavy glass. There are people ahead of him at reception and he is tempted to walk past, but the Ambassade Hotel is too small for him to pass unnoticed and so he waits and drums his fingers together in a manner that, were he able to see himself, would remind him disturbingly of his father.

'Mr Jansen,' he tells the clerk when he has his attention. 'My wife arrived a few hours ago.'

'Certainly Mr Jansen, your wife is in room 95. Shall I show . . . have a nice evening, sir.'

Juliette is at the window. As always he is surprised by how tall she is, how her long, dark hair shines like lacquered walnut. She smiles, and he loves that she can never hide the pleasure she takes in his company.

'I've been watching the mermaid,' she says.

Over her shoulder he sees the tiny woman with the rickety body and long red hair who seems to be sniffing her way over the bridge like a stray dog.

'That old gypsy?' he says. 'She's not very elegant but I hardly think that's a tail she's tottering around on.'

'The clerk downstairs was telling me she's been seen around here since she was a child. She's always by the water so people call her the mermaid.'

Ralf doesn't want to talk about the old woman. 'So how do you like my city?' he asks.

'I like the syrup waffles,' she tells him.

'Waffles?'

'Little flat pancakes. You put them on your coffee cup and the syrup inside starts to melt.'

He loves the feel of the muscles playing in her strong, slim back, the way she smells of rice milk and cherries.

'Yeah, I know what they are. Is that it?'

'And the way it looks drunk.'

'Drunk?'

She wriggles round in his arms to face the narrow, high gabled houses across the canal. 'The houses are all over the place,' she says. 'They're like elegant ladies after a good night out on the town.'

'Syrup waffles and tipsy streets. Anything else?'

'The quiet,' she whispers, tickling his ear. 'Such a quiet city. I think in the middle of the night we can open the window and hear nothing.'

For a second he doesn't answer and she stiffens in his arms.

'What?' she says.

He sighs. 'There's a problem? My wife is very suspicious.'

'Has she gone?'

'She's gone.'

His wife – his real wife, not the woman he occasionally claims is his wife at hotel reception desks – left their home an hour ago. 'She's going to phone me at midnight. At home.'

'You're kidding me?'

He shrugs. 'What can I do? If I'm not there, she'll drive back.'

'I've flown from London for what? Dinner?'

'I'll be back in the morning. I'll come with you to the airport.'

'I've come all this way to spend the night by myself?'

It is a constant irritation to him that a woman so beautiful can be so needy. Over her shoulder he can see the old woman, leaning on the bridge, muttering to the water below. 'Aren't mermaids supposed to be young and pretty?' he says.

Juliette is still sulking. 'Maybe she was, once. Maybe I'll look like that one day.'

He tells himself that if she does, he won't be around to see it. 'We have this evening,' he says, pulling her close again. 'We have now.'

The couple leave the hotel arm in arm, his leather-soled shoes moving slowly to keep pace with her shorter, high-heeled steps. He smells different now. Beneath the synthetic mimicry of flowers and spice, the mermaid can detect the acrid whiff of sex.

'Scarf for your lady friend?' she calls out, more as a taunt than a sales pitch.

Better behaved in front of his woman, he pulls out his wallet. The mermaid misjudges and the money wafts towards the water. She makes her angry sound high in her throat, the rattling hiss of the swan defending its family. The woman's voice, young, sweet and foreign, comes from close to the ground.

'Got it,' she says. As she takes the note the mermaid brushes the woman's hand. So cold, like the ice that forms on the water's edge in January. As the couple walk away, the mermaid makes the sound of the pen swan when her cygnets have been stoned to death by cruel children.

'Thank you,' Juliette says to him at dinner. The piece of brown and orange cloth is around her shoulders. He'd like to tell her it ruins the simple elegance of her dress, but knows he'll probably want her again before the evening is out and Juliette seems to delight in taking what he says the wrong way.

'I'm glad we saw her,' she goes on. 'Some people think she's connected to the Beguines, do you know about them?'

'The catholic not-quite-nuns of the Begijnhof,' he says, referring to the enclosed medieaval square close to the Singel canal that his wife once dragged him around. 'I think the last one died in the 1970s.'

'The story is the mermaid was the illegitimate child of one of the last nuns,' says Juliette. 'So no one could acknowledge her, but they looked after her in the community. People think she still lives somewhere around the Begijnhof but no one ever sees her coming or going, just walking around the canals.'

A text has just arrived on his phone. His wife. When he looks up again, Juliette's face has darkened and he knows he is going to have to work for the sex later on. Maybe he should wait for the morning, when she'll be needy again, dreading the goodbye, eager to make the most of their remaining time together.

'Don't give me a hard time.'
 'I didn't realise I was.'

He sighs. She doesn't need to say anything, the look in her eyes is enough. He wonders whether it might, actually, be time to move on. 'I'll see you in the morning,' he says. 'We'll have breakfast.'
 Downstairs, the gypsy who sold him the scarf has actually made her way inside. She is arguing with the night porter, whose back is turned. As the cold air rushes through the lobby, the mermaid turns to watch him go. Her eyes flash a fluorescent green, like those of a cat caught in a car's headlights and then that tiny, wrinkled nose twitches again, as though she can smell him.

Probably because she is crying, Juliette doesn't see the silk scarf on the bathroom floor. As she steps on it, it slides along the smooth tiles. She falls heavily and her head strikes the stone edge of the bath.
 The pain is nauseating. Hardly aware of what she is doing, Juliette gets to her feet. She grips the basin for balance, waits for the pain to lessen. When she feels she can bear it, she lifts her head. The skin on her temple is bruised but not broken. No blood. She runs a glass of water and walks back to the bedroom. Tears are still falling, but she's no longer sure which pain is causing them. Naked, she lowers her head gingerly to the pillow, telling herself she's OK and that she'll feel better in the morning.
 She is wrong. The internal bleeding of an acute, subdural haematoma has already begun. Five hours after slipping on the mermaid's silk scarf, Juliette is dead.

'She's here, Guv,' the custody sergeant tells his inspector, who has spent the last hour interviewing the prime suspect in that morning's murder. An important Dutch lawyer, married with two young children, kills his mistress in a hotel bedroom and flees the scene. The papers are going to love it.
 The inspector shakes his head. 'They book into a hotel as Mr and Mrs Jansen, they're seen going out to dinner, seen coming back, heard shagging rather enthusiastically and then she's not seen again till the maid goes in to make up the room. His story is that he left just before eleven. Says he went home to take a call from his wife, only she changed her mind. He says he got back before dawn to find the lady-friend stiff as his prick.'
 'Any doubt he did it?'
 'Not really. We'll wait for the pathologist's report but it's pretty clear she died from a blow to the head. I think our friend's going down for a long time.'
 'And what's the mermaid got to do with it?' asks the sergeant.
 'He claims she saw him leave the hotel last night. She's his alibi. His only one.'
 The sergeant was born in the canal district. He has known of the mermaid all his life. 'She saw him?' he repeats.

'She was certainly in the lobby at the right time according to the desk clerks. OK, she in here?'

The mermaid is looking at the floor, but he sees her nostrils twitch. The inspector finds himself wishing he'd taken a shower that morning. She leans forward, definitely sniffing him. Then she relaxes, and the corners of her mouth turn up in the semblance of a smile.

'The man from the hotel,' she says. 'You have been with him just now?'

The inspector ignores this. 'Madam,' he says. 'When you were in the Ambassade Hotel last night, did you see anyone leave?'

'I saw nothing.'

The mermaid lifts her head. He understands now, why the custody sergeant found his request amusing. This frail, elderly woman with the remarkable hair has eyes that are pale and opaque with advanced cataracts. She has been blind for years.

THE HIDDEN APE

Marjorie Bowen

Marjorie Bowen was a pseudonym for Margaret Campbell (1885–1952), a British author most famous for historical romances and popular biographies. She wrote crime and supernatural short stories prolifically and is considered a master of gothic horror. Bowen also proved an unexpected influence on Graham Greene.

"Nothing at all," smiled the Doctor, "but a few bruises and shock. No, really nothing. It was a very brave thing for Joliffe to do," he added; "extremely brave."

"Of course, I understand that," said Professor Awkwright, a little stiffly. He felt that the Doctor thought him lacking in gratitude and sympathy, and he knew that he was indeed incapable of any emotional expression, also that he resented, deeply resented, the intrusion of the violent and sensational into a life that he had contrived to make exactly as he wished it to be.

But, all the same, he did feel immensely grateful to Joliffe, and said so again, snappishly, blinking behind the thick crystal spectacles that distorted his pale eyes.

"Naturally I shall do all in my power to show my deep appreciation."

The Doctor, who did not like the Professor, cheerfully remarked:

"It is rather rare, you know, for a scholar – a man who leads an intellectual and sedentary life – to be so prompt and decisive in action; it's no reflection on Joliffe to say that I would have thought him the last man – not to have the will to, but to have the power – to risk his life for another."

When the Doctor had gone Professor Awkwright rather resentfully considered these words. He agreed with the Doctor; he secretly thought that Joliffe's action was quite amazing and the last thing he would have expected of him.

"I could never have done it," he confessed to himself ruefully. He had always, in a kindly fashion, patronized Joliffe, but now Joliffe was definitely revealed as the superior being. Really, in the Professor's estimation, the whole episode was disagreeable, and what was worse, slightly ridiculous; he was sure that the Doctor had been faintly amused.

Yet, he certainly ought to feel grateful to Joliffe and on many counts.

The incident which had first alarmed, then irritated the Professor, was this: his orphan ward Edmund had been out as usual with his tutor, Samuel Joliffe, and Charles the vicar's son, just one of the usual rambles over the lovely North Wales hills which were undertaken every day as a matter of duty; when Edmund, scrambling on ahead, had slipped, like the clumsy lad he was, over a precipice and hung, stunned, on a ledge overhanging a ravine.

Now the Professor would have thought that the jolly athletic Charles, a stout, trained youth, would really without any fuss at all have gone down the face of the rock and brought up Edmund; but Charles had done nothing of the kind; he had just "lost his head" like a silly girl and could think of nothing better to do than to run and fetch help from the nearest cottage which was some distance away. On the other hand, Samuel Joliffe, middle-aged, stiff-limbed, shortsighted, absent-minded to all appearances, cautious and timid, whom no one would expect to be quick or active, had actually lowered himself down the face of the precipice, supported Edmund till help arrived and then, with great coolness and dexterity, with the aid only of a dubious rope and some frail saplings, hauled up Edmund and himself to safety.

It was all, Professor Awkwright thought, very grotesque, the sort of thing one would so much rather had not happened.

He peeped in at his nephew sleeping heavily on his bed behind a screen. Mrs. Carter, the housekeeper, was in charge; the wretched woman seemed to enjoy the sensation caused by the accident, as Professor Awkwright looked at the boy with the bandaged head, breathing heavily under the influence of the sleeping potion, she began to murmur the praises of Mr. Joliffe.

It was clear that the tutor would be a hero in the eyes of everyone; the Professor resented this as a fuss and an interruption to a very smooth existence, but he was, at bottom, a just, even an amiable man, and he did not wish to evade his obligations to Samuel Joliffe.

So he went downstairs rather nervously to the study where he was sure the tutor would be working and, as he went, he honestly put before himself the extent of his obligations towards Samuel Joliffe; these were very varied and deep and amounted to far more than gratitude for the rather absurd act of heroism yesterday.

Professor Awkwright was a born scholar and solitary; his one interest and passion was the most abstruse branch of archaeology, the deciphering of dead languages; he had always had sufficient means to enable him to devote himself entirely to this fascinating labor and the one interruption in a life otherwise devoid of incident had been when his only brother had died and left in his charge a sullen, unruly boy of ten years of age, of the type known as "difficult and awkward," slightly abnormal and not very lovable, but a boy who had a comfortable income from a nice little fortune that would make him, when he attained his majority, quite a wealthy man.

Professor Awkwright had the conventional ideas of duty and subscribed, to the full, to the codes endorsed by his class and training, so he very scrupulously did his best with his unwelcome charge and made the great sacrifice of keeping with him a boy so obviously unfitted for school.

And after the Professor had found Samuel Joliffe, Edmund was no trouble at all; and the little household in the exceedingly comfortable but lonely Welsh mansion ran very smoothly and with a most agreeable, if eventless, harmony.

For Samuel Joliffe, besides being the perfect tutor, was the perfect secretary, the perfect assistant, and had thrown himself with the greatest ardor into the Professor's enthusiastic labors.

Indeed, Professor Awkwright, pausing at the door of the study, realized, in the emotional upset of the accident, that Joliffe was absolutely essential to him; after eight years of his support, help, assistance and company Joliffe was indeed indispensable; indispensable, that was the word.

"I daresay," said the little scholar to himself, pausing on the threshold, "I never quite appreciated Joliffe – of course, he has been handsomely paid and very well treated, but really I don't believe that I ever quite realized his – his sterling worth."

And Professor Awkwright thought, with a shudder, how ghastly it would have been if poor Edmund had died in that miserable way; he was fond of the unattractive boy who would probably never evoke any other affection in all his futile life.

And with that sharp realization of happiness that comes when happiness is threatened, the Professor cast over with profound gratitude all the blessings he had hitherto taken for granted . . . the smooth, easy life; the congenial, successful work; the way that all four of them, himself, Joliffe, Edmund, Mrs. Carter the housekeeper, all fitted together, like hand in glove – the comfort, the peace, the ordered leisure of it all! And surely much of this was owing to Joliffe – Joliffe who was never out of humor, nor ill, nor wanted a holiday, who was never tired or dull, who had known from the first how to "manage" Edmund, who never crossed Mrs. Carter nor vexed the servants, who worked so diligently, with such enthusiasm and skill under his employer's direction . . .

The Professor opened the door quickly; he crossed to the desk where Joliffe was sitting (as he had known he would be), and said:

"I don't know how to thank you, Joliffe, how to express my gratitude, I really don't."

Joliffe rose and stared; this was the first time since his knowledge of him that Awkwright had expressed himself on impulse; the tutor stood humbly; behind him the huge desk was neatly piled with the manuscripts that embodied their joint labors on the subject of the Minoan language.

"But," added the Professor with even greater warmth, "I am quite resolved that you shall have your name on the book. That is only just – it is your work as much as mine, you have been far more, for years now, than an assistant –"

Joliffe's sandy face flushed.

"I could not think of that, sir, really, I couldn't; what I have done has been the greatest pleasure and honor."

He spoke sincerely, without servility; Awkwright grasped his hand.

"I know. But, of course, we are to go equal shares in this – I ought to have thought of it before."

He glowed with the pleasure of his generous action; it was no ordinary prize, no feeble glory that he offered; he believed that when his, their, book was published it would bring to the authors a fame equal to that of Champollion.

For the two secluded scholars working almost in secret were convinced that they had discovered the clue to the long-dead language of one of the most interesting civilizations of prehistoric Greece, that of Crete.

Joliffe said:

"I hope, sir, yesterday had not put this into your mind. What I did was nothing. Anyone would have done as much."

"I don't think so, Joliffe."

"Anyone, sir, as fond of Edmund as I am."

"Again I disagree. Presence of mind, coolness like that! Rare indeed. But, of course, one can't talk of rewards; absurd, of course; but –"

The Professor sat down in front of the great bow-window; his kindly, conventional and rather simple face, with the thin beard, speckled like his grey tweed coat, and the thinner hair exact and glossy over the large brow was clearly outlined against the shining laurels in the garden and the blue hills beyond.

Joliffe regarded him with meek intentness.

"But, you were saying, sir," he prompted –

"I was about to say," remarked the Professor candidly, "that a shock – like this – clarifies the air, as it were. I suppose we live rather a monotonous, rather an old-fogeyish sort of life, values get a little dimmed, one gets absorbed in the past, in one's work. One's own life gets a little unreal . . . until a thing like this happens . . ."

"I have never felt that," replied Joliffe thoughtfully.

"No? A remarkably clear brain," agreed the other with simple admiration. "I've noticed how you never lose grip on things. That's why you've been so successful with Edmund. But really, for myself, I confess that a – a revelation of this kind – what the loss of Edmund would mean – the sort of man you really are – wakes me up, puts everything clearly."

"I don't see that the fact that I rescued Edmund, in the most ordinary way, reveals the sort of man I am."

"But that kind of prompt action isn't expected of – of our type, Joliffe. It's most unusual; the Doctor said so."

"I don't think Dr. Jones knows very much."

"No, but I agreed with what he meant. And it is settled about the book."

Professor Awkwright felt very content for the rest of that day; the sense of the absurdity of the accident, the irritating, disturbing excitement had passed away. Edmund came down to tea and the household was stolidly normal again; but the Professor continued, as he had himself put it, "to see clearly" – the vast value of Joliffe, for instance, and Edmund's inarticulate and pathetic affection for him, and the very agreeable intimacy that bound them all together; it was surprising how fond he was himself of the unattractive, slightly "mental" youth; why, he believed that if Edmund had really been killed the shock would have prevented him from finishing the book.

When the two men settled down in the study that evening after Edmund had gone to bed Professor Awkwright felt that their relationship had subtly changed; never had they been so intimate, never so frank, as if there was no possibility of any misunderstanding or irritation between them.

Joliffe seemed to "let himself go" intellectually; his usually respectful, almost timid manner mellowed, he was more candid, more brilliant, slightly, though quite unmistakably, different, Awkwright thought, from his habitual self.

One of Mrs. Carter's most tempting dinners had celebrated Edmund's escape; there had been good wine and afterwards, contrary to custom, good brandy.

Perhaps it was the brandy that stimulated the Professor's added sense of clarity, of which he had been aware all day; a most temperate man, he had always, on the few occasions when he had drunk liberally, been teased as to the right naming of his heightened perceptions. Did alcohol give everything an air of caricature, or did it allow you to see everything as it really was?

Was it, for instance, just excitement and then the brandy that made him think what a queer fellow Joliffe was? – or had he, Awkwright, always had his head so in the air that he had never before observed the strangeness of his constant companion? Joliffe sat a little more at his ease than he had ever sat before; a very tall, stiff, long-legged man, with an odd look of being featureless; the only definite object about his face was his glistening spectacles, for the rest a sandy glow seemed to blot out any salient point in his countenance; even his profile seemed to mean nothing; a closer inspection showed his features to be sharp, small and neat, his expression composed and kindly.

He also must have been a little excited that night, also a little stimulated by the occasion and the brandy, for he forgot (to the Professor's amusement) to go up to his room and listen for the wireless news bulletin.

Professor Awkwright had always refused to have wireless, gramophone or telephone; but Joliffe, with meek persistence, had indulged in all in his own room; he had little chance of using any of these inventions and he scrupulously contrived so that they never annoyed the rest of the household; but he liked to "sneak off," as the Professor put it with indulgent irony, to listen to news, a talk, or a concert; but tonight he seemed to have forgotten even the attraction of the evening bulletin which he so seldom missed.

The two elderly men talked of their researches, of the book that was going to bring glory to both, and of the accident of yesterday which the Professor, at least, could by no means dismiss from his mind.

"It was pure impulse," said Joliffe at last; "if I had reflected at all I don't suppose that I should have done it."

"I'm sure that you would."

"No, because I always think that we attach too much importance to human life. And Edmund wouldn't really mind dying; I daresay he'd be better off in another state."

"I didn't know that you had those ideas."

"They aren't ideas. Surely, sir, you don't hold by all the orthodox views –"

"I'd really rather –"

"Oh, the sacredness of human life, et cetera, et cetera?"

"I suppose so, I haven't quite thought it out."

"I have. I can't see, sir, how, after all your researches you can avoid a broader view . . . look at the East, Russia, Mexico, today – look at the Elizabethans, look at America, at Italy – and how they regard and have regarded death –"

"You don't think it matters – violent death?"

"No. An intelligent man should be able to deal with death – give it, withhold it, accept it, avoid it, according to his reason. The world was more worthwhile when this was so."

"But, my dear Joliffe, to argue like that is to condone murder," Awkwright smiled, very comfortable in his chair, "and suicide."

Joliffe did not reply, he seemed sunk in a pleasing reverie; to rouse him Awkwright said:

"I suppose one gets conventional-minded on these subjects, but I think the West is right in the value put on human life – our violences, our indifferences to right and wrong, our cowardices are nothing, I fear, but manifestations of the hidden ape, still lurking within so many of us, alas!"

Joliffe listened to this speech with closed eyes.

"On the contrary," he declared, "I believe that the hidden ape in me made me rescue Edmund."

"My dear Joliffe, as if apes –"

"They do – animal affection – animal devotion, no reason, no logic. I am fond of Edmund."

"Why?" wondered the Professor rather wistfully.

"One doesn't know. The ape again! The boy never pretends, he is very wise about some things, has extraordinary instincts! I believe I understand him as no one else ever will."

Joliffe sat up suddenly. He was smiling, his small eyes looked yellow behind the glasses, his movement seemed to dismiss the subject; they each drank some more brandy and began to discuss the book; but this speedily brought them to the same point; Joliffe remarked on the beauty of some of the Minoan seals he had been copying the very morning of the accident, and Awkwright's comment was that the artist who designed them had an evil mind.

"Why?" challenged the tutor with his new freedom.

"Well, they are evil. The Minoans were, it is acknowledged – cruel; consider their bull-leaping sports – no soul . . ."

"Nonsense!" Never had Joliffe expressed himself so boldly to his employer; he seemed really excited, "They were simply too civilized to put so much value on individual life –"

"The hidden ape wasn't hidden, you mean?" smiled Awkwright.

They argued keenly and at length, remaining in the study long after their usual hour for retiring; to Awkwright it was an entirely academical discussion, but Joliffe seemed to throw more and more feeling into it until he was making quite a personal point of his contention that no civilized people would consider murder a crime.

The Professor did not know how they had got to this subject; it was strange how the accident seemed to have thrown both a little out of their stride, a little off their balance; even Awkwright felt the mental atmosphere becoming distasteful, an unpleasant sense of unreality obscured the familiar cosy room; he wished that Joliffe would not talk so much, so at random (and he had never wished that before). He roused himself out of a disagreeable lethargy to say, with a rather false attempt at authority:

"This sort of stuff is really absurd from a man like you, Joliffe." The tutor rose and stood in front of the fire; his attitude was dogmatic, his habitual featurelessness seemed to have developed into a face that Awkwright did not recognize.

"Pardon me, my dear sir, how do you know what kind of man I am?"

"We have been intimate for eight years."

"But I know you much better than you know me."

"I don't agree."

"Well, what do you know of me? You said yourself that what I did yesterday surprised you."

"But –"

Joliffe talked him down.

"You've always accepted me on my face value, you just met me through an agency. I had excellent credentials and you were quite satisfied. You never asked me why I had no relations, no friends, why I never wanted a holiday –"

"My dear Joliffe," interrupted the Professor testily, "don't try to make yourself out a mysterious person. I know you as just a solitary scholar like myself, one who happens to have drifted away from his relatives and not cared to make friends; come, come, this is all really rather childish."

"Is it?" Joliffe peered over his glasses down on the little man in the chair, his face was sharpened by what seemed a queer vanity. "So you think that you know me through and through?"

"My dear fellow, of course I do."

"Well, to begin with, my name isn't Samuel Joliffe."

The Professor tried to smile; he thought this was a joke, but it was certainly a stupid, vulgar joke, and he wished that the tutor, who must really be a little drunk, would be quiet and go up to bed.

"Do you remember the Hammerton case – ten years ago?" demanded Joliffe.

"As if I ever took the slightest interest –"

"No, I thought you didn't. Well, it was the case of a man, an educated man of means, well-connected, intelligent, being tried for the murder of his wife. The usual arsenic from weed-killer."

"I do recall something – Hammerton was acquitted, wasn't he?"

"Yes. But no one thought he was innocent; the jury just gave him the benefit of a very small doubt. A 'not proven' it would have been in Scotland. He was ruined – he had to disappear."

"But I don't see what all this has got to do with anything –"

"Wait a minute. Though everyone thought Hammerton was guilty, everyone had a secret sympathy with him."

"Morbid sentimentality."

"No, his wife was such an awful woman, she nagged and whined and pestered and was always sickly, and he was a very decent fellow; he just wanted peace and quiet, and then, perhaps, one day she went too far even for his patience –"

"And the hidden ape leaped up in him? A very usual case –"

"Not at all. Perhaps he used his reason and removed a worthless, tiresome, repulsive creature –"

"If he did he was a murderer," snapped the Professor. "And, since he was acquitted, we have no right to assume that."

He rose, hoping to silence Joliffe, but the tutor leaned forward, took him by the lapel of the coat, and said with a smile: "I am Hammerton."

The little Professor twisted and squealed in grotesque (through it all he felt all was grotesque) horror.

"No," he cried, "no, we've both had too much to drink and it's time we went to bed."

But the tutor did not release his calm, steady grasp on the other's lapel.

"A man of your intelligence, sir," he said gently, "should not find my information so surprising, I merely gave it to prove a point; it can't possibly make any difference to our relationship."

"Of course you were acquitted, but, but it is very terrible, very unfortunate. And the false name . . ."

"I had no chance with my own. I waited for two years for an opportunity like you gave me. And I did not deceive you. My credentials were exact save for the name. I had all the attainments, the qualifications you required, and I believe that I have served you faithfully – you and Edmund."

"Of course." The Professor made a show of recovering himself, he twisted away from the other and sat down. "And then yesterday – but I wish that you hadn't told me."

"Why, what difference can it make?"

"Well, it's a shock and you spoke just now as if – as if you were – but it's absurd."

"What's absurd?"

"Didn't you say that you had – that you were –?"

"Guilty? I assumed it, yes. I don't say so definitely – let it go. I was acquitted and no one can touch me now, even if I confessed, and I don't intend to confess. We need not talk of it again."

Professor Awkwright sickened; he sat shrunk together in the big cosy, pleasant chair and felt all the agreeable, safe and familiar places of his life laid bare and devastated.

"I should like to think that it isn't true, Joliffe." The little man's eyes were pathetic behind the thick crystals.

"I can prove it if you wish. What difference can it make? There's the boy, our work, the book, all our years together. Whatever I did can't affect any of that?"

"Quite so. Quite so."

The tutor went to bed; he did not seem in the least disturbed, he spoke of the Minoan seals he hoped to finish copying in the morning, and gave his usual "Good night, sir" cheerfully.

The Professor sat alone with his problem.

What ought he to do?

What did he intend to do?

Joliffe was essential to him, to the boy, to the book . . . where would he find another man who suited him so well, who would be willing to live his kind of life? Who would put up with Edmund?

Professor Awkwright groaned and began to argue speciously with himself.

Joliffe had been acquitted, a victim of a terrible misfortune; it was ten years ago and no one's business; Joliffe had put him under the greatest obligation yesterday – why shouldn't everything go on as before?

"Just forget all about it, eh? Joliffe would never speak of it again."

But there was that stern streak in the Professor that made him soon reject the easy, the convenient way, and all specious, fallacious reasonings.

He grimly tackled himself; the man was almost, on his own confession, a murderer, and one without remorse; the Professor utterly rejected all arguments about the codes of the Cretans, the Elizabethans, Mexico and Chicago and the value of human life; he was an upright, law-abiding man; murder was murder, deceit was deceit; of course it was most extraordinary that a cultured human being like Joliffe . . . He returned to his own theory of the hidden ape, the ape striking down where it hated, rescuing where it loved; he shuddered before the horrid vision of Joliffe, suddenly agile as a monkey, scaling down those rocks after Edmund . . . he had wondered how the stiff-limbed man had done it . . . the Professor checked these crazy, miserable thoughts, he forced himself to be brave and cool.

After all, there was only one thing to be done. Joliffe must go.

Yes, if all the Professor's peace and happiness went with him he must go; that was the only right, reasonable and logical solution of the horrid problem.

And, screwed up to an unnatural courage that he feared would not last till the morning, Professor Awkwright went up at once to Samuel Joliffe's (for so he persisted in naming him) room.

The tutor opened the door to the timid knock of his employer. "I am afraid I must speak to you, Joliffe, at once."

Joliffe wore a camel-hair dressing-gown, rather short in the sleeves, he looked meek, surprised and of an imperturbable innocence; the Professor felt very shaky indeed as he followed him into the neat bedroom.

"Speak to me, sir, at once? About the book?"

Joliffe glanced at a pile of notes on the table by his bedside, but Awkwright glanced at the wireless set, the gramophone, the telephone.

Why had it not occurred to him before that these were outlets for the tutor's personality which was by no means satisfied by the quiet scholarly life that, outwardly, seemed so to content him?

Perhaps he spoke to friends of the old days on the telephone, no doubt he kept in touch with the busy doings of the world by means of the wireless, and indulged personal tastes with the gramophone discs – safety valves all these for a dangerous, complex personality.

"I'm afraid" – Professor Awkwright checked himself with a cowardly clutching at a faint hope – "I suppose it wasn't all a joke about your being Hammerton?"

"It wasn't a joke. I thought I knew you well enough to tell you. But you began to say, 'am afraid' –?"

"I am afraid that you must go."

"I must go? You mean that I am dismissed?"

"I wouldn't put it like that –"

"But that is what it comes to –"

"I'm afraid so."

Joliffe seemed completely amazed; he took off his glasses, fidgeted with them, returned them to his nose, and asked dully:

"What about the boy?"

"It's dreadful, I know – but –"

"What are you going to tell him?"

"Oh, not the truth – some excuse – I know it is all dreadful," repeated the Professor feebly.

"Dreadful?" repeated Joliffe shortly. "It is absurd. It means that we have never understood each other – indeed, totally mistaken each other – all these years. I thought that, under your little mannerisms, you were a broad-minded man –"

"But a question of – of –"

"Of murder? I never admitted to murder, but if I had? It can't be possible that you take the view of the man in the street about that – think of these ancient peoples we are always studying –"

"It is no use, Joliffe." Professor Awkwright was shuddering with anguish. "You must go."

"And the book?"

The little Professor's drawn face took on a livelier expression of grief.

"The book must be sacrificed" – there was heroism in his supreme renunciation. "I quite agree that you have a large share in it – but to publish it under an assumed name – or under your own!"

"Impossible?"

"Quite impossible, you must see it."

"I don't see it."

They stared at each other with the bitter hostility only frustrated affection can assume; Professor Awkwright's dry and trembling fingers stroked his thin grey beard; he felt quite sick with the temptation to "forget all about it" as he put it childishly to himself – why not, for the book's sake, the boy's sake, hush up the whole affair? It was so long ago and who was to care now?

But the little man's innate integrity was too strong for his intense desires; Joliffe was watching him quietly, with dignity, yet as a prisoner may watch a judge about to pronounce sentence. "I'm happy here and useful," he remarked drily. "And you have nothing to go on but bare suspicion – you might consider that."

"I can't tell you quite what it is, Joliffe –" The Professor's anguish was very stressed and Joliffe's glance darkened into some emotion that seemed (the other man thought) pity mingled with disdain.

"Perhaps," he said, "you are afraid? Of me? Of what you call 'the hidden ape'?"

"That's absurd!" Awkwright made a great effort to give the whole nightmare business a commonplace, almost a jovial, air, to reduce what was so fantastically horrible and had indeed changed the aspect of everything for him, into an affair of everyday – just the giving of "notice" to a secretary, a tutor, who had proved unsuitable – a distasteful business, no more, but he shuddered with the desperate futility of this attempt; he made for the door with an uncontrollable need to get away from Joliffe's gaze.

He had said that it was "absurd" for him to be afraid – but of course he was afraid, horribly afraid, of Joliffe, of his own weakness, of something more powerful than either that seemed to fill the room like a fearful miasma.

But nothing sensational happened; Joliffe said in the most ordinary tones:

"Very well. I will go tomorrow. Of course I shall miss the book. And Edmund."

At the door Professor Awkwright mumbled:

"I shall always remind Edmund that you saved his life – what a great deal he owes you."

"Oh, there won't be any need of that – he'll remember me all right – good night, Professor Awkwright."

The Professor closed the door, and went, not to his bedroom, but to his study where he and Joliffe had worked for so long in complete harmony.

"I'm sure I've done right," he kept saying to himself, "I'm quite sure I've done right." But he found it unbearable to look at the other man's notes, at the neat evidences of his long labor, he found it impossible to rest or in any way to consider the situation calmly, and he could not for a second conceive in what manner he should deal with Edmund when that poor youth discovered that Joliffe was gone.

And there was another torturing horror working in Awkwright's mind.

"I say I am quite sure, but I never shall be quite sure – I mean if he is – or not –"

Professor Awkwright sat quite still for a full quarter of an hour; staring at the materials for his book which showed familiar yet horrible in the shaded electric lamp. He was really hardly able to grasp his misery nor the full value of all that he had sacrificed to a principle; he tried to comfort himself by the sheer strength of his integrity of purpose, the blamelessness of his own motives – but it was useless; he could make himself conscious of nothing but his great personal disaster.

The window had been set open to air the room and Awkwright became gradually conscious of the physical discomfort of the cold draft blowing beneath the blind.

He rose at last heavily, and almost without his own volition to remedy this; exhausted by emotion he stood with the blind in his hand and stared stupidly across the lawn and the shrubbery, faintly lit by the beams of a high moon falling through a mist; he soon forgot that he had risen to shut the window, and stood patiently in the cold air which harshly stirred his loose grey hair.

Suddenly his attention was aroused and held by an object which suddenly swung into the circle of his vision and seemed immediately to become the focus of the midnight landscape and of his own mind.

A thin, darkly clad figure was proceeding across the lawn, half leaping, half crawling through the shadows; the arms looked very long, now and then the lanky, uncouth shape appeared to sink to hands and knees in a scrawling effort at haste.

Professor Awkwright dropped the blind; with no more hesitation than if an imperative hand had seized his collar he swung round, ascended the stairs and crept into Edmund's room.

Until he looked on the bed he did not know why the sight of the ape-like figure had sent him to the boy.

The cosy glow of the carefully sheltered night light showed in the warm flickers of soft illumination a lifeless body on the scarcely disarranged pillow; powerful hands had skilfully strangled Edmund in his sleep.

Again Awkwright found himself at the window, trying now to scream, to signal, to express his scattered soul; again he saw the ape-like figure, running over the fields beyond the garden, towards the gloomy hills; it seemed to proceed with a hideous exultation, a dark joy powerfully expressed in the swinging animal movements, in the triumphant haste towards the wilderness, in the challenging thrown back head which seemed to howl at the moon that swung in an unfathomable, dreadful void.

THE HOUSEKEEPER

Marjorie Bowen

Marjorie Bowen was a pseudonym for Margaret Campbell (1885–1952), a British author most famous for historical romances and popular biographies. She wrote crime and supernatural short stories prolifically and is considered a master of gothic horror. Bowen also proved an unexpected influence on Graham Greene.

M r Robert Sekforde, a rather damaged man of fashion, entered with a lurching step his mansion near the tavern of the 'Black Bull', High Holborn. He was still known as 'Beau Sekforde' and was still dressed in the extreme of the fashion of this year 1710, with wide brocade skirts, an immense peruke, and a quantity of lace and paste ornaments that were nearly as brilliant as diamonds.

About Mr Sekforde himself was a good deal of this spurious gorgeousness; from a little distance he still looked the magnificent man he once had been, but a closer view showed him ruddled with powder and rouge like a woman, heavy about the eyes and jaw, livid in the cheeks – a handsome man yet, but one deeply marked by years of idleness, good living, and the cheap dissipations of a nature at once brutal and effeminate. In the well-shaped features and dark eyes there was not a contour or a shadow that did not help towards the presentment of a type vicious and worthless; yet he had an air of breeding, of gallantry and grace that had hitherto never failed to win him facile admiration and help him over awkward places in his career. This air was also spurious – spurious as the diamonds at his throat and in his shoe-buckles; he was not even of gentle birth; the obscurity that hung round his origin was proof of the shame he felt at the dismal beginning of a career that had been so brilliant.

He entered his mansion that was modest but elegant, and called for candles to be brought into his study.

Taking off slowly his white, scented gloves, he stared thoughtfully at his plump, smooth hands and then at the walnut desk, scattered with silver and ebony stand dishes, pens and taper-holders, and a great number of little notes on gilt-edged and perfumed papers.

There were a great many others, neither gilt-edged nor perfumed; Mr Sekforde knew that these last were bills as surely as he knew the first were insipid invitations to rather third-rate balls and routs.

Everything in Mr Sekforde's world was becoming rather third-rate now.

He looked round the room desperately, with that ugly glance of defiance which is not courage but cowardice brought to bay.

Nothing in the house was paid for and his credit would not last much longer; this had been a last venture to float his shaky raft on the waters of London society; he could foresee himself going very comfortably to the bottom.

Unless . . .

Unless he could again carry off some successful 'coup' at cards; and this was unlikely; he was too well known now.

Every resource that could, at any pinch, afford means of livelihood to an unscrupulous rogue and yet permit him to move among the people on whom he preyed, had already been played by Mr Sekforde.

The sound of the opening door caused him to look up; he dreaded duns and was not sure of the unpaid servants.

But it was his wife who entered; at sight of her, Beau Sekforde cursed in a fashion that would have surprised his genteel admirers, over whose tea-tables he languished so prettily.

'Oh, pray keep civil,' said the lady, in a mincing tone.

She trailed to the fireplace and looked discontentedly at the logs that were falling into ashes.

'The upholsterer came,' she added, 'with a bill for near a thousand guineas – I had difficulty in sending him away. Is nothing in the house paid for?'

'Nothing.'

She looked at him with a contempt that was more for herself than for him; she was quite callous and heartless; a sense of humour, a nice appreciation of men and things alone prevented her from being odious.

'Lord!' she smiled. 'To live to be fooled by Beau Sekforde!'

She was a Countess in her own right; her patent was from Charles II and explained her career; she still had the air of a beauty and wore the gowns usually affected by loveliness, but she was old with the terrible old age of a wanton, soulless woman.

Her reputation was bad even for her type; she had cheated at everything from love to cards, and no tenderness or regret had ever softened her ugly actions. At the end of her career as presiding goddess of a gambling saloon she had married Robert Sekforde, thinking he had money or at least the wits to get it, and a little betrayed by his glib tongue, that had flattered her into thinking her beauty not lost, her charm not dead; only to find him an adventurer worse off than herself, who had not even paid for the clothes in which he had come to woo her. Her sole satisfaction was that he had also been deceived.

He had thought her the prudent guardian of the spoils of a lifetime; instead, selfishness had caused her to scatter what greed had gained, and for her too this marriage had been seized as a chance to avert ruin.

Haggard and painted, a dark wig on her head, false pearls round her throat, and a dirty satin gown hanging gracefully round a figure still upright and elegant, she stared at the fire.

'We shall have to disappear,' she remarked drily.

He looked at her with eyes of hate.

'You must have some money,' he said bluntly.

Avarice, the vice of old age, flashed in her glance as jealousy would have gleamed in that of a younger woman.

'What little I have I need,' she retorted. 'The man has turned simple.' She grinned at her reflection in the glass above the fireplace.

'Well, leave me, then,' he said bitterly; could he be rid of her, he felt it would gild his misfortune.

But my lady had come to the end of all her admirers; she could not even any longer dazzle boys with the wicked glory of her past; she had no-one save Mr Sekforde, and she meant to cling to him; he was a man and twenty years younger than herself – he ought, she thought, to be useful.

Besides, this woman who had never had a friend of her own sex shuddered to think of the utter loneliness it would be to live without a man attached to her – better the grave; and of that she had all the horror of the true atheist.

'You talk folly,' she said with a dreadful ogle. 'I shall remain.'

'Then you will starve, my lady!' he flung out violently.

'Oh, fie, sir; one does not starve.'

He could not endure to look at her, but starting at the desk began to tear up the notes before him.

'Will you not go to a mask tonight?' she asked querulously.

'I have no money to pay for a chair,' he sneered.

'We might win something at cards.'

'People are very wary.'

'You were very clever at tricking me,' remarked the Countess, 'cannot you trick someone else, Mr Sekforde?'

He wheeled round on her with concentrated venom.

'Ah, madam, if I were a bachelor –'

She quailed a little before his wrath, but rallied to reply with the spirit of a woman who had been spoilt by a king: 'You think you are so charming? *Wealthy matches are particular. Look in the glass, sir; your face is as ruined as your reputation!*'

He advanced on her and she began to shriek in a dreadful fashion; the town woman showed through the airs of a great lady.

'I'll call the watch!' she shrilled.

He fell back with a heavy step and stood glaring at her.

'A pair of fools,' said my lady bitterly. Then her cynical humour triumphed over her disgust. 'Your first wife would smile to see us now,' she remarked.

Beau Sekforde turned to her a face suddenly livid.

'What do you know about my first wife?' he demanded fiercely.

'Nothing at all,' replied my lady. 'You kept her rather in the background, did you not? But one can guess.'

Mr Sekforde raged; he loathed any reference to the woman whom he had married in his obscurity, and who had been his drudge in the background through all his shifting fortunes – her worn face, her wagging tongue, her rude manners had combined to make the thorn in the rose bed of his softest days.

He had hated her and believed that she had hated him; she was a Scotswoman, a shrew, thrifty, honest, plain, and a good housekeeper; she had always made him very comfortable at home, though she had shamed him on the rare occasions when she had forced him to take her abroad.

She had died only a few months before his present marriage. 'One can guess,' repeated the Countess, showing teeth dark behind her rouged lips in a ghastly grin, 'that you made her life very pleasant.'

He sprang up and faced her, a big, heavy bully for all his satins and French peruke.

'Oh,' she shrilled, frightened but defiant, 'you look like murder.'

He turned away sharply and muttered some hideous words under his breath.

'What are you going to do?' asked my lady, with a quizzical glance round the tawdry splendour that had been hired to lure her into marriage and that now would so shortly be rent away.

Beau Sekforde controlled his wrath against the terrible woman who had deceived him into losing his last chance of retrieving ruin. 'Where are the servants?' he asked.

'All gone. I think they have taken some of the plate and all of the wine. There is some food downstairs.'

Mr Sekforde had seen it as he came up – a hacked piece of fat ham on a dirty dish, a stained cloth, and a jagged loaf had been laid out on the dining-room table.

'I have had my dinner,' remarked the Countess.

Her husband rudely left the room; he was hungry and forced to search for food, but the remembrance of the meal waiting nauseated him. He was delicate in his habits, and as he descended the stairs he thought of his late wife – she had been a wonderful housekeeper – even in poverty she had never failed to secure comfort.

As he opened the door of the dining-room he was agreeably surprised. Evidently one of the servants had remained after all.

The hearth had been swept and a neat fire burnt pleasantly; a clean cloth was on the table, and the service was set out exactly; a fresh loaf, butter, wine, fruit, a dish of hot meat, of cheese, of eggs stood ready; there was wine and brightly polished glasses.

'I did not know,' Mr Sekforde muttered, 'that any of the hussies in the house could work like this.'

He admired the spotless linen, the brilliant china, the gleaming glasses, the fresh and appetising food; and ate and drank with a pleasure that made him forget for the moment his troubles.

One thing only slightly disturbed his meal: among the dishes was a plate of goblin scones; they were of a peculiar shape and taste, and he had never known anyone make them but the late Jane Sekforde.

When he had finished he rang the bell for candles, for the short November day was closing in.

There was no answer. Surprised and slightly curious to see the servant who had been so deft, Mr Sekforde went to the head of the basement stairs and shouted lustily; still there was no reply.

He returned to the dining-room; the candles were lit and set precisely on the table.

Mr Sekforde ran upstairs to his wife. 'Who is in this house?' he asked in a tone of some agitation. The Countess was by the fire, seated on a low chair; before her on the floor was a wheel of playing cards from which she was telling her fortune.

'Who is in the house?' she sneered. 'A drunken ruffian.'

Misery was wearing thin the courtier-like manner from both of them.

'You old, wicked jade,' he replied, 'there is someone hiding in this house.'

She rose; scattering the cards with the worn toe of her little satin shoe. 'There is no-one in the house,' she said, 'not a baggage of them all would stay. I am going out. I want lights and amusement. Your house is to too dull, Mr Sekforde.'

With this speech and an air that was a caricature of the graces of a young and beautiful woman, she swept out of the room.

Even her own maid, a disreputable Frenchwoman, had left her, having moved out of the impending crash; but my lady had never lacked spirit; she attired herself, put all the money she had in her bosom, and left the house to pass the evening with one of her cronies, who kept an establishment similar to that which she had been forced to abandon.

Even the departure of her vindictive presence did not sweeten for Beau Sekforde the house that was the temple of his failure.

He glared at the furniture that should have been paid for by bills on his wife's fortune, and went to his chamber.

He too knew haunts, dark and gleaming, where health and money, wits and time might be steadily consumed, and where one who was bankrupt in all these things might be for the time tolerated if he had a flattering and servile tongue and an appearance that lent some dignity to mean vices and ignoble sins.

He found a fire in his bedchamber, the curtains drawn, his cloak, evening rapier, and gloves put ready for him, the candles lit on his dressing-table. He dressed himself rather soberly and went downstairs.

The meal was cleared away in the dining-room, the fire covered, the chairs put back in their places.

Beau Sekforde swore. 'If I had not seen her fastened down in her coffin I should have sworn that Jane was in this house,' he muttered, and his bloodshot eyes winced a little from the gloom of the empty house.

Again he went to the head of the basement stairs and listened. He could hear faintly yet distinctly the sound of someone moving about – the sound of dishes, of brisk footsteps, of clattering irons.

'Some wench has remained,' he said uneasily, but he did not offer to investigate those concealed kitchen premises.

That evening his companions found him changed – a quiet, sullen, dangerous mood was on him; they could easily understand this, as tales of the disaster of his marriage had already leaked abroad.

But something deeper and more terrible even than his almost accomplished ruin was troubling Robert Sekforde.

He returned very late to the mansion in High Holborn; he had drunk as much wine as his friends would pay for, and there was little of the elegant gallant about the heavy figure in the stained coat, with wig awry and the flushed, sullen face, who stumbled into the wretched place he named home with unconscious sarcasm.

A light stood ready for him in the hall; he took this up and staggered upstairs, spilling the candle-grease over his lace ruffles.

Halfway up he paused, suddenly wondering who had thought to leave the light.

'Not my lady wife – not my royal Countess,' he grinned.

Then a sudden pang of horror almost sobered him. Jane had never forgotten to put a candle in the hall.

He paused, as if expecting to hear her shrill, nagging voice. 'You're drunk,' he said to himself fiercely; 'she is dead, dead, *dead*.' He went upstairs.

The fire in his room was bright, the bed stood ready, his slippers and bed-gown were warming, a cup of posset stood steaming on the side table.

Mr Sekforde snatched up his candle and hurried to the room of the Countess. He violently entered and stood confronting her great bed with the red damask hangings.

With a shriek she sat up; her cheeks were still rouged, the false pearls dangled in her ears, the laced gown was open on her skinny throat; a cap with pink ribbons concealed her scant grey hair.

She flung herself, with claw-like hands, on an embroidered purse on the quilt and thrust it under her pillow; it contained her night's winnings at cards.

'Have you come to rob me?' she screamed.

Terror robbed her of all dignity; she crouched in the shadows of the huge bed, away from the red light cast on her dreadful face by the candle her husband held.

Beau Sekforde was not thinking of money now, and her words passed unheeded.

'Who is in this house?' he demanded.

'You are mad,' she said, a little recovering her composure, but keeping her hands very firmly on the purse beneath the pillow. 'There is no-one in this house.'

Did *you* put a candle for me, and prepare my room and light the fire and place the posset?'

He spoke thickly and leant against the bedpost; the candle, now almost guttered away, sent a spill of grease on the heavy quilt.

'You are drunk, you monstrous man!' screamed my lady. 'If you are not away instantly I'll put my head out of the window and screech the neighbourhood up.'

Beau Sekforde, regarding her with dull eyes, remained at his original point.

'There was someone in the kitchen this afternoon,' he insisted. 'I heard sounds –'

'Rats,' said my lady; 'the house is full of 'em.'

A look of relief passed over the man's sodden features. 'Of course, rats,' he muttered.

'What else could it be?' asked the Countess, sufficiently impressed by his strange manner momentarily to forget her grievance against him.

'What else?' he repeated; then suddenly turned on her with fury, lurching the candle into her face.

'Could rats have set this for me?' he shouted.

The Countess shrank back; when agitated her head trembled with incipient palsy, and now it trembled so that the false pearls rattled hollow against her bony neck.

'You will fire the bed-curtains!' she shrilled desperately.

He trembled with a loathing of her that was like a panic fear of fury. 'You time-foundered creature!' he cried. 'You bitter horror! And 'twas for *you* I did it!'

She sprang to her knees in the bed, her hands crooked as if ready for his face; there was nothing left now of the fine dame nurtured in courts, the beauty nursed in the laps of princes. She had reverted to the wench of Drury Lane, screaming abuse from alley to alley.

'If you are disappointed, what about me?' she shrieked. 'Have I not tied myself to a low, ugly fool?'

He stepped back from her as if he did not understand her, and, muttering, staggered back into his own room.

There he lit all the candles, piled up the fire with more fuel, glanced with horror at the bed, flung off his coat and wig, and settled himself in the chair with arms before the fire to sleep.

The Countess, roused and angered, could sleep no more.

She rose, flung on a chamber-robe, of yellow satin lined with marten's fur, that was a relic of her court days, and threadbare and moth-eaten in places though giving the effect of much splendour.

Without striking a light she went cautiously out into the corridor, saw the door of her husband's room ajar, a bright glow from it falling across the darkness, and crept steadily in.

He was, as she had supposed, in an intoxicated stupor of sleep by the fire.

His head had sunk forward on the stained and untied lace cravat on his breast; his wigless head showed fat and shaven and grey over the temples, his face was a dull purple and his mouth hung open. His great frame was almost as loose as that of a man newly dead, his hands hung slack and his chest heaved with his noisy breathing. My lady was herself a horrid object, but that did not prevent her from giving him a glance of genuine disgust.

'Beau Sekforde indeed!' she muttered.

She put out all the candles save two on the dressing-table, found the coat her husband had flung off, and began going swiftly through the pockets.

He had been, as she had hoped, fortunate at cards that night; he was indeed, like herself, of a type who seldom was unfortunate, since he only played with fools or honest men, neither of whom had any chance against the peculiar talents of the sharper.

The Countess found sundry pieces of gold and silver, which she knotted up in her handkerchief with much satisfaction. She knew that nothing but money would ever be able to be of any service to her in this world.

Pleased with her success, she looked round to see if there were anything else of which she could despoil her husband.

Keeping her cunning old eyes constantly on him, she crept to the dressing-table and went over the drawers and boxes. Most of the ornaments that she turned out glittered and gleamed heavily in the candlelight. But she knew that they were as false as the pearls trembling in her own ears; one or two things, however, she added to the money in the handkerchief, and she was about to investigate further when a little sound, like a cough, caused her to look sharply round.

The room was full of warm shadows, the fire was sinking low and only cast a dim light on the heavy, sleeping figure on the hearth, while the candlesticks on the dressing-table served only to illuminate the bent figure of the Countess in her brilliant wrap.

As she looked round she found herself staring straight at the figure of a woman, who was observing her from the other side of the bed.

This woman was dressed in a grey tabinet fashioned like the dress of an upper servant. Her hair was smoothly banded and her features were pale and sharp; her hands, that she held rather awkwardly in front of her, were rough and work-worn.

Across one cheek was a long scratch.

The Countess dropped her spoils; she remembered her husband's words that she had taken for the babbling of a drunkard.

So there *was* someone in the house.

'How dare you?' she quavered, in a low voice, for she did not wish to rouse her husband. 'How dare you come here?'

Without replying the woman moved across to the sleeping man and looked down at him with an extraordinary expression of mingled malice and protection, as if she would defend him from any evil save that she chose to deal herself.

So sinister was this expression and the woman's whole attitude that the Countess was frightened as she never had been in the course of her wicked life.

She stood staring; the handkerchief, full of money and ornaments, dropped on the dressing-table unheeded.

Beau Sekforde moved in his sleep and fetched a deep groan.

'You impertinent creature!' whispered the Countess, taking courage. 'Will you not go before I wake my husband?'

At these last words the woman raised her head; she did not seem to speak, yet, as if there were an echo in the room, the Countess distinctly heard the words 'My husband!' repeated after her in a tone of bitter mockery.

A sense of unreality such as she had never known before touched the Countess; she felt as if her sight were growing dim and her hearing failing her; she made a movement as if to brush something from before her eyes.

When she looked again at Beau Sekforde he was alone; no-one was beside him.

In dreaming, tortured sleep he groaned and tossed.

'The baggage has slipped off,' muttered the Countess; 'belike it is some ancient dear of his own. I will send her away in the morning.'

She crept back to her own room, forgetting her spoils. She did not sleep, and Mr Sekforde did not wake till the pale winter dawn showed between the curtains.

The Countess looked round on a chamber in disorder, but for Beau Sekforde everything was arranged, shaving water ready, his breakfast hot and tempting on a tray, his clothes laid out.

When he had dressed and come downstairs he found his wife yawning over a copy of the *Gazette*.

She remembered last night quite clearly, and considerably regretted what she had left behind in Beau Sekforde's room in her confusion. She gave him a glance, vicious with the sense of an opportunity lost.

He flung at her the question he had asked last night.

'Who is in this house?'

'Some woman has stayed,' she answered. 'I think it was Joanna – the house-keeper, but I did not see very clearly. She must be out now, as I have rung the bell and there has been no answer.'

'My breakfast was brought up to me,' said Mr Sekforde. 'So it is Joanna Mills, is it?'

The Countess was angry; she had had to go to the kitchen and pick among yesterday's scraps for her own food.

'And who is she?'

'You said, madam, the housekeeper.'

'She must be very fond of you,' sneered the lady.

He stared at that and turned on her a ghastly look.

'Oh, don't think I am jealous!' she grinned cynically.

'It was the word you used,' he muttered. 'I do not think anyone has been *fond* of me save one –'

He paused and passed his hand over his weary, heavy eyes. 'I dreamt of her last night.'

'Who?'

'Jane, my wife.'

The Countess remembered the ugly echo of her words last night. 'Your wife – do you forget that I and no other am your wife?'

'I do,' he replied sullenly; 'to me Jane is always my wife.'

'A pity,' said my lady sarcastically, 'that she did not live longer.' He gave her a queer look.

'And now we have got to think of ourselves,' he said abruptly. 'I cannot keep these things much longer – you had better go.'

'Where?'

'What do I care!' he answered cruelly.

'I stay here,' she replied. 'Is the rent paid?'

'No.'

'Well, they will not disturb us till quarter-day,' said my lady calmly. 'You do not want to be parted from your loving wife, do you, dear?'

He stared at her as if her words had a double meaning.

'Cannot you be quiet about my wife?' he exclaimed.

'La! The man is off his head!' shrilled my lady. 'Jane Sekforde is dead.'

'That is why I think about her,' he retorted grimly.

'A model husband,' jeered the Countess, eyeing him viciously. 'I am sorry I never knew the sweet creature you regret so keenly and so touchingly.'

He raged at her like a man whose nerves are overwrought. 'Will you not let the matter be? Think of yourself, you monstrous horror! You will soon be in the Fleet!'

This picture was sufficiently realistic to make the Countess shiver. 'What are you going to do?' she asked with sudden feebleness.

He did not know; brooding and black-browed, he withdrew to the window-place and stared out at the leaden November sky that hung so heavily over the London streets.

'I suppose if you were free of me you would take your handsome face to market again?' added my lady, with a sudden flash of new fury.

He gave her a red look, at which she shrank away. 'Well, still we do not decide on anything,' she quavered.

He would not answer her, but flung out of the house. His unsteady steps were directed to St. Andrew's Church. It was a long time since Beau Sekforde had been near a church. Even when his wife had been buried here, he had not attended the service.

He stood now in the porch, biting his thumb; then presently he entered. Hesitating and furtive, he went round the walls until he came to the new, cheap tablet with the badly cut draped urn and the florid Latin setting forth the virtues of Jane Sekforde.

'They don't say anything about her being a good housekeeper,' he found himself saying aloud. 'Why, she told me once she would come back from the grave to set her house in order.'

He looked round as if to seek the answer of some companion, then laughed sullenly, drew his hat over his eyes, and left the church. Towards dusk he wandered home.

The dining-room was neat and clean, the fire attended to, the dinner on the table. He managed to eat some of the food, but without appetite. The Countess was out; there was no trace anywhere of her slovenly splendour.

The whole house was as clean and precise as it had been when that neglected drudge Jane Sekforde had ruled over it.

When the Countess returned he was almost glad to see her – he had been thinking so much, too much, of Jane. He had thought of her as he had seen her last, cold in her bed, clothed in her best grey gown, and how he had stared at her and hung over her and drawn suddenly away, so sharply that the button of cut steel on his cuff had left a scratch on her dead cheek.

'Where is Joanna Mills?' he abruptly asked his wife.

She stared at him. In such a moment as this could he think of nothing but the housekeeper? Was he losing his wits?

But she did not now much care; she had found a crony willing to shelter her and exploit her ancient glories.

'I am going away,' she said. 'I do not know who is in the house – I have seen no-one.'

He seemed to pay no attention at all to her first remark. 'What was that woman you saw last night like?'

'A very plain, shrewish-looking creature,' replied my lady, with some bitterness, as she recalled how she had been startled into dropping the filched money.

'Are you sure it was a woman?' asked Beau Sekforde with a ghastly grin.

'Why, what else could it have been?' she replied curiously.

'I do not think it has been a woman for – some months,' he said.

'Why, do you imagine there is a spectre in the place?'

He would not, could not answer; he left her, and went from room to room throwing everything into disorder, taking a horrid pleasure in making a confusion in the neatness of the house. And then he flung himself away from the dreary mansion, leaving the Countess, like an old, weary bird of prey, wandering among the untidy rooms to see if there were anything worth taking away.

When he returned in the dark hours before the dawn he found the candle on the hall table.

'Curse you!' he screamed. 'Cannot you let me alone?'

He hastened upstairs; everything was neat, his bed, his fire, his posset ready, his shoes warming, his candles lit. His terrified eyes cast a horrid glance round the room.

'The medicine cupboard – has she tidied that?' he muttered.

He crossed to where it hung in one corner, opened the door, and looked at the rows of pots and bottles. One he knew well had been stained – had been left with a broken stopper . . . a bottle of a peculiar, ugly look, holding a yellow liquid that stained linen purple.

Such a stain, very tiny, had been on Jane Sekforde's pillow.

As he stared into the cupboard he saw that the bottle had been cleaned and set in its place, while a new, neat label had been pasted on the front.

The writing was the writing of Jane Sekforde – it said in clear letters, 'Poison.'

Beau Sekforde dropped the candle and ran into the Countess's room.

'Wake up!' he shouted. 'Wake up and hear me! She has come back. I want to confess. I murdered her! Let them take me away . . . somewhere where – where she cannot tidy for me.'

The room was empty of the Countess, who had fled; an unnatural light came from the unshuttered windows and showed a woman sitting up in the great bed.

She had a pale, shrewish face, a grey garment on, and a scratch across her cheek.

As the shrieks of Beau Sekforde's confession echoed into the night and drew the watch to thunder on the door, the woman smiled.

THE MYSTERY AT FERNWOOD

Mary Elizabeth Braddon

Mary Elizabeth Braddon (1835–1915) was one of the most popular novelists in Victorian Britain. She is best known for the 1862 sensation novel *Lady Audley's Secret*, but her prolific output included pioneering mystery stories published the same year.

"No, Isabel, I do *not* consider that Lady Adela seconded her son's invitation at all warmly."

This was the third time within the last hour that my aunt had made the above remark. We were seated opposite each other in a first-class carriage of the York express, and the flat fields of ripening wheat were flitting by us like yellow shadows under the afternoon sunshine. We were going on a visit to Fernwood, a country mansion ten miles from York, in order that I might become acquainted with the family of Mr. Lewis Wendale, to whose only son Laurence I was engaged to be married.

Laurence Wendale and I had only been acquainted during the brief May and June of my first London season, which I—orphan heiress of a wealthy Calcutta merchant—had passed under the roof of my aunt, Mrs. Maddison Trevor, the dashing widow of a major in the Life Guards, and my father's only sister. Mrs. Trevor had made many objections to this brief six weeks' engagement between Laurence and me; but the impetuous young Yorkshireman had overruled everything. What objection could there be? he asked. He was to have two thousand a-year and Fernwood at his father's death; forty thousand pounds from a maiden aunt the day he came of age—for he was not yet one-and-twenty, my impetuous young lover. As for his family, let Mrs. Trevor look into Burke's *County Families* for the Wendales of Fernwood. His mother was Lady Adela, youngest daughter of Lord Kingwood, of Castle Kingwood, county Kildare. What objection could my aunt have, then? His family did not know me, and might not approve of the match, urged my aunt. Laurence laughed aloud; a long ringing peal of that merry, musical laughter I loved so well to hear.

"Not approve!" he cried—"not love my little Bella! That is too good a joke!" On which immediately followed an invitation to Fernwood, seconded by a note from Lady Adela Wendale.

To this note my aunt was never tired of taking objection. It was cold, it was constrained; it had been only written to please Laurence. How little I thought of the letter! and yet it was the first faint and shadowy indication of that terrible rock ahead upon which my life was to be wrecked; the first feeble link in the chain of the one great mystery in which the fate of so many was involved.

The letter was cold, certainly. Lady Adela started by declaring she should be most happy to see us; she was all anxiety to be introduced to her charming daughter-in-law. And then my lady ran off to tell us how dull Fernwood was, and how she feared we should regret our long journey into the heart of Yorkshire to a lonely country-house, where we should find no one but a captious invalid, a couple of nervous women, and a young man devoted to farming and field-sports.

But I was not afraid of being dull where my light-hearted Laurence was; and I overruled all my aunt's objections, ordered half a dozen new dresses, and carried Mrs. Maddison Trevor off to the Great Northern Station before she had time to remonstrate.

Laurence had gone on before to see that all was prepared for us; and had promised to meet us at York, and drive us over to Fernwood in his mail-phaeton. He was standing on the platform as the train entered the station, radiant with life and happiness.

Laurence Wendale was very handsome; but perhaps his greatest charm consisted in that wonderful vitality, that untiring energy and indomitable spirit, which made him so different from all other young men whom I had met. So great was this vitality, that, by some magnetic influence, it seemed to communicate itself to others. I was never tired when Laurence was with me. I could waltz longer with him for my partner; ride longer in the Row with him for my cavalier; sit out an opera or examine an exhibition of pictures with less fatigue when he was near. His presence pervaded a whole house; his joyous laugh ran through every room. It seemed as if where he was sorrow could not come.

I felt this more than ever as we drew nearer Fernwood. The country was bleak and bare; wide wastes of moorland stretched away on either side of the by-road down which we drove. The afternoon sunshine had faded out, leaving a cold gray sky, with low masses of leaden cloud brooding close over the landscape, and shutting in the dim horizon. But no influence of scenery or atmosphere could affect Laurence. His spirits were even higher than usual this afternoon.

"They have fitted up the oak-rooms for you, ladies," he said. "Such solemn and stately chambers, with high-canopied beds crowned with funeral plumes; black-oak paneling; portraits of dead-and-gone Wendales: Mistress Aurora, with pannier-hoops and a shepherdess's crook; Mistress Lydia, with ringlets *a la Sevigne* and a pearl necklace; Mortimer Wendale, in a Ramilies wig; Theodore, with love-locks, velvet doublet, and Spanish-leather boots. Such a collection of them! You may expect to see them all descend from their frames in the witching time of night to warm their icy fingers at your seacoal fires. Your expected arrival has made quite a sensation in our dull old abode. My mother has looked up from the last new novel half a dozen times this day, I verily believe, to ask if all due preparations were being made; while my dear, active, patient, indefatigable sister Lucy has been running about superintending the arrangements ever since breakfast."

"Your sister Lucy!" I said, catching at his last words; "I shall so love her, Laurence."

"I hope you will, darling," he answered, almost gravely, "for she has been the best and dearest sister to me. And yet I'm half afraid; Lucy is ten years older than you—grave, reserved, sometimes almost melancholy; but if ever there was a banished angel treading this earth in human form, my sister Lucy surely is that guardian spirit."

"Is she like you, Laurence?"

"Like me! O, no, not in the least. She is only my half-sister, you know. She resembles her mother, who died young."

We were at the gates of Fernwood when he said this,—high wooden gates, with stone pillars moss-grown and dilapidated; a tumble-down-looking lodge, kept by a slatternly woman, whose children were at play in a square patch of ground planted with cabbages and currant-bushes, fenced in with a rotten paling, and ambitiously called a garden. From this lodge entrance a long avenue stretched away for about half a mile, at the end of which a great red-brick mansion, built in the Tudor style, frowned at us, rather as if in defiance than in welcome. The park was entirely uncultivated; the trunks of the trees were choked with the tangled underwood; the fern grew deep in the long vistas, broken here and there by solitary pools of black water, on whose quiet borders we heard the flap of the heron's wing, and the dull croaking of an army of frogs.

Lady Adela was right. Fernwood *was* a dull place. I could scarcely repress a shudder as we drove along the dark avenue, while my poor aunt's teeth chattered audibly. Accustomed to spend three parts of the year in Onslow-square, and the autumn months at Brighton or Ryde, this dreary Yorkshire mansion was a terrible trial to her rather oversensitive nerves.

Laurence seemed to divine the reason of our silence. "The place is frightfully neglected, Mrs. Trevor," he said apologetically; "but I do not mean this sort of thing to last, I assure you. Before I bring my delicate little Bella to reign at Fernwood, I shall have landscape-gardeners and upholsterers down by the score, and do my best to convert this dreary wilderness into a terrestrial paradise. I cannot tell you why the place has been suffered to fall into decay; certainly not for want of money, still less for want of opportunity, for my father is an idle man, to whom one would imagine restoring and rebuilding would afford a delightful hobby. No, there is no reason why the place should have been so neglected."

He said this more to himself than to us, as if the words were spoken in answer to some long train of thought of his own. I watched his face earnestly, for I had seldom seen him look so thoughtful. Presently he said, with more of his usual manner,

"As you are close upon the threshold of Fernwood now, ladies, I ought perhaps to tell you that you will find ours a most low-spirited family. With everything in life to make us happy, we seem for ever under a cloud. Ever since I can remember my poor father, he has been sinking slowly into decay, almost in the same way as this neglected place, till now he is a confirmed invalid, without any positive illness. My mother reads novels all day, and seems to exist upon sal-volatile and spirits of lavender. My sister, the only active person in the house, is always thoughtful, and very often melancholy. Mind, I merely tell you this to prepare you for anything you may see; not to depress you, for you may depend upon my exertions towards reforming this dreary household, which has sunk into habitual despondency from sheer easy fortune and want of vexation."

The phaeton drew up before a broad flight of stone steps as Laurence ceased speaking, and in five minutes more he had assisted my aunt and myself to alight, and had ushered us into the presence of Lady Adela and Miss Lucy Wendale.

We found Lady Adela, as her son's description had given us reason to expect, absorbed in a novel. She threw down her book as we entered, and advanced to meet us with considerable cordiality; rather, indeed, as if she really were grateful to us for breaking in upon her solitary life.

"It is so good of you to come," she said, folding me in her slender arms with an almost motherly embrace, "and so kind of you, too, my dear Mrs. Trevor, to abandon all your town pleasures for the sake of bringing this dear girl to me. Believe me, we will do all in our power to make you comfortable, if you can put up with very limited society; for we have received no company whatever since my son's childhood, and I do not think my visiting-list could muster half-a-dozen names."

Lady Adela was an elegant-looking woman, in the very prime of life; but her handsome face was thin and careworn, and premature wrinkles gathered about her melancholy blue eyes and thoughtful mouth. While she was talking to my aunt, Lucy Wendale and I drew nearer to each other.

Laurence's half-sister was by no means handsome; pale and sallow, with dark hair and rather dull gray eyes, she looked as if some hidden sorrow had quenched out the light of her life long ago, in her earliest youth; some sorrow that had neither been forgotten, nor lessened by time, but that had rather grown with her growth, and strengthened with her strength, until it had become a part of her very self,— some disappointed attachment, I thought, some cruel blow that had shattered a girl's first dream, and left a broken-hearted woman to mourn the fatal delusion. In my utter ignorance of life, I thought these were the only griefs which ever left a woman's life desolate.

"You will try and be happy at Fernwood, Isabel," Miss Wendale said gently, as she drew me into a seat by her side, while Laurence bent fondly over us both. I do not believe, dear as we were to each other, that my Laurence ever loved me as he loved this pale-faced half-sister. "You will try and be happy, will you not, dear Isabel? Laurence has been breaking-in the prettiest chestnut mare in all Yorkshire, I think, that you may explore the country with us. I have heard what a daring horsewoman you are. The pianos have been put in tune for you, and the billiard-table re-covered, that you may have exercise on rainy days; and if we cannot give you much society, we will do all else to prevent your feeling dull."

"I shall be very happy here with you, dear Lucy," I said; "but you tell me so much of the dulness of Fernwood, while, I daresay, you yourself have a hundred associations that make the old place very dear to you."

She looked down as I spoke, and a very faint flush broke through the sallow paleness of her complexion.

"I am not very fond of Fernwood," she said gravely.

It was at Fernwood, then, that the great sorrow of her life came upon her, I thought.

"No, Lucy," said Laurence almost impatiently, "everybody knows this dull place is killing you by inches, and yet nothing on earth can induce you to quit it. When we all go to Scarborough or Burlington, when mamma goes to Harrogate, when I run up to town to rub off my provincial rust, and see what the world is made of outside these dreary gates,—you obstinately persist in staying at home; and the only reason you can urge for doing so is, that you must remain here to take care of that unfortunate invalid of yours, Mr. William."

I was holding Lucy's hand in mine, and I felt the poor wasted little fingers tremble as her brother spoke. My curiosity was strongly aroused.

"Mr. William!" I exclaimed half involuntarily.

"Ah, to be sure, Bella, I forgot to tell you of that member of our household, but as I have never seen him, I may be forgiven the omission. This Mr. William is a poor relative of my father's; a hopeless invalid, bedridden, I believe—is he not, Lucy?— who requires a strong man and an experienced nurse to look after him, and who occupies the entire upper story of one wing of the house. Poor Mr. William, invalid as he is, must certainly be a most fascinating person. My mother goes to see him every day, but as stealthily as if she were paying a secret visit to some condemned criminal. I have often met my father coming away from his rooms, pale and melancholy; and, as for my sister Lucy, she is so attached to this sick dependent of ours, that, as I have just said, nothing will induce her to leave the house, for fear his nurse or his valet should fail in their care of him."

I still held Lucy's hand, but it was perfectly steady now. Could this poor relative, this invalid dependent, have any part in the sorrowful mystery that had overshadowed her life? And yet, no; I thought that could scarcely be, for she looked up with such perfect self-possession as she answered her brother:

"My whole life has gradually fallen into the duty of attendance upon this poor young man, Laurence; and I will never leave Fernwood while he lives."

A young man! Mr. William was a young man, then. Lucy herself led us to the handsome suite of apartments prepared for my aunt and me. My aunt's room was separated from mine by a corridor, out of which opened two dressing-rooms and a pretty little boudoir, all looking on to the park. My room was at the extreme angle of the building; it had two doors, one leading to the corridor communicating with my aunt's apartments, the other opening into a gallery running the entire length of the house. Looking out into this gallery, I saw that the opposite wing was shut in by a baize door. I looked with some curiosity at this heavy baize door. It was most likely the barrier which closed the outer world upon Laurence Wendale's invalid relation.

Lucy left us as soon as we were installed in our apartments. While I was dressing for dinner, the housekeeper, a stout, elderly woman, came to ask me if I found everything I required.

"As you haven't brought your own servant with you, miss," she said, "Miss Lucy told me to place her maid Sarah entirely at your service. Miss gives very little work to a maid herself, so Sarah has plenty of leisure time on her hands, and you'll find her a very respectable young woman."

I told her that I could do all I wanted for myself; but before she left me I could not resist asking her one question about the mysterious invalid.

"Are Mr. William's rooms at this end of the house?" I asked.

The woman looked at me with an almost scared expression, and was silent for a moment.

"Has Mr. Laurence been saying anything to you about Mr. William?" she said, rather anxiously as I thought.

"Mr. Laurence and his sister Miss Lucy were both talking of him just now."

"O, indeed, miss," answered the woman with an air of relief; "the poor gentleman's rooms are at the other end of the gallery, miss."

"Has he lived here long?" I asked.

"Nigh upon twenty years, miss—above twenty years, I'm thinking."

"I suppose he is distantly related to the family."

"Yes, miss."

"And quite dependent on Mr. Wendale?"

"Yes, miss."

"It is very good of your master to have supported him for so many years, and to keep him in such comfort."

"My master is a very good man, miss."

The woman seemed determined to give me as little information as possible; but I could not resist one more question.

"How is it that in all these years Mr. Laurence has never seen this invalid relation?" I asked.

It seemed that this question, of all others, was the most embarrassing to the housekeeper. She turned first red and then pale, and said, in a very confused manner, "The poor gentleman never leaves his room, miss; and Mr. Laurence has such high spirits, bless his dear heart, and has such a noisy, rackety way with him, that he's no fit company for an invalid."

It was evidently useless trying for further information, so I abandoned the attempt, and bidding the housekeeper good afternoon, began to dress my hair before the massive oak-framed looking-glass.

"The truth of the matter is," I said to myself, "that after all there is nothing more to be said about it. I have tried to create a mystery out of the simplest possible family arrangement. Mr. Wendale has a bedridden relative, too poor and too helpless to support himself. What more natural than that he should give him house-room in this dreary old mansion, where there seems space enough to lodge a regiment?"

I found the family assembled in the drawing-room. Mr. Wendale was the wreck of a very handsome man. He must in early life have resembled Laurence; but, as my lover had said, it seemed indeed as if he and the house and grounds of Fernwood had fallen into decay together. But notwithstanding his weak state of health, he gave us a warm welcome, and did the honours of his hospitable dinner-table with the easy grace of a gentleman.

After dinner, my aunt and Lady Adela sat at one of the windows talking; while Laurence, Lucy, and I loitered upon a long stone terrace outside the drawing-room, watching the last low crimson streak of the August sunset fade behind the black trunks of the trees, and melt away into faint red splashes upon the water-pools amongst the brushwood. We were very happy together; Laurence and I talking of a hundred different subjects—telling Lucy our London adventures, describing our fashionable friends, our drives and rides, *fêtes*, balls, and dinners; she, with a grave smile upon her lips, listening to us with almost maternal patience.

"I must take you over the old house to-morrow, Isabel," Laurence said in the course of the evening. "I suppose Lucy did not tell you that she had put you into the haunted room?"

"No, indeed!"

"You must not listen to this silly boy, my dear Isabel," said Miss Wendale. "Of course, like all other old houses, Fernwood can boast its ghost-story; but since no one in my father's lifetime has seen the phantom, you may imagine that it is not a very formidable one."

"But you own there *is* a ghost!" I exclaimed eagerly. "Pray tell me the story."

"I'll tell you, Bella," answered Laurence, "and then you'll know what sort of a visitor to expect when the bells of Fernwood church, hidden away behind the elms yonder, tremble on the stroke of midnight. A certain Sir Humphrey Wendale, who lived in the time of Henry the Eighth, was wronged by his wife, a very beautiful woman. Had he acted according to the ordinary fashion of the time, he would have murdered the lady and his rival; but our ancestor was of a more original turn of mind, and he hit upon an original plan of vengeance. He turned every servant out of Fernwood House; and one morning, when the unhappy lady was sleeping, he locked every door of the mansion, secured every outlet and inlet, and rode away merrily in the summer sunshine, leaving his wife to die of hunger. Fernwood is lonely enough even now, Heaven knows! but it was lonelier in those distant days. A passing traveller may now and then have glanced upward at the smokeless chimneys, dimly visible across the trees, as he rode under the park-palings; but none ever dreamed that the deserted mansion had one luckless tenant. Fifteen months afterwards, when Sir Humphrey rode home from foreign travel, he had some difficulty in forcing the door of the chamber in which you are to sleep: the withered and skeleton form of his dead wife had fallen across the threshold."

"What a horrible story!" I exclaimed with a shiver.

"It is only a legend, dear Isabel," said Lucy; "like all tradition, exaggerated and distorted into due proportions of poetic horror. Pray do not suffer your mind to dwell upon such a fable."

"Indeed I hope it is not true," I answered. "How fond people are of linking mysteries and horrors such as this with the history of an old family! And yet we never fall across any such family mystery in our own days."

I slept soundly that night at Fernwood, undisturbed by the attenuated shadow of Sibyl Wendale, Sir Humphrey's unhappy wife. The bright sunshine was reflected in the oak panels of my room, and the larks were singing aloft in a cloudless blue sky, when I awoke. I found my aunt quite reconciled to her visit.

"Lady Adela is a very agreeable woman," she said; "quiet, perhaps, to a fault, but with that high-bred tone which is always charming. Lucy Wendale seems a dear good girl, though evidently a confirmed old maid. You will find her of in-estimable use when you are married—that is to say, if you ever have to manage this great rambling place, which will of course fall to your lot in the event of poor Mr. Wendale's death."

As for myself, I was as happy at Fernwood as the August days were long. Lucy Wendale rode remarkably well. It was the only amusement for which she cared; and she and her horses were on terms of the most devoted attachment. Laurence, his sister, and I were therefore constantly out together, riding amongst the hills about Fernwood, and exploring the country for twenty miles round.

Indoors, Lucy left us very much to ourselves. She was the ruling spirit of the house, and but for her everything must have fallen utterly to decay. Lady Adela read novels, or made a feeble attempt at amusing my aunt with her conversation. Mr. Wendale kept his room until dinner; while Laurence and I played, sang, sketched, and rattled the billiard-balls over the green cloth whenever bad weather drove us to indoor amusements.

One day, while sketching the castellated facade of the old mansion, I noticed a peculiar circumstance connected with the suite of rooms occupied by the invalid, Mr. William. These rooms were at the extreme left angle of the building, and were lighted by a range of six windows. I was surprised by observing that every one of these windows was of ground glass. I asked Laurence the reason of this.

"Why, I believe the glare of light was too much for Mr. William," he answered; "so my father, who is the kindest creature in Christendom, had the windows made opaque, as you see them now."

"Has the alteration been long made?"

"It was made when I was about six years old; I have rather a vague recollection of the event, and I should not perhaps remember it but for one circumstance. I was riding about down here one morning on my Shetland pony, when my attention was attracted by a child who was looking through one of those windows. I was not near enough to see his face, but I fancy he must have been about my own age. He beckoned to me, and I was riding across the grass to respond to his invitation, when my sister Lucy appeared at the window and snatched the child away. I suppose he was someone belonging to the female attendant upon Mr. William, and had strayed unnoticed into the invalid's rooms. I never saw him again; and the next day a glazier came over from York, and made the alteration in the windows."

"But Mr. William must have air; I suppose the windows are sometimes opened," I said.

"Never; they are each ventilated by a single pane, which, if you observe, is open now."

"I cannot help pitying this poor man," I said, after a pause, "shut out almost from the light of heaven by his infirmities, and deprived of all society."

"Not entirely so," answered Laurence. "No one knows how many stolen hours my sister Lucy devotes to her poor invalid."

"Perhaps he is a very studious man, and finds his consolation in literary or scientific pursuits," I said; "does he read very much?"

"I think not. I never heard of his having any books got for him."

"But one thing has puzzled me, Laurence," I continued. "Lucy spoke of him the other day as a young man, and yet Mrs. Porson, your housekeeper, told me he had lived at Fernwood for upwards of twenty years."

"As for that," answered Laurence carelessly, "Lucy no doubt remembers him as a young man upon his first arrival here, and continues to call him so from mere force of habit. But, pray, my little inquisitive Bella, do not rack your brains about this poor relation of ours. To tell the truth, I have become so used to his unseen presence in the house, that I have ceased to think of him at all. I meet a grim woman, dressed in black merino, coming out of the green-baize door, and I know that she is Mr. William's nurse; or I see a solemn-faced man, and I am equally assured that he is Mr. William's servant, James Beck, who has grown gray in his office; I encounter the doctor riding away from Fernwood on his brown cob, and I feel convinced that he has just looked in to see how Mr. William is going on; if I miss my sister for an hour in the twilight, I know that she is in the west wing talking to Mr. William; but as nobody ever calls upon me to do anything for the poor man, I think no more of the matter."

I felt these words almost a reproof to what might have appeared idle, or even impertinent, curiosity on my part. And yet the careless indifference of Laurence's manner seemed to jar upon my senses. Could it be that this glad and high-hearted being, whom I so tenderly loved, was selfish—heedless of the sufferings of others? No, it was surely not this that prompted his thoughtless words. It is a positive impossibility for one whose whole nature is life and motion, animation and vigour, to comprehend for one brief moment the horror of the invalid's darkened rooms and solitary days.

I had been nearly a month at Fernwood, when, for the first time during our visit, Laurence left us. One of his old schoolfellows, a lieutenant in the army, was quartered with his regiment at York, and Laurence had promised to dine with the mess. Though I had been most earnest in requesting him to accept this invitation, I could not help feeling dull and dispirited as I watched him drive away down the avenue, and felt that for the first time we were to spend the long autumn evening without him. Do what I would, the time hung heavily on my hands. The September sunset was beautiful, and Lucy and I walked up and down the terrace after dinner, while Mr. Wendale slept in his easy-chair, and my aunt and Lady Adela exchanged drowsy monosyllabic sentences on a couch near the fire, which was always lighted in the evening.

It was in vain that I tried to listen to Lucy's conversation. My thoughts wandered in spite of myself,—sometimes to Laurence in the brilliantly-lighted mess-room, enlivening a circle of *blasé* officers with his boisterous gaiety; sometimes, as if in contrast to this, to the dark west rooms in which the invalid counted the long hours; sometimes to that dim future in whose shadowy years death was to claim our weary host, and Laurence and I were to be master and mistress at Fernwood. I had often tried to picture the place as it would be when it fell into Laurence's hands, and architects and landscape-gardeners came to work their wondrous transformations; but, do what I would, I could never imagine it otherwise than as it was,—with straggling ivy hanging forlornly about the moss-stained walls, and solitary pools of stagnant water hiding amongst the tangled brushwood.

Laurence and I were to be married in the following spring. He would come of age in February, and I should be twenty in March,—only a year and a month between our ages, and both a great deal too young to marry, my aunt said. After tea Lucy and I sang and played. Dreary music it seemed to me that night. I thought my voice and the piano were both out of tune, and I left Lucy very rudely in the middle of our favourite duet. I took up twenty books from the crowded drawing-room table, only to throw them wearily down again. Never had Lady Adela's novels seemed so stupid as when I looked into them that night; never had my aunt's conversation sounded so tiresome. I looked from my watch to the old-fashioned timepiece upon the chimney half a dozen times, to find at last that it was scarcely ten o'clock. Laurence had promised to be home by eleven, and had begged Lucy and me to sit up for him.

Eleven struck at last, but Laurence had not kept his promise. My aunt and Lady Adela rose to light their candles. Mr. Wendale always retired a little after nine. I pleaded for half an hour longer, and Lucy was too kind not to comply readily.

"Isabel is right," she said; "Laurence is a spoilt boy, you know, mamma, and will feel himself very much ill-used if he finds no one up to hear his description of the mess-dinner."

"Only half an hour, then, mind, young ladies," said my aunt. "I cannot allow you to spoil your complexions on account of dissipated people who drive ten miles to a military dinner. One half hour; not a moment more, or I shall come down again to scold you both."

We promised obedience, and my aunt left us. Lucy and I seated ourselves on each side of the low fire, which had burned dull and hollow. I was too much dispirited to talk, and I sat listening to the ticking of the clock, and the occasional falling of a cinder in the bright steel fender. Then that thought came to me which comes to all watchers: What if anything had happened to Laurence? I went to one of the windows, and pulled back the heavy shutters. It was a lovely night; clear, though not moonlight, and myriads of stars gleamed in the cloudless sky. I stood at the window for some time, listening for the wheels and watching for the lamps of the phaeton.

I too was a spoilt child; life had for me been bright and smooth, and the least thought of grief or danger to those I loved filled me with a wild panic. I turned suddenly round to Lucy, and cried out, "Lucy, Lucy, I am getting frightened! Suppose anything should have happened to Laurence; those horses are wild and unmanageable sometimes. If he had taken a few glasses of wine—if he trusted the groom to drive—if—"

She came over to me, and took me in her arms as if I had been indeed a little child.

"My darling," she said, "my darling Isabel, you must not distress yourself by such fancies as these. He is only half an hour later than he said; and as for danger, dearest, he is beneath the shelter of Providence, without whose safeguard those we love are never secure even for a moment."

Her quiet manner calmed my agitation. I left the window, and returned shivering to the expiring fire.

"It is nearly three-quarters of an hour now, Bella dear," she said presently; "we must keep our promise; and as for Laurence, you will hear the phaeton drive in before you go to sleep, I daresay."

"I shall not go to sleep until I do hear it," I answered, as I took my candle and bade her good-night.

I could not help listening for the welcome sound of the carriage-wheels as I crossed the hall and went upstairs. I stopped in the corridor to look into my aunt's room; but she was fast asleep, and I closed the door as softly as I had opened it. It was as I left this room that, glancing down the corridor, I was surprised to see that there was a light in my own bed-chamber. I was prepared to find a fire there, but the light shining through the half-open door was something brighter than the red glow of a fire. I had joined Laurence in laughing at the ghost-story; but my first thought on seeing this light was of the shadow of the wretched Lady Sibyl. What if I found her crouching over my hearth!

I was half inclined to go back to my aunt's room, awaken her, and tell her my fears; but one moment's reflection made me ashamed of my cowardice. I went on, and pushed open the door of my room: there was no pale phantom shivering over the open hearth. There was an old-fashioned silver candlestick upon the table, and Laurence, my lover, was seated by the blazing fire; not dressed in the evening costume he had worn for the dinner-party, but wrapped in a loose gray woollen dressing-gown, and wearing a black-velvet smoking cap upon his chestnut hair.

Without stopping to think of the strangeness of his appearance in my room; without wondering at the fact of his having entered the house unknown either to Lucy or myself; without one thought but joy and relief of mind in seeing him once more,—I ran forward to him, crying out, "Laurence, Laurence, I am so glad you have come back!"

He—Laurence, my lover, as I thought—the man, the horrible shadow—rose from his chair, snatched up some papers that lay loosely on the table by his side, crumpled them into a ball with one fierce gesture of his strong hand, and flung them at my feet; then, with a harsh dissonant laugh that seemed a mocking echo of the joyous music I loved so well, he stalked out of the door opening on the gallery. I tried to scream, but my dry lips and throat could form no sound. The oak-panelling of the room spun round, the walls and ceiling contracted, as if they had been crushing in upon me to destroy me. I fell heavily to the floor; but as I fell I heard the phaeton-wheels upon the carriage-drive below, and Laurence Wendale's voice calling to the servants.

I can remember little more that happened upon that horrible night. I have a vague recollection of opening my eyes upon a million dazzling lights, which slowly resolved themselves into the one candle held in Lucy Wendale's hand, as she stood beside the bed upon which I was lying. My aunt, wrapped in her dressing-gown, sat by my pillow. My face and hair were dripping with the vinegar-and-water they had thrown over me, and I could hear Laurence, in the corridor outside my bedroom door, asking again and again, "Is she better? Is she quite herself again?"

But of all this I was only dimly conscious; a load of iron seemed pressing upon my forehead, and icy hands seemed riveted upon the back of my head, holding it tightly to the pillow on which it lay. I could no more have lifted it than I could have lifted a ton weight. I could only lie staring with stupid dull eyes at Lucy's pale face, silently wishing that she and my aunt would go, and leave me to myself.

I suppose I was feverish and a little light-headed all that night, acting over and over again the brief scene of my meeting with the weird shadow of my lover. All the stories I had laughed at might be true, then. I had seen the phantom of the man I loved, the horrible duplicate image of that familiar figure, shaped perhaps out of impalpable air, but as terribly distinct to the eye as if it had been a form of flesh and blood.

Lucy was sitting by my bedside when I awoke from a short sleep which had succeeded the long night of fever. How intensely refreshing that brief but deep slumber was to me! How delicious the gradual fading-out of the sense of horror and bewilderment, with all the hideous confusions of delirium, into the blank tranquillity of dreamless sleep! When I awoke my head was still painful, and my frame as feeble as if I had lain for a week on a sick bed; but my brain was cleared, and I was able to think quietly of what had happened.

"Lucy," I said, "you do not know what frightened me, or why I fainted."

"No, dearest, not exactly."

"But you can know nothing of it, Lucy. You were not with me when I came into this room last night. You did not see—"

I paused, unable to finish my sentence.

"Did not see whom—or what, dear Isabel?"

"The shadow of your brother Laurence."

My whole frame trembled with the recollection of my terror of the night before, as I said this; yet I was able to observe Lucy's face, and I saw that its natural hue had faded to an ashen pallor.

"The shadow, Isabel!" she faltered; not as if in any surprise at my words, but rather as if she merely spoke because she felt obliged to make some reply to me.

"Yes, Lucy," I said, raising myself upon the pillow, and grasping her wrist, "the shadow of your brother Laurence. The living, breathing, moving image of your brother, with every lineament and every shade of colouring reflected in the phantom face as they would be reflected in a mirror. Not shadowy, transparent, or vanishing, but as distinct as you are to me at this very moment. Good heavens! Lucy, I give you my solemn word that I heard the phantom footsteps along that gallery as distinctly as I have ever heard the steps of Laurence himself; the firm heavy tread of a strong man."

Lucy Wendale sat for some time perfectly silent, looking straight before her,— not at me, but out at the half-open window, round which the ivy-leaves were fluttering, to the dim moorland melting into purple distance above the treetops in the park. Her profile was turned towards me; but I could see by her firmly-compressed lips and fixed eyes that she was thinking deeply.

Presently she said, slowly and deliberately, without once looking at me as she spoke, "You must be fully aware, my dearest Isabel, that these delusions are of common occurrence with people of an extremely sensitive temperament. You may be one of these delicately-organised persons; you had thrown yourself last night into a very nervous and hysterical state in your morbid anxiety about Laurence. With your whole mind full of his image, and tormented by all kinds of shadowy terrors about danger to him, what more likely than that you should conjure up an object such as that which you fancy you saw last night?"

"But so palpable, Lucy, so distinct!"

"It would be as easy for the brain to shape a distinct as an indistinct form. Grant the possibility of optical delusion, a fact established by a host of witnesses,—and you cannot limit the character of the delusion. But I must get our doctor, Mr. Arden, to talk to you about this. He is something of a metaphysician as well as a medical man, and will be able to cure your mental ills and regulate this feverish pulse of yours at the same time. Laurence has ridden over to York to fetch him, and I daresay they will both be here directly."

"Lucy, remember you must never tell Laurence the cause of my last night's fainting-fit."

"I never shall, dear. I was about to make the very same request to you. It is much better that he should not know it."

"Much better; for O, Lucy, do you remember that in all ghost-stories the appearance of the shadow, or double, of a living person is a presage of death to that person? The thought of this brings back all my terror. My Laurence, my darling, if anything should happen to him!"

"Come, Bella, Mr. Arden must talk to you. In the mean time, here comes Mrs. Porson with your breakfast. While you are taking it, I will go to the library, and look for Sir Walter Scott's *Demonology*. You will find several instances in that book of the optical delusions I have spoken of."

The housekeeper came bustling into the room with a breakfast-tray, which she placed on a table by the bed. When she had arranged everything for my comfort, and propped me up with a luxurious pile of pillows, she turned round to speak to Lucy.

"O, Miss Lucy," she said, "poor Beck is so awfully cut up. If you'd only just see him, and tell him—"

Lucy silenced her with one look; a brief but all-expressive glance of warning and reproval. I could not help wondering what possible reason there could be for making a mystery of some little trouble of James Beck's.

Mr. Arden, the York surgeon, was the most delightful of men. He came with Lucy into my room, and laughed and chatted me out of my low spirits before he had been with me a quarter of an hour. He talked so much of hysteria, optical delusions, false impressions of outward objects, abnormal conditions of the organ of sight, and other semi-mental, semiphysical infirmities, that he fairly bewildered me into agreeing with and believing all he said.

"I hear you are a most accomplished horsewoman," Miss Morley, "he said, as he rose to leave us; "and as the day promises to be fine I most strongly recommend a canter across the moors, with Mr. Wendale as your cavalier. Go to sleep between this and luncheon; rise in time to eat a mutton-chop and drink a glass of bitter ale; ride for two hours in the sunniest part of the afternoon; take a light dinner, and go to bed early; and I will answer for your seeing no more of the ghost. You have no idea how much indigestion has to do with these things. I daresay if I were to see your bill of fare for yesterday I should discover that Lady Adela's cook is responsible for the phantom, and that he made his first appearance among the *entrées*. Who can wonder that the Germans are a ghost-seeing people, when it is remembered that they eat raspberry-jam with roast veal?"

I followed the doctor's advice to the letter; and at three o'clock in the afternoon Laurence and I were galloping across the moorland, tinged with a yellow hazy light in the September sunshine. Like most impressionable people, I soon recovered from my nervous shock; and by the time I sprang from the saddle before the wide stone portico at Fernwood I had almost forgotten my terrors of the previous night.

A fortnight after this my aunt and I left Yorkshire for Brighton, whither

Laurence speedily followed us. Before leaving I did all in my power to induce Lucy to accompany us, but in vain. She thanked my aunt for her cordial invitation, but declared that she could not leave Fernwood. We departed, therefore, without having won her, as I had hoped to have done, from the monotony of her solitary life; and without having seen Mr. Wendale's invalid dependent, the mysterious occupant of the west wing.

Early in November Laurence was summoned from Brighton by the arrival of a black-bordered letter, written by Lucy, and telling him of his father's death. Mr. Wendale had been found by his servant, seated in an easy-chair in his study, with his head lying back upon the cushions, and an open book on the carpet at his feet, dead. He had long suffered from disease of the heart.

My lover wrote me long letters from Yorkshire, telling me how his mother and sister bore the blow which had fallen upon them so suddenly. It was a quiet and subdued sorrow rather than any tempestuous grief, which reigned in the narrow circle at Fernwood. Mr. Wendale had been an invalid for many years, giving very little of his society to his wife and daughter. His death, therefore, though sudden, had not been unexpected, nor did his loss leave any great blank in that quiet home. Laurence spent Christmas at Fernwood, but returned to us for the new year; and it was then settled that we should go down to Yorkshire early in February, in order to superintend the restoration and alteration of the old place.

All was arranged for our journey, when, on the very day on which we were to start, Laurence came to Onslow-square with a letter from his mother, which he had only just received. Lady Adela wrote a few hurried lines to beg us to delay our visit for some days, as they had decided on removing Mr. William, before the alterations were commenced, to a cottage which was being prepared for him near York. His patron's death did not leave the invalid dependent on the bounty of Laurence or Lady Adela. Mr. Wendale had bequeathed a small estate, worth three hundred a-year, in trust for the sole use and benefit of this Mr. William Wendale.

Neither Laurence nor I understood why the money should have been left in trust rather than unconditionally to the man himself. But neither he nor I felt deeply interested in the subject; and Laurence was far too careless of business matters to pry into the details of his succession. He knew himself to be the owner of Fernwood and of a handsome income, and that was all he cared to know.

"I will not hear of this visit being delayed an hour," Laurence said impatiently, as he thrust Lady Adela's crumpled letter into his pocket. "My poor foolish mother and sister are really too absurd about this first or fifth cousin of ours, William Wendale. Let him leave Fernwood, or let him stay at Fernwood, just as he or his nurse or his medical man may please; but I certainly shall not allow his arrangements to interfere with ours. So, ladies, I shall be perfectly ready to escort you by the eleven-o'clock express."

Mrs. Trevor remonstrated, declaring that she would rather delay our visit according to Lady Adela's wish; but my impetuous Laurence would not hear a word, and under a black and moonless February sky we drove up the avenue at Fernwood.

We met Mr. Arden in the hall as we entered. There seemed something ominous in receiving our first greeting from the family doctor; and Laurence was for a moment alarmed by his presence.

"My mother—Lucy!" he said anxiously; "they are well, I hope?"

"Perfectly well. I have not been attending them; I have just come from Mr. William."

"Is he worse?"

"I fear he is rather worse than usual."

Our welcome was scarcely a cordial one, for both Lucy and Lady Adela were evidently embarrassed by our unexpected arrival. Their black dresses half-covered with crape, the mourning liveries of the servants, the vacant seat of the master, the dismal winter weather, and ceaseless beating of the rain upon the window-panes, gave a more than usually dreary aspect to the place, and seemed to chill us to the very soul.

Those who at any period of their lives have suffered some terrible and crushing affliction, some never-to-be-forgotten trouble, for which even the hand of Time has no lessening influence, which increases rather than diminishes as the slow course of a hopeless life carries us farther from it, so that as we look back we do not ask ourselves why the trial seemed so bitter, but wonder rather how we endured even as we did,—those only who have sunk under such a grief as this can know how difficult it is to dissociate the period preceding the anguish from the hour in which it came. I say this lest I should be influenced by after-feelings when I describe the dismal shadows that seemed to brood over the hearth round which Lady Adela, my aunt, Laurence, and myself gathered upon the night of our return to Fernwood.

Lucy had left us; and when her brother inquired about her, Lady Adela said she was with Mr. William.

As usual, Laurence chafed at the answer. It was hard, he said, that his sister should have to act as sick-nurse to this man.

"James Beck has gone to York to prepare for William," answered Lady Adela, "and the poor boy has no one with him but his nurse."

The poor boy! I wondered why it was that Lady Adela and her stepdaughter always alluded to Mr. William as a young man.

Early the next morning, Laurence insisted upon our accompanying him on a circuit of the house, to discuss the intended alterations. I have already described the gallery, running the whole length of the building, at one end of which was situated the suite of rooms occupied by Mr. William, and at the other extremity those devoted to Aunt Trevor and myself. Lady Adela's apartments were nearest to those of the invalid, Lucy's next, then the billiard-room, and opening out of that the bed-and-dressing-room occupied by Laurence. On the other side of the gallery were servants' and visitors' rooms, and a pretty boudoir sacred to Lady Adela.

Laurence was in very high spirits, planning alterations here and renovations there—bay-windows to be thrown out in one direction, and folding-doors knocked through in another—till we laughed heartily at him on finding that the pencil memorandum he was preparing for the architect resolved itself into an order for knocking down the old house and building a new one. We had explored every nook and corner in the place, with the one exception of those mysterious apartments in the left wing. Laurence Wendale paused before the green baize door, but after a moment's hesitation tapped for admittance.

"I have never seen Mr. William, and it is rather awkward to have to ask to look at his rooms while he is in them; but the necessity of the case will be my excuse for intruding on him. The architect will be here to-morrow, and I want to have all my plans ready to submit to him."

The baize-door was opened by Lucy Wendale; she started at seeing us.

"What do you want, Laurence?" she said.

"To see Mr. William's rooms. I shall not disturb him, if he will kindly allow me to glance round the apartments."

I could see that there was an inner half-glass door behind that at which Lucy was standing.

"You cannot possibly see the rooms to-day, Laurence," she said hurriedly. "Mr. William leaves early to-morrow morning."

She came out into the gallery, closing the baize-door behind her; but as the shutting of the door reverberated through the gallery, I heard another sound that turned my blood to ice, and made me cling convulsively to Laurence's arm.

The laugh, the same dissonant laugh that I had heard from the spectral lips of my lover's shadow!

"Lucy," I said, "did you hear that?"

"What?"

"The laugh, the laugh I heard the night that—"

Laurence had thrown his arm round me, alarmed by my terror. His sister was standing a little way behind him; she put her finger to her lips, looking at me significantly.

"You must be mistaken, Isabel," she said quietly.

There was some mystery, then, connected with this Mr. William—a mystery which for some especial reason was to be concealed from Laurence.

Half an hour after this, Lucy Wendale came to me as I was searching for a book in the library.

"Isabel," she said, "I wish to say a few words to you."

"Yes, dear Lucy."

"You are to be my sister, and I have perhaps done wrong in concealing from you the one unhappy secret which has clouded the lives of my poor father, my stepmother, and myself. But long ago, when Laurence was a child, it was deemed expedient that the grief which was so heavy a load for us should, if possible, be spared to him. My father was so passionately devoted to his handsome light-hearted boy that he shrank day by day from the thought of revealing to him the afflicting secret which was such a source of grief to himself. We found that, by constant care and watchfulness, it was possible to conceal all from Laurence, and up to this hour we have done so. But it is perhaps better that you should know all; for you will be able to aid us in keeping the knowledge from Laurence; or, if absolutely necessary, you may by and by break it to him gently, and reconcile him to an irremediable affliction."

"But this secret—this affliction—it concerns your invalid relation, Mr. William?"

"It does, Isabel."

I know that the words which were to reveal all were trembling upon her lips,—that in one brief moment she would have spoken, and I should have known all. I should have known—in time; but before she could utter a syllable the door was opened by one of the women-servants.

"O miss, if you please," she said, "Mrs. Peters says would you step upstairs this minute?"

Mrs. Peters was the nurse who attended on Mr. William.

Lucy pressed my hand. "To-morrow, dearest, to-morrow I will tell you all."

She hurried from the room, and I sank into a chair by the fire, with my book lying open in my lap, unable to read a line, unable to think, except upon one subject—the secret which I was so soon to learn. If she had but spoken then! A few words more, and what unutterable misery might have been averted!

I was aroused from my reverie by Laurence, who came to challenge me to a game at billiards. On my pleading fatigue as an excuse for refusing, he seated himself on a stool at my feet, offering to read aloud to me.

"What shall it be, Bella?—*Paradise Lost*, De Quincey's Essays, Byron, Shelley, Tennyson—"

"Tennyson by all means! The dreary rain-blotted sky outside those windows, and the bleak moorland in the distance, are perfectly Tennysonian. Read *Locksley Hall*."

His deep melodious voice rolled out the swelling verses; but I heard the sound without its meaning. I could only think of the mystery which had been kept so long a secret from my lover. When he had finished the poem he threw aside his book, and sat looking earnestly at me.

"My solemn Bella," he said, "what on earth are you thinking about?"

The broad glare of the blaze from an enormous sea-coal fire was full upon his handsome face. I tried to rouse myself, and, laying my hands upon his forehead, pushed back his curling chestnut hair. As I did so I for the first time perceived a cicatrice across his left temple—a deep gash, as if from the cut of a knife, but a wound of remote date.

"Why, Laurence," I said, "you tell me you were never thrown, and yet you have a scar here that looks like the evidence of some desperate fall. Did you get it in hunting?"

"No, my inquisitive Bella! No horse is to blame for that personal embellishment. I believe it was done when I was a child of two or three years old; but I have no positive recollection of the event, though I have a vague remembrance of wearing a sticking-plaster bandage across my forehead, and being unconscionably petted by Lucy and my mother."

"But it looks like a scar from a cut—from the cut of a knife."

"I must have fallen upon some sharp instrument,—the edge of one of the stone steps, perhaps, or a metal scraper."

"My poor Laurence, the blow might have killed you!"

He looked grave.

"Do you know, Bella," he said, "how difficult it is to dissociate the vague recollections of the actual events of our childhood from childish dreams that are scarcely more vague? Sometimes I have a strange fancy that I can remember getting this cut, and that it was caused by a knife thrown at me by another child."

"Another child! what child?"

"A boy of my own age and size."

"Was he your playfellow?"

"I can't tell; I can remember nothing but the circumstance of his throwing the knife at me, and the sensation of the hot blood streaming into my eyes and blinding me."

"Can you remember where it occurred?"

"Yes, in the gallery upstairs."

We lunched at two. After luncheon Laurence went to his own room to write some letters; Lady Adela and my aunt read and worked in the drawing-room, while I sat at the piano, rambling through some sonatas of Beethoven.

We were occupied in this manner when Lucy came into the room, dressed for walking.

"I have ordered the carriage, mamma," she said. "I am going over to York to see that Beck has everything prepared. I shall be back to dinner."

Lady Adela seemed to grow more helpless every day,—every day to rely more and more on her stepdaughter.

"You are sure to do all for the best, Lucy," she said. "Take plenty of wraps, for it is bitterly cold."

"Shall I go with you, Lucy?" I asked.

"You! O, on no account, dear Isabel. What would Laurence say to me if I carried you off for a whole afternoon?"

She hurried from the room, and in two minutes the lumbering close carriage drove away from the portico. My motive in asking to accompany her was a selfish one: I thought it possible she might resume the morning's interrupted conversation during our drive.

If I had but gone with her!

It is so difficult to reconcile oneself to the irrevocable decrees of Providence; it is so difficult to bow the head in meek submission to the awful fiat; so difficult not to look back to the careless hours which preceded the falling of the blow, and calculate how it might have been averted.

The February twilight was closing in. My aunt and Lady Adela had fallen asleep by the fire. I stole softly out of the room to fetch a book which I had left upstairs. There was more light in the hall and on the staircase than in the drawing-room; but the long gallery was growing dark, the dusky shadows gathering about the faded portraits of my lover's ancestry. I stopped at the top of the staircase, and looked for a moment towards the billiard-room. The door was open, and I could see a light streaming from Laurence's little study. I went to my own room, contrived to find the book I wanted, and returned to the gallery. As I left my room I saw that the green-baize door at the extreme end of the gallery was wide open.

An irresistible curiosity attracted me towards those mysterious apartments. As I drew nearer to the staircase I could plainly perceive the figure of a man standing at the half-glass door within. The light of a fire shining in the room behind him threw the outline of his head and figure into sharp relief. There was no possibility of mistaking that well-known form—the broad shoulders, the massive head, and clusters of curling hair. It was Laurence Wendale looking through the glass door of the invalid's apartments. He had penetrated those forbidden chambers, then. I thought immediately of the mystery connected with the invalid, and of Lucy's anxiety that it should be kept from her brother, and I hurried forward towards the baize-door. As I advanced, he saw me, and rattled impatiently at the lock of the inner door. It was locked, but the key was on the outside. He did not speak, but rattled the lock incessantly, signifying by a gesture of his head that I was to open the door. I turned the key, the door opened outwards, and I was nearly knocked down by the force with which he flung it back and dashed past me.

"Laurence!" I said, "Laurence! what have you been doing here, and who locked you in?"

He did not answer me, but strode along the gallery, looking at each of the doors till he came to the only open one, that of the billiard-room, which he entered.

I was wounded by his rude manner; but I scarcely thought of that, for I was on the threshold of the apartments occupied by the mysterious invalid, and I could not resist one hurried peep into the room behind the half-glass door.

It was a roomy apartment, very plainly furnished: a large fire burned in the grate, which was closely guarded by a very high brass fender, the highest I had ever seen. There was an easy-chair close to this fender, and on the floor beside it a heap of old childish books, with glaring coloured prints, some of them torn to shreds. On the mantelpiece there was a painted wooden figure, held together by strings, such as children play with. Exactly opposite to where I stood there was another door, which was half open, and through which I saw a bedroom, furnished with two iron bedsteads, placed side by side. There were no hangings either to these bedsteads or to the windows in the sitting-room, and the latter were protected by iron bars. A horrible fear came over me. Mr. William was perhaps a madman. The seclusion, the locked doors, the guarded fireplace and windows, the dreary curtainless beds, the watchfulness of Lucy, James Beck, and the nurse,—all pointed to this conclusion.

Tenantless as the rooms looked, the maniac might be lurking in the shadow. I turned to hurry back to the gallery, and found myself face to face with Mrs. Peters, the nurse, with a small tea-tray in her hands.

"My word, miss," she said, "how you did startle me, to be sure! What are you doing here? and why have you unlocked this door?"

"To let out Mr. Laurence."

"Mr. Laurence!" she exclaimed, in a terrified voice.

"Yes; he was inside this door. Someone had locked him in, I suppose; and he told me to open it for him."

"O miss, what have you done! what have you done! Today, above all things, when we've had such an awful time with him! What have you done!"

What had I done? I thought the woman must herself be half distraught, so unaccountable was the agitation of her manner.

O merciful Heaven, the laugh! the harsh, mocking, exulting, idiotic laugh! This time it rang in loud and discordant peals to the very rafters of the old house.

"O, for pity's sake," I cried, clinging to the nurse, "what is it, what is it?"

She threw me off, and rushing to the balustrades at the head of the staircase, called loudly, "Andrew, Henry, bring lights!"

They came, the two men-servants,—old men, who had served in that house for thirty or forty years,—they came with candles, and followed the nurse to the billiard-room.

The door of communication between that and Laurence Wendale's study was wide open, and on the threshold, with the light shining upon him from within the room, stood the double of my lover; the living, breathing image of my Laurence, the creature I had seen at the half-glass door, and had mistaken for Laurence himself. His face was distorted by a ghastly grin, and he was uttering some strange unintelligible sounds as we approached him,—guttural and unearthly murmurs horrible to hear. Even in that moment of bewilderment and terror I could see that the cambric about his right wrist was splashed with blood.

The nurse looked at him severely; he slunk away like a frightened child, and crept into a corner of the billiard-room, where he stood grinning and mouthing at the blood-stains upon his wrist.

We rushed into the little study. O horror of horrors! the writing-table was overturned; ink, papers, pens, all scattered and trampled on the floor; and in the midst of the confusion lay Laurence Wendale, the blood slowly ebbing away, with a dull gurgling sound, from a hideous gash in his throat.

A penknife, which belonged to Laurence's open desk, lay amongst the trampled papers, crimsoned to the hilt.

Laurence Wendale had been murdered by his idiot twin brother.

There was an inquest. I can recall at any hour, or at any moment, the whole agony of the scene. The dreary room, adjoining that in which the body lay; the dull February sky; the monotonous voice of the coroner and the medical men; and myself, or some wretched, shuddering, white-lipped creature that I could scarcely believe to be myself, giving evidence. Lady Adela was reproved for having kept her idiot son at Fernwood without the knowledge of the murdered man; but every effort was made to hush-up the terrible story. William Wendale was tried at York, and transferred to the county lunatic asylum, there to be detained during her Majesty's pleasure. His unhappy brother was quietly buried in the Wendale vault, the chief mausoleum in a damp moss-grown church close to the gates of Fernwood.

It is upwards of ten years since all this happened; but the horror of that February twilight is as fresh in my mind to-day as it was when I lay stricken— not senseless, but stupefied with anguish—on a sofa in the drawing-room at Fernwood, listening to the wailing of the wretched mother and sister.

The misery of that time changed me at once from a young woman to an old one; not by any sudden blanching of my dark hair, but by the blotting-out of every girlish feeling and of every womanly hope. This change in my own nature has drawn Lucy Wendale and me together with a link far stronger than any common sisterhood. Lady Adela died two years after the murder of her son. The Fernwood property has passed into the hands of the heir-at-law.

Lucy lives with me at the Isle of Wight. She is my protectress, my elder sister, without whom I should be lost; for I am but a poor helpless creature.

It was months after the quiet funeral in Fernwood church before Lucy spoke to me of the wretched being who had been the author of so much misery.

"The idiotcy of my unhappy brother," she said, "was caused by a fall from his nurse's arms, which resulted in a fatal injury to the brain. The two children were infants at the time of the accident, and so much alike that we could only distinguish Laurence from William by the different colour of the ribbons with which the nurse tied the sleeves of the children's white frocks. My poor father suffered bitterly from his son's affliction; sometimes cherishing hope even in the face of the verdict which medical science pronounced upon the poor child's case, sometimes succumbing to utter despair. It was the intense misery which he himself endured that made him resolve on the course which ultimately led to so fatal a catastrophe. He determined on concealing William's affliction from his twin-brother. At a very early age the idiot child was removed to the apartments in which he lived until the day of his brother's murder. James Beck and the nurse, both experienced in the treatment of mental affliction, were engaged to attend him; and indeed the strictest precaution seemed necessary, as, on the only occasion of the two children meeting, William evinced a determined animosity to his brother, and inflicted a blow with a knife the traces of which Laurence carried to his grave. The doctors attributed this violent hatred to some morbid feeling respecting the likeness between the two boys. William flew at his brother as some wild animal springs upon its reflection in a glass. With me, in his most violent fit, he was comparatively tractable; but the strictest surveillance was always necessary; and the fatal deed which the wretched, but irresponsible creature at last committed might never have been done but for the imprudent absence of James Beck and myself."

THE MAN ON THE ROOF

Christianna Brand

Christianna Brand (1907–1988) was born in Malaya and educated in an English convent school. She wrote detective novels featuring Inspector Cockrill for fourteen years before focusing on short fiction, pseudonymous thrillers, and books for children. Films based on her books include *Green for Danger* and *Nanny McPhee*.

Sergeant Crum, who, with the assistance of only a fledgling constable, runs the tiny police station in the village of Hawksmere, rang up Chief Inspector Cockrill in Heronsford. "It's the Duke, sir. Phoned to the station and says he's going to shoot hisself."

"The Duke? What Duke? Your Duke, up at the castle?"

Sergeant Crum took a leisurely moment to reflect that in his own small neck of the woods they were hardly so rich in the gilded aristocracy as to necessitate discrimination. Inspector Cockrill, however, had not waited for an answer.

"What have you done about it?"

"Tried to get my constable, sir. Gets his dinner in the village, he does, being his home is there—the Sardine Tin, they call it these days, since the old people—"

"Yes, well, never mind your constable's domestic arrangements—"

"—and they told me he'd suddenly rushed off," continued Crum placidly. "Said he'd heard a shot or something of that. *They* hadn't heard nothing, but the old people are getting a bit—"

"Well, get after him fast, for goodness sake! I'll be there in half an hour at latest."

The sergeant pursued his unhurried way and at the North Gate leaned out of his car to question the lodgekeeper—and, learning that His Grace had gone down a two–three hours ago towards South Lodge, cursed himself mildly for not having thought of that and started on the long haul round the castle walls to what had once been the opposite entrance. South Lodge, of course! Fisher couldn't have heard a shot fired up at the castle.

The constable met him at the little wooden gate of the graveled path that led up to the lodge, clinging as though for support to his bicycle. Over his large, rather handsome young face was spread a strange pall of grey. He said, "He's dead, Sarge."

"Dead? He's done it?"

"Seems like it. He's lying on the floor in the parlor. Lot of blood around."

"You're sure? You didn't make certain?"

"Door's locked, sir. I looked in at the window, but it's too small to get through. And anyway—"

"I was held up. Started for the castle first. You came here direct?"

"Yessir. I heard the shot, I guessed what it might be. I knew he'd be here—I saw him this morning, turning in at the gate. So I got on me bike and came over."

The lodge was in fact a lodge no longer. In the not too distant past, its magnificent wrought-iron gates had been removed and the gap bricked up except for a small postern door. And the high wall ringing the castle and its grounds, rebuilt in a curve that now left the little house standing outside on its own, in an expanse something under an acre of dull, flat land, was at present covered in a blanket of Christmas snow about two inches deep. A hedge completed a sort of high ring around the building, with a break in it to admit of a small wooden gate leading up to the tiny porch over the front door.

The redundant lodgekeeper had been allowed to remain in residence until the accession of the present Duke about three years ago, when he had been evicted with his poor old wife, so that His Grace, whose single bleak passion was the collection and destruction of butterflies, might convert the place into a sort of playroom for himself and his hobby. Considering that there must, up at the castle, be at least seventy rooms which might equally have served his purpose, the dispossessed might be forgiven for suggesting resentfully—but not to the Duke—that a nook might have been created for him there.

Now, in the light snow, two narrow lines, clearly the marks of the constable's bicycle tires, led up and away from the front door—the return journey having apparently been decidedly wobbly. There was no other mark in the snow.

"No sign of his footsteps."

"No. It hadn't started snowing when I saw him going in through the gate." For whatever reason, the constable had lost more color. "That was a couple of hours ago."

"Oh, well." Sergeant Crum abandoned a secret hope that by delaying his errand until the Inspector should come, he might shift onto other shoulders the onus of the whole alarming affair, for sudden death is not a commonplace in quiet little Hawksmere, nestling under the calm shadow of the castle up the hill. He started off through the light flurry of swirling snow, some vague instinct suggesting that it might be well to avoid the tracks of the bicycle tires. You could see where the constable had propped his machine against the wall of the house and gone up the two or three steps. Snow was shuffled as his footprints came down and appeared to move round to the right.

"I ran round to the side window," said Fisher, following his glance. He indicated a small window to their left. "You can't see in so well from there."

"Yes, well, you'd know, wouldn't you?" said Sergeant Crum.

The door was secured by a Yale lock, the sort that clicks shut of itself, to be opened, when the door is closed, only by its own particular key. "Mm," said the sergeant. He tramped in the constable's footsteps leading round the house, and returned with his rugged countryman's visage the same curious shade of grey. "Certainly *looks* very dead," he said uncomfortably and lifted up his heart in a wordless prayer.

The prayer was answered. There came the throbbing of a car in the snowbound stillness and Chief Inspector Cockrill stood at the little gate. For once his shabby mackintosh was not trailing over one shoulder but was worn with his arms in the sleeves, and pushed back upon his noble head with its spray of fine grey hair was the inevitable ill-fitting hat. Inspector Cockrill is known to pick up any hat that happens to be at hand, to the considerable inconvenience of the true owner. Anything that does not actually deafen and blind him is perfectly acceptable to the Terror of Kent.

He remained for a long time intently surveying the scene: the little house in its flat white circle of snow, ringed in by the wall and the hedge so as to be almost invisible to anyone not looking in over the gate. Nice setting for a locked-room mystery, he thought: which God forbid! Fortunately, it appeared to have been a good, straightforward suicide, heralded in advance by the gentleman himself. And from what he had heard, there would be few to mourn the passing of the sixth Duke of Hawksmere—very few indeed.

A pretty little building, almost fairylike in its present aspect, its highly orna-mental pseudo-Gothic façade aglitter with its dusting of snow. An octagonal room, flat-roofed, with a small side window where the lodgekeeper might sit watching for the first signs of approaching vehicles all ready to leap out and open the gates. Into this room, the door opened directly. There was an opposite door leading to the back of the house—two or three small rooms and the household offices. Only the front had been designed to be seen. The rest was cut off and hidden away behind it, considerably less decorative in appearance. The room was furnished only with a desk and a trestle table, upon which were distributed the tools of the Duke's preoccupation, a typewriter, and sheaves of paperwork. There was no other furniture in the house.

Inspector Cockrill stood quietly, taking it all in. The door leading to the other rooms was locked and bolted on this side. There could be nobody else in the house unless they had entered by a back door or window: and in fact there was nobody there. The body lay across the front door, so that, upon entering, one saw nothing but the head and shoulders (turned away from the door) and an outflung hand and arm. The shot had gone through the right temple and out through the other side of the head, somewhat higher up; a bullet was lodged much where one would have expected it to be, high up on the post of the opposite door. An open thermos jug stood on the desk with a puddle of cooling coffee left inside, and there was a piece of foil that had evidently been wrapped round a packet of sandwiches. The time was still early afternoon.

It was almost an hour before, having set in motion the wheels of investigative law, Mr. Cockrill decided: "Well, I'd better go up to the castle and see them there." But before he went, he summoned the constable to stand before him— very pale, hands hanging faintly twitching at his sides. "So, boy. Fish your name is, is it?"

"Fisher, sir," said the constable, hardly daring to contradict.

Inspector Cockrill conceded the point. "Well, now, once again—you heard this shot?"

"Having me dinner I was, sir, at home with me gran and grandad and Mum and Dad and all. And I heard this shot and I thought, the old bastard has done it at last. I mean," said the constable in a terrible hurry, "His-Grace-has-done-himself-in-at-last, sir!"

"You knew of this habit of the Duke's of constantly threatening suicide?"

"Being as he often rang up the station—which he did today, sir."

"Mm. Who else heard the shot?"

"Well, no one, Mr. Cockrill, sir. Gran and Grandad, they're a bit deaf and me mum and dad was arguing and the kids all quarreling, kicking up a row as usual. Besides—"

"Besides?"

"They'd've only said good riddance, and to leave things be."

"Oh?" said Cockie coldly. "Why would they have said that?"

"Well, account of— I mean, nobody liked the old—I mean, nobody liked the Duke, sir, did they?"

"You, however, stifled your feelings and dashed off to his assistance?"

"Only me duty, sir," said Constable Fisher.

"How did you know he'd be here?"

"Well, I saw him arriving," the constable explained. "And he always did spend most of the day here, brought down his sangwidges and coffee and that."

"And seems to have consumed them. Does that strike you as rather odd?"

"What, like 'the prisoner ate a hearty breakfast'?"

The Inspector bent upon him an appreciative eye. "Exactly. Who eats up his lunch before he sets about killing himself?"

"If a gentleman had—well, like moods, sir. And it was a while ago: the coffee's gone quite cold."

"Yes, well . . . Now once again, Constable. You were at this door within six or seven minutes of your hearing the shot? The door was locked. You went round to the window and looked through. The window round at the side of the room, not to this one next to the door, which is nearest."

"You can't see the whole room from the little window, sir. Even from the other one, I couldn't see much. But I could see a good bit of him. I—well, I got a bit rattled, sir, seeing him lying there like that, sort of dead like."

"Very dead like," said Cockie sardonically. "You didn't think of going in and trying to resuscitate him?"

"But he was dead, sir. His head—" He puffed out his cheeks and put a hand over his mouth.

"You'll get used to it," said the Inspector, more kindly. "It shakes one, the first time. So you got on your bike and rode back to the gate? A bit wobbly, those tire marks, the returning ones."

"Yes, well, I was a bit—I didn't know what to do, sir, till the sergeant came."

"In other words, you lost your head."

To Sergeant Crum he said, grumbling: "A wretched young rookie! The Duke of Hawksmere, no less, announces his forthcoming suicide and who's on the spot? This great, green baby of a rookie constable, not yet dry behind the ears." He glanced up at the castle frowning down, formidable, upon them from the hilltop. "God knows what on earth the Duchess is going to say . . ."

What the Duchess in fact said was, comfortably, "Oh, well, he was always threatening suicide, *wasn't* he? His farewell notes simply litter the place. If the police had always had someone important at the ready, no other work would have got done at all." But that poor boy, she added, must have been scared stiff, all on his own, having to cope. "And you say it's not really quite so simple?"

Not simple at all. But for the moment he dodged it. He said, gratefully: "Your Grace takes it very calmly."

They sat in her private room with its charming pieces of period furniture, made cozy by large, comfortable armchairs. The Duchess had always seemed to him, in many ways, like a comfortable armchair herself: warm and well cushioned and to all the world holding out welcoming arms. "Well, yes—I can't pretend to be heartbroken, he was only a fairly remote cousin, you know, and such a misery, poor man!" Her son, the young Duke, had died in an accident up at his University three years ago and his cousin succeeded to the title.

"I stayed on here at the castle with him, though I longed to retire to the Dower House and be on my own. But he was a mean man, he cared nothing for the estate and the people—he was doing a lot of harm all over the place. Now his brother will succeed him and he's a very different kettle of fish. He loves it, and Rupert, his boy, and darling little Becca, they really do care about it, too. And what a change for them! Poor as church mice they all were till Cousin Hamnet inherited. Everyone thinks that if you belong to a great old family like ours, you must naturally be rich, but of course, apart from the title, that needn't be so at all. And they certainly weren't." It was on account of this, she believed, that Hamnet had never got married; though now, as a matter of fact, there were murmurs about his doing so.

"So Hamnet was pretty happy to succeed?"

"Well—not happy as we've seen. He was not a happy man. A depressive, I suppose the psychiatrists would say, and he certainly got no joy out of being Duke of Hawksmere. But there is a joy, you know, in being at the center of it all and caring about the land—running it properly, looking after the people, one's own people. It sounds condescending, referring to them as 'our people,' but they do become like one's own, so many have been for generations with the family. One gets very protective towards them, and I'm thankful to say that Will, the new Duke, and darling Rupert and Becca have the feeling very strongly. I must confess," said the Duchess, "that I've loved it all. Even the bazaar-opening I've secretly rather enjoyed."

"Nobody opens a bazaar like Your Grace," said Cockie handsomely.

"Well, a new Grace will be opening them now, and they're all so happy to be here—now forever. The children were here a lot in their school hols, inseparable friends with the family down at South Lodge. Poor Dave, a bad attack of calf-love, it was rather touching, all great hands and feet and blushing like a peony every time she came near him."

Inspector Cockrill, unfamiliar with any South Lodge family and ignorant of whoever Dave might be, preferred to probe a little further into the family of the new Duke. "They're all staying here at the moment, I understand?"

"Yes, for Christmas. I'm so happy having them here."

"A handsome pair, I believe. Tall, are they? Take after their father?"

"Oh, my dear, no—ants! I mean, compared with my own beautiful son, they seem so dark and little."

"Pretty lightweight, are they?"

"Both of them." She looked at him warily. "Why should you ask? You've got something up your sleeve, you old devil! You've been holding out on me."

"No, no," said the Inspector, "I just wanted to get the facts from you, un-prejudiced. And so I have. And in return I'll offer Your Grace a fact, which I wouldn't do for most people, so please keep it absolutely to yourself." But he could hardly bring himself to speak it aloud. "Have you ever heard, Duchess, of a locked-room mystery?"

"You mean like detective stories? Doors bolted, windows barred, wastes of untrodden—" She broke off, incredulous. "You don't mean it? The lodge down there in the middle of all that snow?"

"The constable rode up to the front door on his bike. He walked a little way round to a side window and back. He rode back down to the gate. He and his sergeant then walked up to the house. *I* walked up to the house. Apart from those footsteps coming and going and the two lines coming and going of the bicycle tires there isn't a break in the whiteness all round about that place. Ringed round by the wall and the hedge, the lodge sitting like a cherry in the middle of an iced cake. Not a single sign."

"Oh, well," said the Duchess, "what's really so odd about that? Naturally, he'd have let the door close when he went into the lodge—the Duke, I mean. And in this weather he'd keep the windows shut. He went down before the snow began. Had this gun with him—presumably in case he came on suicidal at any time, which he was always doing; and he did come on suicidal. He rang up the police station as usual, sat down and composed yet another note, and this time, for a change, poor old Ham, he really did shoot himself. I mean, you say he was just lying there?"

"Almost right across the doorway," said Cockie. "Right hand flung out, fingers curled as though the gun had just fallen from them. The first thing you saw as you pushed open the door—his hand with his fingers half curled. Death instantaneous, shot at very close range, and no question of one of these medical freaks when a man moves about a bit, even walks a little distance after death. He died at once and lay where he had fallen."

"And in fact the constable even heard the shot. So where's the mystery?" said the Duchess reasonably. "Where's your locked room?"

"The locked room is the lodge," said Cockie, "locked in, as it were, in all that untrodden snow. A man dead in the lodge, very recently dead, death instant-aneous, from a gunshot wound at very close range. And the mystery is very easy to state and not at all easy to answer. The mystery is, where is the gun—?"

"Where—?"

"—because it isn't lying there close to his right hand where it ought to be, and it isn't anywhere else in the lodge, and it isn't anywhere outside in all the snow." The cigarette held in his cupped hand sent its pale smoke spiraling up between his fingers, and he flung the butt suddenly, with an almost violent movement, into the heart of the flickering fire. "So damn the blasted thing," he said. "Where the hell *is* it?" And apologized immediately. "I beg Your Lady-ship's pardon!"

"Oh, no, don't apologize," said the Duchess. "I do see. It's dreadful for you."

Well, and dreadful for all of them, she added with growing recognition of what it must mean.

For if the Duke of Hawksmere hadn't shot himself at last, who had done it for him?

And how did that person get away?

And what did he do with the gun?

They sat for a long time in silence, thinking it over. The Chief Inspector said at last, reluctantly: "There seems to be only the one possible solution."

"Mm," said the Duchess. She looked at him rather unhappily. "Are you thinking what I'm thinking?"

"Just a question of what on earth could have been the motive," said the Inspector, shrugging.

"Motive? Oh!" She looked quite horrified. "You're not thinking what I'm thinking after all, Cockie." And what he *was* thinking was absolutely, absolutely, said the Duchess earnestly, "abso*lutely wrong.*"

The handful of men at the disposal of the police had been supplemented by carefully selected village helpers, and at South Lodge there was much pushing and thrusting and beating about hedges and ditches in search of the missing weapon. Result: exactly nil. By now, in the magical way that such things happen, the local press at least had got wind of the affair and their reporters had come swarming over in a fever of excitement from the neighboring small towns: doubtless Fleet Street would soon be upon them. Already they were creating a dangerous nuisance, slouching about in the inevitable filthy old mackintoshes, humped under the weight of swinging cameras, trampling all over the sacred ground.

"Couldn't do much about it," said the Inspector's own sergeant, Charlie Thomas, from Heronsford. "What with the search and all, there aren't enough men to keep them back. It's like a blob of mercury, you think you've got them all under your thumb and suddenly they're scattering into little blobs all over the place again. But, anyway, with fresh snow falling we couldn't do much more in the way of investigation, Chief. All the tracks are disappearing and we'd sorted out every last detail of what might have been a clue."

The Inspector stood for a long, long time looking outside at the ring of wall and hedge surrounding the flat expanse of white, tramped round through the churned-up snow to the window through which Constable Fisher had peered, trembling, for his first sight of the Duke's dead body. (Later the constable had been hoisted up by way of the same window frame to look over the many-spired parapet for any sign of the revolver. "No, Sarge," he had reported, "nothing up here!" From no other vantage point could it have been thrown there.)

And no gun anywhere else in the house. Not in the room where the Duke had died nor in the empty rooms out at the back. The connecting door had been locked and bolted from this side, all the windows and the back door had been similarly fastened—boarded up in most cases. It was as though someone, having made all safe from within, had come out into the octagonal room and locked the intervening door behind him. Nor was there any sign of anyone having been in the back of the house for many long months. Inspector Cockrill gave vent to a satisfied sigh. He liked things to be exact.

It was late evening when, having left in charge trusted henchmen of his own, he collected his sergeant and drove with him back to Heronsford. The night was dark but star-lit, all aglitter where the headlights picked out the leafless twigs of the hedges, frost-laden. He sat in the passenger seat, the cigarette smoke curling up through his nicotined fingers. "Well, then, Charlie—what do you make of it?"

"Not a lot," said the sergeant, eyes on the unrolling white ribbon of the road.

"Sealed room. No marks in the snow that aren't accounted for."

"Time of death?" prompted the sergeant.

"The doc says very recent. Works out at about the time young Fish says he heard the shot."

"Fisher," said Charlie.

"I don't know why I keep thinking it's Fish. Well—so?"

"Well, so there are questions to be asked," said the sergeant. "No acrobatic leaps possible, or trapeze acts or any of that stuff: the distances between the lodge and anything else are much too great. So number one would be, could anyone have been hiding in the lodge? Answer—we searched it thoroughly, even the roof outside, and positively there was not. Well, we were looking for the gun, but if a man had been there we'd hardly have missed him.

"Question two—and this one I know you're a bit fond of: why were the returning bicycle marks so wobbly? Answer—the wretched lad was scared out of his wits, having been first on the scene and found the Duke dead—his hands were probably shaking like jellies on the handlebars. Even Crum observed that he was pale and distressed. Question three, then: did he really hear the sound of the shot?—no one else did. Answer—sure enough, we have only his word for it. Question four then is: was it really the Duke who telephoned the station? And the answer to that is that Sergeant Crum, who took the message, is so thick he would never think to question it.

"Number five: why did Crum then bat off up to the castle when the constable was supposed to have heard the shot from his home, which he couldn't possibly have done if it had been fired up at the castle? That gets the same answer—the man is as thick as two planks. Question six: did the Duke really write the suicide note which was propped up on the desk? Answer—yes, probably, but it could have been written under coercion. Finally—and this is the sixty-million-dollar one—how did the murderer get away, taking the gun with him? Answer—"

"Or answers . . ."

"Pretty obvious, Mr. Cockrill, don't you think? Only one way, really. Different versions of the same, depending upon who the murderer *was*."

"Except in the case of the one I think of as number four."

"Four?" said the sergeant, almost as though they were playing a word-game. "I've only got three."

Inspector Cockrill ran over them, ascribing to each a motive or motives. "I've only just now decided to add in this fourth one. In that case, the motive could be anything: His Late Grace was a deeply unlovable man." They sat silent a little while, musing over it all, while the little car crept across the light carpet of snow—in this narrow, little-used byroad hardly disturbed at all. The sergeant said at last: "It's odd that with the first three the motive in each case seems to be vicarious—if by that I mean, on behalf of other people."

"Well, I'd hardly say that: other people would benefit, certainly. In the first, it would certainly seem so vicarious, as you call it, as to be very hard to believe." He added rather gloomily that they mustn't forget that the Duchess appeared to have a candidate of her own and one without even a motive. "And that makes five."

The sergeant was hardly impressed. "Oh, well, sir—the Duchess!"

The Inspector had sat all this time nursing the enormous hat on his bony knees. Now, as they reached his gate, he scrambled out, clapping it back onto his head. "Yes, well—'the Duchess' you say, my lad. But the Dowager Duchess of Hawksmere, let me tell you, is an exceedingly shrewd old bird. And I'm a bit scared of her. There's nothing she'd stop at to protect 'our people,' let alone her own family." He slammed-to the door of the car and stood hunting through the pockets of the disreputable old mac in search of his keys. "Oh, thank goodness, here are the damn things. I'm in need of a hot drink and bed. Good night, Charlie. Go off home now and sleep well. Tomorrow is another day."

Another day. For all but the late Duke of Hawksmere, lying so quiet and stiff in his metal cold-box, split like a herring to reveal his body's secrets: with nothing to disclose, however, but the recent consumption of a sandwich meal, and a gunshot wound in the head . . .

The new day was less than gladdened for Inspector Cockrill by the arrival of the Chief Constable of the county. A choleric, ex-military man, he huffed and puffed a good deal, unable to face the grotesquerie of a locked-room mystery right there in their midst, and for comfort settled on the solid facts relating to the missing weapon. Well, yes, said Inspector Cockrill, a common enough type of weapon left over from the last war—impossible to say how many ex-officers might, for one reason or another, have failed to hand back their revolvers at the conclusion of hostilities. The passage through bone, explained the experts, would make it difficult to ascribe the bullet to any one particular gun.

"Was the late Duke known to have possessed such a revolver?"

"If you recall, Sir George, you yourself undertook to question him on the subject."

"Yes, well, so I did call on him and ask him. But delicately, you know, stepping very delicately. He hardly seemed to know what I was talking about. But he certainly didn't deny that he had such a weapon."

Very helpful, reflected Cockie.

"Well, you can't march in with a sniffer-dog and search a place like the castle," said the Chief Constable huffily. Besides, he added, these people who were always threatening suicide never really did it.

"Nosir," said Cockie in the authentic accents of Police Constable Fisher at his most wooden. He explained the probable difficulties in ascribing the bullet to the late Duke's, or indeed to any revolver.

"Which, anyway, you've lost," the Chief Constable reminded him sourly.

"Oh, yessir, so we have," said the Inspector, more in the Sergeant Crum line this time. Sort of thing that could happen to anyone, the voice suggested.

At first light, the search for the missing gun had begun again—village people, tremendously eager and helpful, said Cockie. Although, he added limpidly, none of them had liked the Duke, most of them having understandable grudges against him. To tenants so long accustomed to the cherishing rule of the Dukes of Hawksmere, with the family arms around "our people," he had seemed a mean, to them a dangerous man.

The Chief Constable was as appalled as the Inspector could have wished. "Good God, man, they'll all be on the side of the killer! You don't know *who* may have found the thing and be harboring it somewhere. They must be taken off at once—search them, search their homes, search every house in the village!"

He stumped off angrily to wreak further havoc from the comfortable ambiance of the Heronsford police station and Chief Inspector Cockrill was able to give out, with a lightened heart, that these arbitrary orders came not from himself—as if he would—but from the Chief Constable in his un-wisdom. He must, however, have considerably overrated his superior's enthusiasm—Sir George would never have contemplated an intrusion into the castle itself.

The search there was more easily concluded than might have been expected—by anyone but the Inspector himself. "Under some papers in a drawer of the late Duke's desk," he explained to the Dowager Duchess. "Surprise, surprise!" he added sardonically.

"*Not* a surprise." said the Duchess. "After all, it may not be the one that was used. I hear the bullet may not prove to be traceable. Perhaps he didn't have this one with him. He presumably didn't always lug one around with him."

"So how did he propose to shoot himself down at the lodge? He rang up the station and said he was about to do so."

"Well, someone rang up the station. Would Sergeant Crum necessarily have questioned the voice? And there'd be suicide notes all over the place. Whoever it was could just have used one of those."

"Your Grace ought to be in my job," said the Chief Inspector respectfully.

"Do you know, Cockie," said the Duchess on a note of not very sincere apology, "in this particular case, I really believe I should."

Mr. Cockrill felt in duty bound to report to his Chief Constable, though by no means to unravel matters clearly for him. "Her Grace put the gun there herself, of course, as I knew she would."

"The *Duchess*?"

"The Dowager. It was in a package sent up with her letters this morning. Well, of course, her post has been prodigious. Posted last night here in Hawksmere. Everyone's been in and out of the village, in and out of Heronsford, up and down to London like yoyos, lawyers and so forth: a Duke doesn't die like ordinary men, let alone get himself murdered. The post alone may tell us something," suggested Cockie. "Don't you think?"

It patently told the Chief Constable nothing whatsoever. He huffed and puffed and went off at a tangent. "Why should the Duchess do such a thing?"

"Protecting her family?"

"For heaven's sake—her family! You're not suspecting the new Duke of Hawksmere in a business like this?"

"He had everything to gain. But, well, no—"

"Well, then, young Rupert. You wouldn't—"

"His father has succeeded the sixth Duke. He is now heir to the title. And he loves the place and the people on the estate deeply. The family own half the county. He was horrified by the way the late Duke was treating them. And he was threatening to marry and get an heir for himself. We have to consider young Rupert."

"Good heavens, Cockrill, I shall never live this down!"

"Or there's the girl," continued Cockie remorselessly. "She felt the same about it all. And of course her parents now become Duke and Duchess instead of being just hard-up nobodies."

Sir George looked as though spontaneous combustion were just around the corner. The daughter of the Duke! Or the heir to the dukedom! But comfort was at hand. He demanded triumphantly, "Just explain to me how either of them could have got away from the building? The tire marks, the footmarks, are all accounted for, and there are no others. So how could either of those young people have got away from the place?"

Oh, well, as to that, said Cockie, tremendously offhand, one could think of three or four explanations in each case; surely Sir George must have worked them out for himself? And he suddenly caught sight of Charlie Thomas and must rush off and join his sergeant, if Sir George would excuse him . . .

To Charlie, he said: "I can't resist pulling the old buffer's leg."

"You'll get yourself into trouble one of these days, Boss," said the sergeant, laughing. But what on earth, he wondered, was going to happen next?

"What will happen next," said Cockie prophetically, "is that a letter will arrive, suggesting a new and totally unexpected suspect and a new and totally unexpected method of getting away from the lodge—snow surroundings, bike marks, footprints, and all."

And duly the letter arrived and was handed over to them by the Duchess herself. "In this morning's post. Addressed to me. The postmark? But, Cockie dear, you've no notion what the mails have been like—with the Duke's death, you know, all the business letters and the sympathetics, poor loves, so tricky for them to know just what to say! I mean, 'So sorry to hear that your cousin has been murdered. Whatever will you do about the funeral? Yours affectionately, Aunt Maude.' The children are reading through them in fits of giggles, they are so naughty! But as to the postmarks, I'm afraid we just slit all the envelopes open and threw them away. It's not like the Americans who put their addresses on the back—I never get used to it. But out they've gone, and with this sort of cheap writing paper there wouldn't be a matching envelope, we'd never trace which belonged to which."

Nor had the typewriter proved traceable to anyone in or around Hawksmere. Probably done in a pretense of testing a demonstration model somewhere up in London, Cockie thought. A very old trick. Style, predictably illiterate.

"Dear Dutchess," ran the letter, "I am well away now and soon will be abroad so to save truoble for others I confes to the murder of tghe duke of Hawksmear he was a relaiton of yuors but he was a dead rotter and he deseved to die. I went doun befor the sno began he let me in I told him he mite as well comit suiside but he siad he would not now as he was hopeing to het marrid he did not seam to have a gun but I had bruoght one along with me in case. I cuold not make him write a suiside note but there was one rihgt there on the desk just lying about.

"By now it was snoing and I pushed the gun in his back and mad him ring up the police station and say he was going to shoot hisself then I put tghe gun near his head and shot him. When I opend the door it was very quite I haerd a bycicle bell and I went back and closed the door when I hared the person go away I cam out and I saw footsteps in the snow going round the house and I followed them and there was a window. I climbed up by the window on to the roof and when the jurnalists cam crowding round I showed myself and a policeman came and hauled me down so I said I only wanted to get a shot of the snow with the footmarks, as if I was a jurnalist and they quit beleived me. I better say I saw a policeman was being hoisted up to see if tghe gun was on the roof, so I lay up against the parapet where he would be leaning over to look and unles he bent right over he wuld not see me and he did not he only calld out no gun here. That is all. There was a lot of peeple hated tghe duke long before he was a duke and I was one of them. Yuo need not look any feurther."

"Well, well, well," said Cockie, handing over this effusion to his sergeant. "What did I tell you?" He went on down to the lodge and summoned the constable. "Well, now, Fish—"

"Fisher, sir," said the constable a trifle desperately.

"All right, never mind that. You were the man sent up to see if the gun had been thrown onto the flat roof of this room. Why did you choose to climb up via the side window?"

"It couldn't have been thrown from any other point, sir. There's a porch over the front steps and there weren't any other marks in the snow."

"The gun could have slithered back and come to rest just under the parapet. You didn't think to hook yourself right over the edge and look downwards and inwards?"

"The gun wouldn't have done that, Mr. Cockrill, sir." He made a chucking movement with his hand. "It would slither away, sir, not backwards. But anyway, with the snow it would probably just stay where it fell. So it would be about in the middle of the roof. And it wasn't."

"So if a man were hiding close up under the parapet where you looked over—?"

"I could well have missed seeing him," Fisher admitted. "I wasn't looking there." And come to think of it, he suggested, a man *had* tried to climb up on the roof—two or three in fact—but each time been hauled back before he got there. "Them journalists, sir. If anyone got far enough, he would have seen if a gun had been thrown up there."

In fact, several of the culprits had been traced but none admitted having got up as far as the roof, and the consensus had been that this was true. Still, it might be well for Cockrill to scan the newspapers for press photographs of the snowy ground, taken from a high angle . . .

He came back to Constable Fisher. "The late Duke had a good many enemies? You yourself hardly loved him, I daresay?"

The constable's air of ease gave way to pallor and tensed-up fingers. "I never hardly set eyes on him, sir. Him being the Duke and all."

"Till the day before yesterday?"

"And by then he was dead, sir."

"Yes, so he was. It must have been a shock, peering in at that close-shut window? Now, tell me again—why that particular window?"

"You can't see right into the room from the nearer one, sir. Not into the whole of the room."

"No you can't, can you? But how did you know that?"

"Well, sir, being as my gran and grandad used to live here—"

"They *lived* here?" said Cockrill, and glanced with a sort of gleam towards his sergeant. "They *lived* here? And were chucked out by the Duke, I suppose? And had to squash in with the rest of your big family, all in one little cottage—the old folks cranky and carping, I daresay, as old people are when they see too much of the young—your parents resentful and answering back, all those noisy brothers and sisters worse than ever, and everyone miserable. In other words—the Sardine Tin!"

"Except I think it must be more peaceful, sir, in a sardine tin."

No wonder, reflected the Inspector, that I kept thinking of him as Fish. "Never mind your constable's domestic arrangements," he had said, choking off Sergeant Crum's ill-timed explanations, and all that time . . . "All right for the moment, then, Fisher." But to Charlie he said: "Well, Sarge—the simplest explanation, after all? It was only that being more or less strangers to these parts we had no idea that such a motive existed. But now—"

A shot that nobody else had heard. Down to the lodge on one's bicycle and up to the front door. The Duke, placidly consuming sandwiches, is easily persuaded to admit the uniformed figure of the local rozzer. Some excuse—the police require the handing over of the revolver which His Grace is understood to have illegally in his possession. Gun in hand, force the telephone call to the police station. With any luck, Sergeant Crum will go batting off up to the castle, thus giving one more time. Force the production of the suicide note and then—one shot and it's done.

It's done: but all of a sudden, it's horrible. Back away to the open front door, gun in hand, having forgotten in one's panic to throw it down beside the outflung hand. Stand there, shaking, trying to wipe off one's fingerprints and—horror!— the door is blown shut by the whirl of the wind that is sending the snowflakes aflurry and one is locked out on the step with the gun in one's hand! Round to the window in hopes it may open sufficiently to throw the gun into the room. But it is tightly closed—and at any moment Sergeant Crum may arrive!

Down to the gate, then, awobble with nervousness, on one's bike and when the hue and cry goes forth, join eagerly in. For who will think of looking in the pocket of the heroic discoverer of the crime, for the weapon which brought it about?

Nervous? Yes, of course he would be nervous. But so what? A man is dead whom all the world detested, Gran and Grandad can come back to the cozy little home, Mum and Dad will be free and happy again, and the pack of younger brothers and sisters will be safe from the ceaseless censure of the older generation and settle down happily once more. Her Grace can move out to the dear little Dower House, the new Duke is a kind and generous man, Rupert, friend of one's childhood, will be heir to the dukedom, and long-loved Becca will be rich and happy and always down here at Hawksmere to be adored from afar. And how grateful, could they have known, would everyone for miles around have been to the begetter of all this happiness . . .

But first the gun. One cannot carry it around in a uniform pocket, and where to hide it in the narrow confines of the village to which one is now restricted? Post it off to the castle, then, with a message to the Duchess, "Please put this back where it belongs, for all our sakes." Her Grace must recognize that the thing has been done by someone here on the ducal estates, by one of "our people." Her Grace won't make trouble for anyone who will throw themselves upon her mercy, and Her Grace knows very well how to protect herself . . .

Charlie Thomas had been mulling it over, muttering at intervals into the recital, "Mm, mm." Now he said: "And the letter?"

"Ah," said Cockie, for the first time losing confidence a little. "The letter."

"Very interesting, that letter. Not in fact the work of an illiterate. The mistakes are deliberate. A writer who spells 'brought' as 'bruoght' knows what letters there are in that difficult word. A true illiterate would write 'brort' or something. And this isn't an accomplished typist. It's easy to hit a *g* when you intended an *h* and he keeps putting *tghe*. But Fisher types very well and I don't think he's bright enough to have thought all this up. So that would bring us to—"

"The new heir," said Cockie none too happily. "Young Rupert."

"It's one thing for a lad to want to help his grandparents to get back their old home," said Charlie. "But Rupert's dad becomes a Duke, they're all in the money, and, what's probably the most important point, 'our people' will be safe from the tyrant, who was threatening to marry and spawn a breed of mini-tyrants forever."

"So how do you suggest he got away, leaving no trace in the snow? You don't suggest that Rupert was the man on the roof?"

"There never was any man on the roof, sir, *was* there? Just some damn journalist, trying to be cleverer than the rest; and *he* was hauled down and whoever he may have been, he wasn't Rupert. But we've both thought of ways in which someone other than Fisher could have got away from the lodge . . ."

There was the sound of hooves chiff-chuffing across the grass and a light voice exhorted: "Now, darlings, be good horses and just stay there!" and, with a thump at the door, the two young people came into the room.

"Look here, Inspector, you're *not* accusing poor Dave of murdering Cousin Ham?" demanded Lady Rebecca on a note of scorn.

An ant she might be, but a very pretty ant, the cloud of dark, soft hair crowned by a shabby little riding bowler. The brother was as dark and scarcely taller, very slender, and no less shabbily fitted out. Poor as church mice, the Duchess had said, and clearly their late cousin had not been generous with handouts, despite his sudden acquisition of title and great wealth. Inspector Cockrill said mildly: "Are you referring to Police Constable Fisher?"

"Yes—we've just met him in the lane, and he's petrified."

"If he did kill the Duke, that would be fairly natural."

"He no more killed the Duke than I did!" Rupert said.

"In fact, my boy, we were just discussing that very possibility. That you *did*."

"*Me?* What a lot of rubbish! Why on earth should I want to kill rotten old Cousin Hamnet?"

"Just because he *was* rotten old Cousin Hamnet."

The brother and sister were leaning back negligently against the edge of the table, feet crossed in their well worn riding boots. "Good lord," said Rebecca, "you're not going to suggest that he was the man on the roof, beloved of our Aunt Daisy—the Duchess Daisy," she elaborated. "And if you are, how did he get away from the lodge without leaving great humping footprints in the snow?"

"Well," said the Inspector easily, "we had an idea that he might have used a bicycle."

"Oh, that's great!" said Rupert. "I haven't even got a bicycle."

"But your dear friend Dave—he had a bicycle."

It rocked them a little, but the boy said nonchalantly enough, "Don't tell me— let me guess. I borrowed Dave's bicycle."

"At gun-point," suggested Becca, mocking, her pretty little nose in the air.

"Or by cajolement. He would be very much on your side."

"You seem to have a simple faith in the trustworthiness of your force," said Rupert.

"Well, but—to such a good friend. And it does all seem to fit."

"It doesn't fit at all," said Rebecca. "We were together the whole afternoon, out riding." She saw as she spoke the weakness of this double alibi and added, "My Aunt Daisy saw us from the window. She'll tell you so."

"I'm sure she will," said the Inspector drily.

Rebecca slid down from her perch on the table edge. "So we'll be going home now because I can assure you that Dave didn't do it and neither did Rupert, so just *don't* be silly about it."

"No, indeed, since you put up so convincing a case. On the other hand," suggested Cockie, "you leave yourself undefended."

"*Me?*" said Becca as her brother had said before her.

"You had exactly the same possible motives as your brother. One or the other of you came down here before the snow fell—"

"Why one or the other—why not both of us?"

"Because only one person could have ridden away on that bicycle, with or without Constable Fisher." The sergeant opened his mouth to speak, but Mr. Cockrill quelled him. "You came down here before the snow fell, one or the other of you. You started a long argument with your cousin about the running of the estate—about his possible marriage, perhaps. But it was all no good. You lost your temper, the gun was lying around as usual, ready for use if the fancy took him—and you picked it up. By that time the snow had fallen, but while you stood panicking on the doorstep, there appeared the gallant Saint Dave to the rescue on his trusty bicycle. No need in your case, Lady Rebecca, for any gun-pointing or even cajolement: up you scramble and, wobbling a bit with the extra weight and general insecurity, you duly arrive at the gate. Off you scarper and the friend of your childhood is left, rather scared, but glowing with the knowledge that he has saved—well, I'll still say one or other of those he loves."

"Not bad," said Rupert with a determined air of superiority, but looking, all the same, a little pale. "But surely there must be other candidates, not just Becca and me?"

"There aren't, you know. Your father is too big and heavy to have shared a bike with Fisher, who's a big chap too—I've tried an experiment and the bicycle broke down—and what's more, he has an alibi rather more convincing than that of a brother and sister out riding, watched by Her Grace, your cousin Daisy. Someone from round about? Well, the police aren't entirely idiots, you know, whatever you may believe to the contrary, and we've made very thorough investigations—you can count them all out."

"So you seriously think you have a case against us—against one of us?"

"Or Constable Fisher," said Cockie placidly.

Rupert slid down and stood beside his sister. "Well, we'll be going now, if you'll excuse us. You can bring the handcuffs up to the castle any time. Come on," he said to his sister. "We'll go and lay this mouse at the feet of our ever present help in times of trouble and see what *she* has to say to Mr. Cockrill about it."

The Inspector waited until the shuffle of hooves had trotted off into silence. Then he stretched himself. "Well, Charlie, at least we've got that off our chests." And perhaps another time, he added laughing, his sergeant would refrain from breaking out into expostulation when his superior officer dropped a clanger.

"It was you saying that only one person could have ridden away on the bike—with or without Fisher. Of course, anyone who had ridden the bike up to the lodge could just have ridden it back again—and any bike, for that matter, it needn't be Fisher's. The tire marks were snowed over before we really got at them."

"Well, it doesn't matter either way. The tracks were made by the constable: he'd seen into the room, he described it to Sergeant Crum. The tire marks were made by him, riding his own bike—quite possibly giving a lift back to the gate to someone of a fairly small physique. And we've eliminated everyone except that precious pair." He heaved himself up and shrugged on his dreadful old mac, thrust that hat onto his head, and gave it a thump which brought it down over his eyes. "Damn the thing, it never used to be as big as this," he said, irritably shoving it up to his forehead. "I'll get on up to the castle now and, in my turn, place my poor mouse at the feet of Her Ladyship. Who, however, is their cousin and not their aunt."

"Does it matter?" said Charlie, surprised.

"Not a bit," said the Inspector and folded himself, mac and hat and all, into his little police car. "See you, Sarge!"

"In one piece, I hope," said Charlie rather doubtfully.

The Duchess of Hawksmere met him in the vast hall, where she stood surrounded by his trio of suspects. "Oh, Cockie—how nice to see you! Now you, my loves," she said to the young ones—apparently without affectation on either side, including among her loves the village constable—"go off and get some coffee and buns or something and don't make any more fuss." One freckled hand on the bannisters, she began to haul herself up the stairs. "Sorry to be so slow, Inspector, but my arthritis is giving me hell today." At the door of her sitting room, she ushered him in. "Find a chair for yourself, but first pour me a drop of vodka, like an angel, and help yourself to whatever you like. And no nonsense about being on duty and all that—we're both going to need it, I promise you."

The Chief Inspector thought that upon his side, at any rate, this would certainly prove only too true. He cast the mac and hat upon a chair and sat down with her before the agreeably flickering fire. "Well, Duchess?"

"Well, Cockie! I thought you'd come up after the kids, with all their dramas, and here you are, and we can settle down and have a real good yat."

Only the Duchess of Hawksmere, reflected the Inspector, would refer to a serious discussion of a murder in the family as a good old yat. "I have to walk circumspectly, my lady."

"Oh, not with me. I mean nobody ever does: it's because I'm so dreadfully un-circumspect myself. So I thought," she suggested with her own particular brand of authority and humility, "would it be possible for you to outline for me the cases you have against all these young people? Because I really do think I can help you, you know."

He thought it over. It was all highly unconventional, but he, no more than Her Grace, had never been, would never be, a slave to that sort of thing. Moreover, he was curious about her own so-far-undisclosed candidate. "If it honestly will go no further?"

"Cross my heart and wish to die," said the Duchess, making a sign upon her well upholstered bosom.

"Well, then . . ." Somewhat gingerly and with many ifs and ands, he outlined one by one his suspicions of the young heir, Rupert, and his sister, the Lady Rebecca. "And then as to Fish—"

"Fisher," said the Duchess. "I do think it's so hurtful to get people's names wrong. I do it all the time myself, but I'm old so it doesn't count. Besides, I call everyone darling, such an actressy habit, I simply hate it: but at least they don't realize that half the time it's because I can't think who on earth they are!"

"Duchess, you are trying to charm me," said Cockie severely.

"Am I? Well, perhaps I am—I never know I'm doing it. But we need a little gaiety in all this awfulness, don't we? So, well then, that brings us to the man on the roof—the letter."

Chief Inspector Cockrill expatiated at length upon the letter. Don't let's be silly about that, was the unexpressed burden of his reflections. Aloud he said: "We know that that was just a diversion."

"But a very potent diversion, Chief Inspector, wouldn't you say? I mean—hardly to be denied outright, at least with any certainty. No possible proof for or against, is there?" She fixed him with a quizzical look which told him that he might as well be a bazaar that Her Grace was about to open. He knew he was at her mercy—and would love every minute of it. "But first, Cockie dear—another drink?"

"Not another drop, Duchess, thank you."

"Oh, but you must, or *I* can't. And you know that I can't get weaving till I'm in vodka up to the ankles. I get so tired," said the Duchess, looking as wan as every evidence of robust health would allow, "and when I'm tired, my mind simply won't work—I'm helpless."

It seemed to Inspector Cockrill highly desirable from his own point of view that Her Grace should remain without reviving vodka, but she had him in thrall. He reluctantly poured out two small rations ("Oh, Cockie, for goodness sake!") and more generously topped them up. "So now, my dear, what are we to do? Because you know perfectly well that my two young ones couldn't possibly have killed the man, and neither could poor, dear Dave. So we come back to the letter. And who wrote the letter."

"You wrote the letter yourself, Duchess, and posted it on one of your necessary expeditions up to London. Or didn't post it at all—just 'found it' among your letters."

"Well, what a thing to suggest! But really very perspicacious of you, Cockie. Yes, of course. I thought it might come in nicely for covering every eventuality: because if you could just settle for that—only keeping it to yourself, of course—and never be able to find a trace of the murderer, well, who could say a word against you?"

"My Chief Constable, for one, could say a word against me and would, most vociferously."

"Oh, that pompous old fool! Nobody will listen to a word he says; you just leave him to me. All you need do is cast about like mad, dragging in Scotland Yard and Interpol and all that lot, trying to trace the letter, trying to ferret out all Hamnet's old enemies, which after all would take you back twenty or thirty years—and finally give up and say the case is closed or whatever the expression is."

"No case is ever closed," said Cockie severely.

"Well, keep it a bit open, but just never solve it. Because what the letter says is true. Millions of people simply hated poor old Ham, long before he was ever a Duke. He was a misery to himself, always saying he wanted to die, never having the courage to get around to doing it. And now the lovely man on the roof has done it for him and everyone will simply love him for it and never want him to be caught at all."

"Except me," said the Chief Inspector somberly.

"Well, I do call that rather lacking in appreciation of my efforts to help you!"

"You don't suppose that *I'd* be content with some cooked-up nonsense, no one ever knowing the truth?"

"Well, but someone does know the truth, don't they, Cockie? I mean, I've told you all along, haven't I? *I* do."

"Your Grace has never had the goodness to divulge it to *me*."

"Oh, Cockie, how cross and sarcastic! Well, I'll divulge it now. But only," said the Duchess, downing the last of her second vodka tonic, "if you promise, promise, promise never to do anything about it."

"Are you asking me to let a criminal go free?"

"No, I'm not. I don't think there is any criminal—except the man on the roof. I think Hamnet did at last really go ahead and commit suicide. Ate his lunch, thought things over—he was always a bit dyspeptic after meals—and reached for the gun. And then—" She put out her pudgy hand with its carefully tended, varnished nails and touched his own nicotined fingers. "Trust me. You'll be grateful to me, honestly you will. I'm not practicing any deceit upon you—and it will solve everything."

You are old, he thought, and stout and arthritic and nowadays no beauty, but damn you— "All right," he said grudgingly. "So?"

"So—that boy, Cockie. You kept on saying it yourself—to be first on the scene of the bloody death of the Earl of Hawksmere, no less—a baby, a great, raw green rookie of a baby policeman, not yet dry behind the ears. In a total panic— wouldn't he be? What he said was the truth, my dear—he heard the shot, leapt on his bike, and pedaled like a lunatic down to the lodge and up through the snow to the front door. And the door was open. Hamnet always left an escape route—rang up in advance so that if ever he did take the plunge, someone could get there in time to haul him back to life. The door was open—how would any- one have heard the shot if it had been fired from behind sealed-up windows and doors? He looked inside and the first thing he saw was the Duke's head, dread- fully wounded, and the revolver lying there, fallen from the dead hand. So—what would any of us do? He panicked and, in an automatic impulse bent down and picked up the gun."

"Oh, my God!" said the Inspector.

"Yes, it was a bit Oh-my-God, wasn't it, since the number-one lesson a police- man is taught is never ever to touch anything at the scene of the crime. He would have thrown it down at once, I daresay, but another lesson came into his mind as he began to calm down—watch out for fingerprints! He got out his hankie or whatever and started wiping his own off the gun and—horror of horrors—there comes a flurry of wind and the door blows shut!"

"Leaving him locked out, with the gun still in his hands. Nips round to the side window to see if he can throw it back in, but the window's tight shut. So he shoves the thing into his pocket and, very nervous, wobbles back to the gate, and when Sergeant Crum arrives—not the most observant of men—goes into his act. The door was closed, he could only see the body by looking in through the window . . ."

"Yes. Well, there you are, Cockie—and there *he* was, poor wretched boy, and just think of his state of mind. Marching about all evening searching for the weapon when all the time it was in his uniform pocket. And now, for days, he'll be kept on duty in the village—and where in little Hawksmere can such a thing remain hidden for any length of time, with everyone searching for it? So what does he do? He posts it off to me. Of course, he can't be sure I've guessed the truth, but people have got into a sort of habit of thinking I'll cope. And that's all, really, except for the lovely, convenient man on the roof, made up for you by me."

He sat almost paralyzed in the deep armchair, looking at her smiling face. "Constable Fisher lost his head and just picked up the gun. Is this what you really believe?"

"It's the simple truth, my dear. And simple is the word."

"He's admitted it?"

"I haven't asked him. It was so obvious."

Not to the assembled forces of the law, it hadn't been. "But to prefer to be suspected of murder—?"

"He could always tell the truth in the end."

"Why not have told it from the beginning?"

"My *dear*," said the Duchess, "you'd have had his guts for garters."

He leapt to his feet. "One thing's for certain—I'll have them now."

"Yes, well—the only thing is, if this story gets out you'll look a bit of a fool, old love, won't you?"

Chief Inspector Cockrill, the Terror of Kent—a bit of a fool, right here on his own patch. "Hey, now, Duchess, if you *don't* mind—"

"Oh, but I do mind," she said. "I don't like to think of you looking foolish." And she pleaded, "Let the boy go! He's been through a bad time, you can be pretty sure of that; he won't do it again. There's nothing against Rupert and Becca, there's been no crime! This is what actually happened and that's the end of it. But the man on the roof—there he is, all worked out so nicely for you and it all hangs together perfectly, now doesn't it? Someone out of the past caught up with the wicked Duke and you never had a hope in hell of catching up with the someone from the past. Gradually the whole affair will fade and Chief Inspector Cockrill, for a miracle, has failed to Get his Man; but for the rest, everyone is happy." And one couldn't help thinking, said the Duchess, confiding to the fire-place, that it is less humiliating to fail to solve a very difficult case than to have failed to solve such a very simple one as a young officer losing his head.

"No one must ever know," said the Inspector; and it was capitulation.

"Good heavens, no. I'll talk to Dave Fisher and tell him what I've guessed and that to save his skin I've played a naughty game all round, and just to pipe down and never get it into his head to confess because he'd get me into trouble. I could even suggest that you rather suspect that this might have happened, but you have to investigate every possibility."

"Except the right one," said Chief Inspector Cockrill rather stiffly. He collected his droopy mackintosh from the back of the chair, clapped the hat on his head, and hastily removed it, in the presence of Her Ladyship. "And honest-ly—not one word of this to anyone?"

"Oh, not a word," vowed the Duchess, even now casting about in her mind for someone one could safely confide in. For really it had been rather a bit of fun. "But I *told* you."

"You told me—?"

"That in this case, I really should have been in your job," said the Duchess. She too rose. "I say, Inspector—what about one more little one? I really think we could do with it. Do join me!"

Inspector Cockrill paused a moment and then cast down his hat and coat again. "Do you know, Duchess—I think I will," he said.

KILLING JUSTICE

Alison Brennan

Alison Brennan published her first novel in 2005 and has become a *New York Times* bestseller. Her romantic suspense thrillers have been nominated for five Romance Writers of America awards, the International Thriller Writers award, and twice won the Daphne du Maurier prize. She currently writes two series: one featuring Lucy Kincaid and one featuring Maxine Revere.

I.

Senate Pro Tem Simon Beck sat in his high-back leather chair signing letters, the tall, narrow window behind him framing the Tower Bridge at the far end of Sacramento's Capitol Mall, the morning sun making the elevator bridge appear golden. His secretary Janice escorted Senator Matt Elliott into the office, offered him coffee—which he refused—then quietly retreated.

Simon had been expecting the confrontation since Elliott called him at six in the morning and said nothing, allowing the tension to build.

It didn't take long. Elliott slammed his fist on the antique desk and leaned forward, his knuckles white. "You bastard. You stacked the committee!"

Simon placed the pen precisely on the blotter, sat up straight, and clasped his hands in front of him.

"Sit down, Senator Elliott."

The pulse in Elliott's neck throbbed. He pushed away from the desk and paced, running both hands through his dark hair. "You promised you wouldn't fuck with my bill package."

That was true. Simon had always planned to quash the so-called "children's safety" legislation on the Senate floor at the end of session when it would be too late for Elliott to raise the money and qualify an initiative. Simon hated the fact that in California, when the legislature—which had been given the power to pass or defeat legislation—didn't cater to the cause of the year, the rich and powerful would raise a few million dollars to put their pet project on the ballot.

He hated it except when it benefited his interests.

The truth was, if Senator Matt Elliott had the time, he could have qualified an initiative in time for the November ballot, the worst time for their party to be forced to take a position on so-called "tough on crime" legislation. Didn't Elliott see that? Wasn't the future strength of their party more important than one bill?

Kill the bill now, Simon.

Jamie Tan's words came back to him. The head of the Juvenile Justice Alliance, which operated nearly two hundred group homes for juveniles in the criminal justice system, had made it perfectly clear that if Elliott's bill passed, they'd pull all support. It was an election year and they wanted to take no chances on a vote by the full Senate. The bill had to die in committee.

Worse, Tan had brought the head of a prison reform group and one of the two major trial lawyer organizations into the meeting. The warning was clear: screw them, his election well would run dry.

That was the biggest problem with term limits, Simon realized. Before the electorate put in limits, the leader had real power. Now, special interests had the power. Jamie Tan would be around longer than Simon Beck, and Tan knew it.

Simon had no choice but to back down. If he lost even one seat this election cycle, he'd be unceremoniously dumped as leader.

"Put Paula back on the committee," Elliott demanded, stopping in front of his desk.

"Forget it, Elliott. My decision is final."

"I'll bury you, Beck."

"You? You're the outcast of our party. A maverick. Ha! No one trusts you. You're just as likely to vote with the Republicans as vote with us. So you won Paula over to this issue, but you know damn well she'll never agree with you on your other pet projects."

"This isn't a pet project. My bill will save lives."

Beck waved his hand in the air. "Don't believe your own press releases."

"Damn you, we can make a difference!"

"Do you realize what's at stake? Do you know how many people will lose their jobs if your bill passes? Do you understand that the state is under court order to decrease the prison population? All your bill would do is make the crisis worse."

"Tell that to Timothy Stewart! Wait, you can't. He's dead."

"That's what this has all been about. You want to destroy an entire industry because of one mistake."

"One? The Stewart case is only one example of the problems with the current system."

Simon's phone beeped. On cue. He'd told his secretary to never leave Matt Elliott alone in his office for more than five minutes.

"Yes, Janice? Right, I'll take it."

He covered the mouthpiece. "Get out, shut up, or your career is over."

II.

Senator Matt Elliott hung up with the fiery Paula Ramirez who was as livid as he was that Beck had replaced her on the Public Safety Committee. Matt had spent the entire three years of his legislative term working on Paula, earning her trust and respect. It all came to a head when he asked for her support of this bill, against their party line. Matt was the maverick, the others expected him to vote however he damn well pleased, but Paula was one of theirs: a dyed-in-the-wool, intellectual, steadfast liberal.

And he'd won her over on this issue. He'd also grown to like her, though they still didn't see eye-to-eye on criminal justice reform.

It was Hannah Stewart, the slain boy's mother for which "Timothy's Law" had been named, who'd swayed Paula. Her raw, honest testimony that Matt, a former prosecutor, could only attest to, not recreate. She'd been to hell and back in the five years since her son had been murdered. Matt had been the assistant district attorney when her son's killer had gone to trial; he'd been with Hannah since the very beginning. It was that case that had prompted him to run for office to change the laws that he had vowed to uphold as a prosecutor.

And now he had to tell her that not only was the bill dead as the result of political posturing and corruption, but he didn't think they had the time or resources to qualify an initiative for this year's ballot. It would be put on the back burner until the next election.

His chief of staff, Greg Harper, knocked on the door. "Mrs. Stewart and her sister are here."

"Send them in."

He stood and walked to the door to greet them. Matt felt like a prosecutor again, giving bad news to surviving family. He'd always hated that part of the job, and this was worse because he knew Hannah.

"What's wrong?" she asked as soon as they sat down on the couch facing his desk.

She'd always been perceptive. Even when she was going through the emotional ringer during Rickie Coleman's trial, she'd picked up on the subtleties of the court testimony.

"Paula was removed from the Public Safety Committee," Matt said. "She was replaced by someone who opposes Timothy's Law."

"Why?"

"I told you this was going to be a tough sell."

"But after Senator Ramirez agreed to support Timothy's Law, we had the votes, correct?"

He nodded. Hannah sounded calm, but her eyes were glassy. She knew what this setback meant.

"And she was removed why? Because someone didn't want the bill to pass?"

"Essentially."

"You mean the Senate Leader."

"I'm not going to lie to you, Hannah. Politics reigns supreme in this building. We knew what we were up against—the group home industry is worth tens of millions of dollars and growing. All they are doing is slowing down the tide against them. We will change the system. But I learned this isn't the way."

Hannah said, "Since Timmy, more kids have been hurt. It'll happen again. Are human lives a justifiable cost for these people?"

Matt had nothing to say. He agreed with Hannah. "I'm truly sorry. Paula is sorry, too. We did everything we could."

Hannah turned away from Senator Elliott and looked at her niece in the stroller. Rachel was a beautiful child, perfect in every way, round and plump with chubby hands and deep dimples. The dimples ran in their family—both Hannah and her sister, Meg, had them.

Unlike Rachel's twin indentions, Timmy had had a solitary dimple on his left cheek.

She squeezed her eyes shut as the wave of pain hit her, palatable. Unconsciously, her hand fiercely rubbed her forehead.

"Hannah, are you okay?"

It was the senator speaking. He'd tried. He'd been so kind, so steadfast, he'd worked so hard. But it wasn't enough.

She lied. "I'm fine."

"I know you're disappointed. I'm furious about this, and I promise you I'll take it to the voters. I'm not going to sit back and let this power play go unnoticed. My chief of staff is crafting a press release, and I'm having a press conference—with Paula—immediately after the committee hearing."

Hannah nodded, though she only heard part of what he said. She'd known this could happen. And, really, why had she come to testify in the first place? It wouldn't bring Timothy back. It wouldn't piece together her destroyed marriage.

You did it to save other children.

And now other children were still at risk because of politics. Politics that allowed juvenile sex offenders to move quietly into neighborhoods without anyone knowing. Politics that allowed those perverts to live across the street from an elementary school, to watch the little boys and little girls walking to and from school every day.

They could slip out of the poorly secured houses because people who had no idea how to care for these criminals were put in positions of authority. Did they even understand that their young charges hurt other children? That it was only a matter of time before they escalated from sex crimes to murder?

What was the difference between a seventeen-year-old convicted rapist and an eighteen-year-old rapist? The public was allowed to know when the older predator moved into their neighborhood, but not the younger.

"Hannah?"

It was her sister Meg, in her motherly tone. A sign that she was worried.

Rachel started fussing in her stroller and Meg reached for her. Hannah interrupted.

"Let me take care of her," she said.

Meg agreed, her eyes following Hannah as she left with the baby.

Meg said to Matt, "She needs to do something. Rachel helps, I think."

Matt would never forget the pain in her eyes when he first met her, even though he'd always thought of Hannah as a quietly strong woman. Yet five years later, the agony was still there, a permanent reminder of the uncaring bureaucrats and a callous system that made it more profitable to house sex offenders in middle-class neighborhoods than in prison.

Of course, the group homes were officially "non-profit," but the people who ran the facilities also owned the food supply, laundry services, and transportation companies. Investors quietly bought up houses in middle-class neighborhoods and leased them out to the "non-profits" at inflated rates. Then there was court-ordered counseling, attorney fees, private security companies—Matt had only just begun to trace the money trail of those connected with these facilities.

"How's she holding up?" Matt asked.

"Hannah's strong. She's gotten through the worst of it, and now that the divorce is final, I think she'll be okay. It's just—"

"What?"

"Every time Hannah speaks in public, like in front of the committee, she relives Timmy's murder."

Matt hated thinking he was partly to blame for Hannah's pain. He'd sympathized with her, he took care of her needs, but he'd never failed to use Timmy's murder to advance his goals. And while his goals were for the protection of all children, he'd lost sight of his own humanity in the process. That maybe everything he'd asked Hannah to do had kept the wounds open and festering, instead of healing.

He wished he could help Hannah move forward, reclaim her lost life. Five years was a long time to grieve.

But he'd never lost a child to violence.

III.

Hannah pushed her index fingers into her temple, pushing back the dull, constant ache that she'd learned to live with for the last five years.

She'd lost her only child. Then she'd lost her husband. Eric wasn't dead, but he was dead to her.

"Why weren't you watching him? How could you let this happen?"

He'd apologized, but the damage was done. Eric thought she was responsible. That her actions and inactions had resulted in Timmy being stabbed six times after enduring a rape.

Rickie Coleman said he didn't mean to kill Timmy—that he was scared of going to jail if he was caught. The judge only gave him nine years. For manslaughter, not murder.

The sixteen-year-old Coleman lived right down the street from Timmy's school in a group home for juvenile sex offenders. Timmy had passed by that house every day, unaware of the depravity that hid behind the door.

If she'd only known, she'd never have let Timmy walk home alone. Or even with friends. She would have picked him up. Or arranged a neighborhood carpool.

Dammit! His school was only three blocks from home! He should have been safe.

She worked only ten minutes away and had adjusted her work schedule in order to meet Timmy when he came home from school every day.

But he never came home that day. She called every friend and ran from her house to the school, calling his name, her panic growing.

She ran right past the house where Timmy lay dead in the backyard, to be discovered three hours later when the owner came home from work.

The house next door to the group home.

Rachel let out a yelp and Hannah cleared her head. Remembered where she was . . . in a restroom in the California State Capitol.

"Sorry, sweetheart." She changed the wet infant's diaper. Rachel reached up and pulled Hannah's long brown hair. Hannah was in the handicap stall, which she'd often used when Timmy had been in a stroller. Now, she needed it for privacy more than the room.

"Sorry, Rachel," she murmured as she reached under the stroller. Her hand touched the cold metal.

Are you sure?

Of course she was sure. Her son was dead, her marriage was over, and she had nothing left but distant memories of happiness.

Rachel gurgled in her stroller, reached again for Hannah's hair. She allowed the baby to grab a handful, a tear falling onto Rachel's little pink dress.

"I love you, Rachel," she whispered. "I hope your mommy forgives me."

Hannah loosened the gun, which she had strapped down with duct tape under the stroller that morning when she volunteered to load Rachel's stroller into the car.

She had watched people coming and going through security during her numerous trips to the Capitol. The guards passed the strollers around the metal detector and only took a cursory glance at the contents. Diaper bags and backpacks were run through the X-ray, but not the stroller itself.

She and Meg had grown up on a farm in the Central Valley and their father taught them to shoot at a young age. Hannah never expected to use a gun on a human being.

Senator Beck was anything but human.

"Let's tell your mommy you want a walk," she told Rachel, securing the gun in the small of her back, under her loose-fitting blouse. "Auntie Hannah has a meeting."

IV.

"I'm not going to sit here and pretend none of us know exactly what happened today. Senator Ramirez was unceremoniously removed from the Public Safety Committee after faithfully serving for seven years. Why? Because she supported Timothy's Law."

He stared at his fellow committee members one by one. They in turn looked disgusted, bored and angry. Angry at him, perhaps, because he was shining a high-wattage light on the dark dealings of the Capitol.

Good bills were killed because of special interests every day of the week. Matt's bill was simply another casualty.

"We've heard enough," the Chairman, Senator Thomas, said. "You're getting very close to being censured."

"Censured? You think I care about being censured when you sit there and abstain on a bill that would protect children and save lives?"

"Senator Elliott, that is enough."

Out of the corner of his eye, Matt noticed Hannah Stewart enter the committee hearing room. She came in through the rear entrance and sat in the back row.

He couldn't drag her through another hearing, not like this. Her face was ashen, and she was as skinny as he'd seen her during the trial when her sister told him she'd lost weight, going from one hundred forty pounds to less the one hundred ten.

"It may be enough for you, but I will continue to fight for child safety legislation even if some of the members of this committee believe in politics over human lives."

Thomas stared at him icily as Matt took his seat. He stared back. He wasn't going to let them get away with it. He knew what he would tell the press.

Without fanfare, the committee voted. Three ayes, four abstentions. Failed.

The next time he looked at the audience, Hannah was gone.

V.

Though Hannah had grown up listening to her father's tirades about the corruption of government, she'd always believed in the system. That good people ran for office—people like Matt Elliott, the man who'd prosecuted Timmy's murderer. The man whose eyes teared up when he told her the judge was going to give Coleman a lenient sentence. That Rickie Coleman would be a free man at the same time Timmy should have been graduating from high school.

Senator Elliott was not to blame. He'd done what he could. It just wasn't enough.

It was Beck's fault. Simon Beck, the man who'd stacked the committee for the sole purpose of killing Timothy's Law. A man who cared more about politics than a little boy who'd bled to death, alone, crying for his mommy . . .

Hannah screamed, but no sound escaped her tight throat. She heard Timmy's silent pleas every time she closed her eyes, every time she tried to sleep. But never in daylight, never like this.

She pretended to look through her purse as she watched the traffic in the corridor. It didn't take long before she saw the group she needed. Six women of different ages, walking with briefcases and purpose. She quickly trailed after them, standing only a foot from the rear as they opened the door and piled into the Senator's waiting room.

The short woman of the group announced them. "Betsy Franklin with the Nurses Coalition. We have a meeting with Senator Beck."

The secretary checked the schedule, nodded, and told them to have a seat and she would let the senator know that they'd arrived.

If any of the women noticed her, they must have assumed she also had an appointment with the senate leader. They didn't comment. She didn't offer an explanation.

She sat in a chair while Nurse Betsy Franklin spoke to Beck's secretary. Hannah hadn't been in this office before, but she was a good observer. She watched as the secretary vaguely nodded toward a door behind her and to the left. Was Beck's office right on the other side of the door? Or down a hall?

Now that she'd made her decision, an eerie calm descended around her.

Killing Senator Beck wouldn't bring Timmy back from the dead, but it would punish him for what he'd done to stop justice. It would make a statement: that people who had the lives of others in their hands could not callously disregard the dead, or the living.

"Janice, I'll just be a sec." A tall, lanky man with a boyish face and graying hair walked past the secretary with a half-smile at the nurses. He opened the door, then closed it. But Hannah saw what she needed to see. A short hall, then double doors.

Where that bastard worked.

Rickie Coleman was to blame for killing Timmy. But what about the system that put him in the neighborhood in the first place? Even though Coleman was now in prison and the staff fired, that house was still open and operational in her old neighborhood. Nearly every day she drove by, watched as the so-called "counselors," who looked barely old enough to vote, escorted the six teenage boys from the house to an unmarked van. Followed as they drove across the county to "school." Their school was housed in a recreation center that also held a preschool and several after-school programs. They put those sexual predators in the same building with innocent children.

When she'd gone to the Recreation Board, she was told that, "There have been no reported problems. And they pay their rent on time."

She'd been in the Capitol building enough over the last six months to know that she couldn't simply walk into the Pro Tem's office. The secretary would ask if she had an appointment. And she doubted that Senator Beck would talk to her, even if she did ask for a meeting.

Are you sure you want to do this?

She wasn't sure of anything. She couldn't sleep; she could barely eat. She'd never wanted to move, but she couldn't live in the same house where Timmy had lived. She was in limbo, going through the motions of living while having no real life.

Her soul had died the same day as Timmy.

The man left Beck's office ten minutes later and Hannah jumped up.

"Ma'am, you can't—"

Hannah closed the door and ran to the double doors, opening them at the same time as the secretary opened the outer door.

"Sergeants!" the woman called.

Hannah closed the door.

She'd noticed Matt Elliott had locks on his doors and was pleased to find that so did Senator Beck. She turned it.

"Ms. Franklin?" Senator Beck asked, confused, as he rose from his desk.

Recognition crossed his tanned face as he stared at her.

"Hannah Stewart," she said, though it was unnecessary. "You killed Timothy's Law."

Fists pounded on the door behind Hannah. She drew the gun.

"Senator? Senator?" a muffled voice called through the door. Someone shouted, "Get the Sergeants!"

"Mrs. Stewart—" Beck put his hands up, slowly. He stared at the gun, not at her.

Her enemy cowered in front of her. Sweat formed along his receding hairline. She should kill him now. But her hand trembled, so she held the gun with both hands; her purse fell to the floor with a thud. She jumped, heart pounding.

"You sacrificed innocent children for politics," she said, surprised that her voice sounded normal.

"Mrs. Stewart, put the gun down."

He tried to sound tough, but his voice cracked at the end. He was scared. He feared for his life when the lives of the innocent meant nothing to him.

"That group home, the same one that Rickie Coleman slipped out of to kill my son, is still in operation. And because of you, it will not be shut down."

"That's not the role of state government—"

"Bullshit!" Swearing surprised her as much as her volume. "You stacked the committee! You killed my bill!"

"Mrs. Stewart, it's only legislation—it can't bring your son back."

"Timmy! His name is Timmy! Do you know how many juvenile sex offenders escaped and hurt children? Do you?"

"Mrs. Stewart—"

"We don't know because they're minors and their records are confidential! And because the people who run those homes make millions of dollars off the system, they'll never be shut down. The group home in my own neighborhood? The owner makes three times the market value every month on an inflated lease. Is that the price of a child? Seven thousand dollars a month?"

Beck took a step toward her and Hannah pulled the trigger.

VI.

"Senator, they're evacuating the building," Greg exclaimed as he ran into Matt's office, his lips in a tight, white line.

"What's going on? Bomb threat?"

"There's a gunman in the building."

"They'd lockdown if there was a gunman loose, not evacuate," Matt said. His instincts hummed.

"I'm just relaying what the Sergeants told me. He's in the historic building; the annex has been locked down and is being evacuated. It's mandatory."

Matt waved his hand dismissively at Greg and turned on the television by remote.

". . . Capitol building is being evacuated. Nothing more is known at this time."

The picture switched from a reporter outside the east entrance of the Capitol to the bureau chief. "Sources in the building tell NBC news that every office has been ordered to evacuate immediately. A gunman is in the building. Wait—"

The reporter listened to his earpiece. "A shot has been confirmed fired. Three separate sources report that a shot has been fired on the second floor of the historic building. Sources indicate the shot may have come from Senate Pro Tem Beck's office, a Democrat from Los Angeles."

"Simon," Matt whispered.

He pictured the look on Hannah's face when he told her about the committee.

Suddenly, the last five years became clear. For the first time Matt realized what he'd done. The last major case he tried before filing for office was the Timothy Stewart murder. It was the judge's idiocy that had propelled him to seek the senate seat. He'd wanted to fix the system in a way that a prosecutor couldn't—by changing the laws.

And then he brought Hannah Stewart in to help his cause. She'd seemed the perfect spokeswoman for reform: an eloquent, attractive mother, a person the press and the people could relate to. She joined his bandwagon to change the laws, to ensure that children were protected and violent predators—whatever their age—were locked up where they couldn't hurt anyone.

It had been his cause because he'd lost in court when he hated to lose—and rarely did. Rickie Coleman had been convicted, but the judge threw out the first-degree murder charge—believing Coleman when he said he didn't intend to kill the boy—and Coleman ended up with manslaughter and a nine-year sentence.

Matt had wanted to change the system, fix what was broken, and he used every means possible.

Including a woman so devastated by grief that she hadn't truly lived in five years.

He suddenly knew who the "gunman" was.

He had unwittingly created her.

VII.

The Sergeant-At-Arms, Bob Bush, ran a hand over his mustache, a nervous habit he'd thought he'd broken. In charge of Capitol security for the past twenty years, he'd had his share of situations. But never had a shot been fired in the Capitol under his watch.

"CHP is on alert," Jefferson said.

They stood outside Beck's office, which had been immediately evacuated after the gunshot. He'd just debriefed the secretary, who didn't know anything.

"Where's the damn security tape?"

The security camera outside the senator's office would have recorded who'd passed through the door.

"They're viewing it downstairs right now," Jefferson said, listening to his earpiece. "They have an I.D. Hannah Stewart, Caucasian female, forty-two."

"Who the hell is she?"

A commotion outside the door had Bob turning. He saw Senator Elliott trying to bypass the shield they'd set up around the office.

"Senator, you need to evacuate," Bob said, turning around to talk to Jefferson before he'd finished his sentence.

"I know Hannah."

Bob stopped, turned to him. "She won't pick up the phone. We've been trying to call into the office for the last five minutes."

"She'll talk to me. Please, let me go in."

"I can't do that, we don't even know if Senator Beck is alive. SWAT is getting into position."

"Don't shoot her."

"He's been ordered to assess the situation and report."

"Please, Bob. I can defuse this."

"What's her story?"

"She testified on one of my bills in Public Safety. It was defeated today."

"She's holding Beck hostage because a bill got killed?"

"No. She's holding Beck hostage because her son got killed and she doesn't think anyone cares."

VIII.

The Sergeants would not let him go in, but that didn't faze Matt. He had an idea.

He ran upstairs to the third floor to the Republican leader's office. The floor was oddly deserted. The windows in the gallery were sealed shut, but those in the Member's offices could be opened. Matt walked in through the leader's "escape" door—an unmarked entrance directly into his office from the side hallway. Few legislators kept their private door locked.

Matt crossed to the window behind the desk, directly above Beck's office. He opened the window. A portico traversed the west steps of the Capitol building, but stopped before reaching the office windows.

Matt looked down, swallowed heavily. A three-foot ledge ran under the windows, but if he slipped . . . the drop was already precarious because of the seventeen-foot ceilings. But broken ankles were the least of his concern now. To his left was a spindly palm tree, to his right the top of a tree with long, narrow leaves. It didn't look sturdy enough to climb down, but if he fell from the ledge, the tree would prevent him from hitting ground.

He knew Beck's little secret. After hours, he often opened that window and leaned out to smoke cigars. Not once had Matt seen him lock it.

Without hesitating, Matt flung open the far window and climbed out, holding onto the ledge, his legs dangling over, and assessing the drop. He hung there only a moment before falling . . .

Slam. Right on the ledge. His knees protested, but nothing broke. He teetered a moment, grabbed a thin branch to steady himself. He shook off the pain, shimmied along the ledge to Beck's unlocked window and pushed it open.

Hannah stood over Beck's desk, a gun aimed at his chest. Beck's face was ashen and he lay awkwardly across his chair.

He was too late.

IX.

"What the hell was that?" Bob Bush exclaimed at the faint thump coming from outside the building.

Jefferson listened, then said, "SWAT reports that a man jumped from the third floor onto the balcony and has entered Beck's office."

Bob bit back expletives. "Who?"

"No confirmation yet. He was wearing gray slacks and white button-down, rolled up at the sleeves. Dark hair, approximately six foot one inch—"

"Matt Elliott. Ring the office." Dammit, did the Senator want to get both him and Beck killed?

Bob held the phone to his ear as it rang and rang.

X.

"Let me answer the phone," Matt told Hannah.

"Why are you here?"

"Hannah, please."

She didn't respond, and Matt slowly reached over to Beck's desk, watching Hannah's eyes the entire time. He pressed line one, picked up the phone. "It's Matt Elliott."

"Senator, what are you doing?" Bob Bush exclaimed.

"Beck is alive. Give me five minutes."

He hung up over Bob's protests. "Hannah," he said, "you don't want to do this."

He glanced at the senate leader. There was no blood; she hadn't shot him. Something was still wrong. Beck's mouth moved rapidly, but no words came out.

He was pale and his left eye seemed to look in a different direction than his right. Heart attack? Didn't matter, Beck needed medical attention immediately.

"You don't want to kill him."

Hannah looked at him with blue eyes filled with anguish so tangible Matt's own heart broke.

"No one cares about Timmy," she whispered.

"You care, Hannah. You've done everything you can. I'm not going to let anyone forget about your son."

Tears welled in her eyes. "Today—today he would have been fifteen."

Matt had forgotten. He'd breathed nothing but the Timothy Stewart homicide for five and a half years, but he hadn't remembered the child's birthday.

His mother would never forget.

"I'm so sorry, Hannah. I've done everything I could to make sure no other mother suffers like you have."

She shook her head. "He—" She waved the gun at Beck and swallowed. "People like him don't care. All they see are numbers and statistics. And money. Always the money. Like the life of a child has a price on it! All they had to do was give parents information. Give us a chance to protect our children. I'd have walked Timmy home myself every day if I'd known those sex offenders lived in that house. But no one can protect the children if we don't even know what we're up against!"

Matt was concerned about Beck. His breathing was shallow, his face clammy, and an odd sound emanated from his throat. Maybe it was a stroke, not a heart attack. Hannah seemed oblivious.

If Beck died, she'd be charged with second-degree murder. Matt didn't know if he could live with that on his conscience.

"What about Rachel?"

Hannah blinked, really looked at him for the first time. "Rachel?"

"How can you protect your niece if you go to prison? What is Meg going to tell Timmy's cousin? Rachel needs you. Meg needs you. She's stood by you from the very beginning. She sat next to you during Coleman's trial every single day. Think of how she will feel if you go to prison. Or if SWAT shoots you."

Matt had spied the SWAT team member in the tree across the path, and blocked his direct line of fire. He couldn't let Hannah die, especially not as a criminal.

He couldn't let Beck die.

"I'm nothing," she whispered.

"Hannah, you're living in hell. Let me help bring you back. Please."

She stared at him. "Promise me one thing."

"What?"

"You won't stop until Timothy's Law passes."

"That I can promise you." Arms outstretched, he took a step toward her. "Hand me the gun."

She nodded.

His momentary relief that she was giving up the fight dissipated as Hannah brought the gun to her head.

"No!"

He leaped toward her.

The gun went off.

XI.

Three Months Later.

"Matt, Sandra Cullen is here to see you."

"Thanks, Bonnie."

Bonnie was the last of his staff. When he announced last month that he wasn't seeking reelection, his entire staff found other jobs. He didn't blame them, though there were still six months left in his term. He didn't care that he was staffless. He had nothing he wanted to accomplish—at least in this building.

He'd already done all the damage he could.

Sandy closed the door behind her. She was a petite woman, skinny through excess energy. She'd been the District Attorney of Sacramento County for coming on twelve years, as well as his former boss. He had complete respect for her. It was Sandy who had tried to stop him from running for state senate. He'd accused her of playing politics—he was taking out a member of her party. But in hindsight, she'd wanted to spare him the pain of failure.

An idealist in government simply tilted at windmills, she'd said.

"I'm not going to try to change your mind," she said, "because you're going to make a damn fine D.A."

When Sandy had announced her retirement, Matt had tossed his hat into the ring. She'd endorsed him immediately.

Already, he felt like the world that had crashed down three months ago was rising just enough to allow him to breathe.

"Thought you might like to know that my office just accepted a plea on Hannah Stewart's case. She'll remain at Napa State Hospital for twelve months."

"No jail time?"

Sandy frowned. "I know you think I'm callous, but I couldn't fight for jail time on this one. I would have got it. But in a trial, I think I would have ended with a hung jury. She wanted—and needed—to go to the mental hospital."

"Thank you."

"I read in the paper that Beck was released from the hospital yesterday. Is he coming back? It was unclear."

"He's still incapacitated from the stroke. He doesn't have mobility on his left side at all, though he's regaining his speech."

"Have you seen him?"

"No."

"And Hannah?"

He paused. "Once." It had been awkward for both of them. He thought originally she'd been too embarrassed and grateful that he'd knocked her hand away before she killed herself. Instead, she'd blamed him for her failed suicide attempt.

"I just don't want to live anymore."

"Matt, I always said you were too good for this building."

He shook his head. "Wouldn't it be better if there were more people here like us? Then maybe we could make a difference."

She smiled sadly. "When Hell freezes over."

DEATH OF THE AUTHOR

Alison Bruce

Alison Bruce is the author of the DC Gary Goodhew novels, set in Cambridge, UK, including *Cambridge Blue*, *The Calling*, *The Promise*, and others. Prior to writing, she had an eclectic career. Bruce has lived in Cambridge since 1998.

Charlie Trace leant against the frame of his open front door and let the dregs of the guests squeeze out past him. He was aware that they turned back to wave, but his attention was only on the phone call now. "I don't write anything that I'm not happy to own, and I don't say it either," he growled.

Bill Hammond grunted in reply. He'd been Charlie's agent for almost twenty years and that meant they knew one another well – well enough for Charlie to know what Bill really meant. Then, for good measure, Bill said it anyway, "Charlie, you're full of shit."

Charlie let the words settle. He ran his tongue over his teeth and considered Bill's perspective. "I'm standing in the doorway of my new house, you really should see the view, Bill." Charlie's house faced onto Midsummer Common, which made it prime Cambridge property, and which, come to think of it, pretty much amounted to prime property nationwide. He glanced over his shoulder, the last two guests were undergraduates. Young enough to hang on to his every word, but comfortably old enough to count as legal. "Prime property, Bill. That's what I've earned for both of us."

"And is that," snapped Bill, "the signal for me to kowtow to the best-selling Charlie Trace and just be thankful?"

"You work it out."

"I have. I am severing our agreement. That interview went too far . . ."

"It will blow over, it was a great piece."

"No, it was crass. You went too far and if you're going down I'm not going with you."

Charlie still had the phone to his ear when Bill cut him off. "Bastard," he breathed.

He left the front door open and headed for the kitchen. Alesha and her friend leant close over their flutes of bubbly, they looked less keen and more cunning now. The night had rapidly turned sour. He took their glasses, poured them into the sink and asked them both to leave.

Each patient's television viewing was displayed on a small, flat screen mounted like an anglepoise lamp so that it could twist and tilt its way across the bed.

Miriam Lloyd's had been pushed to one side but the screen was still in Goodhew's line of sight and only a couple of feet from his chair near her bed. It silently displayed the BBC News channel, the same stories rotated every few minutes, flickering in the unmoving room and creating the impression that time had been trapped in a fifteen minute loop.

Goodhew had been in the loop for six hours; since she'd left surgery and been stabilised enough for this bed. Before that she'd belonged to the paramedics as they'd fought to save her from dying on the tarmac of Maids Causeway. The driver who'd hit her had been a breath under the drink-drive limit but a breath under the speed limit too; driver and pedestrian both possibly saved by those two breaths.

She'd *run from nowhere*, but then, the driver would say that. The call had come in at 11.42 but no other motorist on that perpetually busy stretch of road, or any occupant from any of those windows facing onto the street, had seen a thing. Just one student had come forward because she'd heard the bang of car on person. *Like a small explosion.*

The road had been cordoned off, but the saturation of blue pulsing and bright white pools of light would have been visible from the other side of Midsummer Common, drawing the curious until one of them noticed an open doorway and caught sight of the other body.

Goodhew had arrived at five minutes before midnight. Now, a total of eleven hours later, his tired gaze settled back on the national news and he watched a repeat of the first news' footage. A reporter stood in the dark, near a line of police tape, with floodlights and a police tent two hundred yards behind that. A red banner of text rotated at the bottom of the screen. CHARLIE TRACE MURDER. *Celebrated but controversial author killed in Cambridge knife attack.*

Goodhew checked his phone; #CharlieTraceMurder was trending on Twitter too, along with #DeathOfTheAuthor, probably, he guessed, the gleeful creation of a first year English literature student. A new hash-tag had sprung up since he'd last checked; #TraceMurderSuspect followed by variations and re-tweets of a woman being questioned by police.

Being questioned wasn't how he would describe it. He looked up from his phone, to Miriam Lloyd. She had been unconscious at the scene of the accident and remained so. He knew, from her notes, that she was 52 years old and an administrator for one of the many English Language schools in Cambridge centre. She drove an older model VW Golf and lived with her nineteen-year-old daughter in a rented house five miles out, in Barton. On the face of it she seemed to have had little in common with Trace, but the blood-coated knife in her jacket pocket said otherwise.

Just then her lips parted as she tried to form words.

"Mrs Lloyd? Miriam?"

She took a few seconds to respond, then her eyelids flickered. "Tony," she whispered.

Kincaide had led them into the corridor and closed the door behind him. He continued to grip the handle as though he thought it might be pulled open from the other side. Unlikely, Goodhew thought, since Miriam Lloyd was still barely conscious, heavily medicated and attached to a drip.

But, as PC Sue Gully had commented, it was all about effect with Kincaide. There were days when the way Kincaide answered the phone, held a pen and probably even breathed that irritated her too. It was a shame she wasn't here right now; she always enjoyed the moments when Goodhew found it impossible to contain his distaste for Kincaide.

"I'm not prepared to back you up on this," Goodhew told him.

"Gary, her eyes were open, it counts as an arrest."

Goodhew shook his head. "She's not in a fit state."

"She spoke when I asked her if she understood and confirmed her name."

"You can't ask her any questions when she's drugged up like that."

"We would if she was an assault victim about to die. We'd get whatever we could from her and use it in court. I don't see the difference." Kincaide set his jaw and stared past Goodhew, along the corridor towards A and E and the exit. "I'll be speaking to Marks in a few minutes, requesting that we charge her."

DI Marks wouldn't go for it, at least not without more to back it up. Goodhew shook his head but didn't reply, he knew his breath would be wasted and, instead, found himself studying the limp lapel of Kincaide's knock-off suit and its pretentions of being the real thing.

"Stay with her," Kincaide instructed. A smile flickered in one corner of his mouth, "I know I can trust you to keep notes of anything useful."

Goodhew nodded. "I'll grab a coffee and go back in." He turned from Kincaide, he didn't need a drink, just needed to be out of Kincaide's orbit until he was sure that Kincaide really had left the building.

Miriam Lloyd thought she would have known nothing about the time she lay unconscious, but, as she adjusted to the stripes of sunlight that cut between the blinds, she knew that smells of the ward, the footfalls on the hard tiled floor and even her own immobility all made sense.

She wasn't alone either. She didn't see anyone at first but instinctively knew that she only had to turn her head towards the shady corner of the room and she would find someone there.

Not her daughter though. She would have spoken as soon as Miriam stirred, or pulled closer to reach for her hand. She turned her head a little, enough to glance at her fingers and make sure that no one was holding them. Then she looked at the man in the visitor's chair.

He looked almost too young to be there for any genuine reason, young enough to be looking to someone older for answers. She guessed therefore that he'd been told to sit there, to wait for her to wake then fill in whatever pedantic form he might be about to produce.

"Mrs Lloyd?" His voice was firm and clear; her opinion of him wavered and changed almost instantly. "I'm DC Gary Goodhew. How are you feeling?"

"Almost awake." He held her in sharp focus and she could tell then that he'd come for information. She exhaled slowly, hoping to buy enough time to gather her thoughts. Her mind flashed to anecdotes of people in peril, their minds racing and constructing escape routes with only milliseconds to spare, but it flashed a single image back to her; Charlie Trace. Dead. Curled on the floor as though he'd clutched his stomach, fallen to his knees then tipped to one side. He hadn't reached out or attempted to crawl away, he'd just stayed still with his hands wasting their last seconds trying to hold back the blood that slipped effortlessly between his weakening fingers.

The blood had pooled. Miriam blinked as she remembered the smell of his urine as it slid along the channels between the glossy floor tiles.

Charlie Trace had deserved to die.

"Mrs Lloyd?"

She opened her eyes and studied him some more. He leant forwards, resting his elbows on his knees. "I need to ask you some questions about last night." His physique was strong and he seemed serious beyond his years. She revised her estimate of his age up to late-twenties. "Do you know why you are in hospital?"

"Something hit me. Feels like it could have been a bus."

"It was a car. The driver claims you ran into the road. What do you remember before the accident?"

"Feeling crushed and elated all at once. I wasn't the only one who hated him, and I felt as though the world had improved simply because he no longer breathed."

"Who?"

"You know who."

"For my notes."

"Charlie Trace." She expected Goodhew to react at hearing Trace's name spoken so openly, but his expression gave away nothing. "He made a name for himself by humiliating others; I wanted to do something about it."

"Tell me what happened."

"I visited his house." She started her next sentence then paused, her head was rapidly clearing now. It was telling her that she needed to be careful. *Say nothing.*

"Mrs Lloyd?"

She pressed her lips together. *Say nothing.* Say nothing until she had worked out what had happened. And what they knew.

He tried coaxing her with questions, but she succeeded in locking him out until his phone bleeped with an incoming text. He glanced at the screen and, finally, stood to leave.

She relaxed, but a little too soon because he turned back at the door. "So, who's Tony?" he asked.

"My daughter." And, for a moment, her mask slipped. "Has something happened?"

"It was the name you spoke as you were coming round."

He hadn't even realised it had been a female name, let alone her daughter's. She managed a small smile; she was out of her depth already. "Toni, short for Antonia of course. She was Rudy's sister, but she didn't kill Trace."

Before tonight Goodhew had known the name Charlie Trace, he'd never read anything he'd written and never planned to. In the last ten years Charlie Trace's writing career had taken a backseat to his partying and rent-a-gob appearances on TV and radio, debating everything from the future of publishing to the future of the country's youth. He still produced novels, still sold them to a loyal body of fans who seemed to stay with him no matter what scandal followed, despite the claims of plagiarism from a young writer, despite the suicide of that same writer.

"Rudy Costello?" he asked her.

"That was his pen name, Rudy Lloyd to us." She sighed as her head sank back on the pillow. "He is why Charlie Trace deserved to die."

"And is that why you went to his home? To kill him?"

She nodded slowly. "I suppose it is."

"And did you?"

She looked straight at him but didn't reply, no discernible emotion appeared on her face. Not fear, or satisfaction or guilt, just curiosity at what Goodhew might say next; she was clearly hoping that he had the answer to something.

"It was his housewarming, but you weren't a guest. So was it a coincidence that you chose tonight or did someone tell you?" She held his gaze too solidly and he knew he was warm. "Did Toni tell you?"

A small smile touched her lips, curling with an equally subtle tinge of irony. "I heard, that's all."

He needed to find the right topic, and if her daughter was off limits perhaps her son wouldn't be. He settled back in his chair. "So, tell me about Rudy."

The sharp tangent seemed to throw her, but her expression softened immediately. "Rudy?" She tilted her face towards the ceiling and closed her eyes, mouthing his name. She smiled as she remembered. "He was so talented. Funny too. And he adored his sister." Her eyes reopened but her gaze slipped past Goodhew. "His father used to say that Rudy thought in rainbows, that nothing was dull or impossible to him. And I believed Andy, until close to the day Rudy died."

"When Charlie Trace accused him of stealing his work?"

She looked back at him and to Goodhew's surprise, she shook her head. "Not really, well I don't think so. It wouldn't have been so hard for Rudy to prove that the work was his; his writing was as good as his fingerprint. No, it was the betrayal, Rudy loved Trace, he considered him to be his ally and mentor but then Trace turned and humiliated him in public. People who had been his friends refused to speak to him. His agent and publisher dropped him and his career was over barely before it had begun. All Rudy wanted to know was why Trace had done it."

"Professional jealousy perhaps?"

"Maybe. But my ex-husband knew Charlie Trace back when he was plain Gareth Cooper, said he'd do anything for attention."

"So he thinks Trace wanted publicity?"

Her eyes darkened. "I don't know what he *thinks*. He cleared off after Rudy's death. For Toni and me it was like we'd been bereaved twice."

"Does she know you're here?"

Miriam ignored the question and, instead, struggled up onto one elbow. "How could that bastard Trace think he had the right to hold up his head? To push himself right under our noses? The last thing we want is to risk seeing him, or having the press in our faces again, or to be left jumping at shadows in our own home town."

PC Sue Gully found Goodhew in Addenbrooke's Hospital's main concourse. He sat alone with his coffee to one side and a sheet of paper directly in front of him. She glanced at it as she took the seat opposite.

He'd only written two words, *"WHY NOW?"*

"Prolific eh?" He glanced up. "What do you have?"

"We've been in contact with the last couple of guests, Alesha Hart and her friend Emily Malik. They left after Trace had a telephone argument and became verbally abusive."

"To them?"

"Yes and no. He was furious with the caller and continued to vent afterwards, shouting obscenities down the phone even after the man had hung up."

"So they saw a less charming side to him and cleared off?"

"Uh-huh."

"But they knew it was a man?"

Gully grinned. "Yep, Bill Hammond, Literary Agent." She passed a phone number on a Post-it note across to Goodhew.

"Does Marks have this?"

"He's chasing down Miriam Lloyd's daughter Toni, so I left him a message. And unfortunately I can't seem to find Kincaide, so that's all yours."

She watched Goodhew as he moved to a quieter area. He spoke for several minutes, turning his back on the concourse and facing a noticeboard each time he needed to concentrate. He seemed more thoughtful when he returned.

"Well?" she asked.

"Bill Hammond dumped him, he said. Wanted to put as much distance as possible between himself and Trace before the shit hit the fan."

"What shit?"

"What fan more like." Goodhew drew his sheet of paper closer to him. "Trace made a documentary and it was due for broadcast next week. He refers to the aftermath of Rudy Costello's death as a *'career highlight'* and, according to Hammond, when the interviewer gave him the opportunity to show compassion, Trace claimed that the suicide was no more than Costello's admission of guilt. He was unrepentant and Hammond wanted out before his client became a total pariah."

Gully nodded towards Goodhew's two word question. "That answers that then. Now what?"

Goodhew smiled. "Hammond told someone about the interview. We cross our fingers and hope he also tells them that we're about to charge Miriam Lloyd."

"And are we?"

"Only if she's guilty."

Miriam had said little since Goodhew's brief reappearance, this time a policewoman in uniform came with him and it was she who now sat near the window. She was polite when she spoke but mostly silent.

It was almost an hour since they'd spoken, when Miriam had asked again whether her daughter was on her way. PC Gully had promised to find out, had left the room for less than a minute, then returned with the message, *she'll be here soon.*

So this was a waiting game; Miriam could feel it. Her thoughts began to drift, picturing scenarios that filled her with fear, then calming herself a little when she imagined the words she might use if the time came to confess.

Just then she saw PC Gully's attention turn to the door, so she followed her gaze. Goodhew was back. "You have a visitor," he said. "You have two minutes together. You are both under caution and I will be in the room the whole time. Do you understand?"

Miriam nodded as PC Gully slipped quietly outside.

Goodhew held the door a little wider and Miriam managed to push herself into a half-sitting position, expecting for her daughter, Toni, to appear.

"How are you, Miriam?"

She froze with her cannula-free hand halfway through straightening the thin hospital blanket. "Andy?"

He'd lost weight since she'd last seen him, but aside from that he hadn't changed much. He wore a blue shirt with narrow white stripes and it looked like one she'd bought him ten years ago.

Her ex-husband stopped near the foot of her bed. "I'm so glad I reached him first." She glanced at Goodhew, then back at Andy who seemed to read her thoughts. "I've told him what I did," he said. "I had no intention of letting any-one else take the blame for this. Bill told me about the interview and I told Toni. I wanted you both to be prepared for the pain, I should have known you might snap . . ."

"I didn't snap, I calmly decided to kill him."

"Miriam." He repeated her name once more and both times sounded as though it was meant as a full and complete sentence, filled with sentiment. He moved to the side of the bed and she watched him take her hand. "I'm sorry I ever introduced Rudy to Charlie Trace. I couldn't guess what would happen, but I knew Trace, I should have seen it was a bad idea." His hand squeezed hers a little harder. "I'm sorry I left you and Toni, and I'm sorry I haven't been much of a father ever since. But I'm not sorry I killed him. I'm just so glad I got to him before you."

And so glad it wasn't Toni, she added silently. Miriam pressed her free hand over his. "Thank you," she whispered.

THE HIDDEN HARDY, 1926

Chelsea Cain

Chelsea Cain describes her novels and short stories as 'gory thrillers'. A *New York Times* bestseller, her books include *Heartsick*, *Kill You Twice*, and *One Kick*. A noted feminist and columnist, she lives in Oregon, USA.

Readers of Carolyn Keene's version of my life's events may be surprised to learn that Ned Nickerson was not the love of my life. In fact, my heart belonged to another. I first met Frank Hardy in the summer of 1925. He and his younger brother, Joe, had come to town from Bayport, New Jersey, on the trail of a missing waitress. I was walking out of Jackson's Drug Store when I saw them pull up on their red Indian Scout motorcycles. Even soiled from their five-day journey, they were both striking. Frank was wearing khaki pants, a collared shirt, and a maroon sweater. Joe was wearing the same clothes, only his sweater was blue. They even had the same haircut, though Frank's hair was darker. Yet to me they could not have been more different. I could tell immediately that Frank was the older, more experienced of the two brothers. He held himself taller and walked with the subtle swagger of a boy older than his seventeen years. I approached them—they had parked their Scouts in a no-parking zone—and soon found myself swept up in their mystery. We found their missing waitress working the morning shift at Oscar Peterson's Bakery, and the two soon returned to Bayport. I never thought I'd see Frank again. Until that next summer when the doorbell rang.

I had just solved the Mystery at Lilac Inn and was unpacking my tasteful blue luggage when I heard our housekeeper, Hannah Gruen, answer the door. Hannah was only in her mid-thirties then, though a youth spent smoking unfiltered Luckys had aged her prematurely. She wore her fair hair in a bun and her skirts long, though I had seen her more than once leave the house in trousers when my father was away on business. Curious as to the identity of our visitor, I craned to look around the upstairs corner and saw the back of Frank's head as Hannah took his coat. My heart leapt in my chest.

I smoothed my stylish coif, adjusted my loose knit jacket, and went downstairs.

"Frank," I announced maturely. "How good to see you again."

I extended my hand, and Frank took it, grinning.

"Nancy," he responded. "It's a pleasure. It's good to see you looking as slim and attractive as always." Then his face grew grave. "But enough pleasantries. I'm here because something has happened to Joe and I need your help."

I nodded solemnly, but even as I did my heart swelled. He needed my help.

Of all the teen sleuths he knew (and rumor was he knew plenty), he had come to me.

Before we could say another word, the doorbell rang again. Hannah answered it. She turned to me, her cheeks flushed with excitement. "Nancy!" she gasped. "It's a letter for you. Special delivery!"

Hannah Gruen and Frank Hardy gathered around me as I opened the mysterious letter that had just arrived.

"Who's it from?" asked the housekeeper.

"I don't know," I answered. "There's no return address." I opened the letter carefully so as not to destroy any clues. Inside was a typewritten note:

"STAY OUT OF IT," the note warned.

I looked up at Frank, who stood gazing intently at the letter. "Maybe you had better tell me a little more about what happened to Joe," I told him.

Hannah went to the kitchen to make tea while Frank and I sat in the living room, the typed note on the coffee table between us.

"Joe has been penning mash notes to Helen Corning for months. She finally agreed to meet him if he came to River Heights," Frank explained glumly. (Helen was three years older than I so had already graduated from R.H. High and was in heady pursuit of a husband.) "But she had to cancel at the last minute," Frank continued. "I called Jake's Ice Cream Parlor where they were supposed to rendezvous, and Jake said that Joe waited for an hour and then left. This was two days ago, and he has yet to surface!"

I folded my hands neatly in my lap. "Is he a drinker?"

Frank shifted uncomfortably in his seat. "He likes to bend an elbow from time to time."

We locked eyes. I could feel a warm rush of passion swell in my bosom. "We'll find him," I told Frank breathlessly. "We'll find your brother Joe." I stood up and reached for my expensive camel hair coat, cloche hat, and aviator goggles. "Come on," I exclaimed, looking back at Frank. "There's only one place to get an illicit drink in this town: The Green Jade Café. We haven't a moment to lose!"

Frank and I sped along the country road in my custom blue Ford Roadster. We had just passed Riverside Park and the Bridle Path when I heard a piercing scream.

I froze behind the wheel. Had I inadvertently hit someone again? The judge had let me off the first time, but a second would be manslaughter for sure! My heart pounded in fright as I opened the car door to step out.

At that instant a shadowy figure arose from a pile of hay nearby. The attractive young man was wearing a full-length raccoon coat, popular in those days with the college set. "Hi, Nancy," the young man greeted me bashfully.

I removed my goggles. "Ned?"

"You know this fellow?" asked Frank.

"Yes," I pouted. "Ned, what are you doing here? Are you following me again?"

Ned looked at his shoes. "I was just worried about you," he muttered. "I phoned and Mrs. Gruen told me what was going on. I figured you were headed to the Green Jade Café so I thought I'd beat you there. But then my scooter ran out of gas. I was hiding in the hay pile when a chicken startled me. That's when you drove up."

"Who is this cat?" Frank asked me.

Ned stood up a little. "I'm her special friend," he explained. "Omega Chi Epsilon."

Frank looked at me questioningly. I shrugged.

A few minutes later Ned had strapped his scooter to my trunk and the three of us were racing toward our destination.

The Green Jade Café was in Dockville, a slum area near the Muskoka, the river that divides my hometown. A tributary of the Mississippi, the Muskoka of my youth was still crystal clear and I cruised it often as a member of the River Heights Yacht Club. Of course these days most people know the Muskoka as one of the first EPA Superfund cleanup sites in the 1980s.

The pavement in Dockville was poor, and there were rows upon rows of tenement houses punctuated by fortune-tellers and thrift shops. The residents were mostly domestic workers, recent immigrants, petty criminals, and others down on their luck. This was an area rarely mentioned in the River Heights *Morning Record*. (Unlike my own exploits, which were often front-page news. With photos.)

We arrived at the Green Jade Café only to find it closed. As it was early evening on a weekday, using my detective prowess, I deduced that this was suspicious.

"I guess we should just go home," suggested Ned.

But peering through the glass front door, I thought I caught the sight of movement. I tried the door. It opened.

"Nancy!" Ned gasped.

I took a step inside. Frank followed. Ned followed behind Frank.

The Green Jade Café was a speakeasy that specialized in plying patrons with fraudulent palm readings once they had imbibed several ounces of malt whiskey. Everyone knew it existed, including Chief McGinnis, but it was allowed to operate due to the protection of several members of the city council.

Inside, the walls were painted emerald green, and a dark wooden bar loomed huge on one wall. Several chairs were scattered on the floor.

"There's been a fight!" reported Frank.

"Shh!" I ordered. "Listen!"

From deep inside the café came a distant moan.

"Jiminy crickets!" exclaimed Ned.

The three of us moved through the café toward the faint groaning noise coming from what seemed to be the kitchen area.

"There!" Frank cried, pointing to a closet at the back of the room. "The noise seems to be coming from behind that door!"

Putting my finger over my lips, I reached toward the doorknob and turned it. It was locked. I took off my hat, pulled a bobby pin from my smart hairdo and, kneeling in my slimming skirt, quickly and expertly picked the closet lock. Then I stood, took a step back, and opened the door.

A fair-haired young man was curled at the bottom of the closet, his arms and legs bound and a handkerchief tied across his mouth.

"Joe!" wept Frank. He quickly cut the cords that bound his brother and lifted him out of the closet, trembling, into his arms.

My momentary fright gone, I let my guard down. It was a split second later that I felt the blanket come down over my head and wrap tightly around me.

I screamed and struggled as my assailant attempted to drag me backward toward an uncertain fate. I could hear a scuffle and assumed that the boys were facing similar assaults.

My arms were pinned underneath the blanket, and I could feel my attacker's arms wrapped snuggly around my waist, holding the blanket and my own arms in place. Unable to free myself, I bent my knees and flailed my legs in hopes of making contact. I screamed again and a hand wrapped tightly over my mouth. Suddenly my senses were overcome with a strong odor. Chloroform, I thought. Then I blacked out.

I awoke in a small dimly lit room that I identified immediately as a pantry of some sort. I instantly deduced that I was most likely still in the Green Jade Café. My head throbbed, my tongue felt heavy, and my titian hair was mussed, but I was not restrained. I sat up.

"Nancy, are you okay?" asked a voice in the corner.

It was Frank.

"I think so," I answered steadily. "Where are the others?"

"I don't know," he sighed glumly. "I woke up in here."

I got up and tried the door. It was locked. I fumbled for a bobby pin. They were all gone! My hair was completely undone!

I slunk over to Frank and sat down beside him.

"So who's this Ned person?" he asked.

"Oh, we've dated forever," I sighed. "He goes to Emerson. I'm always having to get him out of jams. You know, kidnapping, quicksand, wild dogs. But he's dark haired and handsome, and he's captain of the football team."

"But do you love him?"

"I love rescuing him when he's been taken prisoner."

Frank was very near me now, and I could feel my heart race at his proximity. I cleared my throat.

"And you? Do you have a girlfriend?" I asked.

He smiled. "No one serious," he answered with a twinkle in his eye.

Then he reached his hand behind my head, firmly pulled me toward him, and kissed me.

It was a full hour later when I noticed the ventilator duct above our heads.

"Frank!" I exclaimed, adjusting my blouse. "Look at that! Lift me up, and I bet I'll be able to climb out and open the door."

Frank lifted me by my hips, and I was able to reach up to the vent, remove the grate, and pull myself into the small square duct. I shimmied several feet and found myself at another vent that exited into the kitchen of the Green Jade Café. After ascertaining that the coast was clear, I carefully lowered myself to the floor and, retracing my route through the duct, found the pantry where Frank and I had been held captive. The key was in the lock! Within moments, Frank was free and we set out to find the others.

We found them tied to chairs in a back room behind the kitchen. They were dressed in striped shirts and wool pants, the sailor outfits of the day. Their captors, two mustachioed gentlemen with tattooed forearms and large gold hoop earrings in one ear, hovered over them, scowling. "Gypsy pirates," I mouthed to Frank.

Joe and Ned were being shanghaied!

Without thought to my own personal safety, I rushed in and karate-chopped one of the pirates firmly across the back of the neck. He fell to the ground with a thud. Frank, a few steps behind me, socked the other pirate across the jaw. The pirate stumbled for a moment and then also fell to the floor, unconscious.

Frank and I quickly untied the boys.

"Oh, Ned!" I cried, throwing my arms around him.

"They were going to sell us to a riverboat captain," cried Joe. "He was going to take us to New Orleans and then send us on a ship to the Orient! I came here to get a drink after Helen Corning stood me up, and the next thing I knew I was in that closet where you found me!"

"Helen didn't stand you up," explained Frank gently. "Her great-aunt Rosemary was taken ill. She called, but you didn't get the message."

Joe looked chagrined.

Ned gaped at me gratefully, his eyes wet. "You saved me," he cried.

One of the pirates stirred on the floor.

"I'd better call Chief McGinnis," I exclaimed, heading toward the phone behind the bar.

Ten minutes later the chief and several of River Heights's finest were milling around the cafe, and the pirates were in custody.

"Nancy, you're a hero," declared Chief McGinnis. "You broke up a massive shanghai operation."

"I had plenty of help," I replied, glancing over at Frank. "I'm just happy that we could make a difference."

"What about the note?" Ned asked.

"The pirates must have found out that Frank was coming to town to look for Joe. They sent the note to my house to try to intimidate us," I explained.

"Fat chance," Ned declared adoringly.

I walked over to where Frank was standing. "I guess we did it," I told him.

His brown eyes bored deeply into mine, and I felt my pulse quicken. "Bayport is a bit of a hoof, but I have to say I like the cut of your jib."

I glanced over at Ned talking to the chief. "Ned needs me," I explained. Then I hugged Frank. "We'll meet again," I whispered into his ear.

And we did.

THE INTRUDER AT NUMBER ONE

Louise Candlish

Louise Candlish is the bestselling author of several novels, including *The Swimming Pool* and *The Sudden Departure of the Frasers*. Before writing fiction, she studied English at University College London and worked as an editor and copywriter.

O n a pleasingly sharp blue day in May, Ryan Steer let himself into a vacant house on Vale Road in Lime Park. He was happy to see among the scattered post on the doormat the package he'd taken the liberty of ordering in the owner's name.

Not to mention without the owner's knowledge.

Of course, as precautions went, it was hardly worth the padded envelope it was written on: a child could trace the order back to Mr R. Steer, negotiator at Lime Park Estates, sole agency for the sale of the property in which Ryan now stood. But, still, it seemed necessary to make a token effort to cover his tracks. To commit a crime in plain sight was disrespectful to all concerned.

He stored the unopened packet in his work bag, piled the rest of the post on the hall radiator cover and took a quick look about the place before leaving. He agreed with his manager Deborah's appraisal that it wasn't going to get anywhere near the full asking price in this half-furnished state. People couldn't visualize, which was why the owner needed to bite the bullet and pay to have it staged. The Frasers' interior-designer totty – Hetty was her name – could probably organize that, and it would be Ryan's pleasure to supply her details.

Vale Road was on the outer reaches of Lime Park near St Luke's Primary (another mark against it) and it was a good twenty-minute amble to the north-eastern edge of the park, where he found a free bench and settled to open his package. He was careful to keep the item screened from the passing school-run mums and dog walkers – not that they'd have any reason to doubt that it was anything other than what it appeared to be, but he didn't want anyone noticing even that much.

What it appeared to be was a regular household smoke alarm, mains-operated (that was important: he wouldn't be in a position to recharge batteries). What it in fact *was* was a concealed camera, with no smoke detection capability whatsoever. It was one of the more expensive versions on the market, not MI5 level – no doubt the spooks had their own suppliers at prices to make your hair curl – but costly enough to have put back his personal flat hunt a couple of months. His girlfriend, Julie, had really been the one to suffer: she'd wanted a Tiffany charm bracelet for her birthday and had got a market knock-off, which probably explained why they hadn't had sex since.

She was petty, Julie, and he didn't like pettiness in a woman.

From where he sat he had a clear view of the rear aspect of Lime Park Road, each pair of villas a solid brick square, the sashes satisfyingly uniform thanks to the street's conservation restrictions. His gaze kept straying to the top floor of the building he knew to be number 40, where a light at the window suggested that the new owners continued to base themselves in the upper rooms of the house while their builders invaded below.

Tucking his purchase safely in his jacket pocket, Ryan tore the envelope and delivery note into small pieces and disposed of them in a nearby bin. The portion with the address on it he screwed up and swallowed.

Since he was in the park, he couldn't resist a detour through the south gates and down Lime Park Road and, as always, he scanned the passing faces for the one he longed to see. But someone like her wouldn't be up and about this early. She wasn't one of those stout, strident-voiced mothers who stomped around from the early morning, thinking they owned the place. (Actually, they *did* own the place, most of it anyway. Ninety per cent of properties were being bought by families, even the flats.)

It was getting on for 8.50 a.m. now and the builders were making their usual racket at number 40. With an abruptness that was almost violent, the occupant of the upstairs flat at number 38 lowered his blind – as if *that* would help.

Ryan doubled back to the park and then through the main gates to the high street where, in the café opposite his office, the mothers were gathering after drop-off. They threw themselves into their seats as if they'd just climbed Kilimanjaro, eagerly colluding to make a mountain out of a molehill. Er, walking a few streets to deliver a small child to a school gate? Try selling houses at the back end of a recession, he thought.

He was aware that he was developing a serious squeamishness regarding mothers and that it was somehow related to the ambiguity he was experiencing in his own relationship. So Julie wanted a baby, all right? (She was not so petty on this score – she was pretty fucking intense, in fact.) His protestations that they needed a flat first would buy him only so much time.

In the Lime Park Estates' shop window, one set of details caught his eye, just as it always did: *SOLD! Stunning family home in sought-after Lime Park Road . . .*

Number 40. All the more sought after now *she* was there.

Fingering the alarm in his pocket, he entered the office with a sense of calling, a sense of his true life just beginning.

'Ryan, you still looking for a two-bed?' His colleague Cheryl summoned him over to her desk. 'I'm doing a valuation this morning at 10 Station Road. Want to come with?'

One of the benefits of selling property: when you were buying, you went straight to the top of the list of candidates.

'Actually, I've hit the pause button on that,' he said.

'Oh. Why?'

'Gonna save a bigger deposit, I think.'

'You're not splitting with Julie?'

Now she said it, he saw the inevitability of it. He disappointed Julie and that was only going to continue, possibly even intensify into anger. Her tenacity would not survive what was to come. 'You know something I don't?' he said, straight faced.

Sensing his lack of conviction (estate agents were attuned to the subtlest of false notes and experienced in ignoring them), Cheryl raised an eyebrow. 'Well, make your mind up. The market's going to pick up soon.'

They'd been trotting out that line throughout the recession and sooner or later it would prove true. Twenty-twelve it was now, year of the Olympics, year of London, year of little old Lime Park! Even so, better not to buy a flat locally in case he lost his job or was issued with a restraining order. And you couldn't pay your mortgage from jail, could you?

He returned the Vale Road keys to their cubbyhole and fired up his PC. Six years he had worked at Lime Park Estates as a negotiator. Two minutes it had taken him to decide to risk everything by installing a hidden camera device in Amber Fraser's bedroom.

Pure luck had found him at his desk and at a loose end when she'd walked in one Saturday morning in January. His nine-thirty had failed to show and he'd returned to the office early.

He knew at once what she was, even though her silhouette was obscured by a thick wool coat and the kind of oversized sheepskin boots an Inuit might choose: goddess, muse, supreme being. Hair shiny as copper and bright as a house fire. Broad, generous smile. Green-gold eyes with a complicated history in their depths and rare kindness softening the surface.

(Julie's eyes he would probably describe as, what, 'brown'?)

She'd been with her husband, of course: goddesses didn't roam the place unattended, that would be too easy. What Ryan saw every other man saw too and this one had done the sensible thing and put a ring on her finger. He was predictably well spoken and charming – what was the word? Avuncular (which made Ryan think of tarantula) – and plainly wealthy. Pleased with himself didn't begin to describe his attitude as he placed a protective palm on the small of the goddess's back and steered her towards the seats at Ryan's desk. At least he knew the value of what he had, he wasn't one of those trophy hunters: when he looked at her it was with profound devotion.

Jeremy and Amber Fraser they were called, and they'd just started looking for a family home in Lime Park.

'Your children aren't with you today?' Ryan asked.

'We haven't got any yet,' she said with a shocked giggle, as if he'd said something risqué.

Better get on with it, Ryan thought. Sugar daddy had to be fifty if he was a day. But this was excellent news. Being revealed to have given birth wouldn't necessarily have stripped Mrs Fraser of her godliness, but it would have been an issue he'd have needed to consciously overlook thanks to that aforementioned distaste.

'Is there anything you can show us this morning?' she asked. Her voice was gentle, playful, neutral of accent. The husband was the one with the breeding, evidently; *she* was a blank canvas, as beautifully staged as a high-end apartment in Manhattan. 'Seems a shame to troop back up to Battersea without taking a little peek somewhere.'

'Let me make a couple of calls,' Ryan told her.

Adrenaline oiling his silver tongue, he talked two clients into impromptu viewings. There would be no time to clean the place up, said the Crowboroughs on Trinity Avenue, but they would be happy to take the dogs out so at least the source of the stink was removed, even if the stink itself remained. Similarly, the Lockes on Lime Park Road promised to clear the breakfast table and get the kids out to the park (he hoped they would make the beds and flush the loos, too). Ryan imagined the two householders striking up a conversation in the street, wondering which, if either, would get lucky with the morning's buyers.

He drove the Frasers to the two properties in the company Fiat 500. Considering how he felt – starstruck, moonstruck, one of the two or both – he handled himself pretty well, careful not to focus too obviously on her. Even so, he didn't miss the chance to ogle her skinny-jeaned legs as they unfolded from the car and, likewise, he made sure the couple took all stairs first so he could bring up the rear as closely as was decent. She liked touching things, he noticed; touch was her primary sense: she'd peer at a family photo and then put her fingertips on the glass, tenderly, as if the faces she touched were real; or she'd trail the back of her hand along a scuffed banister. In the Trinity Avenue house there was a cat sleeping on a mohair throw and she stooped to stroke both the animal and its bed. 'Hello, button,' she told it. 'Aren't you a cutie?'

'I think this one's a possibility,' Jeremy Fraser said, as they departed Lime Park Road. 'If you look past the clutter, it's actually pretty sizeable.'

'I like the secret gate to the park,' Amber said.

'It needs work, but you won't find a better location,' Ryan agreed. 'It won't hang around long.' He gave the couple his mobile number, made it sound as if that was the better way to arrange a second viewing than using the office landline that Deborah preferred her negotiators to issue.

As Amber used her index and middle fingers to key in the digits he dictated, he imagined them stepping instead over the bare skin of his chest, heading downwards, a probe identifying a place of interest.

She rang on the Monday. 'Is this Ryan? I don't know if you remember me . . .?'

Was she insane? She must know any man would remember her. The better question was whether he had managed to sleep at night knowing she was in the same city and not sharing his bed. He'd Googled her over the weekend and learned little more than that her last, and possibly current, job was in media – no surprise there. She was not, as he'd hoped, one of those women who constantly posted selfies on social media as if their cleavage didn't exist unless someone was liking it.

'I'd really like to see the Lime Park Road house again,' she purred. 'I'm going to bring my designer Hetty, if that's OK. She's free any time Wednesday.'

'Of course, let me look at the diary and see who's around that day.'

'Oh.' There was a pause. 'To be honest, Ryan, I was hoping *you* might be available again.'

She trusted him, was the implication. So she worked in the old-school way of relationships, voice-to-voice, face-to-face – that made sense (and explained the lack of digital footprint: she recognized herself that she was an experience best had IRL).

He would have cancelled his own wedding to make the viewing.

It was only a shame the temperature continued to hover at zero and she again arrived wrapped up from head to toe.

'I love your shearling coat, Amber,' Hetty the designer said. 'Is it new?' She was no dud herself, with a great cloud of dark hair and make-up that stopped just short of theatrical, but she was a little brittle and entitled in her manner for Ryan's tastes. She knew her own value, that was for sure, like a Premier League footballer's wife (a cricketer's wife, maybe? No, a polo player's). Or one of those high-end escorts you read about who cost ten grand for the weekend but let you do whatever you liked.

Amber Fraser was not for sale. She was sincere and, what's more, had a capacity for humility he was not used to seeing in his wealthier house hunters. She made no distinction between Ryan, Hetty and the cleaner busy at the Lockes' house as they toured, but spoke equally respectfully to all.

'Christmas prezzie from Jeremy,' she told her companion regarding the coat, and she shrugged, causing its shoulders to slip slightly and reveal a perfect creamy collarbone.

Now he clocked the details, he found her outfit to be more pleasing than he'd first thought thanks to some killer accessories. Her gloves were close-fitting black leather, with a little covered button at her narrow wrist, and the boots were a huge improvement on the eskimo ones: also black leather, with a full-length zip up the inside of the calf and high spiky heels. Any other house and he'd have been worried she'd damage the flooring, but the Lockes' place was already so wrecked, it wasn't an issue. The kids were savages, no two ways about it. (Pity the poor cleaner who waded through the heaps of junk to find a piece of carpet to vacuum.)

'Do you still like the place?' Ryan asked Amber as they paused in the kitchen before leaving.

'I *love* it,' she said, and she drew close, conspiratorial. Her hair smelled of cake spices: nutmeg and cinnamon and ginger. 'But I haven't forgotten you work for the seller, not the buyer, so don't try to trap me, Ryan. And don't you *dare* tell them how keen I am. Jeremy wants to get some money off.'

'Tell them it needs a ton of work,' Hetty told him sternly. 'Because that's the truth.'

'They've just put in a new worktop,' Ryan protested.

Hetty dismissed this. 'That's just a spritz of cheap perfume on a body that hasn't been washed for a week.'

'What a charming image,' Amber said. 'But if we're going to get anatomical, guys, the bones *are* great, aren't they?'

'They are,' Hetty agreed. 'But we'll have to rip everything out, Amber, rebuild from scratch. The state of those kids' bedrooms: it's like they've been playing football up there or, I don't know, running a steeplechase.'

'I know, it's totally wrecked. How many kids *are* there in this family? There are so many beds.' Leather fingers brushed Ryan's forearm, thrilling him. 'Tell us they've stopped reproducing, Ryan, *please.*'

Ryan couldn't help the corners of his mouth twitching, but said nothing. Rachel Locke was often in the café across the road and, recently, in the branch, too, checking on progress. She was flustered and sweaty and smelled so *bodily*. When she communicated with her kids, her voice rose to a foghorn, making Ryan cringe. If every Mrs Locke in Lime Park could be replaced by a Mrs Fraser, well, he gave his word that no further work-related complaint would pass his lips as long as he lived.

'Did you notice the man's shirt on the floor in the spare bedroom?' Hetty said. '*And* a pair of socks.'

Amber's gloved fingers flew to her mouth. 'What are you saying? That that's where the husband sleeps?'

'Well, he's not a looker,' Hetty said. 'Did you see the holiday photo in the sitting room? No wonder she's kicked him out of bed.'

'You girls are wicked,' Ryan said, and he enjoyed the wink the comment elicited.

His favourite line of the encounter: *If we're going to get anatomical, guys . . .*

The offer was made and confirmed in writing and Ryan guided the Lockes towards accepting it. They might get more, he conceded, but the market was still more sluggish than they hoped. (It was all very well telling buyers that after the Olympics houses like this would go to sealed bids. They just didn't believe you.) There was a second visit with Hetty, along with an architect, at which measurements were taken and technical specifications discussed. The weather was milder by then and Amber wore a thin jersey dress with those very sheer champagne-coloured tights that were fashionable. Ryan could tell the bra she wore was wafer-thin and lacy.

They exchanged contracts and completed the sale in April. To Ryan's dismay, on the Friday of completion it was Jeremy Fraser who came to pick up the keys. He'd hoped it would be Amber and that she might be moved by the occasion to embrace him. (Still, the commission would be welcome.) Recovering, on the Monday he delivered a gift basket to the house, strolling over at lunchtime when he expected Jeremy to be safely at work.

The builders had already started tearing the place apart and Amber arrived at the door like the miracle survivor of an explosion. 'Ryan, what a lovely gesture! Come upstairs away from all the noise and dust.'

The master bedroom was in use as a storage room, Ryan noticed, en route to the top of the house where Amber installed him in the makeshift living room and made him a coffee from a gleaming new Nespresso machine. There were several other welcome gifts, he saw, including a variety of indoor plants and three quarters of a homemade chocolate cake sitting in a glass dome.

'You're the first person to come into our private chamber,' she said. She was wearing workout clothes a size too small, a gift to outrank any offering the neighbours might have made. 'Would you like some cake? The woman next door made it and Jeremy says it's delicious. I don't allow myself cake, but I like watching other people eat it. I hope you don't mind if I stare?'

'Stare away,' Ryan said. 'Nice of her to bake you a cake. Lime Park's like that, though. Great sense of community.'

She passed him a slice and settled beside him. 'Where do you live, Ryan? I don't think I've ever asked you. Are you local?'

'I'm over in Bexleyheath,' he told her. Though the cake *was* good, sitting next to her was too distracting for eating to be anything but mechanical. 'Looking to buy, been saving for a deposit for ever.'

'Better late than never,' Amber said, sighing. 'It's all so painful, isn't it? You know this is the first place I've owned? Our flat in Battersea was Jeremy's from his bachelor days and before that I always rented.'

'If this is your first rung on the ladder, where will you end up?' Ryan joked, 'Windsor Castle?'

'Oh, Ryan, you make me laugh. I'm going to miss our chats,' she said.

He already knew that she'd make these sorts of remarks to anyone; flirting was like breathing to her. Indeed, there was a sense of an ending for her as she escorted him to the door an hour later. He was under no illusion that he was a casual diversion she would forget the moment the door closed. Which was fine, he accepted that.

What was unacceptable was any suggestion that *he* should forget *her*.

He was a patient man. Between taking delivery of the device and identifying the opportunity to plant it, he was required to wait more than three months. The mission relied on timing: he'd need to go in after the decorators had finished and, most crucially, once Hetty had approved the job. Weekly walk-bys gave him an idea of how the work was progressing, increased to daily once the builders had retreated and the decorators taken up residence. The whole thing was remarkably efficient compared with some of the extension projects you heard about. At the far end of Lime Park Road, a basement had taken two years to be completed and the couple had separated in the process. The house that came back on the market was bigger and deeper and yet mysteriously slow to shift. (It had, according to Cheryl, lost its soul.)

One day in July, he saw Amber at a terrace table at the café across the road. She was with a typical Lime Park denizen – a posh mum in her forties – and a less typical one: an attractive straight man in his thirties, a bit rough around the edges. As the woman rummaged in the tote at her feet, almost putting her head into the bag in her impatience, the man cast an appreciative gaze Amber's way. More than appreciative – carnal, Ryan would say. That was the only time he was tempted to expedite his plan: what if Amber ran off with this guy? All Ryan would be left with was Jeremy, which would be no reward for his perseverance.

Then he saw Hetty's red Beetle at the kerb one August morning and his blood fired. Of course Amber would not be running off with some casual admirer; the man in the café had been no more of a threat to the Fraser marriage than Ryan himself.

He waited till the end of the afternoon and phoned Hetty. 'We have a client looking for an interior designer and I mentioned your beautiful work at the Frasers' place. Is that all finished up now?'

'Almost! I was just there today, in fact. The decorators are all done with the first floor, they're just doing the last bits and pieces at the top now.'

'We all know what they say,' Ryan said chummily. 'The last ten per cent of the job takes ninety per cent of the time.'

'Not these guys,' Hetty said. 'They're on a penalty if they overrun.'

She was a ball-breaker: he'd been right to identify her as potentially danger-ous. She was also, it transpired, his willing accomplice. 'I'll be popping in again on Thursday afternoon if you want to swing by and see the finished article?' she offered. 'I'm sure Amber won't mind.'

'I might take you up on that,' Ryan said.

He arrived half an hour early. Amber was not in, which was disappointing in itself, but also advantageous in that she would not divert his attention from the job at hand. The decorators were not native English speakers and a quick call to Hetty was enough to satisfy them that he was not a violent offender or con man.

'You carry on,' Ryan told them. 'I'll have a look around down here while I wait for Hetty.'

After a safe interval, he slipped off his shoes in consideration of the new carpeting and padded up the stairs to the first floor. The place was unrecogniz-able, so slick and immaculate as to feel unreal. The master bedroom was plushly carpeted in vanilla, the walls, he was relieved to see, helpfully pale (Farrow & Ball Clunch, Hetty clarified, when she arrived). But the furniture was not yet in, nor any curtains or blinds up at the windows, and the Frasers, displaced from their upper quarters by the decorators, were evidently sleeping in a room at the rear of the first floor. Had they changed their minds and decided on a smaller bedroom for themselves? Couples did, sometimes, valuing the garden outlook over the greater square footage at the front. After a few moments' hesitation, he resolved to fit the device in the master as intended and to check with Hetty that there had been no permanent change of plan. If there had, he'd somehow have to find a way to sneak back up and switch the thing before he left.

Shouldering the door closed behind him, he surveyed the empty room, nerves growling like hunger. He clearly recalled Amber and Hetty discussing layout pos-sibilities on their last visit before the sale went through. They'd agreed there were two options for the placement of the bed: opposite the bay against the internal wall, or facing the fireplace against the dividing wall with number 38.

'But what if the couple on the other side have their bed against this wall, too?' Amber had queried. 'The headboards will be *this* close.' Fingers rigid, she held her palms a few inches apart.

'I think it's flats next door, actually,' Hetty said. 'In which case it might be a living room.'

Amber's eyes grew wide. 'So when you're in the middle of, *you know what,* they're sitting a couple of feet away watching *Silent Witness?*'

'Yes,' laughed Hetty. 'Unless they've installed one of those peephole cameras and are watching you, *"you know what".*'

It startled Ryan to remember that last part of the conversation. Had it been what had planted the idea? All at once the reality, the peril, of his trespass tor-pedoed him and he chided himself for dithering even the few minutes he had. Circling the room with new urgency, he found there was an obvious power point on the left-hand side of the fireplace above the double-height skirting. It was a twin socket, which was ideal, because the alarm wouldn't be torn out the moment power was needed for something else.

He slid the prongs into the holes and turned on the switch. There was no light or hum to draw attention to it. Astonishing, in fact, how discreet it looked and how *right*, the sort of thing you might assume someone else had fitted as a legal requirement, in this case one of the builders. Provided it got past Hetty, the worst-case scenario was that the Frasers' aesthetic sensibility was on the OCD side and, deeming it an eyesore, they relocated it or ditched it, in neither case stopping to investigate what it was they were handling.

Actually, that wasn't the worst-case scenario. The worst-case scenario was that Jeremy Fraser would smash it open, identify the surveillance device and call the police. But that was what a risk was, wasn't it?

Hetty arrived soon after and appeared to think nothing of his having waited in the house unaccompanied. 'Oh, Ryan, Amber isn't around today, as you've probably gathered. She had a lunch date she couldn't get out of and won't be back till four. It's just us.'

'That's no problem. I've got to hand it to you, Hetty, from what I've seen down here, you've done a magnificent job.' Ryan oohed and aahed dutifully, pointing out the value she'd added.

'The Frasers aren't worried about that,' Hetty said. 'This is a home, a love nest, not an investment. They won't move for years, if ever.'

'Pleased to hear it,' Ryan said.

But when she led the tour into the master bedroom, he had the sensation of standing on a precipice, gulls sweeping past his face. His voice sounded hollow as he gestured into the emptiness, saying, 'They've decided against this as their master, have they?'

'No, not at all,' Hetty said. 'There's just been a delay with the en suite, we were waiting for the bath to arrive. But we're all set now and they'll be able to move in here as soon as the furniture comes out of storage.'

Excellent.

As for her spotting the device, he needn't have worried, for she had her eyes on a bigger, brighter prize: the famous bathtub. 'You remember our talking about it? I found it in Oaxaca in Mexico? Come and see it, it's *amazing*.' And she hurried past the smoke alarm into the en suite.

It was a monster of a tub, the kind of thing slaves spent years hammering to perfection for Cleopatra – or whoever the Mexican equivalent was. 'Wow, big enough for two,' he said, allowing his fingers to glance off the gleaming near lip.

'The interior is pewter,' Hetty said. 'I've already told Amber, if she *does* ever move, she should take it with her. It's too precious to leave.'

As Ryan departed, an older woman was arriving at the gate of number 38. She wore a blue velour tracksuit and her face was blotched with exertion. Well, if she was the occupant of the flat upstairs, he knew which side of the wall he'd prefer to sleep.

All being well, he'd be able to watch Mrs Fraser in her copper-and-pewter tub, provided she was the sort to leave the bathroom door open, for the camera facilitated 180-degree views with a dewarping function. A motion-detection function would save him trawling through hours of inanimate video. The high-definition images would be streamed direct to his smartphone, a pay-as-you-go procured expressly for the purpose and paid for in cash, though, again, he doubted the efficacy of such a precaution.

Now he'd got the crime underway, he found he was almost pleasurably fatalistic about it.

The footage was, at first, more thrilling for the novelty (excellent definition, great colour) than the content. As Hetty had promised, the furniture was delivered within a few days of Ryan's visit. The bed was positioned facing the window and within close range of the camera; beyond stood an enormous freestanding wardrobe with mirrored doors and, in the window, a pair of armchairs with voluptuously curved arms. As a team of young men hauled these and other items, removing the protective packaging with the flourishes of magicians, he despaired of Amber Fraser appearing at all. Then, speeding through, he found her. As she entered the room, all heads turned as to an emerging sun and she smiled a greeting, running her hands through her hair. Then, right in front of a roomful of men, she jumped onto the bare mattress and stretched out, pantomiming a nap, doing a little roll from side to side. The watching faces laughed now and she sprang up again, gave a little wave, and exited. This, evidently, was how she supervised workmen.

Without sound, the video had an effect that was faintly sinister.

There was nothing for forty-eight hours, but then came the day she moved in the couples' clothes and arranged their wardrobe. It was a fancy item fitted with fussy little his and her drawers and cubbyholes for an exhaustive collection of shoes. She worked at a lazy pace, stopping frequently to text on her phone or fetch herself coffee. Only as Ryan was growing sleepy did she do what he had been waiting over three months to see: she undressed.

Well, her body was hands-down the most erotic and arousing he'd ever laid eyes on, slender and toned but with heavy breasts and a proper behind, like one of those insanely proportioned RealDolls he'd read about (and, OK, dreamed of acquiring). Truly this was a woman born to be worshipped. To be touched, too, of course – but you couldn't have everything.

She devoted an hour to trying on dresses. One, green and lacy, appeared to be her favourite, and she stalked about the room in it (and a pair of heels) before slipping out of it once more and hanging it on the wardrobe door. Then she lay on top of the bed in just her knickers as if wondering what to do next. Not what Ryan would have hoped, sadly, but when she jumped up again her breasts swung a little in the direction of the camera, which was a delightful bonus. She used her left hand to minimize the bounce, smoothing the right one across her face before dropping both hands to her sides. She still had the heels on.

Truly, it was like an opening ceremony just for him.

He was not prepared for the frequency of the marital sex. The Frasers were active in a way he knew to be exclusive to new relationships and couples trying for a baby (they belonged, for all he knew, to both groups). Mostly the action was under the covers and in darkness, but sometimes it was well lit and exposed. The positions varied every once in a while, but it was mostly missionary or her on top. Often, it began with her husband pawing her as she lay on her front, more like a cub that wanted to get a game going rather than an erotic seduction – and then spinning her on to her back. It was mostly fairly fast.

Incredible how quickly you became inured to free pornography. After the first few weeks, Ryan found himself zooming in on their faces, craving human nuance over the mammalian moves of the sexual act itself. Once Jeremy's face was square on to the camera and, as he spoke, Ryan strained to lipread; he was fairly certain Jeremy was simply repeating Amber's name, which was conventional enough. What was odd was *her* face: still, almost closed, as if transported to another place or perhaps lobotomized. She loved her husband but she didn't have any wild, obscene lust for him. *That*, Ryan would have liked to have seen.

In a novel, he would have witnessed some awful domestic violence or other crime, but the reality was the Frasers got on extremely well. On the few occasions that Amber seemed low, Jeremy comforted her. On the rare occasions that he looked angry, she consoled him. Ryan grew to prefer these non-sexual tableaux: they were more revealing, more involving of their (admittedly uninvited) guest.

Best of all was when Amber was alone, unselfconscious, and he had her to himself. Most of the days, she dressed in workout clothes and kept them on until the early evening, changing in good time for the return of her husband. The rest, she dressed properly and did her hair and make-up, often beautifying herself well into the late morning, presumably for a lunch date or outing of some sort. Then, hours later, she'd come back and shower or bathe a second time and she'd be back in front of the mirrored wardrobe doors putting on another dress, retouching her face. Occasionally she'd sigh heavily, as if exhausted by the stipulations of her own beauty.

Ryan followed the strict rule of viewing only at home at night behind closed doors, but it was a time-consuming hobby and, just as he'd willed it, Julie soon arrived at his door and told him she wanted to break up.

'What have you been *doing*?' she demanded, and Ryan found himself regarding her with genuine curiosity. Mid-brown hair, mid-brown eyes, mid-height: how *mid* she was, and how tragic that women – and men, for that matter – were consigned to this ordinariness when you could see how they ached to be special.

'Don't you have *anything* to say?' She spoke in a way that he understood to mean all he had to do was promise to reform and she'd change her mind, but he didn't because the truth was he didn't have time for both her and Amber and of course he was going to choose Amber.

'Not really,' he said.

As he watched – and rewatched – the images on his phone, ears alert for any approaching noises on the landing outside his room, he felt no guilt. Yes, Amber excited predictable baseness in him, he was not made of stone, but she also inspired something higher, even spiritual. Amber was a religion and he was her believer.

*

He was surprised by the relief he felt when, towards Christmastime, the Frasers packed two enormous suitcases and disappeared, presumably for a holiday. (He would not forget the glorious afternoon when Amber had come back from a trip to Selfridges and tried on three new bikinis, one g-string style. In the informal league table of highlights this catapulted straight into his top five.)

Safe in the knowledge that the couple were off-site, he would have liked to have broken into number 40 somehow, taken an item of underwear for himself, but of course the Frasers had a state-of-the-art alarm system. There was risk-taking and then there was walking into the police station and giving yourself up.

He spent Christmas with his mother, scratching constantly at the infestation of thoughts about Ronnie Corbett in *Sorry!* and, more disquietingly, Anthony Perkins in *Psycho*.

One day in January, something new and disturbing happened. Amber appeared in the bedroom sobbing and threw herself violently onto the bed. She clutched her chest and writhed in pain as if suffering a cardiac arrest; she beat her fists against the pillow like a child denied her birthday. Was this emotional or medical, then? He couldn't be sure. Had he been watching the footage live, he might have been tempted to phone for an ambulance, but there was a lag of several hours and all he could do was wait, appalled, to see how it ended.

After an hour or so of this recumbent anguish, Amber got to her feet and stumbled from the room. She didn't come back for days. During this period, a grave-faced Jeremy continued to move in and out of the room, still sleeping there at first, until he too abandoned ship and returned only each morning to select clothes from the wardrobe and get ready for work. Where had Amber gone? Was she still in the house? Ryan suppressed feelings of panic that she might have been hospitalized: no, he'd seen her leave the room on her own two feet, she'd definitely not been injured. Most likely, she was still there, but using a different bedroom. Perhaps she and Jeremy had had a row.

When, finally, Jeremy packed a holdall with clothes, Ryan understood that the couple were separating and Jeremy moving out. Now Amber was back in view. She'd come into the room and stare at herself in the wardrobe mirror. Once, she stood right in front of the camera, tore a bangle from her wrist and flung it into the en suite. Overbalancing, she fell, landing close to the alarm, peering at it with bitter eyes before getting up from the floor. Where she'd previously been helpless, now she was furious, a fury that could not be contained, judging by her pacing. Pained by her pain, Ryan decided to pay a visit, rehearsing a line about it being a courtesy call to follow up the sale (albeit nine months after the event) and ask if she might like the property revalued. He imagined himself saying, 'Everything all right? You look a bit off colour,' prompting a confession of marital breakdown and the grateful acceptance of estate-agently sympathy.

There was no reply at the door.

'She's not answering,' said the neighbour at number 42. Ryan recognized her as the woman Amber had been in the café with, together with the good-looking guy who Ryan had since seen on the high street a few times with a posh blonde.

'I'm not sure she's even in. I think she might have gone to join her husband on his business trip. She hasn't been well recently.'

'I know,' Ryan was about to say, but stopped himself. At least he knew now that the couple had not split up. Knowledge equalled self-preservation for a man in his position.

The courtesy call became a courtesy email. She did not reply.

The next time the camera registered any activity was the following Saturday, when Amber spent half an hour or so at the window watching the street below. She seemed calmer now, content again. In the mirror she cupped her breasts with her hands through her sweater and kept them like that for some time. He wondered if she'd had enlargement surgery, which would explain her previous absence; perhaps that hysteria had been pre-op nerves. But he didn't think so. Her figure, with which he was as minutely familiar as any husband, looked just the same.

Though he didn't realize it then, this was the last time he would see her. Jeremy returned from his work trip and was in and out of the room, showering, dressing, and finally packing again. The leather holdall was the same one he'd used for his work travel but this time he took items for both his wife and himself.

There was nothing for several days and then, at one otherwise unremarkable morning briefing in early February, Deborah made an incredible announcement. The owner of 40 Lime Park Road had just phoned and the house was going back on the market.

'You mean Jeremy and Amber Fraser?' Ryan exclaimed. 'But they've only been there ten months.'

'You've got a good memory,' Deborah said.

She handled the sale personally, allowing several parties to proceed in a race to exchange, an unethical practice that the agency discouraged as a rule. Though it was standard for each client to be assigned a negotiator as a point of contact, it was a small team and the properties themselves were shared. Not this time. Only Deborah and her most senior negotiator, Mark, were allowed to know the burglar alarm code for 40 Lime Park Road and when Ryan made requests to take his own candidates for a viewing, he was told they must be referred to Mark.

The old woman next door was selling up as well, apparently, though she was using a different agent.

Someone had seen a police car on the street, Cheryl whispered.

Well, once he heard *that*, he couldn't sleep. What if the police searched the Frasers' house and found the smoke alarm? Objects that might fool ordinary civilians would surely not fool a forensic investigator. The website from which he'd bought the device had promised no hidden serial numbers, but what good was that if they only sold a handful of the things a month? They could be traced individually in no time at all.

On the other hand, there was a tamper alarm on the device and this had not yet been triggered. Plus Cheryl had eavesdropped on Deborah and Mark and understood that it was the next-door flat that was of police interest, not the Frasers'. 'Wonder if they'll tell people *that* when they're showing them around,' she said, disgruntled for more obvious reasons than Ryan's to have been cut out of the deal.

There was nothing for it but to bide his time and stay calm. Now, when he checked in with the Frasers' master bedroom, it was to watch his colleagues conduct viewings.

Even though, in time, he was aware of the house selling to a young couple from New Cross, it came as a supreme shock when a new figure appeared on video. She was a dowdy woman in her thirties – and possibly quite mad, he soon decided, judging by the frantic way she cleaned the room, going over and over the spotless carpet with her Hoover. One minute she was ill in bed and the next she was up and removing all the furniture. Watching her manhandle the double bed on to its side and edge it through the door, Ryan almost lost the will to live.

No sooner had the mad woman moved herself and her husband (a fretful-looking thing) out of the bedroom than she was back, spending hours a day in a chair by the window. It was like she was convalescing from some debilitating disease and yet she appeared perfectly able-bodied. She must be, he realized with an unexpected pinch of compassion, depressed.

Then, the tamper alarm *did* issue an alert and the connection between 40 Lime Park Road and his secret phone was broken. Sleepless, he berated himself for not having got into the house before somehow (it wasn't as if he hadn't tried to think of a way, but Deborah's defences had been impenetrable and the new owner struck him as the type to escalate it if he were to visit unannounced; after all she'd never met him). Dozens of theories occurred as to what might have deactivated the device, his favourite being that she'd removed it with the intention of fitting it somewhere else in the house, somewhere a fire was more likely to start.

However, two days passed and it had not been reinstalled.

Rubbish collection day in Lime Park was Friday. Late Thursday night, Ryan drove his mother's Micra to Lime Park and located the bin for number 40. At least there were only two sackfuls; these he transferred to the boot of the car, watched only by a fox.

It took over an hour the next evening to sift twice through the disgusting tangle of dust and human hair and God knew what (it was compulsory to recycle food waste in a separate bin, thank the Lord). He hadn't actually expected to find it, the exercise being more in the spirit of elimination than discovery, but, to his great joy, there it was! It had slipped into an empty Tampax box, to all appearances a discarded smoke alarm.

'What are you doing, Ryan?' his mother called through the locked garage door. 'Ros is here with her daughter . . .'

'Coming!'

Since he and Julie had split up, his mother had been hinting about the neighbour's divorced daughter, who was Ryan's age. She'd been going to the gym, apparently, and was 'back in the game'. Meeting her, he saw immediately that she was revolted by the idea of a middle-aged man living with his mother and needing to be persuaded from some unnamed activity in a sealed garage. It probably didn't help that he clutched a crushed Tampax box under his arm as he reached to accept a beer. She was OK-looking, he supposed, soft-bodied and a bit wrinkled, especially around the eyes and mouth. Like him, like Julie, like the new couple in the Frasers' house, she was nothing special.

He couldn't wait to go up to his bedroom and review the Amber highlights. Not that he intended storing them for long, he understood that that was too risky. This would be the last time.

The next day, having stuffed the Lime Park rubbish into his own bin, he walked down to the boating lake in Danson Park. 'Goodbye, Amber,' he mouthed, before hurling the alarm and the phone into the water.

And he imagined her at that exact moment, wherever she was, whoever she was with, reacting as if by extrasensory perception to the sound of his thoughts.

'Oh, Ryan,' she'd say, her voice sticky with sorrow. 'I'm really going to miss you.'

'I'll miss you, too,' he said aloud. His heart hammered dreadfully, his skin was afire, and it took him a minute or two to regain his composure.

And then, chin up, he walked to the station to catch his usual train to work.

TAPE-MEASURE MURDER

Agatha Christie

Agatha Christie (1890–1976) is the bestselling crime writer in history. The creator of Hercule Poirot and Jane Marple, her works include *Murder on the Orient Express, And Then There Were None* and *The Mousetrap*. She wrote non-crime novels as Mary Westmacott, and was made a Dame in 1971.

Miss Politt took hold of the knocker and rapped politely on the cottage door. After a discreet interval she knocked again. The parcel under her left arm shifted a little as she did so, and she readjusted it. Inside the parcel was Mrs. Spenlow's new green winter dress, ready for fitting. From Miss Politt's left hand dangled a bag of black silk, containing a tape measure, a pincushion, and a large, practical pair of scissors.

Miss Politt was tall and gaunt, with a sharp nose, pursed lips, and meagre iron-grey hair. She hesitated before using the knocker for the third time. Glancing down the street, she saw a figure rapidly approaching. Miss Hartnell, jolly, weather-beaten, fifty-five, shouted out in her usual loud bass voice, "Good afternoon, Miss Politt!"

The dressmaker answered, "Good afternoon, Miss Hartnell." Her voice was excessively thin and genteel in its accents. She had started life as a lady's maid. "Excuse me," she went on, "but do you happen to know if by any chance Mrs. Spenlow isn't at home?"

"Not the least idea," said Miss Hartnell.

"It's rather awkward, you see. I was to fit on Mrs. Spenlow's new dress this afternoon. Three thirty, she said."

Miss Hartnell consulted her wrist watch. "It's a little past the half hour now."

"Yes. I have knocked three times, but there doesn't seem to be any answer, so I was wondering if perhaps Mrs. Spenlow might have gone out and forgotten. She doesn't forget appointments as a rule, and she wants the dress to wear the day after tomorrow."

Miss Hartnell entered the gate and walked up the path to join Miss Politt outside the door of Laburnum Cottage.

"Why doesn't Gladys answer the door?" she demanded. "Oh, no, of course, it's Thursday—Gladys's day out. I expect Mrs. Spenlow has fallen asleep. I don't expect you've made enough noise with this thing."

Seizing the knocker, she executed a deafening *rat-a-tat-tat,* and in addition thumped upon the panels of the door. She also called out in a stentorian voice, "What ho, within there!"

There was no response.

Miss Politt murmured, "Oh, I think Mrs. Spenlow must have forgotten and gone out, I'll call round some other time." She began edging away down the path.

"Nonsense," said Miss Hartnell firmly. "She can't have gone out. I'd have met her. I'll just take a look through the windows and see if I can find any signs of life."

She laughed in her usual hearty manner, to indicate that it was a joke, and applied a perfunctory glance to the nearest windowpane—perfunctory because she knew quite well that the front room was seldom used, Mr. and Mrs. Spenlow preferring the small back sitting room.

Perfunctory as it was, though, it succeeded in its object. Miss Hartnell, it is true, saw no signs of life. On the contrary, she saw, through the window, Mrs. Spenlow lying on the hearthrug—dead.

"Of course," said Miss Hartnell, telling the story afterwards, "I managed to keep my head. That Politt creature wouldn't have had the least idea of what to do. 'Got to keep our heads,' I said to her. '*You* stay here, and I'll go for Constable Palk.' She said something about not wanting to be left, but I paid no attention at all. One has to be firm with that sort of person. I've always found they enjoy making a fuss. So I was just going off when, at that very moment, Mr. Spenlow came round the corner of the house."

Here Miss Hartnell made a significant pause. It enabled her audience to ask breathlessly, "Tell me, how did he *look*?"

Miss Hartnell would then go on, "Frankly, I suspected something at once! He was *far* too calm. He didn't seem surprised in the least. And you may say what you like, it isn't natural for a man to hear that his wife is dead and display no emotion whatever."

Everybody agreed with this statement.

The police agreed with it, too. So suspicious did they consider Mr. Spenlow's detachment, that they lost no time in ascertaining how that gentleman was situated as a result of his wife's death. When they discovered that Mrs. Spenlow had been the monied partner, and that her money went to her husband under a will made soon after their marriage, they were more suspicious than ever.

Miss Marple, that sweet-faced—and, some said, vinegar-tongued—elderly spinster who lived in the house next to the rectory, was interviewed very early—within half an hour of the discovery of the crime. She was approached by Police Constable Palk, importantly thumbing a notebook. "If you don't mind, ma'am, I've a few questions to ask you."

Miss Marple said, "In connection with the murder of Mrs. Spenlow?"

Palk was startled. "May I ask, madam, how you got to know of it?"

"The fish," said Miss Marple.

The reply was perfectly intelligible to Constable Palk. He assumed correctly that the fishmonger's boy had brought it, together with Miss Marple's evening meal.

Miss Marple continued gently. "Lying on the floor in the sitting room, strangled—possibly by a very narrow belt. But whatever it was, it was taken away."

Palk's face was wrathful. "How that young Fred gets to know everything—"

Miss Marple cut him short adroitly. She said, "There's a pin in your tunic."

Constable Palk looked down, startled. He said, "They do say, 'See a pin and pick it up, all the day you'll have good luck.'"

"I hope that will come true. Now what is it you want me to tell you?"

Constable Palk cleared his throat, looked important, and consulted his notebook. "Statement was made to me by Mr. Arthur Spenlow, husband of the deceased. Mr. Spenlow says that at two thirty, as far as he can say, he was rung up by Miss Marple, and asked if he would come over at a quarter past three as she was anxious to consult him about something. Now, ma'am, is that true?"

"Certainly not," said Miss Marple.

"You did not ring up Mr. Spenlow at two thirty?"

"Neither at two thirty nor any other time."

"Ah," said Constable Palk, and sucked his moustache with a good deal of satisfaction.

"What else did Mr. Spenlow say?"

"Mr. Spenlow's statement was that he came over here as requested, leaving his own house at ten minutes past three; that on arrival here he was informed by the maidservant that Miss Marple was 'not at 'ome.'"

"That part of it is true," said Miss Marple. "He did come here, but I was at a meeting at the Women's Institute."

"Ah," said Constable Palk again.

Miss Marple exclaimed, "Do tell me, Constable, do you suspect Mr. Spenlow?"

"It's not for me to say at this stage, but it looks to me as though somebody, naming no names, has been trying to be artful."

Miss Marple said thoughtfully, "Mr. Spenlow?"

She liked Mr. Spenlow. He was a small, spare man, stiff and conventional in speech, the acme of respectability. It seemed odd that he should have come to live in the country, he had so clearly lived in towns all his life. To Miss Marple he confided the reason. He said, "I have always intended, ever since I was a small boy, to live in the country someday and have a garden of my own. I have always been very much attached to flowers. My wife, you know, kept a flower shop. That's where I saw her first."

A dry statement, but it opened up a vista of romance. A younger, prettier Mrs. Spenlow, seen against a background of flowers.

Mr. Spenlow, however, really knew nothing about flowers. He had no idea of seeds, of cuttings, of bedding out, of annuals or perennials. He had only a vision—a vision of a small cottage garden thickly planted with sweet-smelling, brightly coloured blossoms. He had asked, almost pathetically, for instruction, and had noted down Miss Marple's replies to questions in a little book.

He was a man of quiet method. It was, perhaps, because of this trait, that the police were interested in him when his wife was found murdered. With patience and perseverance they learned a good deal about the late Mrs. Spenlow—and soon all St. Mary Mead knew it, too.

The late Mrs. Spenlow had begun life as a between-maid in a large house. She had left that position to marry the second gardener, and with him had started a flower shop in London. The shop had prospered. Not so the gardener, who before long had sickened and died.

His widow carried on the shop and enlarged it in an ambitious way. She had continued to prosper. Then she had sold the business at a handsome price and embarked upon matrimony for the second time—with Mr. Spenlow, a middle-aged jeweller who had inherited a small and struggling business. Not long afterwards, they had sold the business and came down to St. Mary Mead.

Mrs. Spenlow was a well-to-do woman. The profits from her florist's establishment she had invested—"under spirit guidance," as she explained to all and sundry. The spirits had advised her with unexpected acumen.

All her investments had prospered, some in quite a sensational fashion. Instead, however, of this increasing her belief in spiritualism, Mrs. Spenlow basely deserted mediums and sittings, and made a brief but wholehearted plunge into an obscure religion with Indian affinities which was based on various forms of deep breathing. When, however, she arrived at St. Mary Mead, she had relapsed into a period of orthodox Church-of-England beliefs. She was a good deal at the vicarage, and attended church services with assiduity. She patronized the village shops, took an interest in the local happenings, and played village bridge.

A humdrum, everyday life. And—suddenly—murder.

Colonel Melchett, the chief constable, had summoned Inspector Slack.

Slack was a positive type of man. When he had made up his mind, he was sure. He was quite sure now. "Husband did it, sir," he said.

"You think so?"

"Quite sure of it. You've only got to look at him. Guilty as hell. Never showed a sign of grief or emotion. He came back to the house knowing she was dead."

"Wouldn't he at least have tried to act the part of the distracted husband?"

"Not him, sir. Too pleased with himself. Some gentlemen can't act. Too stiff."

"Any other woman in his life?" Colonel Melchett asked.

"Haven't been able to find any trace of one. Of course, he's the artful kind. He'd cover his tracks. As I see it, he was just fed up with his wife. She'd got the money, and I should say was a trying woman to live with—always taking up with some 'ism' or other. He cold-bloodedly decided to do away with her and live comfortably on his own."

"Yes, that could be the case, I suppose."

"Depend upon it, that was it. Made his plans careful. Pretended to get a phone call—"

Melchett interrupted him. "No call been traced?"

"No, sir. That means either that he lied, or that the call was put through from a public telephone booth. The only two public phones in the village are at the station and the post office. Post office it certainly wasn't. Mrs. Blade sees everyone who comes in. Station it might be. Train arrives at two twenty-seven and there's a bit of a bustle then. But the main thing is *he* says it was Miss Marple who called him up, and that certainly isn't true. The call didn't come from her house, and she herself was away at the Institute."

"You're not overlooking the possibility that the husband was deliberately got out of the way—by someone who wanted to murder Mrs. Spenlow?"

"You're thinking of young Ted Gerard, aren't you, sir? I've been working on him—what we're up against there is lack of motive. He doesn't stand to gain anything."

"He's an undesirable character, though. Quite a pretty little spot of embezzlement to his credit."

"I'm not saying he isn't a wrong 'un. Still, he did go to his boss and own up to that embezzlement. And his employers weren't wise to it."

"An Oxford Grouper," said Melchett.

"Yes, sir. Became a convert and went off to do the straight thing and own up to having pinched money. I'm not saying, mind you, that it mayn't have been astuteness. He may have thought he was suspected and decided to gamble on honest repentance."

"You have a sceptical mind, Slack," said Colonel Melchett. "By the way, have you talked to Miss Marple at all?"

"What's *she* got to do with it, sir?"

"Oh, nothing. But she hears things, you know. Why don't you go and have a chat with her? She's a very sharp old lady."

Slack changed the subject. "One thing I've been meaning to ask you, sir. That domestic service job where the deceased started her career—Sir Robert Abercrombie's place. That's where that jewel robbery was—emeralds—worth a packet. Never got them. I've been looking it up—must have happened when the Spenlow woman was there, though she'd have been quite a girl at the time. Don't think she was mixed up in it, do you, sir? Spenlow, you know, was one of those little tuppenny-ha'penny jewellers—just the chap for a fence."

Melchett shook his head. "Don't think there's anything in that. She didn't even know Spenlow at the time. I remember the case. Opinion in police circles was that a son of the house was mixed up in it—Jim Abercrombie—awful young waster. Had a pile of debts, and just after the robbery they were all paid off—some rich woman, so they said, but I don't know—Old Abercrombie hedged a bit about the case—tried to call the police off."

"It was just an idea, sir," said Slack.

Miss Marple received Inspector Slack with gratification, especially when she heard that he had been sent by Colonel Melchett.

"Now, really, that is very kind of Colonel Melchett. I didn't know he remembered me."

"He remembers you, all right. Told me that what you didn't know of what goes on in St. Mary Mead isn't worth knowing."

"Too kind of him, but really I don't know anything at all. About this murder, I mean."

"You know what the talk about it is."

"Oh, of course—but it wouldn't do, would it, to repeat just idle talk?"

Slack said, with an attempt at geniality, "This isn't an official conversation, you know. It's in confidence, so to speak."

"You mean you really want to know what people are saying? Whether there's any truth in it or not?"

"That's the idea."

"Well, of course, there's been a great deal of talk and speculation. And there are really two distinct camps, if you understand me. To begin with, there are the people who think that the husband did it. A husband or a wife is, in a way, the natural person to suspect, don't you think so?"

"Maybe," said the inspector cautiously.

"Such close quarters, you know. Then, so often, the money angle. I hear that it was Mrs. Spenlow who had the money, and therefore Mr. Spenlow does benefit by her death. In this wicked world I'm afraid the most uncharitable assumptions are often justified."

"He comes into a tidy sum, all right."

"Just so. It would seem quite plausible, wouldn't it, for him to strangle her, leave the house by the back, come across the fields to my house, ask for me and pretend he'd had a telephone call from me, then go back and find his wife murdered in his absence—hoping, of course, that the crime would be put down to some tramp or burglar."

The inspector nodded. "What with the money angle—and if they'd been on bad terms lately—"

But Miss Marple interrupted him. "Oh, but they hadn't."

"You know that for a fact?"

"Everyone would have known if they'd quarrelled! The maid, Gladys Brent—she'd have soon spread it round the village."

The inspector said feebly, "She mightn't have known—" and received a pitying smile in reply.

Miss Marple went on. "And then there's the other school of thought. Ted Gerard. A good-looking young man. I'm afraid, you know, that good looks are inclined to influence one more than they should. Our last curate but one—quite a magical effect! All the girls came to church—evening service as well as morning. And many older women became unusually active in parish work—and the slippers and scarfs that were made for him! Quite embarrassing for the poor young man.

"But let me see, where was I? Oh, yes, this young man, Ted Gerard. Of course, there has been talk about him. He's come down to see her so often. Though Mrs. Spenlow told me herself that he was a member of what I think they call the Oxford Group. A religious movement. They are quite sincere and very earnest, I believe, and Mrs. Spenlow was impressed by it all."

Miss Marple took a breath and went on. "And I'm sure there was no reason to believe that there was anything more in it than that, but you know what people are. Quite a lot of people are convinced that Mrs. Spenlow was infatuated with the young man, and that she'd lent him quite a lot of money. And it's perfectly true that he was actually seen at the station that day. In the train—the two twenty-seven down train. But of course it would be quite easy, wouldn't it, to slip out of the other side of the train and go through the cutting and over the fence and round by the hedge and never come out of the station entrance at all. So that he need not have been seen going to the cottage. And, of course, people do think that what Mrs. Spenlow was wearing was rather peculiar."

"Peculiar?"

"A kimono. Not a dress." Miss Marple blushed. "That sort of thing, you know, is, perhaps, rather suggestive to some people."

"You think it was suggestive?"

"Oh, no, *I* don't think so, I think it was perfectly natural."

"You think it was natural?"

"Under the circumstances, yes." Miss Marple's glance was cool and reflective.

Inspector Slack said, "It might give us another motive for the husband. Jealousy."

"Oh, no, Mr. Spenlow would never be jealous. He's not the sort of man who notices things. If his wife had gone away and left a note on the pincushion, it would be the first he'd know of anything of that kind."

Inspector Slack was puzzled by the intent way she was looking at him. He had an idea that all her conversation was intended to hint at something he didn't understand. She said now, with some emphasis, "Didn't *you* find any clues, Inspector—on the spot?"

"People don't leave fingerprints and cigarette ash nowadays, Miss Marple."

"But this, I think," she suggested, "was an old-fashioned crime—"

Slack said sharply, "Now what do you mean by that?"

Miss Marple remarked slowly, "I think, you know, that Constable Palk could help you. He was the first person on the—on the 'scene of the crime,' as they say."

Mr. Spenlow was sitting in a deck chair. He looked bewildered. He said, in his thin, precise voice, "I may, of course, be imagining what occurred. My hearing is not as good as it was. But I distinctly think I heard a small boy call after me, 'Yah, who's a Crippen?' It—it conveyed the impression to me that he was of the opinion that I had—had killed my dear wife."

Miss Marple, gently snipping off a dead rose head, said, "That was the impression he meant to convey, no doubt."

"But what could possibly have put such an idea into a child's head?"

Miss Marple coughed. "Listening, no doubt, to the opinions of his elders."

"You—you really mean that other people think that, also?"

"Quite half the people in St. Mary Mead."

"But—my dear lady—what can possibly have given rise to such an idea? I was sincerely attached to my wife. She did not, alas, take to living in the country as much as I had hoped she would do, but perfect agreement on every subject is an impossible idea. I assure you I feel her loss very keenly."

"Probably. But if you will excuse my saying so, you don't sound as though you do."

Mr. Spenlow drew his meagre frame up to its full height. "My dear lady, many years ago I read of a certain Chinese philosopher who, when his dearly loved wife was taken from him, continued calmly to beat a gong in the street—a customary Chinese pastime, I presume—exactly as usual. The people of the city were much impressed by his fortitude."

"But," said Miss Marple, "the people of St. Mary Mead react rather differently. Chinese philosophy does not appeal to them."

"But you understand?"

Miss Marple nodded. "My Uncle Henry," she explained, "was a man of unusual self-control. His motto was 'Never display emotion.' He, too, was very fond of flowers."

"I was thinking," said Mr. Spenlow with something like eagerness, "that I might, perhaps, have a pergola on the west side of the cottage. Pink roses and, perhaps, wisteria. And there is a white starry flower, whose name for the moment escapes me—"

In the tone in which she spoke to her grandnephew, aged three, Miss Marple said, "I have a very nice catalogue here, with pictures. Perhaps you would like to look through it—I have to go up to the village."

Leaving Mr. Spenlow sitting happily in the garden with his catalogue, Miss Marple went up to her room, hastily rolled up a dress in a piece of brown paper, and, leaving the house, walked briskly up to the post office. Miss Politt, the dressmaker, lived in the rooms over the post office.

But Miss Marple did not at once go through the door and up the stairs. It was just two thirty, and, a minute late, the Much Benham bus drew up outside the post office door. It was one of the events of the day in St. Mary Mead. The postmistress hurried out with parcels, parcels connected with the shop side of her business, for the post office also dealt in sweets, cheap books, and children's toys.

For some four minutes Miss Marple was alone in the post office.

Not till the postmistress returned to her post did Miss Marple go upstairs and explain to Miss Politt that she wanted her old grey crepe altered and made more fashionable if that were possible. Miss Politt promised to see what she could do.

The chief constable was rather astonished when Miss Marple's name was brought to him. She came in with many apologies. "So sorry—so very sorry to disturb you. You are so busy, I know, but then you have always been so very kind, Colonel Melchett, and I felt I would rather come to you instead of Inspector Slack. For one thing, you know, I should hate Constable Palk to get into any trouble. Strictly speaking, I suppose he shouldn't have touched anything at all."

Colonel Melchett was slightly bewildered. He said, "Palk? That's the St. Mary Mead constable, isn't it? What has he been doing?"

"He picked up a pin, you know. It was in his tunic. And it occurred to me at the time that it was quite probable he had actually picked it up in Mrs. Spenlow's house."

"Quite, quite. But after all, you know, what's a pin? Matter of fact he did pick the pin up just by Mrs. Spenlow's body. Came and told Slack about it yesterday—you put him up to that, I gather? Oughtn't to have touched anything, of course, but as I said, what's a pin? It was only a common pin. Sort of thing any woman might use."

"Oh, no, Colonel Melchett, that's where you're wrong. To a man's eye, perhaps, it looked like an ordinary pin, but it wasn't. It was a special pin, a very thin pin, the kind you buy by the box, the kind used mostly by dressmakers."

Melchett stared at her, a faint light of comprehension breaking in on him. Miss Marple nodded her head several times, eagerly.

"Yes, of course. It seems to me so obvious. She was in her kimono because she was going to try on her new dress, and she went into the front room, and Miss Politt just said something about measurements and put the tape measure round her neck—and then all she'd have to do was to cross it and pull—quite easy, so I've heard. And then, of course, she'd go outside and pull the door to and stand there knocking as though she'd just arrived. But the pin shows she'd *already been in the house.*"

"And it was Miss Politt who telephoned to Spenlow?"

"Yes. From the post office at two thirty—just when the bus comes and the post office would be empty."

Colonel Melchett said, "But my dear Miss Marple, why? In heaven's name, why? You can't have a murder without a motive."

"Well, I think, you know, Colonel Melchett, from all I've heard, that the crime dates from a long time back. It reminds me, you know, of my two cousins, Antony and Gordon. Whatever Antony did always went right for him, and with poor Gordon it was just the other way about. Race horses went lame, and stocks went down, and property depreciated. As I see it, the two women were in it together."

"In what?"

"The robbery. Long ago. Very valuable emeralds, so I've heard. The lady's maid and the tweeny. Because one thing hasn't been explained—how, when the tweeny married the gardener, did they have enough money to set up a flower shop?

"The answer is, it was her share of the—the swag, I think is the right expression. Everything she did turned out well. Money made money. But the other one, the lady's maid, must have been unlucky. She came down to being just a village dressmaker. Then they met again. Quite all right at first, I expect, until Mr. Ted Gerard came on the scene.

"Mrs. Spenlow, you see, was already suffering from conscience, and was inclined to be emotionally religious. This young man no doubt urged her to 'face up' and to 'come clean' and I daresay she was strung up to do it. But Miss Politt didn't see it that way. All she saw was that she might go to prison for a robbery she had committed years ago. So she made up her mind to put a stop to it all. I'm afraid, you know, that she was always rather a wicked woman. I don't believe she'd have turned a hair if that nice, stupid Mr. Spenlow had been hanged."

Colonel Melchett said slowly, "We can—er—verify your theory—up to a point. The identity of the Politt woman with the lady's maid at the Abercrombies', but—"

Miss Marple reassured him. "It will be all quite easy. She's the kind of woman who will break down at once when she's taxed with the truth. And then, you see, I've got her tape measure. I—er—abstracted it yesterday when I was trying on. When she misses it and thinks the police have got it—well, she's quite an ignorant woman and she'll think it will prove the case against her in some way."

She smiled at him encouragingly. "You'll have no trouble, I can assure you." It was the tone in which his favourite aunt had once assured him that he could not fail to pass his entrance examination into Sandhurst.

And he had passed.

THE FIVE-DOLLAR DRESS

Mary Higgins Clark

Mary Higgins Clark is a bestselling American author of suspense novels, short stories and historical fiction. Each of her fifty-one books has been a bestseller in the United States and across Europe. Five of her novels, including *Where Are the Children?*, have been filmed for television.

It was a late August afternoon, and the sun was sending slanting shadows across Union Square in Manhattan. *It's a peculiar kind of day*, Jenny thought as she came up from the subway and turned east. This was the last day she needed to go to the apartment of her grandmother, who had died three weeks ago.

She had already cleaned out most of the apartment. The furniture and all of Gran's household goods, as well as her clothing, would be picked up at five o'clock by the diocese charity.

Her mother and father were both pediatricians in San Francisco and had intensely busy schedules. Having just passed the bar exam after graduating from Stanford Law School, Jenny was free to do the job. Next week, she would be starting as a deputy district attorney in San Francisco.

At First Avenue, she looked up while waiting for the light to change. She could see the windows of her grandmother's apartment on the fourth floor of 415 East Fourteenth Street. Gran had been one of the first tenants to move there in 1949. *She and my grandfather moved to New Jersey when Mom was five*, Jennie thought, *but she moved back after my grandfather died*. That was twenty years ago.

Filled with memories of the grandmother she had adored, Jenny didn't notice when the light turned green. *It's almost as though I'm seeing her in the window, watching for me the way she did when I'd visit her*, she reminisced. An impatient pedestrian brushed against her shoulder as he walked around her, and she realized the light was turning green again. She crossed the street and walked the short distance to the entrance of Gran's building. There, with increasingly reluctant steps, she entered the security code, opened the door, walked to the elevator, got in, and pushed the button.

On the fourth floor, she got off the elevator and slowly walked down the corridor to her grandmother's apartment. Tears came to her eyes as she thought of the countless times her grandmother had been waiting with the door open after having seen her cross the street. Swallowing the lump in her throat, Jenny turned the key in the lock and opened the door. She reminded herself that, at eighty-six, Gran had been ready to go. She had said that twenty years was a long time without her grandfather, and she wanted to be with him.

And she had started to drift into dementia, talking about someone named Sarah . . . how Barney didn't kill her . . . Vincent did . . . that someday she'd prove it.

If there's anything Gran wouldn't have wanted to live with, it's dementia, Jenny thought. Taking a deep breath, she looked around the room. The boxes she had packed were clustered together. The bookshelves were bare. The tabletops were empty. Yesterday she had wrapped and packed the Royal Doulton figurines that her grandmother had loved, and the framed family pictures that would be sent to California.

She only had one job left. It was to go through her grandmother's hope chest to see if there was anything else to keep.

The hope chest was special. She started to walk down the hallway to the small bedroom that Gran had turned into a den. Even though she had a sweater on, she felt chilled. She wondered if all apartments or homes felt like this after the person who had lived in them was gone.

Entering the room, she sat on the convertible couch that had been her bed there ever since she was eleven years old. That was the first time she had been allowed to fly alone from California and spend a month of the summer with her grandmother.

Jenny remembered how her grandmother used to open the chest and always take out a present for her whenever she was visiting. But she had never allowed her granddaughter to rummage through it. "There are some things I don't want to share, Jenny," she had said. "Maybe someday I'll let you look at them. Or maybe I'll get rid of them. I don't know yet."

I wonder if Gran ever did get rid of whatever it was that was so secret? Jenny asked herself.

The hope chest now served as a coffee table in the den.

She sat on the couch, took a deep breath, and lifted the lid. She soon realized that most of the hope chest was filled with heavy blankets and quilts, the kind that had long since been replaced by lighter comforters.

Why did Gran keep all this stuff? Jenny wondered. Struggling to take the blankets out, she then stacked them into a discard pile on the floor. *Maybe someone can use them,* she decided. *They do look warm.*

Next were three linen tablecloth and napkin sets, the kind her grandmother had always joked about. "Almost nobody bothers with linen tablecloths and napkins anymore, unless it's Thanksgiving or Christmas," she had said. "It's a wash-and-dry world."

When I get married, Gran, I'll use them in your memory on Thanksgiving and Christmas and special occasions, Jenny promised.

She was almost to the bottom of the trunk. A wedding album with a white leather cover, inscribed with *Our Wedding Day* in gold lettering, was the next item. Jenny opened it. The pictures were in black and white. The first one was of her grandmother in her wedding gown arriving at the church. Jennie gasped. *Gran showed this to me years ago, but I never realized how much I would grow to look like her.* They had the same high cheekbones, the same dark hair, the same features. *It's like looking in a mirror,* she thought.

She remembered that when Gran had shown her the album, she'd pointed out the people in it. "That was your father's best friend . . . That was my maid of honor, your great-aunt . . . And doesn't your grandfather look handsome? You were only five when he died, so of course you have no memory of him."

I do have some vague memories of him, Jenny thought. *He would hug me and give me a big kiss and then recite a couple lines of a poem about someone named Jenny. I'll have to look it up someday.*

There was a loose photograph after the last bound picture in the album. It was of her grandmother and another young woman wearing identical cocktail dresses. *Oh, how lovely,* Jenny thought. The dresses had a graceful boat neckline, long sleeves, a narrow waist, and a bouffant ankle-length skirt.

Prettier than anything on the market today, she thought.

She turned over the picture and read the typed note attached to it:

Sarah wore this dress in the fashion show at Klein's only hours before she was murdered in it. I'm wearing the other one. It was a backup in case the original became damaged. The designer, Vincent Cole, called it "The Five-Dollar Dress," because that's what they were going to charge for it. He said he would lose money on it, but that dress would make his name. It made a big hit at the show, and the buyer ordered thirty, but Cole wouldn't sell any after Sarah was found in it. He wanted me to return the sample he had given me, but I refused. I think the reason he wanted to get rid of the dress was because Sarah was wearing it when he killed her. If only there was some proof. I had suspected she was dating him on the sly.

Her hand shaking, Jenny put the picture back inside the album. In her delirium the day before she died, Gran had said those names: Sarah . . . Vincent . . . Barney . . . Or had it just been delirium?

A large manila envelope, its bright yellow color faded with time, was next. Opening it, she found it filled with three separate files of crumbling news clippings. *There's no place to read these here,* Jenny thought. With the manila envelope tucked under her arm, she walked into the dining area and settled at the table. Careful not to tear the clippings, she began to slide them from the envelope. Looking at the date on the top clipping of the three sets, she realized they had been filed chronologically.

"Murder in Union Square" was the first headline she read. It was dated June 8, 1949. The story followed:

The body of twenty-three-year-old Sarah Kimberley was found in the doorway of S. Klein Department Store on Union Square this morning. She had been stabbed in the back by person or persons unknown sometime during the hours of midnight and five a.m. . . .

Why did Gran keep all these clippings? Jenny asked herself. *Why didn't she ever tell me about it, especially when she knew I was planning to go into criminal law? I know she must not have talked with Mom about it. Mom would have told me.*

She spread out the other clippings on the table. In sequence by date, they told of the murder investigation from the beginning. In the late afternoon, Sarah Kimberley had been modeling the dress she was wearing when her body was found.

The autopsy revealed that Sarah was six weeks pregnant when she died.

Up-and-coming designer Vincent Cole had been questioned for hours. He was known to have been seeing Sarah on the side. But his fiancée, Nona Banks, an heiress to the Banks department store fortune, swore they had been together in her apartment all night.

What did my grandmother do with the dress she had? Jenny wondered. *She said it was the prettiest dress she ever owned.*

Jenny's computer was on the table, and she decided to see what she could find out about Vincent Cole. What she discovered shocked her. Vincent Cole had changed his name to Vincenzia and was now a famous designer. *He's up there with Oscar de la Renta and Carolina Herrera,* she thought.

The next pile of clippings was about the arrest of Barney Dodd, a twenty-six-year-old man who liked to sit for hours in Union Square Park. Borderline mentally disabled, he lived at the YMCA and worked at a funeral home. One of his jobs was dressing the bodies of the deceased and placing them in the casket. At noon and after work he would head straight to the park, carrying a paper bag with his lunch or dinner. As Jenny read the accounts, it became clear why he had come under suspicion. The body of Sarah Kimberley had been laid out as though she was in a coffin. Her hands had been clasped. Her hair was in place, the wide collar of the dress carefully arranged.

According to the accounts, Barney was known to try to strike up a conversation if a pretty young woman was sitting near him. *That's not proof of anything,* Jenny thought. She realized that she was thinking like the deputy district attorney she would soon become.

The last clipping was a two-page article from the *Daily News*. It was called "Did Justice Triumph?" It was about "The Case of the Five-Dollar Dress," as the writer dubbed it. At a glance, she could see that long excerpts from the trial were included in the article.

Barney Dobbs had confessed. He signed a statement saying that he had been in Union Square at about midnight the night of the murder. It was chilly, so the park was deserted. He saw Sarah walking across Fourteenth Street. He followed her, and then, when she wouldn't kiss him, he killed her. He carried her body to the front door of Klein's and left it there. But he arranged it so that it looked nice, the way he did in the funeral parlor. He threw away the knife as well as the clothes he was wearing that night.

Too pat, Jenny thought scornfully. *It sounds to me like whoever got that confession was trying to cover every base. Talk about a rush to justice.* Barney certainly didn't get Sarah pregnant. Who was the father of the baby? Who was Sarah with that night? Why was she alone at midnight (or later) in Union Square?

It was obvious the judge also thought there was something fishy about the confession. He entered a plea of not guilty for Barney and assigned a public defender to his case.

Jenny read the accounts of the trial with increasing contempt. It seemed to her that although the public defender had done his best to defend Barney, he was obviously inexperienced. *He should* never *have put Barney on the stand,* she thought. The man kept contradicting himself. He admitted that he had confessed to killing Sarah, but only because he was hungry and the officers who were talking to him had promised him a ham and cheese sandwich and a Hershey bar if he would sign something.

That was good, she thought. *That should have made an impression on the jurors.*

Not enough of an impression, she decided as she continued reading. *Not compared to the district attorney trying the case.*

He had shown Barney a picture of Sarah's body taken at the scene of the crime. "Do you recognize this woman?"

"Yes. I used to see her sometimes in the park when she was having her lunch or walking home after work."

"Did you ever talk to her?"

"She didn't like to talk to me. But her friend was so nice. She was pretty, too. Her name was Catherine."

My grandmother, Jenny thought.

"Did you see Sarah Kimberley the night of the murder?"

"Was that the night I saw her lying in front of Klein's? Her hands were folded, but they weren't folded nice like they are in the picture. So I fixed them."

His attorney should have called a recess, should have told the judge that his client was obviously confused! Jenny raged.

But the defense lawyer had allowed the district attorney to continue the line of questioning, hammering at Barney. "You arranged her body?"

"No. Somebody else did. I only changed her hands."

There were only two defense witnesses. The first was the matron at the YMCA where Barney lived. "He'd never hurt a fly," she said. "If he tried to talk to someone and they didn't respond to him, he never approached them again. I certainly never saw him carry a knife. He doesn't have many changes of clothes. I know all of them, and nothing's missing."

The other witness was Catherine Reeves. She testified that Barney had never exhibited any animosity toward her friend Sarah Kimberley. "If we happened to be having lunch in the park and Sarah ignored Barney, he just talked to me for a minute or two. He never gave Sarah a second glance."

Barney was found guilty of murder in the first degree and sentenced to life without parole.

Jenny read the final paragraph of the article:

Barney Dodd died at age sixty-eight, having served forty years in prison for the murder of Sarah Kimberley. The case of the so-called Five-Dollar Dress Murder has been debated by experts for years. The identity of the father of Sarah's unborn baby is still unknown. She was wearing the dress she had modeled that day. It was a cocktail dress. Was she having a romantic date with an admirer? Whom did she meet and where did she go that evening?
DID JUSTICE TRIUMPH?

I'd say, absolutely not, Jenny fumed. She looked up and realized that the shadows had lengthened.

At the end, Gran had ranted about Vincent Cole and the five-dollar dress. Was it because he couldn't bear the sight of it? Was he the father of Sarah's unborn child?

He must be in his mid-eighties now, Jenny thought. His first wife, Nona Hartman, was a department store heiress. One of the article clips was about her. In an interview in *Vogue* magazine in 1952, she said she had first suggested that Vincent Cole did not sound exotic enough for a designer, and she urged her husband to upgrade his image by changing his name to Vincenzia. Included was a picture of their over-the-top wedding at her grandfather's estate in Newport. It had taken place on August 10, 1949, a few weeks after Sarah was murdered.

The marriage lasted only two years. The complaint had been adultery.

I wonder . . . Jenny thought. She turned back to the computer. The file on Vincent Cole—Vincenzia—was still open. She began searching through the links until she found what she was looking for. Vincent Cole, then twenty-five years old, had been living two blocks from Union Square when Sarah Kimberley was murdered.

If only they had DNA in those days. Sarah lived on Avenue C, just a few blocks away. If she had been in his apartment that night and told him she was pregnant, he easily could have followed her and killed her. Cole probably knew about Barney, a character around Union Square. Could Vincent Cole have arranged the body to throw suspicion on Barney? Maybe he saw him sitting in the park that night?

We'll never know, Jenny thought. *But it's obvious that Gran was sure he was guilty.*

She got up from the chair and realized that she had been sitting for a long time. Her back felt cramped, and all she wanted to do was get out of the apartment and take a long walk.

The charity pick-up truck should be here in fifteen minutes. Let's be done with it, she thought, and went back into the den. Two boxes were left to open. The one with the Klein label was the first she investigated. Wrapped in blue tissue was the five-dollar dress she had seen in the picture.

She shook it out and held it up. *This must be the dress Gran talked about a couple years ago. I had bought a cocktail dress in this color. Gran told me that it reminded her of a dress she had when she was young. She said Grandpa didn't like to see her wearing it.* "A girl I worked with was wearing one like it when she had an accident," she'd said, "and he thought it was bad luck."

The other box held a man's dark blue three-button suit. Why did it look familiar? She flipped open the wedding album. *I'm pretty sure that's what my grandfather wore at the wedding*, she thought. *No wonder Gran kept it. She could never talk about him without crying.* She thought about what her grandmother's old friends had told her at the wake: "Your grandfather was the handsomest man you'd ever want to see. While he was going to law school at night, he worked as a salesman at Klein's during the day. All the girls in the store were after him. But once he met your mother, it was love at first sight. We were all jealous of her."

Jenny smiled at the memory and began to go through the pockets of the suit, in case anything had been left in them. There was nothing in the trousers. She slipped her fingers through the pockets of the jacket. The pocket under the left sleeve was empty, but it seemed as though she could feel something under the smooth satin lining.

Maybe it has one of those secret inner pockets, she thought. *I had a suit with a hidden pocket like that.*

She was right. The slit to the inner pocket was almost indiscernible, but it was there.

She reached in and pulled out a folded sheet of paper. Opening it, she read the contents.

It was addressed to Miss Sarah Kimberley.

It was a medical report stating that the test had confirmed she was six weeks pregnant.

LOST BOY

Alice Clark-Platts

Alice Clark-Platts is a former human rights lawyer who used to work for the UK government. Her first novel, *Warchild*, was published in 2013 and shortlisted for the Impress Prize. In 2015 she created D.I. Erica Martin in *Bitter Fruits*. Clark-Platts lives in Singapore.

This summer is as bleaching hot as any that I can remember. The new tutor on campus says this can't possibly be true because of the La Nina effect which *categorically* is lowering global temperatures and that, by the way, bleaching isn't an adjective. I ignore him. I don't think I've looked at him in the five weeks since we've been here. He might have pierced his nose, dyed his hair, become a woman, and I wouldn't know.

The summer is bleaching hot and anyone who says it isn't or that bleaching isn't the right word hasn't stood on a clay court under the tiny shade that only the brim of a baseball cap can bring whilst Barnes hits yellow balls at you for four hours straight. After a while I can't see his features, he just becomes a thin white line at the other end of the court, a shouting, writhing pencil dick, banging balls like bullets at me over the net.

After coding with the tutor, I go down to the pool to swim laps. I love that pool. It dissolves the bleach, the sun coming off my skin like a sheath disintegrating in the chlorine. Off comes the clay and the dirt and the sweat until underwater, I can only see white patches where the sun has failed to reach, below my sock and short lines.

Barnes lets me swim three times a week. He tried to stop me at first, explaining the anaerobic dividends that are exponentially reached by HIIT sessions *vis a vis* the benefits of swimming laps. I ignored him too. I'm learning that passivity in the face of aggression has remarkably successful results *vis a vis,* for example, crying.

On about my tenth length, I spy Devon's trainers at the edge of the pool, his shape wobbling above the water in the heat. I come to the surface, breathing out water through my nose and resting my arms on the side. He squats down and I lift up my goggles. He's holding a Magnum ice cream in one hand and a cold drop of vanilla makes its way onto the mosaic tiles by my cheek.

"Twenty quid, Sharky," he says, opening his mouth to take a bite.

I look at him, droplets running down my face.

"That's how much your dad paid Fat Lard. You asked me to find out."

He says this as if I don't remember. Three nights ago, sneaking out of the training camp grounds, climbing the gates behind the fifth hole on the golf course. Sitting in the bunker drinking cherry brandy nicked from Fierro's, the tiny supermarket on campus. Devon's face was freckled with stars and I kept on drinking until there were three of him and god knows how many of me. Flexing my knuckles, watching the skin on my hands puckering up and then flattening. I'd asked him to find out because I knew Barnes had given the chubby kid something and I wanted to know how much.

"Not much," I concede, wiping my eyes with a wet hand.

"Enough for Fat Lard. Kid ran right to Fierro's and bought a kilo of sugar." Devon sighs and stands up, shaking out the pins and needles, considering the ice cream before bending his head to it again. "What was it for?"

I look at him.

"The money, Sharky. What did your dad give it to Fat Lard for?"

I snap my goggles on into place and duck my shoulders under, deep into the cool, blue water. "Came up to me before the semi-final."

"Fat Lard did?"

I nod. "Came up to me and said I was going to lose. And when I did – coz they'd decided to only take one of us to the Open – well, then it would be you that went not me." I lean back a little, let the water swill over my ear lobes, rush into my ears, muffling out my voice and Devon's reply. I come to the surface again, shaking the water off.

"But you did win. And that's bullshit – what he said – because they're taking us both," Devon is saying. "So who won doesn't matter, in the scheme of things."

In the scheme of things. I let that one slide. I've played against Devon forever, and he knows as well as I do that winning is what the scheming is all about. Without the winning, there is no scheme.

Devon ignores my silence. "And, fuck. Who cares about Fat Lard saying that? It's what we do anyway." He looks puzzled, saying it again as if to try and work it out. "It's what we do."

And I know he thinks he's right, at first. The notes we put in each other's rooms, in our trainers, in our change bags. Cheap insults, playground stuff. Saying that your mum's a good shag, that I'm the bollocks, you're a loser, you couldn't outrun a fucking blind and deaf quadriplegic. But that's different, I think. Those notes are almost love letters. Devon should understand that as much as I do. They're grist to the Lost Boys' mill. They feed the fires, keep us tight, stream-lined; untouchable.

"But your dad . . ." Devon goes on, as if he's catching up with me as I'm thinking. "He's not . . . that, is he? Coming from him, it's like he's betting against you, trying to make you . . . *lose*." He gives a sort of pained look at that, as if even the *word* lose should be obliterated from his vocabulary.

I give him a bit of a smile then before I flip and jettison myself back into stride, stroking through the water hard and fast. Devon's not a traitorous dick like Fat Lard because he knows. He understands what it is to be us, all of us Lost Boys batting balls to each other, faster and faster: gladiators stomping, muscled and gleaming in the ring, our fathers watching like emperors from the stalls.

Now Devon gets it, that it's not the same. Barnes paying a kid to slam me, right before I go on court, it's not the same as the locker room notes. Because the dude's supposed to be my dad. He's supposed to be gunning for me, buoying me up.

But then, I should never have asked Devon to do anything for me. When it comes to it, he wants to suck me dry as much as Barnes does. If I'm out, he's in, whatever he's just said, however many boys they take to the Open. It's just that, on that night, on the golf course when it was soft and quiet, I felt, just for a second, that we were the same. That maybe, underneath it all, we were actually friends. And I wanted to know how much it was worth, is all. How much fucking with me meant, in cash terms, to my dad.

And it turns out, not that much. Barnes had paid that fat kid pretty much nothing to taunt me, make me angry. Twenty quid was all it took to make me feel shit enough that I would go out onto that court fierce and raging, and win.

The next month, I'm in the hospital.

Barnes is sitting by my bed and he sort of pats me on the shoulder as I try and sit up. "Relax," he says. "Just lie still."

"What happened?"

"You collapsed. On court."

Immediately I'm searching his face, looking for pockets of anger, hard marks under his eyes, across his cheeks. Thoughts flood in, high waves of consummate failure. And memories of the usual heat out on court, but also a different kind this time. Something burning up my insides like acid.

"They don't know if it was food poisoning or what. Some kind of poison though," Barnes looks away from me, out of the window, which is when I know for sure he's mad. "We had to concede the match on your behalf. That was yesterday," he says. "Wednesday. When you're better," he waves his hand over my bed sheets like a magician's reveal, "they'll be sending you home. You're out."

I shut my eyes. The cramping in my stomach, in my lower back, is nothing to the way he's staring out of the window. The blank way he's talking, as if he's reading disconnected words out loud from a newspaper column.

"I'm sorry," I say, because I can't think of anything else to do.

Barnes nods, turns down his mouth. "Seven months," he says, and I know he means the seven months of training, of qualifying to get here to Milan, to the Open, to the possibility of an end of year ranking.

"I'm sorry," I say again, as the sun shifts lower through the blinds in the sudden silence, as Barnes keeps breathing softly by my bed until at last, it's dark, and he leaves.

The next day, as I wake up from a nap, there's a Polizia de Stato standing alongside my bed. He's polished and navy and gold with buttons and a blue-black sheen skimming his hair and eyes.

He asks me when it was I first felt sick and I tell him, a few hours before I went out on court. And did I leave my kit bag unattended, he asks? Yes, I say, everyone does, you leave it in the locker room with all the other boys' bags. Drinks bottle too, he clarifies? Although he calls it a *bottiglia d'aqua* but I know what he means. Yes, I say, even my water bottle.

Barnes appears then, standing in the doorway and I wonder at him and at this policeman. Why would the police be concerned with food poisoning?

The Polizia shrugs in a clownish way. "Maybe," he says, his eyebrows waggling above his impressive nose. "Maybe it's not poisoning by the food? Forse . . .?"

Perhaps . . . he means. Perhaps what?

"What else could it have been?" I shift my gaze to Barnes who leans heavily against the door, his arms folded over his chest. He hasn't shaved and his lips are dry, like he's been biting the skin off them.

"We think it may have been deliberate," he says. "To get you off the tour. Make you sick on purpose. So you couldn't play."

I blink at him as a stomach cramp passes through me. I move my head to a cool patch on the pillow. "Who?" I say. "Who would . . .?"

The Polizia flattens his palms in my direction. "No, no. Non sappiamo nulla ora . . ." *We don't know anything at the moment.*

"They're just investigating Finn," and Barnes' hands are tight around the edges of the door jamb, the muscles in his shoulders pulling under his polo shirt. "We just want to find out what's been going on."

"What did you eat, *mangia? Ieri*, Senor Finn? *Anche* . . . uh, before that day?"

I can say it without thinking. Bran cereal for breakfast, chicken pasta for lunch, protein shake as an afternoon snack, tuna salad for dinner. Every day, without fail. "Athlete's diet. Bring it," I say, a smirk on my lips but I don't look at Barnes as I do. I don't think the Polizia understands sarcasm. I'm not sure he's getting most of what I'm saying to be honest.

"Was Devon in the locker room before the match?" Barnes asks, his voice cutting across my thoughts.

Now I look at him. "Of course he was." I almost want to laugh. "He was getting ready like me."

For a second, I think Barnes is going to heave into the room and smack me across the face. But he stays where he is, bites his lip and says nothing, his eyes like a Taser on me.

The Polizia shrugs again. "So . . ." he says with a kind smile. "Ci siamo."

"No," Barnes nearly spits, jerking forward. "No, we are not *there*, or any-where. Not until we find out how Finn got sick like this. We need to know, subito!"

The Polizia frowns. "Alora," he says sadly. He moves his gaze between me and my father with a small shake of his head, but also – I see it, and it makes the back of my neck prickle with defeat – the empathy for a father's ambition for his son. "I hope you are better soon *ragazzo*." He goes then and I'm not sure if I'm relieved or desperate that he's gone.

In a few days, once I'm off the drip, they move me back to the hotel. I can still hear the thwump, thwump of the yellow balls outside my window so I ask to be moved to another room, round to the front of the hotel where I can only hear the swish of Range Rovers and the BMWs coming up the drive, the muffled Italian greetings of the bell boys.

JP, the Grade A events director, comes to see me. He stands at the end of my bed as if afraid to get any closer. He talks to my calves, can't meet my eyes.

I don't want to judge, but I'm guessing JP isn't a natural nurse. The man is as freaked out by physical disability as I am by eating squid. Don't ask me, I don't know why, but it's true. He calls himself Uncle JP but we all know the rumours about him driving someone you'll know, a very famous, yet pissed-up player to rehab, only he went via the Birmingham Indoor Arena for a quick one-two against McEnroe for an exhibition match. The man is a slave to cash. And god forbid there's even a whiff of a mental breakdown. JP would rather talk to Bin Laden than deal with someone in tears.

"Leptospirosis," he says with a not so hidden revulsion. "You've had Weil's disease, Finn." He checks a look at Barnes who's also there, sitting wide-legged in the Regency chair by the window. There's a nice breeze coming in, it moves my hair across my forehead a little and I try to concentrate on that.

JP takes a step forward, his eyes moving up to my knees. For some reason, this makes them itch and I have to physically stop myself from scratching them under his gaze. "Thing is," he says. "We don't want this coming off badly for the hotel, for the Open. I mean," he shoots a disbelieving laugh in Barnes' direction. "What's the line going to be? The host of the Italian Open is putting rat urine in its Diet Cokes?" He snorts, his eyes closing momentarily.

Barnes' chewed-up lips tighten.

"I mean," JP continues, "do you think you *might* have got it from eating something here?"

From his tone, I know that I'm supposed to answer in the negative. I shrug from my prone position lying on top of the duvet. I hedge a glance at Barnes but he doesn't meet my eyes.

JP sighs and rubs his hand over his face. His jowls sag down like some kind of dog. I can't think of the breed but, you know the one, with the long jowls and the sad expression. Anyway, he looks defeated and, despite myself, I feel like I want to make him feel better.

"I'm sure it wasn't anything I had here, JP," I say.

He brightens at this. "Really? That's good, that's good," he says. "I mean, I think that's *right*. Right? This hotel is *pristine,* for pity's sake. *Pristine.*" He manages to look at me then, until he takes in my sallow complexion, the dark circles under my eyes, and shifts his weight, desperately searching for another, *healthier,* focal point.

"If it's not the hotel food," Barnes says, and I don't like his tone. It's got something in it which isn't pleasant. "Then what was it?"

"Well, exactly," JP answers eagerly, as if he didn't really hear the question, as if he's still clinging on to us all being on the same page. "What exactly could it be?"

"CCTV," Barnes says. "There'll be CCTV in the locker rooms. We can see who went in and out. The police can analyse it. Work out the timings. See the fucker who did this."

JP's face cringes at the swear word at the same time as my stomach contracts. The cramp passes but not before Barnes has noticed me stiffen and clench. It doesn't make him soften. In fact, it makes him frown, as if a thought's just occurred to him.

And something in me knows I'm not going to like what he's thinking.

*

Then Devon asks to see me. And when he comes to my room, he's sweating. Not from the court or the gym, but from being anxious is my guess. He's got a look on his face like he might cry at any second and his hands won't stay still, those hands which spin his racket back and forth in front of the net like a conductor's baton. They're clammy – I can tell just by looking – and jumpy as a bean.

I'm right.

"The fucking *police* came to see me today," he says in an awed, taut kind of whisper. "They're saying something about cameras in the locker room, that it'd be better for me to tell them before they trawl through hours of tape. I mean," he pushes his blonde hair back from his face, "tell them *what*?" He shakes his head. "They didn't want to let me up here. I had to fucking *beg*. What am I going to do, right? Put a pillow over your fucking face?" He checks a glance to the door. "Barnes is outside. Fucking gorilla. Standing there like he's guarding fucking Beyonce or someone."

He breaks off, suddenly noticing me lying on the bed it seems. "Hey, man. I mean, are you alright? I couldn't believe it when they called it. They had to carry you off the court. It's bloody rough for you. I mean, don't get me wrong," his thoughts shift a gear again, back to the flat road of despair. "But what's it got to do with me? I've got to focus. I've got Santoro tomorrow. Quarters."

"Congrats," I say. And I mean it.

"Yeah, well. But this is *fucked up*. My dad's going nuclear. I mean," he stops and takes a breath, eyeballs me good and straight. "You know I didn't have anything to do with it, right? Where would I even get the stuff? I wouldn't have a clue. And why would I anyway?" He splutters a half-laugh. "I mean, I can fucking beat you, Sharky, right? I don't need to fucking poison you."

I watch him, perspiring at the end of my bed. I remember that night, out on the golf course, the brandy and the cigarettes. How I asked him for a favour. So unlike me, to ask anyone for anything. I think of Barnes outside the door. And JP and the Polizia. And I close my eyes. I don't want to look at him anymore.

"I think you'd better leave," I say.

At the press conference, they're in my face. Lepto-this, Weil's disease that. How did it get in the drinks bottle? Was it when I'd left my bag unattended? What is the Open's position on free access to the junior tour locker rooms? Where would anyone get this kind of poison? And why would anyone do this anyway?

Their faces are arched and disbelieving. Was it really poison or did the kid just get sick? Can the kid just not handle the pressure?

"Finn Barnes is an exceptional player," JP says. His hairline alone brings gravitas to the situation. "If he had been able to play, we are in little doubt that he would have ranked high enough to qualify for the professional circuit next year. As it is . . ." He ducks his head, looking sad again.

Barnes cuts in, his anger tight inside him like rope right before it frays and snaps. "He'll be on the back foot going forward, unfortunately. But he'll train. He'll win at Osaka and then in Florida and he'll get through. Despite this . . . setback." His mouth curls down as he says this, his eyes staring forward, bright blue and ice-cold.

I say nothing, chewing gum under the brim of my cap. I look at the fading tan line on my wrist where my watch used to be. They took it off in the hospital and I haven't put it back on. I don't really want to know what the time is. It's not necessary for me.

"Well, if it *was* poison," some woman with a face like a rabbit asks incredulously from the middle of the pack. "Is it possible that Finn ingested it at the Hotel Trebbiano?"

"No, no," JP splutters, his ears turning beetroot red under the lights the television crews are pointing at him. "I'm not sure Finn even ate in the hotel, did you, Finn?" He doesn't wait for me to answer, ploughs on . . . "The police are investigating the footage from cameras in the locker rooms . . ."

I drown him out thinking, who puts cameras in locker rooms anyway? Fucking pervs. I hope those tapes got wiped. I hope they don't get to see who put that stuff in my aqua. Stuff I couldn't taste because of those rank energy gels I have to mix in with it. I hope those tapes got erased and we can just forget this thing ever happened.

I hope, I hope, I think to myself, running my thumb up and down where my watch used to be as the journos scream and shout and JP flusters and Barnes just sits there with his arms folded like fucking Buddha.

I hear Devon leave the next morning. He's crying as he walks down one of the long hotel corridors that smell like flowers or perfume or something. I hear him as he goes past my room. It sounds like he's sniffling and I can imagine him with his arm across his eyes. He won't want to be seen crying like a girl. His dad will be right next to him, sturdy and filled up with bacon from breakfast, his Saucony tracksuit jacket just too tight for his frame.

Trial by media. That's what JP called it, Barnes tells me. Like it was something beyond JP's control, like it isn't what JP wanted – have the blame pitched onto Devon rather than any whiff of wrong doing by the hotel.

The Polizia decided not to press charges. Barnes told me they watched the CCTV footage, all nine hours of it before anything good happens. They saw Devon and me come into the locker room, put our bags on the bench. We talk to each other, they said. They could see it. Then I stretch my arms up high above my head and leave the locker room. Devon is left there alone. He sits down for a bit, then gets something out of his bag. Barnes says it's grainy, the footage, but you can see him stand up and come up to where my stuff is. He leans down, his back to the camera. He's tall, Devon, so you can't see much as he bends over, but he clearly opens up my kit bag and puts something in it. Has a good rummage around. You can't tell what it is. But it's something.

Barnes says that, on that basis, the police didn't have enough to charge Devon. And in light of the competition between us, the fact we were about to play each other, and the common knowledge that we disliked each other, it was their view that he was, in some way, to blame for my illness. This was relayed to JP who made so many allusions to it in his statement to the press that he may as well have had a banner with the words DEVON GILLESPIE IS A POISONER written on it and flown across the length and breadth of Italy.

Trial by media indeed.

When Barnes said that though – about it being common knowledge that Devon and I disliked each other – I didn't say anything. I could have done, I suppose. I could have told him about how it was in Spain at the training camp. About how, often, I felt that Devon was the only one who really got it, got me. And that when I saw him out front, leaving the hotel, passing his racket bag across to the porter like he was Atlas shifting the sky for all eternity, I nearly cried hot tears of injustice and pain.

I *nearly* cried. But I didn't.

And I didn't tell him anything.

Barnes is talking about going back to Spain now. It's been a week since I left the hospital and we should start to think about Osaka, he says. It's in five months which he says is plenty of time to rehabilitate, get strong and get back out there. Then, my feet swell up like piggy-pink water balloons and the docs say I've had a relapse. I have to stay in bed longer and the hotel gets antsy, now the tournament is over. JP comes again to my room and has a hushed conversation with Barnes in the corridor except it's not so hushed because Barnes ends up punching the wall.

They won't let me fly because of the *gonfiore alle estremita*, the swelling in my extremities. Barnes scoffs at this. "Italians don't fucking swim for three hours after lunch because they're scared of getting cramps," he says. But anyway, our insurance won't kick in unless we have medical permission to fly, and now we've missed the tour flights. JP and his crew have gone, off on their gleaming jets into that periwinkle sky, onto the next red and dusty court.

So Barnes and I move into a small *albergo* on the outskirts of Milan. In a room with twin beds where my feet are constantly raised and iced, and Barnes gives me paracetamol every four hours. It's not the Trebbiano, but it's not too bad.

One night a few weeks later, Barnes lifts me up and carries me down to the tiny piazza outside our *albergo*. The jaundice is pretty bad now, I get a few stares from the passing Italians. *Bella figura*, they call it. The *passagiato* in the early evening when they put on their nice clothes and stroll around, taking in the dusky air. My yellow face and me, we don't really fit in but it's okay. It's nice in fact. Sitting here, watching it all go by. It's June already, so it's still hot. But not bleaching hot. It's a peachy, caramel sort of a heat, the kind that creeps back warm in your stomach after you've eaten a gelato.

We sit out there, Barnes and me. I don't have much appetite anymore, but he has a Hawaiian pizza while I have the soup. We sit not saying much which I think makes a change from all the razz of the tour and the training camps but then I realise, we never really spoke to each other then either. Just about tennis and yellow balls and red and dusty courts.

Barnes tops up my glass of water and leans back in his chair as the ultraviolet light of a mosquito zapper sparks suddenly above him. He studies me for a while and then reaches into his pocket. Slides a piece of paper across the table to me. I look back at him for a moment before picking up the paper and reading what's on it. And a chill streaks through me that turns my mouth dry and my eyes have to hide from Barnes' stare like they haven't done in a while since we've been at the *albergo*. Thoughts tumble through my brain like freaking dwarves on acid and I can't make head nor tail of what I'm supposed to think. Because the paper has this message on it:

Hey fuckwit. You chump. You can bang your balls as much you bang your mother but I've got this in the bag lolz . . .

"Ironic, isn't it?" Barnes says. "Him talking about it being *in the bag*."

That's when I snap my head up to look at him, to meet his stare like I'm unafraid.

I can't do it yet, though. I can't speak yet.

"Thing is," Barnes says, picking up his bottle of beer and taking a swig. "The thing is, is the disappointment." He waves his hand across the table. "Not in missing out on the ranking. Not that. But when you got sick, I knew. I knew immediately what you'd done. You think I'm a fucking idiot? I mean . . . Jesus. I thought to myself, well alright then. Boy's got some fucking balls." He points at me suddenly, sharp and contained. "Devon would have beaten you, you know? I'd seen him at practice the day before. He was on his game. And, I thought, well good, let's ramp it up a little. Let's give him something to worry about, a little frisson with the Polizia de Stato."

He's got a nasty smile on him now, Barnes. He's talking like he's not going to stop until this evening's ironed out all the creases. I shift my bad foot on the chair it's resting on and take a sip of water.

"And it worked, right? Devon puts one of his shitty little notes in your bag but everyone thinks he doped your water. Devon gets shipped out, JP was happy, everyone was happy and we could have gone back to Spain and got ready for Osaka. Job done. But then," he says, leaning forward on his elbows, moving his beer around with his thick fingers on the white table cloth. "You went and had a fucking relapse."

A couple walk past us. He's got his arm around the girl's shoulders, dangling past her neck like he's so comfortable with her. And my stomach is so sick all of a sudden, my soup congealed and covered in a gloopy skin in my bowl.

"And I didn't understand, I didn't get it," Barnes says. "Because you were cured, right? The hospital had flushed you out, made you new. Got that shit out your veins, your organs. So how could you relapse? It didn't make sense." He shakes his head, balancing the beer on its bottom edge, teetering it across the table towards me. "And then I realised that there was only one explanation. Only one way in which this whole little holiday we're having in Milan could have been engineered. And it wasn't Devon. It wasn't the hotel not washing its cups properly. Nah uh," he gives a sad sort of smile, placing the beer carefully upright again and meeting my eyes. "It was you."

I try to breathe in so he won't notice. Try to steady the thumping in my chest, the throbbing in my foot. Like all predators, Barnes works best when he can smell fear.

"You poisoned yourself," he says. "But you didn't do it to fit up Devon, to get your main threat in the competition disbarred. You did it," and his face is contorted now, crunched up in absolute bewilderment, "so that you could stop playing." He shakes his head again as the church clock in the piazza begins to toll. It makes him have to raise his voice a little to speak over it. "You've got some frigging little vial of something, somewhere and you're keeping yourself doped up; giving yourself relapses, giving yourself fucking *jaundice!* Just so you won't have to play? I mean . . ." Barnes scrapes his chair back, his hands tight against the edge of the table, his jaw rigid.

A waiter comes up then, tops up our water glasses, assessing Barnes with a considered look. "Va bene?" he asks.

Barnes swallows, dipping his eyes. "Sure."

The waiter retreats and Barnes eyeballs me. "You're going to give me that fucking thing and we're going to throw it down the toilet. You understand? You're killing yourself, Finn. You're sick. Look at you," and he stares at me. And, for once, his face is filled with so much concern, it makes my heart stop.

He leans into me, puts his hand on mine. "I *love* you, Finn. Don't you get it? I don't want you to be sick. You've got to stop this." He takes in a deep breath. "Get it? It ends now."

And I nod. Relief warm as the evening air washes over me, as the church bells chime and the couple reach the fountain, sit down and trail their hands in its waters. I nod again and smile at Barnes, at my Dad.

He lifts his chin and pulls his chair back, tucks his knees under the table, gives me a fleeting smile. Brings the beer bottle to his lips again and takes a good long pull. "Alright then," he says.

We sit there again, in a soft and tranquil silence, watching the *passagiato*, listening to the final calls of the birds wheeling above the city. And the waiter brings the bill and Barnes pays it and then lifts me up into his arms to carry me back inside.

"And the tennis," he says, as he pushes the door open with his back, into the light of the foyer where the Virgin Mary stands in an alcove, watching me with her big eyes as we move past. "I'll talk to JP. We'll work it out. Get you fit. This year was too soon. You're too young. We'll give it some time. A year maybe. Then get back to Spain. Or maybe Switzerland?" He looks at me, bright and burning with ambition. "It's cooler there, right? Better climate and the mountains . . . you'll love the mountains, Finn. Practice playing in altitude. Get you tight and ready. Back on the circuit. Back on it in no time."

The moon is high and white and easy through the window. Barnes is curled into his normal rigid ball of dreamless sleep, I listen to his hard, strong breaths as he powers through sleep like everything else in his life.

He made me flush the vials away. All the ones hidden in the secret pocket of my bag. The internet is a great thing, really. All that coding in Spain with the tutor taught me a lot about getting onto some very interesting sites. After we were back in our room, I showed Barnes the ones in that pocket. They were nearly all I had.

I think about my mother for a moment, watching the moon moving gently across the sky. Think about who she was and why she left. Why, when she held me as a baby, she didn't want to stay. And I think about how that must have made Barnes feel, left all by himself with his son. How could he prove to her that they were good enough? That she had made a terrible mistake?

I watch him clenched there, fixed under his sheet like some freaking kind of ancient statue, never moving, never yielding. And I think about Devon and how

I'm sorry he got fucked by it all. But, I always said it, he understood everything just as well as me, if not more. We're just the players, the Lost Boys. We have no say. We just bat our balls and skid across these surfaces as if they are ice and we are man-made rockets of fire.

Then I pour what I have left, and it's enough, into my glass and drink it down and watch the moon some more.

FROM AN OLD GENTLEMAN'S DIARY

Caroline Clive

Caroline Clive (1801–1872) wrote under the pseudonym 'V' and was a regular contributor to Victorian periodicals. In 1855 she shocked readers with *Paul Ferroll*, a psychological thriller about a man who murders his wife. A serial, a play, and other works about Paul Ferroll followed.

April 27th, 18—. — At church, two pews behind me, there has sat ever since January a family that has caught my fancy. The girl's sweet voice in singing first attracted me, and made me turn half round after the psalm was over to look at her over my spectacles. This I continue to do on most similar occasions, but she does not seem ever to notice me; yet I am become as familiar with her face and those of the family as with any of my own acquaintance. She is sixteen perhaps; hardly so much; and is dressed as a child, with a broad flapping hat; and in cold weather wears a warm dark jacket buttoned up to her throat. It is a sweet childish face, grave as becomes the place, and attentive to what she is doing.

May 4th.—The mother sits at the head of the pew; a soberly splendid matron. There is a pretty little girl, with wavy hair combed down over her back; a young delicate boy; and the father, who often comes later than the rest. The service is but moderately performed in this church. I have been about to leave it for years, and I should have done so now had it not been for this child. As it is I may as well stay another week or two. Except such an occasional motive there is no reason why I should stay or go; therefore, finding a motive, however slight, I stay. Old age has brought indifference with it. I seem to myself to be sitting in the waiting-room of a great house till the carriage shall come up which is to take me away. I watch many arrive and many depart; and simply wait till my turn comes. Comparing this life with the one which I hoped and expected to lead—comparing what I am with what I thought to be, my heart sinks sometimes: however, I have all the more leisure to observe the little incidents which happen to other people. These neighbours at church interest me. I don't want to know their names nor their dwelling; I should not care to be told their history. I like better to argue out what must have happened to them, from what I see does happen. The boy is absent now; gone to school I suppose. He is a frail-looking little fellow, very unlike his companion, the youngest girl, who is perhaps a year younger than he, and fat and rosy as she can be.

May 18th.—Week after week I see the same people doing the same thing. I am always early in church and know the sound of their pew door opening. I am aware that a servant is laying their books on the desk shelf before they come in, and glancing round as the congregation rises, I can see the eldest girl's lilac ribbons and her broad hat hiding the upper half of her face. I catch sight of the mother's feathers soberly ornamenting the edge of her bonnet; and at times can see the little one, who is hidden by her low stature, except when she finds opportunity to rise on a hassock and examine all the objects before and behind. The mother's eye is upon her, and her whisper or the motion of her hand brings back the wandering Christian.

June 2nd.—It is but seldom during the service that I let myself take note of these neighbours of mine. The chief times are, first, when all the congregation rises to begin the service; next, when the psalm-singing is over; and lastly, when we are all going out of church. I see that the little girl appeals to the elder as to a sure succour. I caught sight of her to-day in a puzzle about her ribbons. I could see her head turned appealingly to the elder, the little hat all on one side; the older head bent itself towards her with a gentle shake, as much as to say, 'Keep quiet till the prayer is over.' And as soon as all rose from their knees, the appeal was attended to, the impatient young one was released from whatever it was that vexed her; and it seemed to me, as soon as the elder sister interfered, the other was quite satisfied and confident of being put at her ease. In leaving the church the young one seizes the hand of the elder girl, and is inclined to move her feet more hastily than the progress of the congregation down the aisle permits: her sister keeps her back, but it is all in kindness and good-humour, for they go out of church hand-in-hand.

Monday June 23rd.—The pew is empty. They are all gone, I suppose, for the summer; for two Sundays have passed without them. It is time for me to go, London is very hot, and nobody wants me at their dinners and drums, though they ask me, and I go. But I often think, why do I go? It is weary work, as Lord Bacon says, 'to do the same thing so oft over and over.'

July 14th.—The pew-opener gets less and less work every Sunday. Nearly everybody has left London I should think; yet I am still here. To-day the heat in church was excessive; every window was open, yet not a breath of air. There was a sense of the presence of human beings mixed with an oppressive consciousness of pomatum and Cologne water. I will be at Caswell Bay next Sunday.

July 21st.—Next week I will certainly be there, but last week Saturday came before I had sent my Rubens to the cleaner, so I was obliged to wait another week.

July 28th.—I did not go last week, for I was not ready. I might have hurried and made myself ready, but why should I? If I was easier dawdling, why should I not dawdle? I have nothing to do. I will stay the whole summer if I don't feel inclined to go.

August 4th.—A fat old woman sat to-day in my neighbours' pew—their housekeeper I should think; for she wore, I believe, the very lilac ribbons which I saw all the spring on the broad hat of the young girl: a legacy no doubt when they left London, and gave away the odds and ends of the season. It is my habit of turning round after the psalm which made me see the old woman. If she comes again I shall leave town.

August 11*th.*—The same lilac ribbons this morning at church. I have told Sedley to pack my portmanteau.

February 10*th,* 18—, brought all the—how shall I call them?—to church. Now I am easy. I have been kept a long time waiting for them. I don't know, nor wish to know, their name, but they want some designation. John Morris asked me in the gallery at Dresden what was the date of the great painter Unbekannt. I will call them the Unbekannts. The eldest girl is altered. She is older; her dress is silk of a very small pattern, not exactly like those which the grown-up young ladies wear neither. She has a bonnet instead of a hat, and wears a veil over her face. Perhaps it is the first lace veil she has ever had, and she is unconsciously desirous of letting it be seen. But there is just the same serious attentive air, just the same clear subdued voice singing; and the little one is in the same place between her and her mother. The boy was there to-day; and though the day was fine, had a cloak over his shoulders. He is pretty, but frail; poor mother!

February 17*th.*—The Unbekannts I judge to be people accustomed to good society, by their quiet but careful dress; by their shape, height, and manner of moving; all which the better people may be without, but which reveal good society when present. They are loving people, anxious a little about these nice young creatures. The father holds the little weak hand of the boy, the small girl is taken by the mother, but if possible she clings also to her elder sister; they go without hurry, without delay, with no grain of affectation; and when fairly out of the doors, the mother takes her husband's arm, and they all walk briskly away, daintily over the crossing, down the next street, and then round the corner, and disappear from me till another Sunday.

March 17*th.*—It is the end of Lent, and all the Unbekannts are gone. Gone into the country for Easter, I suppose—a bad practice, for it disturbs the course in which things are moving. When I look round, I see instead of the sweet earnest face, a blank, or else some uninteresting stranger. I dare say they will do the same at Whitsuntide. How absurd to give way thus to fashion!

April 14*th.*—The second Sunday after Easter; and they reappeared only to-day. They are all together. Why does not the boy go to school? I saw an addition to their party this morning, a bald man with spectacles. I fancy he is a tutor for the boy, whose health probably makes them afraid to send him to school. However, they are not a family who can complain of health, for through all weather they are always in their place on Sundays. They either have no colds or coughs like other children, or do not mind them. Wet or dry I never knew the mother and her girls fail. I know the grey cloaks with hoods which they wear on rainy Sundays, and the fresh high colour which testifies to having come through the rain, best pace, consistent with a lady-like passage along the streets.

April 21*st.*—Because I made that observation on the Unbekannts' health last Sunday, the little one has fallen ill, I believe. At all events she was absent to-day. Let children be as healthy as they will, they must have measles and chicken-pox, I suppose. I missed her busy restless shape; her little air of importance with which she carried her parasol, and that of her mother's too, if she could get it.

April 28*th.*—To-day the mother was not in church. The father came in, following the eldest girl, and holding his boy by the hand. Is the little one ill so as to alarm the mother? It is a fortnight since I saw her here in rosy bloom: it will be a week before I can know anything about her—or them, for I am perfectly ignorant where they live. Perhaps the careful mother has taken the little one into the country or to the sea, and they keep these others separate from the sick one.

May 5th.—Nobody in the Unbekannts' pew. All are gone to join the mother and the sick child very likely.

May 19th.—They were in their pew to-day, all except the little girl, and all in deep mourning. Alas! the little blossom has withered, the fresh strong-blowing flower has been plucked. Its strength and bloom were no warrant that it should live and be. There was the pale boy, but the rosy face was gone. The eldest girl, the only girl now, was beside her mother. I did not hear her voice singing to-day. Once I distinguished a smothered sob; it came from the mother; and glancing round I saw the girl press against her mother's side and look up in her face. There was no other sign of emotion. They moved gently out of church after the service, and walked rather slower than usual down the street and out of my sight. When I got home, I looked for the little old copy of Hogg's poems, in the green and gold paper binding. I laid my hand on that, but I could not find the poem I wanted. It ends

> A jewel's wanting in my crown,
>   That never can come back to me:
> There is a blank at my right hand,
>   Which cannot be made up to me.

June 16th.—The mother does not come always now. Sometimes only the daughter, the young son, and the old tutor,—all in deep mourning still. Nevertheless, I saw the brother and sister go gaily together down the street, this fine warm day: they were laughing, and the boy had a leaping joyous step. I, whenever I see them, think of the one event which clothes them in black; but I must not forget that they are living through all the twenty-four hours of various interests: and their painful subject is but one among their thousand thoughts.

July 7th.—It has been a black summer with the Unknown, and a short one. The pew became vacant the first day of June, and was occupied to-day by some commonplace people, who sing too loud, and disturb the congregation. For my part I cannot attend to what I am doing, and perhaps it will be best to pay the visit I promised to Theodore when he married. He was forty-nine when he married, and that's five years ago. He has made me promise every year since then to visit him.

April 15th, 18—.—I see I wrote *promise* last year when I went out of London. That is a mere phrase. It implies that you do something which your friend has been striving to obtain from you, and which renders him a service. I did Theodore and his wife no service by going to see them. I am not cheerful, nor clever, nor powerful, nor pleasant. They invited me because it is a sort of hospitable habit to say to your old chums, 'You *must* come to see us this summer. Promise.' Then the old chum says to himself, and those who will hear him, 'I must go to the so and so's when I leave London. They made me promise.' And ten to one, when you get there, they want your room, or they want to be alone; and, if honest with themselves, say, 'Actually old Bob has taken what we said out of civility for truth.' It struck me so at Edensmore, though it might not be. I came back in November. It has been a foggy winter in London. Yesterday, though it is now in the middle of April, the streets were lost at the end furthest from you in yellow fog. The houses across the square were invisible. The church was lighted with gas, otherwise reading would have been impossible. The Unbekannts were in their pew; all in high colours, though the little one died not yet a year ago.

April 22nd.—The young girl has, I think, made the great step from a child to the ranks of the come-out. She has undergone a change of apparel. What it is I can hardly say, but it suits that hypothesis. This brilliant day there were rosebuds outside and inside of her bonnet; there was a lilac silk gown, intersected with lines of black velvet, and a cobweb kind of lace cloak over her low shoulders. I suppose she has her head full of the balls she goes to, and of those she misses; the matches made by her friends, and which she envies; the fine things she ought to do, and the fine phrases she ought to use. However, I did not perceive that she had changed her grave and earnest simplicity; and when they walked home I saw she took her brother's arm, and elastically tripped behind her father and mother, listening to him with gay replies. That boy is grown, and is wider too than he was.

May 19th.—At least the dissipation of the season does not keep her from church on a Sunday; but to be sure no balls are given on Saturdays, so she can go early to bed that night at least.

June 2nd.—This morning, when the congregation was going out of church, I observed a young man standing up in his pew after the other occupants had left it, who waited till the Unbekannts had passed, making them a very obvious salutation as they did so, and then following them closely. He said a few words to the young girl. A dancing acquaintance, I suppose. A great, good-looking fellow; he can dance doubtless.

June 23rd.—The intimacy of the young man and the Unbekannt family makes great progress. I can see how it advances week by week in the frank way the elders meet him, and in the increased shyness of the girl.

July 1st.—To-day it so happened that I turned my head just as the young Unbekannt was in the momentary act of turning hers. She gave one hurried glance at the place where this young man usually sits. He was not there. I hope they have quarrelled.

July 22nd.—Three Sundays and no stranger youth; but never again have I caught the pretty girl's head turned that way. There is no interest in common between them; and whether he is present or absent makes no difference to her. But, on the other hand, may not an understanding have arisen, which does not want these chance meetings?

July 29th.—I fear it is so. There was the stranger at church to-day, and in the Unknown's pew. He stood beside the young girl, and they read from one hymn-book. They walked out side by side. The father and mother were first. Ah! I see. It must be so.

August 5th.—To-day the pew was full—so full of women friends that the son and that young man found seats elsewhere. Relations perhaps, come to be present at the marriage. A carriage was waiting at the door, into which the young man handed the oldest of the ladies, who was not indeed very old, but weak and unlike my splendid Unbekannt. The lovely daughter got in with her. It was her future mother-in-law, very likely.

Here is certainly a gathering for the wedding. How shall I know? It would be easy enough to ask the clerk. I could hear the name, the fact, the day, from him. He is in the church every Wednesday and Friday.

August 12th.—On Wednesday I put off asking till Friday. On Friday, just after the usual prayer-time, I looked into the church, and found the clerk, as I expected, shutting pew-doors and straightening the benches in the aisle. 'Any weddings this week?' I asked. 'A vast many,' said he. 'The second pew behind you, sir, was married yesterday.' Yes, that was it, I did not want to know more.

August 19th.—Of all the family number that were in the pew last Sunday, there was only one, the solitary mother, to-day. The mother was alone, and the farewells of the past week must have been bitter to her; but though the solitude must have gone to her heart, she showed no outward sign; she went through her duties simply as usual; there was no sign that she thought of herself, and she walked out and home alone, or rather worse than alone, followed by her servant only. Where are they all gone, and she remains behind? 'O thou Adam, what hast thou done?' Surely it is a part of thy transgression that the bonds of familiar affection and first friendship must be rent asunder by the progress of life, and that hearts suffer so habitually as to acquiesce quietly in their sufferings. They were all one when I saw them first. Now the youngest member is turned again to the dust. The girl of eighteen years of hope, care, devoted love is gone to another home, which she loves in the place of the old one. The son is away taking root for himself in the world. The father is carried off by one or other of those new interests, and for the time leaves his home-companion as solitary even as I, the old, lonely, uninterested man, whose pleasures, great and small, pass away one after the other. I won't stay in this church any longer. I'll get a pew in St. George's Church from next Sunday forward.

LUCKY DIP

Liza Cody

Liza Cody created Anna Lee, the first female private eye in British crime fiction. Cody has written a trilogy featuring professional wrestler Eva Wyle. Many of her novels and short stories, including *Backhand*, *Bucket Nut*, and *Lady Bag*, are set in London, UK, where she was raised.

He was sitting against a bit of broken wall, looking almost normal. I could see him because of the full moon. It was a lovely moon with wispy clouds like old lady's hair across its face.

I watched the man for a couple of minutes, but he didn't move. Well, he wouldn't, would he? I could see he didn't belong—he was far too well dressed—and I wondered how he got there. This is not a part of the city men dressed like him go.

He had not been dead long. You could tell that at a glance because he still had his shoes on. If you die here you won't keep your shoes for ten minutes. You won't keep your wallet for ten seconds, dead or alive.

With this in mind I had a quick look, right and left, for anyone lurking in the shadows. If I'd seen anyone bigger than me, I'd have stayed where I was. Moon shadows are blacker than hearses, and I knew I wasn't the only one out that night. But in the Trenches only the big are bold, and someone big would have been rummaging in the remains already. So I hopped out from behind my pile of rubble and made a run for it.

I reached him in no time at all and grabbed his left lapel. Seven out of ten men are right-handed, and the chances are seven to three anything valuable will be in a left-hand inside pocket. I took a swift dip and came up with the winnings.

By now I could hear stirrings—a snap of rotten wood, a slide of brick dust. I flicked his watch off his wrist and almost in the same motion made a dive into his jacket pocket. Then I got on my toes and legged it.

I legged it out of the Trenches completely, because, although there are plenty of places to hide, the people I wanted to hide from know them as well as I do. The Trenches are useful as long as it's only the law you want to avoid. Robbing a corpse isn't nice, and I didn't want to take all that trouble only to be robbed myself.

It was just a quick jog to the High Street. On the way I stopped under a street lamp to look at what I had in my hand. The wallet was fat snakeskin, the watch was heavy gold, and the loose change was all pound coins and fifty-pence pieces. For once in my short life I'd struck oil.

All the same you don't break old habits for the sake of one lucky dip, and when I saw all those plump taxpayers doing their late Christmas shopping on the High Street, I stuck out my hand as usual.

"Got any spare change, please?" I said, as always. "For a cup of tea. For a bed for the night. For a hot meal."

And as always they coughed up like princes or told me to get myself a job. It was nice that night. I perform best when there's no pressure, and by the time I'd worked my way down to the station, I'd made a nice little pile. But it doesn't do to loll around and count your takings in public, so I jumped a tube to Paddington.

My sister has this room in Paddington. She lives in Camberwell with her boyfriend, so this room's just for business. I don't trust my sister's boyfriend, but I do trust my sister, up to a point, which was why I went to her business address. You may meet all sorts of funny blokes there, but you won't meet her boyfriend, and that suits me. It suits him, too, if you want to know the truth: he doesn't like me any more than I like him.

When we first came down to the city, Dawn and me, we relied on each other; we didn't have anyone else to turn to. But after she took up with him and he set her up in business, she didn't need me like she used to, and we drifted apart.

The trouble with Dawn is she always needs a man. She says she doesn't feel real without one. Feeling real is important to Dawn so I suppose I shouldn't criticize. But her men have been nothing but a disappointment. You could say I'm lucky to have an older sister like Dawn: she's an example to me. I'd rather die than turn out like her.

Still, she is my sister, and we've been through a lot together. Especially in this last year when we came down to the city together. And before that, when our mum kicked us out, or rather, kicked Dawn out because of the baby. And after that when Dawn's boyfriend kicked Dawn out because of the baby.

I have never been hungrier than I was last year trying to look after Dawn. She lost the baby in the end, which was a bit of a relief to me. I don't know how we would have managed if she'd had it. I don't think she would have coped very well either. It's much harder to get a man when you've got a little baby to look after.

Anyway, that's all in the past, and now Dawn has business premises in Paddington.

I waited outside until I was sure she was alone, and then I went up and knocked on the door.

"Crystal!" she said when she opened the door. "What you doing here? You got to be more careful—I might've had company."

"Well, you haven't," I said. And she let me in, wrinkling her nose and pulling her kimono tight. I don't like that kimono—it's all hot and slippery. Since she got her hair streaked, Dawn has taken to wearing colors that would look all right on a tree in autumn but turn her hard and brassy.

"Gawd," she said, "you don't half look clatty. Can't you get your hair cut? That coat looks like it's got rats living in it."

I took the coat off, but she didn't like the one underneath either.

"What a pong," she said.

"I had a wash last week," I told her. "But I would like to use your bathroom." I wanted somewhere private to look at what I'd got off the dead man.

"You can't stop around here," she said, worried. "I got someone coming in half an hour." She looked at her watch.

I sat in her bathroom and looked at the dead man's watch. It had *Cartier* written on the face, and it really was proper gold. Quality, I thought, and felt a bit sad. By rights a man with a watch like that shouldn't end up in the Trenches without a stitch on. Because that's how he'd be by now, pale and naked in the moonlight. Nobody would recognize him without his coat and suit and shoes. He'd just look like anyone. We're into recycling in the Trenches.

To cheer myself up I looked at his wallet, and when I counted up I found I had 743 pounds and 89 pence. And I couldn't use half of it.

Imagine me trying to change a fifty-pound note! There's a chance in a million a cat with cream on his whiskers milked a cow, but that's good odds compared to the chance I'd come by a fifty-quid note honestly. I couldn't even pop the watch. One look at a watch like that and any honest pawnbroker would turn me in. A dishonest one would rip me off quick as a wink. Either way the watch was no good for me.

I borrowed my sister's toothbrush and had a fast swipe with her deodorant before I joined her again. You never know when you're going to find clean water next so it pays to make use of what there is.

"Do me a favor, Crystal," she said, when she saw me. "Bugger off before you frighten the horses."

"Brought you a Christmas present," I said and handed her the watch.

"You're barmy, Crystal." She stared at the watch like it was a spider in her bed. "Who'd you nick this off?"

"I never," I told her. "I found it." And it was true because the feller was dead. It wasn't as if it was his property because there wasn't a him anymore for it to belong to. When you're dead you're gone. And that's final. Dead men don't own watches.

Even with a Christmas present, Dawn wouldn't let me stop for the night. It's a funny thing, if I hadn't had 743 pounds, 89 pence in my pocket, I wouldn't have wanted to. If it had just been the 89 pence, I'd've been quite happy sleeping out.

But having things is dangerous. Having things makes you a mark. It's like being pretty. If you don't believe me, look at Dawn. She's pretty and she's been a mark from the time she was eleven. Being pretty brought her nothing but trouble. She's always had to have someone to protect her. I'm glad I'm not pretty.

There's a hospital down the Harrow Road so I went there. I couldn't decide what to do, so I sat in Casualty till they chucked me out. It's a pity there aren't more places you can go and sit in at night to have a quiet think. It's hard to think on the hoof, and if you are cold or hungry, thinking is not on your mind at all.

It seemed to me, after a while, that the best place to go was where I slept last night. Some might say it was a daft idea to go back to a place that was rousted, but I thought if the police had been there last night, it would be deserted tonight.

Twenty-seven Alma-Tadema Road is a condemned house. They say it's unsafe. There are holes in the roof and holes in the floors, but it is perfectly safe if you are sober, tread carefully, and don't light fires. That was what went wrong last night: we had a couple of winos in, and one of them got cold just before day-break.

When I got there, I saw that they had nailed more boards across the front door and downstairs windows. I could get in, but it would take time. There were still people up and about so, to be on the safe side, I would have to come back later if I wanted more than a few minutes' kip.

I walked on past and went down to the Embankment. It is quite a long walk, and by the time I got there I was hungry. Actually, I'm hungry all the time. Dawn says she thinks I must have worms and I probably do, but mostly I think it's just my age. Someone like Bloody Mary does almost as much walking as I do, but she doesn't seem to need half the fuel. She stopped growing years ago.

There are a lot of women like Bloody Mary, but I mention her because she was the one I picked up on the Embankment that night, huffing and puffing along with her basket on wheels.

"Oh, me poor veins," she said, and we walked on together. I slowed down a bit so she could keep up.

"There's a stall open by the Arches," she said. "Couldn't half murder a cuppa."

She used to sing in the streets—walk up and down Oxford Street bellowing "Paper Moon" with her hand held out—but after a bad dose of bronchitis last year her voice went.

At the Arches I got us both a cup of tea and a sausage sandwich.

"Come into money, Crys?" Johnny Pavlova asked. It is his stall and he has a right to ask, because now and then when there's no one around to see, he gives me a cup free. As he always says, he's not a charitable institution, but catch him in the right mood and he'll slip you one like the best of them.

All the same it reminded me to be careful.

"Christmas," I said. "They were feeling generous down the High Street."

"Down the High Street?" he said. "You ain't been on that demolition site, have you? I heard they found this stiff bollock-naked there this evening."

"Did they?" I said as if I couldn't care less. "I didn't hear nothing. I was just working the High Street."

I went over and sat with Bloody Mary under the Arches. Johnny Pavlova doesn't like us hanging too close round his stall. He says we put the respectable people off their hot dogs.

"Will you look at that moon," Bloody Mary said, and she pulled her coats tight.

It was higher in the sky now and smaller, but there was still a good light to see by.

"Where you kipping tonight, Crystal?" she asked. I knew what she meant. A moon like that is a freezing moon this time of year.

Just then, Brainy Brian came slithering in beside us so I didn't have to answer. He was coughing his lungs out as usual, and he didn't say anything for a while. I think he's dying. You can't cough like that and live long. He used to go to college in Edinburgh, but then he started taking drugs and he failed all his exams. He did all right down here in the city because to begin with he was very pretty. But druggies don't keep their looks any longer than they keep their promises. Now he's got a face like a violin and ulcers all over his arms and legs.

When he recovered his breath he said. "Share your tea, Crystal?"

We'd already finished ours so we didn't say anything for a while. But Brian was so sorry-looking, in the end I went to get another two, one for him and one for Bloody Mary. While they were sucking it up I slipped away.

"Watch yourself, Crys," Johnny Pavlova said as I went by. He gave me a funny look.

The first thing you do when you break into a house is find another way out. A good house has to have more than one way out because you don't want to go running like the clappers to get out the same door the Law is coming in.

The house on Alma-Tadema Road has a kitchen door through to the garden. I loosened the boards on that before lying down to sleep. I also made sure I had the snakeskin wallet safe.

I had made the right decision: there was no one but me there. A heap of damp ashes marked the spot where the winos had lit their fire, and they blew in little eddies from the draught. Otherwise nothing stirred.

I went over the house collecting all the paper and rags I could find to build myself a nest, then I curled up in it and shut my eyes.

Nighttime is not the best time for me. It's when I can't keep busy and in control of my thoughts that bad memories and dreams burst out of my brain. It's hard to keep cheerful alone in the dark, so I need to be very, very tired before I'll lie down and close my eyes. Sometimes I say things over and over in my head until I get to sleep—things like the words of a song or a poem I learned at school—over and over so there's no spare room in my brain for the bad stuff.

That night I must have been very tired because I only got part of the way through "What's Love Got to Do with It," when I dropped off. Dawn used to play that song all the time when we were still living at home. She played it so often it used to drive me up the wall. But it is songs like that, songs I didn't even know I'd learned the words to, that help me through the night nowadays.

The next thing I knew someone was coughing. I opened my eyes but it was still dark, and there was this cough, cough, cough coming my way. Brainy Brian, I thought, and relaxed a bit. It's something you have to watch out for—people coming up on you when you're alone in the dark.

"It's cold," he said when he found me. "It's hard, hard cold out there." He crawled into my nest. I was quite warm and I didn't want to leave but I knew his coughing would keep me awake.

"Give us a cuddle, Crystal," he said. "I got to get warm."

"Shove off," I said. His hands remind me of a fork. Some people do it to keep warm. Not me. I've seen too much and I want to die innocent.

He started coughing again. Then he said, "You got any dosh, Crystal?"

"Enough for a tea in the morning," I said. I really did not want to go. It was one of my better nests and it didn't seem fair to give it up to Brian.

"They're looking for you," he said. "Someone saw you in the Trenches."

"Not me," I said. "Who saw me?"

"You know that little kid?" he said. "Marvin, I think he's called. Well, they hurt him bad. He said he saw you."

"Who wants to know?" I sat up.

"Lay down," he said, "I got to get warm." He grabbed me and pulled me down, but he didn't start anything so I kept still.

After a while he said, "Johnny Pavlova says you got dosh. They asked him too."

I waited till he finished coughing. Then I said, "Who's asking? The Law?"

"Not them," he said. He knew something, I thought. And then I thought, he talked to Johnny Pavlova, he's talked to Marvin, and Marvin saw me in the Trenches. Maybe Brian talked to whoever is looking for me.

I said, "Did they send you, Brian? Did they send you to find me?"

He doubled over, coughing. Later he said, "You don't understand, Crystal. I got to get some money. I lost my fixings, and I haven't scored for days."

So that was that. I left him and went out the kitchen way. Brian was right—it was hard cold outside. And I was right, too—having things makes you a mark. I dumped the snake-skin wallet in the garden before I climbed over the fence. And then I climbed right back and picked it up again. Dumping the wallet wouldn't stop anyone looking for me. Not having it would be no protection. Marvin didn't have it and he got hurt. I wondered why they picked on Marvin to clobber. Perhaps he got the dead man's shoes, or his coat. Perhaps they saw a little kid in a big thick coat and they recognized the coat.

No one ever looked for me before. There was no one interested. I thought maybe I should run away—somewhere up north, or maybe to the West Country. But when I ran away the first time, it was me and Dawn together. And it was difficult because we didn't know the city. It took us ages to get sorted.

I thought about it walking down the road. The moon had gone and the sky had that dirty look it gets just before day. My nose was runny from the cold and I was hungry, so I went to the Kashmir takeaway. The Kashmir is a good one because it has a bin not twenty paces away. What happens is that when the pubs close a lot of folks want an Indian takeaway, but because they've been drinking they order too much and chuck what's left over in this bin. I've had breakfast there many times. The great thing about a Kashmir breakfast is that although the food is cold by the time you get it, the spices are still hot, and it warms you up no end. From this point of view Indian food is the best in the city.

I felt much more cheerful after breakfast, and I found a lighted shopwindow with a doorway to sit in. It was there I had a proper look at the wallet. Before, at Dawn's business premises, I only counted the money and redistributed it in the pockets of my coats. Now I studied the credit cards, library cards, and business stuff.

These are not things I am normally interested in. I can't use them. But this time, it seemed to me, the only way out of trouble was to give them back. The dead man in the Trenches might be dead but he was still dangerous.

His name was Philip Walker-Jones. He belonged to a diners club, a bridge club, and a chess club. He had two business cards—Data Services Ltd. and Safe Systems Plc. He was managing director twice over, which seemed quite clever because both companies had the same address in Southwark Road. Southwark Road is not far from where I found him. Maybe he walked out of his office and died on the way to the station. But that didn't explain what he was doing in the Trenches. Nobody like him goes in the Trenches.

I thought about Philip Walker-Jones sitting in the moonlight against the broken brickwork. He had looked as if he'd just sat down for a bit of a breather.

But he wasn't resting. He was dead. There wasn't a mark on him that I could see. It didn't look as if anyone had bumped him—he was just sitting there in all his finery. Quite dignified, really.

Little Marvin would have been there watching like I was, and probably a few others too—waiting to see if it was safe to take a dip. We were wrong, weren't we?

I didn't want to go back too close to the Trenches, but if I was going to give the wallet back I had to. It was too early yet for public transport so I started walking. A good breakfast does wonders for the brain, so while I was walking I went on thinking.

I didn't know anything about data and systems except that they sounded like something to do with computers, but I do know that dining, bridge, and chess are all things you do sitting down. Philip Walker-Jones didn't have any cards saying he belonged to a squash club or a swimming club, and if he spent all that time sitting down, maybe he wasn't very fit. If he wasn't very fit, and he started to run suddenly, he could have had a heart attack.

It was a satisfying bit of thinking that took me down to the river without really noticing. Crossing over, it occurred to me that computers, bridge, and chess were things that really brainy people did, and in my experience brainy people all wear glasses and don't run around much. A really brainy man would not go running into the Trenches after dark, unless he was being chased. A scared, unfit man running in the Trenches would have no bother getting a heart attack. Easy.

The wind off the river was sharp and cold, but it wasn't the only thing making me shiver. Because if Philip Walker-Jones had a reason to be scared to death, so did I.

Give the rotten wallet back, I thought, *and do it double quick. Say, "Here's your money, now leave me be." And then do a runner.* I'm good at that.

I stopped for a pint of milk to fuel up. And I went through my pockets to find some of the fifty-pound notes, which I stuffed back in the wallet to make it look better.

I felt quite good. I had made my plan and it was almost as if I didn't have the wallet anymore. It was as good as gone, and by the time I reached Southwark Road I wasn't bothering much about keeping out of sight. It was daylight now and there were other people in the streets, and cars on the roads, and as usual no one seemed to notice me.

All the same, I gave the Trenches a miss. I walked down Southwark Road bold as brass looking at numbers and signs. And when I found one that read *Safe Systems Plc*, I walked right up to the door.

It was a new door in an old building, and it was locked. Perhaps it was too early. Not having a watch myself, I don't keep track of office hours. I stood there wondering if I should hike on to the station where there's a clock and a cup of tea, and just then the door opened from the inside. It gave me such a fright I nearly legged it. But the person opening the door was a young woman, and usually women don't give me much trouble. This one had red rims to her eyes and a really mournful expression on her face. She also had a nasty bruise on her cheekbone that made me think of Little Marvin.

She said, "Where do you think you're going?" She wasn't friendly but she looked as if she had other things on her mind.

"Safe Systems Plc," I said.

"What do you want?" she said. "The office is closed. And haven't you ever heard of a thing called soap and water?"

"I've got something for Safe Systems," I said, and held out the wallet.

"Jesus Christ!" she said and burst into tears.

We stood there like that—me holding the wallet and her staring at it, crying her eyes out.

At last, she said, "I don't want it. Take it away." And she tried to slam the door.

But I stuck my foot in there. "What do I do with it?" I said.

"Lose it," she said, and because I wouldn't let her close the door, she went on, "Look, you silly little cow, don't you come near me with that thing. Drop it in the river—you can give it to Steve for all I care. I'm finished with all that."

She started banging the door on my foot so I hopped back. The door crashed shut and she was gone.

I was so surprised I stood there gawping at the door and I didn't see the big feller coming up behind until he dropped a hand on my shoulder.

"You the one they call Crystal?" he said from a great height.

"Not me," I said. "Never heard of her." I got the wallet back under my top coat without him noticing.

"What you doing at that office then?" he said, not letting go.

"The lady sometimes gives me her spare change," I said, and watched his feet. It's no good watching their eyes. If you want to know what a bloke's going to do, watch his feet. The big man's feet were planted. I did not like him knowing my name.

"What is your name then?" he said.

I nearly said, "Dawn," but I bit it off just in time.

"What?" he said.

"Doreen," I said. "Who's asking?" If he was Steve, I would give him the wallet and run.

"Detective Sergeant Michael Sussex," he said. It was even worse than I thought. Now even the Law knew my name. It made me sweat in spite of the cold.

"I've got a few questions for you," he said, and he tightened his hand on my shoulder.

"I don't know anything," I said. "What about?"

"About where you was last night," he said. "And who you saw."

"I never saw nothing," I said, really nervous.

"Course you didn't," he said. "Come on. I'll buy you breakfast and then we can talk." And he smiled.

Never, never trust the Law when it smiles.

None of this had ever happened to me before. If you must know, I've hardly ever talked to a policeman in my life. I'm much too fast on my feet.

"Where do you live, Crystal?" he said, starting to walk.

"The name's Doreen," I said, and tried to get out from under the big hand.

"Where do you live . . . Doreen?" he said.

The thing you have to know about the Law is that they ask questions and you answer them. You've got to tell them something or they get really upset. It's the same with social workers. If they want an answer, give them an answer, but keep the truth to yourself. I told Detective Sergeant Michael Sussex the address of a hostel in Walworth.

He was walking us in the direction of the Trenches, and I didn't want to go there. So I said, "I've had my breakfast and I ought to go because I've got an appointment with my social worker."

It was a mistake because then he wanted to know who my social worker was and what time I had to be there. Lies breed. It's much better if you don't talk to the Law because then you can keep to the truth.

After a while he said, "Aren't you a bit young to be living on your own . . . Doreen?"

"I'm eighteen," I said. I felt depressed. I hadn't spoken one honest word to the man since he dropped his big hand on my shoulder. Well, you can't, can you? I talked to a social worker once and she tried to put Dawn and me in care. Never again. They would have split us up and then Dawn would never have found herself a man. Say what you like about Dawn's boyfriend, but he did set her up in business, and she does make good money. She feels real. No one can feel real in care.

We were right next to the Trenches by now. For a change it looked completely deserted—no winos, no bonfires, none of us picking through the rubbish dumped there in the night. It's just a big demolition site, really, but since no one is in any hurry to build there, it's become home to all sorts of people.

Detective Sergeant Michael Sussex stopped. He said, "We found a body in there last night."

I said nothing. I couldn't see the bit of wall the dead man had been sitting by, but I knew where it was.

"Yes," he said, as if he was thinking about something else. "Stripped clean, he was. When it comes my turn I'd like to be somewhere no one can get their thieving hands on me."

I was still watching his feet, and now even his boots looked as if they were thinking about something else. So I took off.

I broke clear of his hand. I dodged between two people passing by and hopped over the wire. Then I dropped down into the Trenches.

It was the last place I wanted to be, but it was the only place I could go.

I heard him come down behind me, and as I ran through the rubble I could feel his feet thudding on the ground. He was awfully fast for a big man.

"Stop!" he yelled, and I kept running. This way, that way, over the brickwork, round the rubbish tips, into cellars, up steps. And all the time I could hear his feet and his breath. I couldn't get free of him.

I was getting tired when I saw the drain. I put on one more sprint and dived head first into it. It was the only thing I could think of to do. It was the only place he couldn't come after me.

It was the only place I couldn't get out of.

I know about the drain. I've been in there before to get out of the wind, but it doesn't go anywhere. There is a bend about ten yards from the opening, and after that it's very wet and all stopped up with earth.

Anyway, like it or not, I dived straight in and crawled down. There wasn't much room even for me. I had to get all the way to the bend before I could turn round.

It was totally dark in the drain. There should have been a circle of light at the opening, but Detective Sergeant Michael Sussex had his head and shoulders wedged in it.

He said, "Don't be a fool, Crystal. Come out of there!" His voice boomed.

"Look, I only want a chat," he said. "I'm not going to hurt you."

He wasn't going to hurt me as long as I stayed in the drain and he stayed out of it.

"Come and get me," I said. I would have felt quite cheerful if it hadn't been so dark and wet.

"I don't know what you think you're up to, Crystal," he said. "But you're in a lot of trouble. I can help you."

I nearly laughed. "I don't know any Crystals," I said. "How can you help me?"

"You've got enemies," he said. "The bloke who died had the same enemies. You took something off him and now they're looking for you. They're rough people, Crystal, and you need my help."

"I don't know any dead blokes," I said. "I didn't take anything. What am I supposed to have nicked?"

"You're wasting my time," he said.

"All right," I said. "Then I'll go." There wasn't anywhere to go, but I didn't think he'd know that.

"Wait," he said. "Don't go anywhere till you've heard what I have to say." He fell silent. It was what I always thought. You tell them things. They'd rather eat worms before they tell you something back.

After a bit he said, "You still there?"

"I'm still here," I said. "But not for long. I'm getting wet."

"All right," he said. "You won't understand this but I'll tell you anyway. The dead bloke was a systems analyst."

"What's one of them?" I asked.

"He was a computer expert." Detective Sergeant Michael Sussex sighed. I could hear it from my end of the drain. Sound travels in a drain.

"He wrote programs for computers. He debugged programs. But most of all he wrote safe programs." He sighed again.

"This doesn't mean anything to you," he said. "Why don't you just come out of there like a good girl and give me the number."

"What number?" I said. He was right. I didn't understand. I was very confused. I thought I was in trouble because I'd taken the wallet. I tried to give it back but the woman wouldn't take it. That was confusing. Whoever heard of anyone not taking money when it was offered.

"It doesn't matter what number," he said, sounding angry. "This bloke, this Philip Walker-Jones, he worked for some very funny types. These types don't keep their dealings in books or ledgers anymore. Oh no. They stick them on computer tape, or discs where your average copper won't know how to find them. It's all bleeding high tech now."

He sounded very fed up, and I couldn't tell if it was because I was in a drain out of reach, or because he didn't understand high tech any more than I did.

Just then I heard footsteps, and someone said, "What you doing down there, boss?"

"Taking a bleeding mudbath," Detective Sergeant Michael Sussex said. "What does it look like I'm doing?"

"Did you lose her, then?" the other voice said.

"Course not. This is a new interview technique. Orders from on high: 'Do it in a bleeding land-drain.'" He sounded so down I almost laughed.

"Are you still there?" he said.

"No," I said. "Good-bye." And I scrambled into the bend of the pipe and pulled my knees up to my chest so that I couldn't be seen.

"Shit!" Detective Sergeant Michael Sussex said. "You've scared her off, you bleeding berk."

I could hear him heaving and cursing, and then he said, "You'd better give me a pull out of here, Hibbard."

There was some more heaving and cursing, and then I heard his voice from further off saying, "Where does this bleeding drain come out?"

"Buggered if I know, boss," Hibbard said. "Could be the river for all I know."

"Well, bleeding go and look," Detective Sergeant Michael Sussex said. "And if you find her don't lose her or I'll have you back in uniform quicker than you can say 'crystal balls.'"

"You sure you had the right one?" Hibbard said. He sounded reluctant to go tramping around the Trenches looking for the other end of a drain.

"You saw the description—there can't be two like her."

I didn't like the way he said that, and I didn't like the way he made fun of my name. I was freezing cold and soaked through, but I wasn't going to come out for anyone with that sort of attitude.

So that's where we stayed, him outside in the Trenches and me scrunched up at the end of the drain waiting for him to give up and go away. Sometimes he shone a torch in—to keep himself busy, I suppose. But I stayed stone-still and never made a sound.

Sometimes he paced up and down and muttered foul language to himself. He reminded me of our mum's boyfriend when he thought I'd pinched something off him. We were all at it in those days. He'd pinch things out of our mum's handbag and Dawn and me pinched things off him. We used to hide under the stairs, Dawn and me, while he raged around swearing he'd leather the lights out of us. Sometimes I'd hide from the truant officer too.

I'm used to hiding. All it takes is a bit of patience and a good breakfast in your belly. Don't try it somewhere wet and cold, though—that calls for real talent and I wouldn't recommend it to beginners.

At one stage Hibbard came back. He didn't sound half so cocky now.

"She'll be long gone," he said. "I can't find where this thing comes out."

"It's got to come out somewhere," Detective Sergeant Michael Sussex said. "Use your radio. Get more bodies. Make a bleeding effort."

He stayed where he was, and I stayed where I was.

Another time, Hibbard said, "Why don't we get in the Borough Engineers to dig this whole fucking site up and be done with it?"

And another time Detective Sergeant Michael Sussex said, "Comb the bleeding area. She could've dropped it or stashed it." He was sounding cold and tired too.

"All this for a bleeding number," he said. "And if we don't get it our whole case goes down the bleeding bog. Why couldn't the silly sod pick somewhere else to pop his clogs?"

Hibbard said, "Why are we so sure he had it on him? And why are we so sure she's got it now?"

"We know he had it because he was bringing it to me," Detective Sergeant Michael Sussex said. "And we know she got it because she swiped his wallet. We've got everything else back except that, and unless he had the number tattooed to his bleeding skull under his bleeding hair that's where it is."

"Couldn't he have just had it in his head?" Hibbard said. "Remembered it."

"Twenty-five bleeding digits? Do me a favor. He said it was written down and he said I could have it. You just want to go indoors for your dinner. Well, no one gets any dinner till I get that kid."

So we all sat there without our dinners. Detective Sergeant Michael Sussex made everyone go hungry for nothing. Because I didn't have any number twenty-five digits long.

But it's no use worrying about what you don't have, especially when what really worries you is what you might get. I was worried I might get pneumonia. If you get sick you can't feed yourself. If you can't feed yourself you get weak, and then either the officials grab you and put you in a hospital, or you die. I've seen it happen.

And I'll tell you something else—a very funny thing happened when I got out of the drain. Well, it wasn't a thing, and it didn't really happen. But I thought it did, and it really frightened me.

I became an old woman.

It was when I looked round the bend and couldn't see the circle of light at the end of the drain. I strained my ears and I couldn't hear anything moving out there. And suddenly I thought I'd gone deaf and blind.

I tried to move, but I was so stiff with cold it took me ages to inch my way along to the opening. I didn't care if Detective Sergeant Michael Sussex caught me. In fact I called out to him, and my voice had gone all weak and husky. I wanted him to be there, if you can believe that. I actually wanted him to help me, see, because I thought I'd gone blind, and I was scared.

But he wasn't there, and it was dark and teeming down with rain. And I couldn't straighten up. My back was bent, my knees were bent. There was no strength in my legs. I couldn't have run if they'd set the dogs on me.

I was an old woman out there in the dark—looking at the puddles in the mud, shuffling along, bent over. And I thought about Bloody Mary and the way she is first thing of a morning. There are some of them even older than she is who never have to bend over to look in dustbins because that's the shape they always are.

Of course I come to my senses soon enough. I got my circulation back and I rubbed the stiffness out of my legs. And I knew it was truly dark. I hadn't gone blind. But I did not stop being scared.

Even standing upright I felt helpless. Even with 743 pounds, 89 pence on me.

The Law was after me. The bastards who beat up Little Marvin were after me. And I had nowhere to go. I was sick and old, and I needed help. What I needed, I thought, was a mark of my own.

Once having thought that, I became a little more cheerful. Not a lot, mind, because I hadn't had anything to eat since that curry before daybreak, and being hungry brings on the blues like nothing else can. But I pulled myself together and went looking for my mark.

I didn't know her name, but I knew where to find her. It was up the other end of the northern line. I couldn't have walked it that night, not for love nor money. So I caught the tube to Chalk Farm, and I hung around outside one of those bookshops.

I thought I had her once, but she tightened her grip on her shopping and hurried away. It was a mistake I put down to hunger. Usually I don't go wrong on middle-aged women.

But I saw her at last. She was wearing a fawn-colored raincoat and a tartan scarf. She had a green umbrella and she was struggling with her Christmas shopping.

I said, "Carry your bags for you, missus?"

She hesitated. I knew her. She's the one who has her handbag open before you even ask. She doesn't give you any mouth about finding a job or spending money on drink. She just looks sort of sorry and she watches you when you walk away.

She hesitated, but then she gave me a bag to carry. Not the heaviest one either. She's nice. She wants to trust me. At least she doesn't want to distrust me. I knew her. She was my mark.

She said, "Thank you very much. The car is just round the corner."

I followed her, and stood in the rain while she fumbled with her umbrella and car keys. I put her bag in the boot and helped her with the other one.

She looked at me and hesitated again. Not that she'd dream of going off without giving me something. This one just wants to find a polite way of doing it.

She said, "Well, thanks very much," and she started to fumble in her handbag again. I let her get her money out, and then I said, "I don't want your money, missus, thanks all the same for the thought."

She said, "Oh, but you must let me give you something."

I just stood there shaking my head, looking pitiful.

"What is it?" she asked, with that sorry expression on her face.

It was the crucial time. I said. "I've got some money, missus, but I can't spend it." And I held out one of the fifty-pound notes.

She looked at the money and she looked at me.

I said, "I know what you're thinking. That's why I can't spend it. I want to get some decent clothes because I can't get a job looking like this. But every time I try they look at me like I stole the money and they go to call the Law. No one trusts people like me."

She went on looking first at me and then at the money, and said, "I don't mean to sound suspicious, but where *did* you get a fifty-pound note?"

"A nice lady give it to me," I said. "She must've thought it was a fiver. She was a really nice lady because no one's ever given me a fiver before. But when I went in to buy a cup of tea and some chips, the man went to call the Law and I saw she must have made a mistake."

"I see," she said.

"You don't," I said. "Having this money is worse than not having anything."

"I can see that," she said. "How can I help?"

I had her. "Please, missus," I said. "Please help me spend it. All I want's a good coat and some shoes. There's a charity shop just round the corner and I been hanging around for ages but I can't bring myself to go in on my own."

She was good as gold, my lady mark. She bought me a big wool coat for only a couple of quid and she talked to the women in the shop while I looked for jeans and jerseys.

It was all quality stuff and probably it was all donated to the charity by women like her. They don't give any old rubbish to charity. And I'll tell you something else—my lady mark was having the time of her life. It was like a dream come true to her. Someone really and truly wanted her help with something she approved of. She didn't have to worry I was spending her money on drink or drugs because it wasn't her money and I was there under her nose spending it on warm clothes.

Even the women behind the counter had a sort of glow on them when I came out from behind the racks with my arms full. She'd probably told them my story in whispers when my back was turned. And that was why I really had needed her help. Because those nice ladies behind the counter would have chased me out if I'd gone in on my own. They'd have been afraid I'd pinch their charity.

It was still coming down in buckets when we left the shop. This time it was me carrying all the bags.

I was about to go when she said, "Look, don't be insulted, but what you need is a hot bath and somewhere to change." She said it in a rush as if she really was afraid of hurting my feelings.

"I live up the hill," she said. "It won't take any time at all."

"Nah," I said. "I'll get your car seats all dirty."

"It doesn't matter," she said. "Please."

And I thought, why not? She deserved the satisfaction.

She ran me a hot bath and squirted loads of scented oil in. She gave me her shampoo and a whole heap of clean towels. And then my lovely lady mark left me alone in her bathroom.

I swear she had tears in her eyes when I came out in my new clothes.

"Crystal," she said, "you look like a new person." This was just what I wanted to hear.

"You look quite like my own daughter when she was younger," she said. Which was a good thing because the Law and the bastards who beat Marvin up weren't looking for someone who looked like my lady mark's daughter. And no one would bat an eyelash if she had a fifty-pound note. My lady mark's daughter would not turn into an old woman who had to bend over to root around in dustbins.

And nor, I thought, would I, if I could help it.

She cooked me eggs and potatoes for my tea, and when I left she gave me a fiver and her green umbrella.

It was a shame really to have pinched her soap. But you can't break old habits all at once.

She even wanted to give me another ride in her car. But I wouldn't let her. She was a lovely lady, but I didn't think she'd understand about Dawn. Lovely ladies don't.

I could give lessons about what to do when you find your mark, and the last one would be—don't push your luck. Because if you push your luck and let them take over, they start giving you what they think you need instead of what you want. If my lady mark knew too much about Dawn and what was really going on, she'd have got in touch with the Social Services all over again. And far from being a lovely lady she'd have turned into an interfering old cow.

I was doing her a favor, really. I'm sure she'd rather be a lovely lady than an interfering old cow.

No one who saw me knocking at Dawn's door in Paddington would have known I'd spent all day down a drain. Dawn didn't.

"'Struth, Crystal," she said when she opened up. "You look like one of those girls from that snob school up the hill from ours."

I knew what she meant and I didn't like it much. But I was lucky really. I'd caught her at a slack time when she was just lying around reading her comic and playing records. And now I was all clean and respectable, she didn't mind if I sat on her bed.

"You still need your hair cut," Dawn said.

She got out her scissors and manicure set, and we sat on her bed while she cut my hair and did my nails. Dawn could be a beautician if she wanted. The trouble is she'd never stand for the training and the money wouldn't be enough. She's used to her creature comforts now, is Dawn.

It was a bit like the old days—Dawn and me together listening to records, and her fiddling with my hair. I didn't want to spoil it but I had to ask about the watch.

Because when I was in the lovely lady's bathroom I'd had another search through Philip Walker-Jones's wallet.

Dawn said, "What about the watch?" And she rubbed round my thumb with her little nail file.

"It was real gold," I said, to remind her. "Your Christmas present."

"I can't wear a man's watch," she said. Dawn likes to be very dainty sometimes.

"Where is it?" I said.

"You want it back?" she asked. "Fine Christmas present if you want it back."

I looked at her and she looked at me. Then she said, "Well, Crystal, if you must know, I was going to give it to my boyfriend for Christmas."

"It wasn't for him," I said. "It was for you."

"A man's watch?" she said, and laughed. "I was going to get his name engraved on the back. 'Eternal love, from Dawn.' But there wasn't room. There were all these numbers on the back, and the man at the jewelers said I'd lose too much gold having them rubbed down."

"Hah!" I said. I felt clever. Because all it takes is some good hot food to help you think. And it had come to me in a flash just after I'd put down my last mouthful of egg and potato.

I said, "Bet there were twenty-five of them."

"Loads of numbers," she said. She put the nail file back in her manicure set.

"If you must know, Crystal," she said, "I popped it. And I bought him a real gold cigarette lighter instead."

And she gave me the pawn ticket.

She hadn't got much for a solid gold watch. Dawn isn't practical like I am, so the pawnbroker cheated her. Not that it mattered. It wasn't her watch in the first place, and besides, it would cost me less to get back. If I wanted it back.

Poor Dawn. She needs me to take care of her. She doesn't think she does because she thinks her boyfriend's doing it. She's not like me. She doesn't want to look after herself. That's not her job. And if I told her what I'd been through today to solve my own problems she'd say I was a fool.

But look at it this way—I'd given Detective Sergeant Michael Sussex the slip. I'd dressed up so he wouldn't know me again if I ran slap-bang into him. Nor would Brainy Brian. So he couldn't finger me to the bastards who beat up little Marvin. I'd had a bath and I'd had eggs and potatoes for my tea. I had enough money to sleep in a bed for as many nights as I wanted. And now I had the watch.

Or I could have it any time I wanted. But it was safer where it was. I still didn't know why the number was so important but I was sure it would be worth something to me sooner or later.

I saw Dawn looking at me.

"Don't get too cocky, Crystal," she said. "You might *look* like a girl from the snob school, but you're still just like me."

That's how much she knew.

MURDER WITHOUT A TEXT

Amanda Cross

Amanda Cross (1926–2003) was a crime-writing pseudonym for the American academic Carolyn Gold Heilbrun. One of the foremost feminists of her time, Heilbrun wrote fourteen novels and several short stories featuring the university lecturer Kate Fansler. With academic settings and feminist themes, her fiction has a scholarly flavour.

A t the time of Professor Beatrice Sterling's arraignment, she had never set foot in a criminal court. As a juror, a duty she performed regularly at the close of whatever academic year she was called, she had always asked to serve in the civil division. She felt too far removed from the world of criminals, and, because of her age (and this was true even when she was younger, referring as it did more to the times in which she had been born than to the years she had lived), too distanced from the ambience of the criminal to judge him (it was almost always a him) fairly. She was, in short, a woman of tender conscience and unsullied reputation.

All that was before she was arrested for murder.

Like most middle-class dwellers in Manhattan, therefore, she had never been through the system, never been treated like the felon the DA's office was claiming her to be. It is a sad truth that those engaged in activity they know to be criminal, shoddy business practices, drug dealing, protection rackets, contract killings, have quicker access to the better criminal lawyers. Those unlikely to be accused of anything more serious than jaywalking often know only the lawyer who made their will or, at best, some pleasant member of a legal firm as distant from the defense of felons as from the legal intricacies of medieval England. Beatrice Sterling's lawyer was a partner in a corporate law firm; long married to a woman who had gone to school with Beatrice, he had some time ago agreed to make her will as a favor to his wife. His usual practice dealt with the mergers or takeovers of large companies; he had never even proffered legal advice to someone getting a divorce, let alone accused of murder. There was not even a member of his firm knowledgeable about how the criminal system worked at the lower end of Manhattan, next door though it might have been to where their elegant law firm had its being. The trouble was, until her arraignment, neither Beatrice nor her sister considered any other lawyer. It is always possible that with the best legal advice in the world, Beatrice would still have been remanded, but as it happened, she never had any chance of escaping rides to and from Riker's Island in a bus reinforced with mesh wiring, and incarceration in a cell with other women, mostly drug dealers and prostitutes. By that time Beatrice was alternately numb or seized with such rage against the young woman she was supposed to have murdered that her guilt seemed, even to her unhappy corporate counsel, likely.

Professor Beatrice Sterling was accused of having murdered a college senior, a student in a class Beatrice had been teaching at the time the young woman was found bludgeoned to death in her dormitory room. The young woman had hated Beatrice; Beatrice had hated the young woman and, in fact, every young woman in that particular class. She would gladly, as she had unfortunately mentioned to a few dozen people, have watched every one of her students whipped out of town and tarred and feathered as well. She had, however, insisted that she had not committed murder or even laid a finger on the dead girl. This counted for little against the evidence of the others in the class who claimed, repeatedly and with conviction, that Beatrice had hated them all and was clearly not only vicious but capable of murder. The police carried out a careful investigation, putting their most reliable and experienced homicide detectives on the case. These, a man and a woman, had decided that they had a better than even case against the lady professor, and, since the case might become high profile, got an arrest warrant and went to her apartment to arrest her and bring her into the precinct.

It is possible, even at this stage, to avoid being sent to jail, but not if the charge is murder in the second degree (first degree murder is reserved for those who kill policepersons). Those accused of minor misdemeanors are issued a Desk Appearance Ticket and ordered to appear in court some three or four weeks hence. (Sometimes they do, sometimes they don't, but such a choice was not offered to Beatrice, who would certainly have appeared anytime she was ordered to). She was allowed one phone call, which she made to her sister to ask for a lawyer, a wasted call since the sister, whose name was Cynthia Sterling, had already called the corporate lawyer husband of Beatrice's school friend. Beatrice was told by the woman detective that it could be anywhere from twenty-four to seventy-two hours until her arraignment and that probably no lawyer could get to her until a half hour before that occurred. Men who go through the system are held during this period in pens behind the courtrooms. Since there are, in the Manhattan criminal system, no pens for women, Beatrice was held in a cell in the precinct. The system happened at that time to be more than usually backed up—and it was usually backed up—so she was not taken directly to Central Booking at One Police Plaza, police headquarters for all the boroughs and Central Booking for Manhattan, until two days had passed.

Neither Beatrice nor her sister Cynthia had ever married, and a more unlikely pair to become caught in the criminal system could not easily be imagined. As Beatrice in jail alternated between numbness and rage, weeping and cold anger, Cynthia came slowly, far too slowly as she later accused herself, to the conclusion that what she needed was help from someone who understood the criminal system. Beatrice's school friend's husband was useless: less than useless, because he did not know how little he knew. A knowledgeable lawyer could not now save Beatrice from her present incarceration and all the shame and humiliation connected with it; but he or she might be able to offer some worthwhile, perhaps even practical, advice.

We all know more people than we at first realize. Cynthia could have sworn that she knew no one connected with law enforcement or criminal defense even four times removed. She forced herself to sit quietly, and upright, in a chair, calming herself in the manner she had read of as recommended for those undertaking meditation in order to lower their blood pressure. She sat with her feet flat on the floor, her back straight to allow a direct line from the top of her head to the base of her spine, and in this position she repeated, as she thought she remembered from her reading, a single word. Any one-syllable word, if simple relaxation as opposed to religious experience were the aim, would suffice. She chose, not without some sense of irony, the word "law." Faith in law was what, above all, she needed. Slowly repeating this word with her eyes closed and her breathing regular, she bethought herself, as though the word had floated to her from outer space, of Angela Epstein.

Cynthia, after continuing her slow breathing and word repetition for a few seconds out of gratitude, contemplated the wonders of Angela Epstein. She had come to Cynthia's office only a week or two ago to say hello. Could fate, were there any such thing, have whispered in her ear? Cynthia was the dean in charge of finances at a large, urban college quite different from the elite suburban institution in which Beatrice taught. In that capacity, Cynthia had, in the past, been able to put Angela Epstein in the way of fellowship aid, and Angela, unlike the greater number of her kind, had continued to be grateful. Finding herself in the area of her old college, she had stopped in to greet Cynthia, to thank her for her past help, and to tell Cynthia about her present life. What Angela did—it was something in the investment line—Cynthia could not precisely remember, but a sentence of Angela's echoed, like the voice of a guardian angel in a legend, in Cynthia's postmeditation ears: "I'm living with a wonderful guy; he's a public defender, and he loves what he does. It's great to live with someone who loves what he does, and who does good things for people caught up in New York's criminal system; between us, we can afford a loft in Manhattan."

From Information, Cynthia got the number of Angela Epstein. Here, as it was night, she got a message machine. She left as passionate a request for Angela to call back as she could muster; indeed, passion quivered in every syllable. But if Angela and lover had retired at midnight, they might not return her call until morning, perhaps not until they returned from work the next day. Cynthia decided—rather, she was seized by a determination—to go and visit Angela herself at that very moment. Perhaps she would not get in; perhaps she would be mugged in the attempt. But with Beatrice behind bars, any action seemed better than no action. She pictured herself banging on the door of their loft until allowed entrance and the chance to plead. She dressed hurriedly, descended to the street, commandeered a taxi, and told the driver to take her to the Lower East Side, insisting over his protests that that was indeed where she wanted to go.

"This time of night, you gotta be outta your mind."

It occurred to Cynthia, even in the midst of her distracted determination, that she had not been driven by an old-fashioned cabdriver for a very long time indeed. He was American, old, shaggy, and wonderfully soothing.

"I have to go now," she said. "Please. Take me."

"It's your funeral, literally. I'm telling you. I wouldn't be out on the streets myself this time of night, except it's my nephew's cab; my nephew's having a baby in the hospital with his wife. It takes two to have a baby these days, I mean to have it, not to start it, if you see what I mean. Me, I drive only by day."

"I see," Cynthia said, blessing him for beginning to drive.

"He's working his way through law school, drives a cab at night. These days, in this city, you don't need to be a lawyer, you need to hire one, and a doctor too while you're at it, I tell him. So he's crazy, so you're crazy. You're not buying drugs, I hope?"

Cynthia assured him that she was not. Was meditation like prayer? Was it answered like prayer? First the name had come to her, then this wonderful cabdriver. Could another miracle happen, that they would hear her pounding on the door and let her in and listen to her story?

Another miracle happened, though not quite that way. As she emerged from the taxi, a couple approached her. They looked at her oddly; she was not, it was to be assumed, a usual type to be seen in this neighborhood at this hour. The couple had also emerged from a taxi, even now departing.

"Dean Sterling!" someone shouted. It was Angela Epstein. "What on earth are you doing here?"

"I'm looking for you," Cynthia said, suddenly unbelievably tired, worn out by all the sudden good fortune that had come her way.

"So ya gonna pay me, or ya forgot and left your purse at home?"

Cynthia came to her senses, apologizing to the cabdriver and the astonished young couple. She reached into her purse and gave the cabdriver a large bill. "For you and your nephew and the baby," she said. "You are wonderful."

"You too," he shouted, taking off with a screech of tires. Cynthia had meant to beg him to return, but she merely shrugged. It was Angela Epstein's young man upon whom she now turned her full attention.

"You are a public defender, you understand the criminal system?" she said, as though he might deny it and turn out to be something wholly useless.

"Yes," he said, taking her arm. "Are you in trouble? Why don't we go upstairs and talk about it?" Over her head, for he was a tall young man, he gave Angela a quizzical look; she made soothing gestures and rushed ahead to open the building door, peering about to see that there were no dangerous types lurking.

"I'm afraid I don't even know your name," Cynthia said.

"My name's Leo," he said. "Leo Fansler. What's yours?"

"Cynthia Sterling. My sister Beatrice Sterling is in jail, accused of murder. And I'm afraid they won't even let her out on bail; that seemed to be the only coherent statement I could get out of the lawyer I called. Will you help us?"

"I'll try," Leo Fansler said.

They got her settled on the couch with a cup of tea and a blanket over her legs because the loft was chilly. Besides, they wanted to do all the easy things they could think of to help her. She had always appeared to Angela as a woman of such power and efficiency, but she now looked the very picture of distraction and disarray, rather—Leo later said to Angela—like the White Queen. (Leo had to explain who the White Queen was. "You've read everything," Angela lovingly accused him. "Not really," he answered. "I just lived for a time with a literary aunt.")

At last Cynthia managed to tell Leo, in answer to his questions, with what her sister was charged, when she had been arrested, whether or not the detectives had had a warrant, and whether she had yet been arraigned. He tried, as gently as possible, to keep her from telling him the whole story from the very beginning. "Not yet," he said. "I'll find out from your sister; I'll talk to her. I'll get the whole story, believe me. But right now all I want to know is where she is, and what's already happened in court."

Cynthia made a noble attempt to be as coherent as possible. To her infinite relief, Leo understood her, interpreted her vague answers, knew what to do.

"Do you know when the arraignment is?" he asked. "Did they tell you, or her?"

"Probably tomorrow, but they can't be sure."

"Okay. I'll be there," Leo said. "Her lawyer will try for bail at the arraignment, but probably won't get it. The chances are she'll be remanded, and we'll try again; we may do better upstairs at the felony arraignment. But if she does get bail for a murder charge, it may be in the neighborhood of a million dollars. Can you raise that much? There are bondsmen. . . ."

"I'll raise it," Cynthia said. "The lawyer already spoke to me about that. The one who doesn't know anything. I think he talked about money because that's all he knows anything about. We'll mortgage our apartment. It's very valuable. It's worth over a million now, though it wasn't when we moved in thirty years ago."

"It takes a while to get a mortgage, even a loan," Leo said, more to himself than her. "I'm going to call you a taxi now; the company will send one if we offer double. Otherwise they avoid this neighborhood at night. You go home and try to get some rest. Meet me in the public defender's office on Centre Street across from the courthouse tomorrow morning at nine. Can you manage that?"

"I could take her," Angela said. "I could be late to work."

"I'll find it," Cynthia said. "Please, you've done enough. I'll meet you there."

"Get off the subway at Chambers Street. Then ask someone the way. Don't take a taxi; you'll be stuck in traffic for hours."

"I'll be there," Cynthia said. "Poor Beatrice. I'll be there. You will let me convince you she's innocent."

"Tomorrow, or maybe even later. The important thing is, you've got someone on your side who knows the system. That's all you have to think about right now. I'm going to try to get you another lawyer for the trial. I know it's impossible, but try not to worry too much."

Cynthia arrived at the public defender's office at nine o'clock. She saw no reason to tell Leo, who came out to the reception desk to meet her, that she had set out at seven, and wandered around the confusing streets of lower Manhattan for at least an hour, until a truck driver finally gave her proper directions. Leo led her off to his office, hung up her coat, sat her down, and tried to tell her what had happened so far.

"Where is Beatrice now?" Cynthia asked, before he began.

"Probably on her way in from Central Booking. We haven't much time, so you must listen."

"I am listening," Cynthia said, drawing together all her powers of attention. The time for action had come.

"All right," Leo said. "She was arrested and taken to your precinct, where pedigree information, name, address, and so on, are taken, and a warrant check is made, that is, to see if she is wanted on any other cases. I know, I know, but we're talking about the system here, not your sister. As you'll see when we go to court, most of those arrested have records, and quite a number do not have an address, so she's ahead on that count. The detectives will have questioned your sister extensively, and we can only pray she had the sense not to say anything at all. Any statement she made upon arrest can and will be read out at her arraignment."

"It all seems very unfair," Cynthia said, "taking advantage of people when they're upset."

"That's exactly the point. And even hardened criminals rarely know enough to shut up. I don't know how long she was held in the precinct—I'll find out— but it was as long as they had to wait before Central Booking was ready to process more bodies." Leo ignored the fact that Cynthia had closed her eyes and gone white. He kept on talking to bring her around. "Her prints were then faxed to Albany, where they are matched by computer against all other prints in the state. The result is a rap sheet, which in your sister's case will be encouragingly blank. I assume she has no record." He looked at Cynthia, who nodded certainly. "That's good news for our side when it comes to pleading for bail," Leo said.

"The reason she's now in jail is because the system was backed up; they had to go to the DA's office for a complaint to be drawn up, and because she had to be interviewed by the Criminal Justice Agency." Leo noticed that Cynthia was beginning to look faint. "Hold on," he said. "We're almost finished with this part. She's got a CJA sheet—for Criminal Justice Agency," he added, as faintness was now joined by bewilderment. "Everyone in court, the judge, the DA, your sister's lawyer, will use that sheet. It gives her years at her address, her employment, length of employment, and so on. That's going to help your sister, because she's obviously been a responsible member of the community with a good employment record and a steady address. We're waiting now until all these papers reach the court. We'll try for bail at the arraignment, but don't be hopeful. On a murder charge like this, she'll almost certainly be remanded at arraignment."

"Will you be at the arraignment arguing for her bail?"

"I can't be," Leo said. "She's not eligible for legal aid. But I've got her a lawyer, a woman I went to law school with. She's first-rate, she has worked for the DA, she knows what she's doing, she's smart, and above all, she'll understand where your sister's coming from. She's already gone to the court to be ready to meet with your sister when she's brought in from Central Booking to the arraignment. That's the whole story. Are you okay for now?"

"Will they put her in a cell when she gets here?"

"No. Women aren't put into pens. She'll sit on a bench with other women prisoners at the front of the courtroom. She'll go into a booth there to talk to her lawyer. We're going over there now; you'll see the setup."

"Will she see me?"

"Yes. But you mustn't try to talk to her or to reach her. Sally, that's her lawyer, will tell her about what you've done so far, including finding me. Ready? Here's your coat. Let's go."

"Don't you need a coat?"

Leo shook his head. Nothing, he thought, would keep a woman from noticing he didn't wear a coat racing around the courts; no man would ever notice it. It had something to do with female nurturing, Angela would say.

"Do you think you could walk down six flights," he asked, "because the elevators take forever? Good. We're off."

There was a lot happening at the court. Cynthia saw the judge, the DAs, and men in white shirts with guns who Leo said were court officers; they carried the papers between the lawyers and the judge. When Beatrice was brought in front of the judge, holding her hands behind her, Cynthia thought she would weep and never stop. She couldn't hear what any of them said, except for the DA who spoke loud and clear: "The people are serving statement notice. Defendant said: 'I didn't kill her. I loathed her but I didn't kill her. I couldn't kill anyone.' No other notices."

Cynthia looked with agony at Leo.

"Never mind. Not exactly inculpatory. It's always better to shut up, but a protest of innocence is not the worst. Listen now; Sally's asking for bail. The DA asked that she be remanded—sent to jail while awaiting trial. Sally's answering."

"With all due respect, your honor, the ADA's position, while predictable, takes no account of my client's position in the community. The case is not strong against my client; the major evidence is circumstantial. We have every intention of fighting this case. My client not only has no record, but is a long-honored professor in a well-established and well-known institution of higher education. She has been a member of the community and has lived at the same address for many years. There can be no question of my client's returning. We ask that bail be set sufficient to insure that return, but not excessive. My client is a woman in her late fifties who is innocent and intends to prove it." There was more, but Cynthia seemed unable any longer to listen. Leo had said there was little hope for bail at this point. She tried to send thought waves of encouragement and support to Beatrice, but the sight of her back with her hands held together behind her was devastating.

The judge spoke with—Cynthia might have felt under other circumstances—admirable clarity. "The defendant is remanded. Adjourned to AP–17, January sixth, for grand jury action."

That was that. Beatrice was led away, and Cynthia wept.

"It won't be too long," Leo said, trying to find some words of comfort. "The law does not allow anyone to be kept more than one hundred forty-four hours after arrest without an indictment. And now she has a lawyer who knows what she's doing, and who will, with any luck, get bail for her after her felony arraignment upstairs. You go home and try to be ready to raise it. At least a million; that's a guess, but probably a good one. Can you get home all right?" Cynthia looked at where Beatrice had been, but she was gone. She saw the booths, like confessionals, she thought, where Beatrice might have talked to her lawyer before Leo had brought her. But Leo hurried her out; he was already late for another hearing in another court.

Later Leo and Sally met for lunch in a Chinese restaurant on Mulberry Street. Sally was not encouraging. "Am I sure she didn't do it? No, I'm not sure, so what is a jury going to make of her? Talk about reasonable doubt: I'd have less doubt if I saw the cat licking its lips before an empty birdcage. Leo, my love, my treasure, take my advice: start thinking about a plea in this case. She'll get eight and a third to twenty-five if she's maxed out on a manslaughter plea, with parole after eight and a third. Otherwise, we're talking fifteen to life. Think of Jean Harris."

"Jean Harris shot her lover."

"That's more excusable than bludgeoning to death a twenty-year-old girl."

"What happened exactly?"

"According to the DA? The girl was found dead in her dormitory room on a Saturday night. The dormitory was close to empty, and no one saw anything, except some boy on his way out who saw an old lady, and picked Professor B out of a lineup. A hell of a lot of good her corporate lawyer did her there. Professor B says she was home; sister away at some institutional revel. Every one of the girl's friends has testified that Professor B hated her, though only slightly more than she hated the other girls in her seminar. Something to do with women's studies, more's the pity."

"That's all the DA's got?"

"An eyewitness, a lack of other suspects, and Professor B's prints all over the girl's notebook. Even Daphne's friends admit she went rather far in goading the old lady, but that hardly excuses murder. It's not as though we're dealing with the battered woman's syndrome here. That's how it is, Leo. We'll have to plead her out."

"Thanks for agreeing to a Japanese restaurant," Leo said. "I know it's not your thing. I needed some raw fish: brain food. Also you like the martinis here; I think you better have two before I start on my story."

Kate Fansler sipped from the one she had already ordered and contemplated Leo. He had said he wanted advice; the question was, about what? Kate considered the role of aunt far superior to that of parent, which did not alter the fact that the young made her nervous. This advice, however, turned out not to be about the young.

"It doesn't sound like a very strong case against her," Kate said, when Leo had told her the story and consumed several yellowback somethings; he went on to eel.

"It's not; but it's the sort of case they'll win. They'll bring on all the girl's friends, and what's on Beatrice's side? A devoted sister, and all the stereotypes in the world to tell you she had a fit of frantic jealousy and knocked the girl's head in."

"You sound rather involved."

"I'm always involved; that's why I'm so good at what I do, and why it's interesting. I also know how to get uninvolved at five o'clock and go home, unlike high-class lawyers."

"So Sally's arguments have a certain cogency."

"Naturally. That's the trouble. It's a little early to tell, but it looks to me like either she cops or, as my clients say, she'll blow trial and get a life term. As far as I can see it's a dilemma with only one way out. Find the real killer. Right up your alley, I rather thought."

Kate, who had decided on only one martini, waved for the waiter and ordered another. "I've known you so long," she said, "that I'm not going to exchange debating points. We can both take it as said. If I wanted to talk with your murderer, would I have to go out to Riker's Island?"

"No. Anyway, I'm pretty sure Sally will get bail after the indictment, if we have any luck at all with the judge. There's every reason not to keep the old gal in jail, and Sally can be very persuasive. In which case you can visit her in the apartment they have just mortgaged to get the bail."

"Leo, I want one thing perfectly clear. . . ."

"As you said, dear Aunt Kate, we know the debating points. Just talk to the elderly sisters, together, separately, and let me know what you decide. End of discussion, unless of course, you decide they're innocent and I can help."

"I thought it was just one of them?"

"It is; but Cynthia's the one I met first, so I sort of think of them as a pair. I've never met Beatrice; just caught sight of her with the other women prisoners at the arraignment. But I have met Cynthia, I've heard Angela on Cynthia, and I'm not ready to believe that Cynthia's sister could have murdered anyone."

Leo had told Kate that for a woman of Professor Beatrice Sterling's background, experience of the criminal system would be a nightmare; indeed, Beatrice, as she asked Kate to call her, had the look of someone who has seen horrors. They were meeting in the sisters' apartment after bail had been granted. Cynthia, now that Beatrice was home, was clearly taking the tack that a good dose of normality was what was needed, and she was providing it, with a kind of courageous pretense at cooperation from Beatrice that touched Kate, who allowed a certain amount of desultory chatter to go on while she reviewed the facts in her mind.

Burglary had always been a possibility, but it was considered an unlikely one. The victim's wallet had not been taken, though the cash, if any, had. Her college ID, credit cards, and a bank card remained. Pictures that had been in the wallet had been vigorously torn apart and scattered over the body. Her college friends, although they knew the most intimate facts of her life as was usual these days, did not know how much money she usually carried or if anything else was missing from her wallet. She had been bludgeoned with a tennis award, a metal statue of a young woman swinging a racket that had been heavily weighted at the base. The assailant had worn gloves. What had doomed Beatrice was not so much these facts, not even the identification by the young man (though this was crushing), but the record of deep dislike between the victim and the accused that no one, not even the accused, denied. Motive is not enough for a conviction, but, as Leo had put it, the grounds for reasonable doubt were also, given the likely testimony of the victim's friends, slim. Kate put down her teacup and began to speak of what faced them.

"You are our last hope," Cynthia said, before Kate could begin.

"If that is true," Kate answered, looking directly into the eyes of first one and then the other, "then you are going to have to put up with my endless questions, and with retelling your story until you think even jail would be preferable. Now, let's start at the beginning, with a description of this seminar itself. How did you come to teach it, were these students you had known before, what was the subject? I want every detail you can think of, and then some. Start at the beginning."

Beatrice took a deep breath, and kept her eyes on her hands folded in her lap. "I didn't know those particular students at all," she said, "and I didn't particularly want to teach that seminar. For two reasons," she added, catching Kate's "Why?" before it was spoken. "It was in women's studies, which I have never taught. I'm a feminist, but my field is early Christian history, and I have not much expertise about contemporary feminist scholarship. The seminar was for writing honors theses in women's studies, which meant there were no texts; in addition, the students were all doing subjects in sociology or political science or anthropology, and I know little of these fields beyond their relation to my own rather ancient interests. I had worked hard, and under some unpleasant opposition, to help establish women's studies at our college, so I had little excuse not to take my turn in directing this seminar; in any case, there was no one else available. There were twelve students, all seniors, and yes, it did occur to me to relate it to the Last Supper, which I mention only because you will then understand what the seminar invoked in me." A sigh escaped, but Beatrice, with an encouraging pat from Cynthia, continued.

"The young are rude today; anyone who teaches undergraduates can tell you that. They are not so much aggressively rude as inconsiderate, as though no perspective but theirs existed. The odd part of this is that the most radical students, those who talk of little but the poor and the racially oppressed, are, if anything, ruder than the others, courtesy being beneath them. Forgive me if I rant a bit, but you wanted to hear all this.

"The point is, they hated me on sight and I them. Well, that's an exaggeration. But when I tried to suggest what seemed to me minimal scholarly standards, they sneered. Quite literally, they sneered. I talked this over with the head of women's studies, and she admitted that they are known to be an unruly bunch, and that they had not wanted me for their seminar, but she couldn't do anything except cheer me on. They spoke about early feminists, like me, as though we were a bunch of co-opted creeps; worst of all, they never talked to me or asked me anything; they addressed each other, turning their backs on me. You're a teacher, so perhaps this will sound less silly to you than to the police. It was the kind of rudeness that is close to rape. Or murder. Oh, don't think I don't usually run quite successful classes; I do. Students like me. Of course, my students are self-selected: they're interested in the subject, which they elect to take. But even when I teach a required history survey, I do well. I'm not as intimate with the students as some of the younger teachers, and I regret that, but I grew up in a different time, and it seems best to be oneself and not pretend to feelings one doesn't have. Do you agree?"

Kate nodded her agreement.

"The dead girl—they called each other only by their first names, and hers was Daphne, but I remembered *her* last name (which the police found suspicious) because it was Potter-Jones, and that sounded to me like something out of a drama from the BBC—she was the rudest of the lot and was writing on prostitutes, or, as they insisted on calling them, sex-workers. I should add that all their subjects were enormous, totally unsuitable to undergraduates, and entirely composed of oral history. All history, all previously published research, was lies. They would talk to real sex-workers, real homeless women, real victims of botched abortions, that sort of thing. When I suggested some academic research, they positively snorted. Daphne said that being a sex-worker was exactly like being a secretary—they were equally humiliating jobs—but at least we might try to see that sex-workers got fringe benefits. My only private conversation, if you can call it that—they never, any of them, came to my office hours or consulted me for a minute—was with Daphne. She had been advised at a seminar to pretend to be a sex-worker and try to get into a 'house' so that she might meet some prostitutes; she had, not surprisingly to me but apparently to her and all the others, found it difficult to get prostitutes to talk to her. I took her aside at the end of the class and told her I thought that might be rather dangerous. She laughed, and said she had told her mother, who thought it was a great idea. I know all this may sound exaggerated or even the wanderings of a demented person, but this is, I promise you, a straightforward rendition of my experience. I have spared you some details, considering them repetitive. No doubt you get the picture. It occurred to me, when I was in Riker's Island, that perhaps I might now be of some interest to the members of the seminar, except of course that they thought I had murdered their friend, so I failed to interest them even as an accused murderer. Cynthia thought I oughtn't to mention that, but my view is if, knowing it all, you can't believe me, I might as well plead to manslaughter as my young but clearly smart lawyer urges."

Kate did not break for some minutes the silence that fell upon them. She was trying to order her perceptions, to analyze her responses. Could the hate Beatrice felt have driven her to violence? Kate put that thought temporarily on hold. "Tell me about the night of the murder," she said. "You were here the whole time alone. Is that the whole truth?"

"All of it. The irony is, Cynthia tried to persuade me to go with her to the party, which she thought might be better than most. I almost went, but I had papers to correct, and in the end I stayed home, thereby sacrificing my perfect alibi. Do you think the moral is: always accept invitations?"

"When did you last see Daphne?"

"I last saw them all the day before, at the meeting of the seminar. I think they had been told that I would give them a grade, and that attendance would count. The director was probably trying to help me, but that of course only increased their resentment, which increased mine. I don't want to exaggerate, but at the same time you should know that this was the worst teaching experience I have ever had."

"Were you shocked when that young man picked you out of the lineup?"

"At the time, yes, shocked and horrified. But soon after it all began to seem like a Kafka novel; I wasn't guilty, but that didn't matter. They would arrange it all so that I was condemned. And they had found my fingerprints on Daphne's notebook; it was like mine, and I had picked it up by mistake at the last seminar.

Daphne always sat next to me, I never knew why, but I supposed because from there, as I was at the head of the table, she could most readily turn her back to me and address her comrades. I had opened her notebook before I saw my mistake; I've no doubt I left my fingerprints all over it. But that also told against me. You might as well hear the worst. Before I was arrested, I would have told you that I was incapable of bludgeoning anyone to death. Now, I think I am quite capable of it."

Some days later Kate summoned Leo to dinner, requesting that he bring along Beatrice's lawyer; they met this time in an Italian restaurant: Kate's tolerance for watching Leo consume raw fish had its limits. Sally had clearly come prepared for Kate's admission that any defense would be quixotic, if not fatal.

"I'm not so sure," Kate told her. "There's nothing easy about this case. Beatrice's reaction to this seminar was unquestionably excessive; on the other hand, had murder not occurred, she would probably have forgotten the whole thing by now. No doubt her words would seem extreme to anyone who had not labored long in the academic vineyards; I'll only mention that when Beatrice took up teaching, she saw respect for the scholar as one of the perks of the job; she has, in addition, risked much and undergone considerable pain as an early feminist. To her, it seems as though all this has become less than nothing. Add that to what may well be a period of personal depression, and you have this reaction. Do we also have murder? I don't think so, and for three reasons.

"First, I think the last thing Beatrice would do would be to go to that girl's room under any pretense whatsoever; Beatrice claims never to have entered a dormitory and I believe her. I know, so far nothing counts that much with you"—Kate held up a cautioning hand to Sally—"but I have two other reasons, both of them, I think, persuasive. One, I purchased a cheap gray wig, donned some rather raggy clothes, and wandered into the dorm where Beatrice was supposedly spotted. I'm prepared to stand in a line and see if that young man or anyone else picks me out: to youth one gray-haired, frumpish woman looks very like another. Doffing my wig, donning my usual dress, I returned to the dormitory half an hour later; needless to say, no one recognized me. I was there this time to interview Daphne's roommate, who was also in the seminar. She told me how close she and Daphne were—they even looked alike—and how devastated she was. She, it turned out, was writing on the homeless and had had almost as much difficulty in interviewing her subjects as had Daphne. Her animus against Beatrice was pronounced, but that was hardly surprising. I asked how her paper was going; she had gotten an extension under the circumstances, but had, in fact, found only one homeless woman to interview. She told me about her. No, don't interrupt. Good pasta, isn't it?

"I tried to find this homeless woman and failed, but I did get a description. I would suggest that when you find her, she and some others similarly dressed be put in the lineup with Beatrice to let that young man reconsider. No, that isn't my clincher. Here's my clincher." Kate took a sip of wine and sat back for a moment.

"I noticed that Daphne had a MasterCard, an American Express card, and no VISA card. Now that's perfectly possible, not all of us carry every card, but I was, as you know, grasping at straws, or at least thinnish reeds. Nudged by me, the police arranged to see every credit card bill that came in after Daphne's death. That merely seemed like another crazy idea of the lady detective, until yesterday. The VISA bill came in yesterday. Here it is." Kate passed it to Sally; Leo looked at it too. "See anything of interest?" Kate asked.

"Yes," Sally said. "There's a charge during the days when Beatrice was in Riker's Island; two, in fact. But these charges aren't always recorded on the day they're charged."

"Those from supermarkets are," Kate said. "I've checked with this particular supermarket, which is in a shopping center near the college; Beatrice never goes there, since she lives in the city, but it's also doubtful that Daphne did; she was, in any case, dead at the time of this charge."

"Let me be sure I have this right," Leo said, as Sally continued to stare at the bill. "You're saying Daphne's roommate's homeless interviewee killed Daphne, tore up the pictures in anger, perhaps mistook Daphne for her roommate or was too full of rage to care, stole the cash and one credit card that she later used to buy food at a supermarket. The police will have to find her, that's for sure."

"I think if the police put their minds to it, they'll find more evidence still. What *you've* got to do, Sally, after you've got the charges against Beatrice dismissed, is take up the defense of the homeless woman. I'll pay the legal costs. Given one of those uppity girls questioning and patronizing her, and probably inviting her once or twice to their comfy dormitory room, I should think you'd get her a suspended sentence at the very least. Extreme provocation."

"Please God she hasn't got previous convictions," Sally said.

"I doubt it," Kate said. "It could well take an undergraduate to send even the most benign homeless person over the edge. The trouble with the police," she added sanctimoniously, "is that they've never tried to teach a class without a text. One can do nothing without the proper equipment, as they should be the first to understand. I have urged Beatrice to write a calm letter to the director of women's studies suggesting an entire revamping of the senior thesis seminar. They must require texts. Under the circumstances, it seems the least they can do.

"More wine?"

THE ADVOCATE'S WEDDING DAY

Catherine Crowe

> **Catherine Crowe** (c.1790–1872) was one of the most popular writers in Victorian Britain, with her short stories and serialised novels appearing in periodals such as Charles Dickens' *Household Words*. Her novel *Susan Hopley* (1841) featured a servant as a detective and is now considered ahead of its time.

Antoine de Chaulieu was the son of a poor gentleman of Normandy, with a long genealogy, a short rent-roll, and a large family. Jacques Rollet was the son of a brewer, who did not know who his grandfather was; but he had a long purse, and only two children. As these youths flourished in the early days of liberty, equality, and fraternity, and were near neighbors, they naturally hated each other. Their enmity commenced at school, where the delicate and refined De Chaulieu, being the only gentilhomme amongst the scholars, was the favorite of the master (who was a bit of an aristocrat in his heart), although he was about the worst dressed boy in the establishment, and never had a sou to spend; whilst Jacques Rollet, sturdy and rough, with smart clothes and plenty of money, got flogged six days in the week, ostensibly for being stupid and not learning his lessons,—which he did not,—but in reality for constantly quarrelling with and insulting De Chaulieu, who had not strength to cope with him.

When they left the academy, the feud continued in all its vigor, and was fostered by a thousand little circumstances, arising out of the state of the times, till a separation ensued, in consequence of an aunt of Antoine de Chaulieu's undertaking the expense of sending him to Paris to study the law, and of maintaining him there during the necessary period.

With the progress of events came some degree of reaction in favor of birth and nobility; and then Antoine, who had passed for the bar, began to hold up his head, and endeavor to push his fortunes; but fate seemed against him. He felt certain that if he possessed any gift in the world, it was that of eloquence, but he could get no cause to plead; and his aunt dying inopportunely, first his resources failed, and then his health. He had no sooner returned to his home than, to complicate his difficulties completely, he fell in love with Miss Natalie de Bellefonds, who had just returned from Paris, where she had been completing her education. To expatiate on the perfections of Mademoiselle Natalie would be a waste of ink and paper; it is sufficient to say that she really was a very charming girl, with a fortune which, though not large, would have been a most desirable addition to De Chaulieu, who had nothing. Neither was the fair Natalie indisposed to listen to his addresses; but her father could not be expected to countenance the suit of a gentleman, however well-born, who had not a ten-sous piece in the world, and whose prospects were a blank.

Whilst the ambitious and love-sick barrister was thus pining in unwelcome obscurity, his old acquaintance, Jacques Rollet, had been acquiring an undesirable notoriety. There was nothing really bad in Jacques; but having been bred up a democrat, with a hatred of the nobility, he could not easily accommodate his rough humor to treat them with civility when it was no longer safe to insult them. The liberties he allowed himself whenever circumstances brought him into contact with the higher classes of society, had led him into many scrapes, out of which his father's money had in one way or another released him; but that source of safety had now failed. Old Rollet, having been too busy with the affairs of the nation to attend to his business, had died insolvent, leaving his son with nothing but his own wits to help him out of future difficulties; and it was not long before their exercise was called for.

Claudine Rollet, his sister, who was a very pretty girl, had attracted the attention of Mademoiselle de Bellefonds's brother, Alphonse; and as he paid her more attention than from such a quarter was agreeable to Jacques, the young men had had more than one quarrel on the subject, on which occasion they had each, characteristically, given vent to their enmity, the one in contemptuous monosyllables, and the other in a volley of insulting words. But Claudine had another lover, more nearly of her own condition of life; this was Claperon, the deputy-governor of the Rouen jail, with whom she had made acquaintance during one or two compulsory visits paid by her brother to that functionary. Claudine, who was a bit of a coquette, though she did not altogether reject his suit, gave him little encouragement, so that, betwixt hopes and fears and doubts and jealousies, poor Claperon led a very uneasy kind of life.

Affairs had been for some time in this position, when, one fine morning, Alphonse de Bellefonds was not to be found in his chamber when his servant went to call him; neither had his bed been slept in. He had been observed to go out rather late on the previous evening, but whether he had returned nobody could tell. He had not appeared at supper, but that was too ordinary an event to awaken suspicion; and little alarm was excited till several hours had elapsed, when inquiries were instituted and a search commenced, which terminated in the discovery of his body, a good deal mangled, lying at the bottom of a pond which had belonged to the old brewery.

Before any investigation had been made, every person had jumped to the conclusion that the young man had been murdered, and that Jacques Rollet was the assassin. There was a strong presumption in favor of that opinion, which further perquisitions tended to confirm. Only the day before, Jacques had been heard to threaten Monsieur de Bellefonds with speedy vengeance. On the fatal evening, Alphonse and Claudine had been seen together in the neighborhood of the now dismantled brewery; and as Jacques, betwixt poverty and democracy, was in bad odor with the respectable part of society, it was not easy for him to bring witnesses to character or to prove an unexceptionable alibi. As for the Bellefonds and De Chaulieus, and the aristocracy in general, they entertained no doubt of his guilt; and finally, the magistrates coming to the same opinion, Jacques Rollet was committed for trial at the next assizes, and as a testimony of good-will, Antoine de Chaulieu was selected by the injured family to conduct the prosecution.

Here, at last, was the opportunity he had sighed for. So interesting a case, too, furnishing such ample occasion for passion, pathos, indignation! And how eminently fortunate that the speech which he set himself with ardor to prepare would be delivered in the presence of the father and brother of his mistress, and perhaps of the lady herself. The evidence against Jacques, it is true, was altogether presumptive; there was no proof whatever that he had committed the crime; and for his own part, he stoutly denied it. But Antoine de Chaulieu entertained no doubt of his guilt, and the speech he composed was certainly well calculated to carry that conviction into the bosom of others. It was of the highest importance to his own reputation that he should procure a verdict, and he confidently assured the afflicted and enraged family of the victim that their vengeance should be satisfied.

Under these circumstances, could anything be more unwelcome than a piece of intelligence that was privately conveyed to him late on the evening before the trial was to come on, which tended strongly to exculpate the prisoner, without indicating any other person as the criminal. Here was an opportunity lost. The first step of the ladder on which he was to rise to fame, fortune, and a wife was slipping from under his feet.

Of course so interesting a trial was anticipated with great eagerness by the public; the court was crowded with all the beauty and fashion of Rouen, and amongst the rest, doubly interesting in her mourning, sat the fair Natalie, accompanied by her family.

The young advocate's heart beat high; he felt himself inspired by the occasion; and although Jacques Rollet persisted in asserting his innocence, founding his defence chiefly on circumstances which were strongly corroborated by the information that had reached De Chaulieu the preceding evening, he was nevertheless convicted.

In spite of the very strong doubts he privately entertained respecting the justice of the verdict, even De Chaulieu himself, in the first flush of success, amidst a crowd of congratulating friends and the approving smiles of his mistress, felt gratified and happy; his speech had, for the time being, not only convinced others but himself; warmed with his own eloquence, he believed what he said. But when the glow was over, and he found himself alone, he did not feel so comfortable. A latent doubt of Rollet's guilt now pressed strongly on his mind, and he felt that the blood of the innocent would be on his head. It was true there was yet time to save the life of the prisoner; but to admit Jacques innocent, was to take the glory out of his own speech, and turn the sting of his argument against himself. Besides, if he produced the witness who had secretly given him the information, he should be self-condemned, for he could not conceal that he had been aware of the circumstance before the trial.

Matters having gone so far, therefore, it was necessary that Jacques Rollet should die; and so the affair took its course; and early one morning the guillotine was erected in the court-yard of the gaol, three criminals ascended the scaffold, and three heads fell into the basket, which were presently afterward, with the trunks that had been attached to them, buried in a corner of the cemetery.

Antoine de Chaulieu was now fairly started in his career, and his success was as rapid as the first step toward it had been tardy. He took a pretty apartment in the Hôtel Marbœuf, Rue Grange Batelière, and in a short time was looked upon as one of the most rising young advocates in Paris. His success in one line brought him success in another; he was soon a favorite in society, and an object of interest to speculating mothers; but his affections still adhered to his old love, Natalie de Bellefonds, whose family now gave their assent to the match,—at least prospectively,—a circumstance which furnished such additional incentive to his exertions, that in about two years from his first brilliant speech he was in a sufficiently flourishing condition to offer the young lady a suitable home.

In anticipation of the happy event, he engaged and furnished a suite of apartments in the Rue de Helder; and as it was necessary that the bride should come to Paris to provide her trousseau, it was agreed that the wedding should take place there, instead of at Bellefonds, as had been first projected,—an arrangement the more desirable, that a press of business rendered Monsieur de Chaulieu's absence from Paris inconvenient.

Brides and bridegrooms in France, except of the very high classes, are not much in the habit of making those honeymoon excursions so universal in this country. A day spent in visiting Versailles, or St. Cloud, or even the public places of the city, is generally all that precedes the settling down into the habits of daily life. In the present instance, St. Denis was selected, from the circumstance of Natalie's having a younger sister at school there, and also because she had a particular desire to see the Abbey.

The wedding was to take place on a Thursday; and on the Wednesday evening, having spent some hours most agreeably with Natalie, Antoine de Chaulieu returned to spend his last night in his bachelor apartments. His wardrobe and other small possessions had already been packed up, and sent to his future home; and there was nothing left in his room now but his new wedding suit, which he inspected with considerable satisfaction before he undressed and lay down to sleep.

Sleep, however, was somewhat slow to visit him, and the clock had struck one before he closed his eyes. When he opened them again, it was broad daylight, and his first thought was, had he overslept himself? He sat up in bed to look at the clock, which was exactly opposite; and as he did so, in the large mirror over the fireplace, he perceived a figure standing behind him. As the dilated eyes met his own, he saw it was the face of Jacques Rollet. Overcome with horror, he sank back on his pillow, and it was some minutes before he ventured to look again in that direction; when he did so, the figure had disappeared.

The sudden revulsion of feeling which such a vision was calculated to occasion in a man elate with joy may be conceived. For some time after the death of his former foe, he had been visited by not infrequent twinges of conscience; but of late, borne along by success and the hurry of Parisian life, these unpleasant remembrances had grown rarer, till at length they had faded away altogether. Nothing had been further from his thoughts than Jacques Rollet when he closed his eyes on the preceding night, or when he opened them to that sun which was to shine on what he expected to be the happiest day of his life. Where were the high-strung nerves now, the elastic frame, the bounding heart?

Heavily and slowly he arose from his bed, for it was time to do so; and with a trembling hand and quivering knees he went through the processes of the toilet, gashing his cheek with the razor, and spilling the water over his well-polished boots. When he was dressed, scarcely venturing to cast a glance in the mirror as he passed it, he quitted the room and descended the stairs, taking the key of the door with him, for the purpose of leaving it with the porter; the man, however, being absent, he laid it on the table in his lodge, and with a relaxed hand and languid step he proceeded to the carriage which quickly conveyed him to the church, where he was met by Natalie and her friends.

How difficult it was now to look happy, with that pallid face and extinguished eye!

"How pale you are! Has anything happened? You are surely ill?" were the exclamations that assailed him on all sides.

He tried to carry the thing off as well as he could, but he felt that the movements he would have wished to appear alert were only convulsive, and that the smiles with which he attempted to relax his features were but distorted grimaces. However, the church was not the place for further inquiries; and whilst Natalie gently pressed his hand in token of sympathy, they advanced to the altar, and the ceremony was performed; after which they stepped into the carriages waiting at the door, and drove to the apartments of Madame de Bellefonds, where an elegant déjeuner was prepared.

"What ails you, my dear husband?" inquired Natalie, as soon as they were alone.

"Nothing, love," he replied; "nothing, I assure you, but a restless night and a little overwork, in order that I might have to-day free to enjoy my happiness."

"Are you quite sure? Is there nothing else?"

"Nothing, indeed, and pray don't take notice of it; it only makes me worse."

Natalie was not deceived, but she saw that what he said was true,—notice made him worse; so she contented herself with observing him quietly and saying nothing; but as he felt she was observing him, she might almost better have spoken; words are often less embarrassing things than too curious eyes.

When they reached Madame de Bellefonds' he had the same sort of scrutiny to undergo, till he grew quite impatient under it, and betrayed a degree of temper altogether unusual with him. Then everybody looked astonished; some whispered their remarks, and others expressed them by their wondering eyes, till his brow knit, and his pallid cheeks became flushed with anger.

Neither could he divert attention by eating; his parched mouth would not allow him to swallow anything but liquids, of which he indulged in copious libations; and it was an exceeding relief to him when the carriage which was to convey them to St. Denis, being announced, furnished an excuse for hastily leaving the table.

Looking at his watch, he declared it was late; and Natalie, who saw how eager he was to be gone, threw her shawl over her shoulders, and bidding her friends good morning they hurried away.

It was a fine sunny day in June; and as they drove along the crowded boulevards and through the Porte St. Denis, the young bride and bridegroom, to avoid each other's eyes, affected to be gazing out of the windows; but when they reached that part of the road where there was nothing but trees on each side, they felt it necessary to draw in their heads, and make an attempt at conversation.

De Chaulieu put his arm round his wife's waist, and tried to rouse himself from his depression; but it had by this time so reacted upon her, that she could not respond to his efforts; and thus the conversation languished, till both felt glad when they reached their destination, which would, at all events, furnish them something to talk about.

Having quitted the carriage and ordered a dinner at the Hôtel de l'Abbaye, the young couple proceeded to visit Mademoiselle de Bellefonds, who was overjoyed to see her sister and new brother-in-law, and doubly so when she found that they had obtained permission to take her out to spend the afternoon with them.

As there is little to be seen at St. Denis but the Abbey, on quitting that part of it devoted to education, they proceeded to visit the church with its various objects of interest; and as De Chaulieu's thoughts were now forced into another direction, his cheerfulness began insensibly to return. Natalie looked so beautiful, too, and the affection betwixt the two young sisters was so pleasant to behold! And they spent a couple of hours wandering about with Hortense, who was almost as well informed as the Suisse, till the brazen doors were open which admitted them to the royal vault.

Satisfied at length with what they had seen, they began to think of returning to the inn, the more especially as De Chaulieu, who had not eaten a morsel of food since the previous evening, confessed to being hungry; so they directed their steps to the door, lingering here and there as they went to inspect a monument or a painting, when happening to turn his head aside to see if his wife, who had stopped to take a last look at the tomb of King Dagobert, was following, he beheld with horror the face of Jacques Rollet appearing from behind a column. At the same instant his wife joined him and took his arm, inquiring if he was not very much delighted with what he had seen. He attempted to say yes, but the word died upon his lips; and staggering out of the door, he alleged that a sudden faintness had overcome him.

They conducted him to the hotel, but Natalie now became seriously alarmed; and well she might. His complexion looked ghastly, his limbs shook, and his features bore an expression of indescribable horror and anguish. What could be the meaning of so extraordinary a change in the gay, witty, prosperous De Chaulieu, who, till that morning, seemed not to have a care in the world? For, plead illness as he might, she felt certain, from the expression of his features, that his sufferings were not of the body, but of the mind; and unable to imagine any reason for such extraordinary manifestations, of which she had never before seen a symptom, but a sudden aversion to herself, and regret for the step he had taken, her pride took the alarm, and, concealing the distress she really felt, she began to assume a haughty and reserved manner toward him, which he naturally interpreted into an evidence of anger and contempt.

The dinner was placed upon the table, but De Chaulieu's appetite, of which he had lately boasted, was quite gone; nor was his wife better able to eat. The young sister alone did justice to the repast; but although the bridegroom could not eat, he could swallow champagne in such copious draughts that erelong the terror and remorse which the apparition of Jacques Rollet had awakened in his breast were drowned in intoxication.

Amazed and indignant, poor Natalie sat silently observing this elect of her heart, till, overcome with disappointment and grief, she quitted the room with her sister, and retired to another apartment, where she gave free vent to her feelings in tears.

After passing a couple of hours in confidences and lamentations, they recollected that the hours of liberty, granted as an especial favor to Mademoiselle Hortense, had expired; but ashamed to exhibit her husband in his present condition to the eyes of strangers, Natalie prepared to reconduct her to the Maison Royal herself. Looking into the dining-room as they passed, they saw De Chaulieu lying on a sofa, fast asleep, in which state he continued when his wife returned. At length the driver of their carriage begged to know if monsieur and madame were ready to return to Paris, and it became necessary to arouse him.

The transitory effects of the champagne had now subsided; but when De Chaulieu recollected what had happened, nothing could exceed his shame and mortification. So engrossing, indeed, were these sensations, that they quite overpowered his previous ones, and, in his present vexation, he for the moment forgot his fears. He knelt at his wife's feet, begged her pardon a thousand times, swore that he adored her, and declared that the illness and the effect of the wine had been purely the consequences of fasting and overwork.

It was not the easiest thing in the world to reassure a woman whose pride, affection, and taste had been so severely wounded; but Natalie tried to believe, or to appear to do so, and a sort of reconciliation ensued, not quite sincere on the part of the wife, and very humbling on the part of the husband. Under these circumstances it was impossible that he should recover his spirits or facility of manner; his gayety was forced, his tenderness constrained; his heart was heavy within him; and ever and anon the source whence all this disappointment and woe had sprung would recur to his perplexed and tortured mind.

Thus mutually pained and distrustful, they returned to Paris, which they reached about nine o'clock. In spite of her depression, Natalie, who had not seen her new apartments, felt some curiosity about them, whilst De Chaulieu anticipated a triumph in exhibiting the elegant home he had prepared for her. With some alacrity, therefore, they stepped out of the carriage, the gates of the hotel were thrown open, the concierge rang the bell which announced to the servants that their master and mistress had arrived; and whilst these domestics appeared above, holding lights over the balusters, Natalie, followed by her husband, ascended the stairs.

But when they reached the landing-place of the first flight, they saw the figure of a man standing in a corner, as if to make way for them. The flash from above fell upon his face, and again Antoine de Chaulieu recognized the features of Jacques Rollet.

From the circumstance of his wife preceding him, the figure was not observed by De Chaulieu till he was lifting his foot to place it on the top stair: the sudden shock caused him to miss the step, and without uttering a sound, he fell back, and never stopped until he reached the stones at the bottom.

The screams of Natalie brought the concierge from below and the maids from above, and an attempt was made to raise the unfortunate man from the ground; but with cries of anguish he besought them to desist.

"Let me," he said, "die here. O God! what a dreadful vengeance is thine! Natalie, Natalie," he exclaimed to his wife, who was kneeling beside him, "to win fame, and fortune, and yourself, I committed a dreadful crime. With lying words I argued away the life of a fellow-creature, whom, whilst I uttered them, I half believed to be innocent; and now, when I have attained all I desired and reached the summit of my hopes, the Almighty has sent him back upon the earth to blast me with the sight. Three times this day—three times this day! Again! Again! Again!" And as he spoke, his wild and dilated eyes fixed themselves on one of the individuals that surrounded him.

"He is delirious," said they.

"No," said the stranger, "what he says is true enough, at least in part." And, bending over the expiring man, he added, "May Heaven forgive you, Antoine de Chaulieu! I am no apparition, but the veritable Jacques Rollet, who was saved by one who well knew my innocence. I may name him, for he is beyond the reach of the law now: it was Claperon, the jailer, who, in a fit of jealousy, had himself killed Alphonse de Bellefonds."

"But—but there were three," gasped Antoine.

"Yes, a miserable idiot, who had been so long in confinement for a murder that he was forgotten by the authorities, was substituted for me. At length I obtained, through the assistance of my sister, the position of concierge in the Hôtel Marbœuf, in the Rue Grange Batelière. I entered on my new place yesterday evening, and was desired to awaken the gentleman on the third floor at seven o'clock. When I entered the room to do so, you were asleep; but before I had time to speak, you awoke, and I recognized your features in the glass. Knowing that I could not vindicate my innocence if you chose to seize me, I fled, and seeing an omnibus starting for St. Denis, I got on it with a vague idea of getting on to Calais and crossing the Channel to England. But having only a franc or two in my pocket, or indeed in the world, I did not know how to procure the means of going forward; and whilst I was lounging about the place, forming first one plan and then another, I saw you in the church, and, concluding that you were in pursuit of me, I thought the best way of eluding your vigilance was to make my way back to Paris as fast as I could; so I set off instantly, and walked all the way; but having no money to pay my night's lodging, I came here to borrow a couple of livres of my sister Claudine, who is a brodeuse and resides au cinquième."

"Thank Heaven!" exclaimed the dying man, "that sin is off my soul. Natalie, dear wife, farewell! Forgive—forgive all."

These were the last words he uttered; the priest, who had been summoned in haste, held up the cross before his failing sight; a few strong convulsions shook the poor bruised and mangled frame; and then all was still.

BAD SUSAN

Fiona Cummins

Fiona Cummins was a journalist for the *Daily Mirror* before she published her debut thriller, *Rattle*, in 2017. Cummins is a graduate of the Faber Academy Write A Novel Course and lives in Essex.

rip. Drip. Drip.

D   Eyes buttoned shut, Joyce Robinson, one stocking collapsed down her calf and cheek sticky against the linoleum floor, half-imagined she was back in the kitchen of her childhood. Even sixty-eight years after the birthday that had changed everything, the sound was as familiar as the liver spots on her hands.

Drip. Drip. Drip.

Joyce sang *Morning Has Broken* under her breath to ward off the memory of that day, but it rushed towards her, demanding to be unwrapped like the brown paper and string the gift had arrived in all those years ago.

Even the pain tightening its grip in the valley between her shoulder blades was not enough to blot it out.

In her mind's eye, she could still see the label with its return address scratched in coloured ink that had bled, sent from a country far, far away and an uncle she would never meet.

The paper had crackled as she had unwrapped it, not tearing at it like her younger brother would have done, but peeling back the layers with careful fingers.

'Fancy him sending you that,' her mother had said, drying her hands on a tea towel. Joyce caught the whiff of carbolic soap. 'Must have cost a small fortune.'

The box was cardboard with a matching lid. Joyce tried out the name that was printed on it: *Susan*. She had eased off the cover, and her heart, newly aged seven, sped up.

A wooden head, cotton wool hair, painted eyes and eyebrows, and a jaunty hat. A sky blue skirt of silk. But it was the strings fixed to the hands and ugly yellow clogs that caught her attention.

'A marionette,' she breathed.

Her mother had rummaged through the wrappings. 'No letter, then?' She hadn't waited for Joyce to reply, but tutted at her own question. 'At least he remembered, I suppose.'

The green eyes of the puppet had stared at Joyce, and the girl had stared back.

Joyce's mother had set about making dumplings, her comfortable back turned away from her children. Joyce was opening a gift from her Cornish cousins, a set of Tiddlywinks. Her younger brother had taken advantage of their distraction, and his greedy hands had dragged the marionette under the kitchen table with him, tangling the strings.

As soon as she had realised what he'd done, Joyce had burned up with anger, and shouted at him, firing flames. 'That's mine. Give it back.'

'No.' A babyish refusal, stubborn.

'Give. It. Back.'

Joyce would later say she had no idea what had happened, because it had unfolded so quickly, and because she couldn't find the words to describe the bad feeling in the hollow of her stomach.

The milk bottle had been standing by the salt and pepper cellars, and then it had fallen on its side, and rolled across the table, the liquid spilling across the cloth and onto the floor.

Drip. Drip. Drip.

As the bottle hit the tiles, the glass had shattered into long, thin shards. One flew up and lacerated her four-year-old brother's pupil, blinding him, although they had not known that at the time.

'You stupid, clumsy girl.' Her mother had grabbed the towel she had used to dry her hands and pressed it to the boy's eye. 'All elbows, aren't you?' Still clutching the boy, she had run into the street, shouting for help.

When Joyce had crawled under the table to retrieve Susan, the spilt blood and milk dampening her tights, the puppet's strings had been as perfect as when she had opened the box.

Sixty-eight years after that birthday, Joyce was now lying on her own kitchen floor, and watching the night dial down into morning. Her body had stopped trembling and she had forced open her eyes, but the cold was bone-deep, and the way the shadows dappled the walls told her it was snowing.

The alarm she was supposed to wear around her neck was by her bed. *Fat lot of use it will do there.* Even though her mother had been dead for forty-two years, Joyce could still hear her voice. She supposed it was because there had never been a husband or children of her own to take its place.

How long until someone noticed? Two days? A week? With no-one to miss her, she wasn't sure she would still be alive by Thursday, when she was due at The Constitutional Club for a gentle dance and her weekly Campari and soda. Or was that Saturday? The days had a habit of blurring together until they were a single, sludgy entity.

There was something sticking out of her back.

Joyce dragged her eyes to the chairs grouped around her modest table. A cardigan hung across the back of one. She glimpsed a pot of hyacinths left over from Christmas. And there she was, dangling by her control bar, her blue silk skirt hanging prettily around her legs, chin pressed against her chest, clogs pointing floorwards.

Always there when something went wrong, turning up like the proverbial bad penny.

Bad Susan.

Joyce was certain she had packed that marionette away for good the night of her mother's death, but how could she be sure she hadn't taken her out again when some days she couldn't remember what she had eaten for breakfast. Her eyelids drooped again. *Don't go to sleep.*

'Don't go to sleep,' her mother had said.

Joyce had tried to lift her head from the sofa, but it was a sweltering day, and she was so tired. She had been up half the night with their cat who had given birth to five kittens, and would have preferred to stay at home, marvelling at their newness, were it not for her brother's wedding.

Her mother checked her reflection again, patting her fat curls. 'You'd better get dressed, Joyce. The cars will be here in an hour.'

'Just a couple more minutes,' she had murmured, but her mother was already climbing the stairs, to straighten her son's tie and kiss him goodbye.

Joyce must have fallen asleep, because the blast of the horn awoke her, and there were footsteps running down the stairs, and her brother, all tall and handsome, despite his milky eye, was filling up the room, and her mother was shrieking at her again.

'I told you to get dressed. You'll make us late. It's always you, isn't it, Joyce? Always bloody you.'

'What's that supposed to mean?' Cornered, Joyce could shriek too.

'Hurting us. Letting us down.'

Her brother had flashed her a sympathetic grin. 'Be quick, sis. OK?'

He had wandered outside to share a nerve-settling smoke with the driver of the Bentley, and so when the police had arrived and asked what had happened, there had been no witnesses in the house apart from Joyce.

'Mother lost her footing and stumbled on the stairs.'

That's what Joyce had told them, and her brother, and she had never wavered from that story. She didn't tell them about her open bedroom door or the marionette dangling over the bannister when she was sure she had boxed her up. She didn't tell them how her young schoolmates had stopped coming to her house because they left with scratches up their arms and compass pricks in their thighs. Or how Peggy Butler – a teenager who had moved into their street and stolen Joyce's first crush - had drowned in their pond.

She didn't tell them how her first – and last – lover had died from a heart attack on a still, hot night when the puppet had begun to sway on its strings. Or her vow to never marry or have children in case they got hurt too.

And she did not share with them her mother's final words as she had tumbled backwards, rolling over and over until the bladed corner of wall caved in her skull.

'You're a bad girl, Joyce. You're going to Hell.'

Joyce Robinson was almost dead by the time the police broke down the door. The knife was still in her back, and the blood from the wound had pooled on the uneven floor, and slid down the two steps that led to the split-level dining area.

Drip. Drip. Drip.

A worried neighbour had called for help after the light in Joyce's kitchen had stayed on for two solid nights and days, and no-one would answer the door.

The police officer stroked the white strands of hair from the victim's face. Her handbag was still on the table, and he could see her purse. A quick inspection of her bungalow had revealed no forced doors or windows.

There was a cold cup of tea on the table with scum around its edges, and next to it, a box with a hinged lid, a padlock and an address for a toy museum in Germany.

The police officer leaned over the old woman, so close she could smell the previous night's garlic.

'Who did this to you?'

Joyce's eyelids fluttered, and closed for the last time. She used her dying breath to push out a name.

'Bad Susan,' she said.

NO REMORSE

Paula Daly

Paula Daly worked as a freelance physiotherapist and briefly lived in France before becoming a writer. Her intense psychological thrillers include *Just What Kind of Mother Are You?*, *Keep Your Friends Close*, and *The Mistake I Made*. Daly lives with her family in Cumbria.

Before today, I have been forced to beg only once in my life, and the circumstances could not have been more different from this.

'Catherine,' he says, sighing, '*oh*, Catherine. How many others did you try before me?'

The office is dingy and soiled, the air contaminated with diesel fumes from the adjoining warehouse. A lone filing cabinet stands alongside his desk, its lowest drawer dented from being kicked shut.

'Two,' I reply.

Sceptically, he raises his eyebrows. 'Only two?'

'Okay, nine.'

He smiles, unoffended, and studies the printout before him. Apart from some loosening of the flesh around his jaw and two wads of fat below his eyes, he is the same. He wears the same crumpled suit: too big on the shoulders, too short in the arms.

'Your skills are certainly up to date,' he says. 'In fact, you're actually overqualified. And I see you've taken care of yourself. You look good, Catherine. But then you always were nicely turned out.'

I nod, accepting the compliment even though he is wrong. Under my woollen overcoat I wear a sheer blouse, yellowed beneath the arms from continual use, and my once good trousers are thinned at the knee. My shoes are also dated. Dated and scuffed at the heel.

'You know I'd love to help,' he says.

'Then help.'

'This is a family business; I depend on the community for trade. If folk get wind of you working here, Catherine . . .' He pauses, shrugging his shoulders. 'Well, who knows what would happen?'

I stand.

Forcing a smile, I extend my hand across the desk. 'Thank you for your time, Bill,' I say, not meeting his eye. 'I understand it's difficult. I understand you can't take the risk.'

And he rises. Leans in, wrapping both hands around mine, squeezing gently. 'No,' he replies softly, 'I can't.'

When I try to pull away, he holds me fast. 'Why'd you come back, Catherine? Surely it'd be easier in another town?'

I shake my head as though that's not an option and he releases my hand, walks around the desk and comes to stand face to face.

'Take care now, love.'

It's my signal to leave, so I dust down my coat. I keep my eyes low to try to spare Bill from further embarrassment.

'I'm sure something'll turn up,' he adds.

I go to move, then hesitate. This was my last hope. 'Bill, please,' I whisper. 'Isn't there anything you can do?'

'There's not.'

I lift my head, meeting his gaze. 'But I'm *begging* you.'

'I know you are. I know you are, love,' he says.

Outside, a sharp January wind funnels through Windermere high street. I turn up my collar, lift my chin and stride along the road as if I have every right to be here. My demeanour shouts confidence. I have the look of the wronged politician's wife, the woman who will not show weakness even though her world is crumbling.

I set my focus ahead, estimating that there are approximately three hundred steps between here and the safety of home.

Home.

Oakleigh House is the last place I'd imagined I would end up. Not the kind of dwelling I'd envisioned for myself at forty-six.

A woman shuffles towards me, loaded with shopping. There is something familiar about her, but I can't recall what so pretend I'm distracted. Wearing a mask of vague confusion I look straight through her, as if I have so much on my mind I'm oblivious to the life around me.

She stops. Regards me with a fury that seems to have come from nowhere and says, 'You've got a bloody cheek.'

Before I can answer, before I can register her words, she drops her bags at her feet. The contents spill across the pavement and pedestrians gather, thinking she's in need of assistance. She's oblivious to their concern. She is busy jabbing her index finger into my left breast. 'Get back where you came from,' she hisses. 'Climb right back down that hole and get away from here.'

I am too embarrassed to speak. I watch as a can of Heinz Mulligatawny rolls into the road, causing a motorist to swerve.

'Sorry,' I stammer. 'I'm so sorry,' and she stares back at me, indignant.

Cheeks burning, I hurry away.

Two hundred steps.

Back at Oakleigh, inside the bedsit, I realize the woman is Judy Harper. I'm ashamed I didn't recognize her as she used to be my cleaner. Judy worked at my house three mornings a week for well over two years. I'm a little thrown by her hostile reception because as far as I recall she has no direct reason to hate me. But, as Bill pointed out, who knows what will happen when people catch on? I'm starting to grasp that I might be unprepared for the potential backlash from this once sedate and dignified community.

I remove my blouse, slip out of my trousers and change into my other outfit: jeans, sweatshirt and trainers. I'm in the habit of pulling the sweatshirt low over my hips in the manner of a body-conscious teenager. The jeans are from the Save the Children charity shop and are a throwback to the early nineties. High-waisted and stonewashed, they are a total disaster – but at a cost of sixty pence, and with the sweatshirt to cover up the worst of them, I make do.

I lie on the bed, close my eyes, and begin the diaphragmatic breathing that has kept me sane for the past decade. Within minutes, sleep approaches. Sleep is my escape. When there *is* no escape, sleep is your friend. My limbs sink into the mattress, my eyes roll back, my jaw slackens, just as the banging begins from below. It's worse than usual, the occupant sounding out what appear to be familiar songs and rhythms. I have complained, but I'm told there is nothing to be done.

I'm in a sort of halfway house – although they don't call it that. As with everything affecting individuals on the margins of society, those in charge see fit to change names and titles every so often in an attempt to destigmatize. It doesn't work. It simply confuses the public, making them more outraged when they finally comprehend that they've been conned.

The banging continues and I cover my ears. I was told not to confront the gentleman downstairs, who suffers from episodes of debilitating depression. 'He's not *considered* dangerous,' the officer laughed when I enquired about the noise, 'but it's probably not wise to antagonize him unnecessarily.' I have been in this shared property for eleven days and I am yet to see the man's face. He leaves under the cover of darkness, takes off in his car – a boxy Kia which I assume was bequeathed by Motability – returning before dawn. It is always around one in the afternoon that the pounding starts.

I fix myself some lunch – two boiled eggs, one slice of toast, an apple – and turn up the volume on the radio alarm at the side of the sofa bed. Everything a person needs is contained inside this space. Bedroom, living area and kitchen are one. The bathroom is adjoining, fitted into a small closet that once housed the hot-water cylinder. Everything is reduced to the absolute basics, but it is warm and clean and safe.

There is some respite from the noise as I eat. There are no eggcups, so I must hold the hot egg inside the tea towel whilst spooning out the contents. Opening the second egg, I am satisfied to see it's gloriously runny, only just cooked, exactly as I like it. I eat this same lunch every day and have become an expert in timings, removing my second egg from the pan forty-five seconds before the first, so it is perfectly cooked by the time I eat it. For a seventy-pence lunch I can remain full until evening.

I check my watch again.

Even though I know exactly what time I must leave, I run through the logistics once more. Five minutes to get ready, twenty-five minutes to walk to my destination, arriving ten minutes early just in case. I've toyed with the idea of making an earlier reconnaissance at lunch, but I'm nervous of attracting attention.

The banging resumes.

This time, I feel it directly beneath my feet. The occupier of the room below is thrusting something hard against his ceiling – the narrow end of a broom, perhaps. The rhythm is uneven, seven beats then eight, and the asymmetry gnaws at me until I am forced to leave the room and descend the stairs. I hesitate for a moment before knocking on his door.

Ten feet along the hallway another door opens an inch and I see an eye. I go to ask the elderly woman who lives there if she knows what the noise is all about, when she closes the door without a sound. A bolt slides across.

Tentatively, I knock on the man's door.

No answer.

I knock again. Firmer this time.

The door opens wide and the man I've seen only from my attic window stands before me, expressionless. He is remarkably unattractive: bulging eyes, thick acned neck, hairline sitting a mere inch above his brow. He wears a polyester tracksuit top – a football club's emblem on the chest – and has the cocky stance of a petty criminal who regards himself to be above the law.

'You're banging,' I say to him.

No response. His wet lips remain closed.

'You're banging on my ceiling,' I repeat.

'You're banging on my door.'

'Because you're banging on my ceiling.'

'I tell you what,' he says, giving me an ugly smile, 'clear off now, and I won't put your head through the fucking ceiling.'

I make my way to the school, the northerly wind in my face. I wear my awful jeans, trainers, and an ankle-length, belted Aquascutum overcoat. The incongruous outfit makes for a bizarre picture, particularly since I have my wallet, keys, tissues and other detritus contained inside a Tesco's carrier bag. When I bought the overcoat, Aquascutum was a place I shopped at regularly. I would spend the day in Manchester, buying new winter boots at Russell & Bromley, woollen dresses and suits at Hobbs, heading to Kendal's for a bite to eat, perhaps buying Julian a tie or some aftershave. Now Aquascutum has gone and so has Julian. The coat was one of the few remaining possessions handed back to me. Everything else – the objects that told the world who I was, that demonstrated my place within society – was reduced to the bare minimum.

All except one thing.

And that's the one thing I can't reclaim. The thing that, no matter how I turn my life around, I can never have back.

Elizabeth.

Let me tell you about Elizabeth. She came early. She was a preemie, a prem, preterm. Lots of different names for a doll of a child. She stayed in hospital for ten weeks – her lungs wouldn't open, she had no surfactant. They were like the tiny wet wings of a butterfly. Julian and I rented a cottage in Lancaster near the hospital so that we could be with her, and for a while time was suspended. It's funny, the things that fall away when you're dealing with something like that. As adults we are addicted to routines. Our routines come to define us. We go to work the same way, wash our body parts in the shower in the same order, arrange our meals, our hair, our lives. A sick child stops all that. A sick child who might not make it changes everything. My whole world fragmented and I barely noticed.

At three months old, Elizabeth weighed just under 6 lbs. When well-meaning people asked how old she was, I would lie, saying she was a newborn, because I became tired of their questions. All I wanted to do was carry Elizabeth next to my heart and gaze at her. Anything which stopped me from this was not worth doing.

The last picture I have of her is at four. We were on the shingled beach at Silecroft and Elizabeth had spent the morning playing with her miniature Teletubbies, placing them inside cups, inside her socks – which doubled up nicely as sleeping bags. She was still in the habit of crouching low as she played, her skinny rump brushing the pebbles beneath, something her friends had ceased to do, and I could watch her for hours as she talked and generally bossed those poor Teletubbies into submission.

The photo shows her squatting in a floppy denim hat, her yellow curls peeping out from beneath, frowning as she watches a black and white Collie bark at the advancing waves. Later, that same Collie, after zigzagging madly along the beach, its nose to the ground following a scent, came to rest beside Elizabeth. And she reached out, cupping her hand beneath its chin with the same gentleness, the same care and concentration you'd use to catch a feather.

That was ten years ago.

Elizabeth was fostered for eighteen months by three different families in and around Carlisle and returned to the Lake District when a couple from Ambleside adopted her. Both my parents were dead, and my brother, stationed at the time in Dusseldorf, flatly refused to take her. It was a closed adoption with consent – those were the terms offered and I accepted. It was not a difficult decision. The alternative – a life in foster care, no guarantee of a proper family for Elizabeth – was enough for me to put my own needs aside in an instant. And with a concrete wall surrounding me for the whole of her childhood, it wasn't exactly difficult to keep my distance. Freedom, on the other hand, has presented more of a challenge. The thought that she is barely a bus ride away torments me to the point where I am unable to breathe.

I've been telling myself I need just a glimpse. One good look at her to know she's doing okay, then I can move on. I've not received any news of Elizabeth for over four years. Before that I would receive one letter per year, in accordance with the Letterbox scheme. The scheme was created to help mothers in prison, the adoptees and their families. It was found that without factual information, children tend to romanticize their pasts, and it can be damaging in later life when they find out their mother is not in fact Madonna, after all, but a strung-out smack addict who left her child unattended for days. The letters pass through Social Services and though I got word that Denise Farley was finding the process too distressing to go on with – writing about Elizabeth's news and development – I continued to write. I tried to give Elizabeth explanations, not excuses. I told her I loved her, but had had no choice. I told her I thought of her every day and that she was never, ever forgotten.

Over the years, I have become resigned to the fact that it's unlikely Denise handed over my letters, and though I requested it many times, she could never quite bring herself to provide me with a photograph of Elizabeth.

As I near the school I cast around furtively, checking for anyone in authority who may notice my presence. I pick a spot to stand – across the road from where I was yesterday. I alternate so as not to arouse suspicion. There are plenty of parents arriving in cars, but the only other person on foot is an outdoorsy type of woman with a black Labrador. She strides down the hill towards me full of vigour and good purpose, as if to say that though she has a clear calendar, she dilly-dallies for no one.

A double-decker bus passes. It does a slow, careful three-point turn before pulling alongside the kerb twenty yards away. This is the Ambleside bus. I worked that out a few days ago when I watched it turn left at the end of the road and set off towards the village. I didn't see Elizabeth board. Of course it's possible that she's not been in school. Or perhaps she stays behind late to play netball or hockey. For all I know, she could be at chess club.

Children pour out of the main doors and the area is awash with navy uniforms. Three girls walk towards me – very overweight, dyed black hair, their roots growing through in various shades of mousy brown. Each wears wrecked ballet pumps on her feet. When I was inside, I would pore over images in the press of models and celebrities, each averaging a weight of around seven stone. Women in the public eye have definitely become thinner in the last ten years. Each morning I would read in both the broadsheets and red tops about the pressures girls face today from the bombardment of sculpted images, Photoshopped thighs. I left prison expecting to see hoards of emaciated, bug-eyed teenage girls following suit. Girls dropping like flies in the street from hunger and dehydration. It's been quite an eye-opener to witness the abundance of overweight teenagers, apparently quite unconcerned about their weight.

The bus driver has yet to open his doors and I watch as the three girls apply black lipstick to one another as they wait. I rise on to my tiptoes, craning my neck to see over them in an attempt to spot Elizabeth. My eyes flit to the bus driver. He is regarding me with cool detachment.

I hang around for another five minutes, waiting for the stragglers to exit the school. When there is no sign of Elizabeth, I head towards home, my heart heavy again with disappointment. I'm just about to cross the road when an unremarkable grey car pulls up alongside, the driver signalling for me to wait. The driver turns off her lights and grabs her coat from the back seat, before removing a band from around her wrist and pulling her hair into an untidy ponytail. Shrugging on her jacket, she walks around the bonnet of the car, withdrawing a wallet from an inside pocket. Very discreetly, she shows me her warrant card, and I nod in response.

'Catherine Rhodes?' she asks.

'Yes.'

'DC Joanne Aspinall. Can I offer you a lift home?'

'I'm okay to walk, thanks.'

DC Aspinall smiles. 'Jump in, Catherine.'

She pulls away and drives towards Windermere. I'm in the front seat beside her. I don't ask how she knows my address or what she wants with me. One thing I've learned is not to open my mouth unless absolutely necessary. We drive over the mini roundabout and when I glance to the right instinctively to check for oncoming traffic, I take in her features fully. Fear had clutched at my insides when she approached and I was unable to look at her earlier.

Now I realize I kind of know her. She used to be a bobby on the beat, visiting schools and neighbourhood-watch meetings. I remember her speaking at Elizabeth's school, instructing the children about fire safety, how to behave sensibly around fireworks. She was in a blue Nato jumper – just about the worst possible thing a large-breasted woman can be forced to wear. It removes a woman's natural curves, making her appear almost cylindrical. DC Aspinall seemed so very young and self-conscious of her shape at that time.

Once we're at Windermere, she drives onto the public car park at the side of the library. 'I won't drop you right by your door,' she says. 'I imagine you've got enough curtain-twitchers without me adding to the situation.'

I smile my thanks, wondering what it is that motivates kindness in some people and not in others. Was this woman born this way? Or did she do it minute by minute – a series of small decisions to try to make the world a little easier for the person in front of her?

'Am I free to go?' I ask.

'You are.'

I reach down for the plastic bag between my feet and am about to pull on the door handle.

'You know you can't keep going to the school, Catherine,' she says.

I stare straight ahead.

'You must give me your word that you won't ever go there again.' Her words are soft, but the message is clear. 'It's a condition of a closed adoption, is it not?'

I sit back in my seat and exhale. After a moment I get up the courage to speak. 'I didn't want to cause any trouble,' I tell her. 'I just needed to know that she's okay.'

'She's okay.'

I turn my head around fast. 'You know her?'

'Not very well, but I do know who she is.'

'How . . . how is she?' I stammer.

Emotion has surged upwards and from nowhere I feel my brain shorting out. I have to concentrate incredibly hard on DC Aspinall's face to hear her words.

'She's had a few problems, but she's doing well now.'

'Problems?'

DC Aspinall's eyes shine with compassion as she gives a small shrug to indicate she's not really at liberty to say any more.

'Has she been loved?' I ask. 'Have they loved her? Can you at least tell me that?'

'Yes. She's had a lot of love. That's probably been part of the problem.'

I nod repeatedly, struggling to speak. 'Thank you,' I whisper. 'Thank you for telling me.'

'You understand I'll be forced to report it to your offender manager next time . . . if you do try to contact Elizabeth?'

I frown.

'So this—' I say, gesturing to the air between us, 'this meeting has *not* been recorded?'

'No.' And then: 'You have a friend looking out for you.'

'Who?' I ask, but she shakes her head.

'A member of the public spotted you waiting,' she says. 'She recognized you and worked out why you were there. She asked me to have a word with you, discreetly, before someone – let's say before someone *less* sympathetic – makes a complaint. Strictly speaking, Catherine, this is not really part of my job.'

'I understand.'

I climb out, brush down my coat and straighten my spine. I am about to walk away when DC Aspinall lowers the window. 'By the way, Catherine,' she calls out, and I'm forced to bend at the waist, dip my head so I can see her face, 'the word from those in the know is that your husband had it coming,' she says. 'Most say he'd had it coming to him for a while.'

I nod. Swallow down something familiar that feels close to remorse, but never ever regret, and reply, 'Yeah. He did.'

The following morning, I wake from another restless night. I have a job interview today. This one came via my offender manager – new name for probation officer – since I was unsuccessful in finding a job myself. It's a maintenance position for a charity which keeps some of the common grounds around Windermere tidy and litter-free and a couple of the lakeshore woodland paths accessible. The charity was set up by a benevolent Friend of The Lake District who wanted to offer good, worthwhile work to those who aren't always considered desirable employees. If I'm successful today, I will be working alongside a young guy in a long-term drug-rehabilitation programme who has anger issues, and a woman who's been imprisoned twice for theft. One thing prison did for me – it got rid of my supercilious streak. I wouldn't say I was ever especially snooty, but given descriptions of my future co-workers, as above, I'd have been horrified. Now I welcome the unpredictable nature of those on the periphery. You never know what you're going to get. Folk surprise you. I witnessed more empathy, more understanding and gentle encouragement from the inmates of Styal Women's Prison than from any other collection of people I've been a part of. Women pulling together, leaning on one another, all trying our upmost to make each other's time in there as pain-free as possible.

They say the first night in prison is the worst. Not so. The *fear* of being sent to prison is the worst. It's almost a relief when the verdict comes. I can't speak for everyone who finds themselves in my shoes, but certainly my terror dissipated substantially when the gavel came down. That was it. No more what-ifs; the rollercoaster ride of the trial was over, there was absolutely no chance of release. By the afternoon of the sentencing I had made my peace with my future and I was composed and calm. I had spent an hour with Elizabeth that morning, held her and loved her until she would take no more, swatting me away, giggling, 'No more kisses, Mummy, *no more*,' and I let her go without drama. I let her go because I always knew this would be the outcome.

I lost my child, my home, my liberty, and any chance of a decent future. I was sentenced to twelve years, ended up serving ten, and said goodbye to my life.

Given the choice, would I shoot him again?

Of course. In a heartbeat.

*

My job turns out better than I could have predicted. I'm supplied with a uniform which includes a warm winter ski jacket with hi-vis stripes, steel-toecapped boots, a woollen hat, a cap, and two pairs of leather gardening gloves. After tax and national insurance, I come out with around one hundred and seventy pounds a week. With this money I'm able to buy a pay-as-you-go mobile and a few other essentials – eggcups and suchlike. Now that I'm earning I must look for a permanent place to live.

The vigour of the work suits me and within days I feel my atrophied, underused muscles responding to the hard labour. I fall on to the sofa bed each night aching and sore, my hands quivering from the continual use of shears or from gripping the hoe, with a sense of profound satisfaction and wellbeing. For the first time since my release my thoughts are not tumbling around inside my head; in fact, for the first time in years I am too physically tired to think at all. It's bliss. Work has become like an opiate. Each night I slide into a deep, black sleep and wake in the morning renewed and ready for more.

And there is another advantage. I am no longer cooped up in the bedsit, hiding from the world outside, going slowly insane from all the hammering and banging courtesy of the crazy man downstairs.

Yesterday, when I returned home, I was in the cellar washing my overalls – mud-caked and stiffened from a day down by the lake – when the elderly woman from the first floor appeared. Upon seeing me she did a fast about-face, scampering back up the cellar steps. She wore a velour skirt, tights the colour of stewed tea and old-fashioned handmade brogues. Her quick ankles moved at the speed of someone a quarter of her age.

'Wait,' I called out, but she didn't. 'Please, wait,' I repeated, and this time she stopped.

I walked to the foot of the stairs and beckoned her down so I could keep my voice low. 'Don't be afraid,' I said.

'I'm not,' she replied.

'So why run away?'

'I keep myself to myself.'

I paused. 'Does keeping yourself to yourself have anything to do with your charming neighbour?'

She surveyed me warily. Went to speak, then changed her mind. 'I'll be leaving here tomorrow,' she said. 'I've found something permanent.'

'Anywhere nice?'

She shook her head. 'A word of advice before I go . . . don't knock on his door. He doesn't appreciate visitors.'

It's now seven fifteen, and I descend the stairs ready for work. I'm picked up at seven thirty each morning by Alan, outside Windermere post office. I am always on time, as is Alan. If Alan were to be late, you could safely assume there had been an accident. But Sandra, the perpetual thief, is late every single day. And Alan, who has a hard time controlling his anger about her timekeeping, gets more riled by the second.

Sandra will climb into the cab of the truck, under a cloud of smoke, anywhere between five and twenty-five minutes late, wickedly delighted at the effect her tardiness is having on Alan's disposition. It's become almost a sport to her.

I nip back upstairs, having left my sandwich in the fridge, and as I come back down the stairs, packing it into my rucksack beside the flask of coffee, I notice that the door to the flat beneath mine is not completely closed. It's not ajar, not even open a centimetre, but if I were to press against it, it would open.

I stand for a moment, unsure of what to do, listening for signs of life.

He doesn't appreciate visitors.

Perhaps I could just take a peek? I mean, the door *is* open. I nudge the wood and a thin slice of white light appears between door and frame. The hallway is in semi-darkness, dawn not having fully broken this bleak winter morning, and the light is an assault on my eyes. Quickly, I pull back.

But where is he? And what does he do in there?

I'm propelled by the need to know. I mean, he could have a slave. What if there's a poor woman chained to the bed, and the tap-tapping I hear is her lone signal to the outside world?

Christ, I could be one of those neighbours you see on the news. The ones who say, all matter-of-fact, 'Now you come to mention it, I *did* see a naked woman at the window, holding up messages like HELP, SOS, that kind of thing. But to be honest, I didn't think much of it at the time.'

Imbued with a sense of righteousness, I push open the door.

And he's right there.

His flat is larger than mine. There is room for a small dining table at the centre. He sits at it, deeply asleep, his head on top of his folded arms. The air smells stagnant with alcohol. An almost empty bottle of Absolut vodka is beside his elbow. In front of him lie his car keys and around ten neat stacks of fifty-pound notes. Each stack is about 6 cm high.

There is no slave.

I stand rooted to the spot and stare, transfixed by all that money.

Ten minutes later I'm in the warm truck, drinking coffee from my flask, as Alan taps on the steering wheel. He wipes his nose with his thumb and forefinger, twists the sleeper earring in his left ear twice, before curling his tongue up around his front teeth, releasing it fast to make a loud, wet, smacking sound. This series of tics, which Alan repeats minute by minute, keeps a lid on his emotions. I find it quite soothing, watching him soothe himself. It's not dissimilar to the array of quirky rituals Rafa Nadal goes through each time he makes a serve.

Now he's back to the tapping.

'Can I see the job sheet, Al?' I ask.

He reaches down and pulls out a rolled-up wad of printer paper from beneath his seat. The sheets are dog-eared at the edges, adorned with muddy fingerprints, and there are also a couple of blood-red smears across the front page – most likely from Alan's nose.

While I'm scanning the page, Alan glances at me out of the corner of his eye. 'We're edging the turf at St Mary's church this morning,' he tells me. 'Litter pick-up along the main road at Troutbeck Bridge after that.'

My stomach turns over at the mention of Troutbeck Bridge. That's where Elizabeth's school is located. 'Easy day, then,' I reply with a casualness belying my inner tumult.

Handing the job sheet back to Alan, I wipe out my coffee cup with a tissue and replace it on top of the flask. Then, under the pretence of returning the flask to my rucksack, I have a good root around in it, trying to locate my cap. It's crammed right at the bottom. Later, my ears will suffer in the bitter air, but pulled low the cap will provide the much needed concealment of my face.

I feel a rush of giddiness as I picture Elizabeth laughing with her friends as I watch from the sidelines. She doesn't notice me at first; perhaps she glances my way and smiles shyly, before continuing on, her yellow curls bouncing with each stride. Her expression quizzical and intent, just as I remember her: interested in everything, wholly in love with life.

'You're fucking late,' Alan spits as Sandra flings open the passenger door.

'Morning, Al. Morning, Cath.'

'Eighteen minutes late,' he adds.

'And you, Alan,' she replies, climbing in, 'are getting tedious. Cath, pass me that *Daily Mirror*, will you?'

I reach forward to the dashboard as Alan slaps his hand down hard on top of it. 'Buy your own fucking newspaper,' he says.

I haven't talked to Alan or Sandra about Elizabeth so I'm unsure if they know I have a daughter. They are both from the area, so know of my shooting Julian, but both are a good deal younger than I, so perhaps they are unaware of the finer details of the case.

Sandra and I have traded prison stories. She has spent two stints at HMP Askham Grange in Yorkshire, an open prison that's soon to close on account of a restructure of the system used to deal with women offenders.

Sandra said, 'Reckon the Ministry of Justice finally cottoned on that *all* women prisoners are there on account of some dickhead man.'

She's not wrong.

Practically every female prisoner I met was inside because her man dealt drugs, dealt in stolen goods, or ran up huge debts in her name. The other common reason for imprisonment amongst women was alcohol-induced violence against a cheating man, or else the cheating man's bit on the side (sometimes both).

Alan parked the truck on the road leading to the school and I'm hurling my third black bagful of litter into the back of it when I hear the faint sound of the bell. This is our signal to leave. But Alan has nipped to the petrol station for his daily energy drink – a disgusting concoction that turns both his tongue and few remaining teeth blue. I pretend to move the gardening equipment around, rearranging for maximum space, all the while glancing from beneath the brim of my cap for any sign of Elizabeth.

Kids make their way past me. Out of the corner of my eye I catch sight of Sandra's hi-vis stripes as she heads back towards the truck. An obese girl with blue-black hair shuffles along on the other side of the road, head down, and I'm horrified when a cocky lad behind her launches a half-eaten Granny Smith straight at her head.

The apple hits her cleanly on the back of her skull and I can tell by her reaction – shock, followed by a reddening of her cheeks and a quickening of her pace – that this is a regular occurrence for her.

Poor kid.

But she's around eighteen stone, an easy target for the teenage clown. Why do parents let them get like that? I've heard people say it's akin to child abuse and I have to agree. Surely you'd want to make your child's passage through school as easy as possible? Surely you'd want to—

'Hey, Elizabeth!' the boy shouts out to her and I freeze.

The girl keeps on walking. She crosses the street right in front of me and my eyes fly to Sandra, who is now almost at the truck also.

Sandra's staring at me. 'That's *her*,' she mouths silently. 'Who?'

'Your daughter,' she says.

So she did know about her.

The girl comes to a stop a little further along the road and waits for the bus driver to open his doors. Her expression is urgent, desperate. *Please open*, I can feel her willing, and my heart is breaking.

Because I now understand that it *is* Elizabeth. My girl. My daughter who is standing there.

I take a couple of steps and Elizabeth turns. She is watching me apprehensively and I realize instantly that she does not want me to approach. She does not know who I am, that much is clear, but her expression warns me off. *I do not want your pity*, her scowl tells me before she snatches her head away and suddenly I, too, am transported back to school. I am the one who is the butt of the jokes that day and, yes, the last thing I want is the attention of a sympathetic onlooker. That would make things so much worse.

I stop and turn. Make my way to the truck and climb into the cab next to Sandra.

Sandra does not speak to me for the entire journey home.

Back at Oakleigh House, there's a builder's van parked on the kerb. Its back doors are open and I hear the sound of machinery – an electric planer, perhaps. The front of the building is shielded by the neighbour's privet fence, which has grown way too high and wild, keeping the small front garden of Oakleigh in an almost permanent state of shade.

I say goodbye to Sandra and Alan. Alan is already checking his wing mirror, ready to pull away to get home, but Sandra glares at me. 'I thought you would have talked to her,' she says.

'Yeah, well, you thought wrong.'

I don't tell Sandra I was so wrong-footed, so slammed by the fact that I didn't recognize my own child that I couldn't move. Let alone approach Elizabeth.

All the hours – hours that stretched into days, and finally into years – that I imagined our reunion, not once did it occur to me that I wouldn't know who she was. Not once did I imagine I would watch Elizabeth – Christ, that I would *judge* Elizabeth – as though she was another woman's overweight child.

I turn into my gateway and two men are busy fitting a new front door to the building. One is in his fifties – small pencil behind each ear, clean shaven, with the neat, wiry build of a fell runner. The other is mid-thirties, and what I notice immediately is his sweatshirt. It's navy-blue, emblazoned with the Reebok emblem. It's covered in paint and smears of silicon sealant, but I find it endearing to see this throwback from an earlier era now used exclusively for work.

'What happened?'

The older one answers. 'The door was forced. They didn't just break the lock but damaged all the casing as well . . . it all needs refitting.'

'Do we know by whom?' I ask.

They shrug, exchanging wry smiles. 'Dunno. But the chap upstairs is a bit agitated.'

I climb the first flight of stairs, apprehensive as I hear shouting from above. I hear my neighbour claim he doesn't have the money. That he *really doesn't* have the money. The layout of the building is such that on reaching the top of the stairs I must pass by his door – along the landing – before climbing the next flight of stairs up to my bedsit in the attic.

There are splinters of wood scattered on the carpet outside his room. I look to my left and see that the door to his flat has been forced open, like the front door. It hangs at a thirty-degree angle where the top hinge is missing. Seems as if whoever wants that money is serious. I hurry upstairs. Bolt the door shut once I'm inside.

I stand with my back to the sink unit and listen.

Within seconds there is the sound of movement on the stairs, the boards creaking under the weight of someone.

There's a knock.

I don't answer.

'I know you're in there,' he says. His voice is quiet. Purposely soft, so no one will hear. 'I just want to speak to you,' he says.

Silently, I turn around and slide open the cutlery drawer behind me. I deposit a small paring knife inside my pocket – it's the one I use to slice apples and carrots, to peel potatoes – then I walk across the room and inch open the door, keeping one steel-toecapped boot against it.

He doesn't bother with hello, getting straight to his point.

'You leave early each day, right?'

I nod.

'What time?' he asks.

'Seven fifteen.'

'You left at seven fifteen this morning?'

'Yes.'

'Did you see anyone near my room?'

'No.'

He pauses. Swallows. He has blood in his hair.

'Okay,' he says, and turns to make his way back down.

'Can I ask a question?'

'Depends what it is,' he replies.

'I can see there's been trouble here today . . . the damage to the property, your head . . . is it safe to stay here?'

'I don't think anyone will bother you.'

'But will they be back?' I ask.

He doesn't answer.

*

That night I sleep in snatches, waking every twenty minutes to listen for sounds on the stairway. Strong winds batter the building in the early hours and a thread of cold air is pulled past my face, drawn as it is to the large gap beneath the door.

When I rise, I open the curtains to see stray leaves circling in the air. A lone wood pigeon tries to swoop from the roof opposite and is instead lifted high on the current.

Last night I packed my rucksack with a few of my belongings. Hardly anything really, as I own hardly anything, but I've purposely left my toothbrush, toothpaste, a photograph of my father next to the bed, so as to make it look as though I plan to return. The flat will be searched. Maybe not today, but some time.

I send a text to Alan informing him of a fantasy illness. If it was anyone else I wouldn't bother, but Alan could very well explode if left to tap, wipe his nose, twist his earring for too long. I tell him I'll contact him when I'm returning to work.

Creeping past my neighbour's room, I hear no signs of life, so make my way to the cellar. My phone is set to silent. Once there, I tip the supersized box of Daz upside-down into the plastic washing-up bowl in the Belfast sink, shaking the items I stowed inside free from specks of washing powder. Then I pour the Daz back into its box.

With my heart jackhammering inside my chest, I make my way up the cellar steps and turn off the light. The hallway is in semi-darkness. The air is stale, heavy with a scorched smell from the cast-iron radiators. And there's something else.

Alcohol.

'A bit early to be doing laundry, isn't it?' he asks. My neighbour is three feet away, but such is the pungency of his breath that it clouds around me like a hideous fog.

'I wasn't doing laundry,' I answer, stalling.

'No?'

I reach along the wall and flick on the light. Both of us squint in response, and when I sense his eyes have adjusted, I lift my leg, gesture to my trousers. 'I needed to get these from the dryer,' I say to him.

He flashes a smile. 'So, what, you went past my room in just your underwear? Shame I missed that.'

I pretend to go bashful. 'You're not normally awake at this hour, so I thought I was pretty safe.'

'I'm awake today.'

'So I see. I'll have to be more careful in future.'

'Don't be too careful,' he whispers and moves towards me.

For one appalling moment I think he may kiss me and I make a fast decision to let him. But he doesn't. He strokes my jaw with his index finger. His skin is coarse and jagged there and I shiver beneath his touch.

He laughs.

'I'm back off to bed,' he says. 'See you tonight.'

'Looking forward to it,' I reply, and have to stop myself from sprinting from the house under his gaze.

Conscious that he may be watching from his first-floor window, I head off in my usual direction. Once out of sight, though, I linger. I lean against the wall of a guest house – closed until Valentine's Day weekend, the sign says – and fiddle with my phone, looking mildly vexed as though my lift is running late. The wind pushes me against the stonework of the building, making my eyes water and the inside of my ears ache.

Ten minutes later, I've circled back and I'm removing his stolen car keys from my rucksack and climbing into his car. The Kia.

Ten minutes after that, I'm discreetly parallel parked between a car and a minibus, just a hundred yards from Elizabeth's school entrance.

Now all I have to do is to wait.

'Elizabeth? Are you Elizabeth Farley?'

'Yes,' she replies uneasily, as if she might be in trouble.

'Can I talk to you?'

'About what?'

Throngs of children are passing the car. Elizabeth stands away from the driver's window, cautious, and the kids jostle and tut as she blocks their way.

'How about you get in the car?' I suggest.

She thinks for a moment and it's only now that I see the features she acquired from both myself and her father begin to emerge. Before, her frown of concentration and everything that made Elizabeth distinctive – the bright, inquisitive eyes, a sense that you were looking into the face of an old soul – were concealed beneath the mask of an obese child. And the prejudices are right here. You cannot see past a fat person, not even when it's your own daughter. I'm filled with a mixture of overwhelming love and fear, the urge to bundle her into the car, kidnap her and get her on a strict regime of healthy food and exercise.

Is that wrong?

Probably. But there it is.

'Who are you?' she asks.

I don't answer immediately. I want to blurt out *Your mother!* But I keep a lid on it for now, saying, 'I'm Catherine Rhodes.'

She shows nothing. No emotion to indicate how she feels upon hearing my name, and I'm left wide open. Nothing to hide behind. Her response is telling me all that I feared. She has no idea who Catherine Rhodes is.

'Do you know who I am, Elizabeth?' I ask tentatively. 'Have you heard my name before?'

She nods, but her face is still devoid of emotion.

'Elizabeth?' I prompt.

And she starts to cry.

'You came,' she says eventually.

'Yes,' I reply, and hold out my hand to her. 'As soon as I possibly could.'

We head towards the motorway. I have no destination in mind, but Elizabeth asked me to drive, so that's what I'm doing. I hadn't actually expected her to get into the car – I was prepared for her to hear my name and keep on walking. But she didn't, she asked me to take her away from school. I have the impression that she's been hoping for someone to pull up outside and take her away for as long as she's attended the place.

'What if I'm not who I say I am?' I ask, as we head towards the dual carriageway.

'Who else would want to talk to me?' she counters. 'And besides,' she says, smiling for the first time, 'you knew my name.'

'That still doesn't mean I am who I say I am.' I shoot her a look, as though to say she should be more careful.

'I'm glad she didn't change it, by the way,' I add. 'Your name, I mean. I'm glad your mum decided to keep it as it is.'

'She wanted to change it,' she replies. 'She wanted to rename me Georgia, but my dad wouldn't allow her. He said it was disrespectful to you.'

'Which name do you prefer?'

'I'm not mad for either,' she says.

We reach the M6 and I cast a glance at Elizabeth. 'Do I keep on driving?' I ask.

She gives a small gesture to indicate yes, she wants to continue, so I join the slip road and head north. As soon as we're on the exposed carriageway the car is buffeted by the wind and I have to hold the wheel firmly to prevent being dragged across the lanes.

'How are your mum and dad?' I ask, once I'm comfortable with my position behind an Eddie Stobart doing sixty-five.

'Dad left when I was eight and—'

'What?'

'He left.'

'I didn't know that,' I say, shocked. 'Do you see him regularly?'

She shakes her head. 'Mum never wanted me to. He went off with a friend of hers from work, someone she knew, and she said she didn't want me going around there.'

'Where does he live?'

'No idea.'

'He doesn't write? He doesn't call you?'

'No.'

We drive for a few minutes. I can't help but feel enraged by this. The only reason I agreed to a closed adoption in the first place was so that Elizabeth would have a family. Denying her access to her adoptive father was never part of the deal.

'You're angry, aren't you?' Elizabeth notes quietly.

'I'm not.'

'You are.'

I turn to her. 'Tell me, did you get *my* letters? I wrote to you all the time . . . they would only pass on one letter a year, but did you get it?'

'No.'

'Not one?'

'No.'

'What did you think?' I ask. 'Did you think that *I'd* abandoned you as well?'

'You *did* abandon me.'

*

Ahead there's a sign for Tebay Services. 'I could do with a coffee,' I murmur, flicking on my indicator as I approach the motorway exit.

I find a parking space right at the front of the building. This service station is a quaint, privately owned affair – the only one of its sort in the UK, the sign claims. There's no McDonald's, no Costa. It has fabulous views and a duck pond. I'm hoping for a good coffee and something stodgy – a pastry, perhaps – to soak up the excess acid that's swilling around my stomach.

'You want anything?' I ask Elizabeth as I grab my rucksack.

'No.'

'Are you coming in?'

'I'll wait here.'

I take a trip to the ladies' and wash my face in the sink. In the mirror I examine my reflection.

What the hell are you doing, Catherine? You realize you've effectively kidnapped her?

I told myself this morning that if I could just talk to her, talk to her before I left Windermere, it would be enough. All I wanted, all I have ever wanted, is for her to be safe and happy. And rather than hang around Windermere until she reaches eighteen, I had been given an unexpected opportunity to leave.

I could go, make a good, decent life for myself elsewhere, and contact her in the proper way later, through Social Services, as the law dictates.

I didn't actually expect her to want to come with me.

Or did I?

Hadn't I kind of prepared for this subconsciously? Hadn't I hoped things would go off at a crazy tangent and she would *want* to come?

I make my way to the café, grab a tray and push it along the shelf, perusing the homemade soups, stews, pies and cakes. There is no one else queuing, so as I reach the barista I'm under pressure to make my choice fast. 'A large coffee and a Danish with almonds on the top, please.'

'Which coffee would you like?' she asks, pointing to the list behind her.

Now ten years ago this didn't happen around here. You asked for a large coffee, that's what you got. And since I haven't had the money to go frivolously drinking my way through Starbucks' offerings, I have no idea what I want.

'Just give me your favourite,' I tell her and she gives a small shudder of delight. 'And a hot chocolate as well, please.'

I pull out a fifty-pound note, apologizing, saying, 'Sorry, I've got nothing smaller,' and turn, pocketing the change. Then I spot Elizabeth over by the window, gazing out at the ducks.

She is too big for the chair, her bulk spilling over the sides. She reads my expression and shifts a little, as though trying to make herself smaller.

I place the tray down between us and without looking at me she says, 'Tell me about my father. My real father. Because I heard you kind of murdered him.'

I sit, remove the lid from my coffee and blow across the surface of it. Some particles – a mixture of ground cloves and cinnamon, I suspect – land on the table-top between us. Elizabeth brushes them away. 'It was manslaughter.'

'How can blowing someone apart with a shotgun be manslaughter?' she asks. 'It's a bit difficult to do that accidentally, isn't it?'

'It's not something I'm proud of.'

She nods as though understanding, but her eyes have taken on a cool, remote quality. 'Mind if I have some of that?' she asks, gesturing to the Danish.

I hesitate and notice she is watching me carefully. Gauging my reaction to her request for food. 'I'll get you something to eat of your own if you like.'

And she smiles. 'That's okay. I can tell you don't really want me to have one.'

''Course I do. Why wouldn't I?'

'It pisses you off that I'm fat.'

'Yeah, well, it pisses *you* off that I shot your dad. We're both pretty pissed off. There you go, now we're even.'

'Nice,' she says with half a smile.

'Nice what?'

'Nice way of dealing with your long-lost kid.'

'Thanks,' I say, 'I've been practising.'

She breaks the Danish into two and licks the buttery grease from her fingertips. Then she removes the lid from the hot chocolate and dips the pastry in twice before popping it into her mouth.

'So why did you do it then?' she asks as she chews.

'Kill him?'

'Uh-huh.'

'He was fast with his fists when he'd had a drink.'

She stops eating. 'That's *it*?'

'Well, it's a bit more complicated, but that's about the size of it.'

She gives me a look as if to say, *Go on.*

'Julian had built up a good business,' I begin. 'He employed around a hundred local people, and was young, dynamic, he'd been voted in as chairman of the council. Everything was going great. But around twelve years ago his business began to fail and he couldn't handle the shame. He'd always been a drinker, not a very nice drunk, but now he started taking his failure out on me. Slapping me when I spoke my mind, slapping me harder when I asked him not to drink too much.

'I was embarrassed that I'd made a mistake by marrying him, because I had been warned,' I say. 'People had told me he was controlling and aggressive when he had had a drink. So I did what a lot of women do under the circumstances – I hid it. I pretended to everyone it wasn't happening, because I didn't want to admit that I'd made a mistake.

'He always kept shotguns in the house,' I continue, 'and one day he drove home completely out of it, after a shoot, ploughing his Land Rover straight into your Wendy house in the front garden. Luckily you weren't inside, but you were close by, and when you started screaming he struck you. He hit you so hard he knocked you straight off your feet.

'I yelled at him to stop, but he got his gun. I was holding you in my arms by then and he aimed it at the two of us. I begged him to stop. I actually got down on my knees and begged him not to shoot. But he did. He pulled the trigger. He pulled the trigger and when the gun didn't fire I realized in that second that it was either him or me. If he didn't kill us now, he was going to at some point.'

I take a sip of coffee and look straight at Elizabeth. 'The moment he put down the gun to get his spare shells from the car, I reloaded it with two from his jacket pocket in the hallway. And then I shot him.'

Elizabeth swallows. She waits before responding and I can't read how she's feeling.

'I was told,' she says after a time, frowning, '. . . well, actually I wasn't told, I searched the news reports. And they all said you waved the gun at him, never meaning to actually shoot him.'

'That was my defence, yes.'

'But that's not what happened?' she asks carefully.

'No. Like I said, it was either him or me. My barrister used the self-defence angle, but the problem was I watched him die. I didn't call an ambulance until he'd bled to death because I wanted to be certain he was gone. That's why I got twelve years.'

She looks down at the table.

'My mum told me you were nuts,' she says quietly. 'She said that you shot him in a rage and took off, leaving me behind because you'd lost your mind and couldn't cope with the responsibilities of being a mother.'

I shrug. Try not to let the hurt show in my face.

'Well, now you know the truth,' I tell her, 'it's up to you what you do with it. Up to you what you believe. Just know that what I did, I did because I had no choice.

'Anyway,' I say, my tone lighter, 'do you want the other half of that Danish?'

She smiles. 'I do, actually.'

I push it towards her. 'Help yourself.'

We sit in silence as she eats. From time to time she looks out of the window, at the clouds casting deep shadows across the fells, and from time to time she looks back to me. It's an odd thing watching her. Not at all how I imagined after the desperate love I felt in her early years. I used to watch her sleep and become so overawed with it all. One second I was awash with love and gratitude, and the next that would be eclipsed by an ominous dread. A fear of something terrible happening. What if she was taken from us? What if she was not really ours to keep?

A sense of peace settles as I realize that she is still mine on some level.

Elizabeth smiles at me, and is just about to say something when her attention is caught by something over my right shoulder. I see unease creep into her eyes and I think I can guess what is over there.

'Are you in trouble?' she asks quietly.

'A bit,' I nod. 'Bringing you here sort of violates the conditions of my parole.'

'Oh,' she says quietly.

'And the car we came in?' I say. 'Well, it's stolen. So there's that. I might have to go away for a while.'

She bites her lip. 'For long?'

'Shouldn't be too long. A couple of months, maybe.'

I turn and see three police officers approaching from the far side of the café.

'This place where you're going,' she says quickly, '. . . could I write to you? Could I come and see you?'

'I'd like that.'

She puts out her hands and holds mine. The officers are now only metres away. Elizabeth leans in and kisses my cheek. 'Thank you for what you did for me,' she whispers.

'A pleasure.'

'Catherine Rhodes?'

I turn to the officers and nod.

'I'm coming,' I tell them and they give me a little space.

Then I stand.

'Don't forget your rucksack,' I say, handing my bag to Elizabeth, and she looks back at me, perplexed.

I lean in. 'There's something at the bottom,' I whisper urgently. 'There's some money in there. Quite a lot, actually. Keep it safe for when I come back, okay?'

GOING ANYWHERE NICE?

Lindsey Davis

Lindsey Davis created the historical Roman detective Falco in 1989. Her many crime novels set in ancient Rome include *The Silver Pigs*, *One Virgin Too Many* and *The Ides of April*, which introduces Falco's adopted daughter Flavia Albia as a detective. Davis has won numerous awards and lives in Birmingham, UK.

'**G**oin' anywhere nice for your 'oliday?'

Immediately, Renzo was summoned by his mobile phone. A computerised trill from *La Forza del Destino* left Mr Grubshaw thwarted. Renzo stepped outside to lean his paunch against the doorframe and engage in impenetrable Sardinian business chat.

According to Renzo, he was the best barber in Deptford. Certainly Mr Grubshaw went into the shop feeling untidy and came out different – though passers-by then peered at him as if he resembled a conman on *Crimewatch* who was being sought by three police forces for emptying old ladies' bank accounts.

Renzo's shop was owned by Halycon Properties, a front for two Lebanese brothers with big ideas and dodgy spelling. They had run a VAT racket on mobile phones until Customs and Excise tightened up the rules; now they were planning to rent out student bedsits. Until they put in place the finance for installing faulty gas water-heaters, Renzo hung on, alongside Cursing Khaleed, whose tiny café was filled with cigarette smoke and thin men of Balkan appearance who did nothing all day.

'Grubby' Grubshaw was sole proprietor of the XYZ Detective Agency, though Renzo, who was curiously uninterested in his customers, had never discovered this. The private eye had wandered into the barber's once when the Department of Social Services, for whom he did occasional fraud enquiries, asked him to watch a Chinese man who seemed to be claiming for a non-existent wife. Mrs Cheung's body then washed up on the bank of the Thames, so the DSS lost interest because she was perfectly entitled to benefits, had Mr Cheung not murdered her. The police hijacked Mr Grubshaw's casenotes, complimenting him on their neatness and detail (he had written them up hastily, with his niece's help, the night before). Then Cheung fled the country, so even the police lost interest. At least Grubby had acquired a barber.

Renzo was cheap. He was gloomy and introspective, but when he bothered he could cut hair well. He made a tasteless joke of 'Don' worry, I no cut your throat!' to anyone who risked a wet shave – but Mr Grubshaw had seen too many films about the Chicago Mob to relax in a chair while lathered up. He only ever braved a trim. Normally, by the time Renzo asked if he had any holiday plans and he replied not really, it was all over. Today, Grubby experienced slight disappointment; the mobile phonecall prevented him announcing that for once he was taking his niece to the Bay of Naples. He had hoped a Mediterranean destination would impress Renzo.

'Business colleagues; big people,' the barber boasted, shoving away the phone and clicking his scissors alarmingly. He seemed put out by the call. He muttered in his home dialect, then flashed a brazen grin. 'Big people who need Renzo! Very special job . . .'

That sounded far too much like Sweeney Todd. Mr Grubshaw avoided discussing his holiday and fled.

Back at his office, his niece was busy at his computer. The XYZ Detective Agency was another Halycon Properties rental, two upstairs rooms with rotten floors, over a bankrupt software firm. It made an unsuitable haven for a twelve-year-old girl, but both her parents worked, so Mr Grubshaw took her in after school. Perdita ('call me Tracey') kept his records in order for him.

'I've booked everything online with Dad's credit card,' she sniggered. It made a change from her buying CDs with Mr Grubshaw's own card. A pale thing with bunches in scrunchies, whose wardrobe was dominated by pink leggings and big black shoes, she vacuumed relatives' PIN numbers from their minds by osmosis. 'He's sending us Business Class.'

'Oh! . . . Does Clive know you use his card?'

'He will!'

Mr Grubshaw's youngest brother, a 'respectable' City broker, had caused the Naples trip. Finding his niece in tears a week earlier, Mr Grubshaw discovered that Clive had left home, to be with his young assistant. 'Fiona – ugh! She's having a baby.' Something worse had caused the tears: 'Dad forgot to pay for my school trip.' Grubby stepped in to take Tracey and her mother Jean to see the archaeological sites.

They were not the only people heading towards Vesuvius: as they entered the airport boarding lounge, Mr Grubshaw was convinced he spotted Renzo, though the barber had his head in a phone booth. Grubby said nothing, a professional habit, and since Business Class was boarded last there was no awkward eye contact.

During the flight, Tracey kept her CD player welded to both ears, listening to Mortal Dread and the Troubled Minds, so her uncle could give her mother legal advice. Clive had money, but allocating any to Tracey's upkeep might become tricky; there were signs that Fiona had spent her time as a finance assistant learning how to ensure *her* life would be a soft one.

'Constant "late business meetings", then he claims *I* lost interest!' ranted Jean, who was still adapting to her loss of status as part of a yuppie couple. They had bought a four-storey Georgian house in Greenwich before the Docklands Light Railway was brought across the river, causing a knee-jerk in prices. 'We were planning to upgrade to a five-storey, cashing in. Now he says I can buy him out – how, exactly, on teaching Conparative Literature four days a week?

They maintain they are slumming in a flat – but it's a flat with Philippe Starck washbasins! All I ever got was Villeroy and Boch, installed by plumbers who took eight months – and we never did get the right loo handle . . .' After years of despising Grubby for his informal lifestyle, she now suspected she had married the wrong brother; it made for an intriguing family atmosphere. 'I've been blind. Do you think there were others?'

'There must have been, Jean.'

'I suppose it's the oldest deceit.'

'It's been known,' Grubby agreed.

'I could kill him!'

'That's been done,' said Grubby sadly.

'Would a private detective suggest a contract killer?'

'My code requires me to advise against it, Jean.'

'I don't even need you to find evidence; he bloody told me everything himself . . . Well, I hope you haven't brought that damned matchbox!' Jean was denouncing the container where Grubby kept a woodlouse who allegedly helped solve cases. When he merely looked innocent, she exploded, 'Oh no! What if we're searched by Customs?'

'Woody has a pet passport,' grinned Tracey, holding an earplug aside.

The pilot was mumbling on the muffly intercom. 'Alter your watches,' deciphered Mr Grubshaw alertly, winding his on an hour. 'Get back to Mort, Trace, while I instruct your mother on how to fleece your father.'

They stayed at a shoreline hotel by the Castel d'Ovo, an old fortress with a harbourful of boats nodding their mast at the foot of the keep. They had splendid views across the bay out to Capri, which was visible on clear nights as a scatter of pale lights. From their balconies, they could turn towards Mount Vesuvius and wonder whether that was a faint trace of smoke threading upwards from the crater . . .

Before dinner, Mr Grubshaw lay on one of the twin beds in his room, reading a free newspaper from the plane. Having assured Jean that all the Vespa-riding bag-snatchers had been cleared out of Naples in Millennium Year, he had concealed from her an article discussing problems with Mafia drug-sellers. There was uproar on some impoverished estates because the local Camorra was trying to impose a new business plan on pushers.

'Must have been on a management course!' Grubby glanced across to the second bed, where a matchbox reposed on the pillow just where chambermaids deposit a chocolate to remind guests to leave a tip. 'Reminds me of that brochure I chucked in the bin: *Participants will learn how to:*

- **Formulate** a strategic market plan
- **Organise** activities to bring in new business
- **Develop** a marketing culture in their organisation
- **Motivate** colleagues to achieve agreed commitments

Pretty straightforward, Woody. Some dealer annoys you with his feeble marketing culture, you shoot dead his young girlfriend.' He read on. 'Guns in the street –

mainly at weekends. The Camorra must all hold down nice jobs . . . No-go tower blocks, where dealers have installed security cameras to show the police arriving; then they've put metal gates on stairwells to hold the officers up . . . Just like home, Woody. Let's hope the Deptford pushers don't take holidays to get ideas.'

Woody said nothing, being a reticent character.

The family set out on foot for dinner. Lights across the causeway to the fortress attracted them, but they decided to head further afield, turning past a row of elegant old hotels. Outside the grandest a limousine pulled up. A chauffeur in a classic blue blazer escorted an elderly couple across the pavement towards a flunkey in a maroon tailcoat. The couple looked like local VIPs on some regular night out at a hotel restaurant.

Tracey marched up, a self-assured child. The woman tolerantly paused to let her pass. Jean smiled their thanks and scuttled out of the way. Lagging in the rear, Mr Grubshaw noticed that Signor looked annoyed at being kept waiting. The man had a quiet manner, yet expected to be given precedence, even by strangers. His chauffeur's attitude was tellingly different.

'The Mayor of Naples?' wondered Jean.

'Gangland racketeer,' her daughter suggested.

'Successful accountant and wife,' murmured Grubby. 'Meeting friends for a bridge party.'

'I don't *think* so!' scoffed Tracey.

Replete after their Business Class dinner earlier, the family settled for pizzas. As they tucked in, Tracey explained the terms on which this holiday was to be conducted: the group from her school were staying at a cheaper hotel along the bay and would pick her up every morning as their coach passed by. Tracey did not want to be embarrassed at archaeological sites by the presence of relatives, so Jean and Grubby had to visit other locations. Nobody wanted Trouble, so this was agreed.

Accordingly, when the schoolgirls visited Pompeii, Jean and Grubby went to Herculaneum using the Circumvesuvio railway. While the school party were at Herculaneum, the others crossed by ferry to Capri. The day the girls saw Poppaea's Villa at Oplontis, Jean and Grubby managed a morning in Naples Museum; they went up there by taxi, then afterwards walked back down a long road towards their hotel, window-shopping. They made one quick foray uphill into narrower alleys, but did not linger. Mr Grubshaw was remembering the newspaper article's description of a drug-dealer being shot in a salami shop, among hams and prosciutto salesmen. Dead meat.

'That's enough backstreet Neapolitan atmosphere! Let's find an ice-cream.'

Returning to the main road, they came across an enormous glass-roofed gallery, its cross-shaped interior lined with banks, cafés, jewellers and incongruous electrical shops. Jean's guide-book identified the Galleria Umberto I. While she admired the grey and pale gold marble floor of one gracious arcade, Mr Grubshaw noticed through the farthermost exit a faded building across the street. Tall rectangular windows were flanked by dark green louvred shutters. Outside one window, two men talked on a balcony, perhaps avoiding eavesdroppers. He realised that there, discreetly placed above a Solarium, was a business close to his heart: an International Detective Agency.

He took a closer look. A man, much like himself, though with a smarter jacket, emerged at street level, hands in pockets. He sauntered into the Galleria. It seemed the wrong place for a detective to spend his lunch break – at least until he stationed himself outside an electrical shop, studying cut-price vacuum cleaners.

Jean had found a pavement table for a cappuccino. She whispered excitedly, 'There's that racketeer from the other evening!'

'Merely a toasted-pannini mogul.' Grubby stuck to his theory that the man was mundane.

'The couple looked too respectable to *be* respectable. I should know. Think of Clive! The bastard is smooching his trophy mistress – believe me.'

Mr Grubshaw mildly followed her gaze. The man they had seen entering the hotel restaurant on their first night was indeed enjoying an expresso with a much-younger woman, though he was not bothering to smooch her. They knew each other *far* better than that. This was their regular lunchtime rendezvous; Grubby conceded that no Italian boss would routinely take his secretary to lunch.

She wore a wide-shouldered tan leather coat loosely over her shoulders, its collar brushed by expensively streaked blonde hair. She had a confident personality and was speaking, not angrily but at length. A chunky gold bracelet pulled the cuff of her cashmere sweater as she gesticulated passionately. Grubby remarked that she looked like a woman who did most things passionately and Jean joked, 'Except the dusting!'

As a bachelor in a solo business, Mr Grubshaw had chosen life on his own terms. To see another male under such pressure made him queasy.

The man remained calm, replying only briefly. Eventually reassured, his companion left half the coffee that had been bought for her, air-kissed her lover, then left. She walked briskly, calling greetings to a female friend outside a boutique. She looked open about her meeting and the man, too, was powerful enough not to be furtive. Well, not unless his wife strolled through the Galleria. She was unlikely to confront him; that couple had plenty of secrets, Grubby thought, and they would keep their arguments private.

The private detective now acted the tourist, and took photographs. He had already snapped the lovers at their café, especially when they kissed farewell. He took a long view of the woman disappearing down the arcade, then sauntered nonchalantly to gaze at a display of slightly trashy art.

The businessman stayed at the café. Grubby encouraged Jean to indulge in a pastry.

'The price is a rip-off.'

'Relax. We're on holiday.'

'You sound like your brother sometimes.'

'Good old Clive!'

Grubby was quietly watching his colleague, who was now chatting to an ice-cream vendor. The businessman grew bored, checked his watch with the waiter, and stood up. He dropped a large euro note on the table, though no bill had been presented.

The detective hung around.

*

Jean wanted to move, but Grubby had seen a familiar paunchy figure. Renzo, his barber, wandered through an arcade, was distracted by a camera shop, stared three times at the café the businessman had vacated, then chose that one for a snack. Casually, one-handed as he licked an ice-cream, the private eye photographed him.

Renzo drank two expressos and demolished a sandwich with the savagery he used on Cursing Khaleed's vegetarian kebabs back in Deptford. Apparently waiting for someone, he glanced repeatedly at his watch, tried to call someone on his mobile, failed, paid up, and mooched off. The detective then went for a word with the waiter, who indicated his own wristwatch; they laughed.

'Alter your watches . . . Renzo's in the wrong time zone, Jean!'

Banned by Tracey from all archaeological sites that day, Jean and Grubby whiled away the afternoon locally. The Piazza del Plebiscito was an elliptical colonnaded public space, with a church modelled on the Pantheon in Rome and a resident group of lazy town dogs; dramatically sited with views of the bay, they found the Palazzo Reale. Since it was free, they took a relaxed circuit through its astonishingly restored rooms. It had all the glamour of Versailles without the crowds. They finally emerged, sated with enormous Sèvres urns and Gobelin tapestries. Desperate to rest their legs, they headed for Gambrinus, Naples' oldest corner café where they could pretend to be genteel amid faded paintings of roses, as Oscar Wilde had done. There were tables outside, but they chose the interior, the better to torment themselves with the sight of delectable chocolate cakes.

'Well, at least Signora gets out!' Jean's angry mutter alerted Mr Grubshaw to three mature ladies with smart carrier bags. 'Do you think she knows he's two-timing her?'

'Yes; here comes the chauffeur with the prints of Signor and his trophy friend.'

'Signora looks such a nice woman.'

'Mafia mommas have a reputation. I wouldn't cross her.'

'I wonder if they have children?'

'Probably.' But how many were dead in the drug wars?

'He must have strayed before,' snarled Jean, with fellow-feeling, as the elderly woman took the stiff envelope her driver had brought and opened it calmly. She half pulled the photos out, glancing at them as if what she found was only what she expected. One of her friends was stirring her cup; the other gathered herself for a trip to the Ladies. They had hardly acknowledged the chauffeur's arrival, but Grubby thought they both knew what he had brought. 'Plenty of times!' Jean was still harping on.

Grubby remembered the businessman's girlfriend, with her strong walk and her air of having life before her. 'This particular young lady wants it all,' he decided.

'Oh, a *Fiona*!' Jean went into a bitter reverie. 'She wasn't as young as she'd like men to think.'

'So she's a worse threat.'

Viewing the evidence, Signora looked as though she wasn't finished yet. Kept separate from her husband's work, no doubt, she probably knew a lot about it even so. In their early years together she would have helped his struggle to establish himself. Grubby sniggered. 'If *Signora* decides she wants it all too, do you think that includes the chauffeur?'

Jean considered, though not for long. 'He's nothing special.'

The other two mature ladies chatted to the waiting driver, informally; they knew him of old. Signora tapped the photo set back into its envelope, which she dropped into her large designer bag. She dismissed the chauffeur with a nod. All three ladies appeared to continue their previous conversation.

'Catholics,' whispered Jean. 'No divorce.'

'I expect the priest will give him a good talking to.' That would not have deterred Clive, when tackled by a determined finance assistant who wanted his baby and his bonds.

'No divorce – but plenty of retribution, Grubby!'

The husband might anticipate the retribution and want to deflect it. Grubby felt chilled.

He considered warning the private detectives that their bourgeois female client, now eating coffee-iced torte, could be the subject of Renzo's 'special job'. But if she were his client, he would frostily refuse any discussion with an out-sider. Maybe it was all right. The detective had photographed Renzo; that was significant. If Signor had plans, Signora was ahead of him.

Another chill caused Grubby to call time and return to the hotel so they were ready to greet Tracey when the coach brought her back.

'Well, that was real interior design! It was like, well, *themed*.' Tracey had enjoyed Poppaea's Villa, a two-thousand-year-old masterpiece of décor. 'There were hun-dreds of rooms and some had, like, spooky masks painted, but the best bit was the outdoor swimming pool. You could hold a *wicked* barbecue—'

'I expect they did,' said Grubby drily.

'What has been your favourite site, Perdita?' The teacher in Jean relied on constant evaluation. (How sad, therefore, that she had spent so little time evaluating Clive . . .)

'Oh Mum. If you had to call me after somebody in Shakespeare, I wish you'd chosen someone with some style.'

'Goneril?' suggested Jean waspishly, immediately regretting it.

'Great!' Tracey was now Goneril. 'The brothel at Pompeii was quite good.' Jean and Grubby exchanged a surreptitious glance. They had not even found the brothel, let alone negotiated an entry price with its legendary smarmy key-holder. 'Capri was *gross*; you could really imagine terrible old Tiberius hurling his enemies off the crag—' Jean nodded, newly eager to hear of men being cast to their deaths unpleasantly. 'The best was Vesuvius and the hot springs at the Phlegraian Fields. A vulcanologist explained how Naples is doomed. Every year that Vesuvius fails to erupt now, means a bigger explosion when it next blows its top. Millions of people are going to be trapped . . .'

Mr Grubshaw wondered if people who lived in the shadow of a recognised future disaster might be more prone to violence. He discarded the theory. The only difference between Naples and Deptford was that the villains in Deptford were multicultural, while the rival clans in Naples came from one gene pool.

Presumably it went all the way back to the peasants who were buried in pumice or molten mud in Pliny's day.

That made him think. Renzo would be a foreigner here. Someone commissioning a special job, a job that broke even the rules of this tightknit community – deleting a *wife and mother*, say, the matriarch of a clan – might well bring in an outside agent. A Sardinian could have the expertise without the local sensitivity. He could settle a domestic issue without causing decades of Neapolitan blood-feud, and afterwards he could fly off back where he came from.

But Renzo, with his vacant manner and so inefficient he had failed to set his watch to local time, was a bad choice. He might share a criminal background and very dangerous skills, but his stubble darkened the wrong-shaped chin. His dialect probably sounded as thick here as it did in Deptford. Word of his presence would whiz around. The women with neatly pressed tweed jackets and straight skirts who toyed with *limoncelli* in smart cafés possessed just as effective networks as their men. And they probably had their own agents of destruction too.

Whether Signor realised he was rumbled would depend on him. The mouthy young woman in the leather coat must be doing her best to undermine Signora's importance in his eyes. An arrogant man, easily flattered by a feisty mistress, might forget that, although Signora had staff at home these days and no longer toiled over *osso bucco* on a hot stove, she still knew the recipe.

That evening Mr Grubshaw rationalised his own position. 'Woody, I could report my suspicions to the police and be laughed at. I could drop a wink at the detective agency and be seen off as a batty menace. I've no proof of anything, and if challenged, Renzo will claim he's on holiday, just like me.'

The woodlouse said nothing, but did it sympathetically.

To give him an airing, Grubby carried the matchbox out into the balcony. Its concrete was unwelcoming to a creature who lived on rotten wood in damp places, but together the two friends gazed at the ocean. A perfect moon had risen above the Castel d'Ovo. Lights from a cruise ship slowly moved out towards Capri in the darkness. To the right of the causeway, a small boat could just be discerned where lethargic fishermen tended lobster-pots every morning in tethered ranks between the shore and the hydrofoil routes.

'We're dreaming, Woody. We come out to Naples, conditioned by fear of its streetcrime. Perdita and her friends are warned to carry their mobiles and money under their sweatshirts – but that would make sense back in London. Jean and I stare up a back alley hung with washing-lines, and we think we're in the nostalgia scenes of *The Godfather*. If we hadn't scurried away, I still think we could have found the right loo handle for her bathroom – there was a promising shop full of chromeware, just before she decided people were giving us the evil eye . . .'

Though keen on the cavities behind lavatory tanks, Woody had no views on fitments. Mr Grubshaw enticed him back into the matchbox, for it was dinnertime.

Perhaps because Grubby thought he saw a limousine turning onto the causeway, they ate out below the Castel d'Ovo, where there were several good-class pizzerias. It was their last night, which they spent in happy talk of archaeology and food, while dodging the attentions of musicians. 'For the *bambina*!' leered a waiter, placing pasta before Jean, who blushed. Grubby walked outside 'to make a phonecall to the office'; flirting with an Italian waiter was just what Jean needed at this stage.

He stayed in sight in case she panicked, leaning on a short harbour wall. A group of town dogs assembled around him, not begging, but sitting on their haunches in a circle as if they recognised a crony. People came and went in couples or groups. Then, oddly, a man alone walked up the shadowed cobbled street; he was short, chunky, had a mobile phone clamped to his ear. He looked like Renzo. A second figure followed him on lighter feet: peak-capped and blazered. Mr Grubshaw would have tailed them, but now Jean was gesticulating. Time to return to the restaurant.

They ate, settled up, bemoaned the end of their holiday. They took a turn around the little square and the dark quays at the foot of the fortress. Among the parked cars were none Grubby recognised, nor did he spot anyone familiar eating outside. Not that he expected to; they had observed that regulars were greeted specially by smiling maitre d's and wafted indoors to private rooms. 'With menus at half-price,' said Jean.

'Same the world over,' replied Grubby.

'These locals behave as if they own the joint.'

'Maybe they do, Jean.'

He slept badly, anxious to ensure they caught their flight. Rising early, he booked out, left his suitcase in the lobby where Jean and his niece would see it, then took a last constitutional along the esplanade. Braving traffic, he crossed the frantic Via Partenope to the shore. Joggers and anglers had gathered in a knot. Normally the fishermen sat on the great slabs of concrete that thrust skywards, as if heaved by volcanic upheaval. They formed a breakwater. There was no beach; the waves lapped imperceptibly against these jagged, jumbled chunks from which hopefuls cast rods every few yards.

Not today. On one of the massive slabs lay a body.

With his conscience pricking, Mr Grubshaw ascertained that it was male. All he could see was dark clothing; he thought of Renzo, habitually in black jeans and a zipped black bomber jacket. 'A vagrant?' he queried discreetly, as the joggers and anglers stared and waited for the police.

'Most likely,' a man explained to him a little too carefully, 'someone who drank too much—' He mimed it. 'And fell from a cruise liner.'

'Not local, then!' said Grubby. His tone was wry.

A police car drew up and switched on its siren. Two officers clambered to the corpse while colleagues joked with bystanders. Soon the body was turned over. From the pavement, it was still impossible to identify the man or see how he died. The nearest policeman straightened up and began serious phoning on his mobile. An angler and a jogger exchanged glances. Mr Grubshaw decided to return to his hotel.

Perhaps troubled by what he had seen, his feet took him too far. He pulled up, outside the grander establishment beyond. A limousine was parked, its chauffeur in a blue blazer leaning on one door, picking his teeth. The man gave him a courteous 'Good morning' nod. On a whim, Grubby entered the hotel and was directed to its restaurant. At the window table a mature woman breakfasted alone. Waiters hovered near her, but she ignored them, mopping her mouth with a napkin as she gazed down outside, watching the kerfuffle on the shore. No expression showed on her face.

Mr Grubshaw glanced at his watch, made his excuses, and returned to his own hotel. Police activity had increased, an ambulance was now in attendance, and a senior officer was looking taut. There was no attempt to halt the traffic, but after he found his companions, getting cases into a taxi was safer than normal as drivers slowed down of their own accord to gape at the crime scene.

'She fixed him, then!'

'Now, Jean; you don't know that.'

At the airport, Mr Grubshaw craned for sightings of Renzo, without result.

All the following week, he checked the barber's shop, but it remained shuttered. He tackled Cursing Khaleed. 'Renzo gone away?'

'Effing Italy.'

'Business?'

''Oliday, he say. Was arrested at the effing airport for carrying a knife.'

'Bloody hell!' Khaleed looked offended by Mr Grubshaw's language. 'How d'you know, Khaleed?'

'Rang me on his mobile. I had to shift some stuff for him in case the effing cops search the shop.'

'What – he went over his allowance for duty-free aftershave?' White powder, more likely, Grubby thought.

'Somebody stitched him up, he say.'

'I was afraid somebody had done him in.'

'Just effing deported . . . Try Mario's, up Greenwich,' Khaleed advised, fingering his own sinister shaved head. 'Does an effing swanky cut. You going away? My cousin's got a nice apartment in Bodrum. Do you an effing good price.'

'Can't get away. Too many family commitments . . .' Clive was terrified of what Jean might have planned for him financially, and Jean was scaring herself with her hardened attitude. Even his niece, despite her insouciance, was starting to look pinched with worry. 'Thanks,' answered Grubby, 'but I think I'll stay at home this year.'

THE HIGHLANDER'S REVENGE

Ellen Davitt

Ellen Davitt (1812–1879) was born in Yorkshire with the grand name Marie Antoinette Hélène Léontine Heseltine. She moved to Australia with her husband in 1845 and became a pioneering crime writer. A sister-in-law to Anthony Trollope, Davitt has an Australian crime-writing award named in her honour.

"Weel, Maister Ellison," said Dr Dubious, "ye've made out a tale, and that's nae a bad thing on a cauld night; the mair that it gies a mon a pretext for sipping his toddy. But I'm no converted to the theory o' dreams; and by your ain showing, ye were in weakly health when ye dreamt o' the ship on fire. And that, nae doubt, accounted for a' the fancies; for ye ken, when the stomach's heavy the head is apt to be licht.'

The doctor then laid down his pipe, and replenished his tumbler, looking the very picture of obstinacy, when Mr Ellison remarked, "But, my dear sir, how can *you* account for the likeness between the creature of my fancy – if you please to call the dream by such a name – and the *actual man* I afterwards saw; the man who proved to be the culprit?"

"It's a'most as unreasonable to expect a mon to account for a thing he thinks agin reason, as to believe in a' the daft nonsense o' dreams."

"*A man convinced against his will – Is of the same opinion still,*" said Mr Lightfoot, *sotto voce*. Then he added, in a louder tone, "But the foundation of half the stories we read of or listen to are as baseless as that of a vision, and sometimes still worse – a complete perversion of facts."

"As the fire is good and the toddy still better, I'll tell you a story, gentlemen, that *has* a more solid foundation than a dream; nor will I pervert facts, though there are some I shall suppress," said a stout-looking Highlander, who had listened in silence to the narratives of the two lawyers.

"Let us have it, Ferguson, for ye're not the man to trouble your head with dreams," said the doctor.

"No; *my* story is a stern reality; and *that* my friend M'Lean can vouch for," replied the Highlander.

"Ay, I can do that, Ferguson. I am not likely to forget those times, though it is long since they passed away," said a man whose countenance bore an expression of deep thought, tinctured perhaps with remorse. His own reference to *those times* caused him to look still more gloomy; and he sighed heavily as he prepared himself a glass of the stimulant which, on that night, seemed to be equally essential to speaker and to listener.

Mr Ferguson, whilst similarly engaged, introduced his story by saying, "It is not a tale of well-dressed miscreants, who might have run the gauntlet with the London police, nor of a rascally digger defrauding and murdering a poor credulous mate, that I am about to tell, but of enemies who caused our lives to be a constant scene of anxiety and a succession of hair-breadth escapes. Ah, but they are not very much to be feared *now*. We took down their mettle, didn't we, M'Lean?"

"Ay, by destroying nine-tenths of them," replied M'Lean, with another sigh.

"Well, you need not look so dismal about it, man; there was no other plan for us to adopt – no other way, gentlemen, to make this land habitable for you. And even if there had been, were we not entitled to our *revenge*? But, M'Lean, do you remember what year it was when you and I first met?"

"No. That business on the Murray seems to have put all dates out of my head. Ferguson, why *will* you force me to think of those days?"

"It is not what we *did* that disturbs my reflections. But as none of you gentlemen were out in this hemisphere at that time – some of you not even in existence – you cannot imagine the place where you are all sitting so comfortably overrun by a set of blackfellows like –"

"Like the man they have got to sweep out the bar and to help the chambermaid with her work?" asked a dandy recently arrived in the colony, who had no idea of Australia beyond that which he had acquired between the limits of Melbourne and its suburbs. Even this colonial experience was chiefly confined to the pit of the theatres, a few cafes and similar places of resort, until destiny compelled him to seek employment as a lawyer's clerk up-country.

"Like that fellow who wears a green-baize apron, and who follows Mary about the house, with a pail in one hand and a broom in the other? No, Mr Skimmile; the blacks *we* had to encounter were as unlike that poor animal as the hammer of a Highlander to the dainty article with which you were driving a few tintacks into your mosquito-net yesterday. Tush! What do you Cockneys know of Australia in the old times? Ha, you may thank *us* for taming the blackfellows, and making them exchange their spears for sweeping brooms."

Mr Skimmile had always admired Highlanders since he became acquainted with the pages of Sir Walter Scott. Inspired by the *Wizard of the North*, he had once spent a fortnight in Scotland, where he experimentalised in grouse shooting till he found that he was putting himself into more danger than the game he tried to bring down. Since then he had worn a kilt at a fancy ball, where he afforded considerable amusement to every Scotchman present by the smallness of his legs, as well as by the adjustment of his pouch. Now, thinking perhaps he could hereafter emulate the prowess of the Highlander on whom he was gazing with admiration mixed with awe, he resolved to try the effect of strong drink; and immediately set about brewing a tumbler of whisky punch. But the experiment was unsuccessful, as it made the adventurous youth cough most piteously for at least a quarter of an hour.

"Gang into the kitchen and ask the cook to gie ye a spoonfu' o' jam; it's mair in your line than toddy an' the like," said Dr Dubious, with a sly wink; and the young man left the room till the violence of his cough abated. Several of the guests laughed heartily at this mischance, and as soon as silence was restored Mr Ferguson commenced his narrative.

"When people walk about the streets of this rising township," he said, "and admire the rapid progress of different institutions, they seldom reflect that a quarter of a century has scarcely elapsed since this spot was trodden only by a few settlers; or by the race they were to exterminate. But it was not in this locality where I became the enemy of the aborigines. I see a gentleman in that corner look rather scandalised at this remark; and it may, perhaps, appear uncharitable to those who came into these colonies long after *we* had tamed or driven away the remnant of the natives. Well, I *was* their enemy – I am so still – and their enemy I shall ever remain; and a very good reason have I for feeling the most deadly hatred towards them.

I had been residing rather more than a year in Sydney – after my arrival in this part of the world – when I became informed of the whereabouts of an uncle, who had settled in a locality to me utterly unknown. It was then a lonely place, and one at that time seldom visited, excepting by a few adventurous explorers; but now a thriving district near to Deniliquin. My uncle had two sons and three daughters – the two younger girls being mere children, the eldest a fine young woman of seventeen. One of her brothers was two years older, the other a year and a half younger than herself.

I was then about twenty; as tall, and nearly as stout as I am now; strong and resolute, and, therefore, not unfit to assist my uncle in clearing his land and looking after his stock. It was to aid him in these undertakings, that I accompanied the men – who had been sent to Sydney with wool – to the district in which my uncle resided. It was a long and hazardous journey; a great portion of it lying through a country that had only been partially explored; a circumstance which compelled us, on several occasions, to make a very circuitous route, in order to avoid an attack from the natives.

At length we reached a hut which had been hastily put up by my uncle as a temporary abode, till a more commodious dwelling could be erected in its stead. This hut was tenanted only by a shepherd and his son, whose business it was to tend the cattle which my uncle had lately bought, together with a few thousand acres; the farther boundary of the land being about twenty five miles from the station.

"Thank God there is the hut – we can rest there," said McTavish, the leader of the party, when the small structure appeared in sight.

"Had we not better push on to the station at once?" I asked, for I thought if I yielded to a growing sense of fatigue, I should have some difficulty in resuming my journey.

"We'd make for the station fast enough, if there was a chance of reaching it," replied McTavish. "But there are blackfellows on our track, and we may think ourselves fortunate if we can obtain shelter in the hut. As I'm alive, I see a dozen or more of their ugly faces behind the scrub. Ride on, my men! We have not an instant to lose!"

We spurred on our jaded horses, and in a few minutes reached the hut. The door was fastened, but the great bar which protected it was at once withdrawn by the shepherd within, who said, "For God's sake, come in quickly, and lead your horses through into the kitchen – there is no other place for them."

Our leader alighted, and led his horse into a portion of the hut designated 'the kitchen' though the whole dwelling consisted merely of two rooms, and there was very little distinction between them. We followed his example, removing our saddles, which was almost all the alleviation we could afford to the weary animals.

"The beasts must e'en take their chance like ourselves, and I canna tell whether I be glad to see ye or no. We have a lot o' blackfellows a great deal nearer to us than is pleasant; and it's odds if ye'll aid us or add to our danger," said the shepherd.

"We'll try to aid ye, Jock," said McTavish, "but I'm afraid that if the defenders are increased in number, the assailants are so likewise, for there are blackfellows on our track."

"The de'il!" exclaimed Jock.

And the next moment the presence of the savages was announced by a frightful yell; and through several crevices between the slabs of the hut appeared the sharp points of our enemies' spears.

We had no means of resisting the attack, neither of adding to our defence; save by raising the beds and the mattresses of the shepherd and his son against the walls on one side of the hut, and the table and all the rugs we could muster on the other. Our position was perilous in the extreme; our only hope being that assistance might arrive from the station before the slabs of the hut gave way, or before we perished with thirst, for the shepherd had but a scanty supply of water to be distributed amongst so many.

It is true that we had provided ourselves with a few bottles of rum; and this liquor served as a stimulant, though it was of little use in allaying our thirst. The sight of a large chest of tea, which Jock had lately received from his employer, added to our irritation, for if we had availed ourselves of it, the appearance of smoke issuing from the chimney would at once have suggested the idea of cooking to the enemy, and caused them to be still more daring in their attack.

In this manner four nights and three days passed away, by which time we were almost mad with thirst. One of our horses had died from a spear wound, the weapon having penetrated the wall against which the poor animal stood. We, apprehensive of a similar fate, sat huddled together in the middle of the room. Still were we horribly conscious of the presence of our foe, and of the incessant shivering of their spears, the points of which had now made fearful rents in the fragile edifice. The moaning of the cattle at a distance also prepared us for another calamity, though I – a stranger then to bush life – was not aware of the cause till McTavish exclaimed, "These infernal savages have speared the poor animals."

Things had now reached a climax, and suddenly the shower of spears ceased, and the sound of firing was heard, followed by a yell. McTavish called an order to retreat, and this announced that the enemy had taken flight.

"Courage, my poor fellows!" said my uncle, as he broke open the door of the hut. "Half your foes are dead, and the other half in no condition to do much harm."

Our deliverance was now effected; for my uncle, alarmed by the delay of our party, had sallied forth, accompanied by his stockmen – and just in time to save us from destruction, as our little fortress could not much longer withstand the attack.

We soon found that three hundred head of cattle had been speared by the savages, and the rest of the herd driven away; although the greater portion found their way to the station.

"So, nephew, this is your first encounter with the blacks, I suppose," said my uncle, when he released me from my captivity.

"I cannot call being bailed-up in a hut by these fellows an encounter with them; but I'll let them see what I can do one of these days," I replied.

And I have kept my word.

After a year spent amongst my uncle's family, I gained some applause for my skill as a bushman – though I had little merit for the same – having taken to that sort of life with the greatest eagerness. At the end of this time I went, with my eldest cousin, to reside at his station; the place where the shepherd's hut had formerly stood.

One evening, as we were going to visit our relatives, we were surprised by perceiving indications of a bush fire in the distance. This should not have seemed an extraordinary circumstance during the heat of summer, but the season was now far too much advanced for such a thing to have happened; excepting by extreme carelessness on the part of those who had lighted a fire in the bush – or by wanton mischief. Whilst we were debating about the strangeness of the occurrence, a boy came running towards us, exclaiming, "The blackfellows have set fire to the station, and have speared some of the men in the stockyard."

We galloped on as fast as our horses could carry us, but arrived too late – for, although the ground was strewn with the corpses of blackfellows, several of the stockmen were also killed. On entering the house, we found my uncle and all his family inhumanly slaughtered.

I am not generally supposed to be a tender-hearted man but, even after this lapse of time, I cannot speak of that occurrence without feeling almost as much anguish as I experienced on that terrible night. I therefore pass over the description of a sight which sufficed to change the whole current of my nature. But I ask, do you wonder that I henceforth became the bitter enemy of the blackfellows? If you had seen that poor old man lying dead, his grey hair dabbled in his blood; if you had seen his beautiful daughter, Isabella, pierced by the spears of these savages; if you had had the cause for hatred that I have, there is not one amongst you who would not likewise have been their enemy.

But do not suppose that one amongst their tribe escaped unpunished; as every settler, for hundreds of miles around, mustered all his men to hunt the scoundrels to death. And in less than two months, there was not a blackfellow in the district.

We did not care *how* we destroyed them. Once, we got an old fieldpiece – that some naval officer had left as a trophy of *his* deeds to his descendants – and it did us good service; for we charged it with broken glass and fired it off amongst the scoundrels. Nicely mangled they were, as you may suppose, and a hideous noise they made; but we soon put a stop to that, for we lighted a good fire, and threw the dying into it. Ha! I shall never forget one old fellow, who had lain on the ground, pretending to be dead; a cunning trick of theirs, for they think white men respect a corpse. However, he did not play his part very well, for he trembled – perhaps he was frightened – and we soon gave him cause to be so, as we threw him into the fire, on the top of his companions. An obstinate old fellow he was, being determined not to die if he could help it; and, hoping to escape, he crawled away from the burning logs like a snake. He had some spirit in him, that blackfellow; but we threw him back again into the flames, and he was burnt *with* a snake, as one lay coiled up amongst the scrub; and so we got rid of two reptiles at the same time.

That was the night which haunts the memory of my friend McLean; but he is only half a Highlander, and does not know how to *hate*.

I did not stop with this exploit. How could I? A pretty thing it would have been to give way to idle sentiment, when I had just taken up land in a district where the blackfellows had not been taught how to behave themselves; and I said so, to some good neighbours of mine, who fancied that savages were to be gained over by kindness. If I had not known to the contrary, I should have found it out, for – just by way of convincing my charitable friends of their mistake – I distributed blankets amongst some of the natives – giving them at the same time both rum and flour. To reward my bounty, they speared some of my cattle. But we soon brought them under subjection.

The next year, I had a narrow escape. As I was rowing down the Murrumbidgee with a couple of friends, a dozen blackfellows lay in ambush amongst the mangroves; and as soon as they thought we were in their power, they assailed us with their spears. It was a miracle how we escaped; and it would have been altogether an impossibility, had not the river been unusually high at the time and the current very strong. Consequently, we were carried out of their immediate reach, and enabled to row away faster than even the nimblest of all nimble blackfellows can run.

Such were the men – animals I should say – whom my righteous friends said I should *trust*. However, we treated our foe of the Murrumbidgee as we had treated others; for we had a good stock of powder and shot in our boat, and we peppered the rascals pretty well with it, giving those who escaped unhurt plenty to do in looking after their wounded companions, without pursuing us any farther.

In a few weeks I reached my station, where I found a well-intentioned gentleman, lately arrived from the Old Country who, knowing very little about any colonial race, and nothing at all of our aborigines, argued as others had done before him, on the advisability of treating them like brothers. By this he meant, as philanthropists generally do, giving away what they did not want themselves. I humoured my well-meaning friend for a little while, and then distributed blankets and bread, as I had formerly done. But, having important business in Sydney, I left my station under the superintendence of my friend McLean. I was absent several months; and, on my return, found that my two compassionate friends had been trying the argument of weak tea, and still weaker talk, on the natives.

"No weak measures will do with these fellows," I said, in answer to their assurances that their plan would succeed. And the result proved that I was in the right; for in the course of a few weeks, our black neighbours, having joined a tribe of their allies, mustered in great numbers, and it required all our exertions to prevent a disaster similar to that I have already described. Fortunately, however, we were well armed, and by this time even McLean admitted that mercy would be madness; and thus, by a vigorous attack, we either killed or dispersed our treacherous enemies.

That district has been safe from their attacks ever since, but the station on the Murrumbidgee continued to be infested by a prowling set of fellows, who were continually pilfering when they did not venture upon acts of greater violence. However, we allowed them to poison themselves with adulterated flour; that is to say, flour adulterated with arsenic.

McLean pretends that the spirits of these fellows haunt him in his sleep; but I can't say that *they* trouble my repose, though I often see the murdered forms of my poor uncle, his amiable wife, his innocent children, and especially the beautiful Isabella; and till I see them no longer, shall I be an enemy to the blackfellows.

Understand, however, I do not mean such miserable creatures as the poor drudge employed about this hotel; though I think even *he* would not be safe from the hatred of my cousin – the only survivor of that unfortunate family.

I have not seen Donald of late, for he now resides in Queensland; but three years have scarcely elapsed since he was the principal agent in exterminating a whole tribe of natives. Nor has this transaction been regarded with horror; for the blackfellows in that particular district had a short time before repaid the hospitality of a charitable man with a cowardly murder. Nevertheless, I think Donald was rather actuated by a determination to revenge the death of his own relations, than that of his Queensland acquaintance.

It is true that many years had passed since the massacre of my uncle and his family, and that the Queensland tribe had no hand in the affair, nor, indeed, anyone in existence, at the time of the latter occurrence; but is it to be supposed that Donald should ever show mercy to a blackfellow, whatever his tribe or district? This is understood by the very authorities, who have proclaimed the shooting of an aborigine to be a felony; for Donald fires at all he may chance to meet, with impunity.

As for myself, I have of late ceased to raise a hand against them; for the remnants of the scattered tribes I occasionally meet are too abject for my revenge. My revenge, you perhaps think, ought to have been appeased by what I have already done. I try to think so sometimes; but when the images of the friends I loved so well arise to my memory, I feel that if I would live apparently at peace with the natives, it must be by avoiding them. For a Highlander can never forgive.

The guests listened in silence to this narrative of a long-cherished hatred; and when the speaker concluded, a long suppressed sigh broke from his auditors. All felt that Ferguson must have sorrowed deeply for the death of his relatives; but the impression the story made was not the same on all.

Some there were who, even whilst living the life of Australian settlers, still felt very much as their fathers had done: that it was the first duty of a clansman to revenge the death of his chief. These men seemed ready to applaud whenever Ferguson spoke of the acts of wholesale extermination in which he had taken part.

Others had shuddered to perceive how relentless he still was in heart; for he appeared to dwell with satisfaction on those portions of his tale which chiefly referred to the cruelties he had practised; and then his eye flashed fire, as if it would say, *I hate them still.*

But amongst the group were a few who fancied those proud dark eyes had glistened with tears at the recollection of Isabella.

Perhaps Mr Lightfoot thought of his wife and children; for at the conclusion of the Highlander's story, he said, "We are not sufficiently thankful to the noble pioneers who cleared our path from so many dangers; for if *they* had not dispersed – and, in some cases, *destroyed* – whole tribes of these blackfellows, should we now be enjoying the blessings of civilised life?"

"Ye're right there, Mr Lightfoot; but these blessings have been purchased at a fearful price, and it's a sore trouble to remember these times," said McLean; who, during the greater part of the story, had sat with his face buried between his hands.

"Civilisation has seldom been introduced by gentle means; nor – in spite of the rigorous measures resorted to by our friend Mr Ferguson – can it be said really to exist where a bushranger is either protected or regarded as a hero," said Mr Ellison.

"Nevertheless, there are lights as well as shades, even in a bushranger's career," remarked Mr Wildman, a barrister, who was often retained in defence of these Australian freebooters. "And, if it were not too late, I could tell you of an adventure that –"

"Was not foreshadowed by a dream, I hope," said the doctor.

"A dream! No, indeed; there is almost as much actual busy life connected with it as in the stirring narrative of our friend Ferguson; but as it is late, I will postpone my story till another night."

"You've frightened that fellow out of his senses, Ferguson. I heard him tell Mary not to let the poor black body into his room," said the doctor, who now returned, after a visit to the bar; for the doctor, as well as Mr Ferguson and a few deep drinkers, often sat over the parlour fire till the small hours of the morning.

Mr Ferguson smiled contemptuously; and he and his countryman then entered into a discussion respecting local topics. Stupid as such may be, they often occupy as much time as more heroic subjects; and whilst the gentlemen were thus engaged, more than an hour slipped away.

Suddenly they were aroused by a dull sound overhead, like that of a man striking with his fists against a door; and presently a voice, naturally weak, but rendered still more so by fear, was heard to exclaim, "Mr Ferguson! Mr Ferguson! The blacks are upon us! The hotel will be burnt, and we shall all be murdered!"

"What has that cockney idiot taken into his head now?" demanded the Highlander.

"Ower much toddy, I'm a thinking," replied the doctor.

"No, no! They *are* here, Ferguson. I had hoped never to see a tribe of blackfellows again!" exclaimed poor McLean.

Mr Ferguson regarded his friend with a look of disdain, asking him if he had lost his senses.

But the recollection of those deeds in which he had formerly taken a part was too much for McLean who, throwing himself on a sofa, endeavoured – by burying his face amongst the pillows – to shut out the vision of the past from his 'mind's eye' as the *actual sounds* met his ear.

But so different was the effect produced upon Ferguson that he said to the landlord, who had now entered the room, "If you want to prevent bloodshed, keep your revolvers out of my way. I do not wish to shoot those blackfellows."

By this time the excitement of Mr Skimmile became so great, that the joint efforts of the landlady and the chambermaid were insufficient to hold him, and he rushed wildly into the parlour, exclaiming that the hotel was attacked by a troop of blacks.

"Keep yourself quiet, sir; they are beating a retreat," said the landlord. "We have sent them some rum and cold meat; for they have been celebrating the moonlight night, by holding a corroboree!"

THE ALIBI

Daphne du Maurier

Daphne du Maurier (1907–1989) is best known as the author of *Rebecca, The Birds, Jamaica Inn, Don't Look Now* and *My Cousin Rachel,* which have all become major films. Part of a prominent Cornish family, she pioneered suspense in fiction, and was made a Dame of the British Empire twenty years before her death.

1.

The Fentons were taking their usual Sunday walk along the Embankment. They had come to Albert Bridge, and paused, as they always did, before deciding whether to cross it to the gardens or continue along past the houseboats; and Fenton's wife, following some process of thought unknown to him, said, "Remind me to telephone the Alhusons when we get home to ask them for drinks. It's their turn to come to us."

Fenton stared heedlessly at the passing traffic. His mind took in a lorry swinging too fast over the bridge, a sports car with a loud exhaust, and a nurse in a grey uniform, pushing a pram containing identical twins with round faces like Dutch cheeses, who turned left over the bridge to Battersea.

"Which way?" asked his wife, and he looked at her without recognition, seized with the overwhelming, indeed appalling impression that she, and all the other people walking along the Embankment or crossing the bridge, were minute, dangling puppets manipulated by a string. The very steps they took were jerking, lopsided, a horrible imitation of the real thing, of what should be; and his wife's face—the china-blue eyes, the too heavily made-up mouth, the new spring hat set at a jaunty angle—was nothing but a mask painted rapidly by a master-hand, the hand that held the puppets, on the strip of lifeless wood, matchstick wood, from which these marionettes were fashioned.

He looked quickly away from her and down to the ground, hurriedly tracing the outline of a square on the pavement with his walking-stick, and pin-pointing a blob in the centre of the square. Then he heard himself saying, "I can't go on."

"What's the matter?" asked his wife. "Have you got a stitch?"

He knew then that he must be on his guard. Any attempt at explanation would lead to bewildered stares from those large eyes, to equally bewildered, pressing questions; and they would turn on their tracks back along the hated Embankment, the wind this time mercifully behind them yet carrying them inexorably towards the death of the hours ahead, just as the tide of the river beside them carried the rolling logs and empty boxes to some inevitable, stinking mud-spit below the docks.

Cunningly he rephrased his words to reassure her. "What I meant was that we can't go on beyond the houseboats. It's a dead-end. And your heels . . ." he glanced down at her shoes . . . "your heels aren't right for the long trek round Battersea. I need exercise, and you can't keep up. Why don't you go home? It's not much of an afternoon."

His wife looked up at the sky, low-clouded, opaque, and blessedly, for him, a gust of wind shivered her too thin coat and she put up her hand to hold the spring hat.

"I think I will," she said, and then with doubt, "Are you sure you haven't a stitch? You look pale."

"No, I'm all right," he replied. "I'll walk faster alone."

Then, seeing at that moment a taxi approaching with its flag up, he hailed it, waving his stick, and said to her, "Jump in. No sense in catching cold." Before she could protest he had opened the door and given the address to the driver. There was no time to argue. He hustled her inside, and as it bore her away he saw her struggle with the closed window to call out something about not being late back and the Alhusons. He watched the taxi out of sight down the Embankment, and it was like watching a phase of life that had gone forever.

He turned away from the river and the Embankment, and, leaving all sound and sight of traffic behind him, plunged into the warren of narrow streets and squares which lay between him and the Fulham Road. He walked with no purpose but to lose identity, and to blot from present thought the ritual of the Sunday which imprisoned him.

The idea of escape had never come to him before. It was as though something had clicked in his brain when his wife made the remark about the Alhusons. "Remind me to telephone when we get home. It's their turn to come to us." The drowning man who sees the pattern of his life pass by as the sea engulfs him could at last be understood. The ring at the front door, the cheerful voices of the Alhusons, the drinks set out on the sideboard, the standing about for a moment and then the sitting down—these things became only pieces of the tapestry that was the whole of his life-imprisonment, beginning daily with the drawing-back of the curtains and early morning tea, the opening of the newspaper, break-fast eaten in the small dining-room with the gas-fire burning blue (turned low because of waste), the journey by Underground to the City, the passing hours of methodical office work, the return by Underground, unfolding an evening paper in the crowd which hemmed him in, the laying down of hat and coat and umbrella, the sound of television from the drawing-room blending, perhaps, with the voice of his wife talking on the 'phone. And it was winter, or it was summer, or it was spring, or it was autumn, because with the changing seasons the covers of the chairs and sofa in the drawing-room were cleaned and replaced by others, or the trees in the square outside were in leaf or bare.

"It's their turn to come to us," and the Alhusons, grimacing and jumping on their string, came and bowed and disappeared, and the hosts who had received them became guests in their turn, jiggling and smirking, the dancing couples set to partners in an old-time measure.

Now suddenly, with the pause by Albert Bridge and Edna's remark, time had ceased; or rather, it had continued in the same way for her, for the Alhusons answering the telephone, for the other partners in the dance; but for him every-thing had changed. He was aware of a sense of power within. He was in control. His was the master-hand that set the puppets jiggling. And Edna, poor Edna, speeding home in the taxi to a predestined role of putting out the drinks, patting cushions, shaking salted almonds from a tin, Edna had no conception of how he had stepped out of bondage into a new dimension.

The apathy of Sunday lay upon the streets. Houses were closed, withdrawn.

"They don't know," he thought, "those people inside, how one gesture of mine, now, at this minute, might alter their world. A knock on the door, and someone answers—a woman yawning, an old man in carpet slippers, a child sent by its parents in irritation; and according to what I will, what I decide, their whole future will be decided. Faces smashed in. Sudden murder. Theft. Fire." It was as simple as that.

He looked at his watch. Half-past three. He decided to work on a system of numbers. He would walk down three more streets, and then, depending upon the name of the third street in which he found himself, and how many letters it contained, choose the number of his destination.

He walked briskly, aware of mounting interest. No cheating, he told himself. Block of flats or United Dairies, it was all one. It turned out that the third street was a long one, flanked on either side by drab Victorian villas which had been pretentious some fifty years ago, and now, let out as flats or lodgings, had lost caste. The name was Boulting Street. Eight letters meant Number 8. He crossed over confidently, searching the front-doors, undaunted by the steep flight of stone steps leading to every villa, the unpainted gates, the lowering basements, the air of poverty and decay which presented such a contrast to the houses in his own small Regency square, with their bright front doors and window-boxes.

Number 8 proved no different from its fellows. The gate was even shabbier, perhaps, the curtains at the long, ugly ground-floor window more bleakly lace. A child of about three, a boy, sat on the top step, white-faced, blank-eyed, tied in some strange fashion to the mud-scraper so that he could not move. The front door was ajar.

James Fenton mounted the steps and looked for the bell. There was a scrap of paper pasted across it with the words "Out of Order". Beneath it was an old-fashioned bell-pull, fastened with string. It would be a matter of seconds, of course, to unravel the knotted strap binding the child, carry him off under his arm down the steps, and then dispose of him according to mood or fancy. But violence did not seem to be indicated just yet: it was not what he wanted, for the feeling of power within demanded a longer term of freedom.

He pulled at the bell. The faint tinkle sounded down the dark hall. The child stared up at him, unmoved. Fenton turned away from the door and looked out on the street, at the plane tree coming into leaf on the pavement edge, the brown bark patchy yellow, a black cat crouching at its foot biting a wounded paw; and he savoured the waiting moment as delicious because of its uncertainty.

He heard the door open wider behind him and a woman's voice, foreign in intonation, ask, "What can I do for you?"

Fenton took off his hat. The impulse was strong within him to say, "I have come to strangle you. You and your child. I bear you no malice whatever. It jus happens that I am the instrument of fate sent for this purpose." Instead, he smiled. The woman was pallid, like the child on the steps, with the same expressionless eyes, the same lank hair. Her age might have been anything from twenty to thirty-five. She was wearing a woollen cardigan too big for her, and her dark, bunched skirt, ankle-length, made her seem squat.

"Do you let rooms?" asked Fenton.

A light came into the dull eyes, an expression of hope. It was almost as if this was a question she had longed for and had believed would never come. But the gleam faded again immediately, and the blank stare returned.

"The house isn't mine," she said. "The landlord let rooms once, but they say it's to be pulled down, with those on either side, to make room for flats."

"You mean," he pursued, "the landlord doesn't let rooms any more?"

"No," she said. "He told me it wouldn't be worth it, not with the demolition order coming any day. He pays me a small sum to caretake until they pull the house down. I live in the basement."

"I see," he said.

It would seem that the conversation was at an end. Nevertheless Fenton continued to stand there. The girl or woman—for she could be either—looked past him to the child, bidding him to be quiet, though he hardly whimpered.

"I suppose," said Fenton," you couldn't sublet one of the rooms in the basement to me? It could be a private arrangement between ourselves while you remain here. The landlord couldn't object."

He watched her make the effort to think. His suggestion, so unlikely, so surprising coming from someone of his appearance, was something she could not take in. Since surprise is the best form of attack, he seized his advantage. "I only need one room," he said quickly, "for a few hours in the day. I shouldn't be sleeping here."

The effort to size him up was beyond her—the tweed suit, appropriate for London or the country, the trilby hat, the walking-stick, the fresh-complexioned face, the forty-five to fifty years. He saw the dark eyes become wider and blanker still as they tried to reconcile his appearance with his unexpected request.

"What would you want the room for?" she asked doubtfully.

There was the crux. To murder you and the child, my dear, and dig up the floor, and bury you under the boards. But not yet.

"It's difficult to explain," he said briskly. "I'm a professional man. I have long hours. But there have been changes lately, and I must have a room where I can put in a few hours every day and be entirely alone. You've no idea how difficult it is to find the right spot. This seems to me ideal for the purpose." He glanced from the empty house down to the child, and smiled. "Your little boy, for instance. Just the right age. He'd give no trouble."

A semblance of a smile passed across her face. "Oh, Johnnie is quiet enough," she said. "He sits there for hours, he wouldn't interfere." Then the smile wavered, the doubt returned. "I don't know what to say . . . We live in the kitchen, with the bedroom next to it. There *is* a room behind, where I have a few bits of furniture stored, but I don't think you would like it. You see, it depends what you want to do . . ."

Her voice trailed away. Her apathy was just what he needed. He wondered if she slept very heavily, or even drugged. Those dark shadows under the eyes suggested drugs. So much the better. And a foreigner too. There were too many of them in the country.

"If you would only show me the room, I should know at once," he said.

Surprisingly she turned, and led the way down the narrow, dingy hall. Switching on a light above a basement stair, murmuring a continual apology the while, she took Fenton below. This had been, of course, the original servants' quarters of the Victorian villa. The kitchen, scullery and pantry had now become the woman's living-room, kitchenette and bedroom, and in their transformation had increased in squalor. The ugly pipes, the useless boiler, the old range, might once have had some pretension to efficiency, with fresh white paint on the pipes and the range polished. Even the dresser, still in position and stretching nearly the full width of one wall, would have been in keeping some fifty years ago, with polished brass saucepans and a patterned dinner-service, while an overalled cook, bustling about with arms befloured, called orders to a minion in the scullery. Now the dirty cream paint hung in flakes, the worn linoleum was torn, and the dresser was bare save for odds and ends bearing no relation to its original purpose—a battered wireless set with trailing aerial, piles of discarded magazines and newspapers, unfinished knitting, broken toys, pieces of cake, a toothbrush, and several pairs of shoes. The woman looked about her helplessly.

"It's not easy," she said, "with a child. One clears up all the time."

It was evident that she never cleared, that she had given in, that the shambles he observed was her answer to life's problems, but Fenton said nothing, only nodded politely, and smiled. He caught a glimpse of an unmade bed through a half-open door, bearing out his theory of the heavy sleeper—his ring at the bell must have disturbed her—but seeing his glance she shut the door hurriedly, and in a half-conscious effort to bring herself to order buttoned her cardigan and combed her hair with her fingers.

"And the room you do not use?" he asked.

"Oh, yes," she replied, "yes, of course . . ." vague and uncertain, as if she had forgotten her purpose in bringing him to the basement. She led the way back across the passage, past a coal cellar—useful, this, he thought—a lavatory with a child's pot set in the open door and a torn *Daily Mirror* beside it, and so to a further room, the door of which was closed.

"I don't think it will do," she said sighing, already defeated. Indeed, it would not have done for anyone but himself, so full of power and purpose; for as she flung open the creaking door, and crossed the room to pull aside the strip of curtain made out of old wartime blackout material, the smell of damp hit him as forcibly as a sudden patch of fog beside the river, and with it the unmistakable odour of escaping gas. They sniffed in unison.

"Yes, it's bad," she said. "The men are supposed to come, but they never do."

As she pulled the curtain to let in air the rod broke, the strip of material fell, and through a broken pane of the window jumped the black cat with the wounded paw which Fenton had noticed beneath the plane tree in front of the house. The woman shooed it ineffectually. The cat, used to its surroundings, slunk into a far corner, jumped on a packing-case and composed itself to sleep. Fenton and the woman looked about them.

"This would do me very well," he said, hardly considering the dark walls, the odd L-shape of the room and the low ceiling. "Why, there's even a garden," and he went to the window and looked out upon the patch of earth and stones—level with his head as he stood in the basement room—which had once been a strip of paved garden.

"Yes," she said, "yes, there's a garden," and she came beside him to stare at the desolation to which they both gave so false a name. Then with a little shrug she went on, "It's quiet, as you see, but it doesn't get much sun. It faces north."

"I like a room to face north," he said abstractedly, already seeing in his mind's eye the narrow trench he would be able to dig for her body—no need to make it deep. Turning towards her, measuring the size of her, reckoning the length and breadth, he saw a glimmer of understanding come into her eye, and he quickly smiled to give her confidence.

"Are you an artist?" she said. "They like a north light, don't they?"

His relief was tremendous. An artist. But of course. Here was the excuse he needed. Here was a way out of all difficulty.

"I see you've guessed my secret," he answered slyly, and his laugh rang so true that it surprised even himself. He began to speak very rapidly. "Part-time only," he said. "That's the reason I can only get away for certain hours. My mornings are tied down to business, but later in the day I'm a free man. Then my real work begins. It's not just a casual hobby, it's a passion. I intend to hold my own exhibition later in the year. So you understand how essential it is for me to find somewhere . . . like this."

He waved his hand at the surroundings, which could offer no inducement to anyone but the cat. His confidence was infectious and disarmed the still doubtful, puzzled enquiry in her eyes.

"Chelsea's full of artists, isn't it?" she said. "At least they say so, I don't know. But I thought studios had to be high up for getting the light?"

"Not necessarily," he answered. "Those fads don't affect me. And late in the day the light will have gone anyway. I suppose there is electricity?"

"Yes . . ." She moved to the door and touched a switch. A naked bulb from the ceiling glared through its dust.

"Excellent," he said. "That's all I shall need."

He smiled down at the blank, unhappy face. The poor soul would be so much happier asleep. Like the cat. A kindness, really, to put her out of her misery.

"Can I move in to-morrow?" he asked.

Again the look of hope that he had noticed when he first stood at the front door enquiring for rooms, and then—was it embarrassment, just the faintest trace of discomfort, in her expression?

"You haven't asked about . . . the cost of the room," she said.

"Whatever you care to charge," he replied, and waved his hand again to show that money was no object. She swallowed, evidently at a loss to know what to say, and then, a flush creeping into the pallid face, ventured, "It would be best if I said nothing to the landlord. I will say you are a friend. You could give me a pound or two in cash every week, what you think fair."

She watched him anxiously. Certainly, he decided, there must be no third party interfering in any arrangement. It might defeat his plan.

"I'll give you five pounds in notes each week, starting to-day," he said.

He felt for his wallet and drew out the crisp, new notes. She put out a timid hand, and her eyes never left the notes as he counted them.

"Not a word to the landlord," he said, "and if any questions are asked about your lodger say your cousin, an artist, has arrived for a visit."

She looked up and for the first time smiled, as though his joking words, with the giving of the notes, somehow sealed a bond between them.

"You don't look like my cousin," she said, "nor much like the artists I have seen, either. What is your name?"

"Sims," he said instantly, "Marcus Sims," and wondered why he had instinctively uttered the name of his wife's father, a solicitor dead these many years, whom he had heartily disliked.

"Thank you, Mr. Sims," she said. "I'll give your room a clean-up in the morning." Then, as a first gesture towards this intention, she lifted the cat from the packing-case and shooed it through the window.

"You will bring your things to-morrow afternoon?" she asked.

"My things?" he repeated.

"What you need for your work," she said. "Don't you have paints and so on?"

"Oh, yes . . . yes, naturally," he said, "yes, I must bring my gear." He glanced round the room again. But there was to be no question of butchery. No blood. No mess. The answer would be to stifle them both in sleep, the woman and her child. It was much the kindest way.

"You won't have far to go when you need tubes of paint," she said. "There are shops for artists in the King's Road. I have passed them shopping. They have boards and easels in the window."

He put his hand over his mouth to hide his smile. It was really touching how she had accepted him. It showed such trust, such confidence.

She led the way back into the passage, and so up the basement stair to the hall once more.

"I'm so delighted," he said, "that we have come to this arrangement. To tell you the truth, I was getting desperate."

She turned and smiled at him again over her shoulder. "So was I," she said. "If you hadn't appeared . . . I don't know what I might not have done."

They stood together at the top of the basement stair. What an amazing thing. It was an act of God that he had suddenly arrived. He stared at her, shocked.

"You've been in some trouble, then?" he asked.

"Trouble?" She gestured with her hands, and the look of apathy, of despair, returned to her face. "It's trouble enough to be a stranger in this country, and for the father of my little boy to go off and leave me without any money, and not to know where to turn. I tell you, Mr. Sims, if you had not come today . . ." She did not finish her sentence, but glanced towards the child tied to the foot-scraper and shrugged her shoulders. "Poor Johnnie . . ." she said, "it's not your fault."

"Poor Johnnie indeed," echoed Fenton, "and poor you. Well, I'll do my part to put an end to your troubles, I assure you."

"You're very good. Truly, I thank you."

"On the contrary, I thank *you*." He made her a little bow and, bending down, touched the top of the child's head. "Goodbye, Johnnie, see you to-morrow." His victim gazed back at him without expression.

"Good-bye, Mrs. . . . Mrs. . . .?"

"Kaufman is the name. Anna Kaufman."

She watched him down the steps and through the gate. The banished cat slunk past his legs on a return journey to the broken window. Fenton waved his hat with a flourish to the woman, to the boy, to the cat, to the whole fabric of the mute, drab villa.

"See you to-morrow," he called, and set off down Boulting Street with the jaunty step of someone at the start of a great adventure. His high spirits did not even desert him when he arrived at his own front-door. He let himself in with his latch-key and went up the stairs humming some old song of thirty years ago. Edna, as usual, was on the telephone—he could hear the interminable conversation of one woman to another. The drinks were set out on the small table in the drawing-room. The cocktail biscuits were laid ready, and the dish of salted almonds. The extra glasses meant that visitors were expected. Edna put her hand over the mouthpiece of the receiver and said, "The Alhusons will be coming. I've asked them to stay on for cold supper."

Her husband smiled and nodded. Long before his usual time he poured himself a thimbleful of sherry to round off the conspiracy, the perfection, of the past hour. The conversation on the telephone ceased.

"You look better," said Edna. "The walk did you good."

Her innocence amused him so much that he nearly choked.

2.

It was a lucky thing that the woman had mentioned an artist's props. He would have looked a fool arriving the following afternoon with nothing. As it was, it meant leaving the office early, and an expedition to fit himself up with the necessary paraphernalia. He let himself go. Easel, canvases, tube after tube of paint, brushes, turpentine—what had been intended as a few parcels became bulky packages impossible to transport except in a taxi. It all added to the excitement, though. He must play his part thoroughly. The assistant in the shop, fired by his customer's ardour, kept adding to the list of paints; and, as Fenton handled the tubes of colour and read the names, there was something intensely satisfying about the purchase, and he allowed himself to be reckless, the very words chrome and sienna and terre-verte going to his head like wine. Finally he tore himself away from temptation, and climbed into a taxi with his wares. No. 8, Boulting Street; the unaccustomed address instead of his own familiar square added spice to the adventure.

It was strange, but as the taxi drew up at its destination the row of villas no longer appeared so drab. It was true that yesterday's wind had dropped, the sun was shining fitfully, and there was a hint in the air of April and longer days to come; but that was not the point. The point was that No. 8 had something of expectancy about it. As he paid his driver and carried the packages from the taxi, he saw that the dark blinds in the basement had been removed and makeshift curtains, tangerine-coloured and a shock to the eye, hung in their place. Even as he noted this the curtains were pulled back and the woman, the child in her arms, its face smeared with jam, waved up at him. The cat leapt from the sill and came towards him purring, rubbing an arched back against his trouser leg. The taxi drove away, and the woman came down the steps to greet him.

"Johnnie and I have been watching for you the whole afternoon," she said. "Is that all you've brought?"

"All? Isn't it enough?" he laughed.

She helped him carry the things down the basement stair, and as he glanced into the kitchen he saw that an attempt had been made to tidy it, besides the hanging of the curtains. The row of shoes had been banished underneath the dresser, along with the child's toys, and a cloth, laid for tea, had been spread on the table.

"You'll never believe the dust there was in your room," she said. "I was working there till nearly midnight."

"You shouldn't have done that," he told her. "It's not worth it, for the time."

She stopped before the door and looked at him, the blank look returning to her face. "It's not for long, then?" she faltered. "I somehow thought, from what you said yesterday, it would be for some weeks?"

"Oh, I didn't mean that," he said swiftly. "I meant that I shall make such a devil of a mess anyway, with these paints, there was no need to dust."

Relief was plain. She summoned a smile and opened the door. "Welcome, Mr. Sims," she said.

He had to give her her due. She had worked. The room did look different. Smelt different, too. No more leaking gas, but carbolic instead—or was it Jeyes? Disinfectant, anyway. The blackout strip had vanished from the window. She had even got someone in to repair the broken glass. The cat's bed—the packing-case—had gone. There was a table now against the wall, and two little rickety chairs, and an armchair also, covered with the same fearful tangerine material he had observed in the kitchen windows. Above the mantelpiece, bare yesterday, she had hung a large, brightly-coloured reproduction of a Madonna and Child, with an almanac beneath. The eyes of the Madonna, ingratiating, demure, smiled at Fenton.

"Well . . ." he began, "well, bless me . . ." and to conceal his emotion, because it was really very touching that the wretched woman had taken so much trouble on what was probably one of her last days on this earth, he turned away and began untying his packages.

"Let me help you, Mr. Sims," she said, and before he could protest she was down on her knees struggling with the knots, unwrapping the paper and fixing the easel for him. Then together they emptied the boxes of all the tubes of colour, laid them out in rows on the table, and stacked the canvases against the wall. It was amusing, like playing some absurd game, and curiously she entered into the spirit of it although remaining perfectly serious at the same time.

"What are you going to paint first?" she asked, when all was fixed and even a canvas set up upon the easel. "You have some subject in mind, I suppose?"

"Oh, yes," he said, "I've a subject in mind." He began to smile, her faith in him was so supreme, and suddenly she smiled too and said, "I've guessed. I've guessed your subject."

He felt himself go pale. How had she guessed? What was she driving at?

"What do you mean, you've guessed?" he asked sharply.

"It's Johnnie, isn't it?"

He could not possibly kill the child before the mother—what an appalling suggestion. And why was she trying to push him into it like this? There was time enough, and anyway his plan was not yet formed . . .

She was nodding her head wisely, and he brought himself back to reality with an effort. She was talking of painting, of course.

"You're a clever woman," he said. "Yes, Johnnie's my subject."

"He'll be good, he won't move," she said. "If I tie him up he'll sit for hours. Do you want him now?"

"No, no," Fenton replied testily. "I'm in no hurry at all. I've got to think it all out."

Her face fell. She seemed disappointed. She glanced round the room once more, converted so suddenly and so surprisingly into what she hoped was an artist's studio.

"Then let me give you a cup of tea," she said, and to save argument he followed her into the kitchen. There he sat himself down on the chair she drew forward for him, and drank tea and ate Bovril sandwiches, watched by the unflinching eyes of the grubby little boy.

"Da . . ." uttered the child suddenly, and put out its hand.

"He calls all men Da," said his mother, "though his own father took no notice of him. Don't worry Mr. Sims, Johnnie."

Fenton forced a polite smile. Children embarrassed him. He went on eating his Bovril sandwiches and sipping his tea.

The woman sat down and joined him, stirring her tea in an absent way until it must have been cold and unfit to drink.

"It's nice to have someone to talk to," she said. "Do you know, until you came, Mr. Sims, I was so alone . . . The empty house above, no workmen even passing in and out. And this is not a good neighbourhood—I have no friends at all."

Better and better, he thought. There'll be nobody to miss her when she's gone. It would have been a tricky thing to get away with had the rest of the house been inhabited. As it was, it could be done at any time of the day and no one the wiser. Poor kid, she could not be more than twenty-six or seven; what a life she must have led.

". . . he just went off without a word," she was saying. "Three years only we had been in this country, and we moved from place to place with no settled job. We were in Manchester at one time, Johnnie was born in Manchester."

"Awful spot," he sympathised, "never stops raining."

"I told him 'You've got to get work'," she continued, banging her fist on the table, acting the moment over again. "I said, 'We can't go on like this. It's no life for me, or for your child.' And, Mr. Sims, there was no money for the rent. What was I to say to the landlord when he called? And then, being aliens here, there is always some fuss with the police."

"Police?" said Fenton, startled.

"The papers," she explained, "there is such trouble with our papers. You know how it is, we have to register. Mr. Sims, my life has not been a happy one, not for many years. In Austria I was a servant for a time to a bad man. I had to run away. I was only sixteen then, and when I met my husband, who was not my husband then, it seemed at last that there might be some hope if we got to England . . ."

She droned on, watching him and stirring her tea the while, and her voice with its slow German accent, rather pleasing and lilting to the ear, was somehow soothing and a pleasant accompaniment to his thoughts, mingling with the ticking of the alarm clock on the dresser and the thumping of the little boy's spoon upon his plate. It was delightful to remind himself that he was not in the office, and not at home either, but was Marcus Sims the artist, surely a great artist, if not in colour at least in premeditated crime; and here was his victim putting her life into his hands, looking upon him, in fact, almost as her saviour—as indeed he was.

"It's queer," she said slowly, "yesterday I did not know you. To-day I tell you my life. You are my friend."

"Your sincere friend," he said, patting her hand. "I assure you it's the truth." He smiled, and pushed back his chair.

She reached for his cup and saucer and put them in the sink, then wiped the child's mouth with the sleeve of her jumper. "And now, Mr. Sims," she said, "which would you prefer to do first? Come to bed, or paint Johnnie?"

He stared at her. Come to bed? Had he heard correctly?

"I beg your pardon?" he said.

She stood patiently, waiting for him to move.

"It's for you to say, Mr. Sims," she said. "It makes no difference to me. I'm at your disposal."

He felt his neck turn slowly red, and the colour mount to his face and forehead. There was no doubt about it, no misunderstanding the half-smile she now attempted, and the jerk of her head towards the bedroom. The poor wretched girl was making him some sort of offer, she must believe that he actually expected . . . wanted . . . It was appalling.

"My dear Madame Kaufman," he began—somehow the Madame sounded better than Mrs., and it was in keeping with her alien nationality—"I am afraid there is some error. You have misunderstood me."

"Please?" she said, puzzled, and then summoned a smile again. "You don't have to be afraid. No one will come. And I will tie up Johnnie."

It was preposterous. Tie up that little boy . . . Nothing he had said to her could possibly have made her misconstrue the situation. Yet to show his natural anger and leave the house would mean the ruin of all his plans, his perfect plans, and he would have to begin all over again elsewhere.

"It's . . . it's extremely kind of you, Madame Kaufman," he said. "I do appreciate your offer. It's most generous. The fact is, unfortunately, I've been totally incapacitated for many years . . . an old war wound . . . I've had to put all that sort of thing out of my life long ago. Indeed, all my efforts go into my art, my painting, I concentrate entirely upon that. Hence my deep pleasure in finding this little retreat, which will make all the difference to my world. And if we are to be friends . . ."

He searched for further words to extricate himself. She shrugged her shoulders. There was neither relief nor disappointment in her face. What was to be, would be.

"That's all right, Mr. Sims," she said. "I thought perhaps you were lonely. I know what loneliness can be. And you are so kind. If at any time you feel you would like . . ."

"Oh, I'll tell you immediately," he interrupted swiftly. "No question of that. But alas, I'm afraid . . . Well now, to work, to work." And he smiled again, making some show of bustle, and opened the door of the kitchen. Thank heaven she had buttoned up the cardigan which she had so disastrously started to undo. She lifted the child from his chair and proceeded to follow him.

"I have always wanted to see a real artist at work," she said to him, "and now, lo and behold, my chance has come. Johnnie will appreciate this when he is older. Now, where would you like me to put him, Mr. Sims? Shall he stand or sit? What pose would be best?"

It was too much. From the frying-pan into the fire. Fenton was exasperated. The woman was trying to bully him. He could not possibly have her hanging about like this. If that horrid little boy had to be disposed of, then his mother must be out of the way.

"Never mind the pose," he said testily. "I'm not a photographer. And if there is one thing I cannot bear, it's being watched when I work. Put Johnnie there, on the chair. I suppose he'll sit still?"

"I'll fetch the strap," she said, and while she went back to the kitchen he stared moodily at the canvas on the easel. He must do something about it, that was evident. Fatal to leave it blank. She would not understand. She would begin to suspect that something was wrong. She might even repeat her fearful offer of five minutes ago . . .

He lifted one or two tubes of paint, and squeezed out blobs of colour on to the pallet. Raw sienna . . . Naples yellow . . . Good names they gave these things. He and Edna had been to Siena once, years ago, when they were first married. He remembered the rose-rust brickwork, and that square—what was the name of the square?—where they held a famous horse-race. Naples yellow. They had never got as far as Naples. See Naples and die. Pity they had not travelled more. They had fallen into a rut, always going up to Scotland, but Edna did not care for the heat. Azure blue . . . made you think of the deepest, or was it the clearest, blue? Lagoons in the South Seas, and flying-fish. How jolly the blobs of colour looked upon the pallet. . .

"So . . . be good, Johnnie." Fenton looked up. The woman had secured the child to the chair, and was patting the top of his head. "If there is anything you want you have only to call, Mr. Sims."

"Thank you, Madame Kaufman."

She crept out of the room, closing the door softly. The artist must not be disturbed. The artist must be left alone with his creation.

"Da," said Johnnie suddenly.

"Be quiet," said Fenton sharply. He was breaking a piece of charcoal in two. He had read somewhere that artists drew in the head first with charcoal. He adjusted the broken end between his fingers, and pursing his lips drew a circle, the shape of a full moon, upon the canvas. Then he stepped back and half-closed his eyes. The odd thing was that it did look like the rounded shape of a face without the features . . . Johnnie was watching him, his eyes large. Fenton realised that he needed a much larger canvas. The one on the easel would only take the child's head. It would look much more effective to have the whole head and shoulders on the canvas, because he could then use some of the azure blue to paint the child's blue jersey.

He replaced the first canvas with a larger one. Yes, that was a far better size. Now for the outline of the face again . . . the eyes . . . two little dots for the nose, and a small slit for the mouth . . . two lines for the neck, and two more, rather squared like a coat-hanger, for the shoulders. It was a face all right, a human face, not exactly that of Johnnie at the moment, but given time . . . The essential thing was to get some paint on to that canvas. He simply must use some of the paint. Feverishly he chose a brush, dipped it in turpentine and oil, and then, with little furtive dabs at the azure blue and the flake white to mix them, he stabbed the result on to the canvas. The bright colour, gleaming and glistening with excess of oil, seemed to stare back at him from the canvas, demanding more. It was not the same blue as the blue of Johnnie's jersey, but what of that?

Becoming bolder, he sloshed on further colour, and now the blue was all over the lower part of the canvas in vivid streaks, making a strange excitement, contrasting with the charcoal face. The face now looked like a real face, and the patch of wall behind the child's head, which had been nothing but a wall when he first entered the room, surely had colour to it after all, a pinkish-green. He snatched up tube after tube and squeezed out blobs; he chose another brush so as not to spoil the brush with blue on it . . . damn it, that burnt sienna was not like the Siena he had visited at all, but more like mud. He must wipe it off, he must have rags, something that wouldn't spoil . . . He crossed quickly to the door.

"Madame Kaufman?" he called. "Madame Kaufman? Could you find me some rags?"

She came at once, tearing some undergarment into strips, and he snatched them from her and began to wipe the offending burnt sienna from his brush. He turned round to see her peeping at the canvas.

"Don't do that," he shouted. "You must never look at an artist's work in the first rough stages."

She drew back, rebuffed. "I'm sorry," she said, and then, with hesitation, added, "It's very modern, isn't it?"

He stared at her, and then from her to the canvas, and from the canvas to Johnnie.

"Modern?" he said. "Of course it's modern. What did you think it would be? Like that?" He pointed with his brush to the simpering Madonna over the mantelpiece. "I'm of my time. I see what I see. Now let me get on."

There was not enough room on one pallet for all the blobs of colour. Thank goodness he had bought two. He began squeezing the remaining tubes on to the second pallet and mixing them, and now all was riot—sunsets that had never been, and unrisen dawns. The Venetian red was not the Doge's palace but little drops of blood that burst in the brain and did not have to be shed, and zinc white was purity, not death, and yellow ochre . . . yellow ochre was life in abundance, was renewal, was spring, was April even in some other time, some other place . . .

It did not matter that it grew dark and he had to switch on the light. The child had fallen asleep, but he went on painting. Presently the woman came in and told him it was eight o'clock. Did he want any supper? "It would be no trouble, Mr. Sims," she said.

Suddenly Fenton realised where he was. Eight o'clock, and they always dined at a quarter to. Edna would be waiting, would be wondering what had happened to him. He laid down the pallet and the brushes. There was paint on his hands, on his coat.

"What on earth shall I do?" he said in panic.

The woman understood. She seized the turpentine and a piece of rag, and rubbed at his coat. He went with her to the kitchen, and feverishly began to scrub his hands at the sink.

"In future," he said, "I must always leave by seven."

"Yes," she said, "I'll remember to call you. You'll be back to-morrow?"

"Of course," he said impatiently, "of course. Don't touch any of my things."

"No, Mr. Sims."

He hurried up the basement stair and out of the house, and started running along the street. As he went he began to make up the story he would tell Edna. He'd dropped in at the club, and some of the fellows there had persuaded him into playing bridge. He hadn't liked to break up the game, and never realised the time. That would do. And it would do again to-morrow. Edna must get used to this business of him dropping into the club after the office. He could think of no better excuse with which to mask the lovely duplicity of a secret life.

3.

It was extraordinary how the days slipped by, days that had once dragged, that had seemed interminable. It meant several changes, of course. He had to lie not only to Edna, but at the office as well. He invented a pressing business that took him away in the early part of the afternoon, new contacts, a family firm. For the time being, Fenton said, he could really only work at the office half-time. Naturally, there would have to be some financial adjustment, he quite understood that. In the meantime, if the senior partner would see his way . . . Amazing that they swallowed it. And Edna, too, about the club. Though it was not always the club. Sometimes it was extra work at another office, somewhere else in the City; and he would talk mysteriously of bringing off some big deal which was far too delicate and involved to be discussed. Edna appeared content. Her life continued as it had always done. It was only Fenton whose world had changed. Regularly now each afternoon, at around half-past three, he walked through the gate of No. 8, and glancing down at the kitchen window in the basement he could see Madame Kaufman's face peering from behind the tangerine curtains. Then she would slip round to the back door, by the strip of garden, and let him in. They had decided against the front door. It was safer to use the back. Less conspicuous.

"Good afternoon, Mr. Sims."

"Good afternoon, Madame Kaufman."

No nonsense about calling her Anna. She might have thought . . . she might have presumed. And the title "Madame" kept the right sense of proportion between them. She was really very useful. She cleaned the studio—they always alluded to his room as the studio—and his paintbrushes, and tore up fresh strips of rag every day, and as soon as he arrived she had a cup of tea for him, not like the stew they used to brew in the office, but piping hot. And the boy . . . the boy had become quite appealing. Fenton had felt more tolerant about him as soon as he had finished the first portrait. It was as though the boy existed anew through him. He was Fenton's creation.

It was now midsummer, and Fenton had painted his portrait many times. The child continued to call him Da. But the boy was not the only model. He had painted the mother too. And this was more satisfying still. It gave Fenton a tremendous sense of power to put the woman upon canvas. It was not her eyes, her features, her colouring—heavens above, she had little enough colouring!—but somehow her shape: the fact that the bulk of a live person, and that person a woman, could be transmuted by him upon a blank canvas. It did not matter if what he drew and painted bore no resemblance to a woman from Austria called Anna Kaufman. That was not the point. Naturally the silly soul expected some sort of chocolate-box representation the first time she acted as his model. He had soon shut her up, though.

"Do you really see me like that?" she asked, disconsolate.

"Why, what's wrong?" he said.

"It's . . . it's just that . . . you make my mouth like a big fish ready to swallow, Mr. Sims."

"A fish? What utter nonsense!" He supposed she wanted a cupid's bow. "The trouble with you is that you're never satisfied. You're no different from any other woman."

He began mixing his colours angrily. She had no right to criticise his work.

"It's not kind of you to say that, Mr. Sims," she said after a moment or two. "I am very satisfied with the five pounds that you give me every week."

"I was not talking about money," he said.

'"What were you talking about, then?"

He turned back to the canvas, and put just the faintest touch of rose upon the flesh part of the arm. "What was I talking about?" he asked. "I haven't the faintest idea. Women, wasn't it? I really don't know. And I've told you not to interrupt."

"I'm sorry, Mr. Sims."

That's right, he thought. Stay put. Keep your place. If there was one thing he could not stand it was a woman who argued, a woman who was self-assertive, a woman who nagged, a woman who stood upon her rights. Because of course they were not made for that. They were intended by their Creator to be pliable, and accommodating, and gentle, and meek. The trouble was that they were so seldom like that in reality. It was only in the imagination, or glimpsed in passing or behind a window, or leaning from a balcony abroad, or from the frame of a picture, or from a canvas like the one before him now—he changed from one brush to another, he was getting quite dexterous at this—that a woman had any meaning, any reality. And then to go and tell him that he had given her a mouth like a fish . . .

"When I was younger," he said aloud, "I had so much ambition."

"To be a great painter?" she asked.

"Why, no . . . not particularly that," he answered, "but to become great. To be famous. To achieve something outstanding."

"There's still time, Mr. Sims," she said.

"Perhaps . . . perhaps . . ." The skin should not be rose, it should be olive, a warm olive. Edna's father had been the trouble, really, with his endless criticising of the way they lived. Fenton had never done anything right from the moment they became engaged: the old man was always carping, always finding fault. "Go and live abroad?" he had exclaimed. "You can't make a decent living abroad. Besides, Edna wouldn't stand it. Away from her friends and all she's been accustomed to. Never heard of such a thing."

Well, he was dead, and a good thing too. He'd been a wedge between them from the start. Marcus Sims . . . Marcus Sims the painter was a very different chap. Surrealist. Modern. The old boy would turn in his grave.

"It's a quarter to seven," murmured the woman.

"Damn . . ." He sighed, and stepped back from the easel. "I resent stopping like this, now it's so light in the evenings," he said. "I could go on for quite another hour, or more."

"Why don't you?" she asked.

"Ah! Home ties," he said. "My poor old mother would have a fit."

He had invented an old mother during the past weeks. Bed-ridden. He had promised to be home every evening at a quarter to eight. If he did not arrive in time the doctors would not answer for the consequences. He was a very good son to her.

"I wish you could bring her here to live," said his model. "It's so lonely when you've gone back in the evenings. Do you know, there's a rumour this house may not be pulled down after all. If it's true, you could take the flat on the ground floor, and your mother would be welcome."

"She'd never move now," said Fenton. "She's over eighty. Very set in her ways." He smiled to himself, thinking of Edna's face if he said to her that it would be more comfortable to sell the house they had lived in for nearly twenty years and take up lodgings in No. 8, Boulting Street. Imagine the upheaval! Imagine the Alhusons coming to Sunday supper!

"Besides," he said, thinking aloud, "the whole point would be gone."

"What point, Mr. Sims?"

He looked from the shape of colour on the canvas that meant so much to him to the woman who sat there, posing with her lank hair and her dumb eyes, and he tried to remember what had decided him those months ago, to walk up the steps of the drab villa and ask for a room. Some temporary phase of irritation, surely, with poor Edna, with the windy grey day on the Embankment, with the fact of the Alhusons coming to drinks. But the workings of his mind on that vanished Sunday were forgotten, and he knew only that his life had changed from then, that this small, confined basement room was his solace, and the personalities of the woman Anna Kaufman and the child Johnnie were somehow symbolic of anonymity, of peace. All she ever did was to make him tea and clean his brushes. She was part of the background, like the cat, which purred at his approach and crouched on the window-sill, and to which he had not as yet given a single crumb.

"Never mind, Madame Kaufman," he said. "One of these days we'll hold an exhibition, and your face, and Johnnie's, will be the talk of the town."

"This year . . . next year . . . sometime . . . never. Isn't that what you say to cherry stones?" she said.

"You've got no faith," he told her. "I'll prove it. Just wait and see."

She began once more the long, tedious story about the man she had fled from in Austria, and the husband who had deserted her in London—he knew it all so well by now that he could prompt her—but it did not bother him. It was part of the background, part of the blessed anonymity. Let her blab away, he said to himself, it kept her quiet, it did not matter. He could concentrate on making the orange she was sucking, doling out quarters to Johnnie on her lap, larger than life, more colourful than life, rounder, bigger, brighter.

And as he walked home along the Embankment in the evening—because the walk was no longer suggestive of the old Sunday but was merged with the new life as well—he would throw his charcoal sketches and rough drawings into the river. They were now transfigured into paint and did not matter. With them went the used tubes of colour, pieces of rag, and brushes too clogged with oil. He threw them from Albert Bridge and watched them float for a moment, or be dragged under, or drift as bait for some ruffled, sooty gull. All his troubles went with his discarded junk. All his pain.

4.

He had arranged with Edna to postpone their annual holiday until mid-September. This gave him time to finish the self-portrait he was working upon, which, he decided, would round up the present series. The holiday in Scotland would be pleasant. Pleasant for the first time for years, because there would be something to look forward to on returning to London.

The brief mornings at the office hardly counted now. He scraped through the routine somehow, and never went back after lunch. His other commitments, he told his colleagues, were becoming daily more pressing: he had practically decided to break his association with the present business during the autumn.

"If you hadn't warned us," said the senior partner drily, "we should have warned you."

Fenton shrugged his shoulders. If they were going to be unpleasant about it, the sooner he went the better. He might even write from Scotland. Then the whole of the autumn and winter could be given up to painting. He could take a proper studio: No. 8, after all, was only a makeshift affair. But a large studio, with decent lighting and a kitchenette off it—there were some in the process of being built, only a few streets away—that might be the answer to the winter. There he could really work. Really achieve something good, and no longer feel he was only a part-time amateur.

The self-portrait was absorbing. Madame Kaufman had found a mirror and hung it on the wall for him, so the start was easy enough. But he found he couldn't paint his own eyes. They had to be closed, which gave him the appearance of a sleeping man. A sick man. It was rather uncanny.

"So you don't like it?" Fenton observed to Madame Kaufman, when she came to tell him it was seven o'clock.

She shook her head. "It gives me what you call the creeps," she said. "No, Mr. Sims, it's not you."

"A bit too advanced for your taste," he said cheerfully. "Avant-garde, I believe, is the right expression."

He himself was delighted. The self-portrait was a work of art.

"Well, it will have to do for the time being," he said. "I'm off for my holiday next week."

"You are going away?"

There was such a note of alarm in her voice that he turned to look at her.

"Yes," he said, "taking my old mother up to Scotland. Why?"

She stared at him in anguish, her whole expression changed. Anyone would think he had given her some tremendous shock.

"But I have no one but you," she said. "I shall be alone."

"I'll give you your money all right," he said quickly. "You shall have it in advance. We shall only be away three weeks."

She went on staring at him, and then, of all things, her eyes filled with tears and she began to cry.

"I don't know what I shall do," she said. "I don't know where I am to go."

It was a bit thick. What on earth did she mean? What should she do, and where should she go? He had promised her the money. She would just go on as she always did. Seriously, if she was going to behave like this the sooner he found himself a studio the better. The last thing in the world he wanted was for Madame Kaufman to become a drag.

"My dear Madame Kaufman, I'm not a permanency, you know," he said firmly. "One of these days I shall be moving. Possibly this autumn. I need room to expand. I'll let you know in advance, naturally. But it might be worth your while to put Johnnie in a nursery school and get some sort of daily job. It would really work out better for you in the end."

He might have beaten her. She looked stunned, utterly crushed.

"What shall I do?" she repeated stupidly, and then, as if she still could not believe it, "When do you go away?"

"Monday," he said, "to Scotland. We'll be away three weeks." This last very forcibly, so that there was no mistake about it. The trouble was that she was a very unintelligent woman, he decided as he washed his hands at the kitchen sink. She made a good cup of tea and knew how to clean the brushes, but that was her limit. "You ought to take a holiday yourself," he told her cheerfully. "Take Johnnie for a trip down the river to Southend or somewhere."

There was no response. Nothing but a mournful stare and a hopeless shrug.

The next day, Friday, meant the end of his working week. He cashed a cheque that morning, so that he could give her three weeks' money in advance. And he allowed an extra five pounds for appeasement.

When he arrived at No. 8 Johnnie was tied up in his old place by this foot-scraper, at the top of the steps. She had not done this to the boy for some time. And when Fenton let himself in at the back door in the basement, as usual, there was no wireless going and the kitchen door was shut. He opened it and looked in. The door through to the bedroom was also shut.

"Madame Kaufman . . .?" he called. "Madame Kaufman . . .?"

She answered after a moment, her voice muffled and weak.

"What is it!" she said.

"Is anything the matter?"

Another pause, and then, "I am not very well."

"I'm sorry," said Fenton. "Is there anything I can do?"

"No."

Well, there it was. A try-on, of course. She never looked well, but she had not done this before. There was no attempt to prepare his tea; the tray was not even laid. He put the envelope containing the money on the kitchen table.

"I've brought you your money," he called. "Twenty pounds altogether. Why don't you go out and spend some of it? It's a lovely afternoon. The air would do you good."

A brisk manner was the answer to her trouble. He was not going to be black-mailed into sympathy.

He went along to the studio, whistling firmly. He found, to his shocked surprise, that everything was as he had left it the evening before. Brushes not cleaned, but lying clogged still on the messed pallet. Room untouched. It really was the limit. He'd a good mind to retrieve the envelope from the kitchen table. It had been a mistake ever to have mentioned the holiday. He should have posted the money over the week-end, and enclosed a note saying he had gone to Scotland. Instead of which . . . this infuriating fit of the sulks, and neglect of her job. It was because she was a foreigner, of course. You just couldn't trust them. They always let you down in the long run.

He returned to the kitchen with his brushes and pallet, the turpentine and some rags, and made as much noise as possible running the taps and moving about, so as to let her know that he was having to do all the menial stuff himself. He clattered the teacup, too, and rattled the tin where she put the sugar. Not a sound, though, from the bedroom. Oh, damn it, he thought, let her stew . . .

Back in the studio, he pottered with the final touches to the self-portrait, but concentration was difficult. Nothing worked. The thing looked dead. She had ruined his day. Finally, an hour or more before his usual time, he decided to go home. He would not trust her to clean up, though, not after last night's neglect. She was capable of leaving everything untouched for three weeks.

Before stacking the canvases one behind the other he stood them up, ranged them against the wall, and tried to imagine how they would look hanging in an exhibition. They hit the eye, there was no doubt about it. You couldn't avoid them. There was something . . . well, something telling about the whole collection! He didn't know what it was. Naturally, he couldn't criticise his own work. But . . . that head of Madame Kaufman, for instance, the one she had said was like a fish, possibly there *was* some sort of shape to the mouth that . . . or was it the eyes, the rather full eyes? It was brilliant, though. He was sure it was brilliant. And, although unfinished, that self-portrait of a man asleep, it had significance.

He smiled in fantasy, seeing himself and Edna walking into one of those small galleries off Bond Street, himself saying casually, "I'm told there's some new chap got a show on here. Very controversial. The critics can't make out whether he's a genius or a madman." And Edna, "It must be the first time you've ever been inside one of these place." What a sense of power, what triumph! And then, when he broke it to her, the dawn of new respect in her eyes. The realisation that her husband had, after all these years, achieved fame. It was the shock of surprise that he wanted. That was it! The shock of surprise . . .

Fenton had a final glance round the familiar room. The canvases were stacked now, the easel dismantled, brushes and pallet cleaned and wiped and wrapped up. If he should decide to decamp when he returned from Scotland—and he was pretty sure it was going to be the only answer, after Madame Kaufman's idiotic behaviour—then everything was ready to move. It would only be a matter of calling a taxi, putting the gear inside, and driving off.

He shut the window and closed the door, and, carrying his usual weekly package of what he called "rejects" under his arm—discarded drawings and sketches and odds and ends—went once more to the kitchen and called through the closed door of the bedroom.

"I'm off now," he said. "I hope you'll be better to-morrow. See you in three weeks' time."

He noticed that the envelope had disappeared from the kitchen table. She could not be as ill as all that.

Then he heard her moving in the bedroom, and after a moment or two the door opened a few inches and she stood there, just inside. He was shocked. She looked ghastly, her face drained of colour and her hair lank and greasy, neither combed nor brushed. She had a blanket wrapped round the lower part of her, and in spite of the hot, stuffy day, and the lack of air in the basement, was wearing a thick woollen cardigan.

"Have you seen a doctor?" he asked with some concern.

She shook her head.

"I would if I were you," he said. "You don't look well at all." He remembered the boy, still tied to the scraper above. "Shall I bring Johnnie down to you?" he suggested.

"Please," she said.

Her eyes reminded him of an animal's eyes in pain. He felt disturbed. It was rather dreadful, going off and leaving her like this. But what could he do? He went up the basement stairs and through the deserted front hall, and opened the front door. The boy was sitting there, humped. He couldn't have moved since Fenton had entered the house.

"Come on, Johnnie," he said. "I'll take you below to your mother."

The child allowed himself to be untied. He had the same sort of apathy as the woman. What a hopeless pair they were, thought Fenton; they really ought to be in somebody's charge, in some sort of welfare home. There must be places where people like this were looked after. He carried the child downstairs and sat him in his usual chair by the kitchen table.

"What about his tea?" he asked.

"I'll get it presently," said Madame Kaufman.

She shuffled out of her bedroom, still wrapped in the blanket, with a package in her hands, some sort of paper parcel, tied up with string.

"What's that?" he asked.

"Some rubbish," she said, "if you would throw it away with yours. The dustmen don't call until next week."

He took the package from her and waited a moment, wondering what more he could do for her.

"Well," he said awkwardly, "I feel rather bad about this. Are you sure there is nothing else you want?"

"No," she said. She didn't even call him Mr. Sims. She made no effort to smile or hold out her hand. The expression in her eyes was not even reproachful. It was mute.

"I'll send you a postcard from Scotland," he said, and then patted Johnnie's head. "So long," he added—a silly expression, and one he never normally used. Then he went out of the back door, round the corner of the house and out of the gate, and so along Boulting Street, with an oppressive feeling in his heart that he had somehow behaved badly, been lacking in sympathy, and that he ought to have taken the initiative and insisted that she see a doctor.

The September sky was overcast and the Embankment dusty, drear. The trees in the Battersea gardens across the river had a dejected, faded, end-of-summer look. Too dull, too brown. It would be good to get away to Scotland, to breathe the clean, cold air.

He unwrapped his package and began to throw his "rejects" into the river. A head of Johnnie, very poor indeed. An attempt at the cat. A canvas that had got stained with something or other and could not be used again. Over the bridge they went and away with the tide, the canvas floating like a match-box, white and frail. It was rather sad to watch it drift from sight.

He walked back along the Embankment towards home, and then, before he turned to cross the road, realised that he was still carrying the paper parcel Madame Kaufman had given him. He had forgotten to throw it away with the rejects. He had been too occupied in watching the disappearance of his own debris.

Fenton was about to toss the parcel into the river when he noticed a policeman watching him from the opposite side of the road. He was seized with an uneasy feeling that it was against the law to dispose of litter in this way. He walked on self-consciously. After he had gone a hundred yards he glanced back over his shoulder. The policeman was still staring after him. Absurd, but it made him feel quite guilty. The strong arm of the law. He continued his walk, swinging the parcel nonchalantly, humming a little tune. To hell with the river—he would dump the parcel into one of the litter baskets in Chelsea Hospital gardens.

He turned into the gardens and dropped the parcel into the first basket, on top of two or three newspapers and a pile of orange peel. No offence in that. He could see the damn fool of a bobby watching through the railings, but Fenton took good care not to show the fellow he noticed him. Anyone would think he was trying to dispose of a bomb. Then he walked swiftly home, and remembered, as he went up the stairs, that the Alhusons were coming to dinner. The routine dinner before the holiday. The thought did not bore him now as it had once. He would chat away to them both about Scotland without any sensation of being trapped and stifled. How Jack Alhuson would stare if he knew how Fenton spent his afternoons! He would not believe his ears!

"Hullo, you're early," said Edna, who was arranging the flowers in the drawing-room.

"Yes," he replied. "I cleared up everything at the office in good time. Thought I might make a start planning the itinerary. I'm looking forward to going north."

"I'm so glad," she said. "I was afraid you might be getting bored with Scotland year after year. But you don't look jaded at all. You haven't looked so well for years."

She kissed his cheek and he kissed her back, well content. He smiled as he went to look out his maps. She did not know she had a genius for a husband.

The Alhusons had arrived and they were just sitting down to dinner when the front-door bell rang.

"Who on earth's that?" exclaimed Edna. "Don't say we asked someone else and have forgotten all about them."

"I haven't paid the electricity bill," said Fenton. "They've sent round to cut us off, and we shan't get the soufflé."

He paused in the middle of carving the chicken, and the Alhusons laughed.

"I'll go," said Edna. "I daren't disturb May in the kitchen. You know the bill of fare by now, it *is* a soufflé."

She came back in a few moments with a half-amused, half-puzzled expression on her face. "It's not the electricity men," she said, "it's the police."

"The police?" repeated Fenton.

Jack Alhuson wagged his finger. "I knew it," he said. "You're for it this time, old boy."

Fenton laid down the carving knife. "Seriously, Edna," he said, "what do they want?"

"I haven't the faintest idea," she replied. "It's an ordinary policeman, and what I assumed to be another in plain clothes. They asked to speak to the owner of the house."

Fenton shrugged his shoulders. "You carry on," he said to his wife, "I'll see if I can get rid of them. They've probably come to the wrong address."

He went out of the dining-room into the hall, but as soon as he saw the uniformed policeman his face changed. He recognised the man who had stared after him on the Embankment.

"Good evening," he said. "What can I do for you?"

The man in plain clothes took the initiative.

"Did you happen to walk through Chelsea Hospital gardens late this afternoon, sir?" he enquired. Both men were watching Fenton intently, and he realised that denial would be useless.

"Yes," he said, "yes, I did."

"You were carrying a parcel?"

"I believe I was."

"Did you put the parcel in a litter basket by the Embankment entrance, sir?"

"I did."

"Would you object to telling us what was in the parcel?"

"I have no idea."

"I can put the question another way, sir. Could you tell us where you obtained the parcel?"

Fenton hesitated. What were they driving at? He did not care for their method of interrogation.

"I don't see what it has to do with you," he said. "It's not an offence to put rubbish in a litter basket, is it?"

"Not ordinary rubbish," said the man in plain clothes.

Fenton looked from one to the other. Their faces were serious.

"Do you mind if I ask you a question?" he said.

"No, sir."

"Do you know what was in the parcel?"

"Yes."

"You mean the policeman here—I remember passing him on the beat—actually followed me, and took the parcel after I had dropped it in the bin?"

"That is correct."

"What an extraordinary thing to do. I should have thought he would have been better employed doing his regular job."

"It happens to be his regular job to keep an eye on people who behave in a suspicious manner."

Fenton began to get annoyed. "There was nothing suspicious in my behaviour whatsoever," he declared. "It so happens that I had been clearing up odds and ends in my office this afternoon, and it's rather a fad of mine to throw rubbish in the river on my way home. Very often I feed the gulls too. To-day I was about to throw in my usual packet when I noticed the officer here glance in my direction. It occurred to me that perhaps it's illegal to throw rubbish in the river, so I decided to put it in the litter basket instead."

The two men continued to stare at him.

"You've just stated," said the man in plain clothes, "that you didn't know what was in the parcel, and now you state that it was odds and ends from the office. Which statement is true?"

Fenton began to feel hunted.

"Both statements are true," he snapped. "The people at the office wrapped the parcel up for me to-day, and I didn't know what they had put in it. Sometimes they put in stale biscuits for the gulls, and then I undo it and throw the crumbs to the birds on my way home, as I told you."

It wouldn't do, though. Their set faces said so, and he supposed it sounded a thin enough tale—a middle-aged man collecting rubbish so that he could throw it in the river on his way home from the office, like a small boy throwing twigs from a bridge to see them float out on the other side. But it was the best he could think of on the spur of the moment, and he would have to stick to it now. After all, it couldn't be a criminal action—the worst they could call him was eccentric.

The plain-clothes policeman said nothing but, "Read your notes, Sergeant."

The man in uniform took out his notebook and read aloud:

"At five minutes past six to-day I was walking along the Embankment and I noticed a man on the opposite pavement make as though to throw a parcel in the river. He observed me looking and walked quickly on, and then glanced back over his shoulder to see if I was still watching him. His manner was suspicious. He then crossed to the entrance to Chelsea Hospital gardens and, after looking up and down in a furtive manner, dropped the parcel in the litter bin and hurried away. I went to the bin and retrieved the parcel, and then followed the man to 14 Annersley Square, which he entered. I took the parcel to the station and handed it over to the officer on duty. We examined the parcel together. It contained the body of a premature new-born infant."

He snapped the notebook to.

Fenton felt all his strength ebb from him. Horror and fear merged together like a dense, overwhelming cloud, and he collapsed on to a chair.

"Oh, God," he said. "Oh, God, what's happened . . .?"

Through the cloud he saw Edna looking at him from the open door of the dining-room, with the Alhusons behind her. The man in plain clothes was saying, "I shall have to ask you to come down to the station and make a statement."

5.

Fenton sat in the Inspector's room, with the Inspector of Police behind a desk, and the plain-clothes man, and the policeman in uniform, and someone else, a medical officer. Edna was there too—he had especially asked for Edna to be there. The Alhusons were waiting outside, but the terrible thing was the expression on Edna's face. It was obvious that she did not believe him. Nor did the policemen.

"Yes, it's been going on for six months," he repeated. "When I say 'going on', I mean my painting has been going on, nothing else, nothing else at all . . . I was seized with the desire to paint . . . I can't explain it. I never shall. It just came over me. And on impulse I walked in at the gate of No. 8, Boulting Street. The woman came to the door and I asked if she had a room to let, and after a few moments' discussion she said she had—a room of her own in the basement—nothing to do with the landlord, we agreed to say nothing to the landlord. So I took possession. And I've been going there every afternoon for six months. I said nothing about it to my wife . . . I thought she wouldn't understand . . ."

He turned in despair to Edna, and she just sat there, staring at him.

"I admit I've lied," he said. "I've lied to everyone. I lied at home, I lied at the office. I told them at the office I had contacts with another firm, that I went there during the afternoon, and I told my wife—bear me out, Edna—I told my wife I was either kept late at the office or I was playing bridge at the club. The truth was that I went every day to No. 8, Boulting Street. Every day."

He had not done anything wrong. Why did they have to stare at him? Why did Edna hold on to the arms of the chair?

"What age is Madame Kaufman? I don't know. About twenty-seven, I should think . . . or thirty, she could be any age . . . and she has the little boy, Johnnie . . . She is an Austrian, she has led a very sad life and her husband has left her . . . No, I never saw anyone in the house at all, no other men . . . I don't know, I tell you . . . I don't know. I went there to paint. I didn't go for anything else. She'll tell you so. She'll tell you the truth. I'm sure she is very attached to me . . . At least, no, I don't mean that; when I say attached I mean she is grateful for the money I pay her . . . that is, the rent, the five pounds for the room. There was absolutely nothing else between us, there couldn't have been, it was out of the question . . . Yes, yes, of course I was ignorant of her condition. I'm not very observant . . . it wasn't the sort of thing I would have noticed. And she did not say a word, not a word."

He turned again to Edna. "Surely you believe me?"

She said, "You never told me you wanted to paint. You've never mentioned painting, or artists, all our married life."

It was the frozen blue of her eyes that he could not bear.

He said to the Inspector, "Can't we go to Boulting Street now, at once? That poor soul must be in great distress. She should see a doctor, someone should be looking after her. Can't we all go now, my wife too, so that Madame Kaufman can explain everything?"

And, thank God, he had his way. It was agreed they should go to Boulting Street. A police car was summoned, and he and Edna and two police officers climbed into it, and the Alhusons followed behind in their car. He heard them say something to the Inspector about not wanting Mrs. Fenton to be alone, the shock was too great. That was kind, of course, but there need not be any shock when he could quietly and calmly explain the whole story to her, once they got home. It was the atmosphere of the police station that made it so appalling, that made him feel guilty, a criminal.

The car drew up before the familiar house, and they all got out. He led the way through the gate and round to the back door, and opened it. As soon as they entered the passage the smell of gas was unmistakable.

"It's leaking again," he said. "It does, from time to time. She tells the men, but they never come."

Nobody answered. He walked swiftly to the kitchen. The door was shut, and here the smell of gas was stronger still.

The Inspector murmured something to his subordinates. "Mrs. Fenton had better stay outside in the car with her friends."

"No," said Fenton, "no, I want my wife to hear the truth."

But Edna began to walk back along the passage with one of the policemen, and the Alhusons were waiting for her, their faces solemn. Then everybody seemed to go at once into the bedroom, into Madame Kaufman's bedroom. They jerked up the blind and let in the air, but the smell of gas was over-powering, and they leant over the bed and she was lying there asleep, with Johnnie beside her, both fast asleep. The envelope containing the twenty pounds was lying on the floor.

"Can't you wake her?" said Fenton. "Can't you wake her and tell her that Mr. Sims is here? Mr. Sims."

One of the policemen took hold of his arm and led him from the room.

When they told Fenton that Madame Kaufman was dead and Johnnie too, he shook his head and said, "It's terrible . . . terrible . . . if only she'd told me, if only I'd known what to do . . ." But somehow the first shock of discovery had been so great, with the police coming to the house and the appalling contents of the parcel, that this fulfilment of disaster did not touch him in the same way. It seemed somehow inevitable.

"Perhaps it's for the best," he said. "She was alone in the world. Just the two of them. Alone in the world."

He was not sure what everyone was waiting for. The ambulance, he supposed, or whatever it was that would take poor Madame Kaufman and Johnnie away. He asked, "Can we go home, my wife and I?"

The Inspector exchanged a glance with the man in plain clothes, and then he said, "I'm afraid not, Mr. Fenton. We shall want you to return with us to the station."

"But I've told you the truth," said Fenton wearily. "There's no more to say. I have nothing to do with this tragedy. Nothing at all." Then he remembered his paintings. "You haven't seen my work," he said. "It's all here, in the room next door. Please ask my wife to come back, and my friends too. I want them to see my work. Besides, now that this has happened I wish to remove my belongings."

"We will take care of that," said the Inspector.

The tone was noncommittal, yet firm. Ungracious, Fenton thought. The officious attitude of the law.

"That's all very well," said Fenton, "but they are my possessions, and valuable at that. I don't see what right you have to touch them."

He looked from the Inspector to his colleague in plain clothes—the medical officer and the other policeman were still in the bedroom—and he could tell from their set expressions that they were not really interested in his work. They thought it was just an excuse, an alibi, and all they wanted to do was to take him back to the police station and question him still further about the sordid, pitiful deaths in the bedroom, about the body of the little, prematurely born child.

"I'm quite ready to go with you, Inspector," he said quietly, "but I make this one request—that you will allow me to show my work to my wife and my friends."

The Inspector nodded at his subordinate, who went out of the kitchen, and then the little group moved to the studio, Fenton himself opening the door and showing them in.

"Of course," he said, "I've been working under wretched conditions. Bad light, as you see. No proper amenities at all. I don't know how I stuck it. As a matter of fact, I intended to move out when I returned from my holiday. I told the poor girl so, and it probably depressed her."

He switched on the light, and as they stood there, glancing about them, noting the dismantled easel, the canvases stacked neatly against the wall, it struck him that of course these preparations for departure must seem odd to them, suspicious, as though he had in truth known what had happened in the bedroom behind the kitchen and had intended a getaway.

"It was a makeshift, naturally," he said, continuing to apologise for the small room that looked so unlike a studio, "but it happened to suit me. There was nobody else in the house, nobody to ask questions. I never saw anyone but Madame Kaufman and the boy."

He noticed that Edna had come into the room, and the Alhusons too, and the other policeman, and they were all watching him with the same set expressions. Why Edna? Why the Alhusons? Surely they must be impressed by the canvases stacked against the wall? They must realise that his total output for the past five and a half months was here, in this room, only awaiting exhibition? He strode across the floor, seized the nearest canvas to hand, and held it up for them to see.

It was the portrait of Madame Kaufman that he liked best, the one which—poor soul—she had told him looked like a fish.

"They're unconventional, I know that," he said, "not picture-book stuff. But they're strong. They've got originality." He seized another. Madame Kaufman again, this time with Johnnie on her lap. "Mother and child," he said, half-smiling, "a true primitive. Back to our origins. The first woman, the first child."

He cocked his head, trying to see the canvas as they would see it, for the first time. Looking up for Edna's approval, for her gasp of wonder, he was met by that same stony frozen stare of misunderstanding. Then her face seemed to crumple, and she turned to the Alhusons and said, "They're not proper paintings. They're daubs, done anyhow." Blinded by tears, she looked up at the Inspector. "I told you he couldn't paint," she said. "He's never painted in his life. It was just an alibi, to get into the house with this woman."

Fenton watched the Alhusons lead her away. He heard them go out of the back door and through the garden to the front of the house. "They're not proper paintings, they're daubs," he repeated. He put the canvas down on the ground with its face to the wall, and said to the Inspector, "I'm ready to go with you now."

They got into the police car. Fenton sat between the Inspector and the man in plain clothes. The car turned out of Boulting Street. It crossed two other streets, and came into Oakley Street and on towards the Embankment. The traffic lights changed from amber to red. Fenton murmured to himself, "She doesn't believe in me—she'll never believe in me." Then, as the lights changed and the car shot forward, he shouted, "All right, I'll confess everything. I was her lover, of course, and the child was mine. I turned on the gas this evening before I left the house. I killed them all. I was going to kill my wife too when we got to Scotland. I want to confess that I did it . . . I did it . . . I did it . . . "

A SERVICE OF DANGER

Amelia B. Edwards

Amelia B. Edwards (1831–1892) was a noted polymath, famously passionate about Egyptology and travel writing. She was also known for her ghost stories and novels, including *My Brother's Wife* and *Lord Brackenbury*. Edwards died of influenza in Bristol.

I, Frederick George Byng, who writes this narrative with my own hand, without help of spectacles, am so old a man that I doubt if I now have a hundred living contemporaries in Europe. I was born in 1780, and I am eighty-nine years of age. My reminiscences date so far back that I almost feel, when I speak of them, as if I belonged to another world. I remember when news first reached England of the taking of the Bastille in 1789. I remember when people, meeting each other in the streets, talked of Danton and Robespierre, and the last victims of the guillotine. I remember how our whole household was put into black for the execution of Louis XVI., and how my mother who was a devout Roman Catholic, converted her oratory for several days into a chapelle ardente. That was in 1793, when I was just thirteen years of age.

Three years later, when the name of General Bonaparte was fast becoming a word of power in European history, I went abroad, and influenced by considerations which have nothing to do with my story, entered the Austrian army.

A younger son of a younger branch of an ancient and noble house, and distantly connected, moreover, with more than one great Austrian family, I presented myself at the Court of Vienna under peculiarly favourable auspices. The Archduke Charles, to whom I brought letters of recommendation, accorded me a gracious welcome, and presented me almost immediately upon my arrival with a commission in a cavalry corps commanded by a certain Colonel von Beust, than whom a more unpopular officer did not serve in the Imperial army.

Hence, I was glad to exchange, some months later, into Lichtenstein's Cuirassiers. In this famous corps which was commanded by his uncle the Prince of Lichtenstein, my far-off cousin, Gustav von Lichtenstein, had lately been promoted to a troop. Serving in the same corps, sharing the same hardships, incurring the same dangers, we soon became sworn friends and comrades. Together we went through the disastrous campaign of 1797, and together enjoyed the brief interval of peace that followed upon the treaty of Campo Formio and the cession of Venice. Having succeeded in getting our leave of absence at the same time, we then travelled through Styria and Hungary. Our tour ended, we came back together to winter quarters in Vienna.

When hostilities were renewed in 1800, we joyfully prepared to join the army of the Inn. In peace or war, at home or abroad, we two held fast by each other. Let the world go round as it might, we at least took life gaily, accepted events as they came, and went on becoming truer and stauncher friends with every passing day. Never were two men better suited. We understood each other perfectly. We were nearly of the same age; we enjoyed the same sports, read the same books, and liked the same people. Above all, we were both passionately desirous of military glory, and we both hated the French.

Gustav von Lichtenstein, however, was in many respects, both physically and mentally, my superior. He was taller than myself, a finer horseman, a swifter runner, a bolder swimmer, a more graceful dancer. He was unequivocally better-looking; and having to great natural gifts superadded a brilliant University career at both Göttingen and Leipzig, he was as unequivocally better educated. Fair-haired, blue-eyed, athletic—half dreamer and poet, half sportsman and soldier—now lost in mists of speculative philosophy—now given up with keen enthusiasm to military studies—the idol of his soldiers—the beau sabreur of his corps—Gustav von Lichtenstein was then, and has ever since remained, my ideal of a true and noble gentleman. An orphan since his early childhood, he owned large estates in Franconia, and was, moreover, his uncle's sole heir. He was just twenty when I first came to know him personally in Vienna in 1796; but his character was already formed, and he looked at least four years older than his age. When I say that he was even then, in accordance with a family arrangement of long standing, betrothed to his cousin, Constance von Adelheim, a rich and beautiful Franconian heiress, I think I shall have told all that need be told of my friend's private history.

I have said that we were rejoiced by the renewal of hostilities in 1800; and we had good reason to rejoice, he as an Austrian, I as an Englishman; for the French were our bitterest enemies, and we were burning to wipe out the memory of Marengo. It was in the month of November that Gustav and I received orders to join our regiment; and, commanded by Prince Lichtenstein in person, we at once proceeded, in great haste and very inclement weather, to fall in with the main body of the Imperial forces near Landshut on the Inn. The French, under Moreau, came up from the direction of Ampfing and Mühldorf; while the Austrians, sixty thousand strong, under the Archduke John, advanced upon them from Dorfen.

Coming upon the French by surprise in the close neighbourhood of Ampfing on the 30th, we fell upon them while in line of march, threw them into confusion, and put them to the rout. The next day they fell back upon that large plateau which lies between the Isar and the Inn, and took up their position in the forest of Hohenlinden. We ought never to have let them so fall back. We ought never to have let them entrench themselves in the natural fastnesses of that immense forest which has been truly described as "a great natural stockade between six and seven leagues long, and from a league to a league and a half broad."

We had already achieved a brilliant coup, and had our General known how to follow up his success, the whole fortune of the campaign would in all probability have been changed. But the Archduke John, though a young man of ability and sound military training, wanted that boldness which comes of experience, and erred on the side of over-caution.

All that day (the 2nd of December) it rained and sleeted in torrents. An icy wind chilled us to the bone. We could not keep our camp-fires alight. Our soldiers, however, despite the dreadful state of the weather, were in high spirits, full of yesterday's triumph, and longing for active work. Officers and men alike, we all confidently expected to be on the heels of the enemy soon after daybreak, and waited impatiently for the word of command. But we waited in vain. At midday the Archduke summoned a council of his generals. But the council by-and-by broke up; the afternoon wore on; the early Winter dusk closed in; and nothing was done.

That night there was discontent in the camp. The officers looked grave. The men murmured loudly, as they gathered round the sputtering embers and tried in vain to fence off the wind and rain. By-and-by the wind ceased blowing and the rain ceased falling, and it began to snow.

At midnight, my friend and I were sitting together in our little tent, trying to kindle some damp logs, and talking over the day's disappointment.

"It is a brilliant opportunity lost," said Gustav, bitterly. "We had separated them and thrown them into confusion; but what of that, when we have left them this whole day to reassemble their scattered forces and reform their broken battalions? The Archduke Charles would never have been guilty of such an oversight. He would have gone on forcing them back, column upon column, till soon they would have been unable to fly before us. They would have trampled upon each other, thrown down their arms, and been all cut to pieces or taken prisoners."

"Perhaps it is not yet too late," said I.

"Not yet too late!" he repeated. "Gott im Himmel! Not too late, perhaps to fight hard and get the worst of the fight; but too late to destroy the whole French army, as we should have destroyed it this morning. But, there! of what use is it to talk? They are all safe now in the woods of Hohenlinden."

"Well, then, we must rout them out of the woods of Hohenlinden, as we routed the wild boars last Winter in Franconia," I said, smiling.

But my friend shook his head.

"Look here," he said, tearing a leaf from his pocket-book, and, with a few bold strokes, sketching a rough plan of the plateau and the two rivers. "The forest is pierced by only two great roads—the road from Munich to Wasserburg, and the road from Munich to Mühldorf. Between the roads, some running transversely, some in parallel lines, are numbers of narrow footways, known only to the peasants, and impassable in Winter. If the French have had recourse to the great thoroughfares, they have passed through ere this, and taken up their position on some good ground beyond; but if they have thrown themselves into the forest on either side, they are either taking refuge in thickets whence it will be impossible to dislodge them, or they are lying in wait to fall upon our columns when we attempt to march through."

I was struck by the clearness of his insight and his perfect mastery of the situation.

"What a general you will make by-and-by, Lichtenstein!" I exclaimed.

"I shall never live to be a general, my dear fellow," he replied gloomily. "Have I not told you before now that I shall die young?"

"Pshaw!—a mere presentiment!"

"Ay—a mere presentiment; but a presentiment of which you will some day see the fulfilment."

I shook my head and smiled incredulously; but Lichtenstein, stooping over the fire, and absorbed in his own thoughts, went on, more, as it were, to himself than to me.

"Yes," he said, "I shall die before I have done anything for which it might be worth while to have lived. I am conscious of power—I feel there is the making of a commander in me—but what chance have I? The times are rich in great soldiers . . . Ah, if I could but once distinguish myself—if I could but achieve one glorious deed before I die! . . . My uncle could help me if he would. He could so easily appoint me to some service of danger; but he will not—it is in vain to ask him. There was last year's expedition—you remember how I implored him to let me lead the assaulting party at Mannheim. He refused me. Von Ranke got it, and covered himself with glory! Now if we do have a battle to-morrow" . . .

"Do you really think we shall have a battle to-morrow?" I said eagerly.

"I fancy so; but who can answer for what the Archduke may do? Were we not confident of fighting to-day?"

"Yes—but the Prince of Lichtenstein was at the council."

"My uncle tells me nothing," replied Gustav, drily.

And then he went to the door of the tent and looked out. The snow was still coming down in a dense drifting cloud, and notwithstanding the heavy rains of the last few days, was already beginning to lie upon the ground.

"Pleasant weather for a campaign!" said Gustav. "I vote we get a few hours' sleep while we can."

And with this he wrapped himself up in his cloak and lay down before the fire. I followed his example, and in a few moments we were both fast asleep.

Next day—the memorable 3rd of December A.D. 1800—was fought the famous battle of Hohenlinden; a day great and glorious in the annals of French military history, yet not inglorious for those who bravely suffered defeat and disaster.

I will not attempt to describe the conflict in detail—that has been done by abler pens than mine. It will be enough if I briefly tell what share we Lichtensteiners bore in the fray. The bugles sounded to arms before daylight, and by grey dawn the whole army was in motion. The snow was still falling heavily; but the men were in high spirits and confident of victory.

Divided into three great columns—the centre commanded by the Archduke, the right wing under Latour, and the left under Riesch—we plunged into the forest. The infantry marched first, followed by the artillery and caissons, and the cavalry brought up the rear. The morning, consequently, had far advanced, and our comrades in the van had already reached the farther extremity of the forest, when we, with the rest of the cavalry, crossed, if I may so express it, the threshold of those fatal woods.

The snow was now some fourteen inches deep upon the ground, and still falling in such thick flakes as made it impossible to see twenty yards ahead. The gloomy pine-trees closed round our steps in every direction, thick-set, uniform, endless. Except the broad chaussée, down which the artillery was lumbering slowly and noiselessly, no paths or side-tracks were distinguishable. Below, all was white and dazzling; above, where the wide-spreading pine-branches roofed out the leaden sky, all was dark and oppressive. Presently the Prince of Lichtenstein rode up, and bade us turn aside under the trees on either side of the road till Kollowrath's reserves had passed on. We did so; dismounted; lit our pipes; and waited till our turn should come to follow the rest.

Suddenly, without a moment's warning, as if they had sprung from the earth, an immense body of the enemy's foot poured in upon us from the very direction in which our left wing, under Riesch, had lately passed along. In an instant the air was filled with shouts, and smoke, and shots, and gleaming sabres—the snow was red with blood—men, horses, and artillery were massed together in inextricable confusion, and hundreds of our brave fellows were cut down before they could even draw their swords to strike a single blow.

"Call up the Bavarian reserve!" shouted the Prince, sitting his horse like a statue and pointing up the road with his sword.

The next instant I was rolling under my own horse's feet, with a murderous grip upon my throat, a pistol at my head, and in my ears a sound like the rushing of a mighty sea. After this I remember nothing more, till by-and-by I came to my senses, and found myself, with some five or six wounded cuirassiers, lying in an open cart, and being transported along a country road apparently skirting the forest. I thought at first that I also was wounded and that we were all prisoners, and so closed my eyes in despair.

But as the tide of consciousness continued to flow back, I discovered that we were in the care of our own people, and in the midst of a long string of ambulances bringing up the rear of the Imperial army. And I also found that, more fortunate than my companions, I had been stunned and badly bruised, but was otherwise unhurt.

Presently Gustav came riding up, and with a cry of joy exclaimed:—

"How now, lieber Freund! No broken bones? All well and safe this time?"

"All well and safe," I replied; "but sore from head to foot, and jolted almost to death. Where's my horse, I wonder?"

"Dead, no doubt; but if you can ride, take mine, and I'll secure the first I can get."

"Is the battle over?"

He shook his head.

"Ay," he said, gloomily. "The battle is over—and lost."

"Lost!—utterly?"

"Utterly."

And then, still riding beside the cart and bending towards me as he rode, he told, in a few bitter sentences, all he knew of the day's disaster.

Moreau, the Generals Groucy and Grandjean, had, it seemed, lain in wait with the main body of his army at the farther end of the forest, where the great Munich and Wasserburg road debouches upon the open plain, in order to drive our forces back as soon as the heads of the first columns should emerge on that side; while Ney, prepared to execute a similar manoeuvre with his division, was stationed for the same purpose at the mouth of the other great chaussée.

Richepanse, meanwhile, separated by an accident from half his brigade, instead of retreating, advanced with great intrepidity, and fell upon us flank and rear, as I have said, when we least expected danger. Thus it was that the Imperial army was attacked and driven back upon itself from three points, and defeated with great slaughter.

"As for our losses," said Lichtenstein, "Heaven only knows what they are! It seems to me that we have scarcely a gun or a baggage-waggon left; while our men, herded together, trampled, cut down by thousands—Herr Gott! I cannot bear to think of it."

That night we retired across the Inn and halted upon the Tyrolean side, making some show of defence along the line of the river, in the direction of Saltzburg. Our men, however, had none of the spirit of resistance left in them. They seemed as if crushed by the magnitude of their defeat. Hundreds deserted daily. The rest clamoured impatiently for a retreat. The whole camp was in dismay and disorder.

Suddenly, none could exactly tell how, a rumour went about that Moreau was about to attempt the passage of the Lower Inn.

This rumour soon became more definite.

The point chosen was distant some three or four marches from that where we were now posted.

All the boats upon the Isar had been seized and sent down the river as far as Munich.

From Munich they were about to be transported overland to the nearest point upon the Inn.

Two bridges of boats were then to be thrown across the river, and the French battalions were to march over to our attack.

Such was the information which the peasantry brought to our camp, and which was confirmed by the scouts whom we sent out in every direction. The enemy's movements were open and undisguised. Confident of success and secure in our weakness, he disdained even the semblance of strategy.

On the 4th of December the Archduke called another council of war; and some hours before daybreak on the morning of the 5th, our whole right wing was despatched to the point at which we anticipated an attack.

At dawn, Gustav, who had been out all night on duty, came in wet and weary, and found me still asleep.

"Rouse up dreamer!" he said. "Our comrades are gone, and now we can sing 'De Profundis' for ourselves."

"Why for ourselves?" I asked, raising myself upon my elbow.

"Because Riesch is gone; and, if I am not very much mistaken, we shall have to fight the French without him."

"What do you mean? Riesch is gone to repulse the threatened attack down the river?"

"I mean that my mind misgives me about that attack. Moreau is not wont to show his cards so plainly. I have been thinking about it all night; and the more I think of it, the more I suspect that the French have laid a trap, and the Archduke has walked into it."

And then, while we lit our fire and breakfasted together off our modest rations of black bread and soup, my friend showed me, in a few words, how unlikely it was that Moreau should conduct any important operation in so ostentatious a fashion. His object, argued Lichtenstein, was either to mislead us with false rumours, and then, in the absence of Riesch's division, to pour across the river and attack us unexpectedly, or, more probably still, it was his design to force the passage of the Upper Inn and descend upon us from the hills to our rear.

I felt a sudden conviction that he was right.

"It is so—it must be so!" I exclaimed. "What is to be done?"

"Nothing—unless to die hard when the time comes."

"Will you not lay your suspicions before the Archduke?"

"The Archduke would not thank me, perhaps, for seeing farther than himself. Besides, suspicions are nothing. If I had proof—proof positive . . . if my uncle would but grant me a party of reconnoissance . . . By Heaven! I will ask him."

"Then ask him one thing more—get leave for me to go with you!"

At this moment three or four drums struck up the rappel—were answered by others—and again by others far and near, and in a few seconds the whole camp was alive and stirring. In the meanwhile, Lichtenstein snatched up his cap and rushed away, eager to catch the Prince before he left his tent.

In about half an hour he came back, radiant with success. His uncle had granted him a troop of twenty men, with permission to cross the Inn and reconnoitre the enemy's movements.

"But he will not consent to let thee join, mein Bruder," said Gustav, regretfully.

"Why not?"

"Because it is a service of danger, and he will not risk the life of a second officer when one is enough."

"Pshaw! as if my life were worth anything! But there—it's just my luck. I might have been certain he would refuse. When do you go?"

"At midday. We are to keep on this side following the road to Neubevern till we find some point narrow enough to swim our horses over. After that, we shall go round by any unfrequented ways and bridle-paths we can find; get near the French camp as soon as it is dusk; and find out all we can."

"I'd have given my black mustang to be allowed to go with you."

"I don't half forgive the Prince for refusing," said Gustav. "But then, you see, not a man of us may come back; and after all, it's more satisfactory to get one's bullet on the open battle-field than to be caught and shot for a spy."

"I should prefer to take my chance of that."

"I am not quite sure that I should prefer it for you," said my friend. "I have gained my point—I am glad to go: but I have an impression of coming disaster."

"Ah! you know I don't believe in presentiments."

"I do know it, of old. But the sons of the house of Lichtenstein have reason to believe in them. I could tell you many a strange story if I had time. . . . But it is already ten, and I must write some letters and put my papers in order before I start."

With this he sat down to his desk, and I went out, in order to leave him alone while he wrote. When I came back, his charger was waiting outside in care of an orderly; the troop had already assembled in an open space behind the tent; and the men were busy tightening their horses' girths, looking to the locks of their pistols, and gaily preparing to be gone.

I found Lichtenstein booted and spurred and ready. A letter and a sealed packet lay upon the table, and he had just opened a locker to take a slice of bread and a glass of kirschwasser before starting.

"Thank heaven you are come!" he said. "In three minutes more I should have been gone. You see this letter and packet?—I entrust them to you. The packet contains my watch, which was my father's, given to him by the Empress Catherine of Russia; my hereditary star and badge as a Count of the early Roman Empire; my will; my commission; and my signet ring. If I fall to-day, the packet is to be given to my uncle. The letter is for Constance, bidding her farewell. I have enclosed in it my mother's portrait and a piece of my hair. You will forward it, lieber Freund. . . ."

"I will."

He took a locket from his bosom, opened it, kissed it, and gave it to me with a sigh.

"I would not have her portrait fall into rude and sacrilegious hands," he said; "if I never come back, destroy it. And now for a parting glass, and good bye!"

We then chinked our glasses together, drank to each other in silence, clasped hands, and parted.

Away they rode through the heavy mire and beating rain, twenty picked men, two and two, with their Captain at their head. I watched them as they trotted leisurely down the long line of tents, and when the last man had disappeared, I went in with a heavy heart, telling myself that I should perhaps never see Gustav von Lichtenstein again.

Throughout the rest of the day it continued to rain incessantly. It was my turn that night to be on duty for five hours; to go the round of the camp, and to visit all the outposts. I therefore made up the best fire I could, stopped indoors, and, following my friend's example, wrote letters all the afternoon.

About six in the evening the rain ceased, and it began to snow. It was just the Hohenlinden weather over again.

At eight, having cooked and eaten my solitary supper, I wrapped myself in my rug, lay down before the fire, and slept till midnight, when the orderly came, as usual, to wake me and accompany me on my rounds.

"Dreadful weather, I suppose, Fritz?" I said, getting up unwillingly, and preparing to face the storm.

"No, mein Herr; it is a beautiful night."

I could hardly believe him.

But so it was. The camp lay around us, one sheet of smooth dazzling snow; the clouds had parted, and were clearing off rapidly in every direction; and just over the Archduke's tent where the Imperial banner hung drooping and heavy, the full moon was rising in splendour.

A magnificent night—cold, but not piercing—pleasant to ride in—pleasant to smoke in as one rode. A superb night for trotting leisurely round about a peaceful camp; but a bad night for a reconnoitring party on hostile ground,—a fatal night for Austrian white-coats in danger of being seen by vigilant French sentries.

Where now were Gustav and his troop? What had they done? What had happened since they left? How soon would they come back? I asked myself these questions incessantly.

I could think of nothing else. I looked at my watch every few minutes. As the time wore on, the hours appeared to grow longer. At two o'clock, before I had gone half my round, it seemed to me that I had been all night in the saddle. From two to three, from three to four, the hours dragged by as if every minute were weighted with lead.

"The Graf von Lichtenstein will be coming back this way, mein Herr," said the orderly, spurring his horse up beside mine, and saluting with his hand to the side of his helmet as he spoke.

"Which way? Over the hill, or down in the hollow?"

"Through the hollow, mein Herr. That is the road by which the Herr Graf rode out; and the river is too wide for them to cross anywhere but upstream."

"Then they must come this way?"

"Yes, mein Herr."

We were riding along the ridge of a long hill, one side of which sloped down towards the river, while on the other side it terminated in an abrupt precipice overhanging a narrow road or ravine, some forty feet below. The opposite bank was also steep, though less steep than that on our side; and beyond it the eye travelled over a wide expanse of dusky pine-woods, now white and heavy with snow.

I reined in my horse the better to observe the scene. Yonder flowed the Inn, dark and silent, a river of ink winding through meadow flats of dazzling silver. Far away upon the horizon rose the mystic outlines of the Franconian Alps. A single sentry, pacing to and fro some four hundred yards ahead, was distinctly visible in the moonlight; and such was the perfect stillness of the night that, although the camp lay at least two miles and a half away, I could hear the neighing of the horses and the barking of the dogs.

Again I looked at my watch, again calculated how long my friend had been absent. It was now a quarter past four A.M., and he had left the camp at midday.

If he had not yet returned—and of course he might have done so at any moment since I had been out on duty—he had now been gone sixteen hours and a quarter.

Sixteen hours and quarter! Time enough to have ridden to Munich and back!

The orderly again brought his horse up abreast with mine.

"Pardon, mein Herr," he said, pointing up the ravine with his sabre; "but do you see nothing yonder—beyond the turn of the road—just where there is a gap in the trees?"

I looked; but I saw nothing.

"What do you think you see?" I asked him.

"I scarcely know, mein Herr;—something moving close against the trees, beyond the hollow way."

"Where the road emerges upon the plain and skirts the pine-woods?"

"Yes, mein Herr; several dark objects—Ah! they are horsemen!"

"It is the Graf von Lichtenstein and his troop!" I exclaimed.

"Nay, mein Herr; see how slowly they ride, and how they keep close under the shade of the woods! The Graf von Lichtenstein would not steal back so quietly."

I stood up in my stirrups, shaded my eyes with my hand, and stared eagerly at the approaching cavalcade.

They were perhaps half-a-mile away as the crow flies, and would not have been visible from this point but for a long gap in the trees on this side of the hill. I could see that they were soldiers. They might be French; but, somehow, I did not think they were. I fancied, I hoped, they were our own Lichtensteiners come back again.

"They are making for the hollow way, mein Herr," said the orderly.

They were evidently making for the hollow way. I watched them past the gap till the last man had gone by, and it seemed to me they were about twenty in number.

I dismounted, flung my reins to the orderly, and went to where the edge of the precipice overhung the road below. Hence, by means of such bushes and tree-stumps as were rooted in the bank, I clambered down a few feet lower, and there lay concealed till they should pass through.

It now seemed to me that they would never come. I do not know how long I waited. It might have been ten minutes—it might have been half an hour; but the time that elapsed between the moment when I dismounted and the moment when the first helmet came in sight seemed interminable.

The road, as I have already said, lay between a steep declivity on the one side and a less abrupt height, covered with pine-trees, on the other—a picturesque winding gorge or ravine, half dark as night, half bright as day; here deep in shadow, there flooded with moonlight; and carpeted a foot deep with fresh-fall-en snow. After I had waited and watched till my eyes ached with staring in the gloom, I at last saw a single horseman coming round the turn of the road, about a hundred yards from the spot where I was lying. Slowly, and as it seemed to me, dejectedly, he rode in advance of his comrades. The rest followed, two and two.

At the first glance, while they were yet in deep shadow, and, as I have said, a hundred yards distant, I recognised the white cloaks and plumes and the black chargers of my own corps. I knew at once that it was Lichtenstein and his troop.

Then a sudden terror fell upon me. Why were they coming back so slowly? What evil tidings did they bring? How many were returning? How many were missing? I knew well, if there had been a skirmish, who was sure to have been foremost in the fight. I knew well, if but three or four had fallen, who was sure to be one of the fallen.

These thoughts flashed upon me in the first instant when I recognised the Lichtenstein uniform. I could not have uttered a word, or have done anything to attract the men's attention, if it had been to save my life. Dread paralyzed me.

Slowly, dejectedly, noiselessly, the first cuirassier emerged into the moonlight, passed on again into the gloom, and vanished in the next turn of the road. It was but for a moment that the moonlight streamed full upon him; yet in that moment I saw there had been a fray, and that the man had been badly wounded.

As slowly, as dejectedly, as noiselessly, with broken plumes and battered hel-mets, and cloaks torn and blood-stained, the rest came after, two and two; each pair, as they passed, shining out momentarily, distinctly, like the images projected for an instant upon the disc of a magic-lantern.

I held my breath and counted them as they went by—first one alone; then two and two, till I had counted eighteen riding in pairs. Then one alone, bringing up the rear. Then . . . .

I waited—I watched—I refused to believe that this could be all. I refused to believe that Gustav must not presently come galloping up to overtake them. At last, long after I knew it was in vain to wait and watch longer, I clambered up again—cramped, and cold, and sick at heart—and found the orderly walking the horses up and down on the brow of the hill. The man looked me in the face, as if he would fain have asked me what I had seen.

"It was the Graf von Lichtenstein's troop," I said, by an effort; "but—but the Graf von Lichtenstein is not with them."

And with this I sprang into the saddle, clapped spurs to my horse, and said no more.

I had still two outposts to visit before finishing my round; but from that moment to this I have never been able to remember any one incident of my homeward ride. I visited those outposts, without doubt; but I was as unconscious of the performance of my duty as a sleeper is unconscious of the act of breathing.

Gustav was the only man missing. Gustav was dead. I repeated it to myself over and over again. I felt that it was true. I had no hope that he was taken prisoner. No—he was dead. He had fallen, fighting to the last. He had died like a hero. But—he was dead.

At a few minutes after five, I returned to camp. The first person I met was von Blumenthal, the Prince of Lichtenstein's secretary. He was walking up and down outside my tent, waiting for me. He ran to me as I dismounted.

"Thank heaven you are come!" he said. "Go at once to the prince—the Graf von Lichtenstein is dying. He has fought a troop of French lancers three times as many as his own, and carried off a bundle of despatches. But he has paid for them with his life, and with the lives of all his men. He rode in, covered with wounds, a couple of hours ago, and had just breath enough left to tell the tale."

"His own life, and the lives of all his men!" I repeated hoarsely.

"Yes, he left every man on the field—himself the only survivor. He cut his way out with the captured despatches in one hand and his sword in the other—and there he lies in the Prince's tent—dying."

He was unconscious—had been unconscious ever since he was laid upon his uncle's bed—and he died without again opening his eyes or uttering a word. I saw him breathe his last, and that was all. Even now, old man as I am, I cannot dwell upon that scene. He was my first friend, and I may say my best friend. I have known other friendships since then; but none so intimate—none so precious.

But now comes a question which I yet ask myself "many a time and oft," and which, throughout all the years that have gone by since that night, I have never yet been able to answer. Gustav von Lichtenstein met and fought a troop of French Lancers; saw his own twenty cuirassiers cut to pieces before his eyes; left them all for dead upon a certain hillside on the opposite bank of the Inn; and rode back into camp, covered with wounds—the only survivor!

What, then, was that silent cavalcade that I saw riding through the hollow way—twenty men without their leader? Were those the dead whom I met, and was it the one living man who was absent?

HOW THE THIRD FLOOR KNEW THE POTTERIES

Amelia B. Edwards

Amelia B. Edwards (1831–1892) was a noted polymath, famously passionate about Egyptology and travel writing. She was also known for her ghost stories and novels, including *My Brother's Wife* and *Lord Brackenbury*. Edwards died of influenza in Bristol.

I am a plain man, Major, and you may not dislike to hear a plain statement of facts from me.

Some of those facts lie beyond my understanding. I do not pretend to explain them. I only know that they happened as I relate them, and that I pledge myself for the truth of every word of them.

I began life roughly enough, down among the Potteries. I was an orphan; and my earliest recollections are of a great porcelain manufactory in the country of the Potteries, where I helped about the yard, picked up what halfpence fell in my way, and slept in a harness-loft over the stable. Those were hard times; but things bettered themselves as I grew older and stronger, especially after George Barnard had come to be foreman of the yard.

George Barnard was a Wesleyan—we were mostly dissenters in the Potteries—sober, clear-headed, somewhat sulky and silent, but a good fellow every inch of him, and my best friend at the time when I most needed a good friend. He took me out of the yard, and set me to the furnace-work. He entered me on the books at a fixed rate of wages. He helped me to pay for a little cheap schooling four nights a week; and he led me to go with him on Sundays to the chapel down by the river-side, where I first saw Leah Payne. She was his sweetheart, and so pretty that I used to forget the preacher and everybody else, when I looked at her. When she joined in the singing, I heard no voice but hers. If she asked me for the hymn-book, I used to blush and tremble. I believe I worshipped her, in my stupid ignorant way; and I think I worshipped Barnard almost as blindly, though after a different fashion. I felt I owed him everything. I knew that he had saved me, body and mind; and I looked up to him as a savage might look up to a missionary.

Leah was the daughter of a plumber, who lived close by the chapel. She was twenty, and George about seven or eight-and-thirty. Some captious folks said there was too much difference in their ages; but she was so serious-minded, and they loved each other so earnestly and quietly, that, if nothing had come between them during their courtship, I don't believe the question of disparity would ever have troubled the happiness of their married lives. Something did come, however; and that something was a Frenchman, called Louis Laroche. He was a painter on porcelain, from the famous works at Sèvres; and our master, it was said, had engaged him for three years certain, at such wages as none of our own people, however skilful, could hope to command. It was about the beginning or middle of September when he first came among us. He looked very young; was small, dark, and well made; had little white soft hands, and a silky moustache; and spoke English nearly as well as I do. None of us liked him; but that was only natural, seeing how he was put over the head of every Englishman in the place. Besides, though he was always smiling and civil, we couldn't help seeing that he thought himself ever so much better than the rest of us; and that was not pleasant. Neither was it pleasant to see him strolling about the town, dressed just like a gentleman, when working hours were over; smoking good cigars, when we were forced to be content with a pipe of common tobacco; hiring a horse on Sunday afternoons, when we were trudging a-foot; and taking his pleasure as if the world was made for him to enjoy, and us to work in.

"Ben, boy," said George, "there's something wrong about that Frenchman."

It was on a Saturday afternoon, and we were sitting on a pile of empty seggars against the door of my furnace-room, waiting till the men should all have cleared out of the yard. Seggars are deep earthen boxes in which the pottery is put, while being fired in the kiln. I looked up, inquiringly.

"About the Count?" said I, for that was the nickname by which he went in the pottery.

George nodded, and paused for a moment with his chin resting on his palms.

"He has an evil eye," said he; "and a false smile. Something wrong about him."

I drew nearer, and listened to George as if he had been an oracle. "Besides," added he, in his slow quiet way, with his eyes fixed straight before him as if he was thinking aloud, "there's a young look about him that isn't natural. Take him just at sight, and you'd think he was almost a boy; but look close at him— see the little fine wrinkles under his eyes, and the hard lines about his mouth, and then tell me his age, if you can! Why, Ben boy, he's as old as I am, pretty near; ay, and as strong, too. You stare; but I tell you that, slight as he looks, he could fling you over his shoulder as if you were a feather. And as for his hands, little and white as they are, there are muscles of iron inside them, take my word for it."

"But, George, how can you know?"

"Because I have a warning against him," replied George, very gravely. "Because, whenever he is by, I feel as if my eyes saw clearer, and my ears heard keener, than at other times. Maybe it's presumption, but I sometimes feel as if I had a call to guard myself and others against him. Look at the children, Ben, how they shrink away from him; and see there, now! Ask Captain what he thinks of him! Ben, that dog likes him no better than I do."

I looked, and saw Captain crouching by his kennel with his ears laid back, growling audibly, as the Frenchman came slowly down the steps leading from his own workshop at the upper end of the yard. On the last step he paused; lighted a cigar; glanced round, as if to see whether anyone was by; and then walked straight over to within a couple of yards of the kennel. Captain gave a short angry snarl, and laid his muzzle close down upon his paws, ready for a spring. The Frenchman folded his arms deliberately, fixed his eyes on the dog, and stood calmly smoking.

He knew exactly how far he dared go, and kepi just that one foot out of harm's way. All at once he stooped, puffed a mouthful of smoke in the dog's eyes, burst into a mocking laugh, turned lightly on his heel, and walked away; leaving Captain straining at his chain, and barking after him like a mad creature.

Days went by, and I, at work in my own department, saw no more of the Count. Sunday came—the third, I think, after I had talked with George in the yard. Going with George to chapel, as usual, in the morning, I noticed that there was something strange and anxious in his voice, and that he scarcely opened his lips to me on the way. Still I said nothing. It was not my place to question him; and I remember thinking to myself that the cloud would all clear off as soon as he found himself by Leah's side, holding the same book, and joining in the same hymn.

It did not, however, for no Leah was there. I looked every moment to the door, expecting to see her sweet face coming in; but George never lifted his eyes from his book, or seemed to notice that her place was empty. Thus the whole service went by, and my thoughts wandered continually from the words of the preacher. As soon as the last blessing was spoken, and we were fairly across the threshold, I turned to George, and asked if Leah was ill?

"No," said he, gloomily. "She's not ill."

"Then why wasn't she—?"

"I'll tell you why," he interrupted, impatiently. "Because you've seen her here for the last time. She's never coming to chapel again."

"Never coming to the chapel again?" I faltered, laying my hand on his sleeve in the earnestness of my surprise. "Why, George, what is the matter?"

But he shook my hand off and stamped with his iron heel till the pavement rang again.

"Don't ask me," said he, roughly. "Let me alone. You'll know soon enough."

And with this he turned off down a by-lane leading towards the hills, and left me without another word.

I had had plenty of hard treatment in my time; but never, until that moment, an angry look or syllable from George. I did not know how to bear it. That day my dinner seemed as if it would choke me; and in the afternoon I went out and wandered restlessly about the fields till the hour for evening prayers came round. I then returned to the chapel, and sat down on a tomb outside, waiting for George. I saw the congregation go in by twos and threes; I heard the first psalm-tune echo solemnly through the evening stillness; but no George came. Then the service began, and I knew that, punctual as his habits were, it was of no use to expect him any longer. Where could he be? What could have happened? Why should Leah Payne never come to chapel again? Had she gone over to some other sect, and was that why George seemed so unhappy?

Sitting there in the little dreary churchyard with the darkness fast gathering around me, I asked myself these questions over and over again, till my brain ached; for I was not much used to thinking about anything in those times. At last,

I could bear to sit quiet no longer. The sudden thought struck me that I would go to Leah, and learn what the matter was, from her own lips. I sprang to my feet, and set off at once towards her home.

It was quite dark, and a light rain was beginning to fall. I found the garden-gate open, and a quick hope flashed across me that George might be there. I drew back for a moment, hesitating whether to knock or ring, when a sound of voices in the passage, and the sudden gleaming of a bright line of light under the door, warned me that someone was coming out. Taken by surprise, and quite unprepared for the moment with anything to say, I shrank back behind the porch, and waited until those within should have passed out. The door opened, and the light streamed suddenly upon the roses and the wet gravel.

"It rains," said Leah, bending forward and shading the candle with her hand.

"And is as cold as Siberia," added another voice, which was not George's, and yet sounded strangely familiar. "Ugh! what a climate for such a flower as my darling to bloom in!"

"Is it so much finer in France?" asked Leah, softly.

"As much finer as blue skies and sunshine can make it. Why, my angel, even your bright eyes will be ten times brighter, and your rosy cheeks ten times rosier, when they are transplanted to Paris. Ah! I can give you no idea of the wonders of Paris—the broad streets planted with trees, the palaces, the shops, the gardens!—it is a city of enchantment."

"It must be, indeed!" said Leah. "And you will really take me to see all those beautiful shops?"

"Every Sunday, my darling—Bah! don't look so shocked. The shops in Paris are always open on Sunday, and everybody makes holiday. You will soon get over these prejudices."

"I fear it is very wrong to take so much pleasure in the things of this world," sighed Leah.

The Frenchman laughed, and answered her with a kiss.

"Good night, my sweet little saint!" and he ran lightly down the path, and disappeared in the darkness. Leah sighed again, lingered a moment, and then closed the door.

Stupefied and bewildered, I stood for some seconds like a stone statue, unable to move; scarcely able to think. At length, I roused myself, as it were mechanically, and went towards the gate. At that instant a heavy hand was laid upon my shoulder, and a hoarse voice close beside my ear, said:

"Who are you? What are you doing here?"

It was George. I knew him at once, in spite of the darkness, and stammered his name. He took his hand quickly from my shoulder.

"How long have you been here?" said he, fiercely. "What right have you to lurk about, like a spy in the dark? God help me, Ben—I'm half mad. I don't mean to be harsh to you."

"I'm sure you don't," I cried, earnestly.

"It's that cursed Frenchman," he went on, in a voice that sounded like the groan of one in pain.

"He's a villain. I know he's a villain; and I've had a warning against him ever since the first moment he came among us. He'll make her miserable, and break her heart some day—my pretty Leah—and I loved her so! But I'll be revenged—as sure as there's a sun in heaven, I'll be revenged!"

His vehemence terrified me. I tried to persuade him to go home; but he would not listen to me.

"No, no," he said. "Go home yourself, boy, and let me be. My blood is on fire: this rain is good for me, and I am better alone."

"If I could only do something to help you—"

"You can't," interrupted he. "Nobody can help me. I'm a ruined man, and I don't care what becomes of me. The Lord forgive me, my heart is full of wickedness, and my thoughts are the promptings of Satan. There go—for Heaven's sake, go. I don't know what I say, or what I do!"

I went, for I did not dare refuse any longer; but I lingered a while at the corner of the street, and watched him pacing to and fro, to and fro in the driving rain. At length I turned reluctantly away, and went home.

I lay awake that night for hours, thinking over the events of the day, and hating the Frenchman from my very soul. I could not hate Leah. I had worshipped her too long and too faithfully for that; but I looked upon her as a creature given over to destruction. I fell asleep towards morning, and woke again shortly after daybreak. When I reached the pottery, I found George there before me, looking very pale, but quite himself, and setting the men to their work the same as usual. I said nothing about what had happened the day before. Something in his face silenced me; but seeing him so steady and composed, I took heart, and began to hope he had fought through the worst of his trouble. By-and-by the Frenchman came through the yard, gay and off-hand, with his cigar in his mouth, and his hands in his pockets. George turned sharply away into one of the workshops, and shut the door. I drew a deep breath of relief. My dread was to see them come to an open quarrel; and I felt that as long as they kept clear of that, all would be well.

Thus the Monday went by, and the Tuesday; and still George kept aloof from me. I had sense enough not to be hurt by this. I felt he had a good right to be silent, if silence helped him to bear his trial better; and I made up my mind never to breathe another syllable on the subject, unless he began.

Wednesday came. I had overslept myself that morning, and came to work a quarter after the hour, expecting to be fined; for George was very strict as foreman of the yard, and treated friends and enemies just the same. Instead of blaming me, however, he called me up, and said:

"Ben, whose turn is it this week to sit up?"

"Mine, sir," I replied. (I always called him "Sir" in working hours.)

"Well, then, you may go home to-day, and the same on Thursday and Friday; for there's a large batch of work for the ovens to-night, and there'll be the same to-morrow night and the night after."

"All right, sir," said I. "Then I'll be here by seven this evening."

"No, half-past nine will be soon enough. I've some accounts to make up, and I shall be here myself till then. Mind you are true to time, though."

"I'll be as true as the clock, sir," I replied, and was turning away when he called me back again.

"You're a good lad, Ben," said he. "Shake hands."

I seized his hand, and pressed it warmly.

"If I'm good for anything, George," I answered with all my heart, "it's you who have made me so. God bless you for it!"

"Amen!" said he, in a troubled voice, putting his hand to his hat.

And so we parted.

In general, I went to bed by day when I was attending to the firing by night; but this morning I had already slept longer than usual, and wanted exercise more than rest. So I ran home; put a bit of bread and meat in my pocket; snatched up my big thorn stick; and started off for a long day in the country. When I came home, it was quite dark and beginning to rain, just as it had begun to rain at about the same time that wretched Sunday evening: so I changed my wet boots, had an early supper and a nap in the chimney-corner, and went down to the works at a few minutes before half-past nine. Arriving at the factory-gate, I found it ajar, and so walked in and closed it after me. I remember thinking at the time that it was unlike George's usual caution to leave it so but it passed from my mind next moment. Having slipped in the bolt, I then went straight over to George's little counting-house, where the gas was shining cheerfully in the window. Here also, somewhat to my surprise, I found the door open, and the room empty. I went in. The threshold and part of the floor was wetted by the driving rain. The wages-book was open on the desk, George's pen stood in the ink, and his hat hung on its usual peg in the corner. I concluded, of course, that he had gone round to the ovens; so, following him, I took down his hat and carried it with me, for it was now raining fast.

The baking-houses lay just opposite, on the other side of the yard. There were three of them, opening one out of the other; and in each, the great furnace filled all the middle of the room.

These furnaces are, in fact, large kilns built of brick, with an oven closed in by an iron door in the centre of each, and a chimney going up through the roof. The pottery, enclosed in seggars, stands round inside on shelves, and has to be turned from time to time while the firing is going on. To turn these seggars, test the heat, and keep the fires up, was my work at the period of which I am now telling you, Major.

Well! I went through the baking-houses one after the other, and found all empty alike. Then a strange, vague, uneasy feeling came over me, and I began to wonder what could have become of George. It was possible that he might be in one of the workshops; so I ran over to the counting-house, lighted a lantern, and made a thorough survey of the yards. I tried the doors; they were all locked as usual. I peeped into the open sheds; they were all vacant. I called "George! George!" in every part of the outer premises; but the wind and rain drove back my voice, and no other voice replied to it. Forced at last to believe that he was really gone, I took his hat back to the counting-house, put away the wages-book, extinguished the gas, and prepared for my solitary watch.

The night was mild, and the heat in the baking-rooms intense. I knew, by experience, that the ovens had been overheated, and that none of the porcelain must go in at least for the next two hours; so I carried my stool to the door, settled myself in a sheltered corner where the air could reach me, but not the rain, and fell to wondering where George could have gone, and why he should not have waited till the time appointed. That he had left in haste was clear—not because his hat remained behind, for he might have had a cap with him—but because he had left the book open, and the gas lighted. Perhaps one of the workmen had met with some accident, and he had been summoned away so urgently that he had no time to think of anything; perhaps he would even now come back presently to see that all was right before he went home to his lodgings.

Turning these things over in my mind, I grew drowsy, my thoughts wandered, and I fell asleep.

I cannot tell how long my nap lasted. I had walked a great distance that day, and I slept heavily; but I awoke all in a moment, with a sort of terror upon me, and, looking up, saw George Barnard sitting on a stool before the oven door, with the firelight full upon his face.

Ashamed to be found sleeping, I started to my feet. At the same instant, he rose, turned away without even looking towards me, and went out into the next room.

"Don't be angry, George!" I cried, following him. "None of the seggars are in. I knew the fires were too strong, and—"

The words died on my lips. I had followed him from the first room to the second, from the second to the third, and in the third—I lost him!

I could not believe my eyes. I opened the end door leading into the yard, and looked out; but he was nowhere in sight. I went round to the back of the baking-houses, looked behind the furnaces, ran over to the counting-house, called him by his name over and over again; but all was dark, silent, lonely, as ever.

Then I remembered how I had bolted the outer gate, and how impossible it was that he should have come in without ringing. Then, too, I began again to doubt the evidence of my own senses, and to think I must have been dreaming.

I went back to my old post by the door of the first baking-house, and sat down for a moment to collect my thoughts.

"In the first place," said I to myself, "there is but one outer gate. That outer gate I bolted on the inside, and it is bolted still. In the next place, I searched the premises, and found all the sheds empty, and the workshop-doors padlocked as usual on the outside. I proved that George was nowhere about, when I came, and I know he could not have come in since, without my knowledge. Therefore it is a dream. It is certainly a dream, and there's an end of it."

And with this I trimmed my lantern and proceeded to test the temperature of the furnaces. We used to do this, I should tell you, by the introduction of little roughly-moulded lumps of common fire-clay. If the heat is too great, they crack; if too little, they remain damp and moist; if just right, they become firm and smooth all over, and pass into the biscuit stage. Well! I took my three little lumps of clay, put one in each oven, waited while I counted five hundred, and then went round again to see the results. The two first were in capital condition, the third had flown into a dozen pieces. This proved that the seggars might at once go into ovens One and Two, but that number Three had been overheated, and must be allowed to go on cooling for an hour or two longer.

I therefore stocked One and Two with nine rows of seggars, three deep on each shelf; left the rest waiting till number Three was in a condition to be trusted;

and, fearful of falling asleep again, now that the firing was in progress, walked up and down the rooms to keep myself awake.

This was hot work, however, and I could not stand it very long; so I went back presently to my stool by the door, and fell to thinking about my dream. The more I thought of it, the more strangely real it seemed, and the more I felt convinced that I was actually on my feet, when I saw George get up and walk into the adjoining room. I was also certain that I had still continued to see him as he passed out of the second room into the third, and that at that time I was even following his very footsteps. Was it possible, I asked myself, that I could have been up and moving, and yet not quite awake? I had heard of people walking in their sleep. Could it be that I was walking in mine, and never waked till I reached the cool air of the yard? All this seemed likely enough, so I dismissed the matter from my mind, and passed the rest of the night in attending to the seggars, adding fresh fuel from time to time to the furnaces of the first and second ovens, and now and then taking a turn through the yards. As for number Three, it kept up its heat to such a degree that it was almost day before I dared trust the seggars to go in it.

Thus the hours went by; and at half-past seven on Thursday morning, the men came to their work. It was now my turn to go off duty, but I wanted to see George before I left, and so waited for him in the counting-house, while a lad named Steve Storr took my place at the ovens. But the clock went on from half-past seven to a quarter to eight; then to eight o'clock; then to a quarter-past eight—and still George never made his appearance. At length, when the hand got round to half-past eight, I grew weary of waiting, took up my hat, ran home, went to bed, and slept profoundly until past four in the afternoon.

That evening I went down to the factory quite early; for I had a restlessness upon me, and I wanted to see George before he left for the night. This time, I found the gate bolted, and I rang for admittance.

"How early you are, Ben!" said Steve Storr, as he let me in.

"Mr. Barnard's not gone?" I asked, quickly; for I saw at the first glance that the gas was out in the counting-house.

"He's not gone," said Steve, "because he's never been."

"Never been?"

"No and what's stranger still, he's not been home either, since dinner yesterday."

"But he was here last night."

"Oh yes, he was here last night, making up the books. John Parker was with him till past six; and you found him here, didn't you, at half-past nine?"

I shook my head.

"Well, he's gone, anyhow. Good night!"

"Good night!"

I took the lantern from his hand, bolted him out mechanically, and made my way to the baking-houses like one in a stupor. George gone? Gone without a word of warning to his employer, or of farewell to his fellow-workmen? I could not understand it. I could not believe it. I sat down bewildered, incredulous, stunned. Then came hot tears, doubts, terrifying suspicions. I remembered the wild words he had spoken a few nights back; the strange calm by which they were followed; my dream of the evening before. I had heard of men who drowned themselves for love; and the turbid Severn ran close by—so close, that one might pitch a stone into it from some of the workshop windows.

These thoughts were too horrible. I dared not dwell upon them. I turned to work, to free myself from them, if I could; and began by examining the ovens. The temperature of all was much higher than on the previous night, the heat having been gradually increased during the last twelve hours. It was now my business to keep the heat on the increase for twelve more; after which it would be allowed, as gradually, to subside, until the pottery was cool enough for removal. To turn the seggars, and add fuel to the two first furnaces, was my first work. As before, I found number Three in advance of the others, and so left it for half an hour, or an hour. I then went round the yard; tried the doors; let the dog loose; and brought him back with me to the baking-houses, for company. After that, I set my lantern on a shelf beside the door, took a book from my pocket, and began to read.

I remember the title of the book as well as possible. It was called Bowlker's Art of Angling, and contained little rude cuts of all kinds of artificial flies, hooks, and other tackle. But I could not keep my mind to it for two minutes together; and at last I gave it up in despair, covered my face with my hands, and fell into a long absorbing painful train of thought. A considerable time had gone by thus—maybe an hour—when I was roused by a low whimpering howl from Captain, who was lying at my feet. I looked up with a start, just as I had started from sleep the night before, and with the same vague terror; and saw, exactly in the same place and in the same attitude, with the firelight full upon him—George Barnard!

At this sight, a fear heavier than the fear of death fell upon me, and my tongue seemed paralysed in my mouth. Then, just as last night, he rose, or seemed to rise, and went slowly out into the next room. A power stronger than myself appeared to compel me, reluctantly, to follow him. I saw him pass through the second room—cross the threshold of the third room—walk straight up to the oven—and there pause. He then turned, for the first time, with the glare of the red firelight pouring out upon him from the open door of the furnace, and looked at me, face to face. In the same instant, his whole frame and countenance seemed to glow and become transparent, as if the fire were all within him and around him—and in that glow he became, as it were, absorbed into the furnace, and disappeared. I uttered a wild cry, tried to stagger from the room, and fell insensible before I reached the door.

When I next opened my eyes, the grey dawn was in the sky; the furnace-doors were all closed as I had left them when I last went round; the dog was quietly sleeping not far from my side; and the men were ringing at the gate, to be let in.

I told my tale from beginning to end, and was laughed at, as a matter of course, by all who heard it. When it was found, however, that my statements never varied, and, above all, that George Barnard continued absent, some few began to talk it over seriously, and among those few, the master of the works. He forbade the furnace to be cleared out, called in the aid of a celebrated naturalist, and had the ashes submitted to a scientific examination. The result was as follows:

The ashes were found to have been largely saturated with some kind of fatty animal matter. A considerable portion of those ashes consisted of charred bone. A semi-circular piece of iron, which evidently had once been the heel of a workman's heavy boot, was found, half fused, at one corner of the furnace. Near it, a tibia bone, which still retained sufficient of its original form and texture to render identification possible. This bone, however, was so much charred, that it fell into powder on being handled.

After this, not many doubted that George Barnard had been foully murdered, and that his body had been thrust into the furnace. Suspicion fell upon Louis Laroche. He was arrested, a coroner's inquest was held, and every circumstance connected with the night of the murder was as thoroughly sifted and investigated as possible. All the sifting in the world, however, failed either to clear or to condemn Louis Laroche. On the very night of his release, he left the place by the mail-train, and was never seen or heard of there, again. As for Leah, I know not what became of her. I went away myself before many weeks were over, and never have set foot among the Potteries from that hour to this.

THE FOUR-FIFTEEN EXPRESS

Amelia B. Edwards

Amelia B. Edwards (1831–1892) was a noted polymath, famously passionate about Egyptology and travel writing. She was also known for her ghost stories and novels, including *My Brother's Wife* and *Lord Brackenbury*. Edwards died of influenza in Bristol.

The events which I am about to relate took place between nine and ten years ago. Sebastopol had fallen in the early spring, the peace of Paris had been concluded since March, our commercial relations with the Russian empire were but recently renewed; and I, returning home after my first northward journey since the war, was well pleased with the prospect of spending the month of December under the hospitable and thoroughly English roof of my excellent friend, Jonathan Jelf, Esq., of Dumbleton Manor, Clayborough, East Anglia. Travelling in the interests of the well-known firm in which it is my lot to be a junior partner, I had been called upon to visit not only the capitals of Russia and Poland, but had found it also necessary to pass some weeks among the trading ports of the Baltic; whence it came that the year was already far spent before I again set foot on English soil, and that, instead of shooting pheasants with him, as I had hoped, in October, I came to be my friend's guest during the more genial Christmas-tide.

My voyage over, and a few days given up to business in Liverpool and London, I hastened down to Clayborough with all the delight of a schoolboy whose holidays are at hand. My way lay by the Great East Anglian line as far as Clayborough station, where I was to be met by one of the Dumbleton carriages and conveyed across the remaining nine miles of country. It was a foggy afternoon, singularly warm for the 4th of December, and I had arranged to leave London by the 4.15 express. The early darkness of winter had already closed in; the lamps were lighted in the carriages; a clinging damp dimmed the windows, adhered to the door-handles, and pervaded all the atmosphere; while the gas-jets at the neighbouring book-stand diffused a luminous haze that only served to make the gloom of the terminus more visible. Having arrived some seven minutes before the starting of the train, and, by the connivance of the guard, taken sole possession of an empty compartment, I lighted my travelling-lamp, made myself particularly snug, and settled down to the undisturbed enjoyment of a book and a cigar. Great, therefore, was my disappointment when, at the last moment, a gentleman came hurrying along the platform, glanced into my carriage, opened the locked door with a private key, and stepped in.

It struck me at the first glance that I had seen him before—a tall, spare man, thin-lipped, light-eyed, with an ungraceful stoop in the shoulders, and scant grey hair worn somewhat long upon the collar. He carried a light waterproof coat, an umbrella, and a large brown japanned deed-box, which last he placed under the seat. This done, he felt carefully in his breast-pocket, as if to make certain of the safety of his purse or pocket-book, laid his umbrella in the netting overhead, spread the waterproof across his knees, and exchanged his hat for a travelling-cap of some Scotch material. By this time the train was moving out of the station and into the faint grey of the wintry twilight beyond.

I now recognized my companion. I recognized him from the moment when he removed his hat and uncovered the lofty, furrowed, and somewhat narrow brow beneath. I had met him, as I distinctly remembered, some three years before, at the very house for which, in all probability, he was now bound, like myself. His name was Dwerrihouse, he was a lawyer by profession, and, if I was not greatly mistaken, was first cousin to the wife of my host. I knew also that he was a man eminently "well-to-do", both as regarded his professional and private means. The Jelfs entertained him with that sort of observant courtesy which falls to the lot of the rich relation, the children made much of him, and the old butler, albeit somewhat surly "to the general", treated him with deference. I thought, observing him by the vague mixture of lamplight and twilight, that Mrs. Jelf's cousin looked all the worse for the three years' wear and tear which had gone over his head since our last meeting. He was very pale, and had a restless light in his eye that I did not remember to have observed before. The anxious lines, too, about his mouth were deepened, and there was a cavernous, hollow look about his cheeks and temples which seemed to speak of sickness or sorrow. He had glanced at me as he came in, but without any gleam of recognition in his face. Now he glanced again, as I fancied, somewhat doubtfully. When he did so for the third or fourth time I ventured to address him.

"Mr. John Dwerrihouse, I think?"

"That is my name," he replied.

"I had the pleasure of meeting you at Dumbleton about three years ago."

"I thought I knew your face," he said; "but your name, I regret to say——"

"Langford—William Langford. I have known Jonathan Jelf since we were boys together at Merchant Taylors', and I generally spend a few weeks at Dumbleton in the shooting season. I suppose we are bound for the same destination."

"Not if you are on your way to the manor," he replied. "I am travelling upon business—rather troublesome business, too—while you, doubtless, have only pleasure in view."

"Just so. I am in the habit of looking forward to this visit as to the brightest three weeks in all the year."

"It is a pleasant house," said Mr. Dwerrihouse.

"The pleasantest I know."

"And Jelf is thoroughly hospitable."

"The best and kindest fellow in the world.

"They have invited me to spend Christmas week with them," pursued Mr. Dwerrihouse, after a moment's pause.

"And you are coming?"

"I cannot tell. It must depend on the issue of this business which I have in hand. You have heard perhaps that we are about to construct a branch line from Blackwater to Stockbridge."

I explained that I had been for some months away from England, and had therefore heard nothing of the contemplated improvement. Mr. Dwerrihouse smiled complacently.

"It will be an improvement," he said, "a great improvement. Stockbridge is a flourishing town, and needs but a more direct railway communication with the metropolis to become an important centre of commerce. This branch was my own idea. I brought the project before the board, and have myself superintended the execution of it up to the present time."

"You are an East Anglian director, I presume?"

"My interest in the company," replied Mr. Dwerrihouse, "is threefold. I am a director, I am a considerable shareholder, and, as head of the firm of Dwerrihouse, Dwerrihouse and Craik, I am the company's principal solicitor."

Loquacious, self-important, full of his pet project, and apparently unable to talk on any other subject, Mr. Dwerrihouse then went on to tell of the opposition he had encountered and the obstacles he had overcome in the cause of the Stockbridge branch. I was entertained with a multitude of local details and local grievances. The rapacity of one squire, the impracticability of another, the indignation of the rector whose glebe was threatened, the culpable indifference of the Stockbridge townspeople, who could not be brought to see that their most vital interests hinged upon a junction with the Great East Anglian line; the spite of the local newspaper, and the unheard-of difficulties attending the Common question, were each and all laid before me with a circumstantiality that possessed the deepest interest for my excellent fellow-traveller, but none whatever for myself. From these, to my despair, he went on to more intricate matters: to the approximate expenses of construction per mile; to the estimates sent in by different contractors; to the probable traffic returns of the new line; to the provisional clauses of the new act as enumerated in Schedule D of the company's last half-yearly report; and so on and on and on, till my head ached and my attention flagged and my eyes kept closing in spite of every effort that I made to keep them open. At length I was roused by these words:

"Seventy-five thousand pounds, cash down."

"Seventy-five thousand pounds, cash down," I repeated, in the liveliest tone I could assume. "That is a heavy sum."

"A heavy sum to carry here," replied Mr. Dwerrihouse, pointing significantly to his breast-pocket, "but a mere fraction of what we shall ultimately have to pay."

"You do not mean to say that you have seventy-five thousand pounds at this moment upon your person?" I exclaimed.

"My good sir, have I not been telling you so for the last half-hour?" said Mr. Dwerrihouse, testily. "That money has to be paid over at half-past eight o'clock this evening, at the office of Sir Thomas's solicitors, on completion of the deed of sale."

"But how will you get across by night from Blackwater to Stockbridge with seventy-five thousand pounds in your pocket?"

"To Stockbridge!" echoed the lawyer. "I find I have made myself very imperfectly understood. I thought I had explained how this sum only carries us as far as Mallingford—the first stage, as it were, of our journey—and how our route from Blackwater to Mallingford lies entirely through Sir Thomas Liddell's property."

"I beg your pardon," I stammered. I fear my thoughts were wandering. "So you only go as far as Mallingford tonight?"

"Precisely. I shall get a conveyance from the Blackwater Arms. And you?"

"Oh, Jelf sends a trap to meet me at Clayborough! Can I be the bearer of any message from you?"

"You may say, if you please, Mr. Langford, that I wished I could have been your companion all the way, and that I will come over, if possible, before Christmas."

"Nothing more?"

Mr. Dwerrihouse smiled grimly. "Well," he said, "you may tell my cousin that she need not burn the hall down in my honour this time, and that I shall be obliged if she will order the blue-room chimney to be swept before I arrive."

"That sounds tragic. Had you a conflagration on the occasion of your last visit to Dumbleton?"

"Something like it. There had been no fire lighted in my bedroom since the spring, the flue was foul, and the rooks had built in it; so when I went up to dress for dinner I found the room full of smoke and the chimney on fire. Are we already at Blackwater?"

The train had gradually come to a pause while Mr. Dwerrihouse was speaking, and, on putting my head out of the window, I could see the station some few hundred yards ahead. There was another train before us blocking the way, and the guard was making use of the delay to collect the Blackwater tickets. I had scarcely ascertained our position when the ruddy-faced official appeared at our carriage door.

"Tickets, sir!" said he.

"I am for Clayborough," I replied, holding out the tiny pink card.

He took it, glanced at it by the light of his little lantern, gave it back, looked, as I fancied, somewhat sharply at my fellow-traveller, and disappeared.

"He did not ask for yours," I said, with some surprise.

"They never do," replied Mr. Dwerrihouse; "they all know me, and of course I travel free."

"Blackwater! Blackwater!" cried the porter, running along the platform beside us as we glided into the station.

Mr. Dwerrihouse pulled out his deed-box, put his travelling-cap in his pocket, resumed his hat, took down his umbrella, and prepared to be gone.

"Many thanks, Mr. Langford, for your society," he said, with old-fashioned courtesy. "I wish you a good-evening."

"Good-evening," I replied, putting out my hand.

But he either did not see it or did not choose to see it, and, slightly lifting his hat, stepped out upon the platform. Having done this, he moved slowly away and mingled with the departing crowd.

Leaning forward to watch him out of sight, I trod upon something which proved to be a cigar-case. It had fallen, no doubt, from the pocket of his waterproof coat, and was made of dark morocco leather, with a silver monogram upon the side. I sprang out of the carriage just as the guard came up to lock me in.

"Is there one minute to spare?" I asked, eagerly. "The gentleman who travelled down with me from town has dropped his cigar-case; he is not yet out of the station."

"Just a minute and a half, sir," replied the guard. "You must be quick."

I dashed along the platform as fast as my feet could carry me. It was a large station, and Mr. Dwerrihouse had by this time got more than half-way to the farther end.

I, however, saw him distinctly, moving slowly with the stream. Then, as I drew nearer, I saw that he had met some friend, that they were talking as they walked, that they presently fell back somewhat from the crowd and stood aside in earnest conversation. I made straight for the spot where they were waiting. There was a vivid gas-jet just above their heads, and the light fell upon their faces. I saw both distinctly—the face of Mr. Dwerrihouse and the face of his companion. Running, breathless, eager as I was, getting in the way of porters and passengers, and fearful every instant lest I should see the train going on without me, I yet observed that the newcomer was considerably younger and shorter than the director, that he was sandy-haired, moustachioed, small-featured, and dressed in a close-cut suit of Scotch tweed. I was now within a few yards of them. I ran against a stout gentleman, I was nearly knocked down by a luggage-truck, I stumbled over a carpet-bag; I gained the spot just as the driver's whistle warned me to return.

To my utter stupefaction, they were no longer there. I had seen them but two seconds before—and they were gone! I stood still; I looked to right and left; I saw no sign of them in any direction. It was as if the platform had gaped and swallowed them.

"There were two gentlemen standing here a moment ago," I said to a porter at my elbow; "which way can they have gone?"

"I saw no gentlemen, sir," replied the man.

The whistle shrilled out again. The guard, far up the platform, held up his arm, and shouted to me to "come on!"

"If you're going on by this train, sir," said the porter, "you must run for it."

I did run for it, just gained the carriage as the train began to move, was shoved in by the guard, and left, breathless and bewildered, with Mr. Dwerrihouse's cigar-case still in my hand.

It was the strangest disappearance in the world; it was like a transformation trick in a pantomime. They were there one moment—palpably there, talking, with the gaslight full upon their faces—and the next moment they were gone. There was no door near, no window, no staircase; it was a mere slip of barren platform, tapestried with big advertisements. Could anything be more mysterious?

It was not worth thinking about, and yet, for my life, I could not help pondering upon it—pondering, wondering, conjecturing, turning it over and over in my mind, and beating my brains for a solution of the enigma. I thought of it all the way from Blackwater to Clayborough. I thought of it all the way from Clayborough to Dumbleton, as I rattled along the smooth highway in a trim dog-cart, drawn by a splendid black mare and driven by the silentest and dapperest of East Anglian grooms.

We did the nine miles in something less than an hour, and pulled up before the lodge-gates just as the church clock was striking half-past seven. A couple of minutes more, and the warm glow of the lighted hall was flooding out upon the gravel, a hearty grasp was on my hand, and a clear jovial voice was bidding me "welcome to Dumbleton".

"And now, my dear fellow," said my host, when the first greeting was over, "you have no time to spare. We dine at eight, and there are people coming to meet you, so you must just get the dressing business over as quickly as may be. By the way, you will meet some acquaintances; the Biddulphs are coming, and Prendergast (Prendergast of the Skirmishers) is staying in the house. Adieu! Mrs. Jelf will be expecting you in the drawing-room."

I was ushered to my room—not the blue room, of which Mr. Dwerrihouse had made disagreeable experience, but a pretty little bachelor's chamber, hung with a delicate chintz and made cheerful by a blazing fire. I unlocked my portmanteau. I tried to be expeditious, but the memory of my railway adventure haunted me. I could not get free of it; I could not shake it off. It impeded me, it worried me, it tripped me up, it caused me to mislay my studs, to mistie my cravat, to wrench the buttons off my gloves. Worst of all, it made me so late that the party had all assembled before I reached the drawing-room. I had scarcely paid my respects to Mrs. Jelf when dinner was announced, and we paired off, some eight or ten couples strong, into the dining-room.

I am not going to describe either the guests or the dinner. All provincial parties bear the strictest family resemblance, and I am not aware that an East Anglian banquet offers any exception to the rule. There was the usual country baronet and his wife; there were the usual country parsons and their wives; there was the sempiternal turkey and haunch of venison. Vanitas vanitatum. There is nothing new under the sun.

I was placed about midway down the table. I had taken one rector's wife down to dinner, and I had another at my left hand. They talked across me, and their talk was about babies; it was dreadfully dull. At length there came a pause. The entrées had just been removed, and the turkey had come upon the scene. The conversation had all along been of the languidest, but at this moment it happened to have stagnated altogether. Jelf was carving the turkey; Mrs. Jelf looked as if she was trying to think of something to say; everybody else was silent. Moved by an unlucky impulse, I thought I would relate my adventure.

"By the way, Jelf," I began, "I came down part of the way today with a friend of yours."

"Indeed!" said the master of the feast, slicing scientifically into the breast of the turkey. "With whom, pray?"

"With one who bade me tell you that he should, if possible, pay you a visit before Christmas."

"I cannot think who that could be," said my friend, smiling.

"It must be Major Thorp," suggested Mrs. Jelf.

I shook my head.

"It was not Major Thorp," I replied; "it was a near relation of your own, Mrs. Jelf."

"Then I am more puzzled than ever," replied my hostess. "Pray tell me who it was."

"It was no less a person than your cousin, Mr. John Dwerrihouse."

Jonathan Jelf laid down his knife and fork. Mrs. Jelf looked at me in a strange, startled way, and said never a word.

"And he desired me to tell you, my dear madam, that you need not take the trouble to burn the hall down in his honour this time, but only to have the chimney of the blue room swept before his arrival."

Before I had reached the end of my sentence I became aware of something ominous in the faces of the guests. I felt I had said something which I had better have left unsaid, and that for some unexplained reason my words had evoked a general consternation. I sat confounded, not daring to utter another syllable, and for at least two whole minutes there was dead silence round the table. Then Captain Prendergast came to the rescue.

"You have been abroad for some months, have you not, Mr. Langford?" he said, with the desperation of one who flings himself into the breach. "I heard you had been to Russia. Surely you have something to tell us of the state and temper of the country after the war?"

I was heartily grateful to the gallant Skirmisher for this diversion in my favour. I answered him, I fear, somewhat lamely; but he kept the conversation up, and presently one or two others joined in, and so the difficulty, whatever it might have been, was bridged over—bridged over, but not repaired. A something, an awkwardness, a visible constraint remained. The guests hitherto had been simply dull, but now they were evidently uncomfortable and embarrassed.

The dessert had scarcely been placed upon the table when the ladies left the room. I seized the opportunity to select a vacant chair next Captain Prendergast.

"In Heaven's name," I whispered, "what was the matter just now? What had I said?"

"You mentioned the name of John Dwerrihouse."

"What of that? I had seen him not two hours before."

"It is a most astounding circumstance that you should have seen him," said Captain Prendergast. "Are you sure it was he?"

"As sure as of my own identity. We were talking all the way between London and Blackwater. But why does that surprise you?"

"Because," replied Captain Prendergast, dropping his voice to the lowest whisper—"because John Dwerrihouse absconded three months ago with seventy-five thousand pounds of the company's money, and has never been heard of since."

John Dwerrihouse had absconded three months ago—and I had seen him only a few hours back! John Dwerrihouse had embezzled seventy-five thousand pounds of the company's money, yet told me that he carried that sum upon his person! Were ever facts so strangely incongruous, so difficult to reconcile? How should he have ventured again into the light of day? How dared he show himself along the line? Above all, what had he been doing throughout those mysterious three months of disappearance?

Perplexing questions these—questions which at once suggested themselves to the minds of all concerned, but which admitted of no easy solution. I could find no reply to them. Captain Prendergast had not even a suggestion to offer. Jonathan Jelf, who seized the first opportunity of drawing me aside and learning all that I had to tell, was more amazed and bewildered than either of us. He came to my room that night, when all the guests were gone, and we talked the thing over from every point of view; without, it must be confessed, arriving at any kind of conclusion.

"I do not ask you," he said, "whether you can have mistaken your man. That is impossible."

"As impossible as that I should mistake some stranger for yourself."

"It is not a question of looks or voice, but of facts. That he should have alluded to the fire in the blue room is proof enough of John Dwerrihouse's identity. How did he look?"

"Older, I thought; considerably older, paler, and more anxious."

"He has had enough to make him look anxious, anyhow," said my friend, gloomily, "be he innocent or guilty."

"I am inclined to believe that he is innocent," I replied. "He showed no embarrassment when I addressed him, and no uneasiness when the guard came round. His conversation was open to a fault. I might almost say that he talked too freely of the business which he had in hand."

"That again is strange, for I know no one more reticent on such subjects. He actually told you that he had the seventy-five thousand pounds in his pocket?"

"He did."

"Humph! My wife has an idea about it, and she may be right——"

"What idea?"

"Well, she fancies—women are so clever, you know, at putting themselves inside people's motives—she fancies that he was tempted, that he did actually take the money, and that he has been concealing himself these three months in some wild part of the country, struggling possibly with his conscience all the time, and daring neither to abscond with his booty nor to come back and restore it."

"But now that he has come back?"

"That is the point. She conceives that he has probably thrown himself upon the company's mercy, made restitution of the money, and, being forgiven, is permitted to carry the business through as if nothing whatever had happened."

"The last," I replied, "is an impossible case. Mrs. Jelf thinks like a generous and delicate-minded woman, but not in the least like a board of railway directors. They would never carry forgiveness so far."

"I fear not; and yet it is the only conjecture that bears a semblance of likelihood. However, we can run over to Clayborough tomorrow and see if anything is to be learned. By the way, Prendergast tells me you picked up his cigar-case."

"I did so, and here it is."

Jelf took the cigar-case, examined it by the light of the lamp, and said at once that it was beyond doubt Mr. Dwerrihouse's property, and that he remembered to have seen him use it.

"Here, too, is his monogram on the side," he added—"a big J transfixing a capital D. He used to carry the same on his note-paper."

"It offers, at all events, a proof that I was not dreaming."

"Ay, but it is time you were asleep and dreaming now. I am ashamed to have kept you up so long. Goodnight."

"Goodnight, and remember that I am more than ready to go with you to Clayborough or Blackwater or London or anywhere, if I can be of the least service."

"Thanks! I know you mean it, old friend, and it may be that I shall put you to the test. Once more, goodnight."

So we parted for that night, and met again in the breakfast-room at half-past eight next morning. It was a hurried, silent, uncomfortable meal; none of us had slept well, and all were thinking of the same subject. Mrs. Jelf had evidently been crying, Jelf was impatient to be off, and both Captain Prendergast and myself felt ourselves to be in the painful position of outsiders who are involuntarily brought into a domestic trouble. Within twenty minutes after we had left the breakfast-table the dog-cart was brought round, and my friend and I were on the road to Clayborough.

"Tell you what it is, Langford," he said, as we sped along between the wintry hedges, "I do not much fancy to bring up Dwerrihouse's name at Clayborough. All the officials know that he is my wife's relation, and the subject just now is hardly a pleasant one. If you don't much mind, we will take the 11.10 to Blackwater. It's an important station, and we shall stand a far better chance of picking up information there than at Clayborough."

So we took the 11.10, which happened to be an express, and, arriving at Blackwater about a quarter before twelve, proceeded at once to prosecute our inquiry.

We began by asking for the station-master, a big, blunt, businesslike person, who at once averred that he knew Mr. John Dwerrihouse perfectly well, and that there was no director on the line whom he had seen and spoken to so frequently. "He used to be down here two or three times a week about three months ago," said he, "when the new line was first set afoot; but since then, you know, gentle-men——"

He paused significantly.

Jelf flushed scarlet.

"Yes, yes," he said, hurriedly; "we know all about that. The point now to be ascertained is whether anything has been seen or heard of him lately."

"Not to my knowledge," replied the station-master.

"He is not known to have been down the line any time yesterday, for instance?"

The station-master shook his head.

"The East Anglian, sir," said he, "is about the last place where he would dare to show himself. Why, there isn't a station-master, there isn't a guard, there isn't a porter, who doesn't know Mr. Dwerrihouse by sight as well as he knows his own face in the looking-glass, or who wouldn't telegraph for the police as soon as he had set eyes on him at any point along the line. Bless you, sir! there's been a standing order out against him ever since the 25th of September last."

"And yet," pursued my friend, "a gentleman who travelled down yesterday from London to Clayborough by the afternoon express testifies that he saw

Mr. Dwerrihouse in the train, and that Mr. Dwerrihouse alighted at Blackwater station."

"Quite impossible, sir," replied the station-master, promptly.

"Why impossible?"

"Because there is no station along the line where he is so well known or where he would run so great a risk. It would be just running his head into the lion's mouth; he would have been mad to come nigh Blackwater station; and if he had come he would have been arrested before he left the platform."

"Can you tell me who took the Blackwater tickets of that train?"

"I can, sir. It was the guard, Benjamin Somers."

"And where can I find him?"

"You can find him, sir, by staying here, if you please, till one o'clock. He will be coming through with the up express from Crampton, which stays at Blackwater for ten minutes."

We waited for the up express, beguiling the time as best we could by strolling along the Blackwater road till we came almost to the outskirts of the town, from which the station was distant nearly a couple of miles. By one o'clock we were back again upon the platform and waiting for the train. It came punctually, and I at once recognized the ruddy-faced guard who had gone down with my train the evening before.

"The gentlemen want to ask you something about Mr. Dwerrihouse Somers," said the station-master, by way of introduction.

The guard flashed a keen glance from my face to Jelf's and back again to mine.

"Mr. John Dwerrihouse, the late director?" said he, interrogatively.

"The same," replied my friend. "Should you know him if you saw him?"

"Anywhere, sir."

"Do you know if he was in the 4.15 express yesterday afternoon?"

"He was not, sir."

"How can you answer so positively?"

"Because I looked into every carriage and saw every face in that train, and I could take my oath that Mr. Dwerrihouse was not in it. This gentleman was," he added, turning sharply upon me. "I don't know that I ever saw him before in my life, but I remember his face perfectly. You nearly missed taking your seat in time at this station, sir, and you got out at Clayborough."

"Quite true, guard," I replied; "but do you not also remember the face of the gentleman who travelled down in the same carriage with me as far as here?"

"It was my impression, sir, that you travelled down alone," said Somers, with a look of some surprise.

"By no means. I had a fellow-traveller as far as Blackwater, and it was in trying to restore him the cigar-case which he had dropped in the carriage that I so nearly let you go on without me."

"I remember your saying something about a cigar-case, certainly," replied the guard; "but——"

"You asked for my ticket just before we entered the station."

"I did, sir."

"Then you must have seen him. He sat in the corner next the very door to which you came."

"No, indeed; I saw no one."

I looked at Jelf. I began to think the guard was in the ex-director's confidence, and paid for his silence.

"If I had seen another traveller I should have asked for his ticket," added Somers. "Did you see me ask for his ticket, sir?"

"I observed that you did not ask for it, but he explained that by saying——" I hesitated. I feared. I might be telling too much, and so broke off abruptly.

The guard and the station-master exchanged glances. The former looked impatiently at his watch.

"I am obliged to go on in four minutes more, sir," he said.

"One last question, then," interposed Jelf, with a sort of desperation. "If this gentleman's fellow-traveller had been Mr. John Dwerrihouse, and he had been sitting in the corner next the door by which you took the tickets, could you have failed to see and recognize him?"

"No, sir; it would have been quite impossible."

"And you are certain you did not see him?"

"As I said before, sir, I could take my oath I did not see him. And if it wasn't that I don't like to contradict a gentleman, I would say I could also take my oath that this gentleman was quite alone in the carriage the whole way from London to Clayborough. Why, sir," he added, dropping his voice so as to be inaudible to the station-master, who had been called away to speak to some person close by, "you expressly asked me to give you a compartment to yourself, and I did so. I locked you in, and you were so good as to give me something for myself."

"Yes; but Mr. Dwerrihouse had a key of his own."

"I never saw him, sir; I saw no one in that compartment but yourself. Beg pardon, sir; my time's up."

And with this the ruddy guard touched his cap and was gone. In another minute the heavy panting of the engine began afresh, and the train glided slowly out of the station.

We looked at each other for some moments in silence. I was the first to speak.

"Mr. Benjamin Somers knows more than he chooses to tell," I said.

"Humph! do you think so?"

"It must be. He could not have come to the door without seeing him; it's impossible."

"There is one thing not impossible, my dear fellow."

"What is that?"

"That you may have fallen asleep and dreamed the whole thing."

"Could I dream of a branch line that I had never heard of? Could I dream of a hundred and one business details that had no kind of interest for me? Could I dream of the seventy-five thousand pounds?"

"Perhaps you might have seen or heard some vague account of the affair while you were abroad. It might have made no impression upon you at the time, and might have come back to you in your dreams, recalled perhaps by the mere names of the stations on the line."

"What about the fire in the chimney of the blue room—should I have heard of that during my journey?"

"Well, no; I admit there is a difficulty about that point."

"And what about the cigar-case?"

"Ay, by jove! there is the cigar-case. That is a stubborn fact. Well, it's a mysterious affair, and it will need a better detective than myself, I fancy, to clear it up. I suppose we may as well go home."

A week had not gone by when I received a letter from the secretary of the East Anglian Railway Company, requesting the favour of my attendance at a special board meeting not then many days distant. No reasons were alleged and no apologies offered for this demand upon my time, but they had heard, it was clear, of my inquiries anent the missing director, and had a mind to put me through some sort of official examination upon the subject. Being still a guest at Dumbleton Hall, I had to go up to London for the purpose, and Jonathan Jelf accompanied me. I found the direction of the Great East Anglian line represented by a party of some twelve or fourteen gentlemen seated in solemn conclave round a huge green baize table, in a gloomy boardroom adjoining the London terminus.

Being courteously received by the chairman (who at once began by saying that certain statements of mine respecting Mr. John Dwerrihouse had come to the knowledge of the direction, and that they in consequence desired to confer with me on those points), we were placed at the table, and the inquiry proceeded in due form.

I was first asked if I knew Mr. John Dwerrihouse, how long I had been acquainted with him, and whether I could identify him at sight. I was then asked when I had seen him last. To which I replied, "On the 4th of this present month, December, 1856." Then came the inquiry of where I had seen him on that fourth day of December; to which I replied that I met him in a first-class compartment of the 4.15 down express, that he got in just as the train was leaving the London terminus, and that he alighted at Blackwater station. The chairman then inquired whether I had held any communication with my fellow-traveller; whereupon I related, as nearly as I could remember it, the whole bulk and substance of Mr. John Dwerrihouse's diffuse information respecting the new branch line.

To all this the board listened with profound attention, while the chairman presided and the secretary took notes. I then produced the cigar-case. It was passed from hand to hand, and recognized by all. There was not a man present who did not remember that plain cigar-case with its silver monogram, or to whom it seemed anything less than entirely corroborative of my evidence. When at length I had told all that I had to tell, the chairman whispered something to the secretary; the secretary touched a silver hand-bell, and the guard, Benjamin Somers, was ushered into the room. He was then examined as carefully as myself. He declared that he knew Mr. John Dwerrihouse perfectly well, that he could not be mistaken in him, that he remembered going down with the 4.15 express on the afternoon in question, that he remembered me, and that, there being one or two empty first-class compartments on that especial afternoon, he had, in compliance with my request, placed me in a carriage by myself. He was positive that I remained alone in that compartment all the way from London to Clayborough. He was ready to take his oath that Mr. Dwerrihouse was neither in that carriage with me, nor in any compartment of that train. He remembered distinctly to have examined my ticket at Blackwater; was certain that there was no one else at that time in the carriage; could not have failed to observe a second person, if there had been one; had that second person been Mr. John Dwerrihouse, should have quietly double-locked the door of the carriage and have at once given information to the Blackwater station-master. So clear, so decisive, so ready, was Somers with this testimony, that the board looked fairly puzzled.

"You hear this person's statement, Mr. Langford," said the chairman. "It contradicts yours in every particular. What have you to say in reply?"

"I can only repeat what I said before. I am quite as positive of the truth of my own assertions as Mr. Somers can be of the truth of his."

"You say that Mr. Dwerrihouse alighted at Blackwater, and that he was in possession of a private key. Are you sure that he had not alighted by means of that key before the guard came round for the tickets?"

"I am quite positive that he did not leave the carriage till the train had fairly entered the station, and the other Blackwater passengers alighted. I even saw that he was met there by a friend."

"Indeed! Did you see that person distinctly?"

"Quite distinctly."

"Can you describe his appearance?"

"I think so. He was short and very slight, sandy-haired, with a bushy moustache and beard, and he wore a closely fitting suit of grey tweed. His age I should take to be about thirty-eight or forty."

"Did Mr. Dwerrihouse leave the station in this person's company?"

"I cannot tell. I saw them walking together down the platform, and then I saw them standing aside under a gas-jet, talking earnestly. After that I lost sight of them quite suddenly, and just then my train went on, and I with it."

The chairman and secretary conferred together in an undertone. The directors whispered to one another. One or two looked suspiciously at the guard. I could see that my evidence remained unshaken, and that, like myself, they suspected some complicity between the guard and the defaulter.

"How far did you conduct that 4.15 express on the day in question, Somers?" asked the chairman.

"All through, sir," replied the guard, "from London to Crampton."

"How was it that you were not relieved at Clayborough? I thought there was always a change of guards at Clayborough."

"There used to be, sir, till the new regulations came in force last midsummer, since when the guards in charge of express trains go the whole way through."

The chairman turned to the secretary.

"I think it would be as well," he said, "if we had the day-book to refer to upon this point."

Again the secretary touched the silver hand-bell, and desired the porter in attendance to summon Mr. Raikes. From a word or two dropped by another of the directors I gathered that Mr. Raikes was one of the under-secretaries.

He came, a small, slight, sandy-haired, keen-eyed man, with an eager, nervous manner, and a forest of light beard and moustache. He just showed himself at the door of the board-room, and, being requested to bring a certain day-book from a certain shelf in a certain room, bowed and vanished.

He was there such a moment, and the surprise of seeing him was so great and sudden, that it was not till the door had closed upon him that I found voice to speak. He was no sooner gone, however, than I sprang to my feet.

"That person," I said, "is the same who met Mr. Dwerrihouse upon the platform at Blackwater!"

There was a general movement of surprise. The chairman looked grave and somewhat agitated.

"Take care, Mr. Langford," he said; "take care what you say."

"I am as positive of his identity as of my own."

"Do you consider the consequences of your words? Do you consider that you are bringing a charge of the gravest character against one of the company's servants?"

"I am willing to be put upon my oath, if necessary. The man who came to that door a minute since is the same whom I saw talking with Mr. Dwerrihouse on the Blackwater platform. Were he twenty times the company's servant, I could say neither more nor less."

The chairman turned again to the guard.

"Did you see Mr. Raikes in the train or on the platform?" he asked. Somers shook his head.

"I am confident Mr. Raikes was not in the train," he said, "and I certainly did not see him on the platform."

The chairman turned next to the secretary.

"Mr. Raikes is in your office, Mr. Hunter," he said. "Can you remember if he was absent on the 4th instant?"

"I do not think he was," replied the secretary, "but I am not prepared to speak positively. I have been away most afternoons myself lately, and Mr. Raikes might easily have absented himself if he had been disposed."

At this moment the under-secretary returned with the day-book under his arm.

"Be pleased to refer, Mr. Raikes," said the chairman, "to the entries of the 4th instant, and see what Benjamin Somers's duties were on that day."

Mr. Raikes threw open the cumbrous volume, and ran a practised eye and finger down some three or four successive columns of entries. Stopping suddenly at the foot of a page, he then read aloud that Benjamin Somers had on that day conducted the 4.15 express from London to Crampton.

The chairman leaned forward in his seat, looked the under-secretary full in the face, and said, quite sharply and suddenly:

"Where were you, Mr. Raikes, on the same afternoon?"

"I, sir?"

"You, Mr. Raikes. Where were you on the afternoon and evening of the 4th of the present month?"

"Here, sir, in Mr. Hunter's office. Where else should I be?"

There was a dash of trepidation in the under-secretary's voice as he said this, but his look of surprise was natural enough.

"We have some reason for believing, Mr. Raikes, that you were absent that afternoon without leave. Was this the case?"

"Certainly not, sir. I have not had a day's holiday since September. Mr. Hunter will bear me out in this."

Mr. Hunter repeated what he had previously said on the subject, but added that the clerks in the adjoining office would be certain to know. Whereupon the senior clerk, a grave, middle-aged person in green glasses, was summoned and interrogated.

His testimony cleared the under-secretary at once. He declared that Mr. Raikes had in no instance, to his knowledge, been absent during office hours since his return from his annual holiday in September.

I was confounded. The chairman turned to me with a smile, in which a shade of covert annoyance was scarcely apparent.

"You hear, Mr. Langford?" he said.

"I hear, sir; but my conviction remains unshaken."

"I fear, Mr. Langford, that your convictions are very insufficiently based," replied the chairman, with a doubtful cough. "I fear that you 'dream dreams', and mistake them for actual occurrences. It is a dangerous habit of mind, and might lead to dangerous results. Mr. Raikes here would have found himself in an unpleasant position had he not proved so satisfactory an alibi."

I was about to reply, but he gave me no time.

"I think, gentlemen," he went on to say, addressing the board, "that we should be wasting time to push this inquiry further. Mr. Langford's evidence would seem to be of an equal value throughout. The testimony of Benjamin Somers disproves his first statement, and the testimony of the last witness disproves his second. I think we may conclude that Mr. Langford fell asleep in the train on the occasion of his journey to Clayborough, and dreamed an unusually vivid and circumstantial dream, of which, however, we have now heard quite enough."

There are few things more annoying than to find one's positive convictions met with incredulity. I could not help feeling impatience at the turn that affairs had taken. I was not proof against the civil sarcasm of the chairman's manner. Most intolerable of all, however, was the quiet smile lurking about the corners of Benjamin Somers's mouth, and the half-triumphant, half-malicious gleam in the eyes of the under-secretary. The man was evidently puzzled and somewhat alarmed. His looks seemed furtively to interrogate me. Who was I? What did I want? Why had I come here to do him an ill turn with his employers? What was it to me whether or not he was absent without leave?

Seeing all this, and perhaps more irritated by it than the thing deserved, I begged leave to detain the attention of the board for a moment longer. Jelf plucked me impatiently by the sleeve.

"Better let the thing drop," he whispered. "The chairman's right enough; you dreamed it, and the less said now the better."

I was not to be silenced, however, in this fashion. I had yet something to say, and I would say it. It was to this effect: that dreams were not usually productive of tangible results, and that I requested to know in what way the chairman conceived I had evolved from my dream so substantial and well-made a delusion as the cigar-case which I had had the honour to place before him at the commencement of our interview.

"The cigar-case, I admit, Mr. Langford," the chairman replied, "is a very strong point in your evidence. It is your only strong point, however, and there is just a possibility that we may all be misled by a mere accidental resemblance. Will you permit me to see the case again?"

"It is unlikely," I said, as I handed it to him, "that any other should bear precisely this monogram, and yet be in all other particulars exactly similar."

The chairman examined it for a moment in silence, and then passed it to Mr. Hunter. Mr. Hunter turned it over and over, and shook his head.

"This is no mere resemblance," he said. "It is John Dwerrihouse's cigar-case to a certainty. I remember it perfectly; I have seen it a hundred times."

"I believe I may say the same," added the chairman; "yet how account for the way in which Mr. Langford asserts that it came into his possession?"

"I can only repeat," I replied, "that I found it on the floor of the carriage after Mr. Dwerrihouse had alighted. It was in leaning out to look after him that I trod upon it, and it was in running after him for the purpose of restoring it that I saw, or believed I saw, Mr. Raikes standing aside with him in earnest conversation."

Again I felt Jonathan Jelf plucking at my sleeve.

"Look at Raikes," he whispered; "look at Raikes!"

I turned to where the under-secretary had been standing a moment before, and saw him, white as death, with lips trembling and livid, stealing towards the door.

To conceive a sudden, strange, and indefinite suspicion, to fling myself in his way, to take him by the shoulders as if he were a child, and turn his craven face, perforce, towards the board, were with me the work of an instant.

"Look at him!" I exclaimed. "Look at his face! I ask no better witness to the truth of my words."

The chairman's brow darkened.

"Mr. Raikes," he said, sternly, "if you know anything you had better speak."

Vainly trying to wrench himself from my grasp, the under-secretary stammered out an incoherent denial.

"Let me go," he said. "I know nothing—you have no right to detain me—let me go!"

"Did you, or did you not, meet Mr. John Dwerrihouse at Blackwater station? The charge brought against you is either true or false. If true, you will do well to throw yourself upon the mercy of the board and make full confession of all that you know."

The under-secretary wrung his hands in an agony of helpless terror.

"I was away!" he cried. "I was two hundred miles away at the time! I know nothing about it—I have nothing to confess—I am innocent—I call God to witness I am innocent!"

"Two hundred miles away!" echoed the chairman. "What do you mean?"

"I was in Devonshire. I had three weeks' leave of absence—I appeal to Mr. Hunter—Mr. Hunter knows I had three weeks' leave of absence! I was in Devonshire all the time; I can prove I was in Devonshire!"

Seeing him so abject, so incoherent, so wild with apprehension, the directors began to whisper gravely among themselves, while one got quietly up and called the porter to guard the door.

"What has your being in Devonshire to do with the matter?" said the chairman. "When were you in Devonshire?"

"Mr. Raikes took his leave in September," said the secretary, "about the time when Mr. Dwerrihouse disappeared."

"I never even heard that he had disappeared till I came back!"

"That must remain to be proved," said the chairman. "I shall at once put this matter in the hands of the police. In the meanwhile, Mr. Raikes being myself a magistrate and used to deal with these cases, I advise you to offer no resistance, but to confess while confession may yet do you service. As for your accomplice——"

The frightened wretch fell upon his knees.

"I had no accomplice!" he cried. "Only have mercy upon me—only spare my life, and I will confess all! I didn't mean to harm him! I didn't mean to hurt a hair of his head! Only have mercy upon me, and let me go!"

The chairman rose in his place, pale and agitated. "Good heavens!" he exclaimed, "what horrible mystery is this? What does it mean?"

"As sure as there is a God in heaven" said Jonathan Jelf, "it means that murder has been done."

"No! no! no!" shrieked Raikes, still upon his knees, and cowering like a beaten hound. "Not murder! No jury that ever sat could bring it in murder. I thought I had only stunned him—I never meant to do more than stun him! Manslaughter—manslaughter—not murder!"

Overcome by the horror of this unexpected revelation, the chairman covered his face with his hand and for a moment or two remained silent.

"Miserable man," he said at length, "you have betrayed yourself!"

"You made me confess! You urged me to throw myself upon the mercy of the board!"

"You have confessed to a crime which no one suspected you of having committed," replied the chairman, "and which this board has no power either to punish or forgive. All that I can do for you is to advise you to submit to the law, to plead guilty, and to conceal nothing. When did you do this deed?"

The guilty man rose to his feet, and leaned heavily against the table. His answer came reluctantly, like the speech of one dreaming.

"On the 22nd of September!"

On the 22nd of September! I looked in Jonathan Jelf's face, and he in mine. I felt my own paling with a strange sense of wonder and dread. I saw his blanch suddenly, even to the lips.

"Merciful heaven!" he whispered. "What was it, then, that you saw in the train?"

What was it that I saw in the train? That question remains unanswered to this day. I have never been able to reply to it. I only know that it bore the living likeness of the murdered man, whose body had then been lying some ten weeks under a rough pile of branches and brambles and rotting leaves, at the bottom of a deserted chalk-pit about half-way between Blackwater and Mallingford. I know that it spoke and moved and looked as that man spoke and moved and looked in life; that I heard, or seemed to hear, things related which I could never otherwise have learned; that I was guided, as it were, by that vision on the platform to the identification of the murderer; and that, a passive instrument myself,

I was destined, by means of these mysterious teachings, to bring about the ends of Justice. For these things I have never been able to account.

As for that matter of the cigar-case, it proved, on inquiry, that the carriage in which I travelled down that afternoon to Clayborough had not been in use for several weeks, and was, in point of fact, the same in which poor John Dwerrihouse had performed his last journey. The case had doubtless been dropped by him, and had lain unnoticed till I found it.

Upon the details of the murder I have no need to dwell. Those who desire more ample particulars may find them, and the written confession of Augustus Raikes, in the files of *The Times* for 1856. Enough that the under-secretary, knowing the history of the new line, and following the negotiation step by step through all its stages, determined to waylay Mr. Dwerrihouse, rob him of the seventy-five thousand pounds, and escape to America with his booty.

In order to effect these ends he obtained leave of absence a few days before the time appointed for the payment of the money, secured his passage across the Atlantic in a steamer advertised to start on the 23rd, provided himself with a heavily loaded "life-preserver", and went down to Blackwater to await the arrival of his victim. How he met him on the platform with a pretended message from the board, how he offered to conduct him by a short cut across the fields to Mallingford, how, having brought him to a lonely place, he struck him down with the life-preserver, and so killed him, and how, finding what he had done, he dragged the body to the verge of an out-of-the-way chalk-pit, and there flung it in and piled it over with branches and brambles, are facts still fresh in the memories of those who, like the connoisseurs in De Quincey's famous essay, regard murder as a fine art. Strangely enough, the murderer, having done his work, was afraid to leave the country. He declared that he had not intended to take the director's life, but only to stun and rob him; and that, finding the blow had killed, he dared not fly for fear of drawing down suspicion upon his own head. As a mere robber he would have been safe in the States, but as a murderer he would inevitably have been pursued and given up to justice. So he forfeited his passage, returned to the office as usual at the end of his leave, and locked up his ill-gotten thousands till a more convenient opportunity. In the meanwhile he had the satisfaction of finding that Mr. Dwerrihouse was universally believed to have absconded with the money, no one knew how or whither.

Whether he meant murder or not, however, Mr. Augustus Raikes paid the full penalty of his crime, and was hanged at the Old Bailey, in the second week in January, 1857. Those who desire to make his further acquaintance may see him any day (admirably done in wax) in the Chamber of Horrors at Madame Tussaud's exhibition, in Baker Street. He is there to be found in the midst of a select society of ladies and gentlemen of atrocious memory, dressed in the close-cut tweed suit which he wore on the evening of the murder, and holding in his hand the identical life-preserver with which he committed it.

THE CAPER

Janet Evanovich
(written with Lee Goldberg)

Janet Evanovich created bounty hunter Stephanie Plum in *One for the Money* (1994), which was later filmed. With Lee Goldberg, she has written a series of mysteries featuring FBI special agent Kate O'Hare and master criminal Nick Fox, including *The Caper*. An international bestseller, Evanovich lives in Florida, USA.

FBI Special Agent Kate O'Hare took a firm grip on her Hazelnut Macchiato Grande and wedged herself into the backseat of the black Suburban. Her shoulder-length brown hair was pulled up into a ponytail, and she was wearing a navy polyester suit that could survive a nuclear blast without wrinkling. She was sharing the seat with two Sasquatch-size agents from the local Seattle office, and she was debating the wisdom of the Starbucks stop. Okay, so Agent Kruger had been up all night with his two-year-old daughter and had desperately needed coffee, but jeez Louise, Kate thought, this was freaking frightening. She was sitting thigh to thigh with two men holding scalding-hot liquid in paper containers, with a driver who thought he was trying out for NASCAR.

"Hey, we've got coffee here," Kate yelled to the agent behind the wheel. "If it spills on one of these guys next to me, he isn't going to be able to have a family."

The driver glanced in the rearview mirror. "We're not too sure if they should reproduce anyway."

Kate had spent the night hastily acquiring a Seattle-based task force, and this morning she'd flown from her home base of L.A. to Sea-Tac, where she'd been picked up by the A-team. A guy named Levine was at the wheel, and Kruger was riding shotgun. Mo Smitt and Andy Munder were flanking her. She was following a lead that Nicolas Fox, the slick international con man and thief she'd been chasing for three years, was in Seattle, running a scam. The lead was more than speculation. She had confirmed visuals, and she had a handle on the scam, thanks to her cousin Cindy. Cindy lived in Seattle, and two days ago she'd spotted Kate's picture on a city bench.

"You're not going to believe this," Cindy had said, "but there's a real estate agent here who's a dead ringer for you. And she's in business with a smoking-hot guy. I'm standing here looking at an ad on a bench in front of a bus stop. I'm sending you a picture now."

Moments later Kate had pulled the ad up on her email. The headline read: "Our Listings Don't Sit on the Market, They Sell! Call Us NOW!" Under the headline was a full-color picture of the Realtors, Eustace and Irma Haney.

Eustace was Nick Fox, looking like sex in a suit, wearing a tux, his bow tie unfurled carelessly at his open collar, his mischievous smile making his brown eyes sparkle. Irma was next to him, sporting a face lifted from Kate's driver's license picture and Photoshopped onto the body of an outrageously big breasted woman in a black dress with a plunging neckline.

After round-the-clock computer work and several phone calls, Kate put it together. The CFO at a big health insurance company had been quietly released from his work obligations while federal officials pored over the company books. The CFO had disappeared from sight, off on a six-month cruise. And like the brilliant opportunistic thief that he was, Nick had swooped in, posed as a Realtor, and sold the CFO's $3.5 mil house out from under him. Closing was scheduled for three o'clock this afternoon. Kate checked her watch. It was almost noon. "Are we sure Nick is in the real estate office?"

"There's a guy with a scope on the roof across the street," Mo said. "He's watching Fox. Positive ID."

Levine stopped at an intersection and gestured to an ad on a bench backboard. "That's him, right?"

Kate gaped at the ad. It was the first time she'd actually seen it in person.

"Holy crap," Levine said to Kate. "That looks like you next to him."

The four men leaned forward, looking from the ad to Kate and back to the ad. All four men gave a simultaneous bark of laughter.

"Nice picture of you," Mo said, smiling wide.

"It's been Photoshopped off my driver's license," Kate said. "Nick Fox humor. The man is evil."

"Sort of a shame," Levine said. "I kind of had a thing for Irma."

"Are those ads all over the city?" Kate asked.

"Pretty much," Levine said. "Out in Bellevue too."

"The names are familiar," Kruger said. "I know them from somewhere."

"Nick thinks it's fun to use names from old TV shows," Kate said. "According to my dog-eared copy of *The Complete Directory of Episodic Television Shows*, Eustace Haney was the con man in Green Acres who sold Eddie Albert and Eva Gabor their dilapidated farm."

A driver behind the Suburban leaned on his horn, and Levine moved through the intersection. "Are agents in position on the scene?" Kate asked.

Mo nodded. "We've surrounded the building and can secure the block in thirty seconds."

"Tell them to stay out of sight. Nobody moves until I give the order. I don't want to spook him."

The Suburban sped south on 1st Street through Pioneer Square, which was the original heart of the city and only a block east of Puget Sound. It was a skid row neighborhood of nineteenth-century Romanesque brick and stone buildings that was slowly being gentrified with art galleries and coffee houses.

Levine parked in the red zone at 1st Street and South Washington, positioning the Suburban so that it was kitty-corner from the ground floor offices of Jet City Realty. Mo took Kate's macchiato and handed her a pair of binoculars. She trained the binoculars on the first-floor reception area, where Nick was talking on his cell phone. Then he slipped his phone into his pocket and moved out of view.

"Yep, that's him," she said. "And he looks clueless."

Kate gave the binoculars back to Mo and slipped a Bluetooth headset into her ear.

"I'm going in," she said.

"Alone?" Mo asked.

"I'm not alone. I have a whole task force behind me."

"What if he's armed?"

"He doesn't use guns," Kate said.

"He might if he's cornered."

"Then I'll have to shoot him before he shoots me."

Kate climbed over Munder and exited the Suburban. She crossed the street, tuning into Mo communicating with the other agents, telling them to hold tight. There was another black Suburban in the alley half a block down, and a few agents posing as civilians on the sidewalk. They acknowledged Kate with a glance, and she glanced back and walked into the real estate office.

The walls were stripped to show off weathered old bricks. The reception desk was a tall counter in front of a glass partition with Jet City Realty etched into it. Behind the glass were cubicles where the Realtors worked.

The receptionist was a sleek blond woman in her thirties whose eyes went wide when she saw Kate. "Mrs. Haney!" she said. "What a wonderful surprise. I thought you were still in Florida recuperating from your goiter reduction. Goodness, the doctors did an amazing job. Your neck looks terrific. And I see you had the wart removed from your nose as well."

Kate could hear the other agents laughing in her earpiece. It would take all her self-control not to shoot Nick on sight.

"And you learned all this from my husband?"

"He's been terribly worried about you."

"I'll bet," Kate said. "Where is my little love bug? He doesn't know I'm back, and I want to surprise him."

"He's in his office. It's the third one on the left, past all the cubbies."

Kate walked the short corridor and whispered an order into her Bluetooth to seal the building. She drew her Glock and tried the doorknob to Nick's office. Locked. She stepped back and put everything she had into a well-placed kick to the left of the doorknob. The door splintered at the jamb and flew open into the room. There was a desk, desk chair, and file cabinet in the room. No Nick. She could see that the single window to the street was locked from the inside.

People were spilling out of their cubicles into the corridor.

"What was that crash?" someone asked.

"Mr. Haney's door," someone else said.

And then someone took a good look at Kate and screamed, "Gun!"

People dove under desks, ran for the front door, and shrieked in panic.

Kate took her badge out of her back pocket and held it above her head for everyone to see. "FBI," she said. "Relax. I'm looking for Haney. Where is he?"

"He never said anything about you being in the FBI," the receptionist said to Kate. "Are you sure you aren't one of those crazy jealous wives? You don't want to kill him, do you?"

"It's a tempting thought, but no," Kate said. "I don't want to kill him."

"I saw him go into his office," a woman said. "He went in and closed his door, and I didn't see him come out."

Kate looked behind the desk and around the file cabinet. She cautiously opened the closet door. The closet was empty, the floorboards had been removed, and a ladder led down into the basement.

"He must be in the basement," Kate said to the agents listening in on Bluetooth. "I'm going after him."

"That's not a basement," Mo told her. "It's the first floor. In the 1890s, to stop the constant flooding, the city built a retaining wall along the shore and raised the streets downtown. The second floor of every building became the new street level, and everything below was covered up."

"So what the heck is down there now?"

"It's a maze," Mo said. "Most of it was sealed and condemned over a hundred years ago. A lot of it was buried. But the part right under Pioneer Square is open for tours, and the homeless use the rest of it for shelter in the winter."

Kate rummaged through Nick's desk drawers, grabbed a mini flashlight keychain with the Jet City Realty logo on it, and climbed down the ladder. Walls were visible in the dusty darkness. Windows had been bricked over. Doorways were open. Thick wood beams supported the street above and were braced against the buildings.

Kate heard the sound of footsteps muffled by more than a century's worth of fine dirt that had sifted down onto the original street, and a flash of light turned a corner about thirty yards in front of her. Kate ran toward the light, gun in hand, trying not to stumble over the bricks and fast-food packaging, beer bottles, soiled mattresses, and remnants of campfires that littered the passageway. Every so often, glass cubes embedded in the sidewalk above cast sunlight into her underground world.

"He's down here," Kate said to Mo. "Cover all exits."

"We don't have the manpower. There are dozens of ways out of there. Every building and manhole cover for blocks is a potential exit."

Kate swore and came to a fork in the underground road. Which way did he go?

She pulled the Bluetooth out of her ear and switched it off. She didn't want Mo and everybody else listening in.

"Nick," she yelled.

"Hey, Kate," Nick yelled back, somewhere in front of her, lost in the darkness.

"How did you know I was coming for you?"

"If you want to be inconspicuous, drive a Ferrari, not a black Suburban with tinted windows." His reply was relaxed and amiable, as if they were two old friends catching up on the phone.

Kate listened carefully, hoping she could place him. "Only you would think a Ferrari is subtle."

"Sometimes being intentionally conspicuous is as good as being invisible. If you'd arrived in a Ferrari, you'd probably have me in handcuffs right now."

"It's not too late."

All of his talking had helped her pinpoint him. She took the path to her right and moved as quickly as she dared toward his voice without turning on her flashlight and revealing her position.

"You'd look good in a Ferrari," he said.

"You'd look good in handcuffs," she said.

"Do you imagine that often?"

"Not as often as I picture you in a jail cell."

Kate saw a shaft of daylight illuminating Nick on a ladder at the far end of the underground street. He blew her a kiss and climbed out. The daylight shut off like a candle being blown out. She switched her Bluetooth back on and worked it into her ear as she ran toward the ladder. "He's up above."

"Which street?" Mo asked.

"I don't know. There are no signs down here."

She came to a ladder leading to a manhole cover. She eased the cover up slowly and peeked out. No cars came rushing at her. She was under a park. She pushed the manhole cover aside and climbed out into the sunlight. There were homeless people lazing around and some skateboarders surfing the railings and flying over steps. No sign of Nick.

She jogged to the nearest street and saw Nick staring at her. Not in the flesh, unfortunately, but from a bus bench advertisement. Nick looked as handsome as ever, but someone had drawn a mustache under his Realtor wife's nose with a Magic Marker.

"O'Hare, are you there?" Mo asked in her ear. "What's your 10–20?"

Kate sat on the bench and sighed. It would be a while before she lived this one down. She glanced at the street sign.

"South Main Street," she said.

Right at the corner of Humiliation Boulevard.

THE STORY OF THE ALCÁZAR

Mary Hallock Foote

Mary Hallock Foote (1847–1938) was lauded for her portrayal of turn-of-the-century American West mining life. A writer and illustrator, Foote led a long and varied life, although her memoir, *A Victorian Woman in the Far West*, was not published until 1972.

It was told by Captain John to a boy from the mainland who was spending the summer on the Island, as they sat together one August evening at sunset, on a broken bowsprit which had once been a part of the Alcázar.

It was dead low water in Southwest Harbor, a land-locked inlet that nearly cut the Island in two, and was the gateway through which the fishing-craft from the village at the harbor head found their way out into the great Penobscot Bay. There were many days during the stern winter and bleak spring months when the gate was blocked with ice or veiled in fog, but nature relented a little toward the Island folk in the fall and sent them sunny days for their late, scant harvesting, and steady winds for the mackerel-fishing, to give them a little hope before the winter set in sharp with the equinoctial. Now, at low tide, the bright gateway shone wide open, as if to let out the waters that rise and fall ten feet in the inlet. You could look far out, beyond the lighthouse on Creenlaw's Neck and the islands that throng the mouth of the harbor, to the red spot of flame the sunset had kindled below the rack of smoke-gray clouds. The color burned in a dull gleam upon the water, broken by the dark shapes of shadowy islands; the sail-boats at anchor in the muddy, glistening flats leaned over disconsolately on their sides, in despair of ever again feeling the thrill of the returning waters beneath their keels; and the gray, weather-beaten houses crowded together on the brink of the cliff above the beach, looking like a group of hooded old women watching for a belated sail, seemed to have caught the expression of their inmates' lives. At high tide the hulk of the Alcázar had been full of water, which was now pouring out through a hole in the planking of her side in a continuous, murmurous stream, like the voice of a persistent talker in a silent company. The old ship looked much too big for her narrow grave at the foot of the green cliff, in which her anchor was deeply sunk and half overgrown with thistles. Her blunt bow and the ragged stump of the figure-head rose, dark and high, above the wet beach where Captain John sat with his absorbed listener. There were rifts about her rail where the red sunset looked through. Her naked sides, that for years had been moistened only by the perennial rains and snows, showed rough and scaly like the armor of some fabled sea-monster. She was tethered to the cliff by her rusty anchor-chain that swung across the space between, serving as a clothes-line for the draggled driftweed left by the receding tide to dry.

"She was a big ship for these parts," Captain John was saying. "There wan't one like her ever come into these waters before. Lord! folks come down from the Neck, and from Green's Landin', and Nor'east Harbor, and I don't know but they come from the main, to see her when she was fust towed in. And such work as they made of her name! Some called it one way and some another. It's a kind of a Cubian name, they say. I expect there ain't anybody round here that can call it right. However 'twas, old Cap'n Green took and pried it off her starboard quarter, and somebody got hold of it and nailed it up over the black-smith's shop; and there you can see it now. The old cap'n named her the Stranger when he had her refitted. May be you could make out the tail of an S on her stern if you could git around there. That name's been gone these forty year; seem's if she never owned to it, and it didn't stick to her. She was never called anythin' but the Alcázar, long as ever I knew her, and I expect I know full's much about her as anybody round here. 'Twas a-settin' here on this very beach at low water, just's we be now, that the old man told me fust how he picked her up. It took a wonderful holt on him, there's no doubt about that. He told it to me more 'n once before the time come when he was to put the finish on to it; but in a gen'ral way the cap'n wa'n't much of a talker, and he was shy of this partic'lar business, for reasons that I expect nobody knows much about. But a man most always likes to talk to somebody, no matter how close-mouthed he may be. 'Twas just about this time o' year, fall of '27, the year Parson Flavor was ordained, Cap'n Green had gone a-mack'rel-fishin' with his two boys off Isle au Haut, and they did think o' cruisin' out into Frenchman's Bay if the weather hel' steady. They was havin' fair luck, hangin' round the island off and on for a matter of a week, when it thickened up a little and set in foggy, and for two days they didn't see the shore. The second evenin' the wind freshened from the south'ard and east'ard and drove the fog in shore a bit, and the sun, just before he set, looked like a big yellow ball through the fog and made a sickly kind of a glimmer over the water. They was a-lyin' at anchor, and all of a sudden, right to the wind'ard of 'em, this old ship loomed up, driftin' in with the wind and flood-tide. They couldn't make her out, and I guess for a minute the old cap'n didn't know but it was the Flyin' Dutchman; but she hadn't a rag o' sail on her, and as she got nearer they could see there wa'n't a man on board. The cap'n didn't like the looks of her, but he knew she wa'n't no phantom, and he and one of his boys down with the punt and went alongside. 'Twa'n't more 'n a quarter of a mile to her. They hailed and couldn't git no answer. They knew she was a furriner by her build, and she must 'a' been a long time at sea by her havin' barnacles on her nigh as big's a mack'rel kit. Finally, they pulled up to her fore-chains and clum aboard of her. I never see a ship abandoned at sea, myself, but I ain't no doubt but what it made 'em feel kind o' shivery when they looked aft along her decks, and not a soul in sight, and every-thin' bleached, and gray, and iron-rusted, and the riggin' all slack and white's though it had been chawed, and nothin' left of her sails but some old rags flappin' like a last year's scarecrow. They went and looked in the fo'k'sel: there wan't nothin' there but some chists, men's chists, with a little old beddin' left in the bunks. They went down the companion-way: cabin-door unlocked, everything in there as nat'ral's though it had just been left, only 'twas kind o' mouldy-smellin'. I expect the cap'n give a kind of a start as he looked around. 'Twa'n't no old greasy whaler's cabin, nor no packet-ship neither. There wa'n't many craft like her on the seas in them days. She was fixed up inside more like a gentleman's yacht is now. Merchantmen in them days didn't have their Turkey carpets and their colored wine-glasses jinglin' in the racks. While they was explorin' round in there, movin' round kind o' cautious, the door of the cap'n's stateroom swung open with a creak, just's though somebody was a-shovin' it slow like, and the ship give a kind of a stir and a rustlin', moanin' sound, as if she was a-comin' to life. The old man never made no secret but what he was scairt when he went through her that night. 'Twa'n't so much what he said as the way he looked when he told it. I expect he thought he'd seen enough, about the time that door blew open. He said he knowed 'twas nothin' but a puff o' wind struck her, and that he'd better be a-gittin' on to his own craft before he lost her in the fog. So he went back and got under weigh, and sent a line aboard of the stranger and took her in tow, and all that night with a good southeast wind they kept a-movin' toward home. The old man was kind o' res'less and wakeful, walkin' the decks and lookin' over the stern at the big ship follerin' him like a ghost. The moonlight was a little dull with fog, but he could see her, plain, a-comin' on before the wind with her white riggin' and bare poles, and hear the water sousin' under her bows. He said 'twas in his mind more 'n a dozen times to cut her adrift. You see he had his misgivin's about her from the fust, though he never let on what they was; but he hung on to her as a man will, sometimes, agin feelin's that have more sense in 'em than reason, like as not. He knew everybody at the Harbor would laugh at him for lettin' go such a prize as that just for a notion, and it wa'n't his way, you may be sure; he didn't need no one to tell him what she was wuth. Anyhow he hung to her, and next day they beached her at high water, right over there by the old ship-yard. He took Deacon S'lvine and his brother-in-law, Cap'n Purse—Pierce they call it nowadays, but in the cap'n's time 'twas Purse. That sounds kind o' broad and comfortable, like the cap'n's wescoat; but the family's thinnin' down a good deal lately and gettin' kind o' sharp and lean, and may be Pierce is more suitable. But 's I was sayin', Cap'n Green took them two—cheerful, loud-talkin' men they was both of 'em—aboard of her to go through her, for he hadn't no notion o' goin' into that cap'n's stateroom alone, even in broad daylight; but 'twa'n't there the secret of her lay; there wa'n't nothin' in there to scare anybody. She was trimmed up, I tell you, just elegant. Real mahogany, none of your veneerin', but the real stuff; lace curt'ins to the berth, lace on the pillows, and a satin coverlid, rumpled up as though the cap'n had just turned out; and there was his slippers handy—the greatest-lookin' slippers for a man you ever saw. They wouldn't 'a' been too big for the neatest-footed woman in the Harbor. But Land! they was just thick with mould, and so was everythin' in the place, even to an old gittar with the strings most rotted off of it, and the picters of fur-rin-lookin' women on the walls,—trinin'-lookin' creeturs most of 'em. They hunted all through his desk, but couldn't find no log. 'Twas plain enough that whoever'd left that ship had took pains that she shouldn't tell no tales, and 'twa'n't long before they found out the reason.

"When they come to go below,—there was considerable of a crowd on deck by that time, standin' round while they knocked out the keys and took off the fore-hatch,—Cap'n Green called on Cap'n Purse and the deacon to go down with him; but they didn't 'pear to be very anxious, and the old man wa'n't goin' to hang back for company with everybody lookin' at him, so he lit a candle and went down, and the folks crowded round and waited for him. I was there myself, 's close to him as I be to that fish barrel, when he come up, his face white 's a sheet and the candle shakin' in his hand, and sot down on the hatch-combin'.

"'Give me room!' says he, kind o' leanin' back on the crowd. 'Give me air, can't you? She's full o' dead niggers. She's a slaver.'

"Now, 'twas the talk pretty gen'rally that the cap'n had had a hand in that business himself in his early days, and that it set uncomfortable on him afterwards. It never was known how he'd got his money. He didn't have any to begin with. He was always a kind of a lone bird and dug his way along up somehow. Nobody knows what was workin' on him while he sot there; he looked awful sick. It was kind of quiet for a minute, but them that couldn't see him kep' pushin' for'ards and callin' out: 'What d'you see? What's down there?' And them close by wanted to know, all talkin' to once, why he thought she was a slaver, and how long the niggers had been dead. Lord! what a fuss there was. Everybody askin' the foolishest questions, and crowdin' and squeezin', and them in front pushin' back away from the hatchway, as if they expected the dead would rise and walk out o' that black hole where they'd laid so long. They couldn't get much out o' the old man, except that there was skel'tons scattered all over the after hold, and that he knew she was a slaver by the way she was fixed up. 'How'd he know?' folks asked amongst themselves; but nobody liked to ask the cap'n. As for how long them Africans had been dead, they had to find that out for themselves,—all they ever did find out,—for the cap'n wouldn't talk about it, and he wouldn't go down in her again. It 'peared's if he was satisfied.

"Wal, it made a terrible stir in the place. As I tell you, they come from fifty mile around to see her. They had it all in the papers. Some had one idee and some another about the way she come to be abandoned, all in good shape and them human bein's in her hold. Some said ship-fever, some said mutiny; but when they come to look her over and found there wa'n't a water-cask aboard of her that hadn't s'runk up and gone to pieces, they settled down on the notion that she was a Spanish or a Cubian slaver, or may be a Portagee, got short o' water in the horse-latitudes; cap'n and crew left her in the boats, and the niggers—Lord! it makes a body sick to think o' them. That was always my the'ry 'bout her—short o' water; but some folks wa'n't satisfied 'thout somethin' more ex-citin'. 'Twa'n't enough for 'em to have all them creeturs dyin' down there by inches. They stuck to it about some blood-stains on the linin' in her hold, but I tell you the difference between old blood-stains and rust that's may be ten or fifteen years old's might' hard to tell.

"Nobody knows what the old cap'n was thinkin' about in them days. 'Twas full three month or more 'fore he went aboard of her ag'in. He let it be known about that he wanted to sell her, but he couldn't git an offer even; nobody seemed to want to take hold of her. Winter set in early and the ice blocked her in, and there she lay, the lonesomest thing in sight. You never see no child'n climbin' 'round on her, and there was a story that queer noises like moanin' and clankin' of chains come out of her on windy nights; but it might 'a' been the ice, crowdin' as she careened over and back with the risin' and fallin' tide. But when spring opened, folks used to see the old cap'n hangin' round the ship-yard and lookin' her over at low tide, where the ice had cut the barnacles off of her.

"One night in the store he figgered up how much lumber she'd carry from the Bangor, and 'twa'n't long 'fore he had a gang o' men at work on her. It seemed's though he was kind of infatuated with her. He was 'fraid of her, but he couldn't let her alone. And she was a mighty well-built craft. Floridy pine and live-oak and mahogany from the Mosquito coast; built in Cadiz, most likely. Look at her now—she don't look to home here, does she? She never did. She's as much like our harbor craft as one o' them big, yellow-eyed, bare-necked buzzards is to one o' these here little sand-peeps. But she was a handsome vessel. Them live-oak ribs'll outlast your time, if you was to live to be old."

The two faces looked up at the hulk of the Alcázar,—the blanched, wave-worn messenger sent by the tropic seas into the far North with a tale that the living had never dared to tell, and that had perished on the lips of the dead. Its shadow, spreading broad upon the beach, made the gathering twilight deeper. Out on the harbor the pale saffron light lingered, long after the red had faded. How many tides had ebbed and flowed since the old ship, chained at the foot of the cliff, had warmed in the waters of the Gulf her bare, corrugated sides, warped by the frosts, stabbed by the ice of pitiless Northern winters! Where were the sallow, dark-bearded faces that had watched from her high poop the brief twilights die on that "unshadowed main," which a century ago was the scene of some of the wildest romances and blackest crimes in maritime history—the bright, restless bosom that warmed into life a thousand serpents whose trail could be traced through the hot, flower-scented Southern plazas and courts into the peaceful white villages of the North!

"Sho! I'd no idee 'twas a-gittin' on so late," said Captain John. "There ain't anybody watchin' out for me. I kin put my family under my hat, but I don' know what your folks'll think's come o' you.

"Wal, the rest on 'twon't take long to tell. The old man had her fitted up in good shape by the time the ice was out of the river, and run her up to Bangor in ballast, and loaded her there for New York. He had an ugly trip down the coast: lost his deck load and three men overboard in a southeaster off Nantucket Shoals. It made the whole ship's company feel pretty solemn, but the old man took it the hardest of any of 'em, and from that time seems as if he lost his grip; the old scare settled back on him blacker 'n ever. There wa'n't a man aboard of her that liked her. They all knew her story, that she was the Alcázar from nobody knows where, instead of the Stranger from Newburyport. The cap'n had Newburyport put on to her because he was a Newburyport man and all his vessels was built there. But she hadn't more 'n touched the dock in New York before every one on 'em left her, even to the cook. 'I'm leery o' this 'ere ship,' says one big Cornishman. 'No better than a floatin' coffin, anyway,' was what they all said of her; and I guess the cap'n would 'a' left her right there himself if it hadn't been for the money he'd put into her. I expect he was a little too fond of money, may be; but I've knowed others just as sharp's the old cap'n that didn't seem to have his luck. The mate saw him two or three times while he was a-lyin' in New York, and noticed he was drinkin' more 'n usual. He come home light and anchored off the bar, just as a southeaster was a-comin' on. It wouldn't 'a' been no trouble for him to have laid there, if he'd had good ground-gear; but there 'twas ag'in, he'd been a leetle too savin'. He'd used the old cables he found in her. The new mate didn't know nothin' about her, and he put out one anchor. The cap'n had taken a kag o' New England rum aboard and been drawin' on it pretty reg'lar all the way up, and as the gale come on he got kind o' wild and went at it harder 'n ever. About midnight the cable parted. They let go the other anchor, but it didn't snub her for a minute, and she swung, broadside to, on to the bar. The men clum into the riggin' before she struck, but the old cap'n was staggerin' 'round decks, kind o' dazed and dumb-like, not tryin' to do anythin' to save himself. The mate tried to git him into the riggin', seein' he wa'n't in no condition to look out for himself; but the old man struck loose from his holt and cried out to him through the noise:—

"'Let me alone! I've got to go with her. I tell ye I've got to go with her!'

"The mate just had time to swing himself back into the mizzen-shrouds before the sea broke over her and left the decks bare. The old ship pounded over the bar in an hour or so, and drifted up here on to the beach where she is now. Every man on board was saved except the cap'n. He 'went with her,' sure enough.

"There was talk enough about that thing before they got done with it to 'a' made the old man roll in his grave. They raked up all the stories about his cruisin' on the Spanish main when he was a young man. They wa'n't stories *he*'d ever told; he wa'n't much of a hand to talk about what he'd seen and done on his v'yages. They never let him rest till 'twas pretty much the gen'ral belief, and is to this day, that he knew more about that slaver from the first than he ever owned to.

"I never had much to say about it, but 'twas plain enough to me. I had my suspicions the mornin' he towed her in. He looked terrible shattered. It 'peared to me he wa'n't ever the same man afterwards.

"'I've got to go with her!' Them was his last words. He knew that ship and him belonged together, same as a man and his sins. He knew she'd been a-huntin' him up and down the western ocean for twenty year, with them dead o' his'n in her hold,—and she'd hunted him down at last."

Captain John paused with this peroration: he dug a hole in the wet sand with the toe of his boot, and watched it slowly fill.

"'Twas a bait most any one would 'a' smelt of, a six-hundred-ton ship and every timber in her sound; but you'd 'a' thought he'd been more cautious, knowin' what he did of her. She was bound to have him, though."

"Captain John," said the boy, a little hoarse from his long silence, "what do you suppose it *was* he did? Anything except just leave them—the negroes, I mean?"

"Lord! Wan't that *enough*? To steal 'em, and then leave 'em there—battened down like rats in the hold! However, I expect there ain't anybody that can tell you the whole of that story. It's one of them mysteries that rests with the dead.

"The new mate—the young fellow he brought on from New York—he married the cap'n's daughter. None o' the Harbor boys ever seemed to jibe in with her. I always had a notion that she was a touch above most of 'em, but she and her mother was as good as a providence to them shipwrecked men when they was throwed ashore, strangers in the place and no money; and it ended in Rachel's takin' up with the mate and the whole family's leavin' the place. It was long after all the talk died away that the widow come back and lived here in the same quiet way she always had, till she was laid alongside the old cap'n. There wa'n't a better woman ever walked this earth than Mary Green, that was Mary Spofford."

Captain John rose from the bowsprit and rubbed his cramped knees before climbing the hill. He parted with his young listener at the top and took a lonely path across the shore-pasture to a little cabin, where no light shone, built like the nest of a sea-bird on the edge of high-water mark.

On the gray beach below, a small, dingy yawl, with one sail loosely bundled over the thwarts, leaned toward the door-latch as if listening for its click. It had an almost human expression of patient though wistful waiting. It was the poorest boat in the Harbor; it had no name painted on its stern, but Captain John, in the solitude of his watery wanderings among the islands and channels of the bay, always called her the Mary Spofford. The boy from the main went home slowly along the village street toward the many-windowed house in which his mother and sisters were boarding. There were voices, calling and singing abroad on the night air, reflected from the motionless, glimmering sheet of dark water below as from a sounding-board. Cow-bells tinkled away among the winding paths along the low, dim shores. The night-call of the heron from the muddy flats struck sharply across the stillness, and from the outer bay came the murmur of the old ground-swell, which never rests, even in the calmest weather.

THE WHITE MANIAC: A DOCTOR'S TALE

Mary Helena Fortune

Mary Helena Fortune (c.1833–c.1910) is known as one of Australia's earliest writers of detective fiction. Born in Belfast, Ireland, she grew up in Canada and subsequently lived in Melbourne, Australia. Fortune authored the longest-running serial in history, *The Detective's Album*, which ran from 1868 to 1908.

In the year 1858 I had established a flourishing practice in London; a practice which I owed a considerable portion of, not to my ability, I am afraid, but to the fact that I occupied the singular position of a man professional, who was entirely independent of his profession. Doubtless, had I been a poor man, struggling to earn a bare existence for wife and family, I might have been the cleverest physician that ever administered a bolus, yet have remained in my poverty to the end of time. But it was not so, you see. I was the second son of a nobleman, and had Honourable attached to my name; and I practised the profession solely and entirely because I had become enamoured of it, and because I was disgusted at the useless existence of a fashionable and idle young man, and determined that I, at least, would not add another to their ranks.

And so I had a handsome establishment in a fashionable portion of the city, and my door was besieged with carriages, from one end of the week to the other. Many of the occupants were disappointed, however, for I would not demean myself by taking fees from some vapourish Miss or dissipated Dowager. Gout in vain came rolling to my door, even though it excruciated the leg of a Duke; I undertook none but cases that enlisted my sympathy, and after a time the fact became known and my levees were not so well attended.

One day I was returning on horseback toward the city. I had been paying a visit to a patient in whom I was deeply interested, and for whom I had ordered the quiet and purer air of a suburban residence. I had reached a spot in the neighbourhood of Kensington, where the villas were enclosed in large gardens, and the road was marked for a considerable distance by the brick and stone walls that enclosed several of the gardens belonging to those mansions. On the opposite side of the road stood a small country-looking inn, which I had patronised before, and I pulled up my horse and alighted, for the purpose of having some rest and refreshment after my ride.

As I sat in a front room sipping my wine and water, my thoughts were fully occupied with a variety of personal concerns. I had received a letter from my mother that morning, and the condition of the patient I had recently left was precarious in the extreme.

It was fortunate that I was thought-occupied and not dependent upon outward objects to amuse them, for although the window at which I sat was open, it presented no view whatever, save the bare, blank, high brick wall belonging to a house at the opposite side of the road. That is to say, I presume, it enclosed some residence, for from where I say not even the top of a chimney was visible.

Presently, however, the sound of wheels attracted my eyes from the pattern of the wall-paper at which I had been unconsciously gazing, and I looked out to see a handsome, but very plain carriage drawn up at a small door that pierced the brick wall I have alluded to; and almost at the same moment the door opened and closed again behind two figures in a most singular attire. They were both of the male sex, and one of them was the servant; but it was the dress of these persons that most strangely interested me. They were attired in white from head to heel; coats, vests, trousers, hats, shoes, not to speak of shirts at all, all were white as white could be.

While I stared at this strange spectacle, the gentlemen stepped into the vehicle; but although he did so the coachman made no movement toward driving onward, nor did the attendant leave his post at the carriage door. At the expiration, however, of about a quarter of an hour, the servant closed the door and re-entered through the little gate, closing it, likewise, carefully behind him. Then the driver leisurely made a start, only, however, to stop suddenly again, when the door of the vehicle was burst open and a gentleman jumped out and rapped loudly at the gate.

He turned his face hurriedly around as he did so, hiding, it seemed to me, meanwhile, behind the wall so as not to be seen when it opened. Judge of my astonishment when I recognised in this gentleman the one who had but a few minutes before entered the carriage dressed in white, for he was now in garments of the hue of Erebus. While I wondered at this strange metamorphosis the door in the wall opened, and the gentleman, now attired in black, after giving some hasty instructions to the servant, sprang once more into the carriage and was driven rapidly toward London.

My curiosity was strangely excited; and as I stood at the door before mounting my horse, I asked the landlord who and what were the people who occupied the opposite dwelling.

"Well, sir," he replied, looking curiously at the dead wall over against him. "They've been there now a matter of six months, I dare say, and you've seen as much of them as I have. I believe the whole crew of them, servants and all, is foreigners, and we, that is the neighbours around, sir, calls them the 'white mad people.'"

"What! do they always wear that singular dress?"

"Always, sir, saving as soon as ever the old gentleman goes outside and puts black on in the carriage, and as soon as he comes back takes it off again, and leaves it in the carriage."

"And why in the name of gracious does he not dress himself inside?"

"Oh, that I can't tell you, sir! only it's just as you see, always. The driver or coachman never even goes inside the walls, or the horses or any one thing that isn't white in colour, sir; and if the people aren't mad after that, what else can it be?"

"It seems very like it, indeed; but do you mean to say that everything inside the garden wall is white? Surely you must be exaggerating a little?"

"Not a bit on it, sir! The coachman, who can't speak much English, sir, comes here for a drink now and then. He don't live in the house, you see, and is idle most of his time. Well, he told me himself, one day, that every article in the house was white, from the garret to the drawing-room, and that everything outside it is white I can swear, for I saw it myself, and a stranger sight surely no eye ever saw."

"How did you manage to get into the enchanted castle, then?"

"I didn't get in, sir, I only saw it outside, and from a place where you can see for yourself too, if you have a mind. When first the people came to the place over there, you see, sir, old Mat the sexton and bell-ringer of the church there, began to talk of the strange goings on he had seen from the belfry; and so my curiosity took me there one day to look for myself. Blest if I ever heard of such a strange sight! no wonder they call them the white mad folk."

"Well, you've roused my curiosity," I said, as I got on my horse, "and I'll certainly pay old Mat's belfry a visit the very next time I pass this way, if I'm not hurried."

It appeared unaccountable to even myself that these mysterious people should make such a singular impression on me; I thought of little else during the next two days. I attended to my duties in an absent manner, and my mind was ever recurring to the one subject—viz. an attempt to account for the strange employ-ment of one hue only in the household of this foreign gentleman. Of whom did the household consist? Had he any family? and could one account for the eccentricity in any other way save by ascribing it to lunacy, as mine host of the inn had already done. As it happened, the study of brain diseases had been my hobby during my noviciate, and I was peculiarly interested in observing a new symptom of madness, if this was really one.

At length I escaped to pay my country patient his usual visit, and on my return alighted at the inn, and desired the landlord to have my horse put in the stable for a bit.

"I'm going to have a peep at your madhouse," I said, "do you think I shall find old Mat about?"

"Yes, doctor; I saw him at work in the churchyard not half an hour ago, but at any rate he won't be farther off than his cottage, and it lies just against the yard wall."

The church was an old, ivy-wreathed structure, with a square Norman belfry, and a large surrounding of grey and grass-grown old headstones. It was essen-tially a country church, and a country churchyard; and one wondered to find it so close to the borders of a mighty city, until they remembered that the mighty city had crept into the country, year by year, until it had covered with stone and mortar the lowly site of many a cottage home, and swallowed up many an acre of green meadow and golden corn. Old Mat was sitting in the middle of the graves; one tombstone forming his seat, and he was engaged in scraping the moss from a headstone that seemed inclined to tumble over, the inscription on which was all but obliterated by a growth of green slimy-looking moss.

"Good-day, friend, you are busy," I said. "One would fancy that stone so old now, that the living had entirely forgotten their loss. But I suppose they have not, or you would not be cleaning it."

"It's only a notion of my own, sir; I'm idle, and when I was a lad I had a sort o' likin' for this stone, Lord only knows why. But you see I've clean forgotten what name was on it, and I thought I'd like to see."

"Well, I want to have a look at these 'white mad folk' of yours, Mat, will you let me into the belfry? Mr. Tanning tells me you can see something queer up there."

"By jove you can, sir!" he replied, rising with alacrity, "I often spend an hour watching the mad folk; faith if they had my old church and yard they'd white-wash 'em, belfry and all!" and the old man led the way into the tower.

Of course my first look on reaching the summit was in the direction of the strange house, and I must confess to an ejaculation of astonishment as I peeped through one of the crevices. The belfry was elevated considerably above the premises in which I was interested, and not at a very great distance, so that grounds and house lay spread beneath me like a map.

I scarcely know how to commence describing it to you, it was something I had never seen or imagined. The mansion itself was a square and handsome building of two stories, built in the Corinthian style, with pillared portico, and pointed windows. But the style attracted my attention but little, it was the universal white, white everywhere, that drew from me the ejaculation to which I have alluded.

From the extreme top of the chimneys to the basement, roof, windows, everything was pure white; not a shade lurked even inside a window; the windows themselves were painted white, and the curtains were of a white muslin that fell over every one of them. Every yard of the broad space that one might reasonably have expected to see decorated with flowers and grass and shrubberies, was covered with a glaring and sparkling white gravel, the effect of which, even in the hot brilliant sun of a London afternoon, was to dazzle, and blind, and aggravate. And as if this was not enough, the inside of the very brick walls was whitewashed like snow, and at intervals, here and there, were placed a host of white marble statues and urns that only increased the, to me, horrible aspect of the place.

"I don't wonder they are mad!" I exclaimed, "I should soon become mad in such a place myself."

"Like enough, sir," replied old Mat, stolidly, "but you see it didn't make they mad, for they did it themselves, so they must 'a been mad afore."

An incontrovertible fact, according to the old man's way of putting it; and as I had no answer for it, I went down the old stone stairs, and having given my guide his donation, left the churchyard as bewildered as I had entered it. Nay, more so, for then I had not seen the extraordinary house that had made so painful an impression upon me.

I was in no humour for a gossip with mine host, but just as I was about to mount my horse, which had been brought round, the same carriage drove round to the mysterious gate, and the same scene was enacted to which I had before been a witness. I drew back until the old gentleman had stepped inside and performed his toilet, and when the carriage drove rapidly toward the city, I rode thoughtfully onward toward home.

I was young, you see, and although steady, and, unlike most young gentlemen of my age and position in society, had a strong vein of romance in my character. That hard study and a sense of its inutility had kept it under, had not rendered it one whit less ready to be at a moment's call; and, in addition to all this, I had never yet, in the seclusion of my student life, met with an opportunity of falling in love, so that you will see I was in the very best mood for making the most of the adventure which was about to befall me, and which had so tragic a termination.

My thoughts were full of the "White mad folk," as I reached my own door; and there, to my utter astonishment, I saw drawn up the very carriage of the white house, which had preceded me. Hastily giving my horse to the groom I passed through the hall and was informed by a servant that a gentleman waited in my private consulting-room.

Very rarely indeed had my well-strung nerves been so troublesome as upon that occasion; I was so anxious to see this gentleman, and yet so fearful of exposing the interest I had already conceived in his affairs, that my hand absolutely trembled as I turned the handle of the door of the room in which he was seated. The first glance, however, at the aristocratic old gentleman who rose on my entrance, restored all my self-possession, and I was myself once more. In the calm, sweet face of the perfectly dressed gentleman before me there was no trace of the lunacy that had created that strange abode near Kensington; the principal expression in his face was that of ingrained melancholy, and his deep mourning attire might have suggested to a stranger the reason of that melancholy. He addressed me in perfect English, the entire absence of idiom alone declaring him to be a foreigner.

"I have the pleasure of addressing Doctor Elveston?" he said.

I bowed, and placed a chair in which he re-seated himself, while I myself took possession of another.

"And Doctor Elveston is a clever physician and a man of honour?"

"I hope to be worthy of the former title, sir, while my position ought at least to guarantee the latter."

"Your public character does, sir," said the old gentleman, emphatically, "and it is because I believe that you will preserve the secret of an unfortunate family that I have chosen you to assist me with your advice."

My heart was beating rapidly by this time. There was a secret then, and I was about to become the possessor of it. Had it anything to do with the mania for white?

"Anything in my power," I hastened to reply, "you may depend on; my advice, I fear, may be of little worth, but such as it is———"

"I beg your pardon, Doctor," interrupted he, "it is your medical advice that I allude to, and I require it for a young lady—a relative."

"My dear sir, that is, of course, an every day affair, my professional advice and services belong to the public, and as the public's they are of course yours."

"Oh, my dear young friend, but mine is not an every day affair, and because it is not is the reason that I have applied to you in particular. It is a grievous case, sir, and one which fills many hearts with a bitterness they are obliged to smother from a world whose sneers are poison."

The old gentleman spoke in tones of deep feeling, and I could not help feeling sorry for him at the bottom of my very heart.

"If you will confide in me, my dear sir," I said, "believe that I will prove a friend as faithful and discreet as you could wish."

He pressed my hand, turned away for a moment to collect his agitated feelings and then he spoke again.

"I shall not attempt to hide my name from, you sir, though I have hitherto carefully concealed it. I am the Duke de Rohan, and circumstances, which it is impossible for me to relate to you, have driven me to England to keep watch and ward over my sister's daughter, the Princess d'Alberville. It is for this young lady I wish your attendance, her health is rapidly failing within the last week."

"Nothing can be more simple," I observed, eagerly, "I can go with you at once—this very moment."

"Dear Doctor, it is unfortunately far from being as simple a matter as you think," he replied, solemnly, "for my wretched niece is mad."

"Mad!"

"Alas! yes, frightfully—horribly mad!" and he shuddered as if a cold wind had penetrated his bones.

"Has this unhappy state of mind been of long duration?" I questioned.

"God knows; the first intimation her friends had of it was about two years ago, when it culminated in such a fearful event that horrified them. I cannot explain it to you, however, for the honour of a noble house is deeply concerned; and even the very existence of the unfortunate being I beg of you to keep a secret for ever."

"You must at any rate tell me what you wish me to do," I observed, "and give me as much information as you can guide me, or I shall be powerless."

"The sight of one colour has such an effect on the miserable girl that we have found out, by bitter experience, the only way to avoid a repetition of the most fearful tragedies, is to keep every hue or shade away from her vision; for, although it is only one colour that affects her, any of the others seems to suggest that one to her mind and produce uncontrollable agitation. In consequence of this she is virtually imprisoned within the grounds of the house I have provided for her, and every object that meets her eye is white, even the ground, and the very roof of the mansion."

"How very strange!"

"It will be necessary for you, my dear sir," the Duke continued, "to attire yourself in a suite of white. I have brought one in the carriage for your use, and if you will now accompany me I shall be grateful."

Of course I was only too glad to avail myself of the unexpected opportunity of getting into the singular household, and becoming acquainted with the lunatic princess; and in a few moments we were being whirled on our way toward Kensington.

On stopping at the gate of the Duke's residence, I myself became an actor in the scene which had so puzzled me on two previous occasions. My companion produced two suits of white, and proceeded to turn the vehicle into a dressing-room, though not without many apologies for the necessity. I followed his example, and in a few moments we stood inside the gate, and I had an opportunity of more closely surveying the disagreeable enclosure I had seen from the church belfry. And a most disagreeable survey it was; the sun shining brilliantly rendered the unavoidable contact with the white glare absolutely painful to the eye; nor was it any escape to stand in the lofty vestibule, save that there the absence of sunshine made the uniformity more bearable.

My companion led the way up a broad staircase covered with white cloth, and balustraded with carved rails, the effect of which was totally destroyed by their covering of white paint. The very stair-rods were of white enamel, and the corners and landing places served as room for more marble statues, that held enamelled white lamps in their hands, lamps that were shaded by globes of ground glass. At the door of an apartment pertaining, as he informed me, to the Princess d'Alberville, the Duke stopped, and shook my hand. "I leave you to make your own way," he said, pointing to the door. "She has never showed any symptoms of violence while under the calm influence of white; but, nevertheless, we shall be at hand, the least sound will bring you assistance," and he turned away.

I opened the door without a word, and entered the room, full of curiosity as to what I should see and hear of this mysterious princess. It was a room of vast and magnificent proportions, and, without having beheld such a scene, one can hardly conceive the strange cold look the utter absence of colour gave it. A Turkey carpet that looked like a woven fall of snow; white satin damask on chair, couch, and ottoman; draped satin and snowy lace around the windows, with rod, rings, and snowy marble, and paper on the walls of purest white; altogether it was a weird-looking room, and I shook with cold as I entered it.

The principal object of my curiosity was seated in a deep chair with her side toward me, and I had an opportunity of examining her leisurely, as she neither moved or took the slightest notice of my entrance; most probably she was quite unaware of it. She was the most lovely being I had ever beheld, a fair and perfect peace of statuary one might have thought, so immobile and abstracted, nay, so entirely expressionless were her beautiful features. Her dress was pure white, her hair of a pale golden hue, and her eyes dark as midnight. Her hands rested idly on her lap, her gaze seemed intent on the high white wall that shot up outside the window near her; and in the whole room there was neither the heavy, white-covered furniture, and the draping curtains. I advanced directly before her and bowed deeply, and then I calmly drew forward a chair and seated myself. As I did so she moved her eyes from the window and rested them on me, but, for all the interest they evinced, I might as well have been the white-washed wall outside. She was once more returning her eyes to the blank window, when I took her hand and laid my fingers on her blue-veined wrist. The action seemed to arouse her, for she looked keenly into my face, and then she laughed sadly.

"One may guess you are a physician," she said, in a musical, low, voice, and with a slightly foreign accent, that was in my opinion a great improvement to our harsh language.

"I am," I replied, with a smile, "your uncle has sent me to see about your health, which alarms him."

"Poor man!" she said, with a shade of commiseration clouding her beautiful face, "poor uncle! But I assure you there is nothing the matter with me; nothing but what must be the natural consequence of the life I am leading."

"Why do you lead one which you know to be injurious then?" I asked, still keeping my fingers on the pulse, that beat as calmly as a sleeping infant's, and was not increased by a single throb though a stranger sat beside her.

"How can I help it?" she asked, calmly meeting my inquisitorial gaze, "do you think a sane person would choose to be imprisoned thus, and to be surrounded by the colour of death ever? Had mine not been a strong mind I should have been mad long ago."

"Mad!" I could not help ejaculating, in a puzzled tone.

"Yes, mad," she replied, "could you live here, month after month, in a hueless atmosphere and with nothing but that to look at," and she pointed her slender finger toward the white wall, "could you, I ask, and retain your reason?"

"I do not believe I could!" I answered, with sudden vehemence, "then, again I repeat why do it?"

"And again I reply, how can I help it?"

I was silent. I was looking in the eyes of the beautiful being before me for a single trace of the madness I had been told of, but I could not find it. It was a lovely girl, pale and delicate from confinement, and was about twenty years old, perhaps, and the most perfect creature, I have already said, that I had ever beheld; and so we sat looking into each other's eyes; and mine expressed I cannot say, but hers were purity, and sweetness itself.

"Who are you?" she asked, suddenly, "tell me something of yourself. It will be at least a change from this white solitude."

"I am a doctor, as you have guessed; and a rich and fashionable doctor," I added, smilingly.

"To be either is to be also the other," she remarked, "you need not have used the repetition."

"Come," I thought to myself, "there is little appearance of lunacy in that observation."

"But you doubtless have a name, what is it?"

"My name is Elveston—Doctor Elveston."

"Your christian name?"

"No, my christian name is Charles."

"Charles," she repeated dreamily.

"I think it is your turn now," I remarked, "it is but fair that you should make me acquainted with your name, since I have told you mine."

"Oh! my name is d'Alberville—Blanche d'Alberville. Perhaps it was in consequence of my christian name that my poor uncle decided upon burying me in white," she added, with a look round the cold room, "poor old man!"

"Why do you pity him so?" I asked, "he seems to me little to require it. He is strong and rich, and the uncle of Blanche," I added, with a bow; but the compliment seemed to glide off her as if it had been a liquid, and she were made of glassy marble like one of the statues that stood behind her.

"And you are a physician," she said, looking wonderingly at me, "and have been in the Duke's company, without discovering it?"

"Discovering what, my dear young lady?"

"That he is mad."

"Mad!" How often had I already ejaculated that word since I had become interested in this singular household; but this time it must assuredly have expressed the utmost astonishment, for I was never more confounded in my life; and yet a light seemed to be breaking in upon my bewilderment, as I stared in wondering silence at the calm face of the lovely maiden before me.

"Alas, yes!" she replied, sadly, to my look, "my poor uncle is a maniac, but a harmless one to all but me; it is I who suffer all."

"And why you?" I gasped.

"Because it is his mania to believe me mad," she replied, "and so he treats me."

"But in the name of justice why should you endure this?" I cried, angrily starting to my feet, "you are in a free land at least, and doors will open!"

"Calm yourself, my friend," she said, laying her white hand on my arm, and the contact, I confess, thrilled through every nerve of my system, "compose yourself, and see things as they are; what could a young, frail girl like me do out in the world alone? and I have not a living relative but my uncle. Besides, would it be charitable to desert him and leave him to his own madness thus! Poor old man!"

"You are an angel!" I ejaculated, "and I would die for you!"

The reader need not be told that my enthusiastic youth was at last beginning to make its way through the crust of worldly wisdom that had hitherto subdued it.

"It is not necessary that anyone should die for me; I can do that for myself, and no doubt shall ere long, die of the want of colour and air," she said, with a sad smile.

There is little use following our conversation to the end. I satisfied myself that there was really nothing wrong with her constitution, save the effects of the life she was obliged to lead; and I determined, instead of interfering with her at present, to devote myself to the poor Duke, with a hope that I might be of service to him, and succeed in gaining the liberation of poor Blanche. We parted, I might almost say as lovers, although no words of affection were spoken; but I carried away her image entwined with every fibre of my heart, and in the deep sweetness of her lingering eyes I fancied I read hope and love.

The Duke was waiting impatiently in the corridor as I left the lovely girl, and he led me into another apartment to question me eagerly. What did I think of the princess's state of health? Had she shown any symptoms of uneasiness during my visit? As the old gentleman asked these questions he watched my countenance keenly; while on my part I observed him with deep interest to discover traces of his unfortunate mental derangement.

"My dear sir, I perceive nothing alarming whatever in the state of your niece; she is simply suffering from confinement and monotony of existence, and wants nothing whatever but fresh air and amusement, and exercise; in short, life."

"Alas! you know that is impossible; have I not told you that her state precludes everything of the sort?"

"You must excuse me, my friend," I said, firmly, "I have conversed for a considerable time with the Princess d'Alberville, and I am a medical man accustomed to dealing with, and the observation of, lunacy, and I give you my word of honour there is no weakness whatever in the brain of this fair girl; you are simply killing her, it is my duty to tell you so, killing her under the influence of some, to me, most unaccountable whim."

The Duke wrung his hands in silence, but his excited eye fell under my steady gaze. It was apparently with a strong effort that he composed himself sufficiently to speak, and when he did his words had a solemnity in their tone that ought to have made a deep impression upon me; but it did not, for the sweetness of the imprisoned Blanche's voice was still lingering in my ears.

"You are a young man, Doctor Elveston; it is one of the happy provisions of youth, no doubt, to be convinced of its own infallibility. But you must believe that one of my race does not lie, and I swear to you that my niece is the victim of a most fearful insanity, which but to name makes humanity shudder with horror."

"I do not doubt that you believe such to be the case, my dear sir," I said, soothingly, for I fancied I saw the fearful light of insanity in his glaring eye at that moment, "but to my vision everything seems different."

"Well, my young friend, do not decide yet too hastily. Visit us again, but God in mercy grant that you may never see the reality as I have seen it!"

And so I did repeat my visits, and repeat them so often and that without changing my opinion, that the Duke, in spite of his mania, began to see that they were no longer necessary. One day on my leaving Blanche he requested a few moments of my time, and drawing me into his study, locked the door. I began to be a little alarmed, and more particularly as he seemed to be in a state of great agitation; but, as it appeared, my alarm of personal violence was entirely without foundation.

He placed a chair for me, and I seated myself with all the calmness I could muster, while I kept my eyes firmly fixed upon his as he addressed me.

"My dear young friend; I hope it is unnecessary for me to say that these are no idle words, for I have truly conceived an ardent appreciation of your character; yet it is absolutely necessary that I should put a stop to your visits to my niece. Good Heavens, what could I say—how could I ever forgive myself if any—any—-"

"I beg of you to go no farther, Duke," I said, interrupting him. "You have only by a short time anticipated what I was about to communicate myself. If your words allude to an attachment between Blanche and myself, your care is now too late. We love each other, and intend, subject to your approval, to be united immediately."

Had a sudden clap of thunder reverberated in the quiet room the poor man could not have been more affected. He started to his feet, and glared into my eyes with terror.

"Married!" he gasped. "Married! Blanche d'Alberville wedded! Oh God!" and then he fell back into his chair as powerless as a child.

"And why should this alarm you?" I asked. "She is youthful and lovely, and as sane, I believe in my mind, as I am myself. I am rich, and of a family which may aspire to mate with the best. You are her only relative and guardian, and you say that you esteem me; whence then this great distaste to hear even a mention of your fair ward's marriage?"

"She is not my ward!" he cried, hoarsely, and it seemed to me angrily, "her father and mother are both in existence, and destroyed for all time by the horror she had brought around them! But, my God, what is the use of speaking—I talk to a madman!" and he turned to his desk and began to write rapidly.

There I sat in bewilderment. I had not now the slightest doubt but that my poor friend was the victim of monomania; his one idea was uppermost, and that idea was that his unfortunate niece was mad. I was fully determined now to carry her away and make her my wife at once, so as to relieve the poor girl from an imprisonment, to which there seemed no other prospect of an end. And my hopes went still farther; who could tell but that the sight of Blanche living and enjoying life as did others of her sex, might have a beneficial effect upon the poor Duke's brain, and help to eradicate his fixed idea.

As I was thus cogitating, the old gentleman rose from his desk and handed me a letter addressed, but unsealed. His manner was now almost unearthly calm, as if he had come to some great determination, to which he had only been driven by the most dreadful necessity.

"My words are wasted, Charles," he said, "and I cannot tell the truth; but if you ever prized home and name, friends or family, mother or wife, send that letter to its address after you have perused it, and await its reply."

I took the letter and put it into my pocket, and then I took his hand and pressed it warmly. I was truly sorry for the poor old gentleman, who suffered, no doubt, as much from his fancied trouble as if it were the most terrible of realities.

"I hope you will forgive me for grieving you, my dear sir; believe me it pains me much to see you thus. I will do as you wish about the letter. But oh, how I wish you could see Blanche with my eyes! To me she is the most perfect of women!"

"You have never seen her yet!"—he responded, bitterly, "could you—dare you only once witness but a part of her actions under one influence, you would shudder to your very marrow!"

"To what influence do you allude, dear sir!"

"To that of colour—one colour."

"And that colour? Have you any objection to name it?"

"It is red!" and as the Duke answered he turned away abruptly, and left me standing bewildered, but still unbelieving.

I hastened home that day, anxious to peruse the letter given me by the Duke, and as soon as I had reached my own study drew it from my pocket and spread it before me. It was addressed to the Prince d'Alberville, Chateau Gris, Melun, France; and the following were its singular contents:—

"DEAR BROTHER.—A terrible necessity for letting another into our fearful secret has arisen. A young gentleman of birth and fortune has, in spite of my assurances that she is insane, determined to wed Blanche. Such a sacrifice cannot be permitted, even were such a thing not morally impossible. You are her parent, it is then your place to inform this unhappy young man of the unspoken curse that rests on our wretched name. I enclose his address. Write to him at once.

"Your afflicted brother.

"DE ROHAN."

I folded up this strange epistle and despatched it; and then I devoted nearly an hour to pondering over the strange contradictions of human nature, and more particularly diseased human nature. Of course I carried the key to this poor man's strangeness in my firm conviction of his insanity, and my entire belief in the martyrdom of Blanche; yet I could not divest myself of an anxiety to receive a reply to this letter, a reply which I was certain would explain the Duke's lunacy, and beg of me to pardon it. That is to say if such a party as the Prince d'Alberville existed at all, and I did not quite lose sight of the fact that Blanche had assured me that, with the exception of her uncle, she had not a living relative.

It seemed a long week to me ere the French reply, that made my hand tremble as I received it, was put into it. I had abstained from visiting my beloved Blanche, under a determination that I would not do so until armed with such a letter as I anticipated receiving; or until I should be able to say, "ample time for a reply to your communication has elapsed; none to come, give me then my betrothed." Here then at last was the letter, and I shut myself into my own room and opened it; the words are engraven on my memory and will never become less vivid.

"SIR,—You wish to wed my daughter, the Princess Blanche d'Alberville. Words would vainly try to express the pain with which I expose our disgrace— our horrible secret—to a stranger, but it is to save from a fate worse than death. Blanche d'Alberville is an anthropophagus, already has one of her own family fallen victim to her thirst for human blood. Spare us if you can, and pray for us.

"D'ALBERVILLE."

I sat like one turned to stone and stared at the fearful paper! An anthropophagus! a cannibal! Good heavens, the subject was just now engaging the attention of the medical world in a remarkable degree, in consequence of two frightful and well authenticated cases that had lately occurred in France! All the particulars of these cases, in which I had taken a deep interest, flashed before me, but not for one moment did I credit the frightful story of my beloved. Some detestable plot had been formed against her, for what vile purpose, or what end in view I was ignorant; and I cast the whole subject from my mind with an effort, and went to attend my daily round of duties. During the two or three hours that followed, and under the influence of the human suffering I had witnessed, a revolution took place in my feelings, God only knows by what means induced; but when I returned home, to prepare for my eventful visit to the "white house," a dreadful doubt had stolen into my heart, and filled it with a fearful determination.

Having ordered my carriage and prepared the white suit, which I was now possessor of, I went directly to the conservatory, and looked around among the brilliant array of blossoms most suitable to my purpose. I chose the flaring scarlet verbena to form my bouquet; a tasteless one it is true, but one decidedly distinctive in colour. I collected quite a large nosegay of this flower, without a single spray of green to relieve its bright hue. Then I went to my carriage, and gave directions to be driven to Kensington.

At the gate of the Duke's residence I dressed myself in the white suit mechanically, and followed the usual servant into the house, carefully holding my flowers, which I had enveloped in a newspaper. I was received as usual also by the Duke, and in a few seconds we stood, face to face in his study. In answer to his look of fearful inquiry I handed him my French epistle, and stood silently by as he read it tremblingly.

"Well, are you satisfied now?" he asked, looking at me pitifully in the face, "has this dreadful exposure convinced you?"

"No!" I answered, recklessly, "I am neither satisfied nor convinced of anything save that you are either a lunatic yourself, or in collusion with the writer of that abominable letter!" and as I spoke I uncovered my scarlet bouquet and shook out its blossoms. The sight of it made a terrible impression upon my companion; his knees trembled as if he were about to fall, and his face grew whiter than his garments.

"In the name of heaven what are you going to do?" he gasped.

"I am simply going to present my bride with a bouquet," I said, and as I said so I laughed an empty, hollow laugh. I cannot describe my strange state of mind at that moment; I felt as if myself under the influence of some fearful mania.

"By all you hold sacred, Charles Elveston, I charge you to desist! Who or what are you that you should set your youth, and ignorance of this woman against my age and bitter experience?"

"Ha, ha!" was my only response, as I made toward the door.

"By heavens, he is mad!" cried the excited nobleman, "young man, I tell you that you carry in your hand a colour which had better be shaken in the eyes of a mad bull than be placed in sight of my miserable niece! Fool! I tell you it will arouse in her an unquenchable thirst for blood, and the blood may be yours!"'

"Let it!" I cried, and passed on my way to Blanche.

I was conscious of the Duke's cries to the servants as I hurried up the broad staircase, and guessed that they were about to follow me; but to describe my feelings is utterly impossible.

I was beginning now to believe that my betrothed was something terrible, and I faced her desperately, as one who had lost everything worth living for, or placed his last stake upon the cast of a die.

I opened the well-known door of the white room, that seemed to me colder, and more death-like than ever; and I saw the figure of Blanche seated in her old way, and in her old seat, looking out of the window. I did not wait to scan her appearance just then, however, for I caught a glimpse of myself in a large mirror opposite, and was fascinated, as it were, by the strange sight.

The mirror reflected, in unbroken stillness, the cold whiteness of the large apartment, but it also reflected my face and form, wearing an expression that half awoke me to a consciousness of physical indisposition. There was a wild look in my pallid countenance, and a reckless air in my figure which the very garments seemed to have imbibed, and which was awry; the collar of my shirt was unbuttoned, and I had even neglected to put on my neck-tie; but it was upon the blood-red bouquet that my momentary gaze became riveted.

It was such a contrast; the cold, pure white of all the surroundings, and that circled patch of blood-colour that I held in my hand was so suggestive! "Of what?" I asked myself "am I really mad?" and then I laughed loudly and turned toward Blanche.

Possibly the noise of the opening door had attracted her, for when I turned she was standing on her feet, directly confronting me. Her eyes were distended with astonishment at my peculiar examination of myself in the mirror, no doubt, but they flashed into madness at the sight of the flowers as I turned. Her face grew scarlet, her hands clenched, and her regards devoured the scarlet bouquet, as I madly held it towards her. At this moment my eye caught a side glimpse of half-a-dozen terrified faces peeping in the doorway, and conspicuous and foremost that of the poor terrified Duke; but my fate must be accomplished, and I still held the bouquet tauntingly toward the transfixed girl. She gave one wild look into my face, and recognised the sarcasm which I felt in my eyes, and then she snatched the flowers from my hand, and scattered them in a thousand pieces at her feet.

How well I remember that picture to-day. The white room—the torn and brilliant flowers—and the mad fury of that lovely being. A laugh echoed again upon my lips, an involuntary laugh it was, for I knew not that I laughed; and then there was a rush, and white teeth were at my throat, tearing flesh, and sinews, and veins; and a horrible sound was in my ears, as if some wild animal was tearing at my body! I dreamt that I was in a jungle of Africa, and that a tiger, with a tawney coat, was devouring my still living flesh, and then I became insensible!

When I opened my eyes faintly, I lay in my own bed, and the form of the Duke was bending over me. One of my medical confreres held my wrist between his fingers, and the room was still and dark.

"How is this, Bernard?" I asked, with difficulty, for my voice seemed lost, and the weakness of death hanging around my tongue, "what has happened?"

"Hush! my dear fellow, you must not speak. You have been nearly worried to death by a maniac, and you have lost a fearful quantity of blood."

"Oh!" I recollected it all, and turned to the Duke, "and Blanche?"

"She is dead, thank God!" he whispered, calmly.

I shuddered through every nerve and was silent.

It was many long weeks ere I was able to listen to the Duke as he told the fearful tale of the dead girl's disease. The first intimation her wretched relatives had of the horrible thing was upon the morning of her eighteenth year. They went to her room to congratulate her, and found her lying upon the dead body of her younger sister, who occupied the same chamber; she had literally torn her throat with her teeth, and was sucking the hot blood as she was discovered. No words could describe the horror of the wretched parents. The end we have seen.

I never asked how Blanche had died, I did not wish to know; but I guessed that force had been obliged to be used in dragging her teeth from my throat, and that the necessary force was sufficient to destroy her. I have never since met with a case of anthropophagy, but I fancy I still feel Blanche's teeth at my throat.

TRACES OF CRIME

Mary Helena Fortune

Mary Helena Fortune (c.1833–c.1910) is known as one of Australia's earliest writers of detective fiction. Born in Belfast, Ireland, she grew up in Canada and subsequently lived in Melbourne, Australia. Fortune authored the longest-running serial in history, *The Detective's Album*, which ran from 1868 to 1908.

There are many who recollect full well the rush at Chinaman's Flat. It was in the height of its prosperity that an assault was committed upon a female of a character so diabolical in itself, as to have aroused the utmost anxiety in the public as well as in the police, to punish the perpetrator thereof.

The case was placed in my hands, and as it presented difficulties so great as to appear to an ordinary observer almost insurmountable, the overcoming of which was likely to gain approbation in the proper quarter, I gladly accepted the task.

I had little to go upon at first. One dark night, in a tent in the very centre of a crowded thoroughfare, a female had been preparing to retire to rest, her husband being in the habit of remaining at the public-house until a late hour, when a man with a crape mask—who must have gained an earlier entrance—seized her, and in the prosecution of a criminal offence, had injured and abused the unfortunate woman so much that her life was despaired of. Although there was a light burning at the time, the woman was barely able to describe his general appearance; he appeared to her like a German, had no whiskers, fair hair, was low in stature, and stoutly built.

With one important exception, that was all the information she was able to give me on the subject. The exception, however, was a good deal to a detective, and I hoped might prove an invaluable aid to me. During the struggle she had torn the arm of the flannel shirt he wore, and was under a decided impression that upon the upper part of the criminal's arm there was a small anchor and heart tattooed.

Now, I was well aware that in this colony to find a man with a tattooed arm was an everyday affair, especially on the diggings, where, I dare say, there is scarcely a person with who has not come in contact more than once or twice with half a dozen men tattooed in the style I speak of—the anchor or heart, or both, being a favourite figure with those "gentlemen" who are in favour of branding. However, the clue was worth something, and even without its aid, not more than a couple of weeks had elapsed when, with the assistance of the local police, I had traced a man bearing in appearance a general resemblance to the man who had committed the offence, to a digging about seven miles from Chinaman's Flat.

It is unnecessary that I should relate every particular as to how my suspicions were directed to this man, who did not live on Chinaman's Flat, and to all appearances, had not left the diggings where he was camped since he first commenced working there. I say "to all appearances," for it was with a certain knowledge that he had been absent from his tent on the night of the outrage that I one evening trudged down the flat where his tent was pitched, with my swag on my back, and sat down on a log not far from where he had kindled a fire for culinary or other purposes.

These diggings I will call McAdam's. It was a large and flourishing gold-field, and on the flat where my man was camped there were several other tents grouped, so that it was nothing singular that I should look about for a couple of bushes, between which I might swing my little bit of canvas for the night.

After I had fastened up the rope, and thrown my tent over it in regular digger fashion, I broke down some bushes to form my bed, and having spread thereon my blankets, went up to my man—whom I shall in future call "Bill"—to request permission to boil my billy on his fire.

It was willingly granted, and so I lighted my pipe and sat down to await the boiling of the water, determined if I could so manage it to get this suspected man to accept me as a mate before I lay down that night.

Bill was also engaged in smoking, and had not, of course, the slightest suspicion that in the rough, ordinary looking digger before him he was contemplating the "make-up" of a Victorian detective, who had already made himself slightly talked of among his comrades by one or two clever captures.

"Where did you come from mate?" inquired Bill, as he puffed away leisurely at a cutty.

"From Burnt Creek," I replied, "and a long enough road it is in such d—— hot weather as this."

"Nothing doing at Burnt Creek?"

"Not a thing—the place is cooked."

"Are you in for a try here, then?" he asked, rather eagerly I thought.

"Well, I think so; is there any chance do you think?"

"Have you got a miner's right?" was his sudden question.

"I have," said I taking it out of my pocket, and handing the bit of parchment for his inspection.

"Are you a hatter?" inquired Bill, as he returned the document.

"I am," was my reply.

"Well, if you have no objections then, I don't mind going mates with you—I've got a pretty fair prospect, and the ground's going to run rather deep for one man, I think."

"All right."

So here was the very thing I wanted, settled without the slightest trouble.

My object in wishing to go mates with this fellow will, I dare say, readily be perceived. I did not wish to risk my character for 'cuteness by arresting my gentleman, without being sure that he was branded in the way described by the woman, and besides, in the close supervision which I should be able to keep over him while working together daily, heaven knows what might transpire as additional evidence against him, at least so I reasoned with myself; and it was with a partially relieved mind that I made my frugal supper, and made believe to "turn in", fatigued, as I might be supposed to be, after my long tramp.

But I didn't turn in, not I, I had other objects in view, if one may be said to have an object in view on one of the darkest nights of a moonless week—for dark enough the night in question became, even before I had finished my supper, and made my apparent preparations for bed.

We were not camped far enough from the business part of the rush to be very quiet, there was plenty of noise—the nightly noise of a rich gold-field—came down our way, and even in some of the tents close to us, card-playing, and drinking, and singing, and laughing, were going on; so it was quite easy for me to steal unnoticed to the back of Bill's little tent, and, by the assistance of a small slit made in the calico by my knife, have a look at what my worthy was doing inside, for I was anxious to become acquainted with his habits, and, of course, determined to watch him as closely as ever I could.

Well, the first specimen I had of his customs was certainly a singular one, and was, it may be well believed, an exception to his general line of conduct. Diggers, or any other class of men, do not generally spend their evenings in cutting their shoes up into small morsels, and that was exactly what Bill was busily engaged in doing when I clapped my eye to the hole. He had already disposed of a good portion of the article when I commenced to watch him: the entire "upper" of a very muddy blucher boot lying upon his rough table in a small heap, and in the smallest pieces that one would suppose any person could have patience to cut up a dry, hard, old leather boot.

It was rather a puzzler to me this, and that Bill was doing such a thing simply to amuse himself was out of the question; indeed, without observing that he had the door of his tent closely fastened upon a warm evening, and that he started at the slightest sound, the instincts of an old detective would alone have convinced me that Bill had some great cause indeed to make away with those old boots; so I continued watching.

He had hacked away at the sole with an old but sharp butcher's knife, but it almost defied his attempts to separate it into pieces, and at length he gave it up in despair, and gathering up the small portions on the table, he swept them with the mutilated sole into his hat, and opening his tent door, went out.

I guessed very truly that he would make for the fire, and as it happened to be at the other side of a log from where I was hiding, I had a good opportunity of continuing my espial. He raked together the few embers that remained near the log, and flinging the pieces of leather thereon, retired once more into his tent, calculating, no doubt, that the hot ashes would soon scorch and twist them up, so as to defy recognition, while the fire he would build upon them in the morning would settle the matter most satisfactorily.

All this would have happened just so, no doubt, if I had not succeeded in scraping nearly every bit from the place where Bill had thrown them, so silently and quickly, that I was in the shelter of my slung tent with my prize and a burn or two on my fingers before he himself had had time to divest himself of his garments and blow out the light.

He did so very soon, however, and it was long before I could get asleep. I thought it over and over in all ways, and looked upon it in all lights that I could think of, and yet, always connecting this demolished boot with the case in the investigation of which I was engaged, I could not make it out at all.

Had we overlooked, with all our fancied acuteness, some clue which Bill feared we had possession of, to which this piecemeal boot was the key? And if so why had he remained so long without destroying it?

It was, as I said before, a regular puzzler to me, and my brain was positively weary when I at length dropped off to sleep.

Well, I worked for a week with Bill, and I can tell you it was work I didn't at all take to. The unaccustomed use of the pick and shovel played the very mischief with my hands; but, for fear of arousing the suspicions of my mate, I durst not complain, having only to endure in silence, or as our Scotch friends would put it, "Grin and bide it." And the worst of it was, that I was gaining nothing—nothing whatever—by my unusual industry.

I had hoped that accidentally I should have got a sight of the anchor and heart, but I was day after day disappointed, for my mate was not very regular in his ablutions, and I had reckoned without my host in expecting that the very ordinary habit of a digger, namely, that of having a "regular wash" at least every Sunday, would be a good and certain one for exposing the brand.

But no, Bill allowed the Sunday to come and go, without once removing what I could observe was the flannel shirt, in which he had worked all the week; and then I began to swear at my own obtuseness—"the fellow must be aware that his shirt was torn by the woman, of course he suspects that she may have seen the tattooing, and will take blessed good care not to expose it, mate or no mate," thought I; and then I called myself a donkey, and during the few following days, when I was trusting to the chapter of accidents, I was also deliberating on the "to be or not to be" of the question of arresting him at once, and chancing it. Saturday afternoon came again, and then the early knock-off time, and that sort of quarter holiday among the miners, namely, four o'clock, was hailed by me with the greatest relief, and it was with the full determination of never again setting foot in the cursed claim that I shouldered my pick and shovel and proceeded tentwards.

On my way I met a policeman, and received from him a concerted signal that I was wanted at the camp, and so telling Bill that I was going to see an old mate about some money that he owed me, I started at once.

"We've got something else in your line, mate," said my old chum, Joe Bennet, as I entered the camp, "and one which, I think, will be a regular poser for you. The body of a man has been found in Pipeclay Gully, and we can scarcely be justified by appearances in giving even a surmise as to how he came by his death."

"How do you mean?" I inquired. "Has he been dead so long?"

"About a fortnight, I dare say, but we have done absolutely nothing as yet. Knowing you were on the ground we have not even touched the body: will you come up at once?"

"Of course I will!" And after substituting the uniform of the force for the digger's costume, in which I was apparelled, in case of an encounter with my "mate," we went straight to "Pipeclay."

The body had been left in charge of one of the police, and was still lying, undisturbed in the position in which it had been discovered; not a soul was about, in fact, the gully had been rushed and abandoned, and bore not the slightest trace of man's handiwork, saving and except the miner's holes and their surrounding little eminences of pipeclay, from which the gully was named. And it was a veritable "gully," running between two low ranges of hills, which hills were covered with an undergrowth of wattle and cherry trees, and scattered over with rocks and indications of quartz, which have, I dare say, been fully tried by this time.

Well, on the slope of one of the hills, where it amalgamated as it were with the level of the gully, and where the sinking had evidently been shallow, lay the body of the dead man. He was dressed in ordinary miner's fashion, and saving for the fact of a gun being by his side, one might have supposed that he had only given up his digging to lie down and die beside the hole near which he lay.

The hole, however, was full of water—quite full; indeed the water was sopping out on the ground around it, and that the hole was an old one was evident, by the crumbling edges around it, and the fragments of old branches that lay rotting in the water.

Close to this hole lay the body, the attitude strongly indicative of the last exertion during life having been that of crawling out of the water hole, in which indeed still remained part of the unfortunate man's leg. There was no hat on his head, and in spite of the considerable decay of the body, even an ordinary observer could not fail to notice a large fracture in the side of the head.

I examined the gun; it was a double-barrelled fowling piece, and one barrel had been discharged, while very apparent on the stock of the gun were blood marks, that even the late heavy rain had failed to erase. In the pockets of the dead man was nothing, save what any digger might carry—pipe and tobacco, a cheap knife, and a shilling or two, this was all; and so leaving the body to be removed by the police, I thoughtfully retraced my way to the camp.

Singularly enough, during my absence, a woman had been there, giving information about her husband, on account of whose absence she was becoming alarmed; and as the caution of the policeman on duty at the camp had prevented his giving her any idea of the fact of the dead body having been discovered that very day, I immediately went to the address which the woman had left, in order to discover, if possible, not only if it was the missing man, but also to gain any information that might be likely to put me upon the scent of the murderer, for that the man had been murdered I had not the slightest doubt.

Well, I succeeded in finding the woman, a young and decidedly good-looking Englishwoman of the lower class, and gained from her the following information:—

About a fortnight before, her husband, who had been indisposed, and in consequence not working for a day or two, had taken his gun one morning in order to amuse himself for an hour or two, as well as to have a look at the ranges near Pipeclay Gully, and do a little prospecting at the same time. He had not returned, but as he had suggested a possibility of visiting his brother who was digging about four miles off, she had not felt alarmed until upon communicating with the said brother she had become aware that her husband had never been there. From the description, I knew at once that the remains of the poor fellow lying in Pipeclay Gully were certainly those of the missing man, and with what care and delicacy I might possess I broke the tidings to the shocked wife, and after allowing her grief to have vent in a passion of tears, I tried to gain some clue to the likely perpetrator of the murder.

"Had she any suspicions?" I asked; "was there any feud between her husband and any individual she could name?"

At first she replied "no," and then a sudden recollection appeared to strike her, and she said that some weeks ago a man had, during the absence of her husband, made advances to her, under the feigned supposition that she was an unmarried woman. In spite of her decidedly repellent manner, he had continued his attentions, until she, afraid of his impetuosity, had been obliged to call the attention of her husband to the matter, and he, of course feeling indignant, had threatened to shoot the intruder if he ever ventured near the place again.

The woman described this man to me, and it was with a violent whirl of emotional excitement, as one feels who is on the eve of a great discovery, that I hastened to the camp, which was close by.

It was barely half-past five o'clock, and in a few minutes I was on my way, with two or three other associates, to the scene of what I had no doubt had been a horrible murder. What my object was there was soon apparent. I had before tried the depth of the muddy water, and found it was scarcely four feet, and now we hastened to make use of the remaining light of a long summer's day in draining carefully the said hole.

I was repaid for the trouble, for in the muddy and deep sediment at the bottom we discovered a deeply imbedded blucher boot; and I dare say you will readily guess how my heart leaped up at the sight.

To old diggers, the task which followed was not a very great one; we had provided ourselves with a "tub," etc., and "washed" every bit of the mud at the bottom of the hole. The only "find" we had, however, was a peculiar bit of wood, which, instead of rewarding us for our exertions by lying like gold at the bottom of the dish in which we "turned off," insisted upon floating on the top of the very first tub, when it became loosened from its surrounding of clay.

It was a queer piece of wood, and eventually quite repaid us for any trouble we might have had in its capture. A segment of a circle it was, or rather a portion of a segment of a circle, being neither more nor less than a piece broken out of one of those old fashioned black wooden buttons, that are still to be seen on the monkey-jacket of many an Australian digger, as well as elsewhere.

Well, I fancied that I knew the identical button from whence had been broken this bit of wood, and that I could go and straightaway fit it into its place without the slightest trouble in the world—singular, was it not?—and as I carefully placed the piece in my pocket, I could not help thinking to myself "Well, this does indeed and most truly look like the working of Providence."

There are many occasions when an apparent chance has effected the unravelling of a mystery, which but for the turning over of that particular page of fatality, might have remained a mystery to the day of judgment, in spite of the most strenuous and most able exertions. Mere human acumen would never have discovered the key to the secret's hieroglyphic, nor placed side by side the hidden links of a chain long enough and strong enough to tear the murderer from his fancied security, and hang him as high as Haman. Such would almost appear to have been the case in the instance to which I am alluding, only that in place of ascribing the elucidation and the unravelling to that mythical power chance, the impulse of some "inner man" writes the word Providence.

I did not feel exactly like moralizing, however, when, after resuming my digger's "make up," I walked towards the tent of the man I have called Bill. No; I felt more and deeper than any mere moralist could understand. The belief that a higher power had especially called out, and chosen, one of his own creatures to be the instrument of his retributive power, has, in our world's history, been the means of mighty evil, and I hope that not for an instant did such an idea take possession of me. I was not conscious of feeling that I had been chosen as a scourge and an instrument of earthly punishment; but I did feel that I was likely to be the means of cutting short the thread of a most unready fellow-mortal's life, and a solemn responsibility it is to bring home to one's self I can assure you.

The last flush of sunlight was fading low in the west when I reached our camping ground, and found Bill seated outside on a log, indulging in his usual pipe in the greying twilight.

I had, of course, determined upon arresting him at once, and had sent two policemen round to the back of our tents, in case of an attempted escape upon his part; and now, quite prepared, I sat down beside him; and, after feeling that the handcuffs were in their usual place in my belt, I lit my pipe and commenced to smoke also. My heart verily went pit-a-pat as I did so, for, long as I had been engaged in this sort of thing, I had not yet become callous either to the feelings of wretched criminal or the excitement attendant more or less upon every capture of the sort.

We smoked in silence for some minutes, and I was listening intently to hear the slightest intimation of the vicinity of my mates; at length Bill broke the silence. "Did you get your money?" he inquired.

"No," I replied, "but I think I will get it soon."

Silence again, and then withdrawing the pipe from my mouth and quietly knocking the ashes out of it on the log, I turned towards my mate and said:

"Bill, what made you murder that man in Pipeclay Gully?"

He did not reply, but I could see his face pale and whiten in the grey dim twilight, and at last stand out distinctly in the darkening like that of the dead man we found lying in the lonely gully.

It was so entirely unexpected that he was completely stunned: not the slightest idea had he that the body had ever been found, and it was on quite nerveless wrists that I locked the handcuffs, as my mates came up and took him in charge.

Rallying a little, he asked huskily, "Who said I did it?"

"No person," I replied, "but I know you did it."

Again he was silent, and did not contradict me, and so he was taken to the lock-up.

I was right about the broken button, and had often noticed it on an old jacket of Bill's. The piece fitted to a nicety; and the cut-up blucher! Verily, there was some powerful influence at work in the discovery of this murder, and again I repeat that no mere human wisdom could have accomplished it.

Bill, it would appear, thought so too, for expressing himself so to me, he made a full confession, not only of the murder, but also of the other offence, for the bringing home to him of which I had been so anxious.

When he found that the body of the unfortunate man had been discovered upon the surface, in the broad light of day, after he had left him dead in the bottom of the hole, he became superstitiously convinced that God himself had permitted the dead to leave his hiding place for the purpose of bringing the murderer to justice.

It is no unusual thing to find criminals of his class deeply impregnated with superstition, and Bill insisted to the last that the murdered man was quite dead when he had placed him in the hole, and where, in his anxiety to prevent the body from appearing above the surface, he had lost his boot in the mud, and was too fearful of discovery to remain to try and get it out.

Bill was convicted, sentenced to death, and hung; many other crimes of a similar nature to that which he had committed on Chinaman's Flat having been brought home to him by his own confession.

JEMIMA SHORE'S FIRST CASE

Antonia Fraser

Antonia Fraser is known for her historical writing and biographies, as well as her detective fiction. She created the television reporter detective Jemima Shore in *Quiet as a Nun* (1977) and wrote her final Shore mystery in 1995. A recipient of several awards, Fraser was made a Dame in 2011.

At the sound of the first scream, the girl in bed merely stirred and turned over. The second scream was much louder and the girl sat up abruptly, pushing back the meagre bedclothes. She was wearing a high-necked white cotton nightdress with long sleeves which was too big for her. The girl was thin, almost skinny, with long straight pale-red hair and oddly shaped slanting eyes in a narrow face.

Her name was Jemima Shore and she was fifteen years old.

The screams came again: by now they sounded quite blood-curdling to the girl alone in the small room – or was it that they were getting nearer? It was quite dark. Jemima Shore clambered out of bed and went to the window. She was tall, with long legs sticking out from below the billowing white cotton of the nightie, legs which like the rest of her body were too thin for beauty. Jemima pulled back the curtain which was made of some unlined flowered stuff. Between the curtain and the glass was an iron grille. She could not get out. Or, to put it another way, whatever was outside in the thick darkness could not get in.

It was the sight of the iron grille which brought Jemima properly to her senses. She remembered at last exactly where she was: sleeping in a ground-floor room at a boarding-school in Sussex called the Convent of the Blessed Eleanor. Normally Jemima was a day-girl at the Catholic boarding-school, an unusual situation which had developed when her mother came to live next door to Blessed Eleanor's in her father's absence abroad. The situation was unusual not only because Jemima was the only day-girl at Blessed Eleanor's but also because Jemima was theoretically at least a Protestant: not that Mrs Shore's vague ideas of religious upbringing really justified such a positive description.

Now Mrs Shore had been called abroad to nurse her husband who was recovering from a bad attack of jaundice, and Reverend Mother Ancilla, headmistress of the convent, had agreed to take Jemima as a temporary boarder. Hence the little ground-floor room – all that was free to house her – and hence for that matter the voluminous nightdress, Mrs Shore's ideas of nightclothes for her teenage daughter hardly according with the regulations at Blessed Eleanor's. To Jemima, still staring uncomprehendingly out into the darkness which lay beyond the grille and the glass, as though she might perceive the answer, none of this explained why she should now suddenly be awakened in the middle of the night by sounds which suggested someone was being murdered or at least badly beaten up: the last sounds you would expect to hear coming out of the tranquil silence which generally fell upon the Blessed Eleanor's after nine o'clock at night.

What *was* the time? It occurred to Jemima that her mother had left behind her own smart little travelling-clock as a solace in the long conventual nights. Squinting at its luminous hands – somehow she did not like to turn on the light and make herself visible through the flimsy curtains to whatever was outside in the night world – Jemima saw it was three o'clock. Jemima was not generally fearful either of solitude or the dark (perhaps because she was an only child) but the total indifference with which the whole convent appeared to be greeting the screams struck her as even more alarming than the noise itself. The big red-brick building, built in the twenties, housed not only a girls' boarding-school but the community of nuns who looked after them; the two areas were divided by the chapel.

The chapel! All of a sudden Jemima realized not only that the screams were coming from that direction but also – another sinister thought – she might conceivably be the only person within earshot. The so-called 'girls' guest-room' (generally old girls) was at the very edge of the lay part of the building. Although Jemima had naturally never visited the nuns' quarters on the other side, she had had the tiny windows of their cells pointed out by her best friend Rosabelle Powerstock, an authority on the whole fascinating subject of nuns. The windows were high up, far away from the chapel.

Was it from a sense of duty, or was it simply due to that ineradicable curiosity in her nature to which the nuns periodically drew grim attention suggesting it might be part of her unfortunate Protestant heritage . . . at all events, Jemima felt impelled to open her door a crack. She did so gingerly. There was a small night-light burning in the long corridor before the tall statue of the Foundress of the Order of the Tower of Ivory – Blessed Eleanor, dressed in the black habit the nuns still wore. The statue's arms were outstretched.

Jemima moved warily in the direction of the chapel. The screams had ceased but she did hear some other sound, much fainter, possibly the noise of crying. The night-light cast a dim illumination and once Jemima passed the statue with its long welcoming arms – welcoming, that is, in daylight; they now seemed to be trying to entrap her – Jemima found herself in virtual darkness.

As Jemima cautiously made her way in to the chapel, the lingering smell of incense began to fill her nostrils, lingering from that night's service of bene-diction, that morning's mass, and fifty other years of masses said to incense in the same place. She entered the chapel itself – the door was open – and perceived a few candles burning in front of a statue to her left. The incense smell was stronger. The little red sanctuary lamp seemed far away. Then Jemima stumbled over something soft and shapeless on the floor of the central aisle.

Jemima gave a sharp cry and at the same time the bundle moved, gave its own anguished shriek and said something which sounded like: 'Zeeazmoof,

Zeeazmoof'. Then the bundle sat up and revealed itself to be not so much a bundle as an Italian girl in Jemima's own form called Sybilla.

At this point Jemima understood that what Sybilla was actually saying between sobs was: 'She 'as moved, she 'as moved', in her characteristic strong Italian accent. There was a total contrast between this sobbing creature and the daytime Sybilla, a plump and rather jolly dark-haired girl, who jangled in illicit gold chains and bracelets, and wore more than a hint of equally illicit make-up. Jemima did not know Sybilla particularly well despite sharing classes with her. She pretended to herself that this was because Sybilla (unlike Jemima and her friends) had no interest in art, literature, history or indeed anything very much except Sybilla herself; pleasure, parties and the sort of people you met at parties, principally male. Sybilla was also old for her form – seventeen already – whereas Jemima was young for it, so that there was a considerable age gap between them. But the truth was that Jemima avoided Sybilla because she was a princess (albeit an Italian one, not a genuine British Royal) and Jemima, being middle class and proud of it, had no wish to be accused of snobbery.

The discovery of Sybilla – Princess Maria Sybilla Magdalena Graffo di Santo Stefano to give her her full title – in the chapel only deepened the whole mystery. Knowing Sybilla, religious mania, a sudden insane desire to pray alone in the chapel at night, to make a novena for example, simply could not be the answer to her presence. Sybilla was unashamedly lazy where religion was concerned, having to be dragged out of bed to go to mass even when it was obligatory on Sundays and feast days, protesting plaintively, like a big black cat ejected from the fireside. She regarded the religious fervour of certain other girls, such as Jemima's friend Rosabelle Powerstock, with good-natured amazement.

'So boring' she was once overheard to say about the Feast of the Immaculate Conception (a holiday of obligation). 'Why do we have this thing? I think we don't have this thing in Italy.' It was fortunate that Sybilla's theological reflections on this occasion had never come to the ears of Reverend Mother Ancilla who would have quickly set to rights this unworthy descendant of a great Roman family (and even, delicious rumour said, of a Pope or two).

Yes, all in all, religious mania in Princess Sybilla could definitely be ruled out.

'Sybilla,' said Jemima, touching her shoulder, 'don't cry –'

At that moment came at last the sound for which Jemima had been subconsciously waiting since she first awoke: the characteristic swoosh of a nun in full habit advancing at high speed, rosary at her belt clicking, rubber heels twinkling down the marble corridor.

'Sybilla, *Jemima?*' The rising note of surprise on the last name was evident in the sharp but controlled voice of Sister Veronica, the Infirmarian. Then authority took over and within minutes nun-like phrases such as 'To bed at once both of you' and 'No more talking till you see Reverend Mother in the morning' had calmed Sybilla's convulsive sobs. The instinctive reaction of nuns in a crisis, Jemima had noted, was to treat teenage girls as children; or perhaps they always mentally treated them as children, it just came to the surface in a crisis. Sybilla after all was nearly grown-up, certainly if her physical appearance was any guide. Jemima sighed; was she to be hustled to bed with her curiosity, now quite rampant, unsatisfied?

It was fortunate for Jemima that before despatching her charges, Sister Veronica did at least make a quick inspection of the chapel – as though to see what other delinquent pupils might be lurking there in the middle of the night.

'What happened, Sybilla?' Jemima took the opportunity to whisper. 'What frightened you? I thought you were being murdered –'

Sybilla extended one smooth brown arm (unlike most of the girls at Blessed Eleanor's, she was perpetually sun-tanned, and unlike Jemima, she had somehow avoided wearing the regulation white nightdress).

'Oh, my God, Jemima!' It came out as 'Omigod, Geemima! I am telling you. She 'as moved!'

'Who moved, Sybilla?'

'The statue. You know, the one they call the Holy Nelly. She moved her arms towards me. She 'as touched me, Jemima. It was *miraculo*. How do you say? A mir-a-cul.'

Then Sister Veronica returned and imposed silence, silence on the whole subject.

But of course it was not to be like that. The next morning at assembly the whole upper school, Jemima realized, was buzzing with excitement in which words like 'miracle', 'Sybilla's miracle' and 'there was a miracle, did you hear' could be easily made out. Compared to the news of Sybilla's miracle – or the Blessed Eleanor's miracle depending on your point of view – the explanation of Sybilla's presence near the chapel in the middle of the night passed almost unnoticed: except by Jemima Shore that is, who definitely did not believe in miracles and was therefore still more avid to hear about Sybilla's experiences than she had been the night before. Jemima decided to tackle her just after Sister Hilary's maths lesson, an experience calculated to leave Sybilla unusually demoralized.

Sybilla smiled at Jemima, showing those dimples in her pinkish-olive cheeks which were her most attractive feature. (Come to think of it, was that pinkish glow due to a discreet application of blush-on? But Jemima, no nun, had other things on her mind.)

'Eet's ridiculous,' murmured Sybilla with a heavy sigh; there was a clank as her gold charm bracelet hit the desk; it struck Jemima that the nuns' rosaries and Sybilla's jewellery made roughly the same sound and served the same purpose, to advertise their presence. 'But you know these nuns, they won't let me write to my father. So boring. Oh yes, they will let me *write*, but it seems they must read the letter. Mamma made them do that, or maybe they did it, I don't know which. Mamma is so holy, Omigod, she's like a nun . . . Papa' – Sybilla showed her dimples again – 'Papa, he is – how do you say – a bit of a bad dog.'

'A gay dog,' suggested Jemima helpfully. Sybilla ignored the interruption. She was busy speaking affectionately even yearningly of Prince Graffo di Santo Stefano's bad (or gay) dog-like tendencies which seemed to include pleasure in many different forms. (The Princess being apparently in contrast a model of austere piety, Jemima realized that Sybilla was very much her father's daughter.) The Prince's activities included racing in famous motor cars and escorting famously beautiful women and skiing down famous slopes and holidaying on famous yachts, and other things, amusing things. 'Papa he 'ates to be bored, he 'ates it!'

These innocuous pursuits had according to Sybilla led the killjoy Princess to forbid her husband access to his daughter: this being Italy there could of course be no divorce either by the laws of the country or for that matter by the laws of Mother Church to which the Princess at least strictly adhered.

'But it's true, Papa, he doesn't want a divorce either,' admitted Sybilla. 'Then he might have to marry – I don't know who but he might have to marry this woman or that woman. That would be terrible for Papa. So boring. No, he just want some money, poor Papa, he has no money, Mamma has all the money, I think it's not fair that, she should *give* him the money, *si*, he is her *marito*, her 'usband, she should give it to him. What do you think, Jemima?'

Jemima, feeling the first stirrings of primitive feminism in her breast at this description of the Santo Stefano family circumstances, remained politely silent on that subject.

Instead: 'And the statue, Sybilla?' she probed gently.

'Ah.' Sybilla paused. 'Well, you see how it is, Jemima. I write to him. I write anything, amusing things. And I put them in a letter but I don't like the nuns to read these things so –' she paused again. 'So I am making an arrangement with Gregory,' ended Sybilla with a slight but noticeable air of defiance.

'Yes, Gregory,' she repeated. 'That man. The gardener, the chauffeur, the odd-things man, whatever he is, the taxi-man.'

Jemima stared at her. She knew Gregory, the convent's new odd-job man, a surprisingly young fellow to be trusted in this all-female establishment, but all the same –

'And I am placing these letters under the statue of the Holy Nelly in the night,' continued Sybilla with more confidence. 'To wake up? Omigod, no problem. To go to sleep early, *that* is the problem. They make us go to bed like children here. And he, Gregory, is collecting them when he brings the post in the morning. Later he will leave me an answer which he takes from the post office. That day there will be one red flower in that big vase under the statue. And so we come to the night when I am having my *miraculo*,' she announced triumphantly.

But Jemima, who did not believe in miracles, fell silent once more at what followed: Sybilla's vivid description of the statue's waving arms, warm touch just as she was about to hide the letter (which she then retrieved) and so forth and so on – an account which Jemima had a feeling was rapidly growing even as she told it.

'So you see I am flinging myself into the chapel,' concluded Sybilla. 'And sc-r-r-reaming and sc-r-r-reaming. Till you, Jemima *cara*, have found me. Because you only are near me!'

Well, that at least was true, thought Jemima: because she had formed the strong impression that Sybilla for all her warmth and confiding charm was not telling her the truth; or not the whole truth. Just as Jemima's reason would not let her believe in miracles, her instinct would not let her believe in Sybilla's story, at any rate not all of it.

Then both Jemima and Sybilla were swirled up in the sheer drama of Sister Elizabeth's lesson on her favourite Wordsworth ('Oh, the lovely man!').

'Once did she hold the gorgeous East in fee,' intoned Sister Liz in a sonorous voice before adding rather plaintively: 'Sybilla, do wake up; this is *your* Venice after all, as well as dear Wordsworth's.' Sybilla raised her head reluctantly from her desk where it had sunk as though under the weight of the thick dark hair, unconfined by any of the bands prescribed by convent rules. It was clear that her thoughts were very far from Venice, 'hers' or anyone else's, and even further from Wordsworth.

Another person who did not believe in miracles or at any rate did not believe in this particular miracle was Reverend Mother Ancilla. Whether or not she was convinced by Sybilla's explanation of sleep-walking – 'since a child I am doing it' – Mother Ancilla dismissed the mere idea of a moving statue.

'Nonsense child, you were asleep at the time. You've just said so. You dreamt the whole thing. No more talk of miracles please, Sybilla; the ways of Our Lord and indeed of the Blessed Eleanor may be mysterious but they are not as mysterious as *that*,' announced Mother Ancilla firmly with the air of one to whom they were not in fact at all that mysterious in the first place. 'Early nights for the next fourteen days – no, Sybilla, that is what I said, you need proper rest for your mind which is clearly, contrary to the impression given by your report, over-active . . .'

Even Sybilla dared do no more than look sulky-faced with Mother Ancilla in such a mood. The school as a whole was compelled to take its cue from Sybilla: with no further grist to add to the mill of gossip, gradually talk of Sybilla's miracle died away to be replaced by scandals such as the non-election of the Clitheroe twins Annie and Pettie (short for Annunziata and Perpetua) as Children of Mary. This was on the highly unfair grounds that they had appeared in a glossy magazine in a series called 'Cloistered Moppets' wearing some Mary Quantish version of a nun's habit.

Jemima Shore did sometimes wonder whether Sybilla's illicit correspondence still continued. She also gazed from time to time at Gregory as he went about his tasks, all those tasks which could not be performed by the nuns themselves (surprisingly few of them as a matter of fact, picking up and delivering the post being one of them). Gregory was a solid-looking individual in his thirties with nice thick curly hair cut quite short, but otherwise in no way striking; were he not the only man around the convent grounds (with the exception of visiting priests in the morning and evening and parents at weekends) Jemima doubted whether she would have remembered his face. But he was a perfectly pleasant person, if not disposed to chat, not to Jemima Shore at least. The real wonder was, thought Jemima, that Sybilla had managed to corrupt him in the first place.

It was Jemima's turn to sigh. She had better face facts. Sybilla was rich – that much was obvious from her appearance – and she was also voluptuous. Another sigh from Jemima at the thought of Sybilla's figure, so much more like that of an Italian film star – if one fed on dollops of spaghetti – than anything Jemima could achieve. No doubt both factors, money and figure, had played their part in enabling Sybilla to capture Gregory. It was time to concentrate on other things – winning the English Prize for example (which meant beating Rosabelle) or securing the part of Hamlet in the school play (which meant beating everybody).

When Sybilla appeared at benediction on Saturday escorted by a middle-aged woman, and a couple of men in camel-haired coats, one very tall and dark, the other merely dark, Jemima did spare some further thought for the Santo Stefano family. Were these relations? The convent rules were strict enough for it to be unlikely they were mere friends, especially when Mamma Principessa was keeping such a strict eye on access to her daughter. Besides, the woman did bear a certain resemblance to Sybilla, her heavily busted figure suggesting how Sybilla's voluptuous curves might develop in middle age.

Jemima's curiosity was satisfied with unexpected speed: immediately after benediction Sybilla waved in her direction, and with wreathed smiles and much display of dimple, introduced her cousin Tancredi, her Aunt Cristiana and her Uncle Umberto.

'Ah now, Jemima, you come with us, yes, you come with us for dinner? Yes, I insist. You have saved me. *Si, si*, it was her' – to her relations. To Jemima she confided: 'What a surprise, they are here. I am not expecting them. They come to spy on the naughty Sybilla,' dimples again. 'But listen, Tancredi, he is very much like my Papa, now you know what Papa looks like, 'andsome, yes? And Papa, he like Tancredi very much, so you come?'

'I don't have a Permission –' began Jemima rather desperately. One look at Tancredi had already told her that he approximated only too wonderfully to her latest ideal of masculine attraction, derived partly from the portrait of Lord Byron at the front of her O-level text, and partly from a character in a Georgette Heyer novel called *Devil's Cub*. (Like many would-be intellectuals, Jemima had a secret passion for Georgette Heyer. Jemima, with Rosabelle, Annie, Pettie and the rest of her coterie, were relieved when from time to time some older indisputably intellectual female would announce publicly in print, tribute perhaps to her own youth, that Georgette Heyer was an important if neglected literary phenomenon.)

Alas, Jemima felt in no way ready to encounter Tancredi, the man of her dreams, at this precise juncture: she was aware that her hair, her best feature, hung lankly, there having been no particular reason in recent days to wash it. Her 'home clothes', in which she would be allowed to emerge from the convent, belonged to a much shorter girl (the girl Mrs Shore had in fact bought the clothes for, twelve months previously), nor could they be passed off as mini-skirted because they were too unfashionable.

One way and another, Jemima was torn between excitement and apprehension when Sybilla, in her most wayward mood, somehow overrode these very real difficulties ('But it's charming, the long English legs; Tancredi has seen you, *ma che bella*! Yes, yes, I am telling you . . .') and also, even more surprisingly, convinced Mother Ancilla to grant permission.

'An unusual friendship, dear Jemima,' commented the Reverend Mother drily, before adding: 'But perhaps you and Sybilla have both something to learn from each other.' Her bright shrewd little eyes beneath the white wimple moved down Jemima's blouse and that short distance covered by her skirt.

'Is that a mini-skirt?' asked Mother Ancilla sharply. 'No, no, I see it is not. And your dear mother away . . .' Mother Ancilla's thoughts were clearly clicking rapidly like the beads of her rosary. 'What will the Marchesa think? Now, child, go immediately to Sister Baptist in the sewing-room, I have a feeling that Cecilia Clitheroe' – she mentioned the name of a recent postulant, some relation to Annie and Pettie – 'is about your size.' Marvelling, not for the first time, at the sheer practical worldliness of so-called unworldly nuns, Jemima found herself wearing not so much a drooping blouse and outmoded skirt as a black suit trimmed in beige braid which looked as if it had come from Chanel or thereabouts.

Without the suit, would Jemima really have captured Tancredi in quite the way she did at the dinner which followed? For undoubtedly, as Jemima related it to Rosabelle afterwards, Tancredi *was* captured and Rosabelle, summing up all the evidence, agreed that it must have been so. Otherwise why the slow burning looks from those dark eyes, the wine glass held in her direction, even on one occasion a gentle pressure of a knee elegantly clad in a silk suit of a particular shade of blue just a little too bright to be English? As for Tancredi himself, was he not well worth capturing, the muscular figure beneath the dandyish suit, nothing effeminate about Tancredi, the atmosphere he carried with him of international sophistication – or was it just the delicious smell of *Eau Sauvage*? (Jemima knew it was *Eau Sauvage* because on Rosabelle's recommendation she had given some to her father for Christmas; not that she had smelt it on him subsequently beyond one glorious whiff at Christmas dinner itself.)

As for Sybilla's uncle and aunt, the Marchesa spoke very little but when she did so it was in careful English, delivered, whether intentionally or not, in a reproachful tone as though Jemima's presence at dinner demanded constant explanation if not apology. Jemima's answers to the Marchesa's enquiries about her background and previous education seemed to disgust her particularly; at one point, hearing that Jemima's father was serving in the British army, the Marchesa simply stared at her. Jemima hoped that the stare was due to national prejudice based on wartime memories, but feared it was due to simple snobbery.

Uncle Umberto was even quieter, a short pock-marked Italian who would have been plausible as a waiter, had he not been an Italian nobleman. Both uncle and aunt, after the first unfortunate interrogation, spoke mainly in Italian to their niece: family business, Jemima assumed, leaving Tancredi free for his pursuit of Jemima while their attention was distracted.

The next day: 'You 'ave made a conquest, Jemima,' related Sybilla proudly. 'Tancredi finds you so int-ell-igent' – she drawled out the word – 'and he asks if all English girls are so int-ell-igent, but I say that you are famous for being clever, so clever that you must find him so stu-pid!'

'I'm not all *that* clever, Sybilla.' Jemima despite herself was nettled; for once she had hoped her attraction lay elsewhere than in her famous intelligence. That might win her the English Prize (she had just defeated Rosabelle) but intelligent was not quite how she wished to be regarded in those sophisticated international circles in which in her secret daydreams she was now dwelling . . .

Tancredi's letter, when it came, did not however dwell upon Jemima's intelligence but more of her particular brand of English beauty, her strawberries-and-cream complexion (Sybilla's blush-on had been liberally applied), her hair the colour of Italian sunshine and so forth and so on in a way that Jemima had to admit could scarcely be bettered even in daydream. The method by which the letter arrived was less satisfactory: the hand of Sybilla, who said that it had been enclosed in a letter from Tancredi's sister Maria Gloria (letters from accredited female relations were not generally opened). Had Sybilla read the letter which arrived sealed with sellotape? If she had, Jemima was torn between embarrassment and pride at the nature of the contents.

Several more letters followed until one day – 'He wants to see you again. Of course he wants to see you again!' exclaimed Sybilla. 'He loves you. Doesn't he say so always?' Jemima shot her a look: so Sybilla did know the letters' contents. To her surprise Jemima found that she was not exactly eager to see Tancredi again, despite the fact that his smuggled letters had become the centre of her emotional existence. Tancredi's passion for Jemima had something of the miraculous about it – Jemima smiled to herself wryly, she who did not believe in miracles – and she couldn't help being worried that the miracle might not happen a second time . . . It was in the end more sheer curiosity than sheer romance which made Jemima continue to discuss Sybilla's daring idea for a rendezvous. This was to be in Jemima's own ground-floor room no less – Tancredi to be admitted through the grille left open for the occasion.

'The key!' cried Jemima. 'No, it's impossible. How would we ever get the key?'

'Oh, Jemima, you who are so clever,' purred Sybilla, looking more than ever like a fat black cat denied its bowl of cream. 'Lovely Jemima . . . I know you will be thinking of something. Otherwise I am thinking that Tancredi goes to Italy and you are not seeing him. So boring. He has so many girls there.'

'Like Papa?' Jemima could not resist asking. But Sybilla merely pouted.

'I could give such a long, long letter to Papa if you say yes,' she sighed. 'I'm frightened to speak to Gregory now, you know. Papa thinks –' She paused. 'He's a bit frightened. And I'm frightened too. That moving statue.' Sybilla shuddered.

'No, Sybilla,' said Jemima.

Nevertheless in her languorously persistent way, Sybilla refused to let the subject of Tancredi's projected daring expedition to Blessed Eleanor's drop. Jemima for her part was torn between a conviction that it was quite impossible to secure the key to the grille in front of her ground-floor window and a pride which made her reluctant to admit defeat, defeat at the hands of the nuns. In the end pride won, as perhaps Jemima had known all along that it would. She found by observing Sister Dympna, who swept her room and was responsible for locking the grille at darkness, that the grille was opened by a key, but snapped shut of its own accord. From there it was a small step to trying an experiment: a piece of blackened cardboard between grille and jamb, and the attention of Sister Dympna distracted at the exact moment the busy little nun was slamming the grille shut.

It worked. Jemima herself had to close the grille properly after Sister Dympna left. That night Jemima lay awake, conscious of the outer darkness and the window through which Tancredi would come if she wanted him to come. She began to review the whole thrilling affair, beginning so unpropitiously as it had seemed at the time, with Sybilla's screams in the night. She remembered that night in the chapel with the terrified girl, the smell of incense in her nostrils, and then switched her thoughts to her first and so far her only encounter with Tancredi . . . Her own personal miracle. She heard Sybilla's voice: *'Miraculo.'*

But I don't believe in miracles, said the coldly reasonable voice of Jemima enclosed in the darkness, away from the seductive Mediterranean charm of Sybilla. And there's something else too: my instinct. I thought she was lying that first night, didn't I? Why did the statue move? A further disquieting thought struck Jemima. She got out of bed, switched on the light, and gazed steadily at her reflection in the small mirror over the basin.

'Saturday,' said Jemima the next morning; she sounded quite cold. 'Maria Gloria had better pass the message.' But Sybilla, in her pleasure at having her own way, did not seem to notice the coldness. 'And Sybilla –' added Jemima.

'Cara?'

'Give me the letter for your father in good time because I've got permission to go over to my own house to borrow some decent dresses of my mother's, she's coming back, you know. As I may not see you later, give me the letter before I go.' Sybilla enfolded Jemima in a soft, warm, highly scented embrace.

By Saturday, Jemima found herself torn between two exactly contradictory feelings. Half of her longed for the night, for the rendezvous – whatever it might bring – and the other half wished that darkness would never come, that she could remain for the rest of her life suspended, just waiting for Tancredi Was this what being in love meant? For Jemima, apart from one or two holiday passions, for her father's young subalterns, considered that she had never been properly in love; although it was a matter much discussed between herself and Rosabelle (of her other friends the Clitheroe twins, Annie and Pettie being too merrily wanton and Bridget too strictly pious to join in these talks). Then there was another quite different side to her character, the cool and rational side, which simply said: I want to investigate, I want to find out what's going on, however painful the answer.

Jemima made her visit to her parents' home driven by the silent Gregory and chaperoned by Sister Veronica who was cross enough at the waste of time to agree with Jemima that the garden was in an awful state, and rush angrily at the neglected branches – 'Come along, Jemima, we'll do it together.' Jemima took a fork to the equally neglected beds and dug diligently out of range of Sister Veronica's conversation. (Gregory made no move to help but sat in the car.) Jemima herself was also extremely quiet on the way back, which with Gregory's enigmatic silence, meant that Sister Veronica could chatter on regarding the unkempt state of the Shore home ('Your poor dear mother . . . no gardener') to her heart's content. For the rest of the day and evening, Jemima had to keep the investigative side of her nature firmly to the fore. She found her emotional longings too painful.

Darkness fell on the convent. From the corner of her window – unbarred or rather with a crack left in the grille, so that only someone who knew it would open would be able to detect it – Jemima could watch as the yellow lights in the high dormitories were gradually extinguished. Sybilla was sleeping somewhere up there in the room which she shared with a monkey-like French girl called Elaine, who even in the summer at Blessed Eleanor's was huddled against the cold: 'She is too cold to wake up. She is like your little mouse who sleeps,' Sybilla had told Jemima. But Sybilla now was certainly watched at night and could not move about freely as she had once done.

On the other side of the building were the nuns, except for those on duty in the dormitories or Sister Veronica in the infirmary. Jemima had no idea where Mother Ancilla slept – alone perhaps in the brief night allowed to nuns before the early morning mass? But Mother Ancilla was another subject about which Jemima preferred not to think; the nun was so famously percipient that it had required some mental daring for Jemima even to say goodnight to her. She feared that the dark shrewd eyes might see right through to her intentions.

In her room, Jemima decided not to change into her convent night gown; she snuggled under the covers in jeans (collected that afternoon from home – strictly not allowed at Blessed Eleanor's) – and a skimpy black polo-necked jersey. In spite of herself, convent habits inspired in her a surprising desire to pray.

Reflecting that to do so, even by rationalist standards, could not exactly do any *harm*, Jemima said three Hail Marys.

Oddly enough it was not until Jemima heard the faint – very faint – sound of someone rapping on the window, which was her clue to wind back the grille, that it occurred to Jemima that what she was doing might not only be foolhardy but actively dangerous. By then of course it was too late. She had no course now but to pull back the grille as silently as possible – since Sybilla's escapade the nuns had taken to patrolling the outside corridor from time to time. She raised the window cautiously.

Over the sill, dressed as far as she could make out entirely in black, at any rate in black jersey (remarkably similar to her own) and black trousers, with black rubber-soled shoes, came Tancredi. The smell of *Eau Sauvage* filled the room: for one wild moment the sweetness of it made Jemima regret . . . then she allowed herself to be caught into Tancredi's arms. He kissed her, his rather thin lips forcing apart her own.

Then Tancredi stood back a little and patted her lightly on her denim-clad thigh. 'What protection! You are certainly not anxious to seduce me, *cara*,' he said softly. Jemima could sense him smiling in the darkness. 'This is a little bit like a nun, yes?' He touched her breast in the tight black jersey. 'This not so much.'

'Tancredi, you mustn't, I mean –' What did she mean? She knew what she meant. She had it all planned, didn't she?

'Tancredi, listen, you've simply got to take Sybilla's packet, her letter that is, it's quite thick, the letter, you must take it and then go. You see, the nuns are very suspicious. I couldn't let you know, but I have a feeling someone suspects . . . Mother Ancilla, she's the headmistress, she's awfully beady.' Jemima was conscious she was babbling on. 'So you must take the letter and *go*.'

'Yes, I will take the letter. In good time. Or now, *tesoro*, if you like. I don't want to make tr-r-rouble for you.' Tancredi sounded puzzled. 'But first, oh I'm so tired, all that walking through this park, its enor-mous, let's sit down a moment on this ridiculous little bed. Now this is really for a nun, this bed.'

'I think you should just collect the letter and go,' replied Jemima, hoping that her voice did not quaver.

'Collect, you mean you don't have it.' Trancredi was now a little brisker, more formal.

'I – I hid it. By the statue outside. You see we have inspection on Saturdays, drawer inspection, cupboard inspection, everything. I didn't dare keep it. So I used her place, Sybilla's place. Look, I'll explain where you go –'

To Jemima's relief, yes, it really was to her relief, she found Tancredi seemed to accept the necessity for speed, and even for a speedy departure. The embrace he gave her as he vanished into the ill-lit corridor was quite perfunctory, only the lingering smell of *Eau Sauvage* in her room reminded her of what a romantic tryst this might under other circumstances have turned out to be. Jemima sat down on the bed suddenly and waited for Tancredi's return. Then there would be one last embrace, perhaps perfunctory, perhaps a little longer, and he would vanish into the darkness from which he had come, out of her life.

She waited.

But things did not turn out quite as Jemima had planned. One moment Tancredi was standing at the door again, with a clear view of the big statue behind him; he had a pencil torch in his hand and a packet opened at one end. The next moment he had leapt towards her and caught her throat in the fingers of one strongly muscled hand.

'Where is it?' he was saying in a fierce whisper. 'Where is it? Have you taken it? Who has taken it?' And then, with more indignation – 'What is *this*?' He was looking at some white Kleenex which protruded from the packet, clearly addressed to the Principe Graffo di Santo Stefano in Sybilla's flowing hand. The fingers tightened on Jemima's throat so that she could hardly speak, even if she had some answer to the fierce questioning.

'Tancredi, I don't know what –' she began. Then beyond Tancredi, at the end of the corridor, to Jemima's horror she saw something which looked to her very much like the statue of the Blessed Eleanor moving. Jemima gave a scream, cut off by the pressure of Tancredi's fingers. After that a lot of things happened at once, so that later, sorting them out for Rosabelle (under very strict oath of secrecy – the Clitheroe twins and Bridget definitely not to be informed) Jemima found it difficult to get the exact order straight. At one moment the statue appeared to be moving in their direction, the next moment a big flashlight, of quite a different calibre from Tancredi's pencil torch, was shining directly on both of them. It must have been then that Jemima heard the voice of Gregory, except that Gregory was saying something like: Detective Inspector Michael Vann, Drugs Squad, and Michael Vann of the Drugs Squad was, it seemed, in the process of arresting Tancredi.

Or rather he might have intended to be in the process, but an instant after Tancredi heard his voice and was bathed in the flashlight, he abandoned his hold on Jemima, dived in the direction of the window, pulled back the grille and vanished.

Then there were more voices, an extraordinary amount of voices for a tranquil convent at night, and phrases were heard like 'Never mind, we'll get him', and words like 'Ports, airports', all of which reverberated in the mind of Jemima without making a particularly intelligible pattern. Nothing seemed to be making much sense, not since the statue had begun to move, until she heard someone – Gregory – say:

'And after all that, he's managed to take the stuff with him.'

'He hasn't,' said Jemima Shore in a small but firm voice. 'It's buried in the garden at home.'

It was so typical of Mother Ancilla, observed Jemima to Rosabelle when the reverberations of that night had at long last begun to die away, so typical of her that the very first thing she should say was: 'You're wearing jeans, Jemima.'

'I suppose she had to start somewhere,' commented Rosabelle. 'Personally, I think it's a bit much having the Drugs Squad moseying round the convent even if it is the biggest haul etc. etc. and even if the Principe is a wicked drug pusher etc. etc. Thank goodness it's all over in time for the school play.' Rosabelle had recently been cast as Hamlet (Jemima was cast as Laertes – 'that dear misguided *reckless* young man, as Sister Elizabeth put it, with a meaning look in Jemima's direction). Rosabelle at least had the school play much on her mind. 'Did Mother Ancilla give any proper explanation?' Rosabelle went on.

'You know Mother Ancilla,' Jemima said ruefully. 'She was really amazingly lofty about the whole thing. That is, until I remarked in a most innocent voice that the nuns obviously agreed with the Jesuits that the ends justify the means.'

'Daring! Then what?'

'Then I was told to write an essay on the history of the Society of Jesus by Friday – you can't win with Mother Ancilla.'

'Sybilla and Co. certainly didn't. Still, all things considered, you were quite lucky, Jem. You did save the cocaine. You didn't get struck down by Tancredi, and you didn't get ravished by him.'

'Yes, I was lucky; wasn't I?' replied Jemima in a tone in which Rosabelle thought she detected just a hint of wistfulness.

The reverberations of that night had by this time included the precipitate departure of Sybilla from the convent, vast amounts of expensive green velvety luggage surrounding her weeping figure in the convent hall the next day. She refused to speak to Jemima beyond spitting at her briefly: 'I *'ate* you, Jemima, and Tancredi, he 'ates you too, he thinks you are *ugly*.' Then Sybilla shook her black head furiously so that the long glittering earrings, which she now openly flaunted, jangled and glinted.

What would happen to Sybilla? The Drugs Squad were inclined to be lenient towards someone who was so evidently under the influence of a father who was both pleasure-loving and poverty-stricken (a bad combination). Besides, thanks to a tip-off, they had had her watched since her arrival in England, and the Prince's foolproof method of bringing drugs into the country via his daughter's school luggage – clearly labelled 'Blessed Eleanor's Convent, Churne, Sussex' – had never in fact been as foolproof as he imagined. For that matter Gregory, the enigmatic gardener, had not been as subornable as Sybilla, in her confident way and Jemima in her envious one, had imagined.

Gregory however, as an undercover operative, had not been absolutely perfect; it had been a mistake for example to let Sybilla glimpse him that night by the statue, provoking that fit of hysterics which had the effect of involving Jemima in the whole affair. Although it could be argued – and was by Jemima and Rosabelle – that it was Jemima's involvement which had flushed out Tancredi, the Prince's deputy, after Sybilla had become too frightened to contact Gregory. Then there was Jemima's valiant entrapment of Tancredi and her resourceful preservation of the cocaine.

All the same, Jemima Shore herself had not been absolutely perfect in the handling of the whole matter, as Mother Ancilla pointed out very firmly, once the matter of the jeans had been dealt with. It was only after some very frank things had been said about girls who kept things to themselves, things best confided to authority, girls who contemplated late-night trysts with males (albeit with the highest motives as Mother Ancilla accepted) that Mother Ancilla put her bird's head on one side: 'But, Jemima dear child, what made you – how did you guess?'

'I just never believed in the second miracle, Mother,' confessed Jemima.

'The second miracle, dear child?'

'I didn't believe in the first miracle either, the miracle of Sybilla's waving statue. The second miracle was Tancredi, the cousin, falling in love with me. I looked in the mirror, and well . . .' Her voice tailed away. Mother Ancilla had the effect of making her confess things she would rather, with hindsight, have kept to herself.

Mother Ancilla regarded Jemima for a moment. Her gaze was quizzical but not unkind.

'Now, Jemima, I am sure that when we have finished with you, you will make a wonder Ca– . . . a wonderful wife and mother' – she had clearly intended to say 'Catholic wife and mother' before realizing who sat before her.

Jemima Shore saw her first and doubtless her last chance to score over Mother Ancilla.

'Oh, no, Reverend Mother,' she answered boldly, 'I'm not going to be a wife and mother. I'm going into television,' and having already mentioned one of Mother Ancilla's pet banes, she was inspired to add another: 'I'm going to be an investigative reporter.'

THE LONG ARM

Mary E. Wilkins Freeman

Mary E. Wilkins Freeman (1852–1930) was one of the most celebrated authors in nineteenth-century America. Originally a children's writer, she developed a distinctive voice, combining naturalistic depictions of New England life with supernatural elements. In 1925, she became the first recipient of the William Deans Howells Medal.

I. The Tragedy

(From notes written by Miss Sarah Fairbanks immediately after the report of the Grand Jury.)

As I take my pen to write this, I have a feeling that I am in the witness-box—for, or against myself, which? The place of the criminal in the dock I will not voluntarily take. I will affirm neither my innocence nor my guilt. I will present the facts of the case as impartially and as coolly as if I had nothing at stake. I will let all who read this judge me as they will.

This I am bound to do, since I am condemned to something infinitely worse than be the life-cell or the gallows. I will try my own self in lieu of judge and jury; my guilt or my innocence I will prove to you all, if it be in mortal power. In my despair I am tempted to say, I care not which it may be, so something be proved. Open condemnation could not overwhelm me like universal suspicion.

Now, first, as I have heard is the custom in the courts of law, I will present the case. I am Sarah Fairbanks, a country school teacher, twenty-nine years of age. My mother died when I was twenty-three. Since then, while I have been teaching at Digby, a cousin of my father's, Rufus Bennett, and his wife have lived with my father. During the long summer vacation they returned to their little farm in Vermont, and I kept house for my father.

For five years I have been engaged to be married to Henry Ellis, a young man whom I met in Digby. My father was very much opposed to the match, and has told me repeatedly that if I insisted upon marrying him in his lifetime he would disinherit me. On this account Henry never visited me at my own home; while I could not bring myself to break off my engagement. Finally, I wished to avoid an open rupture with my father. He was quite an old man, and I was the only one he had left of a large family.

I believe that parents should honour their children, as well as children their parents; but I had arrived at this conclusion: in nine-tenths of the cases wherein children marry against their parents' wishes, even when the parents have no just grounds for opposition, the marriages are unhappy.

I sometimes felt that I was unjust to Henry, and resolved that, if ever I suspected that his fancy turned toward any other girl, I would not hinder it, especially as I was getting older and, I thought, losing my good looks.

A little while ago, a young and pretty girl came to Digby to teach the school in the south district. She boarded in the same house with Henry. I heard that he was somewhat attentive to her, and I made up my mind I would not interfere. At the same time it seemed to me that my heart was breaking. I heard her people had money, too, and she was an only child. I had always felt that Henry ought to marry a wife with money, because he had nothing himself, and was not very strong.

School closed five weeks ago, and I came home for the summer vacation. The night before I left, Henry came to see me, and urged me to marry him. I refused again; but I never before had felt that my father was so hard and cruel as I did that night. Henry said that he should certainly see me during the vacation, and when I replied that he must not come, he was angry, and said—but such foolish things are not worth repeating. Henry has really a very sweet temper, and would not hurt a fly.

The very night of my return home Rufus Bennett and my father had words about some maple sugar which Rufus made on his Vermont farm and sold to father, who made a good trade for it to some people in Boston. That was father's business. He had once kept a store, but had given it up, and sold a few articles that he could make a large profit on here and there at wholesale. He used to send to New Hampshire and Vermont for butter, eggs, and cheese. Cousin Rufus thought father did not allow him enough profit on the maple sugar, and in the dispute father lost his temper, and said that Rufus had given him under weight. At that, Rufus swore an oath, and seized father by the throat. Rufus's wife screamed, "Oh, don't! don't! oh, he'll kill him!"

I went up to Rufus and took hold of his arm.

"Rufus Bennett," said I, "you let go my father!"

But Rufus's eyes glared like a madman's, and he would not let go. Then I went to the desk-drawer where father had kept a pistol since some houses in the village were broken into; I got out the pistol, laid hold of Rufus again, and held the muzzle against his forehead.

"You let go of my father," said I, "or I'll fire!"

Then Rufus let go, and father dropped like a log. He was purple in the face. Rufus's wife and I worked a long time over him to bring him to.

"Rufus Bennett," said I, "go to the well and get a pitcher of water." He went, but when father had revived and got up, Rufus gave him a look that showed he was not over his rage.

"I'll get even with you yet, Martin Fairbanks, old man as you are!" he shouted out, and went into the outer room.

We got father to bed soon. He slept in the bedroom downstairs, out of the sitting-room. Rufus and his wife had the north chamber, and I had the south one. I left my door open that night, and did not sleep. I listened; no one stirred in the night. Rufus and his wife were up very early in the morning, and before nine o'clock left for Vermont. They had a day's journey, and would reach home about nine in the evening. Rufus's wife bade father good-bye, crying, while Rufus was getting their trunk downstairs, but Rufus did not go near father nor me. He ate no breakfast; his very back looked ugly when he went out of the yard.

That very day about seven in the evening, after tea, I had just washed the dishes and put them away, and went out on the north door-step, where father was sitting, and sat down on the lowest step. There was a cool breeze there; it had been a very hot day.

"I want to know if that Ellis fellow has been to see you any lately?" said father all at once.

"Not a great deal," I answered.

"Did he come to see you the last night you were there?" said father.

"Yes, sir," said I, "he did come."

"If you ever have another word to say to that fellow while I live, I'll kick you out of the house like a dog, daughter of mine though you be," said he. Then he swore a great oath and called God to witness. "Speak to that fellow again, if you dare, while I live!" said he.

I did not say a word; I just looked up at him as I sat there. Father turned pale and shrank back, and put his hand to his throat, where Rufus had clutched him. There were some purple finger-marks there.

"I suppose you would have been glad if he had killed me," father cried out.

"I saved your life," said I.

"What did you do with that pistol?" he asked.

"I put it back in the desk-drawer."

I got up and went around and sat on the west doorstep, which is the front one. As I sat there, the bell rang for the Tuesday evening meeting, and Phoebe Dole and Maria Woods, two old maiden ladies, dressmakers, our next-door neighbours, went past on their way to the meeting. Phoebe stopped and asked if Rufus and his wife were gone. Maria went around the house. Very soon they went on, and several other people passed. When they had all gone, it was as still as death.

I sat alone a long time, until I could see by the shadows that the full moon had risen. Then I went to my room and went to bed.

I lay awake a long time, crying. It seemed to me that all hope of marriage between Henry and me was over. I could not expect him to wait for me. I thought of that other girl; I could see her pretty face wherever I looked. But at last I cried myself to sleep.

At about five o'clock I awoke and got up. Father always wanted his breakfast at six o'clock, and I had to prepare it now.

When father and I were alone, he always built the fire in the kitchen stove, but that morning I did not hear him stirring as usual, and I fancied that he must be so out of temper with me, that he would not build the fire.

I went to my closet for a dark blue calico dress which I wore to do housework in. It had hung there during all the school term.

As I took it off the hook, my attention was caught by something strange about the dress I had worn the night before. This dress was made of thin summer silk; it was green in colour, sprinkled over with white rings. It had been my best dress for two summers, but now I was wearing it on hot afternoons at home, for it was the coolest dress I had. The night before, too, I had thought of the possibility of Henry's driving over from Digby and passing the house. He had done this sometimes during the last summer vacation, and I wished to look my best if he did.

As I took down the calico dress I saw what seemed to be a stain on the green silk. I threw on the calico hastily, and then took the green silk and carried it over to the window. It was covered with spots—horrible great splashes and streaks down the front. The right sleeve, too, was stained, and all the stains were wet.

"What have I got on my dress?" said I.

It looked like blood. Then I smelled of it, and it was sickening in my nostrils, but I was not sure what the smell of blood was like. I thought I must have got the stains by some accident the night before.

"If that is blood on my dress," I said, "I must do something to get it off at once, or the dress will be ruined."

It came to my mind that I had been told that blood-stains had been removed from cloth by an application of flour paste on the wrong side. I took my green silk, and ran down the back stairs, which lead—having a door at the foot— directly into the kitchen.

There was no fire in the kitchen stove, as I had thought. Everything was very solitary and still, except for the ticking of the clock on the shelf. When I crossed the kitchen to the pantry, however, the cat mewed to be let in from the shed. She had a little door of her own by which she could enter or leave the shed at will, an aperture just large enough for her Maltese body to pass at ease beside the shed door. It had a little lid, too, hung upon a leathern hinge. On my way I let the cat in; then I went into the pantry and got a bowl of flour. This I mixed with water into a stiff paste, and applied to the under surface of the stains on my dress. I then hung the dress up to dry in the dark end of a closet leading out of the kitchen, which contained some old clothes of father's.

Then I made up the fire in the kitchen stove. I made coffee, baked biscuits, and poached some eggs for breakfast.

Then I opened the door into the sitting-room and called, "Father, breakfast is ready." Suddenly I started. There was a red stain on the inside of the sitting-room door. My heart began to beat in my ears. "Father!" I called out—"father!"

There was no answer.

"Father!" I called again, as loud as I could scream. "Why don't you speak? What is the matter?"

The door of his bedroom stood open. I had a feeling that I saw a red reflection in there. I gathered myself together and went across the sitting-room to father's bedroom door. His little looking-glass hung over his bureau opposite his bed, which was reflected in it.

That was the first thing I saw, when I reached the door. I could see father in the looking-glass and the bed. Father was dead there; he had been murdered in the night.

II. The Knot of Ribbon

I think I must have fainted away, for presently I found myself on the floor, and for a minute I could not remember what had happened. Then I remembered, and an awful, unreasoning terror seized me. "I must lock all the doors quick," I thought; "quick, or the murderer will come back."

I tried to get up, but I could not stand. I sank down again. I had to crawl out of the room on my hands and knees.

I went first to the front door; it was locked with a key and a bolt. I went next to the north door, and that was locked with a key and bolt. I went to the north shed door, and that was bolted. Then I went to the little-used east door in the shed, beside which the cat had her little passage-way, and that was fastened with an iron hook. It has no latch.

The whole house was fastened on the inside. The thought struck me like an icy hand, "The murderer is in this house! "I rose to my feet then; I unhooked that door, and ran out of the house, and out of the yard, as for my life.

I took the road to the village. The first house, where Phoebe Dole and Maria Woods live, is across a wide field from ours. I did not intend to stop there, for they were only women, and could do nothing; but seeing Phoebe looking out of the window, I ran into the yard.

She opened the window.

"What is it?" said she. "What is the matter, Sarah Fairbanks?"

Maria Woods came and leaned over her shoulder. Her face looked almost as white as her hair, and her blue eyes were dilated. My face must have frightened her.

"Father—father is murdered in his bed!" I said.

There was a scream, and Maria Woods's face disappeared from over Phoebe Dole's shoulder—she had fainted. I do not know whether Phoebe looked paler—she is always very pale—but I saw in her black eyes a look which I shall never forget. I think she began to suspect me at that moment.

Phoebe glanced back at Maria, but she asked me another question.

"Has he had words with anybody?" said she.

"Only with Rufus," I said; "but Rufus is gone."

Phoebe turned away from the window to attend to Maria, and I ran on to the village.

A hundred people can testify what I did next—can tell how I called for the doctor and the deputy-sheriff; how I went back to my own home with the horror-stricken crowd; how they flocked in and looked at poor father; but only the doctor touched him, very carefully, to see if he were quite dead; how the coroner came, and all the rest.

The pistol was in the bed beside father, but it had not been fired; the charge was still in the barrel. It was blood-stained, and there was one bruise on father's head which might have been inflicted by the pistol, used as a club. But the wound which caused his death was in his breast, and made evidently by some cutting instrument, though the cut was not a clean one; the weapon must have been dull.

They searched the house, lest the murderer should be hidden away. I heard Rufus Bennett's name whispered by one and another. Everybody seemed to know that he and father had had words the night before; I could not understand how, because I had told nobody except Phoebe Dole, who had had no time to spread the news, and I was sure that no one else had spoken of it.

They looked in the closet where my green silk dress hung, and pushed it aside to be sure nobody was concealed behind it, but they did not notice anything wrong about it. It was dark in the closet, and besides, they did not look for anything like that until later.

All these people—the deputy-sheriff, and afterwards the high sheriff, and other out-of-town officers, for whom they had telegraphed, and the neighbours—all hunted their own suspicion, and that was Rufus Bennett. All believed he had come back, and killed my father. They fitted all the facts to that belief. They made him do the deed with a long, slender screw-driver, which he had recently borrowed from one of the neighbours and had not returned. They made his finger-marks, which were still on my father's throat, fit the red prints of the sitting-room door. They made sure that he had returned and stolen into the house by the east door shed, while father and I sat on the doorsteps the evening before; that he had hidden himself away, perhaps in that very closet where my dress hung, and afterwards stolen out and killed my father, and then escaped.

They were not shaken when I told them that every door was bolted and barred that morning. They themselves found all the windows fastened down, except a few which were open on account of the heat, and even these last were raised only the width of the sash, and fastened with sticks, so that they could be raised no higher. Father was very cautious about fastening the house, for he sometimes had considerable sums of money by him. The officers saw all these difficulties in the way, but they fitted them somehow to their theory, and two deputy-sheriffs were at once sent to apprehend Rufus.

They had not begun to suspect me then, and not the slightest watch was kept on my movements. The neighbours were very kind, and did everything to help me, relieving me altogether of all those last offices—in this case so much sadder than usual.

An inquest was held, and I told freely all I knew, except about the blood-stains on my dress. I hardly knew why I kept that back. I had no feeling then that I might have done the deed myself, and I could not bear to convict myself, if I was innocent.

Two of the neighbours, Mrs. Holmes and Mrs. Adams, remained with me all that day. Towards evening, when there were very few in the house, they went into the parlour to put it in order for the funeral, and I sat down alone in the kitchen. As I sat there by the window I thought of my green silk dress, and wondered if the stains were out. I went to the closet and brought the dress out to the light. The spots and streaks had almost disappeared. I took the dress out into the shed, and scraped off the flour paste, which was quite dry; I swept up the paste, burned it in the stove, took the dress upstairs to my own closet, and bunged it in its old place. Neighbours remained with me all night.

At three o'clock in the afternoon of the next day, which was Thursday, I went over to Phoebe Dole's to see about a black dress to wear at the funeral. The neighbours had urged me to have my black silk dress altered a little, and trimmed with crape.

I found only Maria Woods at home. When she saw me she gave a little scream, and began to cry. She looked as if she had already been weeping for hours. Her blue eyes were bloodshot.

"Phoebe's gone over to—Mrs. Whitney's to—try on her dress," she sobbed.

"I want to get my black silk dress fixed a little," said I.

"She'll be home pretty soon," said Maria.

I laid my dress on the sofa and sat down. Nobody ever consults Maria about a dress. She sews well, but Phoebe does all the planning.

Maria Woods continued to sob like a child, holding her little soaked handkerchief over her face. Her shoulders heaved. As for me, I felt like a stone; I could not weep.

"Oh," she gasped out finally, "I knew—I knew! I told Phoebe—I knew just how it would be, I—knew!"

I roused myself at that.

"What do you mean?" said I.

"When Phoebe came home Tuesday night and said she heard your father and Rufus Bennett having words, I knew how it would be," she choked out. "I knew he had a dreadful temper."

"Did Phoebe Dole know Tuesday night that father and Rufus Bennett had words?" said I.

"Yes," said Maria Woods.

"How did she know?"

"She was going through your yard, the short cut to Mrs. Ormsby's, to carry her brown alpaca dress home. She came right home and told me; and she overheard them."

"Have you spoken of it to anybody but me?" said I.

Maria said she didn't know; she might have done so. Then she remembered hearing Phoebe herself speak of it to Harriet Sargent when she came in to try on her dress. It was easy to see how people knew about it.

I did not say any more, but I thought it was strange that Phoebe Dole had asked me if father had had words with anybody when she knew it all the time.

Phoebe came in before long. I tried on my dress, and she made her plan about the alterations, and the trimming. I made no suggestions. I did not care how it was done, but if I had cared it would have made no difference. Phoebe always does things her own way. All the women in the village are in a manner under Phoebe Dole's thumb. The garments are visible proofs of her force of will.

While she was taking up my black silk on the shoulder seams, Phoebe Dole said—

"Let me see—you had a green silk made at Digby three summers ago, didn't you?"

"Yes," I said.

"Well," said she, "why don't you have it dyed black? those thin silks dye quite nice. It would make you a good dress."

I scarcely replied, and then she offered to dye it for me herself. She had a recipe which she used with great success. I thought it was very kind of her, but did not say whether I would accept her offer or not. I could not fix my mind upon anything but the awful trouble I was in.

"I'll come over and get it to-morrow morning," said Phoebe.

I thanked her. I thought of the stains, and then my mind seemed to wander again to the one subject. All the time Maria Woods sat weeping. Finally Phoebe turned to her with impatience.

"If you can't keep calmer, you'd better go upstairs, Maria," said she. "You'll make Sarah sick. Look at her! she doesn't give way—and think of the reason she's got."

"I've got reason, too," Maria broke out; then, with a piteous shriek, "Oh, I've got reason."

"Maria Woods, go out of the room!" said Phoebe. Her sharpness made me jump, half dazed as I was.

Maria got up without a word, and went out of the room, bending almost double with convulsive sobs.

"She's been dreadfully worked up over your father's death," said Phoebe calmly, going on with the fitting. "She's terribly nervous. Sometimes I have to be real sharp with her, for her own good."

I nodded. Maria Woods has always been considered a sweet, weakly, dependent woman, and Phoebe Dole is undoubtedly very fond of her. She has seemed to shield her, and take care of her nearly all her life. The two have lived together since they were young girls.

Phoebe is tall, and very pale and thin; but she never had a day's illness. She is plain, yet there is a kind of severe goodness and faithfulness about her colourless face, with the smooth bands of white hair over her ears.

I went home as soon as my dress was fitted. That evening Henry Ellis came over to see me. I do not need to go into details concerning that visit. It seemed enough to say that he tendered the fullest sympathy and protection, and I accepted them. I cried a little, for the first time, and he soothed and comforted me.

Henry had driven over from Digby and tied his horse in the yard. At ten o'clock he bade me good night on the doorstep, and was just turning his buggy around, when Mrs. Adams came running to the door.

"Is this yours?" said she, and she held out a knot of yellow ribbon.

"Why, that's the ribbon you have around your whip, Henry," said I.

He looked at it.

"So it is," he said. "I must have dropped It." He put it into his pocket and drove away.

"He didn't drop that ribbon to-night!" said Mrs. Adams. "I found it Wednesday morning out in the yard. I thought I remembered seeing him have a yellow ribbon on his whip."

III. Suspicion is Not Proof

When Mrs. Adams told me she had picked up Henry's whip-ribbon Wednesday morning, I said nothing, but thought that Henry must have driven over Tuesday evening after all, and even come up into the yard, although the house was shut up, and I in bed, to get a little nearer to me. I felt conscience-stricken, because I could not help a thrill of happiness, when my father lay dead in the house.

My father was buried as privately and as quietly as we could bring it about. But it was a terrible ordeal. Meantime word came from Vermont that Rufus Bennett had been arrested on his farm. He was perfectly willing to come back with the officers, and indeed, had not the slightest trouble in proving that he was at his home in Vermont when the murder took place. He proved by several witnesses that he was out of the State long before my father and I sat on the steps together that evening, and that he proceeded directly to his home as fast as the train and stage-coach could carry him.

The screw-driver with which the deed was supposed to have been committed was found, by the neighbour from whom it had been borrowed, in his wife's bureau drawer. It had been returned, and she had used it to put a picture-hook in her chamber. Bennett was discharged and returned to Vermont.

Then Mrs. Adams told of the finding of the yellow ribbon from Henry Ellis's whip, and he was arrested, since he was held to have a motive for putting my father out of the world. Father's opposition to our marriage was well known, and Henry was suspected also of having had an eye to his money. It was found, indeed, that my father had more money than I had known myself.

Henry owned to having driven into the yard that night, and to having missed the ribbon from his whip on his return; but one of the hostlers in the livery stables in Digby, where he kept his horse and buggy, came forward and testified to finding the yellow ribbon in the carriage-room that Tuesday night before Henry returned from his drive. There were two yellow ribbons in evidence, therefore, and the one produced by the hostler seemed to fit Henry's whip-stock the more exactly.

Moreover, nearly the exact minute of the murder was claimed to be proved by the post-mortem examination; and by the testimony of the stable man as to the hour of Henry's return and the speed of his horse, he was further cleared of suspicion; for, if the opinion of the medical experts was correct, Henry must have returned to the livery stable too soon to have committed the murder.

He was discharged, at any rate, although suspicion still clung to him. Many people believe now in his guilt—those who do not, believe in mine; and some believe we were accomplices.

After Henry's discharge, I was arrested. There was no one else left to accuse. There must be a motive for the murder; I was the only person left with a motive. Unlike the others, who were discharged after preliminary examination, I was held to the grand jury and taken to Dedham, where I spent four weeks in jail, awaiting the meeting of the grand jury.

Neither at the preliminary examination, nor before the grand jury, was I allowed to make the full and frank statement that I am making here. I was told simply to answer the questions that were put to me, and to volunteer nothing, and I obeyed.

I know nothing about law. I wished to do the best I could—to act in the wisest manner, for Henry's sake and my own. I said nothing about the green silk dress. They searched the house for all manner of things, at the time of my arrest, but the dress was not there—it was in Phoebe Dole's dye-kettle. She had come over after it one day when I was picking beans in the garden, and had taken it out of the closet. She brought it back herself, and told me this, after I had returned from Dedham.

"I thought I'd get it and surprise you," said she. "It's taken a beautiful black."

She gave me a strange look—half as if she would see into my very soul, in spite of me, half as if she were in terror of what she would see there, as she spoke. I do not know just what Phoebe Dole's look meant. There may have been a stain left on that dress after all, and she may have seen it.

I suppose if it had not been for that flour-paste which I had learned to make, I should have hung for the murder of my father. As it was, the grand jury found no bill against me because there was absolutely no evidence to convict me; and I came home a free woman. And if people were condemned for their motives, would there be enough hang-men in the world?

They found no weapon with which I could have done the deed. They found no blood-stains on my clothes. The one thing which told against me, aside from my ever-present motive, was the fact that on the morning after the murder the doors and windows were fastened. My volunteering this information had of course weakened its force as against myself.

Then, too, some held that I might have been mistaken in my terror and excitement, and there was a theory, advanced by a few, that the murderer had meditated making me also a victim, and had locked the doors that he might not be frustrated in his designs, but had lost heart at the last, and had allowed me to escape, and then fled himself. Some held that he had intended to force me to reveal the whereabouts of father's money, but his courage had failed him.

Father had quite a sum in a hiding-place which only he and I knew. But no search for money had been made, as far as any one could see—not a bureau drawer had been disturbed, and father's gold watch was ticking peacefully under his pillow; even his wallet in his vest pocket had not been opened. There was a small roll of bank-notes in it, and some change; father never carried much money. I suppose if father's wallet and watch had been taken, I should not have been suspected at all.

I was discharged, as I have said, from lack of evidence, and have returned to my home—free, indeed, but with this awful burden of suspicion on my shoulders. That brings me up to the present day. I returned yesterday evening. This evening Henry Ellis has been over to see me; he will not come again, for I have forbidden him to do so. This is what I said to him—

"I know you are innocent, you know I am innocent. To all the world beside we are under suspicion—I more than you, but we are both under suspicion. If we are known to be together that suspicion is increased for both of us. I do not care for myself, but I do care for you. Separated from me the stigma attached to you will soon fade away, especially if you should marry elsewhere."

Then Henry interrupted me.

"I will never marry elsewhere," said he.

I could not help being glad that he said it, but I was firm.

"If you should see some good woman whom you could love, it will be better for you to marry elsewhere," said I.

"I never will!" he said again. He put his arms around me, but I had strength to push him away.

"You never need, if I succeed in what I undertake before you meet the other," said I. I began to think he had not cared for that pretty girl who boarded in the same house after all.

"What is that?" he said. "What are you going to undertake?"

"To find my father's murderer," said I.

Henry gave me a strange look; then, before I could stop him, he took me fast in his arms and kissed my forehead.

"As God is my witness, Sarah, I believe in your innocence," he said; and from that minute I have felt sustained and fully confident of my power to do what I had undertaken.

My father's murderer I will find. Tomorrow I begin my search. I shall first make an exhaustive examination of the house, such as no officer in the case has yet made, in the hope of finding a clue. Every room I propose to divide into square yards, by line and measure, and every one of these square yards I will study as if it were a problem in algebra.

I have a theory that it is impossible for any human being to enter any house, and commit in it a deed of this kind, and not leave behind traces which are the known quantities in an algebraic equation to those who can use them.

There is a chance that I shall not be quite unaided. Henry has promised not to come again until I bid him, but he is to send a detective here from Boston—one whom he knows. In fact, the man is a cousin of his, or else there would be small hope of our securing him, even if I were to offer him a large price.

The man has been remarkably successful in several cases, but his health is not good; the work is a severe strain upon his nerves, and he is not driven to it from any lack of money. The physicians have forbidden him to undertake any new case, for a year at least, but Henry is confident that we may rely upon him for this.

I will now lay aside this and go to bed. Tomorrow is Wednesday; my father will have been dead seven weeks. Tomorrow morning I will commence the work, in which, if it be in human power, aided by a higher wisdom, I shall succeed.

IV. The Box of Clues

(The pages which follow are from Miss Fairbanks's journal begun after the conclusion of the notes already given to the reader.)

Wednesday night.—I have resolved to record carefully each day the progress I make in my examination of the house. I began today at the bottom—that is, with the room least likely to contain any clue, the parlour. I took a chalk-line and a yard-stick, and divided the floor into square yards, and every one of these squares I examined on my hands and knees. I found in this way literally nothing on the carpet but dust, lint, two common white pins, and three inches of blue sewing-silk.

At last I got the dustpan and brush, and yard by yard swept the floor. I took the sweepings in a white pasteboard box out into the yard in the strong sunlight, and examined them. There was nothing but dust and lint and five inches of brown woollen thread—evidently a ravelling of some dress material. The blue silk and the brown thread are the only possible clues which I found to-day, and they are hardly possible. Rufus's wife can probably account for them.

Nobody has come to the house all day. I went down to the store this afternoon to get some necessary provisions, and people stopped talking when I came in. The clerk took my money as if it were poison.

Thursday night.—To-day I have searched the sitting-room, out of which my father's bedroom opens. I found two bloody footprints on the carpet which no one had noticed before—perhaps because the carpet itself is red and white. I used a microscope which I had in my school work. The footprints, which are close to the bedroom door, pointing out into the sitting-room, are both from the right foot; one is brighter than the other, but both are faint. The foot was evidently either bare or clad only in a stocking—the prints are so widely spread. They are wider than my father's shoes. I tried one in the brightest print.

I found nothing else new in the sitting-room. The blood-stains on the doors which have been already noted are still there. They had not been washed away, first by order of the sheriff, and next by mine. These stains are of two kinds; one looks as if made by a bloody garment brushing against it; the other, I should say, was made in the first place by the grasp of a bloody hand, and then brushed over with a cloth. There are none of these marks upon the door leading to the bedroom—they are on the doors leading into the front entry and the china closet. The china closet is really a pantry, although I use it only for my best dishes and preserves.

Friday night.—To-day I searched the closet. One of the shelves, which is about as high as my shoulders, was blood-stained. It looked to me as if the murderer might have caught hold of it to steady himself. Did he turn faint after his dreadful deed? Some tumblers of jelly were ranged on that shelf and they had not been disturbed. There was only that bloody clutch on the edge.

I found on this closet floor, under the shelves, as if it had been rolled there by a careless foot, a button, evidently from a man's clothing. It is an ordinary black enamelled metal trousers-button; it had evidently been worn off and clumsily sewn on again, for a quantity of stout white thread is still clinging to it. This button must have belonged either to a single man or to one with an idle wife.

If one black button had been sewn on with white thread, another is likely to be. I may be wrong, but I regard this button as a clue.

The pantry was thoroughly swept—cleaned, indeed, by Rufus's wife, the day before she left. Neither my father nor Rufus could have dropped it there, and they never had occasion to go to that closet. The murderer dropped the button.

I have a white pasteboard box which I have marked "clues." In it I have put the button.

This afternoon Phoebe Dole came in. She is very kind. She had re-cut the dyed silk, and she fitted it to me. Her great shears clicking in my ears made me nervous. I did not feel like stopping to think about clothes. I hope I did not appear ungrateful, for she is the only soul beside Henry who has treated me as she did before this happened.

Phoebe asked me what I found to busy myself about, and I replied, "I am searching for my father's murderer." She asked me if I thought I should find a clue, and I replied, "I think so." I had found the button then, but I did not speak of it. She said Maria was not very well.

I saw her eyeing the stains on the doors, and I said I had not washed them off, for I thought they might yet serve a purpose in detecting the murderer. She looked closely at those on the entry-door—the brightest ones—and said she did not see how they could help, for there were no plain finger-marks there, and she should think they would make me nervous.

"I'm beyond being nervous," I replied.

Saturday.—To-day I have found something which I cannot understand. I have been at work in the room where my father came to his dreadful end. Of course some of the most startling evidences have been removed. The bed is clean, and the carpet washed, but the worst horror of it all clings to that room. The spirit of murder seemed to haunt it. It seemed to me at first that I could not enter that room, but in it I made a strange discovery.

My father, while he carried little money about his person, was in the habit of keeping considerable sums in the house; there is no bank within ten miles. However he was wary; he had a hiding-place which he had revealed to no one but myself. He had a small stand in his room near the end of his bed. Under this stand, or rather under the top of it, he had tacked a large leather wallet. In this he kept all his spare money. I remember how his eyes twinkled when he showed it to me.

"The average mind thinks things have either got to be in or on," said my father. "They don't consider there's ways of getting around gravitation and calculation."

In searching my father's room I called to mind that saying of his, and his peculiar system of concealment, and then I made my discovery. I have argued that in a search of this kind I ought not only to search for hidden traces of the criminal, but for everything which had been for any reason concealed. Something which my father himself had hidden, something from his past history, may furnish a motive for some one else.

The money in the wallet under the table, some five hundred dollars, had been removed and deposited in the bank. Nothing more was to be found there. I examined the bottom of the bureau, and the undersides of the chair seats. There are two chairs in the room, besides the cushioned rocker—green painted wooden chairs, with flag seats. I found nothing under the seats.

Then I turned each of the green chairs completely over, and examined the bottoms of the legs. My heart leaped when I found a bit of leather tacked over one. I got the tack-hammer and drew the tacks. The chair-leg had been hollowed out, and for an inch the hole was packed tight with cotton. I began picking out the cotton, and soon I felt something hard. It proved to be an old-fashioned gold band, quite wide and heavy, like a wedding-ring.

I took it over to the window and found this inscription on the inside: "Let love abide for ever." There were two dates—one in August, forty years ago, and the other in August of the present year.

I think the ring had never been worn; while the first part of the inscription is perfectly clear, it looks old, and the last is evidently freshly cut.

This could not have been my mother's ring. She had only her wedding-ring, and that was buried with her. I think my father must have treasured up this ring for years; but why? What does it mean? This can hardly be a clue; this can hardly lead to the discovery of a motive, but I will put it in the box with the rest.

Sunday night.—To-day, of course, I did not pursue my search. I did not go to church. I could not face old friends that could not face me. Sometimes I think that everybody in my native village believes in my guilt. What must I have been in my general appearance and demeanour all my life? I have studied myself in the glass, and tried to discover the possibilities of evil that they must see in my face.

This afternoon about three o'clock, the hour when people here have just finished their Sunday dinner, there was a knock on the north door. I answered it, and a strange young man stood there with a large book under his arm. He was thin and cleanly shaved, with a clerical air.

"I have a work here to which I would like to call your attention," he began;

and I stared at him in astonishment, for why should a book agent be peddling his wares upon the Sabbath?

His mouth twitched a little.

"It's a Biblical Cyclopædia," said he.

"I don't think I care to take it," said I.

"You are Miss Sarah Fairbanks, I believe?"

"That is my name," I replied stiffly. "Mr. Henry Ellis, of Digby, sent me here," he said next. "My name is Dix—Francis Dix."

Then I knew it was Henry's first cousin from Boston—the detective who had come to help me. I felt the tears coming to my eyes. "You are very kind to come," I managed to say.

"I am selfish, not kind," he returned, "but you had better let me come in, or any chance of success in my book agency is lost, if the neighbours see me trying to sell it on a Sunday. And, Miss Fairbanks, this is a *bona fide* agency. I shall canvass the town."

He came in. I showed him all that I have written, and he read it carefully. When he had finished he sat still for a long time, with his face screwed up in a peculiar meditative fashion.

"We'll ferret this out in three days at the most," said he finally, with a sudden clearing of his face and a flash of his eyes at me.

"I had planned for three years, perhaps," said I.

"I tell you, we'll do it in three days," he repeated. "Where can I get board while I canvass for this remarkable and interesting book under my arm? I can't stay here, of course, and there is no hotel. Do you think the two dressmakers next door, Phoebe Dole and the other one, would take me in?"

I said they had never taken boarders.

"Well, I'll go over and inquire," said Mr. Dix; and he had gone, with his book under his arm, almost before I knew it.

Never have I seen any one act with the strange noiseless soft speed that this man does. Can he prove me innocent in three days? He must have succeeded in getting board at Phoebe Dole's, for I saw him go past to meeting with her this evening. I feel sure he will be over very early to-morrow morning.

V. The Evidence Points to One

Monday night—The detective came as I expected. I was up as soon as it was light, and he came across the dewy fields, with his cyclopædia under his arm. He had stolen out from Phoebe Dole's back door.

He had me bring my father's pistol; then he bade me come with him out into the back yard.

"Now, fire it," he said, thrusting the pistol into my hands. As I have said before, the charge was still in the barrel.

"I shall arouse the neighbourhood," I said.

"Fire it," he ordered.

I tried; I pulled the trigger as hard as I could.

"I can't do it," I said.

"And you are a reasonably strong woman, too, aren't you?"

I said I had been considered so. Oh, how much I heard about the strength of my poor woman's arms, and their ability to strike that murderous weapon home!

Mr. Dix took the pistol himself, and drew a little at the trigger.

"I could do it," he said, "but I won't. It would arouse the neighbourhood."

"This is more evidence against me," I said despairingly. "The murderer had tried to fire the pistol and failed."

"It is more evidence against the murderer," said Mr. Dix.

We went into the house, where he examined my box of clues long and carefully. Looking at the ring, he asked whether there was a jeweller in this village, and I said there was not. I told him that my father oftener went on business to Acton, ten miles away, than elsewhere.

He examined very carefully the button which I had found in the closet, and then asked to see my father's wardrobe. That was soon done. Beside the suit in which father was laid away there was one other complete one in the closet in his room. Besides that, there were in this closet two overcoats, an old black frock coat, a pair of pepper-and-salt trousers, and two black vests. Mr. Dix examined all the buttons; not one was missing.

There was still another old suit in the closet off the kitchen. This was examined, and no button found wanting.

"What did your father do for work the day before he died?" he then asked.

I reflected and said that he had unpacked some stores which had come down from Vermont, and done some work out in the garden.

"What did he wear?"

"I think he wore the pepper-and-salt trousers and the black vest. He wore no coat, while at work."

Mr. Dix went quietly back to father's room and his closet, I following. He took out the grey trousers and the black vest, and examined them closely.

"What did he wear to protect these?" he asked.

"Why, he wore overalls!" I said at once. As I spoke I remembered seeing father go around the path to the yard, with those blue overalls drawn up high under his arms.

"Where are they?"

"Weren't they in the kitchen closet?"

"No."

We looked again, however, in the kitchen closet; we searched the shed thoroughly. The cat came in through her little door, as we stood there, and brushed around our feet. Mr. Dix stooped and stroked her. Then he went quickly to the door, beside which her little entrance was arranged, unhooked it, and stepped out. I was following him, but he motioned me back.

"None of my boarding mistress's windows command us," he said, "but she might come to the back door."

I watched him. He passed slowly around the little winding footpath, which skirted the rear of our house and extended faintly through the grassy fields to the rear of Phoebe Dole's. He stopped, searched a clump of sweetbrier, went on to an old well, and stopped there. The well had been dry many a year, and was choked up with stones and rubbish. Some boards are laid over it, and a big stone or two, to keep them in place.

Mr. Dix, glancing across at Phoebe Dole's back door, went down on his knees, rolled the stones away, then removed the boards and peered down the well. He stretched far over the brink, and reached down. He made many efforts; then he got up and came to me, and asked me to get for him an umbrella with a crooked handle, or something that he could hook into clothing.

I brought my own umbrella, the silver handle of which formed an exact hook. He went back to the well, knelt again, thrust in the umbrella and drew up, easily enough, what he had been fishing for. Then he came bringing it to me.

"Don't faint," he said, and took hold of my arm. I gasped when I saw what he had—my father's blue overalls, all stained and splotched with blood!

I looked at them, then at him.

"Don't faint," he said again. "We're on the right track. This is where the button came from—see, see!" He pointed to one of the straps of the overalls, and the button was gone. Some white thread clung to it. Another black metal button was sewed on roughly with the same white thread that I found on the button in my box of clues.

"What does it mean?" I gasped out. My brain reeled.

"You shall know soon," he said. He looked at his watch. Then he laid down the ghastly bundle he carried. "It has puzzled you to know how the murderer went in and out and yet kept the doors locked, has it not?" he said.

"Yes."

"Well, I am going out now. Hook that door after me."

He went out, still carrying my umbrella. I hooked the door. Presently I saw the lid of the cat's door lifted, and his hand and arm thrust through. He curved his arm up towards the hook, but it came short by half a foot. Then he withdrew his arm, and thrust in my silver-handled umbrella. He reached the door-hook easily enough with that.

Then he hooked it again. That was not so easy. He had to work a long time. Finally he accomplished it, unhooked the door again, and came in.

"That was how!" I said.

"No, it was not," he returned. "No human being, fresh from such a deed, could have used such patience as that to fasten the door after him. Please hang your arm down by your side."

I obeyed. He looked at my arm, then at his own.

"Have you a tape measure?" he asked.

I brought one out of my work-basket. He measured his arm, then mine, and then the distance from the cat-door to the hook.

"I have two tasks for you to-day and to-morrow," he said. "I shall come here very little. Find all your father's old letters, and read them. Find a man or woman in this town whose arm is six inches longer than yours. Now I must go home, or my boarding-mistress will get curious."

He went through the house to the front door, looked all ways to be sure no eyes were upon him, made three strides down the yard, and was pacing soberly up the street, with his cyclopædia under his arm.

I made myself a cup of coffee, then I went about obeying his instructions. I read old letters all the forenoon; I found packages in trunks in the garret; there were quantities in father's desk. I have selected several to submit to Mr. Dix. One of them treats of an old episode in father's youth, which must have years since ceased to interest him. It was concealed after his favourite fashion—tacked under the bottom of his desk. It was written forty years ago, by Maria Woods, two years before my father's marriage—and it was a refusal of an offer of his hand. It was written in the stilted fashion of that day; it might have been copied from a "Complete Letter-writer."

My father must have loved Maria Woods as dearly as I love Henry, to keep that letter so carefully all these years. I thought he cared for my mother. He seemed as fond of her as other men of their wives, although I did use to wonder if Henry and I would ever get to be quite so much accustomed to each other.

Maria Woods must have been as beautiful as an angel when she was a girl. Mother was not pretty; she was stout, too, and awkward, and I suppose people would have called her rather slow and dull. But she was a good woman, and tried to do her duty.

Tuesday night.—This evening was my first opportunity to obey the second of Mr. Dix's orders. It seemed to me the best way to compare the average length of arms was to go to the prayer-meeting. I could not go about the town with my tape measure, and demand of people that they should hold out their arms. Nobody knows how I dreaded to go to the meeting, but I went, and I looked not at my neighbours' cold altered faces, but at their arms.

I discovered what Mr. Dix wished me to, but the discovery can avail nothing, and it is one he could have made himself. Phoebe Dole's arm is fully seven inches longer than mine. I never noticed it before, but she has an almost abnormally long arm. But why should Phoebe Dole have unhooked that door?

She made a prayer—a beautiful prayer. It comforted even me a little. She spoke of the tenderness of God in all the troubles of life, and how it never failed us.

When we were all going out I heard several persons speak of Mr. Dix and his Biblical Cyclopædia. They decided that he was a theological student, book-canvassing to defray the expenses of his education.

Maria Woods was not at the meeting. Several asked Phoebe how she was, and she replied, "Not very well."

It is very late. I thought Mr. Dix might be over to-night, but he has not been here.

Wednesday.—I can scarcely believe what I am about to write. Our investigations seem to point all to one person, and that person—It is incredible! I will not believe it.

Mr. Dix came as before, at dawn. He reported, and I reported. I showed Maria Woods's letter. He said he had driven to Acton, and found that the jeweller there had engraved the last date in the ring about six weeks ago.

"I don't want to seem rough, but your father was going to get married again," said Mr. Dix.

"I never knew him to go near any woman since mother died," I protested.

"Nevertheless, he had made arrangements to be married," persisted Mr. Dix.

"Who was the woman?"

He pointed at the letter in my hand.

"Maria Woods!"

He nodded.

I stood looking at him—dazed. Such a possibility had never entered my head.

He produced an envelope from his pocket, and took out a little card with blue and brown threads neatly wound upon it.

"Let me see those threads you found," he said.

I got the box and we compared them. He had a number of pieces of blue sewing-silk and brown woollen ravellings, and they matched mine exactly.

"Where did you find them?" I asked.

"In my boarding-mistress's piece-bag." I stared at him.

"What does it mean?" I gasped out. "What do you think?"

"It is impossible!"

VI. The Revelation

Wednesday, continued.—When Mr. Dix thus suggested to me the absurd possibility that Phoebe Dole had committed the murder, he and I were sitting in the kitchen. He was near the table; he laid a sheet of paper upon it, and began to write. The paper is before me.

"First," said Mr. Dix, and he wrote rapidly as he talked, "whose arm is of such length that it might unlock a certain door of this house from the outside?— Phoebe Dole's.

"Second, who had in her piece-bag bits of the same threads and ravellings found upon your parlour floor, where she had not by your knowledge entered?— Phoebe Dole.

"Third, who interested herself most strangely in your blood-stained green silk dress, even to dyeing it?—Phoebe Dole.

"Fourth, who was caught in a lie, while trying to force the guilt of the murder upon an innocent man?—Phoebe Dole."

Mr. Dix looked at me. I had gathered myself together.

"That proves nothing," I said. "There is no motive in her case."

"There is a motive."

"What is it?"

"Maria Woods shall tell you this afternoon."

He then wrote—

"Fifth, who was seen to throw a bundle down the old well, in the rear of Martin Fairbanks's house, at one o'clock in the morning?—Phoebe Dole."

"Was she—seen?" I gasped.

Mr. Dix nodded. Then he wrote—

"Sixth, who had a strong motive, which had been in existence many years ago?—Phoebe Dole."

Mr. Dix laid down his pen, and looked at me again.

"Well, what have you to say?" he asked. "It is impossible!"

"Why?"

"She is a woman."

"A man could have fired that pistol, as she tried to do."

"It would have taken a man's strength to kill with the kind of weapon that was used," I said.

"No, it would not. No great strength is required for such a blow."

"But she is a woman!"

"Crime has no sex."

"But she is a good woman—a church member. I heard her pray yesterday afternoon. It is not in character."

"It is not for you, nor for me, nor for any mortal intelligence, to know what is or is not in character," said Mr. Dix.

He arose and went away. I could only stare at him in a half-dazed manner.

Maria Woods came this afternoon, taking advantage of Phoebe's absence on a dress-making errand. Maria has aged ten years in the last few weeks. Her hair is white, her cheeks are fallen in, her pretty colour is gone.

"May I have the ring he gave me forty years ago?" she faltered. I gave it to her; she kissed it and sobbed like a child.

"Phoebe took it away from me before," she said; "but she shan't this time."

Maria related with piteous sobs the story of her long subordination to Phoebe Dole. This sweet child-like woman had always been completely under the sway of the other's stronger nature. The subordination went back beyond my father's original proposal to her; she had, before he made love to her as a girl, promised Phoebe she would not marry; and it was Phoebe who, by representing to her that she was bound by this solemn promise, had led her to write a letter to my father declining his offer, and sending back the ring.

"And after all, we were going to get married, if he had not died," she said. "He was going to give me this ring again, and he had had the other date put in. I should have been so happy!"

She stopped and stared at me with horror-stricken inquiry.

"What was Phoebe Dole doing in your back-yard at one o'clock that night?" she cried.

"What do you mean?" I returned.

"I saw Phoebe come out of your back shed door at one o'clock that very night. She had a bundle in her arms. She went along the path about as far as the old well, then she stooped down, and seemed to be working at something. When she got up she didn't have the bundle. I was watching at our back door. I thought I heard her go out a little while before, and went down-stairs, and found that door unlocked. I went in quick, and up to my chamber, and into my bed, when she started home across the fields. Pretty soon I heard her come in, then I heard the pump going. She slept downstairs; she went on to her bedroom. What was she doing in your back-yard that night?"

"You must ask her," said I. I felt my blood running cold.

"I've been afraid to," moaned Maria Woods.

"She's been dreadful strange lately. I wish that book agent was going to stay at our house."

Maria Woods went home in about an hour. I got a ribbon for her, and she has my poor father's ring concealed in her withered bosom. Again I cannot believe this.

Thursday.—It is all over, Phoebe Dole has confessed! I do not know now in exactly what way Mr. Dix brought it about—how he accused her of her crime. After breakfast I saw them coming across the fields; Phoebe came first, advancing with rapid strides like a man, Mr. Dix followed, and my father's poor old sweetheart tottered behind, with her handkerchief at her eyes. Just as I noticed them the front door bell rang; I found several people there, headed by the high sheriff. They crowded into the sitting-room just as Phoebe Dole came rushing in, with Mr. Dix and Maria Woods.

"I did it!" Phoebe cried out to me. "I am found out, and I have made up my mind to confess. She was going to marry your father—I found it out. I stopped it once before. This time I knew I couldn't unless I killed him. She's lived with me in that house for over forty years. There are other ties as strong as the marriage one, that are just as sacred. What right had he to take her away from me and break up my home?

"I overheard your father and Rufus Bennett having words. I thought folks would think he did it. I reasoned it all out. I had watched your cat go in that little door, I knew the shed door hooked, I knew how long my arm was; I thought I could undo it. I stole over here a little after midnight. I went all around the house to be sure nobody was awake. Out in the front yard I happened to think my shears were tied on my belt with a ribbon, and I untied them. I thought I put the ribbon in my pocket—it was a piece of yellow ribbon—but I suppose I didn't, because they found it afterwards, and thought it came off your young man's whip. I went round to the shed door, unhooked it, and went in. The moon was light enough. I got out your father's overalls from the kitchen closet; I knew where they were. I went through the sitting-room to the parlour.

"In there I slipped off my dress and skirts and put on the overalls. I put a handkerchief over my face, leaving only my eyes exposed. I crept out then into the sitting-room; there I pulled off my shoes and went into the bedroom.

"Your father was fast asleep; it was such a hot night, the clothes were thrown back and his chest was bare. The first thing I saw was that pistol on the stand beside his bed. I suppose he had had some fear of Rufus Bennett coming back, after all. Suddenly I thought I'd better shoot him. It would be surer and quicker; and if you were aroused I knew that I could get away, and everybody would suppose that he had shot himself.

"I took up the pistol and held it close to his head. I had never fired a pistol, but I knew how it was done. I pulled, but it would not go off. Your father stirred a little—I was mad with horror—I struck at his head with the pistol. He opened his eyes and cried out; then I dropped the pistol, and took these"—Phoebe Dole pointed to the great shining shears hanging at her waist—"for I am strong in my wrists. I only struck twice, over his heart.

"Then I went back into the sitting-room. I thought I heard a noise in the kitchen—I was full of terror then—and slipped into the sitting-room closet. I felt as if I were fainting, and clutched the shelf to keep from falling.

"I felt that I must go upstairs to see if you were asleep, to be sure you had not waked up when your father cried out. I thought if you had I should have to do the same by you. I crept upstairs to your chamber. You seemed sound asleep, but, as I watched, you stirred a little; but instead of striking at you I slipped into your closet. I heard nothing more from you. I felt myself wet with blood. I caught something hanging in your closet, and wiped myself over with it. I knew by the feeling it was your green silk. You kept quiet, and I saw you were asleep, so crept out of the closet, and down the stairs, got my clothes and shoes, and, out in the shed, took off the overalls and dressed myself. I rolled up the overalls, and took a board away from the old well and threw them in as I went home. I thought if they were found it would be no clue to me. The handkerchief, which was not much stained, I put to soak that night, and washed it out next morning, before Maria was up. I washed my hands and arms carefully that night, and also my shears.

"I expected Rufus Bennett would be accused of the murder, and, maybe, hung. I was prepared for that, but I did not like to think I had thrown suspicion upon you by staining your dress. I had nothing against you. I made up my mind I'd get hold of that dress—before anybody suspected you—and dye it black. I came in and got it, as you know. I was astonished not to see any more stains on it. I only found two or three little streaks that scarcely anybody would have noticed. I didn't know what to think. I suspected, of course, that you had found the stains and got them off, thinking they might bring suspicion on you.

"I did not see how you could possibly suspect me in any case. I was glad when your young man was cleared. I had nothing against him. That is all I have to say."

I think I must have fainted away then. I cannot describe the dreadful calmness with which that woman told this—that woman with the good face, whom I had last heard praying like a saint in meeting. I believe in demoniacal possession after this.

When I came to, the neighbours were around me, putting camphor on my head, and saying soothing things to me, and the old friendly faces had returned. But I wish I could forget!

They have taken Phoebe Dole away—I only know that. I cannot bear to talk any more about it when I think there must be a trial, and I must go!

Henry has been over this evening. I suppose we shall be happy after all, when I have had a little time to get over this. He says I have nothing more to worry about. Mr. Dix has gone home. I hope Henry and I may be able to repay his kindness some day.

A month later. I have just heard that Phoebe Dole has died in prison. This is my last entry. May God help all other innocent women in hard straits as He has helped me!

LAST DAY OF SPRING

Celia Fremlin

Celia Fremlin (1914–2009) was a much-garlanded author of British suspense and psychological fiction, beginning with *The Hours Before Dawn* in 1958. Despite being middle-class and Oxford-educated, she worked in domestic service during the Second World War, and was a keen member of the Progressive League. All her books are available and published by Faber.

Even though her eyes were still closed, Martha Briggs knew that the sun was shining. The warmth was creeping slowly, gloriously across the blankets, and any minute now it would reach her face, bathe her in lovely, lovely heat. And after that it would creep across the pillow to Thomas's side of the bed, and wake him too. Now that he couldn't get out of bed any more, it was a shame that the sun didn't get to his side first. He should have had it all, every scrap – she would have pushed her own share over to him if she could! Old though she was, the thought made Martha giggle a little; and the thin dry sound coming from her lips roused her a little further. But she wouldn't open her eyes yet. No, this was the loveliest bit of the whole day, lying here with Thomas, waiting for the sun to reach her face. Strange how the sun seemed to shine every morning now that she was nearly ninety years old. Such lovely sun, too – it must be spring, day after day. If only she could get Thomas into his chair by the window; but he was too heavy, she couldn't lift him any more.

Thomas. . . . What was it that was worrying at the back of her mind, spoiling this lovely lying still in the sunshine?

Then she remembered. Of course! It was Thursday. This was the day when that Welfare woman with the clumping shoes was going to come and take Thomas away.

Take Thomas away, indeed! Martha had never heard such nonsense. As if she couldn't look after Thomas herself while he was ill! Hadn't he ever been ill before during their sixty years together, and hadn't she nursed him then? Of course she had – and before this clumping woman had been born or thought of, too!

She tried her hardest to remember what the creature had said. For a little while she could only remember the great shoes, and the snorting, breathy sort of voice that was so difficult to hear. Then slowly the woman's words came back to her:

'It isn't that we're criticising you, Mrs. Briggs, not for one moment. We know you're doing your very, very best – you've done wonders for your age, I know you have. But you see – well, I'm sure you'll agree with me really – it isn't right, is it, that he should be lying like this at past midday, not been attended to, not even had his breakfast yet! And the room! . . . You *do* see, don't you, Mrs. Briggs? It simply is too much for you – it's *you* we're considering really, you know, just as much as him. And he'll be quite happy, I promise you, he'll have every attention. . . .'

On and on went the voice in Martha's mind, and she almost smiled at the absurdity of it all. As if she and Thomas couldn't have their breakfast when it suited them! If they liked to lie like this in the sun for a little while first, whose business was it but their own?

Still, perhaps it would be a good idea, this morning, to teach that creature a lesson. She'd get up early and cook a good breakfast. Now, what would they have? An egg. Of course. She would fry an egg for Thomas. He would love that, with a bit of fried bread. She knew there was an egg somewhere, and he should have it. Then she would scrub the floor until the boards shone white in the sunlight; she would wash the curtains – she could almost see them now, billowing clean and lovely on the line. She would polish the chest of drawers, and rub the window till it shone. Too much for me, indeed! thought Martha: *I'll* show her!

But the sun was right on her face now, in all its glory. It would be a shame to get up just at this minute, just while it was like this. She would lie and enjoy it for a minute or two longer. . . .

Martha woke with a start. How tiresome! She must have dozed off, and now she would have to hurry to get everything done before that woman arrived.

She climbed stiffly out of bed and fumbled about for her dress. Where *could* it have got to? Then she remembered: of course, she had to sit quite still on the edge of the bed for a bit in the mornings, then things sort of straightened themselves out.

Her head was dropped a little forwards, and she could see lots and lots of floor. It was quite true; it *was* dirty. And what was worse, now that she was up all her enthusiasm for scrubbing it had drained away. The vision of sunlit, white-scrubbed boards was gone, and she could think only of the backbreaking weight of the pail, and the ever more perilous feat of getting down onto one's knees and then, somehow, getting back up again. . . .

But at least she had found her dress. At least that woman would find her up and dressed this time, and Thomas with a good breakfast in front of him. She made her way into the kitchen and set about preparing the meal.

But how had the fat in the frying-pan managed to burn black and smoking in just that moment or two it had taken her to find the egg? How tiresome things were! She poured the blackened mess away and started again, and this time it was wonderful. The egg was fried plump and golden, a little crisp round the edges, just the way Thomas liked it, and the fried bread was delicately brown. *That's* what he needed to build up his strength, a good breakfast like this every morning. It would be quite a job to buy an egg every day out of her tiny pension, but she'd managed it this time, and she'd manage it again. Oh yes, it would be worth it, to watch her Thomas grow strong and well again with good food inside him.

Now to get it into the bedroom. Slowly – oh, so slowly, because the boards had grown so uneven and treacherous of late – she carried it across the landing and into the bedroom. First she must put it down while she got Thomas propped up comfortably on his pillows.

But when she tried to put it down on the chest of drawers she found to her annoyance that there was no room there. It was all cluttered up with stuff – what *was* all this rubbish? She looked more carefully – and a dull bewilderment gripped her. For on the chest of drawers already was a plate with a fried egg on it – ice cold and congealed. And another, and another, and another – each with its loathsome wrinkled egg, staring at her like ancient eyes.

Something, half a memory, half a fear, made her turn, slowly, slowly, to look at the bed. Yes, it was empty. Stark, staring empty. Thomas was gone.

She knew she must sit down on the edge of the bed and think this out. There was something – something she half remembered – something that made sense of all this.

Of course! That was it! It was the wrong Thursday! That woman had already come on some other Thursday – last Thursday? – the Thursday before? – and had taken Thomas away!

Taken Thomas away! The import of the words slowly sank into her. How *could* she have let it happen? She, who had defended her family against all comers; she who in her time had stood up to rent collectors, probation officers, school-attendance officers, bailiffs, all the lot of them – how *could* she have let this flat-footed woman take her Thomas away?

She must think, think. When did they take him? Where would they have taken him to? Where *did* that woman say?

The hospital. Of course, Thomas was ill; it must have been the hospital. She would go there right now and fetch him, fetch him home herself through the spring sunshine.

Such a long, long way to the hospital, and when she got there and sat down at last on the hard bench, how they did talk! One after another of them, flashing about in front of her, snapping out questions like firecrackers.

'No record of it.' 'No such admission' – the senseless words kept tossing about among them like paper balls – like little girls playing ball in a sunlit garden. . . .

Sister spoke a little louder, still patiently:

'Do you understand? You must go to the Enquiry desk, and they'll give you a form. You must fill in the patient's name and address, the date of admission. . . .'

But Martha Briggs was no longer listening to her. Because right now at the far end of the shadowy stone corridor she could see Thomas. How well he looked! and – why – he was *running,* actually running towards her, with his dear, grey hair all rumpled and his arms outstretched!

'Thomas!' she cried, in joy and anxiety, 'Thomas, my darling, you mustn't run! – your heart . . .!'

She drew one breath of sweet, cool air, and then somehow seemed not to need another; for now she too was running, lightly, lightly, like a young girl, like a bird, her feet skimming over the stone floor. How wonderful it was to run, and run, and run to meet your love.

'Will you *please* go to the Enquiry desk——' Sister's voice broke off suddenly. A less expert eye than hers would scarcely have noticed the slight change as the old woman's head dropped a little further towards her chest and the faint breathing stopped.

TALKING TO STRANGERS

Nicci French

Nicci French is a pseudonym for the married journalists Nicci Gerrard and Sean French. Their psychological crime thrillers, including *The Memory Game*, *Killing Me Softly*, and *What to Do When Someone Dies*, are bestsellers. In 2011, they introduced the psychotherapist Frieda Klein in *Blue Monday*.

She had red spots on her tummy and a clammy forehead, but her mother seemed cross when she fetched her from school.

Her mother looked pretty, though. She was wearing a green dress Mattie hadn't seen before, and had red lips and pink nails.

Her hair bounced and she smelt of roses. She said they had to run an errand.

Mattie's skin prickled. Houses blurred past. She wished she could put her head on her cool plump pillow.

"Wait in the car. I won't be long."

Mattie watched her mother walk up to a blue door, smoothing her new green dress.

The door opened, then closed behind her. The sun banged in her head. She watched a fly on the window, making its way slowly along the glass. Could it see her?

Her skin prickled, she had a funny taste in her mouth and it hurt to swallow.

She needed a drink and she needed a wee as well. The blue door didn't open. She closed her eyes.

"Wake up, sweetie."

A hand shaking her. Mattie opened her eyes and blearily made out a woman, sitting in her mother's seat.

She wasn't as pretty as her mother, though. She wasn't wearing nice clothes and she'd spilt something red on her white T-shirt.

Her hair was all messed and her face smeary. She smelt funny too and was making a scratchy panting noise when she breathed.

"Who are you?"

"It's all right."

"Where's my mummy?"

"She can't come at the moment."

"I don't feel well. The teacher says it's chickens. I want mummy."

"I'm going to take you home. Will your daddy be there?"

"Why is your neck scratched?"

"Is it?"

"Did your cat do that?"

"Be quiet now, there's a good girl."

"Why are your hands trembling like that? Can't you make the car go?"

"Be quiet."

The woman switched on the satnav and pressed the home button.

"Thirteen minutes," she said. "Depending on the traffic."

She started the car and pulled away from the kerb.

"Mummy says not to talk to strangers," said Mattie.

"I'm not a stranger," said the woman.

"Not really. I know someone your mummy knows. I know him even better than your mummy knows him. So I'm not a stranger."

When they reached Mattie's home, the woman drove 100 yards past it.

"Can you find your way to the house?" said the woman.

"Yes."

"I'm going away now. You won't see me again and you won't remember where you've been."

"Can I go now?"

"Not yet. I've got a message for your daddy. Tell him that your mummy made a mistake with a man.

"A big mistake. And she said goodbye. Can you remember that?"

"Yes."

"I'm going now. You count to 100. When you've done that, you can go home."

The woman got out of the car and she was gone.

Mattie felt a tear run down her cheek.

A hundred. She wasn't sure if she could count all the way.

3 TRUTHS AND A LIE

Lisa Gardner

Lisa Gardner is a multi-award-winning, internationally bestselling author of crime thrillers, which include *The Killing Hour*, *The Next Accident*, and *Find Her*. She created three series: the FBI Profiler series, books featuring Detective D.D. Warren, and the cases of state police trooper Tessa Leoni. Gardner lives in New Hampshire, USA.

"I don't know if I can do this."

"Really? It's a bunch of fiction writers. I think you've faced tougher opponents."

"Please! Have you read some of these thrillers? Blood and guts every page. Not to mention the keynote speaker's last name is Slaughter. That tells you something."

"You've faced worse."

"I don't know what to say. In their world, detectives only take on serial killers and DNA results are available in a matter of hours. Real-world policing isn't like that."

"Tell them that. Give them the truth."

"Yeah, because I'm going to explain to a bunch of crime addicts who Google things like 'the best way to dispose of a body' everything they're getting wrong in their novels. Try again. You have it easier." She scowled at him. "You get to talk about blood spatter. They're going to love you."

"I am naturally charming. And armed with a graphic crime scene photo. The advantage of having done this before."

D.D. glanced at her watch, scrubbed her palms on her jeans. "Thirty minutes. Thirty minutes till I face forty, fifty—"

"I'd say closer to a hundred."

"—rabid thriller writers. What am I going to say?"

Alex leaned over, kissed her cheek as they stood in line at the coffee bar. "I'm sure you'll think of something."

Then Alex's coffee order was called. And he left her to fend for herself.

"Writers' Police Academy," Boston detective D. D. Warren was muttering fifteen minutes later, coffee in one hand, map of the technical college in the other. "What kind of writers even want to go to a police academy? For the love of God, even cops can't wait to get out." She paused in front of the building that housed the lecture series. This "vacation" had been Alex's idea. Fly out to Wisconsin, of all places, and spend a weekend hanging out with hundreds of thriller writers talking shop. He'd been roped into it years ago by a forensic buddy, who swore it really was fun. Discuss latent prints, blood spatter, and favorite crime scenes with a bunch of aspiring novelists who were not only fascinated by police procedure but determined to get it right. As experts, D.D. and Alex got to attend for free. And as long as they were there, they could also attend some of the more interesting activities.

For example, the yearly Writers' Police Academy not only offered hourly lectures on things such as ballistics 101 but also partnered with the local sheriff's department to provide hands-on workshops: SWAT team training. Evasive driving techniques. Underwater evidence recovery. Alex had brought his wet suit. Personally, D.D. was looking forward to playing on the SWAT team's training course later in the afternoon.

But first she had to survive the morning. Where she got to play the part of the so-called expert, providing day-to-day details of a homicide detective's life. Which, in fact, was not nearly as interesting as most people/writers thought. D.D. read thrillers on occasion—when she had time to read. She enjoyed a good twisty plot. And if fictional detectives spent all their time playing cat-and-mouse with serial killers, all the better for leaving the real cares of her job behind.

Today, however, her job was to provide the truth, the whole truth, and nothing but the truth. She just hoped she didn't bore her students to death.

D.D. walked through glass doors, instantly replacing the hot August sun with frigid institutional temperatures. She'd forgotten this from her own academy days: the tendency to keep classrooms arctic, most likely to keep the occupants awake.

One flight of stairs, a turn here, a turn there, and she arrived at her designated classroom. Outside the sign read: *Boston Detective D. D. Warren's Insider's Guide to Policing.* Within, true to Alex's prediction, easily a hundred people waited, some having arrived early enough to snatch seats, the rest standing valiantly in any available space. Meaning she really had better open strong, or bit by bit, the standing ones would wander out again.

"What am I going to say?"

D.D. smiled bravely, clutched her coffee tighter, and headed for the front of the room. Along the way, she passed a petite blonde whose hairstyle D.D. wouldn't mind trying out for herself—the keynote speaker, Karin Slaughter, whose thrillers did live up to her name. And sitting next to her, a forensic anthropologist, Kathy Reichs, who already wrote things about decomp D.D. never wanted to know. Because a Writer's Police Academy had to offer more than just cops bursting everyone's bubbles, but also a few *New York Times* bestselling authors who already knew how to get the fictional job done.

"Insider's guide to policing," D.D. muttered under her breath. "Not going to work, not going to work, not going to work."

She made it to the front. Set down her coffee. Her bag. Eyed a whiteboard designed for her to write out scintillating details of a detective's job. Turn in your paperwork. Never piss off your boss. *Definitely* turn in your paperwork.

She turned, faced the room.

Yep, at least a hundred faces, all armed with iPads and laptops for note taking. Bestselling authors, new writers, every single one of them obsessed with crime and determined to get it right. What had Alex told her about his presentation last year? The bloodier his slides, the happier his audience.

D.D. took a deep breath. An insider's guide to policing was never going to cut it.

She opened her mouth, heard herself say: "I'm going to share with you today the strangest case I ever worked. It involves a seedy motel, a hooker, and a dismembered leg. What do you think?"

The people standing in the back quietly put down their bags, settled in against the wall.

"All right. Let's begin."

"So you know that game, three truths and a lie? Most of the details of what I'm going to tell you will be the truth. One will be a lie. Since most of you like to write about detectives, this will be your chance to play one. First person to identify the lie will get a special prize."

Hand in the back. Male, six foot four, brown mop top, thick glasses. "What's the prize?" he asked.

"You'll have to win to find out."

Collective groan.

"Hey, aren't you people supposed to be fans of suspense?"

D.D. took a sip of coffee. Collected her thoughts. "All right. Here's a bit of policing one-oh-one. A crime starts with a call—say, to nine-one-one, maybe even a direct complaint to the department. Either way, uniformed patrol officers are the first responders. In this case, the night manager of the Best Getaway hotel in Boston contacted nine-one-one demanding an ambulance. Dispatch tried to get more information, but the man was too busy vomiting to answer questions. So the operator summoned emergency services as well as the first available officer. In this case, a rookie patrolman, Justin, three days on the job, got to be the one to find the body.

"You know what homicide detectives hate? What really, truly gets on our nerves?" D.D. gazed around the room. One by one, her audience members dutifully shook their heads. "First responders who trash our crime scenes. Don't get me wrong. We respect EMTs. Of course we respect EMTs. But have you ever seen what they can do to a crime scene? Trampling across fields of evidence with backboards. Kneeling in blood spatter to check vitals, start CPR. Tossing aside packaging from bandages, gauze, life-saving injections. Hey, I'm not completely petty; I understand trying to save someone's life comes first. The tricky part is that my job begins when, by definition, the EMTs' efforts have failed. Except, of course, now my job is that much more difficult."

Her audience nodded.

"But in this case, the rookie patrolman, Justin, saved me and my team a great deal of grief. He peered inside the motel room, noted the carnage, and, not being an idiot, called *off* the ambulance, as it wasn't going to matter. Justin secured the scene, then notified dispatch to contact my unit instead. Job well done.

"Boston homicide works as three-people squads. I'm a sergeant detective, meaning I'm the so-called leader of my squad, though my teammates, Phil and Neil, would love to argue. Each squad takes a turn being on call. That Saturday night, we were the lucky squad to be summoned at two A.M. to a sleazy motel in downtown Boston where the rooms rent by the hour.

"Now, policing is a matter of playing the odds. Hourly-rate hotel in that area of Boston, I'm already thinking drug overdose, or maybe pimp versus hooker or dealer versus dealer. These things happen. So I wasn't totally shocked to walk into a bloody hotel room and discover the body of a naked man on the floor. What caught me off guard was that the body had been partially dismembered— the right leg hacked off just above the knee.

"Which had then been left behind in the room's bathtub."

"All right." D.D. made her voice brisk. "You guys are the aspiring crime aficionados. Picture yourself as a homicide detective walking into a crime scene. What's the first thing you do?"

Hands shot in the air. She went with a middle-aged woman in the back, who stated immediately: "Secure the perimeter."

"Partial credit," D.D. granted. "In theory, the first responder establishes the perimeter. But screw the perimeter, screw the investigation, which is why I feel a need to at least check things out when I first appear. In this case, our rookie officer Justin had been paying attention during training. He hadn't just cordoned off the room, but most of the parking lot. Aggressive? Maybe. But our DG— dead guy—had to get into the motel room somehow, right? So best to protect all entrances and exits from contamination. Next?"

"Establish a murder log," someone called out.

"Wow, you guys do watch a lot of TV. Partial credit again. Generally, a uniformed patrol officer or district detective will take this job, stationing themselves just inside of the crime scene tape and recording every person who crosses the line into the so-called murder book. Basically, upon arrival, every working officer, myself included, must supply a badge number for the log. You know why?"

"Locard's principle."

D.D. squinted the respondent in the front row. Attractive male, nice jacket, short wavy brown hair. She thought she recognized him as one of the speakers, Joe Finder, known for his clever thrillers.

"Show-off," she informed him. He grinned.

"Joe, here, is being technical about things. But yes, Locard's principle holds that everyone who enters a crime scene will transfer something to that scene— hair, fiber, fingerprints, you name it. It's the basic tenet behind forensic science: By working the scene, forensic experts can identify these transfer elements and then smart detectives like me can use that information to catch the bad guy. Of course, that same principle applies to even the good guys. Sure, we don gloves and, in the case of a really bloody scene, maybe hair caps and foot booties. But that doesn't mean we won't inevitably leave something behind. So the murder log has two functions. One, to help forensics sort out our footprints, maybe even a really stupid officer's fingerprint, from the relevant evidence gathered at the scene. Also, for legal reasons, you need a record of everyone at the scene. Now, here's a question, the rookie officer, having answered his first homicide call, having done a great job of setting up his first perimeter, then snaps a photo to show off to his buddies. One of the perks of the job, or do I now seize his phone?"

"Seize the phone," the room agreed.

"What about the leg?" someone else called out.

"You, sir, are bloodthirsty. The rest of the room gets extra credit. No personal photos of the scene. Any prosecutor will tell you cell phone photos, selfies, whatever, are the bane of their existence. Any photo of the scene is evidence, and all evidence is subject to discovery—meaning it must be turned over to the defense upon request. Rookie officer takes a photo, rookie officer never tells, so the defense never gets a chance to view it, and six months after trial, when the officer shares it to the wrong person at a bar, the defense lawyer now has grounds to overturn the conviction. Definitely no personal photos at the scene. So. I believe our DG is still missing a leg."

D.D. stopped. Took a sip of her coffee. Contemplated her audience. They were leaning forward eagerly. Alex had pegged them correctly. Thriller writers had a thing for gore.

"This is what a homicide detective really does upon entering a scene: prioritize. I have a motel room with a dead body that needs to be analyzed by both the crime scene techs as well as my squad. I have an entire building full of possible witnesses, most of whom will deny everything, but I gotta ask. In this day and age, there's also video somewhere, which, sooner versus later, I want to pull. Lots of things to do, very little time to do it. So, I need to prioritize objectives, then devise strategy.

"In this case, I assigned patrol officers to go door-to-door for witnesses. Who heard what. If there's something of interest, the patrol officer will summon one of my detectives to conduct the actual questioning. In the meantime, I assign my squad mate Phil to meet with the night manager, drill him on what he knows about who checked into this room, and, oh yes, grab any and all video he can. Phil has a way with people, so even without a warrant, I'm sure he'll get the job done.

"That leaves me and my other partner, Neil, to work the room. Two detectives in a space this small are more than enough. Understand I already have crime scene techs everywhere, not to mention a photographer. Too many of us in the room and no one can get anything done. I've also held off the ME. Guy's dead, not going anyplace; the ME can remove the body, and the leg, when we're done. This is crime scene management. And frankly, it's one of the most important parts of my job. Just as with securing the perimeter, screw the management, screw the investigation. I'm not going to mess up my own investigation. Which brings us to . . .

"The leg."

D.D. paused, took another sip of coffee.

"No, see, of course you want the leg. I wanted to stare at the leg; Neil, a former EMT, definitely wanted to stare at the leg. But in my job, just like your novels, you can't skip ahead in the story. Leg is in the bathtub. Body's in front of the door. Meaning first, we gotta deal with the body.

"All right. Basic info. I judged the deceased to be a midfifties male, thinning brown hair, a little paunchy around the middle but decent muscle tone. No, I'm not ogling the dead. I'm trying to figure out who this guy is. Identify the victim. One of the first steps in my investigation. There's also a bunch of things I don't see—for example, needle marks. No way this guy is using. For lack of a better word, he's too healthy. He also has buffed nails, which indicates a level of income I don't expect at an hourly motel. Guy is facedown, and we won't roll him till the last minute. I can make out traces of blood around his neck and shoulders, but for now, the most obvious wound on him is the severed limb—right leg, amputated above the knee.

"Now, here's where things get interesting. For one thing, there's a tourniquet above the knee. And it appears to be a silk tie. My partner Neil does the honors of walking to the foot of the bed, where we can see a pile of clothes in plain sight. The stack includes a neatly folded pair of black slacks and a blue dress shirt. Neil reads off the labels. His best guess, he's looking at a thousand-dollar ensemble. And yeah, the tie is missing.

"I know what you guys want me to do. My husband, Alex Wilson, is a blood spatter expert. He warned me all about you. You want the leg. You're obsessed with the leg. Follow the blood trail back to the bathroom and the severed limb. Because, definitely, if you were writing this scene, some depraved psycho whacked off this guy's leg, then left him to bleed out, at which point our DG—maybe a CIA operative, or corporate informant—valiantly tied off his own bleeding stump and crawled through a trail of his own blood, only to expire right in front of the door, inches from getting help.

"We don't follow the blood trail. Sorry. But this is real-world policing, so I'm stuck with telling you the truth. Instead, we search the man's clothes, then the bed, then the nightstand next to the bed. ID, people. Wallet, cell phone, car keys. We want to know who DG is."

D.D. rolled her eyes, took another sip of coffee. Her audience was disappointed. They really did want the severed limb.

"Fine, you win. I'll speed up. No wallet, no cell phone, no keys. So in addition to our DG being dismembered, we also assume he was robbed. And given the way the clothes are folded neatly on the bed, I already have some theories on that subject. But we'll return to that. Because now, what you've all been waiting for. We follow the blood trail down the grimy carpet. We peer inside the tiny, freezing-cold, misty bathroom, where not one but two cockroaches are already making tracks through the blood.

"And we behold the severed leg. Packed in dry ice, in a plastic-lined tub."

Hand in the air. Mop top from the back.

"Yes," D.D. called on him.

"Dry ice is the lie. I mean, who hacks off a limb and places it in dry ice?"

"Better yet, who brings dry ice to a squalid motel?" D.D. commented, then shook her head. "No, dry ice is not the lie, but I'll be the first to admit, an unusual element at a crime scene. In addition to the dry ice, we found rubber gloves—blood-soaked—and a hacksaw—also blood-spattered—on the floor next to the toilet. In the sink, we discovered several round green pills. Being a savvy detective, my partner Neil ran the number stamped on the pills through the drug ID website and determined they were OxyContin."

Fresh hand in the front.

"Yes."

"The drugs are a lie. Who brings painkillers to a dismemberment?"

"Great question. Who indeed? The pills are not a lie, but a clue. Given the lack of a prescription bottle, most likely they're illegal, a street buy, and, finally, something I would expect to find in this type of motel. Meaning maybe this is why our rich DG ended up in this place—for the narcotics."

"Dry ice and painkillers," someone commented from the back. "Hey, wait a minute—"

"No, no, no," D.D. interrupted. "No skipping ahead. A crime scene is like a novel. One thing at a time here. So by this stage, my partner Phil is back from meeting with the night manager. He has the name DG used to rent the room: George Clooney. We went out on a limb and agreed this was an alias. Man paid cash, of course. And yes, there's a video camera for the parking lot, which the night manager let Phil watch. Unfortunately, all Phil can see is the back of a man, carrying an enormous duffel bag, walking down to the room, then unlocking the door. DG definitely has two legs at this point, and appears to be a well-dressed gentleman, maybe a business executive. But that's about all Phil can tell.

"At this stage, Phil and I exit the motel room to allow the ME to move in. I leave Neil behind, because, being a former EMT, he likes to conduct his own study of the body.

"Neil gets the body. Phil and I fan out around the parking lot to see if we can find DG's vehicle, which would hopefully include registration information with his name. But we strike out. If DG drove, he didn't park out front. I get the bright idea to have a patrol officer canvass the nearby area and shoot photos of the license plates. We can check back in twenty-four hours and see which vehicles have never moved—maybe one of them belongs to the deceased.

"Now, we reach a lull in our investigative efforts. We have an unidentified DG missing a limb. Yeah, we have some leads. Dry ice for one. Can't be that many places where you can buy it. We can visit the nearest distributors, see if one of them can identify our DG, but that'll have to wait till morning business hours and I don't want to wait. I'm a homicide detective. I need leads I can pursue now, because every single hour that goes by decreases the odds of me solving the case."

"What about the duffel bag?" a woman toward the back spoke up. "You said the video shows the man carrying a duffel bag, but you never mentioned it in the room."

"Ah, give that woman a prize. Where is the duffel bag, because it's not in the room. It's missing, much like that man's wallet."

D.D. paused, let her audience think it out.

"Phil has to watch more of the security tape," someone called out. "Someone must've arrived after the man."

"Phil is not an idiot. Phil watched the rest of the tape. No one arrived after our DG."

Karin Slaughter did the honors. "Then the person arrived before. The second person was already waiting for the man. It's not who entered the room after the dead guy. It's who exited."

"And we're back to partial credit. Upon further investigation, turns out the security video is a digital loop. Records over itself every two hours. So it's possible someone arrived before our DG and the security camera had already recorded over it. Your theory is correct: Most likely, our mysterious second person arrived before the deceased."

"Then exited after the murder," someone else in the room prodded.

D.D. shrugged. "You would think so, except here is where things get complicated: On video, we can watch the complete sequence of the DG entering the room with duffel bag, to night manager appearing, then barfing, to rookie officer taking control of the scene. In that entire span, no second person magically exits the room."

"That's not possible." A man in the back of the room.

"Fair enough. No one exited out the front. But the motel room has a rear window. Small. Certainly nothing a grown man could fit through. But when Phil and I reenter the room to address this issue, we discover the window unlocked and slightly ajar. As if, yes, someone had recently opened it. Which is right about the same time that Neil discovers the glitter."

"What do we know at this point? Sometimes in an active investigation, you need to stop, back up, take stock. We have a presumably wealthy DG discovered on the floor of an hourly-rate strip motel. We know he arrived alone, on foot, with a duffel bag. Once inside the room, the man removed his clothes. Given how neatly they're folded, I'm guessing he did it willingly. We know the man had illegally obtained drugs. He wouldn't be the first successful type to develop on addiction to prescription narcotics, so maybe he's an addict. We know something definitely went wrong that resulted in the man's leg being sawed off and stuck in a bathtub. At which point he made a valiant attempt to save his own life by fashioning a tourniquet? This series of events is murky for me. But we definitely know his duffel bag, wallet, personal possessions—say, cell phone and/or keys—are all missing. And now, thanks to Neil, we know the silk tie used to fashion the tourniquet is streaked not with just blood but silver glitter."

"That's the lie." Fresh voice from the front. "If the tie is soaked in blood, how can you see the glitter?"

"Glitter is sparkly. Blood isn't. Now, I'm not an expert in trace evidence. The forensics value of glitter is beyond me. What I do know is there's no obvious *source* of silver glitter in the rest of the motel room. Meaning . . ."

"Locard's principle." Finder again.

"Exactly. The glitter must have come from our perpetrator. Who then exited out of a very small rear window, with the DG's personal possessions in tow. A theory that gains even more credence when we find traces of blood and glitter on the windowsill. Come on, people, tell me what I need to know."

"The hooker," half of the room volunteered.

D.D. nodded her approval. "Told you. This is a story involving a seedy motel, a hooker, and a dismembered leg. And now, it's time to identify our first person of interest, the hooker."

"First thing we do is call the district detectives. In most urban police departments, you have a vice unit, which covers such crimes as prostitution. In Boston, however, 'morality' offenses are handled by the various district offices. Basically, the local detectives. Given that working girls, much like cops, stick to certain beats, all we have to do is provide the address of the motel and we receive a couple of names in a matter of minutes. Now we're off and running again. Phil and I leave Neil with the body, and hit the streets.

"We locate the first potential girl, Sasha, almost immediately, working two blocks from the motel, and pissed that the police presence is scaring off her business. She's too composed to be who we're looking for. Instead, in the interest of getting rid of the patrol cars sooner versus later, she agrees to tell us where several of the girls hole up. There's an apartment building not far away. Falling apart, rotten plumbing, and even shittier management, we're told, but that's where most of the girls live.

"Phil and I head over. We start going door-to-door, knocking, banging, and getting nowhere. Till the third floor. When we come upon a door with blood on the knob.

"We identify ourselves. We order the occupant to open up.

"Then, when nothing happens, Phil races downstairs to wake the manager. Now technically speaking, a landlord doesn't have the authority to grant police access to an apartment without the tenant's permission—that would violate the tenant's expectation of privacy, otherwise known as the Fourth Amendment. But the blood on the doorknob combined with the fact no one is answering our calls works in our favor, providing something called exigent circumstances. We can argue that the blood trail plus lack of response gave us reason to believe the safety of the person inside was at imminent risk, so of course we had to access the apartment. It wasn't for our sake; it was for the occupant's. Honest! Trust me when I say the building manager isn't going to argue with us. And as long as we can make a reasonable argument before a judge . . .

"Manager unlocks the door, mutters about having to clean up blood . . . again . . . then disappears back down the hall. Whatever is going to happen next, he doesn't want to know. Phil assumes the lead, I take his back, and we get down to business.

"First thing we spot upon entering is a black duffel sitting near the door. After that, the dank, one-bedroom appears empty. Neither of us, however, are buying it. Inch by inch, we scour the unit. Sure enough, fifteen minutes later we discover Harmony LaFab, as she's called, hiding under her bed. I do the honors of grabbing her ankle and dragging her out.

"Harmony turns out to be five foot nothing, rail thin, with more poufy blond hair than bones in her body and, yes, arms streaked with blood. She's definitely who we've been looking for.

"Now this is the crazy part: I don't even get a chance to read her her rights before she starts talking.

"'It's not what you think, it's not what you think, it's not what you think,' she babbles immediately.

"'It never is,' I assure her, reaching for my cuffs.

"'But I didn't do nothing. Just brought the Oxy. The leg . . . He did it himself. Swear to God. Fool idiot chewed up a bunch of Oxy, then sawed his own damn leg off!'"

"Back to our game. Three truths and a lie. How are we doing?"

"She's lying," a woman to the left spoke up immediately. "She's covered in blood, has the victim's possessions. Of course she's lying."

"It's a good theory," D.D. agreed. "Certainly, it wouldn't be the first time I've had an obvious murder suspect who still felt a need to deny, deny, deny. Most of the stories I get from suspects, witnesses, even the victim's supposed loved ones, involve at least some lies. But in my experience, it's always a mistake to rush to judgment. Even when dealing with a blood-soaked suspect, first thing a good detective does is listen.

"This is the story we get from Harmony LaFab: The night manager of the seedy motel has a side gig. He sells illegal drugs. Also, he sets up business for the local girls for a fee. Harmony's evening starts with a call from the manager. He has a customer who wants Oxy, plus some companionship. Manager—let's call him Shaggy—told his customer to return in two hours. During this window, Harmony is put in charge of the drugs and goes to the room—allowing enough time to pass to delete her presence from the security video. Eliminating questions for both her and the night manager, right?

"According to Harmony, when our DG first enters, she's a little surprised. Not by the nice clothes—her clientele runs the gamut—but that the guy is beaming. He seems both extremely happy and a bit nervous. The prospect of drugs, sex, who knows, but in Harmony's line of work, very few people are as up as this guy.

"He sets down the duffel bag, then he starts talking. It's the strangest proposition Harmony has ever heard—and trust me when I say a woman in her line of work gets a lot of unusual propositions. First, he wants to see the Oxy. He wants to know the dose, which he then proceeds to look up on his phone. Apparently, far from being an addict, he claims he doesn't have much experience. He'd like to know her professional opinion on how many he should take to effectively dull the worst of the pain but remain conscious.

"Conscious for what, Harmony wants to know.

"DG opens the black duffel bag to reveal a small cooler of dry ice, rubber gloves, a knife, a hacksaw, and a hammer. Harmony starts to freak out. Oh no, oh no, oh no, the guy rushes to assure her. This has nothing to do with her. It's all for him. The whole evening, the Oxy, the setup, it's about his leg. It doesn't belong to him. It never has. From the time he was a toddler, he knew his leg was alien. He's tried to adapt, he assured her. To convince himself, even if he couldn't love it, he should accept it, pretend it was a prosthetic or maybe a plastic leg. He even saw a therapist for a while. But nothing has worked. And he just can't keep living with an alien anymore. The leg must come off. It's time.

"He'll do the hard part. He just needs a little help from her. And in return, he'll pay her five thousand dollars. For one night's work. Deal?

"Harmony doesn't know what to say. She's still pretty confused. Then there's not really time for talking. The man is already in motion. First, he downs three Oxy with a handful of water from the sink. He's worried it'll either be too much or not enough, so he says he must move quickly. He lines the tub with a trash bag, then, donning the rubber gloves, dumps in the dry ice. He's very polite, according to Harmony. Warns her not to touch the dry ice with her bare hands. It freezes at a temperature even lower than regular ice and can cause instant frostbite.

"He positions his tools in the bathtub. Then he comes back out to the main room and carefully removes all his clothing. This is it, Harmony figures. Man'll want a quickie, some sort of last hurrah with both legs intact before he completes his journey to the land of completely crazy.

"But no, he piles his clothes neatly. Carries his phone back to the bathroom and sets it on the toilet seat. Then he comes back and picks up the tie. He's getting a little bit sloppy now, his eyelids heavy as the Oxy starts to kick in, but if anything that seems to make him more determined.

"This is what he's going to do, he explains to Harmony: He's going to fashion a tourniquet with the tie above his right knee to eliminate blood flow to his lower leg. Then, he's going to position himself on the edge of the bathtub, which, having seen green slime rimming the tub, Harmony already knows is the action of a desperate man. He's going to place his lower leg in the bath of dry ice.

"This will hurt, he tells her. Even with the Oxy in his system, it will be excruciating. In fact, maybe he should take another right now. Just to be safe. Because he's got to do it. It's very important. The limb must freeze.

"Because as painful as the dry ice will be, it's nothing compared to how it will feel if he saws through his leg unfrozen.

"Harmony doesn't know what to do. For one thing, she's still not sure she believes him. Who cuts off their own leg? Who goes through life thinking their own limb is an alien? But as she watches, the man calmly wraps his silk tie above his knee and pulls it so tight, she can watch his thigh turn red, while below the knee, his lower leg slowly but surely goes white.

"'Perfect,' the man declares.

"Now, in order for her to earn the five thousand dollars, this is what he needs. He'll do the hard part, don't worry. But . . . this is going to be difficult. He's studied it, researched it, planned it. And based on everything he's read, as much as he wants his own leg gone, the process is agonizing and it's going to come down to a matter of will.

"He'd like her to hold his hand. Perhaps dole out more painkillers, in case he needs them. He'd really appreciate it. For the record, he doesn't want to die. He just wants the leg gone. He's willing to do the amputation part himself, but based on what he's read, he might pass out. It's a distinct possibility. At which time, he needs her to call nine-one-one for him. He has it all programmed in his phone, ready to go. She just needs to hit the button.

"Now here's the catch. When the EMTs arrive, they won't just load him on the stretcher, they'll take his leg, too. Medical protocol. Save the limb to be re-attached. And because the limb will just be frozen, maybe some crack surgeon will be able to sew it back on while the man's unconscious and can't protest.

"Basically, he needs her to take the hammer to the leg. Given its frozen state, it should shatter easily. At least according to what he's read online. So if she could please deliver a couple of good whacks to the offensive body part, that should do it. He'll finally be free.

"Harmony doesn't know what to think. Harmony doesn't know what to say. While she's sitting there, still trying to sort this out in her mind, the man reaches inside the duffel bag and withdraws a stack of cash. Thousand dollars, he tells her. A show of good faith. When he gets out of the hospital, he'll bring her the other four. He's good for it. And frankly, it's a small price to pay to finally feel whole.

"Harmony's pretty sure the guy is nuts. But cash is cash, and no one, not the night manager, not anyone, knows about this money, which makes it even better. The beginnings of a nest egg, maybe even a way out if the idiot actually lives. He seems just crazy enough to be that lucky.

"He gives her the money. Then he limps his way to the bathroom, and positions himself on the edge of the tub. He picks up one of the threadbare wash-cloths, folds it three times—a makeshift gag to keep himself from screaming, he informs her. Can't have the cops, or the ambulance, arriving too soon.

"A final check of tools. Butcher knife, saw, hammer, all within reach. Should he take another Oxy, now that the moment is here? Except he's already feeling loopy, and this will require a steady hand. Plus, he's afraid if he takes too much, not being an experienced user, he'll vomit them back up again. So the four he's already taken will have to do.

"He wants the amputation as clean as possible, he informs her. It will make for a better fit for the prosthetic.

"Harmony doesn't talk. Doesn't say a word. She's got a thousand in cash clutched in her fist as the guy uses both hands to lift his right leg, swing it over the edge of the tub, and dump it in the dry ice.

"It hurts. She can tell immediately. His teeth dig into the washcloth, the cords stand out on his neck. She's sure he's screaming, though no sound comes out. But he doesn't pull his leg out. If anything, he plunges it deeper into the tub, all the way up to his twisted tie.

"It felt cool against her cheeks, that's mostly what she remembers. The ice in the bathtub was smoking, but it felt cool against her cheeks.

"The man thrashes his head, beats it against the walls. At first she thinks this is it, he's having some kind of fit, game over. But apparently, it's just his way of riding through the pain, because next thing she knows, he has the butcher knife in his hands.

"He removes the gag, stares at her wild eyed. 'Hit me. Hit the leg,' he orders her. 'Hard!'

"She does, jabbing a patch of exposed shin with her nail.

"'I don't feel it!' He's excited. 'Try the hammer next.'

"She picks it up, gives the lower limb an experimental tap. Nothing. Crazy guy is a happy camper. He sticks the washcloth back in his mouth, picks up the knife instead.

"Harmony is less certain about this part. Apparently, she's not very good with blood. What she knows is that the second he slices into his thigh, there's blood, skin, and *meat*. Definitely meat. She starts freaking out, already backing up, but the guy keeps on cutting. Deeper and deeper. It's like a traffic accident, she tells us. She can't bear to watch, and yet she can't look away.

"Except all of a sudden, it's too much. And not just for her but for him, as well. He drops the knife, groaning, shaking uncontrollably.

"'I can't, I can't. No, oh no.' It's like the guy is possessed. He wants to cut himself, but he can't cut himself, and now he's pissed off.

"'Smash the leg, smash the leg,' he starts yelling at her, while at the same time he attempts to hit nine-one-one on his phone. 'You can still damage it enough. Come on!'

"But Harmony can't take it anymore. She bolts back into the bedroom, hammer in one hand, cash in the other. She just wants out of here. Right as she hits the door, it occurs to her the video cameras will see her. And given all the blood and madness going on in the bathroom, no way does she want to be tied to this scene. Then she spies the window.

"Harmony is a woman with survival instincts. It only takes her an instant to toss everything in the nearby duffel bag. Then, with both hands free, she pops open the window, tosses out the duffel bag, and shimmies through after it. Thirty seconds later, she's bolting down the street.

"What about her client? We demand to know.

"She assumed an ambulance was already on its way for him.

"And his wallet, his cell phone?"

"She frowns at us, shakes her head. She doesn't have any wallet or cell phone. She has the black duffel bag. Take it, now. Money, too. Take it all. Hell, she never wants to think about that room again. Then, at the last second, she catches herself. And the guy? Did the EMTs get there in time?

"I study her for a while. Guy didn't make it, I inform her. He finished the job, got his leg off. But he must've never completed his call to emergency services because he ended up bleeding out trying to crawl to the door for help.

"Harmony appears puzzled. That doesn't make any sense. She knows he reached nine-one-one. She heard the female operator talking to him. Plus, the man had already thrown the knife to the side. When she shimmied through the window, the guy wasn't trying to hack off his leg anymore. He was fighting to live."

"All right." D.D. surveyed her audience. "Your turn to play detective. If you were me, what would you do next?"

Hands shot in the air. She picked several at random.

"Trace the nine-one-one call" was the first offering.

"Good idea, except you know how many calls are generated per hour in a city the size of Boston? We can get a recording of the call, but that'll take time. Other ideas."

"Arrest the hooker."

"Follow up with the motel manager."

"Return to the scene and find the guy's car so you have his identity."

"Hey, can't you trace his prints?"

D.D. held up a quieting hand. "Actually, the first thing we did was take custody of the black duffel bag. And we did book Harmony LaFab, basically for distributing illegal drugs, to which she'd willingly confessed. Did I think she'd killed the guy? Honestly, I doubted she had the strength, let alone mental fortitude, to hack off anyone's leg. At the same time, however, she was our best lead, and we didn't want her to go anywhere. So we called for a patrol officer to give Miss LaFab a one-way trip to the district office, and then we searched the duffel bag.

"Which turned out to have a name scrawled in black Sharpie on the inside label. Steven Wrobleski. We ran the name through the system, got an address, then Phil and I went for a ride.

"Wrobleski lived out in the burbs, Lexington to be exact. For those of you who don't know Boston, Lexington is a nice town. Kind of place with grand old colonials, white picket fences, a historical town green. Basically, the address fit the suit, which was our first hint we were on the right track.

"Next up was the fact that when we pulled up at four thirty in the morning, the lights were on. We didn't even have to knock before the door opened and a woman appeared. Fifty years of age, expensive hair, even more expensive lounge-wear. The kind of well-kept woman who spends her days doing a lot of yoga and not much else. She took one look at us and said, 'Are you here about my husband? Is Steven okay? Because I've been calling his cell phone for hours now and he won't answer. He always answers. Oh my God, what happened?'

"This is the hard part of the job. Dealing with distraught loved ones. You think it will get easier. It doesn't. And while it's understandable that this woman has questions, that they all have questions, the bottom line is, you're not there to answer their queries. You're there to answer your own.

"We requested to come inside. I escorted the woman into her own kitchen, had her take a seat at the table. Phil, who's a pro at this, went to work making coffee. You don't ask, you just do. Take charge. Which, most of the time, starts to calm people down.

"The woman's name was Eve, and yes, she was Steven's wife. She produced a picture, which resembled our DG. Best she knew, her husband, a partner at a Boston consulting firm, had been staying late to work. But when he still hadn't returned home by midnight, she'd grown concerned. She'd called his cell phone numerous times without receiving an answer. According to her, that was extremely unusual. Steven was responsible and, even when working late, checked in. She'd got an increasingly bad feeling about things. For the past few hours, she'd simply been waiting for either the phone to finally ring or the cops to show up at her door. Then, she looked right at me. 'It was his leg, wasn't it?' she said. 'He finally went and did something awful to that damn leg.'

"Who in this room has heard about BIID?" D.D. looked around.

Older gentleman to the left. "Body integrity identity disorder. Basically, it's people who want to amputate their own limbs."

The room stirred.

"No way!"

"Crazy."

"That's gotta be the lie."

"No lie," D.D. assured them.

"It's real," the man seconded. "I used it in a book."

"Of course you did. The syndrome is rare, but it's genuine. For whatever reason, a person feels part of them isn't real. Maybe a hand, or a foot, or a leg, or even both legs. Some experts consider it a psychological disorder, maybe brought on by trauma. Others are moving more toward a neurological disorder. Kind of the reverse of phantom limb pain. Except, instead of feeling sensation in a limb that's no longer there, sufferers of BIID can't relate to a limb that is present.

"According to Eve, her husband claimed that for as long as he had memory, he was convinced his right leg wasn't his own. When he was a little kid, he thought it might be robotic. Then, for a bit, he worried it was some kind of alien transplant. But he hated it. Wished it to be gone, to such a degree he would only take pictures from the waist up. Even on their wedding day. Because if his leg was in the photo, then it wasn't a picture of him.

"She worried about him, of course, urged him to seek help. As a counselor who specializes in substance abuse, she did some outreach and found him a therapist. For a while, that appeared to be working. He didn't talk about the leg as much, seemed more upbeat. For the record, he was a great husband, successful, smart, considerate. He didn't drink. He didn't do drugs. He just had this one thing: He hated his own leg.

"And tonight, when he didn't answer his phone, and hour turned into hour without him returning home, it had come to her: why he no longer talked about the leg so much. Not because his condition didn't still bother him, but because he'd finally decided to do something about it."

"Suicide high," someone in the room murmured.

D.D. nodded her head. "People with a history of depression often appear happiest right before they commit suicide. Not because their depression has passed, but because they've finally chosen a course of action.

"With Eve's permission, Phil took a look at the computer in Steven's home office. And sure enough, he found in the browser history a chat room devoted to sufferers of BIID. Topics included self-amputation, the recommended method being to tie off the body part with a tourniquet, then submerge it in dry ice. And yeah, it'll take some massive painkillers to see it through, but if you can keep the limb in the dry ice long enough, you can damage it to the point a surgeon will have no choice but to remove it for you. Because reputable doctors won't remove a healthy limb, even if you claim it doesn't belong to you."

"So the DG killed himself?" someone called out. "Because of a psychological disorder?"

D.D. regarded the room. "What do you think? Did the DG kill himself?"

"Where's his wallet, where's his phone?" a woman to her right asked immediately.

"Exactly, where is his wallet, where is his phone? Because we've already searched Harmony LaFab's place. She had his duffel bag and his cash. But no wallet, no phone. And what about her claims of him reaching nine-one-one? Because Eve agrees with Harmony. Sufferers of BIID don't want to die. They just want to get rid of the offending body part. So what exactly went down in that motel room?

"Which is why Phil and I left the victim's wife and returned to the night manager."

"All right." D.D. polished off her coffee, set it aside. She glanced at the clock on the rear wall. Fifteen minutes left, which was about right. "Know how I mentioned a big part of a detective's job is crime scene management? Screw up working the scene, screw up the investigation? Now, welcome to the second half of the job, except this part is more art, less science. Suspect interrogation. This is where a good detective truly earns her paycheck.

"Our first person of interest was Harmony LaFab. Hardly had to work for that one. A traumatized, strung-out prostitute, she *needed* to tell us her story. Our job was simply to listen—though trust me when I tell you some detectives would've still ruined the moment, feeling a need to talk over the witness. Doing less is often doing more, which was the best strategy with Harmony LaFab.

"Now, however, we're returning to the motel night manager, Shaggy. Phil had already talked to the man once, getting permission to watch the video footage. According to Phil, Shaggy, whose real name involves more vowels than consonants, is a stringy, midthirties Eastern European male, most likely raised in a country where cops are the enemies and your best shot at getting ahead involves selling out your own mom. In other words, Shaggy won't be volunteering anything for our benefit. This is going to take work.

"First off, we want to be as prepared as possible. So while I drove, Phil called our other squad mate, Neil, to get the latest on COD—cause of death. The ME wouldn't be making an official ruling for days, but that doesn't mean we can't get some expert guesses to guide our discussion.

"According to Neil, COD appeared to be exsanguination from lower-leg amputation. Now, this is where things get interesting. For one thing, last we'd heard from Harmony LaFab, Wrobleski had started the deed with the butcher knife, but lost heart before ever reaching bone. According to her statement, when she fled the scene he'd already tossed aside the knife and was begging nine-one-one to save him.

"But the leg definitely ended up severed. Furthermore, Neil discovered scratch marks on the bone consistent with the teeth of the bloody hacksaw recovered from the scene. Meaning someone—Wrobleski? our mysterious wallet thief?—finished the job at hand. And to add even more insult to injury, at some point in the leg-removal process, the tourniquet was loosened. For those of you trained in first aid, a proper tourniquet needs to be twisted tightly—you can use, say, a pencil or a stick to twist the knot tight enough to cut off blood flow, then tie it off. In Wrobleski's case, he'd definitely need to pinch off the major arteries in the leg before hacking away at his lower extremity.

"Instead, Neil found only a knotted silk tie serving as the tourniquet. Except this didn't make sense to him. What kind of man goes to the trouble to research dry ice, only to botch a basic tourniquet?

"So he went back to the bathroom and searched the floor on his hands and knees. Where Neil discovered, behind the toilet, a bloody plastic pen bearing the name of the consulting firm where Wrobleski worked. Neil's theory: Wrobleski had fashioned a proper tourniquet using the pen to get the necessary torque. But at some point, someone removed the pen, loosening the knot, and leading to catastrophic blood loss. Needless to say, Neil bagged the pen for prints.

"Phil and I don't want to wait for this report. Not to mention, finding a usable print on a bloody pen is a long shot. But that's okay. One of my favorite interrogation strategies is bluffing. And between Harmony's testimony and Neil's theories, we are good to go.

"Arriving back at the motel, we don't waste any time. We discover Shaggy sitting in the back office, clutching a mug of coffee that, based on smell alone, is spiked with way more than cream and sugar. He's sweaty, clearly agitated and trying not to show it. Like a lot of players watching their house of cards go up in smoke, he decides his best defense is a strong offense.

"Right out of the gate, he states his demands: The police officers need to go. Ambulance, ME, everyone. We're hurting his business, we're infringing upon his rights. Take the security footage, bag the bedding, rip up the carpet, remove whatever we want, but get the hell out. Now, now, now!

"We let him talk. True to Phil's assessment, Shaggy's wound a little tight. Overgrown brown hair, thick brow, hollowed-out cheeks. Man's probably not just supplying illegal narcotics but also using. And with all these cops around, he's behind on his nightly fix. Meaning the more we drag things out, the more strung out our new favorite suspect is about to become.

"We ask stupid questions. Why not? We're detectives, we deserve to have some fun. I ask about childhood pets, favorite brand of coffee. What does he think of *Dancing with the Stars*, and are Bostonians the worst drivers in the world, which has been my theory for a while, or are they truly worse in his homeland of Hungary?

"He chugs his coffee. Practically licks the mug to get out the last remnant of vodka. And then, when the mug starts shaking uncontrollably in his hands, we go in for the kill.

"We know what he did. Everything he did. How he set up Wrobleski with illegal narcotics. How he'd arranged to have Harmony already waiting for Wrobleski in the room, Oxy in hand. Except, how could he have anticipated Wrobleski's true fetish? Come on, a guy who wants to amputate a healthy limb?

"Of course Harmony freaked out and fled from the room. Which left Shaggy on the hook. He's got a crazy, mutilated businessman summoning ambulances and cops to his property. For a guy with Shaggy's interests, no way that's going to end well. Which is why when he went to the room and discovered Wrobleski begging nine-one-one for rescue, Shaggy disconnected the call, then loosened the man's tourniquet, letting Wrobleski's own actions take care of the rest. Better for the EMTs to recover a dead body than one able to testify six months later at a criminal trial.

"Shaggy denies everything. Of course he does. With his hands trembling and his eyes darting everywhere, he's all no, no, no. He did nothing, he knows nothing. Whole thing, very unfortunate, very tragic, but not his fault. Definitely not his fault."

D.D. paused, glanced at her audience. "What do you think? We have eight minutes left. Did Shaggy do it?"

"No," half the room called out. The other half remained silent, hedging their bets.

"Why?"

"The video," an elderly woman in the back called out. "If he'd entered the motel room as you described, you would've seen him on the security tape."

"We do have him entering once, then vomiting. Maybe he was very quick to grab the phone, loosen the tourniquet."

"Blood evidence," another person called out. "On his shoes, but also, there'd be a trail from the room to his office."

"Good point. If Shaggy had walked all the way to the bathroom, the soles of his shoes would've been covered in blood. Sure, he could've changed after the fact, but we'd still see bloody footprints leading from the motel room back to his office. Or, maybe realizing that issue, he could've removed his shoes altogether, except, of course, we'd see that on the video tape—a man walking with shoes in his hands. Basically, it turns out that Shaggy has a pretty decent alibi: the security footage. For that matter, we have a pretty good riddle. Because no matter how many times we watch the video feed, the chain of events remains clear. Only three people enter Wrobleski's room: Wrobleski; then, over an hour later, the night manager, Shaggy; then, fifteen minutes after him, rookie officer Justin."

"What about the rear window?" the elderly woman asked.

"Very tiny. Might work for the Harmony LaFabs of the world, but definitely not for a grown man such as Shaggy."

"So"—D.D. surveyed the room—"who killed Wrobleski? Who finished sawing off his leg, loosened his tourniquet, then grabbed his phone and wallet and fled?"

"What about the EMTs?" someone called out. "If Wrobleski reached nine-one-one the way the girl said, where's the ambulance?"

"The responding officer called off the ambulance," another writer pointed out.

D.D. shook her head. "It's true that Justin called off emergency services upon arriving on the scene—but remember, he wasn't activated by a dying man's call to nine-one-one. Justin was dispatched after the call center was contacted by the vomiting night manager, Shaggy. So your question is the right question: What happened to Wrobleski's call?"

"You need to listen to the nine-one-one recordings," several people called out.

"No. I don't." D.D. glanced at the rear clock again. "Five minutes and counting. Come on, people. At least one of you should know who killed Wrobleski by now. I certainly did."

"Here's a question for you. Do cops read books?"

Apparently, it was a trick question, because her audience regarded her blankly.

D.D. tried again: "Do we read your books?"

A tentative hand in the back. "I've interviewed detectives who are readers, but most of them seem to prefer action and adventure. Or there was this female sergeant who loved romance. But as for thrillers . . . most say they get enough suspense on the job."

"Fair enough. I read. *Goodnight Moon*, mostly. Though lately I've been mixing in some Dr. Seuss—I have a toddler. But before my work life became consumed with homicide and my personal life all about my son, I definitely loved reading mysteries. Arthur Conan Doyle, Agatha Christie, Erle Stanley Gardner, Raymond Chandler. Pretty much any detective on the job loves a good puzzle. First we grew up reading about them, then we trained for jobs where we got to work them. Which is what we have here, right? The classic dead body in a locked room? According to the security tape, Steven Wrobleski entered that motel room alive. Only two other people walk through the door after him: our night mana-ger, Shaggy, and rookie cop, Justin, neither of whom were in there long enough to hack off limbs or loosen tourniquets.

"And yet we know someone else had to be present. Someone who finished the amputation Wrobleski started, then pocketed his cell phone and wallet. Assuming we believe Harmony LaFab's story."

"She's the liar!" Several voices, all at once.

"She was already in the room!"

"Maybe there was even more money. She gave you guys the duffel bag with a thousand dollars cash, but Wrobleski entered with ten grand. She kept the rest."

"Like that theory," D.D. assured the speaker, "and in the coming days, we'll track down the exact amount of Wrobleski's cash withdrawal, just to be sure.

"For the record, however, I believe Harmony. In your books, when you write about detectives having hunches, that part is exactly right. I've never met an experienced homicide detective who didn't have some kind of nose for this job. We definitely go by our gut. Then we back up and prove it, because trust me when I say prosecutors aren't nearly so open-minded about these things. In this case, I believed Harmony's story. She was just plain too fragile to have been our killer.

"But here's the deal, the question we haven't gotten around to asking yet, and surely the question you should all be considering: Harmony is a prostitute. The motel is a seedy rent-by-the-hour joint in the proverbial bad section of town. Then we got the drug dealer–slash–night manager. Now look at our victim. Steven Wrobleski. Successful business consultant, thousand-dollar suit, gorgeous home out in the burbs.

"How did that victim make it to this establishment? How did he even hear of such a place?"

"Internet." First response. "In those chat rooms discussing where to cut off limbs."

"Good guess. But no. Phil read them. Chatter was all about process and, if anything, assumed you were hacking off the offending body part in the comfort of your own house. So why come to a skanky motel? Frankly, it risked infection."

"Drugs," man in front spoke up quietly. "Wrobleski needed narcotics. Can't buy those at the same place as hacksaws and hammers."

D.D. nodded. "Exactly. The final ingredient for this venture was painkillers—and the boards were explicit there was no way the person would be able to withstand the pain of the dry ice without them. So Wrobleski, our successful, high-functioning consultant, needed illegal drugs."

She stared at her audience. Stared and stared and stared. One minute to the end of class. Thirty seconds. Fifteen.

Hand in the back, exactly what she'd been waiting for.

"The wife," a young girl called out. "She worked with addicts, right? A counselor? She would know where to get illegal drugs. Wrobleski asked his wife to help with the drugs. She sent him to the motel."

"Ding, ding, ding, give the woman a prize. What else?"

Buzzer sounded. But no one in the room moved.

"Female operator!" Now they were getting it, the room buzzing with energy. Exactly how D.D. and her squad mates felt with a case that finally came together.

"Wrobleski hadn't reached nine-one-one," someone called out excitedly. "He'd called home!"

"Which we proved by three o'clock the next day," D.D. assured them, "by pulling records of all calls, texts, and voice mails from Wrobleski's cellular provider. We never did find his phone, by the way. But as Wrobleski's wife learned the hard way, we don't need the physical unit. Just the call records, available from any cellular provider company.

"And the final nail in the coffin?" she called out as people gathered up their belongings.

"Silver glitter," volunteered the tall man with the mop top.

"Silver glitter," D.D. agreed. "Recovered from the silk tie forming the tourniquet, remember? Except Harmony never helped tie off the leg. The transfer of evidence came from the killer—when she was pulling out the pen, loosening up the knot in order to hasten her husband's demise. We executed a search warrant on Eve Wrobleski's home and recovered a bloody Canyon Ranch tracksuit from her garbage, complete with glittery trim. After her husband had called her, panic-stricken, she'd told him to wait, she'd come help. Together, they'd get this done. She knew where he was because she'd sent him there. Making it very easy for her to park blocks away, walk down the back alley, and shimmy in the rear window left open by Harmony LaFab. She approached her distressed and doped-up husband, splayed on the edge of the tub. Maybe he thought she'd hold his hand until the ambulance came. Or talk him out of his madness. Instead, she picked up the hacksaw and did it. Sawed through the limb. The damn offending limb that had become the bane of her existence. In her own words, if she had to listen to him talk about his right leg one more time . . .

"Wrobleski might have lost his courage that night. But his wife hadn't. Unfortunately for him, she wasn't just over the leg; She was also over him. Leg off, she loosened the tourniquet around his thigh, picked up his phone, his wallet, and disappeared back through the rear window. Given his long history of actively discussing self-amputation, she figured his death would be ruled accidental. Just another BIID sufferer driven to extremes.

"Her husband would be dead, his leg buried with him, and she could finally get on with her life aided by a multimillion-dollar life insurance policy. Frankly, it wasn't a bad plan. If only she hadn't been so partial to expensive tracksuits with shimmery trim."

D.D. picked up her bag. Time was up, her audience moving toward the door.

"Wait, wait, wait!" Several of the writers halted. "What's the lie? You said three truths and a lie. So what part of the story is a lie?"

"You tell me. That's the deal."

"The wanting to cut off his own leg. That was real."

"BIID is very real," she assured them.

"Seedy motel is probably real."

"Have a couple of those in Boston, definitely."

"Shaggy the drug dealer?"

"Nah, he's both real and still out there. Can't solve all the problems in the world."

"Harmony LaFab?"

"Name is an alias. You're writers—does that count as a lie, or more like an occupational requirement? Last I heard, Harmony was enrolled in beauty school.

Nothing like watching a guy take a knife to his own limb to make someone reconsider her line of work."

"Is it the glitter?" someone else spoke up. "I mean, can you really trace glitter?"

"Want to have some fun? Attend my husband Alex's lecture on blood spatter. Ask him about glitter as trace evidence. I'm telling you now, the man will practically levitate with excitement."

"So what's the lie?"

Time to go now, the doorway and hall stacking up with the next class waiting to enter.

D.D. smiled. Followed her own students to the door.

"The lie was implicit in the story. Why did the wife do what she did? Because she honestly believed she could get away with murder.

"That's the lie. For your savvy detectives in your thrillers, and for me and my squad dedicated to the job. Killers can be as creative and clever as they want. We're always gonna get 'em in the end."

THE SQUIRE'S STORY

Elizabeth Gaskell

Elizabeth Gaskell (1810–1865) is well-known for her detailed depictions of Victorian life in novels such as *Cranford* and *North and South*. While her short stories were more gothic horrors than detective fiction, the influences of crime writers and crime journalists is clear to see.

In the year 1769 the little town of Barford was thrown into a state of great excitement by the intelligence that a gentleman (and 'quite the gentleman', said the landlord of the George Inn) had been looking at Mr. Clavering's old house. This house was neither in the town nor in the country. It stood on the outskirts of Barford, on the roadside leading to Derby. The last occupant had been a Mr. Clavering, a Northumberland gentleman of good family who had come to live in Barford while he was but a younger son; but when some elder branches of the family died, he had returned to take possession of the family estate. The house of which I speak was called the White House, from its being covered with a greyish kind of stucco. It had a good garden to the back, and Mr. Clavering had built capital stables, with what were then considered the latest improvement. The point of good stabling was expected to let the house, as it was in a hunting county; otherwise it had few recommendations. There were many bedrooms; some entered through others, even to the number of five, leading one beyond the other; several sitting-rooms of the small and poky kind, wainscoted round with wood, and then painted a heavy slate colour; one good dining-room, and a drawing-room over it, both looking into the garden, with pleasant bow-windows.

Such was the accommodation offered by the White House. It did not seem to be very tempting to strangers, though the good people of Barford rather piqued themselves on it, as the largest house in the town; and as a house in which 'townspeople' and 'county people' had often met at Mr. Clavering's friendly dinners. To appreciate this circumstance of pleasant recollection, you should have lived some years in a little country town, surrounded by gentlemen's seats. You would then understand how a bow or a courtesy from a member of a county family elevates the individuals who receive it almost as much, in their own eyes, as the pair of blue garters fringed with silver did Mr. Bickerstaff's ward. They trip lightly on air for a whole day afterwards. Now Mr. Clavering was gone, where could town and county mingle?

I mention these things that you may have an idea of the desirability of the letting of the White House in the Barfordites' imagination; and to make the mixture thick and slab, you must add for yourselves the bustle, the mystery, and the importance which every little event either causes or assumes in a small town; and then, perhaps, it will be no wonder to — you that twenty ragged little urchins accompanied the 'gentleman' aforesaid to the door of the White House; and that, although he was above an hour inspecting it, under the auspices of Mr. Jones, the agent's clerk, thirty more had joined themselves on to the wondering crowd before his exit, and awaited such crumbs of intelligence as they could gather before they were threatened or whipped out of hearing distance. Presently, out came the 'gentleman' and the lawyer's clerk. The latter was speaking as he followed the former over the threshold. The gentleman was tall, well-dressed, handsome; but there was a sinister cold look in his quick-glancing, light blue eye, which a keen observer might not have liked. There were no keen observers among the boys, and ill-conditioned gaping girls. But they stood too near; inconveniently close; and the gentleman, lifting up his right hand, in which he carried a short riding-whip, dealt one or two sharp blows to the nearest, with a look of savage enjoyment on his face as they moved away whimpering and crying. An instant after, his expression of countenance had changed.

'Here!' said he, drawing out a handful of money, partly silver, partly copper, and throwing it into the midst of them. 'Scramble for it! fight it out, my lads! come this afternoon, at three, to the George, and I'll throw you out some more.' So the boys hurrahed for him as he walked off with the agent's clerk. He chuckled to himself, as over a pleasant thought. 'I'll have some fun with those lads,' he said; 'I'll teach 'em to come prowling and prying about me. I'll tell you what I'll do. I'll make the money so hot in the fire-shovel that it shall burn their fingers. You come and see the faces and the howling. I shall be very glad if you will dine with me at two; and by that time I may have made up my mind respecting the house.'

Mr. Jones, the agent's clerk, agreed to come to the George at two, but, somehow, he had a distaste for his entertainer. Mr. Jones would not like to have said, even to himself, that a man with a purse full of money, who kept many horses, and spoke familiarly of noblemen—above all, who thought of taking the White House—could be anything but a gentleman; but still the uneasy wonder as to who this Mr. Robinson Higgins could be, filled the clerk's mind long after Mr. Higgins, Mr. Higgins's servants, and Mr. Higgins's stud had taken possession of the White House.

The White House was re-stuccoed (this time of a pale yellow colour), and put into thorough repair by the accommodating and delighted landlord; while his tenant seemed inclined to spend any amount of money on internal decorations, which were showy and effective in their character, enough to make the White House a nine days' wonder to the good people of Barford. The slate-colored paints became pink, and were picked out with gold; the old-fashioned banisters were replaced by newly gilt ones; but, above all, the stables were a sight to be seen. Since the days of the Roman Emperor never was there such provision made for the care, the comfort, and the health of horse. But every one said it was no wonder, when they were led through Barford, covered up to their eyes, but curving their arched and delicate necks, and prancing with short high steps, in repressed eagerness. Only one groom came with them; yet they required the care of three men. Mr. Higgins, however, preferred engaging two lads out of Barford; and Barford highly approved of his preference. Not only was it kind and thoughtful to give employment to the lounging lads themselves, but they were receiving such a training in Mr. Higgins's stables as might fit them for Doncaster or Newmarket. The district of Derbyshire in which Barford was situated, was too close to Leicestershire not to support a hunt and a pack of hounds. The master of the hounds was a certain Sir Harry Manley, who was *aut* a huntsman *aut nullus*. He measured a man by the 'length of his fork', not by the expression of his countenance, or the shape of his head. But as Sir Harry was wont to observe, there was such a thing as too long a fork, so his approbation was withheld until he had seen a man on horseback; and if his seat there was square and easy, his hand light, and his courage good, Sir Harry hailed him as a brother.

Mr. Higgins attended the first meet of the season, not as a subscriber but as an amateur. The Barford huntsmen piqued themselves on their bold riding; and their knowledge of the country came by nature; yet this new strange man, whom nobody knew, was in at the death, sitting on his horse, both well breathed and calm, without a hair turned on the sleek skin of the latter, supremely addressing the old huntsman as he hacked off the tail of the fox; and he, the old man, who was testy even under Sir Harry's slightest rebuke, and flew out on any other member of the hunt that dared to utter a word against his sixty years' experience as stable-boy, groom, poacher, and what not—he, old Isaac Wormeley, was meekly listening to the wisdom of this stranger, only now and then giving one of his quick, up-turning, cunning glances, not unlike the sharp o'er-canny looks of the poor deceased Reynard, round whom the hounds were howling, unadmonished by the short whip, which was now tucked into Wormeley's well-worn pocket. When Sir Harry rode into the copse—full of dead brushwood and wet tangled grass—and was followed by the members of the hunt, as one by one they cantered past, Mr. Higgins took off his cap and bowed—half deferentially, half insolently—with a lurking smile in the corner of his eye at the discomfited looks of one or two of the laggards. 'A famous run, sir,' said Sir Harry. 'The first time you have hunted in our country; but I hope we shall see you often.'

'I hope to become a member of the hunt, sir,' said Mr. Higgins.

'Most happy—proud, I am sure, to receive so daring a rider among us. You took the Copper-gate, I fancy; while some of our friends here'—scowling at one or two cowards by way of finishing his speech. 'Allow me to introduce myself—master of the hounds.' He fumbled in his waistcoat pocket for the card on which his name was formally inscribed. 'Some of our friends here are kind enough to come home with me to dinner; might I ask for the honour?'

'My name is Higgins,' replied the stranger, bowing low. 'I am only lately come to occupy the White House at Barford, and I have not as yet presented my letters of introduction.'

'Hang it!' replied Sir Harry; 'a man with a seat like yours, and that good brush in your hand, might ride up to any door in the county (I'm a Leicestershire man!), and be a welcome guest. Mr. Higgins, I shall be proud to become better acquainted with you over my dinner table.'

Mr. Higgins knew pretty well how to improve the acquaintance thus begun. He could sing a good song, tell a good story, and was well up in practical jokes; with plenty of that keen worldly sense, which seems like an instinct in some men, and which in this case taught him on whom he might play off such jokes, with impunity from their resentment, and with a security of applause from the more boisterous, vehement, or prosperous. At the end of twelve months Mr. Robinson Higgins was, out-and-out, the most popular member of the Barford hunt; had beaten all the others by a couple of lengths, as his first patron, Sir Harry, observed one evening, when they were just leaving the dinner-table of an old hunting squire in the neighbourhood.

'Because, you know,' said Squire Hearn, holding Sir Harry by the button—' I mean, you see, this young spark is looking sweet upon Catherine; and she's a good girl, and will have ten thousand pounds down, the day she's married, by her mother's will; and—excuse me, Sir Harry—but I should not like my girl to throw herself away.'

Though Sir Harry had a long ride before him, and but the early and short light of a new moon to take it in, his kind heart was so much touched by Squire Hearn's trembling, tearful anxiety, that he stopped and turned back into the dining-room to say, with more asseverations than I care to give:

'My good Squire, I may say, I know that man pretty well by this time; and a better fellow never existed. If I had twenty daughters he should have the pick of them.'

Squire Hearn never thought of asking the grounds for his old friend's opinion of Mr. Higgins; it had been given with too much earnestness for any doubts to cross the old man's mind as to the possibility of its not being well founded. Mr. Hearn was not a doubter, or a thinker, or suspicious by nature; it was simply his love for Catherine, his only daughter, that prompted his anxiety in this case; and, after what Sir Harry had said, the old man could totter with an easy mind, though not with very steady legs, into the drawing-room, where his bonny, blushing daughter Catherine and Mr. Higgins stood close together on the hearth-rug—he whispering, she listening with downcast eyes. She looked so happy, so like her dead mother had looked when the Squire was a young man, that all his thought was how to please her most. His son and heir was about to be married, and bring his wife to live with the Squire; Barford and the White House were not distant an hour's ride; and, even as these thoughts passed through his mind, he asked Mr. Higgins if he could stay all night—the young moon was already set—the roads would be dark—and Catherine looked up with a pretty anxiety, which, however, had not much doubt in it, for the answer.

With every encouragement of this kind from the old Squire, it took everybody rather by surprise when, one morning, it was discovered that Miss Catherine Hearn was missing; and when, according to the usual fashion in such cases, a note was found, saying that she had eloped with 'the man of her heart', and gone to Gretna Green, no one could imagine why she could not quietly have stopped at home and been married in the parish church. She had always been a romantic, sentimental girl; very pretty and very affectionate, and very much spoiled, and very much wanting in common sense. Her indulgent father was deeply hurt at this want of confidence in his never-varying affection; but when his son came, hot with indignation from the Baronet's (his future father-in-law's house, where every form of law and of ceremony was to accompany his own impending marriage), Squire Hearn pleaded the cause of the young couple with imploring cogency, and protested that it was a piece of spirit in his daughter, which he admired and was proud of. However, it ended with Mr. Nathaniel Hearn's declaring that he and his wife would have nothing to do with his sister and her husband. 'Wait till you've seen him, Nat!' said the old Squire, trembling with his distressful anticipations of family discord. 'He's an excuse for any girl. Only ask Sir Harry's opinion of him. Confound Sir Harry! So that a man sits his horse well, Sir Harry cares nothing about anything else. Who is this man—this fellow? Where does he come from? What are his means? Who are his family?'

'He comes from the south—Surrey or Somersetshire, I forget which; and he pays his way well and liberally. There's not a tradesman in Barford but says he cares no more for money than for water; he spends like a prince, Nat, I don't know who his family are, but he seals with a coat of arms, which may tell you if you want to know—and he goes regularly to collect his rents from his estates in the south. Oh, Nat! if you would but be friendly, I should be as well pleased with Kitty's marriage as any father in the county.'

Mr. Nathaniel Hearn gloomed, and muttered an oath or two to himself. The poor old father was reaping the consequences of his weak indulgence to his two children. Mr. and Mrs. Nathaniel Hearn kept apart from Catherine and her husband; and Squire Hearn durst never ask them to Levison Hall, though it was his own house. Indeed, he stole away as if he were a culprit whenever he went to visit the White House; and if he passed a night there, he was fain to equivocate when he returned home the next day; an equivocation which was well interpreted by the surly, proud Nathaniel. But the younger Mr. and Mrs. Hearn were the only people who did not visit at the White House. Mr. and Mrs. Higgins were decidedly more popular than their brother and sister-in-law. She made a very pretty, sweet-tempered hostess, and her education had not been such as to make her intolerant of any want of refinement in the associates who gathered round her husband. She had gentle smiles for townspeople as well as county people; and unconsciously played an admirable second in her husband's project of making himself universally popular.

But there is some one to make ill-natured remarks, and draw ill-natured conclusions from very simple premises, in every place; and in Barford this bird of ill-omen was a Miss Pratt. She did not hunt—so Mr. Higgins's admirable riding did not call out her admiration. She did not drink—so the well-selected wines, so lavishly dispensed among his guests, could never mollify Miss Pratt. She could not bear comic songs, or buffo stories—so, in that way, her approbation was impregnable And these three secrets of popularity constituted Mr. Higgins's great charm. Miss Pratt sat and watched. Her face looked immovably grave at the end of any of Mr. Higgins's best stories; but there was a keen, needle-like glance of her unwinking little eyes, which Mr. Higgins felt rather than saw, and which made him shiver, even on a hot day, when it fell upon him. Miss Pratt was a dissenter, and, to propitiate this female Mordecai, Mr. Higgins asked the dissenting minister whose services she attended, to dinner; kept himself and his company in good order; gave a handsome donation to the poor of the chapel. All in vain—Miss Pratt stirred not a muscle more of her face towards graciousness; and Mr. Higgins was conscious that, in spite of all his open efforts to captivate Mr. Davis, there was a secret influence on the other side, throwing in doubts and suspicions, and evil interpretations of all he said or did. Miss Pratt, the little, plain old maid, living on eighty pounds a year, was the thorn in the popular Mr. Higgins's side, although she had never spoken one uncivil word to him; indeed, on the contrary, had treated him with a stiff and elaborate civility.

The thorn—the grief to Mrs. Higgins was this. They had no children! Oh! how she would stand and envy the careless, busy motion of half a dozen children; and then, when observed, move on with a deep, deep sigh of yearning regret. But it was as well.

It was noticed that Mr. Higgins was remarkably careful of his health. He ate, drank, took exercise, rested, by some secret rules of his own; occasionally bursting into an excess, it is true, but only on rare occasions—such as when he returned from visiting his estates in the south, and collecting his rents. That unusual exertion and fatigue—for there were no stage-coaches within forty miles of Barford, and he, like most country gentlemen of that day, would have preferred riding if there had been—seemed to require some strange excess to compensate for it; and rumours went through the town that he shut himself up, and drank enormously for some days after his return. But no one was admitted to these orgies.

One day—they remembered it well afterwards—the hounds met not far from the town; and the fox was found in a part of the wild heath, which was beginning to be enclosed by a few of the more wealthy townspeople, who were desirous of building themselves houses rather more in the country than those they had hitherto lived in. Among these, the principal was a Mr. Dudgeon, the attorney of Barford, and the agent for all the county families about. The firm of Dudgeon had managed the leases, the marriage-settlements, and the wills, of the neighbourhood for generations. Mr. Dudgeon's father had the responsibility of collecting the landowners' rents just as the present Mr. Dudgeon had at the time of which I speak: and as his son and his son's son have done since. Their business was an hereditary estate to them; and with something of the old feudal feeling was mixed a kind of proud humility at their position towards the squires whose family secrets they had mastered, and the mysteries of whose fortunes and estates were better known to the Messrs. Dudgeon than to themselves.

Mr. John Dudgeon had built himself a house on Wildbury Heath; a mere cottage as he called it: but though only two stories high, it spread out far and wide, and workpeople from Derby had been sent for on purpose to make the inside as complete as possible. The gardens too were exquisite in arrangement, if not very extensive; and not a flower was grown in them but of the rarest species. It must have been somewhat of a mortification to the owner of this dainty place when, on the day of which I speak, the fox, after a long race, during which he had described a circle of many miles, took refuge in the garden; but Mr. Dudgeon put a good face on the matter when a gentleman hunter, with the careless insolence of the squires of those days and that place, rode across the velvet lawn, and tapping at the window of the dining-room with his whip-handle, asked permission—no! that is not it—rather, informed Mr. Dudgeon of their intention—to enter his garden in a body, and have the fox unearthed. Mr. Dudgeon compelled himself to smile assent, with the grace of a masculine Griselda; and then he hastily gave orders to have all that the house afforded of provision set out for luncheon, guessing rightly enough that a six hours' run would give even homely fare an acceptable welcome. He bore without wincing the entrance of the dirty boots into his exquisitely clean rooms; he only felt grateful for the care with which Mr. Higgins strode about, laboriously and noiselessly moving on the tip of his toes, as he reconnoitred the rooms with a curious eye.

'I'm going to build a house myself, Dudgeon; and, upon my word, I don't think I could take a better model than yours.'

'Oh! my poor cottage would be too small to afford any hints for such a house as you would wish to build, Mr. Higgins,' replied Mr. Dudgeon, gently rubbing his hands nevertheless at the compliment.

'Not at all! not at all! Let me see. You have dining-room, drawing-room—' he hesitated, and Mr. Dudgeon filled up the blank as he expected.

'Four sitting-rooms and the bedrooms. But allow me to show you over the house. I confess I took some pains in arranging it, and, though far smaller than what you would require, it may, nevertheless, afford you some hints.'

So they left the eating gentlemen with their mouths and their plates quite full, and the scent of the fox over-powering that of the hasty rashers of ham; and they carefully inspected all the ground-floor rooms. Then Mr. Dudgeon said:

'If you are not tired, Mr. Higgins—it is rather my hobby, so you must pull me up if you are—we will go upstairs, and I will show you my sanctum.'

Mr. Dudgeon's sanctum was the centre room, over the porch, which formed a balcony, and which was carefully filled with choice flowers in pots. Inside, there were all kinds of elegant contrivances for hiding the real strength of all the boxes and chests required by the particular nature of Mr. Dudgeon's business: for although his office was in Barford, he kept (as he informed Mr. Higgins) what was the most valuable here, as being safer than an office which was locked up and left every night. But, as Mr. Higgins reminded him with a sly poke in the side, when next they met, his own house was not over-secure. A fortnight after the gentlemen of the Barford hunt lunched there, Mr. Dudgeon's strong-box, in his sanctum upstairs, with the mysterious spring-bolt to the window invented by himself, and the secret of which was only known to the inventor and a few of his most intimate friends, to whom he had proudly shown it; this strong-box, containing the collected Christmas rents of half a dozen landlords (there was then no bank nearer than Derby), was rifled; and the secretly rich Mr. Dudgeon had to stop his agent in his purchases of paintings by Flemish artists, because the money was required to make good the missing rents.

The Dogberries and Verges of those days were quite incapable of obtaining any clue to the robber or robbers; and though one or two vagrants were taken up and brought before Mr. Dunover and Mr. Higgins, the magistrates who usually attended in the court-room at Barford, there was no evidence brought against them, and after a couple of nights' durance in the lock-ups they were set at liberty. But it became a standing joke with Mr. Higgins to ask Mr. Dudgeon, from time to time, whether he could recommend him a place of safety for his valuables; or, if he had made any more inventions lately for securing houses from robbers.

About two years after this time—about seven years after Mr. Higgins had been married—one Tuesday evening Mr. Davis was sitting reading the news in the coffee-room of the George Inn. He belonged to a club of gentlemen who met there occasionally to play at whist, to read what few newspapers and magazines were published in those days, to chat about the market at Derby, and prices all over the country. This Tuesday night it was a black frost; and few people were in the room. Mr. Davis was anxious to finish an article in the *Gentleman's Magazine*; indeed, he was making extracts from it, intending to answer it, and yet unable with his small income to purchase a copy. So he stayed late; it was past nine, and at ten o'clock the room was closed. But while he wrote, Mr. Higgins came in. He was pale and haggard with cold. Mr. Davis, who had had for some time sole possession of the fire, moved politely on one side, and handed to the new-comer the sole London newspaper which the room afforded. Mr. Higgins accepted it, and made some remark on the intense coldness of the weather; but Mr. Davis was too full of his article, and intended reply, to fall into conversation readily. Mr. Higgins hitched his chair nearer to the fire, and put his feet on the fender, giving an audible shudder. He put the newspaper on one end of the table near him, and sat gazing into the red embers of the fire, crouching down over them as if his very marrow were chilled. At length he said:

'There is no account of the murder at Bath in that paper?' Mr. Davis, who had finished taking his notes, and was preparing to go, stopped short, and asked:

'Has there been a murder at Bath? No! I have not seen anything of it—who was murdered?'

'Oh! it was a shocking, terrible murder!' said Mr. Higgins, not raising his look from the fire, but gazing on with his eyes dilated till the whites were seen all round them. 'A terrible, terrible murder! I wonder what will become of the murderer? I can fancy the red glowing centre of that fire—look and see how infinitely distant it seems, and how the distance magnifies it into something awful and unquenchable.'

'My dear sir, you are feverish; how you shake and shiver!' said Mr. Davis, thinking privately that his companion had symptoms of fever, and that he was wandering in his mind.

'Oh, no!' said Mr. Higgins. 'I am not feverish. It is the night which is so cold.' And for a time he talked with Mr. Davis about the article in the *Gentleman's Magazine*, for he was rather a reader himself, and could take more interest in Mr. Davis's pursuits than most of the people at Barford. At length it drew near to ten, and Mr. Davis rose up to go home to his lodgings.

'No, Davis, don't go. I want you here. We will have a bottle of port together, and that will put Saunders into good humour. I want to tell you about this murder,' he continued, dropping his voice, and speaking hoarse and low. 'She was an old woman, and he killed her, sitting reading her Bible by her own fireside!' He looked at Mr. Davis with a strange searching gaze, as if trying to find some sympathy in the horror which the idea presented to him.

'Who do you mean, my dear sir? What is this murder you are so full of? No one has been murdered here.'

'No, you fool! I tell you it was in Bath!' said Mr. Higgins, with sudden passion; and then calming himself to most velvet-smoothness of manner, he laid his hand on Mr. Davis's knee, there, as they sat by the fire, and gently detaining him, began the narration of the crime he was so full of; but his voice and manner were constrained to a stony quietude: he never looked in Mr. Davis's face; once or twice, as Mr. Davis remembered afterwards, his grip tightened like a compressing vice.

'She lived in a small house in a quiet old-fashioned street, she and her maid. People said she was a good old woman; but for all that, she hoarded and hoarded, and never gave to the poor. Mr. Davis, it is wicked not to give to the poor—wicked—wicked, is it not? I always give to the poor, for once I read in the Bible that "Charity covereth a multitude of sins". The wicked old woman never gave, but hoarded her money, and saved, and saved. Some one heard of it; I say she threw temptation in his way, and God will punish her for it. And this man—or it might be a woman, who knows?—and this person heard also that she went to church in the mornings, and her maid in the afternoons; and so—while the maid was at church, and the street and the house quite still, and the darkness of a winter afternoon coming on—she was nodding over the Bible—and that, mark you! is a sin, and one that God will avenge sooner or later; and a step came in the dusk up the stair, and that person I told you of stood in the room. At first he—no! At first, it is supposed—for, you understand, all this is mere guess-work—it is supposed that he asked her civilly enough to give him her money, or to tell him where it was; but the old miser defied him, and would not ask for mercy and give up her keys, even when he threatened her, but looked him in the face as if he had been a baby—Oh, God! Mr. Davis, I once dreamt when I was a little innocent boy that I should commit a crime like this, and I wakened up crying; and my mother comforted me—that is the reason I tremble so now—that and the cold, for it is very very cold!'

'But did he murder the old lady?' asked Mr. Davis. 'I beg your pardon, sir, but I am interested by your story.'

'Yes! he cut her throat; and there she lies yet in her quiet little parlour, with her face upturned and all ghastly white, in the middle of a pool of blood. Mr. Davis, this wine is no better than water; I must have some brandy!'

Mr. Davis was horror-struck by the story, which seemed to have fascinated him as much as it had done his companion.

'Have they got any clue to the murderer?' said he. Mr. Higgins drank down half a tumbler of raw brandy before he answered.

'No! no clue whatever. They will never be able to discover him; and I should not wonder, Mr. Davis—should not wonder if he repented after all, and did bitter penance for his crime; and if so—will there be mercy for him at the last day?'

'God knows!' said Mr. Davis, with solemnity. 'It is an awful story,' continued he, rousing himself; 'I hardly like to leave this warm light room and go out into the darkness after hearing it. But it must be done,' buttoning on his greatcoat—I can only say I hope and trust they will find out the murderer and hang him—If you'll take my advice, Mr. Higgins, you'll have your bed warmed, and drink a treacle-posset just the last thing; and, if you'll allow me, I'll send you my answer to Philologus before it goes up to old Urban.'

The next morning, Mr. Davis went to call on Miss Pratt, who was not very well; and, by way of being agreeable and entertaining, he related to her all he had heard the night before about the murder at Bath; and really he made a very pretty connected story out of it, and interested Miss Pratt very much in the fate of the old lady—partly because of a similarity in their situations; for she also privately hoarded money, and had but one servant, and stopped at home alone on Sunday afternoons to allow her servant to go to church.

'And when did all this happen?' she asked.

'I don't know if Mr. Higgins named the day; and yet I think it must have been on this very last Sunday.'

'And to-day is Wednesday. Ill news travels fast.'

'Yes, Mr. Higgins thought it might have been in the London newspaper.'

'That it could never be. Where did Mr. Higgins learn all about it?'

'I don't know; I did not ask. I think he only came home yesterday: he had been south to collect his rents, somebody said.'

Miss Pratt grunted. She used to vent her dislike and suspicions of Mr. Higgins in a grunt whenever his name was mentioned.

'Well, I shan't see you for some days. Godfred Merton has asked me to go and stay with him and his sister; and I think it will do me good. Besides,' added she, 'these winter evenings—and these murderers at large in the country—I don't quite like living with only Peggy to call to in case of need.'

Miss Pratt went to stay with her cousin, Mr. Merton. He was an active magistrate, and enjoyed his reputation as such. One day he came in, having just received his letters.

'Bad account of the morals of your little town here, Jessy!' said he, touching one of his letters. 'You've either a murderer among you, or some friend of a murderer. Here's a poor old lady at Bath had her throat cut last Sunday week; and I've a letter from the Home Office, asking to lend them "my very efficient aid", as they are pleased to call it, towards finding out the culprit. It seems he must have been thirsty, and of a comfortable jolly turn; for before going to his horrid work he tapped a barrel of ginger wine the old lady had set by to work; and he wrapped the spigot round with a piece of a letter taken out of his pocket, as may be supposed; and this piece of a letter was found afterwards; there are only these letters on the outside, "ns, Esq., -arford, -egwor'h," which some one has ingeniously made out to mean Barford, near Kegworth. On the other side there is some allusion to a race-horse, I conjecture, though the name is singular enough: "Church-and-King-and-down-with-the-Rump."'

Miss Pratt caught at this name immediately; it had hurt her feelings as a dissenter only a few months ago, and she remembered it well.

'Mr. Nat Hearn has—or had (as I am speaking in the witness-box, as it were, I must take care of my tenses), a horse with that ridiculous name.'

'Mr. Nat Hearn,' repeated Mr. Merton, making a note of the intelligence; then he recurred to his letter from the Home Office again.

'There is also a piece of a small key, broken in the futile attempt to open a desk—well, well. Nothing more of consequence. The letter is what we must rely upon.'

'Mr. Davis said that Mr. Higgins told him—' Miss Pratt began.

'Higgins!' exclaimed Mr. Merton, 'ns. Is it Higgins, the blustering fellow that ran away with Nat Hearn's sister?'

'Yes!' said Miss Pratt. 'But though he has never been a favourite of mine—'

'ns,' repeated Mr. Merton. 'It is too horrible to think of; a member of the hunt—kind old Squire Hearn's son-in-law! Who else have you in Barford with names that end in ns?'

'There's Jackson, and Higginson, and Blenkinsop, and Davis, and Jones. Cousin! One thing strikes me—how did Mr. Higgins know all about it to tell Mr. Davis on Tuesday what had happened on Sunday afternoon?'

There is no need to add much more. Those curious in lives of the highway-man may find the name of Higgins as conspicuous among those annals as that of Claude Duval. Kate Hearn's husband collected his rents on the highway, like many another 'gentleman' of the day; but, having been unlucky in one or two of his adventures, and hearing exaggerated accounts of the hoarded wealth of the old lady at Bath, he was led on from robbery to murder, and was hung for his crime at Derby, in 1775.

He had not been an unkind husband; and his poor wife took lodgings in Derby to be near him in his last moments—his awful last moments. Her old father went with her everywhere but into her husband's cell; and wrung her heart by constantly accusing himself of having promoted her marriage with a man of whom he knew so little. He abdicated his squireship in favour of his son Nathaniel. Nat was prosperous, and the helpless silly father could be of no use to him; but to his widowed daughter the foolish fond old man was all in all; her knight, her protector, her companion—her most faithful loving companion. Only he ever declined assuming the office of her councellor—shaking his head sadly, and saying—

'Ah! Kate, Kate! if I had had more wisdom to have advised thee better, thou need'st not have been an exile here in Brussels, shrinking from the sight of every English person as if they knew thy story.'

I saw the White House not a month ago; it was to let, perhaps for the twen-tieth time since Mr. Higgins occupied it; but still the tradition goes in Barford that once upon a time a highwayman lived there, and amassed untold treasures; and that the ill-gotten wealth yet remains walled up in some unknown concealed chamber; but in what part of the house no one knows.

Will any of you become tenants, and try to find out this mysterious closet? I can furnish the exact address to any applicant who wishes for it.

THE YELLOW WALLPAPER

Charlotte Perkins Gilman

Charlotte Perkins Gilman (1860–1935) wrote pioneering feminist non-fiction as well as fiction, of which 'The Yellow Wallpaper' has become iconic. She encouraged social reform for women by founding the magazine *The Forerunner* (1909–1916). Born in Pasadena, California, Gilman committed suicide in 1935.

It is very seldom that mere ordinary people like John and myself secure ancestral halls for the summer.

A colonial mansion, a hereditary estate, I would say a haunted house, and reach the height of romantic felicity – but that would be asking too much of fate!

Still I will proudly declare that there is something queer about it.

Else, why should it be let so cheaply? And why have stood so long untenanted?

John laughs at me, of course, but one expects that in marriage.

John is practical in the extreme. He has no patience with faith, an intense horror of superstition, and he scoffs openly at any talk of things not to be felt and seen and put down in figures.

John is a physician, and PERHAPS – (I would not say it to a living soul, of course, but this is dead paper and a great relief to my mind) – PERHAPS that is one reason I do not get well faster.

You see he does not believe I am sick!

And what can one do?

If a physician of high standing, and one's own husband, assures friends and relatives that there is really nothing the matter with one but temporary nervous depression – a slight hysterical tendency – what is one to do?

My brother is also a physician, and also of high standing, and he says the same thing.

So I take phosphates or phosphites – whichever it is, and tonics, and journeys, and air, and exercise, and am absolutely forbidden to "work" until I am well again.

Personally, I disagree with their ideas.

Personally, I believe that congenial work, with excitement and change, would do me good.

But what is one to do?

I did write for a while in spite of them; but it DOES exhaust me a good deal – having to be so sly about it, or else meet with heavy opposition.

I sometimes fancy that in my condition if I had less opposition and more society and stimulus – but John says the very worst thing I can do is to think about my condition, and I confess it always makes me feel bad.

So I will let it alone and talk about the house.

The most beautiful place! It is quite alone, standing well back from the road, quite three miles from the village. It makes me think of English places that you read about, for there are hedges and walls and gates that lock, and lots of separate little houses for the gardeners and people.

There is a DELICIOUS garden! I never saw such a garden – large and shady, full of box-bordered paths, and lined with long grape-covered arbors with seats under them.

There were greenhouses, too, but they are all broken now.

There was some legal trouble, I believe, something about the heirs and coheirs; anyhow, the place has been empty for years.

That spoils my ghostliness, I am afraid, but I don't care – there is something strange about the house – I can feel it.

I even said so to John one moonlight evening, but he said what I felt was a DRAUGHT, and shut the window.

I get unreasonably angry with John sometimes. I'm sure I never used to be so sensitive. I think it is due to this nervous condition.

But John says if I feel so, I shall neglect proper self-control; so I take pains to control myself – before him, at least, and that makes me very tired.

I don't like our room a bit. I wanted one downstairs that opened on the piazza and had roses all over the window, and such pretty old-fashioned chintz hangings! but John would not hear of it.

He said there was only one window and not room for two beds, and no near room for him if he took another.

He is very careful and loving, and hardly lets me stir without special direction.

I have a schedule prescription for each hour in the day; he takes all care from me, and so I feel basely ungrateful not to value it more.

He said we came here solely on my account, that I was to have perfect rest and all the air I could get. "Your exercise depends on your strength, my dear," said he, "and your food somewhat on your appetite; but air you can absorb all the time." So we took the nursery at the top of the house.

It is a big, airy room, the whole floor nearly, with windows that look all ways, and air and sunshine galore. It was nursery first and then playroom and gymnasium, I should judge; for the windows are barred for little children, and there are rings and things in the walls.

The paint and paper look as if a boys' school had used it. It is stripped off – the paper – in great patches all around the head of my bed, about as far as I can reach, and in a great place on the other side of the room low down. I never saw a worse paper in my life.

One of those sprawling flamboyant patterns committing every artistic sin.

It is dull enough to confuse the eye in following, pronounced enough to constantly irritate and provoke study, and when you follow the lame uncertain curves for a little distance they suddenly commit suicide – plunge off at outrageous angles, destroy themselves in unheard of contradictions.

The color is repellent, almost revolting; a smouldering unclean yellow, strangely faded by the slow-turning sunlight.

It is a dull yet lurid orange in some places, a sickly sulphur tint in others.

No wonder the children hated it! I should hate it myself if I had to live in this room long.

There comes John, and I must put this away – he hates to have me write a word.

We have been here two weeks, and I haven't felt like writing before, since that first day.

I am sitting by the window now, up in this atrocious nursery, and there is nothing to hinder my writing as much as I please, save lack of strength.

John is away all day, and even some nights when his cases are serious.

I am glad my case is not serious!

But these nervous troubles are dreadfully depressing.

John does not know how much I really suffer. He knows there is no REASON to suffer, and that satisfies him.

Of course it is only nervousness. It does weigh on me so not to do my duty in any way!

I meant to be such a help to John, such a real rest and comfort, and here I am a comparative burden already!

Nobody would believe what an effort it is to do what little I am able – to dress and entertain, and order things.

It is fortunate Mary is so good with the baby. Such a dear baby!

And yet I CANNOT be with him, it makes me so nervous.

I suppose John never was nervous in his life. He laughs at me so about this wallpaper!

At first he meant to repaper the room, but afterwards he said that I was letting it get the better of me, and that nothing was worse for a nervous patient than to give way to such fancies.

He said that after the wallpaper was changed it would be the heavy bedstead, and then the barred windows, and then that gate at the head of the stairs, and so on.

"You know the place is doing you good," he said, "and really, dear, I don't care to renovate the house just for a three months' rental."

"Then do let us go downstairs," I said, "there are such pretty rooms there."

Then he took me in his arms and called me a blessed little goose, and said he would go down to the cellar, if I wished, and have it whitewashed into the bargain.

But he is right enough about the beds and windows and things.

It is an airy and comfortable room as any one need wish, and, of course, I would not be so silly as to make him uncomfortable just for a whim.

I'm really getting quite fond of the big room, all but that horrid paper.

Out of one window I can see the garden, those mysterious deepshaded arbors, the riotous old-fashioned flowers, and bushes and gnarly trees.

Out of another I get a lovely view of the bay and a little private wharf belonging to the estate. There is a beautiful shaded lane that runs down there from the house. I always fancy I see people walking in these numerous paths and arbors, but John has cautioned me not to give way to fancy in the least. He says that with my imaginative power and habit of story-making, a nervous weakness like mine is sure to lead to all manner of excited fancies, and that I ought to use my will and good sense to check the tendency. So I try.

I think sometimes that if I were only well enough to write a little it would relieve the press of ideas and rest me.

But I find I get pretty tired when I try.

It is so discouraging not to have any advice and companionship about my work. When I get really well, John says we will ask Cousin Henry and Julia down for a long visit; but he says he would as soon put fireworks in my pillow-case as to let me have those stimulating people about now.

I wish I could get well faster.

But I must not think about that. This paper looks to me as if it KNEW what a vicious influence it had!

There is a recurrent spot where the pattern lolls like a broken neck and two bulbous eyes stare at you upside down.

I get positively angry with the impertinence of it and the everlastingness. Up and down and sideways they crawl, and those absurd, unblinking eyes are everywhere. There is one place where two breadths didn't match, and the eyes go all up and down the line, one a little higher than the other.

I never saw so much expression in an inanimate thing before, and we all know how much expression they have! I used to lie awake as a child and get more entertainment and terror out of blank walls and plain furniture than most children could find in a toy store.

I remember what a kindly wink the knobs of our big old bureau used to have, and there was one chair that always seemed like a strong friend.

I used to feel that if any of the other things looked too fierce I could always hop into that chair and be safe.

The furniture in this room is no worse than inharmonious, however, for we had to bring it all from downstairs. I suppose when this was used as a playroom they had to take the nursery things out, and no wonder! I never saw such ravages as the children have made here.

The wallpaper, as I said before, is torn off in spots, and it sticketh closer than a brother – they must have had perseverance as well as hatred.

Then the floor is scratched and gouged and splintered, the plaster itself is dug out here and there, and this great heavy bed, which is all we found in the room, looks as if it had been through the wars.

But I don't mind it a bit – only the paper.

There comes John's sister. Such a dear girl as she is, and so careful of me! I must not let her find me writing.

She is a perfect and enthusiastic housekeeper, and hopes for no better profession. I verily believe she thinks it is the writing which made me sick!

But I can write when she is out, and see her a long way off from these windows.

There is one that commands the road, a lovely shaded winding road, and one that just looks off over the country. A lovely country, too, full of great elms and velvet meadows.

This wallpaper has a kind of sub-pattern in a different shade, a particularly irritating one, for you can only see it in certain lights, and not clearly then.

But in the places where it isn't faded and where the sun is just so – I can see a strange, provoking, formless sort of figure, that seems to skulk about behind that silly and conspicuous front design.

There's sister on the stairs!

Well, the Fourth of July is over! The people are gone and I am tired out. John thought it might do me good to see a little company, so we just had mother and Nellie and the children down for a week.

Of course I didn't do a thing. Jennie sees to everything now.

But it tired me all the same.

John says if I don't pick up faster he shall send me to Weir Mitchell in the fall.

But I don't want to go there at all. I had a friend who was in his hands once, and she says he is just like John and my brother, only more so!

Besides, it is such an undertaking to go so far.

I don't feel as if it was worth while to turn my hand over for anything, and I'm getting dreadfully fretful and querulous.

I cry at nothing, and cry most of the time.

Of course I don't when John is here, or anybody else, but when I am alone.

And I am alone a good deal just now. John is kept in town very often by serious cases, and Jennie is good and lets me alone when I want her to.

So I walk a little in the garden or down that lovely lane, sit on the porch under the roses, and lie down up here a good deal.

I'm getting really fond of the room in spite of the wallpaper. Perhaps BE-CAUSE of the wallpaper.

It dwells in my mind so!

I lie here on this great immovable bed – it is nailed down, I believe – and follow that pattern about by the hour. It is as good as gymnastics, I assure you. I start, we'll say, at the bottom, down in the corner over there where it has not been touched, and I determine for the thousandth time that I WILL follow that pointless pattern to some sort of a conclusion.

I know a little of the principle of design, and I know this thing was not arranged on any laws of radiation, or alternation, or repetition, or symmetry, or anything else that I ever heard of.

It is repeated, of course, by the breadths, but not otherwise.

Looked at in one way each breadth stands alone, the bloated curves and flourishes – a kind of "debased Romanesque" with delirium tremens – go waddling up and down in isolated columns of fatuity.

But, on the other hand, they connect diagonally, and the sprawling outlines run off in great slanting waves of optic horror, like a lot of wallowing seaweeds in full chase.

The whole thing goes horizontally, too, at least it seems so, and I exhaust myself in trying to distinguish the order of its going in that direction.

They have used a horizontal breadth for a frieze, and that adds wonderfully to the confusion.

There is one end of the room where it is almost intact, and there, when the crosslights fade and the low sun shines directly upon it, I can almost fancy radiation after all, – the interminable grotesques seem to form around a common centre and rush off in headlong plunges of equal distraction.

It makes me tired to follow it. I will take a nap I guess.

I don't know why I should write this.

I don't want to.

I don't feel able.

And I know John would think it absurd. But I MUST say what I feel and think in some way – it is such a relief!

But the effort is getting to be greater than the relief.

Half the time now I am awfully lazy, and lie down ever so much.

John says I musn't lose my strength, and has me take cod liver oil and lots of tonics and things, to say nothing of ale and wine and rare meat.

Dear John! He loves me very dearly, and hates to have me sick. I tried to have a real earnest reasonable talk with him the other day, and tell him how I wish he would let me go and make a visit to Cousin Henry and Julia.

But he said I wasn't able to go, nor able to stand it after I got there; and I did not make out a very good case for myself, for I was crying before I had finished.

It is getting to be a great effort for me to think straight. Just this nervous weakness I suppose.

And dear John gathered me up in his arms, and just carried me upstairs and laid me on the bed, and sat by me and read to me till it tired my head.

He said I was his darling and his comfort and all he had, and that I must take care of myself for his sake, and keep well.

He says no one but myself can help me out of it, that I must use my will and self-control and not let any silly fancies run away with me.

There's one comfort, the baby is well and happy, and does not have to occupy this nursery with the horrid wallpaper.

If we had not used it, that blessed child would have! What a fortunate escape! Why, I wouldn't have a child of mine, an impressionable little thing, live in such a room for worlds.

I never thought of it before, but it is lucky that John kept me here after all, I can stand it so much easier than a baby, you see.

Of course I never mention it to them any more – I am too wise – but I keep watch of it all the same.

There are things in that paper that nobody knows but me, or ever will.

Behind that outside pattern the dim shapes get clearer every day.

It is always the same shape, only very numerous.

And it is like a woman stooping down and creeping about behind that pattern. I don't like it a bit. I wonder – I begin to think – I wish John would take me away from here!

It is so hard to talk with John about my case, because he is so wise, and because he loves me so.

But I tried it last night.

It was moonlight. The moon shines in all around just as the sun does.

I hate to see it sometimes, it creeps so slowly, and always comes in by one window or another.

John was asleep and I hated to waken him, so I kept still and watched the moonlight on that undulating wallpaper till I felt creepy.

The faint figure behind seemed to shake the pattern, just as if she wanted to get out.

I got up softly and went to feel and see if the paper DID move, and when I came back John was awake.

"What is it, little girl?" he said. "Don't go walking about like that – you'll get cold."

I thought it was a good time to talk, so I told him that I really was not gaining here, and that I wished he would take me away.

"Why darling!" said he, "our lease will be up in three weeks, and I can't see how to leave before.

"The repairs are not done at home, and I cannot possibly leave town just now. Of course if you were in any danger, I could and would, but you really are better, dear, whether you can see it or not. I am a doctor, dear, and I know. You are gaining flesh and color, your appetite is better, I feel really much easier about you."

"I don't weigh a bit more," said I, "nor as much; and my appetite may be better in the evening when you are here, but it is worse in the morning when you are away!"

"Bless her little heart!" said he with a big hug, "she shall be as sick as she pleases! But now let's improve the shining hours by going to sleep, and talk about it in the morning!"

"And you won't go away?" I asked gloomily.

"Why, how can I, dear? It is only three weeks more and then we will take a nice little trip of a few days while Jennie is getting the house ready. Really dear you are better!"

"Better in body perhaps—" I began, and stopped short, for he sat up straight and looked at me with such a stern, reproachful look that I could not say another word.

"My darling," said he, "I beg of you, for my sake and for our child's sake, as well as for your own, that you will never for one instant let that idea enter your mind! There is nothing so dangerous, so fascinating, to a temperament like yours. It is a false and foolish fancy. Can you not trust me as a physician when I tell you so?"

So of course I said no more on that score, and we went to sleep before long. He thought I was asleep first, but I wasn't, and lay there for hours trying to decide whether that front pattern and the back pattern really did move together or separately.

On a pattern like this, by daylight, there is a lack of sequence, a defiance of law, that is a constant irritant to a normal mind.

The color is hideous enough, and unreliable enough, and infuriating enough, but the pattern is torturing.

You think you have mastered it, but just as you get well underway in following, it turns a back-somersault and there you are. It slaps you in the face, knocks you down, and tramples upon you. It is like a bad dream.

The outside pattern is a florid arabesque, reminding one of a fungus. If you can imagine a toadstool in joints, an interminable string of toadstools, budding and sprouting in endless convolutions – why, that is something like it.

That is, sometimes!

There is one marked peculiarity about this paper, a thing nobody seems to notice but myself, and that is that it changes as the light changes.

When the sun shoots in through the east window – I always watch for that first long, straight ray – it changes so quickly that I never can quite believe it.

That is why I watch it always.

By moonlight – the moon shines in all night when there is a moon – I wouldn't know it was the same paper.

At night in any kind of light, in twilight, candle light, lamplight, and worst of all by moonlight, it becomes bars! The outside pattern I mean, and the woman behind it is as plain as can be.

I didn't realize for a long time what the thing was that showed behind, that dim sub-pattern, but now I am quite sure it is a woman.

By daylight she is subdued, quiet. I fancy it is the pattern that keeps her so still. It is so puzzling. It keeps me quiet by the hour.

I lie down ever so much now. John says it is good for me, and to sleep all I can.

Indeed he started the habit by making me lie down for an hour after each meal.

It is a very bad habit I am convinced, for you see I don't sleep.

And that cultivates deceit, for I don't tell them I'm awake – O no!

The fact is I am getting a little afraid of John.

He seems very queer sometimes, and even Jennie has an inexplicable look.

It strikes me occasionally, just as a scientific hypothesis – that perhaps it is the paper!

I have watched John when he did not know I was looking, and come into the room suddenly on the most innocent excuses, and I've caught him several times LOOKING AT THE PAPER! And Jennie too. I caught Jennie with her hand on it once.

She didn't know I was in the room, and when I asked her in a quiet, a very quiet voice, with the most restrained manner possible, what she was doing with the paper – she turned around as if she had been caught stealing, and looked quite angry – asked me why I should frighten her so!

Then she said that the paper stained everything it touched, that she had found yellow smooches on all my clothes and John's, and she wished we would be more careful!

Did not that sound innocent? But I know she was studying that pattern, and I am determined that nobody shall find it out but myself!

Life is very much more exciting now than it used to be. You see I have something more to expect, to look forward to, to watch. I really do eat better, and am more quiet than I was.

John is so pleased to see me improve! He laughed a little the other day, and said I seemed to be flourishing in spite of my wallpaper.

I turned it off with a laugh. I had no intention of telling him it was BECAUSE of the wallpaper – he would make fun of me. He might even want to take me away.

I don't want to leave now until I have found it out. There is a week more, and I think that will be enough.

I'm feeling ever so much better! I don't sleep much at night, for it is so interesting to watch developments; but I sleep a good deal in the daytime.

In the daytime it is tiresome and perplexing.

There are always new shoots on the fungus, and new shades of yellow all over it. I cannot keep count of them, though I have tried conscientiously.

It is the strangest yellow, that wallpaper! It makes me think of all the yellow things I ever saw – not beautiful ones like buttercups, but old foul, bad yellow things.

But there is something else about that paper – the smell! I noticed it the moment we came into the room, but with so much air and sun it was not bad. Now we have had a week of fog and rain, and whether the windows are open or not, the smell is here.

It creeps all over the house.

I find it hovering in the dining-room, skulking in the parlor, hiding in the hall, lying in wait for me on the stairs.

It gets into my hair.

Even when I go to ride, if I turn my head suddenly and surprise it – there is that smell!

Such a peculiar odor, too! I have spent hours in trying to analyze it, to find what it smelled like.

It is not bad – at first, and very gentle, but quite the subtlest, most enduring odor I ever met.

In this damp weather it is awful, I wake up in the night and find it hanging over me.

It used to disturb me at first. I thought seriously of burning the house – to reach the smell.

But now I am used to it. The only thing I can think of that it is like is the COLOR of the paper! A yellow smell.

There is a very funny mark on this wall, low down, near the mopboard. A streak that runs round the room. It goes behind every piece of furniture, except the bed, a long, straight, even SMOOCH, as if it had been rubbed over and over.

I wonder how it was done and who did it, and what they did it for. Round and round and round – round and round and round – it makes me dizzy!

I really have discovered something at last.

Through watching so much at night, when it changes so, I have finally found out.

The front pattern DOES move – and no wonder! The woman behind shakes it!

Sometimes I think there are a great many women behind, and sometimes only one, and she crawls around fast, and her crawling shakes it all over.

Then in the very bright spots she keeps still, and in the very shady spots she just takes hold of the bars and shakes them hard.

And she is all the time trying to climb through. But nobody could climb through that pattern – it strangles so; I think that is why it has so many heads.

They get through, and then the pattern strangles them off and turns them upside down, and makes their eyes white!

If those heads were covered or taken off it would not be half so bad.

I think that woman gets out in the daytime!

And I'll tell you why – privately – I've seen her!

I can see her out of every one of my windows!

It is the same woman, I know, for she is always creeping, and most women do not creep by daylight.

I see her on that long road under the trees, creeping along, and when a carriage comes she hides under the blackberry vines.

I don't blame her a bit. It must be very humiliating to be caught creeping by daylight!

I always lock the door when I creep by daylight. I can't do it at night, for I know John would suspect something at once.

And John is so queer now, that I don't want to irritate him. I wish he would take another room! Besides, I don't want anybody to get that woman out at night but myself.

I often wonder if I could see her out of all the windows at once.

But, turn as fast as I can, I can only see out of one at one time.

And though I always see her, she MAY be able to creep faster than I can turn!

I have watched her sometimes away off in the open country, creeping as fast as a cloud shadow in a high wind.

If only that top pattern could be gotten off from the under one! I mean to try it, little by little.

I have found out another funny thing, but I shan't tell it this time! It does not do to trust people too much.

There are only two more days to get this paper off, and I believe John is beginning to notice. I don't like the look in his eyes.

And I heard him ask Jennie a lot of professional questions about me. She had a very good report to give.

She said I slept a good deal in the daytime.

John knows I don't sleep very well at night, for all I'm so quiet!

He asked me all sorts of questions, too, and pretended to be very loving and kind.

As if I couldn't see through him!

Still, I don't wonder he acts so, sleeping under this paper for three months.

It only interests me, but I feel sure John and Jennie are secretly affected by it.

Hurrah! This is the last day, but it is enough. John is to stay in town over night, and won't be out until this evening.

Jennie wanted to sleep with me – the sly thing! but I told her I should undoubtedly rest better for a night all alone.

That was clever, for really I wasn't alone a bit! As soon as it was moonlight and that poor thing began to crawl and shake the pattern, I got up and ran to help her.

I pulled and she shook, I shook and she pulled, and before morning we had peeled off yards of that paper.

A strip about as high as my head and half around the room.

And then when the sun came and that awful pattern began to laugh at me, I declared I would finish it to-day!

We go away to-morrow, and they are moving all my furniture down again to leave things as they were before.

Jennie looked at the wall in amazement, but I told her merrily that I did it out of pure spite at the vicious thing.

She laughed and said she wouldn't mind doing it herself, but I must not get tired.

How she betrayed herself that time!

But I am here, and no person touches this paper but me – not ALIVE!

She tried to get me out of the room – it was too patent! But I said it was so quiet and empty and clean now that I believed I would lie down again and sleep all I could; and not to wake me even for dinner – I would call when I woke.

So now she is gone, and the servants are gone, and the things are gone, and there is nothing left but that great bedstead nailed down, with the canvas mattress we found on it.

We shall sleep downstairs to-night, and take the boat home to-morrow.

I quite enjoy the room, now it is bare again.

How those children did tear about here!

This bedstead is fairly gnawed!

But I must get to work.

I have locked the door and thrown the key down into the front path.

I don't want to go out, and I don't want to have anybody come in, till John comes.

I want to astonish him.

I've got a rope up here that even Jennie did not find. If that woman does get out, and tries to get away, I can tie her!

But I forgot I could not reach far without anything to stand on!

This bed will NOT move!

I tried to lift and push it until I was lame, and then I got so angry I bit off a little piece at one corner – but it hurt my teeth.

Then I peeled off all the paper I could reach standing on the floor. It sticks horribly and the pattern just enjoys it! All those strangled heads and bulbous eyes and waddling fungus growths just shriek with derision!

I am getting angry enough to do something desperate. To jump out of the window would be admirable exercise, but the bars are too strong even to try.

Besides I wouldn't do it. Of course not. I know well enough that a step like that is improper and might be misconstrued.

I don't like to LOOK out of the windows even – there are so many of those creeping women, and they creep so fast.

I wonder if they all come out of that wallpaper as I did?

But I am securely fastened now by my well-hidden rope – you don't get ME out in the road there!

I suppose I shall have to get back behind the pattern when it comes night, and that is hard!

It is so pleasant to be out in this great room and creep around as I please!

I don't want to go outside. I won't, even if Jennie asks me to.

For outside you have to creep on the ground, and everything is green instead of yellow.

But here I can creep smoothly on the floor, and my shoulder just fits in that long smooch around the wall, so I cannot lose my way.

Why there's John at the door!

It is no use, young man, you can't open it!

How he does call and pound!

Now he's crying for an axe.

It would be a shame to break down that beautiful door!

"John dear!" said I in the gentlest voice, "the key is down by the front steps, under a plantain leaf!"

That silenced him for a few moments.

Then he said – very quietly indeed, "Open the door, my darling!"

"I can't," said I. "The key is down by the front door under a plantain leaf!"

And then I said it again, several times, very gently and slowly, and said it so often that he had to go and see, and he got it of course, and came in. He stopped short by the door.

"What is the matter?" he cried. "For God's sake, what are you doing!"

I kept on creeping just the same, but I looked at him over my shoulder.

"I've got out at last," said I, "in spite of you and Jane. And I've pulled off most of the paper, so you can't put me back!"

Now why should that man have fainted? But he did, and right across my path by the wall, so that I had to creep over him every time!

A POINT IN MORALS

Ellen Glasgow

Ellen Glasgow (1873–1945) was born into an elite family in Richmond, Virginia, and educated privately. Towards the end of the century, she became a noted suffragist and developed strong feminist themes in her popular fiction.

"THE question seems to be—" began the Englishman. He looked up and bowed to a girl in a yachting-cap who had just come in from deck and was taking the seat beside him. "The question seems to be—" The girl was having some difficulty in removing her coat, and he turned to assist her.

"In my opinion," broke in a well-known alienist on his way to a convention in Vienna, "the question is simply whether or not civilization, in placing an exorbitant value upon human life, is defeating its own aims." He leaned forward authoritatively, and spoke with a half-foreign precision of accent.

"You mean that the survival of the fittest is checkmated," remarked a young journalist travelling in the interest of a New York daily, "that civilization should practise artificial selection, as it were?"

The alienist shrugged his shoulders deprecatingly. "My dear sir," he protested, "I don't mean anything. It is the question that means something."

"Well, as I was saying," began the Englishman again, reaching for the salt and upsetting a spoonful, "the question seems to be whether or not, under any circumstances, the saving of a human life may become positively immoral."

"Upon that point—" began the alienist: but a young lady in a pink blouse who was seated on the Captain's right interrupted him.

"How could it?" she asked. "At least I don't see how it could; do you, Captain?"

"There is no doubt," remarked the journalist, looking up from a conversation he had drifted into with a lawyer from one of the Western States, "that the more humane spirit pervading modern civilization has not worked wholly for good in the development of the species. Probably, for instance, if we had followed the Spartan practice of exposing unhealthy infants, we should have retained something of the Spartan hardihood. Certainly if we had been content to remain barbarians both our digestions and our nerves would have been the better for it, and melancholia would perhaps have been unknown. But, at the same time, the loss of a number of the more heroic virtues is overbalanced by an increase of the softer ones. Notably, human life has never before been regarded so sacredly."

"On the other side," observed the lawyer, lifting his hand to adjust his eye-glasses, and pausing to brush a crumb from his coat, "though it may all be very well to be philanthropic to the point of pauperizing half a community and of growing squeamish about capital punishment, the whole thing sometimes takes a disgustingly morbid turn. Why, it seems as if criminals were the real American heroes! Only last week I visited a man sentenced to death for the murder of his two wives, and, by Jove, the jailer was literally besieged by women sympathizers. I counted six bunches of heliotrope in his cell, and at least fifty notes."

"Oh, but that is a form of nervous hysteria!" said the girl in the yachting-cap, "and must be considered separately. Every sentiment has its fanatics—philanthropy as well as religion. But we don't judge a movement by a few overwrought disciples."

"That is true," said the Englishman, quietly. He was a middle-aged man, with an insistently optimistic countenance, and a build suggestive of general solidity. "But to return to the original proposition. I suppose we will all accept as a fundamental postulate the statement that the highest civilization is the one in which the highest value is placed upon individual life—"

"And happiness," added the girl in the yachting-cap.

"And happiness," assented the Englishman.

"And yet," commented the lawyer, "I think that most of us will admit that such a society, where life is regarded as sacred because it is valuable to the individual, and not because it is valuable to the state, tends to the non-production of heroes— "

"That the average will be higher and the exception lower," observed the journalist. "In other words, that there will be a general elevation of the mass, accompanied by a corresponding lowering of the few."

"On the whole, I think our system does very well," said the Englishman, carefully measuring the horseradish he was placing upon his oysters. "A mean between two extremes is apt to be satisfactory in results. If we don't produce a Marcus Aurelius or a Seneca, neither do we produce a Nero or a Phocas. We may have lost patriotism, but we have gained cosmopolitanism, which is better. If we have lost chivalry, we have acquired decency; and if we have ceased to be picturesque, we have become cleanly, which is considerably more to be desired."

"I have never felt the romanticism of the Middle Ages," remarked the girl in the yachting-cap. "When I read of the glories of the Crusaders, I can't help remembering that a knight wore a single garment for a lifetime, and hacked his horse to pieces for a whim. Just as I never think of that chivalrous brute, Richard the Lion-Hearted, that I don't see him chopping off the heads of his three thousand prisoners."

"Oh, I don't think that any of us are sighing for a revival of the Middle Ages," returned the journalist. "The worship of the past has usually for its devotees people who have only known the present—"

"Which is as it should be," commented the lawyer. "If man was confined to the worship of the knowable, all the world would lapse into atheism."

"Just as the great lovers of humanity were generally hermits," added the girl in the yachting-cap. "I had an uncle who used to say that he never really loved mankind until he went to live in the wilderness."

"I think we are drifting from the point," said the alienist, helping himself to potatoes. "Was it not—can the saving of a human life ever prove to be an immoral act? I once held that it could."

"Did you act upon it?" asked the lawyer, with rising interest. "I maintain that no proposition can be said to exist until it is acted upon. Otherwise it is in merely an embryonic state—"

The alienist laid down his fork and leaned forward. He was a notable-looking man of some thirty-odd years, who had made a sudden leap into popularity through several successful cases. He had a nervous, muscular face, with singularly penetrating eyes, and hair of a light sandy color. His hands were white and well shaped.

"It was some years ago," he said, bending a scintillant glance around the table. "If you will listen—"

There followed a stir of assent, accompanied by a nod from the young lady upon the Captain's right. "I feel as if it would be a ghost story," she declared.

"It is not a story at all," returned the alienist, lifting his wineglass and holding it against the light. "It is merely a fact."

Then he glanced swiftly around the table as if challenging attention.

"As I said," he began, slowly, "it was some few years ago. Just what year does not matter, but at that time I had completed a course at Heidelberg, and expected shortly to set out with an exploring party for South Africa. It turned out afterwards that I did not go, but for the purpose of the present story it is sufficient that I intended to do so, and had made my preparations accordingly. At Heidelberg I had lived among a set of German students who were permeated with the metaphysics of Schopenhauer, von Hartmann, and the rest, and I was pretty well saturated myself. At that age I was an ardent disciple of pessimism. I am still a disciple, but my ardor has abated—which is not the fault of pessimism, but the virtue of middle age—"

"A man is usually called conservative when he has passed the twenties," interrupted the journalist, "yet it is not that he grows more conservative, but that he grows less radical—"

"Rather that he grows less in every direction," added the Englishman, "except in physical bulk."

The alienist accepted the suggestions with an inclination, and continued. "One of my most cherished convictions," he said, "was to the effect that every man is the sole arbiter of his fate. As Schopenhauer has it, '*that there is nothing to which a man has a more unassailable title than to his own life and person.*' Indeed, that particular sentence had become a kind of motto with our set, and some of my companions even went so far as to preach the proper ending of life with the ending of the power of individual usefulness."

He paused to help himself to salad.

"I was in Scotland at the time, where I had spent a fortnight with my parents, in a small village on the Kyles of Bute. While there I had been treating an invalid cousin who had acquired the morphine habit, and who, under my care, had determined to uproot it. Before leaving I had secured from her the amount of the drug which she had in her possession—some thirty grains—done up in a sealed package, and labelled by a London chemist. As I was in haste, I put it in my bag, thinking that I would add it to my case of medicines when I reached Leicester, where I was to spend the night with an old schoolmate. I took the boat at Tighnabruaich, the small village, found a local train at Gourock to reach Glasgow with one minute in which to catch the first express to London. I made the change and secured a first-class smoking-compartment, which I at first thought to be vacant, but when the train had started a man came from the dressing-room and took the seat across from me. At first I paid no heed to him, but upon looking up once or twice and finding his eyes upon me, I became unpleasantly conscious of his presence. He was thin almost to emaciation, and yet there was a muscular suggestion of physical force about him which it was difficult to account for, since he was both short and slight. His clothes were shabby, but well made, and his cravat had the appearance of having been tied in haste or by nervous fingers. There was a trace of sensuality about the mouth, over which he wore a drooping yellow mustache tinged with gray, and he was somewhat bald upon the crown of his head, which lent a deceptive hint of intellectuality to his uncovered forehead. As he crossed his legs I saw that his boots were carefully blacked, and that they were long and slender, tapering to a decided point."

"I have always held," interpolated the lawyer, "that to judge a man's character you must read his feet."

The alienist sipped his claret and took up his words:

"After passing the first stop I remembered a book at the bottom of my bag, and, unfastening the strap, in my search for the book I laid a number of small articles upon the seat beside me, among them the sealed package bearing the morphine label and the name of the London chemist. Having found the book, I turned to replace the articles, when I noticed that the man across from me was gazing attentively at the labelled package. For a moment his expression startled me, and I stared back at him from across my open bag, into which I had dropped the articles. There was in his eyes a curious mixture of passion and repulsion, and, beyond it all, the look of a hungry hound when he sees food. Thinking that I had chanced upon a victim of the opium craving, I closed the bag, placed it in the net above my head, and opened my book.

"For a while we rode in silence. Nothing was heard except the noise of the train and the clicking of our bags as they jostled each other in the receptacle above. I remember these details very vividly, because since then I have recalled the slightest fact in connection with the incident. I knew that the man across from me drew a cigar from his case, felt in his pocket for an instant, and then turned to me for a match. At the same time I experienced the feeling that the request veiled a larger purpose, and that there were matches in the pocket into which he thrust his fingers.

"But, as I complied with his request, he glanced indifferently out of the window, and following his gaze, I saw that we were passing a group of low-lying hills flecked with stray patches of heather, and that across the hills a flock of sheep were filing, followed by a peasant girl in a short skirt. It was the last faint suggestion of the Highlands.

"The man across from me leaned out, looking back upon the neutral sky, the sparse patches of heather, and the flock of sheep.

"'What a tone the heather gives to a landscape!' he remarked, and his voice sounded forced and affected.

"I bowed without replying, and as he turned from the window, and I sat upon the back seat in the draught of cinders, I bent forward to lower the sash. In a moment he spoke again:

"'Do you go to London?'

"'To Leicester,' I answered, laying the book aside, impelled by a sudden interest. 'Why do you ask?'

"He flushed nervously.

"'I—oh, nothing,' he answered, and drew from me.

"Then, as if with swift determination, he reached forward and lifted the book I had laid upon the seat. It was a treatise of von Hartmann's in German.

"'I had judged that you were a physician,' he said—'a student, perhaps, from a German university?'

"'I am.'

"He paused for an instant, and then spoke in absent-minded reiteration, 'So you don't go on to London?'

"'No,' I returned, impatiently; 'but can I do anything for you?'

"He handed me the book, regarding me resolutely as he did so.

"'Are you a sensible man?'

"I bowed.

"'And a philosopher?'

"'In amateur fashion.'

"With fevered energy he went on more quickly, 'You have in your possession,' he said, 'something for which I would give my whole fortune.' He laid two half-sovereigns and some odd silver in the palm of his hand. 'This is all I possess,' he continued, 'but I would give it gladly.'

"I looked at him curiously.

"'You mean the morphia?' I demanded.

"He nodded. 'I don't ask you to give it to me,' he said; 'I only ask—'

"I interrupted him. 'Are you in pain?'

"He laughed softly, and I really believe he felt a tinge of amusement. 'It is a question of expediency,' he explained. 'If you happen to be a moralist—'

"He broke off. 'What of it?' I inquired.

"He settled himself in his corner, resting his head against the cushions.

"'You get out at Leicester,' he said, recklessly. 'I go on to London, where Providence, represented by Scotland Yard, is awaiting me.'

"I started. 'For what?'

"'They call it murder, I believe,' he returned; 'but what they call it matters very little. I call it justifiable homicide—that also matters very little. The point is—I will arrive, they will be there before me. That is settled. Every station along the road is watched.'

"I glanced out of the window.

"'But you came from Glasgow,' I suggested.

"'Worse luck! I waited in the dressing-room until the train started. I hoped to have the compartment alone, but—' He leaned forward and lowered the window-shade. 'If you don't object,' he said, apologetically; 'I find the glare trying. It is a question for a moralist,' he repeated. 'Indeed, I may call myself a question for a moralist,' and he smiled again with that ugly humor. 'To begin with the beginning, the question is bred in the bone and it's out in the blood.' He nodded at my look of surprise. 'You are an American,' he continued, 'and so am I. I was born in Washington some thirty years ago. My father was a politician of note, whose honor was held to be unimpeachable—which was a mistake. His name doesn't matter, but he became very wealthy through judicious speculations—in votes and other things. My mother has always suffered from an incipient hysteria, which developed shortly before my birth.' He wiped his forehead with his pocket-handkerchief, and knocked the ashes from his cigar with a flick of his finger. 'The motive for this is not far to seek,' he said, with a glance at my travelling-bag. He had the coolest bravado I have ever met. 'As a child,' he went on, 'I gave great promise. Indeed, we moved to England that I might be educated at Oxford. My father considered the atmospheric ecclesiasticism to be beneficial. But while at college I got into trouble with a woman, and I left. My father died, his fortune burst like a bubble, and my mother moved to the country. I was put into a banking office, but I got into more trouble with women—this time two of them. One was a low variety actress, and I married her. I didn't want to do it. I tried not to, but I couldn't help it, and I did it. A month later I left her. I changed my name and went to Belfast, where I resolved to become an honest man. It was a tough job, but I labored and I succeeded—for a time. The variety actress began looking for me, but I escaped her, and have escaped her so far. That was eight years ago. And several years after reaching Belfast I met another woman. She was different. I fell ill of fever in Ireland, and she nursed me. She was a good woman, with a broad Irish face, strong hands, and motherly shoulders. I was weak and she was strong, and I fell in love with her. I tried to tell her about the variety actress, but somehow I couldn't, and I married her.' He shot the stump of his cigar through the opposite window and lighted another, this time drawing the match from his pocket. 'She is an honest woman,' he said—'as honest as the day. She believes in me. It would kill her to know about the variety actress—and all the others. There is one child, a girl—a freckle-faced mite just like her mother—and another is coming.'

"'She knows nothing of this affair?'

"'Not a blamed thing. She is the kind of woman who is good because she can't help herself. She enjoys it. I never did. My mother is different, too. She would die if other people knew of this; my wife would die if she knew of it herself. Well, I got tired, and I wanted money, so I left her and went to Dublin. I changed my name and got a clerkship in a shipping office. My wife thinks I went to America to get work, and if she never hears of me she'll probably think no worse. I did intend going to America, but somehow I didn't. I got in with a man who signed somebody's name to a check and got me to present it. Then we quarrelled about the money, and the man threw the job on me and the affair came out. But before they arrested me I ran him down and shot him. I was ridding the world of a damned traitor.'

"He raised the shade with a nervous hand, but the sun flashed into his eyes, and he lowered it.

"'I suppose I'd hang for it,' he said; 'there isn't much doubt of that. If I waited I'd hang for it, but I am not going to wait. I am going to die. It is the only thing left, and I am going to do it.'

"'And how?'

"'Before this train reaches London,' he replied, 'I am a dead man. There are two ways. I might say three, except that a pitch from the carriage might mean only a broken leg. But there is this—' He drew a vial from his pocket and held it to the light. It contained an ounce or so of carbolic acid.

"'One of the most corrosive of irritants,' I observed.

"'And there is—your package.'

"My first impulse promised me to force the vial from him. He was a slight man, and I could have overcome him with but little exertion. But the exertion I did not make. I should as soon have thought, when my rational humor reasserted itself, of knocking a man down on Broadway and robbing him of his watch. The acid was as exclusively his property as the clothes he wore, and equally his life was his own. Had he declared his intention to hurl himself from the window I might not have made way for him, but I should certainly not have obstructed his passage.

"But the morphia was mine, and that I should assist him was another matter, so I said,

"'The package belongs to me.'

"'And you will not exchange?'

"'Certainly not.'

"He answered, almost angrily:

"'Why not be reasonable? You admit that I am in a mess of it?'

"'Readily.'

"'You also admit that my life is morally my own?'

"'Equally.'

"'That its continuance could in no wise prove to be of benefit to society?'

"'I do.'

"'That for all connected with me it would be better that I should die unknown and under an assumed name than that I should end upon the scaffold, my wife and mother wrecked for life, my children discovered to be illegitimate?'

"'Yes.'

"'Then you admit also that the best I can do is to kill myself before reaching London?'

"'Perhaps.'

"'So you will leave me the morphine when you get off at Leicester?'

"'No.'

"He struck the window-sill impatiently with the palm of his hand.

"'And why not?'

"I hesitated an instant.

"'Because, upon the whole, I do not care to be the instrument of your self-destruction.'

"'Don't be a fool!' he retorted. 'Speak honestly, and say that because of a little moral shrinkage on your part you prefer to leave a human being to a death of agony. I don't like physical pain. I am like a woman about it, but it is better than hanging, or life-imprisonment, or any jury finding.'

"I became exhortatory.

"'Why not face it like a man and take your chances? Who knows—'

"'I have had my chances,' he returned. 'I have squandered more chances than most men ever lay eyes on—and I don't care. If I had the opportunity, I'd squander them again. It is the only thing chances are made for.'

"'What a scoundrel you are!' I exclaimed.

"'Well, I don't know,' he answered; 'there have been worse men. I never said a harsh word to a woman, and I never hit a man when he was down—'

"I blushed. 'Oh, I didn't mean to hit you,' I responded.

"He took no notice.

"'I like my wife,' he said. 'She is a good woman, and I'd do a good deal to keep her and the children from knowing the truth. Perhaps I'd kill myself even if I didn't want to. I don't know, but I am tired—damned tired.'

"'And yet you deserted her.'

"'I did. I tried not to, but I couldn't help it. If I was free to go back to her to-morrow, unless I was ill and wanted nursing, I'd see that she had grown shapeless, and that her hands were coarse.' He stretched out his own, which were singularly white and delicate. 'I believe I'd leave her in a week,' he said.

"Then with an eager movement he pointed to my bag.

"'That is the ending of the difficulty,' he added, 'otherwise I swear that before the train gets to London I will swallow this stuff, and die like a rat.'

"'I admit your right to die in any manner you choose, but I don't see that it is my place to assist you. It is an ugly job.'

"'So am I,' he retorted, grimly. 'At any rate, if you leave the train with that package in your bag it will be cowardice—sheer cowardice. And for the sake of your cowardice you will damn me to this—' He touched the vial.

"'It won't be pleasant,' I said, and we were silent.

"I knew that the man had spoken the truth. I was accustomed to lies, and had learned to detect them. I knew, also, that the world would be well rid of him and his kind. Why I should preserve him for death upon the gallows I did not see. The majesty of the law would be in no way ruffled by his premature departure; and if I could trust that part of his story, the lives of innocent women and children would, in the other case, suffer considerably. And even if I and my unopened bag alighted at Leicester, I was sure that he would never reach London alive. He was a desperate man, this I read in his set face, his dazed eyes, his nervous hands. He was a poor devil, and I was sorry for him as it was. Why, then, should I contribute, by my refusal to comply with his request, an additional hour of agony to his existence? Could I, with my pretence of philosophic latitudinarianism, alight at my station, leaving him to swallow the acid and die like a rat in a cage before the journey was over? I remembered that I had once seen a guinea-pig die from the effects of carbolic acid, and the remembrance sickened me suddenly.

"As I sat there listening to the noise of the slackening train, which was nearing Leicester, I thought of a hundred things. I thought of Schopenhauer and von

Hartmann. I thought of the dying guinea-pig. I thought of the broad-faced Irish wife and the two children.

"Then 'Leicester' flashed before me, and the train stopped. I rose, gathered my coat and rug, and lifted the volume of von Hartmann from the seat. The man remained motionless in the corner of the compartment, but his eyes followed me.

"I stooped, opened my bag, and laid the chemist's package upon the seat. Then I stepped out, closing the door after me." As the speaker finished, he reached forward, selected an almond from the stand of nuts, fitted it carefully between the crackers, and cracked it slowly.

The young lady upon the Captain's right shook herself with a shudder.

"What a horrible story!" she exclaimed; "for it is a story, after all, and not a fact."

"A point, rather," suggested the Englishman; "but is that all?"

"All of the point," returned the alienist. "The next day I saw in the *Times* that a man, supposed to be James Morganson, who was wanted for murder, was found dead in a first-class smoking-compartment of the Midland Railway, Coroner's verdict, 'Death resulting from an overdose of morphia, taken with suicidal intent.'"

The journalist dropped a lump of sugar in his cup and watched it attentively.

"I don't think I could have done it," he said. "I might have left him with his carbolic. But I couldn't have deliberately given him his death-potion."

"But as long as he was going to die," responded the girl in the yachting-cap, "it was better to let him die painlessly."

The Englishman smiled. "Can a woman ever consider the ethical side of a question when the sympathetic one is visible?" he asked.

The alienist cracked another almond. "I was sincere," he said. "Of that there is no doubt. I thought I did right. The question is—did I do right?"

"It would have been wiser," began the lawyer, argumentatively, "since you were stronger than he, to take the vial from him, and to leave him to the care of the law."

"But the wife and children," replied the girl in the yachting-cap. "And hanging is so horrible!"

"So is murder," responded the lawyer, dryly.

The young lady on the Captain's right laid her napkin upon the table and rose. "I don't know what was right," she said, "but I do know that in your place I should have felt like a murderer."

The alienist smiled half cynically. "So I did," he answered; "but there is such a thing, my dear young lady, as a conscientious murderer."

A MYSTERIOUS CASE

Anna Katharine Green

Anna Katharine Green (1846–1935) was one of the first American authors of detective fiction. Her novel *The Leavenworth Case* (1878) is often cited as the first such novel written by a woman. An international bestseller credited with popularising the genre in the United States, she was born and died in New York.

It was a mystery to me, but not to the other doctors. They took, as was natural, the worst possible view of the matter, and accepted the only solution which the facts seem to warrant. But they are men, and I am a woman; besides, I knew the nurse well, and I could not believe her capable of wilful deceit, much less of the heinous crime which deceit in this case involved. So to me the affair was a mystery.

The facts were these:

My patient, a young typewriter, seemingly without friends or enemies, lay in a small room of a boarding-house, afflicted with a painful but not dangerous malady. Though she was comparatively helpless, her vital organs were strong, and we never had a moment's uneasiness concerning her, till one morning when we found her in an almost dying condition from having taken, as we quickly discovered, a dose of poison, instead of the soothing mixture which had been left for her with the nurse. Poison! and no one, not even herself or the nurse, could explain how the same got into the room, much less into her medicine. And when I came to study the situation, I found myself as much at loss as they; indeed, more so; for I knew I had made no mistake in preparing the mixture, and that, even if I had, this especial poison could not have found its way into it, owing to the fact that there neither was nor ever had been a drop of it in my possession.

The mixture, then, was pure when it left my hand, and, according to the nurse, whom, as I have said, I implicitly believe, it went into the glass pure. And yet when, two hours later, without her having left the room or anybody coming into it, she found occasion to administer the draught, poison was in the cup, and the patient was only saved from death by the most immediate and energetic measures, not only on her part, but on that of Dr. Holmes, whom in her haste and perturbation she had called in from the adjacent house.

The patient, young, innocent, unfortunate, but of a strangely courageous disposition, betrayed nothing but the utmost surprise at the peril she had so narrowly escaped. When Dr. Holmes intimated that perhaps she had been tired of suffering, and had herself found means of putting the deadly drug into her medicine, she opened her great gray eyes, with such a look of child-like surprise and reproach, that he blushed, and murmured some sort of apology.

"Poison myself?" she cried, "when you promise me that I shall get well? You do not know what a horror I have of dying in debt, or you would never say that." This was some time after the critical moment had passed, and there were in the room Mrs. Dayton, the landlady, Dr. Holmes, the nurse, and myself. At the utterance of these words we all felt ashamed and cast looks of increased interest at the poor girl.

She was very lovely. Though without means, and to all appearance without friends, she possessed in great degree the charm of winsomeness, and not even her many sufferings, nor the indignation under which she was then laboring, could quite rob her countenance of that tender and confiding expression which so often redeems the plainest face and makes beauty doubly attractive.

"Dr. Holmes does not know you," I hastened to say; "I do, and utterly repel for you any such insinuation. In return, will you tell me if there is any one in the world whom you can call your enemy? Though the chief mystery is how so deadly and unusual a poison could have gotten into a clean glass, without the knowledge of yourself or the nurse, still it might not be amiss to know if there is any one, here or elsewhere, who for any reason might desire your death."

The surprise in the child-like eyes increased rather than diminished.

"I don't know what to say," she murmured. "I am so insignificant and feeble a person that it seems absurd for me to talk of having an enemy. Besides, I have none. On the contrary, every one seems to love me more than I deserve. Haven't you noticed it, Mrs. Dayton?"

The landlady smiled and stroked the sick girl's hand.

"Indeed," she replied, "I have noticed that people love you, but I have never thought that it was more than you deserved. You are a dear little thing, Addie." And though she knew and I knew that the "every one" mentioned by the poor girl meant ourselves, and possibly her unknown employer, we were none the less touched by her words. The more we studied the mystery, the deeper and less explainable did it become.

And indeed I doubt if we should have ever got to the bottom of it, if there had not presently occurred in my patient a repetition of the same dangerous symptoms, followed by the same discovery, of poison in the glass, and the same failure on the part of herself and nurse to account for it. I was aroused from my bed at midnight to attend her, and as I entered her room and met her beseeching eyes looking upon me from the very shadow of death, I made a vow that I would never cease my efforts till I had penetrated the secret of what certainly looked like a persistent attempt upon this poor girl's life.

I went about the matter deliberately. As soon as I could leave her side, I drew the nurse into a corner and again questioned her. The answers were the same as before. Addie had shown distress as soon as she had swallowed her usual quantity of medicine, and in a few minutes more was in a perilous condition.

"Did you hand the glass yourself to Addie?"

"I did."

"Where did you take it from?"

"From the place where you left it — the little stand on the farther side of the bed."

"And do you mean to say that you had not touched it since I prepared it?"

"I do, ma'am."

"And that no one else has been in the room?"

"No one, ma'am."

I looked at her intently. I trusted her, but the best of us are but mortal.

"Can you assure me that you have not been asleep during this time?"

"Look at this letter I have been writing," she returned. "It is eight pages long, and it was not begun when you left us at 10 o'clock."

I shook my head and fell into a deep revery. How was that matter to be elucidated, and how was my patient to be saved? Another draught of this deadly poison, and no power on earth could resuscitate her. What should I do, and with what weapons should I combat a danger at once so subtle and so deadly? Reflection brought no decision, and I left the room at last, determined upon but one point, and that was the immediate removal of my patient. But before I had left the house I changed my mind even on this point. Removal of the patient meant safety to her, perhaps, but not the explanation of her mysterious poisoning. I would change the position of her bed, and I would even set a watch over her and the nurse, but I would not take her out of the house — not yet.

And what had produced this change in my plans? The look of a woman whom I met on the stairs. I did not know her, but when I encountered her glance I felt that there was some connection between us, and I was not at all surprised to hear her ask:

"And how is Miss Wilcox to-day?"

"Miss Wilcox is very low," I returned. "The least neglect, the least shock to her nerves, would be sufficient to make all my efforts useless. Otherwise —"

"She will get well?"

I nodded. I had exaggerated the condition of the sufferer, but some secret instinct compelled me to do so. The look which passed over the woman's face satisfied me that I had done well; and, though I left the house, it was with the intention of speedily returning and making inquiries into the woman's character and position in the household.

I learned little or nothing. That she occupied a good room and paid for it regularly seemed to be sufficient to satisfy Mrs. Dayton. Her name, which proved to be Leroux, showed her to be French, and her promptly paid $10 a week showed her to be respectable — what more could any hard-working landlady require? But I was distrustful. Her face, though handsome, possessed an eager, ferocious look which I could not forget, and the slight gesture with which she had passed me at the close of the short conversation I have given above had a suggestion of triumph in it which seemed to contain whole volumes of secret and mysterious hate. I went into Miss Wilcox's room very thoughtful.

"I am going —"

But here the nurse held up her hand. "Hark," she whispered; she had just set the clock, and was listening to its striking.

I did hark, but not to the clock.

"Whose step is that?" I asked, after she had left the clock, and sat down.

"Oh, some one in the next room. The walls here are very thin — only boards in places."

I did not complete what I had begun to say. If I could hear steps through the partition, then could our neighbors hear us talk, and what I had determined upon must be kept secret from all outsiders. I drew a sheet of paper toward me and wrote:

"I shall stay here to-night. Something tells me that in doing this I shall solve this mystery. But I must appear to go. Take my instructions as usual, and bid me good-night. Lock the door after me, but with a turn of the key instantly unlock it again. I shall go down stairs, see that my carriage drives away, and quietly return. On my re-entrance I shall expect to find Miss Wilcox on the couch with the screen drawn up around it, you in your big chair, and the light lowered. What I do thereafter need not concern you. Pretend to go to sleep."

The nurse nodded, and immediately entered upon the programme I had planned. I prepared the medicine as usual, placed it in its usual glass, and laid that glass where it had always been set, on a small table at the farther side of the bed. Then I said "Good-night," and passed hurriedly out.

I was fortunate enough to meet no one, going or coming. I regained the room, pushed open the door, and finding everything in order, proceeded at once to the bed, upon which, after taking off my hat and cloak and carefully concealing them, I lay down and deftly covered myself up.

My idea was this — that by some mesmeric influence of which she was ignorant, the nurse had been forced to either poison the glass herself or open the door for another to do it. If this were so, she or the other person would be obliged to pass around the foot of the bed in order to reach the glass, and I should be sure to see it, for I did not pretend to sleep. By the low light enough could be discerned for safe movement about the room, and not enough to make apparent the change which had been made in the occupant of the bed. I waited with indescribable anxiety, and more than once fancied I heard steps, if not a feverish breathing close to my bed-head; but no one appeared, and the nurse in her big chair did not move.

At last I grew weary, and fearful of losing control over my eyelids, I fixed my gaze upon the glass, as if in so doing I should find a talisman to keep me awake, when, great God! what was it I saw! A hand, a creeping hand coming from nowhere and joined to nothing, closing about that glass and drawing it slowly away till it disappeared entirely from before my eyes!

I gasped — I could not help it — but I did not stir. For now I knew I was asleep and dreaming. But no, I pinch myself under the clothes, and find that I am very wide awake indeed; and then — look! look! the glass is returning; the hand — a woman's hand — is slowly setting it back in its place, and —

With a bound I have that hand in my grasp. It is a living hand, and it is very warm and strong and fierce, and the glass has fallen and lies shattered between us, and a double cry is heard, one from behind the partition, through an opening in which this hand had been thrust, and one from the nurse, who has jumped to her feet and is even now assisting me in holding the struggling member, upon which I have managed to scratch a tell-tale mark with a piece of the fallen glass. At sight of the iron-like grip which this latter lays upon the intruding member, I at once release my own grasp.

"Hold on," I cried, and leaping from the bed, I hastened first to my patient, whom I carefully reassured, and then into the hall, where I found the landlady running to see what was the matter. "I have found the wretch," I cried, and drawing her after me, hurried about to the other side of the partition, where I found a closet, and in it the woman I had met on the stairs, but glaring now like a tiger in her rage, menace, and fear.

That woman was my humble little patient's bitter but unknown enemy.

Enamoured of a man who — unwisely, perhaps — had expressed in her hearing his admiration for the pretty typewriter, she had conceived the idea that he intended to marry the latter, and, vowing vengeance, had taken up her abode in the same house with the innocent girl, where, had it not been for the fortunate circumstance of my meeting her on the stairs, she would certainly have carried out her scheme of vile and secret murder. The poison she had bought in another city, and the hole in the partition she had herself cut. This had been done at first for the purpose of observation, she having detected in passing by Miss Wilcox's open door that a banner of painted silk hung over that portion of the wall in such a way as to hide any aperture which might be made there.

Afterward, when Miss Wilcox fell sick, and she discovered by short glimpses through her loop-hole that the glass of medicine was placed on a table just under this banner, she could not resist the temptation to enlarge the hole to a size sufficient to admit the pushing aside of the banner and the reaching through of her murderous hand. Why she did not put poison enough in the glass to kill Miss Wilcox at once I have never discovered. Probably she feared detection. That by doing as she did she brought about the very event she had endeavored to avert, is the most pleasing part of the tale. When the gentleman of whom I have spoken learned of the wicked attempt which had been made upon Miss Wilcox's life, his heart took pity upon her, and a marriage ensued, which I have every reason to believe is a happy one.

THE GOLDEN SLIPPER

Anna Katharine Green

Anna Katharine Green (1846–1935) was one of the first American authors of detective fiction. Her novel *The Leavenworth Case* (1878) is often cited as the first such novel written by a woman. An international bestseller, credited with popularizing the genre in the United States, she was born and died in New York.

"She's here! I thought she would be. She's one of the three young ladies you see in the right-hand box near the proscenium."

The gentleman thus addressed – a man of middle age and a member of the most exclusive clubs – turned his opera glass toward the spot designated, and in some astonishment retorted:

"She? Why those are the Misses Pratt and –"

"Miss Violet Strange; no other."

"And do you mean to say –"

"I do –"

"That yon silly little chit, whose father I know, whose fortune I know, who is seen everywhere, and who is called one of the season's belles is an agent of yours; a – a –"

"No names here, please. You want a mystery solved. It is not a matter for the police – that is, as yet – and so you come to me, and when I ask for the facts, I find that women and only women are involved, and that these women are not only young but one and all of the highest society. Is it a man's work to go to the bottom of a combination like this? No. Sex against sex, and, if possible, youth against youth. Happily, I know such a person – a girl of gifts and extraordinarily well placed for the purpose. Why she uses her talents in this direction – why, with means enough to play the part natural to her as a successful debutante, she consents to occupy herself with social and other mysteries, you must ask her, not me. Enough that I promise you her aid if you want it. That is, if you can interest her. She will not work otherwise."

Mr. Driscoll again raised his opera glass.

"But it's a comedy face," he commented. "It's hard to associate intellectuality with such quaintness of expression. Are you sure of her discretion?"

"Whom is she with?"

"Abner Pratt, his wife, and daughters."

"Is he a man to entrust his affairs unadvisedly?"

"Abner Pratt! Do you mean to say that she is anything more to him than his daughters' guest?"

"Judge. You see how merry they are. They were in deep trouble yesterday. You are witness to a celebration."

"And she?"

"Don't you observe how they are loading her with attentions? She's too young to rouse such interest in a family of notably unsympathetic temperament for any other reason than that of gratitude."

"It's hard to believe. But if what you hint is true, secure me an opportunity at once of talking to this youthful marvel. My affair is serious. The dinner I have mentioned comes off in three days and –"

"I know. I recognize your need; but I think you had better enter Mr. Pratt's box without my intervention. Miss Strange's value to us will be impaired the moment her connection with us is discovered."

"Ah, there's Ruthven! He will take me to Mr. Pratt's box," remarked Driscoll as the curtain fell on the second act. "Any suggestions before I go?"

"Yes, and an important one. When you make your bow, touch your left shoulder with your right hand. It is a signal. She may respond to it; but if she does not, do not be discouraged. One of her idiosyncrasies is a theoretical dislike of her work. But once she gets interested, nothing will hold her back. That's all, except this. In no event give away her secret. That's part of the compact, you remember."

Driscoll nodded and left his seat for Ruthven's box. When the curtain rose for the third time he could be seen sitting with the Misses Pratt and their vivacious young friend. A widower and still on the right side of fifty, his presence there did not pass unnoted, and curiosity was rife among certain onlookers as to which of the twin belles was responsible for this change in his well-known habits. Unfortunately, no opportunity was given him for showing. Other and younger men had followed his lead into the box, and they saw him forced upon the good graces of the fascinating but inconsequent Miss Strange whose rapid fire of talk he was hardly of a temperament to appreciate.

Did he appear dissatisfied? Yes; but only one person in the opera house knew why. Miss Strange had shown no comprehension of or sympathy with his errand. Though she chatted amiably enough between duets and trios, she gave him no opportunity to express his wishes though she knew them well enough, owing to the signal he had given her.

This might be in character but it hardly suited his views; and, being a man of resolution, he took advantage of an absorbing minute on the stage to lean forward and whisper in her ear:

"It's my daughter for whom I request your services; as fine a girl as any in this house. Give me a hearing. You certainly can manage it."

She was a small, slight woman whose naturally quaint appearance was accentuated by the extreme simplicity of her attire. In the tier upon tier of boxes rising before his eyes, no other personality could vie with hers in strangeness, or in the illusive quality of her ever-changing expression. She was vivacity incarnate and, to the ordinary observer, light as thistledown in fibre and in feeling. But not to all. To those who watched her long, there came moments – say when the music rose to heights of greatness – when the mouth so given over to laughter took on curves of the rarest sensibility, and a woman's lofty soul shone through her odd, bewildering features.

Driscoll had noted this, and consequently awaited her reply in secret hope.

It came in the form of a question and only after an instant's display of displeasure or possibly of pure nervous irritability.

"What has she done?"

"Nothing. But slander is in the air, and any day it may ripen into public accusation."

"Accusation of what?" Her tone was almost pettish.

"Of – of theft," he murmured. "On a great scale," he emphasized, as the music rose to a crash.

"Jewels?"

"Inestimable ones. They are always returned by somebody. People say, by me."

"Ah!" The little lady's hands grew steady – they had been fluttering all over her lap. "I will see you to-morrow morning at my father's house," she presently observed; and turned her full attention to the stage.

Some three days after this Mr. Driscoll opened his house on the Hudson to notable guests. He had not desired the publicity of such an event, nor the opportunity it gave for an increase of the scandal secretly in circulation against his daughter. But the Ambassador and his wife were foreign and any evasion of the promised hospitality would be sure to be misunderstood; so the scheme was carried forward though with less eclat than possibly was expected.

Among the lesser guests, who were mostly young and well acquainted with the house and its hospitality, there was one unique figure – that of the lively Miss Strange, who, if personally unknown to Miss Driscoll, was so gifted with the qualities which tell on an occasion of this kind, that the stately young hostess hailed her presence with very obvious gratitude.

The manner of their first meeting was singular, and of great interest to one of them at least. Miss Strange had come in an automobile and had been shown her room; but there was nobody to accompany her downstairs afterward, and, finding herself alone in the great hall, she naturally moved toward the library, the door of which stood ajar. She had pushed this door half open before she noticed that the room was already occupied. As a consequence, she was made the unexpected observer of a beautiful picture of youth and love.

A young man and a young woman were standing together in the glow of a blazing wood-fire. No word was to be heard, but in their faces, eloquent with passion, there shone something so deep and true that the chance intruder hesitated on the threshold, eager to lay this picture away in her mind with the other lovely and tragic memories now fast accumulating there. Then she drew back, and readvancing with a less noiseless foot, came into the full presence of Captain Holliday drawn up in all the pride of his military rank beside Alicia, the accomplished daughter of the house, who, if under a shadow as many whispered, wore that shadow as some women wear a crown.

Miss Strange was struck with admiration, and turned upon them the brightest facet of her vivacious nature all the time she was saying to herself: "Does she know why I am here? Or does she look upon me only as an additional guest foisted upon her by a thoughtless parent?"

There was nothing in the manner of her cordial but composed young hostess to show, and Miss Strange, with but one thought in mind since she had caught the light of feeling on the two faces confronting her, took the first opportunity that offered of running over the facts given her by Mr. Driscoll, to see if any reconcilement were possible between them and an innocence in which she must henceforth believe.

They were certainly of a most damaging nature.

Miss Driscoll and four other young ladies of her own station in life had formed themselves, some two years before, into a coterie of five, called the Inseparables. They lunched together, rode together, visited together. So close was the bond and their mutual dependence so evident, that it came to be the custom to invite the whole five whenever the size of the function warranted it. In fact, it was far from an uncommon occurrence to see them grouped at receptions or following one another down the aisles of churches or through the mazes of the dance at balls or assemblies. And no one demurred at this, for they were all handsome and attractive girls, till it began to be noticed that, coincident with their presence, some article of value was found missing from the dressing-room or from the tables where wedding gifts were displayed. Nothing was safe where they went, and though, in the course of time, each article found its way back to its owner in a manner as mysterious as its previous abstraction, the scandal grew and, whether with good reason or bad, finally settled about the person of Miss Driscoll, who was the showiest, least pecuniarily tempted, and most dignified in manner and speech of them all.

Some instances had been given by way of further enlightenment. This is one: A theatre party was in progress. There were twelve in the party, five of whom were the Inseparables. In the course of the last act, another lady – in fact, their chaperon – missed her handkerchief, an almost priceless bit of lace. Positive that she had brought it with her into the box, she caused a careful search, but without the least success. Recalling certain whispers she had heard, she noted which of the five girls were with her in the box. They were Miss Driscoll, Miss Hughson, Miss Yates, and Miss Benedict. Miss West sat in the box adjoining.

A fortnight later this handkerchief reappeared – and where? Among the cushions of a yellow satin couch in her own drawing-room. The Inseparables had just made their call and the three who had sat on the couch were Miss Driscoll, Miss Hughson, and Miss Benedict.

The next instance seemed to point still more insistently toward the lady already named. Miss Yates had an expensive present to buy, and the whole five Inseparables went in an imposing group to Tiffany's. A tray of rings was set before them. All examined and eagerly fingered the stock out of which Miss Yates presently chose a finely set emerald. She was leading her friends away when the clerk suddenly whispered in her ear, "I miss one of the rings." Dismayed beyond speech, she turned and consulted the faces of her four companions who stared back at her with immovable serenity. But one of them was paler than usual, and this lady (it was Miss Driscoll) held her hands in her muff and did not offer to take them out. Miss Yates, whose father had completed a big "deal" the week before, wheeled round upon the clerk. "Charge it! charge it at its full value," said she. "I buy both the rings."

And in three weeks the purloined ring came back to her, in a box of violets with no name attached.

The third instance was a recent one, and had come to Mr. Driscoll's ears directly from the lady suffering the loss. She was a woman of uncompromising integrity, who felt it her duty to make known to this gentleman the following facts: She had just left a studio reception, and was standing at the curb waiting for a taxicab to draw up, when a small boy – a street arab – darted toward her from the other side of the street, and thrusting into her hand something small and hard, cried breathlessly as he slipped away, "It's yours, ma'am; you dropped it." Astonished, for she had not been conscious of any loss, she looked down at her treasure trove and found it to be a small medallion which she sometimes wore on a chain at her belt. But she had not worn it that day, nor any day for weeks. Then she remembered. She had worn it a month before to a similar reception at this same studio. A number of young girls had stood about her admiring it – she remembered well who they were; the Inseparables, of course, and to please them she had slipped it from its chain. Then something had happened – something which diverted her attention entirely – and she had gone home without the medallion; had, in fact, forgotten it, only to recall its loss now. Placing it in her bag, she looked hastily about her. A crowd was at her back; nothing to be distinguished there. But in front, on the opposite side of the street, stood a club-house, and in one of its windows she perceived a solitary figure looking out. It was that of Miss Driscoll's father. He could imagine her conclusion.

In vain he denied all knowledge of the matter. She told him other stories which had come to her ears of thefts as mysterious, followed by restorations as peculiar as this one, finishing with, "It is your daughter, and people are beginning to say so."

And Miss Strange, brooding over these instances, would have said the same, but for Miss Driscoll's absolute serenity of demeanour and complete abandonment to love. These seemed incompatible with guilt; these, whatever the appearances, proclaimed innocence – an innocence she was here to prove if fortune favoured and the really guilty person's madness should again break forth.

For madness it would be and nothing less, for any hand, even the most experienced, to draw attention to itself by a repetition of old tricks on an occasion so marked. Yet because it would take madness, and madness knows no law, she prepared herself for the contingency under a mask of girlish smiles which made her at once the delight and astonishment of her watchful and uneasy host.

With the exception of the diamonds worn by the Ambassadress, there was but one jewel of consequence to be seen at the dinner that night; but how great was that consequence and with what splendour it invested the snowy neck it adorned!

Miss Strange, in compliment to the noble foreigners, had put on one of her family heirlooms – a filigree pendant of extraordinary sapphires which had once belonged to Marie Antoinette. As its beauty flashed upon the women, and its value struck the host, the latter could not restrain himself from casting an anxious eye about the board in search of some token of the cupidity with which one person there must welcome this unexpected sight.

Naturally his first glance fell upon Alicia, seated opposite to him at the other end of the table. But her eyes were elsewhere, and her smile for Captain

Holliday, and the father's gaze travelled on, taking up each young girl's face in turn. All were contemplating Miss Strange and her jewels, and the cheeks of one were flushed and those of the others pale, but whether with dread or longing who could tell. Struck with foreboding, but alive to his duty as host, he forced his glances away, and did not even allow himself to question the motive or the wisdom of the temptation thus offered.

Two hours later and the girls were all in one room. It was a custom of the Inseparables to meet for a chat before retiring, but always alone and in the room of one of their number. But this was a night of innovations; Violet was not only included, but the meeting was held in her room. Her way with girls was even more fruitful of result than her way with men. They might laugh at her, criticize her or even call her names significant of disdain, but they never left her long to herself or missed an opportunity to make the most of her irrepressible chatter.

Her satisfaction at entering this charmed circle did not take from her piquancy, and story after story fell from her lips, as she fluttered about, now here now there, in her endless preparations for retirement. She had taken off her historic pendant after it had been duly admired and handled by all present, and, with the careless confidence of an assured ownership, thrown it down upon the end of her dresser, which, by the way, projected very close to the open window.

"Are you going to leave your jewel there?" whispered a voice in her ear as a burst of laughter rang out in response to one of her sallies.

Turning, with a simulation of round-eyed wonder, she met Miss Hughson's earnest gaze with the careless rejoinder, "What's the harm?" and went on with her story with all the reckless ease of a perfectly thoughtless nature.

Miss Hughson abandoned her protest. How could she explain her reasons for it to one apparently uninitiated in the scandal associated with their especial clique.

Yes, she left the jewel there; but she locked her door and quickly, so that they must all have heard her before reaching their rooms. Then she crossed to the window, which, like all on this side, opened on a balcony running the length of the house. She was aware of this balcony, also of the fact that only young ladies slept in the corridor communicating with it. But she was not quite sure that this one corridor accommodated them all. If one of them should room elsewhere! (Miss Driscoll, for instance). But no! the anxiety displayed for the safety of her jewel precluded that supposition. Their hostess, if none of the others, was within access of this room and its open window. But how about the rest? Perhaps the lights would tell. Eagerly the little schemer looked forth, and let her glances travel down the full length of the balcony. Two separate beams of light shot across it as she looked, and presently another, and, after some waiting, a fourth. But the fifth failed to appear. This troubled her, but not seriously. Two of the girls might be sleeping in one bed.

Drawing her shade, she finished her preparations for the night; then with her kimono on, lifted the pendant and thrust it into a small box she had taken from her trunk. A curious smile, very unlike any she had shown to man or woman that day, gave a sarcastic lift to her lips, as with a slow and thoughtful manipulation of her dainty fingers she moved the jewel about in this small receptacle and then returned it, after one quick examining glance, to the very spot on the dresser from which she had taken it. "If only the madness is great enough!" that smile seemed to say. Truly, it was much to hope for, but a chance is a chance; and comforting herself with the thought, Miss Strange put out her light, and, with a hasty raising of the shade she had previously pulled down, took a final look at the prospect.

Its aspect made her shudder. A low fog was rising from the meadows in the far distance, and its ghostliness under the moon woke all sorts of uncanny images in her excited mind. To escape them she crept into bed where she lay with her eyes on the end of her dresser. She had closed that half of the French window over which she had drawn the shade; but she had left ajar the one giving free access to the jewels; and when she was not watching the scintillation of her sapphires in the moonlight, she was dwelling in fixed attention on this narrow opening.

But nothing happened, and two o'clock, then three o'clock struck, without a dimming of the blue scintillations on the end of her dresser. Then she suddenly sat up. Not that she heard anything new, but that a thought had come to her. "If an attempt is made," so she murmured softly to herself, "it will be by –" She did not finish. Something – she could not call it sound – set her heart beating tumultuously, and listening – listening – watching – watching – she followed in her imagination the approach down the balcony of an almost inaudible step, not daring to move herself, it seemed so near, but waiting with eyes fixed, for the shadow which must fall across the shade she had failed to raise over that half of the swinging window she had so carefully left shut.

At length she saw it projecting slowly across the slightly illuminated surface. Formless, save for the outreaching hand, it passed the casement's edge, nearing with pauses and hesitations the open gap beyond through which the neglected sapphires beamed with steady lustre. Would she ever see the hand itself appear between the dresser and the window frame? Yes, there it comes – small, delicate, and startlingly white, threading that gap – darting with the suddenness of a serpent's tongue toward the dresser and disappearing again with the pendant in its clutch.

As she realizes this – she is but young, you know – as she sees her bait taken and the hardly expected event fulfilled, her pent-up breath sped forth in a sigh which sent the intruder flying, and so startled herself that she sank back in terror on her pillow.

The breakfast-call had sounded its musical chimes through the halls. The Ambassador and his wife had responded, so had most of the young gentlemen and ladies, but the daughter of the house was not amongst them, nor Miss Strange, whom one would naturally expect to see down first of all.

These two absences puzzled Mr. Driscoll. What might they not portend? But his suspense, at least in one regard, was short. Before his guests were well seated, Miss Driscoll entered from the terrace in company with Captain Holliday. In her arms she carried a huge bunch of roses and was looking very beautiful. Her father's heart warmed at the sight. No shadow from the night rested upon her.

But Miss Strange! – where was she? He could not feel quite easy till he knew.

"Have any of you seen Miss Strange?" he asked, as they sat down at table. And his eyes sought the Inseparables.

Five lovely heads were shaken, some carelessly, some wonderingly, and one, with a quick, forced smile. But he was in no mood to discriminate, and he had beckoned one of the servants to him, when a step was heard at the door and the delinquent slid in and took her place, in a shamefaced manner suggestive of a cause deeper than mere tardiness. In fact, she had what might be called a frightened air, and stared into her plate, avoiding every eye, which was certainly not natural to her. What did it mean? and why, as she made a poor attempt at eating, did four of the Inseparables exchange glances of doubt and dismay and then concentrate their looks upon his daughter? That Alicia failed to notice this, but sat abloom above her roses now fastened in a great bunch upon her breast, offered him some comfort, yet, for all the volubility of his chief guests, the meal was a great trial to his patience, as well as a poor preparation for the hour when, the noble pair gone, he stepped into the library to find Miss Strange awaiting him with one hand behind her back and a piteous look on her infantile features.

"O, Mr. Driscoll," she began – and then he saw that a group of anxious girls hovered in her rear – "my pendant! my beautiful pendant! It is gone! Somebody reached in from the balcony and took it from my dresser in the night. Of course, it was to frighten me; all of the girls told me not to leave it there. But I – I cannot make them give it back, and papa is so particular about this jewel that I'm afraid to go home. Won't you tell them it's no joke, and see that I get it again. I won't be so careless another time."

Hardly believing his eyes, hardly believing his ears – she was so perfectly the spoiled child detected in a fault – he looked sternly about upon the girls and bade them end the jest and produce the gems at once.

But not one of them spoke, and not one of them moved; only his daughter grew pale until the roses seemed a mockery, and the steady stare of her large eyes was almost too much for him to bear.

The anguish of this gave asperity to his manner, and in a strange, hoarse tone he loudly cried:

"One of you did this. Which? If it was you, Alicia, speak. I am in no mood for nonsense. I want to know whose foot traversed the balcony and whose hand abstracted these jewels."

A continued silence, deepening into painful embarrassment for all. Mr. Driscoll eyed them in ill-concealed anguish, then turning to Miss Strange was still further thrown off his balance by seeing her pretty head droop and her gaze fall in confusion.

"Oh! it's easy enough to tell whose foot traversed the balcony," she murmured. "It left this behind." And drawing forward her hand, she held out to view a small gold-coloured slipper. "I found it outside my window," she explained. "I hoped I should not have to show it."

A gasp of uncontrollable feeling from the surrounding group of girls, then absolute stillness.

"I fail to recognize it," observed Mr. Driscoll, taking it in his hand. "Whose slipper is this?" he asked in a manner not to be gainsaid.

Still no reply, then as he continued to eye the girls one after another a voice – the last he expected to hear – spoke and his daughter cried:

"It is mine. But it was not I who walked in it down the balcony."

"Alicia!"

A month's apprehension was in that cry. The silence, the pent-up emotion brooding in the air was intolerable. A fresh young laugh broke it.

"Oh," exclaimed a roguish voice, "I knew that you were all in it! But the especial one who wore the slipper and grabbed the pendant cannot hope to hide herself. Her finger-tips will give her away."

Amazement on every face and a convulsive movement in one half-hidden hand.

"You see," the airy little being went on, in her light way, "I have some awfully funny tricks. I am always being scolded for them, but somehow I don't improve. One is to keep my jewelry bright with a strange foreign paste an old French-woman once gave me in Paris. It's of a vivid red, and stains the fingers dread-fully if you don't take care. Not even water will take it off, see mine. I used that paste on my pendant last night just after you left me, and being awfully sleepy I didn't stop to rub it off. If your finger-tips are not red, you never touched the pendant, Miss Driscoll. Oh, see! They are as white as milk.

"But some one took the sapphires, and I owe that person a scolding, as well as myself. Was it you, Miss Hughson? You, Miss Yates? or –" and here she paused before Miss West, "Oh, you have your gloves on! You are the guilty one!" and her laugh rang out like a peal of bells, robbing her next sentence of even a sug-gestion of sarcasm. "Oh, what a sly-boots!" she cried. "How you have deceived me! Whoever would have thought you to be the one to play the mischief!"

Who indeed! Of all the five, she was the one who was considered absolutely immune from suspicion ever since the night Mrs. Barnum's handkerchief had been taken, and she not in the box. Eyes which had surveyed Miss Driscoll askance now rose in wonder toward hers, and failed to fall again because of the stoniness into which her delicately-carved features had settled.

"Miss West, I know you will be glad to remove your gloves; Miss Strange certainly has a right to know her special tormentor," spoke up her host in as natural a voice as his great relief would allow.

But the cold, half-frozen woman remained without a movement. She was not deceived by the banter of the moment. She knew that to all of the others, if not to Peter Strange's odd little daughter, it was the thief who was being spotted and brought thus hilariously to light. And her eyes grew hard, and her lips grey, and she failed to unglove the hands upon which all glances were concentrated.

"You do not need to see my hands; I confess to taking the pendant."

"Caroline!"

A heart overcome by shock had thrown up this cry. Miss West eyed her bosom-friend disdainfully.

"Miss Strange has called it a jest," she coldly commented. "Why should you suggest anything of a graver character?"

Alicia brought thus to bay, and by one she had trusted most, stepped quickly forward, and quivering with vague doubts, aghast before unheard-of possibili-ties, she tremulously remarked:

"We did not sleep together last night. You had to come into my room to get my slippers. Why did you do this? What was in your mind, Caroline?"

A steady look, a low laugh choked with many emotions answered her.

"Do you want me to reply, Alicia? Or shall we let it pass?"

"Answer!"

It was Mr. Driscoll who spoke. Alicia had shrunk back, almost to where a little figure was cowering with wide eyes fixed in something like terror on the aroused father's face.

"Then hear me," murmured the girl, entrapped and suddenly desperate. "I wore Alicia's slippers and I took the jewels, because it was time that an end should come to your mutual dissimulation. The love I once felt for her she has herself deliberately killed. I had a lover – she took him. I had faith in life, in honour, and in friendship. She destroyed all. A thief – she has dared to aspire to him! And you condoned her fault. You, with your craven restoration of her booty, thought the matter cleared and her a fit mate for a man of highest honour."

"Miss West," – no one had ever heard that tone in Mr. Driscoll's voice before, "before you say another word calculated to mislead these ladies, let me say that this hand never returned any one's booty or had anything to do with the restoration of any abstracted article. You have been caught in a net, Miss West, from which you cannot escape by slandering my innocent daughter."

"Innocent!" All the tragedy latent in this peculiar girl's nature blazed forth in the word. "Alicia, face me. Are you innocent? Who took the Dempsey corals, and that diamond from the Tiffany tray?"

"It is not necessary for Alicia to answer," the father interposed with not unnatural heat. "Miss West stands self-convicted."

"How about Lady Paget's scarf? I was not there that night."

"You are a woman of wiles. That could be managed by one bent on an elaborate scheme of revenge."

"And so could the abstraction of Mrs. Barnum's five-hundred-dollar handkerchief by one who sat in the next box," chimed in Miss Hughson, edging away from the friend to whose honour she would have pinned her faith an hour before. "I remember now seeing her lean over the railing to adjust the old lady's shawl."

With a start, Caroline West turned a tragic gaze upon the speaker.

"You think me guilty of all because of what I did last night?"

"Why shouldn't I?"

"And you, Anna?"

"Alicia has my sympathy," murmured Miss Benedict.

Yet the wild girl persisted.

"But I have told you my provocation. You cannot believe that I am guilty of her sin; not if you look at her as I am looking now."

But their glances hardly followed her pointing finger. Her friends – the comrades of her youth, the Inseparables with their secret oath – one and all held themselves aloof, struck by the perfidy they were only just beginning to take in. Smitten with despair, for these girls were her life, she gave one wild leap and sank on her knees before Alicia.

"O speak!" she began. "Forgive me, and –"

A tremble seized her throat; she ceased to speak and let fall her partially up-lifted hands. The cheery sound of men's voices had drifted in from the terrace, and the figure of Captain Holliday could be seen passing by. The shudder which shook Caroline West communicated itself to Alicia Driscoll, and the former rising quickly, the two women surveyed each other, possibly for the first time, with open soul and a complete understanding.

"Caroline!" murmured the one.

"Alicia!" pleaded the other.

"Caroline, trust me," said Alicia Driscoll in that moving voice of hers, which more than her beauty caught and retained all hearts. "You have served me ill, but it was not all undeserved. Girls," she went on, eyeing both them and her father with the wistfulness of a breaking heart, "neither Caroline nor myself are worthy of Captain Holliday's love. Caroline has told you her fault, but mine is perhaps a worse one. The ring – the scarf – the diamond pins – I took them all – took them if I did not retain them. A curse has been over my life – the curse of a longing I could not combat. But love was working a change in me. Since I have known Captain Holliday – but that's all over. I was mad to think I could be happy with such memories in my life. I shall never marry now – or touch jewels again – my own or another's. Father, father, you won't go back on your girl! I couldn't see Caroline suffer for what I have done. You will pardon me and help – help –"

Her voice choked. She flung herself into her father's arms; his head bent over hers, and for an instant not a soul in the room moved. Then Miss Hughson gave a spring and caught her by the hand. "We are inseparable," said she, and kissed the hand, murmuring, "Now is our time to show it."

Then other lips fell upon those cold and trembling fingers, which seemed to warm under these embraces. And then a tear. It came from the hard eye of Caroline, and remained a sacred secret between the two.

"You have your pendant?"

Mr. Driscoll's suffering eye shone down on Violet Strange's uplifted face as she advanced to say good-bye preparatory to departure.

"Yes," she acknowledged, "but hardly, I fear, your gratitude."

And the answer astonished her.

"I am not sure that the real Alicia will not make her father happier than the unreal one has ever done."

"And Captain Holliday?"

"He may come to feel the same."

"Then I do not quit in disgrace?"

"You depart with my thanks."

When a certain personage was told of the success of Miss Strange's latest manoeuvre, he remarked: "The little one progresses. We shall have to give her a case of prime importance next."

THE HOUSE OF CLOCKS

Anna Katharine Green

Anna Katharine Green (1846–1935) was one of the first American authors of detective fiction. Her novel *The Leavenworth Case* (1878) is often cited as the first such novel written by a woman. An international bestseller, credited with popularizing the genre in the United States, she was born and died in New York.

Miss Strange was not in a responsive mood. This her employer had observed on first entering; yet he showed no hesitation in laying on the table behind which she had ensconced herself in the attitude of one besieged, an envelope thick with enclosed papers.

"There," said he. "Telephone me when you have read them."

"I shall not read them."

"No?" he smiled; and, repossessing himself of the envelope, he tore off one end, extracted the sheets with which it was filled, and laid them down still unfolded, in their former place on the table-top.

The suggestiveness of the action caused the corners of Miss Strange's delicate lips to twitch wistfully, before settling into an ironic smile.

Calmly the other watched her.

"I am on a vacation," she loftily explained, as she finally met his studiously non-quizzical glance. "Oh, I know that I am in my own home!" she petulantly acknowledged, as his gaze took in the room; "and that the automobile is at the door; and that I'm dressed for shopping. But for all that I'm on a vacation – a mental one," she emphasized; "and business must wait. I haven't got over the last affair," she protested, as he maintained a discreet silence, "and the season is so gay just now – so many balls, so many – But that isn't the worst. Father is beginning to wake up – and if he ever suspects –" A significant gesture ended this appeal.

The personage knew her father – everyone did – and the wonder had always been that she dared run the risk of displeasing one so implacable. Though she was his favourite child, Peter Strange was known to be quite capable of cutting her off with a shilling, once his close, prejudiced mind conceived it to be his duty. And that he would so interpret the situation, if he ever came to learn the secret of his daughter's fits of abstraction and the sly bank account she was slowly accumulating, the personage holding out this dangerous lure had no doubt at all. Yet he only smiled at her words and remarked in casual suggestion:

"It's out of town this time – 'way out. Your health certainly demands a change of air."

"My health is good. Fortunately, or unfortunately, as one may choose to look at it, it furnishes me with no excuse for an outing," she steadily retorted, turning her back on the table.

"Ah, excuse me!" the insidious voice apologized, "your paleness misled me. Surely a night or two's change might be beneficial."

She gave him a quick side look, and began to adjust her boa.

To this hint he paid no attention.

"The affair is quite out of the ordinary," he pursued in the tone of one rehearsing a part. But there he stopped. For some reason, not altogether apparent to the masculine mind, the pin of flashing stones (real stones) which held her hat in place had to be taken out and thrust back again, not once, but twice. It was to watch this performance he had paused. When he was ready to proceed, he took the musing tone of one marshalling facts for another's enlightenment:

"A woman of unknown instincts –"

"Pshaw!" The end of the pin would strike against the comb holding Violet's chestnut-coloured locks.

"Living in a house as mysterious as the secret it contains. But –" here he allowed his patience apparently to forsake him, "I will bore you no longer. Go to your teas and balls; I will struggle with my dark affairs alone."

His hand went to the packet of papers she affected so ostentatiously to despise. He could be as nonchalant as she. But he did not lift them; he let them lie. Yet the young heiress had not made a movement or even turned the slightest glance his way.

"A woman difficult to understand! A mysterious house – possibly a mysterious crime!"

Thus Violet kept repeating in silent self-communion, as flushed with dancing she sat that evening in a highly-scented conservatory, dividing her attention between the compliments of her partner and the splash of a fountain bubbling in the heart of this mass of tropical foliage; and when some hours later she sat down in her chintz-furnished bedroom for a few minutes' thought before retiring, it was to draw from a little oak box at her elbow the half-dozen or so folded sheets of closely written paper which had been left for her perusal by her persistent employer.

Glancing first at the signature and finding it to be one already favourably known at the bar, she read with avidity the statement of events thus vouched for, finding them curious enough in all conscience to keep her awake for another full hour.

We here subscribe it:

I am a lawyer with an office in the Times Square Building. My business is mainly local, but sometimes I am called out of town, as witness the following summons received by me on the fifth of last October.

DEAR SIR –

I wish to make my will. I am an invalid and cannot leave my room. Will you come to me? The enclosed reference will answer for my respectability. If it satisfies you and you decide to accommodate me, please hasten your visit; I have not many days to live. A carriage will meet you at Highland Station at any hour you designate. Telegraph reply.

A. Postlethwaite, Gloom Cottage, — — N. J.

The reference given was a Mr. Weed of Eighty-sixth Street – a well-known man of unimpeachable reputation.

Calling him up at his business office, I asked him what he could tell me about Mr. Postlethwaite of Gloom Cottage, — — N. J. The answer astonished me:

"There is no Mr. Postlethwaite to be found at that address. He died years ago. There is a Mrs. Postlethwaite – a confirmed paralytic. Do you mean her?"

I glanced at the letter still lying open at the side of the telephone:

"The signature reads A. Postlethwaite."

"Then it's she. Her name is Arabella. She hates the name, being a woman of no sentiment. Uses her initials even on her cheques. What does she want of you?"

"To draw her will."

"Oblige her. It'll be experience for you." And he slammed home the receiver.

I decided to follow the suggestion so forcibly emphasized; and the next day saw me at Highland Station. A superannuated horse and a still more super-annuated carriage awaited me – both too old to serve a busy man in these days of swift conveyance. Could this be a sample of the establishment I was about to enter? Then I remembered that the woman who had sent for me was a helpless invalid, and probably had no use for any sort of turnout.

The driver was in keeping with the vehicle, and as noncommittal as the plod-ding beast he drove. If I ventured upon a remark, he gave me a long and curious look; if I went so far as to attack him with a direct question, he responded with a hitch of the shoulder or a dubious smile which conveyed nothing. Was he deaf or just unpleasant? I soon learned that he was not deaf; for suddenly, after a jog-trot of a mile or so through a wooded road which we had entered from the main highway, he drew in his horse, and, without glancing my way, spoke his first word:

"This is where you get out. The house is back there in the bushes."

As no house was visible and the bushes rose in an unbroken barrier along the road, I stared at him in some doubt of his sanity.

"But –" I began; a protest into which he at once broke, with the sharp direc-tion:

"Take the path. It'll lead you straight to the front door."

"I don't see any path."

For this he had no answer; and confident from his expression that it would be useless to expect anything further from him, I dropped a coin into his hand, and jumped to the ground. He was off before I could turn myself about.

"'Something is rotten in the State of Denmark,'" I quoted in startled comment to myself; and not knowing what else to do, stared down at the turf at my feet.

A bit of flagging met my eye, protruding from a layer of thick moss. Farther on I espied another – the second, probably, of many. This, no doubt, was the path I had been bidden to follow, and without further thought on the subject, I plunged into the bushes which with difficulty I made give way before me.

For a moment all further advance looked hopeless. A more tangled, uninviting approach to a so-called home I had never seen outside of the tropics; and the complete neglect thus displayed should have prepared me for the appearance of the house I unexpectedly came upon, just as the way seemed on the point of closing up before me.

But nothing could well prepare one for a first view of Gloom Cottage. Its location in a hollow which had gradually filled itself up with trees and some kind of prickly brush, its deeply stained walls, once picturesque enough in their grouping but too deeply hidden now amid rotting boughs to produce any other effect than that of shrouded desolation, the sough of these same boughs as they rapped a devil's tattoo against each other, and the absence of even the rising column of smoke which bespeaks domestic life wherever seen – all gave to one who remembered the cognomen Cottage and forgot the pre-cognomen of Gloom, a sense of buried life as sepulchral as that which emanates from the mouth of some freshly opened tomb.

But these impressions, natural enough to my youth, were necessarily transient, and soon gave way to others more business-like. Perceiving the curve of an arch rising above the undergrowth still blocking my approach, I pushed my way resolutely through, and presently found myself stumbling upon the steps of an unexpectedly spacious domicile, built not of wood, as its name of Cottage had led me to expect, but of carefully cut stone which, while showing every mark of time, proclaimed itself one of those early, carefully erected Colonial residences which it takes more than a century to destroy, or even to wear to the point of dilapidation.

Somewhat encouraged, though failing to detect any signs of active life in the heavily shuttered windows frowning upon me from either side, I ran up the steps and rang the bell which pulled as hard as if no hand had touched it in years.

Then I waited.

But not to ring again; for just as my hand was approaching the bell a second time, the door fell back and I beheld in the black gap before me the oldest man I had ever come upon in my whole life. He was so old I was astonished when his drawn lips opened and he asked if I was the lawyer from New York. I would as soon have expected a mummy to wag its tongue and utter English, he looked so thin and dried and removed from this life and all worldly concerns.

But when I had answered his question and he had turned to marshal me down the hall towards a door I could dimly see standing open in the twilight of an absolutely sunless interior, I noticed that his step was not without some vigour, despite the feeble bend of his withered body and the incessant swaying of his head, which seemed to be continually saying No!

"I will prepare madam," he admonished me, after drawing a ponderous curtain two inches or less aside from one of the windows. "She is very ill, but she will see you."

The tone was senile, but it was the senility of an educated man, and as the cultivated accents wavered forth, my mind changed in regard to the position he held in the house. Interested anew, I sought to give him another look, but he had already vanished through the doorway, and so noiselessly it was more like a shadow's flitting than a man's withdrawal.

The darkness in which I sat was absolute; but gradually, as I continued to look about me, the spaces lightened and certain details came out, which to my astonishment were of a character to show that the plain if substantial exterior of this house with its choked-up approaches and weedy gardens was no sample of what was to be found inside. Though the walls surrounding me were dismal because unlighted, they betrayed a splendour unusual in any country house. The frescoes and paintings were of an ancient order, dating from days when life and not death reigned in this isolated dwelling; but in them high art reigned supreme, an art so high and so finished that only great wealth, combined with the most cultivated taste, could have produced such effects. I was still absorbed in the wonder of it all, when the quiet voice of the old gentleman who had let me in reached me again from the doorway, and I heard:

"Madam is ready for you. May I trouble you to accompany me to her room."

I rose with alacrity. I was anxious to see madam, if only to satisfy myself that she was as interesting as the house in which she was self-immured.

I found her a great deal more so. But before I enter upon our interview, let me mention a fact which had attracted my attention in my passage to her room. During his absence my guide evidently had pulled aside other curtains than those of the room in which he had left me. The hall, no longer a tunnel of darkness, gave me a glimpse as we went by, of various secluded corners, and it seemed as if everywhere I looked I saw – a clock. I counted four before I reached the stair-case, all standing on the floor and all of ancient make, though differing much in appearance and value. A fifth one rose grim and tall at the stair foot, and under an impulse I have never understood I stopped, when I reached it, to note the time. But it had paused in its task, and faced me with motionless hands and silent works – a fact which somehow startled me; perhaps, because just then I encountered the old man's eye watching me with an expression as challenging as it was unintelligible.

I had expected to see a woman in bed. I saw instead, a woman sitting up. You felt her influence the moment you entered her presence. She was not young; she was not beautiful; – never had been I should judge – she had not even the usual marks about her of an ultra strong personality; but that her will was law, had always been, and would continue to be law so long as she lived, was patent to any eye at the first glance. She exacted obedience consciously and unconsciously, and she exacted it with charm. Some few people in the world possess this power. They frown, and the opposing will weakens; they smile, and all hearts succumb. I was hers from the moment I crossed the threshold till – But I will relate the happenings of that instant when it comes.

She was alone, or so I thought, when I made my first bow to her stern but not unpleasing presence. Seated in a great chair, with a silver tray before her contain-ing such little matters as she stood in hourly need of, she confronted me with a piercing gaze startling to behold in eyes so colourless. Then she smiled, and in obedience to that smile I seated myself in a chair placed very near her own. Was she too paralysed to express herself clearly? I waited in some anxiety till she spoke, when this fear vanished. Her voice betrayed the character her features failed to express. It was firm, resonant, and instinct with command. Not loud, but penetrating, and of a quality which made one listen with his heart as well as with his ears. What she said is immaterial. I was there for a certain purpose and we entered immediately upon the business of that purpose. She talked and I listened, mostly without comment. Only once did I interrupt her with a suggestion; and as this led to definite results, I will proceed to relate the occurrence in full.

In the few hours remaining to me before leaving New York, I had learned (no matter how) some additional particulars concerning herself and family; and when after some minor bequests, she proceeded to name the parties to whom she desired to leave the bulk of her fortune, I ventured, with some astonishment at my own temerity, to remark:

"But you have a young relative! Is she not to be included in this partition of your property?"

A hush. Then a smile came to life on her stiff lips, such as is seldom seen, thank God, on the face of any woman, and I heard:

"The young relative of whom you speak, is in the room. She has known for some time that I have no intention of leaving anything to her. There is, in fact, small chance of her ever needing it."

The latter sentence was a muttered one, but that it was loud enough to be heard in all parts of the room I was soon assured. For a quick sigh, which was almost a gasp, followed from a corner I had hitherto ignored, and upon glancing that way, I perceived, peering upon us from the shadows, the white face of a young girl in whose drawn features and wide, staring eyes I beheld such evidences of terror, that in an instant, whatever predilection I had hitherto felt

for my client, vanished in distrust, if not positive aversion.

I was still under the sway of this new impression, when Mrs. Postlethwaite's voice rose again, this time addressing the young girl:

"You may go," she said, with such force in the command for all its honeyed modulation, that I expected to see its object fly the room in frightened obedience.

But though the startled girl had lost none of the terror which had made her face like a mask, no power of movement remained to her. A picture of hopeless misery, she stood for one breathless moment, with her eyes fixed in unmistakable appeal on mine; then she began to sway so helplessly that I leaped with bounding heart to catch her. As she fell into my arms I heard her sigh as before. No common anguish spoke in that sigh. I had stumbled unwittingly upon a tragedy, to the meaning of which I held but a doubtful key.

"She seems very ill," I observed with some emphasis, as I turned to lay my helpless burden on a near-by sofa.

"She's doomed."

The words were spoken with gloom and with an attempt at commiseration which no longer rang true in my ears.

"She is as sick a woman as I am myself," continued Mrs. Postlethwaite. "That is why I made the remark I did, never imagining she would hear me at that distance. Do not put her down. My nurse will be here in a moment to relieve you of your burden."

A tinkle accompanied these words. The resolute woman had stretched out a finger, of whose use she was not quite deprived, and touched a little bell standing on the tray before her, an inch or two from her hand.

Pleased to obey her command, I paused at the sofa's edge, and taking advantage of the momentary delay, studied the youthful countenance pressed unconsciously to my breast.

It was one whose appeal lay less in its beauty, though that was of a touching quality, than in the story it told – a story, which for some unaccountable reason – I did not pause to determine what one – I felt it to be my immediate duty to know. But I asked no questions then; I did not even venture a comment; and yielded her up with seeming readiness when a strong but none too intelligent woman came running in with arms outstretched to carry her off. When the door had closed upon these two, the silence of my client drew my attention back to herself.

"I am waiting," was her quiet observation, and without any further reference to what had just taken place under our eyes, she went on with the business previously occupying us.

I was able to do my part without any too great display of my own disturbance. The clearness of my remarkable client's instructions, the definiteness with which her mind was made up as to the disposal of every dollar of her vast property, made it easy for me to master each detail and make careful note of every wish. But this did not prevent the ebb and flow within me of an undercurrent of thought full of question and uneasiness. What had been the real purport of the scene to which I had just been made a surprised witness? The few, but certainly unusual, facts which had been given me in regard to the extraordinary relations existing between these two closely connected women will explain the intensity of my interest. Those facts shall be yours.

Arabella Merwin, when young, was gifted with a peculiar fascination which, as we have seen, had not altogether vanished with age. Consequently she had many lovers, among them two brothers, Frank and Andrew Postlethwaite. The latter was the older, the handsomer, and the most prosperous (his name is remembered yet in connection with South American schemes of large importance), but it was Frank she married.

That real love, ardent if unreasonable, lay at the bottom of her choice, is evident enough to those who followed the career of the young couple. But it was a jealous love which brooked no rival, and as Frank Postlethwaite was of an impulsive and erratic nature, scenes soon occurred between them which, while revealing the extraordinary force of the young wife's character, led to no serious break till after her son was born, and this, notwithstanding the fact that Frank had long given up making a living, and that they were openly dependent on their wealthy brother, now fast approaching the millionaire status.

This brother – the Peruvian King, as some called him – must have been an extraordinary man. Though cherishing his affection for the spirited Arabella to the point of remaining a bachelor for her sake, he betrayed none of the usual signs of disappointed love; but on the contrary made every effort to advance her happiness, not only by assuring to herself and husband an adequate income, but by doing all he could in other and less open ways to lessen any sense she might entertain of her mistake in preferring for her lifemate his self-centred and unstable brother. She should have adored him; but though she evinced gratitude enough, there is nothing to prove that she ever gave Frank Postlethwaite the least cause to cherish any other sentiment towards his brother than that of honest love and unqualified respect. Perhaps he never did cherish any other. Perhaps the change which everyone saw in the young couple immediately after the birth of their only child was due to another cause. Gossip is silent on this point. All that it insists upon is that from this time evidences of a growing estrangement between them became so obvious that even the indulgent Andrew could not blind himself to it; showing his sense of trouble, not by lessening their income, for that he doubled, but by spending more time in Peru and less in New York where the two were living.

However – and here we enter upon those details which I have ventured to characterize as uncommon – he was in this country and in the actual company of his brother when the accident occurred which terminated both their lives. It was the old story of a skidding motor, and Mrs. Postlethwaite, having been sent for in great haste to the small inn into which the two injured men had been carried, arrived only in time to witness their last moments. Frank died first and Andrew some few minutes later – an important fact, as was afterwards shown when the latter's will came to be read.

This will was a peculiar one. By its provisions the bulk of the King's great property was left to his brother Frank, but with this especial stipulation that in case his brother failed to survive him, the full legacy as bequeathed to him should be given unconditionally to his widow. Frank's demise, as I have already stated, preceded his brother's by several minutes and consequently Arabella became the chief legatee; and that is how she obtained her millions. But – and here a startling feature comes in – when the will came to be administered, the secret underlying the break between Frank and his wife was brought to light by a revelation of the fact that he had practised a great deception upon her at the time of his marriage. Instead of being a bachelor as was currently believed, he was in reality a widower, and the father of a child. This fact, so long held secret, had become hers when her own child was born; and constituted as she was, she not only never forgave the father, but conceived such a hatred for the innocent object of their quarrel that she refused to admit its claims or even to acknowledge its existence.

But later – after his death, in fact – she showed some sense of obligation towards one who under ordinary conditions would have shared her wealth. When the whole story became heard, and she discovered that this secret had been kept from his brother as well as from herself, and that consequently no provision had been made in any way for the child thus thrown directly upon her mercy, she did the generous thing and took the forsaken girl into her own home. But she never betrayed the least love for her, her whole heart being bound up in her boy, who was, as all agree, a prodigy of talent.

But this boy, for all his promise and seeming strength of constitution, died when barely seven years old, and the desolate mother was left with nothing to fill her heart but the uncongenial daughter of her husband's first wife. The fact that this child, slighted as it had hitherto been, would, in the event of her uncle having passed away before her father, have been the undisputed heiress of a large portion of the wealth now at the disposal of her arrogant step-mother, led many to expect, now that the boy was no more, that Mrs. Postlethwaite would proceed to acknowledge the little Helena as her heir, and give her that place in the household to which her natural claims entitled her.

But no such result followed. The passion of grief into which the mother was thrown by the shipwreck of all her hopes left her hard and implacable, and when, as very soon happened, she fell a victim to the disease which tied her to her chair and made the wealth which had come to her by such a peculiar ordering of circumstances little else than a mockery even in her own eyes, it was upon this child she expended the full fund of her secret bitterness.

And the child? What of her? How did she bear her unhappy fate when she grew old enough to realize it? With a resignation which was the wonder of all who knew her. No murmurs escaped her lips, nor was the devotion she invariably displayed to the exacting invalid who ruled her as well as all the rest of her household with a rod of iron ever disturbed by the least sign of reproach. Though the riches, which in those early days poured into the home in a measure far beyond the needs of its mistress, were expended in making the house beautiful rather than in making the one young life within it happy, she never was heard to utter so much as a wish to leave the walls within which fate had immured her. Content, or seemingly content, with the only home she knew, she never asked for change or demanded friends or amusements. Visitors ceased coming; desolation followed neglect. The garden, once a glory, succumbed to a riot of weeds and undesirable brush, till a towering wall seemed to be drawn about the house cutting it off from the activities of the world as it cut it off from the approach of sunshine by day, and the comfort of a star-lit heaven by night. And yet the young girl continued to smile, though with a pitifulness of late, which some thought betokened secret terror and others the wasting of a body too sensitive for such unwholesome seclusion.

These were the facts, known if not consciously specialized, which gave to the latter part of my interview with Mrs. Postlethwaite a poignancy of interest which had never attended any of my former experiences. The peculiar attitude of Miss Postlethwaite towards her indurate tormentor awakened in my agitated mind something much deeper than curiosity, but when I strove to speak her name with the intent of inquiring more particularly into her condition, such a look confronted me from the steady eye immovably fixed upon my own, that my courage – or was it my natural precaution – bade me subdue the impulse and risk no attempt which might betray the depth of my interest in one so completely outside the scope of the present moment's business. Perhaps Mrs. Postlethwaite appreciated my struggle; perhaps she was wholly blind to it. There was no reading the mind of this woman of sentimental name but inflexible nature, and realizing the fact more fully with every word she uttered I left her at last with no further betrayal of my feelings than might be evinced by the earnestness with which I promised to return for her signature at the earliest possible moment.

This she had herself requested, saying as I rose:

"I can still write my name if the paper is pushed carefully along under my hand. See to it that you come while the power remains to me."

I had hoped that in my passage downstairs I might run upon someone who would give me news of Miss Postlethwaite, but the woman who approached to conduct me downstairs was not of an appearance to invite confidence, and I felt forced to leave the house with my doubts unsatisfied.

Two memories, equally distinct, followed me. One was a picture of Mrs. Postlethwaite's fingers groping among her belongings on the little tray perched upon her lap, and another of the intent and strangely bent figure of the old man who had acted as my usher, listening to the ticking of one of the great clocks. So absorbed was he in this occupation that he not only failed to notice me when I went by, but he did not even lift his head at my cheery greeting. Such mysteries were too much for me, and led me to postpone my departure from town till I had sought out Mrs. Postlethwaite's doctor and propounded to him one or two leading questions. First, would Mrs. Postlethwaite's present condition be likely to hold good till Monday; and secondly, was the young lady living with her as ill as her step-mother said.

He was a mild old man of the easy-going type, and the answers I got from him were far from satisfactory. Yet he showed some surprise when I mentioned the extent of Mrs. Postlethwaite's anxiety about her step-daughter, and paused, in the dubious shaking of his head, to give me a short stare in which I read as much determination as perplexity.

"I will look into Miss Postlethwaite's case more particularly," were his parting words. And with this one gleam of comfort I had to be content.

Monday's interview was a brief one and contained nothing worth repeating. Mrs. Postlethwaite listened with stoical satisfaction to the reading of the will I had drawn up, and upon its completion rang her bell for the two witnesses awaiting her summons, in an adjoining room. They were not of her household, but to all appearance honest villagers with but one noticeable characteristic, an overweening idea of Mrs. Postlethwaite's importance. Perhaps the spell she had so liberally woven for others in other and happier days was felt by them at this hour. It would not be strange; I had almost fallen under it myself, so great was the fascination of her manner even in this wreck of her bodily powers, when triumph assured, she faced us all in a state of complete satisfaction.

But before I was again quit of the place, all my doubts returned and in fuller force than ever. I had lingered in my going as much as decency would permit, hoping to hear a step on the stair or see a face in some doorway which would contradict Mrs. Postlethwaite's cold assurance that Miss Postlethwaite was no better. But no such step did I hear, and no face did I see save the old, old one of the ancient friend or relative, whose bent frame seemed continually to haunt the halls. As before, he stood listening to the monotonous ticking of one of the clocks, muttering to himself and quite oblivious of my presence.

However, this time I decided not to pass him without a more persistent attempt to gain his notice. Pausing at his side, I asked him in the friendly tone I thought best calculated to attract his attention, how Miss Postlethwaite was to-day. He was so intent upon his task, whatever that was, that while he turned my way, it was with a glance as blank as that of a stone image.

"Listen!" he admonished me. "It still says No! No! I don't think it will ever say anything else."

I stared at him in some consternation, then at the clock itself which was the tall one I had found run down at my first visit. There was nothing unusual in its quiet tick, so far as I could hear, and with a compassionate glance at the old man who had turned breathlessly again to listen, proceeded on my way without another word.

The old fellow was daft. A century old, and daft.

I had worked my way out through the vines which still encumbered the porch, and was taking my first steps down the walk, when some impulse made me turn and glance up at one of the windows.

Did I bless the impulse? I thought I had every reason for doing so, when through a network of interlacing branches I beheld the young girl with whom my mind was wholly occupied, standing with her head thrust forward, watching the descent of something small and white which she had just released from her hand.

A note! A note written by her and meant for me! With a grateful look in her direction (which was probably lost upon her as she had already drawn back out of sight), I sprang for it only to meet with disappointment. For it was no billet-doux I received from amid the clustering brush where it had fallen; but a small square of white cloth showing a line of fantastic embroidery. Annoyed beyond measure, I was about to fling it down again, when the thought that it had come from her hand deterred me, and I thrust it into my vest pocket. When I took it out again – which was soon after I had taken my seat in the car – I discovered what a mistake I should have made if I had followed my first impulse. For, upon examining the stitches more carefully, I perceived that what I had considered a mere decorative pattern was in fact a string of letters, and that these letters made words, and that these words were:

IDONOTWANTTODIEBUTISURELYWILLIF

Or, in plain writing:

"I do not want to die, but I surely will if –"

Finish the sentence for me. That is the problem I offer you. It is not a case for the police but one well worth your attention, if you succeed in reaching the heart of this mystery and saving this young girl.

Only, let no delay occur. The doom, if doom it is, is immanent. Remember that the will is signed.

"She is too small; I did not ask you to send me a midget."

Thus spoke Mrs. Postlethwaite to her doctor, as he introduced into her presence a little figure in nurse's cap and apron. "You said I needed care – more care than I was receiving. I answered that my old nurse could give it, and you objected that she or someone else must look after Miss Postlethwaite. I did not see the necessity, but I never contradict a doctor. So I yielded to your wishes, but not without the proviso (you remember that I made a proviso) that whatever sort of young woman you chose to introduce into this room, she should not be fresh from the training schools, and that she should be strong, silent, and capable. And you bring me this mite of a woman – is she a woman? she looks more like a child, of pleasing countenance enough, but who can no more lift me –"

"Pardon me!" Little Miss Strange had advanced. "I think, if you will allow me the privilege, madam, that I can shift you into a much more comfortable position." And with a deftness and ease certainly not to be expected from one of her slight physique, Violet raised the helpless invalid a trifle more upon her pillow.

The act, its manner, and the smile accompanying it, could not fail to please, and undoubtedly did, though no word rewarded her from lips not much given to speech save when the occasion was imperative. But Mrs. Postlethwaite made no further objection to her presence, and, seeing this, the doctor's countenance relaxed and he left the room with a much lighter step than that with which he had entered it.

And thus it was that Violet Strange – an adept in more ways than one – became installed at the bedside of this mysterious woman, whose days, if numbered, still held possibilities of action which those interested in young Helena Postlethwaite's fate would do well to recognize.

Miss Strange had been at her post for two days, and had gathered up the following:

That Mrs. Postlethwaite must be obeyed.

That her step-daughter (who did not wish to die) would die if she knew it to be the wish of this domineering but apparently idolized woman.

That the old man of the clocks, while senile in some regards, was very alert and quite youthful in others. If a century old – which she began greatly to doubt – he had the language and manner of one in his prime, when unaffected by the neighbourhood of the clocks, which seemed in some non-understandable way to exercise an occult influence over him. At table he was an entertaining host; but neither there nor elsewhere would he discuss the family, or dilate in any way upon the peculiarities of a household of which he manifestly regarded himself as the least important member. Yet no one knew them better, and when Violet became quite assured of this, as well as of the futility of looking for explanation of any kind from either of her two patients, she resolved upon an effort to surprise one from him.

She went about it in this way. Noting his custom of making a complete round of the clocks each night after dinner, she took advantage of Mrs. Postlethwaite's inclination to sleep at this hour, to follow him from clock to clock in the hope of overhearing some portion of the monologue with which he bent his head to the swinging pendulum, or put his ear to the hidden works. Soft-footed and discreet, she tripped along at his back, and at each pause he made, paused herself and turned her ear his way. The extreme darkness of the halls, which were more sombre by night than by day, favoured this attempt, and she was able, after a failure or two, to catch the No! no! no! no! which fell from his lips in seeming repetition of what he heard the most of them say.

The satisfaction in his tone proved that the denial to which he listened, chimed in with his hopes and gave ease to his mind. But he looked his oldest when, after pausing at another of the many time-pieces, he echoed in answer to its special refrain, Yes! yes! yes! yes! and fled the spot with shaking body and a distracted air.

The same fear and the same shrinking were observable in him as he returned from listening to the least conspicuous one, standing in a short corridor, where Violet could not follow him. But when, after a hesitation which enabled her to slip behind the curtain hiding the drawing-room door, he approached and laid his ear against the great one standing, as if on guard, at the foot of the stairs, she saw by the renewed vigour he displayed that there was comfort for him in its message, even before she caught the whisper with which he left it and proceeded to mount the stairs:

"It says No! It always says No! I will heed it as the voice of Heaven."

But one conclusion could be the result of such an experiment to a mind like Violet's. This partly touched old man not only held the key to the secret of this house, but was in a mood to divulge it if once he could be induced to hear command instead of dissuasion in the tick of this one large clock. But how could he be induced? Violet returned to Mrs. Postlethwaite's bedside in a mood of extreme thoughtfulness.

Another day passed, and she had not yet seen Miss Postlethwaite. She was hoping each hour to be sent on some errand to that young lady's room, but no such opportunity was granted her. Once she ventured to ask the doctor, whose visits were now very frequent, what he thought of the young lady's condition. But as this question was necessarily put in Mrs. Postlethwaite's presence, the answer was naturally guarded, and possibly not altogether frank.

"Our young lady is weaker," he acknowledged. "Much weaker," he added with marked emphasis and his most professional air, "or she would be here instead of in her own room. It grieves her not to be able to wait upon her generous benefactress."

The word fell heavily. Had it been used as a test? Violet gave him a look, though she had much rather have turned her discriminating eye upon the face staring up at them from the pillow. Had the alarm expressed by others communicated itself at last to the physician? Was the charm which had held him subservient to the mother, dissolving under the pitiable state of the child, and was he trying to aid the little detective-nurse in her effort to sound the mystery of her condition?

His look expressed benevolence, but he took care not to meet the gaze of the woman he had just lauded, possibly because that gaze was fixed upon him in a way to tax his moral courage. The silence which ensued was broken by Mrs. Postlethwaite:

"She will live – this poor Helena – how long?" she asked, with no break in her voice's wonted music.

The doctor hesitated, then with a candour hardly to be expected from him, answered:

"I do not understand Miss Postlethwaite's case. I should like, with your permission, to consult some New York physician."

"Indeed!"

A single word, but as it left this woman's thin lips Violet recoiled, and, perhaps, the doctor did. Rage can speak in one word as well as in a dozen, and the rage which spoke in this one was of no common order, though it was quickly suppressed, as was all other show of feeling when she added, with a touch of her old charm:

"Of course you will do what you think best, as you know I never interfere with a doctor's decisions. But," and here her natural ascendancy of tone and manner returned in all its potency, "it would kill me to know that a stranger was approaching Helena's bedside. It would kill her. She's too sensitive to survive such a shock."

Violet recalled the words worked with so much care by this young girl on a minute piece of linen, I do not want to die, and watched the doctor's face for some sign of resolution. But embarrassment was all she saw there, and all she heard him say was the conventional reply:

"I am doing all I can for her. We will wait another day and note the effect of my latest prescription."

Another day!

The deathly calm which overspread Mrs. Postlethwaite's features as this word left the physician's lips warned Violet not to let another day go by without some action. But she made no remark, and, indeed, betrayed but little interest in anything beyond her own patient's condition. That seemed to occupy her wholly. With consummate art she gave the appearance of being under Mrs. Postlethwaite's complete thrall, and watched with fascinated eyes every movement of the one unstricken finger which could do so much.

This little detective of ours could be an excellent actor when she chose.

To make the old man speak! To force this conscience-stricken but rebellious soul to reveal what the clock forbade! How could it be done?

This continued to be Violet's great problem. She pondered it so deeply during all the remainder of the day that a little pucker settled on her brow, which someone (I will not mention who) would have been pained to see. Mrs. Postlethwaite, if she noticed it at all, probably ascribed it to her anxieties as nurse, for never had Violet been more assiduous in her attentions. But Mrs. Postlethwaite was no longer the woman she had been, and possibly never noted it at all.

At five o'clock Violet suddenly left the room. Slipping down into the lower hall, she went the round of the clocks herself, listening to every one. There was no perceptible difference in their tick. Satisfied of this and that it was simply the old man's imagination which had supplied them each with separate speech, she paused before the huge one at the foot of the stairs – the one whose dictate he had promised himself to follow – and with an eye upon its broad, staring dial, muttered wistfully:

"Oh! for an idea! For an idea!"

Did this cumbrous relic of old-time precision turn traitor at this ingenuous plea? The dial continued to stare, the works to sing, but Violet's face suddenly lost its perplexity. With a wary look about her and a listening ear turned towards the stair top, she stretched out her hand and pulled open the door guarding the pendulum, and peered in at the works, smiling slyly to herself as she pushed it back into place and retreated upstairs to the sick room.

When the doctor came that night she had a quiet word with him outside Mrs. Postlethwaite's door. Was that why he was on hand when old Mr. Dunbar stole from his room to make his nightly circuit of the halls below? Something quite beyond the ordinary was in the good physician's mind, for the look he cast at the old man was quite unlike any he had ever bestowed upon him before, and when he spoke it was to say with marked urgency:

"Our beautiful young lady will not live a week unless I get at the seat of her malady. Pray that I may be enabled to do so, Mr. Dunbar."

A blow to the aged man's heart which called forth a feeble "Yes, yes," followed by a wild stare which imprinted itself upon the doctor's memory as the look of one hopelessly old, who hears for the first time a distinct call from the grave which has long been awaiting him!

A solitary lamp stood in the lower hall. As the old man picked his slow way down, its small, hesitating flame flared up as in a sudden gust, then sank down flickering and faint as if it, too, had heard a call which summoned it to extinction.

No other sign of life was visible anywhere. Sunk in twilight shadows, the corridors branched away on either side to no place in particular and serving, to all appearance (as many must have thought in days gone by), as a mere hiding-place for clocks.

To listen to their united hum, the old man paused, looking at first a little distraught, but settling at last into his usual self as he started forward upon his course. Did some whisper, hitherto unheard, warn him that it was the last time he would tread that weary round? Who can tell? He was trembling very much when with his task nearly completed, he stepped out again into the main hall and crept rather than walked back to the one great clock to whose dictum he made it a practice to listen last.

Chattering the accustomed words, "They say Yes! They are all saying Yes! now; but this one will say No!" he bent his stiff old back and laid his ear to the unresponsive wood. But the time for no had passed. It was Yes! yes! yes! yes! now, and as his straining ears took in the word, he appeared to shrink where he stood and after a moment of anguished silence, broke forth into a low wail, amid whose lamentations one could hear:

"The time has come! Even the clock she loves best bids me speak. Oh! Arabella, Arabella!"

In his despair he had not noticed that the pendulum hung motionless, or that the hands stood at rest on the dial. If he had, he might have waited long enough to have seen the careful opening of the great clock's tall door and the stepping forth of the little lady who had played so deftly upon his superstition.

He was wandering the corridors like a helpless child, when a gentle hand fell on his arm and a soft voice whispered in his ear:

"You have a story to tell. Will you tell it to me? It may save Miss Postlethwaite's life."

Did he understand? Would he respond if he did; or would the shock of her appeal restore him to a sense of the danger attending disloyalty? For a moment she doubted the wisdom of this startling measure, then she saw that he had passed the point of surprise and that, stranger as she was, she had but to lead the way for him to follow, tell his story, and die.

There was no light in the drawing-room when they entered. But old Mr. Dunbar did not seem to mind that. Indeed, he seemed to have lost all consciousness of present surroundings; he was even oblivious of her. This became quite evident when the lamp, in flaring up again in the hall, gave a momentary glimpse of his crouching, half-kneeling figure. In the pleading gesture of his trembling, outreaching arms, Violet beheld an appeal, not to herself, but to some phantom of his imagination; and when he spoke, as he presently did, it was with the freedom of one to whom speech is life's last boon, and the ear of the listener quite forgotten in the passion of confession long suppressed.

"She has never loved me," he began, "but I have always loved her. For me no other woman has ever existed, though I was sixty-five years of age when I first saw her, and had long given up the idea that there lived a woman who could sway me from my even life and fixed lines of duty. Sixty-five! and she a youthful bride! Was there ever such folly! Happily I realized it from the first, and piled ashes on my hidden flame. Perhaps that is why I adore her to this day and only give her over to reprobation because Fate is stronger than my age – stronger even than my love.

"She is not a good woman, but I might have been a good man if I had never known the sin which drew a line of isolation about her, and within which I, and only I, have stood with her in silent companionship. What was this sin, and in what did it have its beginning? I think its beginning was in the passion she had for her husband. It was not the every-day passion of her sex in this land of equable affections, but one of foreign fierceness, jealousy, and insatiable demand. Yet he was a very ordinary man. I was once his tutor and I know. She came to know it too, when – but I am rushing on too fast, I have much to tell before I reach that point.

"From the first, I was in their confidence. Not that either he or she put me there, but that I lived with them and was always around, and could not help seeing and hearing what went on between them. Why he continued to want me in the house and at his table, when I could no longer be of service to him, I have never known. Possibly habit explains all. He was accustomed to my presence and so was she; so accustomed they hardly noticed it, as happened one night, when after a little attempt at conversation, he threw down the book he had caught up and, addressing her by name, said without a glance my way, and quite as if he were alone with her:

"'Arabella, there is something I ought to tell you. I have tried to find the courage to do so many times before now but have always failed. Tonight I must.' And then he made his great disclosure – how, unknown to his friends and the world, he was a widower when he married her, and the father of a living child.

"With some women this might have passed with a measure of regret, and some possible contempt for his silence, but not so with her. She rose to her feet – I can see her yet – and for a moment stood facing him in the still, overpowering manner of one who feels the icy pang of hate enter where love has been. Never was moment more charged. I could not breathe while it lasted; and when at last she spoke, it was with an impetuosity of concentrated passion, hardly less dreadful than her silence had been.

"'You a father! A father already!' she cried, all her sweetness swallowed up in ungovernable wrath. 'You whom I expected to make so happy with a child? I curse you and your brat. I –'

"He strove to placate her, to explain. But rage has no ears, and before I realized my own position, the scene became openly tempestuous. That her child should be second to another woman's seemed to awaken demon instincts within her. When he ventured to hint that his little girl needed a mother's care, her irony bit like corroding acid. He became speechless before it and had not a protest to raise when she declared that the secret he had kept so long and so successfully he must continue to keep to his dying day. That the child he had failed to own in his first wife's lifetime should remain disowned in hers, and if possible be forgotten. She should never give the girl a thought nor acknowledge her in any way.

"She was Fury embodied; but the fury was of that grand order which allures rather than repels. As I felt myself succumbing to its fascination and beheld how he was weakening under it even more perceptibly than myself, I started from my chair, and sought to glide away before I should hear him utter a fatal acquiescence.

THE HOUSE OF CLOCKS

"But the movement I made unfortunately drew their attention to me, and after an instant of silent contemplation of my distracted countenance, Frank said, as though he were the elder by the forty years which separated us:

"'You have listened to Mrs. Postlethwaite's wishes. You will respect them of course.'"

That was all. He knew and she knew that I was to be trusted; but neither of them has ever known why.

A month later her child came, and was welcomed as though it were the first to bear his name. It was a boy, and their satisfaction was so great that I looked to see their old affection revive. But it had been cleft at the root, and nothing could restore it to life. They loved the child; I have never seen evidence of greater parental passion than they both displayed, but there their feelings stopped. Towards each other they were cold. They did not even unite in worship of their treasure. They gloated over him and planned for him, but always apart. He was a child in a thousand, and as he developed, the mother especially, nursed all her energies for the purpose of ensuring for him a future commensurate with his talents. Never a very conscientious woman, and alive to the advantages of wealth as demonstrated by the power wielded by her rich brother-in-law, she associated all the boy's prospects with money, great money, such money as Andrew had accumulated, and now had at his disposal for his natural heirs.

"Hence came her great temptation – a temptation to which she yielded, to the lasting trouble of us all. Of this I must now make confession though it kills me to do so, and will soon kill her. The deeds of the past do not remain buried, however deep we dig their graves, but rise in an awful resurrection when we are old – old –"

Silence. Then a tremulous renewal of his painful speech.

Violet held her breath to listen. Possibly the doctor, hidden in the darkest corner of the room, did so also.

"I never knew how she became acquainted with the terms of her brother-in-law's will. He certainly never confided them to her, and as certainly the lawyer who drew up the document never did. But that she was well aware of its tenor is as positive a fact as that I am the most wretched man alive tonight. Otherwise, why the darksome deed into which she was betrayed when both the brothers lay dying among strangers, of a dreadful accident?"

"I was witness to that deed. I had accompanied her on her hurried ride and was at her side when she entered the inn where the two Postlethwaites lay. I was always at her side in great joy or in great trouble, though she professed no affection for me and gave me but scanty thanks."

"During our ride she had been silent and I had not disturbed that silence. I had much to think of. Should we find him living, or should we find him dead? If dead, would it sever the relations between us two? Would I ever ride with her again?"

"When I was not dwelling on this theme, I was thinking of the parting look she gave her boy; a look which had some strange promise in it. What had that look meant and why did my flesh creep and my mind hover between dread and a fearsome curiosity when I recalled it? Alas! There was reason for all these sensations as I was soon to learn.

"We found the inn seething with terror and the facts worse than had been represented in the telegram. Her husband was dying. She had come just in time to witness the end. This they told her before she had taken off her veil. If they had waited – if I had been given a full glimpse of her face – But it was hidden, and I could only judge of the nature of her emotions by the stern way in which she held herself.

"'Take me to him,' was the quiet command, with which she met this disclosure. Then, before any of them could move:

"'And his brother, Mr. Andrew Postlethwaite? Is he fatally injured too?'

"The reply was unequivocal. The doctors were uncertain which of the two would pass away first.

"You must remember that at this time I was ignorant of the rich man's will, and consequently of how the fate of a poor child of whom I had heard only one mention, hung in the balance at that awful moment. But in the breathlessness which seized Mrs. Postlethwaite at this sentence of double death, I realized from my knowledge of her that something more than grief was at prey upon her impenetrable heart, and shuddered to the core of my being when she repeated in that voice which was so terrible because so expressionless:

"'Take me to them.'"

They were lying in one room, her husband nearest the door, the other in a small alcove some ten feet away. Both were unconscious; both were surrounded by groups of frightened attendants who fell back as she approached. A doctor stood at the bed-head of her husband, but as her eye met his he stepped aside with a shake of the head and left the place empty for her.

"The action was significant. I saw that she understood what it meant, and with constricted heart watched her as she bent over the dying man and gazed into his wide-open eyes, already sightless and staring. Calculation was in her look and calculation only; and calculation, or something equally unintelligible, sent her next glance in the direction of his brother. What was in her mind? I could understand her indifference to Frank even at the crisis of his fate, but not the interest she showed in Andrew. It was an absorbing one, altering her whole expression. I no longer knew her for my dear young madam, and the jealousy I had never felt towards Frank rose to frantic resentment in my breast as I beheld what very likely might be a tardy recognition of the other's well-known passion, forced into disclosure by the exigencies of the moment.

"Alarmed by the strength of my feelings, and fearing an equal disclosure on my own part, I sought for a refuge from all eyes and found it in a little balcony opening out at my right. On to this balcony I stepped and found myself face to face with a star-lit heaven. Had I only been content with my isolation and the splendour of the spectacle spread out before me! But no, I must look back upon that bed and the solitary woman standing beside it! I must watch the settling of her body into rigidity as a voice rose from beside the other Postlethwaite saying, 'It is a matter of minutes now,' and then – and then – the slow creeping of her hand to her husband's mouth, the outspreading of her palm across the livid lips – its steady clinging there, smothering the feeble gasps of one already moribund, till the quivering form grew still, and Frank Postlethwaite lay dead before my eyes!

"I saw, and made no outcry, but she did, bringing the doctor back to her side with the startled exclamation:

"'Dead? I thought he had an hour's life left in him, and he has passed before his brother.'

"I thought it hate – the murderous impulse of a woman who sees her enemy at her mercy and can no longer restrain the passion of her long-cherished antagonism; and while something within me rebelled at the act, I could not betray her, though silence made a murderer of me too. I could not. Her spell was upon me as in another instant it was upon everyone else in the room. No suspicion of one so self-repressed in her sadness disturbed the universal sympathy; and encouraged by this blindness of the crowd, I vowed within myself never to reveal her secret. The man was dead, or as good as dead, when she touched him; and now that her hate was expended she would grow gentle and good.

"But I knew the worthlessness of this hope as well as my misconception of her motive, when Frank's child by another wife returned to my memory, and Bella's sin stood exposed."

"But only to myself. I alone knew that the fortune now wholly hers, and in consequence her boy's, had been won by a crime. That if her hand had fallen in comfort on her husband's forehead instead of in pressure on his mouth, he would have outlived his brother long enough to have become owner of his millions; in which case a rightful portion would have been insured to his daughter, now left a penniless waif. The thought made my hair rise, as the proceedings over, I faced her and made my first and last effort to rid my conscience of its new and intolerable burden.

"But the woman I had known and loved was no longer before me. The crown had touched her brows, and her charm which had been mainly sexual up to this hour had merged into an intellectual force, with which few men's mentality could cope. Mine yielded at once to it. From the first instant, I knew that a slavery of spirit, as well as of heart, was henceforth to be mine.

"She did not wait for me to speak; she had assumed the dictator's attitude at once.

"'I know of what you are thinking,' said she, 'and it is a subject you may dismiss at once from your mind. Mr. Postlethwaite's child by his first wife is coming to live with us. I have expressed my wishes in this regard to my lawyer, and there is nothing left to be said. You, with your close mouth and dependable nature, are to remain here as before, and occupy the same position towards my boy that you did towards his father. We shall move soon into a larger house, and the nature of our duties will be changed and their scope greatly increased; but I know that you can be trusted to enlarge with them and meet every requirement I shall see fit to make. Do not try to express your thanks. I see them in your face.'

"Did she, or just the last feeble struggle my conscience was making to break the bonds in which she held me, and win back my own respect? I shall never know, for she left me on completion of this speech, not to resume the subject, then or ever.

"But though I succumbed outwardly to her demands, I had not passed the point where inner conflict ends and peace begins. Her recognition of Helena and her reception into the family calmed me for a while, and gave me hope that all would yet be well. But I had never sounded the full bitterness of madam's morbid heart, well as I thought I knew it. The hatred she had felt from the first for her husband's child ripened into frenzied dislike when she found her a living image of the mother whose picture she had come across among Frank's personal effects. To win a tear from those meek eyes instead of a smile to the sensitive lips was her daily play. She seemed to exult in the joy of impressing upon the girl by how little she had missed a great fortune, and I have often thought, much as I tried to keep my mind free from all extravagant and unnecessary fancies, that half of the money she spent in beautifying this house and maintaining art industries and even great charitable institutions was spent with the base purpose of demonstrating to this child the power of immense wealth, and in what ways she might expect to see her little brother expend the millions in which she had been denied all share.

"I was so sure of this that one night while I was winding up the clocks with which Mrs. Postlethwaite in her fondness for old timepieces has filled the house, I stopped to look at the little figure toiling so wearily upstairs, to bed, without a mother's kiss. There was an appeal in the small wistful face which smote my hard old heart, and possibly a tear welled up in my own eye when I turned back to my duty.

"Was that why I felt the hand of Providence upon me, when in my halt before the one clock to which any superstitious interest was attached – the great one at the foot of the stairs – I saw that it had stopped and at the one minute of all minutes in our wretched lives: Four minutes past two? The hour, the minute in which Frank Postlethwaite had gasped his last under the pressure of his wife's hand! I knew it – the exact minute I mean – because Providence meant that I should know it. There had been a clock on the mantelpiece of the hotel room where he and his brother had died and I had seen her glance steal towards it at the instant she withdrew her palm from her husband's lips. The stare of that dial and the position of its hands had lived still in my mind as I believed it did in hers.

"Four minutes past two! How came our old timepiece here to stop at that exact moment on a day when Duty was making its last demand upon me to remember Frank's unhappy child? There was no one to answer; but as I looked and looked, I felt the impulse of the moment strengthen into purpose to leave those hands undisturbed in their silent accusation. She might see, and, moved by the coincidence, tremble at her treatment of Helena.

"But if this happened – if she saw and trembled – she gave no sign. The works were started up by some other hand, and the incident passed. But it left me with an idea. That clock soon had a way of stopping and always at that one instant of time. She was forced at length to notice it, and I remember an occasion when she stood stock-still with her eyes on those hands, and failed to find the banister with her hand, though she groped for it in her frantic need for support.

"But no command came from her to remove the worn-out piece, and soon its tricks, and every lesser thing, were forgotten in the crushing calamity which befell us in the sickness and death of little Richard.

"Oh, those days and nights! And oh, the face of the mother when the doctors told her that the case was hopeless! I asked myself then, and I have asked myself a hundred times since, which of all the emotions I saw pictured there bit the deepest, and made the most lasting impression on her guilty heart? Was it remorse? If so, she showed no change in her attitude towards Helena, unless it was by an added bitterness. The sweet looks and gentle ways of Frank's young daughter could not win against a hate sharpened by disappointment. Useless for me to hope for it. Release from the remorse of years was not to come in that way. As I realized this, I grew desperate and resorted again to the old trick of stopping the clock at the fatal hour. This time her guilty heart responded. She acknowledged the stab and let all her miseries appear. But how? In a way to wring my heart almost to madness, and not benefit the child at all. She had her first stroke that night. I had made her a helpless invalid.

"That was eight years ago, and since then what? Stagnation. She lived with her memories, and I with mine. Helena only had a right to hope, and hope perhaps she did, till – Is that the great clock talking? Listen! They all talk, but I heed only the one. What does it say? Tell! tell! tell! Does it think I will be silent now when I come to my own guilt? That I will seek to hide my weakness when I could not hide her sin?"

"Explain!" It was Violet speaking, and her tone was stern in its command. "Of what guilt do you speak? Not of guilt towards Helena; you pitied her too much –"

"But I pitied my dear madam more. It was that which affected me and drew me into crime against my will. Besides, I did not know – not at first – what was in the little bowl of curds and cream I carried to the girl each day. She had eaten them in her step-mother's room, and under her step-mother's eye as long as she had strength to pass from room to room, and how was I to guess that it was not wholesome? Because she failed in health from day to day? Was not my dear madam failing in health also; and was there poison in her cup? Innocent at that time, why am I not innocent now? Because – Oh, I will tell it all; as though at the bar of God. I will tell all the secrets of that day.

"She was sitting with her hand trembling on the tray from which I had just lifted the bowl she had bid me carry to Helena. I had seen her so a hundred times before, but not with just that look in her eyes, or just that air of desolation in her stony figure. Something made me speak; something made me ask if she were not quite so well as usual, and something made her reply with the dreadful truth that the doctor had given her just two months more to live. My fright and mad anguish stupefied me; for I was not prepared for this, no, not at all; – and unconsciously I stared down at the bowl I held, unable to breathe or move or even to meet her look."

As usual she misinterpreted my emotion.

"'Why do you stand like that?' I heard her say in a tone of great irritation. 'And why do you stare into that bowl? Do you think I mean to leave that child to walk these halls after I am carried out of them forever? Do you measure my hate by such a petty yard-stick as that? I tell you that I would rot above ground rather than enter it before she did?'

"I had believed I knew this woman; but what soul ever knows another's? What soul ever knows itself?

"'Bella!' I cried; the first time I had ever presumed to address her so intimately. 'Would you poison the girl?' And from sheer weakness my fingers lost their clutch, and the bowl fell to the floor, breaking into a dozen pieces.

"For a minute she stared down at these from over her tray, and then she remarked very low and very quietly:

"'Another bowl, Humphrey, and fresh curds from the kitchen. I will do the seasoning. The doses are too small to be skipped. You won't?' – I had shaken my head – 'But you will! It will not be the first time you have gone down the hall with this mixture.'

"'But that was before I knew –' I began.

"'And now that you do, you will go just the same.' Then as I stood hesitating, a thousand memories overwhelming me in an instant, she added in a voice to tear the heart, 'Do not make me hate the only being left in this world who understands and loves me.'

"She was a helpless invalid, and I a broken man, but when that word 'love' fell from her lips, I felt the blood start burning in my veins, and all the crust of habit and years of self-control loosen about my heart, and make me young again. What if her thoughts were dark and her wishes murderous! She was born to rule and sway men to her will even to their own undoing."

"'I wish I might kiss your hand,' was what I murmured, gazing at her white fingers groping over her tray.

"'You may,' she answered, and hell became heaven to me for a brief instant. Then I lifted myself and went obediently about my task.

"But puppet though I was, I was not utterly without sympathy. When I entered Helena's room and saw how her startled eyes fell shrinkingly on the bowl I set down before her, my conscience leaped to life and I could not help saying:

"'Don't you like the curds, Helena? Your brother used to love them very much.'

"'His were –'

"'What, Helena?'

"'What these are not,' she murmured.

"I stared at her, terror-stricken. So she knew, and yet did not seize the bowl and empty it out of the window! Instead, her hand moved slowly towards it and drew it into place before her.

"'Yet I must eat,' she said, lifting her eyes to mine in a sort of patient despair, which yet was without accusation.

"But my hand had instinctively gone to hers and grasped it.

"'Why must you eat it?' I asked. 'If – if you do not find it wholesome, why do you touch it?'

"'Because my step-mother expects me to,' she cried, 'and I have no other will than hers. When I was a little, little child, my father made me promise that if I ever came to live with her I would obey her simplest wish. And I always have. I will not disappoint the trust he put in me.'

"'Even if you die of it?'

"I do not know whether I whispered these words or only thought them. She answered as though I had spoken.

"'I am not afraid to die. I am more afraid to live. She may ask me some day to do something I feel to be wrong.'

"When I fled down the hall that night, I heard one of the small clocks speak to me. Tell! it cried, tell! tell! tell! tell! I rushed away from it with beaded forehead and rising hair.

"Then another's note piped up. No it droned. No! no! no! no! I stopped and took heart. Disgrace the woman I loved, on the brink of the grave? I – who asked no other boon from heaven than to see her happy, gracious, and good? Impossible. I would obey the great clock's voice; the others were mere chatterboxes.

"But it has at last changed its tune, for some reason, quite changed its tune. Now, it is Yes! Yes! instead of No! and in obeying it I save Helena. But what of Bella? and O God, what of myself?"

A sigh, a groan, then a long and heavy silence, into which there finally broke the pealing of the various clocks striking the hour. When all were still again and Violet had drawn aside the portiere, it was to see the old man on his knees, and between her and the thin streak of light entering from the hall, the figure of the doctor hastening to Helena's bedside.

When with inducements needless to name, they finally persuaded the young girl to leave her unholy habitation, it was in the arms which had upheld her once before, and to a life which promised to compensate her for her twenty years of loneliness and unsatisfied longing.

But a black shadow yet remained which she must cross before reaching the sunshine!

It lay at her step-mother's door.

In the plans made for Helena's release, Mrs. Postlethwaite's consent had not been obtained nor was she supposed to be acquainted with the doctor's intentions towards the child whose death she was hourly awaiting.

It was therefore with an astonishment, bordering on awe, that on their way downstairs, they saw the door of her room open and herself standing alone and upright on the threshold – she who had not been seen to take a step in years. In the wonder of this miracle of suddenly restored power, the little procession stopped – the doctor with his hand upon the rail, the lover with his burden clasped yet more protectingly to his breast. That a little speech awaited them could be seen from the force and fury of the gaze which the indomitable woman bent upon the lax and half-unconscious figure she beheld thus sheltered and conveyed. Having but one arrow left in her exhausted quiver, she launched it straight at the innocent breast which had never harboured against her a defiant thought.

"Ingrate!" was the word she hurled in a voice from which all its seductive music had gone forever. "Where are you going? Are they carrying you alive to your grave?"

A moan from Helena's pale lips, then silence. She had fainted at that barbed attack. But there was one there who dared to answer for her and he spoke relentlessly. It was the man who loved her.

"No, madam. We are carrying her to safety. You must know what I mean by that. Let her go quietly and you may die in peace. Otherwise –"

She interrupted him with a loud call, startling into life the echoes of that haunted hall:

"Humphrey! Come to me, Humphrey!"

But no Humphrey appeared.

Another call, louder and more peremptory than before:

"Humphrey! I say, Humphrey!"

But the answer was the same – silence, and only silence. As the horror of this grew, the doctor spoke:

"Mr. Humphrey Dunbar's ears are closed to all earthly summons. He died last night at the very hour he said he would – four minutes after two."

"Four minutes after two!" It came from her lips in a whisper, but with a revelation of her broken heart and life. "Four minutes after two!" And defiant to the last, her head rose, and for an instant, for a mere breath of time, they saw her as she had looked in her prime, regal in form, attitude, and expression; then the will which had sustained her through so much faltered and succumbed, and with a final reiteration of the words "Four minutes after two!" she broke into a rattling laugh, and fell back into the arms of her old nurse.

And below, one clock struck the hour and then another. But not the big one at the foot of the stairs. That still stood silent, with its hands pointing to the hour and minute of Frank Postlethwaite's hastened death.

AN INTANGIBLE CLUE

Anna Katharine Green

Anna Katharine Green (1846–1935) was one of the first American authors of detective fiction. Her novel *The Leavenworth Case* (1878) is often cited as the first such novel written by a woman. An international bestseller, credited with popularizing the genre in the United States, she was born and died in New York.

"Have you studied the case?"

"Not I."

"Not studied the case which for the last few days has provided the papers with such conspicuous headlines?"

"I do not read the papers. I have not looked at one in a whole week."

"Miss Strange, your social engagements must be of a very pressing nature just now?"

"They are."

"And your business sense in abeyance?"

"How so?"

"You would not ask if you had read the papers."

To this she made no reply save by a slight toss of her pretty head. If her employer felt nettled by this show of indifference, he did not betray it save by the rapidity of his tones as, without further preamble and possibly without real excuse, he proceeded to lay before her the case in question. "Last Tuesday night a woman was murdered in this city; an old woman, in a lonely house where she has lived for years. Perhaps you remember this house? It occupies a not inconspicuous site in Seventeenth Street – a house of the olden time?"

"No, I do not remember."

The extreme carelessness of Miss Strange's tone would have been fatal to her socially; but then, she would never have used it socially. This they both knew, yet he smiled with his customary indulgence.

"Then I will describe it."

She looked around for a chair and sank into it. He did the same.

"It has a fanlight over the front door."

She remained impassive.

"And two old-fashioned strips of parti-coloured glass on either side."

"And a knocker between its panels which may bring money some day."

"Oh, you do remember! I thought you would, Miss Strange."

"Yes. Fanlights over doors are becoming very rare in New York."

"Very well, then. That house was the scene of Tuesday's tragedy. The woman who has lived there in solitude for years was foully murdered. I have since heard that the people who knew her best have always anticipated some such violent end for her. She never allowed maid or friend to remain with her after five in the afternoon; yet she had money – some think a great deal – always in the house."

"I am interested in the house, not in her."

"Yet, she was a character – as full of whims and crotchets as a nut is of meat. Her death was horrible. She fought – her dress was torn from her body in rags. This happened, you see, before her hour for retiring; some think as early as six in the afternoon. And" – here he made a rapid gesture to catch Violet's wandering attention – "in spite of this struggle; in spite of the fact that she was dragged from room to room – that her person was searched – and everything in the house searched – that drawers were pulled out of bureaus – doors wrenched off of cupboards – china smashed upon the floor – whole shelves denuded and not a spot from cellar to garret left unransacked, no direct clue to the perpetrator has been found – nothing that gives any idea of his personality save his display of strength and great cupidity. The police have even deigned to consult me – an unusual procedure – but I could find nothing, either. Evidences of fiendish purpose abound – of relentless search – but no clue to the man himself. It's uncommon, isn't it, not to have any clue?"

"I suppose so." Miss Strange hated murders and it was with difficulty she could be brought to discuss them. But she was not going to be let off; not this time.

"You see," he proceeded insistently, "it's not only mortifying to the police but disappointing to the press, especially as few reporters believe in the No-thoroughfare business. They say, and we cannot but agree with them, that no such struggle could take place and no such repeated goings to and fro through the house without some vestige being left by which to connect this crime with its daring perpetrator."

Still she stared down at her hands – those little hands so white and fluttering, so seemingly helpless under the weight of their many rings, and yet so slyly capable.

"She must have queer neighbours," came at last from Miss Strange's reluctant lips. "Didn't they hear or see anything of all this?"

"She has no neighbours – that is, after half-past five o'clock. There's a printing establishment on one side of her, a deserted mansion on the other side, and nothing but warehouses back and front. There was no one to notice what took place in her small dwelling after the printing house was closed. She was the most courageous or the most foolish of women to remain there as she did. But nothing except death could budge her. She was born in the room where she died; was married in the one where she worked; saw husband, father, mother, and five sisters carried out in turn to their graves through the door with the fanlight over the top – and these memories held her."

"You are trying to interest me in the woman. Don't."

"No, I'm not trying to interest you in her, only trying to explain her. There was another reason for her remaining where she did so long after all residents had left the block. She had a business."

"Oh!"

"She embroidered monograms for fine ladies."

"She did? But you needn't look at me like that. She never embroidered any for me."

"No? She did first-class work. I saw some of it. Miss Strange, if I could get you into that house for ten minutes – not to see her but to pick up the loose intangible thread which I am sure is floating around in it somewhere – wouldn't you go?"

Violet slowly rose – a movement which he followed to the letter.

"Must I express in words the limit I have set for myself in our affair?" she asked. "When, for reasons I have never thought myself called upon to explain, I consented to help you a little now and then with some matter where a woman's tact and knowledge of the social world might tell without offence to herself or others, I never thought it would be necessary for me to state that temptation must stop with such cases, or that I should not be asked to touch the sordid or the bloody. But it seems I was mistaken, and that I must stoop to be explicit. The woman who was killed on Tuesday might have interested me greatly as an embroiderer, but as a victim, not at all. What do you see in me, or miss in me, that you should drag me into an atmosphere of low-down crime?"

"Nothing, Miss Strange. You are by nature, as well as by breeding, very far removed from everything of the kind. But you will allow me to suggest that no crime is low-down which makes imperative demand upon the intellect and intuitive sense of its investigator. Only the most delicate touch can feel and hold the thread I've just spoken of, and you have the most delicate touch I know."

"Do not attempt to flatter me. I have no fancy for handling befouled spider webs. Besides, if I had – if such elusive filaments fascinated me – how could I, well-known in person and name, enter upon such a scene without prejudice to our mutual compact?"

"Miss Strange" – she had reseated herself, but so far he had failed to follow her example (an ignoring of the subtle hint that her interest might yet be caught, which seemed to annoy her a trifle), "I should not even have suggested such a possibility had I not seen a way of introducing you there without risk to your position or mine. Among the boxes piled upon Mrs. Doolittle's table – boxes of finished work, most of them addressed and ready for delivery – was one on which could be seen the name of – shall I mention it?"

"Not mine? You don't mean mine? That would be too odd – too ridiculously odd. I should not understand a coincidence of that kind; no, I should not, notwithstanding the fact that I have lately sent out such work to be done."

"Yet it was your name, very clearly and precisely written – your whole name, Miss Strange. I saw and read it myself."

"But I gave the order to Madame Pirot on Fifth Avenue. How came my things to be found in the house of this woman of whose horrible death we have been talking?"

"Did you suppose that Madame Pirot did such work with her own hands? – or even had it done in her own establishment? Mrs. Doolittle was universally employed. She worked for a dozen firms. You will find the biggest names on most of her packages. But on this one – I allude to the one addressed to you – there was more to be seen than the name. These words were written on it in another hand. Send without opening. This struck the police as suspicious; sufficiently so, at least, for them to desire your presence at the house as soon as you can make it convenient."

"To open the box?"

"Exactly."

The curl of Miss Strange's disdainful lip was a sight to see.

"You wrote those words yourself," she coolly observed. "While someone's back was turned, you whipped out your pencil and –"

"Resorted to a very pardonable subterfuge highly conducive to the public's good. But never mind that. Will you go?"

Miss Strange became suddenly demure.

"I suppose I must," she grudgingly conceded. "However obtained, a summons from the police cannot be ignored even by Peter Strange's daughter."

Another man might have displayed his triumph by smile or gesture; but this one had learned his role too well. He simply said:

"Very good. Shall it be at once? I have a taxi at the door."

But she failed to see the necessity of any such hurry. With sudden dignity she replied:

"That won't do. If I go to this house it must be under suitable conditions. I shall have to ask my brother to accompany me."

"Your brother!"

"Oh, he's safe. He – he knows."

"Your brother knows?" Her visitor, with less control than usual, betrayed very openly his uneasiness.

"He does and – approves. But that's not what interests us now, only so far as it makes it possible for me to go with propriety to that dreadful house."

A formal bow from the other and the words:

"They may expect you, then. Can you say when?"

"Within the next hour. But it will be a useless concession on my part," she pettishly complained. "A place that has been gone over by a dozen detectives is apt to be brushed clean of its cobwebs, even if such ever existed."

"That's the difficulty," he acknowledged; and did not dare to add another word; she was at that particular moment so very much the great lady, and so little his confidential agent.

He might have been less impressed, however, by this sudden assumption of manner, had he been so fortunate as to have seen how she employed the three quarters of an hour's delay for which she had asked.

She read those neglected newspapers, especially the one containing the following highly coloured narration of this ghastly crime:

"A door ajar – an empty hall – a line of sinister looking blotches marking a guilty step diagonally across the flagging – silence – and an unmistakable odour repugnant to all humanity – such were the indications which met the eyes of Officer O'Leary on his first round last night, and led to the discovery of a murder which will long thrill the city by its mystery and horror.

"Both the house and the victim are well known." Here followed a description of the same and of Mrs. Doolittle's manner of life in her ancient home, which Violet hurriedly passed over to come to the following:

"As far as one can judge from appearances, the crime happened in this wise: Mrs. Doolittle had been in her kitchen, as the tea-kettle found singing on the stove goes to prove, and was coming back through her bedroom, when the wretch, who had stolen in by the front door which, to save steps, she was unfortunately in the habit of leaving on the latch till all possibility of customers for the day was over, sprang upon her from behind and dealt her a swinging blow with the poker he had caught up from the hearthstone.

"Whether the struggle which ensued followed immediately upon this first attack or came later, it will take medical experts to determine. But, whenever it did occur, the fierceness of its character is shown by the grip taken upon her throat and the traces of blood which are to be seen all over the house. If the wretch had lugged her into her workroom and thence to the kitchen, and thence back to the spot of first assault, the evidences could not have been more ghastly. Bits of her clothing, torn off by a ruthless hand, lay scattered over all these floors. In her bedroom, where she finally breathed her last, there could be seen mingled with these a number of large but worthless glass beads; and close against one of the base-boards, the string which had held them, as shown by the few remaining beads still clinging to it. If in pulling the string from her neck he had hoped to light upon some valuable booty, his fury at his disappointment is evident. You can almost see the frenzy with which he flung the would-be necklace at the wall, and kicked about and stamped upon its rapidly rolling beads.

"Booty! That was what he was after; to find and carry away the poor needlewoman's supposed hoardings. If the scene baffles description – if, as some believe, he dragged her yet living from spot to spot, demanding information as to her places of concealment under threat of repeated blows, and, finally baffled, dealt the finishing stroke and proceeded on the search alone, no greater devastation could have taken place in this poor woman's house or effects. Yet such was his precaution and care for himself that he left no finger-print behind him nor any other token which could lead to personal identification. Even though his footsteps could be traced in much the order I have mentioned, they were of so indeterminate and shapeless a character as to convey little to the intelligence of the investigator.

"That these smears (they could not be called footprints) not only crossed the hall but appeared in more than one place on the staircase proves that he did not confine his search to the lower storey; and perhaps one of the most interesting features of the case lies in the indications given by these marks of the raging course he took through these upper rooms. As the accompanying diagram will show [we omit the diagram] he went first into the large front chamber, thence to the rear where we find two rooms, one unfinished and filled with accumulated stuff most of which he left lying loose upon the floor, and the other plastered, and containing a window opening upon an alley-way at the side, but empty of all furniture and without even a carpet on the bare boards.

"Why he should have entered the latter place, and why, having entered he should have crossed to the window, will be plain to those who have studied the conditions. The front chamber windows were tightly shuttered, the attic ones cumbered with boxes and shielded from approach by old bureaus and discarded chairs. This one only was free and, although darkened by the proximity of the house neighbouring it across the alley, was the only spot on the storey where sufficient light could be had at this late hour for the examination of any object of whose value he was doubtful. That he had come across such an object and had brought it to this window for some such purpose is very satisfactorily demonstrated by the discovery of a worn out wallet of ancient make lying on the floor directly in front of this window – a proof of his cupidity but also proof of his ill-luck. For this wallet, when lifted and opened, was found to contain two hundred or more dollars in old bills, which, if not the full hoard of their industrious owner, was certainly worth the taking by one who had risked his neck for the sole purpose of theft.

"This wallet, and the flight of the murderer without it, give to this affair, otherwise simply brutal, a dramatic interest which will be appreciated not only by the very able detectives already hot upon the chase, but by all other inquiring minds anxious to solve a mystery of which so estimable a woman has been the unfortunate victim. A problem is presented to the police –"

There Violet stopped.

When, not long after, the superb limousine of Peter Strange stopped before the little house in Seventeenth Street, it caused a veritable sensation, not only in the curiosity-mongers lingering on the sidewalk, but to the two persons within – the officer on guard and a belated reporter.

Though dressed in her plainest suit, Violet Strange looked much too fashionable and far too young and thoughtless to be observed, without emotion, entering a scene of hideous and brutal crime. Even the young man who accompanied her promised to bring a most incongruous element into this atmosphere of guilt and horror, and, as the detective on guard whispered to the man beside him, might much better have been left behind in the car.

But Violet was great for the proprieties and young Arthur followed her in.

Her entrance was a coup du theatre. She had lifted her veil in crossing the sidewalk and her interesting features and general air of timidity were very fetching. As the man holding open the door noted the impression made upon his companion, he muttered with sly facetiousness:

"You think you'll show her nothing; but I'm ready to bet a fiver that she'll want to see it all and that you'll show it to her."

The detective's grin was expressive, notwithstanding the shrug with which he tried to carry it off.

And Violet? The hall into which she now stepped from the most vivid sunlight had never been considered even in its palmiest days as possessing cheer even of the stately kind. The ghastly green light infused through it by the coloured glass on either side of the doorway seemed to promise yet more dismal things beyond.

"Must I go in there?" she asked, pointing, with an admirable simulation of nervous excitement, to a half-shut door at her left. "Is there where it happened? Arthur, do you suppose that there is where it happened?"

"No, no, Miss," the officer made haste to assure her. "If you are Miss Strange" (Violet bowed), "I need hardly say that the woman was struck in her bedroom. The door beside you leads into the parlour, or as she would have called it, her work-room. You needn't be afraid of going in there. You will see nothing but the disorder of her boxes. They were pretty well pulled about. Not all of them though," he added, watching her as closely as the dim light permitted. "There is one which gives no sign of having been tampered with. It was done up in wrapping paper and is addressed to you, which in itself would not have seemed worthy of our attention had not these lines been scribbled on it in a man's hand-writing: 'Send without opening.'"

"How odd!" exclaimed the little minx with widely opened eyes and an air of guileless innocence. "Whatever can it mean? Nothing serious I am sure, for the woman did not even know me. She was employed to do this work by Madame Pirot."

"Didn't you know that it was to be done here?"

"No. I thought Madame Pirot's own girls did her embroidery for her."

"So that you were surprised –"

"Wasn't I!"

"To get our message."

"I didn't know what to make of it."

The earnest, half-injured look with which she uttered this disclaimer did its appointed work. The detective accepted her for what she seemed and, oblivious to the reporter's satirical gesture, crossed to the work-room door, which he threw wide open with the remark:

"I should be glad to have you open that box in our presence. It is undoubtedly all right, but we wish to be sure. You know what the box should contain?"

"Oh, yes, indeed; pillow-cases and sheets, with a big S embroidered on them."

"Very well. Shall I undo the string for you?"

"I shall be much obliged," said she, her eye flashing quickly about the room before settling down upon the knot he was deftly loosening.

Her brother, gazing indifferently in from the doorway, hardly noticed this look; but the reporter at his back did, though he failed to detect its penetrating quality.

"Your name is on the other side," observed the detective as he drew away the string and turned the package over.

The smile which just lifted the corner of her lips was not in answer to this remark, but to her recognition of her employer's handwriting in the words under her name: Send without opening. She had not misjudged him.

"The cover you may like to take off yourself," suggested the officer, as he lifted the box out of its wrapper.

"Oh, I don't mind. There's nothing to be ashamed of in embroidered linen. Or perhaps that is not what you are looking for?"

No one answered. All were busy watching her whip off the lid and lift out the pile of sheets and pillow-cases with which the box was closely packed.

"Shall I unfold them?" she asked.

The detective nodded.

Taking out the topmost sheet, she shook it open. Then the next and the next till she reached the bottom of the box. Nothing of a criminating nature came to light. The box as well as its contents was without mystery of any kind. This was not an unexpected result of course, but the smile with which she began to refold the pieces and throw them back into the box, revealed one of her dimples which was almost as dangerous to the casual observer as when it revealed both.

"There," she exclaimed, "you see! Household linen exactly as I said. Now may I go home?"

"Certainly, Miss Strange."

The detective stole a sly glance at the reporter. She was not going in for the horrors then after all.

But the reporter abated nothing of his knowing air, for while she spoke of going, she made no move towards doing so, but continued to look about the room till her glances finally settled on a long dark curtain shutting off an adjoining room.

"There's where she lies, I suppose," she feelingly exclaimed. "And not one of you knows who killed her. Somehow, I cannot understand that. Why don't you know when that's what you're hired for?" The innocence with which she uttered this was astonishing. The detective began to look sheepish and the reporter turned aside to hide his smile. Whether in another moment either would have spoken no one can say, for, with a mock consciousness of having said something foolish, she caught up her parasol from the table and made a start for the door.

But of course she looked back.

"I was wondering," she recommenced, with a half wistful, half speculative air, "whether I should ask to have a peep at the place where it all happened."

The reporter chuckled behind the pencil-end he was chewing, but the officer maintained his solemn air, for which act of self-restraint he was undoubtedly grateful when in another minute she gave a quick impulsive shudder not altogether assumed, and vehemently added: "But I couldn't stand the sight; no, I couldn't! I'm an awful coward when it comes to things like that. Nothing in all the world would induce me to look at the woman or her room. But I should like –" here both her dimples came into play though she could not be said exactly to smile – "just one little look upstairs, where he went poking about so long without any fear it seems of being interrupted. Ever since I've read about it I have seen, in my mind, a picture of his wicked figure sneaking from room to room, tearing open drawers and flinging out the contents of closets just to find a little money – a little, little money! I shall not sleep to-night just for wondering how those high up attic rooms really look."

Who could dream that back of this display of mingled childishness and audacity there lay hidden purpose, intellect, and a keen knowledge of human nature. Not the two men who listened to this seemingly irresponsible chatter. To them she was a child to be humoured and humour her they did. The dainty feet which had already found their way to that gloomy staircase were allowed to ascend, followed it is true by those of the officer who did not dare to smile back at the reporter because of the brother's watchful and none too conciliatory eye.

At the stair head she paused to look back.

"I don't see those horrible marks which the papers describe as running all along the lower hall and up these stairs."

"No, Miss Strange; they have gradually been rubbed out, but you will find some still showing on these upper floors."

"Oh! oh! where? You frighten me – frighten me horribly! But – but – if you don't mind, I should like to see."

Why should not a man on a tedious job amuse himself? Piloting her over to the small room in the rear, he pointed down at the boards. She gave one look and then stepped gingerly in.

"Just look!" she cried; "a whole string of marks going straight from door to window. They have no shape, have they – just blotches? I wonder why one of them is so much larger than the rest?"

This was no new question. It was one which everybody who went into the room was sure to ask, there was such a difference in the size and appearance of the mark nearest the window. The reason – well, minds were divided about that, and no one had a satisfactory theory. The detective therefore kept discreetly silent.

This did not seem to offend Miss Strange. On the contrary it gave her an opportunity to babble away to her heart's content.

"One, two, three, four, five, six," she counted, with a shudder at every count. "And one of them bigger than the others." She might have added, "It is the trail of one foot, and strangely, intermingled at that," but she did not, though we may be quite sure that she noted the fact. "And where, just where did the old wallet fall? Here? or here?"

She had moved as she spoke, so that in uttering the last "here," she stood directly before the window. The surprise she received there nearly made her forget the part she was playing. From the character of the light in the room, she had expected, on looking out, to confront a near-by wall, but not a window in that wall. Yet that was what she saw directly facing her from across the old-fashioned alley separating this house from its neighbour; twelve unshuttered and uncurtained panes through which she caught a darkened view of a room almost as forlorn and devoid of furniture as the one in which she then stood.

When quite sure of herself, she let a certain portion of her surprise appear.

"Why, look!" she cried, "if you can't see right in next door! What a lonesome-looking place! From its desolate appearance I should think the house quite empty."

"And it is. That's the old Shaffer homestead. It's been empty for a year."

"Oh, empty!" And she turned away, with the most inconsequent air in the world, crying out as her name rang up the stair, "There's Arthur calling. I suppose he thinks I've been here long enough. I'm sure I'm very much obliged to you, officer. I really shouldn't have slept a wink to-night, if I hadn't been given a peep at these rooms, which I had imagined so different." And with one additional glance over her shoulder, that seemed to penetrate both windows and the desolate space beyond, she ran quickly out and down in response to her brother's reiterated call.

"Drive quickly! – as quickly as the law allows, to Hiram Brown's office in Duane Street."

Arrived at the address named, she went in alone to see Mr. Brown. He was her father's lawyer and a family friend.

Hardly waiting for his affectionate greeting, she cried out quickly, "Tell me how I can learn anything about the old Shaffer house in Seventeenth Street. Now, don't look so surprised. I have very good reasons for my request and – and – I'm in an awful hurry."

"But –"

"I know, I know; there's been a dreadful tragedy next door to it; but it's about the Shaffer house itself I want some information. Has it an agent, a –"

"Of course it has an agent, and here is his name."

Mr. Brown presented her with a card on which he had hastily written both name and address.

She thanked him, dropped him a mocking curtsey full of charm, whispered "Don't tell father," and was gone.

Her manner to the man she next interviewed was very different. As soon as she saw him she subsided into her usual society manner. With just a touch of the conceit of the successful debutante, she announced herself as Miss Strange of Seventy-second Street. Her business with him was in regard to the possible renting of the Shaffer house. She had an old lady friend who was desirous of living downtown.

In passing through Seventeenth Street, she had noticed that the old Shaffer house was standing empty and had been immediately struck with the advantages it possessed for her elderly friend's occupancy. Could it be that the house was for rent? There was no sign on it to that effect, but – etc.

His answer left her nothing to hope for.

"It is going to be torn down," he said.

"Oh, what a pity!" she exclaimed. "Real colonial, isn't it! I wish I could see the rooms inside before it is disturbed. Such doors and such dear old-fashioned mantelpieces as it must have! I just dote on the Colonial. It brings up such pictures of the old days; weddings, you know, and parties; – all so different from ours and so much more interesting."

Is it the chance shot that tells? Sometimes. Violet had no especial intention in what she said save as a prelude to a pending request, but nothing could have served her purpose better than that one word, wedding. The agent laughed and giving her his first indulgent look, remarked genially:

"Romance is not confined to those ancient times. If you were to enter that house to-day you would come across evidences of a wedding as romantic as any which ever took place in all the seventy odd years of its existence. A man and a woman were married there day before yesterday who did their first courting under its roof forty years ago. He has been married twice and she once in the interval; but the old love held firm and now at the age of sixty and over they have come together to finish their days in peace and happiness. Or so we will hope."

"Married! married in that house and on the day that –"

She caught herself up in time. He did not notice the break.

"Yes, in memory of those old days of courtship, I suppose. They came here about five, got the keys, drove off, went through the ceremony in that empty house, returned the keys to me in my own apartment, took the steamer for Naples, and were on the sea before midnight. Do you not call that quick work as well as highly romantic?"

"Very." Miss Strange's cheek had paled. It was apt to when she was greatly excited. "But I don't understand," she added, the moment after. "How could they do this and nobody know about it? I should have thought it would have got into the papers."

"They are quiet people. I don't think they told their best friends. A simple announcement in the next day's journals testified to the fact of their marriage, but that was all. I would not have felt at liberty to mention the circumstances myself, if the parties were not well on their way to Europe."

"Oh, how glad I am that you did tell me! Such a story of constancy and the hold which old associations have upon sensitive minds! But –"

"Why, Miss? What's the matter? You look very much disturbed."

"Don't you remember? Haven't you thought? Something else happened that very day and almost at the same time on that block. Something very dreadful –"

"Mrs. Doolittle's murder?"

"Yes. It was as near as next door, wasn't it? Oh, if this happy couple had known –"

"But fortunately they didn't. Nor are they likely to, till they reach the other side. You needn't fear that their honeymoon will be spoiled that way."

"But they may have heard something or seen something before leaving the street. Did you notice how the gentleman looked when he returned you the keys?"

"I did, and there was no cloud on his satisfaction."

"Oh, how you relieve me!" One – two dimples made their appearance in Miss Strange's fresh, young cheeks. "Well! I wish them joy. Do you mind telling me their names? I cannot think of them as actual persons without knowing their names."

"The gentleman was Constantin Amidon; the lady, Marian Shaffer. You will have to think of them now as Mr. and Mrs. Amidon."

"And I will. Thank you, Mr. Hutton, thank you very much. Next to the pleasure of getting the house for my friend, is that of hearing this charming bit of news its connection."

She held out her hand and, as he took it, remarked:

"They must have had a clergyman and witnesses."

"Undoubtedly."

"I wish I had been one of the witnesses," she sighed sentimentally.

"They were two old men."

"Oh, no! Don't tell me that."

"Fogies; nothing less."

"But the clergyman? He must have been young. Surely there was some one there capable of appreciating the situation?"

"I can't say about that; I did not see the clergyman."

"Oh, well! it doesn't matter." Miss Strange's manner was as nonchalant as it was charming. "We will think of him as being very young."

And with a merry toss of her head she flitted away.

But she sobered very rapidly upon entering her limousine.

"Hello!"

"Ah, is that you?"

"Yes, I want a Marconi sent."

"A Marconi?"

"Yes, to the Cretic, which left dock the very night in which we are so deeply interested."

"Good. Whom to? The Captain?"

"No, to a Mrs. Constantin Amidon. But first be sure there is such a passenger."

"Mrs.! What idea have you there?"

"Excuse my not stating over the telephone. The message is to be to this effect. Did she at any time immediately before or after her marriage to Mr. Amidon get a glimpse of any one in the adjoining house? No remarks, please. I use the telephone because I am not ready to explain myself. If she did, let her send a written description to you of that person as soon as she reaches the Azores."

"You surprise me. May I not call or hope for a line from you early tomorrow?"

"I shall be busy till you get your answer."

He hung up the receiver. He recognized the resolute tone.

But the time came when the pending explanation was fully given to him. An answer had been returned from the steamer, favourable to Violet's hopes. Mrs. Amidon had seen such a person and would send a full description of the same at the first opportunity. It was news to fill Violet's heart with pride; the filament of a clue which had led to this great result had been so nearly invisible and had felt so like nothing in her grasp.

To her employer she described it as follows:

"When I hear or read of a case which contains any baffling features, I am apt to feel some hidden chord in my nature thrill to one fact in it and not to any of the others. In this case the single fact which appealed to my imagination was the dropping of the stolen wallet in that upstairs room. Why did the guilty man drop it? and why, having dropped it, did he not pick it up again? but one answer seemed possible. He had heard or seen something at the spot where it fell which not only alarmed him but sent him in flight from the house."

"Very good; and did you settle to your own mind the nature of that sound or that sight?"

"I did." Her manner was strangely businesslike. No show of dimples now. "Satisfied that if any possibility remained of my ever doing this, it would have to be on the exact place of this occurrence or not at all, I embraced your suggestion and visited the house."

"And that room no doubt."

"And that room. Women, somehow, seem to manage such things."

"So I've noticed, Miss Strange. And what was the result of your visit? What did you discover there?"

"This: that one of the blood spots marking the criminal's steps through the room was decidedly more pronounced than the rest; and, what was even more important, that the window out of which I was looking had its counterpart in the house on the opposite side of the alley. In gazing through the one I was gazing through the other; and not only that, but into the darkened area of the room beyond. Instantly I saw how the latter fact might be made to explain the former one. But before I say how, let me ask if it is quite settled among you that the smears on the floor and stairs mark the passage of the criminal's footsteps!"

"Certainly; and very bloody feet they must have been too. His shoes – or rather his one shoe – for the proof is plain that only the right one left its mark – must have become thoroughly saturated to carry its traces so far."

"Do you think that any amount of saturation would have done this? Or, if you are not ready to agree to that, that a shoe so covered with blood could have failed to leave behind it some hint of its shape, some imprint, however faint, of heel or toe? But nowhere did it do this. We see a smear – and that is all."

"You are right, Miss Strange; you are always right. And what do you gather from this?"

She looked to see how much he expected from her, and, meeting an eye not quite as free from ironic suggestion as his words had led her to expect, faltered a little as she proceeded to say:

"My opinion is a girl's opinion, but such as it is you have the right to have it. From the indications mentioned I could draw but this conclusion: that the blood which accompanied the criminal's footsteps was not carried through the house by his shoes; – he wore no shoes; he did not even wear stockings; probably he had none. For reasons which appealed to his judgment, he went about his wicked work barefoot; and it was the blood from his own veins and not from those of his victim which made the trail we have followed with so much interest. Do you forget those broken beads; – how he kicked them about and stamped upon them in his fury? One of them pierced the ball of his foot, and that so sharply that it not only spurted blood but kept on bleeding with every step he took. Otherwise, the trail would have been lost after his passage up the stairs."

"Fine!" There was no irony in the bureau-chief's eye now. "You are progressing, Miss Strange. Allow me, I pray, to kiss your hand. It is a liberty I have never taken, but one which would greatly relieve my present stress of feeling."

She lifted her hand toward him, but it was in gesture, not in recognition of his homage.

"Thank you," said she, "but I claim no monopoly on deductions so simple as these. I have not the least doubt that not only yourself but every member of the force has made the same. But there is a little matter which may have escaped the police, may even have escaped you. To that I would now call your attention since through it I have been enabled, after a little necessary groping, to reach the open. You remember the one large blotch on the upper floor where the man dropped the wallet? That blotch, more or less commingled with a fainter one, possessed great significance for me from the first moment I saw it. How came his foot to bleed so much more profusely at that one spot than at any other? There could be but one answer: because here a surprise met him – a surprise so startling to him in his present state of mind, that he gave a quick spring backward, with the result that his wounded foot came down suddenly and forcibly instead of easily as in his previous wary tread. And what was the surprise? I made it my business to find out, and now I can tell you that it was the sight of a woman's face staring upon him from the neighbouring house which he had probably been told was empty. The shock disturbed his judgment. He saw his crime discovered – his guilty secret read, and fled in unreasoning panic. He might better have held on to his wits. It was this display of fear which led me to search after its cause, and consequently to discover that at this especial hour more than one person had been in the Shaffer house; that, in fact, a marriage had been celebrated there under circumstances as romantic as any we read of in books, and that this marriage, privately carried out, had been followed by an immediate voyage of the happy couple on one of the White Star steamers. With the rest you are conversant. I do not need to say anything about what has followed the sending of that Marconi."

"But I am going to say something about your work in this matter, Miss Strange. The big detectives about here will have to look sharp if –"

"Don't, please! Not yet." A smile softened the asperity of this interruption. "The man has yet to be caught and identified. Till that is done I cannot enjoy any one's congratulations. And you will see that all this may not be so easy. If no one happened to meet the desperate wretch before he had an opportunity to retie his shoe-laces, there will be little for you or even for the police to go upon but his wounded foot, his undoubtedly carefully prepared alibi, and later, a woman's confused description of a face seen but for a moment only and that under a personal excitement precluding minute attention. I should not be surprised if the whole thing came to nothing."

But it did not. As soon as the description was received from Mrs. Amidon (a description, by the way, which was unusually clear and precise, owing to the peculiar and contradictory features of the man), the police were able to recognize him among the many suspects always under their eye. Arrested, he pleaded, just as Miss Strange had foretold, an alibi of a seemingly unimpeachable character; but neither it, nor the plausible explanation with which he endeavoured to account for a freshly healed scar amid the callouses of his right foot, could stand before Mrs. Amidon's unequivocal testimony that he was the same man she had seen in Mrs. Doolittle's upper room on the afternoon of her own happiness and of that poor woman's murder.

The moment when, at his trial, the two faces again confronted each other across a space no wider than that which had separated them on the dread occasion in Seventeenth Street, is said to have been one of the most dramatic in the annals of that ancient court room.

THE VOICE IS JACOB'S VOICE

Kerry Greenwood

Kerry Greenwood was a criminal defence lawyer before writing crime fiction full-time. A prolific Australian crime writer, Greenwood created the 1920s flapper Phryne Fisher, who first appears in *Cocaine Blues* (1989). The books have been adapted for television as *Miss Fisher's Murder Mysteries*.

The voice is Jacob's voice, but the hands are the hands of Esau.
Genesis 27:22

'Do come in,' invited Death, and bowed.

Dr Elizabeth MacMillan, who had wrestled many a fall with this august personage, returned the bow and entered the Hon. Miss Phryne Fisher's house. There were lights, a buzz of conversation, and a tinkle suggesting filled glasses. Miss Fisher's Winter Solstice party, to which all of her friends and everyone to whom she owed a favour had been invited, was evidently going well.

Death pushed his mask back onto his forehead, rumpling his fine blond hair, and revealed the ingenuous face of Lindsay Herbert.

'Mr Herbert,' Dr MacMillan exclaimed in her precise Edinburgh accent, 'you have chosen an unchancy disguise!'

'Always wanted to be macabre,' confessed Lindsay, smoothing down his robe and propping his sickle against the door. 'Dashed hot, these draperies! Ever since I read that thing of Poe's . . . what was it called?'

'"The Masque of the Red Death", I believe. I hope that you are not a bad omen.'

'I don't think so—party's going swimmingly as far as I can see, though it's a crush. Who are you masqueradin' as, Doctor? You look forbiddin' in that sheet.'

'This is not a sheet, young man, it is a toga virilis, and I am Julius Caesar—observe my laurel crown.'

'Oh.' Lindsay could never remember who had won between Caesar and Pompey, even though he had been forced to study the Civil War. He was about to offer '*Gallia in tres partes divisa est*', which was all he could remember of the work in question, when Phryne swept into the hall, drew closer to Dr MacMillan and whispered in her ear, 'You are mortal.'

'Correct,' said the doctor. 'And well guessed. Now who are you, I wonder? Magnificent, Phryne!'

Phryne stood back a little to allow the older woman to admire her. The black hair was drawn back under a red wig, and she had a crown bright with emeralds, a gold dress, and ropes of pearls.

Dr MacMillan made an Elizabethan bow. 'Your Majesty Queen Elizabeth, I am honoured.'

'I've even got the petticoat,' said Phryne, displaying it, a fine silk one with gold edging. 'Put me down in any part of my realm in my petticoat and I would be what I am. Lindsay, you can come in now and have a drink. Mr Butler has finished making his next batch of cocktails. Come along.' She laid a jewelled hand on each arm, and Julius Caesar and Death escorted her into the drawing room.

It was full of people. Dr MacMillan was provided with a glass of good Scotch, and Lindsay collared two cocktails made to Mr Butler's own jealously guarded recipe. Jazz, provided by gramophone records, rose above the chatter of thirty guests.

'Who,' demanded the singer tinnily, 'stole my heart away? Who?' He seemed destined to remain unanswered.

Dr MacMillan found herself next to a young woman whom she had previously had as a patient.

'Well, Miss Gately—' she peered beneath a layer of make-up to confirm that this Columbine was indeed Miss Gately—'how are you?'

'Hellish, thank you,' muttered Miss Gately. 'What a press of people! I wonder that Phryne invited half of them.'

'Oh?' Dr MacMillan surveyed the room. 'Why?'

'Well, there's that policeman she's so fond of,' snapped Miss Gately, as a pirate in sea-boots passed. 'Detective Inspector Robinson, isn't he? And I'm sure those three don't belong.'

She indicated a group of people dancing very close together: a cat in a skin-tight theatrical suit, head covered by a full mask; a carnival baby, plumped out with cushions, in lacy drawers; and a sleek and scarlet devil. They were all managing to eat somehow, and by the way they were giggling, had got at the cocktails fairly early. Dr MacMillan recognised in the devil a certain Klara, whom she had treated for venereal disease, and assumed that her companions were also ladies (or indeed gentlemen) of the night. She shrugged.

'They seem to be enjoying themselves.'

'Oh, I expect they are! They wouldn't often get into society like ours.' Miss Gately was generously including Dr MacMillan in this term, and Julius Caesar suppressed a grin. 'And I'm sure that she can't have known about Jacob and Esau Tipping, or she wouldn't have invited both of them.'

'What is wrong with them?' asked the doctor, who had tired of Miss Gately's company some time before she met her.

Two gentlemen were standing at the buffet, which was laden with expensive treats, like champagne ices and smoked salmon sandwiches. One was dressed as a Doge, with the Phrygian cap in red leather and the scarlet robes. His hands were burdened with rings. The other, who resembled him closely, was clad in full Renaissance gear, jewelled chain and rings, flowing heavy, embossed velvet. Both had dark eyes and short black beards. Miss Gately was incandescent with scandal.

'They are brothers, you see, and they hate one another. Their father made a most peculiar will—all the Tippings have been odd, though they are so rich. The grandfather made a killing on the goldfields, I believe, selling grog to the miners, or something, and he only had one son, and that son only had two sons, twins, and they hate each other.'

'Oh, yes?'

'Yes. Jacob is the Doge and Esau is Lorenzo de Medici. So overdone, but they never did have any taste. Their grandmother—' her voice sank—'was a gypsy, see? It's in the blood.'

Dr MacMillan, who had seen enough blood to fill a lake and had deep doubts about heredity, snorted.

'So their father, he was a friend of my mother's, horrible man, all tea and temperance, he died about two years ago and left this ridiculous will . . .'

Across the room, Jilly Henderson, attired as a supreme court judge, which she knew that she would never be, was telling Queen Elizabeth the same story.

'It was a mistake to invite them together, Phryne. Their father left all his property to the one who, by the time he was twenty-five, had never been drunk. They've had it in for each other since they were babies.'

'Oh? And when do they turn twenty-five?'

'Tomorrow—rather, tonight, at midnight. I only know about it because my firm represents the estate, and we had to get counsel's opinion as to whether Esau, who is the elder by one hour, would come into his inheritance before Jacob.'

'And does he?' Phryne settled her brocade skirts, a little taken aback. There were still things that she didn't know in the Melbourne social scene, and she did think that someone might have warned her about the Tipping brothers. She did not want a quarrel to mar her party, which was going particularly well.

'No,' Jilly grinned. 'Counsel found it impossible to give an opinion based on precedent, but gave it as his view that the court would take judicial notice of the fact that each new day begins at one second past midnight. So tonight's their last chance. They have both been very good or very careful,' added Jilly, who was, after all, a lawyer. 'And the trustee hasn't managed to catch either of them tippling.'

'Who is the trustee?'

'Severe old gentleman in the Puritan garb. Just about suits him. And he's nicely named, too. Mr Crabbe. Temperance lecturer. Can't stand the man. Tried to stop us keeping port in the office. Said that Mr Latham's best crusty '86 was an alcoholic poison. You should have heard what old Latham said after Crabbe was gone! "My best port, alcohol!" he sputtered. "Alcohol is what they put in compasses!" Oh dear, he was wild, but we just close the door of the inner office when Crabbe inflicts his instruction on us, and warn all the clerks not to offer him a drop, or breathe on him if they've been imbibing at lunch. He's been dogging the Tipping brothers' footsteps ever since the will was read.'

'What, is he paid to do this?'

'No, he's got a monomania about alcohol. In fact talking about him makes me dry. Let's have another of those delicious cocktails.'

'Who are the women hovering around the brothers? The tall lady in that pre-Raphaelite thing, and the short one in tights?'

'Viola, that's Viola Tipping. She always comes to costume parties as the Shakespeare heroine, though I think that Viola in the play must have been more . . . well, boyish. You'd never take Viola for a boy, would you?'

'God's teeth,' said Phryne in character, 'never! Is she Jacob's wife?'

'Yes, and the beggar maid, as in "King Cophetua and the Beggar Maid", that's Tamar Tipping, Esau's wife. I can't say that I take to either of them, Phryne dear. Viola gushes and is as hard as nails and Tamar is cool and distant and as hard as nails. Never mind. Why, by the way, did you invite them?'

'I owed them both an invitation. This party was to clear all my social debts before the beginning of spring, and of course I invited all my friends so that I should not be distracted with tedium.'

'Well, I do think that someone could have told you,' said Jilly, and summoned a server with a judicial wave.

Despite the Tipping brothers, the party was going well. Phryne drifted from conversation to conversation, smiling on social enemies and providing drinks for friends. She had edged quite close to the Tipping brothers and their guardian, and listened as she danced a foxtrot with the delectable Lindsay. He was wondering how difficult it was going to be to remove Miss Fisher from her armoury of clothes, if she allowed him to stay after the guests went home.

Lindsay looked for Dot, Phryne's companion, and sighted her, a Sèvres shepherdess, blushing like a poppy under the avalanche of compliments which a tall young Grenadier Guard was pouring into her ear. Dot would be able to help. She, presumably, had got Phryne into this mountain of a garment, and she would know how to get her out again.

Lindsay sighed. 'Can I stay tonight?'

The red wig and crown inclined, the green eyes, matching the emeralds on her head, cut through his mask.

'Perhaps, if you merit it,' she said. Lindsay attempted to hold her closer, and was foiled by the density of the brocade gown, and painfully spiked by the stomacher.

'Perhaps?' he whispered.

Phryne smiled. 'Perhaps. Now hush, I'm eavesdropping.'

Esau Tipping as Lorenzo the Magnificent jutted a defiant beard at his brother and said, just above a whisper, 'You're contemptible.'

Jacob Tipping, as the Doge of Venice, swallowed an ice and snapped, 'So are you.'

'And no returns,' whispered Lindsay in Phryne's ear.

'You will never inherit!' said Jacob. 'My father meant the property to go to me!'

'You are wrong, brother,' snarled Esau. 'He loved me best and he meant it to go to me!'

'Loved you best!' sneered Jacob, forgetting to speak softly. 'Who was it looked after the old man? Who visited him every day? You never went near him! You and that wife of yours, you didn't care two straws for him!'

'What about that wife of yours, then?' Esau was also forgetting to keep his voice down. 'You set her on the old man, to flatter him, and pat him, and mother him, and it didn't work, did it, brother? He wasn't convinced by all that coaxing and petting. "Oh, Daddy dear, do leave your Viola something to remember you by."' The voice rose in a scathing imitation of his sister-in-law's gushing manner, and Jacob bristled.

'He didn't get taken in. He left her nothing but his pocket watch, and a few jewels that anyway would have gone to the eldest son's wife. No, my father was no easy touch,' added Esau admiringly.

Phryne, unashamedly listening, thought that the elder Mr Tipping sounded as if he had had a hard life between these brothers. Still, he had made them what they were. Both wives, Phryne noticed, were mortally offended. Viola was attempting to summon suitable tears for a wounded heart, and Tamar had frozen into a pillar of ice. Phryne wondered if, like an iceberg, she was about to sink a few ships.

'How dare you!' demanded Jacob. 'How dare you speak about my wife in that tone! At least I married a real woman, not an armful of granite.'

Phryne was about to intervene before the personalities became more general, but a dry voice cut in. 'You are quarrelling,' it observed. Mr Crabbe in Puritan collar, looking like he was about to order a witch to be burned, was not Phryne's ideal man, but he was effective.

'Yes, so we are. And tomorrow is our birthday,' said Jacob. 'A toast, brother! To our birthday!'

'Now, now,' said Mr Crabbe, in a voice that was probably meant to be soothing but sounded as though he had been told some time ago about the term and had never got around to practising. 'You are brothers and you should be friends.'

'I'd be friends if he would,' smiled Jacob, putting down his glass.

'Withdraw what you said about my wife,' said Esau, and Jacob smiled more widely, showing all his teeth.

'If you withdraw what you said about mine.'

'I withdraw.'

'I withdraw.'

There was an indrawn breath behind both men as their wives realised that the insults were going to go unavenged. Phryne hushed Lindsay, who had been about to suggest that they move away from this uninteresting family quarrel. Both twins' glasses were on the table, in Phryne's line of sight. Mr Crabbe picked them up, turned to the punchbowl to refill them, and handed one to each brother. They stared at each other.

'Change glasses,' said Esau, fumbling with his long sleeve. 'It's not that I don't trust you, brother, but I've known snakes with more integrity.'

Jacob grinned and handed over his glass.

'To our birthday!' they chorused, and drank.

Phryne was about to move away when Lorenzo suddenly clutched at his throat and choked. He fell towards the Doge, who was also giving at the knees, and then there was nothing of the Tipping brothers but a blur of scarlet and ermine as they collapsed onto the floor.

Odd things often happened at Phryne's parties. No particular notice was taken, except by Dr MacMillan, and a pirate who in private life was a Detective Inspector of Police. The pirate and Julius Caesar inspected the fallen.

'Dead,' said Dr MacMillan.

'As doornails,' agreed Detective Inspector Jack Robinson.

'Poison?'

'Yes.'

'In the alcohol.' The doctor sniffed at each glass. 'Very neat alcohol, at that.'

'Thus fall the unbelievers,' exclaimed Mr Crabbe, lifting his hands and his eyes to heaven. 'Look at the time!'

It was ten minutes to midnight.

Phryne detached Lindsay and said, 'Come along, now, we'll send all these people into the other room and close this door.'

She ushered her guests out of the room, gently shoving those who appeared to be incapacitated from surprise or gin. Lindsay shut the door and leaned on it, his robes swishing around his ankles, his mask over his face, rendering him both antic and alarming. Behind him, the music began again, and a flood of talk. This was one of Miss Fisher's most interesting parties.

'Well?' she asked.

'Both dead, and both had taken alcohol, though that is not what killed them,' said Jack Robinson. 'Both as dead as the dodo; something very quick. Curare, perhaps?' The rising inflection was directed towards Dr MacMillan, who shook her head.

'I won't know until there is an autopsy.'

The Tipping wives, who appeared to have suffered the fate of Lot's spouse, began to speak.

'Do you mean that Jacob is dead?' exclaimed Viola, clasping her hands. 'My Jacob?'

'Esau, get up,' implored Tamar, descending to cradle his head in a flowing mass of draperies. 'Oh, Esau, just like you, to die before the time! Now what will become of me?'

Phryne, who was not very shockable, was shocked. She hoped that better obsequies would be spoken over her own corpse.

'Sit down, ladies, there, on the sofa. Mr Crabbe, could you sit down? I recommend this armchair.'

Mr Crabbe paid no attention. Tall and stiff, reminding Phryne of a statue of John Knox, he was denouncing the brothers.

'I told their father,' he said funereally, 'I told him! Bad seed, I said, they have gypsy blood in them, they are unreliable, and they will take to drink! Now look at the harvest of this wicked substance! Two brothers dead in their prime and their wives are widows. The hand of the Lord is upon them!'

'Yes, yes, I'm sure that it is,' agreed Phryne. 'Now you will sit down, please.'

Cold grey eyes glared into hers, alight with the red flare of fanaticism. Phryne stood up straight, set her crown in place, and glared haughtily back, in a manner befitting her disguise. Mr Crabbe, lowering his gaze, sat down as requested.

'Despite what Mr Crabbe says,' Jack Robinson had taken up the gentleman's dominant position in front of the fireplace, 'they didn't die of drink.'

'But they took drink,' observed the doctor. 'Polish spirit, perhaps, or vodka. Pure alcohol, perhaps.'

'Where would one find pure alcohol?'

'A hospital, a pharmacy, even a perfumery, they use it to make scent,' said the doctor. 'Had we not better call the police?'

Jack Robinson grinned at her. 'I am the police,' he reminded the company and stripped off his eye patch and scarf. In the pirate's breeches, loose shirt, and thigh-length sea-boots, he was dramatically effective and oddly at home.

He searched in both brothers' pockets and placed his spoils in his scarf.

'Handkerchiefs, keys, cigarette case and lighter, nothing unusual.'

'What's that?' asked Phryne. 'Keep everyone out, Lindsay.'

Lindsay had a brief conversation, and said over his shoulder, 'Miss Henderson wants to come in.'

'All right.'

Jilly Henderson was admitted and Lindsay shut the door again.

'What's up?'

Phryne answered, 'It looks like the two brothers should have been renamed.'

'Renamed?'

'Not Jacob and Esau, but Cain and Abel.'

This biblical reference woke Mr Crabbe from his trance. He had been sitting as ordered, but on the very edge of the chair, and now he half rose, his denouncing finger boring a hole in the air.

'I told their father!'

'Yes, yes, doubtless,' said Phryne crossly.

'Did they poison each other?'

'So it seems, Jilly. What can you remember about the estate of their father? What was it? Land?'

'No, not that I recall. Shares, mostly, and quite a lot of money. It's in trust, of course.'

'I see.'

Both wives began to stir. The shock was wearing off.

'Oh, Jacob!' wailed Viola. 'I told you it was dangerous and I said that we should just wait!'

'Esau, I knew it wouldn't work,' cried Tamar.

Both women stopped and stared at each other. Phryne held her breath. They were about to give her some useful information.

'What?' asked Tamar. 'Did your husband intend to make my husband drunk and get the money?'

'Did your snake of a husband intend to get my angel drunk and get the money?' echoed Viola.

'Well! I never heard of such a thing!'

'Well! I never heard of such a thing either. How?'

'How?' asked Tamar.

Viola sobbed aloud. 'How did that brute intend to cheat my poor Jacob?'

'The same way that dear Jacob intended to cheat poor silly Esau, I expect.' Tamar was recovering. It was possible that Esau would not be sorely missed.

'Well?'

Tamar, shaken, raised her glass to her lips. Phryne dived across the room and snatched it out of her hand.

'I don't think that the punch would agree with you, Mrs Tipping, she said, sniffing at the glass. 'Bitter almond—now, I don't recall putting that in the punch. Catch him, Lindsay!' she cried, as the black-clad figure broke for the door. There was a brief struggle, then the Puritan was down on his face, and Death was perched jauntily between his shoulderblades.

'Mrs Tipping, tell me how Jacob was going to spike Esau's drink.'

'Simple, I knew it wouldn't work, it was too simple,' wailed Viola, still not following the course of events and wondering why the pirate had removed her glass gently from her hand and stood it on the mantelpiece. 'He was going to supply the stuff—him!' She pointed to the fallen Puritan. 'He has pure alcohol, for his temperance lectures, to demonstrate what happens when you dip an earthworm in it.'

'What does happen?' asked Lindsay, who was floating with events, as he always did, and had no idea why he had been asked to fell the elderly gentleman who was presently serving as his cushion.

'It shrivels up,' said Phryne. 'Do belt up, Lindsay! Mrs Tipping,' she said to Tamar, 'how did Esau mean to get Jacob drunk?'

'The same way. That man came to my husband with an offer . . . to make the old man's will more fair, and Esau agreed. They were to change glasses and the glass which was given to Jacob would be the one with the alcohol in it. Then Jacob was to drink and Mr Crabbe would certify him drunk and the money would go to—'

'I see.' Phryne would have found the situation amusing if it was not for the presence of two dead men on her parlour floor.

'So both brothers meant to do down the other and inherit under this ridiculous will. But Jacob did not mean to kill Esau, did he?' she asked Viola, who shook her head.

'And Esau did not mean to kill Jacob, did he?' she asked Tamar, who snapped, 'Of course not.'

'And John Knox here was to supply the booze.' Phryne was thinking aloud. 'He made the same offer to both brothers, and they both accepted, and if they were both found drunk they would not have inherited. What's the reversion of the estate, Jilly? Do you remember?'

'Oh, yes, the wives get five hundred pounds apiece and the rest goes to some temperance organisation. I forget the name . . . Sons of Water-Drinkers, something like that.'

'So you decided to kill them, Mr Crabbe. I wonder why? It was a risky thing to do, but you would have got the money, all of the estate, because I'll bet that you are the founder and sole member of the Sons of Wowsers.'

The black figure under Death squirmed.

'Oh, but wait a moment.' A thought had struck Phryne. She went to the buffet and found a bottle of Scotch, examined the cork and seal, then stripped it and poured herself a drink to assist cogitation.

'I see,' she said softly.

She strode over to the recumbent Puritan and hauled him to his feet. Glittering in the electric light, the shimmer of her gold dress was hard to look at; but Mr Crabbe seemed to have more difficulty with the furious green eyes.

'You don't have the money, do you?' she said with icy clarity. 'You spent it, didn't you? It wasn't enough to just disinherit the brothers, because then you would have had to pay the wives their husbands' share. You had to kill them.' Phryne had backed Mr Crabbe up against the mantelpiece. 'You monster; you nasty wicked hymn-singing hypocrite!'

'It was the Lord's work,' he faltered. 'The Lord told me to take the infidels' gold and spend it on a temple for the glory of his name and the cause of temperance!'

Mr Crabbe turned from her eyes, grabbed the glass standing on the mantelpiece and gulped it down. Phryne could not stop him. Dr MacMillan watched as the tall man swayed and crumpled.

'Dead?' demanded Phryne, as pirate and Roman bent over the fallen murderer.

'He'll live to hang,' she commented, taking off her laurel wreath and chuckling.

'Wasn't that glass poisoned?'

'Only with alcohol,' she said. 'He's drunk good Scotch whisky for the first time in his life. That was my glass.'

Stretcher bearers came and went. The wives of the dead brothers were taken home by policemen. Lindsay, who had been told that he could stay, was attempting a joyful Charleston and was finding that Death should confine himself to the waltz. Jack Robinson farewelled Phryne at the door.

'Thank you, Phryne, it has been a very nice evening,' he said soberly. 'And a nice solution. Do ask me again when you haven't scheduled a double murder, won't you?'

He bowed, kissed Miss Fisher's hand, and turned to leave.

There was someone at the door. Masked and cowled, Death bowed the Detective Inspector out of Miss Fisher's house.

THE OCTOPUS NEST

Sophie Hannah

Sophie Hannah is a bestselling author of psychological crime fiction, including *Little Face* and *The Carrier*, which feature her series detectives Simon Waterhouse and Charlie Zailer. She has also written two novels featuring Agatha Christie's Hercule Poirot, *The Monogram Murders* and *Closed Casket*. Hannah lives in Cambridge, UK.

It was the sight I had hoped never to see: the front door wide open, Becky, our sitter, leaning out into the darkness as if straining to break free of the doorway's bright rectangle, her eyes wide with urgency. When she saw our car, she ran out into the drive, then stopped suddenly, arms at her sides, looking at the pavement. Wondering what she would say to us, how she would say it.

I assured myself that it couldn't be a real emergency; she'd have rung me on my mobile phone if it were. Then I realised I'd forgotten to switch it on as we left the cinema. Timothy and I had been too busy having a silly argument about the movie. He had claimed that the FBI must have known about the people in the woods, that it must have been a government relocation programme for victims of crime. I'd said there was nothing in the film to suggest that, that he'd plucked the hypothesis out of nowhere. He insisted he was right. Sometimes Timothy latches on to an idea and won't let go.

'Oh, no,' he said now. I tasted a dry sourness in my mouth. Becky shivered beside the garage, her arms folded, her face so twisted with concern that I couldn't look at her. Instead, as we slowed to a halt, I focused on the huddle of bins on the corner of the pavement. They looked like a gang of squat conspirators.

Before Timothy had pulled up the handbrake, I was out of the car. 'What is it?' I demanded. 'Is it Alex?'

'No, he's asleep. He's absolutely fine.' Becky put her hands on my arms, steadying me.

I slumped. 'Thank God. Then . . . has something else happened?'

'I don't know. I think so. There's something you need to have a look at.' I was thinking, as Timothy and I followed her into the house, that nothing else mattered if Alex was safe. I wanted to run upstairs and kiss his sleeping face, watch the rhythmic rise and fall of his Thomas the Tank Engine duvet, but I sensed that whatever Becky wanted us to see couldn't wait. She had not said, 'Don't worry, it's nothing serious.' She did not think it was nothing.

All our photograph albums were on the floor in the lounge, some open, most closed. I frowned, puzzled. Becky was tidier than we were. In all the years she had babysat for us, we had not once returned to find anything out of place.

Tonight, we had left one photo album, the current one, on the coffee table so that she could look at our holiday pictures. Why had she thrown it and all the others on the carpet?

She sank to the floor, crossing her legs. 'Look at this.' Timothy and I crouched down beside her. She pointed to a picture of Alex and me, having breakfast on our hotel terrace in Cyprus. Crumbs from our bread rolls speckled the blue tablecloth. We were both smiling, on the verge of laughing, as Timothy took the photograph.

'What about it?' I said.

'Look at the table behind you. Where the blonde woman's sitting.'

I looked. She was in profile, her hair up in a pony-tail. She wore a sea-green shirt with the collar turned up. Her forehead was pink, as if she'd caught the sun the day before. Her hand, holding a small, white cup, was raised, halfway between the table and her mouth. 'Do you know her?' asked Becky, looking at Timothy, then at me.

'No.'

'No.'

She turned a page in the album and pointed to another photograph, of Timothy reading *Ulysses* on a sun-lounger beside the pool. 'Can't you read John Grisham like everybody else?' I'd said to him. 'We're supposed to be on holiday.' In the pool, the same blonde woman from the previous photograph stood in the shallow end, her hands behind her head. I guessed that she was adjusting her pony-tail before beginning her swim. She wore a one-piece swimsuit the colour of cantaloupe melon.

'There she is again,' said Becky. 'You didn't talk to her at all, in the hotel?'

'No.'

'Didn't even notice her,' said Timothy. 'What's this about, Becky? She's just another guest. What's the big deal?'

Becky sighed heavily, as if, by answering as we had, we'd confirmed her worst fears. I began to feel frightened, as if something unimaginably dreadful was on its way. 'She doesn't look familiar?'

'No,' said Timothy impatiently. 'Should she?'

Becky closed the album, reached for another one. This was one of our earliest, from before Alex was born. She flipped a few pages. Cambridge. Me, Timothy and my brother Richard outside King's College, sitting on a wall. I was eating an ice-cream. The day had been oven-hot. 'Sitting next to you, Claire,' said Becky. 'It's the same person.'

I looked at the blonde head. This woman – I was sure Becky was wrong, she couldn't be the same one – was turned away from the camera towards her bespectacled friend, whose face was animated. They looked as if they were having a lively conversation, utterly unaware of our presence. 'You don't know that,' I said. 'All you can see is her hair.'

'Look at the freckles on her shoulder and arm. And her earring. She's wearing the same ones in Cyprus – gold rings that are sort of square. Not very common.'

I was beginning to feel a creeping unease; otherwise I might have pointed out that rings could not be square. 'It's a coincidence,' I said. 'There must be more than one blonde woman with freckly arms who has earrings like that.'

'Or it's the same woman, and she happened to be in Cambridge and then Cyprus at the same time as us,' said Timothy. 'Though I'm inclined to agree with Claire. It must be a different woman.'

Becky was shaking her head as he spoke. 'It isn't,' she said. 'When I looked at the Cyprus photos, I noticed her. I thought I'd seen her somewhere before, but I couldn't place her. I puzzled over it for ages. Then later, when I was standing by the shelves choosing a DVD, I noticed the picture in the frame.'

All our eyes slid towards it. It had been taken by a stranger, so that all three of us could be in it: Timothy, Alex and me. We were in the grounds of a country house hotel just outside Edinburgh. It was the week of the book festival. Many of our trips, over the years, had revolved around Timothy buying books. Behind us were two large sash windows that belonged to the hotel's dining room. Clearly visible at one of them was the blonde woman from the Cyprus photographs. She was wearing a blue shirt this time, again with the collar turned up. Her face was small, but it was unmistakably her. And the earrings were the same – the square hoops. I felt dizzy. This had to mean something. My brain wouldn't work quickly enough.

'That's why she looked familiar,' said Becky. 'I've seen that photo millions of times. I see it every time I come here. Alex is just a baby in it and . . . I thought it was an amazing coincidence, that the same woman was wherever you were in this picture four years ago and also in Cyprus this summer. It seemed too strange. So I got the other albums out and had a look. I couldn't believe it. In each one, she's in at least nine or ten of the photos. See for yourselves.'

'Jesus.' Timothy rubbed the sides of his face. When he removed his hands there were white spots on his skin. I began to turn the pages of another album. I saw the woman, once, twice. In Siena, at a taverna. Walking behind me in a street market in Morocco. Three times. She stood beside Timothy outside the Tate Modern, again with her short-sighted, frizzy-haired friend.

'But . . . this *can't* be a coincidence!' I said, expecting to have to convince Becky, or Timothy. Nobody disagreed with me. I felt sharp, piercing fear.

'What does it mean?' Timothy asked Becky. He rarely asked anybody for advice or an opinion, let alone a nineteen-year-old babysitter. His lips were thin and pale. 'She must be following us. She's some sort of stalker. But . . . for nearly ten years! I don't like this at all. I'm ringing the police.'

'They'll think you're crazy,' I said, desperate to behave as if there was no need to take the matter seriously. 'She's never done us any harm, never even drawn herself to our attention. She's not looking at us in any of the photos. She doesn't seem aware of our presence at all.'

'Of course not!' Timothy snorted dismissively. 'She'd try to look as innocent as possible as soon as she saw a camera coming out, wouldn't she? That's why we've not spotted her until now.'

I turned to Becky. 'Is every album the same?' I didn't have the courage to look. She nodded. 'Some, she's on nearly every page.'

'Oh, God! What should we do? Why would someone we don't know want to follow us?'

'Timothy's right, you've got to tell the police,' said Becky. 'If something happens . . .'

'Christ!' Timothy marched up and down the lounge, shaking his head. 'I don't need this,' he said. 'I really don't.'

'Tim, are you *sure* you don't know her?' An affair, I was thinking. A jealous ex-girlfriend. I would almost have preferred that; at least there would have been a rational explanation, a clarifying link.

'Of course I'm sure!'

'Do you want me to stay?' asked Becky. What she meant was that she was keen to leave.

'She's not some woman I've slept with and discarded, if that's what you're thinking,' Timothy snapped.

'You have to tell me if she is,' I said. Neither of us cared that Becky was listening.

'Have I ever done anything like that?'

'Not that I know of.'

'Claire, I swear on Alex's life: not only have I never slept with this woman, I've never even *spoken* to her.' I believed him. Alex was sacred.

'I should go,' said Becky. Our eyes begged her not to. She was a symbol of safety, the only one of the three of us who was not dogged by a stalker. We needed her normality to sustain us. I had never been so frightened in my life.

'I'll drive you,' said Timothy.

'No!' I didn't want to be left alone with the photo albums. 'Would you mind if we phoned you a cab?'

'Of course not.'

'I said I'll drive her!'

'But I don't want you to go out!'

'Well, I want to get out. I need some air.'

'What about me?'

'I'll be back in half an hour, Claire. Why don't you ring the police while I'm gone? Then we can talk to them when I get back.'

'I can't.' I began to cry. 'You'll have to do it. I'm in no fit state.'

He frowned. 'All right. Look, don't worry. I won't be long.'

Once he and Becky had left, I went upstairs and looked in on Alex. He was sleeping soundly, his hair covering his face. Despite my pleas, I found that I felt less afraid once Timothy had gone. I thought of one of our honeymoon photographs, one that could not possibly contain the blonde woman: Timothy in our en-suite bathroom at the Grand Hotel Tremezzo. He insisted on lavish holidays. Perhaps that was why we were always short of money. That and his book-collecting. In the picture, there is a mirror in front of him and one behind, reflecting an endless row of Timothies, each smaller than the last, each holding the camera to his eye, pressing the button. They dotted an invisible line that led from the foreground to the background. I knew why the picture had sprung to mind. It was the principle of magnification: seeing my own panic reflected in Timothy's eyes had added to my paranoia.

I went downstairs and began to look through all our photographs. This time I was methodical, unsuperstitious. I found the blonde woman with the upturned collars and the square hoop earrings again and again: on a boat, in a park, walking along a canal tow-path. Sometimes she was right behind us, sometimes nearby. Who was she? Why was she following us? I had no way of knowing. Neither would the police, not with only our photo albums to work from. Of course, they could track her down if they wanted to – they could appeal on television and somebody who knew her would be bound to come forward – but the idea of them doing such a thing was laughable. She had committed no crime. Stalking was against the law, I was fairly certain of that, but the direct accosting of one's prey was surely a pre-requisite. What, I wondered, would the police have to say about a stalker so unobtrusive that, were it not for Becky's meticulous eye, we might never have become aware of her? Her presence in our lives, unnoticed for all these years, felt more ghostly than criminal. I was suddenly very aware of myself, my thoughts and my actions, and looked around the room, up at the ceiling, half expecting to find someone watching me.

I concentrated on the woman's face, trying to see a character or a motive behind it. She was either beautiful in a classical, well-proportioned way, or very bland-looking – I couldn't decide. I found it unsettling that, however hard I stared, I couldn't commit her face to memory; it was almost impossible to take in as a coherent whole. I looked at her features one by one and judged each of them regular, flawless, but together they made no lasting impression. I'd had this feeling before, usually about famous people. Sharon Stone, the late Jill Dando. They too had faces one could study in detail and still not know what they looked like.

In one photograph our blonde ghost was touching me. Her shoulder was pressed against mine in a crowded wine bar. Hay-on-Wye? No, Cheltenham. Another of Timothy's literary holidays. I was holding a tall cocktail, dark red and fizzy, like carbonated blood. I pointed to it, an apprehensive expression on my face. Timothy had labelled the photo 'Am I really expected to drink this?' He assigned titles to all our pictures; his parents did it too. It was a Treharne family tradition.

The blonde woman had a book in her hand. It was on the edge of the picture, some of it missing. I screwed up my eyes to read the title. *The Octopus* – that was all that was visible. My heart jolted. *The Octopus Nest*, I whispered. It was a novel I hadn't thought about for years. Timothy used to own it, probably still did. He'd tried to persuade me to read it, but I gave up. Sometimes it is apparent from the first page of a book that nothing is going to happen. A Timothy book.

I slammed the photo album shut and rang his mobile phone. It was switched off. I paced up and down the lounge, desperate to talk to somebody. I nearly rang Becky's mobile, but I didn't want her to make excuses when I asked her to babysit in the future. If I started to talk to her about obscure novels with strange titles, she'd think I was insane. Timothy had said he'd be back within half an hour. This could wait half an hour.

I forced myself to calm down, sit down, and think about how I was feeling. Was this surge of adrenaline justified? Seven years ago, the blonde woman had been in a wine bar, holding a novel that Timothy once raved about. It was a link, but then, I reminded myself, I did not need to look for a link. A woman we didn't know was in the backgrounds of dozens of our photographs. Wasn't that connection enough?

Still, I was too agitated to do nothing. I searched all the bookshelves in our house. There was no copy of *The Octopus Nest*. I tried Timothy's phone again,

574

swearing under my breath, furious with impatience. How could he not have remembered to switch it on? He knew what a state I was in. Irrationally, I took my not being able to speak to him while he was out as an omen that it would take him much longer to return, that he might never come back. I needed to occupy myself, to drive away these groundless fears. That was when I thought of the internet.

I rushed to Timothy's study and switched on the computer, certain that Amazon, the online bookshop, would have *The Octopus Nest* listed. I wanted to know who it was by, what it was about. It might lead nowhere, but it was the only thing I had to go on. In none of the other photographs did our ghost have any identifiable accessories.

The Octopus Nest was available from Amazon, but not easily. Delivery might take up to six weeks, I read. This didn't matter to me. I didn't necessarily want a copy of the book. I just wanted to know more about it. The author was a K V Hammond. I clicked on the small picture of the novel's cover, a white background with one black tentacle running diagonally across it.

The book was number 756,234 in the Amazon chart. If Timothy and the blonde woman hadn't bought it all those years ago it would probably have been number 987,659, I thought, half-smiling. I was surprised I was able to joke, even inside my head. Somehow our ghost didn't seem quite so threatening, now that I had seen her holding a book that Timothy had once thought highly of, though I didn't understand why this should be the case. The optimist in me reasoned that she hadn't done us any harm in nearly a decade. Maybe she never would.

No description of the novel was offered. I had bought books from Amazon before, and there was usually a short synopsis. I clicked on the 'Google' button and typed 'K V Hammond' into the search box. The first result was the author's own website. Perhaps here I would discover more about *The Octopus Nest*. I drummed my fingers on the desk, impatient for the home page to load.

A photograph began to appear on the screen, from the top down. A blue sky, a tree, a straw hat. Blonde hair. Gold, square hoop earrings. I gasped, pushing my chair away from the computer. It was her. A letter welcomed me to her site, was signed 'Kathryn'. Only minutes ago it had seemed out of the question that we would ever know her identity. Now I knew it beyond the slightest doubt.

I tried Timothy's mobile again, with no luck. 'Please, please,' I muttered, even though no-one could hear me, even though a mechanical voice was already telling me to try again later. I felt as if Timothy had let me down badly, deserted me, though I knew he was probably too preoccupied to think about a detail such as whether his phone was on or off. He would be back soon, in any case.

Fear and excitement rioted in my mind, my whole body. I had to do something. Now that I was in possession of certain knowledge, calling the police did not seem such an absurd proposition. I didn't want to go into the whole story on the phone, so I said only that I wanted to report a stalker, that I knew who it was, that I had evidence. The woman I spoke to said she would send an officer to interview me as soon as possible.

Willing the computer to work faster, I moved from one section of Kathryn Hammond's website to another. She had published no books since 'The Octopus Nest', but her newsletter said she was working on her next novel, the story of fifty years in the life of a ventriloquist's dummy, passed from one owner to another. Another Timothy book, I thought. The newsletter also informed fans (it seemed to take for granted that everyone who visited the site would be a fan) that Kathryn and her sister – the frizzy-haired woman, I assumed – were going on holiday to Sicily early next year.

For a second, I felt as if my blood had stopped moving around my body. We were going to Sicily too. In February. Kathryn Hammond and her sister were staying at the Hotel Bernabei. I had a horrible suspicion we were too. My terror returned, twice as strong as before. This was as real, as inexplicable, as ever.

I rummaged through the drawers of the desk, thinking I might find a letter from Timothy's travel agent or a booking confirmation. There was nothing. I flew round the house like a trapped fly, opening drawers and pulling books off shelves. I couldn't understand it; there had to be some paperwork somewhere relating to our holiday.

I was crying, about to give up, when it occurred to me that Timothy kept a filing cabinet in the garage. 'Why not?' he'd said. 'The thing's hideous and the house is too cluttered.' I rarely went into the garage. It was dusty and messy, and smelled of damp, turpentine and cigarettes; since Alex was born, Timothy hadn't smoked in the house.

I had no choice but to go in there now. If the police arrived before Timothy got back, I wanted to be able to show them our holiday details and Kathryn Hammond's website. What more proof could they ask for? Even as I thought this, I was aware that it was not illegal for a novelist to go on holiday to Sicily. Terror gripped me as it occurred to me for the first time that perhaps we would never be able to stop her following us, never force her to admit to her behaviour or explain it. I didn't think I'd be able to stand that.

The cabinet wasn't locked. I pulled open the first drawer. A strangled moan escaped from my mouth as I stared, stunned, at what was inside. Books. Dozens of them. I saw the title *The Octopus Nest*. Then, underneath it, *Le Nid du poulpe*. The same title, but in French. Numb with dread, I pulled the books out one by one, dropping them on the floor. I saw Hebrew letters, Japanese characters, a picture of a purple octopus, a green one, a raised black one that looked as if it might spin off the cover and hit me in the chest.

Kathryn Hammond's novel had been translated into many languages. I pulled open the next drawer down. More copies of *The Octopus Nest* – hardbacks, paperbacks, hardback-sized paperbacks, book club editions.

'Fifty-two in total.'

I screamed, nearly lost my balance. Timothy stood in the doorway of the garage. 'Timothy, what . . .?'

He stared blankly at me for several seconds, saying nothing. I backed away from him until I was against the wall. I felt its rough texture through my blouse, scratching my skin.

'I was telling the truth,' he said. 'I've never spoken to her. I don't know her at all. She doesn't even know I exist.'

The doorbell rang. The police. I'd said only that I wanted to report a stalker, that I knew who it was, that I had evidence.

AUTHENTIC CARBON STEEL FORGED

Elizabeth Haynes

Elizabeth Haynes received critical acclaim for her debut crime novel, *Into the Darkest Corner*. With *Under a Silent Moon* and *Behind Closed Doors*, she has begun a police procedural thriller series featuring the Briarstone Major Crime team. Haynes grew up in East Sussex, UK.

Funny. I've had that knife such a long time, years.

At university I had a boyfriend who was a bit of a foodie; when I graduated, he bought me a knife set. Quality knives, he'd called them. Something about me never having to cut a tomato with a pound shop blade again. I take a moment to count back – nineteen years. And it's my favourite one out of the block, the eight inch chef's knife, sturdy, riveted into a black handle. Perfect for chopping the veg.

Not that I'll get to do that again, at least not with that particular knife. It's wire-mounted into a cardboard box with a clear plastic window, like a Halloween Barbie doll, and the prosecution counsel is waving it at the jury.

'This is LJJ/1, the knife, now Court Exhibit One,' he says, giving it to the usher who offers it to the judge and then it is passed to the jury. They hand it solemnly along the row – some of them lingering over their examination of it – then it's given back to the usher. A bizarre game of pass-the-parcel, with nobody winning a prize.

After this is over I imagine it will be locked away in some evidence storage facility for some indeterminate period of time, never to see a carrot again. I feel weirdly sorry for it. Purposeless. Done with. Incarcerated. A bit like me.

'She took this knife, ladies and gentlemen, and she stabbed him with it. Not once, but twice, penetrating his liver and causing his right lung to collapse. She missed his heart by a matter of inches . . .'

That makes me want to smile and I have to suck in my cheeks to prevent it. A matter of inches! Nowhere near, in other words. Although the fact that I managed to nick his hepatic artery causing fatal blood loss was more by luck; I wasn't exactly aiming. Can't smile though, can't do anything; can't look interested, mustn't look bored. The only way of coping with all of this is to try and switch off. Blank. Detached.

Here are the things that I remember.

Number One: Cooking a roast one Sunday, the sun shining in from the garden. Looking up because it was so bright; the sunlight reflecting off the rain-soaked patio into the kitchen. Peace in there, the radio on, just me peeling the potatoes. Then the boys coming home from rugby, subdued because they lost. And he had been to the pub of course, collected them from their game afterwards, drove them home and now here he was stinking of beer, all bright and pretending to be alert, his eyelids drooping.

I had told him, more than once, that Bev had offered to drop them home, but he didn't like Bev – he wasn't keen on any of my friends, in fact – and so he carried on regardless.

I remember thinking, at least it isn't far. Praying to a God I only half believed in to keep them safe on the road home.

Number Two: I remember being afraid of burning the meat. He didn't like it pink, he liked it well done, but let me tell you apparently there's a fine line between well done and burned, and that line is never where you think it is, no matter how careful you are.

Number Three: the last time I held my babies, my boys. Hugged them before they went to school that morning. I'm glad I did it, that for once I wasn't rushed; glad they let me. They're not babies any more. Any sign of affection gratefully received. I'm glad I held them because I didn't plan it, for it to be that day in particular; I was waiting for the next assault, knowing I would, this time, fight back.

They're talking about the psychological assessment now. They said I had a dissociative disorder, that I was finding it difficult to connect to the reality of what I did. The prosecution lawyer suggests this demonstrates a lack of remorse, that I am a cold, calculating killer and I had every intention of stabbing my husband to death. The defence counters that dissociation is a trauma coping mechanism, brought about not by the incident itself but by the years of abuse preceding it. Look at them both, as if they have any idea.

I'm finding it increasingly difficult to know what to do with my face. I do cry sometimes, quite often in fact, sniffing into my tissue and clutching my hand over my mouth – but it's rarely as a result of whatever it is they are discussing. It's the memories that take me by surprise. Things like Ryan's face when his dad told him he wished he'd never been born. That one gets me every time. Or having to take the cat to the RSPCA – knowing the likelihood of her finding another home was slim – because she was too old to run out of his way when he was raging.

Funny, the things that make me cry are never the things that happened to me. Perhaps that's what they mean by dissociation.

The members of the jury look at me sometimes, especially when called upon to do so by the prosecution counsel – *look at her, the cold-blooded vicious killer* – he hasn't said that, to be fair to him, just words to that effect – and when they do, I manage to look startled. Afraid.

Or maybe that's just the way my face is fixed now.

If anyone were to ask me, when all this is over, that simplest of questions: 'Any regrets?' I'd answer no, of course not. No matter what happens now, at least I'm free of him, at least my boys are safe.

Or perhaps yes, just one.

I wish I'd used a different knife.

A CURIOUS SUICIDE

Patricia Highsmith

Patricia Highsmith (1921–1995) was a pioneering author of American psychological thrillers. Her first novel, *Strangers on a Train*, was filmed by Alfred Hitchcock, and her five novels featuring the attractive criminal antihero Tom Ripley have gained iconic status. Highsmith's narratives are well-known for their dark psychology and homoerotic subtext.

D r Stephen McCullough had a first-class compartment to himself on the express from Paris to Geneva. He sat browsing in one of the medical quarterlies he had brought from America, but he was not concentrating. He was toying with the idea of murder. That was why he had taken the train instead of flying, to give himself time to think or perhaps merely dream.

He was a serious man of forty-five, a little overweight, with a prominent and spreading nose, a brown moustache, brown-rimmed glasses, a receding hairline. His eyebrows were tense with an inward anxiety, which his patients often thought a concern with their problems. Actually, he was unhappily married, and though he refused to quarrel with Lillian – that meant answer her back – there was discord between them. In Paris yesterday he had answered Lillian back, and on a ridiculous matter about whether he or she would take back to a shop on the Rue Royale an evening bag that Lillian had decided she did not want. He had been angry not because he had had to return the bag, but because he had agreed, in a weak moment fifteen minutes before, to visit Roger Fane in Geneva.

'Go and see him, Steve,' Lillian had said yesterday morning. 'You're so close to Geneva now, why not? Think of the pleasure it'd give Roger.'

What pleasure? Why? But Dr McCullough had rung Roger at the American Embassy in Geneva, and Roger had been very friendly, much too friendly, of course, and had said that he must come and stay a few days and that he had plenty of room to put him up. Dr McCullough had agreed to spend one night. Then he was going to fly to Rome to join Lillian.

Dr McCullough detested Roger Fane. It was the kind of hatred that time does nothing to diminish. Roger Fane, seventeen years ago, had married the woman Dr McCullough loved. Margaret. Margaret had died a year ago in an automobile accident on an Alpine road. Roger Fane was smug, cautious, mightily pleased with himself and not very intelligent. Seventeen years ago, Roger Fane had told Margaret that he, Stephen McCullough, was having a secret affair with another girl. Nothing was further from the truth, but before Stephen could prove anything, Margaret had married Roger. Dr McCullough had not expected the marriage to last, but it had, and finally Dr McCullough had married Lillian whose face resembled Margaret's a little, but that was the only similarity. In the past seventeen years, Dr McCullough had seen Roger and Margaret perhaps three times when they had come to New York on short trips. He had not seen Roger since Margaret's death.

Now as the train shot through the French countryside, Dr McCullough reflected on the satisfaction that murdering Roger Fane might give him. He had never before thought of murdering anybody, but yesterday evening while he was taking a bath in the Paris hotel, after the telephone conversation with Roger, a thought had come to him in regard to murder: most murderers were caught because they left some clue, despite their efforts to erase all the clues. Many murderers wanted to be caught, the doctor realized, and unconsciously planted a clue that led the police straight to them. In the Leopold and Loeb case, one of them had dropped his glasses at the scene, for instance. But suppose a murderer deliberately left a dozen clues, practically down to his calling card? It seemed to Dr McCullough that the very obviousness of it would throw suspicion off. Especially if the person were a man like himself, well thought of, a non-violent type. Also, there'd be no motive that anyone could see, because Dr McCullough had never even told Lillian that he had loved the woman Roger Fane had married. Of course, a few of his old friends knew it, but Dr McCullough hadn't mentioned Margaret or Roger Fane in a decade.

He imagined Roger's apartment formal and gloomy, perhaps with a servant prowling about full time, a servant who slept in. A servant would complicate things. Let's say there wasn't a servant who slept in, that he and Roger would be having a nightcap in the living room or in Roger's study, and then just before saying good night, Dr McCullough would pick up a heavy paperweight or a big vase and— Then he would calmly take his leave. Of course, the bed should be slept in, since he was supposed to stay the night, so perhaps the morning would be better for the crime than the evening. The essential thing was to leave quietly and at the time he was supposed to leave. But the doctor found himself unable to plot in much detail after all.

Roger Fane's street in Geneva looked just as Dr McCullough had imagined it – a narrow, curving street that combined business establishments with old private dwellings – and it was not too well lighted when Dr McCullough's taxi entered it at 9 p.m., yet in law-abiding Switzerland, the doctor supposed, dark streets held few dangers for anyone. The front door buzzed in response to his ring, and Dr McCullough opened it. The door was heavy as a bank vault's door.

'Hullo!' Roger's voice called cheerily down the stairwell. 'Come up! I'm on the third floor. Fourth to you, I suppose.'

'Be right there!' Dr McCullough said, shy about raising his voice in the presence of the closed doors on either side of the hall. He had telephoned Roger a few moments ago from the railway station, because Roger had said he would meet him. Roger had apologized and said he had been held up at a meeting at his office, and would Steve mind hopping a taxi and coming right over? Dr McCullough suspected that Roger had not been held up at all, but simply hadn't wanted to show him the courtesy of being at the station.

'Well, well, Steve!' said Roger, pumping Dr McCullough's hand. 'It's great to see you again. Come in, come in. Is that thing heavy?' Roger made a pass at the doctor's suitcase, but the doctor caught it up first.

'Not at all. Good to see you again, Roger.' He went into the apartment.

There were oriental rugs, ornate lamps that gave off dim light. It was even stuffier than Dr McCullough had anticipated. Roger looked a trifle thinner. He was shorter than the doctor, and had sparse blond hair. His weak face perpetually smiled. Both had eaten dinner, so they drank scotch in the living room.

'So you're joining Lillian in Rome tomorrow,' said Roger. 'Sorry you won't be staying longer. I'd intended to drive you out to the country tomorrow evening to meet a friend of mine. A woman,' Roger added with a smile.

'Oh? Too bad. Yes, I'll be off on the one o'clock plane tomorrow afternoon. I made the reservation from Paris.' Dr McCullough found himself speaking automatically. Strangely, he felt a little drunk, though he'd taken only a couple of sips of his scotch. It was because of the falsity of the situation, he thought, the falsity of his being here at all, of his pretending friendship or at least friendliness. Roger's smile irked him, so merry and yet so forced. Roger hadn't referred to Margaret, though Dr McCullough had not seen him since she died. But then, neither had the doctor referred to her, even to give a word of condolence. And already, it seemed, Roger had another female interest. Roger was just over forty, still trim of figure and bright of eye. And Margaret, that jewel among women, was just something that had come his way, stayed a while, and departed, Dr McCullough supposed. Roger looked not at all bereaved.

The doctor detested Roger fully as much as he had on the train, but the reality of Roger Fane was somewhat dismaying. If he killed him, he would have to touch him, feel the resistance of his flesh at any rate with the object he hit him with. And what was the servant situation? As if Roger read his mind, he said:

'I've a girl who comes in to clean every morning at ten and leaves at twelve. If you want her to do anything for you, wash and iron a shirt or something like that, don't hesitate. She's very fast, or can be if you ask her. Her name's Yvonne.'

Then the telephone rang. Roger spoke in French. His face fell slightly as he agreed to do something that the other person was asking him to do. Roger said to the doctor:

'Of all irritating things. I've got to catch the seven o'clock plane to Zurich tomorrow. Some visiting fireman's being welcomed at a breakfast. So, old man, I suppose I'll be gone before you're out of bed.'

'Oh!' Dr McCullough found himself chuckling. 'You think doctors aren't used to early calls? Of course I'll get up to tell you good-bye – see you off.'

Roger's smile widened slightly. 'Well, we'll see. I certainly won't wake you for it. Make yourself at home and I'll leave a note for Yvonne to prepare coffee and rolls. Or would you like a more substantial brunch around eleven?'

Dr McCullough was not thinking about what Roger was saying. He had just noticed a rectangular marble pen and pencil holder on the desk where the telephone stood. He was looking at Roger's high and faintly pink forehead. 'Oh, brunch,' said the doctor vaguely. 'No, no, for goodness' sake. They feed you enough on the plane.' And then his thoughts leapt to Lillian and the quarrel yesterday in Paris. Hostility smouldered in him. Had Roger ever quarrelled with Margaret? Dr McCullough could not imagine Margaret being unfair, being mean. It was no wonder Roger's face looked relaxed and untroubled.

'A penny for your thoughts,' said Roger, getting up to replenish his glass.

The doctor's glass was still half full.

'I suppose I'm a bit tired,' said Dr McCullough, and passed his hand across his forehead. When he lifted his head again, he saw a photograph of Margaret which he had not noticed before on the top of the highboy on his right. Margaret in her twenties, as she had looked when Roger married her, as she had looked when the doctor had so loved her. Dr McCullough looked suddenly at Roger. His hatred returned in a wave that left him physically weak. 'I suppose I'd better turn in,' he said, setting his glass carefully on the little table in front of him, standing up. Roger had showed him his bedroom.

'Sure you wouldn't like a spot of brandy?' asked Roger. 'You look all in.' Roger smiled cockily, standing very straight.

The tide of the doctor's anger flowed back. He picked up the marble slab with one hand, and before Roger could step back, smashed him in the forehead with its base. It was a blow that would kill, the doctor knew. Roger fell and without even a last twitch lay still and limp. The doctor set the marble back where it had been, picked up the pen and pencil which had fallen, and replaced them in their holders, then wiped the marble with his handkerchief where his fingers had touched it and also the pen and pencil. Roger's forehead was bleeding slightly. He felt Roger's still warm wrist and found no pulse. Then he went out the door and down the hall to his own room.

He awakened the next morning at 8.15, after a not very sound night's sleep. He showered in the bathroom between his room and Roger's bedroom, shaved, dressed and left the house at a quarter past nine. A hall went from his room past the kitchen to the flat's door; it had not been necessary to cross the living room, and even if he had glanced into the living room through the door he had not closed, Roger's body would have been out of sight to him. Dr McCullough had not glanced in.

At 5.30 p.m. he was in Rome, riding in a taxi from the airport to the Hotel Majestic where Lillian awaited him. Lillian was out, however. The doctor had some coffee sent up, and it was then that he noticed his briefcase was missing. He had wanted to lie on the bed and drink coffee and read his medical quarterlies. Now he remembered distinctly: he had for some reason carried his briefcase into the living room last evening. This did not disturb him at all. It was exactly what he should have done on purpose if he had thought of it. His name and his New York address were written in the slot of the briefcase. And Dr McCullough supposed that Roger had written his name in full in some engagement book along with the time of his arrival.

He found Lillian in good humour. She had bought a lot of things in the Via Condotti. They had dinner and then took a carozza ride through the Villa Borghese, to the Piazza di Spagna and the Piazza del Populo. If there were anything in the papers about Roger, Dr McCullough was ignorant of it. He bought only the Paris *Herald-Tribune* which was a morning paper.

The news came the next morning as he and Lillian were breakfasting at Donay's in the Via Veneto. It was in the Paris *Herald-Tribune*, and there was a picture of Roger Fane on the front page, a serious official picture of him in a wing collar.

'Good Lord!' said Lillian. 'Why – it happened the night you were there!'

Looking over her shoulder, Dr McCullough pretended surprise. '"– died some time between eight p.m. and three a.m.",' the doctor read. 'I said good night to him about eleven, I think. Went into my room.'

'You didn't *hear* anything?'

'No. My room was down a hall. I closed my door.'

'And the next morning. You didn't—'

'I told you, Roger had to catch a seven o'clock plane. I assumed he was gone. I left the house around nine.'

'And all the time he was in the living room!' Lillian said with a gasp. 'Steve! Why, this is terrible!'

Was it, Dr McCullough wondered. Was it so terrible for her? Her voice did not sound really concerned. He looked into her wide eyes. 'It's certainly terrible – but I'm not responsible, God knows. Don't worry, Lillian.'

The police were at the Hotel Majestic when they returned, waiting for Dr McCullough in the lobby. They were both plainclothes Swiss police, and they spoke English. They interviewed Dr McCullough at a table in a corner of the lobby. Lillian had, at Dr McCullough's insistence, gone up to their room. Dr McCullough had wondered why the police had not come for him hours earlier than this – it was so simple to check the passenger lists of planes leaving Geneva – but he soon found out why. The maid Yvonne had not come to clean yesterday morning, so Roger Fane's body had not been discovered until 6 p.m. yesterday, when his office had become alarmed by his absence and sent someone around to his apartment to investigate.

'This is your briefcase, I think,' said the slender blond officer with a smile, opening a large manila envelope he had been carrying under his arm.

'Yes, thank you very much. I realized today that I'd left it.' The doctor took it and laid it on his lap.

The two Swiss watched him quietly.

'This is very shocking,' Dr McCullough said. 'It's hard for me to realize.' He was impatient for them to make their charge – if they were going to – and ask him to return to Geneva with them. They both seemed almost in awe of him.

'How well did you know Mr Fane?' asked the other officer.

'Not too well. I've known him many years, but we were never close friends. I hadn't seen him in five years, I think.' Dr McCullough spoke steadily and in his usual tone.

'Mr Fane was still fully dressed, so he had not gone to bed. You are sure you heard no disturbance that night?'

'I did not,' the doctor answered for the second time. A silence. 'Have you any clues as to who might have done it?'

'Oh, yes, yes,' the blond man said matter of factly. 'We suspect the brother of the maid Yvonne. He was drunk that night and hasn't an alibi for the time of the crime. He and his sister live together and that night he went off with his sister's batch of keys – among which were the keys to Mr Fane's apartment. He didn't come back until nearly noon yesterday. Yvonne was worried about him, which is why she didn't go to Mr Fane's apartment yesterday – that plus the fact she couldn't have got in. She tried to telephone at eight-thirty yesterday morning to say she wouldn't be coming, but she got no answer. We've questioned the brother Anton. He's a ne'er-do-well.' The man shrugged.

Dr McCullough remembered hearing the telephone ring at eight-thirty. 'But – what was the motive?'

'Oh – resentment. Robbery maybe if he'd been sober enough to find anything to take. He's a case for a psychiatrist or an alcoholic ward. Mr Fane knew him, so he might have let him into the apartment, or he could have walked in, since he had the keys. Yvonne said that Mr Fane had been trying for months to get her to live apart from her brother. Her brother beats her and takes her money. Mr Fane had spoken to the brother a couple of times, and it's on our record that Mr Fane once had to call the police to get Anton out of the apartment when he came there looking for his sister. That incident happened at nine in the evening, an hour when his sister is never there. You see how off his head he is.'

Dr McCullough cleared his throat and asked, 'Has Anton confessed to it?'

'Oh, the same as. Poor chap, I really don't think he knows what he's doing half the time. But at least in Switzerland there's no capital punishment. He'll have enough time to dry out in jail, all right.' He glanced at his colleague and they both stood up. 'Thank you very much, Dr McCullough.'

'You're very welcome,' said the doctor. 'Thank you for the briefcase.'

Dr McCullough went upstairs with his briefcase to his room.

'What did they say?' Lillian asked as he came in.

'They think the brother of the maid did it,' said Dr McCullough. 'Fellow who's an alcoholic and who seems to have had it in for Roger. Some ne'er-do-well.' Frowning, he went into the bathroom to wash his hands. He suddenly detested himself, detested Lillian's long sigh, an 'Ah-h' of relief and joy.

'Thank God, thank God!' Lillian said. 'Do you know what this would have meant if they'd – if they'd have accused *you*?' she asked in a softer voice, as if the walls had ears, and she came closer to the bathroom door.

'Certainly,' Dr McCullough said, and felt a burst of anger in his blood. 'I'd have had a hell of a time proving I was innocent, since I was right there at the time.'

'Exactly. You couldn't have proved you were innocent. Thank God for this Anton, whoever he is.' Her small face glowed, her eyes twinkled. 'A ne'er-do-well. Ha! He did us some good!' She laughed shrilly and turned on one heel.

'I don't see why you have to gloat,' he said, drying his hands carefully. 'It's a sad story.'

'Sadder than if they'd blamed you? Don't be so – so altruistic, dear. Or rather, think of us. Husband kills old rival-in-love after – let's see – seventeen years, isn't it? And after eleven years of marriage to another woman. The torch still burns high. Do you think I'd like that?'

'Lillian, what're you talking about?' He came out of the bathroom scowling.

'You know exactly. You think I don't know you were in love with Margaret? *Still* are? You think I don't know you killed Roger?' Her grey eyes looked at him with a wild challenge. Her head was tipped to one side, her hands on her hips.

He felt tongue-tied, paralysed. They stared at each other for perhaps fifteen seconds, while his mind moved tentatively over the abyss her words had just spread before him. He hadn't known that she still thought of Margaret. Of course she'd known about Margaret. But who had kept the story alive in her mind? Perhaps himself by his silence, the doctor realized. But the future was what mattered. Now she had something to hold over his head, something by which she could control him for ever. 'My dear, you are mistaken.'

But Lillian with a toss of her head turned and walked away, and the doctor knew he had not won.

Absolutely nothing was said about the matter the rest of the day. They lunched, spent a leisurely hour in the Vatican museum, but Dr McCullough's mind was on other things than Michelangelo's paintings. He was going to go to Geneva and confess the thing, not for decency's sake or because his conscience bothered him, but because Lillian's attitude was insupportable. It was less supportable than a stretch in prison. He managed to get away long enough to make a telephone call at five p.m. There was a plane to Geneva at 7.20 p.m. At 6.15 p.m., he left their hotel room empty-handed and took a taxi to Ciampino airport. He had his passport and travellers cheques.

He arrived in Geneva before eleven that evening, and called the police. At first, they were not willing to tell him the whereabouts of the man accused of murdering Roger Fane, but Dr McCullough gave his name and said he had some important information, and then the Swiss police told him where Anton Carpeau was being held. Dr McCullough took a taxi to what seemed the outskirts of Geneva. It was a new white building, not at all like a prison.

Here he was greeted by one of the plainclothes officers who had come to see him, the blond one. 'Dr McCullough,' he said with a faint smile. 'You have some information, you say? I am afraid it is a little late.'

'Oh? – Why?'

'Anton Carpeau has just killed himself – by bashing his head against the wall of his cell. Just twenty minutes ago.' The man gave a hopeless shrug.

'Good God,' Dr McCullough said softly.

'But what was your information?'

The doctor hesitated. The words wouldn't come. And then he realized that it was cowardice and shame that kept him silent. He had never felt so worthless in his life, and he felt infinitely lower than the drunken ne'er-do-well who had killed himself. 'I'd rather not. In this case – I mean – it's so all over, isn't it? It was something else against Anton, I thought – and what's the use now? It's bad enough—' The words stopped.

'Yes, I suppose so,' said the Swiss.

'So – I'll say good night.'

'Good night, Dr McCullough.'

Then the doctor walked on into the night, aimlessly. He felt a curious emptiness, a nothingness in himself that was not like any mood he had ever known. His plan for murder had succeeded, but it had dragged worse tragedies in its wake. Anton Carpeau. And *Lillian*. In a strange way, he had killed himself just as much as he had killed Roger Fane. He was now a dead man, a walking dead man.

Half an hour later, he stood on a formal bridge looking down at the black water of Lake Leman. He stared down a long while, and imagined his body toppling over and over, striking the water with not much of a splash, sinking. He stared hard at the blackness that looked so solid but would be so yielding, so willing to swallow him into death. But he hadn't even the courage or the despair as yet for suicide. One day, however, he would, he knew. One day when the planes of cowardice and courage met at the proper angle. And that day would be a surprise to him and to everyone else who knew him. Then his hands that gripped the stone parapet pushed him back, and the doctor walked on heavily. He would see about a hotel for tonight, and then tomorrow arrange to get back to Rome.

A HALLOWE'EN TALE

Susi Holliday

Susi Holliday is a Scottish crime writer and the creator of Sergeant Davie Gray. Her novels include *Black Wood*, *Willow Walk* and *The Damselfly*. Her most recent novel is *The Deaths of December*. Holliday lives in London, where she works as a pharmaceutical statistician.

She knew she looked good. Her long dark hair was straightened as smooth as silk, her deep violet eyes ringed with black kohl. She wore a perfect little-black-dress – the type that hugs in all the right places, showing just enough of her milky cleavage to tantalise without looking provocative. A dark cape with deep pockets. Black tights, black lace-up boots . . . and a black velvet hat – not a witch's hat, as such – but some might say that's what it looked like.

It was Hallowe'en, after all.

She left home at seven, the night already dark but for the amber glow of the streetlights and the headlamps of the passing traffic. Almost every pub she passed by was advertising their spooky parties. Ghoulish decoration in the windows, face cobwebs and green fabric tossed over lamps. Nights of scary fun and drinks mixed to look like blood and ooze.

But she wasn't going to the pub. She wasn't even going to a party.

What she loved about Hallowe'en night was the anticipation – the costumes – the crowds of children with their long-suffering parents, carrying pumpkin-shaped buckets to collect their trick or treat wares. The teenagers preparing to scare people in alleyways . . . and the older ones – the pub goers – all set for a night of drinking and dancing and apple bobbing. Witches snogging skeletons in doorways. Zombies smoking fags in beer gardens.

She reached the park, where it became darker, less lit. She hesitated, only briefly. Who might be lurking in the shadows? Not those out for Hallowe'en cheer . . . there were sinister people who hung around at all times of day any night, waiting to see what the darkness might bring them.

The first one was pretty tame. 'Hey, sexy, where's your broom?'

She fought the urge to turn and look. Picked up the pace, just a bit.

'Hello, gorgeous, fancy a drink?'

'Baby . . . where you going all dressed up?'

'Nice hat, sugar . . .'

'Nice tits, baby . . .'

She crossed her arms over her chest, irritated now. Felt the heat in her cheeks. She looked down at the path, kept walking, faster now, faster. Until . . .

Thump.

She felt like she'd walked into a wall. Stumbled back, dazed. Felt arms grabbing at her.

'Hey, darlin', you wanna watch where you're going . . .' She looked up into yellowing eyes, took a step back. 'Fancy a coffee, sexy? You can come back to my place if you like?'

Low whispers. Sniggers from behind the trees. She felt a change in the air.

It was time.

'You know what? That's exactly what I'd like to do. Where's your place?'

Yellow-eyes took a step back. She saw confusion flit across his face, before he smiled at her, revealing a row of rotten teeth.

She felt her heart thumping in her chest. She swallowed.

This is it.

She had to fight hard to control herself, the feeling was so strong. She slid a hand into her pocket. Took a deep breath, trying to steady her nerves. She'd been looking forward to this night for weeks . . . months even. Since the last time she'd walked around the park. Since the last time she'd had to listen to them calling her, beckoning her . . . luring her.

Yellow-eyes placed a hand on her shoulder, guiding her towards the other side of the park.

'This way, gorgeous,' he said.

She said nothing. Let herself be led. She took his hand, gripped it tight.

In her other hand, deep in her pocket, she gripped the carving knife.

'This is going to be *so* much fun,' she said, grinning.

Yellow-eyes grinned back, oblivious.

THE LOTTERY

Shirley Jackson

Shirley Jackson (1916–1965) is one of the most critically acclaimed American writers of the twentieth century. 'The Lottery' is recognized as a classic short story, exploring the interplay of tradition and brutality. She is also known for the ghost novel *The Haunting of Hill House*.

The morning of June 27th was clear and sunny, with the fresh warmth of a full-summer day; the flowers were blossoming profusely and the grass was richly green. The people of the village began to gather in the square, between the post office and the bank, around ten o'clock; in some towns there were so many people that the lottery took two days and had to be started on June 26th, but in this village, where there were only about three hundred people, the whole lottery took only about two hours, so it could begin at ten o'clock in the morning and still be through in time to allow the villagers to get home for noon dinner.

The children assembled first, of course. School was recently over for the summer, and the feeling of liberty sat uneasily on most of them; they tended to gather together quietly for a while before they broke into boisterous play, and their talk was still of the classroom and the teacher, of books and reprimands. Bobby Martin had already stuffed his pockets full of stones, and the other boys soon followed his example, selecting the smoothest and roundest stones; Bobby and Harry Jones and Dickie Delacroix—the villagers pronounced this name "Dellacroy"—eventually made a great pile of stones in one corner of the square and guarded it against the raids of the other boys. The girls stood aside, talking among themselves, looking over their shoulders at the boys, and the very small children rolled in the dust or clung to the hands of their older brothers or sisters.

Soon the men began to gather, surveying their own children, speaking of planting and rain, tractors and taxes. They stood together, away from the pile of stones in the corner, and their jokes were quiet and they smiled rather than laughed. The women, wearing faded house dresses and sweaters, came shortly after their menfolk. They greeted one another and exchanged bits of gossip as they went to join their husbands. Soon the women, standing by their husbands, began to call to their children, and the children came reluctantly, having to be called four or five times. Bobby Martin ducked under his mother's grasping hand and ran, laughing, back to the pile of stones. His father spoke up sharply, and Bobby came quickly and took his place between his father and his oldest brother.

The lottery was conducted—as were the square dances, the teen-age club, the Halloween program—by Mr. Summers, who had time and energy to devote to civic activities. He was a round-faced, jovial man and he ran the coal business, and people were sorry for him, because he had no children and his wife was a scold. When he arrived in the square, carrying the black wooden box, there was a murmur of conversation among the villagers, and he waved and called, "Little late today, folks." The postmaster, Mr. Graves, followed him, carrying a three-legged stool, and the stool was put in the center of the square and Mr. Summers set the black box down on it. The villagers kept their distance, leaving a space between themselves and the stool, and when Mr. Summers said, "Some of you fellows want to give me a hand?," there was a hesitation before two men, Mr. Martin and his oldest son, Baxter, came forward to hold the box steady on the stool while Mr. Summers stirred up the papers inside it.

The original paraphernalia for the lottery had been lost long ago, and the black box now resting on the stool had been put into use even before Old Man Warner, the oldest man in town, was born. Mr. Summers spoke frequently to the villagers about making a new box, but no one liked to upset even as much tradition as was represented by the black box. There was a story that the present box had been made with some pieces of the box that had preceded it, the one that had been constructed when the first people settled down to make a village here. Every year, after the lottery, Mr. Summers began talking again about a new box, but every year the subject was allowed to fade off without anything's being done. The black box grew shabbier each year; by now it was no longer completely black but splintered badly along one side to show the original wood color, and in some places faded or stained.

Mr. Martin and his oldest son, Baxter, held the black box securely on the stool until Mr. Summers had stirred the papers thoroughly with his hand. Because so much of the ritual had been forgotten or discarded, Mr. Summers had been successful in having slips of paper substituted for the chips of wood that had been used for generations. Chips of wood, Mr. Summers had argued, had been all very well when the village was tiny, but now that the population was more than three hundred and likely to keep on growing, it was necessary to use something that would fit more easily into the black box. The night before the lottery, Mr. Summers and Mr. Graves made up the slips of paper and put them into the box, and it was then taken to the safe of Mr. Summers' coal company and locked up until Mr. Summers was ready to take it to the square next morning. The rest of the year, the box was put away, sometimes one place, sometimes another; it had spent one year in Mr. Graves' barn and another year underfoot in the post office, and sometimes it was set on a shelf in the Martin grocery and left there.

There was a great deal of fussing to be done before Mr. Summers declared the lottery open. There were the lists to make up—of heads of families, heads of households in each family, members of each household in each family. There was the proper swearing-in of Mr. Summers by the postmaster, as the official of the lottery; at one time, some people remembered, there had been a recital of some sort, performed by the official of the lottery, a perfunctory, tuneless chant that had been rattled off duly each year; some people believed that the official of the lottery used to stand just so when he said or sang it, others believed that he was supposed to walk among the people, but years and years ago this part of the ritual had been allowed to lapse. There had been, also, a ritual salute, which the official of the lottery had had to use in addressing each person who came up to draw from the box, but this also had changed with time, until now it was felt necessary only for the official to speak to each person approaching. Mr. Summers was very good at all this; in his clean white shirt and blue jeans, with one hand resting carelessly on the black box, he seemed very proper and important as he talked interminably to Mr. Graves and the Martins.

Just as Mr. Summers finally left off talking and turned to the assembled villagers, Mrs. Hutchinson came hurriedly along the path to the square, her sweater thrown over her shoulders, and slid into place in the back of the crowd. "Clean forgot what day it was," she said to Mrs. Delacroix, who stood next to her, and they both laughed softly. "Thought my old man was out back stacking wood," Mrs. Hutchinson went on, "and then I looked out the window and the kids was gone, and then I remembered it was the twenty-seventh and came a-running." She dried her hands on her apron, and Mrs. Delacroix said, "You're in time, though. They're still talking away up there."

Mrs. Hutchinson craned her neck to see through the crowd and found her husband and children standing near the front. She tapped Mrs. Delacroix on the arm as a farewell and began to make her way through the crowd. The people separated good-humoredly to let her through; two or three people said, in voices just loud enough to be heard across the crowd, "Here comes your Mrs., Hutchinson," and "Bill, she made it after all." Mrs. Hutchinson reached her husband, and Mr. Summers, who had been waiting, said cheerfully, "Thought we were going to have to get on without you, Tessie." Mrs. Hutchinson said, grinning, "Wouldn't have me leave m'dishes in the sink, now, would you, Joe?," and soft laughter ran through the crowd as the people stirred back into position after Mrs. Hutchinson's arrival.

"Well, now," Mr. Summers said soberly, "guess we better get started, get this over with, so's we can go back to work. Anybody ain't here?"

"Dunbar," several people said. "Dunbar, Dunbar."

Mr. Summers consulted his list. "Clyde Dunbar," he said. "That's right. He's broke his leg, hasn't he? Who's drawing for him?"

"Me, I guess," a woman said, and Mr. Summers turned to look at her. "Wife draws for her husband," Mr. Summers said. "Don't you have a grown boy to do it for you, Janey?" Although Mr. Summers and everyone else in the village knew the answer perfectly well, it was the business of the official of the lottery to ask such questions formally. Mr. Summers waited with an expression of polite interest while Mrs. Dunbar answered.

"Horace's not but sixteen yet," Mrs. Dunbar said regretfully. "Guess I gotta fill in for the old man this year."

"Right," Mr. Summers said. He made a note on the list he was holding. Then he asked, "Watson boy drawing this year?"

A tall boy in the crowd raised his hand. "Here," he said. "I'm drawing for m'mother and me." He blinked his eyes nervously and ducked his head as several voices in the crowd said things like "Good fellow, Jack," and "Glad to see your mother's got a man to do it."

"Well," Mr. Summers said, "guess that's everyone. Old Man Warner make it?"

"Here," a voice said, and Mr. Summers nodded.

A sudden hush fell on the crowd as Mr. Summers cleared his throat and looked at the list. "All ready?" he called. "Now, I'll read the names—heads of families first—and the men come up and take a paper out of the box. Keep the paper folded in your hand without looking at it until everyone has had a turn. Everything clear?"

The people had done it so many times that they only half listened to the directions; most of them were quiet, wetting their lips, not looking around. Then Mr. Summers raised one hand high and said, "Adams." A man disengaged himself from the crowd and came forward. "Hi, Steve," Mr. Summers said, and Mr. Adams said, "Hi, Joe." They grinned at one another humorlessly and nervously. Then Mr. Adams reached into the black box and took out a folded paper. He held it firmly by one corner as he turned and went hastily back to his place in the crowd, where he stood a little apart from his family, not looking down at his hand.

"Allen," Mr. Summers said. "Anderson . . . Bentham."

"Seems like there's no time at all between lotteries any more," Mrs. Delacroix said to Mrs. Graves in the back row. "Seems like we got through with the last one only last week."

"Time sure goes fast," Mrs. Graves said.

"Clark . . . Delacroix."

"There goes my old man," Mrs. Delacroix said. She held her breath while her husband went forward.

"Dunbar," Mr. Summers said, and Mrs. Dunbar went steadily to the box while one of the women said, "Go on, Janey," and another said, "There she goes."

"We're next," Mrs. Graves said. She watched while Mr. Graves came around from the side of the box, greeted Mr. Summers gravely, and selected a slip of paper from the box. By now, all through the crowd there were men holding the small folded papers in their large hands, turning them over and over nervously. Mrs. Dunbar and her two sons stood together, Mrs. Dunbar holding the slip of paper.

"Harburt . . . Hutchinson."

"Get up there, Bill," Mrs. Hutchinson said, and the people near her laughed.

"Jones."

"They do say," Mr. Adams said to Old Man Warner, who stood next to him, "that over in the north village they're talking of giving up the lottery."

Old Man Warner snorted. "Pack of crazy fools," he said. "Listening to the young folks, nothing's good enough for *them*. Next thing you know, they'll be wanting to go back to living in caves, nobody work any more, live *that* way for a while. Used to be a saying about 'Lottery in June, corn be heavy soon.' First thing you know, we'd all be eating stewed chickweed and acorns. There's *always* been a lottery," he added petulantly. "Bad enough to see young Joe Summers up there joking with everybody."

"Some places have already quit lotteries," Mrs. Adams said.

"Nothing but trouble in *that*," Old Man Warner said stoutly. "Pack of young fools."

"Martin." And Bobby Martin watched his father go forward. "Overdyke . . . Percy."

"I wish they'd hurry," Mrs. Dunbar said to her older son. "I wish they'd hurry."

"They're almost through," her son said.

"You get ready to run tell Dad," Mrs. Dunbar said.

Mr. Summers called his own name and then stepped forward precisely and selected a slip from the box. Then he called, "Warner."

"Seventy-seventh year I been in the lottery," Old Man Warner said as he went through the crowd. "Seventy-seventh time."

"Watson." The tall boy came awkwardly through the crowd. Someone said, "Don't be nervous, Jack," and Mr. Summers said, "Take your time, son."

"Zanini."

After that, there was a long pause, a breathless pause, until Mr. Summers, holding his slip of paper in the air, said, "All right, fellows." For a minute, no one moved, and then all the slips of paper were opened. Suddenly, all the women began to speak at once, saying, "Who is it?," "Who's got it?," "Is it the Dunbars?," "Is it the Watsons?" Then the voices began to say, "It's Hutchinson. It's Bill," "Bill Hutchinson's got it."

"Go tell your father," Mrs. Dunbar said to her older son.

People began to look around to see the Hutchinsons. Bill Hutchinson was standing quiet, staring down at the paper in his hand. Suddenly, Tessie Hutchinson shouted to Mr. Summers, "You didn't give him time enough to take any paper he wanted. I saw you. It wasn't fair!"

"Be a good sport, Tessie," Mrs. Delacroix called, and Mrs. Graves said, "All of us took the same chance."

"Shut up, Tessie," Bill Hutchinson said.

"Well, everyone," Mr. Summers said, "that was done pretty fast, and now we've got to be hurrying a little more to get done in time." He consulted his next list. "Bill," he said, "you draw for the Hutchinson family. You got any other households in the Hutchinsons?"

"There's Don and Eva," Mrs. Hutchinson yelled. "Make *them* take their chance!"

"Daughters draw with their husbands' families, Tessie," Mr. Summers said gently. "You know that as well as anyone else."

"It wasn't *fair*," Tessie said.

"I guess not, Joe," Bill Hutchinson said regretfully. "My daughter draws with her husband's family, that's only fair. And I've got no other family except the kids."

"Then, as far as drawing for families is concerned, it's you," Mr. Summers said in explanation, "and as far as drawing for households is concerned, that's you, too. Right?"

"Right," Bill Hutchinson said.

"How many kids, Bill?" Mr. Summers asked formally.

"Three," Bill Hutchinson said. "There's Bill, Jr., and Nancy, and little Dave. And Tessie and me."

"All right, then," Mr. Summers said. "Harry, you got their tickets back?"

Mr. Graves nodded and held up the slips of paper. "Put them in the box, then," Mr. Summers directed. "Take Bill's and put it in."

"I think we ought to start over," Mrs. Hutchinson said, as quietly as she could. "I tell you it wasn't *fair*. You didn't give him time enough to choose. *Every*body saw that."

Mr. Graves had selected the five slips and put them in the box, and he dropped all the papers but those onto the ground, where the breeze caught them and lifted them off.

"Listen, everybody," Mrs. Hutchinson was saying to the people around her.

"Ready, Bill?" Mr. Summers asked, and Bill Hutchinson, with one quick glance around at his wife and children, nodded.

"Remember," Mr. Summers said, "take the slips and keep them folded until each person has taken one. Harry, you help little Dave." Mr. Graves took the hand of the little boy, who came willingly with him up to the box. "Take a paper out of the box, Davy," Mr. Summers said. Davy put his hand into the box and laughed. "Take just *one* paper," Mr. Summers said. "Harry, you hold it for him." Mr. Graves took the child's hand and removed the folded paper from the tight fist and held it while little Dave stood next to him and looked up at him wonderingly.

"Nancy next," Mr. Summers said. Nancy was twelve, and her school friends breathed heavily as she went forward, switching her skirt, and took a slip daintily from the box. "Bill, Jr.," Mr. Summers said, and Billy, his face red and his feet overlarge, nearly knocked the box over as he got a paper out. "Tessie," Mr. Summers said. She hesitated for a minute, looking around defiantly, and then set her lips and went up to the box. She snatched a paper out and held it behind her.

"Bill," Mr. Summers said, and Bill Hutchinson reached into the box and felt around, bringing his hand out at last with the slip of paper in it.

The crowd was quiet. A girl whispered, "I hope it's not Nancy," and the sound of the whisper reached the edges of the crowd.

"It's not the way it used to be," Old Man Warner said clearly. "People ain't the way they used to be."

"All right," Mr. Summers said. "Open the papers. Harry, you open little Dave's."

Mr. Graves opened the slip of paper and there was a general sigh through the crowd as he held it up and everyone could see that it was blank. Nancy and Bill, Jr., opened theirs at the same time, and both beamed and laughed, turning around to the crowd and holding their slips of paper above their heads.

"Tessie," Mr. Summers said. There was a pause, and then Mr. Summers looked at Bill Hutchinson, and Bill unfolded his paper and showed it. It was blank.

"It's Tessie," Mr. Summers said, and his voice was hushed. "Show us her paper, Bill."

Bill Hutchinson went over to his wife and forced the slip of paper out of her hand. It had a black spot on it, the black spot Mr. Summers had made the night before with the heavy pencil in the coal-company office. Bill Hutchinson held it up, and there was a stir in the crowd.

"All right, folks," Mr. Summers said. "Let's finish quickly."

Although the villagers had forgotten the ritual and lost the original black box, they still remembered to use stones. The pile of stones the boys had made earlier was ready; there were stones on the ground with the blowing scraps of paper that had come out of the box. Mrs. Delacroix selected a stone so large she had to pick it up with both hands and turned to Mrs. Dunbar. "Come on," she said. "Hurry up."

Mrs. Dunbar had small stones in both hands, and she said, gasping for breath, "I can't run at all. You'll have to go ahead and I'll catch up with you."

The children had stones already, and someone gave little Davy Hutchinson a few pebbles.

Tessie Hutchinson was in the center of a cleared space by now, and she held her hands out desperately as the villagers moved in on her. "It isn't fair," she said. A stone hit her on the side of the head.

Old Man Warner was saying, "Come on, come on, everyone." Steve Adams was in the front of the crowd of villagers, with Mrs. Graves beside him.

"It isn't fair, it isn't right," Mrs. Hutchinson screamed, and then they were upon her.

THE AFFAIR

Emma Kavanagh

Emma Kavanagh holds a PhD in psychology and spent many years working as a police and military psychologist. She is the author of tense psychological thrillers *Falling*, *Hidden*, and *The Missing Hours*. Kavanagh lives in South Wales with her husband and sons.

T he bodies are still inside. I'm not even sure how I know that – whether I heard it ripple through the crowd, the whispers carried on the breeze, whether I saw it on the face of the waiting police officers, or whether it is simply that I have been here, or a variant of here, so many times before.

I squeeze my way through the throng of people, wishing that I had remembered my press pass – Charlotte Solomon, *Swansea Times*. That it wasn't currently languishing in amongst the Twix wrappers and the scrambled scraps of paper on my desk. But then in all likelihood my press pass would make very little difference to the crowd that has gathered. So what that I have a job to do? They live here in Harddymaes with its boxed-up council houses and its harsh scrubland, and right here, on their doorstep, they have a murder. Not just a murder. A double murder. They're not moving for anyone.

I shimmy in between a thick-chested man, smelling sickly-sweet of stale booze, and a narrow woman with a large, hook-shaped nose, who has wrapped her arms so tightly around herself that it is a miracle she can breathe. Not for the first time, I thank God for the five-foot-two-inch frame that allows me to slip into places normal-sized people wouldn't be able to go. Rather like a rat up a drainpipe. The booze-soaked man glances at me, leers appreciatively, and I suppress a shudder, instead forming my face into what I'm hoping is a charming smile. You never know who your source is going to be. He winks.

The call came in to the *Swansea Times* offices from a 'concerned' citizen. A believer in the freedom of the press, someone not at all out for a reward – is there one, by the way? The twin dead bodies had been found in a terraced house, in the heart of Harddymaes, a house registered to a Mr Morris Myricks and his wife, Mrs Sian Myricks. Now, said the caller, don't quote me on this, and I couldn't tell you for sure, but it definitely looks like old Morris has had it. My boys, said the caller, well, they were just in the Myricks' back garden to get their football back. Perfectly innocent, like. Only the thing was, they couldn't 'elp looking through the window, and that's when they saw them lying there – two of them, in all that blood.

I've been to these houses before. The back windows are six feet off the garden. Perfectly innocent, my arse.

I glance around the crowd. A couple of teenage boys, younger than they look, hang at the edge of it, leaning against bike handles and trying to look worldly. One of them has been crying. The footballers, I presume.

The police tape lines the front garden, roping off the knee-high grass, the rough concrete path, the window beyond. I bounce on my toes slightly, trying to get a view, to see beyond the cordon into the darkness beyond. But there is nothing. Flowers have been left already, a mass of cheap carnations in cellophane wrap. They have been propped against a neighbouring wall, a makeshift shrine in this most unlikely of temples. It always mystifies me, how these things are gathered so fast. Do people keep a handy supply of carnations and sad-looking teddy bears around, just in case?

My gaze shifts from the flowers to the uniformed officers. There are three of them, standing with arms folded, serious faces. I study them, looking for a face that I recognise, but these ones are young, preternaturally so. The one nearest me has his arms folded across his chest, but his pallor is grey. I'm laying odds on him being the first on the scene. I study him for a moment: double or nothing, it's his first dead body. Two for the price of one. Lucky boy. I sigh, settle back to wait.

I recognise the odd face in the crowd. After all, I am here in Harddymaes a lot. Rampant car-crime; an off-licence that has been knocked over more times than I've had hot dinners. I know the area, I know the wide-splayed roads with their views down to the sea, which anywhere else should cost a fortune, but here come at a budget price. I know the twisting streets with their stacked-up houses, the gardens seeming to spill from one into the other. I know the people; some stumbling through life as best they can, others boiling with anger at the injustice of it all.

I slip my phone from my pocket, run a quick check on Facebook. There was a time when you would have assumed that people of the Myricks' age, approaching fifty, childless, would have sooner climbed Everest than set up a Facebook account. But times are changing. I find Morris first. His account is unprotected, open for anyone to read. In his profile picture he is standing in his garden – I assume it's his garden – bare-chested, face that looks like it's been flattened by a shovel, pulled into a wide grin. I study it for a second. Not an attractive man: small eyes that are far too close together, a nose that looks like it has been broken more than once. He is, however, powerfully built, even though in his photo he is sucking in his stomach so hard it's probably sticking out through his spine. It would have had to be someone pretty strong to get one over on Morris. Or someone he wasn't expecting. I scroll through his posts. A bunch of comedy – or should I say 'comedy' – videos, adverts for a car he was selling. Nothing personal. Nothing that would give any answers. Then I try Sian's. Her profile shot is different, more at a distance. She wears sunglasses and looks uncomfortable, like she would rather there wasn't a camera pointing at her right now. Her account is more personal, a window into her life, new status added most days. I look for Saturday: BBQ with neighbours. Let's hope the rain stays away. LOL.

There are pictures, a knot of people gathered around a tin-can barbecue. A table thick with bottles – vodka, Stella, a cheap white wine. A picture of Sian and Morris, arms around one another, their gazes slack, unfocused. Sian and a woman – thin, a hook-shaped nose – raising a glass to the camera. I sneak a look to my right, trying to be subtle. It is her – the woman beside me sniffing into a tissue. I glance back at the photo, at the dark eye make-up, the cerise lipstick. She looks different now: no make-up that I can see, her black hair pulled up into a rough ponytail. Her eyes are swollen, face puffy from crying. Bingo!

She looks at me, her attention pulled by the intensity of my gaze. I never have been great at subtle. I smile carefully. She stares for a moment, then bites her lip, the flood of tears starting anew. I look away. There is time.

Terrible. That is the word floating on the air. It is muttered by the elderly woman with the coiffured hair, the cherry-red lipstick. It comes from the mother, a slack-jawed baby on her hip, no more than seventeen or so herself. It comes from the man beside me, his breath loaded with Strongbow.

'Well,' mutters the elderly lady in a voice that carries, 'you just wonder who it was that could do such a thing. I mean . . .' A meaningful pause. 'It could be anybody, when you come right down to it.'

Her words ripple through the crowd, feet shifting, as they absorb the implications of that, heads turning, everyone wondering if it is the person standing next to them who is the killer. The woman beside me lets out a quiet sob.

'The thing is, it's not really a surprise, is it?' says the elderly woman.

I wonder who it is that she is talking to? Is she looking for answers from us, or the universe in general?

'I mean, you know Morris. Lovely boy, salt of the earth. But he did like to hang around with some unscrupulous people. I know, I've said to him before, "Now you mind, Morris-boy. You'll get yourself into trouble hanging round with the likes of those."'

I make a note on my phone, through force of habit rather than any real danger that I'll forget. Check Morris's criminal history, convictions. Who were the unscrupulous people? I look back at the elderly woman, wonder if she will talk to me.

'Well, I'll tell you, Muriel . . .' I jot down the name Muriel. Another voice, this one floating from somewhere near the back. 'I heard a car, late – late Saturday night. Was out of here like a bat out of hell. I bet you anything that had something to do with it. I said to you, didn't I, Phil?'

'Aye, you did.'

Phil. Car, late on Saturday.

'See.'

I look back to the front door. It stands open, and every now and again there is a flutter of movement as a white forensic suit crosses the opening. They do not look at us, the waiting audience; just keep their heads down and get on with studying death. I think about Sian Myricks, about the profile picture with the round face, clumsily applied lipstick and the expression that seemed to be slightly surprised. Why are you dead, Sian? Were they coming after you, too? Or were you simply one of the unfortunates, in the wrong place at the wrong time?

Clouds are beginning to mass overhead, dense and grey. The wind has picked up. I suppress a shiver, wonder if the neighbours will have solved the murder before the rain starts. Then I hear the soft squeal of car brakes, the squawk of an opening door.

My feet begin to move before my mind does, because I have done this before and I know how these things work, so I already knew that Del would be here. I push my way through the crowd, get to its edge just as he is climbing his way out of the unmarked Ford Focus. He catches sight of me, grins.

'Might have known you'd be here.'

I smile back. 'You know me too well.'

I've known Del since nursery school, kissed him once in a game of spin-the-bottle. That, however, was the beginning and the end of our romance, and these days we settle for passing gentle barbs back and forth at one another across police lines. He's a good guy, a detective constable for the moment, although scuttlebutt tells me there's a promotion in the offing, a shift back to uniform, but as a sergeant this time. He often tells me more than he should. Fortunately I know how to use his information judiciously. It must be working. He hasn't been fired yet.

'So, you have something for me?'

Del laughs. 'Patience, Charlie. God! All I know so far is it's a married couple . . .'

'Morris and Sian Myricks.'

'Yeah, that's them. Forensics are in, but we've got to wait for Firearms to clear the scene.'

'Firearms? They were shot?'

'No, but Forensics found a gun in the house. So it's got to be checked and removed. Do you know Aden, by the way?'

I hadn't noticed the officer behind him, dressed in dark firearms gear, boots laced up high. Tall, dark-blond hair, good-looking enough that I wished I'd run a comb through my hair before I left the office. 'No, hi. I'm Charlie.'

Aden nods, gives me a swift smile. 'Nice to meet you. I'd better get inside, Del.'

'Yeah, I'm coming. Charlie, I'll call you in a bit?'

The crowd parts before them, heads turning as if on springs to follow this latest development. And I go back to waiting. I do this. A lot.

The elderly lady, Muriel – the one who looks like she has been dipped in make-up – looks across at me, the foundation facade fracturing as she frowns. 'I've seen you before somewhere, 'aven't I?'

I add my best smile. 'Charlotte Solomon, *Swansea Times*. I tend to work around here quite a bit. Can I ask – you knew the Myricks?'

'Aye, well, been here a long time, me. Lovely girl, Sian, lovely.'

The division leaps out at me. 'And Morris?'

She purses her lips. 'Well, let's just say he was lucky to have Sian. What with everything.' She isn't looking at me, is glaring off into the crowd at the narrow woman with the hook-nose. It seems that she feels the force of the gaze, her head lifting slowly, her stare baleful. Muriel shakes her head, a *tchh* sound escaping her.

'You mean . . .'

'No, well, there are others that would need to talk to you about that. It's not my business what people get up to in the privacy of their own homes.'

I study the dark-haired woman. She has looked away now, but it seems that Muriel's glare has done its damage. She has folded in on herself, is sobbing, and I think that someone will come, will detach themselves from the mass of people and put their arms around this woman, comfort her. After all, this is that kind of neighbourhood, where everyone knows everyone else, where people are involved, intimately, in one another's lives. And so I wait. But there is no movement, no concerned looks, no supportive touches, just her crying.

I look back at the house where Morris and Sian lie dead, and I wonder: what did go on in the privacy of these homes?

Then the rain begins. Thick droplets plopping onto the cellophane of the flowers, not a slow build, but a sudden onslaught, rain like it really means it, like it's going to punish us for hanging around outside this house of death. You can see it in people's faces, that they are caught between staying, getting soaked, and leaving and missing what comes next. Beside me, Muriel mutters to herself, something about God-awful British weather, and haven't they all suffered enough. Gradually, slowly, the crowd begins to cave, pushed away by the rain. Muriel folds her arms tight across her chest and marches away without a backward glance. I stand in the rain. I wish to God I had thought to bring a coat.

The thin woman is still standing there. I'm not sure that she has even noticed the rain, too caught up in her own private hell. I shift, uncomfortable, thinking that my car is parked nearby, that I could run, shelter, maybe reply to some emails while I wait. Then I shake my head, sigh, tuck my arms into my armpits and make my way towards the weeping woman. She looks up at me.

'Are you okay?' It is, I acknowledge, a stupid damn question. But it is all I can come up with.

She nods, an uncertain, unconvincing movement.

'Look, you . . . you're getting soaked. You live around here?'

She looks at me, seems to be assessing me – a sensible thing to do, in a community where there has just been a double murder. 'Two doors down. That way.' She gestures down the street.

'Um,' I look to the sky, where the clouds have stacked themselves up into towers, the rain getting heavier and heavier, 'you got a kettle?'

Finally a slight smile breaks through. 'Yes. Come on then.'

I trail behind her, watching as the crowd begin to slip away into their waiting houses. One or two of them watch us as we leave, their faces pursed in disapproval, and my heart sinks. I know what people think of journalists – that we are simply there to cash in on the grief of others. I try to comfort myself with the notion that it isn't only about that; I am offering this woman some sympathy where others have not, I'm getting her in out of the rain. But lying to myself has never been one of my greater skills and, down at the heart of it, I understand my own motivations. That she was Sian's friend. That she saw the Myricks on what was possibly their last day. And something else, tickling at the edges of my awareness – that there are things that happen in the privacy of people's homes, that there are whispers.

She guides me two doors down, pushes open the front door, which even in spite of a double murder she has not locked. It's a strange community, this one. Rough, dangerous sometimes. Yet with an intrinsic feeling of safety, that one is guarded by one's neighbours. What, I wonder, will happen now, though?

'Tea?'

'Thank you.' The house is warm, a relief from the cold rain, the decor a throwback to the 1980s, the carpets marked and thin. It's clean, though – everything in a place of its own. 'My name is Charlie, by the way.'

'Wendy. Sit down. I'll find us some digestives.'

I perch on the end of a sofa.

I study the room. It is large in the way of older council houses, a solid square room with cheap carpets, a Sixties fireplace. A small television in one corner. A bookcase, overstuffed with books – romance mostly, a couple of thrillers.

'I've not seen you round here before – are you new to the area?' Wendy shouts from the kitchen.

'I . . .' My phone begins to ring. Del. 'Sorry, hold on,' I shout to Wendy, and answer the call, 'Hey, that was fast.'

'Well, I do pride myself on speed.'

'Nice. Your wife is very lucky.'

'I know, right? Okay, you want the info? Bearing in mind I could get fired for this?'

'I want the info. And I'll sit on it until you tell me otherwise. You know me.'

'I do. That's the only reason I tell you anything. Right, we've got a stabbing, by the looks of things. The wife has multiple stab-wounds to the back.'

'How many is multiple?'

'I don't know, jeez. Multiple. As in lots.'

'Okay, okay. And the husband?'

'Single stab-wound to the heart.'

'Any sign of forced entry?'

'Nope. Doors all locked up nice and tight.'

'Anything missing?'

'Not obviously. But there's something else.'

'Go on.'

'Husband was found with the knife in his hand.'

'Shit!'

'Yeah. Starting to look like a murder-suicide.'

Wendy comes into the room, balancing a tray with two mugs, a plate of plain digestive biscuits. She is trying not to listen to me – you can see it in the tilt of her head, the conscientious way she sets down the tray. Shit! 'Um, okay, so thanks for that. Let me know – you know, when I'm good to go.' I hang up the phone, deliberately looking away from her, trying to adjust my expression. 'Thank you.' I wait as she sinks into the opposite chair. 'How are you doing?'

She shakes her head. 'Okay. It's hard, you know?'

'You were close to Sian and Morris?'

'We've lived on the same street for most of our lives. I grew up next door to Morris. We went to the same school and everything.' She gives a brittle laugh. 'I feed their cat, when they're on their holidays. I mean, we're all close around here – everyone looks out for everyone else.' I think of the crowd in the street, the ones who watched her cry and did nothing, and I bite my tongue. Maybe it is that British thing, that we are irretrievably uncomfortable in the face of open grief. And I get that, I really do. I mean, I'm not great. I never know what it is you're supposed to say. But still . . . you give it a go, don't you?

'I saw a photo, on Facebook, of you guys together at a barbecue?'

She thinks for a moment. 'Oh, Saturday, you mean? Yeah, they had a load of us round.'

I think of the pictures, the vodka, the Stella. 'Couple of drinks?'

Wendy pulls a face. 'More than a couple, to be honest. I had a stinking head on Sunday.'

'I bet Morris and Sian were steaming?'

'Well . . . no. I mean, yes. We all were. But not, you know, out of their minds or anything. Just enough that you stop caring about what you say and . . .' She stops, looks down in consternation.

I give her a second, try not to push, because often when you push all that you achieve is to slam shut a door that was opening for you. But sometimes, if you wait . . .

'I shouldn't be telling you this.' It is truly astounding how often people say that to me, and how rarely that stops them. 'The thing is, things weren't great. Not if I'm being honest. I mean, you've got to understand. They've been together for a long time, since we were in school, and, you know, things happen. They couldn't have kids, Morris got laid off, so things get tense.'

I think of Morris, with his large frame and his flattened features, the knife clutched in his fingers. Tense.

'They were sniping at each other, at the barbecue. You know the way couples get. Started off as just the usual backbiting stuff, but then, once they'd had some drinks, it got nastier. Sian saying he was a waste of space, that she'd be better off on her own. To be honest, that's why it ended as early as it did; people got uncomfortable, started to slope off. I mean, the thing is, with their arguing, you just aren't comfortable, are you?' She shakes her head. 'If I'd have stayed, maybe I could have . . .'

I study her. Wait.

'I don't know. Maybe I could have done something.'

Her face fluctuates, a medley of emotions dancing across it. And I think: you know; you have already come to the same conclusion as the police have, that there was no one else involved, just the two of them.

I hesitate, choosing my path carefully. 'Did Morris have a temper?'

She looks up, her eyes locking onto mine. Doesn't answer for long moments, and I think that I have gone too far, that I have jumped too soon.

'Yes.' One word, spoken so quietly it is almost lost in the sound of the rain against the windows.

We sit there then, sipping tea, listening to the rain, and it seems there is little else to say. A ray of murky sunlight catches on a thin gold chain that hangs around Wendy's neck. A single tear drifts down her cheek.

Then there is a sound, the front door opening, and my heart leaps to my throat. I rarely think about these things. I go into these houses and I talk to these strangers, and for some reason it never occurs to me that I am unsafe, even in the heart of a murder. The young man stands in the doorway, shaking off the rain. Tall and not what you would call good-looking, he is broadly built, wears his dark hair hanging down to his shoulders, half-covering his face.

'Mam? What's goin' on? There's police all over the place out there.'

Wendy stares at him, her mouth moving like she is trying to figure out how to place these horrors into words.

'Has Morris been arrested or somethin'? I mean, the police . . . they're at his house.'

'No. No, love. Um . . . this is Charlie. Charlie, this is my son, Toby.'

He stares at me, forehead creased into a frown. 'Oh. All right. And you are who, exactly?'

'Toby. Charlie has been very kind to me.'

But still he's staring at me, his mouth a hard line, and I'm about to say something, to justify myself as a journalist crashing his mother's grief, when it hits me. She doesn't know. Shit! I wasn't wearing my press pass. And, with the rain and her tears, I didn't think to tell her. I am floored suddenly. It's like years of driving a car and then suddenly slipping into the driver's seat and forgetting where the key goes. What the hell is the matter with me? I feel my face start to flush. 'Look, I should go.' I make a move to stand, because I have well and truly peed in this particular swimming pool and it is hugely unlikely these people are going to be willing to talk to me, once I do actually tell them who I am. 'Wendy, I'm sorry, I thought I told you. I'm Charlotte Solomon from the *Swansea Times*.'

She stares at me, her mouth moving uselessly. Her son makes a noise, a cross between a growl and a grunt. 'I think you'd better get out of here.' He seems bigger now, has stepped closer to me. Smells of old coffee and cigarettes.

I take a step back. 'Look, I'll let myself out. But I just . . . I'll leave my card here, just in case you decide you'd like a chat.'

The son harrumphs. 'She won't.'

They watch me leave, the house far colder now than it has been. Dammit. Dammit. Dammit. What is the matter with me? I can hear the rhythmic rise and fall of their voices at my back. I am such a moron. I cannot believe I have done this. I pull the door behind me, plunge out into the rain and try to reach for that feeling – let's call it a hunch – that scratches at the back of my brain.

It stays with me as I climb into my car, start the engine, drive down the hill through the town, as I pull up outside the office. What is it? What the hell is bugging me so much? I don't go into the *Swansea Times* office. Not straight away. Just sit in the car, watch the rain and think. What did I see?

I think of Wendy's son. I've seen him somewhere before, I'm almost sure of it. I bite my lip, then pull my phone out, accessing Wendy's Facebook page. This one is better protected. I can't access her main page, can only get to the profile pictures. But there she is, a smile brighter than I would have believed possible. I run through the photos, mentally crossing my fingers. And then I find it – Wendy, her hair styled, lapping around her shoulders, make-up intricately applied, her arm linked through Toby's. His hair is shorter in the picture, his face clearer.

I'm sure I've seen this guy somewhere before.

I flick back through my search history. Go back to the page of Sian Myricks. The picture of her and Wendy, raising a glass to the camera. But this time I'm not looking at them. I'm looking behind them. And there is Toby, his hair tucked back behind his ears, shoulders up. Skulking. That really is the only word for it. I enlarge the picture. And I wonder: what was he doing, late that Saturday night?

I move through the rest of the barbecue pictures to a group shot, unposed

– like the participants do not know they are being photographed. It feels . . . I don't know, weird. Uncomfortable almost. You would expect that the party would have broken down into groups, people talking in pairs, small knots, but instead it appears that within this group of fifteen, twenty people there is a common purpose. I scan the eyes. Those that are not looking at the ground are looking . . . where? At Toby. And at Morris, standing beside him.

Then it hits me – the itch I have needed to scratch coming clear. The boy is the image of the man.

Suddenly I get the looks, the way the crowd seemed to flow around Wendy as if she simply was not there, the way they were able to ignore her tears, her obvious heartbreak. Muriel's frown, her comments. I get the way the crowd's gaze tracked us as we walked towards the house. It wasn't about me. It was about her. They were watching as the mistress grieved. They were judging.

Well, shit!

My mind races. Does the boy know? Did Sian? She'd have to, right? What with the gossip within the community. Or was it one of those situations in which everyone knows, apart from the people it most affects? Is that what happened on that Saturday night, when the Stella had been flowing freely: did suspicion turn to accusations, accusations to murder? Did Sian tackle Morris about it, finally, and did he get angry, punishing her with a knife in the back, for spoiling his good thing? Or was it the son, Toby? The happy family image getting too much for him, so that he snaps?

Of course I can't print any of this. I have no proof. I have nothing on the record, no one willing to spill their guts on the front page of the local rag. In reporting terms, I have naff-all. That's a technical term, by the way.

There will not be a funeral. Not for a while, at least. The police still have not found the killer, haven't finished with the bodies. Instead Harddymaes is holding a candlelight vigil, a way for the community to remember. I pull out onto the Harddymaes road, my headlights picking up the puddles that litter the tarmac ahead of me, and suppress a shiver.

'Look, I shouldn't be telling you this . . .'

'Isn't that my line?' asked Del. I could hear the grin in his voice. I called him as soon as I got into the office, reasoning to myself that the boy wasn't a source, that I wasn't betraying confidences, because no one had told me anything.

'I think you should have a look at Toby.'

'Okay,' said Del slowly. 'Who the hell is Toby?'

'Two doors down from the Myricks, on the left. His mother is Wendy. I just . . . there's something weird about that kid.'

'You know I can't arrest him for being weird, right?'

'Yeah, more's the pity. But there's something else. I have no proof of this, but the thing is, I've got a feeling that he's Morris Myricks' son.'

There was a long silence on the line. 'Interesting.'

'Yeah.'

'Leave it with me, okay?'

I ease the car up the hill, can feel the engine straining. There is a crowd ahead, people already beginning to gather, even though I am early. I park up a little way away and walk the remaining distance, pulling my jacket tight around me. It's hard to make out faces now in the darkness, just ill-defined silhouettes, flickering shadows. People are talking in low tones and I can't help but listen. I am, after all, a journalist. I get paid to be nosy.

'Awful they 'aven't got anyone yet. Just awful.'

'Well, it's Harddymaes, isn't it? Police don't give a shit.'

'Look, there she is. Wonder she can show her face, after everything.'

My heart starts to beat a little faster, and I follow the women's gaze, knowing all too well what I'll see. Wendy. Once again alone, her arms wrapped tight around her, as if that way she can save herself from the slings and arrows.

One of the women leans away from the pack, her voice carrying on the night air. 'Oi! Why don't you get out of it, eh? Slag!'

I can see Wendy, her face briefly crumble, before she pulls it back, ordering her expression. She doesn't look at them, just stares straight ahead towards the house where her lover died. I don't know if I can see the tears or if it's just that I imagine them, but I can't help myself. I duck past the group, their conversation peppered now with words like 'mistress' and 'slut', and make my way to Wendy's side.

'You okay?' I ask her that a lot, I'm starting to realise.

She starts, as if stunned that anyone would speak to her, looks at me. 'Oh, it's you.'

'It's me. Look, I'm sorry about what happened before. I . . . I really had thought I'd told you.'

She stares for a moment, then shrugs. 'Don't matter. It's done now.' She falls silent, then, 'You heard that, I suppose?'

I weigh up my answers, briefly consider lying. 'Yes. You and Morris were . . .'

She doesn't look at me, just nods.

'And Toby?'

'Yes. Toby's his son.'

It had taken less than a day for Del to call me back. 'No good, Charlie. The boy's got an alibi.'

'You're shitting me?'

'Nope, good one, too.'

'What's that?'

'He got arrested for drunk and disorderly on the Kingsway. Spent the night in the cells. No way it could have been him.'

'Thing is,' Wendy goes on, 'what people around here don't understand: Morris and me, we go way back. Long before him and Sian. He was . . .' Her head drops. 'He was my first. I was his. Then Sian came along and, well, he dumped me, see. Left me for her. Only you could tell he was never really happy. Not properly, like. So we just kind of carried on. After they got married even. I just couldn't . . . I never could seem to let him go, see. Then, of course, I got pregnant.' She looks down at her hands. 'I thought he'd leave her then. I really did. Not that I did it on purpose, mind, cos I didn't. But once it happened, I thought it would change things – you know, that we'd be a family.'

'But that didn't happen.'

'No. He talked about it. Especially when Toby was born. But you know how it is, time passes and nothing changes and, well, you just get on with it, don't you?'

'Did Sian know?'

Tears spill down Wendy's cheeks. 'I don't know. I think . . . I think maybe she did. The thing is . . . you think that it's a secret. That it's just between the two of you. But people see things, even when you think they don't. People around here – most of them seem to have figured it out. They don't like me. They don't like what I've done. What Morris has done. They don't say anything to my face, but I can see it when they look at me, and I hear things, them talking when they think I'm not around. "That hussy in number nine." That's what they call me. And Sian . . . I don't know. Over the last couple of years things have changed between us. She's started to be odd. Distant, you know? I mean, I know this sounds weird, but we used to get on. We were, well, friends almost.'

'But you think she suspected?'

'I think so. Just things she said. Nothing obvious, like, but sometimes I would catch her looking at me and I would think: you know, don't you? Then she started drinking at the barbecue, and I mean, she drank a lot – more than I'd ever seen her have before – and she started picking, you know, having a go at Morris. You see,' Wendy says, 'he was going to leave Sian. And he meant it this time, he really did. He was miserable. He told me that. He wanted out, wanted to be with me, with Toby. We were going to get away from here, the three of us. He said it would have to be somewhere lovely, that I deserved that. After all, I had waited so long.' Wendy turns away then, stares out over the sea of candles, starlight in a darkened sky. 'I know what you're thinking about me. I know how it looks. But the thing is, you've got to understand, I loved him. I always have.'

Her face crumples, the weight of her loss hitting her afresh, and she leans forward, tears glassy on her cheeks. I feel useless. Worse than useless. Standing beside this woman and thinking that, even though the life she has settled for has been a half-life at best, still it was hers and, no matter what I thought or what anyone else would think, she loved Morris. And now he is dead.

I look out across the darkened street, try to count the candles. It is an impossible job. There are far too many. Then, as my courage rises and my gaze jolts back to Wendy, I notice something in the candlelight. The necklace. It has slipped forward, so that it rests now just above the zip of her inadequate fleece. From the end of it hangs a band – a gold circle, wide and scuffed.

And I think back to my conversation with Del. 'Yeah, I thought that Toby was looking like a goer, too. I don't know.' Del sighed heavily. 'Starting to look more and more like it was Morris. Neighbours all say they'd been rowing that night, that things had been shaky with them for a while. And if Sian knew about his other woman . . . things could have got out of hand. It's just . . .'

'What?'

'No, well, the only thing that's weird – Morris's wedding ring. He always wore it. It's in every picture we can find of him; friends, neighbours, they all say he had it on at the barbecue . . .'

'And?'

'Well, it's missing. No sign of it anywhere.'

My heartbeat quickens. I stare at Wendy. From across the crowd I hear a tinny cough as someone fires up a microphone, voices dropping away, heads turning towards the sound. But I don't turn. I can't, because all I can see is the wedding ring that Wendy wears around her neck.

She looks at me, dabs at the tears with a handkerchief. Then she gives me a little smile. 'Thing is – what I keep telling myself is – he probably wouldn't have left her anyway. I mean, he'd said that about a thousand times before. And there's only so much you can put up with. Isn't there?' She turns then, towards the sound of the microphone, and her voice drops so low I can barely hear it. 'They said he was stabbed in the heart.' Her hand moves, grips the chain around her neck and, in a swift movement, tucks it back inside her jacket. 'I know what that feels like.'

DISCARDS

Faye Kellerman

Faye Kellerman published the first novel in her Peter Decker and Rina Lazarus series, the Macavity Award-winning *The Ritual Bath*, in 1986. Kellerman trained as a dentist before becoming a bestselling author of mystery thrillers. She lives with her husband, the bestseller Jonathan Kellerman, in California and New Mexico, USA.

Because he'd hung around long enough, Malibu Mike wasn't considered a bum but a fixture. All of us locals had known him, had accustomed ourselves to his stale smell, his impromptu orations and wild hand gesticulations. Malibu preaching from his spot—a bus bench next to a garbage bin, perfect for foraging. With a man that weatherbeaten, it had been hard to assign him an age, but the police had estimated he'd been between seventy and ninety when he died—a decent stay on the planet.

Originally they'd thought Malibu had died from exposure. The winter has been a chilly one, a new arctic front eating through the god-awful myth that Southern California is bathed in continual sunshine. Winds churned the tides gray-green, charcoal clouds blanketed the shoreline. The night before last had been cruel. But Malibu had been protected under layers and layers of clothing—a barrier that kept his body insulated from the low of forty degrees.

Malibu had always dressed in layers even when the mercury grazed the hundred-degree mark. That fact was driven home when the obituary in the Malibu *Crier* announced his weight as 126. I'd always thought of him as chunky, but now I realized it had been the clothes.

I put down the newspaper and turned up the knob on my kerosene heater. Rubbing my hands together, I looked out the window of my trailer. Although it was gray, rain wasn't part of the forecast and that was good. My roof was still pocked with leaks that I was planning to fix today. But then the phone rang. I didn't recognize the woman's voice on the other end, but she must have heard about me from someone I knew a long time ago. She asked for *Detective* Darling.

"Former detective," I corrected her. "This is Andrea Darling. Who am I talking to?"

A throat cleared. She sounded in the range of middle-aged to elderly. "Well, you don't know me personally. I am a friend of Greta Berstat."

A pause allowing me to acknowledge recognition. She was going to wait a long time.

"Greta Berstat," she repeated. "You were the detective on her burglary? You found the men who had taken her sterling flatware and the candlesticks and the tea set?"

The bell went off and I remembered Greta Berstat. When I'd been with LAPD, my primary detail was grand theft auto. Greta's case had come my way during a brief rotation through burglary.

"Greta gave you my phone number?" I inquired.

"Not exactly," the woman explained. "You see, I'm a local resident and I found your name in the Malibu Directory—the one put out by the Chamber of Commerce? You were listed under Investigation right between Interior Design and Jewelers."

I laughed to myself. "What can I do for you, Ms. . . . ."

"Mrs. Pollack," the woman answered. "Deirdre Pollack. Greta was over at my house when I was looking through the phone book. When she saw your name, her eyes grew wide and my-oh-my did she sing your praises, Detective Darling."

I didn't correct her this time. "Glad to have made a fan. How can I help you, Mrs. Pollack?"

"Deirdre, please."

"Deirdre it is. What's up?"

Deirdre hemmed and hawed. Finally, she said, "Well, I have a little bit of a problem."

I said, "Does this problem have a story behind it?"

"I'm afraid it does."

"Perhaps it would be best if we met in person?"

"Yes, perhaps it would be best."

"Give me your address," I said. "If you're local, I can probably make it down within the hour."

"An hour?" Deirdre said. "Well, that would be simply lovely!"

From Deirdre's living room I had a one-eighty-degree view of the coastline. The tides ripped relentlessly away at the rocks ninety feet below. You could hear the surf even this far up, the steady whoosh of water advancing and retreating. Deirdre's estate took up three landscaped acres, but the house, instead of being centered on the property, was perched on the edge of the bluff. She'd furnished the place warmly—plants and overstuffed chairs and lots of maritime knick-knacks.

I settled into a chintz wing chair; Deirdre was positioned opposite me on a loveseat. She insisted on making me a cup of coffee, and while she did I took a moment to observe her.

She must have been in her late seventies, her face scored with hundreds of wrinkles. She was short with a loose turkey wattle under her chin, her cheeks were heavily rouged, her thin lips painted bright red. She had flaming red hair and false eyelashes that hooded blue eyes turned milky from cataracts. She had a tentative manner, yet her voice was firm and pleasant. Her smile seemed genuine even if her teeth weren't. She wore a pink suit, a white blouse, and orthopedic shoes.

"You're a lot younger than I expected," Deirdre said, handing me a china cup.

I smiled and sipped. I'm thirty-eight and have been told I look a lot younger.

But to a woman Deirdre's age, thirty-eight still could be younger than expected.

"Are you married, Detective?" Deirdre asked.

"Not at the moment." I smiled.

"I was married for forty-seven years." Deirdre sighed. "Mr. Pollack passed away six years ago. I miss him."

"I'm sure you do." I put my cup down. "Children?"

"Two. A boy and a girl. Both are doing well. They visit quite often."

"That's nice," I said. "So . . . you live by yourself."

"Well, yes and no," she answered. "I sleep alone but I have daily help. One woman for weekdays, another for weekends."

I looked around the house. We seemed to be alone and it was ten o'clock Tuesday morning. "Your helper didn't show up today?"

"That's the little problem I wanted to tell you about."

I took out my notebook and pen. "We can start now if you're ready."

"Well, the story involves my helper," Deirdre said. "My housekeeper. Martina Cruz . . . that's her name."

I wrote down the name.

"Martina's worked for me for twelve years," Deirdre said. "I've become quite dependent on her. Not just to give me pills and clean up the house. But we've become good friends. Twelve years is a long time to work for someone."

I agreed, thinking: twelve years was a long time to do anything.

Deirdre went on. "Martina lives far away from Malibu, far away from me. But she has never missed a day in all those years without calling me first. Martina is very responsible. I respect her and trust her. That's why I'm puzzled even though Greta thinks I'm being naïve. Maybe I am being naïve, but I'd rather think better of people than to be so cynical."

"Do you think something happened to her?" I said.

"I'm not sure." Deirdre bit her lip. "I'll relate the story and maybe you can offer a suggestion."

I told her to take her time.

Deirdre said. "Well, like many old women, I've acquired things over the years. I tell my children to take whatever they want but there always seem to be leftover items. Discards. Old flower pots, used cookware, out-of-date clothing and shoes and hats. My children don't want those kinds of things. So if I find something I no longer need, I usually give it to Martina.

"Last week, I was cleaning out my closets. Martina was helping me." She sighed. "I gave her a pile of old clothes to take home. I remember it well because I asked her how in the world she'd be able to carry all those items on the bus. She just laughed. And oh, how she thanked me. Such a sweet girl . . . twelve years she worked for me."

I nodded, pen poised at my pad.

"I feel so silly about this," Deirdre said. "One of the robes I gave her . . . it was Mr. Pollack's old robe, actually. I threw out most of his things after he died. It was hard for me to look at them. I couldn't imagine why I had kept his shredded old robe."

She looked down at her lap.

"Not more than fifteen minutes after Martina left, I realized why I hadn't given the robe away. I kept my diamond ring in one of the pockets. I have three different diamond rings—two of which I keep in a vault. But it's ridiculous to have rings and always keep them in a vault. So this one—the smallest of the three—I kept at home, wrapped in an old sock and placed in the left pocket of Mr. Pollack's robe. I hadn't worn any of my rings in ages, and being old, I guess it simply slipped my mind.

"I waited until Martina arrived home and phoned her just as she walked through her door. I told her what I had done and she looked in the pockets of the robe and announced she had the ring. I was *thrilled*—delighted that nothing had happened to it. But I was also extremely pleased by Martina's honesty. She said she would return the ring to me on Monday. I realize now that I should have called my son and asked him to pick it up right at that moment, but I didn't want to insult her."

"I understand."

"Do you?" Deirdre said, grabbing my hand. "Do you think I'm foolish for trusting someone who has worked for me for twelve years?"

Wonderfully foolish. "You didn't want to insult her," I said, using her words.

"Exactly," Deirdre answered. "By now you must have figured out the problem. It is now Tuesday. I still don't have my diamond and I can't get hold of Martina."

"Is her phone disconnected?" I asked.

"No. It just rings and rings and no one answers it."

"Why don't you just send your son down now?"

"Because . . ." She sighed. "Because I don't want him to think of his mother as an old fool. Can you go down for me? I'll pay you for your time. I can afford it."

I shrugged. "Sure."

"Wonderful!" Deirdre exclaimed. "Oh, thank you so much."

I gave her my rates and they were fine with her. She handed me a piece of paper inked with Martina's name, address, and phone number. I didn't know the exact location of the house, but I knew the area. I thanked her for the information, then said, "Deirdre, if it looks like Martina took off with the ring, would you like me to inform the police for you?"

"No!" she said adamantly.

"Why not?" I asked.

"Even if Martina took the ring, I wouldn't want to see her in jail. We have too many years together for me to do that."

"You can be my boss anytime," I said.

"Why?" Deirdre asked. "Do you do housekeeping too?"

I informed her that I was a terrible housekeeper. As I left, she looked both grateful and confused.

Martina Cruz lived on Highland Avenue south of Washington—a street lined by small houses tattooed with graffiti. The address on the paper was a wood-sided white bungalow with a tar paper roof. The front lawn—mowed but devoid of shrubs—was bisected by a cracked red plaster walkway. There was a two-step hop onto a porch whose decking was wet and rotted. The screen door was locked, but a head-size hole had been cut through the mesh. I knocked through the hole but no one answered. I turned the knob and, to my surprise, the door yielded, screen and all.

I called out a "hello," and when no one answered, I walked into the living room—an eight-by-ten rectangle filled with hand-me-down furnishings. The sofa fabric, once gold, had faded to dull mustard. Two mismatched chairs were positioned opposite it. There was a scarred dining table off the living room, its centerpiece a black-and-white TV with rabbit ears. Encircling the table were six folding chairs. The kitchen was tiny, but the counters were clean, the food in the refrigerator still fresh. The trash hadn't been taken out in a while. It was brimming over with Corona beer bottles.

I went into the sole bedroom. A full-size mattress lay on the floor. No closets. Clothing was neatly arranged in boxes—some filled with little-girl garments, others stuffed with adult apparel. I quickly sifted through the piles, trying to find Mr. Pollack's robe.

I didn't find it—no surprise. Picking up a corner of the mattress, I peered underneath but didn't see anything. I poked around a little longer, then checked out the backyard—a dirt lot holding a rusted swing set and some deflated rubber balls.

I went around to the front and decided to question the neighbors. The house on the immediate left was occupied by a diminutive, thickset Latina matron. She was dressed in a floral print muumuu and her hair was tied in a bun. I asked her if she'd seen Martina lately, and she pretended not to understand me. My Spanish, though far from perfect, was understandable, so it seemed as if we had a little communication gap. Nothing that couldn't be overcome by a ten-dollar bill.

After I gave her the money, the woman informed me her name was Alicia and she hadn't seen Martina, Martina's husband, or their two little girls for a few days. But the lights had been on last night, loud music booming out of the windows.

"Does Martina have any relatives?" I asked Alicia in Spanish.

"*Ella tiene una hermana pero no sé a donde vive.*"

Martina had a sister but Alicia didn't know where she lived. Probing further, I found out the sister's name—Yolanda Flores. And I also learned that the little girls went to a small parochial school run by the *Iglesia Evangélica* near Western Avenue. I knew the church she was talking about.

Most people think of Hispanics as always being Catholic. But I knew from past work that Evangelical Christianity had taken a strong foothold in Central and South America. Maybe I could locate Martina or the sister, Yolanda, through the church directory. I thanked Alicia and went on my way.

The Pentecostal Church of Christ sat on a quiet avenue—an aqua-blue stucco building that looked more like an apartment complex than a house of worship. About twenty-five primary-grade children were playing in an outdoor parking lot, the perimeters defined by a cyclone fence. The kids wore green-and-red uniforms and looked like moving Christmas tree ornaments.

I went through the gate, dodging racing children, and walked into the main sanctuary. The chapel wasn't large—around twenty by thirty—but the high ceiling made it feel spacious. There were three distinct seating areas—the Pentecostal triad: married women on the right, married men on the left, and mixed young singles in the middle. The pews faced a stage that held a thronelike chair upholstered in red velvet. In front of the throne was a lectern sandwiched between two giant urns sprouting plastic flowers. Off to the side were several electric guitars and a drum set, the name *Revelación* taped on the bass drum. I heard footsteps from behind and turned around.

The man looked to be in his early thirties with thick dark straight hair and bright green eyes. His face held a hint of Aztec warrior—broad nose, strong cheekbones and chin. Dressed in casual clothing, he was tall and muscular, and I was acutely aware of his male presence. I asked him where I might find the pastor and was surprised when he announced that he was the very person.

I'd expected someone older.

I stated my business, his eyes never leaving mine as I spoke. When I finished, he stared at me for a long time before telling me his name—Pastor Alfredo Gomez. His English was unaccented.

"Martina's a good girl," Gomez said. "She would never take anything that didn't belong to her. Some problem probably came up. I'm sure everything will work out and your *patrona* will get her ring back."

"What kind of problem?"

The pastor shrugged.

"Immigration problems?" I probed.

Another shrug.

"You don't seem concerned by her disappearance."

He gave me a cryptic smile.

"Can you tell me one thing?" I asked. "Are her children safe?"

"I believe they're in school," Gomez said.

"Oh." I brightened. "Did Martina bring them in?"

"No." Gomez frowned. "No, she didn't. Her sister brought them in today. But that's not unusual."

"You haven't seen Martina today?"

Gomez shook his head. I thought he was telling me the truth, but maybe he wasn't. Maybe the woman was hiding from the INS. Still, after twelve years, you'd think she'd have applied for amnesty. And then there was the obvious alternative. Martina had taken the ring and was hiding out somewhere.

"Do you have Martina's husband's work number? I'd like to talk with him."

"José works construction," Gomez said. "I have no idea what crew he's on or where he is."

"What about Martina's sister, Yolanda Flores?" I said. "Do you have her phone number?"

The pastor paused.

"I'm not from the INS." I fished around inside my wallet and came up with my private investigator's license.

He glanced at it. "This doesn't mean anything."

"Yeah, that's true." I put my ID back in my purse. "Just trying to gain some trust. Look, Pastor, my client is really worried about Martina. She doesn't give a hoot about the ring. She specifically told me *not* to call the police even if Martina took the ring—"

Gomez stiffened and said, "Martina wouldn't do that."

"Okay. Then help us both out, Pastor. Martina might be in some real trouble. Maybe her sister knows something."

Silently, Gomez weighed the pros and cons of trusting me. I must have looked sincere because he told me to wait a moment, then came back with Yolanda's work number.

"You won't regret this," I assured him.

"I hope I don't," Gomez said.

I thanked him again, taking a final gander at those beautiful green eyes before I slipped out the door.

I found a pay booth around the corner, slipped a quarter in the slot, and waited. An accented voice whispered hello.

Using my workable Spanish, I asked for Yolanda Flores. Speaking English, the woman informed me that she was Yolanda. In the background I heard the wail of a baby.

"I'm sorry if this is a bad time," I apologized. "I'm looking for your sister."

There was a long pause at the other end of the line.

Quickly, I said, "I'm not from *inmigración*. I was hired by Mrs. Deirdre Pollack to find Martina and was given your work number by Pastor Gomez. Martina hasn't shown up for work in two days and Mrs. Pollack is worried about her."

More silence. If I hadn't heard the same baby crying, I would have thought she'd hung up the phone.

"You work for Missy Deirdre?" Yolanda asked.

"Yes," I said. "She's very worried about your sister. Martina hasn't shown up for work. Is your sister okay?"

Yolanda's voice cracked. "Es no good. Monday *en la tarde*, Martina husband call me. He tell me she don' work for Missy Deirdre and she have new job. He tell me to pick up her girls 'cause Martina work late. So I pick up the girls from the school and take them with me.

"Later, I try to call her, she's not *home*. I call and call but no one answers. I don' talk to José, I don' talk to no one. I take the girls to school this morning. Then José, he call me again."

"When?"

"About two hour. He ask me to take girls. I say jes, but where is Martina? He tell me she has to sleep in the house where she work. I don' believe him."

It was my turn not to answer right away. Yolanda must have been bouncing the baby or something because the squalling had stopped.

"You took the children yesterday?" I asked.

"I take her children, jes. I no mind takin' the kids but I want to talk to Martina. And José . . . he don' give me the new work number. I call Martina's house, no one answer. I goin' to call Missy Deirdre and ask if Martina don' work there no more. *Ahorita*, you tell me Missy Deirdre call *you*. I . . . scared."

"Yolanda, where can I find José?"

"He works *construcción*. I don' know where. Mebbe he goes home after work and don' answer the phone. You can go to Martina's house tonight?"

"Yes, I'll do that," I said. "I'll give you my phone number, you give me yours.

If you find out anything, call me. If I find out something, I'll call you. Okay?"

"Okay."

We exchanged numbers, then said good-bye. My next call was to Deirdre Pollack. I told her about my conversation with Yolanda. Deirdre was sure that Martina hadn't taken a new job. First of all, Martina would never just leave her flat. Secondly, Martina would never leave her children to work as a sleep-in housekeeper.

I wasn't so sure. Maybe Martina had fled with the ring and was lying low in some private home. But I kept my thoughts private and told Deirdre my intention to check out Martina's house tonight. She told me to be careful. I thanked her and said I'd watch my step.

At night, Martina's neighborhood was the mean streets, the sidewalks supporting pimps and prostitutes, pushers and buyers. Every half hour or so, the homeboys cruised by in souped-up low riders, their ghetto blasters pumping out body-rattling bass vibrations. I was glad I had my Colt .38 with me, but at the same time I wished it were a Browning Pump.

I sat in my truck, waiting for some sign of life at Martina's place, and my patience was rewarded two hours later. A Ford pickup parked in front of the framed house, and out came four dark-complexioned males dressed nearly identically: jeans, dark windbreakers zipped up to the neck, and hats. Three of them wore ratty baseball caps; the biggest and fattest wore a bright white painter's cap. Big-and-Fat was shouting and singing. I couldn't understand his Spanish—his speech was too rapid for my ear—but the words I could pick up seemed slurred. The other three men were holding six-packs of beer. From the way all of them acted, the six-packs were not their first of the evening.

They went inside. I slipped my gun into my purse and got out of my truck, walking up to the door. I knocked. My luck: Big-and-Fat answered. Up close he was nutmeg-brown with fleshy cheeks and thick lips. His teeth were rotten and he smelled of sweat and beer.

"I'm looking for Martina Cruz," I said in Spanish.

Big-and-Fat stared at me—at my *Anglo* face. He told me in English that she wasn't home.

"Can I speak to José?"

"He's no home, too."

"I saw him come in." It wasn't really a lie, more of an educated guess. Maybe one of the four men was José.

Big-and-Fat stared at me, then broke into a contemptuous grin. "I say he no home."

I heard Spanish in the background, a male voice calling out the name José. I peered around Big-and-Fat's shoulders, trying to peek inside, but he stepped forward, making me back up. His expression was becoming increasingly hostile, and I always make it a point not to provoke drunk men who outweigh me.

"I'm going," I announced with a smile.

"Pasqual," someone said. A thinner version of Big-and-Fat stepped onto the porch. "Pasqual, *qué pasó?*"

Opportunity knocked. I took advantage.

"I'm looking for José Cruz," I said as I kept walking backward. "I've been hired to look for Martin—"

The thinner man blanched.

"Go away!" Pasqual thundered out. "Go or I kill you!"

I didn't stick around to see if he'd make good on his threat.

The morning paper stated that Malibu Mike, having expired from natural causes, was still in deep freeze, waiting for a relative to claim his body. He'd died buried under tiers of clothing, his feet wrapped in three pairs of socks stuffed into size twelve mismatched shoes. Two pairs of gloves had covered his hands, and three scarves had been wrapped around his neck. A Dodgers' cap was perched atop a ski hat that cradled Malibu's head. In all those layers, there was not one single piece of ID to let us know who he really was. After all these years, I thought he deserved a decent burial, and I guess I wasn't the only one who felt that way. The locals were taking up a collection to have him cremated. Maybe a small service, too—a few words of remembrance, then his ashes would be mixed with the tides.

I thought Malibu might have liked that. I took a twenty from my wallet and began to search the trailer for a clean envelope and a stamp. I found what I was looking for and was addressing the envelope when Yolanda Flores called me.

"Dey find her," she said, choking back sobs. "She *dead*. The police find her in a trash can. She beat to death. Es *horrible*!"

"Yolanda, I'm so sorry." I really was. "I wish I could do something for you."

"You wan' do somethin' for me?" Yolanda said. "You find out what happen to my sister."

Generally I like to be paid for my services, but my mind flashed to little dresses in cardboard boxes. I knew what it was like to live without a mother. Besides, I was still fuming over last night's encounter with Pasqual.

"I'll look into it for you," I said.

There was a silence across the line.

"Yolanda?"

"I still here," she said. "I . . . surprise you help me."

"No problem."

"Thank you." She started to cry. "Thank you very much. I pay you—"

"Forget it."

"No, I work for you on weekends—"

"Yolanda, I live in a trailer and couldn't find anything if you cleaned up my place. Forget about paying me. Let's get back to your sister. Tell me about José. Martina and him get along?"

There was a very long pause. Yolanda finally said, "José no good. He and his brothers."

"Is Pasqual one of José's brothers?"

"How you know?"

I told her about my visit with Pasqual the night before, about Big-and-Fat's threat. "Has he ever killed anyone before?"

"I don' know. He drink and fight. I don' know if he kill anyone when he's drunk."

"Did you ever see Pasqual beating Martina?"

"No," Yolanda said. "I never see that."

"What about José?"

Another moment of silence.

Yolanda said, "He slap her mebbe one or two time. I tell her to leave him but she say no 'cause of the girls."

"Do you think José could kill Martina?"

Yolanda said, "He slap her when he drink. But I don' think he would kill her to kill her."

"He wouldn't do it on purpose."

"Essackly."

"Yolanda, would José kill Martina for money?"

"No," she said firmly. "He's *Evangélico*. A bad *Evangélico*, but not *el diablo*."

"He wouldn't do it for *lots* of money?"

"No, he don' kill her for money."

I said, "What about Pasqual?"

"I don' think so."

"Martina have any *enemigos*?"

"*Nunca persona!*" Yolanda said. "No one want to hurt her. She like sugar. Es so *terrible*!"

She began to cry. I didn't want to question her over the phone. A face-to-face meeting would be better. I asked her when was the funeral service.

"Tonight. *En la iglesia a las ocho.* After the *culto funeral,* we go to *cementerio.* You wan' come?"

"Yes, I think that might be best." I told her I knew the address of the church and would meet her eight o'clock sharp.

I was unnerved by what I had to do next: break the bad news to Deirdre Pollack. The old woman took it relatively well, never even asked about the ring. When I told her I'd volunteered to look into Martina's death, she offered to pay me. I told her that wasn't necessary, but when she insisted, I didn't refuse.

I got to the church by eight, then realized I didn't know Yolanda from Adam. But she picked me out in a snap. Not a plethora of five-foot-eight, blond, blue-eyed Salvadoran women.

Yolanda was petite, barely five feet and maybe ninety pounds tops. She had yards of long brown hair—Evangelical women don't cut their tresses—and big brown eyes moistened with tears. She took my hand, squeezed it tightly, and thanked me for coming.

The church was filled to capacity, the masses adding warmth to the unheated chapel. In front of the stage was a table laden with broth, hot chocolate, and plates of bread. Yolanda asked me if I wanted anything to eat and I declined.

We sat in the first row of the married women's section. I glanced at the men's area and noticed Pasqual with his cronies. I asked Yolanda to point out José: the man who had come to the door with Pasqual. The other two men were also brothers. José's eyes were swollen and bright red. Crying or post-alcohol intoxication?

I studied him further. He'd been stuffed into an ill-fitting black suit, his dark hair slicked back with grease. All the brothers wore dark suits. José looked nervous, but the others seemed almost jocular.

Pasqual caught me staring, and his expression immediately darkened, his eyes bearing down on me. I felt needles down my spine as he began to rise, but luckily the service started and he sank back into his seat.

Pastor Gomez came to the dais and spoke about what a wonderful wife and mother Martina had been. As he talked, the women around me began to let out soft, muted sobs. I did manage to sneak a couple of sidelong glances at the brothers. I met up with Pasqual's dark stare once again.

When the pastor had finished speaking, he gave the audience directions to the cemetery. Pasqual hadn't forgotten about my presence, but I was too quick for him, making a beeline for the pastor. I managed to snare Gomez before Pasqual could get to me. The fat slob backed off when the pastor pulled me into a corner.

"What happened?" I asked.

Gomez looked down. "I wish I knew."

"Do the police—?"

"Police!" The pastor spat. "They don't care about a dead Hispanic girl. One less flea in their country. I was wearing my work clothes when I got the call this morning. I'd been doing some plumbing and I guess they thought I was a wet-back who didn't understand English." His eyes held pain. "They joked about her. They said it was a shame to let such a wonderful body go to waste!"

"That stinks."

"Yes, it stinks." Gomez shook his head. "So you see I don't expect much from the police."

"I'm looking into her death."

Gomez stared at me. "Who's paying you to do it?"

"Not Yolanda," I said.

"Martina's *patrona*. She wants her ring."

"I think she wants justice for Martina."

The pastor blushed from embarrassment.

I said, "I would have done it gratis. I've got some suspicions." I filled him in on my encounter with Pasqual.

Gomez thought a moment. "Pasqual drinks even though the church forbids alcohol. Pasqual's not a bad person. Maybe you made him feel threatened."

"Maybe I did."

"I'll talk to him," Gomez said. "Calm him down. But I don't think you should come to the *cementerio* with us. Now's not the time for accusations."

I agreed. He excused himself as another parishioner approached and suddenly I was alone. Luckily, Pasqual had gone somewhere else. I met up with Yolanda, explaining my reason for not going to the cemetery. She understood.

We walked out to the school yard, into a cold misty night. José and his brothers had already taken off their ties and replaced their suit jackets with warmer windbreakers. Pasqual took a deep swig from a bottle inside a paper bag, then passed the bag to one of his brothers.

"Look at them!" Yolanda said with disgust. "They no even wait till after the funeral. They nothing but *cholos*. Es terrible!"

I glanced at José and his brothers. Something was bothering me and it took a minute or two before it came to me. Three of them—including José—were wearing old baseball caps. Pasqual was the only one wearing a painter's cap.

I don't know why, but I found that odd. Then something familiar began to come up from the subconscious, and I knew I'd better start phoning up bus drivers. From behind me came a gentle tap on my shoulder. I turned around.

Pastor Gomez said, "Thank you for coming, Ms. Darling."

I nodded. "I'm sorry I never met Martina. From what I've heard, she seemed to be a good person."

"She was." Gomez bowed his head. "I appreciate your help and I wish you peace."

Then he turned and walked away. I'd probably never see him again and I felt a little bad about that.

I tailed José the next morning. He and his brothers were part of a crew framing a house in the Hollywood Hills. I kept watch from a quarter block away, my truck partly hidden by the overhanging boughs of a eucalyptus. I was trying to figure out how to get José alone, and then I got a big break. The roach wagon pulled in and José was elected by his brothers to pick up lunch.

I got out of my truck, intercepted him as he carried an armful of burritos, and stuck my .38 in his side, telling him if he said a word, I'd pull the trigger. My Spanish must have been very clear, because he was as mute as Dopey.

After I got him into the cabin of my truck, I took the gun out of his ribs and held it in my lap.

I said, "What happened to Martina?"

"I don' know."

"You're lying," I said. "You killed her."

"I don' kill her!" José was shaking hard. "*Yo juro!* I don' kill her!"

"Who did?"

"I don' know!"

"You killed her for the ring, didn't you, José?" As I spoke, I saw him shrink. "Martina would never tell you she had the ring: she knew you would *take* it from her. But *you* must have found out. You asked her about the ring and she said she didn't have any ring, right?"

José didn't answer.

I repeated the accusation in *español*, but he still didn't respond. I went on.

"You didn't know what to do, did you, José? So you waited and waited and finally, Monday morning, you told your brothers about the ring. But by *that* time, Martina and the ring had already taken the bus to work."

"All we wan' do is talk to her!" José insisted. "Nothin' was suppose to happen."

"What wasn't supposed to happen?" I asked.

José opened his mouth, then shut it again.

I continued. "Pasqual has a truck—a Ford pickup." I read him the license number. "You and your brothers decided to meet up with her. A truck can go a lot faster than a bus. When the bus made a stop, two of you got on it and made Martina get off."

José shook his head.

"I called the bus company," I said. "The driver remembered you and your brother—two men making this woman carrying a big bag get off at the stop behind the big garbage bin. The driver even asked if she was okay. But Martina didn't want to get you in trouble and said todo *está bien*—everything was fine. But everything wasn't fine, was it?"

Tears welled up in José's eyes.

"You tried to force her in the truck, but she fought, didn't she?"

José remained mute.

"But you did get her in Pasqual's truck," I said. "Only you forgot something. When she fought, she must have knocked off Pasqual's Dodgers' cap. He didn't know it was gone until later, did he?"

José jerked his head up. "How you know?"

"How do I know? I *have* that cap, José." Not exactly true, but close enough. "Now, why don't you tell me what happened?"

José thought a long time. Then he said, "It was assident. Pasqual no mean to hurt her bad. Just get her to talk. She no have ring when we take her off the bus."

"Not in her bag—*su bolsa?*"

"*Ella no tiena niuna bolsa.* She no have bags. She tell us she left ring at home. So we took her home, but she don' fin' the ring. That make me mad. I *saw* her with ring. No good for a wife to *lie* to husband." His eyes filled with rage, his nostrils flared. "No good! A wife must always tell husband the truth!"

"So you killed her," I said.

José said, "Pasqual . . . he did it. It was assident!"

I shook my head in disgust. I sat there in my truck, off guard and full of indignation. I didn't even hear him until it was too late. The driver's door jerked open and the gun flew out of my lap. I felt as if I'd been wrenched from my mother's bosom. Pasqual dragged me to the ground, his face looming over me, his complexion florid and furious. He drew back his fist and aimed it at my jaw.

I rolled my head to one side and his hand hit the ground. Pasqual yelled but not as loud as José did, shouting at his brother to *stop*. Then I heard the click of the hammer. Pasqual heard it too and released me immediately. By now, a crowd had gathered. Gun in hand, José looked at me, seemed to speak English for my benefit.

"You kill Martina!" José screamed out to Pasqual. "I'm going to kill you!"

Pasqual looked genuinely confused. He spoke in Spanish. "*You* killed her, you little shit! You beat her to death when we couldn't find the ring!"

José looked at me, his expression saying: do you understand this? Something in my eye must have told him I did. I told him to put the gun down. Instead, he turned his back on me and focused his eyes on Pasqual. "You lie. You get drunk, you kill Martina!"

In Spanish, Pasqual said, "I tried to stop you, you *asshole*!"

"You lie!" José said. And then he pulled the trigger.

I charged him before he could squeeze another bullet out of the chamber, but the damage had been done. Pasqual was already dead when the sirens pulled up.

The two other brothers backed José's story. They'd come to confront Martina about the ring. She told them she had left it at home. But when they returned to the house and the ring wasn't around, Pasqual, in his drunken rage, beat Martina to death and dumped her body in the trash.

José will be charged with second degree murder for Pasqual, and maybe a good lawyer'll be able to bargain it down to manslaughter. But I remembered a murderous look in José's eyes after he'd stated that Martina had lied to him. If I were the prosecutor, I'd be going after José with charges of manslaughter on Martina, Murder One on Pasqual. But that's not how the system works. Anyway, my verdict—rightly or wrongly—wouldn't bring Martina back to life.

I called Mrs. Pollack after it was all over. Through her tears, she wished she'd never remembered the ring. It wasn't her fault but she still felt responsible. There was a small consolation. I was pretty sure I knew where the ring was.

I'm not too bad at guesses—like the one about Pasqual losing his hat in a struggle. That simple snapshot in my mind of the brothers at the church—three with beat-up Dodgers' caps, the fourth wearing a *new* painter's cap. Something off kilter.

So my hunch had been correct. Pasqual had once owned a Dodgers' cap. Where had it gone? Same place as Mr. Pollack's robe. Martina had packed the robe in her bag Monday morning. When she was forced off the bus by José and his brothers, I pictured her quickly dumping the bag in a garbage bin at the bus stop, hoping to retrieve it later. She never got that chance.

As for the ring, it was right where I thought it would be: among the discards that had shrouded Malibu Mike the night he died. The Dodgers' cap on Malibu's head got me thinking in the right direction. If Malibu *had* found Pasqual's cap, maybe he found the other bag left behind by Martina. After all, that bin had been his spot.

Good old Malibu. One of his layers had been a grimy old robe. Wedged into the corner of its pocket, a diamond ring. Had Malibu not died that Monday, José might have been a free man today.

Mrs. Pollack didn't feel right about keeping the ring, so she offered it to Yolanda Flores. Yolanda was appreciative of such generosity, but she refused the gift, saying the ring was cursed. Mrs. Pollack didn't take offense; Yolanda was a woman with pride. Finally, after a lot of consideration, Mrs. Pollack gave the ring to the burial committee for Malibu Mike. Malibu never lived wealthy, but he sure went out in high style.

A DARK TRANSACTION

Marianne Kent

Marianne Kent (1856–1942) was born in London and died in Sussex. She wrote three short stories for the *Strand* magazine in the 1890s, including 'A Dark Transaction'. Kent's writing demonstrates imagination, humour, and a grasp of atmosphere.

If I had described myself when I first started in life, it would simply have been as John Blount, commercial traveller. I was employed by a firm of merchants of very high standing, who only did business with large houses. My negotiations took me to all parts of the United Kingdom, and I enjoyed the life, which was full of change and activity. At least I enjoyed it in my early bachelor days, but while I was still quite young—not more than five-and-twenty—I fell in love and married; and then I found that my roving existence was certainly a drawback to domestic happiness. My wife, Mary, was a bright little creature, always ready to make the best of things, but even she would declare pathetically that she might as well have married a sailor as a landsman who was so seldom at home! Still, as I said, she was one to put a bright face on things, and she and my sister made their home together.

It was in the second year after my marriage, when I had been away on my travels for some weeks, that I heard from my sister that a fever had broken out in the neighbourhood of our home, and that Mary was down with it. Kitty wrote hopefully, saying it was a mild attack, and she trusted by the time I was home her patient would be quite convalescent. I had unbounded faith in Kitty, so that I accepted her cheerful view of things. But, a few evenings later, after a long, tiring day, I returned to the hotel where I was then staying, and found a telegram awaiting me. My heart stood still as I saw the ominous yellow envelope, for I knew my sister would not have sent for me without urgent need. The message was to say that, although Kitty still hoped for the best, a serious change had taken place, and I should return at once.

"Don't delay an hour; come off immediately," she said.

I was not likely to delay. I paid up my reckoning at the hotel, directed that my baggage should be sent on next day, and in less than half an hour from the time I had opened the telegram I rushed, heated and breathless, into the primitive little railway station—the only one which that part of the country boasted for miles round. I gained the platform in time to see the red light on the end of the departing train as it disappeared into the mouth of the tunnel a few hundred yards down the line. For a moment I was unable to realize my ill fortune. I stood gazing stupidly before me in a bewildered way. Then the station-master, who knew me by sight, came up, saying sympathetically:—

"Just missed her, sir, by two seconds!"

"Yes," I answered briefly, beginning to understand it all now, and chafing irritably at the enforced delay. "When is the next train?"

"Six five in the morning, sir. Nothing more to-night."

"Nothing more to-night!" I almost shouted. "There must be! At any rate, there is the evening express from the junction; I have been by it scores of times!"

"Very likely, sir; but that's a through train, it don't touch here—never stops till it reaches the junction."

The man's quiet tone carried conviction with it. I was silent for a moment, and then asked when the express left the junction.

"Nine fifteen," was the answer.

"How far is the junction from this by road; could I do it in time?"

"Out of the question, sir. It would take one who knew the road the best part of three hours to drive."

I looked away to my left, where the green hill-side rose up steep and clear against the evening sky. It was one of the most mountainous quarters of England, and the tunnel that pierced the hill was a triumph of engineering skill, even in these days when science sticks at nothing. Pointing to the brick archway I said, musingly:—

"And yet, once through the tunnel, how close at hand the junction station seems."

"That's true enough, sir; the other side the tunnel it is not half a mile down the line."

"What length is it?"

"The tunnel, sir? Close upon three miles, and straight as a dart."

There was another pause, then I said, slowly:—

"Nothing more goes down the line until the express has passed?"

"Nothing more, sir."

"Anything on the up line?" was my next inquiry.

"No, sir, not for some hours, except, maybe, some trucks of goods, but I have had no notice of them yet."

As the station-master made this last answer he looked at me curiously, no doubt wondering what the object of all these questions could be; but he certainly had no notion of what was passing in my mind, or he would not have turned into his office as he did, and left me there alone upon the platform.

I was young and impetuous, and a sudden wild determination had taken possession of me. In my intense anxiety to get back to my sick wife, the delay of so many hours seemed unendurable, and my whole desire was to catch the express at the junction; but how was that to be accomplished? One way alone presented itself to me, and that was through the tunnel. At another time I should have put the notion from me as a mad impossibility, but now I clung to it as a last resource, reasoning myself out of all my fears. Where was the danger, since nothing was to come up or down the line for hours? A good level road, too, of little more than three miles, and a full hour and a half to do it in. And what would the darkness matter? There was no fear of missing the way; nothing to be done but to walk briskly forward. Yes, it could be, and I was resolved that it should be done.

I gave myself no more time for reflection. I walked to the end of the platform and stepped down upon the line, not very far from the mouth of the tunnel. As I entered the gloomy archway I wished devoutly that I had a lantern to bear me company, but it was out of the question for me to get anything of the kind at the station; as it was, I was fearful each moment that my intentions would be discovered, when I knew for a certainty that my project would be knocked on the head, and, for this reason, I was glad to leave daylight behind me and to know that I was unseen.

I walked on, at a smart pace, for fully ten minutes, trying not to think, but feeling painfully conscious that my courage was ebbing fast. Then I paused for breath. Ugh! how foul the air smelt! I told myself that it was worse even than the impenetrable darkness—and that was bad enough. I recalled to mind how I had gone through tunnels—this very one among others—in a comfortable lighted carriage, and had drawn up the window, sharply and suddenly, to keep out the stale, poisonous air; and this was the atmosphere I was to breathe for the next hour! I shuddered at the prospect. But it was not long before I was forced to acknowledge that it was the darkness quite as much as the stifling air which was affecting me. I had never been fond of the dark in my earliest days, and now it seemed as if the strange, wild fancies of my childhood were forcing themselves upon me, and I felt that, if only for an instant, I must have light of some sort; so, standing still, I took from my pocket a box of vestas, and struck one. Holding the little match carefully, cherishing it with my hand, I gazed about me. How horrible it all looked! Worse, if possible, in reality than in imagination. The outline of the damp, mildewy wall was just visible in the feeble, flickering light. On the brickwork close to me I could see a coarse kind of fungus growing, and there was the silver, slimy trace of slugs in all directions; I could fancy, too, the hundred other creeping things that were about. As the match died out, a noise among the stones near the wall caused me hastily to strike another, just in time to see a large rat whisk into its hole.

A miner, a plate-layer—in fact, anyone whose avocations took them underground—would have laughed to scorn these childish fears; but the situation was so new to me, and also I must confess that I am naturally of a nervous, imaginative turn of mind. Still, I was vexed with myself for my cowardly feelings, and started on my walk again, trying not to think of these gloomy surroundings, but drew a picture of my home, wondering how Mary was, if she was well enough to be told of my coming, and was looking out for me. Then I dwelt upon the satisfaction with which I should enter the express, at the junction, feeling that the troubles of the evening had not been in vain. After a while, when these thoughts were somewhat exhausted, and I felt my mind returning to the horrors of the present moment, I tried to look at it all from a different point of view, telling myself that it was an adventure which I should live to pride myself upon. Then I recalled to mind things I had read of subterranean passages, and naturally stories of the Catacombs presented themselves to me, and I thought how the early Christians had guided themselves through those dim corridors by means of a line or string; the fantastic notion came to me that I was in a like predicament, and the line I was to follow was the steel rail at my feet. For awhile this thought gave me courage, making me realize how straight the way was, and that I had only to go on and on until the goal was reached.

I walked for, perhaps, twenty minutes or half an hour, sometimes passing a small grating for ventilation; but they were so choked by weeds and rubbish that they gave little light and less air. Walking quickly through a dark place, one has the feeling that unseen objects are close at hand, and that at any moment you may come in sharp contact with them. It was this feeling, at least, which made me as I went along continually put out my hand as if to ward off a blow, and suddenly, while my right foot still rested on the smooth steel rail, my left hand struck against the wall of the tunnel. As my fingers grated on the rough brick a new terror took possession of me—or at least, if not a new terror, one of the fears which had haunted me at the outset rushed upon me with redoubled force.

I had faced the possibility of the station-master's having been mistaken, and of a train passing through the tunnel while I was still there, but I told myself I had only to stand close in to the wall, until the train had gone on its way; now, however, I felt, with a sinking horror at my heart, that there was little room to spare. Again and again I tested it, standing with my foot well planted on the rail and my arm outstretched until my fingers touched the bricks. There was a fascination in it—much as in the case of a timid swimmer who cannot bear to think he is out of depth and must keep putting down his foot to try for the bottom, knowing all the while he is only rendering himself more nervous. During the next ten minutes I know I worked myself into a perfect agony of mind, imagining the very worst that could happen. Suppose that the up and the down trains should cross in the tunnel, what chance should I then have? The mere thought was appalling! Retreat was impossible, for I must have come more than half way by this time, and turning back would only be going to meet the express. But surely in the thickness of the wall there must be here and there recesses? I was sure I had seen one, some little time back, when I had struck a light. This was a gleam of hope. Out came the matches once more, but my hands were so shaky that I had scarcely opened the box when it slipped from my fingers and its precious contents were scattered on the ground. This was a new trouble. I was down upon my knees at once, groping about to find them. It was a hopeless task in the dark, and, after wasting much time, I was forced to light the first one I found to look for the others, and, when that died out, I had only four in my hand, and had to leave the rest and go on my way for the time was getting short and my great desire was to find a recess which should afford me shelter in case of need. But, although I grudgingly lit one match after another and walked for some distance with my hand rubbing against the wall, I could find nothing of the kind.

At length, I don't know what time it was, or how far I had walked, I saw before me, a long, long way off, a dim speck of light. At first I thought, with a sudden rush of gladness, that it was daylight, and that the end of the tunnel was in sight; then I remembered that it was now evening and the sun had long set, so that it must be a lamp; and it was a lamp. I began to see it plainly, for it was coming nearer and nearer, and I knew that it was an approaching train. I stood still and looked at it, and it was at that instant that the whole ground beneath me seemed to be shaken. The rail upon which one of my feet was resting thrilled as if with an electric shock, sending a strange vibration through me, while a sudden rush of wind swept down the tunnel, and I knew that the express was upon me!

I shall never forget the feeling that took possession of me: it seemed as if, into that one moment, the experiences of years were crowded—recollections of my childhood—tender thoughts of my wife—dreams of the future, in which I had meant to do so much, all thronged in, thick and fast upon me. Could this be death? I gave a wild, despairing cry for help. I prayed aloud that God would not let me die. I had lost all presence of mind; no thought of standing back against the wall came to me. I rushed madly forward in a frenzy of despair. The sound of my voice, as it echoed through that dismal place, was drowned in an instant by the sharp, discordant scream of the express. On I dashed, right in front of the goods train; the yellow light of the engine shone full upon me; death was at hand. It seemed that nothing short of a miracle could save me, and, to my thinking, it was a miracle that happened.

Only a few yards from the engine and, as I struggled blindly on, a strong hand seized me with a grasp of iron, and I was dragged on one side. Even in my bewilderment I knew that I was not against the wall, but in one of those very recesses I had searched for in vain. I sank upon the ground, only half conscious, yet I saw the indistinct blur of light as the trains swept by.

I am not given to swooning, so that, after the first moment, I was quite alive to my exact situation. I knew that I was crouching on the ground, and that that iron-like grasp was still on my collar. Presently the hand relaxed its hold and a gruff, but not unkindly, voice said:—

"Well, mate, how are you?"

This inquiry unlocked my tongue, and I poured forth my gratitude. I hardly know what I said; I only know I was very much in earnest. I told him who I was and how I came to be there, and in return asked him his name.

"That does not signify," was the answer; "you can think of me as a friend."

"That I shall," I returned, gratefully; "for God knows you have been a friend in need to me!"

"Ah!" he said, musingly, "your life must be very sweet, for you seemed loath enough to part with it!"

I admitted the truth of this—indeed, I had felt it more than once during the last hour. I had been one of those who, in fits of depression, are wont to say that life is not worth living—that we shall be well out of it, and the rest; yet, when it seemed really slipping from my grasp, I had clung to it with a tenacity which surprised myself. And now, with the future once more before me, in which so much seemed possible, I was filled with gratitude to God and to my unknown friend, by whose means I had been saved. There was a short silence; then I asked, rather doubtfully, if there were not some way in which I could prove my gratitude.

"You speak as if you were sincere," my strange companion said, in his gruff, downright way; "so I will tell you frankly that you can do me a good turn if you have a mind to. I don't want your money, understand; but I want you to do me a favour."

"What is it?" I asked, eagerly; "believe me, if it is in my power it shall be done!"

"I would rather you passed your word before I explain more," he said coolly.

"Say my request shall be granted. I take it you are not a man to break your promise."

Here was a predicament! Asked to pledge my word for I knew not what! To be in the dark in more senses than one; for I could not even see my mysterious deliverer's face to judge what manner of man he was. And yet, how could I refuse his request? At last I said, slowly:—

"If what you ask is honest and above-board, you have my word that it shall be done, no matter what it may cost me."

He gave a short laugh. "You are cautious," he said, "but you are right. No, there is nothing dishonest about my request; it will wrong no one, though it may cause you some personal inconvenience."

"That is enough," I said, hastily, ashamed of the half-hearted way in which I had given my promise. "The instant we are out of this place I will take steps to grant your request, whatever it may be."

"But that won't do," he put in, quickly; "what I want must be done here and now!"

I was bewildered, as well I might be, and remained silent while he went on:—

"There is no need to say much about myself, but this you must know. I am in great trouble. I am accused of that which makes me amenable to the law. I am innocent, but I cannot prove my innocence, and my only chance of safety is in flight. That is the reason of my being here: I am hiding from my pursuers."

The poor creature paused, with a deep-drawn sigh, as if he at least had not found his life worth the struggle. I was greatly shocked by his story, and warmly expressed my sympathy; then, on his telling me he had been for two days and nights in the tunnel with scarcely a bit of food, I remembered a packet of sandwiches that had been provided for my journey, and offered them to him. It made me shudder to hear the ravenous manner in which they were consumed. When this was done there was another silence, broken by his saying, with evident hesitation, that the one hope he had was in disguising himself in some way, and thus eluding those who were watching for him. He concluded with:—

"The favour I have to ask is that you will help me in this by allowing me to have your clothes in exchange for mine!"

There was such an odd mixture of tragedy and comedy in the whole thing that for a moment I hardly knew how to answer him. The poor fellow must have taken my silence for anything but consent, for he said, bitterly:—

"You object! I felt you would, and it is my only chance!"

"On the contrary," I returned, "I am perfectly willing to do as you wish—indeed, how could I be otherwise when I have given you my word? I was only fearing that you built too much upon this exchange. Remember, it is no disguise!—the dress of one man is much like that of another."

"That is true enough, as a general rule," was the answer, "but not in this case. I was last seen in a costume not common in these parts. A coarse, tweed shooting-dress, short coat, knee-breeches, and rough worsted stockings—so that an everyday suit is all I want."

After that there was nothing more to be said, and the change was effected without more ado.

It seemed to me that my invisible companion had the advantage over me as far as seeing went, for whereas I was sensible of nothing but touch and sound, his hands invariably met and aided mine whenever they were at fault. He confessed to this, saying that he had been so long in the dark that his eyes were growing accustomed to it.

I never felt anything like the coarseness of those stockings as I drew them on. The shoes, too, were of the clumsiest make; they were large for me, which perhaps accounted for their extreme heaviness. I was a bit of a dandy; always priding myself upon my spick and span get-up. No doubt this made me critical, but certainly the tweed of which the clothes were made was the roughest thing of its kind I had ever handled. I got into them, however, without any comment, only remarking, when my toilet was finished, that I could find no pocket.

My companion gave another of those short laughs.

"No," he said, "that suit was made for use, not comfort!"

From his tone and manner of expressing himself, I had taken him to be a man fairly educated, and when he had declared that he did not require my money, I naturally fancied he was not in want of funds; but the style of his clothes made me think differently, and I decided that he should have my watch—the most valuable thing I had about me. It had no particular associations, and a few pounds would get me another. He seemed pleased, almost touched, by the proposal, and also by my suggesting that the money in my pockets should be divided between us. It was not a large sum, but half of it would take me to my journey's end, I knew. He seemed full of resource, for when I was wondering what to do with my loose change, in my pocketless costume, he spread out my handkerchief, and putting my money and the small things from my pockets into it, knotted it securely up and thrust it into my breast. Then, as we stood facing each other, he took my hand in farewell. I proposed our going on together, but this he would not hear of.

"No," he said, with his grim laugh, "the sooner I and that suit of clothes part company, the better!"

So we wished each other God-speed, and turned on our different ways—he going back through the tunnel, and I keeping on.

The experiences of the last few hours had made a great impression on me, and, although I felt awed and somewhat shaken, my heart was light with the gladness of one who rejoices in a reprieve. The express that I had been so anxious to catch had long since gone on its way; still, in my present hopeful frame of mind, that did not trouble me. I felt a conviction that Mary was mending, that I should find her better, and, comforted by this belief, I walked briskly on; at least, as briskly as my clumsy shoes would allow me, but even in spite of this hindrance, it was not long before I reached the end of the tunnel. The moonlight streaming down upon the rails was a pleasant sight, and showed me, some time before I reached it, that my goal was at hand. When I left the last shadow behind me and stood out under the clear sky I drew a sigh of intense thankfulness, drinking in the sweet fresh air.

I walked down the country road, thinking that I would rest for a few hours at the station hotel and be ready for the first train in the morning. But my adventures were not yet over. As I glanced at my clothes, thinking how unlike myself I looked and felt, something on the sleeve of my coat attracted my attention; it must be tar, which I or the former wearer of the clothes must have rubbed off in the tunnel. But, no. I looked again—my eyes seemed riveted to it—it was unmistakable. There, on the coarse grey material of the coat, was a large broad-arrow.

In an instant the whole truth had flashed upon me. No need to examine those worsted stockings and heavy shoes—no need to take off the coat and find upon the collar the name of one of Her Majesty's prisons, and the poor convict's number. As my eyes rested on the broad-arrow I understood it all.

At first I was very indignant at the position I was in. I felt that a trick had been practised upon me, and I naturally resented it. I sat down by the roadside and tried to think. The cool air blew in my face and refreshed me. I had no hat; the convict—I was beginning to think of him by that name—had given me none, saying he had lost his cap in the tunnel. After a while, when my anger had somewhat subsided, I thought more pitifully of the man whose clothes I wore. Poor wretch, without doubt he had had a hard time of it; what wonder that he had seized upon the first opportunity of escape! He had said that the favour he required would entail personal inconvenience on myself, and that was exactly what it did. I looked at the matter from all sides; I saw the dilemma I was in. It would not do to be seen in this branded garb—the police would lay hands on me at once; nothing would persuade them that I was not the convict. Indeed, who was likely to believe the improbable story I had to tell? I felt that I could expect few to credit it on my mere word, and I had nothing to prove my identity, for I remembered now that my pocket-book and letters were in my coat; I had never given them a thought when making the exchange of clothes. So, as things were, it might take some days for me to establish my real personality, and even when that were done I should still be held responsible for conniving at the prisoner's escape.

All things considered, therefore, I resolved not to get into the hands of the police. But this was no easy matter. There was nothing for it but to walk. I could not face the publicity of railway travelling or of any other conveyance: indeed, it was impossible for me to buy food for myself.

I had many narrow escapes from detection, but by dint of hiding through the day and walking at night, and now and then bribing a small child to buy me something to eat, I contrived to get slowly on my way. It was on the evening of the third day that I reached home. I often thought, somewhat bitterly, of my short cut through the tunnel and all the delay it had caused!

When I actually stood outside the little cottage which I called home, and looked up at the windows, the hope that had buoyed me up for so long deserted me, and I dreaded to enter. At last, however, I opened the gate and walked up the garden. There was a light in the small sitting-room; the curtains were not drawn, and I could see my sister Kitty seated by the table. She had evidently been weeping bitterly, and as she raised her face there was an expression of such hopeless sorrow in her eyes that my heart seemed to stop beating as I looked at her. Mary must be very ill. Perhaps—but no, I could not finish the sentence even in thought. I turned hastily, lifted the latch and went in.

"Kitty!" I said, with my hand on the room door; "it's I, Jack! don't be frightened."

She gave a little scream, and, it seemed to me, shrank back from me, as if I had been a ghost; but the next instant she sprang into my arms with a glad cry of, "Jack, Jack! is it really you?"

"Yes, Kitty, who else should it be?" I said, reassuringly. "But tell me—how is she? How is Mary? Let me hear the truth."

Kitty looked up brightly: "Mary! oh, she is better, much better, and now that you are here, Jack, she will soon be well!"

I drew a breath of intense relief. Then, touching my little sister's pale, tear-stained face, I asked what had so troubled her.

"Oh! Jack," she whispered, "it was you! I thought you were dead!" She handed me an evening paper, and pointed out a paragraph which stated that a fatal accident had occurred in the Blank Tunnel. A man named John Blount, a commercial traveller, had been killed; it was believed while attempting to walk through the tunnel to the junction station. The body had been found, early the previous morning, by some plate-layers at work on the line. The deceased was only identified by a letter found upon him.

And so, poor fellow, he had met his fate in the very death from which he had saved me! In the midst of my own happiness my heart grew very sorrowful as I thought of him, my unknown friend, whose face I had never seen!

KING CLOROX OF THE EASTERN SEABOARD

Caroline Kepnes

Caroline Kepnes is the author of *You* and *Hidden Bodies*. Her first novel was shortlisted for the Crime Writers' Association New Blood award in 2015. She previously worked as a pop culture journalist and now lives in New York.

Nathan poured a tiny drop of Clorox bleach into the lake and watched it force the minnows to swim away. He liked messing with things. He couldn't help it. When he got zits he picked them until they bled, he rejected his mother's Clearasil. "That's for girls," he would say, and slam the door on her. It was just the two of them; always was. Mainly they got along, but his habit of messing with things made him difficult. He knew right now, for instance, that his mother was probably hunting high and low for the bleach. Probably when he got home she would lay into him about wandering off with her things and spending so much time on his own. She'd bring up the time that he put a permanent purple marker into the washing machine full of whites. "Why?" she had asked. "What is this urge to ruin things?"

But he didn't see it that way and he didn't think his mom did either. If she really thought he was a bad kid, wouldn't she ground him and forbid him to touch anything? No, she didn't really care. She let him live as he wanted. He was supposed to be taking karate lessons this summer but after the first class, the teacher had taken him aside and told him to tell his mother that he didn't like rubber checks. Nathan knew about rubber checks from sitcoms and instead of embarrassing his mother he told her that the teacher was a creep, said he'd rather spend his days hanging around. Other mothers might have put a foot down, called the karate teacher at home or demanded to know more. Not her, though. She was always so willing to give up on things and relax.

So here he was, hanging around the dinky beach down the street from his house. You could hear things here, which was cool, frogs, lily pads addled by fish that you couldn't see. The first month or so it was enough to just hang out here and listen and draw the word HELP in the sand with a stick and pick at things. He'd carved his initials in a tree. But the more time he spent, the more the beach became like a scab he wanted desperately to pick. So yesterday he'd snagged the bottle of bleach when his mother wasn't looking. He'd hidden it behind a Sunfish sail boat hull. Nobody had touched the boat in months. When he'd left it there yesterday, he'd thought about that boat while he walked home. Imagine being so rich you had a boat you just abandoned. He couldn't really, not with checks bouncing about his mind.

Bleach had always appealed to Nathan. The smell of it made him feel calm, as if everything wrong in the world could one day be righted. He liked the word Clorox; he liked that there was an X in there and when he and his mom played scrabble, he always hoped for the chance to spell it out. One time he'd gotten lucky, triple word score. He'd leapt off the couch and done a victory dance and she'd sat there, completely stone cold.

"What?" He'd been breathless; jumping up and down even for a few seconds wore him out.

"It's a proper noun, Nathan. You can't use it."

"But it's your favorite." Nathan's mom referred to herself as Queen Clorox of the Eastern Seaboard. Everything in their house, surfaces, sheets, couches, was white, bright white. He got on his hands and knees.

"Nathan no. It's a proper noun. You know the rules."

"But it's just a game. It's just us."

"So what? So if it's just us we don't have to play by the rules?"

Nathan sunk into the carpet. She got up and went for her cigarettes. When she was gone he took the letters off the board one by one. Had she let it go, he would have been ahead by almost sixty points. He wondered about that a lot. Had she really been a stickler for the rules or had she only been a sore loser? His mother was hard to read.

He ran his hand along the fat base of the bottle of Clorox. There was the sturdiness of it, the timelessness; he liked when his mom said how it looked exactly the same when she was a kid. He admired its strength too. Open it and it would take over any room or space. No other smell could beat it. Once his mother bought a puppy and the puppy shat all over the living room floor. His mother had poured bleach onto the stain and it was magical, the way the clear liquid obliterated dog poop, stole its scent, no questions asked. Bleach was power. Nathan's mother would raise the bottle and swing it back and forth, warning her son that the stuff in here was the only cleaning product that could really kill germs. You couldn't live without bleach, she said. Yet it was absolute poison to our bodies. If you drank it, you would die. It was a killer that made life safe and derived all its power from its ability to kill us. Those bottles of Clorox intrigued Nathan; they were like wild tigers he would watch on the Discovery Channel licking their lips and looking into the camera as if to say, "You think you've got me, but I could have you any second I wanted".

Nathan was old enough to realize that pouring the bleach into the lake was illegal, but he knew that the chances of a cop showing up were about zero. This beach wasn't even a beach, really. It only existed because everyone in the neighborhood paid annual dues. Every March a tow truck full of sand arrived and dumped and dumped until the dirt was covered. Most people only came here to feed the ducks. Nobody would be around on a day like this. Clouds hung about the sky like gnats. A cool breeze came off the lake making you think it was September instead of July.

The ducks. Shit. Nathan couldn't stand the idea of hurting ducks and he got nervous and dropped the whole bottle like some kind of a spaz. Maybe he should throw himself into the lake and drink all the water, the bleach too. He stood there frozen, not knowing what to do, to call the 800 number about an emergency? Would he be arrested? Would his mother flip out? Would his dad reemerge in town and spank him?

When he bent over to pick up the bottle, the scope of his world changed. A little girl's body lay no more than fifteen feet away from him. It was around the bend, on the Kinney property, and the first thing he saw was an arm, no bigger than a freshwater bass. He threw the empty bottle in the sand and ran for her. Or was he running for "it"? When something was dead, he wondered, didn't it become a thing?

Nathan and his mother stood over the dead body and waited for the police to arrive. His mother smoked. She wore a thin tank top and cut-offs, the kind of clothes she usually didn't wear outside. They stared at the girl, at her flamingo pink bathing suit, at her open blue eyes. The flies were just starting to come and they'd given up swatting them away.

"She's cute," his mother said.

"You mean she *was* cute."

"So you just found her here?"

Nathan looked at his mother who didn't look back at him. "Yeah. Why?"

She shrugged, sucked on her cigarette and motioned towards the upturned sailboat where Nathan had hidden the bleach. "You better get that bottle of Clorox."

He blushed. How did she know? "What bottle of Clorox?"

"Nathan, honey," she flicked her ashes on the girl and muttered *shit*. "I know you have problems. And I know when a bottle of bleach goes missing. So let's not go and beat around the bush, okay? Not today. Not in front of a dead girl." She turned and looked up at the Kinney house. "For fuck's sake, where are they?"

He followed her directions and walked over to the upside down Sunfish. If the cops asked him what he was doing with a bottle of bleach, he would explain what it was like to grow up on a peninsula. He and his mom lived on Cape Cod, which meant that they were surrounded by four bodies of water. And they lived on this tiny scrap of land, no wider than the length of a football field that jutted into a lake. But only one house sat on the water; the Kinney house. Every other house sat on the marsh, the smelly, fetid, useless marsh.

Living like this was fine for some kids, kids who had dads to take them out on boats, kids who threw end of the year parties and smiled in school pictures. But for Nathan, the sounds of water wore on him year after year. Kids skating in a game of ice hockey, kids playing Marco Polo, kids water skiing, kids creating waves when power boats failed to do it for them. Water brought fun, the mean spirited noise of other people's smiles. His mother had the nerve to adore it here and walk around their house, talking to herself, to him, as if the sound of water shouldn't stop them both from speaking out loud at all. Maybe the cops would think he was crazy if he said all this. And maybe he was. So maybe it would be a better plan to not say anything at all.

When the sirens sounded he and his mother looked at each other. The Kinneys came onto their deck, scratching their eyes. The granddad wore a pink sweater and the grandmother yawned. "What's going on?" she called out. Nathan and his mother said nothing. Soon they would know. Nathan heard her ask her husband, "How long was I asleep?" He held his empty bottle of bleach and wished he'd never gotten it from under the boat. The Kinneys scared him and it was getting colder every second. His mother tossed her cigarette into the sand and buried it with her flip flop. "All right, kid, let's go to it."

At the police station they gave Nathan a room of his own and a strawberry shortcake ice cream bar. He sat alone devouring it, licking the stick, hoping his tongue would get splinters. So this is what it's like to be accused of something really bad. The cop opened the door without knocking and Nathan slid the stick into his pocket.

"Okay, son. Hopefully we'll just get to it."

"Yeah."

"Did you know the little girl?"

Nathan shook his head no. "Where's my mom?"

The cop didn't take his eyes off Nathan, not for a second. "Oh she's just fine. You just don't worry and we'll just have us a talk."

Nathan nodded. His left leg was falling asleep.

"So, the girl." The cop made a church with his fingers, that *here is the church here is the steeple open it up and here are the people* game. "Did you know the girl?"

"Nope."

"You just found her."

"Yep. It scared me bad."

The cop nodded, as if Nathan was boring him. "Your mom tells me that bleach was yours."

"Um," Nathan gulped. Could you go to prison for contaminating a pond? "Well yeah. It was just a stupid thing."

"Nathan, are you gonna tell me you'd never seen that little girl before?"

Nathan shook his head no.

"Did you know her name?"

He shook his head no again. He didn't know what was happening here but it felt like one of those dreams where you go to Spanish class prepared for a Spanish test and the teacher gives you a French test.

"Well her name was April Kinney. Her grandparents live right there on the lake and she was staying with them. Do you know the Kinneys?"

"Yeah sort of." When Nathan used to sell magazine subscriptions for Boy Scouts the Kinneys would always slam the door. Everyone else on Quail's East Avenue had to walk down to the tiny swab of sand if they wanted to go swimming. Maybe that's why most of them caved and got a subscription to *Reader's Digest*. But the Kinneys had a private beach and there were so damn many of them. Every summer, their front yard became a Volvo graveyard, big hulking new station wagons with Kinney kids pouring out of them in brand new bathing suits. Every branch of the Kinney family was whole with a father and a mother. They splashed in the lake and squealed into the wee hours sometimes. He knew them to be catching fireflies and playing badminton. One of his earliest memories was of his mother throwing eggs at the Kinney house when they were away on vacation and she was angry. He'd sat in the car while she egged each Nantucket red window pane. None of the other neighbors woke up. The wind carried the sound of each egg onto the lake, where it disappeared or echoed.

He didn't know.

But these weren't the sort of things you told a cop. You didn't tell a cop that you saw the little girl the day before, in a different bathing suit, that you left your bleach under the boat. You didn't tell the cop that when you walked up the hill to the street you could hear the little girl's parents calling for her, *Kinney Bear! Kinney Bear!* And you didn't tell a cop the way it hurt. Nobody called you bear, did they?

"We did a preliminary biopsy, Nathan. Do you know what that is?"

"It's where you find out what's in her body."

"That's right, son." The cop looked at Nathan very directly now. Nathan could see the pores in his ruddy cheeks and the place where his necktie snapped onto his collar. He wore a wedding band. It was easy to imagining him being one of those fun, active dads to another kid under different circumstances. "Nathan. I need you to be honest with me."

"Okay."

"She had bleach in her blood, Nathan. That's why she died."

"But she was in the water. Didn't she drown? When I saw her, she was like half in the water."

"It looks to us like she was poisoned."

Nathan understood now what was happening. They thought a kid who kills a lake would just as easily kill a little girl in a pink bathing suit. "Where's my mom?"

The cop stood up. "We'll see now if she found you a lawyer." And then he left the room and Nathan started to panic. The floor was so dusty that it was impossible to know the color of the mangy tiles.

Nathan was nineteen the next time he walked down to the lake. He didn't bring any bleach with him. If his mom knew what he was doing she would have his head for breakfast. They'd moved shortly after the accusations hit the papers. His mom said they had to; she'd never get a date ever again, that's what she said every night when they were home from court. The cops lost their case because the jury decided there was enough reason to doubt, or some shit like that. The details were fuzzy. He'd blocked a lot of it out.

"That's what we do," his mother would say. "We throw the trash right out the door and then one day it's just gone."

They had settled outside of Boston in a gray suburb. Nathan had dropped out of high school earlier that year. His mom worked for the cable company and raved about people and their cable. "I hate TV," she would say. "The idea of all these rich bored people sitting around while their brains rot. People who could afford to do anything they wanted. What a waste."

In a way she was trying to talk to Nathan, he supposed. She said these things while he was sitting on the couch, watching hour upon hour of *Full House* and *Roseanne*. He could have told her that he loved sitcoms because of solvable problems. He could have said that TV's not bad, everyone just wants to escape. Watching these programs was like baking a cake out of a box. Add water, eggs, oil and stir. But he always bit his lip around his mother. He listened to her every word, couldn't help but to that, but when he opened his mouth to respond it always felt like whatever he was trying to say would come out all wrong.

Maybe he wasn't nuts. Maybe it was just claustrophobia. Their apartment had one bedroom and one common area that tried to be so many things at once, kitchen, TV room, dining room. Somehow it reminded him of a kid back on the Cape who had shown up midway through the school year and joined every club and team that would have him. So, the apartment. His mother slept in the bedroom and he crashed on the sofa. It was a pull-out, but most of the time he didn't bother. When he did pull out the bed, she complained about tripping over pillows and the coffee table blocking the entrance to the kitchen. And when he didn't pull it out, she said, "This isn't a boarding house, Nathan. It looks awful, you sleeping on a couch."

She eventually tired of him and went to her bedroom and locked the door. Once he'd made a joke about it. "If you're so scared of me you really ought to get a better lock. I could pick that in a heartbeat, ya know?"

She hadn't laughed and when a few days later he got home and saw a hefty guy with a tool belt messing with the bedroom door, he just sat down on the couch as usual. They never spoke of the lock again. Women irritated Nathan. They didn't understand that men were more sensitive, that if you had the genitals that made it weird for you to express your emotions or some bullshit, that you became hyper emotional, sensitive as blind man is to sound.

He threw a rock and watched it skip across the glass water. He missed it here and he felt pretty sure that nobody would recognize him. He was twenty five pounds lighter now, with black hair but he wasn't a punk. He'd tried to be a goth kid; that was why he'd bought the black dye in the first place. The night he did it he expected to look like a different person when he next saw himself in the mirror. But when he stood there rubbing his head dry he saw the same old Nathan looking back at him.

"Only real beauties can get away with black hair," his mother had said.

"You want to use the rest of the dye?" He'd meant it as a compliment, but she'd taken it as an insult and walked away from him. They had a hard time talking about the simplest things. Something kept them together though, some latent instinct of hers to covet him, he supposed. He stuck with her because the world scared the living shit out of him mostly.

A loud shriek and he turned abruptly. It came from the Kinney house and suddenly they were all outside, badminton racquets in their hands. The shriek was a happy one. The lady Kinney carried a pitcher of lemonade and the old man Kinney was pointing out something in the distance to the other couple that must have been friends of theirs. They all looked so happy and relaxed. They looked fine, like their granddaughter had never been killed.

On the way back to his car Nathan picked at a pine cone. Coming here was a mistake. He'd just go now and tell his mother that he'd worked late on account of some upcoming school event. Even when he started the engine he could hear the Kinneys laughing. It was hard to drive away from a sound he'd assumed had become extinct so many years ago.

At the Fall River West Elementary School kids were always throwing up. Nathan spent a good deal of every day pouring Clorox bleach onto the floor and mopping up swabs of kid vomit. He wore a mask over his mouth to block out the stench. He was in the boy's room taking care of an allergic reaction to cafeteria hot dogs when the door opened.

"Nathan Curson?" It was a cop. Shit.

"Yeah."

"You got a minute, son?"

He was twenty four now and still cops were calling him *son*. He knew they weren't to blame. There was something permanently young about him. He almost came off like a retard, he swore.

The cop locked the bathroom door and took a handkerchief from his pocket. He leaned against the short sink and Nathan set his mop in the bucket. He shoved his hands in his pockets and looked at the cop. He hated the waiting game, all the staring.

"All right. I'm from Hyannis."

Nathan's hometown. "Oh yeah?"

"Yep."

Nathan didn't take his eyes off the cop.

"I remember reading about you."

"No shit, Sherlock? You want an autograph or something?" Nathan's face was hot red now. Nobody in Fall River had ever brought it up to him, the incident, the Kinneys, the bleach, the trial. He thought he might throw up.

"I'm not here about that exactly."

"Cuz it was eleven years ago and I was found innocent."

"Very true, son." The cop took off the handkerchief now. "Yes you were."

"Yes I was." Finally Nathan could breathe, almost.

"I'm not supposed to be here and when I leave, you best remember that I never was here. Is that understood?"

Nathan nodded.

"A little girl in this school's mother came to us today. She made an accusation against a teacher here. Said the teacher was doing sick things to her."

"That's horrible."

"What's worse is that the teacher is gonna turn around and need someone else in house to point the finger at. And the teacher's gonna point the finger right at you."

"But I didn't do it."

"Nathan, the teacher's lawyer's gonna look into the history of every single person employed at this school. You get me?"

Nathan gripped the splintered mop. Later that day, he resigned from his job at Fall River West Elementary, packed a backpack of ratty clothes and pulled onto I-95 North. He didn't leave a note for his mother. And he knew that what he was doing made him look guilty. But he didn't let that knowledge stop him from driving to Maine. He arrived late that night in Kennebunkport, home of

L.L. Bean, which he knew to be open 24 hours. He spent his first night walking the aisle of the wilderness store, looking at lanterns and tents and sweatshirts and wool socks. For no reason at all, he tried on a ski suit.

The next few months were no good at all. Maine hated him and he hated it right back. It was like a club that took applications because they had to. He felt shredded every time he made eye contact with someone. It was easy to see why Stephen King was inspired to come up with crazy shit like *The Shining*. As an outsider, with no college education and no girlfriend and no name that rang bells in people's ears, he wasn't welcome. And Maine-iacs weren't afraid to show him that they distrusted him. He drank too much beer at a local dive and grew envious of the rich folk who lived in palaces hanging over the rocky coast. But it was an envy he could handle; he didn't see the point of a rocky shore. The water was too cold for swimming, even in the dog days of summer. And lobster. Jesus Christ. He never wanted to hear or see or smell a lobster ever again.

Fall River pulled him back in that spring. He'd been arrested for molesting the girl at the elementary school and was to be tried by a jury. The day he left Maine, the bartender at the tavern where he scrubbed the floors sneered, "Don't call us, fella. We'll call you"

The first day of the trial, Nathan learned that the "cop" that came at him that day in the bathroom was a townie friend of the accused teacher. He'd played Nathan and now he sat there in the crowd holding hands with his wife. Still, Nathan got off. Again the evidence against him was not sufficient and there was talk of reasonable doubt. He owed his freedom to doubt. The teacher got off too. His lawyer lured in all kinds of psychologists who talked about the girl's emotional problems and antidepressants. She threw up a lot. That much Nathan was able to verify for the court. His mother stayed in Fall River and when they hugged after the jury announced their verdict, she said she'd cook steaks on the grill to celebrate and learn all about what he was up to in Maine. She knew full well that Nathan would be gone by the time she got home from the grocery store. That's why she only bought one steak, which she cooked in the oven. She doused it in ketchup and looked through photo albums and wondered if maybe she should change the locks.

Siesta Key was surrounded by water on all sides in a way that Nathan found soothing. The Gulf of Mexico was a far cry from the moth ridden lake back on the Cape. Seals leaped in the distance. The sand was pink and soft, like someone had laid out a million silken beads. And when it rained, it happened in a way that Nathan found economical and inspiring. Rain poured down for twenty minutes, biblical curtains of it, and then it stopped, abruptly, and the sun returned. Florida made sense to Nathan and he knew that he would stay here forever.

Sometimes, after he ate fish tacos, he cried. He was home at last.

Nathan worked out a lot at a gym and he liked living in a retirement community even though he was only thirty. There was something comforting about it. As an orderly in a retirement home, he had the basic duties of cleaning bed pans and changing sheets. But he liked his job. For the first time in his life, he realized that he had friends. There was a grouchy old Wall Street guy who looked like pictures of F.D.R. in elementary school books that he liked to play checkers with.

There was a woman who'd been a dancer on the strip in Vegas. Through these people, Nathan traveled. He went on excursions to places he'd never dreamt of going. So by day, he listened and lived vicariously through the old folks' stories, many of which they repeated unknowingly. And after work, he lifted weights among other men like him, all of them a little fucked up for living here, a place for the dying.

Nights he walked on the beach and thought about his mother. They spoke once a week, perfunctory conversations that always ended with her promising to visit and him promising to send her a postcard. It was their deal that neither one of them had to go through with these commitments. Finally, they'd figured out how to handle each other. Once in a while, there was a decent souled girl who was in town. He'd see her sitting at a Starbucks, seemingly lost in a village of Early Bird Specials and gargantuan Buicks. So he'd hit on her, take her for fish tacos and fuck her on the outskirts of the key. It was nice the way the girls went away. There were women at work too, huge Jamaican angels who nicknamed him Tiny and played Frank Sinatra songs for the invalid.

"Nathan, baby. I need your ass to some welcoming committee magic in 232. We got a grumpy one on our hands." Sheila was the floor's head nurse, a fat bottomed house of a woman who'd once carried a man on her shoulders down three flights of stairs. Nathan walking behind them, offering to help but she kept laughing, "No tall one. Women were made to feel pain. It's good."

He knocked on the door to 232 and heard a woman groan, "What now?"

The new rooms were always strikingly barren, no matter how many times you walked in knowing what to expect, the sadness of it still kicked you in the gut. He could tell right away that this new girl was here against her will. Someone had covered her lips in dark red gloss but whoever did it hadn't loved her enough to take care of the rest of her face. He picked up her intake sheet: ALZHEIMERS. Kinney. Roberta Kinney. Nathan thought he was going to faint so he got himself seated in the room's only chair. Kinney. Roberta Kinney. And now she was starting in. "I demand to know where I am. I demand to know what this place is. Who are you?"

Nathan closed the door and approached the bed. He ran a hand over her head. Mrs. Roberta Kinney. His head was full of questions. Where was her husband? Was he here too? Had he left her here like an old tennis racquet at the Salvation Army drop off? Was he dead? Did they still have their house on the Cape? Did they place lilies on their granddaughter's grave every year? When was the last time they had friends over for pitchers of lemonade?

"Mrs. Kinney, you're Mrs. Roberta Kinney."

"I am not any such thing."

"Yes," he stroked her hand. "Yes you are."

"Well get me a phone then."

"You need to just relax."

"What I need is a damn phone God damnit."

He leaned in. They had bathed her and she smelled of talcum powder and Jean Nate, the smells he knew from this job. "Mrs. Kinney," he whispered. Talking to the mentally confused was easy. They listened more for tone than for content, so Nathan spoke like a nursery rhyme, ending his short sentences on high notes, high soft cuddly notes. "It's me. It's Nathan from up the street. I killed your granddaughter. April. You called her Kinney Bear." It was the first time he'd said it out loud. He didn't know it was true until the words came out of his mouth. There was clarity and he thought he would faint.

Alzheimer's replaced rational fear with irrational fear. She wasn't scared of him because of his confession. She wasn't angry that he'd escaped the system. She was just looking for facts. She didn't know she was Mrs. Kinney so anything anyone told her was suspect.

"Is that a fact?"

"It is. I left bleach under your boat. On purpose. I knew the little girl would come nosing around. I left the cap off the bleach. I'm sorry. I was in a haze. So many bad things happened to me. And nothing bad ever happened to you. To me, you had so much luck that it seemed logical that the little girl would drink it and survive somehow. I figured you were all above it. Above poison. So that first day, she was watching me. I pretended to gulp it and I left it sitting there and I knew she would come around for a taste when I was gone. I am a murderer, Mrs. Kinney."

"Well, my. What a thing." She squeezed his hand as much as she could. Her blue veins bulged from the tops of her brown leathery hands. Too much sun, he thought.

"What a thing." Nathan kissed her flaxen hair and stroked the nape of her neck. He knew enough to know that Mrs. Kinney wouldn't connect any of this to her own life. When you had Alzheimer's, all talk became a story. It became something outside of yourself.

"What's your name, dear?"

"Nathan Curson."

She pointed at a notepad on the counter. "Write that down for me. You say you killed my granddaughter?"

He nodded and obviously he didn't reach for the notepad. This frenzy would pass. She was only clinging to her last link to memory, the written word. And she pulled her hand back. He pretended to write his name and he slid the notepad beneath the phone.

"Well why exactly would a person do a thing like that? A little girl is a nice thing."

"He was jealous. He was an angry boy."

"Oh my dear, you poor boy."

He opened the mini-refrigerator and the cool air gave him the chills. "Did you want some juice?"

She sat up straight in the bed. It was so easy to read old people's faces. And he looked at her chart. Husband: deceased. Her daughter had put her here. The Kinneys weren't so loving after all. The refrigerator hummed and he knelt there, studying the chart, his left hand shaking slightly and holding the door open.

"Better shut that door," she said. "We don't want all that nice cool air to escape. That's a waste of money."

Nathan shut the door and walked over to Mrs. Kinney. She slid her hands together and picked at her fingernails. Her eyes darted about the bright white room. "Who are you, please? Please have the decency to tell me who you are.

I don't know why you're here. I don't know what's happening. Will you tell me please?"

Nathan left the state of Florida that night and drove for thirteen hours without stopping. When he did finally pull off the road he parked on the outskirts of what appeared to be someone's cornfield. There was no water, not for miles and miles. "Landlocked," he said, to no one in particular.

FEMME FATALE

Laura Lippman

Laura Lippman was a feature journalist when she created the 'accidental PI' Tess Monaghan. Her detective fiction, including *Baltimore Blues*, *Every Secret Thing*, and *What the Dead Know*, explores women's experiences and has received several awards including the Edgar, the Anthony, and the Agatha. Lippman lives in Baltimore, USA.

This is true: there comes a time in the life of a beautiful woman, or even an attractive one with an abundance of charm, when she realizes that she can no longer rely on her looks. If she is unusually, exceedingly self-aware, the realization is a timely one. But, more typically, it lags the physical reality by several years, like a thunderclap when a lightning storm is passing by. One one thousand, two one thousand, three one thousand, four one thousand . . . boom. One one thousand, two one thousand, three one thousand, four one thousand, five one thousand. *Boom.* The lightning is moving out, away, which is a good thing in nature, but not in the life of a beautiful woman.

That's how it happened for Mona. A gorgeous woman at twenty, a stunning woman at thirty, a striking woman at forty, a handsome woman at fifty, she was pretty much done by sixty—but only if one knew what she had been, once upon a time, and at this point that knowledge belonged to Mona alone. A sixty-eight-year-old widow when she moved into LeisureWorld, she was thought shy and retiring by her neighbors in the Creekside Condos, Phase II. She was actually an incurious snob who had no interest in the people around her. People were overrated, in Mona's opinion, unless they were men and they might be persuaded to marry you. *This is not my life*, she thought, walking the trails that wound through the pseudo-city in suburban Maryland. *This is not what I anticipated.*

Mona had expected . . . well, she hadn't thought to expect. To the extent that she had been able to imagine her old age at all, she had thought her sunset years might be something along the lines of Eloise at the Plaza—a posh place in a city center, with twenty-four-hour room service and a concierge. Such things were available—but not to those with her resources, explained the earnest young accountant who reviewed the various funds left by Mona's husband, her fourth, although Hal Wickham had believed himself to be her second.

"Mr. Wickham has left you with a conservative, diversified portfolio that will cover your costs at a comfortable level—but it's not going to allow you to live in a hotel," the accountant had said a little huffily, almost as if he were one of Hal's children, who had taken the same tone when they realized how much of their father's estate was to go to Mona. But she was his wife, after all, and not some fly-by-night spouse. They had been married fifteen years, her personal best.

"But there's over two million, and the smaller units in that hotel are going for less than a million," she said, crossing her legs at the knee and letting her skirt ride up, just a bit. Her legs were still quite shapely, but the accountant's eyes slid away from them. A shy one. These bookish types killed her.

"If you cash out half of the investments, you earn half as much on the remaining principal, which isn't enough to cover your living expenses, not with the maintenance fees involved. Don't you see?"

"I'd be paying cash," she said, leaning forward, so her breasts rested on her elbows. They were still quite impressive. Bras were one wardrobe item that had improved in Mona's lifetime. Bras were amazing now, what they did with so little fabric.

"Yes, theoretically. But there would be taxes to pay on the capital gains of the stocks acquired in your name, and your costs would outpace your earnings. You'd have to dip into your principal, and at that rate, you'd be broke in"—he did a quick calculation on his computer—"seven years. You're only sixty-eight now—"

"Sixty-one," she lied reflexively.

"All the more reason to be careful," he said. "You're going to live a long, long time."

But to Mona, now ensconced in Creekside Condos, Phase II, it seemed only that it would feel that way. She didn't golf, so she had no use for the two courses at LeisureWorld. She had never learned to cook, preferring to dine out, but she loathed eating out alone and the delivery cuisine available in the area was not to her liking. She watched television, took long walks, and spent an hour a day doing vigorous isometric exercises that she had learned in the late sixties. This was before Jane Fonda and aerobics, when there wasn't so much emphasis on sweating. The exercises were the closest thing that Mona had to a religion and they had been more rewarding than most religions, delivering exactly what they promised—and in this lifetime, too. Plus, all her husbands, even the ones she didn't count, had benefited from the final set of repetitions, a series of pelvic thrusts done in concert with vigorous yogic breathing.

One late fall day, lying on her back, thrusting her pelvis in counterpoint to her in-and-out breaths, it occurred to Mona that her life would not be much different in the posh, downtown hotel condo she had so coveted. It's not as if she would go to the theaters or museums; she had only pretended interest in those things because other people seemed to expect it. Museums bored her and theater baffled her—all those people talking so loudly, in such artificial sentences. Better restaurants wouldn't make her like eating out alone, and room service was never as hot as it should be. Her surroundings would be a considerable improvement, with truly top-of-the-line fixtures, but all that would have meant is that she would be lying on a better-quality carpet right now. Mona was not meant to be alone and if she had known that Hal was going to die only fifteen years in, she might have chosen differently. Finding a husband at the age of sixty-eight, even when one claimed to be sixty-one, had to be harder than finding a job at that age. With Hal, Mona had consciously settled. She wondered if he knew that. She wondered if he had died just to spite her.

There was a Starbucks in LeisureWorld plaza and she sometimes ended her afternoon walks there, curious to see what the fuss was about. She found the chairs abominable—had anyone over fifty ever tried to rise from these low-slung traps?—but she liked what a younger person might call the vibe. (Mona didn't actually know any young people and had been secretly glad that Hal's children loathed her so, as it gave her an excuse to have nothing to do with them or the grandchildren.) She treated herself to sweet drinks, chocolate drinks, drinks with whipped cream. Mona had been on a perpetual diet since she was thirty-five, and while the discipline, along with her exercises, had kept her body hard, it had made her face harder still. The coffee drinks and pastries added weight, but no more than five or six pounds, and it was better than Botox, plumping and smoothing Mona's cheeks. She sipped her drink, stared into space, and listened to the curious non-music on the sound system. It wasn't odd to be alone in Starbucks, quite the opposite. When parties of two or three came in, full of conversation and private jokes, they were the ones who seemed out of place. The regulars all relaxed a little when those interlopers finally left.

"I hate to intrude, but I just had to say—ma'am? Ma'am?"

The man who stood next to her was young, no more than forty-five. At first glance, he appeared handsome, well put together. At second, the details betrayed him. There was a stain on his trench coat, flakes of dandruff on his shoulders and down the front of his black turtleneck sweater.

Still, he was a man and he was talking to her.

"Yes?"

"You're . . . someone, aren't you? I'm bad with names, but I don't forget faces and you—well, you were a model, right? One of the new-wave ones in the sixties, when they started going for that coltish look."

"No, you must think—"

"My apologies," he said. "Because you were better known for the movies, those avant-garde ones you did before you chucked it all and married that guy, although you could have been as big as any of them. Julie Christie. She was your only serious competition."

It took Mona a second to remember who Julie Christie was, her brain first detouring through memories of June Christie but then landing on an image of the actress. She couldn't help being pleased, if he was confusing her with someone who was serious competition for Julie Christie. Whoever he thought she was must have been gorgeous. Mona felt herself preening, even as she tried to deny the compliment. He thought she was even younger than she pretended to be.

"I'm not—"

"But you are," he said. "More beautiful than ever. Our culture is so confused about its . . . aesthetic values. I'm not talking about the veneration of age as wisdom, or the importance of experience, although those things are to the good. You are, objectively, more beautiful now than you were back then."

"Perhaps I am," she said lightly. "But I'm not whoever you think I was, so it's hard to know."

"Oh. Gosh. My apologies. I'm such an idiot—"

He sank into the purple velvet easy chair opposite her, twisting the brim of his hat nervously in his hands. She liked the hat, the fact of it. So few men bothered nowadays, and as a consequence, fewer men could pull them off. Mona was old enough, just, to remember when all serious men wore hats.

"I wish you could remember the name," she said, teasing him, yet trying to put him at ease, too. "I'd like to know this stunner that you say I resemble."

"It's not important," he said. "I feel so stupid. Fact is—I bet she doesn't look as good today as you do."

"Mona Wickham," she said, extending her hand. He bowed over it. Didn't kiss it, just bowed, a nice touch. Mona was vain of her hands, which were relatively unblemished. She kept her nails in good shape with weekly manicures and alternated her various engagement rings on the right hand. Today it was the square-cut diamond from her third marriage. Not large, but flawless.

"Bryon White," he said. "With an O, like the poet, only the R comes first."

"Nice to meet you," she said. Two or three seconds passed, and Bryon didn't release her hand and she didn't take it back. He was studying her with intense, dark eyes. Nice eyes, Mona decided.

"The thing is, you could be a movie star."

"So some said, when I was young." Which was, she couldn't help thinking, a good decade before the one in which this Bryon White thought she had been a model and an actress.

"No, I mean now. Today. I could see you as, as—Catherine, the Russian empress."

Mona frowned. Wasn't that the naughty one?

"Or, you know, Lauren Bacall. I think she's gorgeous."

"I didn't like her in that movie with Streisand."

"No, but with Altman—with Altman, she was magnificent."

Mona wasn't sure who Altman was. She remembered a store in New York, years ago, B. Altman's. After her first marriage, she had changed into a two-piece going-away suit purchased there, a dress with matching jacket. She remembered it still, standing at the top of the staircase in that killingly lovely suit, in a houndstooth check of fuchsia and black, readying to throw the bouquet. She remembered thinking: *I look good, but now I'm married, so what does it matter?* Mona's first marriage had lasted two years.

Bryon picked up on her confusion. "In *Prêt à Porter*." This did not clear things up for Mona. "I'm sorry, it translates to—"

"I know the French," she said, a bit sharply. "I used to go to the Paris collections, buy couture." That was with her second husband, who was rich, rich, rich, until he wasn't anymore. Until it turned out he never really was. Wallace just had a high tolerance for debt, higher than his creditors, as it turned out. Mona didn't leave because he filed for bankruptcy, but it didn't make the case for staying, either.

"It was a movie a few years back. The parts were better than the whole, if I can be so bold as to criticize a genius. The thing is, I'm a filmmaker myself."

Mona hadn't been to a movie in ten years. The new ones made her sleepy. She fell asleep, woke up when something blew up, fell back asleep again. "Have you—"

"Made anything you've heard of? No. I'm an indie, but, you know, you keep your vision that way. I'm on the festival circuit, do some direct-to-video stuff.

Digital has changed the equation, you know?"

Mona nodded as if she did.

"Look, I don't want to get all Schwab's on you—"

Finally, a reference that Mona understood.

"—but I'm working on something right now and you would be so perfect. If you would consider reading for me, or perhaps, even, a screen test . . . there's not much money in it, but who knows? If you photograph the way I think you will, it could mean a whole new career for you."

He offered her his card, but she didn't want to put her glasses on to read it, so she just studied it blindly, pretending to make sense of the brown squiggles on the creamy background. The paper was of good stock, heavy and textured.

"In fact, my soundstage isn't far from here, so if you're free right now—"

"I'm on foot," she said. "I walked here from my apartment."

"Oh, and you wouldn't want to get in a car with a strange man. Of course."

Mona hadn't been thinking of Bryon as strange. In fact, she had assumed he was gay. What kind of man spoke so fervently of models and old-time movie stars? But now that he said it—no, she probably shouldn't, part of her mind warned. But another part was shouting her down, telling her such opportunities come along just once. Maybe she looked better than she realized. Maybe Mona's memory of her younger self had blinded her to how attractive she still was to someone meeting her for the first time.

"I'll tell you what. I'll call you a cab, give the driver the address. Tell him to wait, with the meter running, all on me."

"Don't be silly." Mona clutched the arms of the so-called easy chair and willed herself to rise as gracefully as possible. Somehow she managed it. "Let's go."

She was not put off by the fact that Bryon's soundstage was a large locker in one of those storage places. "A filmmaker at my level has to squeeze every nickel until it hollers," he said, pulling the garage-type door behind them. She wasn't sure how he had gotten power rigged up inside, but there was an array of professional-looking lights. The camera was a battery-powered camcorder, set up on a tripod. He even had a "set"—a three-piece 1930s-style bedroom set, with an old-fashioned vanity and bureau to match the ornately carved bed.

He asked Mona to sit on the padded stool in front of the vanity and address the camera directly, saying whatever came into her head.

"Um, testing one, two, three. Testing."

"You look great. Talk some more. Tell me about yourself."

"My name is Mona—" She stumbled for a second, forgetting the order of her surnames. After all, she had five.

"Where did you grow up, Mona?"

"Oh, here, there, and everywhere." Mona had learned long ago to be stingy with the details. They dated one so.

"What were you like as a young woman?"

"Well, I was the . . . bee's knees." An odd expression for her to use, one that pre-dated her own birth by quite a bit. She laughed at its irrelevance and Bryon laughed, too. She felt as if she had been drinking brandy Alexanders instead of venti mochas. Felt, in fact, the way she had that first afternoon with her second husband, when they left the bar at the Drake Hotel and checked into a room. She had been only thirty-five then, and she had let him keep the drapes open, proud of how her body looked in the bright daylight bouncing off Lake Michigan.

"I bet you were. I bet you were. And all the boys were crazy about you."

"I did okay."

"Oh, you did more than okay, didn't you, Mona?"

She smiled. "That's not for me to say."

"What did you wear, Mona, when you were driving those boys crazy? None of those obvious outfits for you, right? You were one of those subtle ones, like Grace Kelly. Pretty dresses, custom fit."

"Right." She brightened. Clothing was one of the few things that interested her. "That's what these girls today don't get. I had a bathing suit, a one-piece, strapless. As modest as it could be. But it was beige, just a shade darker than my own skin, and when it got wet . . ." She laughed, the memory alive to her, the effect of that bathing suit on the young men around the pool at the country club in Atlanta.

"I wish you still had that bathing suit, Mona."

"I'd still fit into it," she said. It would have been true two months ago, before she discovered Starbucks.

"I bet you would. I bet you would." Bryon's voice seemed thicker, lower, slower.

"I never let myself go, the way some women do. They say it's metabolism and menopause"—oh, she wished she could take that word back, one should never even allude to such unpleasant facts of life—"but it's just a matter of discipline."

"I sure wish I could see you in that suit, Mona."

She laughed. She hadn't had this much fun in ages. He was flirting with her, she was sure of it. Gay or not, he liked her.

"I wish I could see you in your *birthday* suit."

"Bryon!" She was on a laughing jag now, out of control.

"Why can't I, Mona? Why can't I see you in your birthday suit?"

Suddenly, the only sound in the room was Bryon's breath, ragged and harsh. It was hard to see anything clearly, with the lights shining in her eyes, but Mona could see that he was steadying the camera with just one hand.

"You want to see me naked?" she asked.

Bryon nodded.

"Just . . . see?"

"That's how we start, usually. Slow like. Everyone has his or her own comfort zone."

"And the video—is that for your eyes only?"

"I told you, I'm an independent filmmaker. Direct to video. A growing market."

"People pay?"

Another shy nod. "It's sort of a . . . niche within the industry."

"Niche."

"It's my niche," he said. "It's what I like. I make other films about, um, things I don't like so much. But I love watching truly seasoned women teach young men about life."

"And you'd pay for this?"

"Of course."

"How much?"

"Some. Enough."

"Just to look? Just to see me, as I am?"

"A little for that. More for . . . more."

"How much?" Mona repeated. She was keen to know her worth.

He came around from behind the camera, retrieved a laminated card from the drawer in the vanity table, then sat on the bed and patted the space next to him. Why laminated? Mona decided not to think about that. She moved to the bed and studied the card, not unlike the menu of services and prices at a spa. She could do that. And that. Not that, but definitely that and that. The fact was, she had done most of these things, quite happily.

"Let me make you a star, Mona."

"Are you my leading man?"

"Our target demographic prefers to see younger men with the women. I just need to get some film of you to take to my partner so he'll underwrite it. I have a very well-connected financial backer."

"Who?"

"Oh, I'll never say. He's very discreet. Anyway, he likes to know that the actresses are . . . up to the challenges of their roles. Usually a striptease will do, a little, um, self-stimulation. But it's always good to have extra footage. I make a lot of films, but these are the ones I like best. The ones I watch."

"Well, then," Mona said, unbuttoning her blouse. "Let's get busy."

Fetish, Mona said to herself as she shopped in the Giant. *Fetish*, she thought as she retrieved her mail from the communal boxes in the lobby. *I am a fetish*. This was the word that Bryon used to describe her "work," which, two months after their first meeting, comprised four short films. She had recoiled at the word at first, feeling it marked her as a freak, something from a sideshow. "Niche" had been so much nicer. But Bryon assured her that the customers who bought her videos were profoundly affected by her performance. There was no irony, no belittling. She was not the butt of the joke, she was the object of their, um, affection.

"Different people like different things," he said to her in Starbucks one afternoon. She was feeling a little odd, as she always did when a film was completed. It was so strange to spend an afternoon having sex and not be taken shopping afterward, just given a cashier's check. "Our cultural definitions of sexuality are simply too narrow."

"But your other films, the other tastes you serve"—Mona by now had familiarized herself with Bryon's catalog, which included the usual whips and chains, but also a surprisingly successful series of films that featured obese women sitting on balloons—"they're sick."

"There you go, being judgmental," Bryon said. "Children is wrong, I'll give you that. Because children can't consent. Everything else is fair game."

"Animals can't consent."

"I don't do animals, either. Adults and inanimate objects, that's my credo."

It was an odd conversation to be having in her Starbucks at the LeisureWorld

Plaza, that much was sure. Mona looked around nervously, but no one was paying attention. The other customers probably thought Mona and Bryon were a mother and son, although she didn't think she looked old enough to be Bryon's mother.

"By the way"—Bryon produced a small stack of envelopes—"we've gotten some letters for you."

"Letters?"

"Fan mail. Your public."

"I'm not sure I want to read them."

"That's up to you. Whatever you do—don't make the mistake of responding to them, okay? The less they know about Sexy Sadie, the better. Keep the mystery." He left her alone with her public.

Keep the mystery. Mona liked that phrase. It could be her credo, to borrow Bryon's word. Then she began to think about the mysteries that Bryon was keeping. If she had already received—she stopped to count, touching the envelopes gingerly—eleven pieces of fan mail, then how many fans must she have? If eleven people wrote, then hundreds—no, thousands—must watch and enjoy what she did.

So why was she getting paid by the job, with no percentage, no profit-sharing? God willing, her health assured, she could really build on this new career. After all, they actually had to make her look older, dressing her in dowdy dresses, advising her to make her voice sound more quavery than it was. Bryon had the equipment, Bryon had the distribution—but only Mona had Mona. How replaceable was she?

"Forget it," Bryon said when she broached the topic on the set a few weeks later. "I was up-front with you from the start. I pay you by the act. By the piece, if you will. No participation. You signed a contract, remember?"

Gone was the rapt deference from that first day at Starbucks. True, Mona had long ago figured out that it was an act, but she had thought there was a germ of authenticity in it, a genuine respect for her looks and presence. How long had Bryon been stalking her? she wondered now. Had he approached her because of her almost lavender eyes, or because she looked vulnerable and lonely? Easy, as they used to say.

"But I have fans," she said. "People who like me, specifically. That ought to be worth a renegotiation."

"You think so? Then sue me in Montgomery County courts. Your neighbors in LeisureWorld will probably love reading about that in the suburban edition of the *Washington Post*."

"I'll quit," she said.

"Go ahead," Bryon said. "You think you're the only lonely old lady who needs a little attention? I'll put the wig and the dress on some other old bag. My films, my company, my concept."

"Some concept," Mona said, trying not to let him see how much the words hurt. So she was just a lonely old lady to him, a mark. "I sit in a room, a young man rings my doorbell, I end up having sex with him. So far, it's been a UPS man, a delivery boy for a florist, a delivery boy for the Chinese restaurant, and a young Mormon on a bicycle. What's next, a Jehovah's Witness peddling the *Watchtower*?"

"That's not bad," Bryon said, pausing to write a quick note to himself. "Look, this is the deal. I pay you by the act. You don't want to do it, you don't have to. I'm always scouting new talent. Maybe I'll find an Alzheimer's patient, who won't be able to remember from one day to the next what she did, much less try to hold me up for a raise. You old bitches are a dime a dozen."

It was the "old bitches" part that hurt.

When Mona's second husband's fortune had proved to be largely smoke and mirrors, she had learned to be more careful about picking her subsequent husbands. That was in the pre-Internet days, when determining a person's personal fortune was much more labor-intensive. She was pleased to find out from a helpful librarian how easy it was now to compile what was once known as a Dun and Bradstreet on someone, how to track down the silent partner in Bryon White's LLC.

Within a day, she was having lunch with Bernard Weinman, a dignified gentleman about her own age. He hadn't wanted to meet with her, but as Mona detailed sweetly what she knew about Bernie's legitimate business interests—more information gleaned with the assistance of the nice young librarian—and his large contributions to a local synagogue, he decided they could meet after all. He chose a quiet French restaurant in Bethesda, and when he ordered white wine with lunch, Mona followed suit.

"I have a lot of investments," he said. "I'm not hands-on."

"Still, I can't imagine you want someone indiscreet working for you."

"Indiscreet?"

"How do you think I tracked you down? Bryon talks. A lot."

Bernie Weinman bent over his onion soup, spilling a little on his tie. But it was a lovely tie, expensive and well made. For this lunch meeting, he wore a black suit and crisp white shirt with large gold cuff links.

"Bryon's very good at . . . what he does. His mail-order business is so steady it's almost like an annuity. I get a very good return on my money, and I've never heard of him invoking my name."

"Well, he did. All I did was make some suggestions about how to"—Mona groped for the odd business terms she had heard on television—"how to grow your business, and he got very short with me, said you had no interest in doing things differently. And when I asked if I might speak to you, he got very angry, threatened to expose me. If he would blackmail me, a middle-class widow with no real money, imagine what he might do to you."

"Bryon knows me well enough not to try that," Bernie Weinman said. After a morning at the Olney branch of the Montgomery County Public Library, Mona knew him pretty well, too. She knew the rumors that had surrounded the early part of his career, the alleged but never proven ties to the numbers runner up in Baltimore. Bernie Weinman had built his fortune from corner liquor stores in Washington, D.C., which eventually became the basis for his chain of party-supply stores. But he had clearly never lost his taste for the recession-proof businesses that had given him his start—liquor, gambling, prostitution. All he had done was live long enough and give away enough money that people were will-ing to forget his past. Apparently, the going price of redemption in Montgomery County was five million dollars to the capital fund at one's synagogue.

"Does Bryon know you so well that he wouldn't risk keeping two sets of books?"

"What?"

"I know what I get paid. I know how cheaply the product is made and produced, and I know how many units are moved. He's cheating you."

"He wouldn't."

"He would—and brag about it, too. He said you were a stupid old man who was no longer on top of his game."

"He said that?"

"He said much worse."

"Tell me."

"I c-c-can't," Mona whispered, looking shyly into her salade niçoise as if she had not made four adult films under the moniker "Sexy Sadie."

"Paraphrase."

"He said . . . he said there was no film in the world that could, um, incite you. That you were . . . starchless."

"That little SOB."

"He laughs at you, behind your back. He practically brags about how he's ripping you off. I've put myself in harm's way, just talking to you, but I couldn't let this go on."

"I'll straighten him out—"

"No! Because he'll know it was me and he'll—he's threatened me, Bernie." This first use of his name was a calculated choice. "He says no one will miss me and I suppose he's right."

"You don't have any children?"

"Just stepchildren, and I'm afraid they're not very kind to me. It was hard for them, their father remarrying, even though he had been a widower for years." Divorced for two years, and Mona had been the central reason, but the kids wouldn't have liked her under any circumstances. "No, no one would miss me. Except my fans."

She let the subject go then, directing the conversation to Bernie and his accom-plishments, the legitimate ones. She asked questions whose answers she knew perfectly well, touched his arm when he decided they needed another bottle of wine, and, although she drank only one glass to his every two, declared herself unfit to drive home. She was going to take a taxi, but Bernie insisted on driving her, and accompanying her to the condo door, to make sure she was fine, and then into her bedroom, where he further assessed her fineness. He was okay, not at all starchless, somewhere between a sturdy baguette and a loaf of Wonder bread. She'd had worse. True, he felt odd, after the series of hard-bodied young men that Bryon had hired for her. But this, at least, did not fall under the cate-gory of fetish. He was seventy-three and she was sixty-eight-passing-for-sixty-one. This was normal. This was love.

Bryon White was never seen again. He simply disappeared, and there was no one who mourned him or even really noticed. And while Bernie Weinman was happily married, he had strong opinions about how his new mistress should spend her time. Mona took over the business but had to retire from performing, at least officially, although she sometimes auditioned the young men, just to be sure. Give Bryon credit, Mona thought, now that she had to scout the coffee shops and grocery stores, recruiting the new talent. It was harder than it looked and Bryon's instincts had been unerring, especially when it came to Mona. She really was a wonderful actress.

ANOTHER KIND OF MAN

Anya Lipska

Anya Lipska trained as a journalist before writing crime thrillers and producing television documentaries. Her first novel, *Where the Devil Can't Go*, detailed the gritty lives of Polish people living in London and introduced Detective Natalie Kershaw and private investigator Janusz Kiszka. Lipska lives in London.

The man sits on a bench at the edge of the cemetery, watching the swallows swooping, jousting with one another among the plane trees. He's in his late thirties – younger than the usual graveyard visitor – and for all his casual air, a sharp-eyed observer might conclude that he has spent the last forty minutes surreptitiously watching the final act of a funeral service unfolding through the trees.

The mourners start to leave the graveside. As they near the cemetery gates, their pace picks up, giving way to relief, to the prospect of a good lunch – *to life*. By the time they reach the street, they're practically skipping.

Only the last knot – an elderly couple and a young woman – tread the slow step of true grief, reluctant to leave this place where they have just committed to the dust someone they loved. *Someone who loved them.*

He turns his head as they pass – but too late: the girl has noticed him. *Kurwa!* he curses to himself.

'*Prosze pana?*' she says. Where do Poles get this unerring knack of recognizing each other, he wondered. 'I couldn't help noticing you were watching. I am guessing that you knew my father?'

He makes a non-committal gesture. She's pretty, he notices – before stifling *that thought* at birth.

'I only wanted to say,' she goes on. 'You're most welcome to come back to the house for the *stypa*.'

Why not, he thinks suddenly, recklessly. *There might be a certain piquancy in toasting the old bastard's memory in his own house.*

'Thank you,' he says. 'I'd be honoured.'

After she's left, he lights a cigar. He probably shouldn't have come. But from the moment he saw the death notice in the paper, it had been inevitable . . . '*Pawel Porecki, peacefully, at home.*' He'd heard, long ago, that the old man had left Poland for London, but to discover that they'd spent the last 17 years living just a few miles from one another . . .! *Peacefully, at home.* The words had tolled in his brain, mockingly, ever since.

The address the girl gave him means a bus ride out to the city's easternmost fringe. On the high street, he spots a Polski *sklep* next to a Tesco Express – a new addition judging by the fresh paint job. Since Poland joined the EU a couple of years back in 2004, he can't barely step out of his front door without hearing the swoop and lilt of his mother tongue. Polish shops have sprouted like wild mushrooms, pubs are selling Tyskie, and in the coffee shops, half the *baristas* seem to hail from Lodz or Poznan.

He wishes they'd all go home. He's spent almost his entire adult life here – trying to live in the present tense – yet now his history dogs him daily down every London street.

He finds the house in a suburban-looking avenue, the trees laced with blossom. Its gables, timbers and leaded glass give off an air of complacent prosperity. Rage rises in his throat. The old man did well for himself – escaping all the damage he'd inflicted, like the sole survivor stepping unharmed from the wreckage of a car he'd written off.

In the front room, the occasional English voice cuts above the Polish hubbub – angular-sounding. Sidestepping conversation, he takes his glass of beer out into the hallway. There his eye falls on a framed family photo: the dead man lounging on a brightly striped garden swing, an arm around his smiling wife, a young girl nestled between them. The daughter. *The picture of a happy family.*

A few minutes later, she finds him there, offers him a small bowl of buckwheat with honey and poppy seed dressing – a traditional funeral feast dish. He takes it with as much grace as he can muster.

'Janina Porecki,' she says, holding out her hand. She pronounces the first name in the English way, with a hard 'J'.

'Janusz Kiszka,' he says, shaking it by the fingers.

'So . . . how did you know my father?' she asks.

'He was a friend of the family, back home.' The lie comes smoothly. 'In Krakow.'

She seems to accept the fabrication. 'I used to love Krakow,' she says. 'Such a beautiful city. I was only 11 when we left but I swore that one day, I'd live in a little attic flat with a view of the square.' Her English is accentless, beautifully modulated: the kind only expensive schooling can buy. She sends him a wry smile. 'But then, I went to university in London, all my friends are here . . . and Mum and Dad are both dead now. You move on, don't you?'

Do you? he thinks. Maybe if you had a privileged upbringing, protected from the realities of life.

'But you must have been back since then to visit, to see . . . family?' he asks.

'No, we don't have any family left over there. And Dad would never go back. He was a civil servant, you see. He always said that there are still people in Poland who are . . . funny about anyone who worked for the government back then, before the elections.'

So blithe, so dismissive. She could only be, what? ten years younger than him, and yet the chasm was unbridgeable.

Taking a sip of beer, he nods, as if in agreement. 'What did he do, in the civil service?'

'Something to do with catering services to public buildings?' She sounds vague yet guileless.

She doesn't even *know*, he realises. Meeting her gaze, he gets a jolt. She has her father's eyes: the irises an unusually light hazel with a darker ring around the outside. *Eyes he's spent the last twenty years trying to forget.*

Just at that moment an older woman comes to find her, to ask if she should pour the *krupnik*, ready for the funeral toasts.

He holds himself together till she's gone. Then he escapes through the front door, his vision darkening. Fumbles his way around the side into a passageway. Drops to a crouch, his back against the wall – the breath clotting in his lungs.

He shouldn't have come.

He had only met Pawel Porecki once, two days after his seventeenth birthday, in '85. After a day dodging tear gas and rubber bullets, he and his mates Tomek and Mariusz had spent the evening in a Krakow cellar bar. The demo had been called to protest against the torture and murder of a dissident priest by the secret police. Everybody was pumped up, drinking to the dead hero – and to a free Poland.

After the bar closed, the three of them decided to strike their own blow for freedom. So it was that he found himself dangling over a railway bridge, Tomek and Mariusz each holding a leg, spray-painting some slogan he couldn't even recall now. Then, a shout as they were spotted by a *milicja* patrol. The boys dragged him back up, but by the time he'd found his feet they'd managed to escape.

It was strange, the things your memory clung to. He had no recollection of what the interrogation room looked like, but the smell of the place – disinfectant with an undernote of blood and sweat – would stay with him forever. That, and the eyes of his interrogator, secret service Lieutenant Pawel Porecki. Porecki locked those eyes on his and gave him a simple choice: reveal the names of his two friends – or leave the place in a body bag.

When he refused, Porecki gave a nod. A pair of *milicja* gorillas started in on Janusz with the rubber truncheons. *Kidneys . . . thighs . . . upper arms.* Then they'd start again. At one stage, he looked up and sent Porecki – a man the same age as his father – a look of silent appeal. The chill gaze in those curious eyes, the half-smile on his lips, were all the answer he needed.

Some people betrayed their fellow Poles because they were 'true believers'. Then there were those who were in it for the fringe benefits – the bigger apartment, the holidays in Yugoslavia, the backhanders . . . Some of these would cut you slack, if it could be done without endangering themselves. And then there were the people like Porecki. The ones who simply enjoyed the wielding of power.

After what felt like hours, the thugs paused, getting their breath back. He lay there, eyes tight closed, trying not to cry. When Porecki asked him again for the names of his friends, he shook his head. Porecki murmured something: the signal for a new act of humiliation. He felt the wet warmth on his skin before he smelt the ammoniac tang and heard the spatter on the floor tiles.

After that, he broke. Blabbed, shamelessly. Gave up Tomek and Mariusz.

Time and time again, Janusz told himself that another kind of man would have gone on resisting, would never have betrayed his friends. The murdered priest for one. But at the age of seventeen, he had to face a shaming truth. *He wasn't that kind of man.*

Crack! He strikes the back of his head against the brick wall of the passageway. Bringing himself to. For twenty years he has consigned what happened to a lead-lined box buried deep in his memory. *Self control. Strength of will.* The only things that have kept him sane all this time.

He pictures Porecki's face in the family photograph again. *Contented. Complacent.* The funeral guests would soon be standing to propose toasts to the old traitor. He makes a decision. He would say a few words of his own. Tell everyone what kind of man Pawel Porecki really was. The willing instrument of a pitiless regime who had never paid the price for his crimes. A man who had never atoned.

In the front room, the speeches are underway. He lets the warm words and the smell of the honey wodka wash over him – awaiting his moment. He won't shout or lose his rag, he'll just open the window and let a bit of truth blow in.

A hand touches his forearm. It's the daughter. *Janina.* Her eyes, Porecki's eyes, red-rimmed now – linger a beat longer than necessary on his. And suddenly he has an idea. A much better instrument of revenge is staring him in the face.

What better way of paying Porecki back than to fuck his darling daughter? She might even fall in love with him. *Yes!* If that could be achieved, and from her look he sensed it might be, then when he told her the truth about her father the *"civil servant"* – how her untroubled life had really been paid for – retribution would taste all the sweeter. It was only right, wasn't it? that she should know the truth about her father.

He puts his hand over hers, presses it gently. Sees the blood rise in her cheeks. She *is* pretty. It would be no hardship. He's gripped by a sudden, euphoric conviction: *this plan of his will dispel the shadow that Pawel Porecki cast over his life.*

When the toasts are finished he makes his apologies, and Janina accompanies him to the door. He hesitates – it's important to get his next step right – but she saves him from having to make the move.

'Maybe we could stay in touch?' she asks, eyes flickering away from his. 'It would be great to chat about Krakow – I really must make it back there one of these days.'

'Sure,' he says. 'I'd like that.' He punches her number into his phone before turning to go.

He's barely halfway down the path when he hears her call out.

'You've hurt your head,' she says. 'Wait a minute.'

He stands there, fingers exploring the sticky patch on the back of his head, from where he cracked it against the brick wall. A minute later, she's back with a tissue, the smell of disinfectant rising from it. Despite his protests, she insists on cleaning the blood from the wound.

'There.' Finally, she lets him go.

The garden gate clangs behind him.

As Janusz heads back down the street lined with blossom trees, he tries to recapture his earlier elation at the idea of settling the score with Porecki. At the entrance to the tube station, he pauses before pulling out his phone. Finding the girl's number, he stands irresolute for a moment, before deleting it.

As he descends the steps to the station, something occurs to him. Another kind of man might be able to carry out such a plan without doubt or hesitation. But he isn't that kind of man.

INSPECTOR BUCKET INVESTIGATES

Sarah Lotz

Sarah Lotz is the author of several thrillers including *The White Road*, *The Three*, and *Day Four*. Under various pseudonyms, Lotz has also written urban horror, young adult zombie fiction, and erotica.

It was the best of times, it was the worst of times . . .

Bollocks is what I say to that. It's always the worst of times in this part of Lambeth, a mess of cobbled alleyways that twist and turn like the devil's intestines. It's going on for nine, the greasy fog muffling the distant clop of hooves, a scream that could be a laugh, and the gloopy splat of a nightsoil bucket being emptied out of a window.

From the outside, the Prince Street poorhouse looks innocuous enough – just another run-down residence a couple of houses down from a tavern – but it'll be a different story inside. I bang my fist on the door, and Crawley eventually pokes his head out.

'Mr Bucket,' he leers, tonguing the remaining tooth in his jaw. 'What brings you to my pretty palace?'

'Heard you've got some new 'uns in for the night. Couple of toffs. Americans. Brought here an hour or so ago.'

'No one of that description 'ere, Mr Bucket.' He goes to shut the door in my face, but I block it with my boot and pull a shilling out of my purse. 'Hmm,' he says, eyes following the coin as I make it dance through my fingers. 'Might be I recall who you're talking about. Them a pair of lunatics?'

'Could be.'

'What you want with them?'

'Need to take 'em out.'

'Says who?'

'Says me.' He lunges for the coin, but I palm it out of his reach. 'Take me to them first.'

He sniffs. 'I put 'em in the shed.'

I shoulder my way in and follow him through the bathhouse – the cracked tubs brimming with murky water the consistency of mutton stew – out into a courtyard and down towards a long low building, the stained roof canvas snapping in the wind. Before I enter, I fire up one of my strongest cigars and surreptitiously smear Vicks below my nose, but it's no match for the reek of gin-soaked vomit roiling out of the shed's open doorway. Most of the Drones stuck here for the night are roaring drunk, and despite the bite of the air, several are shirt-less, sitting on their pallets, smoking cheap tobacco and swapping lewd stories. Others have rolled themselves top to tail in their blankets, looking for all the world like corpses waiting for the cadaver wagon. I attract a couple of dark glances, but most of them keep their heads down when they clock my uniform.

Crawley leads to me to the far end. The tourists are lying huddled on a straw pallet in the draftiest section of the shed. The older of the two – a balding, middle-aged fellow running to fat – is cradling his younger, skinnier partner in his arms. Their feet are turning blue from the cold – some bastard's nicked their coats and boots.

"Ere,' Crawley says, aiming a kick at the skinny one's thigh. 'Mr Bucket's come to take you out.'

The fat fellow looks up at me, cheeks wobbling with relief. 'Oh, thank God.'

'Get their coats, Crawley,' I jump in before the tourists can say anything else. 'Boots as well.'

'Not my fault someone's nicked their boots,' he whines. 'I warned 'em so I did.'

'Just do it.'

Muttering a curse, he scuttles off.

I crouch next to the pallet. The skinny one glances at me, then buries his head in his partner's shoulder. He has the glassy-eyed look of burgeoning PTSD – it wouldn't be the first time a tourist has gone home with a psychological condition. 'You hurt?' I ask, keeping my voice low. 'Raped? Beaten? Rat bites?'

Fatty shakes his head. They were lucky. According to my intel, they slipped away during this morning's A Christmas Carol introductory tour. They were nabbed hours later in the Adelphi, just outside Mrs Crupp's lodging house, giving away their cash and trying to convince a group of jeering Drones that the city is actually a giant theme park built in New Zealand. One of Crawley's blackguards dragged them here, probably hoping for a kick-back; rich lunatics can be good for a bribe. It could have been worse, but my Runners should have been more alert, especially the fucker assigned to watch over them.

Fatty clears his throat. 'Are you . . . are you real?'

'Best to keep your voice down, sir.'

'I mean, you are the Inspector Bucket, aren't you?' he whispers. 'From Bleak House?'

'I am indeed, sir, but I'm no Drone.'

'So what are you? An actor?'

I bristle at this, but it's as good a job description as any. 'In a manner of speak-ing.'

He gestures at the stinking unfortunates lying on the pallets around us. 'But these guys – they're all . . . authentic?'

'They are indeed, sir, and like as not they'll cut your throat soon as look at you.' There are no Runners or Plants in the Prince Street Workhouse. You can't pay anyone enough to put up with the blood, the fights and Crawley's shit.

He smooths his thinning hair over his pate. 'Jesus, man. This place – it's . . . it's sick, inhuman. I've got a mind to sue.'

'Best keep your mouth shut until we're out of here, sir.'

Crawley stalks back towards us and chucks a bundle of clothes at the couple. The coats stink of rat piss and the boots are worn through – they aren't the ones they were wearing when they were brought here, that's for sure – but they're smart enough not to argue. Fatty helps his partner shrug into his coat, fingers fumbling with the buttons.

'These lunatics bound for Bedlam, Mr Bucket?' Crawley asks.

'Mind your own.' I chuck a shilling on the floor, leaving Crawley to dig in the filth to retrieve it, then usher the tourists out of the shed.

It can take days for tourists to acclimatise to the stench – the river, the mounds of horseshit, the unwashed bodies, the coal smoke that makes your lungs ache like you've inhaled eighty fags before breakfast – but after the fetid air inside the workhouse, the evening smells as fresh as a countryside morning.

I stride off through the warren, the tourists puffing behind me, the gaslights doing sod all to cut through the gloom. This late in the season the fog's the real thing – no need to pipe in that atmospheric crap they used when the park first opened.

'Hey,' Fatty tugs at my sleeve. 'Hey, can't we get a carriage? Stephen's traumatised; he needs help.'

Now that we've left Crawley's purgatory behind, Fatty's regaining his confidence. The tourists tend to be mega-rich bastards who are used to being arse-kissed, and it looks like this fellow is part of that tribe. I've instructed an omnibus to meet us in Waterloo Street, but he doesn't need to know that – arse-kissing isn't in my job description. 'Keep moving, sir.'

'You can't treat us like this!' he whines. 'I paid a fortune to come here!'

He grabs at my sleeve again, but this time I catch his hand and bend his fingers back. He squeals like a sow about to have her throat slit. 'Now then,' I murmur in his ear. 'You going to come quietly?'

The bluster leaves him instantly and he nods. I walk them through an alley that runs behind an old boot-blacking factory and leads out into the main thoroughfare. Choosing a lamppost that's casting enough light for my driver to spot us, I lean against it and fire up another cigar.

'Now then,' I say, blowing a plume of smoke into Fatty's face. 'Why don't you tell me what you thought you were doing?'

'Doing?'

'Before you became one of Crawley's special guests.'

'It was Tim.'

'Tim Cratchit?'

'Yeah. It was bad enough when we did the *Little Dorrit* Tour – that foundling hospital was like something out of Sarajevo – but Tim was the last straw. All cold and hungry, his mother ignoring him . . . It was too real, too *horrible*. We had to do something. We had to tell him – and the others – what they *were*.'

Give me strength. Tiny Tim has a lot to answer for – him and bloody Little Nell. Enough pathos between the two of them to melt even the hardest heart. The tourists are screened of course, forced to go through a three-day seminar on 'Dealing with Dickens' London' complete with indemnity forms, antibiotic boosters and guidelines on interacting with the Drones. But every so often a couple of do-gooders like these two show up, not content to just spend a couple of weeks getting pissed on gin, shagging the whores and taunting Scrooge. I can understand the academics being into this sort of thing, but why rich bastards visit 'authentic Victorian London' (as the brochures put it) instead of going to Majorca is beyond me.

'I mean, what you're doing here. It's not right. It's not ethical,' Fatty continues in his whiny New York accent.

I snort. 'You think Victorian London was ethical?' As if to underline my point, a Disaster Beggar Drone looms out of the fog and staggers towards us, brandishing the stump of his right hand. I flip my nightstick out of my belt and he scarpers.

'But these are real people,' Fatty says. 'With feelings. They need help. Medical attention, antibiotics . . . *counselling*.'

'We're giving them a life they wouldn't have had. They don't know any different.' It's the company line, but it's true in a sense as, with the exception of the main players, the majority of the Drones' DNA is filched out of Victorian paupers' graves. 'Besides,' I say, before Fatty can blether on, 'You weren't supposed to end up at Crawley's unsupervised. Places like that are just for local colour, part of the Workhouse and Factory Tour. In any case, you knew what you were getting yourselves into. Why shell out the cash to come here if you didn't want to see this?'

'Stephen did his Ph.D. on *David Copperfield*,' Fatty says, with a slightly resentful glance at his partner. 'We've been saving up to come here for years.' He mumbles something that sounds like, 'I wanted to go to Harry Potter World.'

The omnibus rattles up and pulls to a stop, and I instruct the driver not to let the tourists out of his sight until they're processed and ferried back to the hotel. Fatty can rant on about suing all he likes; he'll be lucky if *he* isn't the one who's slapped with a law suit. The Walt Disney Co. doesn't fuck around. Last thing it needs is a couple of self-important pricks like these two bleating about maltreatment and abuse; it's had enough crap from Amnesty International as it is.

'Aren't you coming with us, Inspector?' Fatty asks, struggling to heave his bulk into the brougham.

'You're in good hands, sir, and I have other matters to attend to.' Like grabbing an eel pie and a pint, then heading back to my lodgings to check my email. I shoot him an ironic salute, then get moving.

'Inspector!' I turn to see the skinny fellow – Stephen – hobbling after me. The shell-shocked glaze has gone from his eyes, replaced by a shrewd intelligence I'm not sure I like. 'Inspector, may I ask you a question?'

'What?'

'What do you think Dickens would think?'

'Think about what?'

'This place. This *theme park*. He spent his whole life railing against social injustice, and here we are, in the twenty-first century, recreating the squalor . . . and for what?'

For profit is what, of course. For the *hell* of it, the novelty of it. But how would I know what bleeding Dickens would think? Far as I can tell from the biographies, the bugger wasn't averse to lining his own pockets. 'Good luck, sir,' I say stiffly. 'Have a safe trip home.'

He suddenly smiles at me – a frankly disturbing grin that has more than a hint of lunacy to it. '"Time and place cannot bind Mr Bucket!"'

Jesus. If I only had a penny every time some pompous academic spouted that in my face.

I'm crossing Chancery Lane, en route to Ye Olde Cheshire Cheese, when my ear-piece buzzes and a tinny voice screeches something unintelligible in my ear. What now? It had better not be another tourist incident; if it is, heads are going to roll. Hopefully it's just a Drone gone AWOL again. Happens occasionally when one of them gets it into his head to cross the river and scale the outer walls. Lab rats say it's an implant malfunction, I'm not so sure. In any case, they don't get far.

'Repeat that?' I say.

'Big fuck-up, guv.'

'Who is this?'

'Oh. Sorry, guv. It's Pete.'

'Who?'

'I mean Tom. Tom . . . er, Chitling.'

It takes me a few seconds to place him, but then I have it. Pete, aka Tom, is the newest of my Plants, assigned a role as a minor member of Fagin's crew. And God, he's a useless bastard if ever there was one. Unlike the rest of my Plants and Runners – most of whom are ex-cops or army men and women – he's an out-of-work Australian soap extra, hired because he can do a passing good Cockney accent. But beggars can't be choosers; staff turnover here is high, there aren't many like me who can stick it here for more than a season. 'What is it?'

'Murder, guv.'

I turn into an alley so that I can talk freely. 'Eh? Nancy's not due to be offed for another week.' And it can't be the Tulkinhorn 'murder' – Inspector Bucket's time in the sun. My miraculous solving of that case is always reserved for the season finale.

'It's not Nancy, guv. It's Fagin.'

'Fagin?'

'Yeah, guv'nor. He's gone got his throat slit.'

'*What?*'

'And lawd love a duck, guv, he's bleeding like a stuck pig.'

'Enough with the Cockney bullshit please.'

'Sorry, guv.'

'Who did it?'

'Dunno. Was out having a slash, heard a commotion, came back and found him.'

'Could it be Sikes?'

'Nah, guv. He's in Newgate for the night.'

'There any Runners in the area?'

'Dunno.'

Christ. 'Look, just stay where you are, try and keep the Drones and Tourists out of the vicinity. I'm on my way.'

I order Bow Street and Scotland Yard to send as many Runners as they can spare, hail a passing cab and instruct the driver to head straight to Clerkenwell. He's none too pleased; it's not likely he'll get a fare on the way back. Fagin's stomping ground makes Lambeth's rookeries look like Bond Street. Still, it shouldn't take longer than five minutes to get there. More experts than you can shake a stick at were consulted to ensure Dickens's London is the most authentic theme park in the world (taking it too far if you ask me; could have done without the stench), but it's still only a fraction of the size of the original. Not even Disney has that much cash to burn.

I instruct the cabbie to wait and hustle over to where Pete's sitting on the steps just outside Fagin's rat-hole. I know we're only talking about a Drone here, but he looks remarkably sanguine for someone who's just discovered a mutilated corpse. He's fidgeting with his cap and humming The Smiths' *Panic on the Streets of London*. Talk about an anachronism. 'Shut your trap, Pete.'

'Sorry, guv.'

'Where is he?'

Pete gestures behind him. 'Up there. But blimey, I didn't think there'd be so much blood.'

'Thought you said his throat was slit?'

'Yeah. But I dunno, guv. I think in me head I'd convinced meself they weren't, you know, actual people. More like them things from that old movie. *Westworld* or whatever.'

Sometimes I wish Disney had gone this route. It would be much easier to police, even if the occasional Drone does go Yul Brynner mental. 'Let's have a look, then.'

Pete clumps up the stairs behind me. To my mind, Fagin's lair is one of the least convincing recreations. Its wooden floorboards and rickety stairs are far too reminiscent of the set from *Oliver! The Musical*.

The stench of blood and shit hits me before I'm through the door. I peer in, eyes adjusting to the sickly glow cast by the gaslamps. Fagin's lying face up on the floor next to a pile of purloined watches, wallets, and jewellery, blood already starting to congeal in his beard. He's a goner, there's no mistake, and whoever did it wasn't after the loot.

We've had quite a lot of trouble with our Fagins in the three years since the park's been up and running, but we've never had one that's had his throat slit before (although he always ends up the same at the end of the season, waiting to be hanged in Newgate prison). In the interests of authenticity, Fagin's supposed to be grown from the DNA of a nineteenth-century money-lender name of Ikey Solomon (the fellow on whom Dickens allegedly based the character) but plundering a Jewish graveyard does not a Fagin make, however much false memory the behaviourists implant into the finished product. Before they came up with the right mix of low cunning and crafty humour, a couple of our former Fagins veered off script. One found religion and decided to become a Rabbi; another became slightly too attached to the children in his care (the ending of *Oliver Twist* doesn't have quite the same ring when its corrupted protagonist ends up selling his arse on Catherine Street).

Still, Fagin will need to be replaced ASAP. They'll probably have to make do with a Plant for a while, so we can count on some complaints from the tourists

– however good the performance it's never as convincing as a Drone that's been programmed to believe it actually is a Victorian fence.

I call through to the station to get them working on the surveillance footage. We'll have to track the Drones by their implants, see who was in the area at the time, but this will take a while. Probably makes sense to start with the known villains, and God knows Dickens didn't skimp on these. My money's on Quilp, a psychopath if ever there was one, but for the life of me I can't think of a motive. And besides, Drones from different novels tend not to interact. It's as if they've got a sixth sense about not mixing up the storylines.

'You think it was a tourist what dunnit, guv?' Pete asks.

'Doubt it, Pete.' But then again, I suppose it's possible that a psychopath might have squeaked through the screening process – some nutter who thinks he can take advantage of the legal loophole where Drones are concerned. But far as I know, the two Americans I dealt with earlier are the only two who have slipped through the net recently, and they would have been well on their way back to the real world when Fagin met his sticky end. No. My money's on another Drone.

A couple of my more reliable Runners show up, and I instruct them to seal the area and inform HQ that we need a replacement Fagin. I drag Pete outside, tell him to head back to his lodgings and keep tonight's balls-up to himself.

'Aw, can't I help, guv? I've always fancied myself a bit of a detective.'

I hesitate. While we wait for the surveillance intel he could have his uses. 'I'm off to talk to Nancy. You round up the kids, see if they saw anything.'

'Aw what? Can't I do Nancy?'

'Have you met her?'

'Not yet. She's always out when I'm on shift.'

'Think yourself lucky.'

'But, guv. Them kids, they're right rotten little bastards.'

He's not wrong. I've never been a fan of the Oliver Drone. Too po-faced for good, and the Artful Dodger and Charley Drones would benefit from a serious dose of Ritalin. 'They know your face, don't they? They're more likely to talk to you. You want to help or not?'

'Alright,' he sulks.

I send a call through to one of my Plants, an ex-Navy Seal with a *The Crimson Petal and the White* obsession and an encyclopedic knowledge of the park's prostitute Drones. She calls back with Nancy's exact location, and five minutes later I'm rolling towards Catherine Street.

It's going on for eleven, and now that the theatres and freak shows have disgorged their punters, the street is teeming with tourists eager to check out 'Victorian London By Night' (or the Whore Tour, as my Runners call it). I spot a few single males allowing themselves to be dragged into the brothels (where they'll be grateful for the strong antibiotics they're made to take). The other tourists are mostly middle-aged couples, their eyes shining with lust or fixed to the pavement in embarrassment or disgust. I spot Nancy outside one of the more disreputable Lounges, trying to distract a tourist with her cleavage while she slips his wallet out of his waistcoat. The second she spots me, she cackles, picks up her skirts and waves them at me, showing off the syphilitic sores that weep along her legs. 'Back for more, Mr Bucket?' she shrieks. 'Hand me a penny and I'll handle you.'

'Not tonight, Nancy.'

'You want me to find you a boy, then, Inspector? Little juicy boy more your thing?' She always says this, knows it gets under my skin. Dicken's Nancy may have been a sweet, loyal character, but they've never yet managed to create a Drone that doesn't turn into a hard-bitten, street-wise harridan after a week of being on the streets. The chemical fug of cheap gin pours out of her pores. Tourists are warned not to drink it – it's potent enough to send you blind; there's another, less dangerous type for them, same with the opium in the dens.

'You hear about Fagin, Nancy?'

'Gone got his throat slit, ain't he?'

'Who told you that?'

'Little bird.'

'You don't seem too concerned.'

'Why would I be? Fagin's nothin' to me, Mr Bucket.'

'You got any idea who'd want to murder him?'

'Ha! Half of London, dearie.' She scratches at her wig and a louse crawls out from behind her ear and skitters across her cheek.

I pull out a shilling – like Crawley, it's the only language she understands. 'Nothing else you want to tell me, Nancy?'

'Well now, Mr Bucket,' she says, eyes glued to the coin. 'I don't know who done it, but there was a strange toff hanging about Field Street earlier. Lunatic, he was. Talking to himself.'

'You recognise him? Seen him before?'

'Nah, Mr Bucket. He looked familiar, but I couldn't make him.'

'Tall, short?'

'Average height I'd say, Mr Bucket.'

Pete shouts something in my ear-piece, and I hand a shilling to Nancy, who bites it, winks at me and moves on to her next victim.

'Say again, Pete,' I say, shielding my lips with my hand.

'Guv! He . . . he bit me! Dodger bit me!'

'Bite him back then.'

'Aw, guv, he's filthy!'

Give me strength. 'Don't let him get away.' It's too late to warn Pete to be more discreet. In any case, Dodger will have seen worse and weirder behavior than some pseudo-Cockney fuckwit talking to himself.

'He says he ain't going to peach, guv.'

'Tell him Inspector Bucket will be round if he doesn't tell what he knows.'

There's a pause. 'Guv! Dodger says he saw a toff leaving Fagin's. Smallish fellow wearing a top hat and long coat.'

'He recognise him?'

'Nah. 'Ang on.' Another pause. 'He says the fella was talking to himself.'

That gels with what Nancy said. 'Dodger hear what he was saying?'

'Yeah, guv. He said it sounded like, "bah, humbug."'

'*What?*'

'Gor blimey,' Pete says. 'Scrooge done it!'

The holographic Marley is still floating above the bed, unaware that the object of its attentions is no longer able to appreciate them.

Scrooge didn't 'do it' after all. The Drone's lying spreadeagled on his bed, the linen black with the arterial blood that's leaking out of the jagged hole in his throat. What a bloody mess. Scrooge is the park's number one attraction, and being derived from John Elwes, a legendary seventeenth-century miser and politician, he's been one of our more reliable Drones, rarely giving us any off-script surprises.

It's going to be hard for the company to bury this one. Seconds after Scrooge was offed, a group of tourists taking part in the *A Christmas Carol* Evening Experience had arrived to peer through the bedroom window. The more bolshy ones are refusing to move on, some of them loudly wondering if this is a postmodern take on the famous fable. The Disney execs are going to shit themselves when they hear about this. That's two pieces of valuable merchandise lost in one night.

I head back outside, instruct my Runners to disperse the crowd, then step to one side so that I can catch up on the latest intel trickling through my ear-piece. It's not promising. The obvious villains – Quilp, Heep, Ralph Nickleby et al. – are all accounted for, and so are the most notorious of the background Drones. And thanks to the bloody CGI Marley interfering with the view of the hidden cameras, all we've got to go on description-wise is a blurry image of a dark-coated bloke wearing a top hat.

Pete comes puffing up towards me. 'Is it true, guv? Is Scrooge really a goner?'

'Looks like it.'

Pete nods towards the throng of protesting tourists, still refusing to move. 'Can't believe he managed to get away through this lot.'

'Tell me about it.'

'You want me to question the Drones what are hanging around the area? See if they saw anything?'

How could it hurt? 'Go on, then.'

Someone's clearly got it in for the character Drones, so what now? Even if I call in all my off-duty Runners, I don't have the staff to tail all the park's main players, not without taking them off tourist duty. And unless a Runner, Plant or tourist is injured I don't have the authority to call in the outside cops. And there's something else niggling at me. The fat tourist's words pop into my head: '*But these are real people . . . with feelings.*' It's one thing for the Drones to live out their lives (and deaths) as Dickens intended, but no one deserves a fate like Scrooge and Fagin have suffered, whatever else they may be.

'Inspector!' An American voice slices through the hubbub. I swing around, spot a burly fellow pushing his way towards me. A few of the Drones are staring at him, wide-eyed, as if he's an escapee from one of the freakshows. The tourists are advised to let themselves go, physically, before they come here – so as not to draw too much attention to themselves. But this guy's sporting a freshly botoxed forehead, bleached teeth, and a bright orange spray-tan. And holy God, he's wearing Nikes below his breeches. A Disney exec if ever there was one.

'Somewhere we can talk?' he says without introducing himself.

I gesture towards a coffee house set back from the street. The proprietor is one of my Plants, and she'll see to it we're undisturbed. She shows us to a table in a dark corner a delightful few feet away from the door leading to the outhouse, slaps a couple of steaming mugs of chicory in front of us and, with a knowing look in my direction, heads off to hang by the door and discourage tourists from entering.

The exec holds a handkerchief to his nose and peers distrustfully at the gloop in the mug. 'Phew. I always forget how much this place stinks. You going to fill me in on this clusterfuck, Inspector?'

'Well, sir, it's simple. Someone's killing off our main characters.'

'What about the surveillance? Tracking?

'We're on it, sir. But I'm thinking, might be best if we evacuated. Get the tourists out of here.'

'We can't do that! The park's rep is hanging by a thread as it is. This is a controlled environment; how hard can it be to track down one bad apple?'

One bad apple indeed! Clearly this is not a man who has explored Clerkenwell's darker elements. 'I've got my best men and women on the job, sir, but I'm thinking that maybe we should call in the outside authorities. We can only track the Drones, sir. What if it's a tourist?' Or one of my Runners. But I'm not going to plant *that* idea in the shill's head.

He snorts. 'Listen to me carefully, Inspector. You *are* a real inspector, as well as playing the part of Mr Bucket, aren't you?'

Christ, is there anything worse than a prick who uses the word eponymous? 'I was a Commander in the Met actually, sir, before I took the job here.'

'Then sort it out. It's a freaking mess, but it's not a disaster. We'll tell the tourists that Scrooge's demise is all part of the fun. The Drone replacements will be here in a couple of days, so if we play our cards right no one need be any the wiser.' He takes a sip of coffee, grimaces and points a finger in my face. 'I heard you had a problem with a couple of tourists earlier.'

'That's dealt with, sir.'

'Good. Hey, you think this whole thing is some sort of publicity stunt? Some bleeding-heart terrorist trying to blackmail us into closing the park?'

'They'd do better to bump off a couple of tourists then, sir. Drones don't have any legal rights, do they?'

'Guv!' Pete pushes past the Plant at the door, and ignoring the company shill, plonks himself on the bench next to me. 'Guv. Cripple I was talking to thinks he saw the killer. Same description and everything.'

The exec opens his mouth to speak, but I gesture to him to keep his trap shut. 'And?'

'Heard 'im saying something, guv. Like before.'

'Well?'

'"Break his heart." What's that mean, guv?'

I don't stop to answer him – I'm already on my feet, ignoring the protestations from the exec and praying that I'm not too late.

I'll give her this. She put up a fight. The yellowing lace of her dress is now dyed crimson, but there are defensive cuts on her palms where she tried to ward off the blows.

Pete is bent double next to the grandfather clock puking his guts up, this scene getting to him where Fagin's murder left him cold. Maybe it's the underlying stench of decaying wedding cake that's affecting him; maybe it's the gut-wrenching sight of a middle-aged woman lying sprawled in the remains of a wedding feast, her skirts rucked up around her hips.

'Pete, call Bow Street, get them to call in the cops.'

He looks up at me, wiping his mouth and struggling to stop himself from gagging again. 'You are the cops, guv.'

'I mean the outside authorities.'

'Seriously, guv?'

'Do it.'

He nods and does as he's told.

I pull Miss Haversham's skirts down to give her some dignity. I've always had a soft spot for the Miss Haversham Drone. Bitter old cow she may be, but despair, loneliness, and revenge are motivations I understand.

Pete joins me, his face slick with sweat, and peers down at her. 'Why's she dressed like that?'

'Didn't you read the novel?'

He squirms. 'Um . . . I downloaded a few of BBC adaptation thingies. Watched *The Muppet Christmas Carol* a few times. The books were . . . I dunno, bit too wordy. I'm more of a Lee Child man myself.'

Idiot.

Pete steps back. 'Blimey, guv. She's breathing!'

He's right. I drop to my knees next to her, grab her wrist. Her pulse is weak, but it's there all right. She sighs, blinks then gazes up at me through muddy eyes. 'He got me in the end,' she whispers.

'The fellow who did this. He say anything before he left?'

She gasps, coughs up a bubble of blood, murmurs: 'Time and place . . .' But the strain is too much. Her eyes lose focus, and then, she's gone.

'What's that mean, guv?' Pete says.

But I know what it means. And I know where to find the fucker.

I pace outside Scotland Yard's entrance, puffing on a cigar. Wondering if I'm right. Wondering if he really is going to come for me. After all, I'm not a Drone, though as the years pass it's getting easier to stay in character. I've instructed my Runners to hang back, keep to the shadows. We still have no idea who we're dealing with and I don't want him to get spooked. The list of suspects is narrowing, but even discounting the tourists there are scores to track and trace. Even a facsimile of Dickens's London is an over-populated mess.

Big Ben chimes out midnight, and between each strike I hear the muffled clump of footsteps getting closer.

It happens fast: a blur of a figure darting towards me, the flash of a blade. But he's no match for me. Unlike the 'real' Inspector Bucket, I've got a black belt in Ninjitsu and six years of SAS training behind me. I grab his wrist, knock the knife from his grip, and twist his arm behind his back with such force I hear his shoulder joint pop. I drag him into the light of a nearby lamppost.

And almost let him go when I clock who it is.

The Runners who've been waiting in the wings race forward and freeze, equally shocked, when they get a look at the fellow writhing in my grasp. Only Pete looks none the wiser.

'Guv! Who is it?'

I ignore him, still not quite believing we've got the right bloke. The David Copperfield Drone has never given us any trouble before – far as I know they've used the same one since the park opened, simply resetting his memory each season. So why would he suddenly go off like this? 'Why did you do it, son?' I ask him.

'Obscenities,' he mutters. 'Abominations. Voices.'

'Eh?' Pete says. 'What voices?'

'In my head,' Copperfield says, tears starting to dribble down his cheeks. 'I had to make them stop.'

'Oh right. Like that Son of Sam bloke,' Pete says. 'Said his dog told him to do it.'

'Very helpful, Pete,' I say.

'So he's not one of them baddies in the books then, guv?'

'He's supposed to be one of the most sympathetic of Dickens's characters. One of the most convincing.' I'm about to launch into *David Copperfield* 101, when it hits me. 'Jesus.'

'What is it, guv?'

'*David Copperfield* is supposed to be Dickens's autobiographical novel.'

'So?'

'Think about it. Where do you think they got the DNA from?'

Even Pete manages to figure this one out. 'Bugger me sideways, guv,' he says, in a broad Sydney drawl, finally slipping out of character.

Copperfield, or Dickens, gives up struggling and allows me to cuff him.

As I watch my Runners dragging him into the Yard, I wonder if it's too late to get hold of that skinny tourist. Let him know that the seed I'm sure he planted when he sneaked off to visit Copperfield's lodgings has sprouted. That now I know the answer to his question.

London's evening soundtrack is suddenly swallowed up by the flik-flack of helicopter blades. I listen to the distant screams of the Drones, panicking as the new world collides with the old one, wondering what they must be thinking. Wondering why truth is always viler than fiction. Wondering what Inspector Bucket is going to do next.

Fuck it.

Maybe Harry Potter World is hiring.

I CAN FIND MY WAY OUT

Ngaio Marsh

Ngaio Marsh (1895–1982) is known as New Zealand's 'Queen of Crime'. Her gentleman police detective Roderick Alleyn appears in thirty-two novels including *A Man Lay Dead* and *A Surfeit of Lampreys*. Marsh also revolutionized the theatre industry in New Zealand and received a Damehood in 1966.

At half-past six on the night in question, Anthony Gill, unable to eat, keep still, think, speak or act coherently, walked from his rooms to the Jupiter Theatre. He knew that there would be nobody backstage, that there was nothing for him to do in the theatre, that he ought to stay quietly in his rooms and presently dress, dine and arrive at, say, a quarter to eight. But it was as if something shoved him into his clothes, thrust him into the street and compelled him to hurry through the West End to the Jupiter. His mind was overlaid with a thin film of inertia. Odd lines from the play occurred to him, but without any particular significance. He found himself busily reiterating a completely irrelevant sentence: "She has a way of laughing that would make a man's heart turn over."

Piccadilly, Shaftesbury Avenue. "Here I go," he thought, turning into Hawke Street, "towards my play. It's one hour and twenty-nine minutes away. A step a second. It's rushing towards me. Tony's first play. Poor young Tony Gill. Never mind. Try again."

The Jupiter. Neon lights: I CAN FIND MY WAY OUT—*by Anthony Gill*. And in the entrance the bills and photographs. *Coralie Bourne with H. J. Bannington, Barry George and Canning Cumberland.*

Canning Cumberland. The film across his mind split and there was the Thing itself and he would have to think about it. How bad would Canning Cumberland be if he came down drunk? Brilliantly bad, they said. He would bring out all the tricks. Clever actor stuff, scoring off everybody, making a fool of the dramatic balance. "In Mr. Canning Cumberland's hands indifferent dialogue and unconvincing situations seemed almost real." What can you do with a drunken actor?

He stood in the entrance feeling his heart pound and his inside deflate and sicken.

Because, of course, it was a bad play. He was at this moment and for the first time really convinced of it. It was terrible. Only one virtue in it and that was not his doing. It had been suggested to him by Coralie Bourne: "I don't think the play you have sent me will do as it is but it has occurred to me—" It was a brilliant idea. He had rewritten the play round it and almost immediately and quite innocently he had begun to think of it as his own although he had said shyly to Coralie Bourne: "You should appear as joint author." She had quickly, over-emphatically, refused. "It was nothing at all," she said. "If you're to become a dramatist you will learn to get ideas from everywhere. A single situation is nothing. Think of Shakespeare," she added lightly. "Entire plots! Don't be silly." She had said later, and still with the same hurried, nervous air: "Don't go talking to everyone about it. They will think there is more, instead of less, than meets the eye in my small suggestion. Please promise." He promised, thinking he'd made an error in taste when he suggested that Coralie Bourne, so famous an actress, should appear as joint author with an unknown youth. And how right she was, he thought, because, of course, it's going to be a ghastly flop. She'll be sorry she consented to play in it.

Standing in front of the theatre he contemplated nightmare possibilities. What did audiences do when a first play flopped? Did they clap a little, enough to let the curtain rise and quickly fall again on a discomforted group of players? How scanty must the applause be for them to let him off his own appearance? And they were to go on to the Chelsea Arts Ball. A hideous prospect. Thinking he would give anything in the world if he could stop his play, he turned into the foyer. There were lights in the offices and he paused, irresolute, before a board of photographs. Among them, much smaller than the leading players, was Dendra Gay with the eyes looking straight into his. *She had a way of laughing that would make a man's heart turn over.* "Well," he thought, "so I'm in love with her." He turned away from the photograph. A man came out of the office. "Mr. Gill? Telegrams for you."

Anthony took them and as he went out he heard the man call after him: "Very good luck for tonight, sir."

There were queues of people waiting in the side street for the early doors.

At six-thirty Coralie Bourne dialed Canning Cumberland's number and waited.

She heard his voice. "It's me," she said.

"O God! darling, I've been thinking about you." He spoke rapidly, too loudly. "Coral, I've been thinking about Ben. You oughtn't to have given that situation to the boy."

"We've been over it a dozen times, Cann. Why not give it to Tony? Ben will never know." She waited and then said nervously, "Ben's gone, Cann. We'll never see him again."

"I've got a Thing about it. After all, he's your husband."

"No, Cann, no."

"Suppose he turns up. It'd be like him to turn up."

"He won't turn up."

She heard him laugh. "I'm sick of all this," she thought suddenly. "I've had it once too often. I can't stand any more. . . . Cann," she said into the telephone. But he had hung up.

At twenty to seven, Barry George looked at himself in his bathroom mirror. "I've got a better appearance," he thought, "than Cann Cumberland. My head's a good shape, my eyes are bigger and my jaw line's cleaner. I never let a show down. I don't drink. I'm a better actor." He turned his head a little, slewing his eyes to watch the effect. "In the big scene," he thought, "I'm the star. He's the feed. That's the way it's been produced and that's what the author wants. I ought to get the notices."

Past notices came up in his memory. He saw the print, the size of the paragraphs; a long paragraph about Canning Cumberland, a line tacked on the end of it. "Is it unkind to add that Mr. Barry George trotted in the wake of Mr. Cumberland's virtuosity with an air of breathless dependability?" And again: "It is a little hard on Mr. Barry George that he should be obliged to act as foil to this brilliant performance." Worst of all: "Mr. Barry George succeeded in looking tolerably unlike a stooge, an achievement that evidently exhausted his resources."

"Monstrous!" he said loudly to his own image, watching the fine glow of indignation in the eyes. Alcohol, he told himself, did two things to Cann Cumberland. He raised his finger. Nice, expressive hand. An actor's hand. Alcohol destroyed Cumberland's artistic integrity. It also invested him with devilish cunning. Drunk, he would burst the seams of a play, destroy its balance, ruin its form and himself emerge blazing with a showmanship that the audience mistook for genius. "While I," he said aloud, "merely pay my author the compliment of faithful interpretation. Psha!"

He returned to his bedroom, completed his dressing and pulled his hat to the right angle. Once more he thrust his face close to the mirror and looked searchingly at its image. "By God!" he told himself, "he's done it once too often, old boy. Tonight we'll even the score, won't we? By God, we will."

Partly satisfied, and partly ashamed, for the scene, after all, had smacked a little of ham, he took his stick in one hand and a case holding his costume for the Arts Ball in the other, and went down to the theatre.

At ten minutes to seven, H. J. Bannington passed through the gallery queue on his way to the stage door alley, raising his hat and saying: "Thanks so much," to the gratified ladies who let him through. He heard them murmur his name. He walked briskly along the alley, greeted the stage-doorkeeper, passed under a dingy lamp, through an entry and so to the stage. Only working lights were up. The walls of an interior set rose dimly into shadow. Bob Reynolds, the stage-manager, came out through the prompt-entrance. "Hello, old boy," he said, "I've changed the dressing-rooms. You're third on the right: they've moved your things in. Suit you?"

"Better, at least, than a black-hole the size of a W.C. but without its appointments," H.J. said acidly. "I suppose the great Mr. Cumberland still has the star-room?"

"Well, yes, old boy."

"And who, pray, is next to him? In the room with the other gas fire?"

"We've put Barry George there, old boy. You know what he's like."

"Only too well, old boy, and the public, I fear, is beginning to find out." H.J. turned into the dressing-room passage. The stage-manager returned to the set where he encountered his assistant. "What's biting *him*?" asked the assistant. "He wanted a dressing-room with a fire."

"Only natural," said the A.S.M. nastily. "He started life reading gas meters."

On the right and left of the passage, nearest the stage end, were two doors, each with its star in tarnished paint. The door on the left was open. H.J. looked in and was greeted with the smell of greasepaint, powder, wet-white, and flowers. A gas fire droned comfortably. Coralie Bourne's dresser was spreading out towels. "Good evening, Katie, my jewel," said H.J. "La Belle not down yet?"

"We're on our way," she said.

H.J. hummed stylishly: *"Bella filia del amore,"* and returned to the passage. The star-room on the right was closed but he could hear Cumberland's dresser moving about inside. He went on to the next door, paused, read the card, "Mr. Barry George," warbled a high derisive note, turned in at the third door and switched on the light.

Definitely not a second lead's room. No fire. A washbasin, however, and opposite mirrors. A stack of telegrams had been placed on the dressing-table. Still singing he reached for them, disclosing a number of bills that had been tactfully laid underneath and a letter, addressed in a flamboyant script.

His voice might have been mechanically produced and arbitrarily switched off, so abruptly did his song end in the middle of a roulade. He let the telegrams fall on the table, took up the letter and tore it open. His face, wretchedly pale, was reflected and endlessly re-reflected in the mirrors.

At nine o'clock the telephone rang. Roderick Alleyn answered it. "This is Sloane 84405. No, you're on the wrong number. *No.*" He hung up and returned to his wife and guest. "That's the fifth time in two hours."

"Do let's ask for a new number."

"We might get next door to something worse."

The telephone rang again. "This is not 84406," Alleyn warned it. "No, I cannot take three large trunks to Victoria Station. No, I am not the Instant All Night Delivery. No."

"They're 84406," Mrs. Alleyn explained to Lord Michael Lamprey. "I suppose it's just faulty dialing, but you can't imagine how angry everyone gets. Why do you want to be a policeman?"

"It's a dull hard job, you know—" Alleyn began.

"Oh," Lord Mike said, stretching his legs and looking critically at his shoes, "I don't for a moment imagine I'll leap immediately into false whiskers and plain-clothes. No, no. But I'm revoltingly healthy, sir. Strong as a horse. And I don't think I'm as stupid as you might feel inclined to imagine—"

The telephone rang.

"I say, do let me answer it," Mike suggested and did so.

"Hullo?" he said winningly. He listened, smiling at his hostess. "I'm afraid—" he began. "Here, wait a bit—Yes, but—" His expression became blank and complacent. "May I," he said presently, "repeat your order, sir? Can't be too sure, can we? Call at 11 Harrow Gardens, Sloane Square, for one suitcase to be delivered immediately at the Jupiter Theatre to Mr. Anthony Gill. Very good, sir. Thank you, sir. Collect. Quite."

He replaced the receiver and beamed at the Alleyns.

"What the devil have you been up to?" Alleyn said.

"He just simply wouldn't listen to reason. I tried to tell him."

"But it may be urgent," Mrs. Alleyn ejaculated.

"It couldn't be more urgent, really. It's a suitcase for Tony Gill at the Jupiter."

"Well, then—"

"I was at Eton with the chap," said Mike reminiscently. "He's four years older than I am so of course he was madly important while I was less than the dust. This'll lam him."

"I think you'd better put that order through at once," said Alleyn firmly.

"I rather thought of executing it myself, do you know, sir. It'd be a frightfully neat way of gate-crashing the show, wouldn't it? I did try to get a ticket but the house was sold out."

"If you're going to deliver this case you'd better get a bend on."

"It's clearly an occasion for dressing up though, isn't it? I say," said Mike modestly, "would you think it most frightful cheek if I—well I'd promise to come back and return everything. I mean—"

"Are you suggesting that my clothes look more like a vanman's than yours?"

"I thought you'd have things—"

"For Heaven's sake, Rory," said Mrs. Alleyn, "dress him up and let him go. The great thing is to get that wretched man's suitcase to him."

"I know," said Mike earnestly. "It's most frightfully sweet of you. That's how I feel about it."

Alleyn took him away and shoved him into an old and begrimed raincoat, a cloth cap and a muffler. "You wouldn't deceive a village idiot in a total eclipse," he said, "but out you go."

He watched Mike drive away and returned to his wife.

"What'll happen?" she asked.

"Knowing Mike, I should say he will end up in the front stalls and go on to supper with the leading lady. She, by the way, is Coralie Bourne. Very lovely and twenty years his senior so he'll probably fall in love with her." Alleyn reached for his tobacco jar and paused. "I wonder what's happened to her husband," he said.

"Who was he?"

"An extraordinary chap. Benjamin Vlasnoff. Violent temper. Looked like a bandit. Wrote two very good plays and got run in three times for common assault. She tried to divorce him but it didn't go through. I think he afterwards lit off to Russia." Alleyn yawned. "I believe she had a hell of a time with him," he said.

"All Night Delivery," said Mike in a hoarse voice, touching his cap. "Suitcase. One." "Here you are," said the woman who had answered the door. "Carry it carefully, now, it's not locked and the catch springs out."

"Fanks," said Mike. "Much obliged. Chilly, ain't it?"

He took the suitcase out to the car.

It was a fresh spring night. Sloane Square was threaded with mist and all the lamps had halos round them. It was the kind of night when individual sounds separate themselves from the conglomerate voice of London; hollow sirens spoke imperatively down on the river and a bugle rang out over in Chelsea Barracks; a night, Mike thought, for adventure.

He opened the rear door of the car and heaved the case in. The catch flew open, the lid dropped back and the contents fell out. "Damn!" said Mike and switched on the inside light.

Lying on the floor of the car was a false beard.

It was flaming red and bushy and was mounted on a chinpiece. With it was incorporated a stiffened mustache. There were wire hooks to attach the whole thing behind the ears. Mike laid it carefully on the seat. Next he picked up a wide black hat, then a vast overcoat with a fur collar, finally a pair of black gloves.

Mike whistled meditatively and thrust his hands into the pockets of Alleyn's mackintosh. His right-hand fingers closed on a card. He pulled it out. "Chief Detective-Inspector Alleyn," he read, "C.I.D. New Scotland Yard."

"Honestly," thought Mike exultantly, "this is a gift."

Ten minutes later a car pulled into the curb at the nearest parking place to the Jupiter Theatre. From it emerged a figure carrying a suitcase. It strode rapidly along Hawke Street and turned into the stage-door alley. As it passed under the dirty lamp it paused, and thus murkily lit, resembled an illustration from some Edwardian spy-story. The face was completely shadowed, a black cavern from which there projected a square of scarlet beard, which was the only note of color.

The doorkeeper who was taking the air with a member of stage-staff, moved forward, peering at the stranger.

"Was you wanting something?"

"I'm taking this case in for Mr. Gill."

"He's in front. You can leave it with me."

"I'm so sorry," said the voice behind the beard, "but I promised I'd leave it backstage myself."

"So you will be leaving it. Sorry, sir, but no one's admitted be'ind without a card."

"A card? Very well. Here is a card."

He held it out in his black-gloved hand. The stage-doorkeeper, unwillingly removing his gaze from the beard, took the card and examined it under the light. "Coo!" he said, "what's up, governor?"

"No matter. Say nothing of this."

The figure waved its hand and passed through the door. "'Ere!" said the door-keeper excitedly to the stage-hand, "take a slant at this. That's a plainclothes flattie, that was."

"*Plain* clothes!" said the stage-hand. "Them!"

"'E's disguised," said the doorkeeper. "That's what it is. 'E's disguised 'isself."

"'E's bloody well lorst 'isself be'ind them whiskers if you arst me."

Out on the stage someone was saying in a pitched and beautifully articulate voice: "*I've always loathed the view from these windows. However, if that's the sort of thing you admire. Turn off the lights, damn you. Look at it.*"

"Watch it, now, watch it," whispered a voice so close to Mike that he jumped. "O.K.," said a second voice somewhere above his head. The lights on the set turned blue. "Kill that working light." "Working light gone."

Curtains in the set were wrenched aside and a window flung open. An actor appeared, leaning out quite close to Mike, seeming to look into his face and saying very distinctly: "God: it's frightful!" Mike backed away towards a passage, lit only from an open door. A great volume of sound broke out beyond the stage. "House lights," said the sharp voice. Mike turned into the passage. As he did so, someone came through the door. He found himself face to face with Coralie Bourne, beautifully dressed and heavily painted.

For a moment she stood quite still; then she made a curious gesture with her right hand, gave a small breathy sound and fell forward at his feet.

Anthony was tearing his program into long strips and dropping them on the floor of the O.P. box. On his right hand, above and below, was the audience; sometimes laughing, sometimes still, sometimes as one corporate being, raising its hands and striking them together. As now; when down on the stage, Canning Cumberland, using a strange voice, and inspired by some inward devil, flung back the window and said: "God: it's frightful!"

"Wrong! Wrong!" Anthony cried inwardly, hating Cumberland, hating Barry George because he let one speech of three words over-ride him, hating the audience because they liked it. The curtain descended with a long sigh on the second act and a sound like heavy rain filled the theatre, swelled prodigiously and continued after the house lights welled up.

"They seem," said a voice behind him, "to be liking your play."

It was Gosset, who owned the Jupiter and had backed the show. Anthony turned on him stammering: "He's destroying it. It should be the other man's scene. He's stealing."

"My boy," said Gosset, "he's an actor."

"He's drunk. It's intolerable."

He felt Gosset's hand on his shoulder.

"People are watching us. You're on show. This is a big thing for you; a first play, and going enormously. Come and have a drink, old boy. I want to introduce you—"

Anthony got up and Gosset, with his arm across his shoulders, flashing smiles, patting him, led him to the back of the box.

"I'm sorry," Anthony said. "I can't. Please let me off. I'm going backstage."

"Much better not, old son." The hand tightened on his shoulder. "Listen, old son—" But Anthony had freed himself and slipped through the pass-door from the box to the stage.

At the foot of the breakneck stairs Dendra Gay stood waiting. "I thought you'd come," she said.

Anthony said: "He's drunk. He's murdering the play."

"It's only one scene, Tony. He finishes early in the next act. It's going colossally."

"But don't you understand—"

"I do. You *know* I do. But you're a success, Tony darling! You can hear it and smell it and feel it in your bones."

"Dendra—" he said uncertainly.

Someone came up and shook his hand and went on shaking it. Flats were being laced together with a slap of rope on canvas. A chandelier ascended into darkness. "Lights," said the stage-manager, and the set was flooded with them. A distant voice began chanting. "Last act, please. Last act."

"Miss Bourne all right?" the stage-manager suddenly demanded.

"She'll be all right. She's not on for ten minutes," said a woman's voice.

"What's the matter with Miss Bourne?" Anthony asked.

"Tony, I must go and so must you. Tony, it's going to be grand. *Please* think so. *Please.*"

"Dendra—" Tony began, but she had gone.

Beyond the curtain, horns and flutes announced the last act.

"Clear please."

The stage hands came off.

"House lights."

"House lights gone."

"Stand by."

And while Anthony still hesitated in the O.P. corner, the curtain rose. Canning Cumberland and H. J. Bannington opened the last act.

As Mike knelt by Coralie Bourne he heard someone enter the passage behind him. He turned and saw, silhouetted against the lighted stage, the actor who had looked at him through a window in the set. The silhouette seemed to repeat the gesture Coralie Bourne had used, and to flatten itself against the wall.

A woman in an apron came out of the open door.

"I say—here!" Mike said.

Three things happened almost simultaneously. The woman cried out and knelt beside him. The man disappeared through a door on the right.

The woman, holding Coralie Bourne in her arms, said violently: "Why have you come back?" Then the passage lights came on. Mike said: "Look here, I'm most frightfully sorry," and took off the broad black hat. The dresser gaped at him, Coralie Bourne made a crescendo sound in her throat and opened her eyes. "Katie?" she said.

"It's all right, my lamb. It's not him, dear. You're all right." The dresser jerked her head at Mike: "Get out of it," she said.

"Yes, of course, I'm most frightfully—" He backed out of the passage, colliding with a youth who said: "Five minutes, please." The dresser called out: "Tell them she's not well. Tell them to hold the curtain."

"No," said Coralie Bourne strongly. "I'm all right, Katie. Don't say anything. Katie, what was it?"

They disappeared into the room on the left.

Mike stood in the shadow of a stack of scenic flats by the entry into the passage. There was great activity on the stage. He caught a glimpse of Anthony Gill on the far side talking to a girl. The call-boy was speaking to the stage-manager who now shouted into space: "Miss Bourne all right?" The dresser came into the passage and called: "She'll be all right. She's not on for ten minutes." The youth began chanting: "Last act, please." The stage-manager gave a series of orders. A man with an eyeglass and a florid beard came from further down the passage and stood outside the set, bracing his figure and giving little tweaks to his clothes. There was a sound of horns and flutes. Canning Cumberland emerged from the room on the right and on his way to the stage, passed close to Mike, leaving a strong smell of alcohol behind him. The curtain rose.

Behind his shelter, Mike stealthily removed his beard and stuffed it into the pocket of his overcoat.

A group of stage-hands stood nearby. One of them said in a hoarse whisper: "'E's squiffy." "Garn, 'e's going good." "So 'e may be going good. And for why? *Becos* 'e's squiffy."

Ten minutes passed. Mike thought: "This affair has definitely not gone according to plan." He listened. Some kind of tension seemed to be building up on the stage. Canning Cumberland's voice rose on a loud but blurred note. A door in the set opened. "Don't bother to come," Cumberland said. "Goodbye. I can find my way out." The door slammed. Cumberland was standing near Mike. Then, very close, there was a loud explosion. The scenic flats vibrated. Mike's flesh leapt on his bones and Cumberland went into his dressing-rooms. Mike heard the key turn in the door. The smell of alcohol mingled with the smell of gunpowder. A stage-hand moved to a trestle table and laid a pistol on it. The actor with the eyeglass made an exit. He spoke for a moment to the stage-manager, passed Mike and disappeared in the passage.

Smells. There were all sorts of smells. Subconsciously, still listening to the play, he began to sort them out. Glue. Canvas. Greasepaint. The call-boy tapped on the doors. "Mr. George, please." "Miss Bourne, please." They came out, Coralie Bourne with her dresser. Mike heard her turn a door handle and say something. An indistinguishable voice answered her. Then she and her dresser passed him. The others spoke to her and she nodded and then seemed to withdraw into herself, waiting with her head bent, ready to make her entrance. Presently she drew back, walked swiftly to the door in the set, flung it open and swept on, followed a minute later by Barry George.

Smells. Dust, stale paint, cloth. Gas. Increasingly, the smell of gas.

The group of stage-hands moved away behind the set to the side of the stage. Mike edged out of cover. He could see the prompt-corner. The stage-manager stood there with folded arms, watching the action. Behind him were grouped the players who were not on. Two dressers stood apart, watching. The light from the set caught their faces. Coralie Bourne's voice sent phrases flying like birds into the auditorium.

Mike began peering at the floor. Had he kicked some gas fitting adrift? The call-boy passed him, stared at him over his shoulder and went down the passage, tapping. "Five minutes to the curtain, please. Five minutes." The actor with the elderly make-up followed the call-boy out. "God, what a stink of gas," he whispered. "Chronic, ain't it?" said the call-boy. They stared at Mike and then crossed to the waiting group. The man said something to the stage-manager who tipped his head up, sniffing. He made an impatient gesture and turned back to the prompt-box, reaching over the prompter's head. A bell rang somewhere up in the flies and Mike saw a stage-hand climb to the curtain platform.

The little group near the prompt corner was agitated. They looked back towards the passage entrance. The call-boy nodded and came running back. He knocked on the first door on the right. "*Mr. Cumberland! Mr. Cumberland!* You're on for the call." He rattled the door handle. "*Mr. Cumberland! You're on.*"

Mike ran into the passage. The call-boy coughed retchingly and jerked his hand at the door. "Gas!"

"Break it in."

"I'll get Mr. Reynolds."

He was gone. It was a narrow passage. From halfway across the opposite room Mike took a run, head down, shoulder forward, at the door. It gave a little and a sickening increase in the smell caught him in the lungs. A vast storm of noise had broken out and as he took another run he thought: "It's hailing outside."

"Just a minute if *you* please, sir."

It was a stage-hand. He'd got a hammer and screwdriver. He wedged the point of the screwdriver between the lock and the doorpost, drove it home and wrenched. The screws squeaked, the wood splintered and gas poured into the passage. "No winders," coughed the stage-hand.

Mike wound Alleyn's scarf over his mouth and nose. Half-forgotten instructions from anti-gas drill occurred to him. The room looked queer but he could see the man slumped down in the chair quite clearly. He stooped low and ran in.

He was knocking against things as he backed out, lugging the dead weight. His arms tingled. A high insistent voice hummed in his brain. He floated a short distance and came to earth on a concrete floor among several pairs of legs. A long way off, someone said loudly: "I can only thank you for being so kind to what I know, too well, is a very imperfect play." Then the sound of hail began again. There was a heavenly stream of clear air flowing into his mouth and nostrils. "I could eat it," he thought and sat up.

The telephone rang. "Suppose," Mrs. Alleyn suggested, "that this time you ignore it."

"It might be the Yard," Alleyn said, and answered it.

"Is that Chief Detective-Inspector Alleyn's flat? I'm speaking from the Jupiter Theatre. I've rung up to say that the Chief Inspector is here and that he's had a slight mishap. He's all right, but I think it might be as well for someone to drive him home. No need to worry."

"What sort of mishap?" Alleyn asked.

"Er—well—er, he's been a bit gassed."

"*Gassed!* All right. Thanks, I'll come."

"*What* a bore for you darling," said Mrs. Alleyn. "What sort of case is it? Suicide?"

"Masquerading within the meaning of the act, by the sound of it. Mike's in trouble."

"What trouble, for Heaven's sake?"

"Got himself gassed. He's all right. Good night darling. Don't wait up."

When he reached the theatre, the front of the house was in darkness. He made his way down the side alley to the stage-door where he was held up.

"Yard," he said, and produced his official card.

"'Ere," said the stage-doorkeeper, "'ow many more of you?"

"The man inside was working for me," said Alleyn and walked in. The door-keeper followed, protesting.

To the right of the entrance was a large scenic dock from which the double doors had been rolled back. Here Mike was sitting in an armchair, very white about the lips. Three men and two women, all with painted faces, stood near him and behind them a group of stage-hands with Reynolds, the stage-manager, and, apart from these, three men in evening dress. The men looked woodenly shocked. The women had been weeping.

"I'm most frightfully sorry, sir," Mike said. "I've tried to explain. This," he added generally, "is Inspector Alleyn."

"I can't understand all this," said the oldest of the men in evening dress irritably. He turned on the doorkeeper. "You said—"

"I seen 'is card—"

"I know," said Mike, "but you see—"

"This is Lord Michael Lamprey," Alleyn said. "A recruit to the Police Department. What's happened here?"

"Doctor Rankin, would you—?"

The second of the men in evening dress came forward. "All right, Gosset. It's a bad business, Inspector. I've just been saying the police would have to be informed. If you'll come with me—"

Alleyn followed him through a door onto the stage proper. It was dimly lit. A trestle table had been set up in the centre and on it, covered with a sheet, was an unmistakable shape. The smell of gas, strong everywhere, hung heavily about the table.

"Who is it?"

"Canning Cumberland. He'd locked the door of his dressing-room. There's a gas fire. Your young friend dragged him out, very pluckily, but it was no go. I was in front. Gosset, the manager, had asked me to supper. It's a perfectly clear case of suicide as you'll see."

"I'd better look at the room. Anybody been in?"

"God, no. It was a job to clear it. They turned the gas off at the main. There's no window. They had to open the double doors at the back of the stage and a small outside door at the end of the passage. It may be possible to get in now."

He led the way to the dressing-room passage. "Pretty thick, still," he said. "It's the first room on the right. They burst the lock. You'd better keep down near the floor."

The powerful lights over the mirror were on and the room still had its look of occupation. The gas fire was against the left hand wall. Alleyn squatted down by it. The tap was still turned on, its face lying parallel with the floor. The top of the heater, the tap itself, and the carpet near it, were covered with a creamish powder. On the end of the dressing-table shelf nearest to the stove was a box of this powder. Further along the shelf, greasepaints were set out in a row beneath the mirror. Then came a wash basin and in front of this an overturned chair. Alleyn could see the track of heels, across the pile of the carpet, to the door immediately opposite. Beside the wash basin was a quart bottle of whiskey, three parts empty, and a tumbler. Alleyn had had about enough and returned to the passage.

"Perfectly clear," the hovering doctor said again. "Isn't it?"

"I'll see the other rooms, I think."

The one next to Cumberland's was like his in reverse, but smaller. The heater was back to back with Cumberland's. The dressing-shelf was set out with much the same assortment of greasepaints. The tap of this heater, too, was turned on. It was of precisely the same make as the other and Alleyn, less embarrassed here by fumes, was able to make a longer examination. It was a common enough type of gas fire. The lead-in was from a pipe through a flexible metallic tube with a rubber connection. There were two taps, one in the pipe and one at the junction of the tube with the heater itself. Alleyn disconnected the tube and examined the connection. It was perfectly sound, a close fit and stained red at the end. Alleyn noticed a wiry thread of some reddish stuff resembling packing that still clung to it. The nozzle and tap were brass, the tap pulling over when it was turned on, to lie in a parallel plane with the floor. No powder had been scattered about here.

He glanced round the room, returned to the door and read the card: "Mr. Barry George."

The doctor followed him into the rooms opposite these, on the left-hand side of the passage. They were a repetition in design of the two he had already seen but were hung with women's clothes and had a more elaborate assortment of greasepaint and cosmetics.

There was a mass of flowers in the star-room. Alleyn read the cards. One in particular caught his eye: "From Anthony Gill to say a most inadequate 'thank you' for the great idea." A vase of red roses stood before the mirror: "To your greatest triumph, Coralie darling. C.C." In Miss Gay's room there were only two bouquets, one from the management and one "From Anthony, with love."

Again in each room he pulled off the lead-in to the heater and looked at the connection.

"All right, aren't they?" said the doctor.

"Quite all right. Tight fit. Good solid grey rubber."

"Well, then—"

Next on the left was an unused room, and opposite it, "Mr. H. J. Bannington." Neither of these rooms had gas fires. "Mr. Bannington's dressing-table was littered with the usual array of greasepaint, the materials for his beard, a number of telegrams and letters, and several bills.

"About the body," the doctor began.

"We'll get a mortuary van from the Yard."

"But—Surely in a case of suicide—"

"I don't think this is suicide."

"But, good God!—D'you mean there's been an accident?"

"No accident," said Alleyn.

At midnight, the dressing-room lights in the Jupiter Theatre were brilliant, and men were busy there with the tools of their trade. A constable stood at the stage-door and a van waited in the yard. The front of the house was dimly lit and there, among the shrouded stalls, sat Coralie Bourne, Basil Gosset, H. J. Bannington, Dendra Gay, Anthony Gill, Reynolds, Katie the dresser, and the call-boy. A constable sat behind them and another stood by the doors into the foyer. They stared across the backs of seats at the fire curtain. Spirals of smoke rose from their cigarettes and about their feet were discarded programs. "Basil Gosset presents I CAN FIND MY WAY OUT by Anthony Gill."

In the manager's office Alleyn said: "You're sure of your facts, Mike?"

"Yes, sir. Honestly. I was right up against the entrance into the passage. They didn't see me because I was in the shadow. It was very dark offstage."

"You'll have to swear to it."

"I know."

"Good. All right, Thompson. Miss Gay and Mr. Gosset may go home. Ask Miss Bourne to come in."

When Sergeant Thompson had gone Mike said: "I haven't had a chance to say I know I've made a perfect fool of myself. Using your card and everything."

"Irresponsible gaiety doesn't go down very well in the service, Mike. You behaved like a clown."

"I *am* a fool," said Mike wretchedly.

The red beard was lying in front of Alleyn on Gosset's desk. He picked it up and held it out. "Put it on," he said.

"She might do another faint."

"I think not. Now the hat: yes—yes, I see. Come in."

Sergeant Thompson showed Coralie Bourne in and then sat at the end of the desk with his notebook.

Tears had traced their course through the powder on her face, carrying black cosmetic with them and leaving the greasepaint shining like snail-tracks. She stood near the doorway looking dully at Michael. "Is he back in England?" she said. "Did he tell you to do this?" She made an impatient movement. "Do take it off," she said, "it's a very bad beard. If Cann had only looked—" Her lips trembled. "Who told you to do it?"

"Nobody," Mike stammered, pocketing the beard. "I mean—As a matter of fact, Tony Gill—"

"*Tony?* But *he* didn't know. Tony wouldn't do it. Unless—"

"Unless?" Alleyn said.

She said frowning: "Tony didn't want Cann to play the part that way. He was furious."

"He says it was his dress for the Chelsea Arts Ball," Mike mumbled. "I brought it here. I just thought I'd put it on—it was idiotic, I know—for fun. I'd no idea you and Mr. Cumberland would mind."

"Ask Mr. Gill to come in," Alleyn said.

Anthony was white and seemed bewildered and helpless. "I've told Mike," he said. "It was my dress for the ball. They sent it round from the costume-hiring place this afternoon but I forgot it. Dendra reminded me and rang up the Delivery people—or Mike, as it turns out—in the interval."

"Why," Alleyn asked, "did you choose that particular disguise?"

"I didn't. I didn't know what to wear and I was too rattled to think. They said they were hiring things for themselves and would get something for me. They said we'd all be characters out of a Russian melodrama."

"Who said this?"

"Well—well, it was Barry George, actually."

"*Barry,*" Coralie Bourne said. "*It was Barry.*"

"I don't understand," Anthony said. "Why should a fancy dress upset everybody?"

"It happened," Alleyn said, "to be a replica of the dress usually worn by Miss Bourne's husband who also had a red beard. That was it, wasn't it, Miss Bourne? I remember seeing him—"

"Oh, yes," she said, "you would. He was known to the police." Suddenly she broke down completely. She was in an armchair near the desk but out of the range of its shaded lamp. She twisted and writhed, beating her hand against the padded arm of the chair. Sergeant Thompson sat with his head bent and his hand over his notes. Mike, after an agonized glance at Alleyn, turned his back. Anthony Gill leant over her: "Don't," he said violently. "Don't! For God's sake, stop."

She twisted away from him and, gripping the edge of the desk, began to speak to Alleyn; little by little gaining mastery of herself. "I want to tell you. I want you to understand. Listen." Her husband had been fantastically cruel, she said. "It was a kind of slavery." But when she sued for divorce he brought evidence of adultery with Cumberland. They had thought he knew nothing. "There was an abominable scene. He told us he was going away. He said he'd keep track of us and if I tried again for divorce, he'd come home. He was very friendly with Barry in those days." He had left behind him the first draft of a play he had meant to write for her and Cumberland. It had a wonderful scene for them. "And now you will never have it," he had said, "because there is no other playwright who could make this play for you but I." He was, she said, a melodramatic man but he was never ridiculous. He returned to the Ukraine where he was born and they had heard no more of him. In a little while she would have been able to presume death. But years of waiting did not agree with Canning Cumberland. He drank consistently and at his worst used to imagine her husband was about to return. "He was really terrified of Ben," she said. "He seemed like a creature in a nightmare."

Anthony Gill said: "This play—was it—?"

"Yes. There was an extraordinary similarity between your play and his. I saw at once that Ben's central scene would enormously strengthen your piece. Cann didn't want me to give it to you. Barry knew. He said: 'Why not?' He wanted Cann's part and was furious when he didn't get it. So you see, when he suggested you should dress and make-up like Ben—" She turned to Alleyn. "You see?"

"What did Cumberland do when he saw you?" Alleyn asked Mike.

"He made a queer movement with his hands as if—well, as if he expected me to go for him. Then he just bolted into his room."

"He thought Ben had come back," she said.

"Were you alone at any time after you fainted?" Alleyn asked.

"I? No. No, I wasn't. Katie took me into my dressing-room and stayed with me until I went on for the last scene."

"One other question. Can you, by any chance, remember if the heater in your room behaved at all oddly?"

She looked wearily at him. "Yes, it did give a sort of plop, I think. It made me jump. I was nervy."

"You went straight from your room to the stage?"

"Yes. With Katie. I wanted to go to Cann. I tried the door when we came out.

It was locked. He said: 'Don't come in.' I said: 'It's all right. It wasn't Ben,' and went on to the stage."

"I heard Miss Bourne," Mike said.

"He must have made up his mind by then. He was terribly drunk when he played his last scene." She pushed her hair back from her forehead. "May I go?" she asked Alleyn.

"I've sent for a taxi. Mr. Gill, will you see if it's there? In the meantime, Miss Bourne, would you like to wait in the foyer?"

"May I take Katie home with me?"

"Certainly. Thompson will find her. Is there anyone else we can get?"

"No, thank you. Just old Katie."

Alleyn opened the door for her and watched her walk into the foyer. "Check up with the dresser, Thompson," he murmured, "and get Mr. H. J. Bannington."

He saw Coralie Bourne sit on the lower step of the dress-circle stairway and lean her head against the wall. Nearby, on a gilt easel, a huge photograph of Canning Cumberland smiled handsomely at her.

H. J. Bannington looked pretty ghastly. He had rubbed his hand across his face and smeared his makeup. Florid red paint from his lips had stained the crepe hair that had been gummed on and shaped into a beard. His monocle was still in his left eye and gave him an extraordinarily rakish look. "See here," he complained, "I've about *had* this party. When do we go home?"

Alleyn uttered placatory phrases and got him to sit down. He checked over H.J.'s movements after Cumberland left the stage and found that his account tallied with Mike's. He asked if H.J. had visited any of the other dressing-rooms and was told acidly that H.J. knew his place in the company. "I remained in my unheated and squalid kennel, thank you very much."

"Do you know if Mr. Barry George followed your example?"

"Couldn't say, old boy. He didn't come near *me*."

"Have you any theories at all about this unhappy business, Mr. Bannington?"

"Do you mean, why did Cann do it? Well, speak no ill of the dead, but I'd have thought it was pretty obvious he was morbid-drunk. Tight as an owl when we finished the second act. Ask the great Mr. Barry George. Cann took the big scene away from Barry with both hands and left him looking pathetic. All wrong artistically, but that's how Cann was in his cups." H.J.'s wicked little eyes narrowed. "The great Mr. George," he said, "must be feeling very unpleasant by now. You might say he'd got a suicide on his mind, mightn't you? Or don't you know about that?"

"It was not suicide."

The glass dropped from H.J.'s eye. "God," he said. "God. I told Bob Reynolds! I told him the whole plant wanted overhauling."

"The gas plant, you mean?"

"Certainly. I was in the gas business years ago. Might say I'm in it still with a difference, ha-ha!"

"Ha-ha!" Alleyn agreed politely. He leaned forward. "Look here," he said: "We can't dig up a gas man at this time of night and may very likely need an expert opinion. You can help us."

"Well, old boy, I was rather pining for a spot of shut-eye. But, of course—"

"I shan't keep you very long."

"God, I hope not!" said H.J. earnestly.

Barry George had been made up pale for the last act. Colorless lips and shadows under his cheek bones and eyes had skilfully underlined his character as a repatriated but broken prisoner-of-war. Now, in the glare of the office lamp, he looked like a grossly exaggerated figure of mourning. He began at once to tell Alleyn how grieved and horrified he was. Everybody, he said, had their faults, and poor old Cann was no exception but wasn't it terrible to think what could happen to a man who let himself go downhill? He, Barry George, was abnormally sensitive and he didn't think he'd ever really get over the awful shock this had been to him. What, he wondered, could be at the bottom of it? Why had poor old Cann decided to end it all?

"Miss Bourne's theory," Alleyn began. Mr. George laughed. "Coralie?" he said. "So she's got a theory! Oh, well. Never mind."

"Her theory is this. Cumberland saw a man whom he mistook for her husband and, having a morbid dread of his return, drank the greater part of a bottle of whiskey and gassed himself. The clothes and beard that deceived him had, I understand, been ordered by you for Mr. Anthony Gill."

This statement produced startling results. Barry George broke into a spate of expostulation and apology. There had been no thought in his mind of resurrecting poor old Ben, who was no doubt dead but had been, mind you, in many ways one of the best. They were all to go to the Ball as exaggerated characters from melodrama. Not for the world—he gesticulated and protested. A line of sweat broke out along the margin of his hair. "I don't know what you're getting at," he shouted. "What are you suggesting?"

"I'm suggesting, among other things, that Cumberland was murdered."

"You're mad! He'd locked himself in. They had to break down the door. There's no window. You're crazy!"

"Don't," Alleyn said wearily, "let us have any nonsense about sealed rooms. Now, Mr. George, you knew Benjamin Vlasnoff pretty well. Are you going to tell us that when you suggested Mr. Gill should wear a coat with a fur collar, a black sombrero, black gloves and a red beard, it never occurred to you that his appearance might be a shock to Miss Bourne and to Cumberland?"

"I wasn't the only one," he blustered. "H.J. knew. And if it had scared him off, *she* wouldn't have been so sorry. She'd had about enough of him. Anyway if this is murder, the costume's got nothing to do with it."

"That," Alleyn said, getting up, "is what we hope to find out."

In Barry George's room, Detective Sergeant Bailey, a fingerprint expert, stood by the gas heater. Sergeant Gibson, a police photographer, and a uniformed constable were near the door. In the centre of the room stood Barry George, looking from one man to another and picking at his lips.

"I don't know why he wants me to watch all this," he said. "I'm exhausted. I'm emotionally used up. What's he doing? Where is he?"

Alleyn was next door in Cumberland's dressing-room, with H.J., Mike and

Sergeant Thompson. It was pretty clear now of fumes and the gas fire was burning comfortably. Sergeant Thompson sprawled in the armchair near the heater, his head sunk and his eyes shut.

"This is the theory, Mr. Bannington," Alleyn said. "You and Cumberland have made your final exits; Miss Bourne and Mr. George and Miss Gay are all on the stage. Lord Michael is standing just outside the entrance to the passage. The dressers and stage-staff are watching the play from the side. Cumberland has locked himself in this room. There he is, dead drunk and sound asleep. The gas fire is burning, full pressure. Earlier in the evening he powdered himself and a thick layer of the powder lies undisturbed on the tap. Now."

He tapped on the wall.

The fire blew out with a sharp explosion. This was followed by the hiss of escaping gas. Alleyn turned the taps off. "You see," he said, "I've left an excellent print on the powdered surface. Now, come next door."

Next door, Barry George appealed to him stammering: "But I didn't know. I don't know anything about it. I don't *know*."

"Just show Mr. Bannington, will you, Bailey?"

Bailey knelt down. The lead-in was disconnected from the tap on the heater. He turned on the tap in the pipe and blew down the tube.

"An air lock, you see. It works perfectly."

H.J. was staring at Barry George. "But I don't know about gas, H.J.. H.J., tell them—"

"One moment." Alleyn removed the towels that had been spread over the dressing-shelf, revealing a sheet of clean paper on which lay the rubber push-on connection.

"Will you take this lens, Bannington, and look at it. You'll see that it's stained a florid red. It's a very slight stain but it's unmistakably greasepaint. And just above the stain you'll see a wiry hair. Rather like some sort of packing material, but it's not that. It's crêpe hair, isn't it?"

The lens wavered above the paper.

"Let me hold it for you," Alleyn said. He put his hand over H.J.'s shoulder and, with a swift movement, plucked a tuft from his false moustache and dropped it on the paper. "Identical, you see, ginger. It seems to be stuck to the connection with spirit-gum."

The lens fell. H.J. twisted round, faced Alleyn for a second, and then struck him full in the face. He was a small man but it took three of them to hold him.

"In a way, sir, it's handy when they have a smack at you," said Detective Sergeant Thompson half an hour later. "You can pull them in nice and straightforward without any 'will you come to the station and make a statement' business."

"Quite," said Alleyn, nursing his jaw.

Mike said: "He must have gone to the room after Barry George and Miss Bourne were called."

"That's it. He had to be quick. The call-boy would be round in a minute and he had to be back in his own room."

"But look here—what about motive?"

"That, my good Mike, is precisely why, at half-past one in the morning, we're still in this miserable theatre. You're getting a view of the duller aspect of homicide. Want to go home"

"No. Give me another job."

"Very well. About ten feet from the prompt-entrance, there's a sort of garbage tin. Go through it."

At seventeen minutes to two, when the dressing-rooms and passage had been combed clean and Alleyn had called a spell, Mike came to him with filthy hands. *"Eureka,"* he said, "I hope."

They all went into Bannington's room. Alleyn spread out on the dressing-table the fragments of paper that Mike had given him.

"They'd been pushed down to the bottom of the tin," Mike said.

Alleyn moved the fragments about. Thompson whistled through his teeth. Bailey and Gibson mumbled together.

"There you are," Alleyn said at last.

They collected round him. The letter that H. J. Bannington had opened at this same table six hours and forty-five minutes earlier, was pieced together like a jig-saw puzzle.

Dear H.J.

Having seen the monthly statement of my account, I called at my bank this morning and was shown a check that is undoubtedly a forgery. Your histrionic versatility, my dear H.J., is only equalled by your audacity as a calligraphist. But fame has its disadvantages. The teller has recognized you. I propose to take action.

"Unsigned," said Bailey.

"Look at the card on the red roses in Miss Bourne's room, signed C.C. It's a very distinctive hand." Alleyn turned to Mike. "Do you still want to be a policeman?"

"Yes."

"Lord help you. Come and talk to me at the office tomorrow."

"Thank you, sir."

They went out, leaving a constable on duty. It was a cold morning. Mike looked up at the façade of the Jupiter. He could just make out the shape of the neon sign: I CAN FIND MY WAY OUT *by Anthony Gill.*

HELLO KITTY

Alex Marwood

Alex Marwood is the pseudonym of Serena Mackesy, a journalist and novelist who lives in London, UK. Her first novel as Marwood, *The Wicked Girls*, won an Edgar Award. Her other books include *The Killer Next Door*, which Stephen King called 'scary as hell', and *The Darkest Secret*.

Things move, in houses. Credit cards, keys, cups of tea. The more so the older you get. Although perhaps that's perceptual, she thinks. I'm only 59, and I'm stressed, with my sister lying on a drip in the hospital. And besides, though I've been here a hundred times over the decades, I don't know this house as well as I feel I do. I'm just putting things back wrong, that's all.

Flora picks the coffee mug off the tea-towel on the draining board and studies it like an archaeologist with a potshard. I just left it the wrong way up, she tells herself. I know I always leave cups upside down to drain, but it's possible to vary the habit of a lifetime when you're under pressure.

But you know you didn't, answers her small internal voice, always there, always nagging at her when she's alone. *You always leave it upside down,* it says. *Every. Single. Time.*

"Hush," she says, out loud. She puts the mug on the countertop and fills the kettle.

A rattle of the scullery door, and Beasley crashes in through the cat flap. Crashes is the only description for what he does. He's the biggest cat she's ever seen. A Maine Coon, huge and ginger, with a ruff like a lion and a body to match, a cross face buried in fur and a pathetic little peeping mew that wrings a laugh from her lips and makes her forget the morning's oddity. He lets out another little peep, then a hiss. He's a funny mix of personalities, like most cats. Sometimes at night he will snuggle in, bury her beneath his giant paws and purr like a distant traction engine, but unsolicited approaches are always greeted in this manner. Flora sighs and gives him breakfast. Two sachets of Purina in a single meal, every meal. He has the appetite of a seven-year-old child.

Deborah is changing day by day, and not for the better. The bruises that marked her injuries have faded to yellow and her lips, half-open to accommodate the feeding tube, are cracked and dry. She has lost weight, though that is probably emphasised by slack facial muscles. On TV, coma victims are beautiful, their faces composed like medieval church memorials. Deborah looks like the skin might slide off her skull like molten wax. Flora has seen two people die in her life, sitting beside this sister as first their father, then their mother, slipped away. That's what she looks like, she thinks, as she takes her seat by the bed, picks up her Deb's hand. She's dead already. She won't be coming back.

"It's Flor, Deb," she says. "Hello, my darling."

Deb doesn't respond. Her hand is cold, though the ward is overheated. Every day it seems a little colder.

Oh, Deb, she thinks as she drives up the lane, I don't want to lose you, but I've realised I also barely know you. Twenty years you've been in this house, all by yourself. How was it? Were you happy? Those were fresh flowers by your bed, with the card from the school, but no-one has visited in all the times I've been. It seems lonely, but I'm not this part of your life. I don't know who your friends are. I thought my bi-annual visits, your trips to London, the weekly phone calls, were keeping us close, but we're not more than friendly acquaintances, really. But when I lose you, and I know that will be soon, everything that *was* will be gone. There will be no-one left who remembers. The shared jokes, the rolling of eyes at Mum's stock phrases, the frosty winter road to school, the sea urchins in the Barmouth rock pools – all of it will be something that only I remember. With you, my past will vanish. Were you afraid, my sister? Did you wish you weren't alone?

The tears that accompanied her on this drive for the first few days no longer come, and replaced by an uneasy numbness. Because of her sister's local standing, head of the local primary, the fact that she'd fallen down her stairs and was in a coma made the local papers, and she's been warned by the police that the deaths and weddings columns give burglars ideas. She feels honour bound to sit the house, and the cat, at least until what she is sure now will be a funeral. But she doesn't like it. The trees that edge the property always feel as though they're creeping inward, at night. Stupid, she knows, but she always feels as though they are watching.

The cottage appears in her headlights. Chocolate box: thatch and beams and little tiny windows, and an unexpected light behind the kitchen blind. How funny, she thinks. I don't remember turning a light on. Why would I turn a light on when I left in daylight? Then Beasley appears before her, mouth open in a yowl, and she forgets about it in the flurry of slamming on brakes, then gathering supermarket bags from the boot and scurrying indoors before the darkness gets her.

The milk's almost empty. She'd thought there was a full pint in there and has only bought one more to get her to the end of the week, but it seems that there's only an inch left in the old container. Flora shakes her head. You think you're coping, she thinks, and then all these weird little things, these misrememberings, show you you're not at all. I could have sworn I'd put the post on the hall shelf this morning, but there it is, on the kitchen table.

The little voice: *someone's been here.*

"Don't be stupid," she chides herself, out loud. "Don't be stupid, Flora. You're overwrought."

But things keep changing, Flora. There was a thumb-print in the butter on Wednesday. The loo roll is unrolling from the back, when Deb and I always hang it forwards. And my coat, this morning. I was sure I'd hung it on a hook, but there it was, on the back of a kitchen chair.

Flora deliberately squeezes her eyes closed, shakes her head. She can't afford to indulge these thoughts. Not when a long night alone stretches out ahead of her.

Beasley hasn't come in. Flora turns on the oven to heat up her lasagne, fills the kettle for frozen peas. Wanders the house calling him, but there is no sign. She doesn't want to go back out again, into the darkness. Hopefully, she picks up his bowl and a teaspoon and goes through to the scullery door. Pushes open his huge cat flap – she remembers Deb having to have it enlarged as he reached adolescence and started looking less like a fluffball than a lion – and taps spoon against bowl as she's seen her sister do.

"Beasley!" she calls, into the darkness, feeling foolish because she's never called a cat before, doesn't know the words. She resorts eventually to a feeble, Ealing Comedy "Here, kitty kitty!" and another tap of the spoon. Her voice sounds dulled by the spongy frozen air.

Something touches the back of her hand: something wet, and raspy. Flora leaps back with a shriek. Then her gigantic companion hurtles into the room, looking, as he always does, surprised, and she realises that what was touching her was his nose and tongue. "Christ," she says, and lays her hand on her breast-bone like a Victorian heroine. I'm jumpy, she thinks.

In the morning, the mail has moved again. This time she knows it for a fact. She didn't touch it last night; remembers it sitting where she saw it when she came in, at the far end of the table, as she ate her ready meal and drank half a bottle of wine to aid uneasy sleep. And now it's sitting in the middle, the four letters neatly lined up parallel with the edge of the table. The sight sends an electric jolt through her. It's not possible, she thinks. I don't believe in poltergeists. This is just –

Someone's been in. They must have been, says the voice.

"Or I'm sleepwalking," she corrects, firmly. She stares at the little pile for a full minute, then she stalks through the house and checks the doors. Front, back, scullery, the French windows that lead out to the patch of lawn that runs down to the woods. Who needs this many doors in a house? How can you need so many doors? She tries the handles, one by one, but nothing gives. The catches are firm and the keys lie, as they are supposed to, in the hall table drawer. She recircles the house, checks the window latches, but all is secure. A couple of the casements are actually painted shut, and clearly have been for years.

Flora goes back to the kitchen and makes her coffee. Sits dumbly at the table, staring at the letters. Should I? she wonders. Should I be worrying? Maybe it *was* me. Maybe I *did* move them myself. Like all the other stuff. I can't really be sure that those paintings at the bottom of the stairs used to hang in each other's spaces. Maybe they did. Maybe Deb swapped them over years ago, and I've only just noticed. And the mug, and the milk, and the fire-irons lying across the hearth rather than propped up, the single lily that was lying on the carpet below the living room vase. They could have just fallen down while I was out; it's not as though I've been in the house every minute of every day. Beasley could have knocked them down. He's clumsy enough, after all. His dishes can go from one side of the kitchen to the other, he's so keen on his food.

Or someone's got a key. That's what it is. She's given someone a key and they've been letting themselves in. Just subtly moving things around, to let me know they've been there. I don't know why. Something stupid. A prank. Or maybe they think they're helping, in some way?

In the middle of the night?

She gulps a mouthful of coffee and has to struggle to get it down her throat. Stop it, Flora. Stop it. You're catastrophising. You're producing all sorts of chemicals because you're upset about Deborah, and your brain's misinterpreting things. It's fine. The doors are locked, the windows are locked.

"Okay," she says, decisively. The voice isn't going to leave her alone, she knows that. She pushes the coffee away and goes to the computer to Google handymen. She doesn't feel entitled to change the locks in someone else's house, but she can, at least, fit bolts.

A man called Andy Hitchin, who sounds the way she imagines Fred West sounded – all rounded Rs and unexpected chortling – agrees to come tomorrow afternoon. She stays in the living room with the cat for most of the day, every light in the house ablaze, doors locked, blinds down, editing an oil-company tender. A wind is getting up, and the trees rustle and groan beyond the garden, blusters of rain hurling against the window, occasional large drips falling down the chimney into the fire with a cat-like hiss.

At ten o'clock, she takes herself to bed. Feeling slightly foolish, she slides the chest of drawers across the painted floorboards to block the bedroom door. She doesn't expect to sleep, but she is, at least, able to be horizontal beneath the covers, her head flying from the pillow each time a gust bursts through the trees, tensing each time a window shakes. Beasley's cat flap goes at 1 a.m. He rattles at the bedroom door ten minutes later, paws and scratches and tries the handle, but eventually he goes away.

Andy Hitchen even looks a bit like Fred West in his dark blue boiler suit, though his mop of unruly hair is washed-out blond rather than black. He whistles his way round the doors, fits heavy bolts top and bottom, drinks mugs of tea and plays the talk shows on LBC through his phone. The sound of angry taxi drivers is comforting to Flora. It sounds, albeit briefly, like home.

"How's Miss Tucker?" he asks, as he washes his hands. "She okay? Sorry to hear about her accident."

"Oh," she says. "You know her?"

He nods. "Everyone round here knows her," he says. "She was my form teacher when I was a nipper, and my McKenzie's just left a couple of years ago. Scary lady."

"Scary?" she asks. The sister she knows is stubborn and maybe, over the last few years, a bit prone to dignity, but she can't imagine her being scary. But then, she's never seen her stalking corridors or running assemblies. In all her adult life she's only ever seen her in relaxation mode. Oh, the things I'll never know, she thinks. She's sixty-one. Even if she does come out of the coma, I doubt she'll be fit to run a school before she's forced into retirement.

He looks a bit abashed. "Sorry," he says. "Just – you know. When you're a kid and that . . ."

"They're not expecting her to recover," she blurts. He blushes, shifts from foot to foot and jabs a hand into his curls. "I'm sorry to hear that," he mumbles. Edges towards the kitchen door and picks up his bag of tools.

"Thank you," she says. "You'll send me the bill?"

He nods, hurriedly, glad of the change of subject. "Yes," he says. "No hurry. I'm sorry. About your sister. People liked her, around here."

Flora stands in the doorway until his headlights vanish from the lane, then goes out to the car. It's pitch-black, but it's only just gone five o'clock and visiting hours at the hospital go on until eight.

It's almost nine when she gets home, but the lights she left blazing are welcoming and, once she's checked the house over and shot the bolts, the place feels transformed. She can't secure it when she's out without changing the locks, but at least now she's in, she knows that no-one can follow. The cottage is warm and, at last, welcoming, cosy; a haven from the darkness. She summons the cat – the embarrassing here-kitty-kitty again, but once again successful – for his supper, builds a fire and eats a frozen pizza curled up on the sofa watching *Made in Chelsea*. Last night she didn't even want to turn the TV on in case she missed a movement beyond the door. Now, she's just tired, fuzzy; numb, still, with looming grief, but sure, at least, of what she has to handle.

Here in the country even the TV seems to be duller once the news is done. By eleven, she's tired out; stumbles up the stairs and flicks off the hall light as she goes. It won't be long, now, she thinks, as she runs the shower to heat up, pulls a towel off the rail and goes to her bedroom to change. I won't be here much longer. I could tell when I saw her tonight. Her skin's gone yellow, she's jaundiced. I won't think about it tonight. But maybe tomorrow I should start sorting the house out. There's something ghoulish about doing it now, but it will have to be done and I might as well use the time while I'm here. Through the floorboards, she hears the cat flap go downstairs; that healthy clunk of a large body coming in from its big night out. I need to think about what to do about *him*, she thinks. Maybe Deb has left instructions. Oh, God, I should start looking out her papers. Start uncovering the chaos beneath the order.

Once it's heated up, the shower is deliciously hot, and the water pressure surprisingly high. Flora heaves a sigh of pleasure as she steps through the curtain into the cubicle, and stands for five minutes letting the jet massage her shoulders as steam builds around her. I must get one of these when I get home. It's really, really nice. I'm amazed I've not thought to treat myself with one before.

She washes her hair, takes time to slough down skin that feels dry with tiredness with her sister's exfoliation mitt. Oh, Deborah, she thinks. I'm so sorry. I wish I knew what happened to you. They said you were in your dressing gown when they found you down on the hall flagstones. Maybe five minutes before, you were doing exactly what I'm doing now.

She turns off the water, reaches past the curtain for the towel she's hung on the hook on the outside of the cubicle. There's nothing there. Annoyed, she feels the floor. Still nothing. She wipes the water from her eyes and pokes her head out. There it is, lying on the chair beneath the window. Flora huffs. At least some of it was forgetfulness, she thinks.

As she's wrapping the towel about herself, she wipes the condensation from the window and looks out at the darkened lawn. To her surprise, in the streak of illumination thrown by her window light, she sees Beasley step out from the trees, a rabbit hanging from his jaws, fierce and noble and . . . outside.

"How funny," she says. "I could have sworn I heard you come in twenty minutes ago. Oh, well. Good hunting, big man."

Flora turns away from the window, picks up her toothbrush from the edge of the basin and squeezes toothpaste onto it. Looks up to see her reflection in the mirror and freezes. In the steam on the glass, someone has written, with a solitary finger,

HERE
KITTY
KITTY

I'VE SEEN THAT MOVIE TOO

Val McDermid

Val McDermid is a leading author of suspense thrillers. Eleven of her thirty-one bestselling and multi-award-winning novels feature clinical psychologist Tony Hill and police officer Carol Jordan. The Hill and Jordan novels, beginning with *The Mermaids Singing*, inspired the television series *Wire in the Blood*. Earlier books feature journalist Lindsay Gordon and PI Kate Brannigan. Her much acclaimed new series is set in Scotland and features DI Karen Pirie.

I truly believed I'd never see her again. That she was gone for good. That the virus she'd planted in my bloodstream would be allowed to lie dormant forever. Which only goes to show how little I really understood about Cerys.

Everybody has an ugly secret. I don't care how righteous you are. Saint or sinner, there's something lurking in your past that looms over every good thing you do, that makes your toes curl in shame, that makes your stomach curdle at the thought of discovery. Don't try to pretend you're the exception. You're not. We all have our skeletons, and Cerys is mine.

The world as I know it falls into two groups. The ones who fall under Cerys's spell and the ones who are immune to the point of bafflement. Over the past three years, I've discovered there were a lot more in the former group than I'd ever suspected. The list of people she'd bewitched ranged from the daughter of a duke to a celebrity midget, from a prizewinning poet to a gay male member of parliament. It mortifies me how many of them I now know she was fucking during the months she was supposed to be my girlfriend. What's extraordinary is how many of them were convinced they were the special one.

For the members of the latter group, the word *even* is crucial to their insistent deconstruction of Cerys. "She isn't even beautiful." "She isn't even interesting." "She isn't even sexy." "She isn't even funny." "She isn't even blonde." But to those of us on the other side of the fence, she's all of those things. The only explanation that makes any sense is the notion of viral infection. The Oxford English Dictionary defines a computer virus as "a piece of code surreptitiously introduced into a system in order to corrupt it." In every sense of the word *corrupt*, that's Cerys.

The one good thing she ever did for me was to walk out of my life three years ago without a goodbye or a forwarding address. I don't think her motive was to destroy me; that would presume my reaction even entered her calculations. No, the suddenness of her departure and the thoroughness of her vanishing had been all about her need to get free and clear before the answers rolled in to the questions other people had started asking. But at the time, I didn't care about the reasons. I was just grateful for the chance to free myself. Deep down, I didn't mind the anguish or the self-loathing or the shame, because it's always easy to endure pain when you understand it's part of the healing process. Even then, I knew that somewhere down the line I would get past all the suffering and resume control over my heart and mind.

And I did. It took me well over a year to drag myself beyond what she'd done to me, but I managed it.

Yet now, in an instant, all that healing was stripped away and I felt as raw and captive as I had the day she'd left. Here, in the unlikely setting of the Finnish consul's Edinburgh residence, I could feel the gears stripping and the wheels coming off my reassembled life.

I shouldn't even have been there. I don't usually bother with the fancy receptions that attach themselves to the movie business like barnacles to a ship's hull. But the three Finnish producers who had become the Coen brothers of the European film industry had optioned a treatment from me, and my agent was adamant that I show my face at the consul's party in their honor at the Edinburgh Film Festival. So I'd turned up forty minutes late, figuring I'd have just enough time for a drink and the right hellos before the diplomats cleared their throats and signaled the party was over.

As soon as I crossed the threshold, I knew something was off-kilter. Cerys had always had that effect on me. Whenever I walked into a room where she was, my senses tripped into overdrive. Now my head swiveled from side to side, my eyes darting round, trying to figure out why I was instantly edgy. She saw me at the same moment I spotted her. She was talking to some guy in a suit and she didn't miss a beat when she caught sight of me. But her eyes widened, and that was enough for my stomach to crash like a severed lift cage.

I felt a ringing in my ears, stilling the loud mutter of conversation in the room. Before I could react, she'd excused herself and snaked through the throng to my side. "Alice," she said, the familiar voice a caress that made the hairs on my arms quiver.

I was determined not to be suckered back in. To put up a fight at least. "What the hell are you doing here?" I tried to make my voice harsh and almost succeeded.

Cerys reached out, circling my wrist with finger and thumb. The touch of her flesh was a band of burning ice. "We need to talk," she said, drawing me to her side and somehow maneuvering me back through the doorway I'd just entered.

"No," I said weakly. "No, we don't need to talk."

She turned to me then and smiled, the tip of her tongue running along the edge of her teeth. "Oh, Alice, you always cut straight to the chase, don't you?" She made a determined break for a staircase at the end of the hall. I couldn't free myself without drawing the wrong kind of attention from the other people milling round in the hallway. The last thing I wanted was for anyone to make a connection between me and Cerys. I'd kept my nose clean on that score and it had saved me from enough of the consequences of our association for me to want to keep it that way.

So I let her lead me up the broad, carpeted stairs without obvious protest. Somehow, she knew where she was going. She opened the second door on the right and pulled me into a small sitting room—a pair of armchairs, a chaise longue, and an antique writing desk with matching chair. She used my momentum to spin me round like a dancer, then closed the door briskly behind her, turning a key in the lock.

"To answer your question, I've been working with the Finnish film agency," she said. At once I understood her apparent familiarity with the layout of the Finnish consul's house. And that the chances were I wasn't the first person she'd been with behind that locked door.

I opened my mouth to protest but I was too late. Cerys took my face between her hands and covered my mouth with dozens of tiny kisses and flicks of the tongue. Her fingertips brushed the skin of my neck, slipping inside my open blouse and over my shoulders. The heat that flushed my skin was nothing to do with the Scottish summer weather. I despised myself even as desire surged through me, but I didn't even consider pushing her away. I knew I wouldn't be able to follow through and I'd only end up humiliating myself by begging for her later.

"This . . . is not . . . a good . . . idea . . ." The words came from my head while every other part of me was willing my mouth to shut the fuck up. Cerys knew this so she just smiled. Her hands moved under my skirt, the backs of her fingernails grazing the insides of my thighs.

"I've missed you," she murmured as her hand moved higher, meeting no resistance. I felt myself falling, the chaise longue behind me, the certainty of pain and trouble ahead.

Not love, not at first sight. I don't want to elevate it to something it wasn't. But it was something, no doubt of that. I'd emerged late one summer evening from Inverness rail station, hoping that someone from the Scottish Film Foundation would be there to drive me to the remote steading where I'd be spending the rest of the week. I'd been supposed to arrive with four other writers for a screenwriting master-class course that morning, but my flight had been canceled and it had taken the rest of the day to travel the length of the country from the West Country to the Highlands by train. I was not in the best of moods.

The woman leaning against the car in the courtyard caught my attention. Her languid pose: long legs crossed at the ankle, right arm folded across her stomach, hand cupping the left elbow, rollie dangling from the fingers of her left hand, a sliver of smoke twisting in the warm evening air, head at an angle, eyes on the middle distance, thick honey-blonde hair cut short . . . She made my breath catch in my throat. It was an image I suspected I would never forget. I feared I would keep on writing scenes for women in that precise pose for the rest of my career. I didn't even dare to hope she was waiting for me.

But she was. Cerys Black, Screenwriting Development Director for the Scottish Film Foundation. It was a fancy title, implying more than a department of one, but I soon learned that Cerys did everything from picking up late arrivals to pitching which projects should win the SFF's backing. That night, though, I wasn't interested in her job description. Only that I'd found myself in the company of a woman who made me dizzy for the first time in years. My grumpiness evaporated in less time than it took to stow my bags in the car boot.

She took me to a bistro by the river. "Everyone's eaten and you won't feel like cooking this late," she said. We ate pasta and drank red wine and talked. I've never been able to piece together the route of the conversation. I only remember that we talked about the women in our past. I now have an inkling of how severely Cerys edited her history, but at the time I had no reason to doubt her tale of a handful of youthful affairs and a single grand passion that had taken her to Hungary before it had finally died a couple of years before. It was the sort of conversation that is really an extended form of deniable flirtation and it kept us occupied until the waitress made it abundantly clear that Inverness had a midnight curfew and we were in danger of breaching it.

We drove out of the city along the side of the loch, the rounded humps of high mountains silhouetted against thin darkness shot with stars. We turned up a steep road that took us away from the mountains to a high valley surrounded by summits. We barely spoke but something was moving forward between us.

The cluster of low buildings that was our base for the week was in darkness when we arrived. Cerys led me to a cottage set to one side. "You're in here," she said. "Downstairs there's a computer room and library and upstairs there are two suites of rooms." We climbed the narrow stairs and Cerys dropped her voice. "Tom Hart's on the right and you're on the left."

She ushered me in and put my backpack by a table facing a pair of long windows. I swung my holdall onto a chair and turned to thank her, suddenly shy.

There was nothing shy about her response. She moved closer, one hand on my hip, the other on my shoulder, and kissed me. Not the air kiss of the media world, not the prim kiss of a distant cousin, not the dry brush of lips friends share. This was the kind of kiss that burns boats and bridges in equal measure.

Time played its tricks and made it last forever and no time at all. When we finally stopped, Cerys looked as astonished as I felt. "I don't think snogging in an open doorway is the most sensible move," she said. "You should shut your door now."

I nodded, numb with disappointment.

Then she smiled, a crooked grin that lifted one side of her mouth higher than the other. "Which side of it would you like me to be on?"

If I could say that sex with Cerys was the most amazing experience of my life, it might make more sense of what happened between us. But that would be a lie. It was enthralling, it was adventurous, it was sometimes dark and edgy. But it never entirely fulfilled me. She always left me not just wanting more but feeling obscurely that somehow it was my fault that I hadn't found total satisfaction in her arms. So I was always eager for the next time, quick to persuade myself that the electricity between us meant the wattage of our sexual connection would rise even higher. I was addicted, no question about it.

I knew by the end of that master-class week that I loved her. I loved her body and her mind, her reticence and her boldness. We'd hadn't spent that much time together—she had other responsibilities, and by the third night, it was clear we both needed some sleep—but I was under her spell. I wanted to see her again, and soon. Her work tied her to Edinburgh, my life was at the other end of the country. But I couldn't see this as an obstacle. We could make it work. We would make it work.

Looking back, I can see all the cracks and gaps of lies and deception. But at the time, I had no reason to mistrust her. I believed in the meetings, the conferences, the working dinners, the trips to film festivals. I was just amazed and grateful that we managed to see each other one night most weeks. We spoke on the phone, though not as much as I craved; Cerys was only comfortable with the phone for professional purposes, she told me. And we made plans. I would sell my house by the sea in Devon and buy a flat in Edinburgh. Not with Cerys—that would have made her claustrophobic. After the disastrous end of her relationship with the Hungarian, she didn't ever want to live with someone else without her own bolt-hole. Given what she'd told me about their last months, I understood that. I'd have felt the same, I thought.

I was anxious about the move, though. Prices in Edinburgh were astronomical. I couldn't see how I was going to afford somewhere half decent. I'd tried to talk to Cerys about it, but she'd stopped my worries with kisses and deft movements of her strong, gentle hands.

And then one night she met me at the airport in the same languid stance. Only the cigarette was missing. As always, my heart seemed to contract in my chest. "I have the answer," she said after she'd kissed my mouth and buried her face in my hair.

"The answer to what?"

"How you can afford a flat."

"How?"

And over dinner, she told me. A legendary Scottish star had died a few months previously. The film foundation had just learned he'd left almost all of his many millions in a trust to benefit Scottish filmmakers. A trust that was to be administered by the SFF. "Instead of giving people piddling little grants of a few grand, we'll be able to fund proper development," Cerys said. "We'll essentially be putting money on the table like the serious players."

"That's fantastic news. But what's that got to do with me?"

The crooked smile and a dark sparkle in her eyes was the only answer I got at first. She sipped her wine and clinked her glass against mine. "You're going to be a star, sweetheart," she finally said.

It was breathtakingly simple but for someone as fundamentally law-abiding as me, unbelievably bad. We were going to set up a fictitious production company. Cerys had access to all the necessary letterheads to make it look as if they had backing from serious Hollywood players. I'd be the screenwriter on the project. We'd go to the SFF for the seed money and come away with a two-million-pound pot. The company would pay me a million via my agent, all aboveboard. And Cerys would siphon off the other million. And then the project would go belly-up because the Hollywood backers had pulled out. A shrug of the shoulders. It happens all the time in the movie business.

"It'll never work," I said. "How will we convince the SFF?"

Again the crooked smile. "Because you're Scottish by birth. Because I'm the person who makes the recommendations to the grant committee. And because you're going to write a brilliant treatment that will sound like it could plausibly be a Hollywood blockbuster."

It's a measure of how Cerys had captivated me that what worried me was not that we were about to embark upon a criminal fraud. What bothered me was whether I could write a good enough treatment to bluff our way past the grants committee.

It took me a month to come up with the idea and another six weeks to get the pitch and treatment in place. And of course Cerys was perfectly placed to help me knock it into shape. I called it *The Whole of the Moon* after the Water-boys track. The opening paragraph of the pitch had taken days to get right, but in the end I was happy with it. *Dominic O'Donnell is an IRA quartermaster who wants to retire from the front line in Belfast; Brigid Fitzgerald is a financial investigator from Seattle. When they meet, their lives change in ways neither of them could ever have imagined.* The Whole of the Moon *is a romantic comedy thriller with a dark edge, strong on sense of place and underpinned by New Irish music.*

I'd have been terrified about pitching the grants committee if Cerys hadn't spent her lunch hour fucking me senseless in the hotel down the street from the SFF office. As it was, I was so dazed I waltzed through it as if a two-million-pound grant was my birthright. Not in an arrogant way, but in that "If Scotland wants to be taken seriously in the international arts community, we need to behave as if we are serious" sort of way.

And it worked. The grants committee was dizzy with its new powers of patronage and Cerys easily persuaded its members that this was the sort of flagship project they needed in order to give the SFF an international profile. The two million pounds was paid into the bank account of the company she'd set up in Panama, which was where we were allegedly going to be doing some of our location filming. My fee was with my agent in days. It took me all of two weeks to close the deal on a New Town flat with views over the Forth estuary to Fife.

Life wasn't quite as perfect as I'd expected. Cerys seemed to be out of town much more than before, and I barely saw more of her than I had when I was living at the other end of the country. And of course we had to keep our relationship under wraps to begin with. Edinburgh's a big city wrapped round a small village, and we didn't want the grants committee members to wonder whether they'd been stitched up. Or worse.

Three months after we'd been given the money, Cerys reported back to her boss that the production company had gone bust. She told me he'd taken it in his stride, and I believed that too.

And then a couple of weeks later, we walked into the breakfast room of a hotel in Newcastle and came face to face with the chairman of the grants committee and his wife. We tried to pretend we'd only just started seeing each other, but my lies were nowhere near as slick as Cerys's.

We were both quiet on the drive back to Edinburgh. I was glum and assumed she was too. A couple of days later, I realized her silence was not because she was worried but because she was planning furiously. She dropped me at my flat that night and went back to her place, where she packed the car with the few things she really cared about—clothes, DVDs, books, her Mac, and half a dozen paintings—and left. When I hadn't heard from her for three days, I borrowed the emergency key to her flat from her neighbor and let myself in. I knew as soon as I walked through the door that she was gone. The air was empty of her presence.

Sprawled on the chaise longue, I could smell her and taste her. If I'd been struck blind and deaf, my senses would still have recognized her. Having her back in my arms again drew me back under her command. I hated the terrible longing that possessed me but I didn't know how to make it stop. Before, only her absence had taken the edge off the craving. I thought I was cured but now I knew I was one of the backsliders. Just like those smokers who have given up for so long they think they can afford the risk of the occasional cigarette. And before they know it, they're back on a pack and a half a day. One fuck and I was no longer my own woman.

"Are you not taking a hell of a chance, coming back here?"

She pushed her sweat-damp hair out of her eyes. She'd let it grow and now it was like a shaggy helmet streaked a dozen different shades by the sun. Not what you'd call a disguise, but a difference. "If they had anything on me, I'd never have got another job in the industry. They can think what they like. It makes no odds without proof."

"So why did you run?"

She closed her eyes and ran her fingertips over my face, as if reminding herself of a tactile memory. "I couldn't be bothered answering the questions."

I felt a faint stirring of what might have been outrage if it had been allowed to take root. "You left me high and dry because you couldn't be bothered answering questions?"

She opened her eyes and sighed. "Alice, you know I hate to be pinned down."

"But you came back." I knew I was clutching at shadows, but apparently I couldn't prevent myself from going into pathetic mode.

Cerys shifted her weight to pin me down more completely, her thigh between my legs exerting a delicious pleasure. "I came back because of you."

I couldn't keep the joy and amazement from my face and voice. "You came back for me?"

A dry little laugh. "Not for you. Because of you."

"I don't understand."

"Because of what you've done. Because you owe me."

Now I was puzzled. "I owe you? You walked out on me, and I owe you?"

"I'm not talking metaphorically, Alice. I'm not talking about emotions. I'm talking about money."

It was a familiar Cerys roller coaster moment and it left me sour. "Money? You got your share. More than your share. You didn't have an agent taking fifteen percent off the top."

"I'm not talking about the grant money. I'm talking about the movie. You might have changed the title but I'm not stupid. As soon as I saw the advance publicity in the trade press, I knew what you'd done. You changed the name from

The Whole of the Moon to *A Man Is In Love* and sold it to Hollywood for real."

"It's not a secret, Cerys. And it's my work to sell."

"It's work that wouldn't exist without me. You'd never have come up with the idea and developed it without me. According to my sources, you cleared another couple of million from the studio. The way I see it, that means you owe me at least another million."

I tried to tell myself she was joking, but I knew her better than that. "That's not how I see it."

"No, but if I can't persuade you to see it my way, the world is going to know how you got your first million. And how much of the work on that treatment was mine."

I managed a strangled laugh. "You can't drop me in it without dropping yourself in it," I protested, trying to shift my body away from hers but confounded by the arm of the chaise.

"I'll throw myself on their mercy. Tell them how I was so besotted by you that I did what you told me. It's what they'll want to hear because it lets them off the hook. Better to employ some woman led astray by her emotions than a crook, don't you think?"

Cerys telling lies would be far more convincing than me telling the truth. I knew that. And even as I listened to her duplicity, I knew I was still her prisoner. The thought of finding myself her enemy was intolerable. "I thought you cared about me. I can't believe you'd blackmail me."

"Blackmail is such an ugly word," she said, finally pushing herself on to her knees and moving away from me.

I shivered, disgust and desire mingling in an unholy alliance. "But an accurate one."

"I like to think of it as sharing. A down payment of fifty grand by the end of the week would be acceptable." She buttoned her shirt, picked her jeans and underwear off the floor, and slipped back into her public persona. "In cash."

"How am I supposed to explain that to my accountant? To my bank?"

She shrugged. "Your problem, Alice. You're good at solving problems. That's what makes your scripts work so well. Call me tomorrow and I'll let you know where to drop the money off."

I sat up. "No. If I'm handing over that kind of money, I want something in exchange. If you want the money, you have to meet me."

Cerys cocked her head, appraising me. It felt like a health and safety risk assessment. "Somewhere public," she said at last.

"No." I seldom managed any kind of assertiveness with her, but the understanding that had blossomed in the past few minutes made it necessary. "I want us to fuck one last time. Like the song says, for the good times."

I could see contempt in her face, but her voice betrayed none of it. She sounded warm and amused. "Why not? Shall I come to your flat?"

I'm not strong. Carrying a body down two flights of stairs and down the back lane to my garage would be beyond me. "I'll pick you up at your hotel. I've got a cabin in Perthshire, we can drive up there and have dinner. You can stay the night. One last night, Cerys, please. I've missed you so much."

A long, calculating pause. Then Cerys made the first miscalculation I'd seen from her. "Why not?" she repeated. We arranged that we would meet in the car park near her hotel on Friday afternoon. "I might as well check out then," she said. "You need to have me at the airport by eleven on Saturday morning so I can make the Helsinki flight."

Perfect. "No problem," I lied, surprised at how easy it was. But then I'd had the best possible teacher.

That left me five days to make my plans. I arranged to withdraw the money from the bank because I wanted to reassure Cerys that she was still in the driving seat. I'd show it to her before we drove off to Perthshire, the magnet that would keep her on board.

Working out the details of murder was a lot harder. Once I'd made the decision, once I'd realized that I'd never be free of her demands or my desire while she was still alive, it wasn't hard to accept that murder was the only possible answer. Cerys had already transformed me from law-abiding citizen to successful criminal, after all.

Body disposal, the usual trip wire for killers in films, was the least of my worries. The Scottish highlands contain vast tracts of emptiness where small predatory animals feed on all sorts of carrion. Forestry tracks lead deep into isolated woodland where nobody sets foot from one year's end to the next. And of course Cerys had walked away from her life before—in Hungary and in Edinburgh that I knew of, which probably meant she'd also done it in other places, other times. Nobody would be too surprised if she did it again. I didn't imagine anyone would seriously go looking for her, especially since she would have checked out of her hotel under her own steam.

How to kill her was a lot harder to figure out. Poison or drugs would have been my weapons of choice. But in her shoes, I wouldn't eat a crumb or drink a drop I hadn't brought with me. I didn't think she would be suspicious of me—I thought she was confident in the power she had over me—but I didn't want to take any chances.

If movies have taught me anything, it's that blunt instruments, blades, and guns are too chancy. They're all capable of missing their targets, they all tend to leave forensic traces you can never erase, and they're all concrete pieces of evidence you have to dispose of. So they were all out of the question.

I thought of smothering her while she slept, but I wasn't convinced I could carry that through, not flesh to flesh and heart to heart. Strangling had the same problems, plus my fear that I wasn't strong enough to carry it through.

Murder, it turned out, was a lot easier in the movies.

I woke up on the Wednesday morning without an idea in my head. When I went through to the kitchen and turned on the light, a bulb popped, tripping the fuse in the main box. And a light went on inside my head.

Back when I bought my house in Devon, I didn't have much money. I'd only been able to afford the house because it was practically derelict and I learned enough of all the building trades to do the restoration and renovation myself. I can lay bricks, plaster walls, install plumbing, and do basic carpentry.

I also know how electricity works.

Cerys may be able to last overnight without eating and drinking. She won't be able to make it without going to the toilet. My cabin on the loch has been fitted out in retro style, with an old-fashioned high-level toilet cistern with a long chain that you have to yank hard to generate a flush. It turned out to be a simple task to replace the ceramic handle with a metal one and to wire the whole lot into the main supply. As her fist closes round the handle, two hundred and forty volts will course through her body, her hand will clench tighter, and her heart will freeze.

Part of my heart will also freeze. But I can live with that. And because nothing is ever wasted, I will find a way to make a script out of it. Such a pity Cerys won't be around to see that movie too.

CONTROLLED EXPLOSIONS

Claire McGowan

Claire McGowan was born in Northern Ireland in 1981 and now lives in London. McGowan created the forensic psychologist Paula Maguire in *The Lost* (2013) and has written several other thrillers, including *The Fall* (2012). Under the name Eva Woods, she writes contemporary women's fiction.

Ballyterrin, Northern Ireland, June 1998

The town was burning.

Sergeant Bob Hamilton felt the heat on his face, scorching through the sides of the armoured jeep – someone had held a light to the line of cars dragged across the road. When the flames went up, licking and hungry, you could hear the shouts. Pure joy. Like weans burning grass under a magnifying glass. That was the worst, how much they were all enjoying it. He raised a hand to his head, mopped the sweat off on the sleeve of his uniform. Hottest day of the year and they were gussied up in full riot gear inside the oven of the jeep. Four grown men – five if you counted the other. The smell of sweaty oxters and burning tyres. The jeep rocking to and fro as the crowd battered it, pushing, shouting. Every time a stone hit, Bob flinched. It was hard not to.

'Which is it this time?' The man next to Bob had to shout to make himself heard over the noise outside. He looked round at the police officers, who all stared straight ahead into their visors, ignoring him. 'Is it going ahead or is it cancelled? What are they angry about?'

No one answered.

Bob could hear the weariness in his own voice. 'This parade was meant to go ahead.'

'So why aren't they moving?'

One of the other officers grunted. 'Because there's a feckin' bomb in the way, that's why.'

The man perked up. 'A bomb? Really?' He reached for his tape recorder, holding it higher.

'There's a suspicious device on the route.' Bob gave the official version. 'Bomb disposal are in. It'll be made safe, it's just . . . causing a wee bit of tension.'

Someone laughed, a short, bitter bark in the confined space.

The man with the tape recorder swung round for a second at the sound, then back again, like a dog with a bone it couldn't crack into. 'So these are Protestants out there? Orangemen?'

Journalists. Always trying to make sense of it, why one half of the population wanted to walk down the road in orange sashes, beating drums, just because they'd done it for the last three hundred years since some battle had been fought on that site. Why the other side, after all this time, had decided they didn't really want men in sashes and bowler hats coming down their road, and in order to make this point were setting the town on fire and planting bombs on their own streets.

The truth was, it didn't make any sense. It wasn't even a very interesting street. A row of houses and a bookie's on the corner, a run-down corner shop. The giant plastic ice cream outside it had bent over in the riot, and looked like it was about to melt all over the pavement. Bob knew the feeling.

He tried to explain. 'They're some of both. Catholics who didn't want it going ahead, Protestants annoyed at the hold-up.' Personally he thought they were all scum, anyone from either side who'd set fire to the place they lived in. It was their town. Not much, but all they had. For the past three days, if you looked out the windows of the police station, at the sun reflecting on metal jeeps and plexiglass riot shields, it had seemed as if all of Ballyterrin was on fire. The town was in stand-off, some parades going, some parades cancelled, someone angry with every decision, and like as not showing that anger by setting fire to a few cars or trashing a few shops or even firing a few wee shots at the police. Businesses had put down their shutters and closed, roads were blocked with burnt-out cars, and half the town gone away on holiday to escape it. The Twelfth Fortnight, they called it. Traditionally it was the Catholic population fleeing overseas, letting the Orange Order get on with it for a few weeks, marching their marches and singing their songs and beating their drums. This year, with the Good Friday Agreement just signed in April and the new Parades Commission getting involved, well, things were . . . mixed up.

The journalist, some English fella with an accent like grating machinery, was taking notes by hand now. Maybe, God willing, the batteries on his wee machine were dead. 'And you, Sergeant, are you Protestant?' They always pronounced it like that, with the *t* stuttering in the middle, instead of softened into a *d* like you did if you were local. Bob met the gaze of his partner – no, his *deputy*, he had to stop forgetting that – over the man's head, and they both shrugged. Then PJ Maguire looked away. It was a hard habit to break, thinking of PJ as his partner, though they hadn't been that for years. Not since Bob's promotion, and everything else that happened in 1993. PJ was a Catholic, and for various reasons Bob wasn't his favourite person, but dear God, the English. They hadn't a notion what went on here. 'Aye, I am,' he said, thinking of the sash in the wardrobe back home, pressed and under plastic. One year he'd led this parade himself, now he was shutting it down. 'But right now I'm just a police officer.'

PJ's radio buzzed and he listened for a moment. 'They're doing a controlled explosion. We better move on back.'

'Can we watch it blow up?' asked the journalist, scribbling excitedly in his notebook. 'That would be amazing.'

Bob Hamilton sighed, and watched his town burn.

'*Tout.*'

She could hear the word behind her, hissing in her ear. At the front of the class, the teacher was droning on about abortion.

'*Your ma was a tout.*'

Paula spun around, teeth bared. Everyone's head was down, writing, but she knew who'd said it all the same. 'Shut up!'

'What's that racket?' The teacher, Mrs Reilly, was fat, like really fat. Once she was wedged into her seat she didn't get out for anything. 'Paula? Is that you talking?'

She felt the red sweep up her face, the unfairness of it, as behind her a breeze of giggling broke out. 'No, miss.'

'In that case can you tell me why the Catholic Church doesn't support abortion?'

Paula sighed. The file paper in front of her was covered in doodles, stars and hearts. No notes on the lesson at all.

'Well? I knew you weren't listen—'

Paula said, bored: 'It's because of the scripture verse "before I formed you in the womb I knew you", that shows life starts at the moment of conception. Jeremiah one, five.'

Another faint giggle, this time not aimed at Paula. She looked down at her paper again.

The teacher said nothing for a few moments. 'Well. That's right. Now keep it down, please.'

Behind her, Paula could feel Catriona's beady eyes bore into her.

Tout. Your ma was a tout.

The worst thing about it: it was probably true.

'Bunch of cows,' said Saoirse, scowling, when Paula caught up with her in the science corridor. 'You should tell someone.'

Paula made a noise that was almost a laugh. You never told on people. Everyone knew that. The teachers did nothing, and you just got in more trouble on top of the bullying. 'Yeah, sure I'll do that. Duh.'

'Anyway, what did you reckon to *ER* last night? Wasn't it brilliant? I wish Dr Carter would marry me. He's sooooo gorgeous.' Saoirse was going to be a doctor; she'd always known it. Paula wondered sometimes if she knew it wouldn't be exactly like *ER*.

'Yeah . . . it was good.'

'Listen. Forget about Catriona O'Keeffe. She's just a little Provo bitch. Come on.' Saoirse put her arm through Paula's as they wandered down the hot corridor, with its reek of Impulse and PE kits. 'We're getting out of here, remember? One more year! Then we'll be in Belfast, we can get our own flat, we can have people round for dinner . . .'

But there'd be no getting out. There'd be Catrionas in Belfast too, lots of them. And everyone would know Paula's da was a Catholic policeman and her ma was maybe a tout and maybe dead but maybe not. Sometimes she couldn't stand it. She'd been starting to think, though she had no idea how to tell Saoirse, that maybe she'd go even further away than Belfast. Further than Dublin too. Maybe she'd go as far away as she could. Maybe she'd just keep running until it wasn't possible to find her way back.

'What've you now? I've Statistics, FUN.'

'Eh . . . I've a free.'

'Lucky. See you on the bus then.'

'Yeah. See ya.'

Saoirse had a normal life. She had both her parents, she had three brothers and two sisters. On Sundays they sat in a little row in Mass, all of them going up to Communion with clean faces and crossed hands. Paula, she had . . . well, nothing.

'We put him inside. Didn't we?'

Detective Inspector Alec Johnson stared round the table. No one answered. He glared at the man furthest from him, who was tipped back in his chair, shirt-sleeves rolled up. 'Patrick. It was you made the arrest.'

PJ Maguire didn't like being called by his first name, Bob knew. Couldn't blame him. If your name was Patrick, you may as well wear a T-shirt saying 'I'm a Taig, please set fire to my house'. 'Aye, sir, it was. Red Hugh's in the Maze and he hasn't put a foot outside it in three years. That's a fact.'

'So why are we still finding his signature bombs all over the routes of Orange Order parades?' Johnson slapped the paper down on the table. It was the analysis of the device from earlier that day, the fifth they'd found that summer. A list of chemicals as long as your arm. Johnson liked to pace up and down behind you in meetings – kept you on your toes. Bob tried to concentrate. Johnson was talking. 'See those long names? That's fertiliser. We all know Red Hugh favoured fertiliser – he used to get subsidies for it on his farm. From the British Government. Then he put it into bombs to blow up British Army patrols.'

'I doubt he appreciated the irony,' PJ muttered. Bob stared down at the table. He could still picture the man at his trial. Mad eyes and a straggly beard like some Russian Commie – they called him Red Hugh because he'd got into the Provos via a dalliance with radical Marxism. That, and the brand of fertiliser he used leaked a red dye that was exactly the colour of blood.

Johnson went on. 'He uses these same detonators. He even uses this brand of copper wiring, but he's in the Maze. So what's going on? How is this possible?'

No one had any answers.

'Sir?' A female voice, quiet but clear. It said – *listen to me. I've got as much right to speak as you.* 'Do you not think maybe someone's taken over Red Hugh's bomb factory?'

Johnson looked annoyed. 'That's where I was going next, Miss Corry.'

'It's Detective Constable.'

Bob looked at her from the corner of his eye, which was close enough. It wasn't right, all that blond hair and the short skirts. This Corry girl was from Belfast and had been pushed up the ranks, though she was barely even thirty. She'd appeared in the station at the start of parade season, after they'd found the first bomb. They didn't even have a vacancy but there she was. And she had a baby, he'd heard. Who was looking after it while she was sitting here telling her elders what to do? Bob had been still on traffic at that age. Of course, things were different then.

Bob had started at the station in 1968, on the same day as Alec Johnson, and Sergeant Ian Robinson had trained them both, showed them how to survive, how to look for car bombs, how to vary your route to work, how to get answers out of some cocky wee IRA shite with a balaclava in his back pocket and a bent lawyer on speed-dial. Until the day Robinson forgot his own rules, and started his BMW in the car park.

They'd heard the bang three storeys up. Cups fell off tables and shattered. The windows bubbled in. Bob had frozen, tea soaking into his shirt and blood on his fingers from trying to catch the broken mug.

Blood. There'd been a lot more of it on the lower windows of the station. They'd had to get in a wee man with a squeegee, who did the job with a fag hanging out of his mouth, not a bother on him. Bob had called his son after his dead sergeant – it felt like the very least he could do. He thought about Robinson every day, even without that. Every time he turned the key in his own car, that half-second where you held your breath, waiting for it all to be over. Hoping at least it would be quick.

'So we'll investigate Red Hugh's farm then? See if the materials are still there?' The Corry girl was upright, alert. She might be a mother but to Bob's mind she could still be in school, putting her hand up for the teacher.

'Yes.' Johnson was doing his best not to look at her. 'Miss Corry, in this station we wait until people have finished before we give our views.'

She didn't bat an eyelid. 'Do we also wait until the whole town knows what we're about to do?'

'I beg your pardon?'

'There's been no physical evidence at any of the bomb sites, no prints or DNA, just clear signs that link them to someone who can't have done it. Am I right?'

'What are you suggesting?'

'It all seems too neat. Someone knows what we'll be looking for and that we'll make the connection to Red Hugh. Sir.'

The silence that fell on the conference room was heavy. It was the kind of silence that came from ten forty-plus men looking at one girl barely out of her twenties. Bob thought of the rumours she'd brought with her from Belfast – that the Corry girl was there to check up on them all, some kind of Professional Standards review. That she took her orders right from the top. He hadn't believed it. The girl wasn't much more than a wean.

She didn't seem to mind the silence. 'I think we should go to the farm soon. Today, ideally. Tomorrow morning at the latest.'

Johnson paused. Bob could see the grey in the hair cut neatly around his collar. He was pushing fifty, both of them were. Did Bob look old too? They'd both be out when everything changed, most likely. Letting weans and women run the place. 'The farm is dead set on the border, so we need to set up liaison with that lot first. It won't be today.'

'*An Garda Síochána?*' The Corry girl rolled off the Irish name of the Southern police force. Definitely Catholic. Had to be. 'I can set that up for you.'

'Oh you can, can you?'

'Of course. It's no bother.' She didn't even ask if she could go out to the farm – and why would she want to, a wet-behind-the-ears girl? It was easy enough to criticise when you were safe in the office, not out in the field afraid someone would shoot the head off your shoulders any minute. Would this be the way now, taking orders from people behind desks, who'd never chased after a wee gobshite with a grenade in his hand, never carried the coffin of yet another colleague shot in the head or blown up? Who'd never washed their friend's blood off their car windows, scrubbing and scrubbing with a sponge, then throwing the sponge and everything you were wearing into the bin, then hosing down your driveway, then selling the car anyway because you couldn't stand to see it outside your house.

She stood up and put on her suit jacket, flipping her yellow ponytail out behind her so it swung like a scythe. 'I'll get on to that now, sir.'

It was amazing how you could use the word to someone while still managing to convey you had no respect for them at all. The girl walked out of the room, clacking on the heels of her shoes, and all the men in the room looked after her, but she didn't turn around.

Paula was tall for seventeen, nearly five foot ten already, but there were four of them, and only one of her.

'Fuck off,' she said, trying to look hard. What were they even doing in her street? Catriona lived out in the country somewhere with the mud and the cows and the mad Provos. But there she was, standing in the road as Paula got home from school, with her little minions Mary and Brid. A boy was sitting on next door's wall, smoking.

Catriona blocked her way. 'Going home to tout on us too? Guess it runs in the family.'

She tried to walk past them, head bowed, but they were everywhere. Her house was only three along. If she could run . . . They were just girls, three of them in the same maroon uniform as her, socks pushed down as far as they'd go, skirts rolled up, sports tops zipped over their blazers – none of it official school uniform. Paula was pretty sure Mary and Brid wouldn't be passing their A-levels – they were both thick as the pigshit they shovelled on their farms – but Catriona was smart. Smart and mean.

The boy was older, maybe nineteen, wearing jeans and Army boots. He had acne down the side of his face. She didn't know who he was.

'Your ma was a tout,' Catriona repeated. 'That's why she snuffed it, isn't it? Couldn't keep her mouth shut.'

'She's not—'

'Is she not? Then did she just go off and leave you? No surprise really. And where's your da? Off harassing his own people? He's a fucking traitor too. Him and your dead ma.'

'Fuck off!' The tears in Paula's eyes were stinging. 'She might be dead, I don't know! I don't know anything and neither do you, you stupid cow. At least I'm going to pass my A-levels. At least I'm getting out of this fucking stupid town. You'll be stuck here forever, milking the cows and signing on the dole.'

'Bitch.'

She hadn't thought they'd actually hurt her – though words could hurt enough, and she'd never believed that crap about them being gentler than sticks and stones – but suddenly there was a scuffle, and Catriona's chipped nails were scratching at Paula's face, and she could smell the girl's BO and bubblegum, and she was fighting back with no plan, just instinct, slapping and pulling, grabbing at Catriona's hair and making a noise like an angry cat.

'Fuck off! Fuck off!'

'Hey, hey, come on now!' Someone was pulling her back. She couldn't see for a moment from the hair in her eyes, just feel someone's hands on her waist. Then – it was Aidan O'Hara. What was he doing here? She pulled away, breathing hard.

'What the fuck's going on?'

'None of your effing business.' Catriona was panting, straightening her clothes. 'Guess all you touts stick together.'

Aidan didn't say anything about that, but he stood very still. 'Her da's a cop, you know. You better piss off or you'll get a record. Silly wee bitch.'

The other girls were juking off down the road, but Catriona was still shouting, standing her ground. Her dyed blond hair had fallen out of its tight bun and her eyes behind their seven coats of mascara were wild. The boy got down off the wall, held her by the arm. He hadn't said a word during the whole thing. She was screeching, 'Whole fucking family are traitors. And your da too, O'Hara. I know who you are. Your da got what was coming to him, and so will hers.'

'Come on, feck's sake.' The boy bundled Catriona off down the street, with a last slitted-eye look at Paula that made her feel sick.

'You know him?' said Aidan, looking after them.

'N-no.' She was trying to blink back the angry tears in her eyes.

'Peadar O'Keeffe is the name. Nasty wee fecker. Year above me in school.'

Catriona's brother, then. The whole family must be out to get her.

'You OK?'

'Fine.' She couldn't meet his eye. Though his mother and hers had been best friends, Aidan never talked to Paula if he could help it. 'What're you even here for?' She saw he'd parked his Clio, a present from his adoring mammy for his eighteenth birthday, outside the door of her house.

'Ma sent me – you know.' He waved his hand in frustration at the plastic container under his arm. Pat O'Hara had been sending food ever since Paula's mother disappeared five years ago. As if that was the main thing missing from their lives – Irish stew and lasagne. 'Said your da'd be busy with all these riots, so maybe youse'd need dinner.'

'Oh. Right so. Yeah, em . . . bring it in.'

They trudged to the door, keeping a foot of distance between them. Aidan was in the grey uniform of St Luke's, the boys' school, his tie loose, blazer over his shoulder. He'd be going off to university in a few months – he'd applied to Dublin, she knew. Pat kept Paula up to date with his life, and she'd see him out and about the odd time, but they'd never been friends. Sometimes that was the way of it, when you knew each other from when you were wee kids. The last time Aidan had spoken this much to her was at her mother's memorial service.

Don't think about that.

She put her key in the lock, trying not to let him see that every day she came home and opened the door, it happened again for her a little bit. Every single day. As if one day it would be different. Maybe – no, of course not. Her mother hadn't been there on that last day in 1993 or any other day since. And she wouldn't be here today.

Paula put the food container in the fridge. It looked like some kind of stew, too hot for the weather. Aidan stood leaning against the counter, flicking his curtains haircut. She could smell his aftershave – Lynx Africa – and cigarettes too. Of course he smoked, all the cool boys did. She thought about bolting upstairs and bucking on some more Impulse O2. 'Eh . . . do you want some tea, or – like, coffee or something?'

'Don't drink it.'

Neither did she. There was a total of one coffee shop in town, and it was the kind of place that served it in little metal pots with leaking lids.

She looked in the fridge. 'Juice?' Her dad wouldn't buy minerals. Her mum hadn't allowed it. *Think of your teeth, Paula.* They were both still trying to keep to Margaret's rules, long after she was gone.

'OK.'

She poured him a glass of Kia Ora and one for herself, and they stood drinking them in silence. It was a hot day and she felt sweat trickling down her back, under her pink shirt and plain M&S bra. Paula had been buying her own bras since she was thirteen – her mother had gone before she'd even needed to wear one. It was Pat who'd taken her that first time, hugely embarrassed but hugely kind. Pat, Aidan's mother. Oh God. She couldn't think of a single thing to say to him. He wouldn't be interested in any of the crap she talked to Saoirse about, mostly TV and which boys they fancied. Neither of them had said anything for a minute. Two minutes. Paula started to panic, opened her mouth. Nothing came out.

Aidan cleared his throat. 'Eh . . . you going to Magnum's Saturday?'

'Dunno. Maybe.' She was officially too young to get into Magnum PI's, the local disco, but they usually turned a blind eye if you were seventeen and had a provisional driving licence.

'It's shite, but like it's the only place round here.'

'Yeah, God, it's awful, isn't it?' She loved Magnum's. She loved the cheap sugary cocktails, she loved the music, S Club 7 and Steps and Spice Girls, and she loved dancing with her friends in a big circle, too loud for anyone to ask her about her missing ma or her cop da, too dark for anyone to recognise her as *that wee Maguire girl, you know, the one whose mother . . .*

'Might see you there then.'

She breathed in, hard. 'Yeah, might do.' God, he was practically *asking her out.*

Aidan was moving now, rearranging his hair again. 'You don't have a mobile, do you?'

'Nah.' Some people at school were getting them now, but not her yet. PJ wasn't keen on the idea or the expense.

'Well. If anything happens . . . get me at school or something.' His school finished ten minutes later than hers. They did it to keep the girls and boys apart, which didn't work at all. 'You know . . . if they give you shit again.'

'OK. See you.'

He didn't look at her as he went out the door, jiggling his car keys in his school trouser pocket. 'See ya.'

OH MY GOD. She was ringing Saoirse right now, before *Neighbours* came on.

*

'Sergeant Hamilton, I'm sorry—'

'What is it?' Bob didn't turn around from where he stood, gazing out of the high windows of the incident room at the town below. In the afternoon sun, it looked like it was still on fire, though the riot had been broken up for now and the device made safe. That's what they called it. Making safe. As if such a thing was possible.

'Sir—'

The admin girl was trying to get his attention. Aoife or something her name was. Why could none of them spell their names right? Let them go and live in Eire if they wanted, with too many letters in the words and not enough money, the potholed roads full of donkeys and unlicensed drivers. It was a mystery to Bob. You gave people benefits and free dentists and roads and hospitals and all they did was complain. You sent your soldiers, your sons, in to protect them, and they blew them up in the street. And now what? You let the terrorists out of prison, while the police officers who'd bled and died to keep the peace . . . you fired them. Bob wasn't stupid. He knew all about the list.

The List. That was the word going round the place, whispered through the walls, gusting under the bottoms of doors, lurking in the car park. The list of officers who'd be put out when the Policing bill went through. A condition of the Good Friday Agreement. They'd been weighed, the RUC, and found wanting. Up there with parades and prisoners, an abomination, a part of the peace process that the other side had demanded gone before they would stop their shooting and bombing. And it had been agreed. They were going to scrap the uniform, the staff, even the name. All those dead officers, killed by cowards in the dark – this was how you rewarded them. You swept them under the carpet of history. You made them shameful.

'Sergeant Hamilton!'

'What is it, Miss Riordan?' He wouldn't say her Christian name. His mouth couldn't mould to those letters. 'I'm busy here. We're going out on an operation first thing tomorrow.'

'But you're wanted on the phone.'

'I'm busy.' Busy watching his town burn.

'It's your wife, sir. There's been . . . I really think you should come.'

Everything was burning.

'Linda?' She never rang him at work. Never. She knew better, none of these personal calls in work time that the younger officers were always getting.

'I'm sorry, I wouldn't have bothered you except—'

'What's wrong, love?'

'Bob, I'm up at the place. I . . .' She didn't want to ask but he could hear it in her voice. 'I know you're busy, but—'

'Is it Ian?'

'Yes.'

'Is it bad?'

'Bob . . .'

'I'm coming. Just wait there for me.' He wrenched open the door to the incident room. 'DC Maguire?'

PJ was at a desk, waiting for the phone call to say they were authorised to go out in the morning. 'Aye, sir?' He was always polite. You could never accuse him of being insubordinate, not in his words or his actions or anything concrete. Bob just wished things were different. So much bad blood there. Robinson, and Bob getting the sergeant job over PJ's head, and everything that happened in 1993, that terrible year. No wonder he couldn't meet PJ's eyes.

'I need to get away. Can you take over?'

PJ had a wee girl of Ian's age. Seventeen. Bob remembered the daughter – terrible height for a girl, and all that red hair. She'd be going to university next year, off out of the town like all the kids did. Whereas Ian . . .

'You're away?' PJ was surprised.

'Aye. Can you handle things here?'

'Well, aye, sure I can handle them, but—'

'Right so.' Bob was aware he was moving quickly, gathering his jacket and wallet and radio. It didn't come naturally to him, to be quick. Important things took time, but sometimes there wasn't any. His car was in its parking space and he was trotting over to it so fast he almost forgot to check. But you had to, whatever the emergency was. Remember what happened to Robinson. Remember the blood on the windows. He got down and peered under it, then stood up, breathing hard. Had to keep breathing, drive slow. No sense in having an accident. He started the engine and nosed his car into the heavy lunchtime traffic.

As he drove, slow, so slow, he found he was thinking of the woman. Her red hair, her pale face. Bob didn't like to think of Margaret Maguire if he could help it. It hadn't been good, that time, for any of them. He'd done his best, but sometimes the fact was people were better off not being found – maybe because they didn't want to be, or maybe because finding them would be worse than losing them. The case was filed away in some drawer now, thank God, but PJ wouldn't let it rest. And Bob could see the looks PJ gave him. So full of blame. Sometimes Bob would have liked to shout at him – *you think you knew her, but you didn't, you didn't know her at all* – but he never would. Not in a million years. He'd take the blame, and it was no more than he deserved.

People thought policing was about finding the truth. Bob could have told them it was often in fact about *managing* the truth, keeping it damped down so it didn't rise up and burn the place to the ground. Fire-fighting. His job was closer to that than people knew.

He didn't know why he was thinking about these things. It passed the drive, he supposed. Stopped him thinking about what he'd find at the end. Anyway, he was there now and parking, shocking prices they charged these days. He could claim it back as police business – some would do that, but not him. The rules mattered. He hadn't even asked Linda what ward they were on. His feet took him there anyway. Acute medicine. So many years trailing up to the hospital, ever since the day in 1980, a summer's day, hot and clear as butter, and he wasn't meant to be there – you didn't go, in those days – but suddenly the station phone was ringing and they were saying, *is that Mr Hamilton*, and he wanted to tell them *it's DC*, but he didn't, and they were saying, *could you come please, come now, there's been some complications with the birth.*

Complications. He'd always thought of it that way after. Ian wasn't well. Ian had complications.

Ian would be eighteen next month. Other weans, like PJ's girl, for example, they'd be getting cars, having parties, smoking, kissing, driving their parents to distraction.

'I'm sorry,' said Linda, as he went in. 'You were busy.' She'd been saying sorry since the day Ian was born, half-dead herself as she was. *I'm sorry, Bob, I tried, I tried.* When it wasn't her fault at all, it was—

Ian was on the bed. He was a big lad, despite it all. He'd be taller than Bob if he could stand up.

'Hello, son. Are you all right?' They always talked to him. It was more for each other than for him. Bob had often wondered what his son's voice would sound like. It didn't seem right that they'd never heard it.

The breathing tube was in Ian's nose again, his skin that sick yellow colour of wax. His breathing like a wet sponge.

Linda looked haggard. 'Another one?' he said. That was how many this month – three? The seizures were getting worse.

'Aye. We'll need to up his medicine, they said. He—' Her shoulders shook, just a wee bit. 'He stopped breathing for a long time, Bob. Nothing worked. I had to do the mouth to mouth. I . . . it wasn't working.'

He dropped his hand onto Linda's shoulder, feeling the wool of the cardigan she wore despite the heat. Her hair was nearly all grey now, and lines ate into her face.

'Well,' he said. 'You brought him back, love. You did it again.' He wasn't sure what he meant by that, whether he was praising her or whether it was something else.

The corner of her Ash poster was peeling off, distorting Tim Wheeler's handsome face. Paula stared up at it. It was ten to seven – her alarm would be going off any minute. She could hear her dad moving about downstairs, clearing his throat, clattering dishes. She didn't know if she'd been to sleep at all.

Why was this happening now? Her mother had been gone nearly five years, five years in October. Of course there'd been comments at the time, people staring when she got on the bus or girls whispering behind her back as she got changed in PE, but she was only just thirteen then and she didn't understand. She'd thought bad people had taken her mother. What other explanation could there possibly be? The police would find her, and she'd be fine and back home making breakfast in the kitchen. Even in the worst moments, when Paula had heard her dad up late at night on the phone, his voice thick with terror, or when they'd found the first body that could have been her mother, but wasn't, she'd only begun to think about funerals and that kind of ending to it all.

She'd never thought it could be five years on and they'd still just know nothing. Nothing at all.

The alarm beeped. She blinked a few times, trying to clear away thoughts of Aidan, and Catriona and the look in her brother's mean eyes. She'd never be able to concentrate on her Sociology mock today. It didn't matter. She could pretty much do it in her sleep, and that was the truth. She got up and washed, put out her uniform for the day, the scratchy maroon skirt and socks, the pink blouse, the heavy blazer even though it was the hottest week of the year. Thank God she'd only another year of this. Aidan would be out soon, of course. Away to Dublin. She wondered how that would work if they . . .

God, get a grip, Paula. He was only being nice.

She was packing her files and pencil case for the exam when she felt something in the bottom of her school bag, a hard lump. It was cold against her fingers as she pulled it out, held it up in the morning light of her bedroom.

It was gold-coloured, shiny, heavy, pointing in at the end. It looked like . . .

'Dad?' She was standing in the kitchen, holding the thing hidden in her hand. The feel of it seemed to leach into her, the coldness of metal and hard stares.

'Aye?' He was rushing about like every morning, late, trying to put the washing on and iron shirts and find a tie and make her eat breakfast.

'There's a girl at school.' She didn't mention the bullet. She thought that's what it was, anyway. Someone had put a bullet in her school bag. It made her heart race, a sick feeling in her stomach.

'Aye?' PJ was trying to read the instructions on the washing machine. Nearly five years since her mother had gone, and he still hadn't figured out how to wash jumpers so that they didn't shrink. He was wearing his work suit, the tie thrown back over his shoulder. She wondered again how he'd cope when she went to university – and how to tell him the only places she'd looked at were in England. Not Belfast, like all her friends. Just . . . away.

'She's been saying things.'

'Um-hum?' His head was in the fridge now. 'Pet, would you get milk on your way home? I'm swamped, we're up to our eyeballs at the station.'

Parade season was always busy, and she knew they'd had a problem with someone bombing the routes of ones that were allowed ahead. 'I've my Sociology mock today.'

'Oh right so. We should have something nice for dinner . . .' She could see the wheels of his brain turning. 'Or I could take you out at the weekend when you're all finished . . . eh . . .' She could see he was about to say they'd invite Pat, since PJ would have no idea where to go to eat in the town, and then she'd have to sit there with Aidan when maybe that same night they'd be at the disco and . . .

'I'll get something in the shops,' she said quickly.

'OK, pet,' he said gratefully. 'Take the cash out of my wallet there. What were you saying before then? Some girl giving you grief?' he asked, shutting the fridge door.

She could feel the bullet in her hand behind her back, heavy as bad news. 'Nothing, Dad. It's OK.'

Bob made it into the station just in time that morning. Johnson was in the incident room, which was now empty. He looked at his watch pointedly. 'The car's out back. You better get your skates on, the lads are ready to go.'

'Sorry, sir.' It was still strange to call him that, the boy with the nervous swallow who'd started alongside Bob thirty years ago. 'There was an emergency at home.'

'This whole summer's an emergency.' Johnson looked out the windows. 'Whole bloody town's a mess. Whole bloody country.'

'Alec . . .' He didn't know he was going to ask it until he did. 'All this talk of a list.'

Johnson didn't turn around. 'You shouldn't listen to talk, Sergeant.'

'It's just I need to know what will happen. I've Ian and Linda to think of. Things . . . things are not too good.'

A pause. 'I'm sorry to hear that, Sergeant. You should of course always say if family matters are likely to impede you in the performance of your duties.'

'It's not—'

'Because this is a major operation and we're very short-handed, and I'm sure DC Maguire would jump at the chance to lead it by himself.'

'There's no need for that.' Bob matched the same official tone. As if they'd never been friends. As if he hadn't come across Alec sobbing in the kit room on the day they'd cleaned Robinson's remains off the station windows. 'I'm ready now.'

'Good. You should get a move on then.'

'Yes. Sir.'

The question had not been answered, Bob noted. Though perhaps that was a kind of answer in itself.

'Yo, P!' Saoirse was bearing down on her across the school lobby. She was red-faced from the heat, and she'd tied her jumper round her waist and rolled up the sleeves of her pink school shirt. Her glasses were smudgy and her dark hair falling out of its ponytail. 'P! Hold up!'

Paula stopped walking. 'Hiya.'

'Right, tell me *everything*.'

'I told you on the phone.' The Aidan stuff from yesterday didn't feel so exciting now she'd found that bullet. It seemed to have lodged itself in her stomach, hard and cold.

'Tell me again! This is big, big news! He asked you out?'

'Well, sort of. Not really. He said he'd maybe see me in Magnum's.'

'Right, so we have to go. I mean, *duh*.'

'Would we get in, though?'

'We can try. As long as you've your provisional. I'll see if Jennifer and that lot want to go too. Mammy thinks she's a good influence – she's no idea they all smoke out the back every lunchtime.'

'OK.'

'What's up?' Saoirse stared at Paula in bafflement – the sun was out, it was the last week of school before the summer holidays, and a cute boy had as good as declared his love for her. What was there to be worried about? 'You're not upset about Bitchface Catriona? She's not even in today. Carmel told me she didn't show up for her English mock. She's gonna get kicked out, I reckon.'

'I know. It's OK. I've got Sociology now, anyway, I better go.'

'OK. Do you want my lucky pen?'

'No, I'm grand, thanks.'

'Good luck. Mammy's collecting me, I have to go to the optician's. I'll ask her can I go out Saturday. You can stay at mine. This is going to be soooo cool!'

'Yeah. Bye.'

Paula watched her friend run out to her mum's old Toyota, flapping with her blazer and bag and violin case, off home to her nice family. There was no way she could understand any of this. Sometimes Paula felt like she was on a little island, where she could hear and see her friends doing normal teenage stuff, fancying boys and listening to Steps and getting their driving licences, while she was stuck there. She swallowed, hard, but the lump would not go away.

'That it? The white one?'

'Aye.' It had to be, there was nothing else for miles. Bob had a bad feeling, itching in the middle of his shoulder blades. It was too quiet out here. Only the fields, stretching on either side of the narrow country road. There was grass down the middle of it and a stink of silage in the air, rotting and sweet. Sometimes you'd hear a bellow from a cow, that was it. The car bumped over the potholes, drawing slowly up to the farmhouse, rattling over the cattle grid and up the long concrete driveway. Plenty of time for whoever was there to see them coming.

PJ was shifting uneasily in his car seat, his hand clasped on his gun. He was certain the local IRA had taken his wife away, probably killed her, and here they were at the farm of one of the worst of them, their former chief bomb maker. Red Hugh. Bob was trying not to think about the man's mad eyes. He was locked up in the Maze, he wasn't here. If Bob was honest with himself, deep down inside he was glad to have PJ at his side again, the only person he ever really thought of as his partner. They'd worked well together, despite all their differences. Until what happened.

'Everyone ready?' They hadn't taken the riot squad – every officer with extreme situation training was out on the streets, trying to stop the town from burning to the ground. This was just one farmhouse, white paint peeling from its walls, no curtains in the windows, a collection of muddy outbuildings. There was no sign of any livestock. So it was just Bob, PJ, and a uniformed officer, no more than twenty-five. Bob didn't know all their names any more. He hadn't even the heart to ask. Everything was changing. 'As far as we know it's just Red Hugh's missus and two weans here. So go easy. Might be nothing to find.' He'd seen PJ's hand twitch to his gun. The air felt heavy and charged. Bob had been in the RUC long enough to know that this was the kind of day when things went wrong.

They parked in the front yard. The stink of silage was stronger here; it seemed to lie low and pressing over the house. Bob shielded his eyes. The light was dazzling. He motioned to the officer to get in position on the other side of the door and moved in front of PJ, who was at his shoulder, itching to get in. Bob was the sergeant; it was his job to lead. He knocked at the peeling door. 'Open up! RUC.'

Not for much longer. The RUC wouldn't be anything. A footnote in a bloody history.

No answer. A gate swung in some unfelt breeze, creaking.

'We should—' PJ was speaking when there was a commotion from the back of the house. A door slammed. Then the officer was running, and Bob and PJ followed, drawing their weapons. Bob wondered if that would change too. If, like other police forces in the UK, they'd have to fight criminals and murderers with only rubber truncheons as defence. His gun in his hand felt cool despite the heat, its weight keeping him anchored.

At the back of the farm a steep hill sloped down to a shed. Someone was running away from them, a figure disappearing in a blur of heat haze. 'Stop!' PJ was shouting. 'You there! Come back here! Stop!' It should have been Bob shouting. He was the one in charge. But he couldn't seem to move.

The young officer had separated off already, going down the side of the hill towards the farm buildings there. 'Sir!' He shouted up from the open door of the nearest shed – its paint was red, peeling off in spots like the skin of a burn victim. Like a woman Bob had helped after a fire bomb once. When was that? 1973? The IRA again.

'Sir? Sir!'

Bob was rooted to the spot. There was the constable at the shed door, going inside, seeing what was there. There was the person running away – it looked like a man. There was PJ following, running towards him as he ran away. The three of them and Bob standing on the hill, still not moving.

'Sir! You need to see this!' The constable was out of the shed again, waving his arms. Bob stood there for a minute more. The sun was blinding on the barn roof. *Everything was burning.*

He walked down the hill. Carefully, didn't want to fall. Time seemed to have slowed. One, two, three . . .

'*Sir!*'

It was so hot. It was never hot like this in Northern Ireland. The kind of day to go to the beach, drive around in a convertible car with the top down, jump into swimming pools. Shame she lived in Ballyterrin, not California. Paula regretted this intensely. Instead she had to spend the afternoon in the gym with its smell of rubber mats and sweat, doing her Sociology paper. Afterwards, rather than getting the bus home, she walked across town, feeling the heat beat down on her. She carried her blazer over her bag, the sleeves of her shirt rolled up. She stopped in a shop and bought an ice-pop, cola flavour, sucking up the cold sweetness, squeezing the tube then letting the melted bit at the bottom run into her mouth. Before she got to the boys' school she stopped again and sprayed herself with Impulse O2, hoping it would cover the sweat that was running down between her shoulders and under her bra. She waited on the wall outside, aware of the boys passing, loud and shoving each other, throwing bits of paper, their eyes crawling over her. She pretended to read *Mansfield Park*, which she was doing for her English A-level.

'It's not a library!' one boy shouted. Laughing. She ignored him.

Aidan came out last, on his own. A fag already in his mouth, sleeves up, tie loose, hair a mess. He stopped in front of her, and she could see he was aware of the other boys looking, all of them seeing her and seeing him stop to talk to her. 'You're brave.'

She put the book away, slowly. 'You said if something happened. You said to get you here.'

'Aye?'

'It happened. There was something in my bag when I got home.'

'What's that?' He looked worried, as if she might show him a tampon or something. She'd almost do it, for the laugh. Except she couldn't imagine laughing right now.

The bullet was in the pocket of her bag, where her dad would be sure never to look in a million years. Aidan weighed it in his hand. 'Four calibre.'

'Is it?'

He laughed. 'I haven't a baldy, Maguire.'

Maguire. He'd never called her that before. She liked it. 'I think maybe Catriona . . . I think it was her. It wasn't there before.'

'Come on,' he said, shrugging his bag over his shoulder. The fag dangled from his lip, and she wondered how it didn't fall. 'I'll walk you home in case they're there.'

The ground was dry under his feet and Bob was not as fit as he'd been ten years ago, five years ago. He was panting when he reached the door of the shed; could already smell the place, something else squirming under the farmyard stink of silage and animals.

Inside was too much to look at all at once. A bench with papers all over it, wires, what looked like little clocks. Bags of Semtex, crumbling like white cheese. Along one back wall, a chest freezer. The smell was coming from there.

The constable looked at Bob for a nod. He closed his eyes. 'Open it, son.'

The young officer wrenched open the lid and the smell rolled out, so thick you could almost see it in the air. An evil yellow smell. 'Jesus,' said the officer. Bob said nothing. He took a step towards it, one more. He looked at what was inside. The officer had gone pale. 'What'll we do?'

'Follow procedure, Constable. Just follow procedure.'

Bob went outside. His partner, ex-partner, had appeared at the brow of the hill, still running, shouting, 'Lost him. He's only a wean. Not even twenty, I'd say. He'll be back.'

Bob called up to him. 'DC Maguire. Could you radio the station and say we've found remains?'

PJ froze on the hill. His shadow lengthened out in front of him. 'There's a body?'

Too late, Bob realised his mistake.

PJ was moving down. 'How old is it? How old a body?'

'Not long,' shouted the officer from inside the shed, his voice strained. 'There's flies . . . God – she's . . . she's rotting.'

'She?' said PJ.

If it hadn't been so hot, if the sun wasn't dazzling in his eyes, Bob might have been faster to stop him. 'DC Maguire . . . PJ – *no* . . .'

Too late. Always too late. His partner – his ex-partner – was running down the hill, his legs windmilling under him on the parched earth.

Bob couldn't move when it happened. Even when PJ fell, sliding down the hill, and the crack of the gunshot was followed closely by the crack of his leg breaking, and his blood began to feed the thirsty ground, even then Bob couldn't do a thing.

PJ was making a noise he'd never heard come out of a person before, not even during the fire that time, not even on the day Robinson died, and a different figure was running out of the grove of trees behind them. Too far away, running too fast, there was no way to catch them . . . her. Because Bob could now see it was a young girl, probably still at school, clutching a very old shotgun and with her hair wild about her head. He recognised the uniform she had on – it was the same school PJ's own daughter went to. The sun seemed to flame in her fair hair. As if she was on fire, too.

'Sir?' The officer was beside him, urgent, panicked. 'Sir, what do we do? It's your call, sir.' A good lad, that. Bob really should learn his name. But was there any point if he was getting put out soon? His mind stretched ahead, a prison guard uniform, back at the bottom of the heap, the pay cut . . .

Very slowly, Bob reached for his radio. 'Back-up requested to Richhill Farm – we have female remains, two fleeing suspects, possibly underage, and an officer shot.' He paused for a minute, and on the hill, PJ had gone silent, and that was somehow worse than the screaming. 'As quick as possible, please.'

From the front of the farm, there was the sound of an engine starting up.

'Catriona,' said Aidan, flicking his cigarette. 'Her da's in the Ra, aye?' They were trailing through the town in the heat, the waves of it rolling up from the tarmac. Paula was walking as slowly as she could. She hoped some of those bitches from school would see her. Aidan was quite the heartthrob at St Clare's, not that he'd ever gone steady with anyone.

'Supposed to be, yeah.'

'Red Hugh, they call him. Red Hugh O'Keeffe.'

'Do they?'

'Aye. And your da put him away three years ago. He's in the Maze, so he is.'

'Did he?' Paula never knew anything about what her father did all day. He'd made sure of it. How did Aidan find these things out?

'Aye.'

'What are you, like, Sherlock Holmes?'

Aidan flicked back his hair so she could see the pale underneath of his wrist, just for a second. She imagined how it would feel, the pulse of the blood beating there. 'They let me hang out at the paper, like. In the office.'

She didn't know what to say to that. John O'Hara had been shot in that office, when Aidan was only seven. He'd been there to see it, watch his dad die in front of him. Someone else was editor now but they never had the heart to send him away. Aidan was going off to do journalism in Dublin, never wanted anything else out of life. She still had no idea what she might do. She liked Sociology, but only the crime bits, and English and Biology, but they didn't let you do that combination. Saoirse knew she would be a doctor, was going to do all the A-levels you needed for that. Everyone knew where they were going to end up – except Paula. She couldn't imagine what her life would be like when she grew up.

'So. That's probably why she's being such a bitch to you.' Aidan tapped away his cigarette ash.

'But why's she started now? I mean, she was always a bitch, but she used to leave me alone before this.'

'I dunno, Maguire.'

That name again. 'Should I tell Dad?'

'Are you scared of her?'

'No. But that boy with her . . . I think he's her brother. He's freaky. And that thing in my bag, that's really weird.'

'Aye. Well, I can . . . if you want you can walk home with me for the next week. Then she'll be out of your hair till next year. Won't she?'

'Yeah. OK.' She acted like it was no big deal. So did he. They kept on walking, heading for home.

Johnson said, 'Tell me again what happened.'

Bob rubbed a hand over his face. His skin felt crumbly, dry as the ground around that farm. 'There were two of them. Red Hugh's weans. Seventeen and nineteen, they are.'

'And the boy shot at DC Maguire?'

'The girl. The younger one.'

'I see. And you let her escape.'

'We . . . we didn't know she was there. She got round to a car, drove off.'

Johnson looked cool and collected. No sweat on his forehead, his collar stiff as if he'd just ironed it an hour before. He was behind his desk and hadn't asked Bob to take a seat. That was deliberate, Bob was sure.

'And DC Maguire? What's his prognosis?'

'He's in surgery. The bullet went through his leg.'

The ambulance had found them in time, thank the Lord, and PJ had been escorted off. He'd been breathing and awake, though his face was white as the walls and his blood was still soaking into the parched ground.

'And you've got the boy in the cells. The girl's brother.'

'Aye. Yes.' They'd caught up with the young fella in the woods, handcuffed him. He'd been shouting terrible things, you bastards, you effing traitors, you dirty Brit-licking scum. But they had him.

'That's something, I suppose.' Bob wondered who would do the interview. So far Johnson hadn't said. 'And the body?'

Bob said, 'It's their ma, we think. Red Hugh's missus. The boy's not talking so far, though.'

Johnson turned, buttoning his smart suit. Not like Bob's, acrylic out of Burton's, creased and shiny in the heat. 'Well, we better change that. Come with me.'

Red Hugh's boy was slumped in the plastic chair. He wore sports gear like all the kids had now, the stripes going down the side of his legs.

'Is this his first arrest?' asked Johnson.

'Aye,' said Bob. 'He's been keeping his head down.'

'Doesn't look old enough to build bombs.'

'He's nineteen, sir.'

'That's good.' Johnson put his hand to the door. 'That means we can stick him in the adult jail with his crazy da.'

He marched in, barrelling the door aside. It was important, how you walked in. Show them you mean business, that you've no respect for their fake army of murderers. It was one of the first things he and Johnson had learned. One of the things Ian Robinson had taught them.

'Peadar,' said Johnson. 'That's your name, is it?'

The boy shrugged. 'Aye.'

'Peadar O'Keeffe. Red Hugh's your da.'

Another shrug.

'Son, we know you've been planting those devices on the parade routes. That's ten years you're looking at right there. But we can be reasonable people, if you tell us why we found a body in your shed.'

'Cos she's dead, I reckon.'

Smart-arse. Johnson leaned forward. He was almost smiling. Bob wondered if Johnson missed this now he was the boss, the rush of it, just you and them and the desk between you, and one of you was going to win. 'Is it your mammy, Peadar? Your mammy's dead?'

He shrugged again. 'Suppose so.'

'She'd been shot in the head, so we hear. Now who'd do a thing like that? It wouldn't be the same person who shot our colleague, would it?'

'Dunno.'

'Your sister. Isn't that right? Catriona?'

'Aye, that's her name.' He looked bored, picking flecks of paints off his hands.

'Where is she, Peadar?'

'How would I know? If you're telling me you can't even catch up to a wee girl, youse aren't much fecking use as a police force, are youse?'

'Oh, we'll catch up to her, don't you worry. What I'm wondering is what will happen when we do. She's armed, and she's a murder suspect – our officers would need to be very careful with her. They'll have their own guns. Only, ours are a lot bigger.'

Bob glanced at Johnson from the corner of his eye. Was he threatening to kill a teenage girl? There'd been a lot of talk over the years about the RUC's Shoot to Kill policy. In truth it was more that when you'd been shot at enough times, you stopped worrying about the rules and started wondering how long you had before a bullet found its mark, in your chest maybe, or the back of your head.

Peadar had gone very still. Sounding bored again, he said: 'Catriona never shot that gun until today.'

'So she didn't kill your mammy.'

'Course not. She's only a wean.'

'So who did?'

Nothing. Peadar folded his arms. He looked casual but Bob knew the pose: he'd run out of road and he knew it.

Johnson leaned in with a big shark smile on his gub: he knew it too. 'Peadar, did your da shoot your mammy? Red Hugh?'

'Don't call him that.'

'All right. But did he shoot her?'

'No. He's in jail, duh.'

'Then who did, Peadar?'

A moment's silence. Then, bored again: 'I did, you fecking eejits.'

Johnson leaned back as if he'd always known it. 'Why would you kill your mammy, son?'

'She was going to give you lot more evidence. Keep Da inside longer. She didn't want him back. He'll be out under the Agreement, see. Then he can do his job – getting rid of the imperialist Brits. And you lot, you fucking Huns. So I shut her up.'

Johnson slapped the table lightly. Job done. He turned to Bob as if to say, *that's how you do it*. 'Mind your language, son. We'll be charging you formally. You just sit tight for a minute. Sergeant Hamilton, would you step outside?'

There was a creak, the boy was leaning back in his chair. 'Youse better catch up to her soon. My sister.'

'And why's that?'

He smiled. 'You didn't find the list, then?'

For a moment, Bob thought the boy was talking about *the* list – the one he was so afraid of, the one he'd been imagining for months now.

'What list's that, son?' Johnson spoke casually, on his way out the door, but Bob had known him long enough to hear the tension underneath.

'Have a wee look at what was in the shed. We know where you live. Where all of you live. She'll be on her way to one of your houses right now.'

Johnson shut the door, and then someone was running up the corridor. The officer from earlier. Bob wished again he knew his name. 'Sir! We've tracked the girl's car.'

'She's on her way to an officer's home?' Johnson spoke casually again.

Bob was moving slowly, like a diver on the bottom of the sea. 'It's me. It's my house, isn't it?' He thought of Ian. Linda would be on her way home with him now, in the car adapted for his wheelchair. He could see it all so clearly it was as if it had already happened: the girl with the gun, Linda slowing down, thinking maybe she needed help, and she'd help anyone, Linda would . . . he was rooted to the spot again.

The officer was still speaking, his words getting louder and faster. 'Sir, it's not you. It's DC Maguire. The girl's gone to his house. They know he's Catholic. They've got his address. She has a gun.'

The relief was like the dazzle of the sun. 'But PJ's not there. He's in the hospital. We can get there in time and . . .'

Johnson spoke. 'Does he not have a daughter?'

Paula was disappointed when they reached her road. She'd have to go in now, let him leave. 'So . . . see you Saturday maybe.'

'Yeah. Might be there.'

She scuffed her Kickers along the dry pavement. There was something else to say, there had to be, but she had no idea what it was.

Aidan wasn't looking at her. He was finishing his cigarette, dropping the butt under the sole of his DM, crushing it. He said nothing.

She glanced at the house; her dad wouldn't be home for hours. She'd have to go in alone, maybe eat a Pot Noodle, watch TV. The house would be cool inside, and lonely, but never empty. Her mother was still in every room, after all.

She put her hand on the gate. 'Well, I better head in, s'pose.'

'Maguire.'

Her heart blurred in her chest. 'Yeah?'

'Come here a minute.'

She couldn't look at him. It was all too much, the sun beating down and him in his uniform, the cigarette dropped from his mouth, his hair falling over his head, his tie loose, and the smell of him, tobacco and aftershave and a tiny bit of sweat. 'What?'

'Paula.'

She still couldn't look. He put his finger under her chin, lifted it. He was taller than she was, just by a few inches.

Oh my God oh my God.

Aidan was suddenly closer than he'd ever been, and his mouth was on hers, warm and soft, tasting of bubblegum. It took her a few seconds to kiss back – she was stunned, reeling. Aidan, who she'd known forever. This was how he tasted. This was how he smelled. This was the sound of his breathing. That was his mouth, pressed on hers.

He broke away. 'I . . .'

She felt like she'd just woken up, confused, fuzzy. 'What . . .' They stared at each other for a moment, dazed.

Nearer and nearer came a sound everyone in Northern Ireland was born knowing, as well as you knew the pulse of your own blood in your ears. Sirens. Coming closer. Aidan was peering down the street, frowning, shading his eyes against the sun. 'Is that not that girl from your school?'

'Catriona?' Paula looked to the sound of running feet, and there she was, her blond hair flying, still in her school uniform. She was holding something in her hand. 'Is that . . .?'

'Shit!' Aidan was suddenly tense, grabbing her arm. 'It's a gun. She's got a fecking gun.'

Paula had never seen a gun before, not up close, just when you passed the police in the street. But Aidan had, of course. He'd seen guns when they shot his dad.

Catriona ran at them so fast it seemed she wasn't going to stop. Her breath was coming in ragged gasps. The light glinted on the gun. She stopped in front of them. Paula felt Aidan's arm tremble – he was shaking. A stab of fear went through her, but somehow her voice was calm. 'What's going on, Catriona?'

'Why didn't you help me?' The girl was almost crying. 'Why didn't you listen?'

'What do you mean?' She tried to speak quietly.

'I kept trying to ask you, talk to you . . . I thought you'd understand . . . your ma's gone too, everyone says she's dead . . . and he killed her. I was trying to tell you.'

'Who killed who?' Still Paula managed to sound OK. She reached for Aidan's arm, squeezed it. Trying to tell him it was going to be all right, though she was far from sure herself.

'He killed my ma. She's dead, in the freezer. He made the bombs . . . I don't know what to do. I kept trying to tell you, but he followed me everywhere, he even put that thing in your bag . . .'

'Who did, Catriona? Your brother?'

She was crying hard now. 'They're all gone. He killed her. Your da's a cop. Why didn't you help me? I thought you'd know what to do. I thought you'd be able to.'

This was crazy. All Catriona's bullying, she'd just been trying to *talk* to Paula? Paula hardly knew what she was doing. She took a step away from Aidan, who seemed to have gone somewhere inside himself, frozen. She put out her hand to Catriona. The gun looked old, and heavy, an evil petrol shade of black. 'Come on. Give it to me. It's going to be all right.'

'It's not. She's dead. She's not coming back.' Tears stuttered from the girl's eyes.

'I know. But . . . it will be OK all the same. Trust me, Catriona. If anyone knows, it's me.'

She reached out her hand to the gun. The noise of sirens got louder and louder, until it was right on top of them.

'That was good work,' said Johnson. 'Maguire's daughter was nearly on the doorstep, I hear. The O'Keeffe girl had a gun. Could have been nasty if we hadn't broken the brother in time.'

'Is Paula all right?' Bob was sitting in Johnson's office, overlooking the town. The riot had at last burned itself out, like a fire starved of fuel. The protestors had wandered home, the streets empty except for torched cars and litter and stones. The last rays of sun touched the roofs of the town. It looked peaceful, a huddle of buildings cradled in the green hills. It looked like nothing bad ever happened there.

'Aye, she's grand. Upset, though. We took her down to see her da. She's at her wee friend's now.'

Bob waited to hear why he'd been called in here, after such a long day, the blood and the bones and the sun burning into his head.

'You were asking about the list,' Johnson said.

Bob readied himself. This was it. He'd had a good career. There were other things you could do at forty-eight . . . prisons, security . . . when you had no choice but to face something, you faced it. 'There is one, then?'

'Aye. Off the record.' Johnson slapped something down on the table. Bob looked. For a moment he didn't understand what he was seeing. That wasn't his name. It was . . .

'But he's . . .'

'He's a liability. We couldn't get him on that thing with his wife, but you saw him today. He's a loose cannon. He'll get someone killed sooner or later. Maybe himself.'

'He's Ca—'

Johnson glanced at him. 'The new police force of Northern Ireland will not be gerrymandered, Sergeant Hamilton. We need to be beyond reproach. We need to weed out the bad apples. And he is rotten. Him and that editor pal of his, they used to leak more than the bloody *Titanic*.'

John O'Hara was eleven years dead and it didn't seem right to impugn the man. 'But the daughter,' Bob said. 'He's bringing her up all by himself. Her mother—'

'There'll be a generous award,' said Johnson. 'And I'm sure the wean would like her da around more. Since he's all she has.'

Bob could hardly get the words out. 'But he's . . . no, sir, this can't be. He's the best officer I ever worked with. And he never gives up, not on a case, not on his wife, not on . . .' He tailed off. PJ hadn't given up on Bob, not even when the investigation into Margaret Maguire's death went cold, tailed off into nothing. But Bob had given up on him.

There was a silence. Johnson just looked at him.

'Does he know?' Bob looked down at the desk. It was arranged the way it had been for years, the phone, the jotter, the pencil tin. They were putting in computers now. He'd have to learn how to use one, and have a mobile phone and all that like the young ones did. If he wasn't being put out, he'd have to learn to work in this new world.

'We thought you could tell him. You were partners, after all.'

Until the day Bob had gone round to arrest PJ in his own house. More of Johnson's dirty work. He'd never forgotten the look on PJ's face when he'd come to the door with the uniformed constable. That bad day back in 1993. And the wee lassie, staring at him with accusing eyes. Her mother's eyes.

'He's in ward eight,' said Johnson, passing Bob an envelope. 'Send him our best. He can take his notice as sick leave.'

'He's out? Just like that?'

Johnson gave him a look. It said – *I know you wanted this.* And Bob had, God help him, sometimes he had wanted PJ gone. Wanted it on the day in 1972 when they'd sent a Belfast Catholic to fill the vacant place left by Robinson getting blown to bits. Wanted it when PJ's wife had gone and he'd refused to cooperate, refused to believe there were no signs of forced disappearance. Refused to see what was there, if only you looked.

'Make your choice, Bobby boy. It's this way or the high way.'

Bob found he was nodding. He would do it. Of course he would.

'Head on home after,' said Johnson. 'Pick up some flowers for Linda, she'll like that.' Bob couldn't bear the way he said it. The network. The old boys. In it together. He stood up, taking the envelope in his hand. That was how you got through the job – you did what you were told. You never asked was it right, because that way you'd never have any peace, ever again.

Bob made his way down the corridors of the police station. He put out his hands to the walls, the carpet tiles fraying and falling off, as if they might close in on him. It was hot still, so hot, a stale, sweaty layer of it pressing all over your skin.

Outside in the car park he breathed in, but the air was no better – smoky, with the tang of burnt-out fires. The sky was burning red too, the exact shade of blood. What was it Linda used to say to Ian? *Red sky at night, shepherd's delight.* It would be hot again tomorrow.

'. . . has to be soon, he's getting spooked, I think . . .'

Bob turned instinctively at the sound of the voice. For a moment he was confused – who was she talking to? – then he realised the Corry girl had a mobile phone tucked up in her hand, hidden under her fall of hair. She started for a second, then recovered. 'Give me a minute,' she said into the phone, and then, to Bob: 'Sergeant Hamilton. I'm awful sorry to hear about DC Maguire. Is he all right?'

'Bullet in the leg. I'm away down to see him now.'

'Tell him I was asking for him, will you?'

He looked at her. Her face was flushed, as if he'd caught her out, but she had herself in hand all the same. A cool customer. 'I will. Goodnight, miss.'

'It's DC.'

He felt the anger rise. 'I have to head on.'

She stepped forward, pushing back her fair hair where it had fallen loose around her face. 'Sergeant – can I ask you something? How long have you worked with DI Johnson?'

'Nigh on thirty years or so. We started out together.'

'You trust him?'

He looked at her. Apart from the hair, she was composed, her black suit neat and pressed. No sign she'd been working all day in the oven of the police station. Cold and sharp as a nail. 'With my life,' he said.

'Has he ever asked you to do anything you felt wasn't right?'

Yes. This. Fire a good man when he's down. 'Miss Corry. It's not appropriate for us to be having this discussion about a senior officer.'

She just looked at him. 'It's Detective Constable Corry. And I'm afraid that if you won't have it now, you'll be having it later, with some more . . . significant people than me. Does that make sense to you?'

'That's not for me to say.'

'Bob. Did you not wonder how those kids had a list of police home addresses? It's not such an easy thing to get hold of, is it?'

'I don't know what you're saying.'

'I think you do. Am I making myself clear here, Bob? I'm trying to help you.'

He looked away. 'Excuse me. I have to go.'

PJ was on the secure ward, the one with soldiers outside. If anyone got wind there was a police officer in hospital, it wouldn't be beneath the IRA to smuggle in guns, finish the job. Even in this so-called ceasefire. Bob showed his pass to the very young, very nervous squaddie on the door, whose gun was nearly bigger than himself. 'Thanks, Sergeant, that's fine.' Liverpool accent. Shaving cuts on his neck. All this might be over soon. Hospitals without guards. Getting into your car without checking beneath it. A new world. And Bob would have to be part of it, since he wasn't on the list. It was hard to take in, life on this side of the mirror. Bob pushed open the swing doors.

PJ was all alone in the eight-person ward. He was staring at the wall, his leg covered in plaster, hoicked up in a metal cage. There was no sign of the daughter, for which Bob was deeply grateful. He couldn't have dealt with her today, looking at him with her mother's eyes in her face. PJ barely acknowledged Bob sitting down.

'Well, PJ. Anything you need?'

'Aye, a femur that's not banjaxed.'

'I'm sorry for what happened.'

'What did you do with them? Red Hugh's weans?'

'The girl's under age, so it'll be young offenders for her. At least they caught up to her in time . . . Paula OK?'

PJ looked away. 'She'll be grand. She's been through worse.'

True. Bob paused for a moment. 'The brother's remanded in custody. He could be seeing his da in the Maze before too long.'

'What about the – remains?'

Bob tried to speak gently. 'It's their mother, we think. She'd been shot in the head. Been there a few weeks.'

'And he killed her? Her own son?'

'Looks that way. God knows how they've kept going, the girl's only the same age as your Paula. She's at her school.'

PJ frowned at the mention of his girl. 'They always said we should move house. Too dangerous, staying in the one place. I thought it'd be OK. But Paula . . .' He tailed off.

Bob heard the distant sounds of the hospital, beeps and running feet, and if you listened hard enough, crying. Hearts breaking. After the baked heat of outside, there was a chill in here that settled on your skin like mist. Bob wondered how it would be to lie in bed here with that trussed-up wean outside and wait for someone to come and shoot you. He knew exactly why PJ had never moved house, even though RUC officers were supposed to shift about every few years, for security. He was waiting in case she came back. Margaret. Bob could have told him what he knew, but he never would. He'd promised.

'So what's the craic?' PJ scratched at his thigh. 'You're here with some work for me, I hope. I'm going spare.'

'PJ,' said Bob, sitting up straight in his plastic chair. The envelope was sweaty in his hand. 'I'm very sorry. Believe me.'

Paula lay awake on the camp bed in Saoirse's room. On either side of her, Saoirse and her younger sister Niamh slept in single beds. Niamh's side of the room was all boy bands, puppies, posters of the cast of *Friends*. Saoirse's had pictures of Noah Wyle, and diagrams of the human body she'd drawn on in highlighter pen to help with her exam revision. The house was full of people, all together, all safe, all asleep. Except for Paula.

She stared up at the ceiling, which the girls had decorated in softly glowing stars. It was hard to sleep on the camp bed, but that wasn't what kept her awake. She was thinking of her dad, shot in the leg. How she'd nearly lost him too, really lost everything. She was thinking of Catriona, and what the other girl had been living with all this time – her mother dead in the shed, they said, killed by her brother – and now she was going to prison, they said. She was thinking of her own mother and that was dangerous; those were the kinds of thoughts that once you started you couldn't stop and they'd pull you under sure as a strong current in the sea. She was thinking of Saoirse, sound asleep, and how she'd spent the evening trying to cheer Paula up, putting on stupid videos of *The Little Mermaid* and *Annie* and singing along like they were eight; of Pat, who'd come straight to the hospital when she heard, all tears and hugs; and Aidan . . . Aidan. How he'd pulled her into him when the van came round the corner and the policemen jumped out in their body armour and helmets, shouting at Catriona to get away, get back. The feel of his arms round her back, shaking. She could still feel his kiss on her mouth, as if he'd stamped it there. And the gun in Catriona's hand. Nearly every RUC family had been attacked at one time or another, but still. This was her house. This was her family.

In the dark, her fists were clenched. She was thinking this: *as soon as I can, I'm going to leave. I'm going to leave and I am never going to come back.*

But now there was Aidan. She wasn't going to think about that. She had to try to keep at least one thought straight in her head. And maybe, after everything they'd been through, he might feel the same.

Bob was sitting in the car outside his house. It was dark, the orange of street lights shining over the little cul-de-sac. Linda asleep in the room upstairs, Ian downstairs in his adapted bed, with the low sides to make it easier to move him. He'd been sent home with an oxygen tank. He was hooked up to it, to life, his chest moving up and down in the dark. Bob's hands tightened on the steering wheel. He couldn't go inside, to the smell of sickness and the sound of Ian's wet breath. He just couldn't.

At that time of night, he was back at the station in ten minutes. He didn't know what he was going to do. Sit at his desk, look through the notes from to-day, try to make sense of what had happened. Of the farm, and those kids, and Johnson, and PJ . . . He nodded to the desk sergeant, who was reading a thriller under the desk, and went up to the incident room, expecting it to be empty.

'Sergeant Hamilton!' Helen Corry was there, along with two men he didn't recognise, both in suits. They were sitting around her desk, talking in low voices, and jumped as if he'd disturbed them in something illegal.

'What are you doing here, miss?'

'I'm working late. These are some . . . colleagues from Belfast.'

'Oh.' Bob stood there. For some reason he was very aware of the gun in his holster.

Then Corry was up and moving across the room to him. She was still in the suit from earlier, her hair hanging loose. She looked no older than the girl from the farm today. 'Bob, you shouldn't be here.' Her voice was low and urgent. 'Go now and we'll say no more. I know you've nothing to do with it.'

'With what?' Bob didn't bother to lower his voice. The two men were up now, moving in a way that showed they had combat training, their hands shifting to their holsters as well.

'Look, there's not much time, but if you go . . .'

'I'm going nowhere.'

There was a noise. Footsteps in the corridor. The whistle of a tune: 'The Sash My Father Wore'.

For a moment Helen Corry looked regretful. 'I did try,' she said. 'Remember I tried to help you.'

Then the door was opening and Johnson was coming in, dressed in slacks and a shirt like he'd just come from home, papers under his arm. He stopped when he saw them all, Bob and Helen Corry and the strangers. 'What's going on?'

The Corry girl faced him. Her voice was clear, her chin raised. 'DI Johnson.

I'm afraid these men are here from Professional Standards. We need to have a chat with you.'

'Don't be silly, girl. How dare you call me in for this? I'm going home.'

'No, you aren't.' Steel in her voice, for all her youth. 'We know all about it, Alec. We know it was you.'

'I've no idea what you're talking about.'

'Peadar O'Keeffe, he didn't get the addresses out of thin air, or know the parades that were going ahead before they were even announced . . . did he? Somebody gave him the information. We know it was you.'

'This is ridiculous.' Johnson made as if to brush past her, then the men were moving, and then something had changed. Bob didn't know what for a moment. He watched Johnson's papers fall slowly to the grey office carpet, like the flap of a bird's wings. Then he saw what Johnson was holding in his hand.

Afterwards, when they were done with all the interviews and the paperwork and talking to more men in suits in small, hot rooms, Bob would never speak about what happened that night. But he knew in himself: he hadn't seen the Corry girl blink once. Not even with the gun pointing between her eyes. The other men had theirs drawn too, but it was too late, they were on the wrong side of her, Johnson was too close.

'Let's not do this, Alec,' she said quietly. 'It's over.'

'And what would you know about it?' He was shaking. His voice, his hand. The gun. 'Slip of a girl like you. Coming in here saying we're doing it all wrong. Lassie, we've been doing this job since you were in nappies. Men have died, good men. Blown to bits by your kind. And now you want to destroy us, drag our good name through the mud . . . People like you, you should be down on your knees thanking the RUC for what we did. We kept you safe in your bed all these years.'

'But why the bombs, Alec? What good does that do?' Still she didn't falter. Even though the gun was so close it almost brushed the skin of her face.

'Making us cancel our parades. Ask for permission to walk when we've been doing it three hundred years. Letting those – those murderers out of jail when we put them there. It isn't right.'

'So you thought you'd stir things up a bit.'

'They're scum, these people. We're letting them walk free – bombers, killers. They'd kill you as soon as look at you, and we're going to let them run the country? It's treachery, is what it is.'

'Was that the idea . . . show everyone the Catholics won't stop bombing, so we shouldn't share power with them? Go back to the bad old days?'

'Well, they won't! We're going into government with murderers! You'll see what'll happen. There's a wave of blood about to break over us, lassie, and we're walking right into it.'

'But this was you, Alec. You may have used those young kids, but it was all you. People could have been hurt. Officers, and their families. Innocent people. Weans, even. You're as bad as the IRA.'

There was movement; she'd got to him. Johnson made an angry noise in his throat, stepped closer to her. For a moment, the girl closed her eyes. Bob didn't know what he was doing until he'd done it. He was standing behind Johnson, so close he could see the strands of white in his old friend's hair, the lines on his face. They'd both changed. Long, long years of bloodshed behind them. 'It's over, Alec,' he said, his voice rusty. 'For God's sake let her go. It's over.'

Johnson turned slowly, and as he saw the gun Bob was pointing at him, a strange look came over his face. Almost like peace. 'You made your choice then, Bobby boy.'

'There is no choice.' Bob cleared his throat. 'There's only backwards, or this. I know that now.'

As the two men grabbed Johnson's arms and cuffed him, Helen Corry met Bob's eyes, and he thought he saw something new there. It might have been respect.

The music was loud. Spice Girls, 'Stop'. Saoirse was over with some girls from school, bopping in a big protective ring. Paula saw him by the bar; went to buy a peach schnapps and lime, her favourite drink.

'Hiya.' He had a fag hanging out of his mouth; she breathed in the smell. She had on her Boots 17 silver Disco Queen nail varnish and a short skirt and a shiny top. She'd so much Impulse body spray on it could have knocked out a horse at twenty paces – or so Saoirse had informed her as they were getting ready.

'Hi.' She leaned her elbows on the bar, wrinkling her nose at the spilled-beer smell.

'Your da OK?'

She shrugged. 'He says he is. His leg's not good.'

'Ma wants you to come and stay. She's worried, with that . . . with Catriona and all.'

She looked away, embarrassed. Trying not to remember it, the darts of fear in her stomach, the heat rising up from the pavement and the sheen of the gun . . . but wanting to remember it too, the feel of his arms and his mouth and . . . 'I'm OK. I'm going to Saoirse's for a few days, like. And you . . . you . . .' She couldn't say it. *You saved me*. If he hadn't kissed her when he had, held her back for those few seconds, who knew what would have happened.

Aidan couldn't meet her eyes either. She wondered if he was thinking it too. 'Fair enough.'

The music changed, just like that. Robbie Williams, 'Angels'. And it was dark and the lights swirled and it smelled of smoke and perfume and aftershave, and all across the room couples were moving in to each other.

She shut her eyes for a second. 'I love this song.'

'Ah no, you don't.'

'What? It's nice!'

'It's shite is what it is.' He paused, stubbing out his cigarette under his foot. 'Wanna dance?'

She pretended for a minute she was thinking about it, like she might say no. But she couldn't help smiling. 'OK.'

From MURDER AT THE OLD VICARAGE: A CHRISTMAS MYSTERY

Jill McGown

Jill McGown (1947–2007) wrote thirteen traditional whodunits featuring Chief Inspector Danny Lloyd and Sergeant Judy Hill, and five standalone mystery novels. *A Shred of Evidence* was filmed for television in 2001. As a child, McGown was taught Latin by the crime writer Colin Dexter.

Lloyd finished the last chapter of his library book, and closed it with relief, wishing that it was in his power to abandon books half-way through. But no matter how obvious the plot, how stilted the dialogue, he was obliged by some natural law to finish them. The worse they were, the more likely he was to devour them, reading into the small hours to get them out of the way. Good books relaxed him, and he would fall asleep with them in his hand, but no such luck with the lousy ones.

He balanced the book on top of the others on his bedside table, and ran his hand over his hair to smooth it down. It was habit – he couldn't get used to his hair being so short now. He had decided that people who were rapidly losing their hair should not draw attention to the fact by keeping the remaining hair long. He still thought it looked odd; Judy said she liked it. He had wondered about growing a moustache, to make up for the shortfall on his head – he craned his neck to see himself in the dressing-table mirror, and pulled a face. His unshaven face held the ghost of what a moustache might look like, and he didn't think it would do. Tall, military types could carry off moustaches, but he had come in at the low end of the regulation height. Too small and dark, he decided. He'd look like a bookie's runner.

He lay back, wide awake, aware that the pile of work which awaited him was being added to as he lay doing nothing. Added to by pre-Christmas burglars who helped themselves to the presents under someone else's tree – added to by the ones who stole the trees, come to that; the chain-saws got stolen around August, the trees in December. Added to by the drunks, added to by the jolly Christmas spirit that brought out the pickpockets and the handbag snatchers, the credit-card frauds and the conmen in the market square.

One small, striped package and the odd Christmas card were the only hint of Christmas in Acting Chief Inspector Lloyd's flat. Not that he had any objection to glitter and tinsel – in fact, if he were truthful with himself, which he quite often was, he was a bit of a sucker for jingle bells. But there was another natural law which decreed that no man be alone at Christmas, and he would once again be made welcome by Jack Woodford and his nice, comfortable wife in their nice, comfortable house. Lloyd didn't really know if they actively desired his presence at their festivities, but they knew that they had to ask him, and he knew that he had to accept. And he would give their grandchildren presents that their parents would insist were too expensive, as he had done for the past three Christmases, and the collective Woodfords would give him a bottle of malt whisky.

He liked buying presents for the children; his own were grown up now, and just got presents like everyone else's. He had missed his annual excursion into the magic world of children's toys. His Christmas visit to his own offspring consisted of an hour or two on Boxing Day, with Barbara making polite conversation as though they hadn't been married for over eighteen years before it all came to pieces in their hands. So he was glad of the Woodfords' goodwill, and he enjoyed the cheerful, noisy family Christmas. Especially this year, now that his father was beginning to get used to the idea of being a widower, and had decided to go back to Wales to live, which he'd wanted to do ever since he'd left. What with that, and Judy about to have her in-laws staying with her, Lloyd would have been very much alone.

Judy was the detective sergeant with whom he'd worked, off and on, for seven of the fifteen years since he'd met her. He had been married then, and the twenty-year-old Judy had rejected his advances, her eyes sad. Eventually, she herself had married, and moved away. Because Barbara had wanted it, and because it might have saved his marriage, Lloyd had requested a return to Stansfield, but the divorce had happened anyway. Then, eighteen months ago, Judy had arrived back in his life, a brand new detective sergeant. Since then they had, with a sense of inevitability, become lovers. Occasional lovers, he thought, with an audible sigh. Very occasional.

When Michael was at home, he and Judy weren't lovers. And Michael's promotion had ensured that he was home for considerably longer periods than before. Michael, a computer salesman turned sales director; Michael, to whom Judy professed an unexplained wish to remain married.

The covert nature of their relationship was beginning to irk Lloyd, though Judy seemed happy enough with things as they were. He wished she was with him now, in his three o'clock in the morning wakefulness, though even that pleasure would have been qualified by her ability, figuratively at least, to keep him at arm's length. He looked at the little gift-wrapped parcel on the dressing table. It ought to be tied with ribbon, he decided. And under a tree. He'd get one tomorrow. And some lights. Tomorrow was Christmas Eve; today, he corrected himself. Judy was on leave to play hostess to Michael's parents. He probably wouldn't even see her until after the holiday, but her present would be under a bloody tree if he had to keep it there until March.

He switched off the light, and closed his eyes. He wondered if it was still snowing, as it had been when he'd retired with his dreadful book. A white Christmas – it looked pretty, but the roads hadn't been gritted, and the traffic lads would be busy. His thoughts dwelt on work until at last his mind began to shunt itself into a siding for what was left of the night. Filtered through the fog of sleep, the sighing of the wind reached his ears, and his last conscious thought was for the traffic division, if the snow drifted.

George Wheeler rubbed his eyes as the early morning sun glinted on the snow. Not so early morning, he realised. It was ten o'clock, and he still hadn't written a word.

'I'm sure *you* understand, Vicar, being a Christian.'

Perhaps it was when those words were addressed to him by someone whose motives he had no desire to understand, and with whose values he had no desire to be aligned, that George Wheeler had stopped believing. Not in God, for he knew that he had never honestly believed in God as a being, an entity. As a force for good, perhaps – something inherent in man – but not as some sort of super-caretaker.

Stopped believing in himself? No, that wasn't right either. George believed in himself, for there he was, flesh, blood and bodily functions. And bodily desires – was it perversion to find himself appreciatively eyeing the young mothers at the church play group, or mere perversity? Was it middle-aged conceit that made him imagine that young Mrs Langton was seeing past his clerical collar to the man, or a sign that soon he would be roaming the streets of Soho, a *News of the World* headline *manqué*?

He put down his pen, and sat back in his chair, the better to contemplate the prospect. He had played a bit of soccer in his youth, and he still did some refereeing when he got the time. He'd kept in shape, more or less. Good enough shape for the lovely Mrs Langton to fancy him? He smiled to himself. Chance would be a fine thing. Though he still had all his hair – its sand colour was diluted here and there by silver, but that was distinguished, according to his wife. George believed in himself enough to be vain about his appearance, so that wasn't it.

No, he had stopped believing that he believed. It wasn't something that it had ever crossed his mind to wonder before. His family went into the Church. His grandfather had made it to Bishop, and there had even been rumours that he was on course to make it all the way to Canterbury, but George rather thought that his grandfather had started those himself. At any rate, he didn't. It was taken for granted – by George as much as anyone else – that he would go into the Church. It was a career decision, if decision it could be called, not a spiritual one. There was the Church, the armed services, the Civil Service. George had chosen the Church.

He addressed himself once more to the pale lines of the A4 pad in front of him, but inspiration, divine or otherwise, eluded him. George had been expected to do well, to rise through the ranks as had his grandfather before him, and as his nephew was doing even now. But George wasn't a company man. He was well enough connected to have secured a living in one of the prettiest villages in England, complete with a vicarage about which anyone might be moved to write poetry. Verdant lawns, bushes, shrubs, climbers; light-filled rooms with elegant lines, and old, good furniture. Wonderful views from its hilltop site, across three counties which today all lay under a shifting blanket of snow. And just twenty-five minutes from Stansfield, with its new-town bustle, its supermarkets and cinema, trains, and buses. The best of both worlds, and for twenty-nine years George had clung tenaciously to his well-behaved flock and his uncomplicated life. Lack of ambition, said his superiors. Pure selfishness, George knew now.

It would take rather longer than usual to get into Stansfield today, George thought, glancing out of the window as the wind whipped up the fallen snow. It was drifting badly on the road, and the cars were already having trouble on the hill.

It was no crisis of faith, for there never had been faith, but it was a crisis of the heart, and the words for the midnight service simply wouldn't come. He put down his pen, and stood up, holding out his hands to the one-bar electric fire. Central heating would make the vicarage truly a poem. As it was, there was still a sliver of ice on the inside of the study window. The parish couldn't afford central heating, and neither could he. Until now, he had accepted that as his lot, just as he had accepted everything else.

He had accepted God, to the extent of praying to him in church, and sometimes out of it. Praying for the rescue of people in peril: physical, in intensive care, or spiritual, in the back of a Vauxhall Chevette. Prayer perhaps helped those who prayed, but that was all. And then there was worship. George had never worshipped God. He had taken part in acts of worship – if saying a few words about the sanctity of life and tossing off a couple of hymns to the less than talented Jeremy Bulstrode's organ accompaniment counted as worship. But it didn't. Not in George's book.

Worship was naked, open adulation, to the point of total selflessness. George had never lost his sense of self, not even on a morning like this, when the elements combined to put man firmly in his place. Not even when he had fallen hopelessly in love, at thirteen, with his cousin from Canada, five years his senior and only in the country for a fortnight. Not in the throes of more mature passion, or grief, or anger. And not, certainly not, in the pulpit of St Augustus.

And yet he knew how it felt, this loss of self, this giving over. Once, long ago, he had felt it. He walked to the window, and ran his finger down the sliver of ice, which melted to his touch. It wasn't a woman, he thought, with a smile at himself. A few courteous and cautious walkings-out before Marian, and marriage. A happy, fulfilled marriage, but not worship. Joanna? No, not even her. He loved his daughter with all his heart, but it was still *his* heart. It was long ago, before any of that, before adulthood.

The dog. Of course, of course. His grandfather's dog, whom he had had the privilege to know all his life until the old soldier died, when George was eleven. Perhaps only a child could truly worship, for he would have died instead, if he could have. So, he thought, as the sun shone blindingly on the white carpet below him, he had broken the first commandment.

Come to that, he had spent all summer spraying greenfly in a deliberate act of destruction. Did greenfly count? Birds did.

His father had shot birds; George had joined him once or twice on shoots, but he was a miserably bad shot, and had barely inconvenienced the game.

He had loved his father and mother, but that was no big deal. It wasn't hard to love people who loved you, and it certainly wasn't an honour to be thus loved. If honouring them meant putting flowers on their grave on the infrequent trips to his remaining relatives, then it was Marian who did the honouring. If it meant being straight with them, then he had dishonoured them by joining the Church.

And *by* joining the Church, he broke one commandment regularly, every Sunday. The Bible might not count taking Sunday services as work, but he certainly did. Standing in the pulpit, in the ever-present draught that gave him a stiff neck, seeing the same old faces staring back at him, not expecting anything from him. They were there, like him, from habit and custom; presumably they did find something that they needed in the chill air and the stained-glass light, but he never had. Whatever kind of fulfilment he sought, it was not to be found in St Augustus on a Sunday morning.

Could Mrs Langton provide it, he wondered? VICAR IN PLAY GROUP LOVE TANGLE. Except that she probably hadn't given him the eye; it had probably never occurred to her that his mind ever dwelt on such things. But it had. Not *News of the World* stuff, then. A question on a game show, perhaps.

'*We asked one hundred vicars: Do you ever have sexual fantasies about the mothers in your church play group? How many vicars said yes, they did have sexual fantasies about . . .*'

'I've brought you some coffee. You must be frozen.'

He jumped at the sound of Marian's voice, and turned from the window.

'Sorry,' she said. 'Were you working or day-dreaming?'

He smiled. 'Oh, day-dreaming,' he said, walking back to the electric warmth.

'I've got the fire going in Joanna's room,' Marian said, handing him the mug. 'It took about six fire-lighters, but it's caught now. And George,' she said, in her scolding voice, 'must you leave your overalls in a heap on the hall floor?'

'Sorry. I was looking at the car.'

'What's wrong with it?' Marian asked.

'Nothing. I was just—' But she had never understood his love for things mechanical, so he didn't try to explain. He put both hands round the mug of coffee, and stared at the empty pad on the desk.

'Are you having trouble?' she asked.

'You could say that.'

Marian wasn't what he thought of as a vicar's wife. Even he saw the situation comedy notion of Vicar's Wife, when he thought of the actual words. Vicars' wives were either dowdy, shy and full of good works, or blue-rinsed, tweedy and full of good sense. Marian had short, curly, dark blonde hair, and mischievous eyes. Her fiftieth birthday had just passed, and those eyes had tiny wrinkles that he supposed had once not been there, but which were a part of her that he felt he had always known. She had the suggestion of freckles on her nose, and a wide, generous smile. She wasn't tall, and seemed even less so once Joanna had grown up to become three full inches taller than her. He smiled. His adulterous thoughts had made him feel quite frisky, and vicars weren't supposed to feel frisky at ten-thirty on a Wednesday morning, especially not on Christmas Eve.

'Which one?' Marian asked.

'Sorry?'

'Tonight's or this afternoon's?'

He stared blankly at her. 'Sorry?' he said again.

'Which sermon are you having trouble with?'

'Oh. Tonight's. This afternoon's for the children really. It's easy to talk to children.'

'Well, I hate to break it to you, but Jeremy Bulstrode's on his way over, in a state about something. He can't play this afternoon.'

'He can't play, period.'

'Something to do with his wife's brother,' she went on. 'He's on his way over for high-level discussions. What will you do?'

'See him,' George said, with a sigh. Ah well, it was highly unlikely that the vicar's wife would want to know at ten-thirty on Christmas Eve morning anyway. And it just wouldn't do for Jeremy Bulstrode to come in and find the vicar and his wife *in flagrante delicto* on the study floor. Would that interest the *News of the World*, he wondered? Or would it have to be the vicar's wife who found him and Jeremy Bulstrode?

'I mean about this afternoon. Shall I fix up the record player?'

'Oh – no, that might not be necessary. Mrs . . .' He hesitated over the surname, not in deliberate deception, but none the less deceptively. 'Mrs Langton plays,' he said. 'I believe.'

'Oh, good,' said Marian.

Mrs Langton was a newcomer to Byford; eight weeks ago she had moved into the cottage at Byford Castle, with her two-year-old daughter.

'I'll pop round and ask her,' George said.

'But Jeremy's coming.'

'After Jeremy,' he said.

'I can go, if you're busy.'

'No,' he said. 'I'll go. It'll be a good excuse to get rid of Jeremy.' He pushed away his pad. 'Maybe visiting someone will give me an idea for this,' he said.

'What about tomorrow? Have you still got to write tomorrow's as well?'

'No. I say the same things every Christmas Day.'

'Do you?' She frowned. 'I hadn't noticed.'

'More or less,' he said. 'It's the midnight service I like to get my teeth into. But the one I'd written won't do.'

'Why not?'

He looked at her. He couldn't tell her she was married to a fraud. He couldn't tell his congregation that they had been listening to a fraud all these years. He didn't know what to say to her, or them. Perhaps seeing Eleanor Langton would help. He found it easy to talk to her, to be himself with her, and not the character actor that he had become, even with Marian.

Eleanor had told him a little of herself – she had been a research assistant, and was now employed by Byford Castle to work during the winter on preparing their archives for publication, and to oversee the guided tours in the summer. She was a widow, and she was lonely. She had told him that because he was a vicar, he assured himself; that's what vicars were for. But he felt as though it was vaguely guilty knowledge, because he *hadn't* imagined her interest in him, and she had seen and recognised his in her. Unspoken, unacknowledged, but it was there, and it had been for weeks.

'George? Are you feeling all right?'

He smiled, almost laughed, at himself. 'Just considering my suitability for getting into the *News of the World*,' he said.

'Do you *want* to get into the *News of the World*?'

'Other vicars do,' he replied.

She smiled. 'You haven't developed a passion for choir boys, have you?'

'Good Lord, no. Nasty little brutes. Can't think what all those unfrocked vicars see in them.' He moved reluctantly from the arc of warmth, back to his desk. 'And that's another commandment gone,' he said, sitting down.

Marian bent down and sniffed. 'You've not been drinking,' she said.

'No. But I took the Lord's name in vain. I do it quite a lot.'

'Yes,' said Marian.

'I suppose,' he mused, 'if I worked my way through all ten commandments – that might qualify me for inclusion.'

'Well,' Marian said, picking up his empty mug. 'I don't care how much you covet it, you're not bringing that ox in here.'

THE PEARL

L.T. Meade

L.T. Meade (1844–1914) is best known for writing hundreds of stories and books for girls, of which the most famous is *A World of Girls* (1886). Meade also published hundreds of mysteries and other titles, sometimes teaming up with Dorothy L. Sayers' future collaborator, Dr Robert Eustace.

On the 5th of October, in the year 1896, I received, on returning from my morning round of visits, the following letter:—

24A, Bayswater Gardens, W.
Dear Dr. Lonsdale,
Will you give us the pleasure of your company to dinner to-morrow at eight o'clock? Mr. Tempest, who has quite recovered from his late illness, is staying with us, and I know would much like to see you.
Yours very truly,
Ella Forrester

Ella was the only daughter of a patient of mine, Ralph Forrester, a precious stone merchant of some fame, but whose speciality was in the pearl trade. I had personally no liking for the man. Though I had no direct evidence against him, certain rumours from time to time had reached my ears that in his dealings with others he was utterly unscrupulous, but perhaps the real reason of my dislike lay in the fact that he treated his motherless daughter in a rough and heartless manner.

Ella was a pretty and charming girl of about nineteen years of age. I had attended her during her childish illnesses, and she and I were always great friends. For some reason also Forrester seemed to take a certain pleasure in my society. He often confided some of his troubles to me, and let me into one or two secrets of his trade. I was a constant guest at their house, and Ella's letter by no means took me by surprise. For her sake, whenever possible, I accepted Forrester's invitations, as I felt that in some sort of way I protected her from his rough and cruel treatment. I was glad to see also that I was to meet my friend Tempest. I had long ago learned the great secret of his life. He loved Ella Forrester, and I felt sure the attachment was reciprocal. Tempest was a nice fellow of about thirty years of age, a Colonial by birth. He had spent much of his early years in pearl-fishing on the coral reefs off the Queensland coast. In this rôle Forrester had employed him several times with great success.

Eighteen months before this story opens he had gone out on a pearling expedition on Forresters's behalf. Early in the year I was told that Cyril Tempest had met with an accident. Particulars of this accident had not reached me. Whatever it was no doubt I should hear all about it the following evening, and I at once accepted Ella's invitation, and presented myself in due course at Bayswater Gardens.

As I entered the room Forrester and Ella both came forward. The latter greeted me warmly. As I shook hands with her I could not help noticing that her face did not wear its accustomed look of vivacity. I also observed that she glanced nervously towards the door, and while I was still speaking to her I saw a curious expression of absolute repulsion cross her face.

Another visitor was announced, and the next moment I found myself introduced to a very vulgar-looking man of the name of Sutherland.

"Mr. Sutherland is one of my greatest friends, Lonsdale," said Forrester, who now came up and spoke in an effusive and almost disagreeable manner. "He accompanied Ella and myself on a charming cruise to Norway during the past summer. I have no doubt you will meet him again here."

Sutherland laughed loudly and glanced at Ella, and then turned away, accompanied by his host.

I looked again at the girl, who still remained near my side. Her face was now very white.

"You know that Mr. Tempest is staying with us," she said, in a low voice.

"Yes," I answered, "and I am glad he is home again; he will have many adventures to tell us."

Her face clouded.

"He has indeed some thrilling experiences," she said. "He told us one this morning. Hark, I think that must be his ring."

Her eyes brightened and the colour returned to her face. The door was thrown open once more, and Mr. Tempest was announced.

I could not help being struck by the change in his appearance since I had last seen him.

Tempest smiled when he saw me, and a look of more than pleasure flitted across his face as he glanced at Ella.

"I am delighted to see you back again safe and sound," I said to him. "You must come and see me soon and tell me your adventures."

"I want to, Lonsdale, I want to see you badly," he said in a low voice.

"Come round to-night, then," I replied with a sudden impulse, as I noticed an anxious ring in his voice.

Dinner was announced, and a few moments later I found myself seated near Miss Forrester, with an elderly lady on my left hand and Mr. Sutherland exactly opposite. The conversation soon became animated, but I noticed that Ella Forrester took little or no part in it. Indeed, Sutherland completely claimed her attention. He was evidently trying to make himself pleasant to her, and she was forced to answer his somewhat pointed questions, and to listen to the anecdotes with which he tried to beguile the time.

Tempest, who was at the other end of the table, was, to my surprise, almost silent, although, as a rule, he was gay and bright and a good conversationalist.

I began to put two and two together, and came to the conclusion that Tempest had a rival in Sutherland, although there was not the least doubt that Ella Forrester greatly disliked the man.

After the ladies left the room and we had drawn our chairs closer to the fire, I perceived further, to my surprise, that the relations between Tempest and Forrester were by no means cordial. The elder man scarcely spoke to his guest, and when he did it was with a look and a few words of such pointed rudeness that I hated him more than I had ever done before, and vowed that, notwithstanding Ella's existence, this was the very last time I would enter his house.

The evening that followed was a dreary one, although Ella did her utmost to make it lively. Soon after eleven o'clock I rose to go, and Tempest followed my example.

"Well, old chap," I said, as we entered my brougham, "what is the matter with you? I never saw you so gloomy in my life. And as for Miss Forrester, she seems to have lost her old gaiety. Is there anything wrong?"

"There is," he replied gravely, "something very wrong, I am sorry to say, and I want to tell you about it. It is a long story, so I won't begin till we get to your house."

"I was afraid it was so," I answered, "I only trust it is nothing very bad."

My companion remained silent till we reached home. When we had settled ourselves in my smoking room he began—

"I don't believe anyone in this world has ever been in such a position as I am in now, but I will tell you the whole thing from beginning to end. You heard from Forrester that I had had an accident?"

"Ella told me about it," I answered, "but you seem to have got over it, whatever it may have been."

"I believe I have got over it as far as my health is concerned," he replied, "but other consequences have arisen on account of it which are far more difficult to cope with. It was a terrible experience, and, as my present story is a sequel to it, I will start right away. It was on the 18th of May this year that I was pearling on the coral reef off the Queensland coast, 150° by 20° rough bearings. It was late in the afternoon, and my Kanakas and I had been working in about five fathoms with fair success. We were just going to put back to the schooner when I thought I would have one more dive. I had just got my foot on the sinker stone with the rope in my hand when one of the Kanakas touched my arm and pointed to a large dark fin that had shouldered up on the crest of a wave and then disappeared. Familiarity with sharks had, however, bred contempt. I determined to take my dive and trust to my proverbial good luck to escape the cruel teeth of the brute. I took some deep breaths, and the next instant was plunging down and down through the green waters to the coral fairyland below. I had just collected a fair quantity of shells into my net when suddenly a huge rough black body struck me with terrific force, sending me reeling back with a blow as if a bayonet had been thrust through my back. I just had sense to spring from the bottom, and came in safety to the surface with the net still in my hand I remembered being hauled into the boat, and then I fainted. When I came to I was back in the schooner. My clothes were soaked with blood, which had come from a terrible wound in my chest, and I felt sick and faint. One of my men was beside me, a half-caste black, a faithful fellow and my best man.

"'Ha, Mr. Tempest, you seem better, eh,' he cried. 'Big fellow, shark I take it, hit you. Lucky dive, though, my word! Look here!'

"He opened his great hand as he spoke, and I gave a gasp when I saw what it contained. In the palm of his hand lay an enormous pink pearl of such splendid size and colour that I had never seen the like before in my life.

"'You mean that I brought that up with me?' I cried, as I took it into my hand. The man nodded.

"Holding it still in my hand, I fell back on my pillow, and an ecstatic wave of delight, in spite of the pain I was suffering, passed through me, for I knew that if I survived my fortune was made. At the lowest computation that pearl was worth thirty thousand pounds. Of course, it really belonged to Forrester, for whom I was working, but as my commission was always twenty per cent., I should have my winnings, and considerable they would be. How badly I was injured I could not tell, but I suddenly felt a wild desire to live, to bring the pearl home with me and marry Ella Forrester, whom, as you know, I have long loved devotedly. The first thing to get was surgical aid. This I knew was no easy matter. I sent for the skipper, an old German named Schiller, and told him to put in at once at Leuville Cove, when I would send for the doctor at the township some eight miles off.

"This was done, and I was carried ashore with the great pink pearl safe in my pocket, for I would trust it to no one. I felt more than anxious about it in my prostrate condition, for Leuville abounded with the lowest form of scoundrel, and the news of my great prize would quickly get abroad. I sent a messenger to the township to cable home the news of the great find to Forrester, and also to bring out the doctor. He came in a few hours.

"He was a young fellow, fresh from England and the London hospitals. I took a fancy to him at once, and, weak as I was, told him my story. I even shewed him the pink pearl.

"'You are in danger with that about you,' he said, 'where can you hide it?'

"'I will take care of the pearl for myself,' I replied; 'I shall not let it out of my grip you may be certain of that, but you must make me live.'

"'I will do my utmost for you,' he replied, and then he examined my chest with great skill and tenderness. He told me that the blow from the shark had considerably injured the breast bone, a portion of which was broken away and must be instantly removed. He had brought chloroform with him, said he would put me under its influence, and perform the operation at once. I was in fearful agony, and, you may be sure, did not wish for a moment's delay. Robertson, the young doctor, immediately set to work. He put me under the influence of the anaesthetic, and I floated off into a delicious dream, in which I had a confused sense that I was leading Ella to the altar and that she was decked with pink pearls.

"Now comes the horrible part of my story. As I was coming to (you know how dazed one is at such times) I became conscious of a confused noise and loud cries. I remember the doctor bending over me, and I noticed a panic-stricken look on his pale face. He was saying something in a low and emphatic voice which I have never since been able to recall. I feel certain that if I could only recall those words they would solve all this terrible mystery and worry. The next instant the noise increased. There was the sound of a struggle, followed by a hoarse cry and a pistol shot outside the tent. I fought against my drowsy sensations, and, startled and terrified, raised myself. The doctor was nowhere to be seen. I struggled up and crawled out. You can imagine what my feelings were when I saw the dead body of poor young Robertson lying only a few feet from the tent door. He had been shot through the heart, doubtless in his efforts to save me from the attack of the scoundrels who wanted to rob me of my treasure.

"A moment later the old skipper was at my side. He helped me back to the tent, put me into bed, and gave me a restorative. He then told me that a party of pearlers had got wind of the great pink pearl and had attacked the tent. The doctor and he had both resisted them, the former losing his life in his attempt to save me and my new treasure, and afterwards the scoundrels had got clear away with the pearl.

"The old skipper's words stunned me. I tried to fancy that I was still under the influence of chloroform and that all this hideous story was but a terrible dream, but I soon discovered that it was only too true.

"For a fortnight I lay there raging in fever and impotent fury at my loss. Then, in spite of everything, I began to get better, and did what I could to trace the villains. All my efforts were useless, and in despair I returned to England, saw Forrester, and told him everything. Imagine my surprise when he said in the coldest, most sneering voice, that he did not believe a word of my story. He followed up this extraordinary sentence by continuing in the following words:

"'I not only refuse to believe what you have just told me, but I am certain you have trumped up this story to cover your own theft. You are the thief who has stolen the great pink pearl.'

"I tried to argue that if such had been my intention I should never have cabled the news of having found it. He would listen to no reason, abused me like a pickpocket with the most insulting language, for which I should have struck him had it not been for Ella's sake. I know now how much he wanted that pearl, and how its possession would have saved him from the ruin which is threatening him. He refused to allow me to see Ella, but to this injustice I would not submit. We managed to meet. I told her my entire story and of course she believed me. She even went further; she spoke to her father and told him that if I was refused admittance to the house she would also leave it and marry me. As she is of age, Forrester knew he could not prevent her.

"'You can cut me off with a shilling,' said my brave girl, 'but I will not desert Cyril. I would rather be his wife than the wife of the richest man on earth.'

"Forrester, brute as he is, is more or less influenced by Ella. I believe his present hope is to induce her to marry that rich scoundrel whom you met there to-night, Sutherland. He hopes to effect this by guile, for in no other way could he get Ella to consent to it. Now I am allowed there on sufferance, hence my appearance on the scene this evening. There, now you have the whole situation, Lonsdale. What do you think of it?"

"My dear fellow, I don't know what to think of it," I replied. "You must give me time to clearly take in your story. It is an extraordinary one. What an awful escape you had of your life! And then for your luck to end with all this misery and suspicion is a bitter reward indeed. But as to the pearl, that seems to me to be the crucial point. What do you yourself think became of it?"

"That is the puzzle of all puzzles," he answered. "Personally, I distrust that skipper's story. I believe it was he who stole it; I believe also that he shot the doctor, who saw him take it, and then made up the story. He was a great rascal, I knew, but I could not get so good a man for my work, as he knew every inch of the Reef."

"But if the pearl was of such exceptional value and unique appearance, could it be disposed of in any market without comments on it leaking out?" I asked.

"No, certainly not; and that is also a very queer point. Of course, it is possible that some private deal might have been made. Any way, it is gone now, and I shall never see it again. There is no use crying over spilt milk. Ella is true to me, that is my one and only comfort; and if I could only persuade her to marry me, poor as I am, I believe I should have heart enough to leave the country and start afresh somewhere else. Luckily, I know all about the pearling business, and may come across another treasure on my own account."

Although his words were brave enough, there was a bitter ring in his voice. I looked at him and saw that to a great extent his spirit was broken.

"It is Forrester's suspicion of me which makes things so hard," he said, meeting my eyes. "Of course, I know only too well that the man is unscrupulous himself, but his attitude towards me is almost intolerable."

"Well, you have but to keep up your courage," I said, after a pause. "The girl is true to you, which is the main point. I grant that things look dark now, but you never know how quickly the cloud may lift. Forrester's accusation is, of course, infamous, and I would not dwell on it if I were you. I suppose you know best, but I think you should have spent more time in trying to regain that pearl, and I think still, granting what you say about its unique appearance, you should still make strenuous efforts to trace it. Surely it would not be impossible to pick up the thread again."

"You speak without knowledge," he answered testily, "I did everything that man could while on the spot. I spent a whole month's earnings in cables and enquiries. There was no use throwing more good money after bad. The maddening thing is this, Lonsdale—I cannot recall those last words of poor young Dr. Robertson just as he bent over me in the tent. God only knows how I have tried to bring back that lost memory. Another moment and I should have been sufficiently conscious to have retained each word. I am absolutely certain that he was telling me about the pearl, because that was the word I could alone distinctly recall."

"Yes, it is indeed maddening," I answered. "Well, I can only give you the hackneyed advice not to give way, old chap. I am afraid I must ask you to leave me now, as I have to visit some patients, late as it is, but will you promise to come and dine with me at 7.30 to-morrow evening?"

"Yes," he replied, "I will with pleasure."

As soon as Tempest had gone, I went out to see my patient, an old man dying of paralysis in the next street. I returned soon after midnight, built up my fire, and sat down to think over the strange story which had been confided to me. It was curious enough, in all conscience.

"What tiny events and moments alter the whole current of affairs of a life," I thought. If Tempest could only recall the words whispered to him by the doctor as consciousness was struggling back all would, I felt certain, be explained. The mystery of the lost pearl would be made clear.

The more I thought over the circumstance, the more inclined I was to the belief that the scoundrel who had shot the doctor might not, after all, have discovered the pearl.

Tempest had heard certain words when returning to the world of sense after the unconsciousness produced by chloroform. Might a similar condition start the same train of thought, and automatically reproduce the words impressed on his brain by the doctor just before his death?

The more I thought over this the more it seemed feasible. I felt intensely excited as the possibility grew vividly before me. It was a subject upon which I had often thought, and apart from the tremendous issues which might depend upon the result, here was the very chance to try it.

I determined to think the matter over carefully, and, if I decided on attempting it, to broach the subject to Tempest the next evening.

The whole of the following day I was haunted by this thought, and definitely determined to propose the experiment when my friend arrived. It was with some anxiety, therefore, I awaited his coming.

He arrived about a quarter to eight, and I went to the door myself to let him in. As I glanced at his face I saw that he had gone through a depressing day, and had doubtless not been able to persuade Ella Forrester to run away with him. His face was drawn and pale, and there were heavy rings round his eyes.

"It's all over, Lonsdale," he said, sinking into a chair and looking the picture of despair.

"She has refused your suggestion then?" I said. "Well, Tempest, I must confess I am scarcely surprised. I have known Ella for years, and I do not think she is the sort of girl willingly to desert her father, even for the man she loves."

His face relaxed into the ghost of a smile.

"She does love me, there is no doubt of that," he answered. Then he rose, the stern lines came back to his mouth and brow. He clenched one of his hands.

"My very worst fears are realised," he said; "I don't blame her, poor darling, she is driven to it. Her father is forcing her to marry Sutherland, and after months of opposition she is beginning to yield. She told me that her father absolutely went on his knees to her last night and implored of her to save him from ruin. What could a girl do under such circumstances?"

"Listen, Tempest," I said, "I have something to say to you. You must keep quiet; I do not believe all hope is over. Here is dinner. Sit down and see whether a glass of this old Heidseck won't smooth away some of those wrinkles from your face."

He approached the table; we sat down and dinner proceeded. By the time we had reached dessert I saw that Tempest had sufficiently regained his self-control for me to enter on the business which now occupied all my thoughts.

"I have a proposal to make to you, and I want your closest attention," I said.

"What is that?" he asked.

Then I began to unfold the idea I had formulated on the previous evening. I watched him closely as I spoke, noting the effect of my words. At first he listened with a listless air, as if wondering why I was troubling him with a psychological theory that did not in the least interest him, but as I came to the point, and at last blurted out the naked fact that if he were once more put under the influence of chloroform the memory he was in vain struggling to grip might return, he started back, stared at me, his eyes dilated, and his lips parted in wonder.

"Do you mean it, Lonsdale?" he cried, "do you really think it possible; it sounds too good to be true."

"It is by no means impossible, my dear fellow," I answered. "Mind, I don't say for a moment it will be successful, but I tell you as a medical man I think it worth trying."

"Then try to-night, don't lose a moment, try now."

The sudden revulsion from despair to a possible hope had sent the colour to his cheeks. He was all on fire with excitement.

"There is no earthly reason why we should not try to-night," I said. "You have taken very little dinner, luckily. We will try within the next couple of hours. I have only one concession to ask on your part."

"What is that?"

"As there is always a very slight element of danger in the administration of chloroform, will you hand me a written note that the experiment is at your wish, and for the purpose stated?"

"Of course I will," he replied. He went straight over to the writing table, drew up a short note at my dictation, and signed it.

It was with the greatest difficulty I could restrain his impatience during the time that intervened between then and eleven o'clock, as I did not care to experiment sooner. At that hour I took him into my consulting room, told him to undo his collar and shirt and lie down on the sofa. I examined his chest with curiosity. I could see plainly what had been done. A piece of bone from the breast bone had been removed, and there was a scar.

His excitement certainly had infected me, and I lost no time in commencing the experiment. I administered the chloroform slowly, and he gradually sank under its influence. It was in the second stage, the stage of excitement, that I expected the result, if any, and I watched him passing into this with the utmost interest. His limbs began to move and his face to flush, and then his voice broke into incoherent words. I strained my ears, listening intently. What was he saying? He was murmuring certain words over and over again, saying them thickly, monotonously; they sounded like a mere jumble.

I grew impatient and anxious, for I knew that this stage lasted but a minute. Then he became quieter, and I had abandoned all hope of success when, in a low murmur that dwindled almost to a whisper, yet with perfect distinctness, I caught the words—

"The pearl is safe in the wound. I have put it there for safety. It is your only chance."

The next instant I had snatched the chloroform from his face, and was standing motionless beside him, as the meaning of his words struck home. The pearl put for safety in the wound in his chest. Was it possible?

At first I could scarcely believe the evidence of my own ears. If, indeed, Tempest was uttering the truth, he had for months, ever since that fatal moment, carried the pink pearl always with him and yet not known it. In an instant of inspiration when the tent was attacked, the doctor must have dipped the pink pearl in his anaesthetic and slipped it into the cavity made by the wound, where it had remained without causing pain or giving any sign of its presence.

Such things had, I knew, been done experimentally with success. What news I had for him when he awoke, or would it not be better for me to go right on with matters now, push him again under the chloroform, open the wound in his chest, and finish the whole thing? Yes, I would do it.

I immediately continued the chloroform, and then quickly got out my instruments. Was I right in doing this single-handed? I determined to risk it. In less than five minutes my preliminary work was done, and in less than another minute my labour had its reward, and the pearl lay in my forceps on the table.

I rapidly completed the operation, put on the dressings, fixing them with a bandage, and then I sat down beside my patient and waited quietly till he should come round.

It is needless to add much more. The pink pearl was its own harbinger of peace, of success, of fortune.

Two months later Cyril Tempest married the girl he loved, severed his partnership with Forrester, and went away with her to Queensland. There he commenced his pearling operations on his own account with marked success, and writes to me that he is the happiest man in the world.

CHRIS TAKES THE BUS

Denise Mina

Denise Mina wrote her first crime novel as a PhD student. A key figure in the Scottish Noir tradition, several of her books, including *The End of the Wasp Season*, feature troubled Glasgow DI Alex Morrow. Mina has adapted Stieg Larsson's *The Girl With the Dragon Tattoo* as a graphic novel.

They stood outside the plate glass window at the bus station, because inside was so bright and cheerful, so full of happy milling people, that neither could bear it.

The cold was channelled here, into a snaking stream that lapped at their ankles, a bitter snapping cold that chilled them both. His eyes were fixed on the ground and she could feel him shrinking, sinking into the concrete.

'Jees-ho!' She shivered theatrically, trying to bring his attention back to her.

Chris looked at her and pulled the zip up at his neck, making a defiant face that said, see? I can look after myself, I know to do my coat up against the cold. They were huddled in their coats, shoulders up at their ears, each alone.

He tried to smile at her but she glanced down at the bag on the floor because his eyes were so hard to look into. The backlit adverts tinged the ground an icy pink and she saw that Chris had put the heel of his bag in a puddle.

'Bag's getting soggy,' she smiled nervously, keeping her eyes averted.

He looked at it, dismayed at yet another fuck-up, and then shrugged, shaking his head a little, as if trying to shake off the concern she must be feeling. 'Dry out on the bus.'

She nodded, 'Yeah, it'll get hot in there.'

'Phew,' he looked away down the concrete fairway. 'Last time I only had a T-shirt and jeans on and I was sweating like a menopausal woman.'

His turn of phrase made her mouth twitch.

'When I got off I had salt rings under my arms.'

She tutted disbelievingly.

'True,' he insisted. 'I stood still at King's Cross and a couple of deer came up and licked me.'

She smirked away from him, felt her eyes brimming up at the same time and frowned to cover it up.

'One of them offered me a tenner for a gobble, actually.'

She was crying and laughing at the same time, spluttering ridiculously, the pink glow from the adverts glinting off her wet cheeks. His whole fucking venture depended on a lie and she wasn't a good liar.

'So,' she wiped her face and turned back to him, 'so when you get there you're off to –'

'My Auntie Margie's, yeah.' He had done her the courtesy of looking away, giving her the chance to get it together before he looked back. 'Yeah, she'll be waiting in for me, got my room ready.'

'D'you get on with her?'

Chris shrugged, 'She's my auntie . . .'

He tipped gently forward on his heels, leaning out into the brutal wind beyond the shelter. A coach pulled past the mouth of the bus station, slowly, dim yellow lights behind the shaded windows. They both saw the rabbit-ear side mirrors. It was a luxury coach, luxury in as much as coaches ever could be. Full of fat tourists coming to see the Castle and the Mile, the pantomime of the city. Not the London Bus, not Chris's bus.

He stepped back and they watched the bus pass, heads swinging around in unison like a pair of kittens watching a ball swing in front of them.

'I'll not get that one,' he said, joking that he had a choice. 'I'll just wait for the shit bus and get that one.'

'Yeah,' she said cheerfully, and looking up saw him flinch, arcing his head back as his neck stiffened. He was still bleeding, she knew, had asked her if it was showing through the seat of his jeans, made her look. It wasn't showing. She'd given him a fanny pad to put down there and he joked about having a period. She didn't know who'd raped him, but it was someone they both knew, or else he wouldn't be leaving. He confided in her because she was mousey, would give him the money for the ticket without asking too much detail, wouldn't make him go to the police.

It came suddenly, a hot molten gush of dread from the base of her gut, rolling up her chest until it bubbled and burst out of her mouth: 'Don't go.' Her voice was flat and loud, ridiculous, a voice from the middle of a heated argument.

Chris looked at her, eyebrows tented pitifully. 'I have tae . . .'

She nodded, looked away.

'I have,' he whispered. 'Have to. You'll come and visit me.'

'Of course. Of course, and we'll phone all the time.'

'Yeah, phone. We'll phone.'

As a coach slowly eased its way around the sharp turn into the St Andrew Bus Station, the destination lit up brightly above the windscreen.

The passengers who had waited inside, in the warm, filtered out behind them, talking excitedly, swinging bags, forming a messy queue.

Conscious of the company, Chris shifted his weight, brushing her shoulder lightly, shifting away. She felt the loss quite suddenly, a wrench, another cherished friend swallowed by the promise of London, loading the coach boot with bags stuffed with the offal of their own history.

DAISY BELL

Gladys Mitchell

Gladys Mitchell (1901–1983) wrote sixty-six novels featuring the psychoanalyst detective Mrs Adela Bradley. Mitchell was, at one time, considered Agatha Christie's closest rival. Many of her books, including *Speedy Death*, *Death at the Opera* and *The Saltmarsh Murders*, are now being republished by Harvill Secker.

> *Daisy, give me your answer, do!*
> *I've gone crazy, all for the love of you!*
> *It won't be a stylish marriage—*
> *We can't afford a carriage—*
> *But you'll look neat upon the seat*
> *Of a bicycle made for two.*

In the curved arm of the bay the sea lay perfectly still. Towards the horizon was reflected back the flashing light of the sun, but under the shadow of huge cliffs the dark-green water was as quiet as a lake at evening.

Above, riding over a ridge between two small villages, went the road, a dusty highway once, a turnpike on which the coach had changed horses three times in twenty miles. That dusty road was within the memory of the villagers; in the post office there were picture postcards, not of the coaches, certainly, but of the horse-drawn station bus on the shocking gradients and hairpin bends of the highway.

The road was now slightly wider—not much, because every extra foot had to be hacked from the rocky hillside, for on one side the road fell almost sheer to the sea. A humped turf edge kept this seaward boundary (insufficiently, some said, for there had been motoring accidents, especially in the dark), and beyond the humped edge, and, treacherously, just out of sight of motorists who could see the rolling turf but not the danger, there fell away a Gadarene descent of thirteen hundred feet.

George took the road respectfully, with an eye for hairpin bends and (although he found this irksome) an occasional toot on the horn. His employer, small, spare, and upright, sat beside him, the better to admire the rolling view. Equally with the moorland scenery she admired her chauffeur's driving. She was accustomed to both phenomena, but neither palled on her. In sixteen crawling miles she had not had a word to say.

At the County Boundary, however, she turned her head slightly to the right.

'The next turning, George. It's narrow.'

His eyes on the road ahead, the chauffeur nodded, and the car turned off to the left down a sandy lane, at the bottleneck of which it drew up courteously in face of a flock of lively, athletic, headstrong moorland sheep. The shepherd saluted Mrs Bradley, passed the time of day with the chauffeur, said it was a pity all they motors shouldn't have the same danged sense, and urged his charges past the car, and kept them within some sort of bounds with the help of a shaggy dog.

At the bottom of the slope, and wedged it seemed in the hollow, was a village with a very small church. Mrs Bradley went into the churchyard to inspect the grave of an ancestress (she believed) of her own who had died in the odour of sanctity, but, if rumour did not lie, only barely so, for she had enjoyed a reputation as a witch.

Mrs Bradley, looking (with her black hair, sharp black eyes, thin hands, and beaky little mouth) herself not at all unlike a witch, spent an interesting twenty minutes or so in the churchyard, and then went into the church.

Its architectural features were almost negligible. A fourteenth-century chancel (probably built on the site of the earliest church), a badly restored nave, a good rood screen, and the only remaining bit of Early English work mutilated to allow for an organ loft, were all obvious. There seemed, in fact, very little, on a preliminary investigation, to interest even the most persistent or erudite visitor.

In the dark south wall, however, of what had been the Lady Chapel, Mrs Bradley came upon a fourteenth-century piscina whose bowl had been carved in the likeness of a hideous human head. She took out a magnifying glass and examined the carving closely. Montague Rhodes James, with his genius for evoking unquiet imaginings and terrifying, atavistic fears, might have described the expression upon its horrid countenance. All that Mrs Bradley could accomplish was a heathenish muttering indicative of the fact that, in her view, the countenance betrayed indication of at least two major Freudian complexes and a Havelock Ellis regression into infantile criminology.

'A murderer's face, ma'am,' said a voice behind her. 'Ay, as I stand, that be a murderer's face.'

She turned and saw the verger with his keys. 'Ay, they do tell, and vicar he do believe it, as carver was vouchsafed a true, just vision of Judas Iscariot the traitor, and carved he out for all to look upon.'

He smiled at her—almost with the sinister leer of the carving itself, thought Mrs Bradley, startled by the change in his mild and previously friendly expression. He passed on into the vestry, dangling his keys.

Shaking her head, Mrs Bradley dropped some money into the offertory box on the pillar nearest the porch, and took the long sloping path between the headstones of the graves to the lych-gate. Here she found George in conversation with a black-haired woman. George had always given himself (with how much truth his employer had never troubled herself to find out) the reputation of being a misogynist, and on this occasion, seated on the step of the car, he was, in his own phrase, 'laying down the law' with scornful masculine firmness. The girl had her back to the lych-gate. She was plump and bareheaded, and was wearing brown corduroy shorts, a slightly rucked-up blouse on elastic at the waist, and—visible from the back view which Mrs Bradley had of her—a very bright pink vest which showed between the rucked-up blouse and the shorts. For the rest she was brown-skinned and, seen face to face, rather pretty.

A tandem bicycle, built to accommodate two men, was resting against the high, steep, ivy-grown bank of the lane. The young woman, seeing Mrs Bradley, who had in fact strolled round to get a view of her, cut short George's jeremiads by thanking him. Then she walked across the road, set the tandem upright, pushed it sharply forward, and, in spite of the fact that the slope of the road was against her, mounted with agility and ease on to the front saddle. Then she tacked doggedly up the hill, the tandem, lacking any weight on the back seat, wagging its tail in what looked to Mrs Bradley a highly dangerous manner as it zigzagged up to the bend in the lane and wobbled unwillingly round it.

George had risen to his feet upon the approach of his employer, and now stood holding the door open.

'A courageous young woman, George?' suggested Mrs Bradley, getting into the car.

'A foolish one, madam, in my opinion,' George responded primly, 'and so I was saying to her when she was asking the way. Looking for trouble I call it to cycle one of them things down these roads. Look at the hill she's coming to, going to Lyndale this route. Meeting her husband, she says; only been married a month, and having their honeymoon now and using the tandem between them; him having to work thereabouts, and her cycling that contraption down from London, where she's living with her mother while he gets the home for her. Taken three days to do it in, and meeting him on top of Lyndale Hill this afternoon. More like a suicide pact, if you ask me what I think.'

'I not only ask you, George, but I am so much enthralled by what you think that I propose we take the same route and follow her.'

'We were due to do so in any case, madam, if I can find a place to turn the car in this lane.'

It took him six slow miles to find a suitable place. During the drive towards the sea, the big car brushing the summer hedgerows almost all the time, Mrs Bradley observed,

'I don't like to think of that young woman, George. I hope you advised her to wheel the bicycle on all dangerous parts of the road?'

'As well advise an errand boy to fit new brake-blocks, madam,' George austerely answered. 'I did advise her to that effect, but not to cut any ice. She fancies herself on that jigger. You can't advise women of that age.'

'Did you offer her any alternative route to Lyndale?'

'Yes, madam; not with success.'

At the top of the winding hill he turned to the left, and then, at the end of another five miles and a quarter of wind and the screaming seabirds, great stretches of moorland heather, bright green tracks of little peaty streams, and, south of the moor, the far-off ridges and tors, he engaged his lowest gear again and the car crept carefully down a long, steep, dangerous hill. There were warning notices on either side of the road, and the local authority, laying special emphasis on the subject of faulty brakes, had cut a parking space from the edge of the stubborn moor. The gradient of the steepest part of the hill was one in four. The car took the slant like a cat in sight of a bird.

'What do you think of our brakes, George?' Mrs Bradley inquired. George replied, in the reserved manner with which he received her more facetious questions, that the brakes were in order, or had been when the car was brought out of the garage.

'Well, then, pull up,' said his employer. 'Something has happened on the seaward side of the road. I think someone's gone over the edge.'

Her keen sight, and a certain sensitivity she had to visual impressions, had not deceived her. She followed the track of a bicycle to the edge of the cliff, crouched, lay flat, and looked over.

Below her the seagulls screamed, and, farther down, the sea flung sullenly, despite the brilliant day, against the heavy rocks, or whirl-pooled, snarling, about the black island promontories, for the tide was on the turn and coming in fast. Sea-pinks, some of them brown and withered now, for their season was almost past, clung in the crevices or grew in the smallest hollows of the cliff-face. Near one root of them a paper bag had lodged. Had it been empty, the west wind, blowing freshly along the face of the cliff (which looked north to the Bristol Channel), must have removed it almost as soon as it alighted, but there it perched, not wedged, yet heavy enough to hold its place against the breeze. To the left of it, about four yards off, was a deep, dark stain, visible because it was on the only piece of white stone that could be seen.

'Odd,' said Mrs Bradley, and began to perform the feat which she would not have permitted to anyone under her control—that of climbing down to reach the dark-stained rock.

The stain was certainly blood, and was still slightly sticky to the touch. She looked farther down (having, fortunately, a mountaineer's head for heights) and thought that, some thirty feet below her, she could see a piece of cloth. It was caught on the only bush which seemed to have found root and sustenance upon the rocky cliff. It resembled, she thought, material of which a man's suit might be made.

She left it where it was and scrambled across to the bag.

'George,' she said, when she had regained the dark, overhanging lip of the rough turf edge of the cliff and had discovered her chauffeur at the top, 'I think I saw a public telephone marked on the map. Somebody ought to search the shore below these cliffs, I rather fancy.'

'It would need to be by boat, then, madam. The tide comes up to the foot,' replied the chauffeur. He began to walk back up the hill.

Mrs Bradley sat down at the roadside and waited for him to return. While she was waiting she untwisted the top of the screwed-up paper bag and examined the contents with interest.

She found a packet of safety-razor blades, a tube of toothpaste half-full, a face flannel, a wrapped cake of soap of the dimensions known euphemistically in the advertisements as 'guest-size', a very badly worn toothbrush, a set of small buttons on a card, a pipe-cleaner, half a bicycle bell, two rubber patches for mending punctures, and a piece of wormlike valve-rubber.

'Calculated to indicate that whoever left the bag there was a cyclist, George,' she observed, when her chauffeur came back from the telephone. 'Of course, nobody may have fallen over the cliff, but—what do you make of the marks?'

'Palmer tyres, gent's model—not enough clearance for a lady's—see where the pedal caught the edge of the turf?'

'Yes, George. Unfortunately one loses the track a yard from the side of the road. I should have supposed that the bicycle would have left a better account of itself if it had really been ridden over. Besides, what could have made anybody ride it over the edge? The road is wide enough, and there does not seem to be much traffic. I think perhaps I'll retrieve that piece of cloth before we go.'

'I most seriously hope you will not, madam, if you'll excuse me. I've no head for heights myself or I would get it. After all, we know just where it is. The police could get it later, with ropes and tackle for their men, if it *should* be required at an inquest.'

'Very true, George. Let us get on to the village to see whether a boat has put out. How much farther is it?'

'Another three miles and a half, madam. There's another hill after this—a smaller one.'

The car descended decorously. The hill dropped sheer and steep for about another half-mile, and then it twisted suddenly away to the right, so that an inn which was on the left-hand side at the bend appeared, for an instant, to be standing in the middle of the road.

So far as the black-haired girl on the smashed and buckled tandem was concerned, that was where it might as well have stood, Mrs Bradley reflected. The tandem had been ridden straight into a brick wall—slap into it as though the rider had been blind or as though the machine she was riding had been completely out of her control. Whatever the cause of the accident, she had hurtled irrevocably to her death, or so Mrs Bradley thought when first she knelt beside her.

'Rat-trap pedals, of all things, madam,' said George. The plump large feet in the centre-seamed cycling shoes were still caught in the bent steel traps. George tested the brakes.

'The brakes don't act,' he said. 'Perhaps a result of the accident, madam, although I shouldn't think so.' He released the girl's feet and lifted the tandem away. Mrs Bradley, first delicately and then with slightly more firmness, sought for injuries.

'George,' she said, 'the case of instruments. And then go and get some cold water from somewhere or other.'

The girl had a fractured skull. Her left leg was slightly lacerated, but it was not bruised and the bone was not broken. Her face was unmarked, except by the dirt from the roadside. It was all a little out of the ordinary, Mrs Bradley thought, seizing the thermos flask full of icy water which the resourceful George had brought from a moorland stream.

'She's alive, George, I think,' she said. 'But there have been some very odd goings-on. Are the tandem handlebars locked?'

'No, madam. They move freely.'

'Don't you think the front wheel should have been more seriously affected?'

'Why, yes, perhaps it should, madam. The young woman can't go much less than ten or eleven stone, and with the brakes out of order . . .'

'And although her feet were caught in the rat-trap pedals, her face isn't even marked. It was only a little dirty before I washed it.'

'Sounds like funny business, madam, to me.'

'And to me, too, George. Is there a hospital near? We must have an ambulance if possible. I don't think the car will do. She ought to lie flat. That skull wants trepanning and at once. Mind how you go down the hill, though. I'll stay here with her. You might leave me a fairly heavy spanner.'

Left alone with the girl, Mrs Bradley fidgeted with her case of instruments, took out gouge forceps, sighed, shook her head, and put them back again. The wound on the top of the head was extremely puzzling. A fracture of the base of the skull would have been the most likely head injury, unless the girl had crashed head-first into the wall, but, from the position in which the body had been lying, this seemed extremely unlikely. One other curious point Mrs Bradley noticed which changed her suppositions into certainty. The elastic-waisted white blouse and the shorts met neatly. It was impossible to believe that they could do so unless they had been pulled together after the girl had fallen from the saddle.

Mrs Bradley made a mental picture of the girl leaning forward over the low-slung sports-type handlebars of the machine. She must, in the feminine phrase, have 'come apart' at the back. That blouse could never have overlapped those shorts.

Interested and curious, Mrs Bradley turned up the edge of the soiled white blouse. There was nothing underneath it but the bare brown skin marked with two or three darker moles at the waist. Of the bright pink vest there was no sign; neither had the girl a knapsack or any kind of luggage into which she could have stuffed the vest supposing that she had taken it off for coolness.

'Odd,' said Mrs Bradley again, weighing the spanner thoughtfully in her hand. 'I wonder what's happened to the husband?'

At this moment there came round the bend an AA scout wheeling a bicycle. He saluted as he came nearer.

'Oh dear, madam! Nasty accident here! Poor young woman! Anything I can do?'

'Yes,' said Mrs Bradley very promptly. 'Get an ambulance. I'm afraid she's dead, but there might be a chance if you're quick. No, don't touch her. I'm a doctor. I've done all that can be done here. Hurry, please. Every moment is important.'

'No ambulance in the village, madam. Couldn't expect it, could you? I might perhaps be able to get a car. How did you get here? Was you with her when she crashed?'

'Go and get a car. A police car, if you like. Dead or alive, she'll have to be moved as soon as possible.'

'Yes, she will, won't she?' said the man. He turned his bicycle, and, mounting it, shot away round the bend.

Mrs Bradley unfolded an Ordnance Survey map of the district and studied it closely. Then she took out a reading glass and studied it again. She put out a yellow claw and traced the line of the road she was on, and followed it into the village towards which first George and then the AA scout had gone.

The road ran on uncompromisingly over the thin red contour lines of the map, past nameless bays on one side and the shoulder of the moor on a rising hill on the other. Of deviations from it there were none; not so much as the dotted line of a moorland track, not even a stream, gave any indication that there might be other ways of reaching the village besides crossing the open moorland or keeping to the line of the road. There was nothing marked on the map but the cliffs and the shore on the one hand, the open hill country on the other.

She was still absorbed when George returned with the car.

'The village has no ambulance, madam, but the bus has decanted its passengers on to the bridge and is getting here as fast as it can. It was thought in the village, madam, that the body could be laid along one of the seats.'

'I hope and trust that "body" is but a relative term. The young woman will live, George, I fancy. Somebody has had his trouble for nothing.'

'I am glad to hear that, madam. The villagers seem well-disposed, and the bus is the best they can do.'

He spoke of the villagers as though they were the aboriginal inhabitants of some country which was still in the process of being explored. Mrs Bradley gave a harsh little snort of amusement and then observed,

'Did the AA scout stop and speak to you? Or did you ask him for information?'

'No, madam, neither at all. He was mending a puncture when I passed him.'

'Was that on your journey to the village or on the return here?'

'Just now, madam. I saw no one on my journey to the village.'

'Interesting,' said Mrs Bradley, thinking of her Ordnance map. 'Punctures are a nuisance, George, are they not? If you see him again you might ask him whether *Daisy Bell* met her husband on top of the hill.'

Just then the bus arrived. Off it jumped a police sergeant and a constable, who, under Mrs Bradley's direction, lifted the girl and placed her on one of the seats, of which the bus had two, running the whole of the inside length of the vehicle.

'You take the car to the hotel, George. I'll be there as soon as I can,' said his employer. 'Now, constable, we have to hold her as still as we can. Sergeant, kindly instruct the driver to avoid the bumps in the road, and then come in here and hold my coat to screen the light from her head. Is there a hospital in the village?'

'No, ma'am. There's a home for inebriates, though. That's the nearest thing. We're going to take her there, and Constable Fogg is fetching Doctor MacBain.'

'Splendid,' said Mrs Bradley, and devoted herself thenceforward entirely to her patient.

One morning some days later, when the mist had cleared from the moors and the sun was shining on every drop of moisture, she sent for the car, and thus addressed her chauffeur:

'Well, did you give the scout my message?'

'Yes, madam, but he did not comprehend it.'

'Indeed? And did you explain?'

'No, madam, not being instructed.'

'Excellent, child. We shall drive to the fatal spot, and there we shall see—what we shall see.'

George, looking haughty because he felt befogged, held open the door of the car, and Mrs Bradley put her foot on the step.

'I'll sit in front, George,' she said.

The car began to mount slowly to the bend where the accident had come to their notice. George was pulling up, but his employer invited him to go on.

'Our goal is the top of the hill, George. That is where they were to meet, you remember. That is the proper place from which to begin our inquiry. Is it not strange and interesting to consider all the motives for murder and attempted murder that come to men's minds? To women's minds, too, of course. The greater includes the less.'

She cackled harshly. George who (although he would have found it difficult to account for his opinion) had always conceived her to be an ardent feminist, looked at the road ahead, and did not relax his expression of dignified aloofness.

Prevented, by the fact that he was driving, from poking him in the ribs (her natural reaction to an attitude such as the one he was displaying), Mrs Bradley grinned tigerishly, and the car crawled on up the worst and steepest part of the gradient.

George then broke his silence.

'In my opinion, madam, no young woman losing her brakes on such a hill could have got off so light as *she* did, nor that tandem either.'

'True, George.'

'If you will excuse the question, madam, what put the idea of an attempt on her into your mind?'

'I suppose the piscina, George.'

George concluded that she was amusing herself at his expense and accepted the reply for what it was worth, which to him was nothing, since he did not know what a piscina was (and was habitually averse to seeking such information). He drove on a little faster as the gradient eased to one in seven and then to one in ten.

'Just here, George,' said his employer. 'Run off on to the turf on the right-hand side.'

George pulled up very close to the AA telephone which he had used before. Here the main road cut away from the route they had traversed and an AA scout was on duty at the junction.

' "*Behind the barn, down on my knees*," ' observed Mrs Bradley, chanting the words in what she fondly believed to be accents of their origin, ' "*I thought I heard a chicken sneeze*"—and I did, too. Come and look at this, George.'

It was the bright pink vest. There was no mistaking it, although it was stained now, messily and rustily, with blood.

'Not *her* blood, George; *his*,' remarked Mrs Bradley. 'I wonder he dared bring it back here, all the same. And I wonder where the young woman the first time fell off the tandem?' She looked again at the blood-stained vest. 'He must have cut himself badly, but, of course, he had to get enough blood to make the white stone look impressive, and he wanted the vest to smear it on with so that he need use nothing of his own. Confused thinking, George, on the whole, but murderers do think confusedly, and one can feel for them, of course.'

She sent George to fetch the AA scout, who observed,

'Was it the young woman as fell off bottom of Countsferry? Must have had a worse tumble just here by the box than Stanley seemed to think. He booked the tumble in his private log. Would you be the young woman's relatives, ma'am?'

'We represent her interests,' said Mrs Bradley, remarking afterwards to George that she thought they might consider themselves as doing so since they had saved her life.

'Well, he's left the log with me, and it do seem to show the cause of her shaking up. Must have been dazed like, and not seen the bend as it was coming, and run herself into the wall. And Stanley, they do say, must have gone over the cliff in trying to save her, for he ain't been back on duty any more. Cruel, these parts, they be.'

'Did her fall upset both her brakes, then?' Mrs Bradley inquired. She read the laconic entry in the exercise book presented for her inspection and, having earned the scout's gratitude in the customary simple manner, she returned to the car with the vest (which the scout had not seen) pushed into the large pocket of her skirt.

'Stop at the scene of the accident, George,' she said. 'She seemed,' said George admiringly later on to those who were standing him a pint in exchange for the story, 'like a bloodhound on the murderer's trail.'

'For a murderer he was, in intention, if not in fact,' continued George, taking, without his own knowledge, a recognized though debatable ecclesiastical view. 'She climbed up the bank and on to the moor as if she knew just what to look for, madam did. She showed me the very stone she reckoned he hit the young woman over the head with, and then where he sunk in the soft earth deeper than his first treads, because he was carrying the body back to the tandem to make out she crashed and fell off.'

'And didn't she crash?' his hearers wanted to know.

'Crash? What her? A young woman who, to give her her due (although I don't hold with such things), had cycled that tandem—sports model and meant for two men—all the way down there from London? No. He crashed the tandem himself after he'd done her in. That was to deceive the police or anybody else that found her. He followed her on his bike down the hill with the deed in his heart. You see, he was her husband.

'But he didn't deceive me and madam, not by a long chalk he didn't! Why, first thing I said to her, I said, "Didn't it ought to be buckled up more than that if she came down that hill without brakes?" 'Course, that was his little mistake. That, and using her vest. I hope they give him ten years!

'Well, back we went up the hill to where madam found the paper bag and its etceteras. The only blood we could see was on the only white stone.'

The barmaid at this point begged him to stop. He gave her the horrors, she said.

'So what?' one listener inquired.

'Well, the whole bag of tricks was to show that *someone*, and that someone a man and a cyclist, had gone over the cliff and was killed, like the other scout said. That was going to be our scout's alibi if the police ever got on his track, so madam thinks, but he hoped he wouldn't need to use that; it was just his stand-by, like. The other AA man had seen him go off duty. That was his danger, or so he thought, not reckoning on madam and me. He'd fixed the head of the young woman's machine while she stood talking to him at the AA telephone, so that when she mounted it threw her. That was to show (that's why he logged it, see?) as she mightn't have been herself when she took the bend. Pretty little idea.'

Three days later Mrs Bradley said to him,

'They will be able to establish motive at the trial, George. Bell—I call him that—was arrested yesterday evening. He had insured his wife, it appears, as soon as they were married, and wished to obtain possession of the money.'

'But what I would still like to know, madam,' George observed, 'is what put the thought of murder into your mind before ever we saw the accident or even the bag and the blood.'

'The bag and the blood, for some reason, sounds perfectly horrible, George.'

'But, madam, you spotted the marks he'd made on that edge with his push-bike as though you'd been *waiting* to spot them. And you fixed on him as the murderer, too, straight away.'

'Ah, that was easy, George. You see, he never mentioned that he'd seen you go by in the car, and you told me that on your journey to the village to find assistance you had not seen him either. Therefore, since he must have been some-where along that road, I asked myself why, even if he should have left the road-side himself, his bicycle should not have been visible. Besides, he was the perfect answer to several questions which, up to that time, I had had to ask myself. One was: why did they choose to meet at the top of that hill? Another was: why did he risk bending over the injured girl to fix her feet back in those rat-trap pedals we saw and out of which, I should imagine, her feet would most certainly have been pulled if she'd had such a very bad crash?'

'Ah, yes, the AA box and the AA uniform, madam. In other words, Mr G. K. Chesterton's postman all over again.'

'Precisely, George. The obvious meeting place, in the circumstances, and the conspicuous yet easily forgotten uniform.'

'But, madam, if I may revert, what *did* turn your mind to murder?'

'The piscina, George,' Mrs Bradley solemnly reminded him. George looked at her, hesitated, then overrode the habit of years and inquired,

'What *is* a piscina, madam?'

'A drain, George. Merely a drain.

' "Now, body, turn to air,
Or Lucifer will bear thee quick to hell!
O soul, be chang'd into little water drops,
And fall into the ocean, ne'er be found!" '

NAIN ROUGE

Barbara Nadel

Barbara Nadel was born in the East End of London, where some of her crime novels are set. Others are set in Turkey, which she visits regularly. Her many books include *Deadly Web*, which was awarded the Crime Writers Association Silver Dagger, *On the Bone*, and *The House of Four*.

Ritchie was as drunk as a sack when he first saw it out of the corner of his eye. Shuffling down Selden towards Woodward Avenue, it was talking and laughing to itself and knitting its tiny fingers in a nervous sort of a way. Ritchie's first thought was that he was seeing things. It had been a long time since he'd put away anything apart from the odd bottle of Bud, much less nine . . . or was it thirteen? . . . beefy great shots of vodka. His body was clearly in some sort of revolt at the violence he had done to it, but Ritchie's attitude was just simply, "Deal with it, bastard!" If his body didn't like the booze he'd tipped into it, then that was its problem. He had much bigger issues to deal with than whether or not his guts wanted to tolerate spirits, or whether his arteries were hardening every time he put a cigarette into his mouth. Now he was seeing the freaking Nain Rouge, which could only mean one thing. He'd lost his mind.

Through all of Detroit's many and various vicissitudes, Ritchie Carbone had always managed, somehow, to cling on to his business. It wasn't much! It *hadn't* been much. A Coney Dog joint on 2nd Avenue. Detroiters loved Coney Hotdogs. What wasn't to like? Nothing! So a lot of people had moved out of the Cass Corridor over the years? So there was a reason for that, namely drug-fuelled and gang-sanctioned violence, but, hey, it was Detroit! Tough city, tough crowd.

But then as Ritchie knew very well, that only worked up to a point. When some little shit who called himself "Da Man" had pumped a bullet into old Freddie's head, that had been enough for Ritchie. That had been it . . . through, finished, gone. No more Coney Dogs on 2nd and a whole heap of trouble about how he was going to explain how he voluntarily made himself unemployed to Welfare. And now, to top it all, a crazy little mythical freak laughing at him from underneath a lamp post. Instinctively he put one hand up to his face so that it wouldn't be able to recognize him. But it was probably way too late.

Of all the many badasses that Detroit had endured over the centuries, the Nain Rouge, or Red Dwarf, had to be the baddest. It was just legend, of course, but it was a legend that went back a long, long way. A small, child-like creature with brown fur, red boots, blazing eyes and rotten teeth was said to have attacked Detroit's founder, Antoine de la Mothe Cadillac, in 1701. Shortly afterwards,

Cadillac, a wealthy French businessman, suffered a downturn in his fortunes from which he never recovered. His altercation with the Nain is said to have rocked Cadillac to his core. But then the Nain Rouge was a creature that he would have recognized from his native country. A variety of lutin, the Nain Rouge was a common figure in the folklore, myths and legends of Normandy. Ritchie Carbone knew of it from the annual Marche du Nain Rouge, an old Detroit custom that had been revived in 2010.

His buddy, Jigsaw, had told him about it first. Jigsaw had been a Ford employee back in the day; now he made his living ripping copper and other metals out of derelict buildings to sell for scrap. He'd walked into Ritchie's place almost a year ago and said, "You heard they gonna banish the Nain this year?"

Ritchie had frowned; he remembered it well. "What? You mean they gonna have that march where everyone gets dressed up so they can fool some thing that don't even exist into walking into a fire?"

"That's the thing." Jigsaw had had his usual; a large dog, fries and a bottle of cherry pop. "Hey, Ritchie, this what you think they call gentrification?"

Reviving the old Marche du Nain Rouge was something that, to Ritchie, certainly smacked of middle-class people amusing themselves. Although most people with money had moved out of the city years ago, a new type of urban elite was trickling back into pretty old buildings like the Fyffes place on the corner of Adams Avenue and Woodward. They liked old customs like the banishing of the Nain Rouge every springtime. It was said that if the Nain could be banished on the nearest Sunday to the Vernal Equinox, the city would be safe from misfortune for another year. Heaven knew it needed it!

Ritchie Carbone, in spite of having a father from Italy, was Detroit through and through. His mother, Agnes, could trace her ancestry back to Cadillac's French compatriots and her folks, the Blancs, had stayed in the city ever since. At fifty-eight, Ritchie had seen the riots of '67, the many vicissitudes of the automobile industry, the urban ruins, and, more latterly, the first little flickers of possible city renewal. He knew that the place needed every bit of help it could get, and if that included banishing an evil fantasy figure from its streets then so be it. But that had been before that little shit Da Man had taken over large swathes of 2nd; before he'd put a gun to Freddie's head and pulled the trigger without Ritchie even having a chance to consider his offer of "protection".

Still with his hand in front of his face – to let the Nain see you was dangerous, lest it come back sometime to take its revenge – Ritchie yelled at the creature. "Hey, you!" he said. "Get out of my city! Don't you think we got enough problems, huh?"

But the little bastard just laughed, bared its rotten teeth at him and then began to scamper off at speed towards Woodward. Why Ritchie Carbone decided to stagger off after the Nain wasn't really clear to him at the time, apart from the notion that he was generally angry. But this was actually at Da Man as opposed to the mythical Nain. Not that that mattered a bean! Ritchie drained his last shot of vodka down to the very last drip and then he got up and ran.

Laughing all the while, the little freak quickly got to Woodward and then turned right. It was, or appeared to be, heading back into the city. Ritchie, adamant that

that shouldn't be allowed to happen, followed. So, it was just some supernatural fairy or whatever – if it meant to sock what remained of Detroit in the guts once again, he was going to give it a hammering it would never forget. His mind had clearly gone, what the hell did it matter if he smacked around some bastard that wasn't really there! What did he have left to lose anyway? The business had gone, his wife had left him, the freaking gangstas had even shot his freaking dog, for God's sake!

Apart from the odd bus, the cars on Woodward seemed to fall into two categories: junk wagons just about held together by rust, and great big gleaming gangsta mobiles, brimming with blacked-out windows, guns, and the odd diamond-encrusted finger just glanced through the windshield. Someone like Ritchie couldn't relate to any of that! Apart from his friendships with junkies like Jigsaw and Black Bottom Boo, he'd always been a straight-down-the-line, middle-of-the-road kind of person. Being white in a majority black neighbourhood had never bothered him. He'd got on with everyone, just like he had when Cass had been largely white. God rest her soul, his momma had even had him take Coneys up to the hookers on Cass Avenue when he was little more than an infant.

"Those girls gotta make a dollar just like everyone," Agnes Carbone had said whenever she'd made up a bag of food for the ladies of the night. White, black, Jew or Gentile, she'd never cared and neither had Ritchie – until Da Man had come into his life. All swagger and crazy jewellery, tooled up homies and attitude, Da Man had started their "conversation" by calling Ritchie "white trash". For the sake of his customers, as well as himself, he'd taken it. Until Da Man had shot Freddie.

There'd been no need to kill the dog like that! Hound was old and blind and he hadn't known what the hell had been going on. The customers had high-tailed out, screaming. Not long afterwards Da Man and his crew left as well, but not before they'd told Ritchie that he had to somehow find a thousand dollars a week to pay for his own "protection". It had been after that that Ritchie had impotently thrown all of his hotdogs, his bread and his French fries after the gangstas. They'd just landed on the sidewalk, the waste inherent in their disposal making him want to weep. Since when had he become this hopelessly vulnerable and impotent old man?

The Nain started to cross over Woodward, dodging between the cars and laughing uproariously as it did so. Sometimes a Focus or a Hummer or a Jeep would look as if it was about to barrel into the Nain, but it would always, somehow, evade a collision and come up smiling. At one point it even climbed on to the hood of some great big gangsta mobile and tapped its clawed fingers against the wind shield, but then it slid off again and landed on the tarmac, giggling. The car went on its way, its driver seemingly oblivious to the danger he or she had been in.

Still on the sidewalk, Ritchie swayed on rubber legs, looking for a gap in the traffic. In New York crossing anywhere but a designated point would have had him up for jaywalking, but in Detroit nobody cared. He launched himself out into the wide road just before he got to Martin Luther King Jr Boulevard. The Nain, across Woodward now, flicked him the finger and Ritchie, at that moment, decided that, real or not, the Nain Rouge was history. Even if he couldn't prove his manhood with some teenage gangsta, he could at least vent his spleen on this little shit!

The Nain Rouge skipped, hopped and babbled its way into the old middle-class professional district of Brush Park. Once a place where doctors, attorneys, auto executives and lumber barons lived, Brush Park was now a wasteland of spectres, a graveyard for old houses that were rotten, abused, and haunted by the shades of lifestyles long since over with. Ritchie Carbone remembered it well. He'd had an old grade-school friend from Brush Park, a Jewish attorney's son called Ron Sachs. His family had moved out in the sixties and Ron had eventually gone to Harvard. Last Ritchie had heard of him, he'd been practising law in LA. Good for him.

Up ahead, the Nain stopped outside the moonlit remains of a Gothic mansion and bent double. Then it pulled its pants down and it farted at him. Infuriated by its rudeness, Ritchie could feel his blood-pressure go through the roof as his head began to pound with anger and with booze and with the unaccustomed exercise he was getting. His father had died from a stroke back in the eighties; he'd have to be careful. But what for? The Nain, fart over, shuffled on, grunting and babbling and laughing through its awful, cracked teeth.

What for? Ritchie thought again. *What am I breathing, what am I existing, what am I living for?* Even before he'd sold the business, his marriage had been on the skids. Maria, his wife, had been so over serving Coneys, she'd run off with a professional poker player back in 2008. Now, apparently, she and this Ralph were holed up somewhere outside Reno. Her kids wouldn't see her, but then neither Kathy nor Frank came to see Ritchie that often either and he was the so-called "injured" partner. No one lived in Detroit any more, no one dared.

Old Jigsaw had offered to buy him some apparently very fierce German Shepherd off a junkie from Eastern Market, but Ritchie had passed. Freddie hadn't been a guard dog, he'd been a friend. Ritchie didn't want to have some beast he was terrified of stopping him from leaving his own apartment.

He followed the Nain on to John R Street and then stopped to catch his breath. This part of Brush Park was completely gone to urban prairie. There was nothing. No wrecked houses, no vegetation – apart from grass – and no objects but litter. People reported seeing skunks in such places, even coyotes. The nothingness of it made Ritchie shudder. This was a district where he'd played as a kid, where he'd had tea with Ron Sachs and his family in his dad's elegant, turreted mansion. All gone. He looked around for the Nain and just saw a void. Even the creature that traditionally presaged doom for the city couldn't stand this. Maybe Brush Park represented "job done" to the evil little freak. After all, the destruction of Detroit was its final aim.

Over the centuries since Cadillac had founded the city, almost every disaster that had befallen it had been heralded by a sighting of the Nain. Back in '67 during the riots there had been a lot of sightings. Then Detroit had survived, but it had changed too. Black folks had had enough and so they'd expressed their anger and they'd forced change. Ritchie had cheered them all the way. So what Da Man had done to him hit still harder. As he'd tried to tell the boy at the time,

"This white trash has always been on your side!" But it hadn't meant squat. Not to Da Man or to any of his crew.

There was a frigid late-February moon in the sky and the frost on the ground was so hard it was almost ice. Cold as unwilling charity, it was too bitter to snow and all but the most desperate addicts, the dying junkies, the most deprived of the deprived, were inside their homes, their squats or their crack shacks. No one was about and the silence, with the exception of the blood pounding through Ritchie's head, was complete. Come March it would be Nain-banishing time again – unless of course he could get the little prick dealt with early. But it had disappeared. Not that it had ever really been anywhere in the first place. A product of vodka shots, the Nain was just bile-scented vomit from his sick, tired and bitter mind. It wasn't Detroit that was falling apart, at least not completely and not yet, but Ritchie Carbone. With no savings, no pension and only a small apartment on Cass by way of assets, he was pretty much finished. With Welfare he could exist, but he couldn't live. His pa had died when he was only two years older than Ritchie was now, and he'd been ready to go. Agnes, his wife, had been dead for almost thirty years by the time old Salvatore died at sixty. Ritchie still remembered how the old man had cried for her every single day.

Then something sharp jabbed into one of his buttocks and he turned around to see the Nain, its vile fingers jabbing into his butt. When he looked at it, it screamed with laughter and Ritchie, furious, said, "You are so freaking dead!"

The Nain took off like a rocket back towards Erskine Street, whooping and chuntering and waving its disgusting furry arms in the air. It was having a high old time!

Heavy, breathless and now seeing stars in front of his eyes, Ritchie Carbone pulled his unwilling body after it, his mind seething with visions of carnage and revenge. Nobody jabbed him in the butt! Not even Da Man and his crew had stooped to that. Some freaky thing from his subconscious wasn't going to get away with it! He ran after the thing and was about to follow it into some rotting house when he recognized exactly where he was. He stopped. At one time there had been two turrets attached to the old Sachs house, now there was only one. But it was definitely where Ron and his family had lived. Ritchie put a hand up to his chest as he gasped for air and tried to deal with the shock. Mrs Sachs had been house-proud crazy! What would she make of the place now? Ritchie knew that it would break her heart and it made him want to cry in sympathy. Mrs Sachs had always made chocolate refrigerator cake, which had tasted so wonderful he'd closed his eyes with pleasure every time he'd eaten it. He'd been young and he and Ron had often talked about what they wanted to do when they grew up. Ritchie hadn't wanted to go into his Pa's Coney Dog business, he'd wanted to be a US Air Force pilot . . . not just a broken dream, but one literally hammered out of him by necessity, by recession, by the systematic destruction of his city.

As he ran up the teetering staircase to the place where the Sachses' front door had once been, Ritchie let out a howl like a wounded wolf. But then suddenly he stopped because it was in front of him. The Nain, scowling and spitting and yet at the same time laughing at him too. He wanted to pull its rotten head off, reach down its neck and pull its wicked heart out.

It laughed one more time and then he was upon it, tearing at its ghastly red flesh with his fingers and with his teeth.

In spite of the cold, Ritchie slept better in that terrible skeleton of the old Sachs house than he'd done in his apartment for months. The Nain had fought, of course it had, it was well known throughout history for its viciousness. But he must have prevailed because he was still alive even though his body hurt and he could see a spider's web of small scratches on his hands. Amazingly, to Ritchie, he'd had neither a stroke nor a heart attack. Maybe killing the Nain had some-how, magically, restored him to full health again.

But then what did he mean by "killing the Nain"? Now that he was sober, there was surely no more craziness and so therefore no more Nain? He had a bunch of small cuts all over the backs of his hands, but then he probably got those scrambling up into the old Sachs place. How he'd remembered where to find the house after so many years, especially drunk out of his gourd, was hard to work out – until he remembered. He'd followed the Nain. But then that wasn't really possible, because the Nain Rouge didn't exist. It was just a folk tale.

Ritchie stood up and felt the rotted floorboards splinter underneath his feet. If he remembered correctly, the Sachses had had a basement. Ritchie moved as carefully as he could until he felt he was on rather more solid footing. He'd just congratulated himself on surviving that particular ordeal when his eyes were caught by the sight of a tattered, miserable bundle underneath the remains of a great bay window. It was very, very red, and although Ritchie knew that it couldn't possibly be the Nain, because the Nain didn't really exist, he knew that he feared examining it.

For what seemed like hours he tried to formulate an excuse he could give to himself for not seeing what the bundle contained. But he couldn't. On the one hand he never wanted to see what was in there, while on the other he wanted to do that more than anything else in the world. If it was the Nain all his precon-ceptions about reality and the world he thought he lived in would be shattered. If it wasn't . . .

As quickly as he could, before fear consumed him, Ritchie reached down with one shaking hand and pulled the thing apart. When his hands came away, they were covered in thick, crimson arterial blood. In slow motion, or so it seemed at the time, the tiny head rolled out of the rags that had once constituted the little girl's tattered clothes and fell to the floor at Ritchie's feet. Her long, thick, bright red hair had been hiding the terrible stump that had been her neck, that he had hacked and hacked and hacked at until it came away in his hands . . .

Ritchie Carbone dropped to his knees as the thundering of his own blood threatened to deafen him. She had to be seven years old at the most! A tiny child, probably the daughter of some spaced-out junkie, playing with him, taunting him, being the Nain Rouge and . . . But had it been like that, or had *he* made *her* run?

He didn't know! He couldn't remember! Not like that, not in any detail! He looked down into her glassy-eyed, horrified little face, and the hammering in his head became a wild, discordant cacophony. Suddenly weak, Ritchie Carbone tipped forward and lay across the tiny body, twitching and unable to speak.

Later it snowed and so neither of them were discovered for well over a week. A ghastly and macabre tableau that the police, when they attended, could only speculate about.

Come the Vernal Equinox, the Marche du Nain Rouge still managed to banish the little horror for another year. Everyone saw the evil dwarf burn, in effigy, on a big bonfire in Cass Park, just minutes from where Carbone's old Coney Dog place used to be. A lot of the revellers said that it was a pity there was nowhere left in the Cass Corridor to get a decent Coney any more. But then they all agreed that it had probably been meant to be. Why, after all, should anyone get a lovely hotdog treat after burning even a mythical being, in effigy, to death?

A CHRISTMAS TRAGEDY

Baroness Orczy

Baroness Orczy (1865–1947) was a prolific Hungarian-English writer, best known for her *Scarlet Pimpernel* series. Her stories featuring Lady Molly of Scotland Yard and the Old Man in the Corner, who solves mysteries in a tea shop, are considered pioneering examples of short detective fiction.

1.

IT was a fairly merry Christmas party, although the surliness of our host somewhat marred the festivities. But imagine two such beautiful young women as my own dear lady and Margaret Ceely, and a Christmas Eve Cinderella in the beautiful ball-room at Clevere Hall, and you will understand that even Major Ceely's well-known cantankerous temper could not altogether spoil the merriment of a good, old-fashioned, festive gathering.

It is a far cry from a Christmas Eve party to a series of cattle-maiming outrages, yet I am forced to mention these now, for although they were ultimately proved to have no connection with the murder of the unfortunate Major, yet they were undoubtedly the means whereby the miscreant was enabled to accomplish the horrible deed with surety, swiftness, and – as it turned out afterwards – a very grave chance of immunity.

Everyone in the neighbourhood had been taking the keenest possible interest in those dastardly outrages against innocent animals. They were either the work of desperate ruffians who stick at nothing in order to obtain a few shillings, or else of madmen with weird propensities for purposeless crimes.

Once or twice suspicious characters had been seen lurking about in the fields, and on more than one occasion a cart was heard in the middle of the night driving away at furious speed. Whenever this occurred the discovery of a fresh outrage was sure to follow, but, so far, the miscreants had succeeded in baffling not only the police, but also the many farm hands who had formed themselves into a band of volunteer watchmen, determined to bring the cattle maimers to justice.

We had all been talking about these mysterious events during the dinner which preceded the dance at Clevere Hall; but later on, when the young people had assembled, and when the first strains of "The Merry Widow" waltz had set us aglow with prospective enjoyment, the unpleasant topic was wholly forgotten.

The guests went away early, Major Ceely, as usual, doing nothing to detain them; and by midnight all of us who were staying in the house had gone up to bed.

My dear lady and I shared a bedroom and dressing-room together, our windows giving on the front. Clevere Hall is, as you know, not very far from York, on the other side of Bishopthorpe, and is one of the finest old mansions in the neighbourhood, its only disadvantage being that, in spite of the gardens being very extensive in the rear, the front of the house lies very near the road.

It was about two hours after I had switched off the electric light and called out "Good-night" to my dear lady, that something roused me out of my first sleep. Suddenly I felt very wide-awake, and sat up in bed. Most unmistakably – though still from some considerable distance along the road – came the sound of a cart being driven at unusual speed.

Evidently my dear lady was also awake. She jumped out of bed and, drawing aside the curtains, looked out of the window. The same idea had, of course, flashed upon us both, at the very moment of waking: all the conversations anent the cattle-maimers and their cart, which we had heard since our arrival at Clevere, recurring to our minds simultaneously.

I had joined Lady Molly beside the window, and I don't know how many minutes we remained there in observation, not more than two probably, for anon the sound of the cart died away in the distance along a side road. Suddenly we were startled with a terrible cry of "Murder! Help! Help!" issuing from the other side of the house, followed by an awful, deadly silence. I stood there near the window shivering with terror, while my dear lady, having already turned on the light, was hastily slipping into some clothes.

The cry had, of course, aroused the entire household, but my dear lady was even then the first to get downstairs, and to reach the garden door at the back of the house, whence the weird and despairing cry had undoubtedly proceeded.

That door was wide open. Two steps lead from it to the terraced walk which borders the house on that side, and along these steps Major Ceely was lying, face downwards, with arms outstretched, and a terrible wound between his shoulder-blades.

A gun was lying close by – his own. It was easy to conjecture that he, too, hearing the rumble of the wheels, had run out, gun in hand, meaning, no doubt, to effect, or at least to help, in the capture of the escaping criminals. Someone had been lying in wait for him; that was obvious – someone who had perhaps waited and watched for this special opportunity for days, or even weeks, in order to catch the unfortunate man unawares.

Well, it were useless to recapitulate all the various little incidents which occurred from the moment when Lady Molly and the butler first lifted the Major's lifeless body from the terrace steps until that instant when Miss Ceely, with remarkable coolness and presence of mind, gave what details she could of the terrible event to the local police inspector and to the doctor, both hastily summoned.

These little incidents, with but slight variations, occur in every instance when a crime has been committed. The broad facts alone are of weird and paramount interest.

Major Ceely was dead. He had been stabbed with amazing sureness and terrible violence in the back. The weapon used must have been some sort of heavy, clasp knife. The murdered man was now lying in his own bedroom upstairs, even as the Christmas bells on that cold, crisp morning sent cheering echoes through the stillness of the air.

We had, of course, left the house, as had all the other guests. Everyone felt the deepest possible sympathy for the beautiful young girl who had been so full of the joy of living but a few hours ago, and was now the pivot round which revolved the weird shadow of tragedy, of curious suspicions and of an ever-growing mystery. But at such times all strangers, acquaintances, and even friends in a house, are only an additional burden to an already overwhelming load of sorrow and of trouble.

We took up our quarters at the "Black Swan," in York. The local superintendent, hearing that Lady Molly had been actually a guest at Clevere on the night of the murder, had asked her to remain in the neighbourhood.

There was no doubt that she could easily obtain the chiefs consent to assist the local police in the elucidation of this extraordinary crime. At this time both her reputation and her remarkable powers were at their zenith, and there was not a single member of the entire police force in the kingdom who would not have availed himself gladly of her help when confronted with a seemingly impenetrable mystery.

That the murder of Major Ceely threatened to become such no one could deny. In cases of this sort, when no robbery of any kind has accompanied the graver crime, it is the duty of the police and also of the coroner to try to find out, first and foremost, what possible motive there could be behind so cowardly an assault; and among motives, of course, deadly hatred, revenge, and animosity stand paramount.

But here the police were at once confronted with the terrible difficulty, not of discovering whether Major Ceely had an enemy at all, but rather which, of all those people who owed him a grudge, hated him sufficiently to risk hanging for the sake of getting him out of the way.

As a matter of fact, the unfortunate Major was one of those miserable people who seem to live in a state of perpetual enmity with everything and everybody. Morning, noon and night he grumbled, and when he did not grumble he quarreled either with his own daughter or with the people of his household, or with his neighbours.

I had often heard about him and his eccentric, disagreeable ways from Lady Molly, who had known him for many years. She – like everybody in the county who otherwise would have shunned the old man – kept up a semblance of friendship with him for the sake of the daughter.

Margaret Ceely was a singularly beautiful girl, and as the Major was reputed to be very wealthy, these two facts perhaps combined to prevent the irascible gentleman from living in quite so complete an isolation as he would have wished.

Mammas of marriageable young men vied with one another in their welcome to Miss Ceely at garden parties, dances and bazaars. Indeed, Margaret had been surrounded with admirers ever since she had come out of the schoolroom. Needless to say, the cantankerous Major received these pretenders to his daughter's hand not only with insolent disdain, but at times even with violent opposition.

In spite of this the moths fluttered round the candle, and amongst this venturesome tribe none stood out more prominently than Mr. Laurence Smethick, son of the M.P. for the Pakethorpe division. Some folk there were who vowed that the young people were secretly engaged, in spite of the fact that Margaret was an outrageous flirt and openly encouraged more than one of her crowd of adorers.

Be that as it may, one thing was very certain – namely, that Major Ceely did not approve of Mr. Smethick any more than he did of the others, and there had been more than one quarrel between the young man and his prospective father-in-law.

On that memorable Christmas Eve at Clevere none of us could fail to notice his absence; whilst Margaret, on the other hand, had shown marked predilection for the society of Captain Glynne, who, since the sudden death of his cousin, Viscount Heslington, Lord Ullesthorpe's only son (who was killed in the hunting field last October, if you remember), had become heir to the earldom and its £40,000 a year.

Personally, I strongly disapproved of Margaret's behaviour the night of the dance; her attitude with regard to Mr. Smethick – whose constant attendance on her had justified the rumour that they were engaged – being more than callous.

On that morning of December 24th – Christmas Eve, in fact – the young man had called at Clevere. I remember seeing him just as he was being shown into the boudoir downstairs. A few moments later the sound of angry voices rose with appalling distinctness from that room. We all tried not to listen, yet could not fail to hear Major Ceely's overbearing words of rudeness to the visitor, who, it seems, had merely asked to see Miss Ceely, and had been most unexpectedly confronted by the irascible and extremely disagreeable Major. Of course, the young man speedily lost his temper, too, and the whole incident ended with a very unpleasant quarrel between the two men in the hall, and with the Major peremptorily forbidding Mr. Smethick ever to darken his doors again.

On that night Major Ceely was murdered.

2.

Of course, at first, no one attached any importance to this weird coincidence. The very thought of connecting the idea of murder with that of the personality of a bright, good-looking young Yorkshireman like Mr. Smethick seemed, indeed, preposterous, and with one accord all of us who were practically witnesses to the quarrel between the two men, tacitly agreed to say nothing at all about it at the inquest, unless we were absolutely obliged to do so on oath.

In view of the Major's terrible temper, this quarrel, mind you, had not the importance which it otherwise would have had; and we all flattered ourselves that we had well succeeded in parrying the coroner's questions.

The verdict at the inquest was against some person or persons unknown; and I, for one, was very glad that young Smethick's name had not been mentioned in connection with this terrible crime.

Two days later the superintendent at Bishopthorpe sent an urgent telephonic message to Lady Molly, begging her to come to the police-station immediately. We had the use of a motor all the while that we stayed at the "Black Swan," and in less than ten minutes we were bowling along at express speed towards Bishopthorpe.

On arrival we were immediately shown into Superintendent Etty's private room behind the office. He was there talking with Danvers – who had recently come down from London. In a corner of the room, sitting very straight on a high-backed chair, was a youngish woman of the servant class, who, as we entered, cast a quick, and I thought suspicious, glance at us both.

She was dressed in a coat and skirt of shabby-looking black, and although her face might have been called good-looking – for she had fine, dark eyes – her entire appearance was distinctly repellent. It suggested slatternliness in an unusual degree; there were holes in her shoes and in her stockings, the sleeve of her coat was half unsewn, and the braid on her skirt hung in loops all round the bottom. She had very red and very coarse-looking hands, and undoubtedly there was a furtive expression in her eyes, which, when she began speaking, changed to one of defiance.

Etty came forward with great alacrity when my dear lady entered. He looked perturbed, and seemed greatly relieved at sight of her.

"She is the wife of one of the outdoor men at Clevere," he explained rapidly to Lady Molly, nodding in the direction of the young woman, "and she has come here with such a queer tale that I thought you would like to hear it."

"She knows something about the murder?" asked Lady Molly.

"Noa! I didn't say that!" here interposed the woman, roughly, "doan't you go and tell no lies, Master Inspector. I thought as how you might wish to know what my husband saw on the night when the Major was murdered, that's all; and I've come to tell you."

"Why didn't your husband come himself?" asked Lady Molly.

"Oh, Haggett ain't well enough – he –" she began explaining, with a careless shrug of the shoulders, "so to speak –"

"The fact of the matter is, my lady," interposed Etty, "this woman's husband is half-witted. I believe he is only kept on in the garden because he is very strong and can help with the digging. It is because his testimony is so little to be relied on that I wished to consult you as to how we should act in the matter."

"What is his testimony, then?"

"Tell this lady what you have just told us, Mrs. Haggett, will you?" said Etty, curtly.

Again that quick, suspicious glance shot into the woman's eyes. Lady Molly took the chair which Danvers had brought forward for her, and sat down opposite Mrs. Haggett, fixing her earnest, calm gaze upon her.

"There's not much to tell," said the woman, sullenly. "Haggett is certainly queer in his head sometimes – and when he is queer he goes wandering about the place of nights."

"Yes?" said my lady, for Mrs. Haggett had paused awhile and now seemed unwilling to proceed.

"Well!" she resumed with sudden determination, "he had got one of his queer fits on Christmas Eve, and didn't come in till long after midnight. He told me as how he'd seen a young gentleman prowling about the garden on the terrace side. He heard the cry of 'Murder' and 'Help' soon after that, and ran in home because he was frightened."

"Home?" asked Lady Molly, quietly, "where is home?"

"The cottage where we live. Just back of the kitchen garden."

"Why didn't you tell all this to the superintendent before?"

"Because Haggett only told me last night, when he seemed less queer-like. He is mighty silent when the fits are on him."

"Did he know who the gentleman was whom he saw?"

"No, ma'am – I don't suppose he did – leastways he wouldn't say – but –"

"Yes? But?"

"He found this in the garden yesterday," said the woman, holding out a screw of paper which apparently she had held tightly clutched up to now, "and maybe that's what brought Christmas Eve and the murder back to his mind."

Lady Molly took the thing from her, and undid the soiled bit of paper with her dainty fingers. The next moment she held up for Etty's inspection a beautiful ring composed of an exquisitely carved moonstone surrounded with diamonds of unusual brilliance.

At the moment the setting and the stones themselves were marred by scraps of sticky mud which clung to them; the ring obviously having lain on the ground, and perhaps been trampled on for some days, and then been only very partially washed.

"At any rate you can find out the ownership of the ring," commented my dear lady after awhile, in answer to Etty's silent attitude of expectancy. "There would be no harm in that."

Then she turned once more to the woman.

"I'll walk with you to your cottage, if I may," she said decisively, "and have a chat with your husband. Is he at home?"

I thought Mrs. Haggett took this suggestion with marked reluctance. I could well imagine, from her own personal appearance, that her home was most unlikely to be in a fit state for a lady's visit. However, she could, of course, do nothing but obey, and, after a few muttered words of grudging acquiescence, she rose from her chair and stalked towards the door, leaving my lady to follow as she chose.

Before going, however, she turned and shot an angry glance at Etty.

"You'll give me back the ring, Master Inspector," she said with her usual tone of sullen defiance. "'Findings is keepings' you know."

"I am afraid not," replied Etty, curtly; "but there's always the reward offered by Miss Ceely for information which would lead to the apprehension of her father's murderer. You may get that, you know. It is a hundred pounds."

"Yes! I knew that," she remarked dryly, as, without further comment, she finally went out of the room.

3.

My dear lady came back very disappointed from her interview with Haggett.

It seems that he was indeed half-witted – almost an imbecile, in fact, with but a few lucid intervals, of which this present day was one. But, of course, his testimony was practically valueless.

He reiterated the story already told by his wife, adding no details. He had seen a young gentleman roaming on the terraced walk on the night of the murder. He did not know who the young gentleman was. He was going homewards when he heard the cry of "Murder," and ran to his cottage because he was frightened. He picked up the ring yesterday in the perennial border below the terrace and gave it to his wife.

Two of these brief statements made by the imbecile were easily proved to be true, and my dear lady had ascertained this before she returned to me. One of the Clevere under-gardeners said he had seen Haggett running home in the small hours of that fateful Christmas morning. He himself had been on the watch for the cattle-maimers that night, and remembered the little circumstance quite plainly. He added that Haggett certainly looked to be in a panic.

Then Newby, another outdoor man at the Hall, saw Haggett pick up the ring in the perennial border and advised him to take it to the police.

Somehow, all of us who were so interested in that terrible Christmas tragedy felt strangely perturbed at all this. No names had been mentioned as yet, but whenever my dear lady and I looked at one another, or whenever we talked to Etty or Danvers, we all felt that a certain name, one particular personality, was lurking at the back of all our minds.

The two men, of course, had no sentimental scruples to worry them. Taking the Haggett story merely as a clue, they worked diligently on that, with the result that twenty-four hours later Etty appeared in our private room at the "Black Swan" and calmly informed us that he had just got a warrant out against Mr. Laurence Smethick on a charge of murder, and was on his way even now to effect the arrest.

"Mr. Smethick did *not* murder Major Ceely," was Lady Molly's firm and only comment when she heard the news.

"Well, my lady, that's as it may be!" rejoined Etty, speaking with that deference with which the entire force invariably addressed my dear lady; "but we have collected a sufficiency of evidence, at any rate, to justify the arrest, and, in my opinion, enough of it to hang any man. Mr. Smethick purchased the moonstone and diamond ring at Nicholson's in Coney Street about a week ago. He was seen abroad on Christmas Eve by several persons, loitering round the gates at Clevere Hall, somewhere about the time when the guests were leaving after the dance, and, again, some few moments after the first cry of 'Murder' had been heard. His own valet admits that his master did not get home that night until long after 2.0 a.m., whilst even Miss Granard here won't deny that there was a terrible quarrel between Mr. Smethick and Major Ceely less than twenty-four hours before the latter was murdered."

Lady Molly offered no remark to this array of facts which Etty thus pitilessly marshalled before us, but I could not refrain from exclaiming:

"Mr. Smethick is innocent, I am sure."

"I hope, for his sake, he may be," retorted Etty, gravely, "but somehow 'tis a pity that he don't seem able to give a good account of himself between midnight and two o'clock that Christmas morning."

"Oh!" I ejaculated, "what does he say about that?"

"Nothing," said the man dryly; "that's just the trouble."

Well, of course, as you who read the papers will doubtless remember, Mr. Laurence Smethick, son of Colonel Smethick, M.P., of Pakethorpe Hall, Yorks, was arrested on the charge of having murdered Major Ceely on the night of December 24th–25th, and, after the usual magisterial inquiry, was duly committed to stand his trial at the next York assizes.

I remember well that, throughout his preliminary ordeal, young Smethick bore himself like one who had given up all hope of refuting the terrible charges brought against him, and, I must say, the formidable number of witnesses which the police brought up against him more than explained that attitude.

Of course, Haggett was not called, but, as it happened, there were plenty of people to swear that Mr. Laurence Smethick was seen loitering round the gates of Clevere Hall after the guests had departed on Christmas Eve. The head gardener, who lives at the lodge, actually spoke to him, and Captain Glynne, leaning out of his brougham, was heard to exclaim:

"Hello, Smethick, what are you doing here at this time of night?"

And there were others, too.

To Captain Glynne's credit, be it here recorded, he tried his best to deny having recognized his unfortunate friend in the dark. Pressed by the magistrate, he said obstinately:

"I thought at the time that it was Mr. Smethick standing by the lodge gates, but on thinking the matter over I feel sure that I was mistaken."

On the other hand, what stood dead against young Smethick was, firstly, the question of the ring, and then the fact that he was seen in the immediate neighbourhood of Clevere, both at midnight and again at about two, when some men, who had been on the watch for the cattle-maimers, saw him walking away rapidly in the direction of Pakethorpe.

What was, of course, unexplainable and very terrible to witness was Mr. Smethick's obstinate silence with regard to his own movements during those fatal hours on that night. He did not contradict those who said that they had seen him at about midnight near the gates of Clevere, nor his own valet's statements as to the hour when he returned home. All he said was that he could not account for what he did between the time when the guests left the Hall and he himself went back to Pakethorpe. He realized the danger in which he stood, and what caused him to be silent about a matter which might mean life or death to him could not easily be conjectured.

The ownership of the ring he could not and did not dispute. He had lost it in the grounds of Clevere, he said. But the jeweller in Coney Street swore that he had sold the ring to Mr. Smethick on the 8th of December, whilst it was a well-known and an admitted fact that the young man had not openly been inside the gates of Clevere for over a fortnight before that.

On this evidence Laurence Smethick was committed for trial. Though the actual weapon with which the unfortunate Major had been stabbed had not been found, nor its ownership traced, there was such a vast array of circumstantial evidence against the young man that bail was refused.

He had, on the advice of his solicitor, Mr. Grayson – one of the ablest lawyers in York – reserved his defence, and on that miserable afternoon at the close of the year, we all filed out of the crowded court, feeling terribly depressed and anxious.

4.

My dear lady and I walked back to our hotel in silence. Our hearts seemed to weigh heavily within us. We felt mortally sorry for that good-looking young Yorkshireman, who, we were convinced, was innocent, yet at the same time seemed involved in a tangled web of deadly circumstances from which he seemed quite unable to extricate himself.

We did not feel like discussing the matter in the open streets, neither did we make any comment when presently, in a block in the traffic in Coney Street, we saw Margaret Ceely driving her smart dog-cart, whilst sitting beside her, and talking with great earnestness close to her ear, sat Captain Glynne.

She was in deep mourning, and had obviously been doing some shopping, for she was surrounded with parcels; so perhaps it was hypercritical to blame her. Yet somehow it struck me that just at the moment when there hung in the balance the life and honour of a man with whose name her own had oft been linked by popular rumour, it showed more than callous contempt for his welfare to be seen driving about with another man who, since his sudden access to fortune, had undoubtedly become a rival in her favours.

When we arrived at the "Black Swan," we were surprised to hear that Mr. Grayson had called to see my dear lady, and was upstairs waiting.

Lady Molly ran up to our sitting-room and greeted him with marked cordiality. Mr. Grayson is an elderly dry-looking man, but he looked visibly affected, and it was some time before he seemed able to plunge into the subject which had brought him hither. He fidgeted in his chair, and started talking about the weather.

"I am not here in a strictly professional capacity, you know," said Lady Molly presently, with a kindly smile and with a view to helping him out of his embarrassment. "Our police, I fear me, have an exaggerated view of my capacities, and the men here asked me unofficially to remain in the neighbourhood and to give them my advice if they should require it. Our chief is very lenient to me and has allowed me to stay. Therefore, if there is anything I can do –"

"Indeed, indeed there is!" ejaculated Mr. Grayson with sudden energy. "From all I hear, there is not another soul in the kingdom but you who can save this innocent man from the gallows."

My dear lady heaved a little sigh of satisfaction. She had all along wanted to have a more important finger in that Yorkshire pie.

"Mr. Smethick?" she said.

"Yes; my unfortunate young client," replied the lawyer. "I may as well tell you," he resumed after a slight pause, during which he seemed to pull himself together, "as briefly as possible what occurred on December 24th last and on the following Christmas morning. You will then understand the terrible plight in which my client finds himself, and how impossible it is for him to explain his actions on that eventful night. You will understand, also, why I have come to ask your help and your advice. Mr. Smethick considered himself engaged to Miss Ceely. The engagement had not been made public because of Major Ceely's anticipated opposition, but the young people had been very intimate, and many letters had passed between them. On the morning of the 24th Mr. Smethick called at the Hall, his intention then being merely to present his *fiancée* with the ring you know of. You remember the unfortunate *contretemps* that occurred: I mean the unprovoked quarrel sought by Major Ceely with my poor client, ending with the irascible old man forbidding Mr. Smethick the house.

"My client walked out of Clevere feeling, as you may well imagine, very wrathful; on the doorstep, just as he was leaving, he met Miss Margaret, and told her very briefly what had occurred. She took the matter very lightly at first, but finally became more serious, and ended the brief interview with the request that, since he could not come to the dance after what had occurred, he should come and see her afterwards, meeting her in the gardens soon after midnight. She would not take the ring from him then, but talked a good deal of sentiment about Christmas morning, asking him to bring the ring to her at night, and also the letters which she had written him. Well – you can guess the rest."

Lady Molly nodded thoughtfully.

"Miss Ceely was playing a double game," continued Mr. Grayson, earnestly. "She was determined to break off all relationship with Mr. Smethick, for she had transferred her volatile affections to Captain Glynne, who had lately become heir to an earldom and £40,000 a year. Under the guise of sentimental twaddle she got my unfortunate client to meet her at night in the grounds of Clevere and to give up to her the letters which might have compromised her in the eyes of her new lover. At two o'clock a.m. Major Ceely was murdered by one of his numerous enemies; as to which I do not know, nor does Mr. Smethick. He had just parted from Miss Ceely at the very moment when the first cry of 'Murder' roused Clevere from its slumbers. This she could confirm if she only would, for the two were still in sight of each other, she inside the gates, he just a little way down the road. Mr. Smethick saw Margaret Ceely run rapidly back towards the house. He waited about a little while, half hesitating what to do; then he reflected that his presence might be embarrassing, or even compromising to her whom, in spite of all, he still loved dearly; and knowing that there were plenty of men in and about the house to render what assistance was necessary, he finally turned his steps and went home a broken-hearted man, since she had given him the go-by, taken her letters away, and flung contemptuously into the mud the ring he had bought for her."

The lawyer paused, mopping his forehead and gazing with whole-souled earnestness at my lady's beautiful, thoughtful face.

"Has Mr. Smethick spoken to Miss Ceely since?" asked Lady Molly, after a while.

"No; but I did," replied the lawyer.

"What was her attitude?"

"One of bitter and callous contempt. She denies my unfortunate client's story from beginning to end; declares that she never saw him after she bade him 'good-morning' on the doorstep of Clevere Hall, when she heard of his unfortunate quarrel with her father. Nay, more; she scornfully calls the whole tale a cowardly attempt to shield a dastardly crime behind a still more dastardly libel on a defenceless girl."

We were all silent now, buried in thought which none of us would have cared to translate into words. That the *impasse* seemed indeed hopeless no one could deny.

The tower of damning evidence against the unfortunate young man had indeed been built by remorseless circumstances with no faltering hand.

Margaret Ceely alone could have saved him, but with brutal indifference she preferred the sacrifice of an innocent man's life and honour to that of her own chances of a brilliant marriage. There are such women in the world; thank God I have never met any but that one!

Yet am I wrong when I say that she alone could save the unfortunate young man, who throughout was behaving with such consummate gallantry, refusing to give his own explanation of the events that occurred on that Christmas morning, unless she chose first to tell the tale. There was one present now in the dingy little room at the "Black Swan" who could disentangle that weird skein of coincidences, if any human being not gifted with miraculous powers could indeed do it at this eleventh hour.

She now said, gently:

"What would you like me to do in this matter, Mr. Grayson? And why have you come to me rather than to the police?"

"How can I go with this tale to the police?" he ejaculated in obvious despair. "Would they not also look upon it as a dastardly libel on a woman's reputation? We have no proofs, remember, and Miss Ceely denies the whole story from first to last. No, no!" he exclaimed with wonderful fervour. "I came to you because I have heard of your marvellous gifts, your extraordinary intuition. Someone murdered Major Ceely! It was not my old friend Colonel Smethick's son. Find out who it was, then! I beg of you, find out who it was!"

He fell back in his chair broken down with grief. With inexpressible gentleness Lady Molly went up to him and placed her beautiful white hand on his shoulder.

"I will do my best, Mr. Grayson," she said simply.

5.

We remained alone and singularly quiet the whole of that evening. That my dear lady's active brain was hard at work I could guess by the brilliance of her eyes, and that sort of absolute stillness in her person through which one could almost feel the delicate nerves vibrating.

The story told her by the lawyer had moved her singularly. Mind you, she had always been morally convinced of young Smethick's innocence, but in her the professional woman always fought hard battles against the sentimentalist, and in this instance the overwhelming circumstantial evidence and the conviction of her superiors had forced her to accept the young man's guilt as something out of her ken.

By his silence, too, the young man had tacitly confessed; and if a man is perceived on the very scene of a crime, both before it has been committed and directly afterwards; if something admittedly belonging to him is found within three yards of where the murderer must have stood; if, added to this, he has had a bitter quarrel with the victim, and can give no account of his actions or whereabouts during the fatal time, it were vain to cling to optimistic beliefs in that same man's innocence.

But now matters had assumed an altogether different aspect. The story told by Mr. Smethick's lawyer had all the appearance of truth. Margaret Ceely's character, her callousness on the very day when her late *fiancé* stood in the dock, her quick transference of her affections to the richer man, all made the account of the events on Christmas night as told by Mr. Grayson extremely plausible.

No wonder my dear lady was buried in thought.

"I shall have to take the threads up from the beginning, Mary," she said to me the following morning, when after breakfast she appeared in her neat coat and skirt, with hat and gloves, ready to go out, "so, on the whole, I think I will begin with a visit to the Haggetts."

"I may come with you, I suppose?" I suggested meekly.

"Oh, yes!" she rejoined carelessly.

Somehow I had an inkling that the carelessness of her mood was only on the surface. It was not likely that she – my sweet, womanly, ultra-feminine, beautiful lady – should feel callously on this absorbing subject.

We motored down to Bishopthorpe. It was bitterly cold, raw, damp, and foggy. The chauffeur had some difficulty in finding the cottage, the "home" of the imbecile gardener and his wife.

There was certainly not much look of home about the place. When, after much knocking at the door, Mrs. Haggett finally opened it, we saw before us one of the most miserable, slatternly places I think I ever saw.

In reply to Lady Molly's somewhat curt inquiry, the woman said that Haggett was in bed, suffering from one of his "fits."

"That is a great pity," said my dear lady, rather unsympathetically, I thought, "for I must speak with him at once."

"What is it about?" asked the woman, sullenly. "I can take a message."

"I am afraid not," rejoined my lady. "I was asked to see Haggett personally."

"By whom, I'd like to know," she retorted, now almost insolently.

"I dare say you would. But you are wasting precious time. Hadn't you better help your husband on with his clothes? This lady and I will wait in the parlour."

After some hesitation the woman finally complied, looking very sulky the while.

We went into the miserable little room wherein not only grinding poverty but also untidiness and dirt were visible all round. We sat down on two of the cleanest-looking chairs, and waited whilst a colloquy in subdued voices went on in the room over our heads.

The colloquy, I may say, seemed to consist of agitated whispers on one part, and wailing complaints on the other. This was followed presently by some thuds and much shuffling, and presently Haggett, looking uncared-for, dirty, and unkempt, entered the parlour, followed by his wife.

He came forward, dragging his ill-shod feet and pulling nervously at his forelock.

"Ah!" said my lady, kindly; "I am glad to see you down, Haggett, though I am afraid I haven't very good news for you."

"Yes, miss!" murmured the man, obviously not quite comprehending what was said to him.

"I represent the workhouse authorities," continued Lady Molly, "and I thought we could arrange for you and your wife to come into the Union tonight, perhaps."

"The Union?" here interposed the woman, roughly. "What do you mean? We ain't going to the Union?"

"Well! but since you are not staying here," rejoined my lady, blandly, "you will find it impossible to get another situation for your husband in his present mental condition."

"Miss Ceely won't give us the go-by," she retorted defiantly.

"She might wish to carry out her late father's intentions," said Lady Molly with seeming carelessness.

"The Major was a cruel, cantankerous brute," shouted the woman with unpremeditated violence. "Haggett had served him faithfully for twelve years, and –"

She checked herself abruptly, and cast one of her quick, furtive glances at Lady Molly.

Her silence now had become as significant as her outburst of rage, and it was Lady Molly who concluded the phrase for her.

"And yet he dismissed him without warning," she said calmly.

"Who told you that?" retorted the woman.

"The same people, no doubt, who declare that you and Haggett had a grudge against the Major for this dismissal."

"That's a lie," asserted Mrs. Haggett, doggedly; "we gave information about Mr. Smethick having killed the Major because –"

"Ah," interrupted Lady Molly, quickly, "but then Mr. Smethick did not murder Major Ceely, and your information therefore was useless!"

"Then who killed the Major, I should like to know?"

Her manner was arrogant, coarse, and extremely unpleasant. I marvelled why my dear lady put up with it, and what was going on in that busy brain of hers. She looked quite urbane and smiling, whilst I wondered what in the world she meant by this story of the workhouse and the dismissal of Haggett.

"Ah, that's what none of us know!" she now said lightly; "some folks say it was your husband."

"They lie!" she retorted quickly, whilst the imbecile, evidently not understanding the drift of the conversation, was mechanically stroking his red mop of hair and looking helplessly all round him.

"He was home before the cries of 'Murder' were heard in the house," continued Mrs. Haggett.

"How do you know?" asked Lady Molly, quickly. .

"How do I know?"

"Yes; you couldn't have heard the cries all the way to this cottage – why, it's over half a mile from the Hall!"

"He was home, I say," she repeated with dogged obstinacy.

"You sent him?"

"He didn't do it –"

"No one will believe you, especially when the knife is found."

"What knife?"

"His clasp knife, with which he killed Major Ceely," said Lady Molly, quietly; "see, he has it in his hand now."

And with a sudden, wholly unexpected gesture she pointed to the imbecile, who in an aimless way had prowled round the room whilst this rapid colloquy was going on.

The purport of it all must in some sort of way have found an echo in his enfeebled brain. He wandered up to the dresser whereon lay the remnants of that morning's breakfast, together with some crockery and utensils.

In that same half-witted and irresponsible way he had picked up one of the knives and now was holding it out towards his wife, whilst a look of fear spread over his countenance.

"I can't do it, Annie, I can't – you'd better do it," he said.

There was dead silence in the little room. The woman Haggett stood as if turned to stone. Ignorant and superstitious as she was, I suppose that the situation had laid hold of her nerves, and that she felt that the finger of a relentless Fate was even now being pointed at her.

The imbecile was shuffling forward, closer and closer to his wife, still holding out the knife towards her and murmuring brokenly:

"I can't do it. You'd better, Annie – you'd better –"

He was close to her now, and all at once her rigidity and nerve-strain gave way; she gave a hoarse cry, and snatching the knife from the poor wretch, she rushed at him ready to strike.

Lady Molly and I were both young, active and strong; and there was nothing of the squeamish *grande dame* about my dear lady when quick action was needed. But even then we had some difficulty in dragging Annie Haggett away from her miserable husband. Blinded with fury, she was ready to kill the man who had betrayed her. Finally, we succeeded in wresting the knife from her.

You may be sure that it required some pluck after that to sit down again quietly and to remain in the same room with this woman, who already had one crime upon her conscience, and with this weird, half-witted creature who kept on murmuring pitiably:

"You'd better do it, Annie –"

Well, you've read the account of the case, so you know what followed. Lady Molly did not move from that room until she had obtained the woman's full confession. All she did for her own protection was to order me to open the window and to blow the police whistle which she handed to me. The police-station fortunately was not very far, and sound carried in the frosty air.

She admitted to me afterwards that it had been foolish, perhaps, not to have brought Etty or Danvers with her, but she was supremely anxious not to put the woman on the alert from the very start, hence her circumlocutory speeches anent the workhouse, and Haggett's probable dismissal.

That the woman had had some connection with the crime, Lady Molly, with her keen intuition, had always felt; but as there was no witness to the murder itself, and all circumstantial evidence was dead against young Smethick, there was only one chance of successful discovery, and that was the murderer's own confession.

If you think over the interview between my dear lady and the Haggetts on that memorable morning, you will realise how admirably Lady Molly had led up to the weird finish. She would not speak to the woman unless Haggett was present, and she felt sure that as soon as the subject of the murder cropped up, the imbecile would either do or say something that would reveal the truth.

Mechanically, when Major Ceely's name was mentioned, he had taken up the knife. The whole scene recurred to his tottering mind. That the Major had summarily dismissed him recently was one of those bold guesses which Lady Molly was wont to make.

That Haggett had been merely egged on by his wife, and had been too terrified at the last to do the deed himself was no surprise to her, and hardly one to me, whilst the fact that the woman ultimately wreaked her own passionate revenge upon the unfortunate Major was hardly to be wondered at, in the face of her own coarse and elemental personality.

Cowed by the quickness of events, and by the appearance of Danvers and Etty on the scene, she finally made full confession.

She was maddened by the Major's brutality, when with rough, cruel words he suddenly turned her husband adrift, refusing to give him further employment. She herself had great ascendency over the imbecile, and had drilled him into a part of hate and of revenge. At first he had seemed ready and willing to obey. It was arranged that he was to watch on the terrace every night until such time as an alarm of the recurrence of the cattle-maiming outrages should lure the Major out alone.

This effectually occurred on Christmas morning, but not before Haggett, frightened and pusillanimous, was ready to flee rather than to accomplish the villainous deed. But Annie Haggett, guessing perhaps that he would shrink from the crime at the last, had also kept watch every night. Picture the prospective murderer watching and being watched!

When Haggett came across his wife he deputed her to do the deed herself.

I suppose that either terror of discovery or merely desire for the promised reward had caused the woman to fasten the crime on another.

The finding of the ring by Haggett was the beginning of that cruel thought which, but for my dear lady's marvellous powers, would indeed have sent a brave young man to the gallows.

Ah, you wish to know if Margaret Ceely is married? No! Captain Glynne cried off. What suspicions crossed his mind I cannot say; but he never proposed to Margaret, and now she is in Australia – staying with an aunt, I think – and she has sold Clevere Hall.

A QUESTION OF FAITH

Edith Pargeter

Edith Pargeter (1913–1995) is better known by her pseudonym Ellis Peters, under which she created the medieval monk detective Brother Cadfael in *A Morbid Taste for Bones* (1977). An expert in history and the classics, Pargeter published widely across several genres and was awarded an OBE in 1994.

The last train was due at 9.50, and the walk from the station to the prison gate took about a quarter of an hour. From the moment when he heard the train whistling its way distantly round the curve, the Governor became a little distracted, and his replies to his friend's questions shrank to monosyllables. When the clock pushed an indifferent hand over the rim of ten and caught its breath for the chime, he began to listen with an intent and sharply-focused eagerness which made conversation impossible.

Wyndham sat back into silence and watched him steadily for several minutes, but whatever it was he waited to hear, the night still did not provide it.

He was young to be in charge of a regional training prison, and in himself he was as much an experiment as the closed stone world he ruled. To be three years in office and still on trial is a tightrope act for any man to have to perform. The Governor showed the signs, Wyndham thought, studying him affectionately after two years of absence, in his too finely drawn thinness, the instant passion of his reactions to sound and movement, his burning weariness of eye.

No doubt they had argued, when he was appointed, that a young and enthusiastic man was needed for such a social revolution as this, a man with a vocation, as well as legal qualifications and academic honours. This kind of life ate men. The Governor was a keeper who fed himself daily to his animals, but, like all sacramental meals, his substance remained inexhaustible.

The clock smoothed its face as complacently as a cat, and now it said a quarter past ten, and still the expected, whatever it was, did not happen. The Governor leaned back from the fireside chair to take the telephone from its cradle.

'Excuse me, won't you? One of my fellows was due in by that train. Hullo, Willetts, has Bayford checked in yet?' His face mirrored the negative reply. 'Yes, I heard it – it seemed to be well on time. He may have missed the connection at Lowbridge. No doubt he'll be in later on. No, we'll give him a few hours grace. I'll call you.'

He hung up, and sat frowning into the fire for a moment under his tired eye-lids.

'One of your home leavers?' asked Wyndham.

'Yes. He has two months of a five-year sentence left to run, and he's been home on the usual ice-breaking trip. It saves them from dying of gate fever – terror of not being wanted back, not finding any place waiting for them.'

'Supposing one of them failed to report back?'

'No one ever has.'

'What's the matter, then? Are you afraid this fellow might be the first?'

'Oh, no. I have absolute faith in him,' said the Governor simply.

'It's a lucky man who can say that of his best friend. What's he like, this chap Bayford?'

'Oh, young – unlucky – unhappy. His care history reads like a tract for the times. He's illegitimate, never knew his father. Mother was never much use to him. When he was three she got the county authorities to take the kid, and went more or less candidly on the streets. Married some miserably bad lot of her own calibre, and when Harry was in his last year of school and looked as if he might be profitable, they suddenly began taking an interest in him.

'You'd hardly credit,' said the Governor, in a detached tone which was belied by his shadowed eyes, 'how easy it is for worthless parents to win their children back again. Every boy wants his mother, I suppose he'll go to quite a lot of trouble to shut his eyes to the suspicion that she might not be worth having. And he'd never been officially taken from her, she had only to claim him and he was hers. Only the boy himself could have saved himself, and then only if he'd been the most exceptional of boys. They lived on him, and neglected him, and knocked him about for three years, and by that time he could hardly keep his eyes shut any longer.

'So he looked for a bit of companionship and pleasure somewhere else, and found it in the wrong places, like so many others. At eighteen he went to Borstal. He'd already been on probation and made a mess of that. The magistrate went out of his way to lecture him about what the younger generation owes to its elders, and how it's letting them down.' A faint smile touched his lips at the thought.

'At twenty-one he got five years for his share in a gang job. The only piece of luck he ever had was that the gun failed to go off, otherwise it might have been murder. Two years ago he was transferred to us.'

'And you think you've done well with him? He doesn't sound desperately promising material to me.'

'He's earned full remission since he's been here. It's been hard going, but it was worth it.'

The Governor recalled with a flash of intense pain the closed, inimical face, so young, so withdrawn, and the burning of the half-veiled eyes, terribly resigned yet more terribly vulnerable, which had confronted him at his first interview with Harry Bayford.

'He was intact morally, you see. He'd understood everything he did; there was a mind there to appeal to. All that was really necessary was to be utterly honest oneself – not always an easy thing to do.'

'I'm not completely sold on this idea of agreeing with young thugs who plead that the whole world's against them.' Wyndham softened his dissension with a smile, for they were old friends.

'He never pleaded anything, he just endured us. But the whole world *has* been against him, you know. I did what might have been the wrong thing with another man,' confessed the Governor. 'I grew fond of him. With Harry it was the right thing. It surprised him when he'd thought he was past surprise, and it disarmed him when he'd thought his armour was complete. Generosity is Harry's vice and virtue – he pays you back double whatever you offer him, whether it's trust or violence.'

'Well, if you have absolute faith in him, what are you afraid of?'

The Governor did not attempt to deny the anxiety which filled him, but only looked up under his thin hand with a wry smile, and said: 'To tell you the truth, I have not quite so absolute a trust in society as I have in Bayford.'

'I can quite see,' said Wyndham, laughing, 'why you still have the twenty-foot wall. It's to defend your children from the world outside.'

A quarter to eleven, and still nothing, no ringing of the telephone bell, no knock at the door, to break the tension of this waiting. Wyndham wondered if it was like this every time one of the prisoners went out to take his first distrustful look at the world again, and how, if it was, his friend's constitution could stand the strain. He wished a message would come soon, before the Governor disintegrated before his eyes.

'It would be a serious blow to you, apart from your concern for the boy himself, if he should fail to report back,' he said sympathetically.

'There are plenty of people and organizations waiting for something like that to happen,' admitted the Governor. 'I doubt if one lapse could provide enough capital for them to damage us, but I'd rather not give them the chance to try.'

He started up abruptly from his chair as the telephone rang, and scooped it from its cradle with an eagerness he did not attempt to disguise. 'This will be him. Excuse me!'

He identified himself briefly, and then sat listening, the relief in his face stiffening into a new and grave anxiety. He was silent for several minutes with the receiver at his ear, and then he said sharply: 'Please hold everything until I get out there myself. Yes, I'll come at once. I should appreciate it very much if you'll let me talk to him.'

Wyndham was on his feet and at his friend's elbow as he pressed down the rest and held it there for a minute. 'What's happened? Not an accident?'

'No. No accident.' He lifted the receiver again. 'Get my car out at once, please. I shall be away a couple of hours or so. No, thanks, I'm driving myself.'

And to Wyndham he continued, as he hung up once more: 'The police picked him up for housebreaking at Hampton's Corner, about an hour ago. Householder caught him on the premises, apparently. He's gone to earth inside himself, and won't say anything. I've got to go.'

'But my dear chap, what can you do about it? If he's let you down like that.'

'I'm not convinced that he has. That's why I've got to go.'

'But Hampton's Corner – that isn't on his way here from Lowbridge at all, it's on the Stapleton road. And if he was actually caught in the house.'

'Yes, all that! The place is ten miles out of his way; the police are sure of their man. Only I'm sure of my man, too. But even if I believed we'd got all the facts, I should still have to go. Look, don't wait up for me, old man, I may be some time. I'm sorry your first night here had to be broken up like this.'

'Like me to come with you?' offered Wyndham, out of sheer unwillingness to see him drive off alone with his bitter disappointment.

'That's uncommonly kind of you, Tom, but no, thanks, I'd better go alone. Wish me luck!'

But so far as belief in his luck was concerned, he knew that his friend's wish was fruitless. And as he slid behind the wheel of the big car and drove it out through the slowly unfolding gates in the high wall, he knew that he was the one creature in the world who believed in Harry Bayford's innocence of all intent to offend. His loneliness did not frighten him; he was used to being alone. No wife, no family, no hierarchies of friends; he belonged to his vocation more exclusively, more rigidly, than any monastic to his cloister.

In his anxiety to have all the details, to confront and confute them, he drove at considerably more than thirty even through the town. Speed was terribly important, for he was like a vital witness trying to forestall an execution; all he knew was that Harry Bayford, whatever his past record, would not, for any inducement which could have been offered him, have committed a crime this night. But he knew that so well that it was all the evidence he needed. Others, the sceptical Stapleton police for instance, who did not love the new prison methods, would need a great deal more convincing.

The little town was half-asleep already, but within the police station there was a bright, gratified wakefulness. They were waiting for him, they ushered him in at once to the Superintendent, who tempered the triumph of his smile with a sympathetic regret, so far as he was able, and told him the whole story.

'It's a large house, right on the corner there, where the lane from the junction comes out on the high road. The constable going off duty was cycling by the gates when he heard somebody blowing a police whistle, and he dived back and in at the gate just in time to see this fellow Bayford vaulting out of a ground-floor window, left of the front door – it's the living room. The lights were on in the room, and the householder – he's our local bank manager, name of Simpson – came to the window after him, still blowing away for help. Our man collared Bayford, and between them they got him back into the house.

'This was just about ten o'clock, according to the constable. Simpson says he was just putting on some coffee in the kitchen, which is at the back of the house, and waiting for his wife to come home from a bridge party at a friend's up the road, and when it struck ten he thought he'd stroll along and meet her – it's only a hundred yards or so. As he came through the hall he heard somebody moving about softly in the living room in the dark, and having his suspicions he went and got the whistle before he crashed into the room and switched the lights on.

'Bayford was at the bureau, but as soon as the lights went on he streaked for the window, which was open. Obviously he got in that way. That's all. Nothing missing, so far as Simpson's been able to judge yet – seems he was interrupted too soon.'

The Governor, balancing his hat with absent care upon his crossed knees, asked in a mild tone: 'And what does Bayford say?'

'Hardly a word. At first he did babble that he wasn't stealing, that he hadn't taken anything, but by the time they got him inside again he'd turned dumb and sulky. All he'll say now is what's the use, nobody's going to believe him. He's made up his mind he's had it, you know, sir. I'm sorry, this is a bad letdown for you. We got his name and record from the papers and letters he had on him, and that's why we got on to you. But he won't add anything. We've been trying to get him to tell his side of it for half an hour now.'

The Governor nodded resigned understanding of this silence.

'I appreciate your calling me, and letting me butt in like this. I'd like to ask you to try and keep an open mind about Bayford. That's all I'm asking. I don't expect you to take my word for it that if he says he wasn't there to steal he's telling you the simple truth. But I will ask you to take my word for it that if he says that to me, *I* shall believe it. And I'll ask you to do us both the justice of assuming that I have solid reasons for feeling so sure of him. I've known him intimately for two years now, and what I feel about him is the result of experience, not sentiment.'

'That's understood, sir. I respect your evidence, and in return you'll realize that I have my duty to do, on the facts as I know them.'

'Good! Would it be in order for me to talk to him alone?'

'Certainly, if you think it's any good. He's in the next room.'

'But first,' said the Governor, checking at the door, 'may I point out one thing? This boy was on his way back to us after a five-day home leave. He should have caught the connection at Lowbridge at 9.25, and by his being here at all he must have fulfilled his bargain up to that point. When he didn't arrive I assumed, as I'm still assuming, that he missed that connection. Now he turns up here, ten miles out of his way by your reckoning, but, by mine, on the nearest point on the road between Stapleton and Mordenfield. There's a bus from Stapleton at 9.45. My estimate is that when he missed his train he begged a lift on the first car he saw heading in the direction of the Stapleton road, to try and catch that bus.'

'It would make a good story,' agreed the Superintendent, solidly entrenched against believing in it.

'In which case it should be possible to trace the car.'

'If he'll give us a description, we'll try. But I'm afraid he's going to need more that that.'

'That's evidently what he thinks, too,' said the Governor, and went into the room where the boy was.

His heart chilled with dismay at the sight of him. He was sitting compactly and resignedly upon an upright chair, his feet planted neatly together, his hands clenched tightly upon the brim of the new trilby in his lap, his eyes roving with narrowed, stoical despair from the constable who kept him company to the window and the door. These were not possible means of escape to him now, they were tunnels to the other, the forfeited world.

He had receded far down the subterranean passage from freedom to the dark anonymity out of which he had been coaxed with so much pain, and so extraordinary a delight, during the last two years. The thin, intense face, lately wildly responsive to every recognition, had congealed into a formal mask of withdrawal and loneliness, as though he defied anyone ever to touch him again; but the alert eyes were frenzied with despair.

Even when he saw the Governor enter his expression did not change; only the eyes fixed on the newcomer hopelessly, almost indifferently, as though from a great distance.

This was the very face they had seen turned upon them when first he came to Mordenfield. Could everything be undone in one hour, like this?

The constable looked over the Governor's shoulder into the Superintendent's face, and got up and went out, closing the door after him.

The Governor said: 'Hullo, Harry.' He had never called him that before, and after tonight he probably never would again, but there is a time for everything, and now it seemed so inevitable that he did not even notice it. 'You'd better tell me all about it,' he said. 'I'd tell you some of it myself, but they might not like it that way round, so you tell me.'

The boy said in a slightly lame voice, as though the effort of silence had already partly disabled him from speech: 'I bet they've told you all that matters to them. I got picked up in a house where I'd no right to be. What more do you want?'

The Governor lifted a chair, and set it opposite to the one on which Harry sat. When he found himself compelled to meet someone else's eyes so closely, the boy turned his head away, but the gesture, instead of being defiant, was indescribably revealing, and more like a convulsion of pain than a gesture of rejection.

'I want to know *why* you went in there,' said the Governor. 'I could make a guess, but they wouldn't be interested in my guesses. So you tell me. Why did you go into the house? Because, of course, it wasn't to steal.'

The head turned again, abruptly, the eyes flared wide. 'I haven't said it wasn't, have I?' His thin hands, nervous as a girl's, tightened violently on the brim of the hat.

'You don't have to say it. I know it.'

'You think you can kid me with a confidence trick like that?' said the boy unpleasantly. 'I've had all that once. I'm over it.' But he began to shake, and had to dig his heels into the floor and his teeth into his lip to suppress the weakness.

The Governor didn't argue; he said instead: 'You missed your connection at Lowbridge, and went up the lane to see if you could hop a car to Hampton's Corner, to try and catch a bus. I don't suppose you made a note of the number – why should you? – but you could describe the car and the driver. It should be possible to find him, and the station staff will be able to confirm how you missed your train. All right, so we've got you to Hampton's Corner. The bus had beaten you to it, after all, and you were still eight miles from home.'

The boy had begun to breathe hard, and the frozen calm of his face was shaken with painful tremors of hope.

'It wasn't a car, it was a van. A bloke from the beet factory – they work all night in the season.'

'Better still! Finding the man will be easy, now we know just where to look. Go on from there, then. You were eight miles from home, and getting worried, because it was getting round to the time when we would be expecting you, and you didn't want us to think you'd welshed on us—'

Harry shut his eyes and rolled his head back as if from a punch. 'What's the use? They won't believe me! Nobody'll ever believe me! I could have told them, but what the hell's the good? Let me alone, can't you? I was all set to take it, and you come beggaring in here and unwind me—'

'You wanted us to know,' said the Governor patiently, as if there had been no interruption, 'that you were on your way, before you walked the eight miles, or hitched a lift if you were lucky. You're making me tell it all for you, Harry. You might make just a small contribution yourself.'

The thin hands came up and clenched the short dark hair at the temples and out of the trembling mouth speech came pouring in jerks and recoveries, like arterial blood.

'I wanted to phone you and tell you why I was late – and that I was coming as quick as I could. There's no call box all along that road, and anyhow, I didn't have any coppers. I saw the phone wires went to that house, so I went up to the door and rang the bell, to ask if I could use their line – but nobody answered, and there was this room, with the curtains not drawn, and a bit of fire still in – and I could see the phone in there on top of the bureau. I tried the window – I know it was daft. I wish I'd never touched it, but I did – and it went up, and I thought, it'll only take me a minute, so I shinned over the sill and went and started to dial. I know I shouldn't have gone in – but it looked so easy, and there was no-where else to ring from, and I thought for sure there was nobody in. They never answered the door, and all the front lights was off.

'But I no sooner got a couple of numbers dialled when I heard him in the hall, and I put the phone back, quick, and stood still, hoping he'd go away. I knew then I'd been a fool – I was scared to go out and come clean to him. And the next minute he was in on me, whistling like mad, and the lights all on, and – and I run for it. With my record, what else could I do but run? Nobody's going to believe *that* for a tale – not from me! With my record, what else could I do but run?'

Listening to him bleed, himself weak with an exquisite, singing relief, the Governor thought: Now it's up to me to get him out of this!

And he found time, between the pulsations of his gratitude, to be deeply afraid; for it was certainly he who had stripped the boy's armour of loneliness from him, and unless something better could be put in its place he might die of the cold.

To know truth when you hear it is one thing, to prove it to the police quite another. And what kind of evidence had he to offer, except the station staff at Lowbridge, and the van driver, though the latter was certainly a godsend? He prayed that Harry might have talked about himself to this chance acquaintance in the dark, but he knew how unlikely that was.

No, it was up to him to put out his hand, and pluck proof out of the air. If one has faith enough, it ought to be possible, and he had claimed an absolute faith. His mind began to read over, word for word, all the things Harry had told him, looking with particular industry for the minute revelations he did not know he had made.

'You must repeat all that to the Superintendent, just as you've told it to me.'

'What's the use? There's nobody to bear me out, after I got out of the van. And *he* doesn't know but what I come there just to lift whatever was lying around.'

'You'll tell him, all the same. Do as I ask you. You know you can rely on me.'

He did not add, but he knew that Harry heard: 'As I knew I could rely on you.'

'I am promising him a miracle,' he thought to himself, 'and he believes me. And now I have got to produce one.'

He went to the door and opened it. The Superintendent looked up knowingly from his desk, rather surprised, even rather disappointed, that the enthusiast should have given up so soon.

'I wonder if you would hear Bayford's story now? He's ready to tell it.'

The boy went through it again almost word for word, his eyes returning always to the Governor's face, and resting there with such trust and such terror that it seemed altogether too much for one man to carry.

'We'll certainly make enquiries for the driver of the factory van,' said the Superintendent at the end of the recital. 'For the rest of the story, it holds together, but you'll allow there's been time for thinking it out, and I should have been more impressed if it had been told immediately. It's a pity there can't be independent confirmation. I'm sure you accept it, sir, and I take it for granted you're in good faith in urging it upon me. But I have to deal with evidence, and you'll agree there's very little possibility of finding any to support this version of what happened.'

The Governor said, aware of the eyes which held fast to him as to life: 'I think I can supply you with two pieces of evidence which will go a very long way towards confirming Bayford's story. I start with the advantage, you see, of having no doubts at all about his honesty in the matter, so I can explore the details of what he's told us even more closely than he can, in his present state. You know this man Simpson? He isn't, by any chance, deaf?'

'Good Lord, no,' said the Superintendent, astonished. 'He hears as well as any of us.'

'And he was in the house when it was entered, so he must have been there when Harry rang the bell. Make no mistake, if he says he rang the bell and got no answer, that's exactly what happened. I don't expect you to be sure, but I am sure. Therefore I think it very probable that you can tell Mr Simpson something he doesn't know about his own house. The front door bell is out of order. At least you can send a constable round to test it, can't you?'

The Superintendent gave him a long look of mingled patience and derision. 'We can settle it from here. I'll ring up Simpson, and ask him to try it.'

'But I'd rather the constable went and did it himself – with all respect to Mr Simpson, but in fairness to Bayford. And at the same time, would you ask him to look into something else there? Knowing Bayford as I do, I know something he hasn't even remembered to tell us. He says he went into the room to telephone, and had already begun to dial when he was interrupted. It didn't occur to him to say that he fully intended to pay for his call, but I tell you so for him—'

The boy's face had suddenly flushed and softened into a wild relief. He opened his lips with a gasp, but the Governor restrained him with a quick pressure of his hand upon the tight fingers that clutched the new hat.

'If he had already begun to dial his number, he had already paid. The price of a call from Hampton's Corner to Mordenfield is fivepence. Somewhere in that room, unless he had time to pick them up again as he ran for it – which I very much doubt – your constable will find five pennies.'

'Sixpence!' stammered the boy, faint and sick with eagerness. 'I told you, I didn't have no coppers – it was a sixpence. I put it inside the top drawer of the bureau, and I never thought about it afterwards.'

He clamped his knees hard together and clenched his hands, to prevent himself from trembling all over.

'If your constable finds the bell out of action, and the sixpence in the drawer, Superintendent—'

'If he does,' said the Superintendent, politely tempering his incredulity, 'it looks as if we shan't have to detain Bayford any longer. That would be clear enough.'

He rose and went out, and they waited in silence, without looking at each other, because there was nothing they had to look for with any uncertainty, it was only other people they had to fear now, and ungentle circumstances.

The Superintendent came back into the room, and sat down again at his desk, staring at the telephone. And once, when the silence had lasted almost ten minutes, he looked up suddenly into the Governor's eyes, and seemed about to ask him something, but thought better of it.

It seemed to him criminal recklessness to go about the world staking your life on other people, like this, but it was none of his business, and the bubble was due to burst any moment, without any pricks from him.

The telephone rang.

They sat breathlessly still, watching and listening as the confident hand lifted it, and the sceptical voice said: 'Well, what results?'

Then there was a silence. 'All right,' said the Superintendent flatly, 'that's all, you can come on back now.'

He laid the telephone resentfully in its cradle; it offended him to see the probabilities disarranged.

'Well, I should have lost my money. The bell doesn't ring. The sixpence was in the drawer. Bayford, you'll probably never know what a lucky lad you are!'

The boy sat with his eyes closed, and the colour ebbing and flowing in his thin cheeks, and all the lines of his body growing languid and eased.

When he opened his eyes, the Governor was leaning over him, smiling, a hand under his forearm to lift him gently out of the chair.

'Come on, Harry! We're going home.'

GUTTER SNIPES

P.J. Parrish

P.J. Parrish is the pseudonym of Detroit-born sisters Kelly Nichols and Kristy Montee. Their bestselling thriller series featuring the biracial Louis Kincaid, including *Dead of Winter* and *Heart of Ice*, has garnered an International Thriller Award, two Anthony Awards, two Shamus Awards and an Edgar nomination.

The Neon was a slash of red in the oily puddles of the asphalt, and every time a car went by it sent the red quivering.

It looked just like Helen's mouth, he thought.

Moon Renfro tossed his butt out the window and leaned back in the seat. He didn't need to be thinking about Helen. There was too much other stuff he needed to be using his brain for right now and there was just no extra space for trying to figure out what the hell he had done this time to set those lips of hers flapping again.

The neon sign was making this annoying buzzing sound. He looked up at it.

PAUL STROFFMAN'S LUCKY STRIKE

A couple of the letters were flickering, getting ready to die. He stared at the sign in admiration. It was original, put up there in the '60s when Paulie "Sour Kraut" Stroffman bought the place. It was big and flashy and when it was working right, a neon ball would roll across the top of the letters, knock down the pins at the end, and the red letters STRIKE would turn to yellow. The sign never worked right since back in '79, but then the city passed some dumb-ass ordinance so Paulie couldn't replace it even if he could afford to. So it kept breaking and Paulie just kept trying to fix it.

It was a fucking work of art after all. They didn't make 'em like that anymore.

Just like the Lucky Strike. He had to admit the place wasn't much to look at on the outside. Just a brick slab in a dying strip mall. But inside . . .

Paulie kept the insides up real good, kept the lanes oiled with the best stuff, and stripped them down twice instead of once a year. Had the best computerized scoring program that not only marked your score, but flashed these cartoons of grinning turkeys and pins being sucked to dust. Things that really made you feel good about what you had just done.

Moon had been bowling at the Lucky Strike every Tuesday and Thursday night for ten years, and he loved it. Loved the sharp smell of acetone, beer, and smoke. Loved the constant clattering of the wood. Loved the feel of that old bowling shirt on his back and the idea that only four other guys in the whole world had one just like it.

It was his life, and for ten years it had been a good life, one that provided him with friends, beer, and even sex from the alley kittens who worked the snack bar. But best of all, he was somebody here. He carried the second highest average in the house, a 239. Only Bulldog Baker had a higher one at 240.

Moon sucked on his cigarette.

One goddamn pin.

It started to drizzle so he cranked the window up halfway. He exhaled and watched the smoke swirl in the clammy air of the truck. His eyes were locked on the front door of the bowling alley and his insides were churning as he considered what he was about to do.

He had gone over every detail in his head, thought about every angle, asked himself every question. Well, every question but one: Did he have the balls to really go through with this?

A sudden noise made him jump. The neon sign was spitting and flickering. He leaned forward and looked up at the sign.

PAUL STROFFMAN'S LUCKY STRIKE

Then, suddenly, with a loud *pop!* some of the letters were gone. Moon stared through the wet windshield at the sign, frowning. He switched on the wipers.

U MU STRIKE

His mouth fell open and he had to grab at his crotch to slap away the cigarette. He found the butt on the floor mat and then swung back up to look at the sign again. Damn. The letters were still there, big as life against the black sky. U Must Strike? Shit . . . it was a sign. It had to be.

The clatter of falling pins drew his eyes back to the entrance of the bowling alley. A guy had come out and was slinking across the lot.

Moon stuck a hand out the window. "Shaky!"

Shaky Cruthers slumped toward Moon's car. He opened the passenger door and climbed inside, flipping his stringy black hair like a wet dog.

"Whatcha doing here, Moon?" Shaky asked. "You didn't bowl tonight, did you?"

"No," Moon said. "I came to talk to you."

Shaky pulled a crumpled pack of Camels from his shirt pocket and started patting at himself, looking for a match. Moon tossed him a book from the bowling alley. Shaky lit his cigarette and settled into the seat, drawing one knee up.

"So, what did you want to talk about?" he asked.

"I want to win the championship for the Triple J Doubles," Moon said. "I want that thousand dollars prize money and that trophy."

Shaky laughed. He had a weird laugh, like one of those little dolls with the talking strings in their necks. "You better run that by Bulldog first," he said.

Moon almost reached out and choked Shaky for his bad joke, but he didn't want to piss him off right now. But he did throw him a sneer and Shaky mumbled an apology.

"Hell, we're in good shape," Shaky said. "We're tied for first."

"But we've been sucking hind tit most of the year," Moon said. "We got only next week. I want you to do something for me."

"Anything, Moon."

"I want you to make sure we win."

Shaky almost laughed again, but he caught Moon's eyebrow slant and he sucked it back in. "What do you want me to do? Stand back there and blow the pins down?"

"I want you to fuck with Bulldog Baker."

Shaky choked on his cigarette smoke. His hacking filled the car and Moon looked away, out to the darkness to tune him out.

"You done coughing?" Moon finally asked.

"Yeah," Shaky gagged. "Yeah. But man . . . I thought you was serious there for a minute."

"I am serious."

"Bulldog is big as a damn semi, Moon," Shaky said. "How am I suppose to fuck him up?"

"Not him, asshole," Moon said. "His equipment."

Shaky stared at him, and suddenly Moon could see the reflection of the sign in his big brown eyes.

"Listen," Moon said. "Bulldog bought a pair of Kangaroo Ultras at the beginning of the season. Second week he wore those shoes, he bowled a 300. He calls them his magic slippers."

"So?"

"I want you to steal them just before we start. It'll mess up his head."

"What? How?"

"It'll be easy," Moon said. "Before practice, Bulldog always goes in the bar to get his beer and play that stupid poker machine. That's when you steal his shoes."

"I dunno, Moon," Shaky said, tossing his cigarette butt out the window. "Why don't you do it?"

"Because it'd be bad karma for me to do it," Moon said. "You know how important karma is in bowling. I'll be plagued with ten pins the rest of my life."

Shaky fell quiet, picking at his fingers, trying to peel off the little pieces of rubber left from his thumb tape.

Moon looked down at his cigarette, trying to decide if he could get one more puff out of it. It was important to get all the puffs you could, just like it was important to always get one of the pins of the 7-10 split because that's what a lot of games came down to. And a lot averages, too. One goddamn pin.

Moon slid a glance to Shaky. "I'll give you my old Red Inferno ball," he said.

"That ball has so many potholes it rolls down the alley like a moon rock," Shaky said.

"Okay, what then?"

"Man . . ."

"Okay, the Inferno and my Brunswick three-baller bag. But you'll have to fix the right wheel. It keeps falling off."

Shaky pulled a long string of thumb tape from his hand and started rolling it between his fingers. When he had it into a tiny ball, he tossed it out the window.

"What about your Atomic Revolution?" he asked. "Can I have that?"

"No fucking way," Moon said. "I worked three weeks OT to get that damn ball. It's a friggin' two-hundred-dollar piece of art. No way. No way."

"Buy a new one with the prize money," Shaky said.

Moon shook his head again, trying to find his cigarettes. His hands were trembling so badly, he couldn't pull one out and when he did, he broke it.

"I got other bills to pay," Moon said, ripping open the pack to get the last smoke. "I'm two months behind on the mortgage and one month on this friggin' truck. And Helen's bitching at me to get her a new washing machine. I can't give you no money."

Shaky was still staring at his fingers and Moon finally tossed the cigarette pack to the dash and grabbed Shaky's collar, jerking him toward the windshield.

"See that up there?" Moon asked.

"What?"

"The sign," Moon said, pointing up. "See the sign? Don't you get it? It's telling us something. It's telling us to strike."

Shaky blinked up at the sky. "Yoo . . . moo. .stttt . . . kee?" he said slowly.

Moon tapped the windshield. "No, stupid, can't you fucking read? You . . . Must . . . Strike. It's talking about Bulldog."

Shaky's eyes widened. "Wow," he whispered.

They both stared at the sign for a few moments, then Shaky slumped back against the door. His eyes stayed glued on the flickering neon.

"Just steal the shoes, huh?" he asked. "That's all I have to do?"

"That's all you have to do."

It rained on position night, like it did most nights in May in Memphis. For some teams, the downpour would mean a forfeit since half the streets would be flooded and most bowlers—those that didn't have a true heart—would stay home. After all, the league was ending and if you weren't one of the top few teams, you were already a loser anyway, so why risk your life driving through a lake just to win games no one cared about?

Moon was sitting at one of the tall back tables, a beer in his hand, his eyes scanning the emptiness. Moon couldn't imagine not showing up every week, rain or sleet. It was what being a purist was all about.

He hadn't known that until a few years ago, when in a drunken bar conversation, the pro shop guy, Al "The Hawk" Hawkins, had first called Moon a purist. Moon had gotten mad until he looked up "purist" in the dictionary and realized The Hawk had paid him a helluva compliment.

Shaky had a good heart, but he wasn't a purist. Like his average. For as long as Moon had known him, Shaky had never gotten above a 199, and he seemed content to let that one pin stay beyond his reach, like there was absolutely no difference between a 199 and 200 average.

Now Bulldog Baker. Not even close to a purist.

Yeah, he wore the silver Dyno-Thane Kangaroo Tour Ultras, and a glove called the Power Paw, and had made a name for himself a few years back by throwing a ball called The Thing. One day The Thing cracked in half on its way to the seven pin, only because Bulldog hadn't respected it enough to take it out of his car trunk all summer. Bulldog tried to get another Thing but it was out of stock, so he bought The Thing's new version, a purple and orange monstrosity called The Thing Lives.

Jesus. Having a ball with that stupid name was bad enough. But Bulldog also liked to act the fool out there, sometimes wearing a dog mask, or bowling with his eyes closed, or clipping a rubber chicken to his teammate's ass and then laughing like hell as it swung and bounced during the guy's approach.

You didn't do stuff like that in a league.

Moon took a drink and spun his chair to look around. On the wall above the alleys was another version of PAUL STROFFMAN'S LUCKY STRIKE sign. Moon stared at it for a moment, waiting for a message, but he knew none would come. This sign was newer, and not the classic symbol the one outside was.

A few dripping bowlers were straggling in. Tony Valleni, who had memorized every page of the ABC rule book, and Bald Leo, whose thumb was sliced off a few years back but who had worked real hard to learn to throw a helluva curve using just his two fingers in the holes. True hearts at their best.

At five thirty-seven, Bulldog came through the front door, lugging his rain-speckled bag. Bulldog always carried two balls—The Thing Lives and a second ball he used only for spares. After he was done hugging the girls, shaking hands with the guys, and talking about last night's scores, he made his way toward alleys eleven and twelve. He had small, penny-colored eyes pressed into a catcher's mitt face and they glinted with something Moon read as victory, even though not a ball had been thrown yet.

"You're here early," Bulldog said. "What are you doing, soaking up the atmosphere for inspiration?"

Moon drew hard on his cigarette and just stared.

Bulldog gave him a smile, then set his bag against the rack that held the ugly pink and green house balls. He glanced up at the computerized scoreboards. The teams and names were already up there. THE STEEL BALLS VS. BULLDOG'S BEST.

"I didn't know we were playing you," Bulldog said.

"It's friggin' roll-off night," Moon said dryly.

"Good Lord," Bulldog said, giving Moon a wink. "Is the season almost over already?"

Moon stubbed out his cigarette, crunching his teeth to avoid saying anything that would get him punched. Besides, he needed to stay focused.

Bulldog unzipped his bag and pulled out The Thing Lives and started toward the ball return to place it on the rack. Moon gaped. Bulldog was going to walk on the polished approach with wet shoes.

"Hey!" Moon called. "Watch it, your feet are wet."

Bulldog looked down at his black work shoes, then came back to his bag. He set The Thing Lives back inside then bent to untie his shoes.

"My apologies, Moon," he said. "Last thing I'd want is someone sticking on the approach and getting hurt on my account."

Bulldog took off his street shoes. Then to Moon's surprise, he pulled out his Dyno-Thane Kangaroo Tour Ultras and started to put them on.

He was putting the shoes on now . . . before he went to the bar. Shit! Shit!

"You going to walk around this whole place in your bowling shoes?" Moon asked. "They'll be soaked."

Bulldog unzipped a pocket on the bag and held up a limp pair of red leather slip-on shoe covers. "Have no fear, my friend," he said. "I always use protection."

Then he laughed, that horrid hoarse chuckle that always sounded like he had a rag caught in his throat. He was still laughing as he pulled the covers over the Kangaroos and sauntered off into the bar to play his poker machine.

Moon couldn't stand it, couldn't sit still, and he pushed away from the counter so fast he almost tipped his beer. Winding his way between bowlers, he shoved the front doors open and stepped outside.

Shit! Fuck! Motherfucker! Tits!

How could he have been so stupid? Why didn't he just keep his mouth shut? Why couldn't he just let some stuff go instead of worrying about a few drops of water getting on the approach?

Because you can't, he thought. It's who you are. You're a purist.

The red neon of the sign cracked and buzzed, drawing his gaze up to the gray sky. Moon stepped out from under the overhang and looked up. Different letters were struggling to stay aglow in the rain. Suddenly, the sign steadied itself, and a handful of letters grew bright and solid.

T OFF   LUC

Moon squinted up into the rain. A new message.

Toff luc? Tough luck?

He stared harder, waiting for something else, waiting for the sign to show him the rest, tell him what to do now. But the letters just stood there, tall and fuzzy and red in the mist.

Tough luck. Tough luck. Tough luck.

Moon spat on the ground. This was bullshit. The sign wasn't some mystical crystal ball that was going to help him beat Bulldog and light the way for a re-purification of the greatest game ever invented. It was just a rusty old relic of a vanishing era.

He reached for the door. The boom of a blown electrical transformer snapped his head back toward the sign. With a groan and a crackle, three new letters came to life. TRI

T OFF   LUC   TRI

The last three—TRI—were blinking on and off.

TRI? Try? Try . . . that was it. Try. Try. Try!

Moon looked up to the clouds, his heart swelling with wonder and gratitude. His eyes filled with tears.

"You okay, Moon?"

Moon jumped, then looked at the man who had spoken. It was Al 'The Hawk' Hawkins, the pro shop guy. Moon's eyes slid back to the sign, but he knew The Hawk couldn't read it.

"I'm cool," Moon said.

The Hawk motioned to his van. "I had to close the shop early. My old lady's in labor again. Good luck tonight. Seven years in a row finishing second, that's gotta hurt after a while."

Moon couldn't even fake a smile. The Hawk hurried off across the parking lot. After a few seconds, a yellow Camaro with confederate flag window decals swung in. Shaky was here.

Moon waited under the overhang until Shaky was almost to the doors then he stopped him with a palm to his chest. Shaky stared at him, his black hair looking like leeches stuck to his forehead.

"What?" Shaky asked. "What's wrong?"

"He's already wearing the shoes," Moon hissed. "You got to do something else."

"Like what?"

"Go to my truck. Inside is a full tube of epoxy. Bring it to me and don't let anyone see you with it."

"Huh?"

"Just go. I'll explain inside."

Moon pushed him out from under the overhang. Shaky planted his feet, blinking like he was figuring something out. "I do something with that epoxy then you gotta give me something better than your old Red Inferno."

"What?" Moon demanded. "What the fuck else I got you want?"

"What about a roll with Helen?"

"What? She would never sleep with you."

"Get her drunk enough, she might."

Moon came off the concrete, fist clenched and Shaky quickly back-pedaled. "I was just kidding, man."

Moon stopped himself, and for a few seconds, both of them stood in the rain, silent. Moon sighed. Man, he had to give Shaky something better than the pitted Red Inferno. Shaky didn't have much else. Hell, maybe the thrill of winning this was enough. Maybe Helen's new washer could wait.

"All right," Moon said. "I'll give you my Atomic Revolution."

In the gray mist, Shaky's face lit up like a headlight. He loped off toward Moon's truck. A few seconds later, he was back.

"You get it?" Moon asked.

Shaky patted his dripping shirt, his voice low. "I'm pack-in' man."

It was crowded by the time they got back to alley eleven. Beefy men hunched over black bowling bags. Shoes scattered everywhere. The counters covered with the fine white powder from tiny bags of Easy-Slide. Paulie had music playing from the speakers, the kind Moon knew would give him a headache if he listened to it too long.

They had both dried off in the john, changed into their yellow and black shirts, and Shaky had opened the epoxy inside the stall, making sure it would be warm and ready when he needed it. He was only going to get one good squeeze per hole.

Back at alley eleven, Moon provided the cover for Shaky. He heard Shaky unzipping Bulldog's bag.

"Good luck tonight, Moon!" someone called.

Moon gave the man a tight nod, keeping his eyes on the alleys. The smell of epoxy was everywhere.

"Hurry up," Moon hissed.

"Do you want I should do the spare ball, too?"

"Yeah."

Moon heard the draw of a zipper and suddenly Shaky appeared in front of him, a tight smile on his face. "Mission accomplished."

Moon watched as Shaky wandered off and dropped the epoxy into a full trash can, then he looked toward the bar. Bulldog was coming out the door.

It was time to get ready.

As Moon put on his shoes, he snuck a look at Bulldog. He hadn't touched his bag yet. Still busy jawing about his recent 300 game and wondering when his award ring would come from ABC.

Moon's eyes slipped quickly to the only ring on his hand, his wedding ring, but he didn't like thinking about that. He set his Atomic Revolution on the rack and looked down at the pins. They stood like polished teeth at the end of the gleaming wood tongue. Pearly and ripe.

"Who's been fucking with my ball?"

Bulldog had pulled The Thing Lives from his bag and was jabbing at the thumb hole with his finger.

"It's . . . filled up with something."

Moon resisted the urge to walk over. Bulldog poked at the clogged hole a few more times, then the copper eyes came up. Right at Moon.

"You," Bulldog whispered.

Moon gave him a dry smile. "Things happen to balls when you leave them in hot car trunks," he said. "Maybe it melted."

Bulldog stared at him, The Thing Lives cradled in his hands like a dead pet.

People started to gather around, taking turns sticking fingers inside Bulldog's thumb hole and mumbling about how the new kind of resin used to make balls nowadays just didn't hold up very well in the southern heat.

"Maybe Al the Hawk can drill it out for you real quick," someone said.

Moon let Bulldog take a few steps toward the pro shop before he called out. "Hey, Bulldog," Moon said. "I saw Al leaving about thirty minutes ago."

Bulldog turned slowly back to Moon. The mumbling all around them grew louder. Everyone knew what this meant.

"You want to borrow one of my balls, Bulldog?" someone asked.

"You know I can't," Bulldog said. "I got fat fingers."

"Maybe you can use one of those pink house balls," Moon offered.

Bulldog glared at Moon, so hard he didn't even notice that Bald Leo had walked up. "Man, that's tough luck," Leo said. "Want me to show you how to throw it without sticking your thumb in?"

Bulldog's head jerked to Bald Leo. "Yeah," he said quickly. "Show me."

They were allowed fifteen minutes of practice. With only two on a team, that gave everyone a chance to throw at least twenty shots. Normally Moon took every one he could, but not tonight. He was watching Bulldog.

At first, Bulldog threw a couple of gutters, then Bald Leo worked on his grip, showing him how to cup the ball to get it to stay on his hand. Eight practice balls later, The Thing Lives, with the clogged holes, was rolling down the alley and getting strikes.

Moon was pissed. No one could learn to bowl with two fingers instead of three that quick. In fact, unless you were thumbless, there ought to be a rule against it. They put three holes on a ball for a reason.

"This sucks," Shaky said, coming up next to him.

"What now?"

Moon's gut was so hard, he couldn't speak. He shoved Shaky aside and ripped into his bag for his shoe covers. He was still struggling to get them on as he hobbled away from the alleys.

Moon shoved open the front doors. He stepped out from under the overhang and into the hard rain. Every damn letter was off.

"Okay!" Moon shouted at the sign. "Okay! Now what? What do I do now?"

The sign stood dark and silent.

"Dammit!" he screamed. "I did everything you wanted me to! Talk to me. C'mon, one more time!"

Nothing.

"You fucking piece of shit!" Moon shouted, fist raised. "You lousy, stinking piece of cheap neon! Talk to me!"

It started with a buzz, then a crackle and a few letters began to glow. First a K, then a second K.

"C'mon," Moon said. "I'm running out of time here!"

More letters. Then the sign stopping buzzing, leaving only a handful of letters lit.

M A K   SIK.

What did that mean?

Ma..k . . . Make? S..i..K . . . Sick.

Make sick.

Yes! That was it. He would make Bulldog sick.

Moon rushed back inside, dripping all the way back to alley twelve. The whole place was alive now with clatter, but to Moon, it seemed strangely muted, like it did sometimes at the end of a one-pin game when he had to tune everything else out in order to throw the perfect ball.

Bulldog was humping strikes every time now and his teammate stood in awe, watching him. Everyone was watching him.

Moon grabbed Shaky's sleeve and pulled him over to the counter.

"Get your acetone," he whispered.

Shaky reached down into his bag and pulled out a small plastic squeeze bottle. Moon glanced at the crowd around Bulldog, then tipped his head toward Bulldog's Rum and Coke.

"Pour some in there," he said.

"You want me to poison him?" Shaky asked.

"He won't die," Moon said. "He'll just get sick."

"I dunno, Moon. This is bad stuff."

"Just do it!" Moon hissed.

Shaky hesitated, then took the cap off the bottle. "I want a bigger pay-off," he said.

"You already got my Revolution. I ain't got nothing else!" Moon said.

"But I could go to jail for this."

Moon looked up, his throat tight. Behind him, he heard the smash of a sure strike, followed by laughter. Man, could he really do this? Yes. He could. He would make it up to her somehow.

"Okay," he said, looking back at Shaky. "If you want Helen—and I mean for one quickie—I'll get her to do it."

Shaky's eyes widened, then he slurped the acetone into the drink and quickly put the bottle away. The scoreboards suddenly turned a bright blue, indicating practice was over. Everyone started back to their own lanes. Moon turned to look at Bulldog.

He was standing by the approach, holding The Thing Lives in his arm. He made a sweeping gesture toward the lanes.

"You're up, Moon."

Bulldog threw up in the wastebasket in frame nine of the first game, and no one was sure if he was going to be able to continue, but right after, he got back up and threw another strike—a Moses ball—the kind that hits the head pin and divides the pins right down the middle.

It was the kind of thing that always happened to unpure bowlers when they found themselves up against real talent. Moon called them ugly strikes, the ones that never should have been and although everyone took them—you had to take them—Moon thought there was an element of shame in having too many. Bulldog didn't seem to think so.

Moon glanced up at the scoreboard. Dammit.

They were going to lose this game. Shaky wasn't concentrating. His shots were laden with guilt, and he was having a hard time keeping his eyes off Bulldog's drink.

Shaky apologized five times for losing the game, even though he had bowled a 218, nineteen pins above his average. Moon had bowled a 266. Any other night, it would have been more than enough. But not tonight.

Bulldog spent most of the second game in the bathroom. Moon wanted to call Tony Valleni and his rule book down to see if there was a set number of minutes someone could delay a game before they forfeited. But half the damn league was in the john, worried about Bulldog, and Moon didn't want to come off as a jerk, so he stayed quiet, just sitting at the table, staring at the scoreboard, which by the end of the second game read: THE STEEL BALLS 521, BULLDOG'S BEST 499.

It was even up. All they needed to do was to win the third game, and the league, the thousand dollars and that big-ass gold trophy would be his.

Moon rubbed his face, wishing the knot in his belly would go away. He looked out at the lanes. Most of the bowlers had stopped their own games to gather behind eleven and twelve to watch the championship. The alleys were so quiet, Moon could hear his own heart.

Someone called his name and he looked to see Bulldog and his entourage heading back to the alleys. Bulldog's fat face was sweaty and white as the pins, and he was walking unsteady, but he managed to find his way to the approach and grab The Thing Lives.

Shaky started off the third game with a Moses ball strike. Moon followed with a perfect pocket hit, but so did Bulldog and his partner. By the middle of the game, amidst rolls of thunder and flickering lights, the game was tied, with X's in every box on the scoreboard. The crowd behind was thickening.

The score stayed almost tied through the ninth, even though Bulldog was staggering, with sweat running down his face and only the cheers of the faithful behind him to give him strength.

Moon looked up at the scoreboard. They were a few pins behind, but it was not out of reach. He was calculating up how many pins he would need if Bulldog struck out when he heard a groan from the spectators and he looked at the alley.

Bulldog had done the unthinkable. The Thing Lives was rolling down the gutter.

Moon watched the ball until it disappeared into the black abyss behind the pins, then his eyes flicked up to the scoreboard. His brain worked like lightning. All Moon had to do was get a spare. Two balls to get all ten pins. It was theirs. Goddammit. The whole thing was theirs!

Bulldog lofted his final ball, a weak hook that toppled the pins in slow motion. He stumbled back to his chair, holding his stomach, falling into the arms of a dozen other bowlers.

It was time to end this.

Moon picked up his Atomic Revolution and took his place on the approach. Lowering his head and concentrating on every step, he threw his first ball. It was perfect—absolutely fucking perfect—and he felt a surge of greatness as the Revolution exploded into the pins and scattered them.

Wait . . . there was one left. One damn pin. The ten pin.

Dammit. Dammit to hell.

Moon grabbed the Atomic Revolution off the return and cradled it, staring at the ten pin. If he missed this, it was over. Everything was over.

He set himself, his heart starting to pound, beads of sweat forming on his palms. Just as he started his first step, thunder rolled overhead. Moon stopped, waiting for it to pass before he set himself again.

He wiggled his fingers into the ball, then slipped in his thumb and stared down at the pin. It stood gleaming and silent, waiting for him.

As he took a step, another explosion from outside vibrated through the building, sending the lights flickering and the pin trembling. He stopped again.

The sign outside must be flickering, too, trying to talk to him, and he wished he could go look at it to see what the message was, but he couldn't leave now.

But then, suddenly, imaginary letters started flashing in his head. They made no sense, like one of those scrambled word puzzles in the newspaper that he couldn't do.

He set himself again, trying not to think about the letters. But now words were starting to form in his head and with every step he took, another letter would drop into place.

S . . . T . . . A

Third step and the swing of his arm.

Y . . . P . . .

It amazed him that he could see his messages now in his mind, and that realization, more than the letters themselves, filled him with a sense of magical power as his arm started forward.

U . . . R . . .

The ball was cupped in his hand like a perfect size C boob, and as he started to lay it down, the last letter dropped into place in his head.

E.

In an instant, he saw it, all the letters blinking as sure and strong in his head as he knew they were blinking outside.

STAY PURE

What? That wasn't the right message. It couldn't be the right message. He was already pure.

Wasn't he?

The Atomic Revolution was just coming off the tips of his fingers when something pulled at him, something powerful and creepy and irresistible, and he did something he never thought he would do. He flipped the ball just a half-inch to the left. The moment it hit the wood, he knew it would miss the pin.

And it did.

The ball disappeared into the dark bowels of the alley, and Moon stood and stared at the ten pin.

It stared back, silent and defiant.

Somewhere in his brain, he could hear cheering and then the rattle of the Revolution coming up the ball return. But everything he expected to feel—rage and disappointment—were not there. All that was there was a scary kind of peace.

He turned slowly and packed up his stuff. Shaky was talking about next year and Bulldog was shaking hands and someone was on the loudspeaker announcing that BULLDOG'S BEST were league champs. In the corner of his eye, Moon caught sight of the huge, gold trophy coming through the crowd.

He headed outside, Shaky hustling along behind him, still yakking about next year and summer leagues and tournaments, but Moon wasn't hearing him. He wanted to see the sign and he wanted to make sure the message he had seen in his head was the right one because if it wasn't, then everything that had happened to him in those last few seconds had been fake.

He stopped under the overhang and told Shaky to shut up. They both stood there, staring at the sign, watching and waiting.

With a crack of thunder, all the letters went out. A few seconds later, they flickered back on.

U L

U L O

U LOSR

Moon stared, and blinked, and kept staring. Then he started slowly off across the parking lot. Shaky trailed behind.

"Do I still get your Atomic Revolution, Moon?"

"No."

"What about Helen?"

"No."

"Well, then do I get the old red Inferno?"

"No."

"Well, then, what do I get out of all this?"

Moon stopped and faced him. "Purity, my friend. We get purity."

THE PROBLEM OF THE KENTISH GHOST

Sarah Perry

Sarah Perry is the author of *After Me Comes the Flood* and the hugely successful *The Essex Serpent*. She holds a PhD in Creative Writing from Royal Holloway University, London, where she was supervised by Andrew Motion. Perry's gothic style is influenced by a deeply religious family background.

I.

I have lately been in the habit of looking over those notebooks in which I have recorded the adventures that befell me in the company of my friend, Mr Sherlock Holmes. Though much has been already brought to the public's attention, I find there remain some incidents which – though scarcely plumbing the depths of human transgression evidenced in the problem of the divided manuscript, or reaching the bewildering complexity of the bells of Hanham Mount – may nonetheless bear witness to an extraordinary career which bestowed upon a retired army surgeon the most singular and fascinating episodes of his life. The adventure of the Kentish Ghost is one such episode; and though Holmes himself has long considered the leaps of deduction which it required to be so scant as to pass without notice, I must allow the reader to conclude for himself whether I err in at last making a public record of that curious adventure.

Towards the end of summer '87 I found myself in the vicinity of my old lodgings at Baker Street. I had attended a lecture on developments in the nomenclature of diseases at the Royal College of Physicians, and my wife being then out of town to attend a relation of indifferent constitution, I decided to call upon my old friend in the hope of passing a pleasant evening of reminiscence. I was thus displeased to find, upon being shown up to those familiar rooms, that *Sherlock* Holmes already played host to a gentleman of middle years whose naturally forbidding aspect was rendered still more forbidding by the black vestments of mourning. He was accompanied by a lady whose fresh countenance, and attractive yet modest attire, brought into the stuffy rooms something of the country air from which the two had so evidently come.

"My dear fellow!" said Holmes, grasping me by the hand; and remarking that he trusted Mrs Watson's health fared better than that of the aunt for whose benefit I had been temporarily deprived of a helpmeet. He was prevented from expanding on the methods by which these deductions had been reached by the visiting gentleman coughing into his handkerchief, in that manner by which the well-brought-up Englishman signals his impatience. "Forgive me, Sir James," said Holmes. "Permit me to introduce my friend and colleague Dr John Watson. You may rely upon his discretion and good character as fully as I have always done. Dr Watson, you find me in the company of Sir James Scott Denys, Bart., and of Miss Amelia Beaumont, who travelled this morning from Kent in order to bring to my attention some problem with which I hope to offer assistance. Sir James, I trust you will accept my condolences on your recent bereavement; and that you will not think it impertinent of me to applaud the wisdom of deriving solace from the art of Orpheus."

Miss Beaumont suppressed an exclamation with a pretty motion of her hand, and thereupon began to twist the fine grey gloves she held with a nervous motion which my friend at once observed. "I did not say when we had travelled, or where from," said Sir James, "and certainly I have not yet confided any matters relating to my personal circumstances!" It was evident the baronet was unaccustomed to being taken by surprise.

"Mere trifles, I assure you," said Holmes smoothly. "The burrs which adhere to the cuff of Miss Beaumont's charming gown must certainly have been acquired during a country walk of the variety this great metropolis cannot provide: thus you have travelled from beyond the capital. One may deduce from the dried mud upon your own attire that a portion of the journey was undertaken in poor weather; and since yesterday's *Times* forecast no rainfall within one hundred miles of London save in the county of Kent, and since you exhibit all the marks of a man in mourning, I arrived at conclusions which could scarcely escape even a schoolboy's attention. Dr Watson will doubtless have observed at once the sore visible above your collar, which is known in vulgar orchestral parlance as 'Fiddler's neck', and which signals the devoted violinist. I further perceive," said Holmes, with a smile, "that I must also offer my congratulations to you both; but perhaps your narrative will furnish me with the details at the proper time." Indicating that his visitors should avail themselves of the pair of arm-chairs set beneath the window, and that I should take up my old post beside the fire, he said, "Now, Sir James: perhaps you would set before Dr Watson and me the facts of the case?"

"Mr Holmes," said the baronet, "you must understand that it is far from natural to me to discuss family matters with a stranger. Indeed, I have long resisted the temptation to consult you, but have been urged to do so by a relation whose reputation was salvaged solely due to your intervention on a matter of the utmost sensitivity."

"Ah! I had thought your name familiar," said my friend: "I recall the incident, and trust that your cousin has turned his hand to more edifying accomplishments. But continue."

"You were correct to suppose that we journeyed this morning from Kent. My family has been resident in that county for five generations, at Boxley Grange, which sits some miles east of Canterbury by the village of Long Marcham. I inherited the baronetcy at thirty, and shortly thereafter married Elizabeth Ghillies, whose family has always been intimately connected with my own. I was devoted to my wife, Mr Holmes, and her peculiarly fair beauty was justly celebrated throughout the county. The early years of our marriage were as happy as any man might reasonably hope, not least when at last Lady Denys bore me a son, Charles. He has demonstrated, I might say almost from birth, those qualities which I should wish always to be associated with our name. Within the year, however, my wife began to display signs of a distressing weakness of spirit which in due course became the defining feature of her character. I recall observing her pluck strands of her own hair, which she then placed within a silver locket. This she gave to my son."

Holmes appeared somewhat struck by this; for he opened a single eye, with which he surveyed Sir James for a moment, before indicating that he should continue.

"Altogether," said our guest, "an unwholesome preoccupation with mortality, and a desire to withdraw from her maternal duties and place herself in absolute seclusion within her own rooms and there to devote herself to spiritual study, were a source of some anxiety to me. You may imagine my gratitude when Miss Beaumont responded to an advertisement placed seeking a governess of exceptional abilities to attend to my son, and to offer that feminine companionship to my wife which I had hoped might prove beneficial to her spirits. In this hope I have been richly rewarded."

Sir James paused in this narrative, and it was possible to detect in that reserved and humourless countenance a warmth at which I could not have guessed. Then he went on: "In the latter part of May, Lady Denys was taken ill. Despite the attentions of Dr Martin – a cousin of Miss Beaumont, at that time a guest at Boxley Grange – complications of the illness, together with a constitution which had never been strong, caused a fatal disease of the lung. She passed from this life to the next as though in a deep sleep, and was buried two months ago in the small churchyard which abuts our property. I need not enter into the sadness occasioned by this loss. You may imagine my pleasure when Miss Beaumont accepted my proposal not five days ago, thus ensuring that the sole remaining source of feminine care and affection on which my son may rely is secured."

Holmes murmured his congratulations, and looked keenly at Miss Beaumont, whose modest smile spoke more eloquently than Sir James himself of the attachment which had formed between them.

"My chief duty now lay in ensuring that my son, who is not yet seven years old, was vouchsafed a youth which would fit him for the responsibilities which are the burden of all those born into an ancient English family. It is thus with the deepest distress that I come at last to the nature of my visit. Mr Holmes, my son believes himself to be haunted by his mother's ghost. I assure you nothing could be more repulsive to my sensibilities. Naturally I dismissed the tale as childish sport: indeed he was punished for a duplicity which could only cause distress to his father. Yet in the weeks that followed he has refused either to retract, or to apologise.

"I must now describe the position of the house. It is situated but half a mile from Long Marcham. Eastward lies six hundred acres of land, tended by some dozen tenant farmers in whom my family has placed their trust for generations. Westward lies the church of St Andrew, its churchyard, and a single tied cottage which for some years has been the residence of Harries, our verger. Behind the house is a large walled garden, which my wife took the greatest pride in tending herself. It may be accessed only through the house itself, or through the western wall into the churchyard. It is an iron gate, to which I alone hold the key."

"And this key is securely kept?"

"It is indeed, Mr Holmes: there is no copy, and it is kept upon my watch-chain. My own rooms are on the upper floor. Miss Beaumont sleeps on the ground floor, as does my son; their apartments are awarded a view of the garden itself. It is in this garden, and there alone, in which Charles claims to have witnessed an apparition. He describes a woman whose fair hair is uncovered to the elements, who wears a white nightgown, and who walks back and forth across the lawn. I should certainly not have troubled you with the prattlings of children had not two further peculiar incidents occurred. We keep a Pekinese, which had been the particular pet of my wife, and which has begun to exhibit what one might almost call symptoms of madness. It will not be kept within doors, but rather insists upon pacing back and forth across a small portion of the garden, pawing senselessly within the thicket that covers the garden wall."

"It does not do so beside the gate?"

"Indeed not: it pays attention only to the thicket at the further end of the wall. There is one last fact I must put before you. Not two days ago, Miss Beaumont and I were seated in the drawing room. Miss Beaumont was attending to house-hold mending, while I played on the violin, as is my habit in the evenings. We were disturbed by violent screaming from the servants' quarters, and on hurrying below stairs we discovered the maid, Sarah, indulging in hysterics. She declared that she had heard a tapping upon the window; that she had there discovered a fair woman in a white gown walking in the garden; and that it was certain to be the ghost. You may be certain, Mr Holmes, that I put her to the test; and on further questioning she confessed that she had spoken of such apparitions with my son. Naturally she was dismissed without notice, and I believed the removal of so foolish an influence would put an end to the matter. And yet last night, as he spoke with me before supper, Charles repeated most insistently his bizarre assertions. It was then that I resolved to seek the counsel of the detective of whom I had heard, both personally and publicly, such extraordinary reports."

I feared there was little in this tale to invigorate that steadfast and pene-trating intelligence, which had been brought hard up against every conceivable vicissitude of humanity. Upon looking at Holmes I perceived that I was correct: rising impatiently from his chair, he stood at the window and gazed down at the thoroughfare below. "It seems to me, Sir James," he said, "that your case is rather better suited to the attentions of a man of the cloth than to a consulting detective. The ravages of grief, the imaginations of children, and the trickery of maids, may readily account for all you have described. Now: I do not say you cannot consult me upon some further demonstration that your case demands the applications of those methods to which I have devoted years of refinement. At present, however, I regret that problems more infinitely pressing must take precedence."

It was evident the baronet was unused to finding requests met with refusal, for he began to demur. Miss Beaumont, who had remained until this moment silent, placed a hand upon the gentleman's arm. "Let us return home," she said, "and take the advice of Mr Holmes. I do not think there is any danger; and with

Sarah's removal from the house, I am certain we shall find ourselves once more at peace."

"Sir James," said I, "I have the deepest sympathy both for your bereavement, and for the strange circumstances which brought you to these apartments. I feel certain Mr Holmes would welcome further communication should there be any further incident which you believe to place your child in danger . . ."

"Oh, certainly, certainly," said Holmes; but it was evident that the engine of that extraordinary mind had moved already onto matters more suited to its intricate machinery. One further interaction, however, proved of some small interest to my friend. On making a courteous bow to the displeased baronet, and clasping the lady's hand in farewell, Holmes remarked upon the splendour of Miss Beaumont's ring. She wore on a weighty sapphire ornament of the sort which is handed down through the great families of England, bestowing upon successive wives the family honour. She blushed, and held up the stone as if to admire it anew. "A handsome gem indeed," said Holmes smoothly, "but it was the ring upon your right hand which commanded my attention. A gift, perhaps?" Miss Beaumont drew on a pair of grey silk gloves, with a demonstration of modesty which I found most appealing.

"A present from an aunt on the occasion of my twenty-first birthday," she said; and with a smile she conducted Sir James away.

"Curious," said Holmes. "Doubtless you noticed the stones which were set into her ring, and their significance?"

"At such a distance!" said I, "I confess I did not. What an extraordinarily charming young lady; Sir James must count himself a blessed man indeed."

"My good Watson!" said Holmes, returning to his customary seat beside the fire, and withdrawing a pouch of shag from its resting-place. "It was ever your way to permit your wits to be blunted in the presence of a pair of fine eyes, and a dimpled cheek. But let us set aside the mystery of the Kentish Ghost for the present; for I count myself fortunate to have retrieved my friend from the demands of uxoriousness for an afternoon, and we shall pass the time swiftly enough. Ring that bell, Watson, for your presence invigorates me, and I find myself equal to one of Mrs Hudson's excellent pies."

II.

I thought little more of this episode for some weeks, for I returned to the demands of home and practice. I was seated at breakfast with my wife when a telegraph was brought, summoning me at once to Baker St. "Curious circumstances at Boxley Grange," it read. "Kentish Ghost returns. Medical man required: come at once."

"I did not expect Mr Holmes to return to a problem which he so thoroughly dismissed!" said Mary, on reading this brusque summons. "Naturally you must go: for am I not first to derive pleasure from your accounts of the episodes which often follow such a missive?" Bestowing a thankful kiss upon my wife, I packed a small valise with items both personal and medical, and presented myself at Baker St within the hour. There I discovered Holmes pacing back and forth with that alert expression which signalled the arrival of some problem capable of arousing his penetrating curiosity, and which roused in me a corresponding anticipation.

"A letter!" said Holmes, without pausing to offer the customary greetings. "From Sir James himself; and it presents two small points which I find myself unable to dismiss entirely. Perhaps you would care to read it yourself?" He handed me the first of two sheets of foolscap, and I sat to read:

Dear Mr Holmes,

I trust you will recall a visit which I made to your chambers in the company of my fiancée, Miss Beaumont, and the bizarre circumstances which led me to your door. For some weeks I believed that a distressing period in the life of my household was indeed at an end; but two events have demonstrated that I have been mistaken. You will recall the extraordinary behaviour of the Pekinese which had been the pet of my wife. No threats or entreaties could dissuade the animal from keeping its post beside the garden wall, at times making such noises of distress as to be audible within the house. Four days ago the wretched animal, having been missing for some time, was discovered to have perished halfway between house and garden. It had shown no signs of disease. I should not have given this incident further thought had not my son claimed to have seen the dog playing with an object in the grass in the hours preceding its death. This object he described as "red beads, like a lady's necklace"; of this we have found no sign, nor can we guess as to who might have placed such an object within the grounds, when the gate is kept secure. The following day, Mr Holmes, my son was taken suddenly ill with a fever, and in his delirium speaks often of the Kentish Ghost, describing in detail its long hair and dark coat, and of the red beads which he saw upon the lawn. I beg . . .

At this the page ended; and Holmes, with a smile hardly fitted to so grave a report, handed me the second sheet of foolscap. I read on:

. . . however that you will think no further of these strange events, which indeed I blush to think of having brought to your attention. My son's illness has proved but brief, and he is in the care of the local physician. It seems likely he has long been subject to a mild fever which contributed to the visions which caused me such distress. Boxley Grange returns to its accustomed peace, and it only remains for me to offer my gratitude, and my hope that you remain in good health.

Thus ended the epistle. "Happy news indeed," I said, recollecting the peculiarly serene picture presented by Miss Beaumont. "I trust the good baronet may now turn his attention to a happier future!"

Holmes folded the letter within its envelope, which he then shook before me with a gesture of admonition. "Come, Watson: do you not perceive the two very striking elements of this note which must suggest – to even the meanest intelligence! – that a happy future must elude the good baronet for some days yet?"

Accustomed as I was to finding my intellect diminished in the presence of my friend, I could not help responding with some acidity. "I merely take the word of an English gentleman," said I. "One might wonder at the child recovering in such short order; but one must equally suppose that a father will place the highest imperative on securing the well-being of his heir!"

"Indeed, one must! I do not propose to burden you at present with the small deductions which occur to me; they are scarcely worth repeating. I observe you come prepared for travel, and applaud your foresight; for I took the liberty of notifying Sir James to expect a visit from the good John Watson, MD, shortly to catch the 11.15 from Greenwich. I have requested that arrangements be made to conduct you onward from Faversham to Boxley Grange." At this I exclaimed, for I had not imagined that I would be required to undertake any tasks in a solitary capacity.

"I cannot myself attend at present – I am preoccupied with assisting a junior minister with a matter attended as much by tedium as by secrecy. It may be that I am able to quit the capital myself in the coming days; but in the meantime can offer no greater help and consolation to our embattled baronet than the offices of my good Watson."

"You wish me to attend to the child?"

"I do. Further, you are to observe, with all the diligence which you have witnessed in my own methods; and two days hence you are to furnish me with a report delineating those aspects of the household which seem to you most striking, not neglecting the below-stairs staff. God speed, Watson: I fear I must now turn my full attention to a certain honourable gentleman." At that, my friend bid me farewell, and took up a scarlet box file which bore the insignia of the Lower House.

III.

I passed the journey happily enough, for autumn dressed the Garden of England in shades of russet and gold, and it was delightful to see fruit bowing the branches of the apple orchards which passed the carriage window. I was greeted at the station by a dog-cart, which conveyed me deep into the Kentish countryside. It was that time of year which will ever recall to me the longing for home which was the constant companion of my years of service in Afghanistan; and I observed with the greatest pleasure the effect of the declining sun on the oaks and elms. At last we passed through a small village which I took to be Long Marcham, and came to a halt before a pair of mighty iron gates. Here Sir James himself awaited me. It was evident he regretted his attempt to dissuade Holmes from any further interest in the case, for he wrung his hands in distress.

"Dr Watson," said he, drawing me through the gate, and towards a great grey house which lay a hundred yards distant. "Welcome to Boxley Grange. Naturally I had hoped that Mr Holmes would find himself able to attend; but I am grateful indeed for the presence of a medical man, for Charles has again begun to show signs of a sickness which I am afraid may prove fatal – might I ask you to attend to him directly, once you have been shown your apartments?"

I said that he might indeed ask; and I was conducted by an unspeaking man-servant to a pleasantly furnished room on the upper floor. The house itself was some three hundred years old, and though it possessed a degree of grandeur in its central staircase, and in the clock-tower which crowned the pediment upon the roof, was nonetheless of modest size and homely aspect. My own room over-looked the walled garden below, which retained the colour of late summer, and testified to the care and imagination of the lady who once had tended it. I noted at once, however, a curious feature of the lawn. From my vantage point it was possible to perceive two paths which marked the passage of footsteps. The first terminated, as one might expect, at the iron gate, which was locked; the other led only to a corner of the garden wall, which was heavily overgrown with some creeping vine. Pondering the significance of this observation I departed my room, valise in hand, and discovered Sir James awaiting me. With agitated haste I was conveyed along a broad hall to the child's nursery. Here the patient was confined to a narrow white bed set beneath an open window, through which a cool air drifted to alleviate the atmosphere of the sickroom.

Miss Beaumont was seated beside the bed, and rose at once to greet me. "Dr Watson," she said. "How grateful we are that you have come; for Dr Reed, who has attended the child since birth, professes himself baffled as to the cause."

I made a brief examination of the child, whose fair curls and peculiarly lam-bent eyes surely recalled the features of his late mother. I noted an accelerated pulse, and that the skin of his forearm was notably cold to the touch; though listless, he responded to my request that he should raise his arm above the cov-erlet. Thus was I able to observe the trembling in his hand. Recalling that the Grange abutted the church of St Andrew, and that Sir James in his letter had made reference to the child's having found scarlet beads upon the lawn, I was struck at once by the diagnosis.

"How many days have passed since the boy was taken ill?"

"This is the third morning."

"And prior to the child being confined to his bed, did you observe anything unusual in his manner?"

"Miss Beaumont observed that he staggered as he walked, as though he were on board ship: it was then that the alarm was raised, and Dr Reed brought from the village."

I addressed myself directly to my patient. "And how do you do, young man? Might we persuade you to take a little food?"

The boy lifted his head from the pillow. "I saw my mother," he said plaintive-ly; then he slept.

"It is distressing, I know," said I, turning from patient to father; "but your son has merely contracted a fever. This must be countered with rest, and with nourishment; and I see it is well to leave matters in the hands of Miss Beaumont, who is evidently an excellent nurse. Nonetheless we must ensure your son is neither disturbed by sudden noises, nor exposed to a chill. Keep the window fastened, and do not permit any visitors into the sickroom, save of course for Miss Beaumont and myself."

Returning to my quarters I made note of my observations, then passed a quiet afternoon in the company of Sir James, who evidently took modest pride in the Grange and its surrounding lands. With a key upon his watch-chain he opened the iron gate which led from the garden into a portion of grassed acreage. This gave, in turn, onto the churchyard of St Andrew, where Lady Denys had been buried. Though breeding forbade the widower any display of grief, we paused there for a moment, and I observed the costly though modest gravestone, on which was carved the commendation WELL DONE THOU GOOD AND FAITHFUL SERVANT. I was then led by Sir James to the handsome church, where a pair of great yew trees were so heavily burdened it was possible to hear the fall of berries on the stone path, and on the flat tombstones which lay all around.

On returning to the Grange, our path was crossed by two men who scarcely could have been less alike in size, aspect and demeanour. The first was the vicar of the parish, a Reverent Ashwood, so advanced in years that his voice trembled as if with suppressed emotion. With a myopic smile he wished the blessing of the Almighty on us both, and vanished within the dim confines of the nave. Hardly five minutes passed before we encountered, walking swiftly in the opposite direction, a man whose height and bulk was that of a prize-fighter, yet who walked the stooped gait of a man with much to conceal. Though he wore the plain black robes of a verger these were not maintained in a manner befitting an officer of the church: they were somewhat stained about the hem, and more-over were surmounted with a muffler of dubious quality, and an evil-looking hat pressed well down upon the brow. This apparition bid us a grudging good evening, before hurrying on towards a small cottage set so deeply within a thicket of hedge and thorn that I had not spied it on first arriving. "That is Harries," said Sir James. "An unprepossessing man, to be sure; but with Ash-worth so far gone in years, much of the burden of parish work falls upon his shoulders." Then he gestured that we should return whence we had come.

The evening meal passed agreeably enough; and mindful of Holmes' instruc-tions that I should not neglect the household staff I praised an excellent pair of partridges with such force that I was able to beg leave to congratulate the cook in person, and perhaps to secure the recipe for the use of my wife. Miss Beaumont, though perhaps bemused by my request, conducted me down to the kitchen, where I discovered a woman, rather gaunt, cleaning a magnificent iron range. I at once observed a chill in the exchange between governess and cook; for the former made a swift introduction, and equally swift apologies.

"I trust you will forgive my intrusion into your kingdom," said I. "But it is a good many years since I've dined so well, and I have insisted on saying so in person."

At once the woman softened a little. I was offered a seat, and a little more of the syllabub which had ended the meal. We spoke in a desultory fashion for a few moments, in which the new companion deplored the scarcity of good eggs, and likewise of asparagus. I was then able to turn my attention to the question of the Kentish Ghost, and it was immediately apparent that the cook was a woman of doughty English sensibility, who could no more countenance the notion of a ghostly visitation than take flight above the Boxley clock-tower.

"I don't give it a moment's thought, sir, and no more should you. Sarah never had an ounce more sense than she was born with, and good riddance to her says I, on account of I could scarcely trust her to walk from one end of the kitchen to the other without she broke six plates and a teacup. As to the boy, God bless and keep him: well, let him have his fancies, poor mite, what with my poor Lady hardly cold in the ground, and he taking sick of a sudden."

"I am sure Miss Beaumont is a great comfort," I said.

"Confidentially, sir, I can't say as I trust her."

"Not trust her!" I ejaculated, recalling the lady's fresh and open countenance, and the charming image which she had presented beside her small patient's bed.

"A hoity-toity miss! Marrying the master, indeed: and she as much a servant as I! Why: down she comes, requesting the little dishes I used to prepare for my Lady, to be taken in her rooms: I never heard of such a thing! Then there's the letters, and all from that French gentleman, I'll be bound. I didn't much take to him while he was here. Oily, as my father might have said. You might have fried an egg off the grease on his palm!"

I recalled Sir James' first narrative. "Doctor Martin," said I, "who attended Lady Denys in her final illness?" But she would say no more; and thus I bade her farewell, and repaired to the comfort of my rooms, where I prepared the report which I was to set before Mr Sherlock Holmes.

It was evident (said I) that the child suffered the effects of *taxus baccata* poisoning, having consumed the scarlet berry of the yew. This I deduced both from the presentation of symptoms, and from the child's belief he had found a lady's necklace, for the yew berry is notable for having a solid, waxen appearance, moreover pierced as if for a length of ribbon. Having lived three days beyond ingesting the noxious substance, he would certainly recover; it was likely the dog had not been so fortunate. Whether each had been poisoned by accident or by design I could not say. Holmes, on his arrival, should scarcely want for candidates upon whom to turn his scrutiny: the dismissed and evidently unreliable maid, the silent manservant, the evil-looking verger and the disgruntled cook I delineated as possible conspirators in this curious and distressing tale, only adding that I had not myself met Dr Reed, but could personally testify that the parish priest was a harmless, if wholly decrepit, servant of God. Concluding with a brief description of the cook's pique, and the curious markings left upon the lawn, I took my rest.

I despatched this communiqué from the post office in the adjoining village. Then passed another day in the Kentish countryside. Sir James being absent on business, I took lunch with Miss Beaumont, in whose charming company the hour passed swiftly indeed. I attended my patient in the afternoon, observing an improvement in his pallor and listless demeanour; and after a modest evening meal begged leave to retire early to my rooms. Sleep nonetheless eluded me; and having read in a desultory fashion for a while, it occurred to me to keep watch a while at the window, in hope of witnessing for myself the phenomenon of the Kentish Ghost. Yet all was quiet below; and in time the folly of this endeavour drove me to the comfort of my bed, and I slept until morning.

I was greeted at breakfast by a telegraph from Sherlock Holmes. If I had hoped to receive a word of praise for my endeavours I was disappointed, for it read: "The case is solved. Confirm postmark on letters arriving from France by return. Expect my arrival." Repellent as it was to intrude upon a lady's correspondence, fate was favourable; for that same morning, as if Holmes himself by some means could direct the postal service, a letter lay in the silver dish set upon an oak cabinet in the great hall. Under pretence of pausing there to wind my pocket-watch, I scrutinised the envelope. It was addressed to Miss Beaumont in a fine masculine hand; and despite indistinctness where poor weather had interposed upon the ink, I was able to read the postmark, which declared the correspondent to be resident in France, in the town of Ververs. Of what significance this detail might be I could not guess; but I did as I was bade, and sent Holmes a telegraph bearing that word alone.

Thus passed another day. I grew restive, and no further shocks or misadventures broke the autumn peace at Boxley Grange. My patient rallied, and there was no mention of the apparition which had precipitated my visit. I thought fondly of my busy practice, and of my wife; and wished fervently that the morrow would come, and bring with it Sherlock Holmes, and thus an end to my unwitting rustication. I awoke the following morning with a curious sensation of foreboding, though could not guess at the source: the room in which I slept was quite as well-appointed as it had been when I'd turned in, yet all seemed altered. It was as if some faint presence pervaded the room, casting a strange and yellowish light upon each object; and though the chorus of garden birds which had greeted me each morning had fallen silent it seemed to me that I heard, from all quarters, the faint tolling of bells. I lit the lamp and cast aside the bedclothes, and confess that I thought briefly of the Kentish Ghost: might this singular atmosphere signal the apparition's approach? I drew aside the curtains, and saw at once the cause: an autumn fog had drifted west from the Downs, and clad the house in a pale haze. It was scarcely possible to make out the walled garden below, and the gate and its lock were obscured entirely. I laughed at my own susceptibility to superstition, and having partaken of breakfast, I satisfied myself that my small patient would shortly quit his chambers, and return to the schoolroom. Mindful of Holmes' instructions, I accompanied Sir James and Miss Beaumont to the church of St Andrews, marvelling at the bells tolling in a tower concealed within a dense pall of fog. As our small party passed through the iron gate, Miss Beaumont looked towards the cottage I had observed two days before, and which was home to the evil-looking verger. There, it was possible to discern the ruddy glow of a lamp set in the window. It was a look both furtive and fearful, and quite unlike the frank and steady gaze with which I had come to associate her. Perhaps she knew that I saw; for suddenly she smiled, and said: "I cannot help being just a little afraid of Harries, for he is so large, and not at all clean." We came then to the stone which marked the final resting-place of Lady Denys, and at that moment the wind stirred the enclosing mist, so that for a moment the inscription appeared to glow in rich autumnal sunshine. We gentlemen bared our heads, and Miss Beaumont stooped to lay a posy on the grave.

It was then that I saw it – and shall I never forget the sight? Scarce ten yards distant, pressed somewhat against the wall which divided the churchyard from the garden, stood a wraith dressed all in white.

"Why – it is the Kentish Ghost!" I cried, for the apparition was just as I had heard described. Its face was ghastly white, though scarcely visible beneath a veil of fair hair, and its pale lips writhed. It wore a robe of some gauzy fabric, which stirred in the breeze, and seemed one with the coils of mist which occluded the air. Its feet were bare, and in its right hand it held a lily flower. It seemed the wraith had seen us, for it raised its left arm, which trembled as though with a mortal chill, towards the party which now stood silent and aghast beside the tomb.

"Great God!" cried Sir James: "Great God! Watson, do you see? It is she! It is she!"

The spectre drew closer, and I perceived clearly the unblinking eyes set deep within their bony sockets, and the awful pallor of its sunken cheek. Then the eyes closed, and it spoke in a soft and feminine voice which carried clearly through the mist: "Though she were dead, yet shall she live."

Sir James shuddered, and gave a terrible cry; he moved as though to reach out and grasp that ghostly hand, but was forestalled by Miss Beaumont, who moved with a swiftness of which I had not thought her capable, and interposed herself between man and vision. "Why, James," she said: "Do not be afraid – there is nothing to trouble us – nothing but the wind stirring the fog among the branches! Look! What do you see? It is nothing; take my arm, for we are late to church: listen, do you hear the bells?" I started in astonishment, and began to remonstrate; for I, too, had seen the white-clad figure standing there; but when I looked again, I saw nothing but mist rising in the long grass, and a thicket of branches stirring against the wall.

"Good God!" I said; "what trickery is at play – Sir James, I believe you have been subject to a deception – I must insist you return with me to the Grange, and await the arrival of Sherlock Holmes, who shall certainly be interested to hear all that has happened this morning!"

"It was she!" said Sir James, shaking off the restraining hand which Miss Beaumont had placed upon his sleeve: "It was Elizabeth, as I stand here before you – it was my wife!"

"Do not trouble yourself so," said Miss Beaumont; and I saw for a moment an expression upon that charming countenance which spoke of an iron resolve. "Do not trouble yourself . . . why, here is Harries! Mr Harries, Sir James has been taken ill – kindly take his arm, and lead him to the church."

I turned and perceived the verger approaching silently, and with that hunched and secretive gait. No officer of the church could have presented a less godly appearance: the black vestments of his calling flapped about him; and the muffler wound about his gaunt neck, and the hat pressed down above a pair of glittering eyes, spoke of a man whose purposes were far from sacred. Stepping past me with scarcely a glance, he heeded Miss Beaumont's plea, and grasped Sir James' arm.

"Stand back!" said I, raising my stick: "Stand back, I tell you – Sir James, I fear this man is a scoundrel, and may not be trusted: Miss Beaumont, I beg you take care!"

"A scoundrel, he says!" said the verger, speaking indistinctly through the vile muffler: "What, old Harries? Who buried Lady Denys, who cast the soil upon her grave?" Then he began to laugh, so that I grew quite enraged. "Get back!" I said again. "Sir James, I assure you I will let no harm come to you; stand by me –"

"A scoundrel, I? For shame, Watson!" cried the verger, and raised a hand to the muffler. That harsh voice was subtly altered; I looked, and saw a pair of eyes fixed upon me with amusement. Then the verger lifted his hat, and with a courteous movement which sat bizarrely on that unwholesome apparition made a bow before the gaunt and startled baronet.

"I trust you will forgive my small deception, Sir James," he said, in a voice quite altered from the verger's indistinct utterances; and removing the muffler revealed himself to be none other than Sherlock Holmes.

"Holmes!" said I, in astonishment. "You gave me no word! – what can you be about; and did you see it – is the problem solved?"

"It is solved," said Holmes, gravely. "Sir James, I beg that you will wait a moment here, and prepare yourself; for I must bring before you facts which can do little but disturb the tranquillity which you have so diligently sought to bring to your family. Watson, attend to Miss Beaumont, for I fear I have startled her somewhat; do me the goodness of ensuring she remains within your care."

I looked to the lady, and was astonished to perceive that her face was set in an expression of the utmost rage. What caused this sudden alteration I could not guess, for it seemed to me certain that Harries – perhaps already in the custody of the village constable – had been the architect of this extraordinary deceit. Then Holmes took a step back behind a bank of rising mist, and appeared to vanish at once behind the dangling thicket that hung over the garden wall, as swiftly and silently as had the Kentish Ghost. Struck quite dumb by this conjuror's trick, we three stood awhile unspeaking, as the bells of St Andrews bid the devout attend their worship. A moment passed, and Holmes again appeared, stepping forward with a quick decisive step; but he was not alone, for with a gentle and courteous motion he drew before us a lady clothed in a white garment, which was surmounted by a dark coat. Her fair hair lay upon her shoulders, and within the fair locks were fragments of branch and leaf, and the scarlet berries of the yew. "Your wife, Sir James," said Holmes. "Though she were dead, yet shall she live: you are no widower, sir."

At this, Miss Beaumont gave a shriek, and might have swooned had I not prevented her from doing so.

"Elizabeth?" said Sir James, in whose voice hope and disbelief mingled equally; and I saw how deep had been the love and grief which lay behind that cool reserve.

I cannot adequately convey what then passed: how the baronet took his wife by the hand, and spoke gently to her; how she lay her head upon his shoulder, and asked for her child; how Miss Beaumont fell senseless upon the damp grass; how she was roused, and conveyed to the verger's cottage. There I sat beside the fire, the governess white and silent beside me. Sir James and his wife stood before the window, the lady's hand returned at last to her husband's; and Holmes threw off the vast coat which covered him, and with it every last vestige of the verger. I saw within the room a narrow bed with a white coverlet, and a white robe hanging on the wall. White lilies were placed upon the windowsill, beside holy books bound in white. The effect was partly that of a church, and partly of some well-kept mausoleum, and I perceived at once that Lady Denys had made this her dwelling-place; though whether willingly or under duress I could not say. In the glow of the lamp the lady, though thin and gaunt, retained much of the beauty which had once been so celebrated in the county.

Sir James, returned at last to his senses, turned to the detective. "Mr Holmes," he said, "I am in your debt, for you have returned to me what I thought was lost; yet I remain at a loss as to what kind of evil has befallen my family. I beg you to set before us all that you have deduced."

"It is the simplest of matters," said Holmes, "and though no capital crime has yet been committed, it is my belief that I have forestalled the gravest of outrages against the laws of man and of God.

"I confess I was not at first compelled to turn my attention to this problem: I do not concern myself with the petty upheavals of household intrigue, nor with the delusions of children. Nonetheless my interest was somewhat piqued on observing that Miss Beaumont wore a ring set with small stones, in the following sequence: amethyst; diamond; opal; ruby; emerald. You see at once, do you not, the significance of such an item?" Holmes looked keenly at us all, and perceiving that any significance eluded us, said: "Come, come! It is child's play! It is the fashion, is it not, for ladies to sport jewels which spell out words of affection? Miss Beachamp's ring reads, to the astute observer, ADORE – an endearment which may indicate a lover either English or French by birth. On being quizzed about the ring, however, the lady informed me that it was a gift from an aunt: a certain lie, for what aunt would be so ardent? It was therefore evident that the lady's affection lay elsewhere, and that her engagement to Sir James was based on a deceit."

"Amelia!" cried Sir James; but could say no more.

"I thought little more of the matter, for the intrigues of governesses do not concern me. Then came your letter, Sir James, which provided me with three points of interest. First, the curious behaviour of Lady Denys' unfortunate Pekinese. Second, that the apparition was perceived to have worn a coat; from which one may deduce at once that here was no childish deceit, but rather a person of flesh and blood – for what spirit exchanges summer garments for the warmth of a coat in winter? Third, the letter was written across two pages. The first of these was expressive of the deepest anxiety; and yet the second sought to rebuff my attentions. Naturally I made a study of the document, and I must tell you, Miss Beaumont, that your skills in forgery leave much to be desired, for it was evident immediately that I was looking at two quite distinct hands. The second page – in which I daresay Sir James begged my assistance – had been substituted for note designed to prevent my coming to the Grange; and I assure you that where my presence is least wanted, it is certainly most needed. Thus I despatched my good Watson, in whose medical skills I place the greatest trust, and who carried out my instructions to watch and to observe with some diligence, though with a degree of imprecision as to the details. Never mind, Watson: you did what you could. Thus was I furnished by letter with the following facts: that the lawn was marked with a second path terminating within the thicket which overlays the wall; that the child suffered *taxus baccata* poisoning, and could not have done so by accident; that a maid had been dismissed upon seeing a ghostly apparition; that this apparition was beyond doubt a being as carnal as you and I; that Miss Beaumont had offended the cook by requesting dishes which had been the particular fancy of Lady Denys; that the governess received letters from the French doctor who had attended her mistress in her final illness, and that these were postmarked Ververs; that only Sir James possessed the key to the gate dividing churchyard from garden; that the parish priest was so elderly as to be beyond use; and that the verger was of so evil an aspect that he could certainly be relied upon to have a hand in villainy. (This last point I might well have discarded, for Watson has ever fallen into error, believing fine features to conceal fine morals, and crooked features to conceal crooked minds.) You perceive of course the conclusions which I inevitably reached?" Again the great detective looked in vain for comprehension; encountering none, he addressed himself to the baronet. "Sir James, it was your own testament that your wife has long been subject to a very particular weakness of the mind. It may perhaps console you to learn that this phenomenon has been noted in others by the French neurological physician, Dr Jules Cotard. His findings have been well reported in the English medical journals; indeed I am surprised that Dr Watson did not immediately note the symptoms."

At this I started, for the name was indeed familiar. "It is the Cotard Delusion!" I said. "Holmes! She believes herself to be dead – oh, had I only made the connection myself!"

"Quite so," said Holmes. "Fantastic as it may seem, Sir James, your wife believes herself to have passed away during her last sickness: thus her desire to sequester herself in her rooms, and to fashion mourning-jewellery from a lock of her own hair. Those afflicted in this fashion are known to display an attachment to churches and their grounds, and I have no doubt Lady Denys frequented the churchyard of St Nicholas, since it is so conveniently situated."

"I should say not," said Sir James, somewhat affronted. "For I have always been sole custodian of the key, and the gate is kept locked, save on those occasions when members of the household attend church."

"Nonetheless, it is so," said Holmes, placidly. "From his vantage point above the garden Watson was able to observe a curious effect upon the lawn. There is, in addition to a path worn from house to gate, an additional track, rather more faint, which appears to terminate against the wall. It was here that Lady Denys discovered a point of egress, from which to slip unseen between garden and churchyard. Did you not think it curious that there, and there alone, a thicket of bramble and thorn was permitted to grow in a garden which otherwise might rival those at Versailles?"

"Great heaven!" said Sir James.

"The behaviour of the lady's dog was thus no madness, but the actions of a creature of habit. We turn now to events immediately preceding the supposed death of Lady Denys. The details must remain ever beyond our ken, but we may be certain of these facts: that Miss Beaumont's relation, Dr Martin, is the source of Miss Beaumont's ornament, which made its silent declaration not in English, but in French. Being resident in Ververs, the very hospital where Cotard himself undertakes his work, he would certainly have observed the phenomenon in your wife. What a happy circumstance it was when Lady Denys fell ill! With her treatment confined solely to his care, what could be simpler than to induce in her a state of insensibility, by the application of chloroform or some other drug; and to pronounce that she had succumbed to a fever. Upon waking, a skilled dissembler such as Miss Beaumont would have small trouble in banking the fires of the lady's delusion, and keeping her sequestered among the accoutrements of mourning. The plan should certainly have failed had it not been for two facts: the parson has grown so old that he is content to rely on the verger for all but the most sacred of duties, and the verger was susceptible to corruption. Do not underestimate, Sir James, the powerful lure of money for those accustomed to little. Thus was a weighted coffin buried with all the reverence due to a Lady; and thus was a Lady kept a cottage unfit to her stature."

"Monstrous!" said Sir James: "To think that I placed my wife in the care of a man who would have done her such ill!" He rose from his seat, as if to reach Miss Beaumont, and remonstrate with the woman who had so cruelly deceived him.

"I was quite content," murmured Lady Denys. "For I had my holy things about me; though I missed my child, and did not like to see him mourn."

"A few further details served to persuade me of my theory. Doubtless perturbed by the extraordinary behaviour of the Pekinese, which a diligent observer might well think suspicious, Miss Beaumont, making use of the concealed passage between garden and churchyard, administered a poison: that provided by the berries with which the yews are so heavily burdened. It is likely these were deposited in the portion of the garden to which the dog was so attached; and that the child, having first mistaken them for the scarlet beads of a lady's necklace, consumed sufficient to induce a brief illness. I need hardly expand upon the nature of the supposed ghost: for it was Lady Denys herself, perhaps in those moments of lucidity to which such patients are subject, seeking to return again to the family home where she had once lived in such contentment. Thus I departed London this morning, with sufficient money in my pocket to persuade Harries to exchange his outer garments for mine, that I may play a trick; for the venal are as changeable as the weathervane, with no loyalty save to coin and coffer."

"Monstrous!" said Sir James again; and was by the hand of his wife upon his sleeve.

"My son," said Lady Elizabeth, in that serene and melodious voice. "I rather liked to see my son, and to walk in my garden again."

"Wretched woman!" cried Miss Beaumont. "Had it not been for your restlessness, all should have been well!"

"Mr Holmes," said Sir James. "It is clear that I am in your debt; yet one thing remains beyond my grasp. What motive might there be for so complex and cruel a plan?"

"It is my belief that Miss Beaumont and Dr Martin saw in you the opportunity to secure for themselves the comfort which they lack. You are a man of both means and of sense; and have spoken often of your desire to secure a future both for your son, and for your intended wife. I daresay you made provisions that upon your death Miss Beaumont, once married, would retain her title, and remain mistress of Boxley Grange until your son attains his majority?"

Sir James threw off the last remnants of his confusion. "I did," he said, keenly: "Not two days past; for I have wanted nothing more than Charles to grow up free from the disruptions which have blighted his childhood thus far!" The full significance of the facts appeared then to strike him anew, for he turned to Miss Beaumont with an expression in which the righteous anger and the most profound distress fought for mastery. "Amelia! What then was your plan – what new deceits lay in store, once so favourable a marriage was attained?"

Beside me the governess was silent, that once smiling countenance now unmoving as that of the stone angels which thronged the churchyard beyond the cottage door. "Do not ask," said Holmes, "for the danger is averted, and your wife returned; and Miss Beaumont's testimony, and in due course that of both her lover and of the faithless Harries, must be reserved for those officers of the law already venturing east from the precincts of Scotland Yard. Indeed I hear their footsteps now – for who else would dare disrupt the very Garden of England with so heavy a tread. Well, Watson: we must depart, and leave Sir James to the family which has ever been the sole focus of his affections. It remains for me to observe that love and money go hand-in-hand more often than either a poet or a consulting detective might wish; and happy indeed is the man who finds himself indifferent to both."

Within the hour, my friend and I were seated in a railway-carriage. Dusk had begun to fall across Kent, and the remnants of the day's fog rolled against the window as we rattled towards the capital.

"The Cotard Delusion!" said I, shaking my head. "If only I had made the connection! I seem able to perceive incidents in isolation, yet am unable to find the thread which joins them!"

Holmes gestured with the stem of his pipe to my pocket-watch, which I had withdrawn from my pocket, and had begun to wind. "Have you ever paid close attention to the workings of a mechanical clock?" he said. "It is little short of a miracle of invention, imprecision, and correction. The wheels require the weight to supply their energy; the weight requires the escapement in its turn; likewise the chime requires the fly, which must be corrected by the weights; and the whole is regulated by the pendulum. So it is with all human endeavour, both benevolent and malign. A plot devised in secret must bend and alter once put into play; for the first deceit requires another, which must soon be attended by another; and it is only the most diligent watchmaker that may discern the chain which links each motion to the other." He drew upon the pipe, and pulling at the blind which covered the carriage window said: "Now let us put all thought of deceit and cupidity from our minds; for I have here my pocket Petrarch, with which we shall pass the time until we find ourselves once again in the good hands of Mrs Hudson."

THE BLACK BAG LEFT ON A DOORSTEP

Catherine Louisa Pirkis

Catherine Louisa Pirkis (1839–1910) started publishing her Loveday Brooke short stories in 1894. Like her first novel, *Disappeared from Her Home* (1877), they were early examples of mystery fiction by British women. Shortly after creating Brooke, Pirkis retired from writing to focus on animal welfare.

"It's a big thing," said Loveday Brooke, addressing Ebenezer Dyer, chief of the well-known detective agency in Lynch Court, Fleet Street; "Lady Cathrow has lost £30,000 worth of jewellery, if the newspaper accounts are to be trusted."

"They are fairly accurate this time. The robbery differs in few respects from the usual run of country-house robberies. The time chosen, of course, was the dinner-hour, when the family and guests were at table and the servants not on duty were amusing themselves in their own quarters. The fact of its being Christmas Eve would also of necessity add to the business and consequent distraction of the household. The entry to the house, however, in this case was not effected in the usual manner by a ladder to the dressing-room window, but through the window of a room on the ground floor – a small room with one window and two doors, one of which opens into the hall, and the other into a passage that leads by the back stairs to the bedroom floor. It is used, I believe, as a sort of hat and coat room by the gentlemen of the house."

"It was, I suppose, the weak point of the house?"

"Quite so. A very weak point indeed. Craigen Court, the residence of Sir George and Lady Cathrow, is an oddly-built old place, jutting out in all directions, and as this window looked out upon a blank wall, it was filled in with stained glass, kept fastened by a strong brass catch, and never opened, day or night, ventilation being obtained by means of a glass ventilator fitted in the upper panes. It seems absurd to think that this window, being only about four feet from the ground, should have had neither iron bars nor shutters added to it; such, however, was the case. On the night of the robbery, someone within the house must have deliberately, and of intention, unfastened its only protection, the brass catch, and thus given the thieves easy entrance to the house."

"Your suspicions, I suppose, centre upon the servants?"

"Undoubtedly; and it is in the servants' hall that your services will be required. The thieves, whoever they were, were perfectly cognizant of the ways of the house. Lady Cathrow's jewellery was kept in a safe in her dressing-room, and as the dressing-room was over the dining-room, Sir George was in the habit of saying that it was the 'safest' room in the house. (Note the pun, please; Sir George is rather proud of it.) By his orders the window of the dining-room immediately under the dressing-room window was always left unshuttered and without blind during dinner, and as a full stream of light thus fell through it on to the outside terrace, it would have been impossible for anyone to have placed a ladder there unseen."

"I see from the newspapers that it was Sir George's invariable custom to fill his house and give a large dinner on Christmas Eve."

"Yes. Sir George and Lady Cathrow are elderly people, with no family and few relatives, and have consequently a large amount of time to spend on their friends."

"I suppose the key of the safe was frequently left in the possession of Lady Cathrow's maid?"

"Yes. She is a young French girl, Stephanie Delcroix by name. It was her duty to clear the dressing-room directly after her mistress left it; put away any jewellery that might be lying about, lock the safe, and keep the key till her mistress came up to bed. On the night of the robbery, however, she admits that, instead of so doing, directly her mistress left the dressing-room, she ran down to the housekeeper's room to see if any letters had come for her, and remained chatting with the other servants for some time – she could not say for how long. It was by the half-past-seven post that her letters generally arrived from St. Omer, where her home is."

"Oh, then, she was in the habit of thus running down to enquire for her letters, no doubt, and the thieves, who appear to be so thoroughly cognizant of the house, would know this also."

"Perhaps; though at the present moment I must say things look very black against the girl. Her manner, too, when questioned, is not calculated to remove suspicion. She goes from one fit of hysterics into another; contradicts herself nearly every time she opens her mouth, then lays it to the charge of her ignorance of our language; breaks into voluble French; becomes theatrical in action, and then goes off into hysterics once more."

"All that is quite Français, you know," said Loveday. "Do the authorities at Scotland Yard lay much stress on the safe being left unlocked that night?"

"They do, and they are instituting a keen enquiry as to the possible lovers the girl may have. For this purpose they have sent Bates down to stay in the village and collect all the information he can outside the house. But they want someone within the walls to hob-nob with the maids generally, and to find out if she has taken any of them into her confidence respecting her lovers. So they sent to me to know if I would send down for this purpose one of the shrewdest and most clear-headed of my female detectives. I, in my turn, Miss Brooke, have sent for you – you may take it as a compliment if you like. So please now get out your note-book, and I'll give you sailing orders."

Loveday Brooke, at this period of her career, was a little over thirty years of age, and could be best described in a series of negations.

She was not tall, she was not short; she was not dark, she was not fair; she was neither handsome nor ugly. Her features were altogether nondescript; her one noticeable trait was a habit she had, when absorbed in thought, of dropping her eyelids over her eyes till only a line of eyeball showed, and she appeared to be looking out at the world through a slit, instead of through a window.

Her dress was invariably black, and was almost Quaker-like in its neat primness.

Some five or six years previously, by a jerk of Fortune's wheel, Loveday had been thrown upon the world penniless and all but friendless. Marketable accomplishments she had found she had none, so she had forthwith defied convention, and had chosen for herself a career that had cut her off sharply from her former associates and her position in society. For five or six years she drudged away patiently in the lower walks of her profession; then chance, or, to speak more precisely, an intricate criminal case, threw her in the way of the experienced head of the flourishing detective agency in Lynch Court. He quickly enough found out the stuff she was made of, and threw her in the way of better-class work – work, indeed, that brought increase of pay and of reputation alike to him and to Loveday.

Ebenezer Dyer was not, as a rule, given to enthusiasm; but he would at times wax eloquent over Miss Brooke's qualifications for the profession she had chosen.

"Too much of a lady, do you say?" he would say to anyone who chanced to call in question those qualifications. "I don't care twopence-halfpenny whether she is or is not a lady. I only know she is the most sensible and practical woman I ever met. In the first place, she has the faculty – so rare among women – of carrying out orders to the very letter: in the second place, she has a clear, shrewd brain, unhampered by any hard-and-fast theories; thirdly, and most important item of all, she has so much common sense that it amounts to genius – positively to genius, sir."

But although Loveday and her chief, as a rule, worked together upon an easy and friendly footing, there were occasions on which they were wont, so to speak, to snarl at each other. Such an occasion was at hand now.

Loveday showed no disposition to take out her note-book and receive her "sailing orders."

"I want to know," she said, "if what I saw in one newspaper is true – that one of the thieves, before leaving, took the trouble to close the safe-door, and to write across it in chalk: 'To be let, unfurnished'?"

"Perfectly true; but I do not see that stress need be laid on the fact. The scoundrels often do that sort of thing out of insolence or bravado. In that robbery at Reigate, the other day, they went to a lady's Davenport, took a sheet of her note-paper, and wrote their thanks on it for her kindness in not having had the lock of her safe repaired. Now, if you will get out your note-book—"

"Don't be in such a hurry," said Loveday calmly: "I want to know if you have seen this?" She leaned across the writing-table at which they sat, one either side, and handed to him a newspaper cutting which she took from her letter-case.

Mr. Dyer was a tall, powerfully-built man with a large head, benevolent bald forehead and a genial smile. That smile, however, often proved a trap to the unwary, for he owned a temper so irritable that a child with a chance word might ruffle it.

The genial smile vanished as he took the newspaper cutting from Loveday's hand.

"I would have you to remember, Miss Brooke," he said severely, "that although I am in the habit of using dispatch in my business, I am never known to be in a hurry; hurry in affairs I take to be the especial mark of the slovenly and unpunctual." Then, as if still further to give contradiction to her words, he very deliberately unfolded her slip of newspaper and slowly, accentuating each word and syllable, read as follows: –

"Singular Discovery.

"A black leather bag, or portmanteau, was found early yesterday morning by one of Smith's newspaper boys on the doorstep of a house in the road running between Easterbrook and Wreford, and inhabited by an elderly spinster lady. The contents of the bag include a clerical collar and necktie, a Church Service, a book of sermons, a copy of the works of Virgil, a *facsimile* of Magna Carta, with translations, a pair of black kid gloves, a brush and comb, some newspapers, and several small articles suggesting clerical ownership. On the top of the bag the following extraordinary letter, written in pencil on a long slip of paper, was found:

'The fatal day has arrived. I can exist no longer. I go hence and shall be no more seen. But I would have Coroner and Jury know that I am a sane man, and a verdict of temporary insanity in my case would be an error most gross after this intimation. I care not if it is *felo de se*, as I shall have passed all suffering. Search diligently for my poor lifeless body in the immediate neighbourhood – on the cold heath, the rail, or the river by yonder bridge – a few moments will decide how I shall depart. If I had walked aright I might have been a power in the Church of which I am now an unworthy member and priest; but the damnable sin of gambling got hold on me, and betting has been my ruin, as it has been the ruin of thousands who have preceded me. Young man, shun the bookmaker and the race-course as you would shun the devil and hell. Farewell, chums of Magdalen. Farewell, and take warning. Though I can claim relationship with a Duke, a Marquess, and a Bishop, and though I am the son of a noble woman, yet am I a tramp and an outcast, verily and indeed. Sweet death, I greet thee. I dare not sign my name. To one and all, farewell. O, my poor Marchioness mother, a dying kiss to thee. R.I.P.'

"The police and some of the railway officials have made a 'diligent search' in the neighbourhood of the railway station, but no 'poor lifeless body' has been found. The police authorities are inclined to the belief that the letter is a hoax, though they are still investigating the matter."

In the same deliberate fashion as he had opened and read the cutting, Mr. Dyer folded and returned it to Loveday.

"May I ask," he said sarcastically, "what you see in that silly hoax to waste your and my valuable time over?"

"I wanted to know," said Loveday, in the same level tones as before, "if you saw anything in it that might in some way connect this discovery with the robbery at Craigen Court?"

Mr. Dyer stared at her in utter, blank astonishment.

"When I was a boy," he said sarcastically as before, "I used to play at a game called 'what is my thought like?' Someone would think of something absurd –

say the top of the monument – and someone else would hazard a guess that his thought might be – say the toe of his left boot, and that unfortunate individual would have to show the connection between the toe of his left boot and the top of the monument. Miss Brooke, I have no wish to repeat the silly game this evening for your benefit and mine."

"Oh, very well," said Loveday, calmly; "I fancied you might like to talk it over, that was all. Give me my 'sailing orders,' as you call them, and I'll endeavour to concentrate my attention on the little French maid and her various lovers."

Mr. Dyer grew amiable again.

"That's the point on which I wish you to fix your thoughts," he said; "you had better start for Craigen Court by the first train to-morrow – it's about sixty miles down the Great Eastern line. Huxwell is the station you must land at. There one of the grooms from the Court will meet you, and drive you to the house. I have arranged with the housekeeper there – Mrs. Williams, a very worthy and discreet person – that you shall pass in the house for a niece of hers, on a visit to recruit, after severe study in order to pass board-school teachers' exams. Naturally you have injured your eyes as well as your health with overwork; and so you can wear your blue spectacles. Your name, by the way, will be Jane Smith – better write it down. All your work will be among the servants of the establishment, and there will be no necessity for you to see either Sir George or Lady Cathrow – in fact, neither of them have been apprised of your intended visit – the fewer we take into our confidence the better. I've no doubt, however, that Bates will hear from Scotland Yard that you are in the house, and will make a point of seeing you."

"Has Bates unearthed anything of importance?"

"Not as yet. He has discovered one of the girl's lovers, a young farmer of the name of Holt; but as he seems to be an honest, respectable young fellow, and entirely above suspicion, the discovery does not count for much."

"I think there's nothing else to ask," said Loveday, rising to take her departure. "Of course, I'll telegraph, should need arise, in our usual cipher."

The first train that left Bishopsgate for Huxwell on the following morning included, among its passengers, Loveday Brooke, dressed in the neat black supposed to be appropriate to servants of the upper class. The only literature with which she had provided herself in order to beguile the tedium of her journey was a small volume bound in paper boards, and entitled, "The Reciter's Treasury." It was published at the low price of one shilling, and seemed specially designed to meet the requirements of third-rate amateur reciters at penny readings. Miss Brooke appeared to be all-absorbed in the contents of this book during the first half of her journey. During the second, she lay back in the carriage with closed eyes, and motionless as if asleep or lost in deep thought.

The stopping of the train at Huxwell aroused her, and set her collecting together her wraps.

It was easy to single out the trim groom from Craigen Court from among the country loafers on the platform. Someone else beside the trim groom at the same moment caught her eye – Bates, from Scotland Yard, got up in the style of a commercial traveler, and carrying the orthodox "commercial bag" in his hand. He was a small, wiry man, with red hair and whiskers, and an eager, hungry expression of countenance.

"I am half-frozen with cold," said Loveday, addressing Sir George's groom; "if you'll kindly take charge of my portmanteau, I'd prefer walking to driving to the Court."

The man gave her a few directions as to the road she was to follow, and then drove off with her box, leaving her free to indulge Mr. Bate's evident wish for a walk and confidential talk along the country road.

Bates seemed to be in a happy frame of mind that morning.

"Quite a simple affair, this, Miss Brooke," he said: "a walk over the course, I take it, with you working inside the castle walls and I unearthing without. No complications as yet have arisen, and if that girl does not find herself in jail before another week is over her head, my name is not Jeremiah Bates."

"You mean the French maid?"

"Why, yes, of course. I take it there's little doubt but what she performed the double duty of unlocking the safe and the window too. You see I look at it this way, Miss Brooke: all girls have lovers, I say to myself, but a pretty girl like that French maid, is bound to have double the number of lovers than the plain ones. Now, of course, the greater the number of lovers, the greater the chance there is of a criminal being found among them. That's plain as a pikestaff, isn't it?"

"Just as plain."

Bates felt encouraged to proceed.

"Well, then, arguing on the same lines, I say to myself, this girl is only a pretty, silly thing, not an accomplished criminal, or she wouldn't have admitted leaving open the safe door; give her rope enough and she'll hang herself. In a day or two, if we let her alone, she'll be bolting off to join the fellow whose nest she has helped to feather, and we shall catch the pair of them 'twixt here and Dover Straits, and also possibly get a clue that will bring us on the traces of their accomplices. Eh, Miss Brooke, that'll be a thing worth doing?"

"Undoubtedly. Who is this coming along in this buggy at such a good pace?"

The question was added as the sound of wheels behind them made her look round.

Bates turned also. "Oh, this is young Holt; his father farms land about a couple of miles from here. He is one of Stephanie's lovers, and I should imagine about the best of the lot. But he does not appear to be first favourite; from what I hear someone else must have made the running on the sly. Ever since the robbery I'm told the young woman has given him the cold shoulder."

As the young man came nearer in his buggy he slackened pace, and Loveday could not but admire his frank, honest expression of countenance.

"Room for one – can I give you a lift?" he said, as he came alongside of them.

And to the ineffable disgust of Bates, who had counted upon at least an hour's confidential talk with her, Miss Brooke accepted the young farmer's offer, and mounted beside him in his buggy. As they went swiftly along the country road, Loveday explained to the young man that her destination was Craigen Court, and that as she was a stranger to the place, she must trust to him to put her down at the nearest point to it that he would pass.

At the mention of Craigen Court his face clouded.

"They're in trouble there, and their trouble has brought trouble on others," he said a little bitterly.

"I know," said Loveday sympathetically; "it is often so. In such circumstances as these suspicions frequently fasten on an entirely innocent person."

"That's it! that's it!" he cried excitedly; "if you go into that house you'll hear all sorts of wicked things said of her, and see everything setting in dead against her. But she's innocent. I swear to you she is as innocent as you or I are."

His voice rang out above the clatter of his horse's hoofs. He seemed to forget that he had mentioned no name, and that Loveday, as a stranger, might be at a loss to know to whom he referred.

"Who is guilty Heaven only knows," he went on after a moment's pause; "it isn't for me to give an ill name to anyone in that house; but I only say she is innocent, and that I'll stake my life on."

"She is a lucky girl to have found one to believe in her, and trust her as you do," said Loveday, even more sympathetically than before.

"Is she? I wish she'd take advantage of her luck, then," he answered bitterly. "Most girls in her position would be glad to have a man to stand by them through thick and thin. But not she! Ever since the night of that accursed robbery she has refused to see me – won't answer my letters – won't even send me a message. And, great Heavens! I'd marry her to-morrow, if I had the chance, and dare the world to say a word against her." He whipped up his pony. The hedges seemed to fly on either side of them, and before Loveday realized that half her drive was over, he had drawn rein, and was helping her to alight at the servants' entrance to Craigen Court.

"You'll tell her what I've said to you, if you get the opportunity, and beg her to see me, if only for five minutes?" he petitioned before he re-mounted his buggy. And Loveday, as she thanked the young man for his kind attention, promised to make an opportunity to give his message to the girl.

Mrs. Williams, the housekeeper, welcomed Loveday in the servants' hall, and then took her to her own room to pull off her wraps. Mrs. Williams was the widow of a London tradesman, and a little beyond the average housekeeper in speech and manner.

She was a genial, pleasant woman, and readily entered into conversation with Loveday. Tea was brought in, and each seemed to feel at home with the other. Loveday, in the course of this easy, pleasant talk, elicited from her the whole history of the events of the day of the robbery, the number and names of the guests who sat down to dinner that night, together with some other apparently trivial details.

The housekeeper made no attempt to disguise the painful position in which she and every one of the servants of the house felt themselves to be at the present moment.

"We are none of us at our ease with each other now," she said, as she poured out hot tea for Loveday, and piled up a blazing fire. "Everyone fancies that everyone else is suspecting him or her, and trying to rake up past words or deeds to bring in as evidence. The whole house seems under a cloud. And at this time of year, too; just when everything as a rule is at its merriest!" and here she gave a doleful glance to the big bunch of holly and mistletoe hanging from the ceiling.

"I suppose you are generally very merry downstairs at Christmas time?" said Loveday. "Servants' balls, theatricals, and all that sort of thing?"

"I should think we were! When I think of this time last year and the fun we all had, I can scarcely believe it is the same house. Our ball always follows my lady's ball, and we have permission to ask our friends to it, and we keep it up as late as ever we please. We begin our evening with a concert and recitations in character, then we have a supper and then we dance right on till morning; but this year!" – she broke off, giving a long, melancholy shake of her head that spoke volumes.

"I suppose," said Loveday, "some of your friends are very clever as musicians or reciters?"

"Very clever indeed. Sir George and my lady are always present during the early part of the evening, and I should like you to have seen Sir George last year laughing fit to kill himself at Harry Emmett dressed in prison dress with a bit of oakum in his hand, reciting the 'Noble Convict!' Sir George said if the young man had gone on the stage, he would have been bound to make his fortune."

"Half a cup, please," said Loveday, presenting her cup. "Who was this Harry Emmett then – a sweetheart of one of the maids?"

"Oh, he would flirt with them all, but he was sweetheart to none. He was footman to Colonel James, who is a great friend of Sir George's, and Harry was constantly backwards and forwards bringing messages from his master. His father, I think, drove a cab in London, and Harry for a time did so also; then he took it into his head to be a gentleman's servant, and great satisfaction he gave as such. He was always such a bright, handsome young fellow and so full of fun, that everyone liked him. But I shall tire you with all this; and you, of course, want to talk about something so different;" and the housekeeper sighed again, as the thought of the dreadful robbery entered her brain once more. "Not at all. I am greatly interested in you and your festivities. Is Emmett still in the neighbourhood? I should amazingly like to hear him recite myself."

"I'm sorry to say he left Colonel James about six months ago. We all missed him very much at first. He was a good, kind-hearted young man, and I remember he told me he was going away to look after his dear old grandmother, who had a sweet-stuff shop somewhere or other, but where I can't remember." Loveday was leaning back in her chair now, with eyelids drooped so low that she literally looked out through "slits" instead of eyes.

Suddenly and abruptly she changed the conversation.

"When will it be convenient for me to see Lady Cathrow's dressing-room?" she asked.

The housekeeper looked at her watch. "Now, at once," she answered: "it's a quarter to five now and my lady sometimes goes up to her room to rest for half an hour before she dresses for dinner."

"Is Stephanie still in attendance on Lady Cathrow?" Miss Brooke asked as she followed the housekeeper up the back stairs to the bedroom floor.

"Yes, Sir George and my lady have been goodness itself to us through this trying time, and they say we are all innocent till we are proved guilty, and will have it that none of our duties are to be in any way altered."

"Stephanie is scarcely fit to perform hers, I should imagine?"

"Scarcely. She was in hysterics nearly from morning till night for the first two or three days after the detectives came down, but now she has grown sullen, eats nothing and never speaks a word to any of us except when she is obliged. This is my lady's dressing-room, walk in please."

Loveday entered a large, luxuriously furnished room, and naturally made her way straight to the chief point of attraction in it – the iron safe fitted into the wall that separated the dressing-room from the bedroom.

It was a safe of the ordinary description, fitted with a strong iron door and Chubb lock. And across this door was written with chalk in characters that seemed defiant in their size and boldness, the words: "To be let, unfurnished."

Loveday spent about five minutes in front of this safe, all her attention concentrated upon the big, bold writing.

She took from her pocket-book a narrow strip of tracing-paper and compared the writing on it, letter by letter, with that on the safe door. This done she turned to Mrs. Williams and professed herself ready to follow her to the room below.

Mrs. Williams looked surprised. Her opinion of Miss Brooke's professional capabilities suffered considerable diminution.

"The gentlemen detectives," she said, "spent over an hour in this room; they paced the floor, they measured the candles, they—"

"Mrs. Williams," interrupted Loveday, "I am quite ready to look at the room below." Her manner had changed from gossiping friendliness to that of the business woman hard at work at her profession.

Without another word, Mrs. Williams led the way to the little room which had proved itself to be the "weak point" of the house.

They entered it by the door which opened into a passage leading to the back-stairs of the house. Loveday found the room exactly as it had been described to her by Mr. Dyer. It needed no second glance at the window to see the ease with which anyone could open it from the outside, and swing themselves into the room, when once the brass catch had been unfastened.

Loveday wasted no time here. In fact, much to Mrs. Williams's surprise and disappointment, she merely walked across the room, in at one door and out at the opposite one, which opened into the large inner hall of the house.

Here, however, she paused to ask a question:

"Is that chair always placed exactly in that position?" she said, pointing to an oak chair that stood immediately outside the room they had just quitted.

The housekeeper answered in the affirmative. It was a warm corner. "My lady" was particular that everyone who came to the house on messages should have a comfortable place to wait in.

"I shall be glad if you will show me to my room now," said Loveday, a little abruptly; "and will you kindly send up to me a county trade directory, if, that is, you have such a thing in the house?"

Mrs. Williams, with an air of offended dignity, led the way to the bedroom quarters once more. The worthy housekeeper felt as if her own dignity had, in some sort, been injured by the want of interest Miss Brooke had evinced in the rooms which, at the present moment, she considered the "show" rooms of the house. "Shall I send someone to help you unpack?" she asked, a little stiffly, at the door of Loveday's room.

"No, thank you; there will not be much unpacking to do. I must leave here by the first up-train to-morrow morning."

"To-morrow morning! Why, I have told everyone you will be here at least a fortnight!"

"Ah, then you must explain that I have been suddenly summoned home by telegram. I'm sure I can trust you to make excuses for me. Do not, however, make them before supper-time. I shall like to sit down to that meal with you. I suppose I shall see Stephanie then?"

The housekeeper answered in the affirmative, and went her way, wondering over the strange manners of the lady whom, at first, she had been disposed to consider "such a nice, pleasant, conversable person!"

At supper-time, however, when the upper-servants assembled at what was, to them, the pleasantest meal of the day, a great surprise was to greet them.

Stephanie did not take her usual place at table, and a fellow-servant, sent to her room to summon her, returned, saying that the room was empty, and Stephanie was nowhere to be found. Loveday and Mrs. Williams together went to the girl's bedroom. It bore its usual appearance: no packing had been done in it, and, beyond her hat and jacket, the girl appeared to have taken nothing away with her.

On enquiry, it transpired that Stephanie had, as usual, assisted Lady Cathrow to dress for dinner; but after that not a soul in the house appeared to have seen her.

Mrs. Williams thought the matter of sufficient importance to be at once reported to her master and mistress; and Sir George, in his turn, promptly dispatched a messenger to Mr. Bates, at the "King's Head," to summon him to an immediate consultation. Loveday dispatched a messenger in another direction – to young Mr. Holt, at his farm, giving him particulars of the girl's disappearance.

Mr. Bates had a brief interview with Sir George in his study, from which he emerged radiant. He made a point of seeing Loveday before he left the Court, sending a special request to her that she would speak to him for a minute in the outside drive.

Loveday put her hat on, and went out to him. She found him almost dancing for glee.

"Told you so! told you so! Now, didn't I, Miss Brooke?" he exclaimed. "We'll come upon her traces before morning, never fear. I'm quite prepared. I knew what was in her mind all along. I said to myself, when that girl bolts it will be after she has dressed my lady for dinner – when she has two good clear hours all to herself, and her absence from the house won't be noticed, and when, without much difficulty, she can catch a train leaving Huxwell for Wreford. Well, she'll get to Wreford safe enough; but from Wreford she'll be followed every step of the way she goes. Only yesterday I set a man on there – a keen fellow at this sort of thing – and gave him full directions; and he'll hunt her down to her hole properly. Taken nothing with her, do you say? What does that matter? She thinks she'll find all she wants where she's going – 'the feathered nest' I spoke to you about this morning. Ha! ha! Well, instead of stepping into it, as she fancies she will, she'll walk straight into a detective's arms, and land her pal there into the bargain. There'll be two of them netted before another forty-eight hours are over our heads, or my name's not Jeremiah Bates."

"What are you going to do now?" asked Loveday, as the man finished his long speech.

"Now! I'm back to the 'King's Head' to wait for a telegram from my colleague at Wreford. Once he's got her in front of him he'll give me instructions at what point to meet him. You see, Huxwell being such an out-of-the-way place, and only one train leaving between 7.30 and 10.15, makes us really positive that Wreford must be the girl's destination and relieves my mind from all anxiety on the matter."

"Does it?" answered Loveday gravely. "I can see another possible destination for the girl – the stream that runs through the wood we drove past this morning. Good night, Mr. Bates, it's cold out here. Of course so soon as you have any news you'll send it up to Sir George."

The household sat up late that night, but no news was received of Stephanie from any quarter. Mr. Bates had impressed upon Sir George the ill-advisability of setting up a hue and cry after the girl that might possibly reach her ears and scare her from joining the person whom he was pleased to designate as her "pal."

"We want to follow her silently, Sir George, silently as the shadow follows the man," he had said grandiloquently, "and then we shall come upon the two, and I trust upon their booty also." Sir George in his turn had impressed Mr. Bates's wishes upon his household, and if it had not been for Loveday's message, dispatched early in the evening to young Holt, not a soul outside the house would have known of Stephanie's disappearance.

Loveday was stirring early the next morning, and the eight o'clock train for Wreford numbered her among its passengers.

Before starting, she dispatched a telegram to her chief in Lynch Court. It read rather oddly, as follows: –

"Cracker fired. Am just starting for Wreford. Will wire to you from there. L. B."

Oddly though it might read, Mr. Dyer did not need to refer to his cipher book to interpret it. "Cracker fired" was the easily remembered equivalent for "clue found" in the detective phraseology of the office.

"Well, she has been quick enough about it this time!" he soliquised as he speculated in his own mind over what the purport of the next telegram might be.

Half an hour later there came to him a constable from Scotland Yard to tell him of Stephanie's disappearance and the conjectures that were rife on the matter, and he then, not unnaturally, read Loveday's telegram by the light of this information, and concluded that the clue in her hands related to the discovery of Stephanie's whereabouts as well as to that of her guilt.

A telegram received a little later on, however, was to turn this theory upside down. It was, like the former one, worded in the enigmatic language current in the Lynch Court establishment, but as it was a lengthier and more intricate message, it sent Mr. Dyer at once to his cipher book.

"Wonderful! She has cut them all out this time!" was Mr. Dyer's exclamation as he read and interpreted the final word.

In another ten minutes he had given over his office to the charge of his head clerk for the day, and was rattling along the streets in a hansom in the direction of Bishopsgate Station.

There he was lucky enough to catch a train just starting for Wreford.

"The event of the day," he muttered, as he settled himself comfortably in a corner seat, "will be the return journey when she tells me, bit by bit, how she has worked it all out."

It was not until close upon three o'clock in the afternoon that he arrived at the old-fashioned market town of Wreford. It chanced to be cattle-market day, and the station was crowded with drovers and farmers. Outside the station Loveday was waiting for him, as she had told him in her telegram that she would, in a four-wheeler.

"It's all right," she said to him as he got in; "he can't get away, even if he had an idea that we were after him. Two of the local police are waiting outside the house door with a warrant for his arrest, signed by a magistrate. I did not, however, see why the Lynch Court office should not have the credit of the thing, and so telegraphed to you to conduct the arrest."

They drove through the High Street to the outskirts of the town, where the shops became intermixed with private houses let out in offices. The cab pulled up outside one of these, and two policemen in plain clothes came forward, and touched their hats to Mr. Dyer.

"He's in there now, sir, doing his office work," said one of the men pointing to a door, just within the entrance, on which was printed in black letters, "The United Kingdom Cab-drivers' Beneficent Association." "I hear, however, that this is the last time he will be found there, as a week ago he gave notice to leave."

As the man finished speaking, a man, evidently of the cab-driving fraternity, came up the steps. He stared curiously at the little group just within the entrance, and then chinking his money in his hand, passed on to the office as if to pay his subscription.

"Will you be good enough to tell Mr. Emmett in there," said Mr. Dyer, addressing the man, "that a gentleman outside wishes to speak with him."

The man nodded and passed into the office. As the door opened, it disclosed to view an old gentleman seated at a desk apparently writing receipts for money. A little in his rear at his right hand sat a young and decidedly good-looking man, at a table on which were placed various little piles of silver and pence. The get-up of this young man was gentleman-like, and his manner was affable and pleasant as he responded, with a nod and a smile, to the cab-driver's message.

"I sha'n't be a minute," he said to his colleague at the other desk, as he rose and crossed the room towards the door.

But once outside that door it was closed firmly behind him, and he found himself in the centre of three stalwart individuals, one of whom informed him that he held in his hand a warrant for the arrest of Harry Emmett on the charge of complicity in the Craigen Court robbery, and that he had "better come along quietly, for resistance would be useless."

Emmett seemed convinced of the latter fact. He grew deadly white for a moment, then recovered himself.

"Will someone have the kindness to fetch my hat and coat," he said in a lofty manner. "I don't see why I should be made to catch my death of cold because some other people have seen fit to make asses of themselves."

His hat and coat were fetched, and he was handed into the cab between the two officials.

"Let me give you a word of warning, young man," said Mr. Dyer, closing the cab door and looking in for a moment through the window at Emmett. "I don't suppose it's a punishable offence to leave a black bag on an old maid's doorstep, but let me tell you, if it had not been for that black bag you might have got clean off with your spoil."

Emmett, the irrepressible, had his answer ready. He lifted his hat ironically to Mr. Dyer; "You might have put it more neatly, guv'nor," he said; "if I had been in your place I would have said: 'Young man, you are being justly punished for your misdeeds; you have been taking off your fellow-creatures all your life long, and now they are taking off you.'"

Mr. Dyer's duty that day did not end with the depositing of Harry Emmett in the local jail. The search through Emmett's lodgings and effects had to be made, and at this he was naturally present. About a third of the lost jewellery was found there, and from this it was consequently concluded that his accomplices in the crime had considered that he had borne a third of the risk and of the danger of it.

Letters and various memoranda discovered in the rooms eventually led to the detection of those accomplices, and although Lady Cathrow was doomed to lose the greater part of her valuable property, she had ultimately the satisfaction of knowing that each one of the thieves received a sentence proportionate to his crime.

It was not until close upon midnight that Mr. Dyer found himself seated in the train, facing Miss Brooke, and had leisure to ask for the links in the chain of reasoning that had led her in so remarkable a manner to connect the finding of a black bag, with insignificant contents, with an extensive robbery of valuable jewellery.

Loveday explained the whole thing, easily, naturally, step by step in her usual methodical manner.

"I read," she said, "as I dare say a great many other people did, the account of the two things in the same newspaper, on the same day, and I detected, as I dare say a great many other people did not, a sense of fun in the principal actor in each incident. I notice while all people are agreed as to the variety of motives that instigate crime, very few allow sufficient margin for variety of character in the criminal. We are apt to imagine that he stalks about the world with a bundle of deadly motives under his arm, and cannot picture him at his work with a twinkle in his eye and a keen sense of fun, such as honest folk have sometimes when at work at their calling."

Here Mr. Dyer gave a little grunt; it might have been either of assent or dissent.

Loveday went on:

"Of course, the ludicrousness of the diction of the letter found in the bag would be apparent to the most casual reader; to me the high falutin' sentences sounded in addition strangely familiar; I had heard or read them somewhere I felt sure, although where I could not at first remember. They rang in my ears, and it was not altogether out of idle curiosity that I went to Scotland Yard to see the bag and its contents, and to copy, with a slip of tracing paper, a line or two of the letter. When I found that the handwriting of this letter was not identical with that of the translations found in the bag, I was confirmed in my impression that the owner of the bag was not the writer of the letter; that possibly the bag and its contents had been appropriated from some railway station for some distinct purpose; and, that purpose accomplished, the appropriator no longer wished to be burthened with it, and disposed of it in the readiest fashion that suggested itself. The letter, it seemed to me, had been begun with the intention of throwing the police off the scent, but the irrepressible spirit of fun that had induced the writer to deposit his clerical adjuncts upon an old maid's doorstep had proved too strong for him here, and had carried him away, and the letter that was intended to be pathetic ended in being comic."

"Very ingenious, so far," murmured Mr. Dyer: "I've no doubt when the contents of the bag are widely made known through advertisements a claimant will come forward, and your theory be found correct."

"When I returned from Scotland Yard," Loveday continued, "I found your note, asking me to go round and see you respecting the big jewel robbery. Before I did so I thought it best to read once more the newspaper account of the case, so that I might be well up in its details. When I came to the words that the thief had written across the door of the safe, 'To be Let, Unfurnished,' they at once connected themselves in my mind with the 'dying kiss to my Marchioness Mother,' and the solemn warning against the race-course and the book-maker, of the black-bag letter-writer. Then, all in a flash, the whole thing became clear to me. Some two or three years back my professional duties necessitated my frequent attendance at certain low class penny-readings, given in the South London slums. At these penny-readings young shop-assistants, and others of their class, glad of an opportunity for exhibiting their accomplishments, declaim with great vigour; and, as a rule, select pieces which their very mixed audience might be supposed to appreciate. During my attendance at these meetings, it seemed to me that one book of selected readings was a great favourite among the reciters, and I took the trouble to buy it. Here it is."

Here Loveday took from her cloak-pocket "The Reciter's Treasury," and handed it to her companion.

"Now," she said, "if you will run your eye down the index column you will find the titles of those pieces to which I wish to draw your attention. The first is 'The Suicide's Farewell;' the second, 'The Noble Convict;' the third, 'To be Let, Unfurnished.'"

"By Jove! so it is!" ejaculated Mr. Dyer.

"In the first of these pieces, 'The Suicide's Farewell,' occur the expressions with which the black-bag letter begins – 'The fatal day has arrived,' etc., the warnings against gambling, and the allusions to the 'poor lifeless body.' In the second, 'The Noble Convict,' occur the allusions to the aristocratic relations and the dying kiss to the marchioness mother. The third piece, 'To be Let, Unfurnished,' is a foolish little poem enough, although I dare say it has often raised a laugh in a not too-discriminating audience. It tells how a bachelor, calling at a house to enquire after rooms to be let unfurnished, falls in love with the daughter of the house, and offers her his heart, which, he says, is to be let unfurnished.

She declines his offer, and retorts that she thinks his head must be to let unfurnished, too. With these three pieces before me, it was not difficult to see a thread of connection between the writer of the black-bag letter and the thief who wrote across the empty safe at Craigen Court. Following this thread, I unearthed the story of Harry Emmett – footman, reciter, general lover and scamp. Subsequently I compared the writing on my tracing paper with that on the safe-door, and, allowing for the difference between a bit of chalk and a steel nib, came to the conclusion that there could be but little doubt but that both were written by the same hand. Before that, however, I had obtained another, and what I consider the most important, link in my chain of evidence – how Emmett brought his clerical dress into use."

"Ah, how did you find that out now?" asked Mr. Dyer, leaning forward with his elbows on his knees.

"In the course of conversation with Mrs. Williams, whom I found to be a most communicative person, I elicited the names of the guests who had sat down to dinner on Christmas Eve. They were all people of undoubted respectability in the neighbourhood. Just before dinner was announced, she said, a young clergyman had presented himself at the front door, asking to speak with the Rector of the parish. The Rector, it seems, always dines at Craigen Court on Christmas Eve. The young clergyman's story was that he had been told by a certain clergyman, whose name he mentioned, that a curate was wanted in the parish, and he had traveled down from London to offer his services. He had been, he said, to the Rectory and had been told by the servants where the Rector was dining, and fearing to lose his chance of the curacy, had followed him to the Court. Now the Rector had been wanting a curate and had filled the vacancy only the previous week; he was a little inclined to be irate at this interruption to the evening's festivities, and told the young man that he didn't want a curate. When, however, he saw how disappointed the poor young fellow looked – I believe he shed a tear or two – his heart softened; he told him to sit down and rest in the hall before he attempted the walk back to the station, and said he would ask Sir George to send him out a glass of wine. The young man sat down in a chair immediately outside the room by which the thieves entered. Now I need not tell you who that young man was, nor suggest to your mind, I am sure, the idea that while the servant went to fetch him his wine, or, indeed, so soon as he saw the coast clear, he slipped into that little room and pulled back the catch of the window that admitted his confederates, who, no doubt, at that very moment were in hiding in the grounds. The housekeeper did not know whether this meek young curate had a black bag with him. Personally I have no doubt of the fact, nor that it contained the cap, cuffs, collar, and outer garments of Harry Emmett, which were most likely redonned before he returned to his lodgings at Wreford, where I should say he repacked the bag with its clerical contents, and wrote his serio-comic letter. This bag, I suppose, he must have deposited in the very early morning, before anyone was stirring, on the door-step of the house in the Easterbrook Road."

Mr. Dyer drew a long breath. In his heart was unmitigated admiration for his colleague's skill, which seemed to him to fall little short of inspiration. By-and-by, no doubt, he would sing her praises to the first person who came along with a hearty good will; he had not, however, the slightest intention of so singing them in her own ears – excessive praise was apt to have a bad effect on the rising practitioner.

So he contented himself with saying:

"Yes, very satisfactory. Now tell me how you hunted the fellow down to his diggings?"

"Oh, that was mere ABC work," answered Loveday. "Mrs. Williams told me he had left his place at Colonel James's about six months previously, and had told her he was going to look after his dear old grandmother, who kept a sweet stuff shop; but where she could not remember. Having heard that Emmett's father was a cab-driver, my thoughts at once flew to the cabman's vernacular – you know something of it, no doubt – in which their provident association is designated by the phase, 'the dear old grandmother,' and the office where they make and receive their payments is styled 'the sweet-stuff shop.'"

"Ha, ha, ha! And good Mrs. Williams took it all literally, no doubt?"

"She did; and thought what a dear, kind-hearted fellow the young man was. Naturally I supposed there would be a branch of the association in the nearest market town, and a local trades' directory confirmed my supposition that there was one at Wreford. Bearing in mind where the black bag was found, it was not difficult to believe that young Emmett, possibly through his father's influence and his own prepossessing manners and appearance, had attained to some position of trust in the Wreford branch. I must confess I scarcely expected to find him as I did, on reaching the place, installed as receiver of the weekly moneys. Of course, I immediately put myself in communication with the police there, and the rest I think you know."

Mr. Dyer's enthusiasm refused to be longer restrained.

"It's capital, from first to last," he cried; "you've surpassed yourself this time!"

"The only thing that saddens me," said Loveday, "is the thought of the possible fate of that poor little Stephanie."

Loveday's anxieties on Stephanie's behalf were, however, to be put to flight before another twenty-four hours had passed. The first post on the following morning brought a letter from Mrs. Williams telling how the girl had been found before the night was over, half dead with cold and fright, on the verge of the stream running through Craigen Wood – "found too" – wrote the housekeeper, "by the very person who ought to have found her, young Holt, who was, and is so desperately in love with her.

"Thank goodness! at the last moment her courage failed her, and instead of throwing herself into the stream, she sank down, half-fainting, beside it. Holt took her straight home to his mother, and there, at the farm, she is now being taken care of and petted generally by everyone."

THE MURDER AT TROYTE'S HILL

Catherine Louisa Pirkis

> Catherine Louisa Pirkis (1839–1910) started publishing her Loveday Brooke short stories in 1894. Like her first novel, *Disappeared from Her Home* (1877), they were early examples of mystery fiction by British women. Shortly after creating Brooke, Pirkis retired from writing to focus on animal welfare.

"Griffiths, of the Newcastle Constabulary, has the case in hand," said Mr. Dyer; "those Newcastle men are keen-witted, shrewd fellows, and very jealous of outside interference. They only sent to me under protest, as it were, because they wanted your sharp wits at work inside the house."

"I suppose throughout I am to work with Griffiths, not with you?" said Miss Brooke.

"Yes; when I have given you in outline the facts of the case, I simply have nothing more to do with it, and you must depend on Griffiths for any assistance of any sort that you may require."

Here, with a swing, Mr. Dyer opened his big ledger and turned rapidly over its leaves till he came to the heading "Troyte's Hill" and the date "September 6th."

"I'm all attention," said Loveday, leaning back in her chair in the attitude of a listener.

"The murdered man," resumed Mr. Dyer, "is a certain Alexander Henderson – usually known as old Sandy – lodge-keeper to Mr. Craven, of Troyte's Hill, Cumberland. The lodge consists merely of two rooms on the ground floor, a bedroom and a sitting-room; these Sandy occupied alone, having neither kith nor kin of any degree. On the morning of September 6th, some children going up to the house with milk from the farm noticed that Sandy's bed-room window stood wide open. Curiosity prompted them to peep in; and then, to their horror, they saw old Sandy, in his night-shirt, lying dead on the floor, as if he had fallen backwards from the window. They raised an alarm; and on examination, it was found that death had ensued from a heavy blow on the temple, given either by a strong fist or some blunt instrument. The room, on being entered, presented a curious appearance. It was as if a herd of monkeys had been turned into it and allowed to work their impish will. Not an article of furniture remained in its place: the bed-clothes had been rolled into a bundle and stuffed into the chimney; the bedstead – a small iron one – lay on its side; the one chair in the room stood on the top of the table; fender and fire-irons lay across the washstand, whose basin was to be found in a farther corner, holding bolster and pillow. The clock stood on its head in the middle of the mantelpiece; and the small vases and ornaments, which flanked it on either side, were walking, as it were, in a straight line towards the door. The old man's clothes had been rolled into a ball and thrown on the top of a high cupboard in which he kept his savings and whatever valuables he had. This cupboard, however, had not been meddled with, and its contents remained intact, so it was evident that robbery was not the motive for the crime. At the inquest, subsequently held, a verdict of 'willful murder' against some person or persons unknown was returned. The local police are diligently investigating the affair, but, as yet, no arrests have been made. The opinion that at present prevails in the neighbourhood is that the crime has been perpetrated by some lunatic, escaped or otherwise and enquiries are being made at the local asylums as to missing or lately released inmates. Griffiths, however, tells me that his suspicions set in another direction."

"Did anything of importance transpire at the inquest?"

"Nothing specially important. Mr. Craven broke down in giving his evidence when he alluded to the confidential relations that had always subsisted between Sandy and himself, and spoke of the last time that he had seen him alive. The evidence of the butler, and one or two of the female servants, seems clear enough, and they let fall something of a hint that Sandy was not altogether a favourite among them, on account of the overbearing manner in which he used his influence with his master. Young Mr. Craven, a youth of about nineteen, home from Oxford for the long vacation, was not present at the inquest; a doctor's certificate was put in stating that he was suffering from typhoid fever, and could not leave his bed without risk to his life. Now this young man is a thoroughly bad sort, and as much a gentleman-blackleg as it is possible for such a young fellow to be. It seems to Griffiths that there is something suspicious about this illness of his. He came back from Oxford on the verge of delirium tremens, pulled round from that, and then suddenly, on the day after the murder, Mrs. Craven rings the bell, announces that he has developed typhoid fever and orders a doctor to be sent for."

"What sort of man is Mr. Craven senior?"

"He seems to be a quiet old fellow, a scholar and learned philologist. Neither his neighbours nor his family see much of him; he almost lives in his study, writing a treatise, in seven or eight volumes, on comparative philology. He is not a rich man. Troyte's Hill, though it carries position in the county, is not a paying property, and Mr. Craven is unable to keep it up properly. I am told he has had to cut down expenses in all directions in order to send his son to college, and his daughter from first to last has been entirely educated by her mother. Mr. Craven was originally intended for the church, but for some reason or other, when his college career came to an end, he did not present himself for ordination – went out to Natal instead, where he obtained some civil appointment and where he remained for about fifteen years. Henderson was his servant during the latter portion of his Oxford career, and must have been greatly respected by him, for although the remuneration derived from his appointment at Natal was small, he paid Sandy a regular yearly allowance out of it. When, about ten years ago, he succeeded to Troyte's Hill, on the death of his elder brother, and returned home with his family, Sandy was immediately installed as lodge-keeper, and at so high a rate of pay that the butler's wages were cut down to meet it."

"Ah, that wouldn't improve the butler's feelings towards him," ejaculated Loveday.

Mr. Dyer went on: "But, in spite of his high wages, he doesn't appear to have troubled much about his duties as lodge-keeper, for they were performed, as a rule, by the gardener's boy, while he took his meals and passed his time at the house, and, speaking generally, put his finger into every pie. You know the old adage respecting the servant of twenty-one years' standing: 'Seven years my servant, seven years my equal, seven years my master.' Well, it appears to have held good in the case of Mr. Craven and Sandy. The old gentleman, absorbed in his philological studies, evidently let the reins slip through his fingers, and Sandy seems to have taken easy possession of them. The servants frequently had to go to him for orders, and he carried things, as a rule, with a high hand."

"Did Mrs. Craven never have a word to say on the matter?"

"I've not heard much about her. She seems to be a quiet sort of person. She is a Scotch missionary's daughter; perhaps she spends her time working for the Cape mission and that sort of thing."

"And young Mr. Craven: did he knock under to Sandy's rule?"

"Ah, now you're hitting the bull's eye and we come to Griffiths' theory. The young man and Sandy appear to have been at loggerheads ever since the Cravens took possession of Troyte's Hill. As a schoolboy Master Harry defied Sandy and threatened him with his hunting-crop; and subsequently, as a young man, has used strenuous endeavours to put the old servant in his place. On the day before the murder, Griffiths says, there was a terrible scene between the two, in which the young gentleman, in the presence of several witnesses, made use of strong language and threatened the old man's life. Now, Miss Brooke, I have told you all the circumstances of the case so far as I know them. For fuller particulars I must refer you to Griffiths. He, no doubt, will meet you at Grenfell – the nearest station to Troyte's Hill, and tell you in what capacity he has procured for you an entrance into the house. By-the-way, he has wired to me this morning that he hopes you will be able to save the Scotch express to-night."

Loveday expressed her readiness to comply with Mr. Griffiths' wishes.

"I shall be glad," said Mr. Dyer, as he shook hands with her at the office door, "to see you immediately on your return – that, however, I suppose, will not be yet awhile. This promises, I fancy, to be a longish affair?" This was said interrogatively.

"I haven't the least idea on the matter," answered Loveday. "I start on my work without theory of any sort – in fact, I may say, with my mind a perfect blank."

And anyone who had caught a glimpse of her blank, expressionless features, as she said this, would have taken her at her word.

Grenfell, the nearest post-town to Troyte's Hill, is a fairly busy, populous little town – looking south towards the black country, and northwards to low, barren hills. Pre-eminent among these stands Troyte's Hill, famed in the old days as a border keep, and possibly at a still earlier date as a Druid stronghold.

At a small inn at Grenfell, dignified by the title of "The Station Hotel," Mr. Griffiths, of the Newcastle constabulary, met Loveday and still further initiated her into the mysteries of the Troyte's Hill murder.

"A little of the first excitement has subsided," he said, after preliminary greetings had been exchanged; "but still the wildest rumours are flying about and repeated as solemnly as if they were Gospel truths. My chief here and my colleagues generally adhere to their first conviction, that the criminal is some suddenly crazed tramp or else an escaped lunatic, and they are confident that sooner or later we shall come upon his traces. Their theory is that Sandy, hearing some strange noise at the park gates, put his head out of the window to ascertain the cause and immediately had his death blow dealt him; then they suppose that the lunatic scrambled into the room through the window and exhausted his frenzy by turning things generally upside down. They refuse altogether to share my suspicions respecting young Mr. Craven."

Mr. Griffiths was a tall, thin-featured man, with iron-grey hair, but so close to his head that it refused to do anything but stand on end. This gave a somewhat comic expression to the upper portion of his face and clashed oddly with the melancholy look that his mouth habitually wore.

"I have made all smooth for you at Troyte's Hill," he presently went on. "Mr. Craven is not wealthy enough to allow himself the luxury of a family lawyer, so he occasionally employs the services of Messrs. Wells and Sugden, lawyers in this place, and who, as it happens, have, off and on, done a good deal of business for me. It was through them I heard that Mr. Craven was anxious to secure the assistance of an amanuensis. I immediately offered your services, stating that you were a friend of mine, a lady of impoverished means, who would gladly undertake the duties for the munificent sum of a guinea a month, with board and lodging. The old gentleman at once jumped at the offer, and is anxious for you to be at Troyte's Hill at once."

Loveday expressed her satisfaction with the programme that Mr. Griffiths had sketched for her, then she had a few questions to ask.

"Tell me," she said, "what led you, in the first instance, to suspect young Mr. Craven of the crime?"

"The footing on which he and Sandy stood towards each other, and the terrible scene that occurred between them only the day before the murder," answered Griffiths, promptly. "Nothing of this, however, was elicited at the inquest, where a very fair face was put on Sandy's relations with the whole of the Craven family. I have subsequently unearthed a good deal respecting the private life of Mr. Harry Craven, and, among other things, I have found out that on the night of the murder he left the house shortly after ten o'clock, and no one, so far as I have been able to ascertain, knows at what hour he returned. Now I must draw your attention, Miss Brooke, to the fact that at the inquest the medical evidence went to prove that the murder had been committed between ten and eleven at night."

"Do you surmise, then, that the murder was a planned thing on the part of this young man?"

"I do. I believe that he wandered about the grounds until Sandy shut himself in for the night, then aroused him by some outside noise, and, when the old man looked out to ascertain the cause, dealt him a blow with a bludgeon or loaded stick, that caused his death."

"A cold-blooded crime that, for a boy of nineteen?"

"Yes. He's a good-looking, gentlemanly youngster, too, with manners as mild as milk, but from all accounts is as full of wickedness as an egg is full of meat. Now, to come to another point – if, in connection with these ugly facts, you take into consideration the suddenness of his illness, I think you'll admit that it bears a suspicious appearance and might reasonably give rise to the surmise that it was a plant on his part, in order to get out of the inquest."

"Who is the doctor attending him?"

"A man called Waters; not much of a practitioner, from all accounts, and no doubt he feels himself highly honoured in being summoned to Troyte's Hill. The Cravens, it seems, have no family doctor. Mrs. Craven, with her missionary experience, is half a doctor herself, and never calls in one except in a serious emergency."

"The certificate was in order, I suppose?"

"Undoubtedly. And, as if to give colour to the gravity of the case, Mrs. Craven sent a message down to the servants, that if any of them were afraid of the infection they could at once go to their homes. Several of the maids, I believe, took advantage of her permission, and packed their boxes. Miss Craven, who is a delicate girl, was sent away with her maid to stay with friends at Newcastle, and Mrs. Craven isolated herself with her patient in one of the disused wings of the house."

"Has anyone ascertained whether Miss Craven arrived at her destination at Newcastle?"

Griffiths drew his brows together in thought.

"I did not see any necessity for such a thing," he answered. "I don't quite follow you. What do you mean to imply?"

"Oh, nothing. I don't suppose it matters much: it might have been interesting as a side-issue." She broke off for a moment, then added:

"Now tell me a little about the butler, the man whose wages were cut down to increase Sandy's pay."

"Old John Hales? He's a thoroughly worthy, respectable man; he was butler for five or six years to Mr. Craven's brother, when he was master of Troyte's Hill, and then took duty under this Mr. Craven. There's no ground for suspicion in that quarter. Hales's exclamation when he heard of the murder is quite enough to stamp him as an innocent man: 'Serve the old idiot right,' he cried: 'I couldn't pump up a tear for him if I tried for a month of Sundays!' Now I take it, Miss Brooke, a guilty man wouldn't dare make such a speech as that!"

"You think not?"

Griffiths stared at her. "I'm a little disappointed in her," he thought. "I'm afraid her powers have been slightly exaggerated if she can't see such a straightforward thing as that."

Aloud he said, a little sharply, "Well, I don't stand alone in my thinking. No one yet has breathed a word against Hales, and if they did, I've no doubt he could prove an *alibi* without any trouble, for he lives in the house, and everyone has a good word for him."

"I suppose Sandy's lodge has been put into order by this time?"

"Yes; after the inquest, and when all possible evidence had been taken, every-thing was put straight."

"At the inquest it was stated that no marks of footsteps could be traced in any direction?"

"The long drought we've had would render such a thing impossible, let alone the fact that Sandy's lodge stands right on the graveled drive, without flower-beds or grass borders of any sort around it. But look here, Miss Brooke, don't you be wasting your time over the lodge and its surroundings. Every iota of fact on that matter has been gone through over and over again by me and my chief. What we want you to do is to go straight into the house and concentrate atten-tion on Master Harry's sick-room, and find out what's going on there. What he did outside the house on the night of the 6th, I've no doubt I shall be able to find out for myself. Now, Miss Brooke, you've asked me no end of questions, to which I have replied as fully as it was in my power to do; will you be good enough to answer one question that I wish to put, as straightforwardly as I have answered yours? You have had fullest particulars given you of the condition of Sandy's room when the police entered it on the morning after the murder. No doubt, at the present moment, you can see it all in your mind's eye – the bed-stead on its side, the clock on its head, the bed-clothes half-way up the chimney, the little vases and ornaments walking in a straight line towards the door?"

Loveday bowed her head.

"Very well. Now will you be good enough to tell me what this scene of con-fusion recalls to your mind before anything else?"

"The room of an unpopular Oxford freshman after a raid upon it by under-grads," answered Loveday promptly.

Mr. Griffiths rubbed his hands.

"Quite so!" he ejaculated. "I see, after all, we are one at heart in this matter, in spite of a little surface disagreement of ideas. Depend upon it, by-and-by, like the engineers tunneling from different quarters under the Alps, we shall meet at the same point and shake hands. By-the-way, I have arranged for daily commu-nication between us through the postboy who takes the letters to Troyte's Hill. He is trustworthy, and any letter you give him for me will find its way into my hands within the hour."

It was about three o'clock in the afternoon when Loveday drove in through the park gates of Troyte's Hill, past the lodge where old Sandy had met with his death. It was a pretty little cottage, covered with Virginia creeper and wild honeysuckle, and showing no outward sign of the tragedy that had been enacted within.

The park and pleasure-grounds of Troyte's Hill were extensive, and the house itself was a somewhat imposing red brick structure, built, possibly, at the time when Dutch William's taste had grown popular in the country. Its frontage presented a somewhat forlorn appearance, its centre windows – a square of eight – alone seeming to show signs of occupation. With the exception of two win-dows at the extreme end of the bedroom floor of the north wing, where, possibly, the invalid and his mother were located, and two windows at the extreme end of the ground floor of the south wing, which Loveday ascertained subsequently were those of Mr. Craven's study, not a single window in either wing owned blind or curtain. The wings were extensive, and it was easy to understand that at the extreme end of the one the fever patient would be isolated from the rest of the household, and that at the extreme end of the other Mr. Craven could secure the quiet and freedom from interruption which, no doubt, were essential to the due prosecution of his philological studies.

Alike on the house and ill-kept grounds were present the stamp of the smallness of the income of the master and owner of the place. The terrace, which ran the length of the house in front, and on to which every window on the ground floor opened, was miserably out of repair: not a lintel or door-post, window-ledge or balcony but what seemed to cry aloud for the touch of the painter. "Pity me! I have seen better days," Loveday could fancy written as a legend across the red-brick porch that gave entrance to the old house.

The butler, John Hales, admitted Loveday, shouldered her portmanteau and told her he would show her to her room. He was a tall, powerfully-built man, with a ruddy face and dogged expression of countenance. It was easy to understand that, off and on, there must have been many a sharp encounter between him and old Sandy. He treated Loveday in an easy, familiar fashion, evidently considering that an amanuensis took much the same rank as a nursery governess – that is to say, a little below a lady's maid and a little above a house-maid.

"We're short of hands, just now," he said, in broad Cumberland dialect, as he led the way up the wide stair case. "Some of the lasses downstairs took fright at the fever and went home. Cook and I are single-handed, for Moggie, the only maid left, has been told off to wait on Madam and Master Harry. I hope you're not afeared of fever?"

Loveday explained that she was not, and asked if the room at the extreme end of the north wing was the one assigned to "Madam and Master Harry."

"Yes," said the man; "it's convenient for sick nursing; there's a flight of stairs runs straight down from it to the kitchen quarters. We put all Madam wants at the foot of those stairs and Moggie herself never enters the sick-room. I take it you'll not be seeing Madam for many a day, yet awhile."

"When shall I see Mr. Craven? At dinner to-night?"

"That's what naebody could say," answered Hales. "He may not come out of his study till past midnight; sometimes he sits there till two or three in the morning. Shouldn't advise you to wait till he wants his dinner – better have a cup of tea and a chop sent up to you. Madam never waits for him at any meal."

As he finished speaking he deposited the portmanteau outside one of the many doors opening into the gallery.

"This is Miss Craven's room," he went on; "cook and me thought you'd better have it, as it would want less getting ready than the other rooms, and work is work when there are so few hands to do it. Oh, my stars! I do declare there is cook putting it straight for you now." The last sentence was added as the opened door laid bare to view, the cook, with a duster in her hand, polishing a mirror; the bed had been made, it is true, but otherwise the room must have been much as Miss Craven left it, after a hurried packing up.

To the surprise of the two servants Loveday took the matter very lightly.

"I have a special talent for arranging rooms and would prefer getting this one straight for myself," she said. "Now, if you will go and get ready that chop and cup of tea we were talking about just now, I shall think it much kinder than if you stayed here doing what I can so easily do for myself."

When, however, the cook and butler had departed in company, Loveday showed no disposition to exercise the "special talent" of which she had boasted.

She first carefully turned the key in the lock and then proceeded to make a thorough and minute investigation of every corner of the room. Not an article of furniture, not an ornament or toilet accessory, but what was lifted from its place and carefully scrutinized. Even the ashes in the grate, the debris of the last fire made there, were raked over and well looked through.

This careful investigation of Miss Craven's late surroundings occupied in all about three quarters of an hour, and Loveday, with her hat in her hand, descended the stairs to see Hales crossing the hall to the dining-room with the promised cup of tea and chop.

In silence and solitude she partook of the simple repast in a dining-hall that could with ease have banqueted a hundred and fifty guests.

"Now for the grounds before it gets dark," she said to herself, as she noted that already the outside shadows were beginning to slant.

The dining-hall was at the back of the house; and here, as in the front, the windows, reaching to the ground, presented easy means of egress. The flower-garden was on this side of the house and sloped downhill to a pretty stretch of well-wooded country.

Loveday did not linger here even to admire, but passed at once round the south corner of the house to the windows which she had ascertained, by a careless question to the butler, were those of Mr. Craven's study.

Very cautiously she drew near them, for the blinds were up, the curtains drawn back. A side glance, however, relieved her apprehensions, for it showed her the occupant of the room, seated in an easy-chair, with his back to the windows. From the length of his outstretched limbs he was evidently a tall man. His hair was silvery and curly, the lower part of his face was hidden from her view by the chair, but she could see one hand was pressed tightly across his eyes and brows. The whole attitude was that of a man absorbed in deep thought. The room was comfortably furnished, but presented an appearance of disorder from the books and manuscripts scattered in all directions. A whole pile of torn fragments of foolscap sheets, overflowing from a waste-paper basket beside the writing-table, seemed to proclaim the fact that the scholar had of late grown weary of, or else dissatisfied with his work, and had condemned it freely.

Although Loveday stood looking in at this window for over five minutes, not the faintest sign of life did that tall, reclining figure give, and it would have been as easy to believe him locked in sleep as in thought.

From here she turned her steps in the direction of Sandy's lodge. As Griffiths had said, it was graveled up to its doorstep. The blinds were closely drawn, and it presented the ordinary appearance of a disused cottage.

A narrow path beneath over-arching boughs of cherry-laurel and arbutus, immediately facing the lodge, caught her eye, and down this she at once turned her footsteps.

This path led, with many a wind and turn, through a belt of shrubbery that skirted the frontage of Mr. Craven's grounds, and eventually, after much zig-zagging, ended in close proximity to the stables. As Loveday entered it, she seemed literally to leave daylight behind her.

"I feel as if I were following the course of a circuitous mind," she said to herself as the shadows closed around her. "I could not fancy Sir Isaac Newton or Bacon planning or delighting in such a wind-about-alley as this!"

The path showed greyly in front of her out of the dimness. On and on she followed it; here and there the roots of the old laurels, struggling out of the ground, threatened to trip her up. Her eyes, however, had now grown accustomed to the half-gloom, and not a detail of her surroundings escaped her as she went along.

A bird flew from out the thicket on her right hand with a startled cry. A dainty little frog leaped out of her way into the shriveled leaves lying below the laurels. Following the movements of this frog, her eye was caught by something black and solid among those leaves. What was it? A bundle – a shiny black coat? Loveday knelt down, and using her hands to assist her eyes, found that they came into contact with the dead, stiffened body of a beautiful black retriever. She parted, as well as she was able, the lower boughs of the evergreens, and minutely examined the poor animal. Its eyes were still open, though glazed and bleared, and its death had, undoubtedly, been caused by the blow of some blunt, heavy instrument, for on one side its skull was almost battered in.

"Exactly the death that was dealt to Sandy," she thought, as she groped hither and thither beneath the trees in hopes of lighting upon the weapon of destruction.

She searched until increasing darkness warned her that search was useless. Then, still following the zig-zagging path, she made her way out by the stables and thence back to the house.

She went to bed that night without having spoken to a soul beyond the cook and butler. The next morning, however, Mr. Craven introduced himself to her across the breakfast-table. He was a man of really handsome personal appearance, with a fine carriage of the head and shoulders, and eyes that had a forlorn, appealing look in them. He entered the room with an air of great energy, apologized to Loveday for the absence of his wife, and for his own remissness in not being in the way to receive her on the previous day. Then he bade her make herself at home at the breakfast-table, and expressed his delight in having found a coadjutor in his work.

"I hope you understand what a great – a stupendous work it is?" he added, as he sank into a chair. "It is a work that will leave its impress upon thought in all the ages to come. Only a man who has studied comparative philology as I have for the past thirty years, could gauge the magnitude of the task I have set myself."

With the last remark, his energy seemed spent, and he sank back in his chair, covering his eyes with his hand in precisely the same attitude as that in which Loveday had seen him over-night, and utterly oblivious of the fact that breakfast was before him and a stranger-guest seated at table. The butler entered with another dish. "Better go on with your breakfast," he whispered to Loveday, "he may sit like that for another hour."

He placed his dish in front of his master.

"Captain hasn't come back yet, sir," he said, making an effort to arouse him from his reverie.

"Eh, what?" said Mr. Craven, for a moment lifting his hand from his eyes.

"Captain, sir – the black retriever," repeated the man.

The pathetic look in Mr. Craven's eyes deepened.

"Ah, poor Captain!" he murmured; "the best dog I ever had."

Then he again sank back in his chair, putting his hand to his forehead.

The butler made one more effort to arouse him.

"Madam sent you down a newspaper, sir, that she thought you would like to see," he shouted almost into his master's ear, and at the same time laid the morning's paper on the table beside his plate.

"Confound you! leave it there," said Mr. Craven irritably. "Fools! dolts that you all are! With your trivialities and interruptions you are sending me out of the world with my work undone!"

And again he sank back in his chair, closed his eyes and became lost to his surroundings.

Loveday went on with her breakfast. She changed her place at table to one on Mr. Craven's right hand, so that the newspaper sent down for his perusal lay between his plate and hers. It was folded into an oblong shape, as if it were wished to direct attention to a certain portion of a certain column.

A clock in a corner of the room struck the hour with a loud, resonant stroke. Mr. Craven gave a start and rubbed his eyes.

"Eh, what's this?" he said. "What meal are we at?" He looked around with a bewildered air. "Eh! – who are you?" he went on, staring hard at Loveday. "What are you doing here? Where's Nina? – Where's Harry?"

Loveday began to explain, and gradually recollection seemed to come back to him.

"Ah, yes, yes," he said. "I remember; you've come to assist me with my great work. You promised, you know, to help me out of the hole I've got into. Very enthusiastic, I remember they said you were, on certain abstruse points in comparative philology. Now, Miss – Miss – I've forgotten your name – tell me a little of what you know about the elemental sounds of speech that are common to all languages. Now, to how many would you reduce those elemental sounds – to six, eight, nine? No, we won't discuss the matter here, the cups and saucers distract me. Come into my den at the other end of the house; we'll have perfect quiet there."

And utterly ignoring the fact that he had not as yet broken his fast, he rose from the table, seized Loveday by the wrist, and led her out of the room and down the long corridor that led through the south wing to his study.

But seated in that study his energy once more speedily exhausted itself.

He placed Loveday in a comfortable chair at his writing-table, consulted her taste as to pens, and spread a sheet of foolscap before her. Then he settled himself in his easy-chair, with his back to the light, as if he were about to dictate folios to her.

In a loud, distinct voice he repeated the title of his learned work, then its sub-division, then the number and heading of the chapter that was at present engaging his attention. Then he put his hand to his head. "It's the elemental sounds that are my stumbling-block," he said. "Now, how on earth is it possible to get a notion of a sound of agony that is not in part a sound of terror? or a sound of surprise that is not in part a sound of either joy or sorrow?"

With this his energies were spent, and although Loveday remained seated in that study from early morning till daylight began to fade, she had not ten sentences to show for her day's work as amanuensis.

Loveday in all spent only two clear days at Troyte's Hill.

On the evening of the first of those days Detective Griffiths received, through the trustworthy post-boy, the following brief note from her:

"I have found out that Hales owed Sandy close upon a hundred pounds, which he had borrowed at various times. I don't know whether you will think this fact of any importance. – L.B."

Mr. Griffiths repeated the last sentence blankly. "If Harry Craven were put upon his defence, his counsel, I take it, would consider the fact of first importance," he muttered. And for the remainder of that day Mr. Griffiths went about his work in a perturbed state of mind, doubtful whether to hold or to let go his theory concerning Harry Craven's guilt.

The next morning there came another brief note from Loveday which ran thus:

"As a matter of collateral interest, find out if a person, calling himself Harold Cousins, sailed two days ago from London Docks for Natal in the *Bonnie Dundee*?"

To this missive Loveday received, in reply, the following somewhat lengthy dispatch:

"I do not quite see the drift of your last note, but have wired to our agents in London to carry out its suggestion. On my part, I have important news to communicate. I have found out what Harry Craven's business out of doors was on the night of the murder, and at my instance a warrant has been issued for his arrest. This warrant it will be my duty to serve on him in the course of to-day. Things are beginning to look very black against him, and I am convinced his illness is all a sham. I have seen Waters, the man who is supposed to be attending him, and have driven him into a corner and made him admit that he has only seen young Craven once – on the first day of his illness – and that he gave his certificate entirely on the strength of what Mrs. Craven told him of her son's condition. On the occasion of this, his first and only visit, the lady, it seems, also told him that it would not be necessary for him to continue his attendance, as she quite felt herself competent to treat the case, having had so much experience in fever cases among the blacks at Natal.

"As I left Waters's house, after eliciting this important information, I was accosted by a man who keeps a low-class inn in the place, McQueen by name. He said that he wished to speak to me on a matter of importance. To make a long story short, this McQueen stated that on the night of the sixth, shortly after eleven o'clock, Harry Craven came to his house, bringing with him a valuable piece of plate – a handsome epergne – and requested him to lend him a hundred pounds on it, as he hadn't a penny in his pocket. McQueen complied with his request to the extent of ten sovereigns, and now, in a fit of nervous terror, comes to me to confess himself a receiver of stolen goods and play the honest man! He says he noticed that the young gentleman was very much agitated as he made the request, and he also begged him to mention his visit to no one. Now, I am curious to learn how Master Harry will get over the fact that he passed the lodge at the hour at which the murder was most probably committed; or how he will get out of the dilemma of having repassed the lodge on his way back to the house, and not noticed the wide-open window with the full moon shining down on it?

"Another word! Keep out of the way when I arrive at the house, somewhere between two and three in the afternoon, to serve the warrant. I do not wish your professional capacity to get wind, for you will most likely yet be of some use to us in the house. – S.G."

Loveday read this note, seated at Mr. Craven's writing-table, with the old gentleman himself reclining motionless beside her in his easy-chair. A little smile played about the corners of her mouth as she read over again the words – "for you will most likely yet be of some use to us in the house."

Loveday's second day in Mr. Craven's study promised to be as unfruitful as the first. For fully an hour after she had received Griffiths' note, she sat at the writing-table with her pen in her hand, ready to transcribe Mr. Craven's inspirations. Beyond, however, the phrase, muttered with closed eyes – "It's all here, in my brain, but I can't put it into words" – not a half-syllable escaped his lips.

At the end of that hour the sound of footsteps on the outside gravel made her turn her head towards the window. It was Griffiths approaching with two constables. She heard the hall door opened to admit them, but, beyond that, not a sound reached her ear, and she realized how fully she was cut off from communication with the rest of the household at the farther end of this unoccupied wing.

Mr. Craven, still reclining in his semi-trance, evidently had not the faintest suspicion that so important an event as the arrest of his only son on a charge of murder was about to be enacted in the house.

Meantime, Griffiths and his constables had mounted the stairs leading to the north wing, and were being guided through the corridors to the sick-room by the flying figure of Moggie, the maid.

"Hoot, mistress!" cried the girl, "here are three men coming up the stairs – policemen, every one of them – will ye come and ask them what they be wanting?"

Outside the door of the sick-room stood Mrs. Craven – a tall, sharp-featured woman with sandy hair going rapidly grey.

"What is the meaning of this? What is your business here?" she said haughtily, addressing Griffiths, who headed the party.

Griffiths respectfully explained what his business was, and requested her to stand on one side that he might enter her son's room.

"This is my daughter's room; satisfy yourself of the fact," said the lady, throwing back the door as she spoke.

And Griffiths and his confrères entered, to find pretty Miss Craven, looking very white and scared, seated beside a fire in a long flowing robe de chambre.

Griffiths departed in haste and confusion, without the chance of a professional talk with Loveday. That afternoon saw him telegraphing wildly in all directions, and dispatching messengers in all quarters. Finally he spent over an hour drawing up an elaborate report to his chief at Newcastle, assuring him of the identity of one Harold Cousins, who had sailed in the *Bonnie Dundee* for Natal, with Harry Craven, of Troyte's Hill, and advising that the police authorities in that far-away district should be immediately communicated with.

The ink had not dried on the pen with which this report was written before a note, in Loveday's writing, was put into his hand.

Loveday evidently had had some difficulty in finding a messenger for this note, for it was brought by a gardener's boy, who informed Griffiths that the lady had said he would receive a gold sovereign if he delivered the letter all right.

Griffiths paid the boy and dismissed him, and then proceeded to read Loveday's communication.

It was written hurriedly in pencil, and ran as follows:

"Things are getting critical here. Directly you receive this, come up to the house with two of your men, and post yourselves anywhere in the grounds where you can see and not be seen. There will be no difficulty in this, for it will be dark by the time you are able to get there. I am not sure whether I shall want your aid to-night, but you had better keep in the grounds until morning, in case of need; and above all, never once lose sight of the study windows." (This was underscored.) "If I put a lamp with a green shade in one of those windows, do not lose a moment in entering by that window, which I will contrive to keep unlocked."

Detective Griffiths rubbed his forehead – rubbed his eyes, as he finished reading this.

"Well, I daresay it's all right," he said, "but I'm bothered, that's all, and for the life of me I can't see one step of the way she is going."

He looked at his watch: the hands pointed to a quarter past six. The short September day was drawing rapidly to a close. A good five miles lay between him and Troyte's Hill – there was evidently not a moment to lose.

At the very moment that Griffiths, with his two constables, were once more starting along the Grenfell High Road behind the best horse they could procure, Mr. Craven was rousing himself from his long slumber, and beginning to look around him. That slumber, however, though long, had not been a peaceful one, and it was sundry of the old gentleman's muttered exclamations, as he had started uneasily in his sleep, that had caused Loveday to open, and then to creep out of the room to dispatch, her hurried note.

What effect the occurrence of the morning had had upon the household generally, Loveday, in her isolated corner of the house, had no means of ascertaining. She only noted that when Hales brought in her tea, as he did precisely at five o'clock, he wore a particularly ill-tempered expression of countenance, and she heard him mutter, as he set down the tea-tray with a clatter, something about being a respectable man, and not used to such "goings on."

It was not until nearly an hour and a half after this that Mr. Craven had awakened with a sudden start, and, looking wildly around him, had questioned Loveday who had entered the room.

Loveday explained that the butler had brought in lunch at one, and tea at five, but that since then no one had come in.

"Now that's false," said Mr. Craven, in a sharp, unnatural sort of voice; "I saw him sneaking round the room, the whining, canting hypocrite, and you must have seen him, too! Didn't you hear him say, in his squeaky old voice: 'Master, I knows your secret – '" He broke off abruptly, looking wildly round. "Eh, what's this?" he cried. "No, no, I'm all wrong – Sandy is dead and buried – they held an inquest on him, and we all praised him up as if he were a saint."

"He must have been a bad man, that old Sandy," said Loveday sympathetically.

"You're right! you're right!" cried Mr. Craven, springing up excitedly from his chair and seizing her by the hand. "If ever a man deserved his death, he did. For thirty years he held that rod over my head, and then – ah where was I?"

He put his hand to his head and again sank, as if exhausted, into his chair.

"I suppose it was some early indiscretion of yours at college that he knew of?" said Loveday, eager to get at as much of the truth as possible while the mood for confidence held sway in the feeble brain.

"That was it! I was fool enough to marry a disreputable girl – a barmaid in the town – and Sandy was present at the wedding, and then – " Here his eyes closed again and his mutterings became incoherent.

For ten minutes he lay back in his chair, muttering thus; "A yelp – a groan," were the only words Loveday could distinguish among those mutterings, then suddenly, slowly and distinctly, he said, as if answering some plainly-put question: "A good blow with the hammer and the thing was done."

"I should like amazingly to see that hammer," said Loveday; "do you keep it anywhere at hand?"

His eyes opened with a wild, cunning look in them.

"Who's talking about a hammer? I did not say I had one. If anyone says I did it with a hammer, they're telling a lie."

"Oh, you've spoken to me about the hammer two or three times," said Loveday calmly; "the one that killed your dog, Captain, and I should like to see it, that's all."

The look of cunning died out of the old man's eye – "Ah, poor Captain! splendid dog that! Well, now, where were we? Where did we leave off? Ah, I remember, it was the elemental sounds of speech that bothered me so that night. Were you here then? Ah, no! I remember. I had been trying all day to assimilate a dog's yelp of pain to a human groan, and I couldn't do it. The idea haunted me – followed me about wherever I went. If they were both elemental sounds, they must have something in common, but the link between them I could not find; then it occurred to me, would a well-bred, well-trained dog like my Captain in the stables, there, at the moment of death give an unmitigated currish yelp; would there not be something of a human note in his death-cry? The thing was worth putting to the test. If I could hand down in my treatise a fragment of fact on the matter, it would be worth a dozen dogs' lives. So I went out into the moonlight – ah, but you know all about it – now, don't you?"

"Yes. Poor Captain! did he yelp or groan?"

"Why, he gave one loud, long, hideous yelp, just as if he had been a common cur. I might just as well have let him alone; it only set that other brute opening his window and spying out on me, and saying in his cracked old voice: 'Master, what are you doing out here at this time of night?'"

Again he sank back in his chair, muttering incoherently with half-closed eyes.

Loveday let him alone for a minute or so; then she had another question to ask.

"And that other brute – did he yelp or groan when you dealt him his blow?"

"What, old Sandy – the brute? he fell back – Ah, I remember, you said you would like to see the hammer that stopped his babbling old tongue – now didn't you?"

He rose a little unsteadily from his chair, and seemed to drag his long limbs with an effort across the room to a cabinet at the farther end. Opening a drawer in this cabinet, he produced, from amidst some specimens of strata and fossils, a large-sized geological hammer.

He brandished it for a moment over his head, then paused with his finger on his lip.

"Hush!" he said, "we shall have the fools creeping in to peep at us if we don't take care." And to Loveday's horror he suddenly made for the door, turned the key in the lock, withdrew it and put it into his pocket.

She looked at the clock; the hands pointed to half-past seven. Had Griffiths received her note at the proper time, and were the men now in the grounds? She could only pray that they were.

"The light is too strong for my eyes," she said, and rising from her chair, she lifted the green-shaded lamp and placed it on a table that stood at the window.

"No, no, that won't do," said Mr. Craven; "that would show everyone outside what we're doing in here." He crossed to the window as he spoke and removed the lamp thence to the mantelpiece.

Loveday could only hope that in the few seconds it had remained in the window it had caught the eye of the outside watchers.

The old man beckoned to Loveday to come near and examine his deadly weapon. "Give it a good swing round," he said, suiting the action to the word, "and down it comes with a splendid crash." He brought the hammer round within an inch of Loveday's forehead.

She started back.

"Ha, ha," he laughed harshly and unnaturally, with the light of madness dancing in his eyes now; "did I frighten you? I wonder what sort of sound you would make if I were to give you a little tap just there." Here he lightly touched her forehead with the hammer. "Elemental, of course, it would be, and —"

Loveday steadied her nerves with difficulty. Locked in with this lunatic, her only chance lay in gaining time for the detectives to reach the house and enter through the window.

"Wait a minute," she said, striving to divert his attention; "you have not yet told me what sort of an elemental sound old Sandy made when he fell. If you'll give me pen and ink, I'll write down a full account of it all, and you can incorporate it afterwards in your treatise."

For a moment a look of real pleasure flitted across the old man's face, then it faded. "The brute fell back dead without a sound," he answered; "it was all for nothing, that night's work; yet not altogether for nothing. No, I don't mind owning I would do it all over again to get the wild thrill of joy at my heart that I had when I looked down into that old man's dead face and felt myself free at last!

Free at last!" his voice rang out excitedly – once more he brought his hammer round with an ugly swing.

"For a moment I was a young man again; I leaped into his room – the moon was shining full in through the window – I thought of my old college days, and the fun we used to have at Pembroke – topsy turvey I turned everything — " He broke off abruptly, and drew a step nearer to Loveday. "The pity of it all was," he said, suddenly dropping from his high, excited tone to a low, pathetic one, "that he fell without a sound of any sort." Here he drew another step nearer. "I wonder – " he said, then broke off again, and came close to Loveday's side. "It has only this moment occurred to me," he said, now with his lips close to Loveday's ear, "that a woman, in her death agony, would be much more likely to give utterance to an elemental sound than a man."

He raised his hammer, and Loveday fled to the window, and was lifted from the outside by three pairs of strong arms.

"I thought I was conducting my very last case – I never had such a narrow escape before!" said Loveday, as she stood talking with Mr. Griffiths on the Grenfell platform, awaiting the train to carry her back to London. "It seems strange that no one before suspected the old gentleman's sanity – I suppose, however, people were so used to his eccentricities that they did not notice how they had deepened into positive lunacy. His cunning evidently stood him in good stead at the inquest."

"It is possible," said Griffiths thoughtfully, "that he did not absolutely cross the very slender line that divided eccentricity from madness until after the murder. The excitement consequent upon the discovery of the crime may just have pushed him over the border. Now, Miss Brooke, we have exactly ten minutes before your train comes in. I should feel greatly obliged to you if you would explain one or two things that have a professional interest for me."

"With pleasure," said Loveday. "Put your questions in categorical order and I will answer them."

"Well, then, in the first place, what suggested to your mind the old man's guilt?"

"The relations that subsisted between him and Sandy seemed to me to savour too much of fear on the one side and power on the other. Also the income paid to Sandy during Mr. Craven's absence in Natal bore, to my mind, an unpleasant resemblance to hush-money."

"Poor wretched being! And I hear that, after all, the woman he married in his wild young days died soon afterwards of drink. I have no doubt, however, that Sandy sedulously kept up the fiction of her existence, even after his master's second marriage. Now for another question: how was it you knew that Miss Craven had taken her brother's place in the sick-room?"

"On the evening of my arrival I discovered a rather long lock of fair hair in the unswept fireplace of my room, which, as it happened, was usually occupied by Miss Craven. It at once occurred to me that the young lady had been cutting off her hair and that there must be some powerful motive to induce such a sacrifice. The suspicious circumstances attending her brother's illness soon supplied me with such a motive."

"Ah! that typhoid fever business was very cleverly done. Not a servant in the house, I verily believe, but who thought Master Harry was upstairs, ill in bed, and Miss Craven away at her friends' in Newcastle. The young fellow must have got a clear start off within an hour of the murder. His sister, sent away the next day to Newcastle, dismissed her maid there, I hear, on the plea of no accommodation at her friends' house – sent the girl to her own home for a holiday and herself returned to Troyte's Hill in the middle of the night, having walked the five miles from Grenfell. No doubt her mother admitted her through one of those easily-opened front windows, cut her hair and put her to bed to personate her brother without delay. With Miss Craven's strong likeness to Master Harry, and in a darkened room, it is easy to understand that the eyes of a doctor, personally unacquainted with the family, might easily be deceived. Now, Miss Brooke, you must admit that with all this elaborate chicanery and double dealing going on, it was only natural that my suspicions should set in strongly in that quarter."

"I read it all in another light, you see," said Loveday. "It seemed to me that the mother, knowing her son's evil proclivities, believed in his guilt, in spite, possibly, of his assertions of innocence. The son, most likely, on his way back to the house after pledging the family plate, had met old Mr. Craven with the hammer in his hand. Seeing, no doubt, how impossible it would be for him to clear himself without incriminating his father, he preferred flight to Natal to giving evidence at the inquest."

"Now about his alias?" said Mr. Griffiths briskly, for the train was at that moment steaming into the station. "How did you know that Harold Cousins was identical with Harry Craven, and had sailed in the *Bonnie Dundee*?"

"Oh, that was easy enough," said Loveday, as she stepped into the train; "a newspaper sent down to Mr. Craven by his wife, was folded so as to direct his attention to the shipping list. In it I saw that the *Bonnie Dundee* had sailed two days previously for Natal. Now it was only natural to connect Natal with Mrs. Craven, who had passed the greater part of her life there; and it was easy to understand her wish to get her scapegrace son among her early friends. The alias under which he sailed came readily enough to light. I found it scribbled all over one of Mr. Craven's writing pads in his study; evidently it had been drummed into his ears by his wife as his son's alias, and the old gentleman had taken this method of fixing it in his memory. We'll hope that the young fellow, under his new name, will make a new reputation for himself – at any rate, he'll have a better chance of doing so with the ocean between him and his evil companions. Now it's good-bye, I think."

"No," said Mr. Griffiths; "it's au revoir, for you'll have to come back again for the assizes, and give the evidence that will shut old Mr. Craven in an asylum for the rest of his life."

THE REDHILL SISTERHOOD

Catherine Louisa Pirkis

Catherine Louisa Pirkis (1839–1910) started publishing her Loveday Brooke short stories in 1894. Like her first novel, *Disappeared from Her Home* (1877), they were early examples of mystery fiction by British women. Shortly after creating Brooke, Pirkis retired from writing to focus on animal welfare.

"They want you at Redhill, now," said Mr. Dyer, taking a packet of papers from one of his pigeon-holes. "The idea seems gaining ground in manly quarters that in cases of mere suspicion, women detectives are more satisfactory than men, for they are less likely to attract attention. And this Redhill affair, so far as I can make out, is one of suspicion only."

It was a dreary November morning; every gas jet in the Lynch Court office was alight, and a yellow curtain of outside fog draped its narrow windows.

"Nevertheless, I suppose one can't afford to leave it uninvestigated at this season of the year, with country-house robberies beginning in so many quarters," said Miss Brooke.

"No; and the circumstances in this case certainly seem to point in the direction of the country-house burglar. Two days ago a somewhat curious application was made privately, by a man giving the name of John Murray, to Inspector Gunning, of the Reigate police—Redhill, I must tell you, is in the Reigate police district. Murray stated that he had been a greengrocer somewhere in South London, had sold his business there, and had, with the proceeds of the sale, bought two small houses in Redhill, intending to let the one and live in the other. These houses are situated in a blind alley, known as Paved Court, a narrow turning leading off the London and Brighton coach road. Paved Court has been known to the sanitary authorities for the past ten years as a regular fever nest, and as the houses which Murray bought—numbers 7 and 8—stand at the very end of the blind alley, with no chance of thorough ventilation, I dare say the man got them for next to nothing. He told the Inspector that he had had great difficulty in procuring a tenant for the house he wished to let, number 8, and that consequently when, about three weeks back, a lady, dressed as a nun, made him an offer for it, he immediately closed with her. The lady gave her name simply as 'Sister Monica,' and stated that she was a member of an undenominational Sisterhood that had recently been founded by a wealthy lady, who wished her name kept a secret. Sister Monica gave no references, but, instead, paid a quarter's rent in advance, saying that she wished to take possession of the house immediately, and open it as a home for crippled orphans."

"Gave no references—home for cripples," murmured Loveday, scribbling hard and fast in her note-book.

"Murray made no objection to this," continued Mr. Dyer, "and, accordingly, the next day, Sister Monica, accompanied by three other Sisters and some sickly children, took possession of the house, which they furnished with the barest possible necessaries from cheap shops in the neighbourhood. For a time, Murray said, he thought he had secured most desirable tenants, but during the last ten days suspicions as to their real character have entered his mind, and these suspicions he thought it his duty to communicate to the police. Among their possessions, it seems, these Sisters number an old donkey and a tiny cart, and this they start daily on a sort of begging tour through the adjoining villages, bringing back every evening a perfect hoard of broken victuals and bundles of old garments. Now comes the extraordinary fact on which Murray bases his suspicions. He says, and Gunning verifies his statement, that in whatever direction those Sisters turn the wheels of their donkey-cart, burglaries, or attempts at burglaries, are sure to follow. A week ago they went along towards Horley, where, at an out-lying house, they received much kindness from a wealthy gentleman. That very night an attempt was made to break into that gentleman's house—an attempt, however, that was happily frustrated by the barking of the house-dog. And so on in other instances that I need not go into. Murray suggests that it might be as well to have the daily movements of these sisters closely watched, and that extra vigilance should be exercised by the police in the districts that have had the honour of a morning call from them. Gunning coincides with this idea, and so has sent to me to secure your services."

Loveday closed her note-book. "I suppose Gunning will meet me somewhere and tell me where I'm to take up my quarters?" she said.

"Yes; he will get into your carriage at Merstham—the station before Redhill—if you will put your hand out of window, with the morning paper in it. By-the-way, he takes it for granted that you will take the 11.5 train from Victoria. Murray, it seems, has been good enough to place his little house at the disposal of the police, but Gunning does not think espionage could be so well carried on there as from other quarters. The presence of a stranger in an alley of that sort is bound to attract attention. So he has hired a room for you in a draper's shop that immediately faces the head of the court. There is a private door to this shop of which you will have the key, and can let yourself in and out as you please. You are supposed to be a nursery governess on the lookout for a situation, and Gunning will keep you supplied with letters to give colour to the idea. He suggests that you need only occupy the room during the day, at night you will find far more comfortable quarters at Laker's Hotel, just outside the town."

This was about the sum total of the instructions that Mr. Dyer had to give.

The 11.5 train from Victoria, that carried Loveday to her work among the Surrey Hills, did not get clear of the London fog till well away on the other side of Purley. When the train halted at Merstham, in response to her signal a tall, soldier-like individual made for her carriage, and, jumping in, took the seat facing her. He introduced himself to her as Inspector Gunning, recalled to her memory a former occasion on which they had met, and then, naturally enough, turned the talk upon the present suspicious circumstances they were bent upon investigating. .

"It won't do for you and me to be seen together," he said; "of course I am known for miles round, and anyone seen in my company will be at once set down as my coadjutor, and spied upon accordingly. I walked from Redhill to Merstham on purpose to avoid recognition on the platform at Redhill, and half-way here, to my great annoyance, found that I was being followed by a man in a workman's dress and carrying a basket of tools. I doubled, however, and gave him the slip, taking a short cut down a lane which, if he had been living in the place, he would have known as well as I did. By Jove!" this was added with a sudden start, "there is the fellow, I declare; he has weathered me after all, and has no doubt taken good stock of us both, with the train going at this snail's pace. It was unfortunate that your face should have been turned towards that window, Miss Brooke."

"My veil is something of a disguise, and I will put on another cloak before he has a chance of seeing me again," said Loveday.

All she had seen in the brief glimpse that the train had allowed was a tall, powerfully-built man walking along a siding of the line. His cap was drawn low over his eyes, and in his hand he carried a workman's basket.

Gunning seemed much annoyed at the circumstance. "Instead of landing at Redhill," he said, "we'll go on to Three Bridges and wait there for a Brighton train to bring us back, that will enable you to get to your room somewhere between the lights; I don't want to have you spotted before you've so much as started your work." Then they went back to their discussion of the Redhill Sisterhood. "They call themselves 'undenominational,' whatever that means," said Gunning. "They say they are connected with no religious sect whatever, they attend sometimes one place of worship, sometimes another, sometimes none at all. They refuse to give up the name of the founder of their order, and really no one has any right to demand it of them, for, as no doubt you see, up to the present moment the case is one of mere suspicion, and it may be a pure coincidence that attempts at burglary have followed their footsteps in this neighbourhood. By-the-way, I have heard of a man's face being enough to hang him, but until I saw Sister Monica's, I never saw a woman's face that could perform the same kind office for her. Of all the lowest criminal types of faces I have ever seen, I think hers is about the lowest and most repulsive."

After the Sisters, they passed in review the chief families resident in the neighbourhood.

"This," said Gunning, unfolding a paper, "is a map I have specially drawn up for you—it takes in the district for ten miles round Redhill, and every country house of any importance is marked with it in red ink. Here, in addition, is an index to those houses, with special notes of my own to every house."

Loveday studied the map for a minute or so, then turned her attention to the index.

"Those four houses you've marked, I see, are those that have been already attempted. I don't think I'll run them through, but I'll mark them 'doubtful;' you see the gang—for, of course, it is a gang—might follow our reasoning on the matter, and look upon those houses as our weak point. Here's one I'll run through, 'house empty during winter months,' that means plate and jewellery sent to the bankers. Oh! and this one may as well be crossed off, 'father and four sons all athletes and sportsmen,' that means firearms always handy—I don't think burglars will be likely to trouble them. Ah! now we come to something! Here's a house to be marked 'tempting' in a burglar's list. 'Wootton Hall, lately changed hands and re-built, with complicated passages and corridors. Splendid family plate in daily use and left entirely to the care of the butler.' I wonder, does the master of that house trust to his 'complicated passages' to preserve his plate for him? A dismissed dishonest servant would supply a dozen maps of the place for half-a-sovereign. What do these initials, 'E.L.,' against the next house in the list, North Cape, stand for?"

"Electric lighted. I think you might almost cross that house off also. I consider electric lighting one of the greatest safeguards against burglars that a man can give his house."

"Yes, if he doesn't rely exclusively upon it; it might be a nasty trap under certain circumstances. I see this gentleman also has magnificent presentation and other plate."

"Yes. Mr. Jameson is a wealthy man and very popular in the neighbourhood; his cups and epergnes are worth looking at."

"Is it the only house in the district that is lighted with electricity?"

"Yes; and, begging your pardon, Miss Brooke, I only wish it were not so. If electric lighting were generally in vogue it would save the police a lot of trouble on these dark winter nights."

"The burglars would find some way of meeting such a condition of things, depend upon it; they have reached a very high development in these days. They no longer stalk about as they did fifty years ago with blunderbuss and bludgeon; they plot, plan, contrive and bring imagination and artistic resource to their aid. By-the-way, it often occurs to me that the popular detective stories, for which there seems to be a large demand at the present day, must be, at times, uncommonly useful to the criminal classes."

At Three Bridges they had to wait so long for a return train that it was nearly dark when Loveday got back to Redhill. Mr. Gunning did not accompany her thither, having alighted at a previous station. Loveday had directed her portmanteau to be sent direct to Laker's Hotel, where she had engaged a room by telegram from Victoria Station. So, unburthened by luggage, she slipped quietly out of the Redhill Station and made her way straight for the draper's shop in the London Road. She had no difficulty in finding it, thanks to the minute directions given her by the Inspector. Street lamps were being lighted in the sleepy little town as she went along, and as she turned into the London Road, shopkeepers were lighting up their windows on both sides of the way. A few yards down this road, a dark patch between the lighted shops showed her where Paved Court led off from the thoroughfare. A side-door of one of the shops that stood at the corner of the court seemed to offer a post of observation whence she could see without being seen, and here Loveday, shrinking into the shadows, ensconced herself in order to take stock of the little alley and its inhabitants. She found it much as it had been described to her—a collection of four-roomed houses of which more than half were unlet. Numbers 7 and 8 at the head of the court presented a slightly less neglected appearance than the other tenements. Number 7 stood in total darkness, but in the upper window of number 8 there showed what seemed to be a night-light burning, so Loveday conjectured that this possibly was the room set apart as a dormitory for the little cripples.

While she stood thus surveying the home of the suspected Sisterhood, the Sisters themselves—two, at least, of them—came into view, with their donkey-cart and their cripples, in the main road. It was an odd little cortège. One Sister, habited in a nun's dress of dark blue serge, led the donkey by the bridle; another Sister, similarly attired, walked alongside the low cart, in which were seated two sickly-looking children. They were evidently returning from one of their long country circuits, and unless they had lost their way and been belated—it certainly seemed a late hour for the sickly little cripples to be abroad.

As they passed under the gas lamp at the corner of the court, Loveday caught a glimpse of the faces of the Sisters. It was easy, with Inspector Gunning's description before her mind, to identify the older and taller woman as Sister Monica, and a more coarse-featured and generally repellant face Loveday admitted to herself she had never before seen. In striking contrast to this forbidding countenance was that of the younger Sister. Loveday could only catch a brief passing view of it, but that one brief view was enough to impress it on her memory as of unusual sadness and beauty. As the donkey stopped at the corner of the court, Loveday heard this sad-looking young woman addressed as "Sister Anna" by one of the cripples, who asked plaintively when they were going to have something to eat.

"Now, at once," said Sister Anna, lifting the little one, as it seemed to Loveday, tenderly out of the cart, and carrying him on her shoulder down the court to the door of number 8, which opened to them at their approach. The other Sister did the same with the other child; then both Sisters returned, unloaded the cart of sundry bundles and baskets, and, this done, led off the old donkey and trap down the road, possibly to a neighbouring costermonger's stables. A man, coming along on a bicycle, exchanged a word of greeting with the Sisters as they passed, then swung himself off his machine at the corner of the court, and walked it along the paved way to the door of number 7. This he opened with a key, and then, pushing the machine before him, entered the house.

Loveday took it for granted that this man must be the John Murray of whom she had heard. She had closely scrutinized him as he had passed her, and had seen that he was a dark, well-featured man of about fifty years of age.

She congratulated herself on her good fortune in having seen so much in such a brief space of time, and coming forth from her sheltered corner turned her steps in the direction of the draper's shop on the other side of the road.

It was easy to find it. "Golightly" was the singular name that figured above the shop-front, in which were displayed a variety of goods calculated to meet the wants of servants and the poorer classes generally. A tall, powerfully-built man appeared to be looking in at this window. Loveday's foot was on the door-step of the draper's private entrance, her hand on the door-knocker, when this individual, suddenly turning, convinced her of his identity with the journeyman workman who had so disturbed Mr. Gunning's equanimity. It was true he wore a bowler instead of a journeyman's cap, and he no longer carried a basket of tools, but there was no possibility for anyone, with so good an eye for an outline as Loveday possessed, not to recognize the carriage of the head and shoulders as that of the man she had seen walking along the railway siding. He gave her no time to make minute observation of his appearance, but turned quickly away, and disappeared down a by-street.

Loveday's work seemed to bristle with difficulties now. Here was she, as it were, unearthed in her own ambush; for there could be but little doubt that during the whole time she had stood watching those Sisters, that man, from a safe vantage point, had been watching her.

She found Mrs. Golightly a civil and obliging person. She showed Loveday to her room above the shop, brought her the letters which Inspector Gunning had been careful to have posted to her during the day. Then she supplied her with pen and ink and, in response to Loveday's request, with some strong coffee that she said, with a little attempt at a joke, would "keep a dormouse awake all through the winter without winking."

While the obliging landlady busied herself about the room, Loveday had a few questions to ask about the Sisterhood who lived down the court opposite. On this head, however, Mrs. Golightly could tell her no more than she already knew, beyond the fact that they started every morning on their rounds at eleven o'clock punctually, and that before that hour they were never to be seen outside their door.

Loveday's watch that night was to be a fruitless one. Although she sat, with her lamp turned out and safely screened from observation, until close upon midnight, with eyes fixed upon numbers 7 and 8 Paved Court, not so much as a door opening or shutting at either house rewarded her vigil. The lights flitted from the lower to the upper floors in both houses, and then disappeared somewhere between nine and ten in the evening; and after that, not a sign of life did either tenement show.

And all through the long hours of that watch, backwards and forwards there seemed to flit before her mind's eye, as if in some sort it were fixed upon its retina, the sweet, sad face of Sister Anna.

Why it was this face should so haunt her, she found it hard to say. "It has a mournful past and a mournful future written upon it as a hopeless whole," she said to herself. "It is the face of an Andromeda! 'here am I,' it seems to say, 'tied to my stake, helpless and hopeless.'"

The church clocks were sounding the midnight hour as Loveday made her way through the dark streets to her hotel outside the town. As she passed under the railway arch that ended in the open country road, the echo of not very distant footsteps caught her ear. When she stopped they stopped, when she went on they went on, and she knew that once more she was being followed and watched, although the darkness of the arch prevented her seeing even the shadow of the man who was thus dogging her steps.

The next morning broke keen and frosty. Loveday studied her map and her country-house index over a seven o'clock breakfast, and then set off for a brisk walk along the country road. No doubt in London the streets were walled in and roofed with yellow fog; here, however, bright sunshine played in and out of the bare tree-boughs and leafless hedges on to a thousand frost spangles, turning the prosaic macadamized road into a gangway fit for Queen Titania herself and her fairy train.

Loveday turned her back on the town and set herself to follow the road as it wound away over the hill in the direction of a village called Northfield. Early as she was, she was not to have that road to herself. A team of strong horses trudged by on their way to their work in the fuller's-earth pits. A young fellow on a bicycle flashed past at a tremendous pace, considering the upward slant of the road. He looked hard at her as he passed, then slackened pace, dismounted, and awaited her coming on the brow of the hill.

"Good morning, Miss Brooke," he said, lifting his cap as she came alongside of him. "May I have five minutes' talk with you?"

The young man who thus accosted her had not the appearance of a gentleman. He was a handsome, bright-faced young fellow of about two-and-twenty, and was dressed in ordinary cyclists' dress; his cap was pushed back from his brow over thick, curly, fair hair, and Loveday, as she looked at him, could not repress the thought how well he would look at the head of a troop of cavalry, giving the order to charge the enemy.

He led his machine to the side of the footpath.

"You have the advantage of me," said Loveday; "I haven't the remotest notion who you are."

"No," he said; "although I know you, you cannot possibly know me. I am a north country man, and I was present, about a month ago, at the trial of old Mr. Craven, of Troyte's Hill—in fact, I acted as reporter for one of the local papers. I watched your face so closely as you gave your evidence that I should know it anywhere, among a thousand."

"And your name is—?"

"George White, of Grenfell. My father is part proprietor of one of the Newcastle papers. I am a bit of a literary man myself, and sometimes figure as a reporter, sometimes as leader-writer, to that paper." Here he gave a glance towards his side pocket, from which protruded a small volume of Tennyson's poems.

The facts he had stated did not seem to invite comment, and Loveday ejaculated merely:

"Indeed!"

The young man went back to the subject that was evidently filling his thoughts. "I have special reasons for being glad to have met you this morning, Miss Brooke," he went on, making his footsteps keep pace with hers. "I am in great trouble, and I believe you are the only person in the whole world who can help me out of that trouble."

"I am rather doubtful as to my power of helping anyone out of trouble," said Loveday; "so far as my experience goes, our troubles are as much a part of ourselves as our skins are of our bodies."

"Ah, but not such trouble as mine," said White eagerly. He broke off for a moment, then, with a sudden rush of words, told her what that trouble was. For the past year he had been engaged to be married to a young girl, who, until quite recently, had been fulfilling the duties of a nursery governess in a large house in the neighbourhood of Redhill.

"Will you kindly give me the name of that house?" interrupted Loveday.

"Certainly; Wootton Hall, the place is called, and Annie Lee is my sweetheart's name. I don't care who knows it!" He threw his head back as he said this, as if he would be delighted to announce the fact to the whole world. "Annie's mother," he went on, "died when she was a baby, and we both thought her father was dead also, when suddenly, about a fortnight ago, it came to her knowledge that instead of being dead, he was serving his time at Portland for some offence committed years ago."

"Do you know how this came to Annie's knowledge?"

"Not the least in the world; I only know that I suddenly got a letter from her announcing the fact, and at the same time, breaking off her engagement with me. I tore the letter into a thousand pieces, and wrote back saying I would not allow the engagement to be broken off, but would marry her to-morrow if she would have me. To this letter she did not reply; there came instead a few lines from Mrs. Copeland, the lady at Wootton Hall, saying that Annie had thrown up her engagement and joined some Sisterhood, and that she, Mrs. Copeland, had pledged her word to Annie to reveal to no one the name and whereabouts of that Sisterhood."

"And I suppose you imagine I am able to do what Mrs. Copeland is pledged not to do?"

"That's just it, Miss Brooke," cried the young man enthusiastically. "You do such wonderful things; everyone knows you do. It seems as if, when anything is wanted to be found out, you just walk into a place, look round you and, in a moment, everything becomes clear as noonday."

"I can't quite lay claim to such wonderful powers as that. As it happens, however, in the present instance, no particular skill is needed to find out what you wish to know, for I fancy I have already come upon the traces of Miss Annie Lee."

"Miss Brooke!"

"Of course, I cannot say for certain, but it is a matter you can easily settle for yourself—settle, too, in a way that will confer a great obligation on me."

"I shall be only too delighted to be of any—the slightest service to you," cried White, enthusiastically as before.

"Thank you. I will explain. I came down here specially to watch the movements of a certain Sisterhood who have somehow aroused the suspicions of the police. Well, I find that instead of being able to do this, I am myself so closely watched—possibly by confederates of these Sisters—that unless I can do my work by deputy I may as well go back to town at once."

"Ah! I see—you want me to be that deputy."

"Precisely. I want you to go to the room in Redhill that I have hired, take your place at the window—screened, of course, from observation—at which I ought to be seated—watch as closely as possible the movements of these Sisters and report them to me at the hotel, where I shall remain shut in from morning till night—it is the only way in which I can throw my persistent spies off the scent. Now, in doing this for me, you will be also doing yourself a good turn, for I have little doubt but that under the blue serge hood of one of the sisters you will discover the pretty face of Miss Annie Lee."

As they had talked they had walked, and now stood on the top of the hill at the head of the one little street that constituted the whole of the village of Northfield.

On their left hand stood the village schools and the master's house; nearly facing these, on the opposite side of the road, beneath a clump of elms, stood the village pound. Beyond this pound, on either side of the way, were two rows of small cottages with tiny squares of garden in front, and in the midst of these small cottages a swinging sign beneath a lamp announced a "Postal and Telegraph Office."

"Now that we have come into the land of habitations again," said Loveday, "it will be best for us to part. It will not do for you and me to be seen together, or my spies will be transferring their attentions from me to you, and I shall have to find another deputy. You had better start on your bicycle for Redhill at once, and I will walk back at leisurely speed. Come to me at my hotel without fail at one o'clock and report proceedings. I do not say anything definite about remuneration, but I assure you, if you carry out my instructions to the letter, your services will be amply rewarded by me and by my employers."

There were yet a few more details to arrange. White had been, he said, only a day and night in the neighbourhood, and special directions as to the locality had to be given to him. Loveday advised him not to attract attention by going to the draper's private door, but to enter the shop as if he were a customer, and then explain matters to Mrs. Golightly, who, no doubt, would be in her place behind the counter; tell her he was the brother of the Miss Smith who had hired her room, and ask permission to go through the shop to that room, as he had been commissioned by his sister to read and answer any letters that might have arrived there for her. "Show her the key of the side door—here it is," said Loveday; "it will be your credentials, and tell her you did not like to make use of it without acquainting her with the fact."

The young man took the key, endeavoured to put it in his waistcoat pocket, found the space there occupied and so transferred it to the keeping of a side pocket in his tunic.

All this time Loveday stood watching him.

"You have a capital machine there," she said, as the young man mounted his bicycle once more, "and I hope you will turn it to account in following the movements of these Sisters about the neighbourood. I feel confident you will have something definite to tell me when you bring me your first report at one o'clock."

White once more broke into a profusion of thanks, and then, lifting his cap to the lady, started his machine at a fairly good pace. Loveday watched him out of sight down the slope of the hill, then, instead of following him as she had said she would "at a leisurely pace," she turned her steps in the opposite direction along the village street.

It was an altogether ideal country village. Neatly-dressed chubby-faced children, now on their way to the schools, dropped quaint little curtsies, or tugged at curly locks as Loveday passed; every cottage looked the picture of cleanliness and trimness, and although so late in the year, the gardens were full of late flowering chrysanthemums and early flowering Christmas roses.

At the end of the village, Loveday came suddenly into view of a large, handsome, red-brick mansion. It presented a wide frontage to the road, from which it lay back amid extensive pleasure grounds. On the right hand, and a little in the rear of the house, stood what seemed to be large and commodious stables, and immediately adjoining these stables was a low-built, red-brick shed, that had evidently been recently erected.

That low-built, red-brick shed excited Loveday's curiosity.

"Is this house called North Cape?" she asked of a man, who chanced at that moment to be passing with a pickaxe and shovel.

The man answered in the affirmative, and Loveday then asked another question: could he tell her what was that small shed so close to the house—it looked like a glorified cowhouse—now what could be its use?

The man's face lighted up as if it were a subject on which he liked to be questioned. He explained that that small shed was the engine-house where the electricity that lighted North Cape was made and stored. Then he dwelt with pride upon the fact, as if he held a personal interest in it, that North Cape was the only house, far or near, that was thus lighted.

"I suppose the wires are carried underground to the house," said Loveday, looking in vain for signs of them anywhere.

The man was delighted to go into details on the matter. He had helped to lay those wires, he said: they were two in number, one for supply and one for return, and were laid three feet below ground, in boxes filled with pitch. These wires were switched on to jars in the engine-house, where the electricity was stored, and, after passing underground, entered the family mansion under its flooring at its western end.

Loveday listened attentively to these details, and then took a minute and leisurely survey of the house and its surroundings. This done, she retraced her steps through the village, pausing, however, at the "Postal and Telegraph Office" to dispatch a telegram to Inspector Gunning.

It was one to send the Inspector to his cipher-book. It ran as follows:

"Rely solely on chemist and coal-merchant throughout the day.—L. B."

After this, she quickened her pace, and in something over three-quarters of an hour was back again at her hotel.

There she found more of life stirring than when she had quitted it in the early morning. There was to be a meeting of the "Surrey Stags," about a couple of miles off, and a good many hunting men were hanging about the entrance to the house, discussing the chances of sport after last night's frost. Loveday made her way through the throng in leisurely fashion, and not a man but what had keen scrutiny from her sharp eyes. No, there was no cause for suspicion there: they were evidently one and all just what they seemed to be—loud-voiced, hard-riding men, bent on a day's sport; but—and here Loveday's eyes traveled beyond the hotel court-yard to the other side of the road—who was that man with a billhook hacking at the hedge there—a thin-featured, round-shouldered old fellow, with a bent-about hat? It might be as well not to take it too rashly for granted that her spies had withdrawn, and had left her free to do her work in her own fashion.

She went upstairs to her room. It was situated on the first floor in the front of the house, and consequently commanded a good view of the high road. She stood well back from the window, and at an angle whence she could see and not be seen, took a long, steady survey of the hedger. And the longer she looked the more convinced she was that the man's real work was something other than the bill-hook seemed to imply. He worked, so to speak, with his head over his shoulder, and when Loveday supplemented her eyesight with a strong field-glass, she could see more than one stealthy glance shot from beneath his bent-about hat in the direction of her window.

There could be little doubt about it: her movements were to be as closely watched to-day as they had been yesterday. Now it was of first importance that she should communicate with Inspector Gunning in the course of the afternoon: the question to solve was how it was to be done?

To all appearance Loveday answered the question in extraordinary fashion. She pulled up her blind, she drew back her curtain, and seated herself, in full view, at a small table in the window recess. Then she took a pocket inkstand from her pocket, a packet of correspondence cards from her letter-case, and with rapid pen, set to work on them.

About an hour and a half afterwards, White, coming in, according to his promise, to report proceedings, found her still seated at the window, not, however, with writing materials before her, but with needle and thread in her hand with which she was mending her gloves.

"I return to town by the first train to-morrow morning," she said as he entered, "and I find these wretched things want no end of stitches. Now for your report."

White appeared to be in an elated frame of mind. "I've seen her!" he cried, "my Annie—they've got her, those confounded Sisters; but they sha'n't keep her—no, not if I have to pull the house down about their ears to get her out."

"Well, now you know where she is, you can take your time about getting her out," said Loveday. "I hope, however, you haven't broken faith with me, and betrayed yourself by trying to speak with her, because, if so, I shall have to look out for another deputy."

"Honour, Miss Brooke!" answered White indignantly. "I stuck to my duty, though it cost me something to see her hanging over those kids and tucking them into the cart, and never say a word to her, never so much as wave my hand."

"Did she go out with the donkey-cart to-day?"

"No, she only tucked the kids into the cart with a blanket, and then went back to the house. Two old Sisters, ugly as sin, went out with them. I watched them from the window, jolt, jolt, jolt, round the corner, out of sight, and then I whipped down the stairs, and on to my machine, and was after them in a trice and managed to keep them well in sight for over an hour and a half."

"And their destination to-day was?"

"Wootton Hall."

"Ah, just as I expected."

"Just as you expected?" echoed White.

"I forgot. You do not know the nature of the suspicions that are attached to this Sisterhood, and the reasons I have for thinking that Wootton Hall, at this season of the year, might have an especial attraction for them."

White continued staring at her. "Miss Brooke," he said presently, in an altered tone, "whatever suspicions may attach to the Sisterhood, I'll stake my life on it, my Annie has had no share in any wickedness of any sort."

"Oh, quite so; it is most likely that your Annie has, in some way, been inveigled into joining these Sisters—has been taken possession of by them, in fact, just as they have taken possession of the little cripples."

"That's it!" he cried excitedly; "that was the idea that occurred to me when you spoke to me on the hill about them, otherwise you may be sure—"

"Did they get relief of any sort at the Hall?" interrupted Loveday.

"Yes; one of the two ugly old women stopped outside the lodge gates with the donkey-cart, and the other beauty went up to the house alone. She stayed there, I should think, about a quarter of an hour, and when she came back, was followed by a servant, carrying a bundle and a basket."

"Ah! I've no doubt they brought away with them something else beside old garments and broken victuals."

White stood in front of her, fixing a hard, steady gaze upon her.

"Miss Brooke," he said presently, in a voice that matched the look on his face, "what do you suppose was the real object of these women in going to Wootton Hall this morning?"

"Mr. White, if I wished to help a gang of thieves break into Wootton Hall to-night, don't you think I should be greatly interested in procuring from them the information that the master of the house was away from home; that two of the men servants, who slept in the house, had recently been dismissed and their places had not yet been filled; also that the dogs were never unchained at night, and that their kennels were at the side of the house at which the butler's pantry is not situated? These are particulars I have gathered in this house without stirring from my chair, and I am satisfied that they are likely to be true. A the same time, if I were a professed burglar, I should not be content with information that was likely to be true, but would be careful to procure such that was certain to be true, and so would set accomplices to work at the fountain head. Now do you understand?"

White folded his arms and looked down on her.

"What are you going to do?" he asked, in short, brusque tones. Loveday looked him full in the face. "Communicate with the police immediately," she answered; "and I should feel greatly obliged if you will at once take a note from me to Inspector Gunning at Reigate."

"And what becomes of Annie?"

"I don't think you need have any anxiety on that head. I've no doubt that when the circumstances of her admission to the Sisterhood are investigated, it will be proved that she has been as much deceived and imposed upon as the man, John Murray, who so foolishly let his house to these women. Remember, Annie has Mrs. Copeland's good word to support her integrity."

White stood silent for awhile.

"What sort of a note do you wish me to take to the Inspector?" he presently asked.

"You shall read it as I write it, if you like," answered Loveday. She took a correspondence card from her letter-case, and, with an indelible pencil, wrote as follows—

"Wootton Hall is threatened to-night—concentrate attention there.

"L. B."

White read the words as she wrote them with a curious expression passing over his handsome features.

"Yes," he said, curtly as before. "I'll deliver that, I give you my word, but I'll bring back no answer to you. I'll do no more spying for you—it's a trade that doesn't suit me. There's a straight-forward way of doing straight-forward work, and I'll take that way—no other—to get my Annie out of that den."

He took the note, which she sealed and handed to him, and strode out of the room.

Loveday, from the window, watched him mount his bicycle. Was it her fancy, or did there pass a swift, furtive glance of recognition between him and the hedger on the other side of the way as he rode out of the court-yard?

Loveday seemed determined to make that hedger's work easy for him. The short winter's day was closing in now, and her room must consequently have been growing dim to outside observation. She lighted the gas chandelier which hung from the ceiling and, still with blinds and curtains undrawn, took her old place at the window, spread writing materials before her and commenced a long and elaborate report to her chief at Lynch Court.

About half-an-hour afterwards, as she threw a casual glance across the road, she saw that the hedger had disappeared, but that two ill-looking tramps sat munching bread and cheese under the hedge to which his bill-hook had done so little service. Evidently the intention was, one way or another, not to lose sight of her so long as she remained in Redhill.

Meantime, White had delivered Loveday's note to the Inspector at Reigate, and had disappeared on his bicycle once more.

Gunning read it without a change of expression. Then he crossed the room to the fire-place and held the card as close to the bars as he could without scorching it.

"I had a telegram from her this morning," he explained to his confidential man, "telling me to rely upon chemicals and coals throughout the day, and that, of course, meant that she would write to me in invisible ink. No doubt this message about Wootton Hall means nothing—"

He broke off abruptly, exclaiming: "Eh! what's this!" as, having withdrawn the card from the fire, Loveday's real message stood out in bold, clear characters between the lines of the false one.

Thus it ran:

"North Cape will be attacked to-night—a desperate gang—be prepared for a struggle. Above all, guard the electrical engine-house. On no account attempt to communicate with me; I am so closely watched that any endeavour to do so may frustrate your chance of trapping the scoundrels. L. B."

That night when the moon went down behind Reigate Hill an exciting scene was enacted at "North Cape." The *Surrey Gazette*, in its issue the following day, gave the subjoined account of it under the heading, "Desperate encounter with burglars."

"Last night, 'North Cape,' the residence of Mr. Jameson, was the scene of an affray between the police and a desperate gang of burglars. 'North Cape' is lighted throughout with electricity, and the burglars, four in number, divided in half—two being told off to enter and rob the house, and two to remain at the engine-shed, where the electricity is stored, so that, at a given signal, should need arise, the wires might be unswitched, the inmates of the house thrown into sudden darkness and confusion, and the escape of the marauders thereby facilitated. Mr. Jameson, however, had received timely warning from the police of the intended attack, and he, with his two sons, all well armed, sat in darkness in the inner hall awaiting the coming of the thieves. The police were stationed, some in the stables, some in out-buildings nearer to the house, and others in more distant parts of the grounds. The burglars effected their entrance by means of a ladder placed to a window of the servants' stair case which leads straight down to the butler's pantry and to the safe where the silver is kept. The fellows, however, had no sooner got into the house than the police, issuing from their hiding-place outside, mounted the ladder after them and thus cut off their retreat. Mr. Jameson and his two sons, at the same moment, attacked them in front, and thus overwhelmed by numbers, the scoundrels were easily secured. It was at the engine-house outside that the sharpest struggle took place. The thieves had forced open the door of this engine-shed with their jimmies immediately on their arrival, under the very eyes of the police, who lay in ambush in the stables, and when one of the men, captured in the house, contrived to sound an alarm on his whistle, these outside watchers made a rush for the electrical jars, in order to unswitch the wires. Upon this the police closed upon them, and a hand-to-hand struggle followed, and if it had not been for the timely assistance of Mr. Jameson and his sons, who had fortunately conjectured that their presence here might be useful, it is more than likely that one of the burglars, a powerfully-built man, would have escaped.

"The names of the captured men are John Murray, Arthur and George Lee (father and son), and a man with so many aliases that it is difficult to know which is his real name. The whole thing had been most cunningly and carefully planned. The elder Lee, lately released from penal servitude for a similar offence, appears to have been prime mover in the affair. This man had, it seems, a son and a daughter, who, through the kindness of friends, had been fairly well placed in life: the son at an electrical engineers' in London, the daughter as nursery governess at Wootton Hall. Directly this man was released from Portland, he seems to have found out his children and done his best to ruin them both. He was constantly at Wootton Hall endeavouring to induce his daughter to act as an accomplice to a robbery of the house. This so worried the girl that she threw up her situation and joined a Sisterhood that had recently been established in the neighbourhood. Upon this, Lee's thoughts turned in another direction. He induced his son, who had saved a little money, to throw up his work in London, and join him in his disreputable career. The boy is a handsome young fellow, but appears to have in him the makings of a first-class criminal. In his work as an electrical engineer he had made the acquaintance of the man John Murray, who, it is said, has been rapidly going downhill of late. Murray was the owner of the house rented by the Sisterhood that Miss Lee had joined, and the idea evidently struck the brains of these three scoundrels that this Sisterhood, whose antecedents were a little mysterious, might be utilized to draw off the attention of the police from themselves and from the especial house in the neighbourhood that they had planned to attack. With this end in view, Murray made an application to the police to have the Sisters watched, and still further to give colour to the suspicions he had endeavoured to set afloat concerning them, he and his confederates made feeble attempts at burglary upon the houses at which the Sisters had called, begging for scraps. It is a matter for congratulation that the plot, from beginning to end, has been thus successfully unearthed, and it is felt on all sides that great credit is due to Inspector Gunning and his skilled coadjutors for the vigilance and promptitude they have displayed throughout the affair."

Loveday read aloud this report, with her feet on the fender of the Lynch Court office.

"Accurate, as far as it goes," she said, as she laid down the paper.

"But we want to know a little more," said Mr. Dyer. "In the first place, I would like to know what it was that diverted your suspicions from the unfortunate Sisters?"

"The way in which they handled the children," answered Loveday promptly. "I have seen female criminals of all kinds handling children, and I have noticed that although they may occasionally—even this is rare—treat them with a certain rough sort of kindness, of tenderness they are utterly incapable. Now Sister Monica, I must admit, is not pleasant to look at; at the same time, there was something absolutely beautiful in the way in which she lifted the little cripple out of the cart, put his tiny thin hand round her neck, and carried him into the house. By-the-way, I would like to ask some rapid physiognomist how he would account for Sister Monica's repulsiveness of feature as contrasted with young Lee's undoubted good looks—heredity, in this case, throws no light on the matter."

"Another question," said Mr. Dyer, not paying much heed to Loveday's digression: "how was it you transferred your suspicions to John Murray?"

"I did not do so immediately, although at the very first it had struck me as odd that he should be so anxious to do the work of the police for them. The chief thing I noticed concerning Murray, on the first and only occasion on which I saw him, was that he had had an accident with his bicycle, for in the right-hand corner of his lamp-glass there was a tiny star, and the lamp itself had a dent on the same side, had also lost its hook, and was fastened to the machine by a bit of electric fuse. The next morning as I was walking up the hill towards Northfield, I was accosted by a young man mounted on that self-same bicycle—not a doubt of it—star in glass, dent, fuse, all three."

"Ah, that sounded an important keynote, and led you to connect Murray and the younger Lee immediately."

"It did, and, of course, also at once gave the lie to his statement that he was a stranger in the place, and confirmed my opinion that there was nothing of the north-countryman in his accent. Other details in his manner and appearance gave rise to other suspicions. For instance, he called himself a press reporter by profession, and his hands were coarse and grimy as only a mechanic's could be. He said he was a bit of a literary man, but the Tennyson that showed so obtrusively from his pocket was new, and in parts uncut, and totally unlike the well-thumbed volume of the literary student. Finally, when he tried and failed to put my latch-key into his waistcoat pocket, I saw the reason lay in the fact that the pocket was already occupied by a soft coil of electric fuse, the end of which protruded. Now, an electric fuse is what an electrical engineer might almost unconsciously carry about with him, it is so essential a part of his working tools, but it is a thing that a literary man or a press reporter could have no possible use for."

"Exactly, exactly. And it was no doubt, that bit of electric fuse that turned your thoughts to the one house in the neighbourhood lighted by electricity, and suggested to your mind the possibility of electrical engineers turning their talents to account in that direction. Now, will you tell me, what, at that stage of your day's work, induced you to wire to Gunning that you would bring your invisible-ink bottle into use?"

"That was simply a matter of precaution; it did not compel me to the use of invisible ink, if I saw other safe methods of communication. I felt myself being hemmed in on all sides with spies, and I could not tell what emergency might arise. I don't think I have ever had a more difficult game to play. As I walked and talked with the young fellow up the hill, it became clear to me that if I wished to do my work I must lull the suspicions of the gang, and seem to walk into their trap. I saw by the persistent way in which Wootton Hall was forced on my notice that it was wished to fix my suspicions there. I accordingly, to all appearance, did so, and allowed the fellows to think they were making a fool of me."

"Ha! ha! Capital that—the biter bit, with a vengeance! Splendid idea to make that young rascal himself deliver the letter that was to land him and his pals in jail. And he all the time laughing in his sleeve and thinking what a fool he was making of you! Ha, ha, ha!" And Mr. Dyer made the office ring again with his merriment.

"The only person one is at all sorry for in this affair is poor little Sister Anna," said Loveday pityingly; "and yet, perhaps, all things considered, after her sorry experience of life, she may not be so badly placed in a Sisterhood where practical Christianity—not religious hysterics—is the one and only rule of the order."

BLACK BETTY

Sheila Quigley

Sheila Quigley was the subject of a BBC documentary when her first book, *Run for Home*, was published in 2004. Her first novels were set around a council housing estate in her home county of Tyne and Wear, UK. In 2010, she created a series detective, DI Mike York.

Staring out of the bus window, Betty impatiently tapped her foot. The bus had been late again and would be even later dropping her at the stop she wanted, the way this flaming slow coach was driving. The bloody Seahills, God she hated the place, everyone so friendly, and so bloody nosy. You couldn't even fart in peace.

She nodded in the right places, not really listening to Doris Musgrove or Dolly Smith rabbiting on about poor Mr Skillings' heart attack and if the old sod would make it out of hospital or not.

Like she gave a flying fuck?

The nine months she'd stood this place was nine months too long.

Completely unaware that the neighbours she despised had given her the nick name Black Betty, mostly because she nearly always wore black as if she was for ever in mourning, but also because of her permanent scowl, she was thinking, time to go, time to leave this place behind. Everyone was far too friendly, she didn't need their nosiness, or their helpfulness, didn't want it. God even most of the kids were helpful, and that friggin Lumsdon lot!

Her plans had been made for a while, they always were, but she usually hung around a bit longer than this.

Just to be on the safe side. But claustrophobia was beginning to set in, if she heard one more good morning on a miserable rainy fucking day, she'd scream.

She caught sight of her reflection in the opposite window, she quite liked the new hair do, and whatever chemicals and sprays the hairdresser had used made her dark hair really shine.

She fastened the top button on her black coat, the nights had cut in and the clocks had just gone back, though not quite winter there was a definite nip in the air.

At last her stop appeared, squeezing past the other passengers in a drastic hurry to escape her neighbours, not caring that she stepped on an old woman's toes, and nearly winded a teenager wearing a hoodie that was the same colour as her coat, as she elbowed herself past him and got off the bus.

She noticed the poster outside of the paper shop simply because the wind had managed to loosen two corners, one at the top and one at the bottom, and the poster was flapping about every so often exposing the same few words, ESCAPED SERIAL KILLER.

For a brief second she contemplated taking the long way, it was well lit, then decided against it. If she went up the back lane behind the shops she would get home much quicker.

It's not like the murderer, whoever he or she was, would be here in the God-forsaken Seahills.

She grinned to herself as she entered the dark tree-covered lane, but that's what she was, wasn't it . . . A murderer, here in the Seahills . . . And a very profitable one too!

Gary was number three and God was she pleased to get rid of this one. She shuddered, his habits were disgusting, to keep him sweet she'd let him perform the most perverted acts, the self same ones she'd endured as a child at the hands of her stepfather.

Did these perverts all do exactly the same?

Is there a handbook on it some bloody where?

And the violence! Night after night of black market gore videos, he had more than one snuff video too.

The creep.

She sighed, then her smile returned, he would get his comeuppance tonight alright. And the next one would be a helpless cripple in a wheel chair. No doubt about that.

The poison had been slowly doing its damage for over a month now, tonight would finish him off, so what if his friends got a little sick, that was all in the plan, she herself was a past master at acting out sickness. Everyone would re-cover, the creep wouldn't though. No way.

A fine rain began to fall. Damn. Just had my hair done as well. She always had a cut and blow wave to celebrate, it had become a custom.

She picked up speed, her heels clacking on the pavement as she mentally ticked off a list to make sure she had everything she needed, the strongest curry powder available that would certainly cover any lingering bitterness the poison might leave, avocados for sweet, to clean the palette. Nodding to herself, her smile grew wider.

No one could say she never gave her men a fucking good send off.

Too busy congratulating herself she failed to notice the figure detach its self from the large oak tree as she passed by; it was the unexpected sound of heavy footsteps behind her that caused her heart to go into overdrive. As the footsteps drew closer, so her heart beat faster.

A phrase she'd heard more than once surfaced from the jangled panicked thoughts in her head, 'Those that live by the sword die by the sword.'

Was this it?

What some would call poetic justice.

A murderer to be murdered!

Unable to stop herself she looked over her right shoulder and got quite a shock to see a tall youth nearly abreast of her, in that one glance she took in the inked spider web covering half his face, the nose and eyebrow rings, the muscular set to his tall body, and gasped as he stepped sideways bringing himself in front of her.

This was it she thought panicking, all that money hidden away and no one left to enjoy it, all her plans dead!

She froze as he pulled something out of his pocket.

A knife?

A gun?

'Have yer got a light Mrs?' he asked holding a cigarette to his lips.

'Wha. . . No . . . Go away.' She started to move, her heart pounding against her ribs. Asking for a light was just an excuse.

Of course it was.

'Sorry . . . Only asking.' He put the cigarette back in the packet then transferred the packet from hand to pocket.

'Go away.' She started to hurry, but he easily kept pace with her.

'I was gonna ask if you'd want me to walk to the end of the lane with yer like, only there's some street lights out further along, soon be real dark yer know Mrs.'

She resisted the urge to tell him to fuck off, for all she knew he could be unstable and anything could set him off, he could also be the murderer.

'No thank you.'

'Suit yerself Mrs, only trying to help, yer look a bit frightened, that's all.'

And who wouldn't be, looking at that hideous tattoo. She thought but again kept quiet.

She couldn't help but feel a bit foolish as he hurried off in front of her, he might be alright she thought, that's the problem these days, you never can tell.

She took a step forward, staring at his retreating figure she failed to see the brick lying in the middle of the path. Suddenly she was down, her body sprawled across the path, her bag with the precious dinner surprises burst open and scattered every which way. Pain blazed white hot in her ankle.

'Please.' She pleaded as she sat up and rubbed it. 'Don't be broken. Not tonight, please not tonight.'

She snorted, foolish to think God would even listen to her never mind help her. A vision of a hospital waiting room superimposed itself over that of her dinner guests sitting round her dining room table.

'Bastard!!!' then she jerked her head up as she heard a noise. Had he come back?

He was playing with her.

He was the murderer after all.

She closed her eyes and shrank in on herself, the pain from her ankle momentarily forgotten as her body cringed waiting for the blow.

'Are you alright dear?' The voice had an Irish lilt to it.

She opened her eyes, it was full dark now and she had to strain to see, her night vision had never been much good.

A man was coming towards her.

Was that a dog collar he was wearing?

Her heart lit up with hope. God hadn't deserted her at all in her hour of need, he'd sent a priest to help her.

'Betty. What the hell?' All pretence at an Irish accent disappeared as quickly as her sinking heart.

'Gary!' What was that fool doing out here dressed as a priest?

'I fell over that stupid brick . . . I thought, I thought you were a real bloody priest for a minute there.'

He bent to help her up. 'You've forgotten again haven't you, it's role play tonight, you know priests and tarts.'

She sighed, yes she had forgotten about the dress up part, seemed she was forgetting a lot these days.

Fully upright she watched impatiently while he picked the strewn packages up. 'Do hurry up will you, this foot's bloody well killing me.'

'Last one dear.'

The last one, she was sure it was the parcel with the poison in, had managed to roll right to the end of the path. 'For God's sake,' she snapped. 'I can't stand up much longer.'

'I'm here now.' He took hold of her arm and placed it over his shoulder. 'It's not too far, if you lean on me do you think you can make it or shall I carry you?'

'No,' she almost shouted, her mind working over time.

What if he insists on making the curry, she could see her plans swiftly going down the drain, perhaps if she sent him on some errand she would be able to slip into the kitchen. She stopped for a moment and tested her foot, then yanking it up yelped with the pain.

'Shit.'

'Don't fret dear, soon you won't feel the pain.'

'Huu.'

She'd been so busy thinking and fretting that she had not realised how close to the trees they were.

'Where are you going stupid, this isn't the way home.'

He sighed heavily. 'Well it's your home now dear.'

'Wha . . .' She got no further, his hands were round her throat, squeezing, squeezing, as she slid down the length of his body.

'Pity about the insurance money dear, it would have kept me going for a while but in this job you have to keep your wits about you, and never, never talk in your sleep.'

The owner of the newsagents shop carefully pinned the latest bulletin to the board.

TREBLE WIFE KILLER GARY WILKINSON
WHO ESCAPED FROM A TOP SECURITY
PRISON TWO YEARS AGO WAS SPOTTED IN
THE AREA YESTERDAY BY HIS LAST VICTIM'S
DAUGHTER. OVER HERE FROM IRELAND ON HOLIDAY.

STILL LIFE

Lori Rader-Day

Lori Rader-Day won an Anthony Award for her debut mystery, *The Black Hour*, in 2014 and a Mary Higgins Clark Award for her second, *Little Pretty Things*, in 2015. Her third novel, *The Day I Died*, was published in 2017. Rader-Day lives in Chicago.

February 14, 1929

Aphotograph could never tell the entire story. How the chill of the garage's stone floor seeped through the bottoms of our shoes into our bones. How the room smelled of raw meat and tin, like a storage locker of beef down in Back of the Yards in the middle of winter, only the cold keeping the stench at bay.

The same principle was at work here on Clark Street, of course, except the butchering had been of men.

Camera stand over my shoulder, I followed an officer into the high-ceilinged garage past men in uniforms, men in hats and coats, men with notebooks, cameras, and grave faces. I recognized photographers from the *Daily News* and the *Daily Tribune*, among others. We nodded to one another and looked away.

Up against a white brick wall at the back of the garage lay six corpses. One man, still breathing, had been taken to the hospital. As the officer led me through the room toward the bodies, I heard another officer talking about this last man as though he, too, were already dead. Seven, then. Seven dead in a single morning.

My escort, a young officer in a uniform still deep blue, still crisp at the seams, directed me toward a spot several feet away from the bodies, next to a dusty Ford. "There was a dog," he said. His breath formed quick clouds as he spoke. "A dog howling when the boys got here. Just the dog. The only living thing in the place." He scratched at the side of his face until a pink welt rose on his cheek.

I backed up to the car and telescoped the stand to the height of my chin. I kept my gloves on.

"I heard the dog belonged to the mechanic," the officer continued, looking over his shoulder at the dead.

He didn't have to tell me which was the mechanic. Five were career men, the sort often found in their own cars with blood trailing from holes put in their heads. They wore suits and vests, pocket watches still in place. They had worn wool overcoats. Chicago's winter sent a chill that seemed to come from within, as though inside the human body was a hollow space that answered when the bitter wind bit the skin. The men had kept their great coats wrapped around them and now sprawled in them, all but the mechanic who wore his over-alls and worn boots. He had been working, only working as I was now. But he lay side by side with the rest of them, his head opened with a bullet and the contents of his skull spilled onto the hard floor. Beside the new void at his temple, a buff tan hat meant for another's head rested on its side, empty.

Inside the bucket of the empty hat lay a poem. I worked in images—on film for the *Post*, of course, but for myself in poetry. In spare words committed to paper with a thin thread of ink that reminded me of the artists back home in Hiroshima. As I worked, as I rode the train, as I sat down to my dinner in my basement apartment and told Florence all the foolish and untidy things I had seen that day as I tramped around the city, in my mind I was trimming the full and vibrant colors and smells into a bare branch with a single blossom: a poem. In my desk at home, I kept the results of my life's art, a book of my slim poems and loose sheets of those I still labored to finish. In another drawer, I stored prints of particular photos of mine from the *Post*. A life's work, which is not the same as a life's art.

The empty hat in the garage was a poem that I did not wish to write. I nodded to the officer to step to the side. He blinked at the camera and shifted to my elbow.

"Does it look any better from in there?" he said.

"The same."

"Is this the worst you ever saw, Togo?"

Every Japanese man was Togo, so I was Togo. The officers knew me that way, even the ones I did not know. The criminals knew me. Even the ones I did not want to know me. If Al Capone himself walked in to take credit for this day, he would greet me as Togo. I was the only Japanese news photographer in the city, but one would believe the only Japanese man in the country from how easily everyone called to me by name.

Was it the worst I'd seen? I turned to the camera, viewing the scene anew. Four men lay in a row, as though they had been tucked into a large bed. One slept at their feet, face down. The last hunched on his knees at a round-backed wooden chair. Blood ran toward the center of the room. Later that day when I returned to the newsroom, I would release the image from the machine in my hands, like a dragon from a cage. The city would see the blood, black, and no one would remember that someone—call him Togo or call him Fujita, the name will not be printed—had stood in the dust of men's bones to face the dragon so that they did not have to.

This was not the worst I had seen. In '15, I had stood on the side of the *Eastland*, a ship overturned in the Chicago River. My camera found a fireman carrying a dead child up from the water, one of hundreds of corpses that day. Men, women, and children—whole families. This was the worst, and the worst of it all was how innocent I had been, how eager to take pictures, how willing to crawl upon the sideways ship while everyone else crawled off.

My camera jostled as the young officer bumped my arm. Trying to see what I could see through the camera, he breathed his cabbage smell into my neck. Cabbage, even at this early hour.

"Sir," I said.

He stood back. "The *Tribune* was here first," he said.

"The *Tribune* pays its many photographers enough to buy cars and also gas to fill the tanks." The men from the *Tribune* had finished with the crime scene but were nearby, already slipping cigarettes to the uniforms for information. I had taken the elevated to the scene, but I would not rush only to keep up with the *Tribune* men. Photography was not poetry, but there was still dignity to a job well done. I studied the light falling across the floor, the mechanic's face and brains. In the corner, the body kneeling at the chair looked as though he had been shot praying.

"And," I said. "The *Tribune* has the money to build a castle in which their photo men put up their feet after doing one-fifth the day's work I do. Kings, every last one of them."

I let my camera droop in my arms. I couldn't get it all—the six bodies, the white wall chipped away by a spray of bullets, the blood running in rivulets from the backs of their heads toward my feet. The empty hat. If I had a larger lens, or more room to back up, I might show it as it really was. I pressed flat against the car, but it was no use. "Where did the *Tribune* photographers stand—never mind." I would find a better place.

At the front of the garage, a door opened and a woman's voice reached out and turned my head. At once I thought of Florence, but of course it was not her. The door closed. The voice was clipped to silence.

The officer chewed at a fingernail and watched a knot of his fellows just inside the door.

"What did she say?" I said.

He dropped his hand from his mouth. "Police business." He turned back to me, squared his shoulders. Such a young one. Such a young one that I remembered, shaking my head, what it had meant to be so young. To be released upon the world. I had left Japan at sixteen to be free of everything Hiroshima held for me—failed romance and humiliation being the largest part, but I will not speak of it—and found myself, after a bit of wandering, here, with a camera in my hands. Nearly thirty years had gone. I hardly remembered the streets I once walked every day.

I let the camera rest heavily on my shoulder and flapped at the pockets of my coat for a cigarette. The match offered a brief glow, a brief warmth. The flash of a match head burning—here, also, a poem lived in each flare and in each tiny death that followed.

"What is your name, Officer?"

He glanced uneasily at the bodies. "I can't tell you anything."

I wondered what he thought he knew. Did he know, for instance, what had happened to the dog that had been found? I didn't know, but I could suppose. One more bullet in a day filled with bullets. One more body in a day stacked high with bodies. I waved the cigarette in the air between us. "Not for the paper. What do the men call you?"

"McCormick. They call me something else."

"Ah." This I understood. "Are you related to the newspaper man, then?"

"I wouldn't be standing here freezing my arse off with you if I was one of them rich ones, would I?" His own name seemed to remind him that he stood in a cold situation in a cold town.

I smoked, nodding as though the brat had said something worth considering.

I said, "I believe that woman at the door said that the men she saw leaving this place with guns wore police uniforms."

The boy paled and looked away. I followed his eyes toward the other officers, who shuffled their feet and discussed matters in low voices. Occasionally, one of them broke away to peer at the bodies. I wondered what they saw that I could not. McCormick said nothing. His mouth tightened into a straight line.

"An interesting turn of events, isn't it, Officer McCormick?" I gestured toward the group of police. "Which one do you suspect?"

He frowned. "You can't report what she said."

"I am not a reporter. May I look about for a better place to shoot?"

McCormick blinked at my camera again. "Shoot?"

"Shoot the film. I will look. You have much to do." I gave a bit of a bow, the sort of thing Americans seemed to expect, hitched the equipment onto my back, and edged past the boy and the trunk of the car. When I glanced back, Officer McCormick stood in the same place, nothing to do, chewing on his fingers.

"Stay away from the—" He gestured toward the blood on the floor.

"Of course."

I had already decided that where I needed to be was on top of the car. I would probably find footprints from the *Tribune* men who had been there before me, but blast it—*Post* readers needed to see this spectacle, too. Arriving to their dinner tables this evening, our gentlemen would unfold their *Post* to find the city under fire and their stomachs turned. Our ladies would have already seen, or perhaps they would have tried not to see. They would have shielded the children's eyes, fed them dinner early, and sent them up to bed so that when Father came home, the matter could be openly discussed.

This was in other households. In mine, Florence would have read the paper front to back before I arrived. She would have a drink ready for me, and there being no children and, in fact, no marriage, we would discuss the massacre up and down. How the city was overrun by hoodlums and opportunistic beasts, and how one never knew who might be a cousin or godson to one of them. "Keep clear of it, Jun," Florence would advise. "Of course," I would reply, but not everyone could steer clear of it. How could I stay out of the picture, when as soon as someone was shot in the street, I came along on the elevator to lean a camera down into the man's missing face?

My job made it difficult for me to lead the quiet life I desired. In '19, I had gone out to cover the riots on the south side. A black man, swimming at the black beach, had ventured across an invisible line in the water into the white area, and another man—need I say that he was white?—threw a rock and caused the black man to drown. In the neighborhoods nearby, men of both colors started fires, beat and shot one another. I took my camera to the streets, the most conspicuous of witnesses. In the drawer of my work at home, there was now a print of a black man, unnamed, lying dead in an alley. I took this photo. Also in the drawer was a print of some uniformed militia stopping men on the street for the simple blackness of their skin. I took this photo.

Sometimes in the evenings, I accepted the drink from Florence and, instead of going to the dinner table, went to the desk. Reading my poems again, I would be greeted as if by old friends, friends as dear to me as Florence's lovely lily face. But when I re-viewed the photographs, I was ill at ease. I had not shot myself standing in these scenes, but I was there, nonetheless. I am there in the alley with the man killed for the color given him by nature. I, whose color was also not white. I am there on the street with the men harangued for walking to work or to the store. I, who had also been questioned for being on that street on that day. I, who drew stares when walking down any street on any day with dear Florence's pale arm through my brown one.

I was an imperfect witness to the events of my city. Every image I created failed. Every image I created reflected back to me what I was and what I was not. Perhaps others could read the impersonal news from my photos. I only saw that I was there, off to the side, out of the frame. I saw it, but no one else did. No one would remember.

In the garage, I slid my camera onto the flat roof of the Ford. I used the hub over the wheel to propel myself up onto the car. At once I knew that I had found the right location. I brought myself and the camera upright and quickly set about framing the situation before anyone could tell me to get down.

"Togo," the young officer said, his voice quiet. He tapped the toe of my shoe. "I don't think you ought to be up there."

"Do you have a girl, Officer McCormick?"

He turned his face up to me, eyebrows furrowed.

I turned to the camera, at last satisfied by how the room opened up, how the six men's bodies could be singled out, how the poor mechanic's face—he had been a good-looking man and certainly someone had loved him—looked up from the floor.

"What does that have to do with the price of tea in—"

"Find yourself a girl, Officer McCormick. No, not a girl. A woman, a woman of passions and intellect with whom you can pass the days of your life. Also find yourself an art. So that your hours are not empty. So that your life is full, no matter how it ends or when."

The boy glanced at the bodies, then away. He left me to my work. In a few minutes I had captured the scene and was done. Next, I would drag my camera to all the dank corners of the garage and burn more images, and then, once the police forced me and my fellows out the door, I would climb another car outside, or perhaps find a tenant at home in the building across the street and lean my camera out her window. And then back to the train and down to the *Post* in time for the evening's deadline. This harsh day would be done soon enough, and I might find myself at home, at my desk. Perhaps there were a few words yet to be written in the thin black ink. Perhaps I could crawl into the dead man's empty hat and have something, however small, to say.

Across the garage I saw a bustle. One of the men from the *Tribune* was climbing atop another car. A second man passed a camera up to him. From the front of the garage, two more with equipment raced to join him, and soon the top of the other car held all three men with their cameras turned on the bodies from above. I leaned into my own camera and took one last image of the room, the photo men hanging over the bloody floor like martyrs in stained glass looking down from a cathedral window. The *Tribune* man raised his flashbulb into the air. In the pop of the bright light lived a poem. A handful of words about quick life and quick death. If only I could write it, if only I could say with certainty which emotions rose within the hollow space in my body when I realized that in their images—in all of their images—it was I who would be standing over the dead men. It was I who would be the only living thing in the place.

THE VENUS FLY TRAP

Ruth Rendell

Ruth Rendell (1930–2015) was a major British crime writer. She wrote seventy-eight novels and short-story collections, including *From Doon with Death* and *A Judgement in Stone*. Twenty-four of her novels featured Chief Inspector Wexford, and fifteen, including *A Dark-Adapted Eye*, were psychological thrillers written as Barbara Vine.

As soon as Daphne had taken off her hat and put it on Merle's bed, Merle picked it up and rammed it on her own yellow curls. It was a red felt hat and by chance it matched Merle's red dress.

'It's a funny thing, dear,' said Merle, looking at herself in the dressing table mirror, 'but anyone seeing us two – any outsider, I mean – would never think that I was the single one and you'd had all those husbands and children.'

'I only had two husbands and three children,' said Daphne.

'You know what I mean,' said Merle, and Daphne, standing beside her friend, had to admit that she did. Merle was so big, so pink and overflowing and female, while she – well, she had given up pretending she was anything but a little dried-up widow, seventy years old and looking every day of it.

Merle took off the hat and placed it beside the doll whose yellow satin skirts concealed her nightdress and her bag of hair rollers. 'I'll show you the flat and then we'll have a sherry and put our feet up. I got some of that walnut brown in. You see I haven't forgotten your tastes even after forty years.'

Daphne didn't say it was dry sherry she had then, and still, preferred. She trotted meekly after Merle. She was just beginning to be aware of the intense heat. Clouds of warmth seemed to breathe out of the embossed wallpaper and up through the lush furry carpets.

'I really am thrilled about you coming to live in this block, dear. This is my little spare room. I like to think I can put up a friend if I want. Not that many of them come. Between you and me, dear, people rather resent my having done so well for myself and all on my own initiative. People are so mean-spirited, I've noticed that as I've got older. That's why I was so thrilled when you agreed to come here. I mean, when *someone* took my advice.'

'You've made it all very nice,' said Daphne.

'Well, I always say the flat had the potential and I had the taste. Of course, yours is much smaller and, frankly, I wouldn't say it lends itself to a very ambitious décor. In your place, the first thing I'd do is have central heating put in.'

'I expect I will if I can afford it.'

'You know, Daphne, there are some things we owe it to ourselves to afford.

But you know your own business best and I wouldn't dream of interfering. If the cold gets you down you're welcome up here at any time. *Any* time, I mean that. Now this is my drawing room, my *pièce de résistance.*'

Merle opened the door with the air of a girl lifting the lid of a jewel case that holds a lover's gift.

'What a lot of plants,' said Daphne faintly.

'I was always mad about plants. My first business venture was a florist's. I could have made a little goldmine out of that if my partner hadn't been so wickedly vindictive. She was determined to oust me from the first. D'you like my suite? I had it completely re-done in oyster satin last year and I do think it's a success.'

The atmosphere was that of a hothouse. The chairs, the sofa, the lamps, the little piecrust tables with their load of bibelots, were islanded in the centre of the large room. No, not an island perhaps, Daphne thought, but a clearing in a tropical jungle. Shelves, window sills, white troughs on white wrought iron legs, were burgeoned with lush trailing growth, green, glossy, frondy, all quite immobile and all giving forth a strange green scent.

'They take up all my time. It's not just the watering and watching the temperature and so on. Plants know when you love them. They only flourish in an atmosphere of love. I honestly don't believe you'd find a better specimen of an *opuntia* in London than mine. I'm particularly proud of the *peperomias* and the *xygocacti* too of course, I expect you've seen them growing in their natural habitat with all your mad rushing around those foreign places.'

'We were mostly in Stockholm and New York, Merle.'

'Oh, were you? So many years went by when you never bothered to write to me that I really can't keep pace. I thought about you a lot, of course. I want you to know you really had my sympathy, moving house all the time and that awful divorce from what's-his-name, and babies to cope with and then getting married again and everything. I used to feel how sad it was that I'd made so much of my life while you . . . What's the matter?'

'That plant, Merle, it moved.'

'That's because you touched it. When you touch one of its mouths it closes up. It's called *Dionaea Muscipula.*'

The plant stood alone in a majolica pot contained in an elaborate white stand. It looked very healthy. It had delicate shiny leaves and from its heart grew five red-gold blossoms. As Daphne peered more closely she saw that these resembled mouths, as Merle had put it, far more than flowers, whiskery mouths, soft and ripe and luscious. One of these was now closed.

'Doesn't it have a common name?'

'Of course it does. The Venus Fly Trap. *Muscipula* means fly-eater, dear.'

'Whatever *do* you mean?'

'It eats flies. I've been trying to grow one for years. I was absolutely thrilled when I succeeded.'

'Yes, but what d'you mean, it eats flies? It's not an animal.'

'It is in a way, dear. The trouble is there aren't many flies here. I feed it on little bits of meat. You've gone rather pale, Daphne. Have you got a headache? We'll have our sherry now and then I'll see if I can catch a fly and you can see it eat it up.'

'I'd really much rather not, Merle,' said Daphne, backing away from the plant. 'I don't want to hurt your feelings but I don't – well, I hate the idea of catching free live things and feeding them to – to that.'

'*Free live things?* We're talking about flies.' Merle, large and perfumed, grabbed Daphne's arm and pulled her away. Her dress was of red chiffon with trailing sleeves and her fingernails matched it. 'The trouble with you,' said Merle, 'is that you're a mass of nerves and you're much worse now than you were when we were girls. I thank God every day of my life I don't know what it is to be neurotic. Here you are, your sherry. I've put it in a big glass to buck you up. I'm going to make it my business to look after you, Daphne. You don't know anybody else in London, do you?'

'Hardly anybody,' said Daphne, sitting down where she couldn't see the Venus Fly Trap. 'My boys are in the States and my daughter's in Scotland.'

'Well, you must come up here every day. No, you won't be intruding. When I first knew you were definitely coming I said to myself, I'm going to see to it Daphne isn't lonely. But don't imagine you'll get on with the other tenants in this block. Those of them who aren't standoffish snobs are – well, not the sort of people you'd want to know. But we won't talk about them. We'll talk about us. Unless, of course, you feel your past has been too painful to talk about?'

'I wouldn't quite say . . .'

'No, you wouldn't care to rake up unpleasant memories. I'll just put a drop more sherry in your glass and then I'll tell you all about my last venture, my agency.'

Daphne rested her head against a cushion, brushed away an ivy frond, and prepared to listen.

From a piece of fillet steak Merle was scraping slivers of meat. She was all in diaphanous gold today, an amber chain around her neck, the finery half-covered by a frilly apron.

'I used to do that for my babies when they first went on solids,' said Daphne.

'Babies, babies. You're always on about your babies. You've been up here every day for three weeks now and I don't think you've once missed an opportunity to talk about your babies and your men. Oh, I'm sorry, dear, I don't mean to upset you, but one really does get so weary of women like you talking about that side of life as if one had actually *missed* something.'

'Why are you scraping that meat, Merle?'

'To feed my little Venus. That's her breakfast. Come along. I've got a fly I caught under a sherry glass but I couldn't catch more than one.'

The fly was very small. It was crawling up the inside of the glass, but when Merle approached it, it began to fly and buzz frenziedly against the transparent dome of its prison. Daphne turned her back. She went to the window, the huge plant-filled bay window, and looked out, pretending to be interested in the view. She heard the scrape of glass and from Merle a triumphant gasp. Merle trod very heavily. Under the thick carpet the boards creaked. Merle began talking to the plant in a very gentle maternal voice.

'This really is a wonderful outlook,' said Daphne brightly. 'You can see for miles.'

Merle said, '*C'est Vénus toute entière à sa proie attachée.*'

'I beg your pardon?'

'You never were any good at languages, dear. Oh, don't pretend you're so mad about that view. You're just being absurdly sensitive about what really amounts to *gardening*. I can't bear that sort of dishonesty. I've finished now, anyway. She's had her breakfast and all her mouths are shut up. Who are you waving to?'

'A rather nice young couple who live in the flat next to me.'

'Well, please don't.' Merle looked down and then drew herself up, all golden pleats and stiff gold curls. 'You couldn't know, dear, but those two people are the very end. For one thing, they're not a couple, they're not married, I'm sure of that. Of course, that's no business of mine. What is my business is that they've been keeping a dog here – look, that spaniel thing – and it's strictly against the rules to keep animals in these flats.'

'What about your Fly Trap?'

'Oh, don't be so silly! As I was saying, they keep that dog and let it foul the garden. I wrote to the managing agents, but those agents are so lax – they've no respect for me because I'm a single woman, I suppose. But I wrote again the day before yesterday and now I understand they're definitely going to be turned out.'

Forty feet below the window, on the parking space between the block and the garden, the boy who wore jeans and a leather jacket picked up his dog and placed it on the back seat of a battered car. His companion, who had waist-length hair much the colour of Merle's dress, got into the passenger seat, but the boy hesitated. As Merle brought her face close to the glass, he looked up and raised two wide-splayed fingers.

'Oaf!' said Merle. 'The only thing to do with people like that is to ignore them. Can you imagine it, he lets that dog of his relieve itself up against a really beautiful specimen of *Cryptomeria japonica*. Let's forget him and have a nice cup of coffee.'

'Merle, how long will those flowers last on that Venus thing of yours? I mean, they'll soon die away, won't they?'

'No, they won't. They'll last for ages. You know, Daphne, fond as I am of you, I wouldn't leave you alone in this flat for anything. You've a personal hatred of my *muscipula*. You'd like to destroy it.'

'I'll put the coffee on,' said Daphne.

Merle phoned for a taxi. Then she put her little red address book with all the phone numbers in it into her scarlet patent leather handbag along with her lip-stick and her gold compact and her keys, her cheque book and four five-pound notes.

'We could have walked,' said Daphne.

'No, we couldn't, dear. When I have a day at the shops I like to feel fresh. I don't want to half-kill myself walking there. It's not the cost that's worrying you, is it? Because you know I'll pay. I appreciate the difference between our incomes, Daphne, and if I don't harp on it it's only because I try to be tactful. I want to buy you something, something really nice to wear. It seems such a wicked shame to me those men of yours didn't see to it you were well-provided for.'

'I've got quite enough clothes, Merle.'

'Yes, but all grey and black. The only bright thing you've got is that red hat and you've stopped wearing that.'

'I'm old, Merle dear. I don't want to get myself up in bright colours. I've had my life.'

'Well, I haven't had mine! I mean, I . . .' Merle bit her lip, getting scarlet lipstick on her teeth. She walked across the room, picked her ocelot coat off the back of the sofa, and paused in front of the Fly Trap. It's soft flame-coloured mouths were open. She tickled them with her fingertips and they snapped shut. Merle giggled. 'You know what you remind me of, Daphne? A fly. That's just what you look like in your grey coat and that funny bit of veil on your hat. A fly.'

'There's the taxi,' said Daphne.

It deposited them outside a large overheated store. Merle dragged Daphne through the jewellery department, the perfumery, past rotary stands with belts on them, plastic models in lingerie. They went up in the lift. Merle bought a model dress, orange chiffon with sequins on the skirt. They went down in the lift and into the next store. Merle bought face bracer and cologne and a gilt choker. They went up the escalator. Merle bought a brass link belt and tried to buy Daphne a green and blue silk scarf. Daphne consented at last to be presented with a pair of stockings, power elastic ones for her veins.

'Now we'll have lunch on the roof garden,' said Merle.

'I should like a cup of tea.'

'And I'll have a large sherry. But first I must freshen up. I'm dying to spend a penny and do my face.'

They queued with their pennies. The ladies' cloakroom had green marble dressing tables with mirrors all down one side and green washbasins all down the other. Daphne sat down. Her feet had begun to swell. There were twenty or thirty other women in the cloakroom, doing their faces, re-sticking false eyelashes. One girl, whose face seemed vaguely familiar, was actually brushing her long golden hair. Merle put her handbag down on a free bit of green marble. She washed her hands, helped herself to a gush of *Calèche* from the scent-squirting machine, came back, opening and shutting her coat to fan herself. It was even hotter than in her flat.

She sat down, drew her chair to the mirror.

'Where's my handbag?' Merle screamed. 'I left my handbag here! Someone's stolen my handbag. Daphne, Daphne, someone's stolen my handbag!'

The oyster satin sofa sagged under Merle's weight. Daphne smoothed back the golden curls and put another pad of cottonwool soaked in cologne on the red corrugated forehead.

'Bit better now?'

'I'm quite all right. I'm not one of your neurotic women to get into a state over a thing like that. Thank God I'd left my spare key with the porter and I hadn't locked the mortice.'

'You'll have to have both locks changed, Merle.'

'Of course I will, eventually. I'll see to it next week. Nobody can get in here, can they? They don't know who I am. I mean, they don't know whose keys they've got.'

'They've got your handbag.'

'Daphne dear, I do wish you wouldn't keep stating the obvious. *I know they have got my handbag.* The point is, there was nothing in my handbag to show who I am.'

'There was your cheque book with your name on it.'

'My name, dear, in case it's escaped your notice, is M Smith. I haven't gone about changing it all my life like you.' Merle sat up and took a gulp of walnut brown sherry. 'The store manager was charming, wasn't he, and the police? I daresay they'll find it, you know. It's a most distinctive handbag, not like that great black thing you cart about with you. My little red one could have gone inside yours. I wish I'd thought to put it there.'

'I wish you had,' said Daphne.

Daphne's phone rang. It was half-past nine and she was finishing her breakfast, sitting in front of her little electric fire.

Merle sounded very excited. 'What do you think? Isn't it marvellous? The store manager's just phoned to say they've found my bag. Well, it wasn't him, it was his secretary, stupid-sounding woman with one of those put-on accents. However, that's no concern of mine. They found my bag fallen down behind a radiator in that cloakroom. Isn't it an absolute miracle? Of course the money had gone, but my cheque book was there and the keys. I'm very glad I didn't take your advice and change those locks yesterday. It never does to act on impulse, Daphne.'

'No, I suppose not.'

'I've arranged to go down and collect my bag at eleven. As soon as I ring off, I'm going to phone for a taxi and I want you to come with me, dear. I'll have a bath and see to my plants – I've managed to catch a bluebottle for Venus – and then the taxi will be here.'

'I'm afraid I can't come,' said Daphne.

'Why on earth not?'

Daphne hesitated. Then she said, 'I said I hardly know anybody in London but I do know this one man, this – well, he was a friend of my second husband, and he's a widower now and he's coming to lunch with me, Merle. He's coming at twelve and I must be here to see to things.'

'A *man?*' said Merle. '*Another* man?'

'I'll look out for your taxi and when I see you come in I'll just pop up and hear all about it, shall I? I'm sorry I can't . . .'

'Sorry? Sorry for what? I can collect my handbag by myself. I'm quite used to standing on my own feet.' The receiver went down with a crash.

Merle had a bath and put on the orange dress. It was rather showy for day wear with its sequins and its fringes, but she could never bear to have a new dress and not wear it at once. The ocelot coat would cover most of it. She watered the *peperomias* and painted a little leaf gloss on the ivy. The bluebottle had died in the night, but *dionaea muscipula* didn't seem to mind. She opened her orange strandy mouths for Merle and devoured the dead bluebottle along with the shreds of fillet steak.

Merle put on her cream silk turban and a long scarf of flame-coloured silk. Her spare mortice key was where she always kept it, underneath the *sanseveria* pot. She locked the Yale and the mortice and then the taxi took her to the store. Merle sailed into the manager's office, and when the manager told her he had no secretary, had never phoned her flat and had certainly not found her handbag, she deflated like a fat orange balloon into which someone has stuck a pin.

'You've been the victim of a hoax, Miss Smith.'

Merle pulled herself together. She could always do that, she had superb control. She didn't want aspirins or brandy or policemen or any of the other aids to quietude offered by the manager. When she had told him he didn't know his job, that if there was a conspiracy against her – as she was sure there must be – he was in it, she floundered down the stairs and flapped her mouth and her arms for a taxi.

When she got home the first thing that struck her as strange was that the door was only locked on the Yale. She could have sworn she had locked it on the mortice too, but no doubt her memory was playing her tricks – and no wonder, the shock she had had. There was a little bit of earth on the hall carpet. Merle didn't like that, earth on her gold Wilton. Inside her ocelot she was sweating. She took off her coat and opened the drawing room door.

Daphne saw the taxi come and Merle bounce out of it, an orange orchid springing from a black bandbox. Merle looked wild with excitement, her turban all askew. Daphne smiled to herself and shook her head. She laid the table and finished making the salad she knew her friend would like with his lunch, and then she went upstairs to see Merle.

There was a mirror on each landing. Daphne was so small and thin that she didn't puff much when she had to climb stairs. As she came to the top of each flight she saw a little grey woman trotting to meet her, a woman with smooth white hair and large, rather diffident, grey eyes, who wore a grey wool dress partly covered by a cloudy stole of lace. She smiled at her reflection. She was old now but she had had her moments, her joy, her gratification, her intense pleasures. And soon there was to be a new pleasure, a confrontation she had looked forward to for weeks. Who could tell what would come of it? With a last smile at her grey and fluttery image, Daphne pushed open the unlatched door of Merle's flat.

In the Garden of Eden, the green paradisal bower, someone had dropped a bomb. No, they couldn't have done that, for the ceiling was still there and the carpet and the oyster satin furniture, torn now and plastered all over with earth. Every plant had been broken and torn apart. Leaves lay scattered in heaps like the leaves of autumn, only these were green, succulent, bruised. In the rape of the room, in the midst of ripped foliage, stems bleeding sap, shards of china, lay the Venus Fly Trap, its roots wrenched from their pot and its mouths closed for ever.

Merle tried to scream but the noise came out only as a gurgle, the glug-glug agonized gasp of a scream in a nightmare. She fell on her knees and crawled about. Choking and muttering, she scrabbled among the earth and, picking up torn leaves, tried to piece them together like bits of a jigsaw puzzle. She crouched over the Fly Trap and nursed it in her hands, keening and swaying to and fro.

She didn't hear the door click shut. It was a long time before she realized Daphne was standing over her, silent, looking down. Merle lifted her red streaming face. Daphne had her hand over her mouth, the hand with the two wedding rings on it. Merle thought Daphne must be covering her mouth to stop herself from laughing out loud.

Slowly, heavily, she got up. Her long orange scarf was in her hands, stretched taut, twisting, twisting. She was surprised how steady her voice was, how level and sane.

'You did it,' she said. 'You did it. You stole my handbag and took my keys and got me out of here and came in and did it.'

Daphne quivered and shook her head. Her whole body shook and her hand flapped against her mouth. Quite whom Merle began to talk to then she didn't know, to herself or to Daphne, but she knew that what she said was true.

'You were so jealous! You'd had nothing, but I'd had success and happiness and love.' Her voice went up and the scarf with it. 'How you hated me, hated, hated . . .! Merle screamed. 'Hate, hate, poisonous jealous hate!' Huge and red and frondy, she descended on Daphne, engulfing her with musky orange petals, twisting the scarf round the frail insect neck, devouring the fly until the fly quivered into stillness.

An elderly man in a black homburg hat crossed the forecourt and went up the steps, a bunch of flowers in his hand. The boy in the leather jacket took no notice of him. He brushed earth and bits of leaf off his hands and said to the girl with the long hair, 'Revenge is sweet.' Then he tossed the scarlet handbag into the back of his car and he and the girl and the dog got in and drove away.

THE INSIDE STORY

Mary Roberts Rinehart

Mary Roberts Rinehart (1876–1958) was often described as the American Agatha Christie. A prolific novelist and short-story writer, she invented the 'Had I But Known' school of crime writing and popularised the cliché 'the butler did it'. One of her criminals was an unlikely inspiration for the superhero Batman.

I.

Andy blinked at the nurse through his heavy spectacles. He had no official right to blink at her, and he knew it. He had even no right to be where he was. He was there because when the alarm came and the chief barged out into the street, the only car in sight was Andy's old Ford.

"For Gawsake!" shouted the chief. "Where's my car? And whose teakettle is that?"

"It's mine," said Andy humbly. "It's mine. And it goes. It doesn't look it, but——"

"Let's see if it goes," said the chief, and crawled in, followed by Jenkins and a plainclothes man. "Let's see how fast it can go without breaking my neck."

And in such fashion did Andy, whose real name was Andrews, enter the Livingstone house and the Livingstone case; the former through a dark back garden, and the latter through a pair of spectacles and a perfectly good pair of eyes. He had been accepted by the household as a part of the police group later gathered surreptitiously in the library, and, with one exception, had been ignored by the chief. That exception, however, had been brief and to the point: "Keep your car in the alley and your mouth shut. That goes until I'm ready to break this story; if it doesn't, I'll break you."

And Andy, young and lowly apprentice of crime at the 21st Precinct station house, had been only too happy to agree.

So now Andy, forgotten by everybody else, was on the top, and nursery, floor of the Livingstone house, blinking at a semi-hysterical trained nurse in a white uniform and with a cap on the back of her head, and using his own methods to restore her to normality.

"I've been wanting to ask you something ever since I saw you in the library, Miss Murray," he said. "I hope you don't mind."

"Mind? Everybody else has asked me questions, why not you?"

"Then tell me," he said gently, "does that cap of yours never come off? It seems so—well, so precarious."

"I suppose you think you are being funny. That cap has stayed where it is for twenty years."

He appeared to consider that statement, still blinking at the cap. "Dear me!" he said. "You should make a note of that. It must be almost a record. But I suppose you take it off at night. Or do you?"

"If you are trying to make me angry——"

"But you are angry already, aren't you?" he inquired. "You are really extremely angry. You were angry down in the library, and you still are. Best thing under those circumstances is to get it off the chest; ask any psychiatrist. He smiled at her. "Come on now, tell papa. You'll feel a lot better."

"Why shouldn't I be angry?" she said, with rising color. "I've been the child's mother ever since he was born. Nothing ever happened to him when I was around. Then I go down town on an errand and——"

Suddenly she began to cry. She was frightened then. He watched her with interest through his spectacles. She cried quite openly, without even fumbling for a handkerchief. Women only cried like that, he considered, when they had lost either all vanity or all hope.

"I wish you wouldn't," he said finally. "It takes so much time, and we need all we have. You went down town and——"

"She sent him out to the park with that girl. That's all. She didn't want him around: she never did, except to show off now and then."

Andy took off his spectacles and wiped them. Without them he looked extremely young and very mild. He put them on again quickly.

"I see. She was like that, was she?"

"She?" The nurse laughed, not pleasantly. There were still tears on her cheeks. "They're all like that these days. Most of them don't even know they're having their babies. They get a pain or two, and then somebody gives them a shot of something, and when they wake up they just say, 'Boy or girl?' and ask for a cigarette. It's not normal, I say. A woman's got to suffer for her children to value them."

"She's taking it hard enough now."

"She's scared," said the nurse. "A lot of grief is remorse, Mr.——"

"Andrews is the name. My friends call me Andy." He gave her a rather charming smile, but she ignored it. "How about the father?" he asked. "He like that too?"

"Better, but not too good," said the nurse laconically. "Business all week, golf Saturdays and Sundays. Came in once in a while before dinner, if Larry wasn't asleep." And she added, inconsequentially: "He gave her a diamond bracelet when he was born."

He studied her carefully. There was nothing subtle about her. Her anger was partly helpless fury at the loss of the child, and possibly, too, the resentment of the middle-aged spinster for the woman who had taken so lightly the maternity which could never be hers. Nevertheless, she was keeping something back. She looked rather like his sister when she was hiding an unpaid bill.

He tried another tack: "They had a good many friends, I suppose?"

"Friends? Well, if you call people friends who are in and out all the time, drinking their cocktails and burning the furniture with cigarettes. No intimates, if that's what you mean. That is——"

"Yes?"

"Well, she's pretty and young, and of course there were plenty of men around."

"No one man in particular, I suppose?"

"I don't think so. They came and went."

"Nobody," he persisted, "who would know Mr. Livingstone's affairs? How much ransom he could pay, and so on."

"Ransom!" she smiled grimly. "They're in debt up to their necks. His mother has some money, but not so much any more."

"Then you don't think he was taken for a ransom?"

"How do I know?" she retorted, and rustled starchily out of the room.

He was still thinking that over when he moved to the nursery window. He had a habit of noiseless whistling when he was thinking, and now he was whistling furiously. Beneath him in the back garden, Murphy, on watch for a note thrown over the fence, was only a deeper shadow near the gate.

"Phony somewhere," he thought, blinking into the darkness. "Too many people not telling all they know, too many coincidences, and no money for a ransom. The chief's off on the wrong foot."

He felt vaguely disloyal to the chief, sitting in the library waiting for the telephone call which had not come. "But the story's right here in the house," he reflected stubbornly, and once again in his mind went over that long inquisition in the library, young Livingstone wild-eyed and truculent, his wife collapsed in a corner, the procession of servants, the emotional grief of the maid, Mary Anne, and her frantic denial of any complicity. The reiteration over and over:

"No, sir, I never saw the man before. . . . Yes, sir, the street was crowded. . . . Yes, he knew his name; he said: I'll carry you over, Larry, just like that. And he told me to go ahead. Then, when I got across and turned, he wasn't coming. I couldn't see either of them. . . . Oh, yes, sir, quite a respectable-looking man."

And that was all. A middle-aged man, neatly dressed, a crowded street, a mass of cars and a missing child. They had given it up at last when the girl finally collapsed, and Andy had slid out of the room after her, too unimportant even to be missed. He had helped her to her small rather untidy room and left her there.

Now, on impulse, he turned and went back there again. There was one question he wanted to ask her.

So now he tapped at her closed and locked door.

"Let me in, please, Mary Anne," he called softly. "It's a poor thing to be alone when you're in trouble."

"I want to be alone."

"Nobody wants to be alone when they're in trouble. Come along now, open the door. I'm not going to worry you."

He heard the girl's slow movements as she crawled out of bed, and then the key turned in the lock. She was back in bed when he entered, and the room was dark and stuffy. He threw up a window and turned on the ceiling light before he drew up a chair and sat down beside the untidy bed.

"Now listen," he said, smiling into the swollen eyes that stared at him. "Get this, my child: If you've been a good girl, nothing is going to happen to you.

Nothing! That's a promise. And I believe you've told a straight story. Does that help any?"

She nodded, trying to smile.

"Good. Next, have you had any dinner?"

She shook her head. "I couldn't eat, sir."

"I'll send up some tea and toast anyhow. And now, Mary Anne, let's go over this quietly again. Tell me something about Larry. Was he a friendly child? You know what I mean. Would he go to strangers easily?"

"I don't know him very well, sir. I don't think so."

"But yet he let this man pick him up? He didn't cry out, or anything like that?"

"No, sir. I looked around before I started, and he was smiling as if he knew him."

He sat up in his chair.

"You didn't tell them downstairs that the boy was smiling."

"I was frightened. I guess I forgot."

He nodded, thinking hard. "And you're sure you have never seen this man before? Not here in the house, for instance?"

She stared at him. "Here in the house? Oh, no, sir."

He promised to send up the tea and toast, and went out again. Well, that was something. If the man knew the child, that meant nothing; but if the child knew the man—— After all, how many men would a child of that age be likely to know? Half a dozen? A dozen? He wondered, standing at the head of the staircase. Then he turned quickly and opened the door of the day nursery again. The nurse had come back. He found her standing idle in the center of the room, as though, like the rest, she had been brought to a sudden stop in mid-career. The whole house gave him that impression, as a matter of fact—as though the disappearance of the child had struck them all still and silent in the midst of some secret turmoil. Only the library was alive.

Perhaps that, too, was usual in such families. His only previous experience had been with the noisy grief of the humble and the poor.

"Just thought of something else," he said briskly. "I suppose this is your usual day off duty, isn't it?"

"What's that got to do with it?" She was suspicious.

"Don't answer if you don't want to," he told her. "If there is any secret about it——"

"Secret?" she blazed. "I have no secrets."

"Only the one about the cap," he said gently. "How you keep it on, and so on. By the way, I forgot to ask if you sleep in it, and how. Like the man with the beard, you know. So it wasn't your regular day out."

"Day off," she corrected him. "No, if that matters. I went down town to do an errand."

"For yourself?"

"For her."

"Oh," he said, still cheerfully. "And just why didn't you tell that before?"

"What difference did it make?"

"Difference! Listen, my dear woman. Could this have happened if you had had Larry out today? No? Well, then, here's the point: Who knew, besides yourself, that you were going on those errands? In addition to Mrs. Livingstone."

"It wasn't any secret."

"But who else knew, long enough ahead to plan this thing? Now think a moment. It ought to be a man, and a man that the boy knew. That shouldn't be hard. How many men does he know? Six? Ten? Not many. But I'm telling you this: He went to somebody he knew."

"Nobody knew I was going, outside of this house," she said fiercely. "Nobody. Unless she——"

"Yes?" he said. "Unless she told somebody herself. Is that it? That's the thing you've been keeping back, isn't it? You're afraid she told somebody you were out, aren't you? And that this person——"

"I don't believe it," she said wildly. "Why would she do such a thing? It isn't true, Mr. Andrews. She's young and foolish, but she wouldn't have done that."

He blinked at her, mildly surprised.

"Look here," he said. "Do you think I'm intimating that Mrs. Livingstone stole her own child?"

"That's what you said," she retorted sullenly.

"Is it? Think back."

Now, however, she was angry again. She shook her head.

"I've said all I am going to say," she told him. "And if you policemen would get out of this house and do some honest work on this case, you might get somewhere. Standing around talking, or smoking around that telephone downstairs—and my baby gone! Get out and bring him back. That's all I have to say. What good are you here? Don't you suppose we want him back? Do you think we've stolen him ourselves?"

"No. But I believe that is what you're afraid of," he told her; and wandered out again after his casual fashion, leaving her staring after him, alarmed and resentful.

II.

He stopped in the hall outside. On the floor below, he heard the doctor taking his departure with that spurious air of cheerfulness which deceives no one.

"I'll look in again in a couple of hours," he boomed from a doorway. "Probably everything will be all right by that time. Take another dose if you need it, and try to relax, like a good girl."

But as Andy moved down the stairs he saw that the doctor was not leaving. Instead he crossed the hall and threw open the door of what was apparently an upstairs sitting room. The detective had a momentary glimpse of a brightly furnished room, and of Livingstone himself standing by a table. Then the door closed.

He stopped dead. Now, that was odd, certainly. He had not seen either of the two young people since that frantic hour after the police had arrived, but he had supposed they were together. Now he recalled that they had not been together even then. The girl, white to her painted lips, had remained, sunk and strained, in a low chair. The young husband had stood facing the police with desperate eyes and an inner fury that fairly burned him.

He reflected, resuming his soundless whistling, that it must be something fairly grave which kept the two apart in a situation of this sort.

Suddenly he was conscious of the nurse at his elbow.

"The old fool," she muttered, evidently referring to the doctor. "Telling her to relax! Relax! And giving her that stuff to take herself. She knows no more about medicine than a baby."

She pushed him aside and went rapidly down the stairs, moving with a certain defiance toward the closed door the doctor had left; and as the detective watched her, he saw that her face had softened. Incredible, this woman, he considered, so full of rage and even suspicion against the girl inside, and yet filled with pity. She opened the door quietly, stepped inside and closed it firmly behind her.

Thus shut out, the detective made his way slowly down the stairs and toward the back of the house. Beyond a door he heard the muffled rattling of dishes and silver, and a woman's voice, high and excited. The parlormaid's voice, he recognized. He flattened himself against the wall for a moment, looking alertly from right to left as he did so.

"Well, you can't say she isn't taking it hard, Riggs," she was saying. "I didn't know she had it in her. Nothing off this tray but a cup of coffee."

"That's not your affair, or mine," said the butler's voice. "You'd better get finished here and get to bed. No one's to leave the house tonight. Remember that."

Andy edged slightly toward the pantry door.

"I'm not wanting to get out," said the woman. "I've been fair sick to my stomach all evening. When I think of that lamb out in the night——"

"Go on. Enjoy yourself," said Riggs morosely.

"Listen, Riggs. Has she seen him yet?"

"How do I know?"

"Well, if two young people can't get together when a thing like this happens, then I'd say it's all over. . . . Don't you touch me, Riggs. What have I said? Let go of my arm."

"You damned little fool!" Riggs said in a voice of suppressed fury. "Do you want to make things worse? This house is full of policemen. Can't you keep your tongue quiet? I've warned you before and I warn you now——"

Andy slid open the pantry door and stepped cheerfully inside. The butler, his face contorted with fury, was just releasing the maid's arm, and she was rubbing it vigorously. Both figures froze into immobility as he entered.

"Well, well," he said. "And what's the trouble here? Everybody excited tonight, eh?"

"Nothing's the trouble, sir," said Riggs. "I lost my temper, that's all. I'm not myself, and that's the truth. I suppose I am a bit worked up, sir."

"Natural enough," said Andy, blinking furiously. "We're all a trifle on edge."

The parlormaid, still rubbing her arm, slid out of the room with a vindictive glance at Riggs; and Andy sat down on a chair and lighted a cigarette. The butler eyed him glumly.

"Been here long, Riggs?"

"Ever since they were married, sir. Before that I was with his mother."

"Get along all right, do they? The young people?"

Riggs looked shocked, and Andy grinned cheerfully.

"Yes, Riggs," he said blandly. "That's what I asked. And," he added, "don't tell me it isn't nice to listen behind doors. That's what I'm paid for. Now, what's been the trouble? Don't bother to deny that there is trouble. Trouble is my business too."

The butler avoided his eyes.

"There's always talk in a house like this, sir," he said. "The servants haven't much life of their own and so they—well, you may say the life of the family has a great deal of interest for them. It's hard to avoid it, sir," he added apologetically.

"That's human nature, Riggs."

"Yes, sir. Well, there's nothing to it, of course, but lately the women have thought there was some trouble between the two of them. Mr. and Mrs. Livingstone, that is. I don't credit it myself, but——"

"But you warned that maid just now that the house was full of policemen, and to keep her mouth shut. Just so." And when the butler remained silent: "Don't be a fool, Riggs. Don't you suppose we'd get that story sooner or later? And what has it got to do with the child?"

"With the child!" The man was either a good actor or was actually surprised. "Why, nothing, sir. It was entirely a matter of keeping this gossip to ourselves. If it ever got to the elder Mrs. Livingstone out in the country——"

"I see. What's this gossip about, Riggs? We needn't be squeamish. There's a good bit at stake. Or wait. I'll put it another way. Was there anybody intimate enough with this family to cause gossip? Anyone who came and went, and who knew all about the household? Think a minute. It's important."

The butler was silent. Andy shrewdly surmised that he was in no doubt as to the answer, but in grave doubt as to its expediency.

"Well, sir," he said at last, "there was no one in particular, that's certain. But a good many young men came and went, and Mr. Livingstone didn't like it much. He wasn't raised to that sort of thing. His father and mother were old-fashioned people."

"About how many?"

"Maybe a dozen or so. Just foolish, you understand, sir. He would come home and——"

"That happen every day, Riggs?"

"Practically every day, sir."

"I see. I'd like the names anyhow, Riggs."

But when he had got them they meant little or nothing. "Like a page out of the Social Register," he thought to himself disgustedly. "Lot of brainless young playboys, and whoever did this had brains."

He slid the list into his pocket and got up.

"So you don't think it was any one of these polo players who caused the trouble between Mr. and Mrs. Livingstone today?" he asked blandly.

"Trouble today, sir? What trouble?"

Andy grinned cheerfully.

"All right, Riggs," he said. "Hold the fort!" and went out noiselessly whistling.

III.

In the hall he hesitated. He was uncertain as to the wisdom of recalling to the chief that he was still in the house. In the end he decided against it, and instead slipped quietly into the room across the hall from the library and closed the door.

Once inside, he inspected it through his glasses. It was lighted, but empty, and it was in perfect order.

"No party here this afternoon, that's sure," he thought. "That's curious. And nobody came after we got here. Looks as if everybody had been called off."

He reflected on that, moving about the room. In the strong upper light he could see that Riggs had been right. Here and there a scorched spot marked a forgotten cigarette, or a circle showed the mark of a glass. Hard lines on an old lady who had given her carefully tended house to be abused in this fashion. Hard lines, too, on young Livingstone, coming home day after day to his crowded home, to slip upstairs now and then for a few minutes with his boy. Andy's face hardened. He remembered the nurse's words: "A lot of grief is remorse." Well, if this taught her anything, it might be worth it—that is, provided they found the boy.

Standing there, the house and even the street were surprisingly silent. It had been agreed that the house should be unwatched, to facilitate any effort at communication from the abductors. But Andy knew that it was only the silent center of a hurricane; that local constables and state policemen were patrolling the roads everywhere, that a determined search was going on in the city, and that a hundred, maybe a thousand, men were sitting, like the chief across the hall, over telephone instruments and waiting for news. He felt small and unimportant in the center of that network of radio, wires and armed men in uniform. Conscious, too, that he had no business to be there.

But he shook that off. "Too many coincidences," he repeated to himself, and stealthily moved out into the hall again. The door into the library was still closed, but from overhead came the muffled booming of the doctor's voice and the restless sound of young Livingstone pacing the floor.

As he stood there, however, he heard a bell ring in the pantry, followed by the butler's deliberate footsteps as he climbed the back staircase. Instantly he was on the move, and this time he had a bit of luck. The parlormaid was in the pantry, and alone.

"Well, well," he said cheerily. "Aren't you working rather late tonight?"

She looked at him coldly.

"You've got us shut up in here, haven't you?" she demanded. "What did you expect? This is Mary Anne's night to relieve me, but with her lying in bed and maybe arrested—and a better girl never lived, Mr. Detective——"

"Where did you get that idea?" he asked. "Mary Anne's not under arrest. As a matter of fact, I thought I'd take her some tea and toast, if someone would get it ready. Even the best girl that ever lived needs nourishment, you know."

He lighted another cigarette while, filled with remorse, she bustled into the kitchen. His ears were alert for Riggs' return, but the butler had not come back when she reëntered with a tray. Andy watched her; to all appearances, idly.

"Good place here, I suppose," he said conversationally.

"Fair. I've known better. Too much company to my taste. You get ready for four and you have eight or ten. And as for the afternoons——"

"Nobody here today, was there?"

She got a quick glance at him, but he only blinked at her owlishly through his glasses, the picture of a bored young man with nothing to do. She relaxed somewhat.

"There's a reason for that." She lowered her voice: "He cleared them all out yesterday. Came home and said he wasn't running a hotel, and his child ought to grow up in a happy home and not a free bar. Not that she drinks, but the rest of them—— You'd think, to watch them, that they'd swallowed blotting paper before they came."

He gave a real whistle at that.

"And was home happy after that?"

"Not so you could notice it. He banged out and went to his club for the night. And she had hysterics. Don't say I told you this," she added cautiously. "Riggs would be crazy. But it's the truth, and I don't care what he thinks."

"Still," he said idly, "that hardly accounts for the boy being taken, does it?"

But she had said all she meant to say, and probably more. She disappeared again into the kitchen, and when Riggs came back he found only Andy there, holding a tray and beaming at him with the face of a cheerful child.

"Mary Anne's supper, Riggs," he said. "I have a heart, if no one else has one."

But as he moved carefully toward the door with his tray, he was aware that something had happened to the man. He looked relieved. He even favored Andy with a faint but benevolent smile.

"I'll carry it up, sir."

"No, you don't, Riggs. This is my tray and I'm sticking to it."

He was still wondering as he climbed the stairs. The door into Mrs. Livingstone's room was still closed and across the hall the doctor was about to depart, booming cheer and hope to the weary young man behind him. "Give them time, man; give them time. It's only five hours or so. He's all right, depend on it."

He closed the door, and in the sudden silence Andy saw that he looked tired and rather deflated, as though he had given out more than he had to give. His voice no longer boomed as they met.

"Bad business, this," he said.

"It is, doctor."

"Any news?"

"Not so far. At least," he added truthfully, "I haven't heard any."

The doctor nodded and went on down, and Andy had a quick feeling of pity for him. He was an actor with a difficult part. All doctors were actors.

He did not move until he had heard the front door slam. He was still puzzled. There was nothing here to account for the change in Riggs. Maybe he had imagined it. He turned and carried his tray up to the third floor.

IV.

Mary Anne was looking slightly better. Nevertheless, her face puckered when she saw him.

"Tell me, Mr. Andrews, am I under arrest?"

"God bless my soul, no. Whatever put that into your head?"

He put the tray on a chair beside the bed. "You've just got notions," he told her. "Lying here alone is what does it. Nobody's been up, I suppose, since I left?"

"Nobody but Mr. Riggs."

"Oh, he came?"

"Not to see me." The grievance revived in her face. "I thought it was the tea and toast, so I opened the door a little. But it was only Riggs with a suitcase."

"A suitcase?"

"Yes, sir. He just put it in the trunk room and went away."

He blinked behind his glasses. A suitcase! Well, after all, why not? He supposed a butler's duty might comprise carrying a suitcase to a trunk room without undue suspicion. Besides, hadn't Livingstone spent the previous night at his club?

"You didn't notice whose suitcase it was, I suppose?"

She looked doubtful.

"Hers, I think. It was black, and Mr. Livingstone's is yellow."

So that was it! That was why Riggs was relieved. That was what lay behind the nurse's anger. He cursed himself for a fool, standing alone later in the dark upper hall. His case, if he had ever had one, had blown up in his face; a family row, nothing more or less, with the wife packing to leave and maybe Reno in the offing.

"You're the hell of a detective," he told himself with disgust, and felt suddenly as deflated as the doctor had looked. "Digging around backstairs for hours, and then turning up a squabble!" He could see the chief if he knew; hear Jenkins' ironic laughter. Jenkins had held out all along for a professional job. Well, maybe it was. But was it?

He ran again over the story as he knew it, and some of his old confidence returned. Someone in the house knew something. There were still too many coincidences. He resumed his silent whistling and wandering back along the hall to the trunk room, went in and turned on the light. The suitcase was there, just inside the door, and it was black, as Mary Anne had said.

He closed the door and inspected it. It was unlocked and empty, and he stood staring at it for some time. Suppose she had meant to go and to take the boy with her? That was possible, certainly, but why stage a kidnaping to do it? Why not simply have taken him? Nevertheless, he had to know, and turning abruptly, he switched off the light and went down the stairs to the second floor.

His face was grim as he knocked at the door of Mrs. Livingstone's room, and still grim when the nurse opened it.

"I want to see Mrs. Livingstone," he said. And he added: "Alone, if you please."

The nurse stared at him. This was not the cheerful young man of an hour or so ago. He looked determined and severe, and her protest died on her lips. But she looked back over her shoulder.

"It's a detective," she said. "He wants to see you."

"All right. Let him come in," said a tired young voice; and Andy entered, closing the nurse out with considerable firmness. Then he faced the bed, and some of his new-found confidence suddenly deserted him. In her bed the girl looked young and desperately tragic. Very lovely, too, but crushed and defeated. His voice softened.

"I wanted to ask a question or two, if you don't mind."

"There's no news, then?"

"Not yet. It's rather soon." He blinked at her through his spectacles. She looked like a child herself, he thought; and that, added to his knowledge that he had no business there, made him uncomfortable. But he pulled himself together.

"You see, Mrs. Livingstone," he said in a fair imitation of the chief's voice, "what we have to do is to get at this thing from the bottom, to—well, to clear the air, if you know what I mean."

She merely looked at him. It was as though her mind was busy somewhere else, and he a thin and unimportant shadow.

"Now, about that suitcase of yours," he went on briskly. "If you'll tell me a little about it, for instance———" His voice broke off, for he saw suddenly that she was trembling.

"What about my suitcase?"

"That's what I'm asking you, Mrs. Livingstone. Isn't it true that you contemplated leaving the house today and going—well, somewhere else?"

She closed her eyes and drew a long breath.

"What has that to do with Larry?" she asked faintly.

"Well, I'll say it like this: Did you or did you not intend to take him with you?"

"No," she said, in a flat voice. "I've been a rotten mother. Ask my husband. Ask Miss Murray. But if you think I stole Larry—well, look at me!"

"But you did intend to go?"

"I did. That hasn't anything to do with what has happened. That is a family matter. My husband thinks I am both a bad mother and a bad wife, if you care to know. Probably he's right. But I didn't plan to take Larry, and if I had I needn't have stolen him." She moved restlessly. "If you want to know any more, ask him."

"Ask him what?"

"I don't know. Ask him if he took Larry." And when he said nothing, she sat up in bed and looked at him wildly. "I suppose I am going crazy," she said, "but I keep wondering if he did. He may have known I was leaving and tried to scare me. But he isn't like that. He'd have let me go. He doesn't care enough. Not any more." And she added, as if to herself: "What a fool I've been! What a fool!" She lay back again, exhausted. "Just forget I said that," she told him. "He hates me, but he would never have done a thing like this. Not to Larry."

Andy was blinking wildly through his glasses. It was all wrong somewhere. She shouldn't be alone here, eating her heart out. Maybe she had been foolish, but it was no crime to be young and gay. She didn't even drink, somebody had said. Well, that was one up for her anyhow; and she looked, as she lay there, just a little like his sister.

Suddenly and to his utter consternation he found himself bending over the bed and giving her a reassuring pat on the shoulder.

"Listen," he said. "You get both those ideas out of your head. He didn't take the boy, and he doesn't hate you. I'm betting all I've got on that." And he felt quite incredibly elated when she rewarded him with a faint smile.

Outside in the hall again, however, his cheerfulness faded. It was one thing to move around backstairs, as it were; it was another to approach the principals. Like a freshman slapping a senior on the back, he thought uncomfortably, going back to his college days. The chief would certainly give him hell if he knew. And he had got precisely nowhere.

His disquiet was not removed by the sudden opening of the sitting-room door and young Livingstone's appearance in it. He was disheveled and pale, and he gave a glance at his wife's door before he saw Andy. Then he stiffened.

"Anything new?"

"Nothing yet. Sorry. It ought to be coming along pretty soon." And when Livingstone showed signs of retreating into the room again: "I'd like a few words with you, if you don't mind."

"Words! That's all I've had so far. My God, don't you fellows do anything in a case like this but sit around and wear out the seats of your pants?"

Andy, who had hardly sat down for the past three hours, smiled rather ruefully as he followed him in. "There's plenty doing," he said. "It's outside, of course."

"And I'm to sit here and wait for that damned telephone while God knows what's happening!"

"Well, they'll want to talk to you, you see."

"They?" Young Livingstone stared at him. "So you think it's an outside job, too, do you?"

"Don't you?"

"I'm damned if I know." He ran his hand through his heavy hair. "Somebody knew a lot, that's certain."

He lapsed into silence, and Andy lighted a cigarette. When he spoke again, it was in a milder voice. The fellows downstairs, as he called them, wanted to issue a general broadcast at eleven o'clock. He wanted that, too, but he was worried about his mother.

"She listens in at night," he said, "and she's not young and she has a bad heart. I'm damned if I know what to do. So far, we haven't told her. I haven't dared to."

But Andy was hardly listening. He was making an important decision.

"I ought to tell you," he said, blinking nervously through his glasses, "that I'm not definitely connected with the case. I brought the others over, and that's about all. But I've been looking around a bit and—well, it doesn't look like a professional job to me."

Livingstone looked up quickly.

"What makes you think that?"

"Well, look at it. Whoever it was took a lot of chances, that's sure. Off-hand you might say that he took too many. How was he to know that the boy would go to him? Or that the girl would cross the street ahead, as he told her to? Or that she wouldn't turn and look back until she got across? What I mean is, no professional would take all those chances at once. One, maybe, not three or four."

Rather surprisingly, young Livingstone seemed to brace himself. "All right," he said roughly. "Come out with it. Who took him, and why?"

"That's going pretty fast, isn't it? D'you mind if I sit down? I've climbed so many stairs I feel like a mountain goat. Well, take it like this. The boy's shy, so the chances are he knew who picked him up. As a matter of fact, I'm pretty sure he did. Then what? Remember, if the girl turns around and sees this fellow making off, there will be the devil to pay. But suppose there is a car right there, and this man doesn't cross. He shows the child to somebody in the car. That's innocent enough, isn't it? Even if the girl howls and there's an officer on hand, the thing ceases to be a kidnaping. 'Is that the Livingstones' little boy? Do let me see him.'

Get it? But the girl hasn't turned, so he simply hands the boy in and gets in himself, and goes away. I'll bet you that by tomorrow we'll find a half dozen people who saw something just like that."

"And who was in the car?"

"No professional crook, depend on it. Somebody who can qualify, in case of an alarm by the girl; can say that they asked to see the child. Very likely someone who knew the child."

"My God," said the young man softly.

"It has its cheerful side at that, you know," Andy went on. "It simplifies the thing, you see. After all, how many men did the boy know? Not so many, probably. And who was in the car? That's what it comes down to. I—you understand, of course, that this is only my own idea. The chief doesn't know it, and he probably wouldn't agree if he did."

There was a brief silence. Livingstone still stood, leaning on a table and thinking intently. All at once he flushed and straightened.

"Look here," he said. "You don't think this was a kidnaping for ransom at all, do you?"

"I haven't said that. I'm trying to find out."

"Then what the hell do you think? That I am guilty? Or my wife?"

"Well," said Andy reasonably, "each of you apparently suspects the other. I suppose you can't both be guilty!"

"Are you telling me," said Livingstone incredulously, "that she thinks I took Larry?"

"Something like that; that she's been all wrong about a lot of things, and that you don't care for her any more. You know the sort of thing. Of course, she's pretty nervous, alone and all——"

But he received no reply. Livingstone had shot across the hall and into his wife's room, and Andy smiled to himself. He sat there for some time, resting his aching feet and keeping an eye on the staircase; for he had no intention of letting Jenkins or the chief find him there. But although his story had blown up and he had no idea of where to turn next, the song he silently whistled was a cheerful one.

V.

Sometime later he made his way to the pantry again. It had suddenly occurred to him that he had had no dinner, and he was carefully inspecting an open refrigerator when Riggs entered. Andy looked up with a grin.

"Been carrying another suitcase, Riggs?"

Riggs looked blank. "I don't understand, sir."

Andy smiled cheerfully. "Never mind," he said. "Hold the fort, as I said before. What's that?"

For the butler had produced a small piece of paper and was holding it out.

"The doctor left a prescription for Mrs. Livingstone. Will it be all right for me to go to the drug store?"

"Probably, but you'll have to get an O.K. from the library first."

But he had lost all interest in food for the moment. He closed the refrigerator door and, while Riggs changed his coat, made his way rather uneasily forward to the library, shutting the door behind him. The men looked up in surprise as he entered.

"For God's sake look who's here," Jenkins said. "I thought you were home and in bed hours ago, Andy."

"I've just been hanging around in case I was needed."

"Needed is good!" said Jenkins. But Andy gave him no time for more. He addressed the chief, smoking his old pipe behind the desk, the telephone in front of him.

"The butler wants to take a prescription to the drug store," he said. "Probably all right, but I might keep an eye on him. He'll be here for an O.K."

The chief, looking tired and anxious, nodded absently. "All right, Andy," he said. "But he's probably all right. Been in the family for thirty years."

Jenkins was grinning when Andy turned and went out, but he did not notice it. The chief's permission had given him his first status on the case, and he was warmed and glowing with recognition. Actually he expected nothing from tailing Riggs to the corner drug store; nor did anything happen at first. It was only after the prescription had been handed in that Andy across the street saw the butler give a quick look around and then move quickly into the telephone booth and close the door.

He bolted across the street and in by a side door. Luckily the shop was empty and the clerk had retired behind the partition, but Andy, edging close to the booth, could hear only the butler's voice, low and cautious, and after a moment he flung open the door and put a hand on Riggs' suddenly rigid arm. He was not quick enough, however. With his left hand Riggs had hung up the receiver, and Andy's frenzied attempts to locate the call resulted only in the usual "Number, please."

The butler had made no move, and finally he turned to him.

"All right, Riggs," he said cheerfully. "Get your little bottle and let's go. You can talk when we get back to the house. That's all they've got to do there—listen."

But Riggs managed to retain his dignity. He even smiled, although he was pale.

"It is all very simple, sir," he said. "You can discover, if you like, who I called. As soon as we learned this afternoon that Master Larry was gone, I telephoned to Barnes, old Mrs. Livingstone's chauffeur, and told him to warn the household. The old lady isn't very well, and the idea was to keep the news from her and reporters out of the house. Then tonight, when I learned that there was to be a radio broadcast at eleven——"

"How did you learn that?"

"I understood it to be the case," said Riggs impassively. "And as we were forbidden to use the house telephone, I called Barnes at Rosedale to cut the aerial out there, or whatever was necessary. There is no crime in that. You can verify it by Barnes himself, if you like. Call the garage. He lives over it."

And that, as was developed a few minutes later in the library again, was that. Andy, waiting nervously while the call was made, was sure that it would be. Barnes himself answered the telephone. Yes, Riggs had called him. . . . Yes, he knew the boy was gone. Very sorry too. Terrible for the old lady if she heard it. . . . Yes, sir, that was why Riggs had called. He had cut the aerial on the roof, but he wasn't sure that it would do any good. . . . No, no reporters so far.

Through it all, Riggs had stood, pale but impassive. All the faces in the room had been turned toward him, intent and suspicious. He was ringed in by suspicion. Four men, all tense, all ready to leap if he made a move, but only when it was over did he move at all. Then he shrugged slightly.

"If that's all, gentlemen——"

But Andy watched him as he went out, and he saw that beads of fine sweat had sprung out on his forehead. They looked as though they had developed spontaneously with the end of his ordeal, out of sheer relief. Men did that, he knew; held out through torment, dry and burning, and then sweated with relief.

Inside the room the tension had been broken, however. They looked at Andy with a sort of amusement.

"Full of tips as a package of cigarettes, Andy, aren't you?"

He grinned back.

"I'm a detective, not a clairvoyant."

"A detective! Who says so?"

But he stood his ground, although he himself was moist with anxiety.

"It's like this, chief," he said: "What's the matter with this Barnes making the snatch? If the boy knew who picked him up——"

"Who says so?"

"Well, it sort of looks like it, doesn't it? And he'd know Barnes, while Mary Anne wouldn't. She's only been here a week."

The chief listened to him patiently. His eyes were red with the smoke which filled the room, and before him was an empty coffee cup and a pad on which he had done considerable aimless scribbling. He watched Andy with a sort of benevolent indulgence.

"Not bad, Andy," he said. "But we've covered that already. Barnes had the old lady out for a drive in the country all afternoon. Didn't get in until five."

So that also was that. Andy turned and went out into the hall, and after a moment's thought, climbed the stairs again. Something stubborn in him refused to acknowledge defeat, was still convinced that the story lay inside the house. But where? The nurse? He did not believe it. And yet—women had been known to steal children—especially childless women.

He thought about her, pausing on the stairs to do so. After all, she was unaccounted for that afternoon. Livingstone had been at his office, his wife in the house. Even Riggs had not been out for any purpose. And according to his theory, whoever had been in the abducting car must have known the boy; must have been there with some semblance of legitimacy.

Nevertheless, he weakened somewhat when he saw her in the hall on the second floor, sitting alone on a stiff chair. She had taken off her cap, and with it had gone some of her austerity. She looked elderly and lonely and rather pitiful, but he had no time to consider that.

"Listen, Miss Murray," he said. "I want you to go over this day bit by bit. What did you do? Where did you go? Who knew you were out, or saw you while you were out?"

"Not more than five thousand people," she said scornfully. "How many recognized me is different." She picked up her cap again and set it defiantly on her head, anchoring it there with pins and keeping her eyes on him. "What are you getting at, anyhow? Asking me for an alibi?"

"Not at all," he said hastily. "I just want the facts. You didn't use the car, I suppose?"

"They drive their own car. If you want any more facts, the old lady wanted some knitting wool. Riggs got the message and brought it up to Mrs. Livingstone; but she wasn't thinking about wool just then. She sent me, and if you don't believe that, ask her. She's got the stuff in there now."

He stood very still, blinking. He had not expected much, but he had run up another blind alley. But was it a blind alley? There was something there; he was just missing it, but it was there. It was just around the corner of his mind.

"Tell me something," he said suddenly. "Did Riggs know that Mrs. Livingstone was planning to go away today?"

She looked startled. "I suppose he did. He had carried down her suitcase."

He was blinking wildly now. "He wouldn't want that to happen, I suppose. He's still devoted to the old lady, and it would be a blow to her. That's true, isn't it?"

"If you think Riggs did it, you are an idiot," she said contemptuously. "He never left the house all day. As for her going, she's not going now. If you don't believe me, go in there and look." She indicated the bedroom door. "It takes trouble to bring some people to their senses."

But Andy was not listening. He was standing still, noiselessly whistling and staring at the closed door. Suddenly he leaned down and put a hand on her rigid arm.

"Listen to me," he said. "I've got a hunch this thing's about to break wide open. Just a hunch, but I get 'em now and then. So you cheer up."

Down in the lower hall again, he picked up his hat and made his way to the door into the yard. Murphy moved out from the shadow, recognized him and fell back again.

"Everything quiet, Murphy?"

"Nobody's tried to leave. The butler's been out on the steps once or twice, but he just smoked a cigarette and went in again."

"Keeping an eye on you, eh?"

"Looks like it," said Murphy, grinning.

He went on, looking right and left along the alley before he left the gate. It was still and empty, however, and he got into his car and took out his road map. About ten miles, he figured; say twenty minutes if the road patrols didn't hold him too long. Every road, of course, was being patrolled.

As he started his engine he found that his hands were sweating, and smiled to himself as he wiped them dry. Hell of a detective, he was! Then he stepped on the gas and shot through the town as though he had been fired out of a gun.

VI.

The trip took more time, however, than he had expected. The road seemed lined with uniformed men in cars, on motorcycles and afoot. A waving lantern would stop him; he would slide to a stop, and from some place of concealment he would be surrounded by a half dozen officers, their faces grim and determined.

The doors of his car would be jerked open and he would be conscious of the light on dark-blue automatics.

He began to be nervous. "Listen, boys. Can't you telephone ahead and clear the road for me? I'm in the hell of a hurry."

"What's the matter, Andy? Got a dead line to beat?"

"Something like it."

Once a car loaded with reporters picked him up and followed him, but he got the troopers to hold it at the next stop. However, he saw with relief, as he turned into the drive of the Livingstone house, that it was only half-past ten. He had still a half hour until that eleven-o'clock broadcast. To his surprise, he found that he was sweating profusely.

He did not go to the house. Instead he left his car in the shadow of some trees, and five minutes later he had skirted the house and was close to the garage. Like the house, it was dark, but there was a young moon, and by its light he saw that the doors were wide open and that a man was sitting inside, smoking a pipe. As he watched he knocked out its ashes onto the floor, and rising, yawned heavily. Then he struck a match to consult his watch, and Andy stepped forward.

"That you, Barnes?"

The man whirled, then stiffened.

"Who is it?"

"It's all right. I didn't want you pulling a gun on me, that's all. You are Barnes, I suppose?"

"That's my name. And who are you?"

The tone was definitely hostile, and Andy smiled as the lights went on over his head.

"It's all right, Barnes," he said. "After Riggs called you, it seemed a good idea to see you, that's all. Nice car you've got there. Just cleaned it, haven't you?"

"Always clean it after we come in, sir. Mrs. Livingstone's orders."

Andy opened the door and glanced inside. "Nice and clean, outside and inside," he said casually. Then he turned suddenly and confronted the chauffeur. "Now see here, Barnes," he said, "I want to know what you know about what happened this afternoon. You know something, and I know you know it. Now, what is it?" And when Barnes said nothing: "What is it that Riggs and you cooked up together when he called you up this morning?"

"Nothing. He didn't call me."

"You are willing to swear to that?"

"On a stack of Bibles."

"You haven't got the boy here?"

"Go up and look, if you like."

Andy stood stock-still, staring at him. He looked solid, middle-aged and respectable. More than that, he looked calm, almost judicial.

"And this afternoon? What about that?"

"I've told you fellows that already. I took Mrs. Livingstone out for a drive."

"Into the city?"

"What business is it of yours where I went? If you think I'd hurt a hair of that child's head——"

But suddenly Andy had had an electrifying, a shocking idea. It began in his head and worked its way all over him. It was so violent that it almost shook him. He gazed at Barnes with his half-whimsical smile; then he did a surprising thing. He reached out solemnly and shook the chauffeur's unresisting hand.

"Had a pretty hard day of it, Barnes, haven't you?" he said. "Always a bad thing to tamper with the law, Barnes. Or to underestimate the police. Now, if Riggs hadn't telephoned tonight, you'd have been all right."

"Yes, sir," said Barnes tonelessly. "I told him he was a fool."

"And now," said Andy, "I'd better see the old lady herself. She'll need a bit of cheering, I imagine."

He whistled soundlessly but gayly on his way to the house. He knew now, knew the story from start to finish. It had always been there, only he hadn't seen it. Mingled with this was an enormous sense of relief that the boy was safe—safe and warm and fed. "I've been scared," he thought to himself. "Scared for the kid." But in the back of his mind was the chief, red-eyed and waiting. He would have something to tell the chief.

Nevertheless, he was slightly uneasy as he entered the house. It was a big house, filled with dignity and fastidious living, and when Barnes at last rapped and then threw open a door on the lower hall, he had to stop and wipe his hands again. Then, blinking furiously, he stepped inside and confronted a little elderly lady, knitting by a fire.

She glanced up quickly, surveying them both with a certain amusement.

"Good gracious, Barnes!" she said. "What is the matter now?"

"There's a gentleman here to see you, from the police," said Barnes.

"From the police? How interesting! What in the world have you been doing, Barnes?"

Andy came forward, still blinking, while her bright birdlike eyes darted over him.

"You don't look at all like a policeman," she announced. "Now tell me about it. What have we done, out here in the country? And do sit down. It's such a long time since I have talked with a policeman."

Barnes had gone out and closed the door. All at once Andy felt dubious and uneasy. She had a bad heart, they said, and he was here without authority. What if she fell over, or whatever it was that people did when they had hearts?

But she gave no indication at the moment of being anything but interested.

"Well?" she said. "And what have we done?"

He sat forward in his chair, looking young and rather absurd, but frightfully earnest.

"Would it mean anything to you, Mrs. Livingstone," he said carefully, "if I told you that everything is all right in town? I mean—well, that your son and his wife are on good terms again?"

She had picked up her knitting again, but now she stopped and looked up.

"Dear me!" she said. "How much you know of our family affairs! I had no idea the police knew so much." And then: "Yes," she said softly. "It would mean a great deal to me, of course. They are such children, you know; playing with life now, but really caring very much for each other."

"And you could understand, I suppose," said Andy, still carefully, "that an interested person might go to considerable lengths to keep them together?"

She eyed him.

"Do you know," she said, "that this is really quite a remarkable talk? Are you trying to tell me that some member of my family is in trouble with the police, after all these years? And what have my son and his wife to do with it?"

But he refused to be put off.

"I'll say it another way," he said, blinking earnestly through his glasses. "Would an interested person, in such a case, feel justified in doing something rather drastic in order to bring them together. Do you think he would?"

"What an odd question!" she said, glancing at him again with her bright eyes. "So psychological! Well, I can only say that in my time we didn't take our marriages for granted. We tried everything we could, legitimate and illegitimate. I remember once that I thought my husband was drinking too much and I got some pills from the doctor. I gave them to him in his coffee one night, and I didn't sleep a wink; but he never even sneezed."

"In other words," he said, "when everything else fails, you believe in direct action. Is that it? In the pill in the coffee and so on?"

"I believe in action. Certainly."

Then at last he smiled.

"I wish you'd tell me about it," he said. "It's costing the state about a million dollars a minute just now, and likely as not, they've arrested a good many innocent people already."

Suddenly he saw that her hands were shaking. For an instant the mask was down, and he saw her for what she was—a tired little elderly woman who had done a desperate and heroic thing in defiance of the law. But she was calm again almost at once.

"It was all very simple," she said quietly. "And something had to be done. They have been drifting apart, and she's a good girl. She'll make a good mother eventually. But they were young and impatient. They wouldn't build; and today, when Riggs telephoned me that she was going to Reno, I—well, I decided to do it."

"And he is here?"

"He is upstairs, sound asleep, after a perfectly proper supper of cereal and stewed fruit." He saw with relief that her color was coming back, and her humor. She was smiling. "Even Miss Murray would approve of that supper," she said.

He looked at the clock. It was fifteen minutes to eleven, and he wanted to shut off the broadcast as soon as possible. No use getting the public excited. The thing was over. But he was still curious.

"I suppose it was Barnes who picked up the boy?"

"Yes. I was waiting in the car. You see, I knew Miss Murray was out. As a matter of fact, I had asked my son's wife to send her on an errand for me. And Mary Anne had never seen Barnes. It might work or it might not, but I had to try."

"I suppose Riggs knew all along?"

"Oh, yes, Riggs knew." She smiled faintly. "He knew, but he didn't approve. He very often doesn't approve of me. Just now he is worrying about getting the boy back. Without involving me," she added. "That's important, you see. The children must never know. Now that you are here, of course——"

Andy got up and looked down at her small and valiant figure.

"Now that I am here," he said, smiling, "I'm to get him back. Is that it?"

"That has been the idea, more or less, ever since you entered that door."

He had a swift vision of those patrolled roads, of the vast machinery she had so simply set in operation, but he only said casually: "Well, I suppose Barnes and I can manage it somehow. And now, if you will get him——"

He watched her out of the room rather ruefully. He could see the chief's face when he told him, the necessity of keeping the story out of the press; a dozen anxieties sat heavy on him. But he would not let her down.

"All right, Barnes," he called. "Come in. You and I have a job to do, and heaven help us. Now, where's the telephone?"

VII.

At half-past eleven that night a shabby Ford came to a stop in the alley behind the house, and a young man with horn-rimmed spectacles and carrying something wrapped in blankets made his way through the gate and confronted the man on watch there.

"Got him, Murphy," he said in a low voice. "Go ahead and open the door."

"My God, Andy!" said Murphy fervently. "What happened to him?"

"Case of direct action," said Andy cheerfully, and left Murphy, looking confounded, staring after him.

It was a half hour later when, behind closed doors and in a library filled with smoke, Andy faced the chief and the others with a determined glint in his eyes.

"Our story's this," he said, "and I for one am going to stick to it. The kidnapers got frightened and dumped the boy in the grandmother's carriage drive. I'd been out to break the news to her, and found the child where he'd been left, rolled in a blanket and still asleep."

One of the men groaned.

"Oh, for God's sake," he said, "why bring in a blanket? We'll be tracing the thing for the next six months."

"All right," Andy agreed. "Not rolled in a blanket, then. But that story has to go, chief; not only for the outside but for this house too."

This was a new Andy, self-confident and stubborn. For the first time they had to recognize him for what he had done, and if there was resentment in their faces, there was respect also.

"Certainly did get a break, Andy."

"Sure. Might have been a fracture."

"What started you off, anyhow?"

"Well," he said modestly, "it was just a bit here and there. Up to the time I got out to the house I thought it was Riggs and Barnes, and I thought I knew why. But after I got there——"

"Yeah? Barnes told you, did he?"

"No. It just struck me all of a heap. The old lady had to have been in that car."

Suddenly he was very tired. He had sat down very little for a number of hours, and his whole body ached. He yawned, and found the chief's eyes on him, kindly and faintly amused.

"Better go home and get to bed," he said. "It was a good job, Andy. Pity the press can't have it, but the commissioner can. However," he added, "it wouldn't hurt the next time to take me into your confidence. I've been known to have an idea or two of my own."

In the hall as they left, Andy saw the nurse, radiant with happiness, coming along from the pantry with a glass of milk. He tried to catch her eye, but she did not even see him. Well, that was a policeman's job, he thought, and strutting slightly, went back to the alley and crawled into his old Ford car.

But before he left he took a final survey of the house, now lighted and alive again. He sat there for some little time, soundlessly whistling. Then he stepped on the starter and, after his usual fashion, shot toward home as though he was going to a fire.

THE ODDS

Angela Savage

Angela Savage is an award-winning and critically respected Australian crime writer. Her thrillers include *Behind the Night Bazaar*, *The Half-Child*, and *The Dying Beach*, which was shortlisted for the Davitt award in 2014.

Doctor Dawn Fethers has fresh flowers delivered twice weekly to her reception area. Her bathroom smells of designer lotions, and her consulting rooms are fragrant with the perfect blend of essential oils and antiseptic. Perfumed and professional, like the doctor herself.

Doctor Dawn Fethers. Her very name seems to hold promise, a dove-grey night ceding to a new day. No doubt I'm not the only one drawn subliminally into her ambit. When you come to rely on hope over experience, you invest all kinds of significance in signs. Doctor Dawn Fethers has an impressive sign, too: a brass plaque, her propitious name resting on a plinth of acronyms signifying her medical credentials.

The plaque is fastened to the brick wall of what was probably once a mansion, now her consulting rooms, located in a street off the beach road. A leadlight bay window illuminates the waiting area, where Doctor Dawn Fethers displays magazines with headlines like 'My miracle baby', 'Mum at 45', 'Surprise twins joy'.

The mansion is not where Doctor Dawn Fethers works her magic. That takes place in a clinic she's attached to in the CBD. The mansion is for the sensitive business of discussing results and options. The paintings on the walls are suitably abstract, nebulous clouds of colour that neither inspire nor offend. I know every image by heart.

I've stopped seeing Doctor Dawn Fethers, but I've been watching her for months. Monday to Wednesday, she works at the clinic, commuting by car from her deluxe bayside apartment with its state of the art security. Thursdays and Fridays are her days at the mansion. Every second weekend, two golden haired boys are deposited at her apartment, and every second Monday, she drops them off at a private school en route to work. Otherwise, she lives alone and unfettered. Two beautiful boys, and she gives them two days a fortnight. It's enough to make my blood boil.

Doctor Dawn Fethers is less parsimonious with her time when it comes to keeping fit. Monday to Wednesday, she works out at a gym near the clinic. Thursday and Friday, she leaves the car at home and walks to the mansion along the coastal trail. The walk takes fourteen minutes, the path always busy. On Fridays, she stays back in her rooms after Gracie, her unflappable receptionist, goes home. I gaze at the yellow light emanating from her window and imagine Doctor Dawn Fethers counting stacks of gold coins like a fairytale witch.

I know Gracie locks the door on her way out because I've tried it a few times. No matter.

Doctor Dawn Fethers wears an ivory suit and a tight smile. Her scalpel-grey eyes register the extravagant bouquet – white orchids and lilies in a cloud of Baby's Breath, against a glossy-green shield of philodendron – and her frown vanishes.

'Are these for me?'

Feigned surprise. I've witnessed such tributes arrive regularly from grateful patients.

'You are Doctor Dawn Fethers?'

I keep my face obscured behind the flowers, though I'm fairly confident she won't recognise me. I've lost a lot of weight since coming off the hormones. I also bleached my mousy hair white, swapped my contact lenses for hipster glasses, and started wearing lipstick in the bloodiest shade of red I could find. My own mother, may she rest in peace, wouldn't recognise me. I look more like the arty type I was at university, than the middle-aged divorcée and recently retrenched public servant I've become.

'You'd better bring them inside. I'll get a vase.'

She returns with a tall glass cylinder half-filled with water. She takes the flowers and I ask if I might photograph her holding them as part of a new quality assurance measure. I point at the logo on my apron, 'Budding Hopes Florist', wondering if she'll see the irony.

'Of course.' She puts on her best salesperson's smile.

I raise the phone. 'Just a moment –'

Doctor Dawn Fethers says, 'God, I love my job.'

Her words are a slap in the face. But Doctor Dawn Fethers, distracted by the flowers, doesn't notice when I fumble. I regain my composure and hold my breath, before sending a stream of capsicum spray into her eyes. Doctor Dawn Fethers screams, drops the flowers and falls to the ground. The screaming continues. I need to make it stop. I make a fist.

But Doctor Dawn Fethers isn't moving.

I realise the screams are mine.

Before you start thinking I'm some kind of psycho, let me be clear: I'm not mad, I'm enraged. There's a big difference. Rage is a rational response to what I've been through. I spent more than ten years of my life and all the money I had for nothing. By contrast, fading quietly from view, bereft, childless, in debt and uncomplaining – that's madness.

I wouldn't have hit Doctor Dawn Fethers. I didn't mean to knock her out. When she emits a sound like a squeaky toy being stepped on, I almost cry with relief.

Doctor Dawn Fethers remains unconscious. I unclench my fist and wipe my eyes, determined not to let my emotions get the better of me. I reach into my bag for the latex gloves and handcuffs.

As a woman who spent years trying to get pregnant, I know how to wait and I know how to plan. I've acquired the necessary meds, assembled the tools, determined optimal sequencing, thought about the environment and planned for contingencies. I've calculated the odds of success and concluded they are, for once, in my favour.

Besides, I have nothing to lose.

I tend to Doctor Dawn Fethers with the same clinical detachment and efficiency she's shown me over the years. I ease her into the recovery position and handcuff her right wrist to a radiator. I remove her shoes and empty her pockets, but leave her watch. I want her to be conscious of time ticking away.

I decide against gagging her. It will only mean having to remove the gag later. And I doubt her voice will carry through the brick walls and double-glazing, across the garden and through the camellia hedge to the street.

I clear the floor, leaving only a couple of plastic bags within her reach. I lower the blinds and turn off all the lights apart from a desk lamp, which I angle so the light falls on her face. Her eyes are red and swollen as though stung by bees, her nose leaks mucous, and there's a wet patch on the front of her skirt where the vase water has spilt.

I take a cushion from the couch. Doctor Dawn Fethers moans as I place it under her head. My fingertips graze a bump on her temple. I straighten her skirt, which has risen above her knees. Restoring order.

Doctor Dawn Fethers comes to slowly, coughing and wincing. She rolls on to her back and cries out, crow-like, when she realises her hand is trapped. She lifts her head and groans, peering at me through eye-slits.

'Who are you? W-what do you want?'

The alarm in her voice carries into the coughing fit that follows. I put my hand under her head and hold a plastic bottle to her lips. She hesitates, but only for a moment, drinking greedily, water spilling from the sides of her mouth and on to the pillow. She raises her free hand to take the bottle but I snatch it back.

'I want to douse my eyes. Please. They're killing me.'

'Water won't help. You've got to keep blinking. Try not to touch them.'

Oozing tears, Doctor Dawn Fethers tries to sit, but doesn't get far. She touches her free hand to the side of her head. 'God, that hurts.'

'You fell before I could stop you, knocked yourself out. Can I get you something for the pain?'

She ignores my question, inching herself up until her back is against the radiator. 'What do you want from me?'

I want you to be focused, I think, not distracted by pain.

'Please, let me get you something.'

She sighs and glances at Gracie's desk. 'Top drawer.'

Panadeine Forte. A prescription drug. Overkill for the office first aid kit. I toss her the packet and, in a further show of trust, roll the plastic bottle of water to her. She holds it between her knees, removes the lid with her left hand and washes down a couple of tablets.

'Now, what do you want?' She keeps her head back when she speaks and though her eyes look closed, I suspect they're not.

'I want to give you the same chances you gave me.'

She turns her head in my direction. 'I don't understand.'

'You're going to start with the odds you gave me when we first met.'

I place a cardboard tray on the floor and open a tin.

'What is it? I can't see. What are you doing?'

'I'm putting two chocolates on this tray. One is impregnated –' I smile at the unintended pun '– with TTX.'

'Tetrodotoxin? Really?' She sounds sceptical.

'Extracted it myself from toadfish livers. Caught the toadies quite close to here, as a matter of fact. Did you know they're a kind of pufferfish?'

I push the tray into the light beside her. 'Pick a chocolate and eat it. You have a fifty per cent chance.'

'You can't be serious.'

'When I first started IVF, you told me my chances of conception were better than one in three. Practically fifty per cent, you said. Same chance I'm giving you now.'

She tilts her head, still trying to get a look at me. 'And when was that again?'

Nice try, I think. 'It doesn't matter.'

'It's Jill, isn't it? The marine biologist.'

I raise my eyebrows. Jill isn't my name, but it suits me for her to think it is. I'm surprised, but then I'm not, to think she might have more than one patient capable of pulling a stunt like this.

'You're not making any sense, Jill. I was offering you a chance at a baby. At life. And you repay me with death threats?'

'Oh, I'm not repaying you. I'm punishing you.'

'Punishing me for what?'

'Extortion.'

'What are you talking about?'

'You coerced me into continuing treatment, kept taking my money long after it was clear that IVF wasn't working for me. That's extortion.'

'Don't be ridiculous, Jill. You were the client. The choice to continue, or not to continue, was yours. Now turn me loose and we'll forget all about this sorry incident.'

I reach into my bag. She nods and smiles, thinking she's talked me around, acting like she's still the one in charge.

Her smile vanishes when she sees the syringe.

'Fair enough,' I say. 'You can have the certainty of the syringe, or take your chances with the chocolate. The choice is yours.'

Doctor Dawn Fethers sticks out her chin, but her face grows pale beneath her make-up. 'You wouldn't –'

'TTX poisoning results in numbness, paralysis, mental impairment. Pretty much how I felt every time I did a pregnancy test and got a big fat negative.'

I uncap the syringe, look past the point of the needle into her puffy eyes. 'You poisoned all my hopes.'

'Don't do this.'

'It's much more deadly if injected.' I flick the barrel of the syringe with my fingernail, making the viscous dark liquid dance. 'Just saying.'

She lifts up the tray of chocolates and sniffs them. She puts the tray back down. Her hand trembles as she selects one and puts it in her mouth. She moans and places her hand to her lips.

'Wash it down.' I gesture at the water bottle with the syringe. 'Don't even think about spitting it out.'

Her throat undulates like a snake as she swallows. I retrieve the tray.

'Okay, there.' She wipes her mouth with the back of her hand. 'I've played along with your twisted little experiment. Let me go now, Jill, and I promise I won't take this any further.'

'You're one to talk about twisted little experiments. Just how long would you have kept me hanging on? Did it ever occur to you to take me aside and say, you know, it might be time to think about a different pathway to parenthood?'

'You know what you would've done if I'd said that? You'd have found yourself another doctor.'

The handcuffs clang against the radiator as she straightens up, warming to her subject. The painkillers have evidently kicked in.

'You wanted to keep going. You all do. It doesn't matter what I try and tell you about your dwindling chances. You all think you're the exception to the rule.'

'You tantalise us. Just look at this.' I toss the magazines from the waiting area at her feet. 'You give us false hope.'

'You wouldn't call it false hope if it worked for you.'

'That's just it. The ones who go through years of treatment and finally get a baby forgive you for everything. Well, I didn't get a baby, I don't forgive you, and I refuse to go quietly.'

In the pause that follows, I hear an insect battering itself against a window.

I add more chocolates and push the tray back to her.

'One in four. Twenty-five per cent. Back when I was thirty-five, I thought those odds were still okay. How do they look from where you're sitting?'

Doctor Dawn Fethers doesn't look at the tray. 'You can't possibly think you'll get away with this.'

I shrug. 'Your business, the IVF business, has failure rate of, what, seventy-five, eighty per cent? Yet you keep turning a profit. You get away with it.' I nod at the tray. 'Now choose.'

She shakes her head.

I pick up the syringe. 'I've had lots of practice, remember. All those hormone injections.'

She manages to look indignant, even with the red puffy eyes. Again, she sniffs the selection before choosing one. She shudders as she takes it and washes it down with water.

I take back the tray. 'Back in my late-thirties, you gave me a one in five chance at a baby. Twenty per cent. The beginning of the end, really, although I didn't want to admit it at the time.'

'Look, I understand you're disappointed.' Doctor Dawn Fethers holds her hands up, palms out, an attempt at a placating gesture perverted by the handcuffs. 'Please, Jill. I understand the grief of infertility.'

'Don't bullshit me. I've seen your children.'

'What children?'

'The ones you can't be bothered spending more than two days a fortnight with.'

She frowns. 'You must mean my stepsons. My ex-husband's boys.' She leans forward. 'You see, Jill, I really do understand.'

I feel my cheeks flush. Is Doctor Dawn Fethers implying that she, too, is infertile? Is that what drove her into her field?

'You're obviously very distressed. I can refer you to specialists who can help with that.'

I recognise the cloying tone she uses to deliver bad news. Low ovarian reserve. Poor quality embryos. Falling beta levels. Miscarriage. No matter how poor the prognosis, Doctor Dawn Fethers always has another specialist to see, another option to try. She's played me for years. She's still playing me. To think, I almost felt sorry for her.

'Nice try, but the younger boy is the image of you.'

'What? How do you know –'

'And you're forgetting, I saw your counsellors for years. None of them ever suggested I give up either.' I push over the tray. 'Take your chance.'

'This is insane.' She bites her lower lip. 'Look, maybe we can still work something out. Did we try egg donation? What about surrogacy?'

'I'll tell you what's insane,' I snap. 'I'm a forty-two-year-old divorcée, who's spent twelve years and all my savings on IVF without success, and you're still trying to sell me something.'

I nod at the chocolates. 'Stop wasting my fucking time.'

Doctor Dawn Fethers flinches. There are tears as she takes another truffle, sniffs and eats. I feel bad for having lost my temper.

'Look, maybe I was insane to put up with what I did for so long,' I say gently. 'But rest assured, I've come to my senses now. I feel better than I have in years.'

Doctor Dawn Fethers makes a noise like something's caught in her throat.

'Need a tissue?'

She nods and I hand her the box from Gracie's desk. While she blows her nose, I add more chocolates.

'Two years ago, you put my chances of getting pregnant at one in ten. Same chance I'm giving you now.'

The tears start up again. At this rate, she'll have her eyes cleared in no time.

She sobs. 'Why are you torturing me like this?'

'Interesting choice of word, torture. Perhaps now you understand how it felt for me, having my body subjected to all those painful and humiliating procedures, ceding to your authority, being encouraged to hope each time that this time would be different –'

I stop myself. Those memories can still unhinge me if I'm not careful and I want to stay calm.

'And if I'd told you there was no hope?' She sounds tired.

'I would've resented you, maybe even hated you. But in the long run, I'd have been grateful. I'd have moved on a lot sooner.' I glance at my watch and slide the tray closer. 'Now, choose.'

Her eyes are starting to open. This time when she picks up the tray, she scrutinises as well as sniffs the contents. She swallows, drinks, looks up at me.

'Can you tell if I've eaten the poison?'

'You seem fine to me. Maybe you'll be luckier than I was.'

I take back the tray, count out eleven more chocolates, and slide them over to her. She catches sight of it and gasps.

'Overwhelming, isn't it. The odds on my last round of IVF. One in twenty. A five per cent chance.'

Another tear slithers down Doctor Dawn Fethers's cheek.

'This is it. Last one.'

She picks up a chocolate, sniffs it, puts it down. 'I c-can't.'

'The syringe then.'

'No, please. But . . . one in twenty –'

'Not great odds, are they.'

Doctor Dawn Fethers shakes her head.

I check my watch again. 'We need to get this over with.'

Doctor Dawn Fethers's hand shakes violently as she inspects four more chocolates. She knocks one from the tray. I pick it up and put it back. When at last she makes her choice, forces it down, she seems to deflate. Her body slumps against the wall and her skirt creeps up above her knees.

I retrieve the tray, tip it and the leftovers into a zip-lock bag. I recap the syringe and add it to the bag, together with the fake phone. I check for anything I've forgotten.

'What happens now?'

I jump at the sound of her voice, assuming she'd fallen unconscious again.

'I'm leaving you with plastic bags, tissues and bottled water. The TTX, if you've ingested it, takes effect anywhere between thirty minutes and four hours.'

She whimpers.

'Not nearly as agonising as the two-week waits I had to go through to find out if I was pregnant.'

'But that wasn't my fault,' she says in a voice like a child's.

I can't help it. I lose my temper again. I kick one of the water bottles across the office, watch it bounce off the wall. 'For fuck's sake, Dawn, take some responsibility.'

She stares at me then, red eyes wide, and I think finally I've gotten through to her.

'It's not Jill, is it?' Doctor Dawn Fethers says. 'Who are you?'

I take my bag and head for the door.

'Mandy? Tara? Stephanie, is that you?'

I spring the deadlock.

'Don't go –'

The cicadas cheer as I cross the garden. I peel off my gloves and add them to the stash I plan to toss in the customs bin at the airport. I retrieve my suitcase from behind the bush where I hid it and drag it four blocks to the Brighton Baths café. I change in the toilets, leaving my fake florist's uniform in a bin, and call a taxi.

En route to the airport, I check my itinerary. My flight to Bangkok leaves at eleven and takes just over nine hours. I assume Doctor Dawn Fethers will induce herself to vomit. But she'll still need to drink, which was why I laced the water with tranquilizers. Took ages to grind so they'd dissolve. But I had the patience to pull it off. I just need her quiet until I leave the country. I'll tip off the police once I land.

I did toy with the idea of poisoning the chocolates for real. But I realised I didn't want to kill Doctor Dawn Fethers. I could tell you I wanted to teach her a lesson, to make a difference to the lives of the women who came after me. And that's true, although it assumes a change of heart on Doctor Dawn Fethers's part, and I honestly can't see that happening, can you? So I'll settle for revenge.

Australia doesn't have an extradition treaty with Thailand. I checked. So even if Doctor Dawn Fethers does manage to figure out who I am, I doubt there's much anyone can do about it.

My plan is to make my way overland to Cambodia. My redundancy payout will last years longer there than it would back home. And while I'm too old to adopt a baby in Australia, it's possible in Cambodia, if you're prepared to wait.

And waiting is something I'm very good at.

THE FASCINATING PROBLEM OF UNCLE MELEAGER'S WILL

Dorothy L. Sayers

> **Dorothy L. Sayers** (1893–1957) was the author of the Lord Peter Wimsey mysteries, including *Strong Poison*, *The Nine Tailors*, and *Busman's Honeymoon*. The Oxford-educated President of the Detection Club, she did much to raise detective fiction's intellectual calibre but eventually tired of it and focused on theology.

"You look a little worried, Bunter," said his lordship kindly to his manservant. "Is there anything I can do?"

The valet's face brightened as he released his employer's grey trousers from the press.

"Perhaps your lordship could be so good as to think," he said hopefully, "of a word in seven letters with S in the middle, meaning two."

"Also," suggested Lord Peter thoughtlessly.

"I beg your lordship's pardon. T-w-o. And seven letters."

"Nonsense!" said Lord Peter. "How about that bath?"

"It should be just about ready, my lord."

Lord Peter Wimsey swung his mauve silk legs lightly over the edge of the bed and stretched appreciatively. It was a beautiful June that year. Through the open door he saw the delicate coils of steam wreathing across a shaft of yellow sunlight. Every step he took into the bathroom was a conscious act of enjoyment. In a husky light tenor he carolled a few bars of *"Maman, dîtes-moi."* Then a thought struck him, and he turned back.

"Bunter!"

"My lord?"

"No bacon this morning. Quite the wrong smell."

"I was thinking of buttered eggs, my lord."

"Excellent. Like primroses. The Beaconsfield touch," said his lordship approvingly.

His song died into a rapturous crooning as he settled into the verbena-scented water. His eyes roamed vaguely over the pale blue-and-white tiles of the bathroom walls.

Mr. Bunter had retired to the kitchen to put the coffee on the stove when the bell rang. Surprised, he hastened back to the bedroom. It was empty. With increased surprise, he realised that it must have been the bathroom bell. The words "heart-attack" formed swiftly in his mind, to be displaced by the still more alarming thought, "No soap." He opened the door almost nervously.

"Did you ring, my lord?" he demanded of Lord Peter's head, alone visible.

"Yes," said his lordship abruptly; "Ambsace."

"I beg your lordship's pardon?"

"Ambsace. Word of seven letters. Meaning two. With S in the middle. Two aces. Ambsace."

Bunter's expression became beatified.

"Undoubtedly correct," he said, pulling a small sheet of paper from his pocket, and entering the word upon it in pencil. "I am extremely obliged to your lordship. In that case the 'indifferent cook in six letters ending with *red*' must be Alfred."

Lord Peter waved a dismissive hand.

On re-entering his bedroom, Lord Peter was astonished to see his sister Mary seated in his own particular chair and consuming his buttered eggs. He greeted her with a friendly acerbity, demanding why she should look him up at that unearthly hour.

"I'm riding with Freddy Arbuthnot," said her ladyship, "as you might see by my legs, if you were really as big a Sherlock as you make out."

"Riding," replied her brother, "I had already deduced, though I admit that Freddy's name was not writ large, to my before-breakfast eye, upon the knees of your breeches. But why this visit?"

"Well, because you were on the way," said Lady Mary, "and I'm booked up all day, and I want you to come and dine at the Soviet Club with me to-night."

"Good God, Mary, why? You know I hate the place. Cooking's beastly, the men don't shave, and the conversation gets my goat. Besides, last time I went there, your friend Goyles plugged me in the shoulder. I thought you'd chucked the Soviet Club."

"It isn't me. It's Hannah Marryat."

"What, the intense young woman with the badly bobbed hair and the brogues?"

"Well, she's never been able to afford a good hair-dresser. That's just what I want your help about."

"My dear child, I can't cut her hair for her. Bunter might. He can do most things."

"Silly. No. But she's got—that is, she used to have—an uncle, the very rich, curmudgeony sort, you know, who never gave anyone a penny. Well, he's dead, and they can't find his will."

"Perhaps he didn't make one."

"Oh, yes, he did. He wrote and told her so. But the nasty old thing hid it, and it can't be found."

"Is the will in her favour?"

"Yes."

"Who's the next of kin?"

"She and her mother are the only members of the family left."

"Well, then, she's only got to sit tight and she'll get the goods."

"No—because the horrid old man left two wills, and, if she can't find the latest one, they'll prove the first one. He explained that to her carefully."

"Oh, I see. H'm. By the way, I thought the young woman was a Socialist."

"Oh, she is. Terrifically so. One really can't help admiring her. She has done some wonderful work——"

"Yes, I dare say. But in that case I don't see why she need be so keen on getting uncle's dollars."

Mary began to chuckle.

"Ah! but that's where Uncle Meleager——"

"Uncle *what*?"

"Meleager. That's his name. Meleager Finch."

"Oh!"

"Yes—well, that's where he's been so clever. Unless she finds the new will, the old will comes into force and hands over every penny of the money to the funds of the Primrose League."

Lord Peter gave a little yelp of joy.

"Good for Uncle Meleager! But, look here, Polly, I'm a Tory, if anything. I'm certainly not a Red. Why should I help to snatch the good gold from the Primrose Leaguers and hand it over to the Third International? Uncle Meleager's a sport. I take to Uncle Meleager."

"Oh, but Peter, I really don't think she'll do that with it. Not at present, anyway. They're awfully poor, and her mother ought to have some frightfully difficult operation or something, and go and live abroad, so it really is ever so important they should get the money. And perhaps Hannah wouldn't be quite so Red if she'd ever had a bean of her own. Besides, you could make it a condition of helping her that she should go and get properly shingled at Bresil's."

"You are a very cynically-minded person," said his lordship. "However, it would be fun to have a go at Uncle M. Was he obliging enough to give any clues for finding the will?"

"He wrote a funny sort of letter, which we can't make head or tail of. Come to the club to-night and she'll show it to you."

"Right-ho! Seven o'clock do? And we could go on and see a show afterwards. Do you mind clearing out now? I'm going to get dressed."

Amid a deafening babble of voices in a low-pitched cellar, the Soviet Club meets and dines. Ethics and sociology, the latest vortices of the Whirligig school of verse, combine with the smoke of countless cigarettes to produce an inspissated atmosphere, through which flat, angular mural paintings dimly lower upon the revellers. There is painfully little room for the elbows, or indeed for any part of one's body. Lord Peter—his feet curled under his chair to avoid the stray kicks of the heavy brogues opposite him—was acutely conscious of an unbecoming attitude and an over-heated feeling about the head. He found it difficult to get any response from Hannah Marryat. Under her heavy, ill-cut fringe her dark eyes gloomed sombrely at him. At the same time he received a strong impression of something enormously vital. He had a sudden fancy that if she were set free from self-defensiveness and the importance of being earnest, she would exhibit unexpected powers of enjoyment. He was interested, but oppressed. Mary, to his great relief, suggested that they should have their coffee upstairs.

They found a quiet corner with comfortable chairs.

"Well, now," said Mary encouragingly.

"Of course you understand," said Miss Marryat mournfully, "that if it were not for the monstrous injustice of Uncle Meleager's other will, and mother being so ill, I shouldn't take any steps. But when there is £250,000, and the prospect of doing real good with it——"

"Naturally," said Lord Peter, "it isn't the money you care about, as the dear old bromide says, it's the principle of the thing. Right you are! Now supposin' we have a look at Uncle Meleager's letter."

Miss Marryat rummaged in a very large handbag and passed the paper over.

This was Uncle Meleager's letter, dated from Siena twelve months previously:

"My dear Hannah,—When I die—which I propose to do at my own convenience and not at that of my family—you will at last discover my monetary worth. It is, of course, considerably less than you had hoped, and quite fails, I assure you, adequately to represent my actual worth in the eyes of the discerning. I made my will yesterday, leaving the entire sum, such as it is, to the Primrose League—a body quite as fatuous as any other in our preposterous state, but which has the advantage of being peculiarly obnoxious to yourself. This will will be found in the safe in the library.

"I am not, however, unmindful of the fact that your mother is my sister, and you and she my only surviving relatives. I shall accordingly amuse myself by drawing up to-day a second will, superseding the other and leaving the money to you.

"I have always held that woman is a frivolous animal. A woman who pretends to be serious is wasting her time and spoiling her appearance. I consider that you have wasted your time to a really shocking extent. Accordingly, I intend to conceal this will, and that in such a manner that you will certainly never find it unless by the exercise of a sustained frivolity.

"I hope you will contrive to be frivolous enough to become the heiress of your affectionate

"UNCLE MELEAGER."

"Couldn't we use that letter as proof of the testator's intention, and fight the will?" asked Mary anxiously.

"'Fraid not," said Lord Peter. "You see, there's no evidence here that the will was ever actually drawn up. Though I suppose we could find the witnesses."

"We've tried," said Miss Marryat, "but, as you see, Uncle Meleager was travelling abroad at the time, and he probably got some obscure people in some obscure Italian town to witness it for him. We advertised, but got no answer."

"H'm. Uncle Meleager doesn't seem to have left things to chance. And, anyhow, wills are queer things, and so are the probate and divorce wallahs. Obviously the thing to do is to find the other will. Did the clues he speaks of turn up among his papers?"

"We hunted through everything. And, of course, we had the whole house searched from top to bottom for the will. But it was quite useless."

"You've not destroyed anything, of course. Who were the executors of the Primrose League will?"

"Mother and Mr. Sands, Uncle Meleager's solicitor. The will left mother a silver teapot for her trouble."

"I like Uncle Meleager more and more. Anyhow, he did the sporting thing. I'm beginnin' to enjoy this case like anything. Where did Uncle Meleager hang out?"

"It's an old house down at Dorking. It's rather quaint. Somebody had a fancy to build a little Roman villa sort of thing there, with a verandah behind, with columns and a pond in the front hall, and statues. It's very decent there just now, though it's awfully cold in the winter, with all those stone floors and stone stairs and the skylight over the hall! Mother said perhaps you would be very kind and come down and have a look at it."

"I'd simply love to. Can we start to-morrow? I promise you we'll be frivolous enough to please even Uncle Meleager, if you'll do your bit, Miss Marryat. Won't we, Mary?"

"Rather! And, I say, hadn't we better be moving if we're going to the Pallambra?"

"I never go to music halls," said Miss Marryat ungraciously.

"Oh, but you must come to-night," said his lordship persuasively. "It's so frivolous. Just think how it would please Uncle Meleager."

Accordingly, the next day found the party, including the indispensable Mr. Bunter, assembled at Uncle Meleager's house. Pending the settlement of the will question, there had seemed every reason why Mr. Finch's executrix and next-of-kin should live in the house, thus providing every facility for what Lord Peter called the "Treasure-hunt." After being introduced to Mrs. Marryat, who was an invalid and remained in her room, Lady Mary and her brother were shown over the house by Miss Marryat, who explained to them how carefully the search had been conducted. Every paper had been examined, every book in the library scrutinised page by page, the walls and chimneys tapped for hiding-places, the boards taken up, and so forth, but with no result.

"Y'know," said his lordship, "I'm sure you've been going the wrong way to work. My idea is, old Uncle Meleager was a man of his word. If he said frivolous, he meant really frivolous. Something beastly silly. I wonder what it was."

He was still wondering when he went up to dress. Bunter was putting studs in his shirt. Lord Peter gazed thoughtfully at him, and then enquired:

"Are any of Mr. Finch's old staff still here?"

"Yes, my lord. The cook and the housekeeper. Wonderful old gentleman they say he was, too. Eighty-three, but as up-to-date as you please. Had his wireless in his bedroom, and enjoyed the Savoy bands every night of his life. Followed his politics, and was always ready with the details of the latest big law-cases. If a young lady came to see him, he'd like to see she had her hair shingled and the latest style in fashions. They say he took up cross-words as soon as they came in, and was remarkably quick at solving them, my lord, and inventing them. Took a £10 prize in the *Daily Yell* for one, and was wonderfully pleased to get it, they say, my lord, rich as he was."

"Indeed."

"Yes, my lord. He was a great man for acrostics before that, I understood them to say, but, when cross-words came in, he threw away his acrostics and said he liked the new game better. Wonderfully adaptable, if I may say so, he seems to have been for an old gentleman."

"Was he, by Jove?" said his lordship absently, and then, with sudden energy:

"Bunter, I'd like to double your salary, but I suppose you'd take it as an insult." The conversation bore fruit at dinner.

"What," enquired his lordship, "happened to Uncle Meleager's cross-words?"

"Cross-words?" said Hannah Marryat, knitting her heavy brows. "Oh, those puzzle things! Poor old man, he went mad over them. He had every newspaper sent him, and in his last illness he'd be trying to fill the wretched things in. It was worse than his acrostics and his jig-saw puzzles. Poor old creature, he must have been senile, I'm afraid. Of course, we looked through them, but there wasn't anything there. We put them all in the attic."

"The attic for me," said Lord Peter.

"And for me," said Mary. "I don't believe there was anything senile about Uncle Meleager."

The evening was warm, and they had dined in the little viridarium at the back of the house, with its tall vases and hanging baskets of flowers and little marble statues.

"Is there an attic here?" said Peter. "It seems—such a—well, such an un-attic thing to have in a house like this."

"It's just a horrid, poky little hole over the porch," said Miss Marryat, rising and leading the way. "Don't tumble into the pond, will you? It's a great nuisance having it there, especially at night. I always tell them to leave a light on."

Lord Peter glanced into the miniature impluvium, with its tiling of red, white, and black marble.

"That's not a very classic design," he observed.

"No. Uncle Meleager used to complain about it and say he must have it altered. There was a proper one once, I believe, but it got damaged, and the man before Uncle Meleager had it replaced by some local idiot. He built three bay windows out of the dining-room at the same time, which made it very much lighter and pleasanter, of course, but it looks awful. Now, this tiling is all right; uncle put that in himself."

She pointed to a mosaic dog at the threshold, with the motto, "Cave canem," and Lord Peter recognised it as a copy of a Pompeian original.

A narrow stair brought them to the "attic," where the Wimseys flung themselves with enthusiasm upon a huge heap of dusty old newspapers and manuscripts. The latter seemed the likelier field, so they started with them. They consisted of a quantity of cross-words in manuscript—presumably the children of Uncle Meleager's own brain. The square, the list of definitions, and the solution were in every case neatly pinned together. Some (early efforts, no doubt) were childishly simple, but others were difficult, with allusive or punning clues; some of the ordinary newspaper type, others in the form of rhymed distichs. They scrutinised the solutions closely, and searched the definitions for acrostics or hidden words, unsuccessfully for a long time.

"This one's a funny one," said Mary, "nothing seems to fit. Oh! it's two pinned together. No, it isn't—yes, it is—it's only been pinned up wrong. Peter, have you seen the puzzle belonging to these clues anywhere?"

"What one's that?"

"Well, it's numbered rather funnily, with Roman and Arabic numerals, and it starts off with a thing that hasn't got any numbers at all:

"Truth, poor girl, was nobody's daughter;
She took off her clothes and jumped into the water."

"Frivolous old wretch!" said Miss Marryat.

"Friv—here, gimme that!" cried Lord Peter. "Look here, I say, Miss Marryat, you oughtn't to have overlooked this."

"I thought it just belonged to that other square."

"Not it. It's different. I believe it's our thing. Listen:

"Your expectation to be rich
Here will reach its highest pitch.

That's one for you, Miss Marryat. Mary, hunt about. We *must* find the square that belongs to this."

But, though they turned everything upside-down, they could find no square with Roman and Arabic numerals.

"Hang it all!" said Peter, "it must be made to fit one of these others. Look! I know what he's done. He's just taken a fifteen-letter square, and numbered it with Roman figures one way and Arabic the other. I bet it fits into that one it was pinned up with."

But the one it was pinned up with turned out to have only thirteen squares.

"Dash it all," said his lordship, "we'll have to carry the whole lot down, and work away at it till we find the one it *does* fit."

He snatched up a great bundle of newspapers, and led the way out. The others followed, each with an armful. The search had taken some time, and the atrium was in semi-darkness.

"Where shall I take them?" asked Lord Peter, calling back over his shoulder.

"Hi!" cried Mary; and, "Look where you're going!" cried her friend.

They were too late. A splash and a flounder proclaimed that Lord Peter had walked, like Johnny Head-in-Air, over the edge of the impluvium, papers and all.

"You ass!" said Mary.

His lordship scrambled out, spluttering, and Hannah Marryat suddenly burst out into the first laugh Peter had ever heard her give.

"Truth, they say, was nobody's daughter;
She took off her clothes and fell into the water"

she proclaimed.

"Well, I couldn't take my clothes off with you here, could I?" grumbled Lord Peter. "We'll have to fish out the papers. I'm afraid they've got a bit damp."

Miss Marryat turned on the lights, and they started to clear the basin.

"Truth, poor girl——" began Lord Peter, and suddenly, with a little shriek, began to dance on the marble edge of the impluvium.

"One, two, three, four, five, six——"

"Quite, quite demented," said Mary. "How shall I break it to mother?"

"Thirteen, fourteen, *fifteen*!" cried his lordship, and sat down, suddenly and damply, exhausted by his own excitement.

"Feeling better?" asked his sister acidly.

"I'm well. I'm all right. Everything's all right. I *love* Uncle Meleager. Fifteen squares each way. Look at it. *Look* at it. The truth's in the water. Didn't he say so. Oh, frabjous day! Calloo! callay! I chortle. Mary, what became of those definitions?"

"They're in your pocket, all damp," said Mary.

Lord Peter snatched them out hurriedly.

"It's all right, they haven't run," he said. "Oh, *darling* Uncle Meleager. Can you drain the impluvium, Miss Marryat, and find a bit of charcoal. Then I'll get some dry clothes on and we'll get down to it. Don't you see? *There's* your missing cross-word square—on the floor of the impluvium!"

It took, however, some time to get the basin emptied, and it was not till next morning that the party, armed with sticks of charcoal, squatted down in the empty impluvium to fill in Uncle Meleager's cross-word on the marble tiles. Their first difficulty was to decide whether the red squares counted as stops or had to be filled in, but, after a few definitions had been solved, the construction of the puzzle grew apace. The investigators grew steadily hotter and more thickly covered with charcoal, while the attentive Mr. Bunter hurried to and fro between the atrium and the library, and the dictionaries piled up on the edge of the impluvium.

Here was Uncle Meleager's cross-word square:

"Truth, poor girl, was nobody's daughter;
She took off her clothes and jumped into the water."

Across.

I.1.   Foolish or wise, yet one remains alone,
         'Twixt Strength and Justice on a heavenly throne.

XI.1.   O to what ears the chink of gold was sweet!
         The greed for treasure brought him but defeat.

"That's a hint to us," said Lord Peter.

I.2.   One drop of vinegar to two of oil
         Dresses this curly head sprung from the soil.

X.2.   Nothing itself, it needs but little more
         To be that nothingness the Preacher saw.

I.3.   Dusty though my fellows be,
         We are a kingly company.

IV.3.   Have your own will, though here, I hold,

The new is *not* a patch upon the old.

XIV.3. Any loud cry would do as well,
Or so the poet's verses tell.

I.4. This is the most unkindest cut of all,
Except your skill be mathematical.

X.4. Little and hid from mortal sight,
I darkly work to make all light.

I.5. The need for this (like that it's cut off short)
The building of a tower to humans taught.

XI.5. "More than mind discloses and more than men believe"
(A definition by a man whom Pussyfoot doth grieve).

II.6. Backward observe her turn her way,
The way of wisdom, wise men say.

VII.6. Grew long ago by river's edge
Where grows to-day the common sedge.

XII.6. One of three by which, they say,
You'll know the Cornishmen alway.

VI.7. Blow upon blow; five more the vanquished Roman shows;
And if the foot slip one, on crippled feet one goes.

I.8. By this Jew's work the whole we find,
In a glass clearly, darkly in the mind.

IX.8. Little by little see it grow
Till cut off short by hammer-blow.

VI.9. Watch him go, heel and toe,
Across the wide Karroo!

II.10. In expectation to be rich
Here you reach the highest pitch.

VII.10. Of this, concerning nothing, much—
Too often do we hear of such!

XII.10. O'er land and sea, passing on deadly wings,
Pain to the strong, to weaklings death it brings.

I.11. Requests like these, however long they be,
Stop just too soon for common courtesy.

XI.11. Cæsar, the living dead salute thee here,
Facing for thy delight tooth, claw, and spear.

I.12. One word had served, but he in ranting vein
"Lend me your ears" must mouth o'er Cæsar slain.

X.12. Helical circumvolution
Adumbrates correct solution.

I.13. One that works for Irish men
Both by word and deed and pen.

"That's an easy one," said Miss Marryat.

IV.13. Seven out of twelve this number makes complete
As the sun journeys on from seat to seat.

XIV.13. My brothers play with planets; Cicero,

Master of words, my master is below.

I.14. Free of her jesses let the falcon fly,
With sight undimmed into the azure sky.

X.14. And so you dine with Borgia? Let me lend
You this as a precaution, my poor friend.

I.15. Friendship carried to excess
Got him in a horrid mess.

XI.15. Smooth and elastic and, I guess,
The dearest treasure you possess.

Down.

1.I. If step by step the Steppes you wander through
Many of those in this, of these in those you'll view.

"Bunter," said Lord Peter, "bring me a whisky-and-soda!"

11.I. If me without my head you do,
Then generously my head renew,
Or put it to my hinder end—
Your cheer it shall nor mar nor mend.

1.II. Quietly, quietly, 'twixt edge and edge,
Do this unto the thin end of the wedge.

10.II. "Something that hath a reference to my state?"
Just as you like, it shall be written straight.

1.III. When all is read, then give the world its due,
And never need the world read this of you.

"That's a comfort," said Lady Mary. "It shows we're on the right lines."

4.III. Sing Nunc Dimittis and Magnificat—
But look a little farther back than that.

14.III. Here in brief epitome
Attribute of royalty.

1.IV. Lo! at a glance
The Spanish gipsy and her dance.

10.IV. Bring me skin and a needle or a stick—
A needle does it slowly, a stick does it quick.

1.V. It was a brazen business when
King Phalaris made these for men.

11.V. This king (of whom not much is known),
By Heaven's mercy was o'erthrown.

2.VI. "Bid ᾿ον και μη ᾿ον farewell?" Nay, in this
The sterner Roman stands by that which is.

7.VI. This the termination is
Of many minds' activities.

12.VI. I mingle on Norwegian shore,
With ebbing water's backward roar.

6.VII.	I stand, a ladder to renown,
	Set 'twixt the stars and Milan town.
1.VIII.	Highest and lowliest both to me lay claim,
	The little hyssop and the king of fame.

"That makes that point about the squares clear," said Mary.
"I think it's even more significant," said her brother.

9.VIII.	This sensible old man refused to tread
	The path to Hades in a youngster's stead.
6.IX.	Long since, at Nature's call, they let it drop,
	Thoughtlessly thoughtful for our next year's crop.
2.X.	To smallest words great speakers greatness give;
	Here Rome propounded her alternative.
7.X.	We heap up many with toil and trouble,
	And find that the whole of our gain is a bubble.
12.X.	Add it among the hidden things—
	A fishy tale to light it brings.
1.XI.	"Lions," said a Gallic critic, "are not these."
	Benevolent souls—they'd make your heart's blood freeze.
11.XI.	An epithet for husky fellows,
	That stand, all robed in greens and yellows.
1.XII.	Whole without holes behold me here,
	My meaning should be wholly clear.
10.XII.	Running all around, never setting foot to floor,
	If there isn't one in this room, there may be one next door.
1.XIII.	Ye gods! think also of that goddess' name
	Whose might two hours on end the mob proclaim.
4.XIII.	The Priest uplifts his voice on high,
	The choristers make their reply.
14.XIII.	When you've guessed it, with one voice
	You'll say it was a golden choice.
1.XIV.	Shall learning die amid a war's alarms?
	I, at my birth, was clasped in iron arms.
10.XIV.	At sunset see the labourer now
	Loose all his oxen from the plough.
1.XV.	Without a miracle it cannot be—
	At this point, Solver, bid him pray for thee!
11.XV.	Two thousand years ago and more
	(Just as we do to-day),
	The Romans saw these distant lights—
	But, oh! how hard the way!

The most remarkable part of the search—or so Lord Peter thought—was its effect on Miss Marryat. At first she hovered disconsolately on the margin, aching with wounded dignity, yet ashamed to dissociate herself from people who were toiling so hard and so cheerfully in her cause.

"I think that's so-and-so," Mary would say hopefully.

And her brother would reply enthusiastically, "Holed it in one, old lady. Good for you! We've got it this time, Miss Marryat"—and explain it.

And Hannah Marryat would say with a snort:

"That's just the childish kind of joke Uncle Meleager *would* make."

Gradually, however, the fascination of seeing the squares fit together caught her, and, when the first word appeared which showed that the searchers were definitely on the right track, she lay down flat on the floor and peered over Lord Peter's shoulder as he grovelled below, writing letters in charcoal, rubbing them out with his handkerchief and mopping his heated face, till the Moor of Venice had nothing on him in the matter of blackness. Once, half scornfully, half timidly, she made a suggestion; twice, she made a suggestion; the third time she had an inspiration. The next minute she was down in the mélée, crawling over the tiles flushed and excited, wiping important letters out with her knees as fast as Peter could write them in, poring over the pages of Roget, her eyes gleaming under her tumbled black fringe.

Hurried meals of cold meat and tea sustained the exhausted party, and towards sunset Peter, with a shout of triumph, added the last letter to the square.

They crawled out and looked at it.

"All the words can't be clues," said Mary. "I think it must be just those four."

"Yes, undoubtedly. It's quite clear. We've only got to look it up. Where's a Bible?"

Miss Marryat hunted it out from the pile of reference books. "But that isn't the name of a Bible book," she said. "It's those things they have at evening service."

"That's all you know," said Lord Peter. "I was brought up religious, I was. It's Vulgate, that's what that is. You're quite right, of course, but, as Uncle Meleager says, we must 'look a little further back than that.' Here you are. Now, then."

"But it doesn't say what chapter."

"So it doesn't. I mean, nor it does."

"And, anyhow, all the chapters are too short."

"Damn! Oh! Here, suppose we just count right on from the beginning—one, two, three——"

"Seventeen in chapter one, eighteen, nineteen—this must be it."

Two fair heads and one dark one peered excitedly at the small print, Bunter hovering decorously on the outskirts.

"O my dove, that art in the clefts of the rock, in the covert of the steep place."

"Oh, dear!" said Mary, disappointed, "that does sound rather hopeless. Are you sure you've counted right? It might mean *anything*."

Lord Peter scratched his head.

"This is a bit of a blow," he said. "I don't like Uncle Meleager half as much as I did. Old beast!"

"After all our work!" moaned Mary.

"It must be right," cried Miss Marryat. "Perhaps there's some kind of an anagram in it. We can't give up now!"

"Bravo!" said Lord Peter. "That's the spirit. 'Fraid we're in for another outburst of frivolity, Miss Marryat."

"Well, it's been great fun," said Hannah Marryat.

"If you will excuse me," began the deferential voice of Bunter.

"I'd forgotten you, Bunter," said his lordship. "Of course you can put us right—you always can. Where have we gone wrong?"

"I was about to observe, my lord, that the words you mention do not appear to agree with my recollection of the passage in question. In my mother's Bible, my lord, it ran, I fancy, somewhat differently."

Lord Peter closed the volume and looked at the back of it.

"Naturally," he said, "you are right again, of course. This is a Revised Version. It's your fault, Miss Marryat. You *would* have a Revised Version. But can we imagine Uncle Meleager with one? No. Bring me Uncle Meleager's Bible."

"Come and look in the library," cried Miss Marryat, snatching him by the hand and running. "Don't be so dreadfully calm."

On the centre of the library table lay a huge and venerable Bible—reverend in age and tooled leather binding. Lord Peter's hands caressed it, for a noble old book was like a song to his soul. Sobered by its beauty, they turned the yellow pages over:

"In the clefts of the rocks, in the secret places of the stairs."

"Miss Marryat," said his lordship, "if your Uncle's will is not concealed in the staircase, then—well, all I can say is, he's played a rotten trick on us," he concluded lamely.

"Shall we try the main staircase, or the little one up to the porch?"

"Oh, the main one, I think. I hope it won't mean pulling it down. No. Somebody would have noticed if Uncle Meleager had done anything drastic in that way. It's probably quite a simple hiding-place. Wait a minute. Let's ask the housekeeper."

Mrs. Meakers was called, and perfectly remembered that about nine months previously Mr. Finch had pointed out to her a "kind of a crack like" on the under surface of the staircase, and had had a man in to fill it up. Certainly, she could point out the exact place. There was the mark of the plaster filling quite clear.

"Hurray!" cried Lord Peter. "Bunter—a chisel or something. Uncle Meleager, Uncle Meleager, we've *got* you! Miss Marryat, I think yours should be the hand to strike the blow. It's your staircase, you know—at least, if we find the will, so if any destruction has to be done it's up to you."

Breathless they stood round, while with a few blows the new plaster flaked off, disclosing a wide chink in the stonework. Hannah Marryat flung down hammer and chisel and groped in the gap.

"There's something," she gasped. "Lift me up; I can't reach. Oh, it is! it is! it *is* it!" And she withdrew her hand, grasping a long, sealed envelope, bearing the superscription:

Positively the Last Will and Testament of Meleager Finch.

Miss Marryat gave a yodel of joy and flung her arms round Lord Peter's neck. Mary executed a joy-dance. "I'll tell the world," she proclaimed.

"Come and tell mother!" cried Miss Marryat.

Mr. Bunter interposed.

"Your lordship will excuse me," he said firmly, "but your lordship's face is all over charcoal."

"Black but comely," said Lord Peter, "but I submit to your reproof. How clever we've all been. How topping everything is. How rich you are going to be. How late it is and how hungry I am. Yes, Bunter, I will wash my face. Is there anything else I can do for anybody while I feel in the mood?"

"If your lordship would be so kind," said Mr. Bunter, producing a small paper from his pocket, "I should be grateful if you could favour me with a South African quadruped in six letters, beginning with Q."

WHERE THEIR FIRE IS NOT QUENCHED

May Sinclair

May Sinclair (1863–1946) coined the term 'stream of consciousness' and was an important part of the modernist and suffragist movements. She is best known for her novel *The Life and Death of Harriett Frean* and her short stories famously explored the uncanny.

There was nobody in the orchard. Harriott Leigh went out, carefully, through the iron gate into the field. She had made the latch slip into its notch without a sound.

The path slanted widely up the field from the orchard gate to the stile under the elder tree. George Waring waited for her there.

Years afterwards, when she thought of George Waring she smelt the sweet, hot, wine-scent of the elder flowers. Years afterwards, when she smelt elder-flowers she saw George Waring, with his beautiful, gentle face, like a poet's or a musician's, his black-blue eyes, and sleek, olive-brown hair. He was a naval lieutenant.

Yesterday he had asked her to marry him and she had consented. But her father hadn't, and she had come to tell him that and say goodbye before he left her. His ship was to sail the next day.

He was eager and excited. He couldn't believe that anything could stop their happiness, that anything he didn't want to happen could happen.

'Well?' he said.

'He's a perfect beast, George. He won't let us. He says we're too young.'

'I was twenty last August,' he said, aggrieved.

'And I shall be seventeen in September.'

'And this is June. We're quite old, really. How long does he mean us to wait?'

'Three years.'

'Three years before we can be engaged even – Why, we might be dead.'

She put her arms round him to make him feel safe. They kissed; and the sweet, hot, wine-scent of the elderflowers mixed with their kisses. They stood, pressed close together, under the elder tree.

Across the yellow fields of charlock they heard the village clock strike seven. Up in the house a gong clanged.

'Darling, I must go,' she said.

'Oh stay – Stay *five* minutes.'

He pressed her close. It lasted five minutes, and five more. Then he was running fast down the road to the station, while Harriott went along the field-path, slowly, struggling with her tears.

'He'll be back in three months,' she said. 'I can live through three months.'

But he never came back. There was something wrong with the engines of his ship, the *Alexandra*. Three weeks later she went down in the Mediterranean, and George with her.

Harriott said she didn't care how soon she died now. She was quite sure it would be soon, because she couldn't live without him.

Five years passed.

The two lines of beech trees stretched on and on, the whole length of the Park, a broad green drive between. When you came to the middle they branched off right and left in the form of a cross, and at the end of the right arm there was a white stucco pavilion with pillars and a three-cornered pediment like a Greek temple. At the end of the left arm, the west entrance to the Park, double gates and a side door.

Harriott, on her stone seat at the back of the pavilion, could see Stephen Philpotts the very minute he came through the side door.

He had asked her to wait for him there. It was the place he always chose to read his poems aloud in. The poems were a pretext. She knew what he was going to say. And she knew what she would answer.

There were elder bushes in flower at the back of the pavilion, and Harriott thought of George Waring. She told herself that George was nearer to her now than he could ever have been, living. If she married Stephen she would not be unfaithful, because she loved him with another part of herself. It was not as though Stephen were taking George's place. She loved Stephen with her soul, in an unearthly way.

But her body quivered like a stretched wire when the door opened and the young man came towards her down the drive under the beech trees.

She loved him; she loved his slenderness, his darkness and sallow whiteness, his black eyes lighting up with the intellectual flame, the way his black hair swept back from his forehead, the way he walked, tiptoe, as if his feet were lifted with wings.

He sat down beside her. She could see his hands tremble. She felt that her moment was coming; it had come.

'I wanted to see you alone because there's something I must say to you. I don't quite know how to begin . . .'

Her lips parted. She panted lightly.

'You've heard me speak of Sybill Foster?'

Her voice came stammering, 'N-no, Stephen. Did you?'

'Well, I didn't mean to, till I knew it was all right. I only heard yesterday.'

'Heard what?'

'Why, that she'll have me. Oh, Harriott – do you know what it's like to be terribly happy?'

She knew. She had known just now, the moment before he told her. She sat there, stone-cold and stiff, listening to his raptures; listening to her own voice saying she was glad.

Ten years passed.

*

Harriott Leigh sat waiting in the drawing-room of a small house in Maida Vale. She had lived there ever since her father's death two years before.

She was restless. She kept on looking at the clock to see if it was four, the hour that Oscar Wade had appointed. She was not sure that he would come, after she had sent him away yesterday.

She now asked herself, why, when she had sent him away yesterday, she had let him come today. Her motives were not altogether clear. If she really meant what she had said then, she oughtn't to let him come to her again. Never again.

She had shown him plainly what she meant. She could see herself, sitting very straight in her chair, uplifted by a passionate integrity, while he stood before her, hanging his head, ashamed and beaten; she could feel again the throb in her voice as she kept on saying that she couldn't, she couldn't; he must see that she couldn't; that no, nothing would make her change her mind; she couldn't forget he had a wife; that he must think of Muriel.

To which he had answered savagely: 'I needn't. That's all over. We only live together for the look of the thing.'

And she, serenely, with great dignity: 'And for the look of the thing, Oscar, we must leave off seeing each other. Please go.'

'Do you mean it?'

'Yes. We must never see each other again.'

And he had gone then, ashamed and beaten.

She could see him, squaring his broad shoulders to meet the blow. And she was sorry for him. She told herself she had been unnecessarily hard. Why shouldn't they see each other again, now he understood where they must draw the line? Until yesterday the line had never been very clearly drawn. Today she meant to ask him to forget what he had said to her. Once it was forgotten, they could go on being friends as if nothing had happened.

It was four o'clock. Half-past. Five. She had finished tea and given him up when, between the half-hour and six o'clock, he came.

He came as he had come a dozen times, with his measured, deliberate, thoughtful tread, carrying himself well braced, with a sort of held-in arrogance, his great shoulders heaving. He was a man of about forty, broad and tall, lean-flanked and short-necked, his straight, handsome features showing small and even in the big square face and in the flush that swamped it. The close-clipped, reddish-brown moustache bristled forwards from the pushed-out upper lip. His small, flat eyes shone, reddish-brown, eager and animal.

She liked to think of him when he was not there, but always at the first sight of him she felt a slight shock. Physically, he was very far from her admired ideal. So different from George Waring and Stephen Philpotts.

He sat down, facing her.

There was an embarrassed silence, broken by Oscar Wade.

'Well, Harriott, you said I could come.' He seemed to be throwing the responsibility on her. 'So I suppose you've forgiven me,' he said.

'Oh, yes, Oscar, I've forgiven you.'

He said she'd better show it by coming to dine with him somewhere that evening.

She could give no reason to herself for going. She simply went.

He took her to a restaurant in Soho. Oscar Wade dined well, even extravagantly, giving each dish its importance. She liked his extravagance. He had none of the mean virtues.

It was over. His flushed, embarrassed silence told her what he was thinking. But when he had seen her home he left her at her garden gate. He had thought better of it.

She was not sure whether she were glad or sorry. She had had her moment of righteous exaltation and she had enjoyed it. But there was no joy in the weeks that followed it. She had given up Oscar Wade because she didn't want him very much; and now she wanted him furiously, perversely, because she had given him up. Though he had no resemblance to her ideal, she couldn't live without him.

She dined with him again and again, till she knew Schnebler's Restaurant by heart, the white panelled walls picked out with gold; the white pillars, and the curling gold fronds of their capitals; the Turkey carpets, blue and crimson, soft under her feet; the thick crimson velvet cushions, that clung to her skirts; the glitter of silver and glass on the innumerable white circles of the tables. And the faces of the diners, red, white, pink, brown, grey and sallow, distorted and excited; the curled mouths that twisted as they ate; the convoluted electric bulbs pointing, pointing down at them, under the red, crinkled shades. All shimmering in a thick air that the red light stained as wine stains water.

And Oscar's face, flushed with his dinner. Always, when he leaned back from the table and brooded in silence she knew what he was thinking. His heavy eyelids would lift; she would find his eyes fixed on hers, wondering, considering.

She knew now what the end would be. She thought of George Waring, and Stephen Philpotts, and of her life, cheated. She hadn't chosen Oscar, she hadn't really wanted him; but now he had forced himself on her she couldn't afford to let him go. Since George died no man had loved her, no other man ever would. And she was sorry for him when she thought of him going from her, beaten and ashamed.

She was certain, before he was, of the end. Only she didn't know when and where and how it would come. That was what Oscar knew.

It came at the close of one of their evenings when they had dined in a private sitting-room. He said he couldn't stand the heat and noise of the public restaurant.

She went before him, up a steep, red-carpeted stair to a white door on the second landing.

From time to time they repeated the furtive, hidden adventure. Sometimes she met him in the room above Schnebler's. Sometimes, when her maid was out, she received him at her house in Maida Vale. But that was dangerous, not to be risked too often.

Oscar declared himself unspeakably happy. Harriott was not quite sure. This was love, the thing she had never had, that she had dreamed of, hungered and thirsted for; but now she had it she was not satisfied. Always she looked for something just beyond it, some mystic, heavenly rapture, always beginning to come, that never came. There was something about Oscar that repelled her. But because she had taken him for her lover, she couldn't bring herself to admit that it was a certain coarseness. She looked another way and pretended it wasn't there. To justify herself, she fixed her mind on his good qualities, his generosity, his strength, the way he had built up his engineering business. She made him take her over his works and show her his great dynamos. She made him lend her the books he read. But always, when she tried to talk to him, he let her see that *that* wasn't what she was there for.

'My dear girl, we haven't time,' he said. 'It's waste of our priceless moments.'

She persisted. 'There's something wrong about it all if we can't talk to each other.'

He was irritated. 'Women never seem to consider that a man can get all the talk he wants from other men. What's wrong is our meeting in this unsatisfactory way. We ought to live together. It's the only sane thing. I would, only I don't want to break up Muriel's home and make her miserable.'

'I thought you said she wouldn't care.'

'My dear, she cares for her home and her position and the children. You forget the children.'

Yes. She had forgotten the children. She had forgotten Muriel. She had left off thinking of Oscar as a man with a wife and children and a home.

He had a plan. His mother-in-law was coming to stay with Muriel in October and he would get away. He would go to Paris, and Harriott should come to him there. He could say he went on business. No need to lie about it; he *had* business in Paris.

He engaged rooms in an hotel in the rue de Rivoli. They spent two weeks there.

For three days Oscar was madly in love with Harriott and Harriott with him. As she lay awake she would turn on the light and look at him as he slept at her side. Sleep made him beautiful and innocent; it laid a fine, smooth tissue over his coarseness; it made his mouth gentle; it entirely hid his eyes.

In six days reaction had set in. At the end of the tenth day, Harriott, returning with Oscar from Montmartre, burst into a fit of crying. When questioned, she answered wildly that the Hotel Saint Pierre was too hideously ugly; it was getting on her nerves. Mercifully Oscar explained her state as fatigue following excitement. She tried hard to believe that she was miserable because her love was purer and more spiritual than Oscar's; but all the time she knew perfectly well she had cried from pure boredom. She was in love with Oscar, and Oscar bored her. Oscar was in love with her, and she bored him. At close quarters, day in and day out, each was revealed to the other as an incredible bore.

At the end of the second week she began to doubt whether she had ever been really in love with him.

Her passion returned for a little while after they got back to London. Freed from the unnatural strain which Paris had put on them, they persuaded themselves that their romantic temperaments were better fitted to the old life of casual adventure.

Then, gradually, the sense of danger began to wake in them. They lived in perpetual fear, face to face with all the chances of discovery. They tormented themselves and each other by imagining possibilities that they would never have considered in their first fine moments. It was as though they were beginning to ask themselves if it were, after all, worth while running such awful risks, for all they got out of it. Oscar still swore that if he had been free he would have married her. He pointed out that his intentions at any rate were regular. But she asked herself: Would I marry *him*? Marriage would be the Hotel Saint Pierre all over again, without any possibility of escape. But, if she wouldn't marry him, was she in love with him? That was the test. Perhaps it was a good thing he wasn't free. Then she told herself that these doubts were morbid, and that the question wouldn't arise.

One evening Oscar called to see her. He had come to tell her that Muriel was ill.

'Seriously ill?'

'I'm afraid so. It's pleurisy. May turn to pneumonia. We shall know one way or another in the next few days.'

A terrible fear seized upon Harriott. Muriel might die of her pleurisy; and if Muriel died, she would have to marry Oscar. He was looking at her queerly, as if he knew what she was thinking, and she could see that the same thought had occurred to him and that he was frightened too.

Muriel got well again; but their danger had enlightened them. Muriel's life was now inconceivably precious to them both; she stood between them and that permanent union, which they dreaded and yet would not have the courage to refuse.

After enlightenment the rupture.

It came from Oscar, one evening when he sat with her in her drawing-room.

'Harriott,' he said, 'do you know I'm thinking seriously of settling down?'

'How do you mean, settling down?'

'Patching it up with Muriel, poor girl ... Has it never occurred to you that this little affair of ours can't go on for ever?'

'You don't want it to go on?'

'I don't want to have any humbug about it. For God's sake, let's be straight. If it's done, it's done. Let's end it decently.'

'I see. You want to get rid of me.'

'That's a beastly way of putting it.'

'Is there any way that isn't beastly? The whole thing's beastly. I should have thought you'd have stuck to it now you've made it what you wanted. When I haven't an ideal, I haven't a single illusion, when you've destroyed everything you didn't want.'

'What didn't I want?'

'The clean, beautiful part of it. The part *I* wanted.'

'My part at least was real. It was cleaner and more beautiful than all that putrid stuff you wrapped it up in. You were a hypocrite, Harriott, and I wasn't. You're a hypocrite now if you say you weren't happy with me.'

'I was never really happy. Never for one moment. There was always something I missed. Something you didn't give me. Perhaps you couldn't.'

'No. I wasn't spiritual enough,' he sneered.

'You were not. And you made me what you were.'

'Oh, I noticed that you were always very spiritual *after* you'd got what you wanted.'

'What I wanted?' she cried. 'Oh, my God –'

'If you ever knew what you wanted.'

'What – I – wanted,' she repeated, drawing out her bitterness.

'Come,' he said, 'why not be honest? Face facts. I was awfully gone on you. You were awfully gone on me – once. We got tired of each other and it's over. But at least you might own we had a good time while it lasted.'

'A good time?'

'Good enough for me.'

'For you, because for you love only means one thing. Everything that's high and noble in it you dragged down to that, till there's nothing left for us but that. *That's* what you made of love.'

Twenty years passed.

It was Oscar who died first, three years after the rupture. He did it suddenly one evening, falling down in a fit of apoplexy.

His death was an immense relief to Harriott. Perfect security had been impossible as long as he was alive. But now there wasn't a living soul who knew her secret.

Still, in the first moment of shock Harriott told herself that Oscar dead would be nearer to her than ever. She forgot how little she had wanted him to be near her, alive. And long before the twenty years had passed she had contrived to persuade herself that he had never been near to her at all. It was incredible that she had ever known such a person as Oscar Wade. As for their affair, she couldn't think of Harriott Leigh as the sort of woman to whom such a thing could happen. Schnebler's and the Hotel Saint Pierre ceased to figure among prominent images of her past. Her memories, if she had allowed herself to remember, would have clashed disagreeably with the reputation for sanctity which she had now acquired.

For Harriott at fifty-two was the friend and helper of the Reverend Clement Farmer, Vicar of St Mary the Virgin's, Maida Vale. She worked as a deaconess in his parish, wearing the uniform of a deaconess, the semi-religious gown, the cloak, the bonnet and veil, the cross and rosary, the holy smile. She was also secretary to the Maida Vale and Kilburn Home for Fallen Girls.

Her moments of excitement came when Clement Farmer, the lean, austere likeness of Stephen Philpotts, in his cassock and lace-bordered surplice, issued from the vestry, when he mounted the pulpit, when he stood before the altar rails and lifted up his arms in the Benediction; her moments of ecstasy when she received the Sacrament from his hands. And she had moments of calm happiness when his study door closed on their communion. All these moments were saturated with a solemn holiness.

And they were insignificant compared with the moment of her dying.

She lay dozing in her white bed under the black crucifix with the ivory Christ. The basins and medicine bottles had been cleared from the table by her pillow; it was spread for the last rites. The priest moved quietly about the room, arranging the candles, the Prayer Book and the Holy Sacrament. Then he drew a chair to her bedside and watched with her, waiting for her to come up out of her doze.

She woke suddenly. Her eyes were fixed upon him. She had a flash of lucidity.

She was dying, and her dying made her supremely important to Clement Farmer.

'Are you ready?' he asked.

'Not yet. I think I'm afraid. Make me not afraid.'

He rose and lit the two candles on the altar. He took down the crucifix from the wall and stood it against the foot-rail of the bed.

She sighed. That was not what she had wanted.

'You will not be afraid now,' he said.

'I'm not afraid of the hereafter. I suppose you get used to it. Only it may be terrible just at first.'

'Our first state will depend very much on what we are thinking of at our last hour.'

'There'll be my – confession,' she said.

'And after it you will receive the Sacrament. Then you will have your mind fixed firmly upon God and your Redeemer . . . Do you feel able to make your confession now, Sister? Everything is ready.'

Her mind went back over her past and found Oscar Wade there. She wondered: Should she confess to him about Oscar Wade? One moment she thought it was possible; the next she knew that she couldn't. She could not. It wasn't necessary. For twenty years he had not been part of her life. No. She wouldn't confess about Oscar Wade. She had been guilty of other sins.

She made a careful selection.

'I have cared too much for the beauty of this world . . . I have failed in charity to my poor girls. Because of my intense repugnance to their sin . . . I have thought, often, about – people I love, when I should have been thinking about God.'

After that she received the Sacrament.

'Now,' he said, 'there is nothing to be afraid of.'

'I won't be afraid if – if you would hold my hand.'

He held it. And she lay still a long time, with her eyes shut. Then he heard her murmuring something. He stooped close.

'This – is – dying. I thought it would be horrible. And it's bliss . . . Bliss.'

The priest's hand slackened, as if at the bidding of some wonder. She gave a weak cry.

'Oh – don't let me go.'

His grasp tightened.

'Try,' he said, 'to think about God. Keep on looking at the crucifix.'

'If I look,' she whispered, 'you won't let go my hand?'

'I will not let you go.'

He held it till it was wrenched from him in the last agony.

She lingered for some hours in the room where these things had happened.

Its aspect was familiar and yet unfamiliar, and slightly repugnant to her. The altar, the crucifix, the lighted candles, suggested some tremendous and awful experience the details of which she was not able to recall. She seemed to remember that they had been connected in some way with the sheeted body on the bed; but the nature of the connection was not clear; and she did not associate the dead body with herself. When the nurse came in and laid it out, she saw that it was the body of a middle-aged woman. Her own living body was that of a young woman of about thirty-two.

Her mind had no past and no future, no sharp-edged, coherent memories, and no idea of anything to be done next.

Then, suddenly, the room began to come apart before her eyes, to split into shafts of floor and furniture and ceiling that shifted and were thrown by their commotion into different planes. They leaned slanting at every possible angle; they crossed and overlaid each other with a transparent mingling of dislocated perspectives, like reflections fallen on an interior seen behind glass.

The bed and the sheeted body slid away somewhere out of sight. She was standing by the door that still remained in position.

She opened it and found herself in the street, outside a building of yellowish-grey brick and freestone, with a tall slated spire. Her mind came together with a palpable click of recognition. This object was the Church of St Mary the Virgin, Maida Vale. She could hear the droning of the organ. She opened the door and slipped in.

She had gone back into a definite space and time, and recovered a certain limited section of coherent memory. She remembered the rows of pitch-pine benches, with their Gothic peaks and mouldings; the stone-coloured walls and pillars with their chocolate stencilling; the hanging rings of lights along the aisles of the nave; the high altar with its lighted candles, and the polished brass cross, twinkling. These things were somehow permanent and real, adjusted to the image that now took possession of her.

She knew what she had come there for. The service was over. The choir had gone from the chancel; the sacristan moved before the altar, putting out the candles. She walked up the middle aisle to a seat that she knew under the pulpit. She knelt down and covered her face with her hands. Peeping sideways through her fingers, she could see the door of the vestry on her left at the end of the north aisle. She watched it steadily.

Up in the organ loft the organist drew out the Recessional, slowly and softly, to its end in the two solemn, vibrating chords.

The vestry door opened and Clement Farmer came out, dressed in his black cassock. He passed before her, close, close outside the bench where she knelt. He paused at the opening. He was waiting for her. There was something he had to say.

She stood up and went towards him. He still waited. He didn't move to make way for her. She came close, closer than she had ever come to him, so close that his features grew indistinct. She bent her head back, peering, short-sightedly, and found herself looking into Oscar Wade's face.

He stood still, horribly still, and close, barring her passage.

She drew back; his heaving shoulders followed her. He leaned forward, covering her with his eyes. She opened her mouth to scream and no sound came.

She was afraid to move lest he should move with her. The heaving of his shoulders terrified her.

One by one the lights in the side aisles were going out. The lights in the middle aisle would go next. They had gone. If she didn't get away she would be shut up with him there, in the appalling darkness.

She turned and moved towards the north aisle, groping, steadying herself by the book ledge.

When she looked back, Oscar Wade was not there.

Then she remembered that Oscar Wade was dead. Therefore, what she had seen was not Oscar; it was his ghost. He was dead; dead seventeen years ago. She was safe from him for ever.

When she came out on to the steps of the church she saw that the road it stood in had changed. It was not the road she remembered. The pavement on this side was raised slightly and covered in. It ran under a succession of arches. It was a long gallery walled with glittering shop windows on one side; on the other a line of tall grey columns divided it from the street.

She was going along the arcades of the rue de Rivoli. Ahead of her she could see the edge of an immense grey pillar jutting out. That was the porch of the Hotel Saint Pierre. The revolving glass doors swung forward to receive her; she crossed the grey, sultry vestibule under the pillared arches. She knew it. She knew the porter's shining, wine-coloured mahogany pen on her left, and the shining wine-coloured mahogany barrier of the clerk's bureau on her right; she made straight for the great grey carpeted staircase; she climbed the endless flights that turned round and round the caged-in shaft of the well, past the latticed doors of the lift, and came up on to a landing that she knew, and into the long, ash-grey, foreign corridor lit by a dull window at one end.

It was there that the horror of the place came on her. She had no longer any memory of St Mary's Church, so that she was unaware of her backward course through time. All space and time were here.

She remembered she had to go to the left, the left.

But there was something there; where the corridor turned by the window; at the end of all the corridors. If she went the other way she would escape it.

The corridor stopped there. A blank wall. She was driven back past the stair-head to the left.

At the corner, by the window, she turned down another long ash-grey corridor on her right, and to the right again where the night-light sputtered on the table-flap at the turn.

This third corridor was dark and secret and depraved. She knew the soiled walls and the warped door at the end. There was a sharp-pointed streak of light at the top. She could see the number on it now, 107.

Something had happened there. If she went in it would happen again.

Oscar Wade was in the room waiting for her behind the closed door. She felt him moving about in there. She leaned forward, her ear to the key-hole, and listened. She could hear the measured, deliberate, thoughtful footsteps. They were coming from the bed to the door.

She turned and ran; her knees gave way under her; she sank and ran on, down the long grey corridors and the stairs, quick and blind, a hunted beast seeking for cover, hearing his feet coming after her.

The revolving doors caught her and pushed her out into the street.

The strange quality of her state was this, that it had no time. She remembered dimly that there had once been a thing called time; but she had forgotten altogether what it was like. She was aware of things happening and about to happen; she fixed them by the place they occupied, and measured their duration by the space she went through.

So now she thought: If I could only go back and get to the place where it hadn't happened.

To get back farther –

She was walking now on a white road that went between broad grass borders. To the right and left were the long raking lines of the hills, curve after curve, shimmering in a thin mist.

The road dropped to the green valley. It mounted the humped bridge over the river. Beyond it she saw the twin gables of the grey house pricked up over the high, grey garden wall. The tall iron gate stood in front of it between the ball-topped stone pillars.

And now she was in a large, low-ceilinged room with drawn blinds. She was standing before the wide double bed. It was her father's bed. The dead body, stretched out in the middle under the drawn white sheet, was her father's body.

The outline of the sheet sank from the peak of the upturned toes to the shin bone, and from the high bridge of the nose to the chin.

She lifted the sheet and folded it back across the breast of the dead man. The face she saw then was Oscar Wade's face, stilled and smoothed in the innocence of sleep, the supreme innocence of death. She stared at it, fascinated, in a cold, pitiless joy.

Oscar was dead.

She remembered how he used to lie like that beside her in the room in the Hotel Saint Pierre, on his back with his hands folded on his waist, his mouth half-open, his big chest rising and falling. If he was dead, it would never happen again. She would be safe.

The dead face frightened her, and she was about to cover it up again when she was aware of a light heaving, a rhythmical rise and fall. As she drew the sheet up tighter, the hands under it began to struggle convulsively, the broad ends of the fingers appeared above the edge, clutching it to keep it down. The mouth opened; the eyes opened; the whole face stared back at her in a look of agony and horror.

Then the body drew itself forwards from the hips and sat up, its eyes peering into her eyes; he and she remained for an instant motionless, each held there by the other's fear.

Suddenly she broke away, turned and ran, out of the room, out of the house.

She stood at the gate, looking up and down the road, not knowing by which way she must go to escape Oscar. To the right, over the bridge and up the hill and across the downs she would come to the arcades of the rue de Rivoli and the dreadful grey corridors of the hotel. To the left the road went through the village.

If she could get further back she would be safe, out of Oscar's reach. Standing by her father's deathbed she had been young, but not young enough. She must get back to the place where she was younger still, to the Park and the green drive under the beech trees and the white pavilion at the cross. She knew how to find it. At the end of the village the high road ran right and left, east and west, under the Park walls; the south gate stood there at the top, looking down the narrow street.

She ran towards it through the village, past the long grey barns of Goodyer's farm, past the grocer's shop, past the yellow front and blue sign of the 'Queen's Head', past the post office, with its one black window blinking under its vine, past the church and the yew trees in the churchyard, to where the south gate made a delicate black pattern on the green grass.

These things appeared insubstantial, drawn back behind a sheet of air that shimmered over them like thin glass. They opened out, floated past and away from her; and instead of the high road and park walls she saw a London street of dingy white façades, and instead of the south gate the swinging glass doors of Schnebler's Restaurant.

The glass doors swung open and she passed into the restaurant. The scene beat on her with the hard impact of reality: the white and gold panels, the white pillars and their curling gold capitals, the white circles of the tables, glittering, the flushed faces of the diners, moving mechanically.

She was driven forward by some irresistible compulsion to a table in the corner, where a man sat alone. The table napkin he was using hid his mouth, and jaw, and chest; and she was not sure of the upper part of the face above the straight, drawn edge. It dropped; and she saw Oscar Wade's face. She came to him, dragged, without power to resist; she sat down beside him, and he leaned to her over the table; she could feel the warmth of his red, congested face; the smell of wine floated towards her on his thick whisper.

'I knew you would come.'

She ate and drank with him in silence, nibbling and sipping slowly, staving off the abominable moment it would end in.

At last they got up and faced each other. His long bulk stood before her, above her; she could almost feel the vibration of its power.

'Come,' he said. 'Come.'

And she went before him, slowly, slipping out through the maze of the tables, hearing behind her Oscar's measured, deliberate, thoughtful tread. The steep, red-carpeted staircase rose up before her.

She swerved from it, but he turned her back.

'You know the way,' he said.

At the top of the flight she found the white door of the room she knew. She knew the long windows guarded by drawn muslin blinds; the gilt looking-glass over the chimney-piece that reflected Oscar's head and shoulders grotesquely between two white porcelain babies with bulbous limbs and garlanded loins, she knew the sprawling stain on the drab carpet by the table, the shabby, infamous couch behind the screen.

They moved about the room, turning and turning in it like beasts in a cage, uneasy, inimical, avoiding each other.

At last they stood still, he at the window, she at the door, the length of the room between.

'It's no good your getting away like that,' he said.

'There couldn't be any other end to it – to what we did.'

'But that *was* ended.'

'Ended there, but not here.'

'Ended for ever. We've done with it for ever.'

'We haven't. We've got to begin again. And go on. And go on.'

'Oh, no. No. Anything but that.'

'There isn't anything else.'

'We can't. We can't. Don't you remember how it bored us?'

'Remember? Do you suppose I'd touch you if I could help it? . . . That's what we're here for. We must. We must.'

'No. No. I shall get away – now.'

She turned to the door to open it.

'You can't,' he said. 'The door's locked.'

'Oscar – what did you do that for?'

'We always did it. Don't you remember?'

She turned to the door again and shook it; she beat on it with her hands.

'It's no use, Harriott. If you got out now you'd only have to come back again. You might stave it off for an hour or so, but what's that in an immortality?'

'Immortality?'

'That's what we're in for.'

'Time enough to talk about immortality when we're dead . . . Ah –'

They were being drawn towards each other across the room, moving slowly, like figures in some monstrous and appalling dance, their heads thrown back over their shoulders, their faces turned from the horrible approach. Their arms rose slowly, heavy with intolerable reluctance; they stretched them out towards each other, aching, as if they held up an overpowering weight. Their feet dragged and were drawn.

Suddenly her knees sank under her; she shut her eyes; all her being went down before him in darkness and terror.

It was over. She had got away, she was going back, back, to the green drive of the Park, between the beech trees, where Oscar had never been, where he would never find her. When she passed through the south gate her memory became suddenly young and clean. She forgot the rue de Rivoli and the Hotel Saint Pierre; she forgot Schnebler's Restaurant and the room at the top of the stairs. She was back in her youth. She was Harriott Leigh going to wait for Stephen Philpotts in the pavilion opposite the west gate. She could feel herself, a slender figure moving fast over the grass between the lines of the great beech trees. The freshness of her youth was upon her.

She came to the heart of the drive where it branched right and left in the form of a cross. At the end of the right arm the white Greek temple, with its pediment and pillars, gleamed against the wood.

She was sitting on their seat at the back of the pavilion, watching the side door that Stephen would come in by.

The door was pushed open; he came towards her, light and young, skimming between the beech trees with his eager, tiptoeing stride. She rose up to meet him. She gave a cry.

'Stephen!'

It had been Stephen. She had seen him coming. But the man who stood before her between the pillars of the pavilion was Oscar Wade.

And now she was walking along the field-path that slanted from the orchard door to the stile; further and further back, to where young George Waring waited for her under the elder tree. The smell of the elder flowers came to her over the field. She could feel on her lips and in all her body the sweet, innocent excitement of her youth.

'George, oh, George!'

As she went along the field-path she had seen him. But the man who stood waiting for her under the elder tree was Oscar Wade.

'I told you it's no use getting away, Harriott. Every path brings you back to me. You'll find me at every turn.'

'But how did you get *here*?'

'As I got into the pavilion. As I got into your father's room, on to his death bed. Because I *was* there. I am in all your memories.'

'My memories are innocent. How could you take my father's place, and Stephen's, and George Waring's? You?'

'Because I did take them.'

'Never. My love for *them* was innocent.'

'Your love for me was part of it. You think the past affects the future. Has it never struck you that the future may affect the past? In your innocence there was the beginning of your sin. You *were* what you *were to be*.'

'I shall get away,' she said.

'And, this time, I shall go with you.'

The stile, the elder tree, and the field floated away from her. She was going under the beech trees down the Park drive towards the south gate and the village, slinking close to the right-hand row of trees. She was aware that Oscar Wade was going with her under the left-hand row, keeping even with her, step by step, and tree by tree. And presently there was grey pavement under her feet and a row of grey pillars on her right hand. They were walking side by side down the rue de Rivoli towards the hotel.

They were sitting together now on the edge of the dingy white bed. Their arms hung by their sides, heavy and limp, their heads drooped, averted. Their passion weighed on them with the unbearable, unescapable boredom of immortality.

'Oscar – how long will it last?'

'I can't tell you. I don't know whether *this* is one moment of eternity, or the eternity of one moment.'

'It must end some time,' she said. 'Life doesn't go on for ever. We shall die.'

'Die? We *have* died. Don't you know what this is? Don't you know where you are? This is death. We're dead, Harriott. We're in hell.'

'Yes. There can't be anything worse than this.'

'This isn't the worst. We're not quite dead yet, as long as we've life in us to turn and run and get away from each other; as long as we can escape into our memories. But when you've got back to the farthest memory of all and there's nothing beyond it – When there's no memory but this – In the last hell we shall not run away any longer; we shall find no more roads, no more passages, no more open doors. We shall have no need to look for each other.

'In the last death we shall be shut up in this room, behind that locked door, together. We shall lie here together, for ever and ever, joined so fast that even

God can't put us asunder. We shall be one flesh and one spirit, one sin repeated for ever, and ever; spirit loathing flesh, flesh loathing spirit; you and I loathing each other.'

'Why? Why?' she cried.

'Because that's all that's left us. That's what you made of love.'

The darkness came down swamping, it blotted out the room. She was walking along a garden path between high borders of phlox and larkspur and lupin. They were taller than she was, their flowers swayed and nodded above her head. She tugged at the tall stems and had no strength to break them. She was a little thing.

She said to herself then that she was safe. She had gone back so far that she was a child again; she had the blank innocence of childhood. To be a child, to go small under the heads of the lupins, to be blank and innocent, without memory, was to be safe.

The walk led her out through a yew hedge on to a bright green lawn. In the middle of the lawn there was a shallow round pond in a ring of rockery cushioned with small flowers, yellow and white and purple. Goldfish swam in the olive brown water. She would be safe when she saw the goldfish swimming towards her. The old one with the white scales would come up first, pushing up his nose, making bubbles in the water.

At the bottom of the lawn there was a privet hedge cut by a broad path that went through the orchard. She knew what she would find there; her mother was in the orchard. She would lift her up in her arms to play with the hard red balls of the apples that hung from the tree. She had got back to the farthest memory of all; there was nothing beyond it.

There would be an iron gate in the wall of the orchard. It would lead into a field.

Something was different here, something that frightened her. An ash-grey door instead of an iron gate.

She pushed it open and came into the last corridor of the Hotel Saint Pierre.

THE BLESSING OF BROKENNESS

Karin Slaughter

Karin Slaughter is a global bestseller, whose crime thrillers include *Blindsighted*, *Triptych*, *Pretty Girls*, and several more. She has created two notable series: the Grant County books and a series featuring Will Trent of the Georgia Bureau of Investigation. Slaughter lives in Atlanta, USA.

Mary Lou Dixon sat in the front pew of the church, her eyes raised as she watched the cross over the pulpit being slowly lowered to the floor. She fiddled with the bracelet on her wrist as the cross, which had seemed so small hanging a few inches from the ceiling, began to grow larger as it descended in front of her like a broken bird.

'Hold up,' the foreman said, and the three men working the pulleys stopped. The cross shook in the air, its broken right arm dangling by a few slivers of wood as it tapped ominously against the side. The noise reminded Mary Lou of a clock, ticking away time.

'Easy, now,' the foreman instructed, using his hands to illustrate. He was the only English speaking person in the four-man crew and the Mexicans were slow to understand his orders. They finally seemed to comprehend, though, because the cross began its journey to the floor once again, finally coming to a gentle resting point on the carpet.

The Mexicans genuflected, and Mary Lou wondered if that was entirely appropriate in the Christ Holiness Baptist Church of Elawa, Georgia. The cross was a simple wooden affair, lacking a Jesus, but with a fine polish that shone in the morning sun. It was hardly the ornamental icon most Catholics were used to exalting, if that was what Catholics did – Mary Lou had no idea. She had been Christ Holiness for the last twenty years and before that Lord and Saviour, which was two steps below Primitive and one above snake handling.

Although plenty of contractors attended the church, none had volunteered their time to repair the ailing cross. Bob Harper, who had been a deacon for the last ten years, owned his own construction company, but he was still over five hundred dollars more expensive than the black man and his crew. The job was too small to make it worth his time, he had said. Mary Lou had commented she was glad Jesus had not felt the same way about dying for Bob's sins, but the deacon had not been swayed by her remark.

So, here Mary Lou was with a black foreman and his Catholic Mexicans, trying to get the cross repaired before Easter Sunday – at considerable expense

– with no help whatsoever from the more capable men of the congregation. This sort of thing was typical of the church lately. Long gone were the times when people happily volunteered to do routine maintenance or send out mailers to collect donations for foreign missionaries. No one visited the sick in the hospital anymore. No one wanted to go on bible retreats unless they were assured there would be a pool and twenty-four-hour room service. The last two anti-abortion rallies down to Atlanta had been cancelled because the weather report had predicted rain, and Lord knew no one wanted to stand out in the rain.

'Mrs Dixon?' the black man asked. His name was Jasper Goode, she knew. He was a dark-skinned older man with a bald head that showed a significant amount of perspiration despite the air-conditioning in the church. Mary Lou did not trust this show of over-perspiration, as if it somehow made him shifty. He had done nothing but stand and direct the crew all morning, yet he was sweating as if he had been running a marathon.

'Ma'am?' he prompted.

'Yes?' Mary Lou answered, shifting in the hard pew. She put her hand to her stomach to calm it.

Jasper walked towards her, down the stairs that lined the stage. He kept walking until he was about three feet away, looming over her.

Mary Lou squared her shoulders, willing herself not to fidget. He was a tall man and knew it. She could not help but glance down at the floor before bracing herself to look back up at him.

'Sorry,' he said, smiling as he kneeled down on one knee in front of her.

'What is it?' she snapped, aware she had no reason to. The truth was she did not like him standing so close to her. The sight of him was almost too much to bear.

The man had been badly burned, and up close his face was a synthetic looking mess, his skin stretched unnaturally tight in places, the pigment a patchwork quilt of varying skin tones around his cheeks so that from afar he looked as if someone had stitched his face together from borrowed flesh. He had no eyebrows or eyelashes, giving his eyes a perpetually startled look. His hands, too, were scarred, and the skin that bunched around his wrists resembled a slouching sock. Even in this heat, he wore his sleeves long, tightly buttoned at the wrists, hiding what Mary Lou imagined was an even more horrific sight.

He said something to his crew, and she tried not to watch him speak. The most startling thing about the man's appearance was his lips – an unnatural shade of pink, like the bright pinkness of a mouse's nose, and delicate looking, more suited for a maiden than an old black man with no facial hair to speak of. The lips had a constant sheen, as if they had been made for him only recently. Mary Lou had seen on television where a child's ear had been grown from scratch on the back of a living mouse. She wondered if the man's lips had been grown under similar circumstances.

The burns were not the kind of thing that could go unremarked upon. The first time they had met, the black man had explained to Mary Lou without her asking that he had been in an automobile accident. The car had exploded, burning alive his wife and child. He had barely escaped with his own life, and subsequent surgeries had healed his body if not his heart; he said the memories of that night still haunted him, and the part he played in the death of both his wife and child was something he could not forgive himself for, let alone forget. Drunk, Mary Lou suspected, but did not say.

Jasper Goode told her, 'We'll leave it here, then take it into the parking lot after lunch.' Mary Lou made a point of looking at her watch, and he added, 'They work better on a full belly.'

'I'm sure they do,' Mary Lou answered, hoping her tone conveyed her displeasure.

'She don't look as bad as I thought she would,' the black man offered, as if the cross were a ship and not a symbol of Jesus's sacrifice.

'Well, good,' she returned, wondering if this meant they would charge less. She doubted it.

As if sensing her thoughts, he added, 'She'll still take a while.'

'You promised it would be ready for Sunday,' Mary Lou reminded him, trying to keep the tremor out of her voice. She didn't think Jasper Goode was the type who went to church on Sundays, and if the decision had been left to Mary Lou, she would have hired Bob Harper instead. Five hundred dollars was a small price to pay to employ someone who was invested in his own salvation.

Jasper stared at her. 'I wants to thank you, ma'am, for giving me this job. It's kind of hard to get work for me now, and I appreciate it.'

She nodded, slightly taken aback by his admission.

Jasper held her gaze. 'You feelin' all right, ma'am?'

'I'll feel better when the cross is fixed,' she told him.

His mouth grimaced into what might be a smile. 'We'll have it on time,' Jasper assured her. He took out a white handkerchief to wipe at his sweating, bald head. He said something Mexican to the crew, and they scampered off, showing more hustle than they had shown thus far on the job.

Mary Lou shifted in the pew again, trying to find a comfortable position. Her office was over the old chapel, which was now the gymnasium, and the air conditioner there left much to be desired. If not for the fact that she could not afford to miss another day of work, she would have just stayed home today.

She let out a heavy sigh, staring at the pulpit. The blank space where the cross had been made the chapel feel hollow, as if the heart had been removed from its chest. It was a mystery how the cross had become damaged. A parishioner had mentioned something about the cross looking 'off' one Sunday, and Mary Lou and Pastor Stephen had come in after the service, both staring up until their necks kinked. There had been a definite tilt to the side, but from the ground they had not been able to tell why.

A week later, Mary Lou was in the church office stuffing envelopes when Randall, the church custodian, burst into her office, mumbling something about a sign from God. This was not the first time that Randall, whose own mother admitted that he was slightly touched in the head, had claimed such a vision, but Mary Lou had followed him into the chapel to stretch her legs. They found the cross tilting almost sideways, the thick cables that anchored it to the ceiling vibrating as if under great pressure. As Mary Lou and Randall stood there, a great cracking sound filled the room, followed by a terrible, low moan, as if Jesus Himself was on the cross, His arm being ripped from His body. She could still see it play in her mind in slow motion: the arm of the cross snapping, the cables twisting and bending as the weight shifted. Sometimes at night, she could hear that awful low moan of the wood breaking, and she would begin to sweat uncontrollably, knowing that the breaking cross had something to do with her.

As a girl, her Uncle Buell had been what was called a lay minister, which meant he had received no special ordination from Christ, yet still chose to teach the Bible. His following had dwindled as Mary Lou got older, but there was always a core group of people who listened to his teachings. They worshipped Buell as they worshipped the Lord Himself.

Every Sunday and Wednesday, the basement of Buell's ranch-style house would be filled with ten to twenty people, all come to hear Buell speak on the Word. His favourite theme was what he called the insidiousness of sin. Sin was a heavy burden, Buell said, and it would eventually break you one way or another. A good man might beat his wife. A good woman might lie to her husband. These were simple ways that sin could break you in two. This split gave easy entry to more sin, more evil, into your heart. It was up to the sinner to seek out Jesus, to ask for redemption, to seek His help in becoming whole again. God never gave a sinner more than he could carry, Buell insisted. That was His gift to man: He would never break you beyond repair. In every aspect of man's life, even at the end of it, there existed God's opportunity for redemption.

'Only Jesus can put you back together once you've been broken by sin,' Buell had preached. 'And that part of you that is broken becomes all the stronger for it.' He called this strengthening the blessing of brokenness. Even on his hospital bed, dying of bone cancer, he had refused treatment, insisting God had broken his bones only to heal them and make Buell stronger. In the end, the morphine had convinced him there were angels in the room. Or maybe not. Buell was known to see angels without the benefit of drugs, too.

Mary Lou turned in the pew as she heard footsteps in the foyer. Pastor Stephen entered the chapel, his shirtsleeves rolled up, his hands tucked into his pockets. Stephen Riddle was the exact opposite of her Uncle Buell. His sermons were not about working for redemption, but being blessed with it. There was no burden Jesus would not take from you, no problem He would not solve. Stephen's favourite admonition was that it was a sin to worry, whereas Buell's charge at the end of every service was to go home and worry, to pick through your life and find out what you were doing wrong and pray to Jesus that He would help you correct it.

Of course, Buell never lacked volunteers for even the smallest task. Such was the devotion of his flock that when his truck broke down, a mechanic appeared to fix it. When his house needed a new roof, the men of the congregation banded together and installed a new one over the weekend. Stephen Riddle would watch the church crumble to the ground around him before the thought even entered his mind to ask his parishioners to carry their proper load.

'Hot day,' Stephen said, then gave her a sideways glance. 'You doing OK?'

Mary Lou nodded, feeling a bead of sweat on her upper lip. She suddenly wanted to go home and lie down in bed so badly that she could almost feel the sheets across her body. Her sick days were used up, though. She could not afford to lose the money. While she accepted that Stephen was genuinely concerned about her health, she also knew that he would dock her pay if she left a minute before she was supposed to. After what had happened between them, Mary Lou should have had power over the preacher. She should have been able to exert this power any way she chose. For some unknown reason, she could not.

'How's our project going?' he asked, gesturing to the empty space above the pulpit. 'Do you feel good about this contractor?'

She knew what he was getting at. Mary Lou had not been in her office all day. 'I thought it best to keep an eye on them.'

'You look like you've lost a little weight,' he said, offering her a polite smile.

'I have,' she said, not pointing out that it was not just some, but a considerable amount. Food did not agree with her lately. Everything she ate sat in her stomach like a piece of coal, waiting to burn her from inside.

Stephen nodded, tucking his chin into his chest as he raised his eyebrows. He did this when there was more to say, but he could not find words. The trick was a good one, and it made him seem thoughtful and introspective when the truth was that he was simply incapable of expressing himself. 'A man of words,' Buell would have said, 'though none of them good.'

'Well,' she said, meaning to move Stephen along, but she could see his lips twisted to the side, his eyes focused on her wrist. The bracelet suddenly felt like an albatross.

He looked up quickly, offering a pained smile. The smile was familiar, too. He was a man well-versed in gestures that brought him compassion under the guise of giving it.

Mary Lou watched him as he walked over to the cross, laying his hand on it with some sort of reverence. His fingers gently glided along the wood, softer than they had ever been on her. She thought of Anne Riddle, his wife, and hated her with a bright searing hate that burned her up inside. Anne was serene and beautiful, her hips jutting out into the air, her skin the finest porcelain. She was the perfect preacher's wife: reverent, righteous, reserved.

'Cleaned up nice,' Stephen mumbled.

Mary Lou did not tell him that the cross had not yet been cleaned. Instead, she nodded, and tried to smile when he looked up at her.

He asked, 'How's Pud doing?'

'Still in school,' she answered, her voice as quiet as his.

'You get that roof fixed yet?'

She frowned, thinking about the money it would take to fix her roof. Nothing short of the lottery would bail her out of the hole she found herself in.

'Think we'll get those fliers mailed out today?' he asked, meaning the anti-abortion leaflets, the church's bread and butter. Their mailing list was one of the largest in the nation, and people from as far away as Michigan contributed money to the cause. This was what had brought Mary Lou to the chapel this morning, the thought that she could not stuff one more colour copy into one more envelope without wanting to slit her wrists. Her stomach rolled when she thought about the photograph on the flyers, the foetus ripped in two, the head caved in by some sharp, foul instrument, the headline above beseeching, 'Why did you let my mommy kill me?'

'Mary Lou?'

She shook her head and tears came to her eyes.

'Mary Lou,' Stephen repeated, but she waved him off, the ridiculous charm bracelet jingling against her wrist. 'Why are you still wearing that?' he asked, obviously resigned to what her answer would be.

'A memento,' she said, sliding the bracelet around her wrist.

'They're supposed to be lucky,' he said, glancing back at the cross, stroking the soft wood again.

'Supposedly,' she said. The worst news of her life had come on the day she had been given the trinket, and Mary Lou could not help but shiver at the evil that discharged from the thing like poisonous gas.

Stephen stared at his hand on the cross, his displeasure evident. The bracelet, like so many things between them, was a secret. Stephen had told the church he was taking a sabbatical to minister to the poor in the Blue Ridge Mountains when in fact he had joined his brother in Las Vegas for a convention of the Greater West Coast Waste Management Association.

That his brother was a garbage man was not something that Stephen liked to brag about – by different accounts the brother was a neurosurgeon, a banker, a missionary – but Mary Lou had been pleased enough when Stephen had brought back the charm bracelet for her. He'd said that he had used all his blackjack winnings to buy it especially for Mary Lou. The bracelet had been displayed in one of the shop windows at the Venetian and he had passed by and instantly thought of her. It was only later that she had noticed the flaws: at some point, the bracelet had been broken and inexpertly welded back together; some of the charms had sharp points that tore her clothes. The snake got caught on her sleeve all the time and the tiny cross's Jesus was horrible to witness, His pain so evident in his features that Mary Lou could not stand to look at it.

Despite all of this, she had taken to wearing it at night and her dreams when she managed to sleep were filled with horrible visions: a bear traversing the darkness in search of human prey; a grown man slit stem to stern; severed hands reaching out as if to strangle her in her sleep. Even when she woke screaming, the skeleton key caught in her hair as if to unlock some horrible secret in her brain, Mary Lou had refused to remove the bracelet.

As if knowing all of this, Stephen suggested, 'Maybe you shouldn't wear it.'

'Why?' she asked, knowing he would not have an answer. It was a reminder; her own Scarlet Letter.

Stephen stood there uncertain, then finally left her with a slight bow, as if he was conceding this round. She listened as his footsteps receded, first a dull thud against the carpeted aisle, then a sharp clicking on the tiles in the foyer, and he was gone. Stephen was better at exiting than most men.

Brian, Mary Lou's ex-husband, had stuck around about ten years too long. She had known for some time that he was cheating on her, but her Uncle Buell's words about a divorced woman still hung heavy on her shoulders. So, she had left it to Brian to do the leaving, and Brian had hated her for that, as had their son. Both men had come to see Mary Lou as weak, a punching bag who would take any amount of abuse but still hang in there, waiting for more.

Pud was worse. Not that she thought of her teenage son as 'Pud'. She had named him William when he was born, and insisted most of his life that it not be shortened to anything crude like Willy or Bill. Pud was the name William had given himself two years ago, around the time puberty had hit and he had started listening to rap music and wearing his pants so that the crack of his ass showed when he bent over. She had watched her darling son change into an unknown creature, a pseudo piccaninny with his blond hair tightly braided in corn rows and his clothes hanging off his body like a wet paper bag on a stick. His language changed, so that she could not understand a word he said, and he sang along to that awful music, saying 'nigga' this and 'nigga' that, a word Mary Lou had never used round him and was ashamed to hear coming from his mouth. At the same time, William could not stand black people, and went out of his way to make derogatory comments about them, even when Mary Lou had people from the church over.

Though she loved her son, the smile William had given Mary Lou when he told her that from now on he would only answer to 'Pud' made her want to slap him for the first time in her life. That mischievous set to his lips as he said the word, as if Mary Lou was an idiot and did not know that 'pulling your pud' was slang for male masturbation. She had been a substitute teacher for the first few years of William's life. She had heard worse than pud in the teacher's lounge.

Her biggest problem with William was his anger, though she had no idea what he had to be angry about. Brian spoiled him, even as he refused to be seen in public with the boy. Anything his son wanted, he got. Two-hundred-dollar tennis shoes and an eighty-dollar skateboard (no helmet) that William had tried once and never again were just a few of the things Brian used to justify paying less child support to Mary Lou. They were constantly arguing over this, with Brian screaming and Mary Lou crying because her anger was such a tight knot inside her that it could only squeeze out tears. Child support was not the only thing Brian was supposed to pay. By court order, he was responsible for half of the up-keep of the house. Still the roof leaked when it rained and there were not enough buckets in the world to catch the water. No matter how much Mary Lou cleaned, mildew grew on the cabinets in the kitchen and walking into the house was like walking across a loaf of moulded bread. Thank God Pud had his two-hundred-dollar tennis shoes to keep his feet from having to touch the ground.

The sound of hammering came from outside the chapel, and Mary Lou slowly moved to the edge of the pew so that she could stand. The bracelet clunked against the armrest, and she glanced around before grinding the edge of the praying angel into the soft wood until it bit out a small gouge. Cramps seized her belly as she tried to rise, and Mary Lou thought for the first time about going to the doctor. A quick calculation of the remaining money in her chequebook convinced her that was not a possibility, even if she sent William to his father's to eat.

She gritted her teeth as she pushed herself up, groaning from the movement. Sweat dripped down her back, and she tried to think about something cool to counteract the sensation. What came to mind was the church retreat she went on last Christmas, and how her life had been unalterably damaged by what had happened there.

Gatlinburg, Tennessee, was about as close as the South came to having a ski resort, even if they still had to blow fake snow on to the mountains most days just so people could slide down on their skis. Brian had agreed to take William for a week, a miracle in itself, and Mary Lou had managed to get the church to help pay some of the cost in exchange for extra help with the youth group.

She had gone to Gatlinburg with no illusions that she would ski. Mary Lou had never been athletic. She was a large woman who did not embrace the outdoors unless it was on a beach somewhere with a pina colada close by and a trashy book. What she had envisioned for herself was sitting in front of a roaring fire, her feet propped up as she read a romance where the women were strong and the men were worshipful. In the evenings, there would be dinners with various members of the congregation, then some socializing. The event was billed as a religious retreat for singles. As a recent single, Mary Lou qualified for this, but she had not gone with the intention of meeting anyone. There were far too many complications in her life without putting another person in the picture.

Of course, Pastor Stephen Riddle was not a new person in her life, and despite the strictures of their employer–employee relationship, she had long thought of him as a trusted counsellor if not a friend. Anne, his wife, was also an acquaintance, and Mary Lou had helped out at birthday parties for their children and even volunteered to clean the house when Anne's father had passed away. That Mary Lou and Stephen had ended up going back to her room the third night of the retreat still surprised her. Ostensibly, they had gone upstairs to talk away from the crowd. Mary Lou knew that her ex-husband had not taken William without strings attached, and that this latest kindness would mean less child support at the end of the month. She had wanted to broach the subject of an advance with the pastor. She had been hoping Stephen would see her plight and volunteer a raise.

When Stephen had moved closer to her, Mary Lou had invited the comfort. When his gentle touching had turned more insistent, and she had felt him stiffen against her, Mary Lou had proceeded as if she was in a fog. Sex with Brian had always been something to endure, and though she had read enough about orgasms in her women's magazines, Mary Lou had considered them much as she considered the recipes and craft suggestions: interesting, but nothing she would ever have time to do. Stephen had not delivered in that area, either, but it felt so good to be held, to have the solid weight of him on top of her, to watch his face contort in pleasure, that she had found herself crying out, biting her lip so that she would not scream.

Stephen had mistaken this for ardour, and though he had slinked out the door a few minutes later, making excuses about being in his room in case Anne or one of the children called, the next evening he had knocked at her door again. She had let him in, somewhat thrilled with the wrongness of what they were doing. Mary Lou had never done anything bad. Her life was spent being as good as she could manage for fear of some greater retribution in the afterlife. To her surprise, there was a certain pleasure to be had from breaking a cardinal rule: not just sex, but sex with a married man. Not just a married man, but her pastor.

The ensuing nights, when Stephen had suggested things he wanted to do, positions he wanted to try, she had encouraged him. In fact, she had begged him, the thought that he had never tried these things with Anne making her almost giddy with power. Even as she leaned on her elbows, her hind end high in the air like a dog on heat, she had encouraged him, thinking in some perverse way that she deserved this degradation.

After the retreat, Stephen had pretended as if nothing had happened, his polite demeanour a slap in her face. Twice she had tried to talk to him, but it was not until he had returned from Las Vegas, holding the charm bracelet in his hand as if he held the world for her, that she had got the message. To put a finer point on it, he had told her, 'I cannot do this. I am a man of God.'

When she had cried, he had held her, then shushed her with his kisses, more gentle than any she had known their few times together. This had made her cry even harder; not for the loss of him but for the loss of the gentleness she could have had. Big, racking sobs took hold, and she had started to hate Anne, because she understood that Stephen's gentleness belonged to Anne, and Mary Lou had been nothing but his whore.

'Ma'am?' a voice interrupted her thoughts.

Mary Lou startled, aware that tears were threatening to fall.

'Yes?' she managed, wiping her eyes as she turned to see the black man standing behind her. He was patting the top of his head again with the now not so white handkerchief. She could see the Mexicans behind him, waiting for orders.

'We just about ready to start,' he said.

She nodded, her hand on the back of the pew, trying to remember what he was talking about. The cross. Of course, the cross.

Mary Lou looked at her watch, as if she had something important scheduled. 'How much longer?'

''Bout ten minutes, I s'pose.' He nodded to the Mexicans. 'Take us that long to get'er set up.'

'You're in the north parking lot?' she queried, though she had seen his beaten-up old truck and tools set up there, and knew they would do as she instructed for fear of being discharged.

'Yes'm,' he told her, then again nodded to the men.

They all proceeded down the aisle as if for a wedding, their footsteps slow and deliberate. Mary Lou watched the Mexicans lift the broken cross, which seemed heavier than she had thought, or maybe they were putting on a show. There was much straining and groaning before the thing was high enough to be carried away, and Mary Lou wondered if Jesus had made as much of a commotion carrying the damn thing up the mountain.

''Bout ten minutes,' Jasper repeated.

After they left, Mary Lou thought about sitting back down again, but she knew if she did she would have an even harder time standing up again. Instead, she walked over to the window and leaned against the glass as she watched the men carrying the cross to the back parking lot. It was just as she had thought: they moved much more quickly when they thought that she was not looking.

There were six sawhorses already set up in an approximate pattern of the cross, and Jasper moved them into position as the cross was lowered on to them. He held the broken right arm in one hand as he did this, pushing the sawhorses with his feet, tugging them with his free hand. The chapel window was higher than the parking lot, and Mary Lou was afforded an aerial view of the proceedings. The cross seemed smaller again now that it was further away. Distance could do that to things, make them seem smaller. Time could do the same. When Mary Lou thought about Gatlinburg, for instance, it seemed like a smaller event in her life. What had ensued of course loomed larger, because it had yet to come to any sort of conclusion.

Uncle Buell was fond of saying that a woman can run faster with her skirt up than a man can with his pants down, but he had failed to point out that when both of them finally stopped trying to run, it was the woman who could not escape the consequences. Stephen Riddle, Mary Lou was sure, had prayed to the Lord for forgiveness and been granted it. Mary Lou had prayed for redemption and been given a child.

Her periods had always been erratic. Working at the church so closely with Stephen, going to the school twice a week to beg them not to expel William, had taken all of her energy, so that when months had gone by without any blood in the toilet, Mary Lou had not noticed. She was a large woman on top of this, and when her stomach began to swell, she had attributed this to too much fast food and late nights eating chips in front of the television. It might be menopause, she had found herself reasoning. She had even welcomed the Change as one less thing she would have to worry about.

Still, part of her must have known, because when she had finally managed to go to the doctor, she did not go to Dr Patterson, who had delivered William, but to a doctor in Ormewood, two towns over, who was just setting up his practice.

'Congratulations,' the doctor had said when Mary Lou had called for the results. He had then given a long list of instructions on diet and exercise, and offered the name of a good midwife as well as the hospital he preferred for the delivery.

Mary Lou had written all this down on a stack of bills by the phone in the church office, all the while praying that no one would walk in. For a panicked few seconds, she had wondered if the phone was tapped, but then realized the church would be too cheap to pay for such a thing. They were more likely to tell Randall to stand at the door and listen. As far as Mary Lou could tell, no one was outside lurking.

The doctor had asked, 'Do you have any questions?'

'What about,' Mary Lou had begun, her voice lowered, still afraid of an unseen listener. 'What about other options?'

Even as she had asked the question, Mary Lou had known exactly what she meant. She had been stuffing envelopes all day, putting the same colour photocopy of that twisted child into a crisp, white envelope, sticking on a label from their national mailing list, then running it through the postage meter so that the letter would get there as soon as possible.

'Mrs Riddle,' the doctor had said, using the name Mary Lou had given him. 'I don't think you understand. You're in your third trimester.'

'Yes,' she had said, wondering what the problem was.

The doctor had got haughty. 'Third trimester abortions are illegal in the state of Georgia, Mrs Riddle.' Then, he had gone on to tell Mary Lou that he did not think he would have time to see her as a regular patient and suggested someone else across town.

She had kept her hand on the receiver long after putting it down, dumbstruck by the doctor's words. Third trimester abortions were routinely performed all over America. She had over ten thousand pamphlets on her desk talking about cases around the nation where viable foetuses – infants, children, really – had been aborted in the womb, their skulls punctured so they could collapse, their brains sucked out through little vacuum hoses so their parts could be sold to medical researchers. Partial-birth abortions were the scourge of the United States. They were as common as night and day.

After a moment's thought, Mary Lou had locked her office door and sat on the floor behind her desk with the Atlanta phone book. Routinely, the church organized protests where they all piled into the church van and, barring unexpected rain, picketed in front of different abortionaries in Atlanta. They carried signs that said, 'MURDERERS!' and 'STOP KILLING BABIES!'. The doctors who worked at the clinics were so ashamed they could not look at the church members. They kept their heads down, their ears covered as the chanting began. 'Save the babies! Kill the doctors!'

Mary Lou had called these places first. When they had all explained to her the same thing that the doctor had earlier said, she had moved on to the yellow pages, trying all the gynaecologists whose names looked like they might be open to helping her out. She had started with the Jewish doctors, followed by a couple of Polish-sounding ones, then a Hispanic doctor's office where the woman answering the phone barely spoke English, yet managed to convey to Mary Lou that not only was what Mary Lou was asking illegal, it was against God's law.

Those names exhausted, Mary Lou had called the obvious places, the clinics with the word 'women' in their names, then the 'feminist' centres. She had searched the Internet and found numbers for places relatively close by in Tennessee and Alabama, but all of them, down to the last, had told her in no uncertain terms that such a procedure could not be performed. One woman who sounded sympathetic had told her that there were a handful of states that did allow abortions this late in the term, but there had to be clear evidence that the mother's life was in danger.

Mary Lou had considered the phrase, finally coming to the conclusion that her life *was* in danger. She could not continue working at the church as an unwed mother. There was barely enough money to feed William and herself, let alone a child. What's more, babies were always sick, always needing medicine and office visits and God; the thought of it made her feel as if she had swallowed glass. The church was exempt from the law that would have required them to give her health insurance and the private plan she had looked into years ago was six hundred dollars a month. After paying the mortgage and car insurance so she could drive to work, Mary Lou barely had six hundred dollars left over from her pay cheque. The visit to the doctor across town had meant peanut butter and jelly sandwiches for two weeks.

The last phone call she had made to a clinic nearly sent her over the edge. The woman on the other end of the line had actually preached to her, said there were good Christian organizations that would help her through this difficult time. Mary Lou had bitten her tongue to keep from screaming that she was part of that Christian organization, and she would be out on the street if they found out.

Instead, she had slammed down the phone, furious. She was not a crack addict, for God's sake. She was not like those women who used abortion for birth control. She wasn't some career minded whore who did not have time for a child. She loved children. She volunteered at the church nursery the last Sunday of every month. She was a *mother*.

Tears sprang into her eyes, and she found herself putting her wrist to her mouth, sucking it as she had done as a child. The charms on the bracelet chattered against her teeth, and the metallic taste burned her throat. She worked each charm into her mouth, sucking it as if to draw some sort of power. She had always seen the thing as evil, a nasty reminder of her sin, but now she found herself counting off the charms – the locket, the ballet slippers, the lighthouse, the cross – like a rosary.

Mary Lou had been teasing the cross with the tip of her tongue when it had occurred to her that of course these places would refuse to say anything incriminating over the phone. She could be anyone, after all. A state regulator, a detective, a pro-life activist trying to trap them into saying something while the phone call was secretly being recorded. Mary Lou would have to go in and meet them face-to-face. She had no doubt that they would help her then. They would see she was not someone out to trick them, but someone who genuinely needed their help.

Stephen had seemed surprised when Mary Lou had asked for a day off. She was given a certain number of sick days every quarter, but at that point in time she had taken no more than a handful of them over the course of her ten years at the church. Still, he had given her a look that said, 'Don't make a habit of this.'

She could have said something about the affair then, something that would have given her the upper hand, but they both knew she would not do it. The church was all that she had left. It was literally her life. She worked here and worshipped here and what few remaining friendships she had were through the church. Mary Lou spent more hours in this place than she did in her own home. If the affair got out, it would not be Stephen they blamed. They would all point the finger at her. Even when Brian had left her, cheating on her in such an obvious way that his own mother had called him worthless, people had still blamed Mary Lou. What had she done to make her husband stray? Was she not a good wife? Surely the fault could not lie with Brian. He was a good man who always provided well for his family, right up until the day he left them.

Much the same logic would come to the defence of Stephen. Not only was he a married man with two adorable children, neither of them insisting they be called Pud, he was a man of God, a learned man. Stephen Riddle had attended Seminary in Atlanta. He had a doctorate in biblical studies. He was not the type to be hurt by this kind of exposure. Knowing the congregation, Mary Lou suspected they would love him even more for having been through such a trial while still remaining loyal to his family. She could even imagine the sermon he would get out of it. 'God tested me, and I failed,' he would say, spreading the blame even as he waited for his sins to be washed away.

Regret bit into her every time she thought about the way Stephen had treated her as she stood in his office, asking for what was rightly hers. The groundwork giving him all the power had been laid that very moment, and unsurprisingly he had been a much more skilful engineer. When he had challenged her with a curt, 'Is that all?' Mary Lou had been unable to do anything but nod. He had then looked down at his desk, at his open bible, dismissing her with the top of his head.

The clinic in Atlanta was tucked out of the way, but Mary Lou had known how to find it. She had driven there several times, actually, with anywhere from twenty to fifty people, most of them women, holding small coolers or sandwiches or thermoses of coffee, as if they were going on a field trip instead of going to prevent what amounted to murder.

It was murder, after all. There was no way around that. Mary Lou had avoided this basic truth as she drove to Atlanta, a considerable distance. As it had so many times the last few months, her mind had wandered back to her childhood. She had imagined herself sitting in the basement of her Uncle Buell's house, listening to the gospel. How simple things had seemed back then, how black and white everything had been. There was nothing that hard work and prayer could not eventually overcome. There was nothing the spirit could not embrace. God never gave you more than you could bear, and even if you broke from the stress, he would build you back and make you stronger. That was his blessing. That was his gift.

Having never been inside the abortion clinic, Mary Lou had been shocked to find how welcoming everyone was. From the outside, the building had seemed gloomy and forbidding, like the death chamber it was. The bars on the windows and the guard at the door certainly lent to this air, as if the women passing through the heavy wooden door were prisoners on death row. Inside, there were cheerful posters of children and animals covering the brightly painted walls. Most surprisingly, there were pamphlets on fertility treatments, adoption and post-natal care. She had never realized that the clinic was also a gynaecological office, where women got routine pap smears and received counselling. Most shocking of all, there were pictures of children on a crowded bulletin board by the door, living children delivered by doctors who worked at the clinic.

Looking at the pictures of children, with sudden clarity, Mary Lou had realized she could not go through with this. Her stomach had pitched, but not with morning sickness. Instead, what she had felt was fear so intense that her bowels seized as if they had been clamped into a vice.

When the nurse called for 'Mrs Riddle', Mary Lou had bolted out the door, gasping for air as she had walked across the street to her car. Still mindful that she was in Atlanta, Mary Lou had kept her keys in her fist, the sharpest one pointed out in case she was attacked. She was not attacked, but there was a man leaning against her car when she had got to it.

He had said, 'Good morning, sister,' looking her up and down the way a farmer might appraise a cow he was thinking of buying. He was filthy-looking, obviously homeless. His arms were crossed over his chest the way her father's used to be when Mary Lou had done something to displease him.

'Please move,' she had said, though there was no threat in her voice. She was exhausted, emotionally spent and incapable of articulating anything but defeat.

'You come from that place,' he had said, indicating the clinic. 'I seen you leaving.'

'No,' she had lied, trying to breathe through her mouth as the wind shifted and she smelled him. 'Please move aside or I'll be forced to call the police.'

He had given her that look again, the same look she had been getting all of her life: you're worthless. You won't stand up to me because you know you deserve this. William looked at her this way and Brian before him and now Stephen Riddle. She was suddenly fed up, and decided then and there that she would not take it from a seedy stranger. Anger had welled up inside her, and without thinking, Mary Lou had lunged at the homeless man, scratching wildly with the key, a startlingly primal yell coming from her mouth as she gouged his face, his neck, his hands as he held them up in an attempt to protect himself.

The attack was still fresh in her mind as she had driven home to Elawa. She had actually drawn blood. Mary Lou had jumped on the disgusting homeless man with more vengeance than she had ever known, anger washing over her like a flood, eroding her better judgement, leaving nothing in its wake but a loose silt of hatred that would not come clean. Part of her had wanted to kill the man. Most surprisingly, part of her had been *capable* of killing him. Mary Lou had never even thought it possible for her to have the strength to defend herself, let alone to be the kind of person someone should have to defend themselves against.

When she had looked into the rear-view mirror, she had been surprised to see blood on her cheek. This wasn't from the homeless man, she knew. The blood was her own. Mary Lou had scratched herself with the charm bracelet as she drew back the key and aimed for his eyes. Had he not turned away his head in that split second, she would have blinded him. Had he not managed to crawl under the closest car when she had raised her foot to kick him, Mary Lou had no doubt that she would have strangled him with her own hands.

How had that happened, she wondered. What had gotten into her? The poor man had probably wanted nothing more than money, a few dollars for a cup of coffee or whatever rotgut had made him homeless in the first place. What had turned inside her that made Mary Lou Dixon capable of murder?

She had put her wrist to her mouth as she drove, her mind reeling with possibilities. She could taste her blood on the charms, and she had suckled them like a child. There was something bad inside of her, something that was turning her into a monster. She had nearly slammed into an eighteen-wheeler in the next lane when she had realized what it was. Mary Lou had dropped her hand, shifting the gears and pulling on to the shoulder of the highway to a cacophony of car horns.

The bad thing inside of her was Stephen's child. The child was her sin, working against her, trying to break her. The solution was simple: the only way to rid herself of her sin was to dispel the child.

Prayer had come to her like salvation. Around the time William was born, she had lost her connection to God. Being a mother had become the focus of her life and she had found herself bowing her head only during the difficult times. Chest rattling coughs from William's room in the middle of the night. High fevers that would not go away. Inexplicable scrapes and bruises. Meningitis at the neighbouring playschool.

When Stephen called for silence in the chapel, Mary Lou merely went through the motions, bowing her head and waiting, the possibility of actually convening with God far from her mind as she glanced at her watch, took note of who was wearing what and sitting with whom. Working for the church as she did made everything more about the business than the church, so that when she was sitting in church, all she could think was that the upholstery on the deacon's chairs needed mending, or that Randall needed to be reminded to dust the baseboard around the stage.

After her sexual encounters with Stephen, even the thought of prayer had seemed blasphemous. Buell had set it in her mind early on that the preacher was the conduit through which God could be reached. Mary Lou could not see Stephen as a conduit. As a matter of fact, whenever she imagined him, all she could see was the time he was behind her, moaning in pleasure, and she had opened her eyes to see what all the excitement was about, only to glimpse her breasts hanging down like the udders of a cow that had not been milked in some time.

Sitting in her car on the highway outside Atlanta, Mary Lou had felt lifted up by the possibility of salvation. She had kept the bracelet in her mouth, nestling the tiny cross on her tongue, praying to God to release her from her sins. As the car shook from passing traffic, she had squeezed her eyes tightly shut and begged Him to break her no more. It had to be possible that God would forgive her without completely ripping her in two. She had prayed for His understanding of her situation and when prayer failed, she had prayed for the strength to do what she knew she had to do.

With sudden clarity, she had understood what she needed to do. The only way to redeem herself was death. As she had merged back on to the highway, Mary Lou had justified the act, knowing William would be happier living with his father. Brian certainly would be ecstatic to be rid of her and Stephen was desperately looking for a way to get Mary Lou out of the church office and out of his life. She was to them a constant reminder of their disappointments. She was not a good wife, a good mother, or even a particularly good lover.

What she had prayed for as she drove was wisdom in the act. Her hands had begun to sweat as she had considered driving off one of the many bridges between Atlanta and Elawa, and she had reasoned that ramming her car into another vehicle would have been incredibly selfish.

Over the course of the next few days, she had read up on suicide, considering her options the same way she consulted *Consumer's Digest* back in the fall to see which was the better refrigerator to buy. The best course of action, she had decided, would be to use a gun, but she did not have enough money to buy one, and besides, buying a gun in Elawa was almost as difficult as getting an abortion. They wanted fingerprints. There was a waiting period. There were so many obstacles, as a matter of fact, that Mary Lou had begun to wonder if the people writing all these pamphlets about America going to hell in a handbasket were aware that the things they were warning about were actually harder to do than you'd think.

Pills were an obvious means to her end, but she did not know where to get the right kind, and was afraid that if she asked William he would know, maybe even give her some of his own. Even if she did know where to get pills, surely illegal drugs cost a lot of money, and after two doctor's visits – the clinic had demanded payment up front – Mary Lou had none. She had Valium from the time when Brian divorced her, but there were only ten left, hardly enough to accomplish the act. There was no garage to her house or she would have left the car running, letting the exhaust do the trick. Passing away in her sleep seemed like the easiest way out, but perhaps that was why it was the hardest to actually accomplish.

Cutting her wrists seemed like a good idea for about an hour's time, but then she had thought about William finding her, and the blood he would see. It wasn't so much that she had worried he would be emotionally scarred from finding his mother dead in a pool of her own blood, but that he might like it, and that by killing herself in such a way, she was creating the next Ted Bundy or Jeffrey Dahmer.

Again Mary Lou had suckled the cross on the bracelet and again she had prayed to God that He would show her how to kill herself. Oddly enough, His sign had come in the form of a flyer. Exactly seven days had passed since she had nearly killed the homeless man, and Mary Lou was not yet back to herself. Normally, she threw out junk mail, but for some reason she had started reading everything that came through the church's post office box as if her life depended on it.

She had scanned the offers from Reader's Digest and American Clearinghouse from start to finish, and entered the youth minister in a sweepstakes for a million dollar prize (even knowing that should he win, the church would never see a penny of it). Then, she had come across a bright pink flyer folded in on itself. The colour should have alerted Mary Lou, but she was beyond alerts since returning from Atlanta. Absently, she opened the folded sheet of paper, her eyes immediately going to the image of an unwound clothes hanger, the tip blackened with little sparks of lines around it because of course these pro-abortion organizations could not afford full colour copies like the church could. The headline asked, 'Do you want women to go back to back-alley abortions?'

Mary Lou had opened her mouth, the charm dropping out and slapping wetly against her chin. She knew His answer. She knew what had to be done.

The startling part of the whole procedure was the pain. Something had made Mary Lou think that she was beyond pain, but such was the intensity that she had passed out during the middle of it. How long she was out, she had no idea. It was dark outside when she had finally come to, and Mary Lou did not think to look at the clock. Like a splinter, it was more painful taking out the clothes hanger than when she had jammed it in. There was blood, but not as much as Mary Lou had anticipated. It was dark and viscous, not at all like the blood on television and therefore not as real.

She had cramped the whole night, but still did not pass the child. What she wanted above all was sleep, and though it had occurred to her that perhaps she had succeeded in killing herself now that God wanted her to live, Mary Lou was fine with this. All she wanted in the world, all she needed in the world, was sleep. She needed peace.

A week had passed, and her sick days were up. If William noticed his mother was unwell, he said nothing. She had heard him come and go by the music being played at full decibel in his room. For all she knew, the stereo was on a timer. There was no telling what her son was up to.

She had gone back to the church because she had to, not because she could. There was a lesson in doing things out of duty, she knew, but the first day back had been so difficult that Mary Lou had actually considered her suicide plans again. She had felt an infection burning in her like a smouldering fire. She had not bled enough. She had not seen fingers or toes in the toilet. There should have been something by now, and if there wasn't, that could only mean that it was still up there, still festering inside of her.

What could she do? A physician at the hospital would know instantly what had happened. She could not go to her regular doctor because he was a deacon at the church. The only thing she could think to do was to call his office and tell them she had a sinus infection but did not have time to come in for an appointment. Thankfully, the nurse had called in some antibiotics without asking any more questions. Mary Lou was not certain that the pills were working, though. Antibiotics were tricky. There were certain kinds for certain infections. Was a sinus infection the same as the infection that boiled in her lower regions? Was this slow, rotting sickness the thing that would finally kill her? Had she gone through all of this, dishonoured her family, her God, coveted her neighbour, committed mortal sins, all for nothing?

She had longed to pray, to talk to God and ask again for His guidance, but she could not bring her mind to do it. Even when she had taken the bracelet into her mouth as a sacrament, thoughts refused to form. She had contemplated speaking aloud to the Lord, confessing her predicament, but what if someone heard? What if Stephen Riddle overheard her confession and renounced her from the pulpit? What if the entire church found out what she had done and cast her out? She would lose what friends she had, and William would be taken away from her. She would have nothing left, nothing, not even a place of worship.

Slowly, she had felt herself begin to fade from the life she had known. After years of unsuccessful dieting, she had suddenly lost weight. Food did not appeal. She no longer read, no longer watched television. When the school suspended William, she had hardly had the strength to shrug. When Brian had told her he would not be able to pay his half of the mortgage, she had simply hung up the phone without another word.

'Ma'am?' Jasper called from the doorway, and Mary Lou realized she had let herself begin to fade yet again. She turned away from the window, her fingers going to the charm bracelet as she looked at the black man. He stood at the edge of the chapel, and if he'd had a hat, it would have been in his mauled hands. She wondered if he was uncomfortable being in a church. He certainly seemed like it, his toes just at the edge of the carpet, not quite crossing back into the room.

'Coming,' she said, clasping the bracelet as she walked towards him. He looked like he might offer her his hand when she reached the foyer, but Mary Lou crossed her arms over her chest making it clear she did not need help. She could tell from the expression on his contorted face that she did not look well. She had chills despite the heat in the foyer, and the back of her legs felt prickly, like a thousand needles stinging into her skin at the same time.

They crossed the parking lot, the heat enveloping them like a blanket. The sun was so intense that it appeared to be black against the blue afternoon sky. Mary Lou kept her eyes on the sawhorses, unable to make out the pattern of the cross. She stumbled, grabbing on to Jasper so she would not fall. His skin was warm under the long sleeves, and she could feel the sinew of his damaged arm, the muscles contracting as he tried to support her. She fell to her knees anyway, her arms flailing out beside her, grasping at the dry air. The pain in her belly was too much now, and she pitched forward, the hot asphalt slapping her face, penetrating her clothes like hellfire.

A racking pain overcame her, as if something was living inside her belly, clawing its way out. She grasped her stomach, screaming in agony, closing her eyes against the black hole that was the sun as her bowels seized and her womb contracted, expelling her sin on to the asphalt. The blood that she had not bled before seeped out between her legs like honey, and she could feel the heavy liquid and tissue dripping down her thighs like great chunks of wet clay.

Mary Lou rolled on to her back and the Mexicans stepped back quickly, as if acid had been poured at their feet. The hand she put over her mouth was covered in her own blood and something else she could not name. The ground was rich with it, a slick black oil. She looked to find the sun in the sky, to stare at the black dot until the image was forever burned into her eyes, but her vision was blocked by the enormous arm of the cross. They had fixed it, a small seam showing where the cross had been rejoined. The point of fracture had been healed like a fresh wound, the scar toughening the wood, making it stronger.

'Holy Mother,' one of the Mexicans said, and she felt more liquid explode between her legs.

Pain shot through Mary Lou again, a knife cutting from the inside. The throbbing between her legs seized her, and she screamed so loud that her throat ached as if she were being choked. Inch by inch, she felt her flesh ripping apart, being clawed open from the inside.

'Steady,' Jasper said, his ugly hands reaching between her legs. She was bared to them all, her dress up above her waist, wet panties around her knees. She could see a figure standing in the window of the chapel. Was it Stephen? Was he watching this, waiting to see what happened? She called out to him, but the figure moved away.

'It's OK,' Jasper soothed, his mauled hands inside her now, trying to pull something out. She felt a final rip, then just as suddenly, a dull ache replaced the pain, blood flowing freely with the obstruction removed.

'Lord, Jesus,' the Mexicans prayed, speaking English as if for her benefit. They took off their hats and bowed their heads.

Jasper held up a tiny bundle of legs and arms, all attached to a torso that moved up and down in rapid beats as the child screamed at the top of his lungs. His cries were an accusation, a condemnation to the whore who had brought him into this world.

One of the Mexicans kneeled beside Mary Lou, holding out a dirty towel for the baby. He gently cradled the baby boy in his arms, cooing.

Jasper stayed beside her, rummaging through his tool box. She saw him take out an old, beaten-up pocketknife, and he used this to cut through the cord that attached Mary Lou to the child. One of the Mexicans caught the cord, tying it with a piece of twine. Jasper did not bother with the end that was connected to Mary Lou. She could tell from the look in his eyes that there was nothing that could stop the flow. Her spirit was being drawn out from between her legs, and anything that made to slow it down would only be postponing the inevitable.

Jasper's big black hand grasped hers, his lips moving almost imperceptibly. The skin on his face was tighter than she had ever noticed, and the discoloration more prominent than before. Her eyes were again drawn to his unnaturally coloured lips as he closed his eyes and began to whisper. She strained to hear what he was saying, and was so surprised by his words that for just a moment she forgot the pain. A sudden lightness filled her chest, and she felt the power of Jasper's words flow through her like a cleansing balm. The drumbeat of her blood pounding in her ears began to recede. As she drew breath, she drew in the man's words, holding them in her lungs until they felt full enough to carry her away.

'Lord God,' Jasper said through his beautiful, pink lips. 'Please welcome this woman into Your house. Shine Your light down upon her to lead the way. Help her see Your power and glory.'

Mary Lou tried to thank him even as she felt herself slip away. She wanted to let Jasper know that his words had brought her peace. The child continued to scream, and she reached her hand out to him, the gold bracelet on her wrist scraping across the asphalt. The sun caught the chain, illuminating where the link had been broken and mended like new.

'For him,' she said. She was broken so the child could be strong.

'For him,' Jasper repeated, his bloody hands working the clasp of the bracelet.

'No,' she said, but her voice was gone now, the word only spoken in her head.

Jasper removed the bracelet and placed it in the blanket beside the boy, telling Mary Lou, 'He'll remember his mother. He'll always have this.'

'No,' she tried again, then she looked into her son's face, and it did not matter. Nothing mattered but the fact that her son had lived. He had fought for his life, challenged the will of his mother to honour the will of God.

Yes, she thought. He would be strong because the bracelet would teach him the lessons that had broken those before him. The many charms would forever tell their stories: the key to vanity, the gluttony of the monkey, the greed of the dollar sign, the envious ballerina, the angry goblin, the lustful tiger and even the cross, which Mary Lou suddenly understood represented her own indolence.

As her fingers slipped from Jasper Goode's hand, Mary Lou felt herself smile. She looked up at the heavens, at the black sun. The child would be good. Like Jesus, he would wash away her sins. He would be strong where his mother was not. He would realize the gift of her death, that only through Mary Lou's sacrifice could he be born, and born again. He would be strong because of her weakness. One day, he would look at the bracelet and know her story.

One day, he would understand the blessing of brokenness.

HOMECOMING

Cath Staincliffe

Cath Staincliffe is the author of mysteries featuring private eye Sal Kilkenny, and the creator of the ITV series *Blue Murder*. She has also written novels based on the television series *Scott & Bailey* and stand-alone psychological thrillers. Staincliffe lives in Manchester, UK.

The day was ending as he reached the house.

The roof still held but the windows had gone, the doors too. And in front where the path had once been, a cloud of gnats danced over a large puddle. A few more years and the whole lot would collapse, the stone return to the earth, the foundations become choked by rough grass and bracken and briars.

'*I had a little nut tree, nothing would it bear, but a silver nutmeg and a golden pear.*'

He hadn't thought of the song for years. Susan singing. Whirling round in the snow, her new purple herringbone coat, the colour of the heather on the moor, flecked with white and black, spinning out as she turned. Her raven hair whipping about. Always dancing, like she couldn't keep still. She would learn the latest moves in the playground and teach Hugh.

'Giddy goat,' their father would say, smiling.

But their mother called her wilful and impudent.

'This dump,' Susan used to call it, 'I'm going to leave this dump and go to London.' She would be a dancer or a singer. Hugh didn't want her to go and leave him behind but she promised to send for him.

'We could share a flat.'

'And have parties.'

'And go travelling in a bus with all our friends.'

'And never go to chapel again.'

The chapel, Mother's passion, dominated their lives. Mother had come to Wales as an evacuee from Liverpool. Her family were killed in the Blitz and so she had stayed on with the old minister and his housekeeper. He was of the fire and brimstone school and taught Mother his ways. Hugh remembered her voice, going on and on and on about the wickedness of people, how corrupt and immoral they were, perverted and shameless, degenerates living in the gutter. On and on until Father would get up and walk out. He'd be gone for hours. And Hugh would have a sick ache inside of him in case Father didn't come home but he always did.

Hugh stepped inside the cottage. The place was stripped bare, he wondered who'd done that, removed beds and the dresser, the table and chairs. It smelled of mice and mould. The paint on the walls was mottled and flaking, chunks of plaster littered the floor. In the back room were signs that people had sheltered here: old fires, cans and crisp packets. Tramps, perhaps, too far off the beaten track for anyone else.

Out the back, wilderness had taken over. He walked, treading down brambles thick as rope, the fruit on them glistening fat and black. Glass and guttering snapping underfoot. This was a kitchen garden once, the soil was poor but his mother had coaxed potatoes and leeks, raspberries and peas from it.

The hazel tree was still there at the end beside the hawthorn. He and Susan would pick the cobnuts, once the bright green shells turned brown, cracking them in their back teeth and fishing out the sweet nut meat.

Hugh loved Susan, she was the warmth of the house, so when she went off to Cardiff he had for a time resented her. He wondered if she would send for him once he was finished with school. But no word came and eventually he took up the apprenticeship in the Merchant Navy.

He'd sent a postcard or two at first, from new continents, new countries, out of a sense of duty. He wrote, once he was settled in New Zealand, so they'd have an address for him, but got no reply.

Forty-seven years since he had left. Nearly half a century.

His mother posted a note, brief and formal, in 2001, after his father's funeral. And once she'd gone, the solicitor had written to say the cottage, with its two acres, was his. Nothing left to Susan, all to him.

Let it rot, he thought, but then he got the diagnosis. The only treatment palliative. He needed to put his affairs in order while they'd still let him travel. Straightforward enough in Auckland: no dependents, no property to dispose of. Raymond and he had built a life together but Raymond had died far too young – before they'd developed the antiretrovirals – and Hugh had never found anyone else. He would leave his savings to Susan and the same with the cottage, it wasn't worth much but it would be hers. After floundering himself, he'd hired an investigator to trace her. No news as yet. According to the records she'd not married but Hugh took heart from the fact that she hadn't died either.

Hugh looked across the moorland to the horizon. You could see for fifteen miles, and no other building in view. Rushes marked the paths of streams descending the hills from the limestone crags, and here and there were lone trees forced to grow sideways by the wind. Sheep dotted the landscape, and lower down the valley the slopes were divided by dry-stone walls. None of it had changed.

He was eleven when Susan fell pregnant. She was fifteen. She never went back to school after Christmas, she had to stay in: no chapel, no trips to town. Hidden if anyone called, though barely anyone ever did. Glandular fever, that's what Hugh had to say if he was asked. She had told him about Gwyn Davies, in the year above her, how he was sweet on Susan, how he wanted to go to London too. She swore Hugh to silence.

He knew it was a terrible thing, a sin. An abomination, his mother called it, one of the few times she mentioned the fact. It was a secret. Even in the house, between the four of them, it was a secret. Everybody pretending that it wasn't there, wasn't happening. When the time came the child would go to a decent Christian family, he'd overheard his mother tell Susan.

Susan never talked about the baby. One time Hugh asked: a Sunday when they were alone, their parents at the morning service. Hugh had been sick with tonsillitis, he was almost better but claimed he still felt ill so he could stay behind. They had switched the radio over to the Light Programme, *Easy Beat*. The reception was crackly, Billy J Kramer, Gerry and The Pacemakers, The Beatles, *I Saw Her Standing There,* but Susan sang along and Hugh joined in. He danced too and she cheered him on. Susan was stroking her stomach which was big by then and Hugh said, 'Does it feel strange?' And she'd flinched, like he'd pinched her, and she moved her hand away. He had felt stupid. But then she'd started on knock-knock jokes and he felt better.

It was July, hot and airless, and Hugh had woken in the middle of the night, thirsty, to hear his parents arguing.

'I'll fetch the doctor—' his father said.

'No,' his mother said.

'If we call the hospital—'

'It's nature's way,' she said.

'It's too soon,' his father said.

'Do you want us shamed, vilified? Do you want the whole valley to know we have a daughter who's no better than a bitch in heat?' his mother said.

'But if—'

'It's God's will,' she said, 'and nature's way.'

'Jean—'

'No.'

Hugh heard steps, the creak of boards by Susan's door.

'Leave her,' Mother said, 'I'll see to her.'

The front door shut, and then there was the bang of the gate as his father left.

Susan was moaning.

When it got light Hugh had to stay outside all day, weeding the vegetable patch, which was full of couch grass and dock and thistle.

His mother called Hugh for tea. Just the two of them at the table. 'Your sister is ill, so you leave her alone, you hear?' she said.

'Yes,' he said. 'Is it the baby coming?'

'There is no baby,' his mother said.

And later still, as the dusk came in, his father was back.

Hugh heard him digging, the crisp cut of the spade, the chink when it struck rock. Peering out of his bedroom window, Hugh saw his father with the spade, at the end of the vegetable beds, along from the hazel tree.

Susan never sang again, not that he heard. She was sullen, refusing to speak, not eating or washing, her face to the wall. Now and then exploding with an anger that seemed too large for the house. Shouting and swearing, calling his mother awful names and hitting out. Raving that if Mother had sent for help the baby might have lived, that she was no better than a murderer. His mother would slap her quiet. And Susan still ranted his mother would reach for the stick.

Hugh had been camping with the scouts in August, a brief respite. His father collected him from the hall in town after finishing his shift at the quarry. He told Hugh on the drive back that Susan had run away. That Mother was furious but there was nothing to be done about it.

Hugh was cross too, that she'd gone without telling him.

'Did she go to London?' Hugh said.

'I don't know,' his father said, 'Cardiff probably.'

When he got the chance, Hugh sneaked into her room to check, and it was true. Her coat and bag were gone. She'd not even left a note for him but then if Mother had discovered the note she might have found a way to stop Susan going.

Hugh waited for news, a letter, but none came. Or if it did, his mother got to it first and threw it on the fire.

Word got round school that Susan had gone to Cardiff. Boys would come up to him saying, 'Your sister's working the docks, isn't she?' Sniggering. He puzzled over that, a fifteen-year-old girl hired as a stevedore, until Thomas Vaughan told him, in the crudest possible terms, how she was earning a living. Hugh's face burned up and he wanted to thump Thomas Vaughan but he just walked off. After that, school was a torture to be endured. The days, the months, stretched out, aching into the distance.

The house was a miserable place with Susan gone. Hugh thought his father missed her too, silent on their morning drives when he'd drop Hugh off on the road to walk the rest of the way to school. Silent all the time. Away from the house even more. His father looked older, smaller, like an apple shrinking with age. If Father had only stood up to Mother then maybe the doctors could have saved the baby and Susan wouldn't have gone just yet.

As soon as he could, Hugh left it all behind.

Hugh found a stone, almost level, where he could sit and watch the sun bleed across the sky and sink beyond the horizon.

As the darkness fell, the bats came out to feed, spinning and swooping not far above his head. Stars glittered and a waxing crescent moon hung, the other way around from at home.

The pain was back, it was time for his tablets, so he rose slowly and used the light on his phone to guide his way through the undergrowth and the shell of the house back to the car where he would sleep. No doubt the hire company would charge him for the state of it, mud and scratches from bucking up the old lane.

The temperature soon dropped, his breath misted the windows but he had a blanket and a flask of coffee so he drank half of it and then pushed the seat back as far as it would go and pulled the blanket up to his chin.

He wondered if she had made it to London, had become a singer or a dancer. If she had any more children. Then he'd be an uncle. That thought made him feel odd, nice though.

As first light crept over the land, Hugh took his tablets and finished the coffee.

He got the things out of the boot. He had called at a large DIY store on the new ring road outside of town where he'd bought the spade and a plastic storage box in case he did find anything. A bundle of bones he guessed by now. Hugh hoped that Susan wouldn't think he was acting out of turn, wanting to find the child and give him a burial, when it was her baby after all. He'd intended to discuss it with her, plan it together. What if they couldn't track her down? What would he put on the headstone? *Baby born too soon.* Was it a boy or a girl? Had she named the child? He wasn't even sure of the date, he only knew it was July, 1963. It would be so much easier to do all this with her.

The day was fair, a breeze from the west, clear blue sky and the promise of warmth to come. He saw rabbits scatter as he walked to the hazel tree.

The ground was hard to dig, tangled thick with roots and he hadn't the strength that he used to have. He stopped several times, sweat stinging his eyes, blisters breaking on his palms. After half an hour, he'd found nothing. Had he been wrong, guessing his father had buried the stillborn baby? Was his memory playing tricks?

Hugh began again, a new hole further along. The sun burned the back of his neck and he heard the burbling song of skylarks, and grasshoppers cricking, then the whistling cry of a red kite. He straightened up and narrowed his eyes to watch the raptor circling the hillside.

He kept digging. He found a tiny hand first, like a monkey's paw, and then the rest of it, not much bigger than a rabbit's skeleton, along with scraps of fabric, a towel or something. He lifted the bones out and placed them in the plastic box. He thought it was all there but decided to dig another foot to the right to make sure. When his shovel hit resistance, he tested the soil around, driving the spade in until he got purchase, digging it out. Scooping back more earth. Panting, his throat parched.

Herringbone cloth, the colours still clear.

Hanks of black hair.

His blood froze.

Trembling he dug some more and found a skull, a jagged line fractured the temple.

Susan spinning, her arms wide, her voice strong and clear, '*I skipped over water, I danced over sea and all the birds in the air they couldn't catch me.*'

Hugh saw the cotton grass shiver in the wind and heard the song of the skylarks rejoicing above.

He set down his spade and knelt and lifted his face to the sky.

THE AMBUSH

Donna Tartt

Donna Tartt is a major American literary novelist and worldwide best-seller. She has won several awards including the Pulitzer Prize in 2014. Her novels include the inverted detective story *The Secret History*, *The Little Friend*, and *The Goldfinch*.

Before I met Tim – who, in spite of everything I'm about to tell you, would be my best friend for the next four or five years – my mother warned me on the way over to his grandmother's house that I had to be nice to him. "I mean it, Evie. And don't mention his father."

"Why?" I said. I was expecting to hear: Because his parents are divorced. (This was why I had to be nice to John Kendrick, who I couldn't stand.)

"Because," my mother said, "Tim's father was killed in Vietnam."

"Did he get shot?"

"I don't know," said my mother. "And don't you ask him."

I was eight, and small for my age. Tim was seven. As my mother and his grandmother chatted above my head in the doorway of his grandmother's house, we looked at each other silently, from a distance, like two little animals: me, standing in the bright doorway between the grown-ups; Tim, from the remote wood-paneled darkness of the hallway. I couldn't see him clearly, but he was my height, which pleased me.

My mother put her hand on my shoulder. "Did you know," she said to me, in the stagy voice she used when she spoke to me in front of other people, "that Mrs. Cameron is good friends with your grandmother?"

I twisted away, shyly, under the broad pink-gummed smile of Mrs. Cameron. Every old lady in town was friends with my grandmother: if she didn't play cards with them, she went to church with them. The card-playing friends dyed their hair and dressed more stylishly, with cocktail rings and handbags that matched their shoes. The church friends were stouter, and friendlier to children; they wore flower prints, and pearls instead of diamonds, if they wore jewelry at all. Mrs. Cameron was clearly a church friend: compact, pony-built, with shiny pink cheeks. Her hair was grey and she had very black eyebrows, but they were naturally black, like a man's – not drawn on with pencil.

"Hello, honey," she said to me. "I've got a nice swing-set out in the backyard. Tim, why don't you take her out to see it?"

As soon as we were alone, the very first thing Tim said to me was: "My dad's dead."

"I know," I said.

He didn't seem surprised that I knew. We stood facing each other, over the water hydrant in his grandmother's back yard: a long way away from the house. He was a snub-nosed, well-rounded little boy, burned brown from the sun, with eerie yellow-brown eyes and a plump, satisfying tummy like a rabbit's. He reached inside his shirt and showed me some dog tags on a metal chain.

"These were his," he said. "They're mine now."

The dog tags had a name stamped on them that was Tim's last name, and they said US MARINES, but didn't look like they really belonged to his dad. They looked like something he'd had made at a fair or at a booth at the mall.

"See, my dad was trying to chase down this Vietnamese that shot his friend," said Tim. "And then the Vietnamese killed him, too. I can act it out for you if you want. I'll be my dad and you be his buddy. OK. Here we are in the jungle." He walked away a few steps, and then looked back at me. "You're walking with me. Keep up. We can't get separated."

"What's my name?"

"Hank," he said, with gratifying swiftness. "Hank Madigan. All right, here we go. We're walking down the path towards camp, we're talking, OK?"

"OK," I said. I caught up with him, and together we crept – heads down, a pair of cautious infantrymen – towards a tangle of shrubbery at the edge of his grandmother's yard. He'd said we were supposed to be talking, and I wondered if maybe I should ask something soldierly ("How far to camp, sir?") but Tim had such a grim, determined look on his face that I was slightly afraid to say anything at all, even in character. He ploughed straight ahead, towards the shrubbery, while I kept my eyes on the side of his face.

"Now – all of a sudden, these shots come out the jungle, eck eck eck BOOM. You're dead," he said, after a moment or two when I still stood looking at him.

Obediently I clutched my chest and crumpled to the grass. Tim – gratifyingly – dropped to his knees beside me and began to shake my shoulders.

"Oh my God!" he said. "Stay with me, Hank! You can't die, you son of a bitch!"

I grimaced and tossed my head from side to side in agony as Tim – in a desperate effort to revive me – pounded on my chest. I was impressed by his profanity, but even more impressed that he had taken the Lord's name in vain on my behalf.

Far away, from the back porch, Tim's grandmother called out to us in a thin, irritating voice: "Do you all want lemonade?"

"No," shouted Tim, plainly annoyed. He sat back on his heels, on the grass, and looked at me. "You're hurt too bad to live," he said to me, matter-of-factly. "There's nothing I can do for you."

I coughed a little and said: "Goodbye." Then I shut my eyes and fell back on the lawn.

In the silence following my death, as I lay still with my cheek against the scratchy warm grass, I heard Tim's grandmother call: "Why don't yall go play on the swings?"

"Because we don't want to," screamed Tim.

I raised up on my elbows obligingly. "Wait until she leaves," said Tim under his breath to me. He was angry, staring fixedly into the yard next door.

At last, Tim's grandmother called: "All right." The childish quiver of her voice as it trailed away made me feel bad. She went back inside the house, and I heard the door shut, with a forlorn, final sound.

I started to get up but Tim pushed me down on the grass again. "You're dead," he said. "You can't raise up on your elbow or talk to me or do anything like that. Anyway. So then," – Tim unslung a pretend rifle from his shoulder – "my dad screams: 'You shot my buddy! I'm gonna get you!'" He ran across the grass to the bank of privet hedge that bordered the lawn, mouth twisted, fanning his imaginary rifle, spitting imaginary bullets: eck eck eck eck eck

"Ha! Got you!" he cried. And then his face went empty; he reeled back, winced and jerked under a burst of automatic gunfire, then clutched his own chest and went down.

We lay there in silence for a few moments, staring blankly at the sky, before Tim got up and looked at me. "That's how my dad died," he said.

I sat up. Then I looked back at his grandmother's house – and saw a hand parting a curtain at a tiny upstairs window.

"Somebody's up there watching us," I said, and pointed. "See?"

"Oh, don't worry," said Tim, without looking, "that's just my mother," and as he spoke, I saw the curtain drop back down slowly over the window.

"Let's act it out again," said Tim.

From then on, I ran down the street to play with Tim almost every day – in his grandmother's yard but also in the tall weeds of an empty lot next door. If for some reason I was late slipping away to his house in the morning, he came down the street and pounded manfully on the back door for me. Then we ran away together down the bright sidewalk without speaking, crashing through back yards and hedges down to the jungle-flanked path where the assassin waited for us. All day long we dodged bullets in rank suburban tangles of elderberry and ailanthus and day-lilies run wild, scrambling on our hands and knees, running doubled over, darting in breathless zigzags from point to point, cover to cover, running and freezing and running again, barraged by fire from an enemy we never saw. And again and again we staggered and fell before him – first me, then Tim; for though our battles became daily more elaborate and complicated (firefights; booby-traps; mortar-rocket attacks) the end of the game was always the same. Contorted in our separate agonies, we lay face-up in the buzzing heat, just long enough for our deaths to settle over us and soak in. And even after we rubbed our eyes, stretched and sat up again, we sometimes sat quietly for a little while without saying much, like people just waking from sleep.

"One more time," Tim would say – standing suddenly, breaking the spell. "But better this time."

I was used to playing with children like Tim – holiday visitors whose grandparents were friends with my grandparents – and when it was time for them to go home it was easy for me to say goodbye and run down the street without looking back. For a week every Christmas I played chess with timid Robby Millard, whose parents were missionaries in Mexico, and who had all kinds of stomach problems and took all kinds of medicine because he'd gotten an intestinal parasite from eating improperly washed fruit in Mexico City. And every Easter vacation I looked forward to Jackie and Sherilyn – twins, blonde and freckled, older than me – who loved little kids and were constantly begging their parents for a baby brother or sister. The first time they'd met me, they had each taken me by a hand and led me up to the remote attic bedroom in their grandmother's house where they had set up housekeeping, kindly explaining that we were destitute orphans and I was their baby sister ("Hannah") who they were bringing up on their own. So every spring, for a few days, I was "Hannah", and Jackie and Sherilyn cooked and washed and swept and sewed for me and sang me to sleep in the "garret" where we all lived.

But Tim was different. We were the same size. His yellow-brown eyes were like the eyes of an intensely interested house-cat. There was nothing silly or frivolous about him and I felt that his seriousness made him my natural soulmate. I felt, too – intuitively – that somehow he wasn't quite as temporary as Jackie and Sherilyn and the others, and as it turned out, I was right.

Tim's father – the Lieutenant Robert Allan Cameron whose name was printed on the dog tags – had been Mrs. Cameron's only son. But what had been announced by Mrs. Cameron (at church) as a post-funeral visit from her grandson and daughter-in-law soon stretched beyond the usual two-week limit. A month passed; then two months. Painters were seen trooping into Mrs. Cameron's house. Then a child's bed was ordered from the furniture store downtown. My mother – in an overly casual tone which did not conceal her curiosity – asked me if I knew when Tim and his mother were going back to Dallas (which was where they lived) or if I ever saw Tim's mother when I went over to Mrs. Cameron's house.

"No," I said, and ran off. I was still little enough that I could deal with questions I didn't want to answer or didn't know how to answer by literally turning and running away.

Vietnam. The war was on the news every night but I couldn't understand it, even when my mother tried to explain it to me. The pictures flashed by in no particular order: bad roads, explosions, fires burning in jungle blackness; schoolgirls riding bicycles, and deserted-looking cities where paper blew down the street. An American prisoner of war bowed from the waist in all four directions like a maniac. The place-names (Haiphong, Dak To, Ia Drang, Dong Ha) were like something from a ghost story. Some of the far country places didn't even have names, only numbers, and some of the soldiers – mud-caked, grinning, staggering and falling, their helmets scrawled with ugly black writing – looked crazy.

There was something nightmarish about the dusty green gloss of the camellia bushes, deep deep cover where our sniper lay and waited for us. Every day, he drew us in as if by a poisonous charm; every day we dove from the trap and crawled for cover, as round after round of fire cracked over our heads. The skirmish took on very different moods, depending on the time of day: damp, overcast mornings, with dew and frantic birdsong; shadowless noons where the sun beat down empty and white; violent afternoon downpours that swept in on us in moments, no warning but a sudden blackening of the sky, and then a gust that sent the leaves flying. Together we hid under the trees as Tim's grandmother called us uselessly from the back porch, the strong wind snatching the words from her mouth. But the rains blew over us and pattered away almost as quickly as they came – sometimes in less than a minute – and then the sun poured out with almost unimaginable brilliance on the rainwashed greenery.

With dripping hair, clothes plastered to our bodies, we dropped to our knees and crawled from beneath our tree and commenced our battle again. It was only a matter of time before I was struck, then Tim, before we clutched the grass and died on the ground together in blood-smeared agony – but still we fought every day until the fireflies came out, until it was almost too dark to see. And even when I was supposed to be dead, sometimes I opened my eyes to sneak a look over at Tim because he was so locked-in, face turned up and staring raptly over the twilit garden and out into some different reality; and though I was never sure exactly what he saw (white smoke? incoming helicopters? tracer rounds, orange sparks?), whatever it was, it shone off his face and left it luminous, like reflected light from a movie screen.

I began to grow bold around Mrs. Cameron. Though I didn't dare shout at her or order her around as Tim did, I often ran past her without answering when she spoke to me, and – following Tim's lead – no longer bothered with thank you or please. If I'd behaved so badly at my own house, I would have got a spanking – but somehow I understood that Mrs. Cameron wasn't going to tell. When Tim and I burst thundering into the house, with mud and leaves in our hair and dirty knees from crawling on the ground, she often looked up at us with a bright, slightly alarmed smile, all long teeth and pink gums, as if we were a pair of snappy terriers who might bite. We gulped down her lemonade without a word, snatched away the oatmeal cookies she offered us and stuffed them into our pockets and ran back out to the field again.

Then one day we galloped into the kitchen, hot and dirty, and there – at the table with Mrs. Cameron, glancing up at us with a quick, flinching movement – was Tim's mother. She was young and very thin, with pale lipstick and a nervous mouth. Her collarbones stood out at the neckline of her sleeveless top; her hair was teased stiff, and back-combed; and her eyes (heavily done, with lots of dark make-up) had a bruised and slightly pleading look. She was the kind of mother that made you want to jump at her from behind a door and yell BOO.

I stopped. "Hello," I said, for I still hadn't quite forgotten my manners.

Tim's mother looked over at me and smiled, with a sort of grateful surprise; and something about the smile made me angry. It was a comradely, confidential smile, as if she assumed that I was her ally and not Tim's.

"Hiya, cutie," she said. "You're a little doll, aren't ya?" Her voice was warm and rough and startling, entirely at odds with her frail-looking person. I'd never heard a Brooklyn accent before, except on The Honeymooners or The Jackie Gleason Show.

"What's wrong, doll? Cat gotcha tongue? Listen up, buddy," she said to Tim, "what's with all the screaming and yellin' out there?"

"Oh, Gali!" said Mrs. Cameron. "Let him play! He's just a little boy!" But as she reached around and drew Tim close to her I noticed – with surprise – that her eyes were pink, that she was blinking back the tears.

Tim shrugged away from her and turned to me with an expression that meant: let's go. And out we ran from the kitchen, clattering down the back steps, running faster than usual because we were both embarrassed by the scene (though I doubt either of us could have said quite why) and because we wanted to get back down to our palmy little Vietnam where our ambush awaited.

"Wonder what Mrs. Cameron thought," my father said at dinner a few nights later, "when Bobby Cameron come back from up north married to a Jewish girl?"

I started to ask what Jewish meant, but before I could, my mother gave me a quick glance and said: "Well, I expect Mrs. Cameron's glad enough to have her now that Bobby's dead."

My father reached for the salt. "Roger Bell over at the barber shop?" he said pleasantly. "He was in for a root canal the other day and he said she used to sell newspapers and magazines from a stand on the street. That's how Bobby met her."

"What's wrong with selling newspapers?" I said.

"Nothing," said my mother. "There's nothing wrong with working for a living."

"I'm just saying." Busily, my father shook salt over his food. "You know it's got to kill Mrs. Cameron. If Bobby had stayed home and married Kitty Teasdale, I can tell you Ogden Teasdale would have kept him out of it. Ogden's in the legislature," he said, when my mother kept on looking at him like she wanted him to shut up. "He isn't going to have any son-in-law of his going off to Vietnam."

"Well," said my mother, "all I can say is, if you went to Vietnam and got killed, I sure wouldn't be taking the children and going to live with your mother."

My father shrugged. "You might," he said. "If you didn't have anyplace else to go."

Both my mother and my grandmother seemed vaguely troubled that Tim and his mother were living at Mrs. Cameron's, but for reasons I didn't understand. Mainly they seemed bothered that Mrs. Cameron hadn't given an official explanation or made a formal announcement of any sort. ("Why hasn't anybody met her yet?" I heard my mother's friend Virginia ask. "It looks like Mrs. Cameron would throw a little party or something for her, doesn't it?")

Some days, Tim's mother stayed in her room and listened to the radio – baseball games, Motown hits turned up so loud that we could hear them outside. But she was also starting to spend a lot more time downstairs. She and Mrs. Cameron called each other by their first names: Rose and Gali. They sat together at the kitchen table; they drank coffee and tea; they talked, mostly in voices too low to hear. ("Sure, I was poor, growing up," I heard her say to Mrs. Cameron, her husky voice rising louder than usual. "But not poor poor.") They looked at magazines and cookbooks; they looked at a scrapbook which was of things Tim's father had done in high school. Once or twice, Tim and I ran in the kitchen while Mrs. Cameron was trying to teach Tim's mother how to knit, but she couldn't seem to get the hang of it ("Nah," she said, flopping her hands at the tangle of yarn, "looka this thing, I got it all screwed up. I mean, all fouled up," she added, when she saw the expression on Mrs. Cameron's face).

By now it was full summer, and the days were almost unbearably hot. And maybe it was only the heat, but the old adrenaline punch of the game wasn't nearly so strong any more. So Tim and I played even harder, trying to pump it all up again, anything to draw fire and beat back our boredom. We tore pickets from the fence to build a stockade; we lobbed mud-clod grenades into the enemy stronghold; we trampled the garden in our desperate retreats, knocked over flowerpots and broke them. Sometimes Tim's mother got up from the kitchen table and came to watch us from the back porch with a strange expression on her face – but once or twice, when it looked like she was about to come out and say something, Mrs. Cameron came over and took her by the arm and whispered in her ear. Then they both went inside, back to the kitchen table again.

"You see?" said Tim triumphantly, as we were carrying the "stakes" we'd torn from Mrs. Cameron's cherry tree back to our position, in order to lay a trap for our enemy. "They don't mind. It's because my dad's dead."

One evening, when my grandmother came over to our house to return a book she'd borrowed, she announced: "Mrs. Cameron brought that little daughter-in-law of hers to the Garden Club party yesterday."

"Oh really?" said my mother. She put down her needlework; she looked at my grandmother. "And how was that?"

"She's a pretty little thing," said my grandmother, "with a trim little figure, but my Lord! Of course she's perfectly pleasant."

"What do you mean?"

"It's just –" My grandmother's voice trailed away, and she made a sort of vague, meaningless gesture. We were used to these pauses of hers; she was one of those ladies who tried never to say anything about anybody if it wasn't nice.

"Well, she tries very hard indeed," she said at last, as if that was an end to it.

It took a while, but finally my mother managed to get a bit more information out of her. For one thing: Tim's mother had worn black stretch pants and spike heeled shoes; and she had also used some coarse language, though my grandmother wouldn't repeat it. Moreover, Tim had been brought to the party (my mother looked startled; this wasn't something people did) and his mother and Mrs. Cameron had had a hard time controlling him.

"They won't lay a hand on him, either one of them," my grandmother said. "He ran wild all over the garden. The mother is lax, but it's not all her fault. Rose Cameron won't let her touch him."

"I wonder why?"

"Well, I don't know if you remember, but Bobby Cameron was spoiled, too."

I listened uneasily as my mother and my grandmother talked about how hard things must be for poor Mrs. Cameron, and how terrible they felt for her. Then, with an uncomfortable start, I realized that my mother was giving me a look.

"What exactly do you and Tim do over at Mrs. Cameron's all day?" she said.

"Nothing."

"You don't ever play rough or misbehave over at her house, do you?"

"No, ma'am," I said.

"I'd better not find out that you do."

I was troubled all the rest of that evening, and that night, as I lay in bed, I resolved to act better at Mrs. Cameron's house. Even if Tim was bad, I would be good. But by the next day – when Tim and I dragged out house-paint and brushes from Mrs. Cameron's garage and began to paint a landing strip on the grass – I had forgotten all about it.

"I'm bored," said Tim one hot afternoon in July.

It was the first time either of us had said it aloud. But I was starting to get bored, too. Our firefights had slowed. Now, when we died, we took longer and longer getting up to fight again. Sometimes now, in Mrs. Cameron's wrecked yard, we lay on the ground for hours, as still as a pair of fallen trees, as clouds of tiny black bugs hummed all around us.

"Without an enemy," said Tim, "it's not a real war."

I knew what he meant. The problem with the artillery barrages we endured all day long was that they weren't actually coming from anywhere; we had ground fire, plenty of it, but no shooter. And what was the fun of that? We had tried splitting up, chasing each other, but we were already too much of a team: it felt fake. There were other kids in the neighbourhood, but they were all much older or much younger; the younger kids were no fun to play with, and the older ones wouldn't have anything to do with us, even when we threw pebbles and tried to make them chase us.

"Let's go play under the hose," I said. I was forbidden to touch the hose and the outdoor faucets at my own house, and I couldn't understand Tim's lack of interest in water fights, especially since it was so hot.

"What about that little kid Brannon who lives in the white brick house?" suggested Tim.

"He's way too little. His mother doesn't let him go out of his own yard."

There was a long silence. Up front, we heard the door creak open – and all of a sudden, Tim's face lit up.

"Hey!" he said, in a hushed voice. He sat up; he listened. I sat up, too. A flash of excitement crackled through me at the tense bright expression on his face. And when we looked at each other, I realized that we were thinking the same thing.

Tim – trembling all over – put a finger to his lips. Then, silently, he motioned for me to follow. Quickly – in his doubled-up Marine crouch – he ran out of our brushy cover and out on to the lawn, and I ran out behind him, blood pounding with a fierce joy.

I've played and replayed this moment a lot in my mind over the years; and it all happened so quickly that even in memory it goes by too fast, I wince at it, knowing I can't stop it. We rounded the corner of the house – and then Tim, with his imaginary machine-gun, charged up the stairs to the front porch with me rushing in tight at his flank, bearing in fast, both of us spraying fire, eck eck eck eck eck. Of course, we knew very well that we were rushing either Tim's mother or Mrs. Cameron, and we meant to scare the hell out of them. But what we didn't know was that Mrs. Cameron wasn't on the porch, but halfway down the front stairs; and she was coming down them rather carefully, because she was wearing shoes with heels and carrying a plate of white-frosted cake in both hands.

We stopped short; but we didn't stop short enough. Her eyes rounded in horror and she reached for a railing that wasn't there, and then Mrs. Cameron – with a faint gasping cry – fell backwards and slid down the stairs, all the way down to the concrete walk at the bottom, as the plate crashed on the ground.

Tim – as if it was all just part of the game – immediately dropped to his knees beside her: the perfect little field medic. "Don't worry," he said to her, bending low, in the tender but businesslike voice he sometimes used with me when I got hit. "Lie still. We'll get you to a doctor."

Frozen at the foot of the stairs, beside them, I found myself staring hard at the cake plate, which lay broken in big pieces on the ground. Blood pooled dark on the gritty concrete walk and – in a sick daze – I noticed that the pool was spreading out bigger and bigger every second.

Tim raised his head. "Mother?" he shouted. Then, to me, with admirable cool, he said: "Go get her."

I ran up the steps – bold with my mission, but also with a weird exhilarating sense of putting some sort of hard-earned emergency training into action – and collided with Tim's mother, who grabbed me by the shoulders and shoved me aside. As soon as she saw Mrs. Cameron lying all bloody on the ground, she pressed her hands on both sides of her head and shrieked: "Oh my God!"

Mrs. Cameron was crying, too, but in a way I didn't think grown-ups ever cried: wetly, noisily, with big gulps of air. Her forearm was cut, on the tender white underside; she'd cut it on the cake plate. That was where all the blood was coming from. The blood pumped out from it in a diagonal slash, streamed down her arm and dripped red off her fingertips, so much red it looked like Mrs. Cameron was wearing a scarlet elbow glove.

"Oh my God!" screamed Tim's mother, looking frantically up into the tree branches, as if she expected to find help there.

"Go call, Evie!" said Tim, over his mother's shrieks. "911!"

I ducked behind Tim's mother – there was a telephone on a table in the front hall – but much to my shock, she caught me by the arm and whirled me around. "Don't you dare go in there!" Her face was bright red. I tried to pull my wrist away, but – almost before I could blink – she whacked me hard with her open hand across the face.

"Little goyische girl," she screamed. "Run around over here like you own the damn place, eh? Lemme tell you something, girlie." She prodded me in the chest with her sharp forefinger. "Ya no good. This boy was never bad a day in his life."

Mrs. Cameron, at the bottom of the steps, was raising a frightened cry: "Gali? Gali?" She was struggling to get up. Tim was trying to hold her down.

"Ah, the hell with it." Tim's mother kicked the board game (Operation) which Tim and I had left spread out on the porch; and the pieces went flying – plastic funny bone, wishbone, heart.

She let go of me; and I backed away from her, down the stairs. She was crying, too.

"It's an ugly world," she said. "An ugly, stinking world."

Edging away from her – edging away from them all – at the bottom of the stairs I felt something slick touch my bare ankle, and I jumped. It was Mrs. Cameron, her hand all bloody. She didn't say anything, but the look on her face was enough. I turned away from them and ran, out from Mrs. Cameron's yard and the shadows of the oak trees into the hard shimmering heat of the sidewalk, no cover, just open space and open sky, streets so hostile in the midday sun that even my panic was drowned in all that emptiness and shrunk down to something flimsy and ridiculous.

Later, people said I'd been smart to run up to Main Street for help instead of toward my own house, which was blocks farther away. I never told anybody the truth: that my fear had spun me around and thrown me blindly off in the wrong direction.

But it wasn't just fear; it was a sick, bitter exaltation. And as I ran, the word she'd shouted at me pounded in my head: goyische goyische goyische, a strange word, screamed in a high, bad voice, a word that sounded like it had to mean something terrible, even if I didn't know what it was. Saigon would not fall for another year. And I was only eight; and Mrs. Cameron would be home from the hospital in a couple of days with 17 stitches in her arm, but still – I knew it even then – I was as close at that moment to the real war as I was ever going to get.

TROUBLE IS A LONESOME TOWN

Cathi Unsworth

Cathi Unsworth has made contributions to the neo-Noir movement in crime fiction, with novels including *The Not Knowing*, *Weirdo*, *Bad Penny Blues*, and *Without the Moon*, the latter two both based on real cases. She edited the award-winning *London Noir* anthology in 2006.

King's Cross

Dougie arrived at the concourse opposite the station just half an hour after it had all gone off. He'd had the cab driver drop him down the end of Gray's Inn Road, outside a pub on the corner there, where he'd made a quick dive into the gents to remove the red hood he'd been wearing over the black one, pulled on a Burberry cap he'd had in his bag so that the visor was down over his eyes. That done, he'd worked his way through the mass of drinkers, ducked out another door, and walked the rest of the way to King's Cross.

The Adidas bag he gripped in his right hand held at least twenty grand in cash. Dougie kind of wished it was hand-cuffed to him, so paranoid was he about letting go of it even for a second that he'd had trouble just putting it on the floor of the taxi between his feet. He'd wanted it to be on his knee, in his arms, more precious than a baby. But Dougie knew that above all else now, he had to look calm, unperturbed. Not like a man who'd just ripped off a clip joint and left a man for dead on a Soho pavement.

That's why he'd had the idea of making the rendezvous at the Scottish restaurant across the road from the station. He'd just blend in with the other travellers waiting for their train back up north, toting their heavy bags, staring at the TV with blank, gormless expressions as they pushed stringy fries smothered in luminous ketchup into their constantly moving mouths. The way he was dressed now, like some hood rat, council estate born and bred, he'd have no trouble passing amongst them.

He ordered his quarter-pounder and large fries, with a supersize chocolate lard shake to wash it all down, eyes wandering around the harshly lit room as he waited for it all to land on his red plastic tray. All the stereotypes were present and correct. The fat family (minus Dad, natch) sitting by the window, mother and two daughters virtually indistinguishable under the layers of flab and identical black-and-white hairstyles by Chavettes of Tyneside to match the colours of their footie team. The solitary male, a lad of maybe ten years and fifteen stone, staring sullenly out the window through pinhole eyes, sucking on the straw of a soft drink that was only giving him back rattling ice cubes. On the back of his shirt read his dreams: 9 *SHEARER*. But he was already closer to football than footballer.

Then there was the pimp and his crack whore; a thin black man sat opposite an even thinner white woman with bruises on her legs and worn-down heels on her boots. Her head bowed like she was on the nod, while he, all angles and elbows and knees protruding from his slack jeans and over-size Chicago Bulls shirt, kept up a steady monologue of abuse directed at her curly head. The man's eyes were as rheumy as a seventy-year-old's, and he sprayed fragments of his masticated fries out as he kept on his litany of insults. Sadly for Iceberg Slim, it looked like the mother-fuckingbitchhocuntcocksucker he was railing at had already given up the ghost.

Oblivious to the psychodrama, the Toon Army had half of the room to themselves, singing and punching the air, reliving moment by moment the two goals they'd scored over Spurs – well, thank fuck they had, wouldn't like to see this lot disappointed. They were vile enough in victory, hugging and clasping at each other with tears in their eyes, stupid joker's hats askew over their gleaming red faces, they might as well have been bumming each other, which was obviously what they all wanted.

Yeah, Dougie liked to get down among the filth every now and again, have a good wallow. In picking over the faults of others, he could forget about the million and one he had of his own.

Handing over a fiver to the ashen bloke behind the counter, who had come over here thinking nothing could be worse than Romania, Dougie collected his change and parked himself inconspicuously in the corner. Someone had left a copy of the *Scum* on his table. It was a bit grubby and he really would have preferred to use surgical gloves to touch it, but it went so perfectly with his disguise and the general ambience of the joint that he forced himself. Not before he had the bag firmly wedged between his feet, however, one of the handles round his ankle so if anyone even dared to try . . .

Dougie shook his head and busied himself instead by arranging the food on his plastic tray in a manner he found pleasing: the fries tipped out of their cardboard wallet into the half of the Styrofoam container that didn't have his burger in it. He opened the ketchup so that he could dip them in two at a time, between mouthfuls of burger and sips of chocolate shake. He liked to do everything methodically.

Under the headline "*STITCHED UP*", the front page of the *Scum* was tirelessly defending the good character of the latest batch of rapist footballers who'd all fucked one girl between the entire team and any of their mates who fancied it. Just so they could all check out each other's dicks while they did it, Dougie reckoned. That sort of shit turned his stomach almost as much as the paper it was printed on, so he quickly flipped the linen over, turned to the racing pages at the back. That would keep his mind from wandering, reading all those odds, totting them up in his head, remembering what names went with what weights and whose colours. All he had to do now was sit tight and wait. Wait for Lola.

Lola.

Just thinking about her name got his fingertips moist, got little beads of sweat breaking out on the back of his neck. Got a stirring in his baggy sweatsuit trousers so that he had to look up sharply and fill his eyes with a fat daughter chewing fries with her mouth open to get it back down again.

Women didn't often have this effect on Dougie. Only two, so far, in his life. And he'd gone further down the road with this one than anyone else before.

He could still remember the shock he felt when he first saw her, when she sat herself down next to him at the bar with a tired sigh and asked for a whisky and soda. He caught the slight inflection in her accent, as if English wasn't her first language, but her face was turned away from him. A mass of golden-brown curls bobbed on top of her shoulders, she had on a cropped leopardskin jacket and hipster jeans, a pair of pointy heels protruding from the bottom, wound around the stem of the bar stool. The skin on her feet was golden-brown too; mixed-race she must have been, and for a minute Dougie thought he knew what she would look like before she turned her head, somewhere between Scary Spice and that bird off *Holby City*. An open face, pretty and a bit petulant. Maybe some freckles over the bridge of her nose.

But when she did turn to him, cigarette dangling between her lips and long fingers wound around the short, thick glass of amber liquid, she looked nothing so trite as "pretty".

Emerald-green eyes fixed him from under deep lids, fringed with the longest dark lashes he had ever seen. Her skin was flawless, the colour of the whisky in her glass, radiating that same intoxicating glow.

For a second he was taken back to a room in Edinburgh a long time ago. An art student's room, full of draped scarves and fake Tiffany lamps and a picture on the wall of Marlene Dietrich in *The Blue Angel*. This woman looked strangely like Marlene. Marlene with an afro. *Black Angel*.

She took the cigarette from between her red lips and asked: "Could you give me a light?" Her glittering eyes held his brown ones in a steady gaze, a smile flickered over her perfect lips.

Dougie fumbled in the sleeve of his jacket for his Zippo and fired it up with shaking fingers. Black Angel inhaled deeply, closing her bronze-coloured eyelids as she sucked that good smoke down, blowing it out again in a steady stream.

Her long lashes rose and she lifted her glass to him simultaneously.

"Cheers!" she said, and he caught that heavy inflection again. Was he going mad, or did she even sound like Marlene too? "Ach," she tossed back her mane of curls, "it's so good to be off vork!"

"I'll drink to that," Dougie said, feeling like his tongue was too big for his head, his fingers too big for his hands, that he was entirely too big and clumsy. He slugged down half his bottle of Becks to try and get some kind of equilibrium, stop this weird teenage feeling that threatened to paralyse him under the spell of those green eyes.

She looked amused.

"What kind of vork do you do?" she asked.

Dougie gave his standard reply. "Och, you know. This an' that."

It pleased her, this answer, so she continued to talk. Told him in that smoky, laconic drawl all about the place she worked. One of the clip joints off Old Compton Street, the ones specifically geared up to rip off the day-trippers.

"It izz called Venus in Furs," she told him. "Is fucking tacky shit, yeah?"

He started to wonder if she was Croatian, or Serbian. Most of the girls pouring into Soho now were supposed to be ones kidnapped from the former Yugoslavia. *Slavic* was a word that suited the contours of her cheeks, the curve of her green eyes. But how could that be? Dougie didn't think there was much of a black population in Eastern Europe. And he couldn't imagine anyone having the balls to kidnap this one. Maybe she was here for a different reason. Images raced through his mind. Spy films, Checkpoint Charlie, the Cold War. High on her accent, he didn't really take the actual words in.

Until at some point close to dawn, she lifted a finger and delicately traced the outline of his jaw. "I like you, Dougie." She smiled. "I vill see you here again, yes?"

Dougie wasn't really one for hanging out in drinking clubs. He was only in this one because earlier that evening he'd had to have a meet in Soho and he couldn't stand any of the pubs round there. Too full, too noisy, too obvious. This was one of the better places. Discreet, old-fashioned, not really the sort of place your younger generation would go for, it was mainly populated by decaying actors skulking in a dimly lit world of memory. It was an old luvvie who'd first shown him the place. An old luvvie friend of a friend who'd been ripped off for all his Queen Anne silver and a collection of Penny Blacks by the mercenary young man he'd been silly enough to invite back for a nightcap. Dougie had at least got the silver back, while the guy was sleeping off what he'd spent the proceeds of the stamps on. He really didn't come here often, but as he watched the woman slip off her stool and shrug on her furry jacket, he felt a sudden pang and asked, "Wait a minute – what's your name?"

She smiled and said: "It's Lola. See you again, honey." And then she was gone.

Dougie found himself drifting back to the club the next evening.

It was weird, because he'd kept to himself for so long he felt like his heart was a hard, cold stone that no one could melt. It was best, he had long ago told himself, not to form attachments in his line of work. Attachments could trip you up. Attachments could bring you down. It was better that no one knew him outside his small circle of professional contacts and the clients they brought. Safer that way. He'd done six months' time as a teenager, when he was stupid and reckless, and had vowed he'd never be caught that way again.

He was mulling over all these facts as he found himself sitting at the bar. He didn't quite know what he thought he was doing there, just that he felt his heart go each time the buzzer went and a new group of people clattered down the steps. Lola had come into the place alone. He supposed he could ask the guvnor what he knew about her, but that didn't seem very gentlemanly. After all, he wasn't a regular himself, who knew how long she'd been making her way down here after the grind of an evening "huzzling the schmucks" under Venus's neon underskirts?

At half past one she had wound her way down the stairs towards him. A smile already twitching at the corners of her mouth, she was pleased to see him. One look up her long, bare, perfect legs to her leather miniskirt and that same leopardskin jacket and he felt the same.

"Hel-*looo*, Dougie," she said.

Dougie felt drunk, as he had ever since.

Gradually, over whisky and sodas with the ice crinkling in the glass, she'd told him her story. It was all very intriguing. Her father was Russian, she said, ex-KGB, who since the fall of communism had managed to create an empire for himself in electronic goods. He was a thug, but a charming one – he had named her after a character in a Raymond Chandler book that he'd read, contraband, as a teenager.

They had a lot of money, but he was very strict. Made her study hard and never go out. There was not a lot of emotion between him and her mother.

Her mother was an oddity, a Somalian. Lola didn't know how they met, but she suspected. Back in the old days, it was quite possible her father had bought her out of semi-slavery in a Moscow brothel. Her mother always claimed she was a princess, but she was also a drunk, so what was Lola to believe? She was beautiful, that was for sure. Beautiful and superstitious, always playing with a deck of strange cards and consulting patterns in tea leaves. She might have mastered dark arts, but never managed to speak Russian – probably she never wanted to. So Lola grew up speaking two languages, in one big, empty apartment in Moscow.

Right now, she was supposed to be in Switzerland. She looked embarrassed when she told Dougie this. "At finishing school. Can you believe? Vot a cliché." Lola had done a bunk six months ago. She'd crossed Europe, taking cash-in-hand work as she did, determined to get to London. She wanted to escape while she was in the "free West" rather than go back to what she knew would be expected of her in Russia. Marriage to some thick bastard son of one of her father's ex-comrades. A life of looking nice and shutting up, just like her mother.

But she feared her father's arm was long. There were too many Russians in London already. Someone was bound to rat her out, the reward money would be considerable. So she had to get together a "travelling fund" and find somewhere else to go. Somewhere safe.

"Vere are you from, Dougie?" she purred. "Not from round here, eh?"

"What do you reckon?" he said archly. "Where d'you think I got a name like Dougie from, hell?"

Lola laughed, put her finger on the end of his nose.

"You are from Scotland, yes?"

"Aye," nodded Dougie.

"Where in Scotland?"

"Edinburgh."

"Vot's it like in Edinburgh?"

A warning voice in Dougie's head told him not to even give her that much. This story she had spun for him, it sounded too much like a fairy tale. She was probably some down-on-her-luck Balkans hooker looking for a sugar daddy. No one could have had the lifestyle she described. It was too far-fetched, too mental.

The touch of her finger stayed on the end of his nose. Her green eyes glittered under the optics. Before Dougie knew what he was doing, words were coming out of his mouth.

She had given him the germ of an idea. The rest he filled in for himself.

Venus in Furs was not run by an established firm, even by Soho standards.

Its ostensible owners were a bunch of chancy Jamaican wide boys whose speciality was taking over moody drinking dens by scaring the incumbents into thinking that they were Yardies. Dougie doubted that was the case. They could have been minor players, vaguely connected somehow, but Yardie lands were south of the river. Triads and micks ran Soho. He doubted these fellas would last long in the scheme of things anyway, so he decided to help Lola out and give fate a hand.

Trying to help her, or trying to impress her?

It helped that her shifts were regular. Six nights a week, six till twelve. Plenty of time to observe who came and went on a routine basis. Maybe her old man really was KGB cos she'd already worked out that the day that the Suit came in would be the significant one.

There was this office, behind the bar, where they did all their business. Three guys worked the club in a rotation, always two of them there at the same time. Lynton, Neville and Little Stevie. They had a fondness for Lola, her being blood, so it was usually her they asked to bring drinks through when they had someone to impress in there. She said the room had been painted out with palm trees and a sunset, like one big Hawaiian scene.

Like everyone, Dougie thought, *playing at gangsters – they're playing* Scarface.

Once a week, a bald white guy in a dowdy brown suit came in with an attaché case. Whichever of the Brothers Grimm were in at the time would make themselves scarce while he busied himself in the office for half an hour. One of them would hang at the bar, the other find himself a dark corner with one of the girls. Then the bald man would come out, speak to no one and make his own way out of the club.

Every Thursday, 8 p.m., punctual as clockwork he came.

That proved it to Dougie. The lairy Jamaicans were a front to terrify the public. The bald man collected the money for their unseen offshore master. With his crappy suit and unassuming exterior, he was deliberately done up like a mark to blend in with the rest of the clientele.

Dougie had a couple of guys that owed him favours. They weren't known faces, and it would be difficult to trace them back to him – their paths crossed infrequently and they moved in different worlds. On two successive Thursdays, he gave them some folding and sent them in as marks. They confirmed Lola's story and gave him more interesting background on the Brothers Grimm. Both weeks, it was the same pair, Steve and Neville, little and large. Large Neville, a tall skinny guy with swinging dreads and shades who was always chewing on a toothpick, sat behind the bar when the bald man showed up. He practised dealing cards, played patience, drank beer and feigned indifference to the world around him, nodding all the while as if a different slow-skanking sound-track was playing in his head – not the cheesy Europop on the club's PA.

Little Stevie, by comparison, always grabbed himself a girl and a bottle and made his way over to the corner booth. While Neville looked like a classic stoner, Little Stevie was mean. He wore a black suit and a white shirt, with thick gold chains around his bulldog neck. A porkpie hat and thick black shades totally obscured his eyes. Occasionally, like when the girl slipped underneath the table, he would grin a dazzling display of gold and diamond dental work. Neville always drank proper champagne – not the pear fizz served to the punters as such – and both Dougie's contacts copped the telltale bulge in his pocket.

Neville's booth was the one from which the whole room could be surveyed, and even while receiving special favours, he never took his eye off the game. The minute the office door clicked open and the bald man slipped away, he would knee his girl off him, adjust his balls and whatever else was down there, and swagger his way back over to the office all puffed-up and bristling, Neville following at his heels.

Yeah, Stevie, they all agreed, was the one to watch.

While they were in there playing punters, Dougie was watching the door.

The Venus was based in a handy spot, in a dingy alley between Rupert Street and Wardour Street. There was a market on Rupert and all he had to do was pretend to be examining the tourist tat on the corner stall. The bald man went the other way. Straight to a waiting cab on Wardour. Each time the same.

On the night it all happened, Dougie felt a rush in his blood that he hadn't felt since Edinburgh, like every platelet was singing to him the old songs, high and wild as the wind.

God, he used to love that feeling, used to let it guide him in the days when he was *Dougie the Cat*, the greatest burglar in that magical city of turrets and towers.

But now he was Dougie Investigates, the private eye for the sort of people who couldn't go to the police. He had changed sides on purpose after that first prison jolt, never wanting to be in close proximity to such fucking filth ever again. If you couldn't be a gentleman thief these days, he reckoned, then why not be a Bad Guys' PI? His methods may have differed from those used by the Old Bill, but Dougie had kept his nose clean for eighteen years, built up his reputation by word of mouth, and made a good living from sorting out shit without causing any fuss. Filled a proper gap in the market, he had.

His blood had never sung to him in all that time. He supposed it must have awakened in him that first night he met Lola, grown strong that night she'd finally allowed him back to her dingy flat above a bookie's in Balham, where she had so studiously drawn out the map of the Venus's interior before unzipping his trousers and taking him to a place that seemed very close to heaven.

Bless her, he didn't need her map. He didn't even need to know what Neville and Stevie got up to, only that they were good little gangsters and stayed where they were, in that little palace of their imagination where they could be Tony Montana every day.

He wasn't going to take them on.

All he needed was the thirty seconds between the Venus's door and Wardour Street. And the curve in the alley that meant the taxi driver wouldn't be able to see. All he needed was the strength of his arm and the fleetness of his feet and the confusion of bodies packed into a Soho night.

At the end of the alley he slipped a balaclava over his head, put the blue hood over the top of that, and began to run.

He was at full sprint as the bald man came out of the door, fast enough to send him flying when he bowled into his shoulder. The man's arms spread out and he dropped his precious cargo to the floor. Dougie was just quick enough to catch the look of astonishment in the pale, watery eyes, before he coshed him hard on the top of his head and they rolled up into whites. He had another second to stoop and retrieve the case before he was off again, out of the alley, across Wardour Street, where the taxi was waiting, its engine running, the driver staring straight ahead.

Dougie was already in the downstairs bogs of the Spice of Life before the cabbie was checking his watch to make sure he hadn't turned up early. Had pulled out his sports bag from the cistern where he'd stashed it and busted the lock on the attaché case by the time the cabbie turned the engine off and stepped out of the car to take a look around. Dougie's deftness of touch was undiminished by his years on the other side. He counted the bundles of cash roughly as he transferred them into his sports bag, eyebrows rising as he did. It was quite a haul for a weekly skim off a clip joint. He briefly wondered what else they had going on down there, then chased the thought away as excess trouble he didn't need to know.

By the time the cabbie was standing over the crumpled heap in the alleyway, he had put the attaché case in the cistern and taken off the blue hood, rolling it into a ball when he nipped out the side door of the pub. He junked it in a bin as he came out onto Charing Cross Road and hailed himself a ride up to King's Cross.

Dougie looked up from his racing pages. As if struck by electrodes, he knew Lola was in the room. She walked towards him, green eyes dancing, clocking amusedly his stupid cap and the bag that lay between his feet. Sat down in front of him and breathed, "Is it enough?"

"Aye," nodded Dougie. "It's enough."

He hadn't wanted there to be any way in which Lola could be implicated in all this. He'd had her phone in sick for two days running, told her just to spend her time packing only the essentials she needed, and gave her the money for two singles up to Edinburgh.

The night train back to the magic city, not even the Toon Army could ruin that pleasure for him.

"You ready?" he asked her.

Her grin stretched languidly across her perfect face.

"Yes," she purred. "I'm ready."

Dougie gripped the Adidas bag, left his floppy fries where they lay.

As they stepped out onto the road, St. Pancras was lit up like a fairy-tale castle in front of them. "See that," he nudged her shoulder, "that's bollocks compared to where we're going."

His heart and his soul sang along with his blood. He was leaving the Big Smoke, leaving his life of shadows, stepping into a better world with the woman he loved by his side. He took her hand and strode towards the crossing, towards the mouth of King's Cross Station.

Then Lola said: "Oooh, hang on a minute. I have to get my bag."

"You what?" Dougie was confused. "Don't you have it with you?"

She laughed, a low tinkling sound. "No, honey, I left it just around the corner. My friend, you know, she runs a bar there and I didn't want to lug it around with me all day. She's kept it safe for me, behind the bar. Don't vorry, it von't take a minute."

Dougie was puzzled. He hadn't heard about this friend or this bar before. But in his limited experience of women, this was typical. Just when you thought you had a plan, they'd make some little amendment. He guessed that was just the way their minds worked.

She leaned to kiss his cheek and whispered in his ear: "Ve still have half an hour before the train goes."

The pub was, literally, around the corner. One of those horrible, bland chain brewery joints heaving with overweight office workers trying to get lucky with their sniggering secretaries in the last desperate minutes before closing time.

He lingered by the door as Lola hailed the bored-looking blonde bartender. Watched her take a small blue suitcase from behind the bar, kiss the barmaid on each cheek, and come smilingly back towards him.

A few seconds before she reached him, her smile turned to a mask of fear.

"Oh shit," she said, grabbing hold of his arm and dragging him away from the doorway. "It's fucking Stevie."

"What?"

"This vay." She had his arm firmly in her grasp now, was propelling him through to the other side of the bar, towards the door marked *Toilets*, cursing and talking a million miles an hour under her breath.

"Stevie was standing right outside the door. I svear to God it was him. I told you, he is bad luck that one, he's voodoo, got a sixth sense – my mama told me about *sheiit* like him. Ve can't let him see us! I'm supposed to be off sick, the night he gets ripped off – he's gonna know! He's gonna kill me if he sees me."

"Hen, you're seeing things," Dougie tried to protest as she pushed him through the door, down some steps into a dank basement that smelled of piss and stale vomit.

"I'm not! It vos him, it vos him!" She looked like she was about to turn hysterical, her eyes were flashing wildly and her nails were digging into his flesh. He tried to use his free hand to extricate himself from her iron grip, but that only served to make her cling on harder.

"Hen, calm down, you're hurting me . . ." Dougie began.

"There's someone coming!" she screamed, and suddenly began to kiss him passionately, smothering him in her arms, grinding her teeth against his lips so that he tasted blood.

And then he heard a noise right behind him.

And the room went black.

"Fucking hell." Lola looked down on Dougie's prone body. "That took long enough."

"I told you he was good," her companion pouted, brushing his hands on his trousers. "But I thought you'd enjoy using all your skills on him."

"Hmm." Lola bent down and pried Dougie's fingers away from the Adidas bag. "I knew this would be the hardest part. Getting money out of a tight fucking jock."

The slinky Russian accent had disappeared like a puff of smoke. She sounded more like a petulant queen.

"Come on." She stepped over her would-be Romeo and the pile of shattered ashtray glass he lay in. "Let's get out of here."

The car was parked near by. As Lola got into the passenger seat, she pulled the honey-gold Afro wig off her head and ran her fingers through the short black fuzz underneath.

"I am *soooo* tired of that bitch," she said, tossing it on the back seat.

Her companion started the car with a chuckle.

"He fucking believed everything, didn't he?" He shook his head as he pulled out.

"Yeah . . . and you said he was a private detective. Well, let me tell you, honey, you wouldn't believe what I suckered that dick with. My dad was a Russian gangster. My mother was a Somalian princess. I was on the run from Swiss finishing school. Can you believe it?"

Lola hooted with derision. "Almost like the fairy tales I used to make up for myself," she added. "You know, I thought he might fucking twig when I told him I was named after a character in a Raymond Chandler novel. But I couldn't resist it."

"Well," her companion smiled at her fondly, "you certainly made up for the loss of that Queen Anne silver. We've got enough to keep us going for months now. So where do you fancy?"

"Not back to Soho," Lola sniffed, as the car pulled into the slipstream of Marylebone Road. "I've fucking had it with those poseur thugs. I know. I fancy some sea air. How does Brighton sound to you?"

"The perfect place," her companion agreed, "for a couple of actors."

Dougie came around with his face stuck to a cold stone floor with his own blood. Shards of glass covered him. He could smell the acrid stench of piss in his nostrils, and from the pub above he could hear a tune, sounding like it was coming from out of a long tunnel of memory. He could just make out the lyrics:

"*I met her in a club down in old Soho/Where you drink champagne and it tastes just like cherry cola . . .*"

WEB DESIGN

Emma Viskic

Emma Viskic won the 2016 Ned Kelly Award for her debut novel *Resurrection Bay*. 'Web Design', published here for the first time, won the 2014 Ned Kelly (S.D. Harvey) short story competition. Viskic is the creator of Caleb Zelic, a deaf outsider with a strong sense of justice, who also appears in *And Fire Came Down*. Viskic is also a classically trained clarinettist, and lives in Melbourne, Australia.

Lisa was singing *Eency Weency Spider* for the thousandth time when she saw the car. A white Commodore a couple of car lengths back. Something about the way it had swung around the corner, was tailing her up the hill. Her foot pressed harder on the accelerator.

'Eency Spider, Eency Spider,' Abby's voice rose from the back seat.

'Shhh,' Hamish said. 'Mummy's worried.'

He was watching her in the mirror. Old-man eyes in the face of a four-year-old. She'd done that to him—her and bloody Billy.

'I'm just concentrating, sweetie.' She kept her voice light, light, light.

The Commodore was metres from her bumper now. She could see the driver. A fleshy face half-hidden by a baseball cap and dark glasses. Familiar. One of Billy's mates? She gripped the wheel with suddenly damp hands. OK, get off the highway and lose him in the back roads. A vision of dirt-track emptiness, her bleeding body.

'Eency Spider, Eency Spider!'

Lisa slipped her hand beside the seat and felt for the pry bar.

'Eency Weency Spider,' she sang as her fingers closed around the cold metal. 'Climbed up the water spout.' She straightened, keeping her hand low. 'Down came the rain and washed poor Eency out.'

She'd smash his windscreen, his face, his kneecaps. She stomped on the brake and pulled over in a squeal of tyres, had the door open, one foot on the road before he drew level.

He didn't stop.

Didn't slow down.

A glimpse of a *Hawks* bumper sticker as he flew by. Just a local, the guy who'd flirted with her in the supermarket car park yesterday. He'd commented on her dress, made a joke about Abby's curls. God, what an idiot. She lowered herself to her seat with trembling legs. Abby was screaming; her dumpling cheeks streaked with snot and tears. Bad mother. Bad, terrible, horrible mother. Lisa dropped the bar onto the passenger seat and started the car.

'Out came the sunshine and dried up all the rain. And Eency Weency Spider climbed up the spout again.'

She put Abby straight to bed and carried the toolbox out to the back yard. Hamish shadowed her, one hand clutching Blue Bear, the other tucked down his pants. He'd started wetting the bed after their third move. She gave him the toolbox to mind and got to work on the back step. Each cat-piss rental house was filled with lurking dangers. She lay awake each night cataloguing the ways the kids could die: a loose step, an old fuse box, an unearthed lamp. Their house, their real house, had been perfect.

'*My little homebody*,' Billy used to say, running a thumb along her calloused palm. '*My heart and hearth.*'

But there was no more beautiful house, no more beautiful Billy, no more beautiful money.

'Are we moving again?' Hamish asked.

'Not yet.'

His hand fossicked deeper in his pants. 'It's nice here.'

'I like it, too. Can you pass me a Phillips head screw?' Funny, she'd never thought of herself as a country girl, but this town had everything going for it.

She tightened the screw and sat back. 'Okay, apprentice, give it a go.'

Hamish stomped up and down the steps and gave her solemn thumbs up. 'Solid as a rock.'

Billy's saying, only the rocks he meant were sold by the gram and turned out not to be such a solid investment after all. Crack cocaine, for God's sake. He'd cried when he told her how much he owed. Half a million . . . If he hadn't done a runner, she probably would have killed him herself.

She pulled out her notepad and checked her list. Stupid to spend so much time on the house, on getting Hamish settled at kindy, on meeting the neighbours; putting down roots that they'd just have to rip out again.

'OK, apprentice, let's have a look at that lamp.'

She was counting out the coins for the kids' ice creams when someone came up behind her. A large, tanned hand slid a ten dollar note across the milk bar counter.

'I've got it, Leese,' a man's voice said. 'My treat for the kids.'

The guy from the supermarket smiled down at her. His cap and dark glasses were gone, revealing dark eyes and short, blond hair. Something reptilian about the eyes.

'Thanks,' she said. Steady voice, easy smile. 'That's kind of you.'

She swung the stroller around and strode out. It was a small town; not that weird she kept seeing him. Except that Billy was the only person who'd ever called her *Leese*.

She started stuffing bedding into suitcases as soon as they got back to the house. Hamish followed, his hand toying with the waistband of his shorts.

'Are we going?'

'Yes.'

The emergency bags were in the boot, her hard-earned savings in the spare wheel. She'd replace everything else when they got to Adelaide/Perth/Broome. She picked up the suitcases and ushered the kids down the hallway.

He was standing in the open doorway.

She snatched up Abby and pulled Hamish to her side.

'Nice house you got here, Leese. Not as flash as your last one, though. Pity that burned down. Glad you and the kids got out—be a fucken horrible way to die.'

Couldn't run with the kids. A weapon, something heavy. She scanned the hallway.

He smiled down at Hamish. 'This one's a good little footy player, isn't he? I've been watching him play at kindy.'

Jesus, fuck. Heart hammering so hard she might vomit it up.

'Where's Billy, Leese? I've been hoping he'd turn up.'

'I don't know. He took everything and ran.'

'That's a bad habit of his, isn't it?' He stroked Abby's plump cheek. 'Your daddy's a naughty, naughty man, isn't he, Abby? Stealing things that don't belong to him.' His snake eyes fixed on Lisa. 'Tell Billy that Detective Sergeant Manning wants his money by Sunday. All five hundred, plus an extra ten for fucking me around.'

'I don't know where he is.'

'Then I guess I'll be paying you a visit on Sunday. You and the kiddies.' He gave Abby's cheek a pinch and sauntered away.

Lisa slammed the door and turned the deadlock. Detective Sergeant. There was no getting away from a cop: a trail of electronic breadcrumbs showing their every move. Bloody Billy—ripping off a cop. The stupid bastard.

'Are we going now?' Hamish asked.

'Not yet, sweetie.'

The dog hadn't died easily: there were burnt patches on its flanks, foam around its mouth. Sick. Just fucking sick. Poor old fella. This is where trusting men had got her—dead dogs in the backyard. She sobbed as she swaddled its limp form in an old sheet. Please God, let it be a stray, let her bury it deep enough before the kids woke up.

On Saturday night, she parked the car in the backyard and put the kids to bed in it. Hamish had been dubious at first, but she'd brought him around with tales of camping and adventure. When they were asleep, she slipped back inside the house to wait. He came in the dull-witted hours before dawn. Not there one minute, in the darkened living room the next. She clambered to her feet, the streetlight glinting on the knife as she whipped it behind her back. Just a flash, but it was enough.

'Leese, Leese, I thought you were smarter than that.'

'I've got the money.' Her voice was too high. 'It's all there. Over by the table.'

'Glad to hear it.' He patted the wall and found the light switch. A click, but no light.

'Bulb's gone,' she said.

'I'm sure it is.' A tone as dry as kindling.

She took a step towards him. 'I'll turn the lamp on.'

'Stay the fuck where you are, sweetheart.'

He shuffled towards the lamp, his hand reaching for the switch. She stood poised, not breathing. A burst of light, a bang, and he thudded face-down on the floor. The smell of charred meat and piss. She edged closer, the squeak of her rubber-soled shoes loud in the silence. The old lamp had blown a fuse, but she kept well away from its exposed wiring as she knelt to feel for his pulse. Nothing. And she breathed again. She hadn't been sure if the wire she'd run from the unearthed switch to the power point would hold enough current, but it had worked perfectly. Wetting the floor had been a good idea, too—he'd died a lot faster than the dog.

Hamish blinked sleepily as she opened the car door.

'Go back to sleep,' she said. 'I'm just putting something in the boot.'

'Are we going?'

She paused with her hand on the boot lever. She'd known as soon as she pulled off the highway that this was the place. Couldn't say why, just that it seemed like a town where they could flourish. She'd been right, too—she'd built up a nice little trade in eccies and ice. And there'd be no stopping her now Billy and his fuckups were gone. They could settle themselves properly, let their roots grow deep.

'No, sweetheart,' she said. 'I think we'll stay.'

ENGLISH AUTUMN – AMERICAN FALL

Minette Walters

Minette Walters published her first novel, *The Ice House*, in 1992. She has written thirteen novels of psychological suspense, the first five of which were televised. Her gritty crime fiction has received many awards from the Crime Writers Association and Mystery Writers of America. Her latest book, *The Last Hours*, is an historical adventure set in 1348.

I remember thinking that Mrs Newberg's problem was not so much her husband's chronic addiction to alcohol as her dreary pretence that he was a man of moderation. They were a handsome couple, tall and slender with sweeps of snow-white hair, always expensively dressed in cashmere and tweeds. In fairness to her, he didn't look like a drunk, or indeed behave like one, but I cannot recall a single occasion in the two weeks I knew them when he was sober. His wife excused him with clichés. She hinted at insomnia, a death in the family, even a gammy leg – a legacy of war, naturally – which made walking difficult. Once in a while an amused smile would cross his face as if something she'd said had tickled his sense of humour, but most of the time he sat staring at a fixed point in front of him afraid of losing his precarious equilibrium.

I guessed they were in their late seventies, and I wondered what had brought them so far from home in the middle of a cold English autumn. Mrs Newberg was evasive. Just a little holiday, she trilled in her birdlike voice with its hint of Northern Europe in the hard edge she gave to her consonants. She cast nervous glances towards her husband as she spoke as if daring him to disagree. It may have been true but an empty seaside hotel in a blustery Lincolnshire resort in October seemed an unlikely choice for two elderly Americans. She knew I didn't believe her, but she was too canny to explain further. Perhaps she understood that my willingness to talk to her depended on a lingering curiosity.

'It was Mr Newberg who wanted to come,' she said *sotto voce*, as if that settled the matter.

It was an unfashionable resort out of season and Mrs Newberg was clearly lonely. Who wouldn't be with only an uncommunicative drunk for company? On odd evenings a rep would put in a brief appearance in the dining-room in order to fuel his stomach in silence before retiring to bed, but for the most part conversations with me were her single source of entertainment. In a desultory fashion, we became friends. Of course, she wanted to know why I was there, but I, too, could be evasive. Looking for somewhere to live, I told her.

'How nice,' she said, not meaning it. 'But do you want to be so far from London?' It was a reproach. For her, as for so many, capital cities were synonymous with life.

'I don't like noise,' I confessed.

She looked towards the window where rain was pounding furiously against the panes. 'Perhaps it's people you don't like,' she suggested.

I demurred out of politeness. 'I don't have a problem with individuals,' I said, casting a thoughtful glance in Mr Newberg's direction, 'just humanity *en masse*.'

'Yes,' she agreed vaguely. 'I think I prefer animals as well.'

She had a habit of using non-sequiturs, and I did wonder once or twice if she wasn't quite 'with it'. But if that were the case, I thought, how on earth had they found their way to this remote place when Mr Newberg had trouble negotiating the tables in the bar? The answer was straightforward enough. The hotel had sent a car to collect them from the airport.

'Wasn't that very expensive?' I asked.

'It was free,' said Mrs Newberg with dignity. 'A courtesy. The manager came himself.' She tut-tutted at my look of astonishment. 'It's what we expect when we pay full rate for a room.'

'I'm paying full rate,' I said.

'I doubt it,' she said, her bosom rising on a sigh. 'Americans get stung wherever they go.'

During the first week of their stay, I saw them only once outside the confines of the hotel. I came across them on the beach, wrapped up in heavy coats and woollen scarves and sitting in deckchairs staring out over a turbulent sea which laboured beneath the whip of a bitter east wind from Siberia. I expressed surprise to see them, and Mrs Newberg, who assumed for some reason that my surprise was centred on the deckchairs, said the hotel would supply anything for a small sum.

'Do you come here every morning?' I asked her.

She nodded. 'It reminds us of home.'

'I thought you lived in Florida.'

'Yes,' she said cautiously, as if trying to remember how much she'd already divulged.

Mr Newberg and I exchanged conspiratorial smiles. He spoke rarely but when he did it was always with irony. 'Florida is famous for its hurricanes,' he told me before turning his face to the freezing wind.

After that I avoided the beach for fear of becoming even more entangled with them. It's not that I disliked them. As a matter of fact I quite enjoyed their company. They were the least inquisitive couple I had ever met, and there was never any problem with the long silences that developed between us. But I had no wish to spend the daylight hours being sociable with strangers.

Mrs Newberg remarked on it one evening. 'I wonder you didn't go to Scotland,' she said. 'I'm told you can walk for miles in Scotland without ever seeing a soul.'

'I couldn't live in Scotland,' I said.

'Ah, yes. I'd forgotten.' Was she being snide or was I imagining it? 'You're looking for a house.'

'Somewhere to live,' I corrected her.

'An apartment then. Does it matter?'

'I think so.'

Mr Newberg stared into his whisky glass. '"*Das Gehimniss, um die grosste Fruchtbarkeit und den grossten Genuss vom Dasein einzuernten, heisst: gefahrlich leben*",' he murmured in fluent German. 'The secret of reaping the greatest fruitfulness and the greatest enjoyment from life is to live dangerously. Friedrich Nietzsche.'

'Does it work?' I asked.

I watched him smile secretly to himself. 'Only if you shed blood.'

'I'm sorry?'

But his eyes were awash with alcohol and he didn't answer. 'He's tired,' said his wife. 'He's had a long day.'

We lapsed into silence and I watched Mrs Newberg's face smooth from sharp anxiety to its more natural expression of resigned acceptance of the cards fate had dealt her. It was a good five minutes before she offered an explanation.

'He enjoyed the war,' she told me in an undertone. 'So many men did.'

'It's the camaraderie,' I agreed, remembering how my mother had always talked fondly about the war years. 'Adversity brings out the best in people.'

'Or the worst,' she said, watching Mr Newberg top up his glass from the litre bottle of whisky which was replaced, new, every evening on their table. 'I guess it depends which side you're on.'

'You mean it's better to win?'

'I expect it helps,' she said absentmindedly.

The next day Mrs Newberg appeared at breakfast with a black eye. She claimed she had fallen out of bed and knocked her face on the bedside cabinet. There was no reason to doubt her except that her husband kept massaging the knuckles of his right hand. She looked wan and depressed, and I invited her to come walking with me.

'I'm sure Mr Newberg can amuse himself for an hour or two,' I said, looking at him disapprovingly.

We wandered down the esplanade, watching seagulls whirl across the sky like wind-blown fabric. Mrs Newberg insisted on wearing dark glasses which gave her the look of a blind woman. She walked slowly, pausing regularly to catch her breath, so I offered her my arm and she leaned on it heavily. For the first time I thought of her as old.

'You shouldn't let your husband hit you,' I said.

She gave a small laugh but said nothing.

'You should report him.'

'To whom?'

'The police.'

She drew away to lean on the railings above the beach. 'And then what? A prosecution? Prison?'

I leant beside her. 'More likely a court would order him to address his behaviour.'

'You can't teach an old dog new tricks.'

'He might have a different perspective on things if he were sober.'

'He drinks to forget,' she said, looking across the sea towards the far off shores of Northern Europe.

I turned a cold shoulder towards Mr Newberg from then on. I don't approve of men who knock their wives about. It made little difference to our relationship. If anything, sympathy for Mrs Newberg strengthened the bonds between the three of us. I took to escorting them to their room of an evening and pointing out in no uncertain terms that I took a personal interest in Mrs Newberg's well-being. Mr Newberg seemed to find my solicitude amusing. 'She has no conscience to trouble her,' he said on one occasion. And on another: 'I have more to fear than she has.'

During the second week he tripped at the top of the stairs on his way to breakfast and was dead by the time he reached the bottom. There were no witnesses to the accident, although a waitress, hearing the crash of the falling body, rushed out of the dining-room to find the handsome old man sprawled on his back at the foot of the stairs with his eyes wide open and a smile on his face. No one was particularly surprised although, as the manager said, it was odd that it should happen in the morning when he was at his most sober. Some hours later a policeman came to ask questions, not because there was any suggestion of foul play but because Mr Newberg was a foreign national and reports needed to be written.

I sat with Mrs Newberg in her bedroom while she dabbed gently at her tears and explained to the officer that she had been sitting at her dressing table and putting the finishing touches to her make-up when Mr Newberg left the room to go downstairs. 'He always went first,' she said. 'He liked his coffee fresh.'

The policeman nodded as if her remark made sense, then inquired tactfully about her husband's drinking habits. A sample of Mr Newberg's blood had shown a high concentration of alcohol, he told her. She smiled faintly and said she couldn't believe Mr Newberg's moderate consumption of whisky had anything to do with his fall. There was no elevator in the hotel, she pointed out, and he had had a bad leg for years. 'Americans aren't used to stairs,' she said, as if that were explanation enough.

He gave up and turned to me instead. He understood I was a friend of the couple. Was there anything I could add that might throw some light on the accident? I avoided looking at Mrs Newberg who had skilfully obscured the faded bruise around her eye with foundation. 'Not really,' I said, wondering why I'd never noticed the scar above her cheek that looked as if it might have been made by the sharp corner of a bedside cabinet. 'He told me once that the secret of fulfilment is to live dangerously so perhaps he didn't take as much care of himself as he should have done.'

He flicked an embarrassed glance in Mrs Newberg's direction. 'Meaning he drank too much?'

I gave a small shrug which he took for agreement. I might have pointed out that Mr Newberg's carelessness lay in his failure to look over his shoulder, but I couldn't see what it would achieve. No one doubted his wife had been in their room at the time.

She bowed graciously as the officer took his leave. 'Are English policemen always so charming?' she asked, moving to the dressing table to dust her lovely face with powder.

'Always,' I assured her, 'as long as they have no reason to suspect you of anything.'

Her reflection looked at me for a moment. 'What's to suspect?' she asked.

CHRISTABEL'S CRYSTAL

Carolyn Wells

Carolyn Wells (1862–1942) was a prolific American author known for her mysteries, children's fiction, and humorous verses. Her detective Fleming Stone first appeared in *The Clue* (1909) and featured in dozens of novels and short stories, including *The Maxwell Mystery* (1913) and *Who Killed Caldwell?* (1942).

O f all the unexpected pleasures that have come into my life, I think perhaps the greatest was when Christabel Farland asked me to be bridesmaid at her wedding.

I always had liked Christabel at college, and though we hadn't seen much of each other since we were graduated, I still had a strong feeling of friendship for her, and besides that I was glad to be one of the merry house party gathered at Farland Hall for the wedding festivities.

I arrived the afternoon before the wedding-day, and found the family and guests drinking tea in the library. Two other bridesmaids were there, Alice Fordham and Janet White, with both of whom I was slightly acquainted. The men, however, except Christabel's brother Fred, were strangers to me, and were introduced as Mr. Richmond, who was to be an usher; Herbert Gay, a neighbor, who chanced to be calling; and Mr. Wayne, the tutor of Christabel's younger brother Harold. Mrs. Farland was there too, and her welcoming words to me were as sweet and cordial as Christabel's.

The party was in frivolous mood, and as the jests and laughter grew more hilarious, Mrs. Farland declared that she would take the bride-elect away to her room for a quiet rest, lest she should not appear at her best the next day.

"Come with me, Elinor," said Christabel to me, "and I will show you my wedding-gifts."

Together we went to the room set apart for the purpose, and on many white-draped tables I saw displayed the gorgeous profusion of silver, glass and bric-a-brac that are one of the chief component parts of a wedding of to-day.

I had gone entirely through my vocabulary of ecstatic adjectives and was beginning over again, when we came to a small table which held only one wedding-gift.

"That is the gem of the whole collection," said Christabel, with a happy smile, "not only because Laurence gave it to me, but because of its intrinsic perfection and rarity."

I looked at the bridegroom's gift in some surprise. Instead of the conventional diamond sunburst or heart-shaped brooch, I saw a crystal ball as large as a fair-sized orange.

I knew of Christabel's fondness for Japanese crystals and that she had a number of small ones of varying qualities; but this magnificent specimen fairly took my breath away. It was poised on the top of one of those wavecrests, which the artisans seem to think appropriately interpreted in wrought-iron. Now, I haven't the same subtle sympathy with crystals that Christabel always has had; but still this great, perfect, limpid sphere affected me strangely. I glanced at it at first with a calm interest; but as I continued to look I became fascinated, and soon found myself obliged (if I may use the expression) to tear my eyes away.

Christabel watched me curiously. "Do you love it too?" she said, and then she turned her eyes to the crystal with a rapt and rapturous gaze that made her appear lovelier than ever. "Wasn't it dear of Laurence?" she said. "He wanted to give me jewels of course; but I told him I would rather have this big crystal than the Koh-i-nur. I have six others, you know; but the largest of them isn't one-third the diameter of this."

"It is wonderful," I said, "and I am glad you have it. I must own it frightens me a little."

"That is because of its perfection," said Christabel simply. "Absolute flawless perfection always is awesome. And when it is combined with perfect, faultless beauty, it is the ultimate perfection of a material thing."

"But I thought you liked crystals because of their weird supernatural influence over you," I said.

"That is an effect, not a cause," Christabel replied. "Ultimate perfection is so rare in our experiences that its existence perforce produces consequences so rare as to be dubbed weird and supernatural. But I must not gaze at my crystal longer now, or I shall forget that it is my wedding-day. I'm not going to look at it again until after I return from my wedding-trip; and then, as I tell Laurence, he will have to share my affection with his wedding-gift to me."

Christabel gave the crystal a long parting look, and then ran away to don her wedding-gown. "Elinor," she called over her shoulder, as she neared her own door, "I'll leave my crystal in your special care. See that nothing happens to it while I'm away."

"Trust me!" I called back gaily, and then went in search of my sister bridesmaids.

The morning after the wedding began rather later than most mornings. But at last we all were seated at the breakfast-table and enthusiastically discussing the events of the night before. It seemed strange to be there without Christabel, and Mrs. Farland said that I must stay until the bridal pair returned, for she couldn't get along without a daughter of some sort.

This remark made me look anywhere rather than at Fred Farland, and so I chanced to catch Harold's eye. But the boy gave me such an intelligent, mischievous smile that I actually blushed and was covered with confusion. Just at that moment Katy the parlor-maid came into the dining-room, and with an anxious expression on her face said: "Mrs. Farland, do you know anything about Miss Christabel's glass ball? It isn't in the present-room."

"No," said Mrs. Farland; "but I suppose Mr. Haley put it in the safe with the silver and jewelry."

"I don't think so, ma'am; for he asked me was he to take any of the cut glass, and I told him you had said only the silver and gold, ma'am."

"But that crystal isn't cut glass, Katy; and it's more valuable than all Miss Christabel's silver gifts put together."

"Oh, my! is it, ma'am? Well, then, won't you please see if it's all right, for I'm worried about it."

I wish I could describe my feelings at this moment. Have you ever been in imminent danger of a fearful catastrophe of any kind, and while with all your heart and soul you hoped it might be averted, yet there was one little, tiny, hidden impulse of your mind that craved the excitement of the disaster? Perhaps it is only an ignoble nature that can have this experience, or there may be a partial excuse for me in the fact that I am afflicted with what sometimes is called the "detective instinct." I say afflicted, for I well know that anyone else who has this particular mental bias will agree with me that it causes far more annoyance than satisfaction.

Why, one morning when I met Mrs. Van Allen in the market, I said "It's too bad your waitress had to go out of town to attend the funeral of a near relative, when you were expecting company to luncheon." And she was as angry as could be, and called me an impertinent busy-body.

But I just had deduced it all from her glove. You see, she had on one brand-new black-kid glove, and the other, though crumpled up in her hand, I could see never had been on at all. So I knew that she wouldn't start to market early in the morning with such gloves if she had any sort of half-worn black ones at all.

And I knew that she had given away her next-best pair recently – it must have been the night before, or she would have tried them on sooner; and as her cook is an enormous woman, I was sure that she had given them to her waitress. And why would she, unless the maid was going away in great haste? And what would require such a condition of things except a sudden call to a funeral. And it must have been out of town, or she would have waited until morning, and then she could have bought black gloves for herself. And it must have been a near relative to make the case so urgent. And I knew that Mrs. Van Allen expected luncheon guests, because her fingers were stained from paring apples, and why would she pare her own apples so early in the morning except to assist the cook in some hurried preparations? Why, it was all as plain as could be, and every bit true; but Mrs. Van Allen wouldn't believe my explanation, and to this day she thinks I made my discoveries by gossiping with her servants.

Perhaps all this will help you to understand why I felt a sort of nervous ex-hilaration that had in it an element of secret pleasure, when we learned that Christabel's crystal really was missing.

Mr. Haley, who was a policeman, had remained in the present room during all of the hours devoted to the wedding celebration, and after the guests had gone he had packed up the silver, gold and jewels and put them away in the family safe, which stood in a small dressing-room between Mrs. Farland's bedroom and Fred's. He had worn civilian's dress during the evening, and few if any of the guests knew that he was guarding the valuable gifts. The mistake had been in not telling him explicitly to care for the crystal as the most valuable gem of all; but this point had been overlooked, and the ignorant officer had assumed that it was merely a piece of cut glass, of no more value than any of the carafes or decanters. When told that the ball's intrinsic value was many thousands of dollars, and that it would be next to impossible to duplicate it at any price, his amazement was unbounded and he appeared extremely grave.

"You ought to have told me," he said. "Sure, it's a case for the chief now!" Haley had been hastily telephoned for to come to Farland Hall and tell his story, and now he telephoned for the chief of police and a detective.

I felt a thrill of delight at this, for I always had longed to see a real detective in the act of detecting.

Of course everybody was greatly excited, and I just gave myself up to the enjoyment of the situation, when suddenly I remembered that Christabel had said that she would leave her crystal in my charge, and that in a way I was responsible for its safety. This changed my whole attitude, and I realized that, instead of being an idly curious observer, I must put all my detective instinct to work immediately and use every endeavor to recover the crystal.

First, I flew to my own room and sat down for a few moments to collect my thoughts and lay my plans. Of course, as the windows of the present-room were found in the morning fastened as they were left the night before, the theft must have been committed by someone in the house. Naturally it was not one of the family or the guests of the house. As to the servants, they all were honest and trustworthy – I had Mrs. Farland's word for that. There was no reason to suspect the policeman, and thus my process of elimination brought me to Mr. Wayne, Harold's tutor.

Of course it must have been the tutor. In nine-tenths of all the detective stories I ever have read the criminal proved to be a tutor or secretary or some sort of gentlemanly dependent of the family; and now I had come upon a detective story in real life, and here was the regulation criminal ready to fit right into it. It was the tutor of course; but I should be discreet and not name him until I had collected some undeniable evidence.

Next, I went down to the present-room to search for clues. The detective had not arrived yet, and I was glad to be first on the ground, for I remembered how much importance Sherlock Holmes always attached to the search. I didn't really expect that the tutor had left shreds of his clothing clinging to the table-legs, or anything absurd like that; but I fully expected to find a clue of some sort. I hoped that it wouldn't be cigar ashes; for though detectives in fiction always can tell the name and price of cigar from a bit of ash, yet I'm so ignorant about such things that all ashes are alike to me.

I hunted carefully all over the floor; but I couldn't find a thing that seemed the least bit like a clue, except a faded white carnation. Of course that wasn't an unusual thing to find, the day after a wedding; but it was the very flower I had given to Fred Farland the night before, and he had worn it in his buttonhole. I recognized it perfectly, for it was wired and I had twisted it a certain way when I adjusted it for him. This didn't seem like strong evidence against the tutor; but it was convincing to me, for if Mr. Wayne was villain enough to steal Christabel's crystal, he was wicked enough to manage to get Fred's boutonniere and leave it in the room, hoping thereby to incriminate Fred. So fearful was I that this trick might make trouble for Fred that I said nothing about the carnation; for I knew that it was in Fred's coat when he said good-night, and then we all went directly to our rooms. When the detective came he examined the room, and I know that he didn't find anything in the way of evidence; but he tried to appear as if he had, and he frowned and jotted down notes in a book after the most approved fashion.

Then he called in everybody who had been in the house over night and questioned each one. I could see at once that his questions to the family and guests were purely perfunctory, and that he too had his suspicions of the tutor.

Finally, it was Mr. Wayne's turn. He always was a nervous little man, and now he seemed terribly flustered. The detective was gentle with him, and in order to set him more at ease began to converse generally on crystals. He asked Mr. Wayne if he had traveled much, if he had ever been to Japan, and if he knew much about the making and polishing of crystal balls.

The tutor fidgeted around a good deal and seemed disinclined to look the detective in the eye; but he replied that he never had been to Japan, and that he never had heard of a Japanese rock crystal until he had seen Miss Farland's wedding-gift, and that even then he had no idea of its great value until since its disappearance he had heard its price named.

This sounded well; but his manner was so embarrassed, and he had such an effect of a guilty man, that I felt sure my intuitions were correct and that he himself was the thief.

The detective seemed to think so too, for he said at last: "Mr. Wayne, your words seem to indicate your innocence; but your attitudes do not. Unless you can explain why you are so agitated and apparently afraid, I shall be forced to the conclusion that you know more about this than you have admitted."

Then Mr. Wayne said: "Must I tell all I know about it, sir?"

"Certainly," said the detective.

"Then," said Mr. Wayne, "I shall have to state that when I left my room late last night to get a glass of water from the ice-pitcher, which always stands on the hall-table, I saw Mr. Fred Farland just going into the sitting-room, or present-room, as it has been called for the last few days."

There was a dead silence. This, then, was why Mr. Wayne had acted so embarrassed; this was the explanation of my finding the white carnation there; and I think the detective thought that the sudden turn affairs had taken incriminated Fred Farland.

I didn't think so at all. The idea of Fred's stealing his own sister's wedding-gift was too preposterous to be considered for a moment.

"Were you in the room late at night, Mr. Farland?" asked the detective.

"I was," said Fred.

"Why didn't you tell me this before?"

"You didn't ask me, and as I didn't take I saw no reason for referring to the fact that I was in the room."

"Why did you go there?"

"I went," said Fred coolly, "with the intention of taking the crystal and hiding it, as a practical joke on Christabel."

"Why did you not do so?"

"Because the ball wasn't there. I didn't think then that it had been stolen, but that it had been put away safely with the other valuables. Since this is not so, and the crystal is missing, we all must get to work and find it somehow before my sister returns."

The tutor seemed like a new man after Fred had spoken. His face cleared, and he appeared intelligent, alert and entirely at his ease. "Let me help," he said. "Pray command my services in any way you choose."

But the detective didn't seem so reassured by Fred's statements. Indeed, I believe he really thought that Christabel's brother was guilty of theft.

But I believed implicitly every word Fred had uttered, and begging him to come with me, I led the way again to the sitting-room. Mr. Wayne and Janet White came too, and the four of us scrutinized the floor, walls and furniture of the room over and over again. "There's one thing certain," I said thoughtfully: "The crystal was taken either by someone in the house or someone out of it. We've been confining our suspicions to those inside. Why not a real burglar?"

"But the windows are fastened on the inside," said Janet.

"I know it," I replied. "But if a burglar could slip a catch with a thin-bladed knife – and they often do – then he could slip it back again with the same knife and so divert suspicion."

"Bravo, Miss Frost!" said Mr. Wayne, with an admiring glance at me. "You have the true detective instinct. I'll go outside and see if there are any traces."

A moment later he was on the veranda and excitedly motioning us to raise the window. Fred pushed back the catch and opened the long French window that opened on the front veranda.

"I believe Miss Frost has discovered the mystery," said Mr. Wayne, and he pointed to numerous scratches on the sash-frame. The house had been painted recently, and it was seen easily that the fresh scratches were made by a thin knife-blade pushed between the sashes.

"By Jove!" cried Fred, "that's it, Elinor; and the canny fellow had wit enough to push the catch back in place after he was outside again."

"I said nothing, for a moment. My thoughts were adjusting themselves quickly to the new situation from which I must make my deductions. I realized at once that I must give up my theory of the tutor, of course, and anyway I hadn't had a scrap of evidence against him except his fitness for the position. But, given the surety of burglars from outside, I knew just what to do: look for footprints, to be sure.

I glanced around for the light snow that always falls in detective stories just before the crime is committed, and is testified, usually by the village folk, to have stopped just at the crucial moment. But there wasn't a sign of snow or rain or even dew. The veranda showed no footprints, nor could the smooth lawn or flagged walks be expected to. I leaned against the veranda railing in despair, wondering what Sherlock Holmes would do in a provoking absence of footprints, when I saw in the flower-bed beneath several well-defined marks of a man's shoes.

"There you are, Fred!" I cried, and rushed excitedly down the steps.

They all followed, and, sure enough, in the soft earth of the wide flower-bed that surrounded the veranda were strong, clear prints of large masculine foot-gear.

"That clears us, girls," cried Janet gleefully, as she measured her daintily shod foot against the depressions.

"Don't touch them!" I cried. "Call Mr. Prout the detective."

Mr. Prout appeared, and politely hiding his chagrin at not having discovered these marks before I did, proceeded to examine them closely.

"You see," he said in a pompous and dictatorial way, "there are four prints pointing toward the house, and four pointing toward the street. Those pointing to the street are superimposed upon those leading to the house, hence we deduce that they were made by a burglar who crossed the flower-bed, climbed the veranda, stepped over the rail and entered at the window. He then returned the same way, leaving these last footprints above the others."

As all this was so palpably evident from the facts of the case, I was not impressed much by the subtlety of his deductions and asked what he gathered from the shape of the prints.

He looked at the well-defined prints intently. "They are of a medium size," he announced at last, "and I should say that they were made by a man of average height and weight, who had a normal-sized foot."

Well, if that wasn't disappointing! I thought of course that he would tell the man's occupation and social status, even if he didn't say that he was left-handed or that he stuttered, which is the kind of thing detectives in fiction always discover.

So I lost all interest in that Prout man, and began to do a little deducing on my own account. Although I felt sure, as we all did, that the thief was a burglar from outside, yet I couldn't measure the shoes of an absent and unidentified burglar, and somehow I felt an uncontrollable impulse to measure shoes.

Without consulting anybody, I found a tape-measure and carefully measured the footprints. Then I went through the house and measured all the men's shoes I could find, from the stable-boy's up to Fred's.

It's an astonishing fact, but nearly all of them fitted the measurements of the prints on the flower-bed. Men's feet are so nearly universal in size, or rather their shoes are, and too, what with extension soles and queer-shaped lasts, you can't tell anything about the size or style of a man from his footprints.

So I gave up deducing and went to talk to Fred Farland.

"Fred," I said simply, "did you take Christabel's crystal?"

"No," he answered with equal simplicity, and he looked me in the eyes so squarely and honestly that I knew he spoke the truth.

"Who did?" I next inquired.

"It was a professional burglar," said Fred, "and a mighty cute one; but I'm going to track him and get that crystal before Christabel comes home."

"Let me help!" I cried eagerly. "I've got the true detective instinct, and I know I can do something."

"You?" said Fred incredulously. "No, you can't help; but I don't mind telling you my plan. You see I expect Lord Hammerton down to make me a visit. He's a jolly young English chap that I chummed with in London. Now, he's a first-rate amateur detective, and though I didn't expect him till next month, he's in New

York, and I've no doubt that he'd be willing to come right off. No one will know he's doing any detecting; and I'll wager he'll lay his hands on that ball in less than a week."

"Lovely!" I exclaimed. "And I'll be here to see him do it!"

"Yes, the mater says you're to stay a fortnight or more; but mind, this is our secret."

"Trust me," I said earnestly; "but let me help if I can, won't you?"

"You'll help most by not interfering," declared Fred, and though it didn't altogether suit me, I resolved to help that way rather than not at all.

A few days later Lord Hammerton came. He was not in any way an imposing-looking man. Indeed, he was a typical Englishman of the Lord Cholmondeley type, and drawled and used a monocle most effectively. The afternoon he came we told him all about the crystal. The talk turned to detective work and detective instinct.

Lord Hammerton opined in his slow languid drawl that the true detective mind was not dependent upon instinct, but was a nicely adjusted mentality that was quick to see the cause back of an effect.

Herbert Gay said that while this doubtless was so, yet it was an even chance whether the cause so skilfully deduced was the true one.

"Quite so," agreed Lord Hammerton amiably, "and that is why the detective in real life fails so often. He deduces properly the logical facts from the evidence before him; but real life and real events are so illogical that his deductions, though true theoretically, are false from mere force of circumstances."

"And that is why," I said, "detectives in story-books always deduce rightly, because the obliging author makes the literal facts coincide with the theoretical ones."

Lord Hammerton put up his monocle and favored me with a truly British stare. "It is unusual," he remarked slowly, "to find such a clear comprehension of this subject in a feminine mind."

They all laughed at this; but I went on: "It is easy enough to make the spectacular detective of fiction show marvelous penetration and logical deduction when the antecedent circumstances are arranged carefully to prove it all; but place even Sherlock Holmes face to face with a total stranger, and I, for one, don't believe that he could tell anything definite about him."

"Oh, come now! I can't agree to that," said Lord Hammerton, more interestedly than he had spoken before. "I believe there is much in the detective instinct besides the exotic and the artificial. There is a substantial basis of divination built on minute observation, and which I have picked up in some measure myself."

"Let us test that statement," cried Herbert Gay. "Here comes Mr. Wayne, Harold's tutor. Lord Hammerton never has seen him, and before Wayne even speaks let Lord Hammerton tell us some detail, which he divines by observation."

All agreed to this, and a few minutes later Mr. Wayne came up. We laughingly explained the situation to him and asked him to have himself deduced.

Lord Hammerton looked at Arthur Wayne for a few minutes, and then said, still in his deliberate drawl: "You have lived in Japan for the past seven years, in Government service in the interior, and only recently have returned."

A sudden silence fell upon us all – not so much because Lord Hammerton made deductions from no apparent evidence, but because we all knew Mr. Wayne had told Detective Prout that he never had been in Japan.

Fred Farland recovered himself first, and said: "Now that you've astonished us with your results, tell us how you attained them."

"It is simple enough," said Lord Hammerton, looking at young Wayne, who had turned deathly white. "It is simple enough, sir. The breast-pocket on the outside of your coat is on the right-hand side. Now it never is put there. Your coat is a good one – Poole, or some London tailor of that class. He never made a coat with an outer breast-pocket on the right side. You have had the coat turned – thus the original left-hand pocket appears now on the right side.

"Looking at you, I see that you have not the constitution which could recover from an acute attack of poverty. If you had it turned from want, you would not have your present effect of comfortable circumstances. Now, you must have had it turned because you were in a country where tailoring is not frequent, but sewing and delicate manipulation easy to find. India? You are not bronzed. China? The same. Japan? Probable; but not treaty ports – there are plenty of tailors there. Hence, the interior of Japan.

"Long residence, to make it incumbent on you to get the coat turned, means Government service, because unattached foreigners are allowed only as tourists. Then the cut of the coat is not so very old, and as contracts run seven or fourteen years with the Japanese, I repeat that you probably resided seven years in the interior of Japan, possibly as an irrigation engineer."

I felt sorry then for poor Mr. Wayne. Lord Hammerton's deductions were absolutely true, and coming upon the young man so suddenly he made no attempt to refute them.

And so as he had been so long in Japan, and must have been familiar with rock crystals for years, Fred questioned him sternly in reference to his false statements.

Then he broke down completely and confessed that he had taken Christabel's crystal because it had fascinated him.

He declared that he had a morbid craving for crystals; that he had crept down to the present-room late that night, merely to look at the wonderful, beautiful ball; that it had so possessed him that he carried it to his room to gaze at for awhile, intending to return with it after an hour or so. When he returned he saw Fred Farland, and dared not carry out his plan.

"And the footprints?" I asked eagerly.

"I made them myself," he explained with a dogged shamefacedness. "I did have a moment of temptation to keep the crystal, and so tried to make you think that a burglar had taken it; but the purity and beauty of the ball itself so reproached me that I tried to return it. I didn't do so then, and since –"

"Since?" urged Fred, not unkindly.

"Well, I've been torn between fear and the desire to keep the ball. You will find it in my trunk. Here is the key."

There was a certain dignity about the young man that made him seem unlike a criminal, or even a wrong-doer.

As for me, I entirely appreciated the fact that he was hypnotized by the crystal and in a way was not responsible. I don't believe that man would steal anything else in the world.

Somehow the others agreed with me, and as they had recovered the ball, they took no steps to prosecute Mr. Wayne.

He went away at once, still in that dazed, uncertain condition. We never saw him again; but I hope for his own sake that he never was subjected to such a temptation.

Just before he left, I said to him out of sheer curiosity: "Please explain one point, Mr. Wayne. Since you opened and closed that window purposely to mislead us, since you made those footprints in the flower-bed for the same reason, and since to do it you must have gone out and then come back, why were the outgoing footprints made over the incoming ones?"

"I walked backward on purpose," said Mr. Wayne simply.

THE ADVENTURE OF THE CLOTHES-LINE

Carolyn Wells

> **Carolyn Wells** (1862–1942) was a prolific American author known for her mysteries, children's fiction, and humorous verses. Her detective Fleming Stone first appeared in *The Clue* (1909) and featured in dozens of novels and short stories, including *The Maxwell Mystery* (1913) and *Who Killed Caldwell?* (1942).

The members of the Society of Infallible Detectives were just sitting around and being socially infallible in their rooms in Fakir Street, when President Holmes strode in. He was much saturniner than usual, and the others at once deduced there was something toward.

"And it's this," said Holmes, perceiving that they had perceived it. "A reward is offered for the solution of a great mystery – so great, my colleagues, that I fear none of you will be able to solve it, or even to help me in the marvelous work I shall do when ferreting it out."

"Humph!" grunted the Thinking Machine, riveting his steel-blue eyes upon the speaker.

"He voices all our sentiments," said Raffles, with his winning smile. "Fire away, Holmes. What's the prob?"

"To explain a most mysterious proceeding down on the East Side."

Though a tall man, Holmes spoke shortly, for he was peeved at the inattentive attitude of his collection of colleagues. But of course he still had his Watson, so he put up with the indifference of the rest of the cold world.

"Aren't all proceedings down on the East Side mysterious?" asked Arsène Lupin with an aristocratic look.

Holmes passed his brow wearily under his hand.

"Inspector Spyer," he said, "was riding on the Elevated Road – one of the small numbered Avenues – when, as he passed a tenement-house district, he saw a clothes-line strung from one high window to another across a courtyard."

"Was it Monday?" asked the Thinking Machine, who for the moment was thinking he was a washing machine.

"That doesn't matter. About the middle of the line was suspended –"

"By clothes-pins?" asked two or three of the Infallibles at once.

"Was suspended a beautiful woman."

"Hanged?"

"No. Do listen! She hung by her hands and was evidently trying to cross from one house to the other. By her exhausted and agonized face, the inspector feared she could not hold on much longer. He sprang from his seat to rush to her assistance, but the train had already started, and he was too late to get off."

"What was she doing there?" "Did she fall?" "What did she look like?" and various similar nonsensical queries fell from the lips of the great detectives.

"Be silent, and I will tell you all the known facts. She was a society woman, it is clear, for she was robed in a chiffon evening gown, one of those roll-top things. She wore rich jewelry and dainty slippers with jeweled buckles. Her hair, unloosed from its moorings, hung in heavy masses far down her back."

"How extraordinary! What does it all mean?" asked M. Dupin. ever straight-forward of speech.

"I don't know yet," answered Holmes, honestly. "I've studied the matter only a few months. But I will find out, if I have to raze the whole tenement block. There must be a clue somewhere."

"Marvelous! Holmes, marvelous!" said a phonograph in the corner, which Watson had fixed up, as he had to go out.

"The police have asked us to take up the case and have offered a reward for its solution. Find out who was the lady, what she was doing, and why she did it."

"Are there any clues?" asked M. Vidocq, while M. Lecoq said simultaneously, "Any footprints?"

"There is one footprint; no other clue."

"Where is the footprint?"

"On the ground, right under where the lady was hanging."

"But you said the rope was high from the ground."

"More than a hundred feet."

"And she stepped down and made a single footprint. Strange! Quite strange!" and the Thinking Machine shook his yellow old head.

"She did nothing of the sort," said Holmes, petulantly. "If you fellows would listen, you might hear something. The occupants of the tenement houses have been questioned. But, as it turns out, none of them chanced to be at home at the time of the occurrence. There was a parade in the next street, and they had all gone to see it."

"Had a light snow fallen the night before?" asked Lecoq, eagerly.

"Yes, of course," answered Holmes. "How could we know anything else? Well, the lady had dropped her slipper, and although the slipper was not found, it having been annexed by the tenement people who came home first, I had a chance to study the footprint. The slipper was a two and a half D. It was too small for her."

"How do you know?"

"Women always wear slippers too small for them."

"Then how did she come to drop it off?" This from Raffles, triumphantly.

Holmes looked at him pityingly.

"She kicked it off because it was too tight. Women always kick off their slippers when playing bridge or in an opera box or at a dinner."

"And always when they're crossing a clothes-line?" This in Lupin's most sarcastic vein.

"Naturally," said Holmes, with a taciturnine frown. "The footprint clearly denotes a lady of wealth and fashion, somewhat short of stature, and weighing about one hundred and sixty. She was of an animated nature."

"Suspended animation," put in Luther Trant, wittily, and Scientific Sprague added, "Like the Coffin of Damocles, or whoever it was."

But Holmes frowned on their light-headedness.

"We must find out what it all means," he said in his gloomiest way. "I have a tracing of the footprint."

"I wonder if my seismospygmograph would work on it," mused Trant.

"I am the Prince of Footprints," declared Lecoq, pompously. "*I* will solve the mystery."

"Do your best, all of you," said their illustrious president. "I fear you can do little; these things are unintelligible to the unintelligent. But study on it, and meet here again one week from tonight, with your answers neatly typewritten on one side of the paper."

The Infallible Detectives started off, each affecting a jaunty sanguineness of demeanor, which did not in the least impress their president, who was used to sanguinary impressions.

They spent their allotted seven days in the study of the problem; and a lot of the seven nights, too, for they wanted to delve into the baffling secret by sun or candlelight, as dear Mrs. Browning so poetically puts it.

And when the week had fled, the Infallibles again gathered in the Fakir Street sanctum, each face wearing the smug smirk and smile of one who had quested a successful quest and was about to accept his just reward.

"And now," said President Holmes, "as nothing can be hid from the Infallible Detectives, I assume we have all discovered *why* the lady hung from the clothes-line above that deep and dangerous chasm of a tenement courtyard."

"We have," replied his colleagues, in varying tones of pride, conceit, and mock modesty.

"I cannot think," went on the hawk-like voice, "that you have, any of you, stumbled upon the real solution of the mystery; but I will listen to your amateur attempts."

"As the oldest member of our organization, I will tell my solution first," said Vidocq, calmly. "I have not been able to find the lady, but I am convinced that she was merely an expert trapezist or tight-rope walker, practising a new trick to amaze her Coney Island audiences."

"Nonsense!" cried Holmes. "In that case the lady would have worn tights or fleshings. We are told she was in full evening dress of the smartest set."

Arsène Lupin spoke next.

"It's too easy," he said boredly; "she was a typist or stenographer who had been annoyed by attentions from her employer, and was trying to escape from the brute."

"Again I call your attention to her costume," said Holmes, with a look of intolerance on his finely cold-chiseled face.

"That's all right," returned Lupin, easily. "Those girls dress every old way! I've seen 'em. They don't think anything of evening clothes at their work."

"Humph!" said the Thinking Machine, and the others all agreed with him.

"Next," said Holmes, sternly.

"I'm next," said Lecoq. "I submit that the lady escaped from a nearby lunatic asylum. She had the illusion that she was an old overcoat and the moths had got at her. So of course she hung herself on the clothes-line. This theory of lunacy also accounts for the fact that the lady's hair was down like *Ophelia's*, you know."

"It would have been easier for her to swallow a few good moth balls," said Holmes, looking at Lecoq in stormy silence. "Mr. Gryce, you are an experienced deducer; what did *you* conclude?"

Mr. Gryce glued his eyes to his right boot toe, after his celebrated habit. "I make out she was a-slumming. You know, all the best ladies are keen about it. And I feel that she belonged to the Cult for the Betterment of Clothes-lines. She was by way of being a tester. She had to go across them hand over hand, and if they bore her weight, they were passed by the censor."

"And if they didn't?"

"Apparently that predicament had not occurred at the time of our problem, and so cannot be considered."

"I think Gryce is right about the slumming," remarked Luther Trant, "but the reason for the lady hanging from the clothes-line is the imperative necessity she felt for a thorough airing, after her tenemental visitations; there is a certain tenement scent, if I may express it, that requires ozone in quantities."

"You're too material," said the Thinking Machine, with a faraway look in his weak, blue eyes. "This lady was a disciple of New Thought. She had to go into the silence, or concentrate, or whatever they call it. And they always choose strange places for these thinking spells. They have to have solitude, and, as I understand it, the clothes-line was not crowded?"

Rouletabille laughed right out.

"You're way off, Thinky," he said. "What ailed that dame was just that she wanted to reduce. I've read about it in the women's journals. They all want to reduce. They take all sorts of crazy exercises, and this crossing clothes-lines hand over hand is the latest. I'll bet it took off twenty of those avoirdupois with which old Sherly credited her."

"Pish and a few tushes!" remarked Raffles, in his smart society jargon. "You don't fool me. That clever little bear was making up a new dance to thrill society next winter. You'll see. Sunday-paper headlines: Stunning New Dance! The Clothes-Line Cling! Caught On Like Wildfire! *That's* what it's all about. What do you know, eh?"

"Go take a walk, Raffles," said Holmes, not unkindly; "you're sleepy yet. Scientific Sprague, you sometimes put over an abstruse theory, what do you say?"

"I didn't need science," said Sprague, carelessly. "As soon as I heard she had her hair down, I jumped to the correct conclusion. She had been washing her hair, and was drying it. My sister always sticks her head out of the skylight; but this lady's plan is, I should judge, a more all-round success."

As they had now all voiced their theories, President Holmes rose to give them the inestimable benefit of his own views.

"Your ideas are not without some merit," he conceded, "but you have overlooked the eternal-feminine element in the problem. As soon as I tell you the real solution, you will each wonder why it escaped your notice. The lady thought she heard a mouse, so she scrambled out of the window, preferring to risk her life on the perilous clothes-line rather than stay in the dwelling where the mouse was also. It is all very simple. She was doing her hair, threw her head over forward to twist it, as they always do, and so espied the mouse sitting in the corner."

"Marvelous! Holmes, marvelous!" exclaimed Watson, who had just come back from his errand.

Even as they were all pondering on Holmes's superior wisdom, the telephone bell rang.

"Are you there?" said President Holmes, for he was ever English of speech.

"Yes, yes," returned the impatient voice of the chief of police. "Call off your detective workers. We have discovered who the lady was who crossed the clothes-line and why she did it."

"I can't imagine you really know," said Holmes into the transmitter; "but tell me what you think."

"A-r-r-rh! Of course I know! It was just one of those confounded moving-picture stunts!"

"Indeed! And why did the lady kick off her slipper?"

"A-r-r-r-h! It was part of the fool plot. She's Miss Flossy Flicker of the Flim-Flam Film Company, doin' the six-reel thriller, At the End of Her Rope."

"Ah," said Holmes suavely, "my compliments to Miss Flicker on her good work."

"Marvelous, Holmes, marvelous!" said Watson.

THE ADVENTURE OF THE "MONA LISA"

Carolyn Wells

Carolyn Wells (1862–1942) was a prolific American author known for her mysteries, children's fiction, and humorous verses. Her detective Fleming Stone first appeared in *The Clue* (1909) and featured in dozens of novels and short stories, including *The Maxwell Mystery* (1913) and *Who Killed Caldwell?* (1942).

In their rooms on Fakir Street, the members of the International Society of Infallible Detectives were holding a special meeting.

"If any one of you," said President Sherlock Holmes, speaking from the chair, "has any suggestions to offer –"

"My dear Holmes," interrupted Arsène Lupin, "we don't offer or accept suggestions any more than you do."

"No," agreed the Thinking Machine; "we merely observe the clues, deduce the truth, and announce the criminal."

"What are the clues?" inquired M. Lecocq of the company at large.

Raffles looked gravely at the old gentleman and then smiled.

"The clues," he said, "are the frame thrown down a back staircase, the wall vacancy in the Louvre, and the nails on which the picture hung."

"Is the wall vacancy just the size of the 'Mona Lisa'?" asked M. Dupin.

"That cannot be ascertained, since the picture is not available to measure by," returned Raffles. "But the 'Mona Lisa' is gone, and there is no other unexplained wall vacancy."

"The evidence seems to me inconclusive," murmured M. Dupin. "Is there not a law concerning the *corpus delicti*?"

"That's neither here nor there," interrupted Arsène Lupin, and Raffles wittily observed, "Neither is the picture."

Sherlock Holmes passed his white hand wearily across his brow.

"This meeting must come to order," he said. "Now, gentlemen, you have heard a description of the clues – the discarded frame, the vacant space, the empty nails. From these I deduce that the thief is five feet, ten inches tall, and weighs 160 pounds. He has dark hair and one gold tooth. He is fairly healthy, but he has a second cousin who was subject to croup as a child."

"Marvelous, Holmes! Marvelous!" exclaimed Dr. Watson, clasping his hands in ecstasy. "He is already the same as behind bars."

"I don't agree with you, Holmes," declared Arsène Lupin. "It is clearly evident to me that the thief was a blond, rather short and thick-set, and looked like his great-aunt on his mother's side."

Holmes looked thoughtful. "I can't think it, Lupin," he said at last; "and if you'll go over the clues again *carefully*, you'll perceive your fallacious inference."

"Munsterberg says," began Luther Trant; but President Holmes cut him off, and said, with his saturnine smile, "Gentlemen, we must get to work scientifically on this problem. Unless we find the stolen picture, and convict the thief, we are not worthy of our professional fame. Now, how much time do you think we should take to accomplish our purpose?"

"I could find the old daub in a week," said M. Dupin "you only have to reason this way. If –"

"There now, there now," said the Thinking Machine, querulously, "who wants to hear another man's advice? Let us all go to work independently of one another. A week will be more than enough time for me to produce both picture and thief."

"A week, bah!" scoffed Raffles. "I can accumulate the missing canvas and the missing miscreant in three days' time. I'm sure of it."

President Holmes kept on with his saturnine smile, and said, "Arsène, how much time do you require for the job?"

"Two days and carfare," replied Arsène Lupin. "And you yourself, Holmes?"

The smile of Sherlock Holmes became a little saturniner as he returned quietly, "I already know where it is; I've only to go and get it."

"That isn't fair," broke in Luther Trant, cutting short Dr. Watson's appreciative remark.

"Perfectly fair," declared Holmes; "I've had no more advantage than the rest of you. We've all heard a list of the clues; I've deduced the solution of the mystery. If you other fellows haven't, it's because you're blind to the obvious."

"Always distrust the obvious," began M. Dupin, didactically.

President Holmes paid his usual lack of attention to this speech, and went on:

"There's no use of further conversation. We're not a lot of consulting amateurs. We're each famous, unique, and infallible. Let us go our various ways, work by our various methods, and see who can find the picture first. Let us meet here one week from tonight, and whoever brings with him the 'Mona Lisa' will receive the congratulations of the rest of us, and incidentally the offered reward."

"Marvelous, Holmes! Marvelous!" cried Dr. Watson before any one else could speak.

But there wasn't much to be said. Famous detectives are ever taciturn, silent, and thoughtful, but looking as if the universe is to them an open primer.

After saying good night in their various fashions, the detectives went away to detect, and Sherlock Holmes got out his violin and played "Her Bright Smile Haunts Me Still."

A week slowly disengaged itself from the future and transferred its attachment to the past. Again the rooms in Fakir Street were cleared up nice and tidy for the meeting. Eight o'clock was the hour appointed, but no one came.

"Hah!" muttered Holmes, "they have all failed, and they dare not come and admit it. I alone have succeeded in the quest, I alone have the priceless 'Joconde' safe in my possession."

"Marv –" began Dr. Watson; but even as he spoke the door opened, and M. Dupin entered, with a large canvas under his arm. The picture was wrapped in an old shawl, but from its size and from the size of the smile on Dupin's face, even Watson deduced that the canvas was the one at which Leonardo had slung paint for four years.

"But, yes," said M. Dupin, carelessly, "I have it. Only I will wait for the others, that I may display my prize amid greater applause than I expect from you, M. Holmes."

Holmes's smile was only slightly saturnine, but before he could make a caustic reply, Lecocq came in, bearing a large roll carefully wrapped in paper. He beamed genially, and then catching sight of the shawled object leaning against the wall, he frowned.

"What have you there?" he cried. "Is it perhaps the gilded frame for the picture I bring?"

Goaded beyond endurance by these scathing words, Dupin sprang to the shawl and tore it off.

"Behold the 'Mona Lisa'! Found! Oh, the glory of it!"

"Ha!" cried Lecocq, and unrolling his roll, he, too, showed the original, the indisputably genuine Leonardo da Vinci masterpiece!

Holmes looked at the twin pictures with interest.

"They are doubtless the real thing," he declared – "both of them. There is no question of the genuineness of either. It must be that da Vinci painted the lady twice."

"Marvelous, Holmes! Marvelous!" chanted Watson.

But the two Frenchmen were not willing to accept Holmes's statement. They were volubly quarreling in their own picturesque tongue, and the purport of their excellent French was that each believed his own find to be the real picture and the other a copy.

Into this controversy shambled the queer old figure of the Thinking Machine.

"Squabble if you like," he shrilled at them. "It doesn't matter which wins, for I have the real 'Mona Lisa' at home. I wouldn't risk bringing it here. Both of yours are copies, and poor ones at that."

Just then appeared Luther Trant, followed by three messenger-boys. Each bore a picture of the "Mona Lisa," which he set down beside the ones already there.

"One of these is the real one," declared Trant. "I hadn't time to decide which, and my seismospygmatograph is broken. But I'll find that out later. Anyway, it's one of the three, and I've found it."

Into the hubbub caused by this announcement Raffles bounded, his face shining with hilarity.

"I've got it!" he cried, and his followers entered.

There were five messenger-boys, whose burden aggregated eight "Mona Lisas"; three sandwich-men wore two "Jocondes" each; and two washer-women brought a clothes-basket containing four.

"These are all vouched for by experts," declared Raffles, "so one of 'em must be the real thing."

"Oh," said Arsène Lupin, sauntering in, "*do* you think so? Well, I have a dray below, piled up with 'Mona Lisas' for each of which I have a signed guaranty by the best experts."

Sherlock Holmes stood looking on, his smile growing saturniner and saturniner.

"Now, gentlemen," he said, in his most cold-chisel tones – "*Now*, gentlemen, will you please step into the next room?"

They stepped, but delicately, like Agag, for the floor was knee-deep in "Mona Lisas," and as they entered the next room, behold, it was like stepping into a multiscope; for the four walls were lined – *lined*, mind you – with "Mona Lisas." And every one – every single one – bore indisputable, indubitable, impeccable, incontrovertible evidence of being the real Simon-Pure article.

Quite aside from the chagrin of the detectives at knowing Holmes had outnumbered them, conceive of the delight of being able to gaze on scores of "Mona Lisas" at once! Remember the thrills that thrilled you when you stood in the Louvre and looked upon just one masterpiece of the great painter; then imagine those thrills multiplied until it was like fever and ague! It was indeed a great psychological moment.

"Are they *all* genuine?" at last whispered M. Dupin, while Raffles began to compute their collective value to collectors.

"All guaranteed by experts," declared Holmes; and just then the telephone sounded.

"Mr. Holmes?" said the chief of police.

"Yes," replied Sherlock, saturninely.

"I have to inform you, Mr. Holmes, that we have the 'Mona Lisa.' The thief, who is a paramaranoiac, has returned it to us, and confessed his crime. He is truly penitent, and though he must be punished, there will doubtless be found extenuating circumstances in his full confession and his return of the picture unharmed. I'm sure you will rejoice with us at the restoration of our treasure."

"Huh!" said Holmes, a little more saturninely than usual, as he hung up the receiver, "when a picture has been restored as often and as poorly as that has, one restoration more or less doesn't matter. Now, gentlemen, you will please begin to give me a successful imitation of a moving-picture show."

AN UNLOCKED WINDOW

Ethel Lina White

Ethel Lina White (1876–1944) was born in Wales but became famous in America when she started publishing crime fiction in 1931. One of the best-known writers of her age, her books included *Some Must Watch* and *The Wheel Spins*, which was filmed by Alfred Hitchcock as *The Lady Vanishes*.

"Have you locked up, Nurse Cherry?"

"Yes, Nurse Silver."

"Every door? Every window?"

"Yes, yes."

Yet even as she shot home the last bolt of the front door, at the back of Nurse Cherry's mind was a vague misgiving.

She had forgotten—*something*.

She was young and pretty, but her expression was anxious. While she had most of the qualities to ensure professional success, she was always on guard against a serious handicap. She had a bad memory.

Hitherto, it had betrayed her only in burnt Benger and an occasional overflow in the bathroom. But yesterday's lapse was little short of a calamity.

Late that afternoon she had discovered the oxygen-cylinder, which she had been last to use, empty—its cap carelessly unscrewed.

The disaster called for immediate remedy, for the patient, Professor Glendower Baker, was suffering from the effects of gas-poisoning. Although dark was falling, the man, Iles, had to harness the pony for the long drive over the mountains, in order to get a fresh supply.

Nurse Cherry had sped his parting with a feeling of loss. Iles was a cheery soul and a tower of strength.

It was dirty weather with a spitting rain blanketing the elephant-grey mounds of the surrounding hills. The valley road wound like a muddy coil between soaked bracken and dwarf oaks.

Iles shook his head as he regarded the savage isolation of the landscape.

"I don't half like leaving you—a pack of women—with *him* about. Put up the shutters on every door and window, Nurse, and don't let *no one* come in till I get back."

He drove off—his lamps glow-worms in the gloom.

Darkness and rain. And the sodden undergrowth seemed to quiver and blur, so that stunted trees took on the shapes of crouching men advancing towards the house.

Nurse Cherry hurried through her round of fastening the windows. As she carried her candle from room to room of the upper floors, she had the uneasy feeling that she was visible to any watcher.

Her mind kept wandering back to the bad business of the forgotten cylinder. It had plunged her in depths of self-distrust and shame. She was overtired, having nursed the patient single-handed, until the arrival, three days ago, of the second nurse. But that fact did not absolve her from blame.

"I'm not fit to be a nurse," she told herself in bitter self-reproach.

She was still in a dream when she locked the front door. Nurse Silver's questions brought her back to earth with a furtive sense of guilt.

Nurse Silver's appearance inspired confidence, for she was of solid build, with strong features and a black shingle. Yet, for all her stout looks, her nature seemed that of Job.

"Has he gone?" she asked in her harsh voice.

"Iles? Yes."

Nurse Cherry repeated his caution.

"He'll get back as soon as he can," she added, "but it probably won't be until dawn."

"Then," said Nurse Silver gloomily, "we are *alone*."

Nurse Cherry laughed.

"Alone? Three hefty women, all of us able to give a good account of ourselves."

"*I'm* not afraid." Nurse Silver gave her rather a peculiar look. "*I'm* safe enough."

"Why?"

"Because of *you*. He won't touch me with you here."

Nurse Cherry tried to belittle her own attractive appearance with a laugh.

"For that matter," she said, "we are all safe."

"Do you think so? A lonely house. No man. And two of *us*."

Nurse Cherry glanced at her starched nurse's apron. Nurse Silver's words made her feel like special bait—a goat tethered in a jungle, to attract a tiger.

"Don't talk nonsense," she said sharply.

The countryside, of late, had been chilled by a series of murders. In each case, the victim had been a trained nurse. The police were searching for a medical student—Sylvester Leek. It was supposed that his mind had become unhinged, consequent on being jilted by a pretty probationer. He had disappeared from the hospital after a violent breakdown during an operation.

Next morning, a night-nurse had been discovered in the laundry—strangled. Four days later, a second nurse had been horribly done to death in the garden of a villa on the outskirts of the small agricultural town. After the lapse of a fortnight, one of the nurses in attendance on Sir Thomas Jones had been discovered in her bedroom—throttled.

The last murder had taken place in a large mansion in the very heart of the country. Every isolated cottage and farm became infected with panic. Women barred their doors and no girl lingered late in the lane, without her lover.

Nurse Cherry wished she could forget the details she had read in the newspapers. The ingenuity with which the poor victims had been lured to their doom and the ferocity of the attacks all proved a diseased brain driven by malignant motive.

It was a disquieting thought that she and Nurse Silver were localized. Professor Baker had succumbed to gas-poisoning while engaged in work of national importance and his illness had been reported in the Press.

"In any case," she argued, "how could—*he*—know that we're left tonight?"

Nurse Silver shook her head.

"*They* always know."

"Rubbish! And he's probably committed suicide by now. There hasn't been a murder for over a month."

"Exactly. There's bound to be another, *soon*."

Nurse Cherry thought of the undergrowth creeping nearer to the house. Her nerve snapped.

"Are you trying to make me afraid?"

"Yes," said Nurse Silver, "I am. I don't trust you. You forget."

Nurse Cherry coloured angrily.

"You might let me forget that wretched cylinder."

"But you might forget again."

"Not likely."

As she uttered the words—like oil spreading over water—her mind was smeared with doubt.

Something forgotten.

She shivered as she looked up the well of the circular staircase, which was dimly lit by an oil-lamp suspended to a cross-bar. Shadows rode the walls and wiped out the ceiling like a flock of sooty bats.

An eerie place. Hiding-holes on every landing.

The house was tall and narrow, with two or three rooms on every floor. It was rather like a tower or a pepper-pot. The semi-basement was occupied by the kitchen and domestic offices. On the ground-floor were a sitting-room, the dining-room and the Professor's study. The first floor was devoted to the patient. On the second floor were the bedrooms of the nurses and of the Iles couple. The upper floors were given up to the Professor's laboratorial work.

Nurse Cherry remembered the stout shutters and the secure hasps. There had been satisfaction in turning the house into a fortress. But now, instead of a sense of security, she had a feeling of being caged.

She moved to the staircase.

"While we're bickering," she said, "we're neglecting the patient."

Nurse Silver called her back.

"I'm on duty now."

Professional etiquette forbade any protest. But Nurse Cherry looked after her colleague with sharp envy.

She thought of the Professor's fine brow, his wasted clear-cut features and visionary slate-grey eyes, with yearning. For after three years of nursing children, with an occasional mother or aunt, romance had entered her life.

From the first, she had been interested in her patient. She had scarcely eaten or slept until the crisis had passed. She noticed, too, how his eyes followed her around the room and how he could hardly bear her out of his sight.

Yesterday he had held her hand in his thin fingers.

"Marry me, Stella," he whispered.

"Not unless you get well," she answered foolishly.

Since then, he had called her "Stella." Her name was music in her ears until her rapture was dashed by the fatal episode of the cylinder. She had to face the knowledge that, in case of another relapse, Glendower's life hung upon a thread.

She was too wise to think further, so she began to speculate on Nurse Silver's character. Hitherto, they had met only at meals, when she had been taciturn and moody.

To-night she had revealed a personal animus against herself, and Nurse Cherry believed she guessed its cause.

The situation was a hot-bed for jealousy. Two women were thrown into close contact with a patient and a doctor, both of whom were bachelors. Although Nurse Silver was the ill-favoured one, it was plain that she possessed her share of personal vanity. Nurse Cherry noticed, from her painful walk, that she wore shoes which were too small. More than that, she had caught her in the act of scrutinizing her face in the mirror.

These rather pitiful glimpses into the dark heart of the warped woman made Nurse Cherry uneasy.

The house was very still; she missed Nature's sounds of rain or wind against the window-pane and the cheerful voices of the Iles couple. The silence might be a background for sounds she did not wish to hear.

She spoke aloud, for the sake of hearing her own voice.

"Cheery if Silver plays up to-night. Well, well! I'll hurry up Mrs. Iles with the supper."

Her spirits rose as she opened the door leading to the basement. The warm spicy odour of the kitchen floated up the short staircase and she could see a bar of yellow light from the half-opened door.

When she entered, she saw no sign of supper. Mrs. Iles—a strapping blonde with strawberry cheeks—sat at the kitchen-table, her head buried in her huge arms.

As Nurse Cherry shook her gently, she raised her head.

"Eh?" she said stupidly.

"Gracious, Mrs. Iles. Are you ill?"

"Eh? Feel as if I'd one over the eight."

"What on earth d'you mean?"

"What *you* call 'tight.' Love-a-duck, my head's that swimmy—"

Nurse Cherry looked suspiciously at an empty glass upon the dresser, as Mrs. Iles's head dropped like a bleached sunflower.

Nurse Silver heard her hurrying footsteps on the stairs. She met her upon the landing.

"Anything wrong?"

"Mrs. Iles. I think she's drunk. Do come and see."

When Nurse Silver reached the kitchen, she hoisted Mrs. Iles under the armpits and set her on unsteady feet.

"Obvious," she said. "Help get her upstairs."

It was no easy task to drag twelve stone of protesting Mrs. Iles up three flights of stairs.

"She feels like a centipede, with every pair of feet going in a different direction," Nurse Cherry panted, as they reached the door of the Ileses' bedroom. "I can manage her now, thank you."

She wished Nurse Silver would go back to the patient, instead of looking at her with that fixed expression.

"What are you staring at?" she asked sharply.

"Has nothing struck you as *strange*?"

"What?"

In the dim light, Nurse Silver's eyes looked like empty black pits.

"To-day," she said, "there were four of us. First, Iles goes. Now, Mrs. Iles. That leaves only two. If anything happens to you or me, there'll only be *one*."

As Nurse Cherry put Mrs. Iles to bed, she reflected that Nurse Silver was decidedly not a cheerful companion. She made a natural sequence of events appear in the light of a sinister conspiracy.

Nurse Cherry reminded herself sharply that Iles's absence was due to her own carelessness, while his wife was addicted to her glass.

Still, some unpleasant suggestion remained, like the sediment from a splash of muddy water. She found herself thinking with horror of some calamity befalling Nurse Silver. If she were left by herself she felt she would lose her senses with fright.

It was an unpleasant picture. The empty house—a dark shell for lurking shadows. No one on whom to depend. Her patient—a beloved burden and responsibility.

It was better not to think of that. But she kept on thinking. The outside darkness seemed to be pressing against the walls, bending them in. As her fears multiplied, the medical student changed from a human being with a distraught brain, to a Force, cunning and insatiable—a ravening blood-monster.

Nurse Silver's words recurred to her.

"*They* always know." Even so. Doors might be locked, but *they* would find a way inside.

Her nerves tingled at the sound of the telephone-bell, ringing far below in the hall.

She kept looking over her shoulder as she ran downstairs. She took off the receiver in positive panic, lest she should be greeted with a maniac scream of laughter.

It was a great relief to hear the homely Welsh accent of Dr. Jones.

He had serious news for her. As she listened, her heart began to thump violently.

"Thank you, doctor, for letting me know," she said. "Please ring up directly you hear more."

"Hear more of what?"

Nurse Cherry started at Nurse Silver's harsh voice. She had come downstairs noiselessly in her soft nursing-slippers.

"It's only the doctor," she said, trying to speak lightly. "He's thinking of changing the medicine."

"Then why are you so white? You are shaking."

Nurse Cherry decided that the truth would serve her best.

"To be honest," she said, "I've just had bad news. Something ghastly. I didn't want you to know, for there's no sense in two of us being frightened. But now I come to think of it, you ought to feel reassured."

She forced a smile.

"You said there'd have to be another murder soon. Well—there has been one."

"Where? Who? Quick."

Nurse Cherry understood what is meant by the infection of fear as Nurse Silver gripped her arm.

In spite of her effort at self-mastery, there was a quiver in her own voice.

"It's a—a hospital nurse. Strangled. They've just found the body in a quarry and they sent for Dr. Jones to make the examination. The police are trying to establish her identity."

Nurse Silver's eyes were wide and staring.

"Another hospital nurse? That makes *four*."

She turned on the younger woman in sudden suspicion.

"Why did he ring you up?"

Nurse Cherry did not want that question.

"To tell us to be specially on guard," she replied.

"You mean—he's near?"

"Of course not. The doctor said the woman had been dead three or four days. By now, he'll be far away."

"Or he may be even nearer than you think."

Nurse Cherry glanced involuntarily at the barred front door. Her head felt as if it were bursting. It was impossible to think connectedly. But—somewhere—beating its wings like a caged bird, was the incessant reminder.

Something forgotten.

The sight of the elder woman's twitching lips reminded her that she had to be calm for two.

"Go back to the patient," she said, "while I get the supper. We'll both feel better after something to eat."

In spite of her new-born courage, it needed an effort of will to descend into the basement. So many doors, leading to scullery, larder and coal-cellar, all smelling of mice. So many hiding-places.

The kitchen proved a cheerful antidote to depression. The caked fire in the open range threw a red glow upon the Welsh dresser and the canisters labelled "Sugar" and "Tea." A sandy cat slept upon the rag mat. Everything looked safe and homely.

Quickly collecting bread, cheese, a round of beef, a cold white shape, and stewed prunes, she piled them on a tray. She added stout for Nurse Silver and made cocoa for herself. As she watched the milk froth up through the dark mixture and inhaled the steaming odour, she felt that her fears were baseless and absurd.

She sang as she carried her tray upstairs. She was going to marry Glendower.

The nurses used the bedroom which connected with the sick chamber for their meals, in order to be near the patient. As the night-nurse entered, Nurse Cherry strained her ears for the sound of Glendower's voice. She longed for one glimpse of him. Even a smile would help.

"How's the patient?" she asked.

"All right."

"Could I have a peep?"

"No. You're off duty."

As the women sat down, Nurse Cherry was amused to notice that Nurse Silver kicked off her tight shoes.

"You seem very interested in the patient, Nurse Cherry," she remarked sourly.

"I have a right to feel rather interested." Nurse Cherry smiled as she cut bread. "The doctor gives me the credit for his being alive."

"Ah! But the doctor thinks the world of you."

Nurse Cherry was not conceited, but she was human enough to know that she had made a conquest of the big Welshman.

The green glow of jealousy in Nurse Silver's eyes made her reply guardedly.

"Dr. Jones is decent to every one."

But she was of too friendly and impulsive a nature to keep her secret bottled up. She reminded herself that they were two women sharing an ordeal and she tried to establish some link of friendship.

"I feel you despise me," she said. "You think me lacking in self-control. And you can't forget that cylinder. But really, I've gone through such an awful strain. For four nights, I never took off my clothes."

"Why didn't you have a second nurse?"

"There was the expense. The Professor gives his whole life to enrich the nation and he's poor. Then, later, I felt I *must* do everything for him myself. I didn't want you, only Dr. Jones said I was heading for a break-down."

She looked at her left hand, seeing there the shadowy outline of a wedding-ring.

"Don't think me sloppy, but I must tell some one. The Professor and I are going to get married."

"*If* he lives."

"But he's turned the corner now."

"Don't count your chickens."

Nurse Cherry felt a stab of fear.

"Are you hiding something from me? Is he—worse?"

"No. He's the same. I was thinking that Dr. Jones might interfere. You've led him on, haven't you? I've seen you smile at him. It's light women like you that make the trouble in the world."

Nurse Cherry was staggered by the injustice of the attack. But as she looked at the elder woman's working face, she saw that she was consumed by jealousy. One life lay in the shadow, the other in the sun. The contrast was too sharp.

"We won't quarrel to-night," she said gently. "We're going through rather a bad time together and we have only each other to depend on. I'm just clinging to *you*. If anything were to happen to you, like Mrs. Iles, I should jump out of my skin with fright."

Nurse Silver was silent for a minute.

"I never thought of that," she said presently. "Only us two. And all these empty rooms, above and below. What's that?"

From the hall, came the sound of muffled knocking.

Nurse Cherry sprang to her feet.

"Some one's at the front door."

Nurse Silver's fingers closed round her arm, like iron hoops.

"Sit down. It's *him*."

The two women stared at each other as the knocking continued. It was loud and insistent. To Nurse Cherry's ears, it carried a message of urgency.

"I'm going down," she said. "It may be Dr. Jones."

"How could you tell?"

"By his voice."

"You fool. Any one could imitate *his* accent."

Nurse Cherry saw the beads break out round Nurse Silver's mouth. Her fear had the effect of steadying her own nerves.

"I'm going down, to find out who it is," she said. "It may be important news about the murder."

Nurse Silver dragged her away from the door.

"What did I say? *You* are the danger. You've forgotten already."

"Forgotten—what?"

"Didn't Iles tell you to open to no one? *No one?*"

Nurse Cherry hung her head. She sat down in shamed silence.

The knocking ceased. Presently they heard it again at the back door. Nurse Silver wiped her face.

"He *means* to get in." She laid her hand on Nurse Cherry's arm. "You're not even trembling. Are you never afraid?"

"Only of ghosts."

In spite of her brave front, Nurse Cherry was inwardly quaking at her own desperate resolution. Nurse Silver had justly accused her of endangering the household. Therefore it was her plain duty to make once more the round of the house, either to see what she had forgotten, or to lay the doubt.

"I'm going upstairs," she said. "I want to look out."

"Unbar a window?" Nurse Silver's agitation rose in a gale. "You shall not. It's murdering folly. Think! That last nurse was found dead *inside* her bedroom."

"All right. I won't."

"You'd best be careful. You've been trying to spare me, but perhaps I've been trying to spare you. I'll only say this. *There is something strange happening in this house.*"

Nurse Cherry felt a chill at her heart. Only, since she was a nurse, she knew that it was really the pit of her stomach. Something wrong? If through her wretched memory, she again were the culprit, she must expiate her crime by shielding the others, at any risk to herself.

She had to force herself to mount the stairs. Her candle, flickering in the draught, peopled the walls with distorted shapes. When she reached the top landing, without stopping to think, she walked resolutely into the laboratory and the adjoining room.

Both were securely barred and empty. Gaining courage, she entered the attic. Under its window was a precipitous slope of roof without gutter or water-pipe, to give finger-hold. Knowing that it would be impossible for any one to gain an entry, she opened the shutter and unfastened the window.

The cold air on her face refreshed her and restored her to calm. She realized that she had been suffering to a certain extent from claustrophobia.

The rain had ceased and a wind arisen. She could see a young harried moon flying through the clouds. The dark humps of the hills were visible against the darkness, but nothing more.

She remained at the window for some time, thinking of Glendower. It was a solace to remember the happiness which awaited her once this night of terror was over.

Presently the urge to see him grew too strong to be resisted. Nurse Silver's words had made her uneasy on his behalf. Even though she offended the laws of professional etiquette, she determined to see for herself that all was well.

Leaving the window open so that some air might percolate into the house, she slipped stealthily downstairs. She stopped on the second floor to visit her own room and that of Nurse Silver. All was quiet and secure. In her own quarters, Mrs. Iles still snored in the sleep of the unjust.

There were two doors to the patient's room. The one led to the nurses' room where Nurse Silver was still at her meal. The other led to the landing.

Directly Nurse Cherry entered, she knew that her fear had been the premonition of love. Something was seriously amiss. Glendower's head tossed uneasily on the pillow. His face was deeply flushed. When she called him by name, he stared at her, his luminous grey eyes ablaze.

He did not recognize her, for instead of "Stella," he called her "Nurse."

"Nurse, Nurse." He mumbled something that sounded like "man" and then slipped back in her arms, unconscious.

Nurse Silver entered the room at her cry. As she felt his pulse, she spoke with dry significance.

"We could do with oxygen now."

Nurse Cherry could only look at her with piteous eyes.

"Shall I telephone for Dr. Jones?" she asked humbly.

"Yes."

It seemed like the continuation of an evil dream when she could get no answer to her ring. Again and again she tried desperately to galvanize the dead instrument.

Presently Nurse Silver appeared on the landing.

"Is the doctor coming?"

"I—I can't get any answer." Nurse Cherry forced back her tears. "Oh, whatever can be wrong?"

"Probably a wet creeper twisted round the wire. But it doesn't matter now. The patient is sleeping."

Nurse Cherry's face registered no comfort. As though the shocks of the last few minutes had set in motion the arrested machinery of her brain, she remembered suddenly what she had forgotten.

The larder window.

She recollected now what had happened. When she entered the larder on her round of locking up, a mouse had run over her feet. She ran to fetch the cat which chased it into a hole in the kitchen. In the excitement of the incident, she had forgotten to return to close the window.

Her heart leapt violently at the realization that, all these hours, the house had been open to any marauder. Even while she and Nurse Silver had listened, shivering, to the knocking at the door, she had already betrayed the fortress.

"What's the matter?" asked Nurse Silver.

"Nothing. Nothing."

She dared not tell the older woman. Even now it was not too late to remedy her omission.

In her haste she no longer feared the descent into the basement. She could hardly get down the stairs with sufficient speed. As she entered the larder the wire-covered window flapped in the breeze. She secured it and was just entering the kitchen, when her eye fell on a dark patch on the passage.

It was the footprint of a man.

Nurse Cherry remembered that Iles had been in the act of getting fresh coal into the cellar when he had been called away to make his journey. He had no time to clean up and the floor was still sooty with rain-soaked dust.

As she raised her candle, the footprint gleamed faintly. Stooping hastily, she touched it.

It was still damp.

At first she stood as if petrified, staring at it stupidly. Then as she realized that in front of her lay a freshly-made imprint, her nerve snapped completely. With a scream, she dropped her candle and tore up the stairs, calling on Nurse Silver.

She was answered by a strange voice. It was thick, heavy, indistinct. A voice she had never heard before.

Knowing not what awaited her on the other side of the door, yet driven on by the courage of ultimate fear, she rushed into the nurses' sitting-room.

No one was there save Nurse Silver. She sagged back in her chair, her eyes half-closed, her mouth open.

From her lips issued a second uncouth cry.

Nurse Cherry put her arm around her.

"What is it? Try to tell me."

It was plain that Nurse Silver was trying to warn her of some peril. She pointed to her glass and fought for articulation.

"Drugs. Listen. When you lock out, you lock *in*." Even as she spoke her eyes turned up horribly, exposing the balls in a blind white stare.

Almost mad with terror, Nurse Cherry tried to revive her. Mysteriously, through some unknown agency, what she had dreaded had come to pass.

She was alone.

And somewhere—within the walls of the house—lurked a being, cruel and cunning, who—one after another—had removed each obstacle between himself and his objective.

He had marked down his victim. *Herself.*

In that moment she went clean over the edge of fear. She felt that it was not herself—Stella Cherry—but a stranger in the blue print uniform of a hospital nurse, who calmly speculated on her course of action.

It was impossible to lock herself in the patient's room, for the key was stiff from disuse. And she had not the strength to move furniture which was sufficiently heavy to barricade the door.

The idea of flight was immediately dismissed. In order to get help, she would have to run miles. She could not leave Glendower and two helpless women at the mercy of the baffled maniac.

There was nothing to be done. Her place was by Glendower. She sat down by his bed and took his hand in hers.

The time seemed endless. Her watch seemed sometimes to leap whole hours and then to crawl, as she waited—listening to the myriad sounds in a house at nightfall. There were faint rustlings, the cracking of wood-work, the scamper of mice.

And a hundred times, some one seemed to steal up the stairs and linger just outside her door.

It was nearly three o'clock when suddenly a gong began to beat inside her temples. In the adjoining room was the unmistakable tramp of a man's footsteps.

It was no imagination on her part. They circled the room and then advanced deliberately towards the connecting door.

She saw the handle begin to turn slowly.

In one bound, she reached the door and rushed on to the landing and up the stairs. For a second, she paused before her own room. But its windows were barred and its door had no key. She could not be done to death there in the dark.

As she paused, she heard the footsteps on the stairs. They advanced slowly, driving her on before them. Demented with terror, she fled up to the top storey, instinctively seeking the open window.

She could go no higher. At the attic door, she waited.

Something black appeared on the staircase wall. It was the shadow of her pursuer—a grotesque and distorted herald of crime.

Nurse Cherry gripped the balustrade to keep herself from falling. Everything was growing dark. She knew that she was on the point of fainting, when she was revived by sheer astonishment and joy.

Above the balustrade appeared the head of Nurse Silver.

Nurse Cherry called out to her in warning.

"Come quickly. There's a man in the house."

She saw Nurse Silver start and fling back her head, as though in alarm. Then occurred the culminating horror of a night of dread.

A mouse ran across the passage. Raising her heavy shoe, Nurse Silver stamped upon it, grinding her heel upon the tiny creature's head.

In that moment, Nurse Cherry knew the truth. Nurse Silver was a man.

Her brain raced with lightning velocity. It was like a searchlight, piercing the shadows and making the mystery clear.

She knew that the real Nurse Silver had been murdered by Sylvester Leek, on her way to the case. It was her strangled body which had just been found in the quarry. And the murderer had taken her place. The police description was that of a slightly-built youth, with refined features. It would be easy for him to assume the disguise of a woman. He had the necessary medical knowledge to pose as nurse. Moreover, as he had the night-shift, no one in the house had come into close contact with him, save the patient.

But the patient had guessed the truth.

To silence his tongue, the killer had drugged him, even as he had disposed of the obstructing presence of Mrs. Iles. It was he, too, who had emptied the oxygen-cylinder, to get Iles out of the way.

Yet, although he had been alone with his prey for hours, he had held his hand.

Nurse Cherry, with her new mental lucidity, knew the reason. There is a fable that the serpent slavers its victim before swallowing it. In like manner, the maniac—before her final destruction—had wished to coat her with the foul saliva of fear.

All the evening he had been trying to terrorize her—plucking at each jangled nerve up to the climax of his feigned unconsciousness.

Yet she knew that he in turn was fearful lest he should be frustrated in the commission of his crime. Since his victim's body had been discovered in the quarry, the establishment of her identity would mark his hiding-place. While Nurse Cherry was at the attic window, he had cut the telephone-wire and donned his own shoes for purposes of flight.

She remembered his emotion during the knocking at the door. It was probable that it was Dr. Jones who stood without, come to assure himself that she was not alarmed. Had it been the police, they would have effected an entry. The incident proved that nothing had been discovered and that it was useless to count on outside help.

She had to face it—alone.

In the dim light from the young moon, she saw the murderer enter the attic. The grotesque travesty of his nursing disguise added to the terror of the moment.

His eyes were fixed on the open window. It was plain that he was pretending to connect it with the supposed intruder. She in her turn had unconsciously deceived him. He probably knew nothing of the revealing footprint he had left in the basement passage.

"Shut the window, you damned fool," he shouted.

As he leaned over the low ledge to reach the swinging casement window, Nurse Cherry rushed at him in the instinctive madness of self-defence—thrusting him forward, over the sill.

She had one glimpse of dark distorted features blotting out the moon and of arms sawing the air, like a star-fish, in a desperate attempt to balance.

The next moment, nothing was there.

She sank to the ground, covering her ears with her hands to deaden the sound of the sickening slide over the tiled roof.

It was a long time before she was able to creep down to her patient's room. Directly she entered, its peace healed her like balm. Glendower slept quietly—a half-smile playing round his lips as though he dreamed of her.

Thankfully she went from room to room, unbarring each window and unlocking each door—letting in the dawn.

CHEESE

Ethel Lina White

Ethel Lina White (1876–1944) was born in Wales but became famous in America when she started publishing crime fiction in 1931. One of the best-known writers of her age, her books included *The Spiral Staircase* and *The Wheel Spins*, which was filmed by Alfred Hitchcock as *The Lady Vanishes*.

This story begins with a murder. It ends with a mousetrap.

The murder can be disposed of in a paragraph. An attractive girl, carefully reared and educated for a future which held only a twisted throat. At the end of seven months, an unsolved mystery and a reward of £500.

It is a long way from a murder to a mouse-trap—and one with no finger-posts; but the police knew every inch of the way. In spite of a prestige punctured by the press and public, they had solved the identity of the killer. There remained the problem of tracking this wary and treacherous rodent from his unknown sewer in the underworld into their trap.

They failed repeatedly for lack of the right bait.

And unexpectedly, one spring evening, the bait turned up in the person of a young girl.

Cheese.

Inspector Angus Duncan was alone in his office when her message was brought up. He was a red-haired Scot, handsome in a dour fashion, with the chin of a prize-fighter and keen blue eyes.

He nodded.

'I'll see her.'

It was between the lights. River, government offices and factories were all deeply dyed with the blue stain of dusk. Even in the city, the lilac bushes showed green tips and an occasional crocus cropped through the grass of the public-gardens, like strewn orange-peel. The evening star was a jewel in the pale green sky.

Duncan was impervious to the romance of the hour. He knew that twilight was but the prelude to night and that darkness was a shield for crime.

He looked up sharply when his visitor was admitted. She was young and flower-faced—her faint freckles already fading away into pallor. Her black suit was shabby, but her hat was garnished for the spring with a cheap cowslip wreath.

As she raised her blue eyes, he saw that they still carried the memory of country sweets . . . Thereupon he looked at her more sharply for he knew that of all poses, innocence is easiest to counterfeit.

'You say Roper sent you?' he enquired.

'Yes, Maggie Roper.'

He nodded. Maggie Roper—Sergeant Roper's niece—was already shaping as a promising young Stores' detective.

'Where did you meet her?'

'At the Girls' Hostel where I'm staying.'

'Your name?'

'Jenny Morgan.'

'From the country?'

'Yes. But I'm up now for good.'

For good? . . . He wondered.

'Alone?'

'Yes.'

'How's that?' He looked at her mourning. 'People all dead?'

She nodded. From the lightning sweep of her lashes, he knew that she had put in some rough work with a tear. It prejudiced him in her favour. His voice grew more genial as his lips relaxed.

'Well, what's it all about?'

She drew a letter from her bag.

'I'm looking for work and I advertised in the paper. I got this answer. I'm to be companion-secretary to a lady, to travel with her and be treated as her daughter—if she likes me. I sent my photograph and my references and she's fixed an appointment.'

'When and where?'

'The day after tomorrow, in the First Room in the National Gallery. But as she's elderly, she is sending her nephew to drive me to her house.'

'Where's that?'

She looked troubled.

'That's what Maggie Roper is making the fuss about. First, she said I must see if Mrs Harper—that's the lady's name—had taken up my references. And then she insisted on ringing up the Ritz where the letter was written from. The address was *printed*, so it was bound to be genuine, wasn't it?'

'Was it? What happened then?'

'They said no Mrs Harper had stayed there. But I'm sure it must be a mistake.' Her voice trembled. 'One must risk something to get such a good job.'

His face darkened. He was beginning to accept Jenny as the genuine article.

'Tell me,' he asked, 'have you had any experience of life?'

'Well, I've always lived in the country with Auntie. But I've read all sorts of novels and the newspapers.'

'Murders?'

'Oh, I love those.'

He could tell by the note in her childish voice that she ate up the newspaper accounts merely as exciting fiction, without the slightest realisation that the printed page was grim fact. He could see the picture: a sheltered childhood passed amid green spongy meadows. She could hardly cull sophistication from clover and cows.

'Did you read about the Bell murder?' he asked abruptly.

'Auntie wouldn't let me.' She added in the same breath, 'Every word.'

'Why did your aunt forbid you?'

'She said it must be a specially bad one, because they'd left all the bad parts out of the paper.'

'Well, didn't you notice the fact that that poor girl—Emmeline Bell—a well-bred girl of about your own age, was lured to her death through answering a newspaper advertisement?'

'I—I suppose so. But those things don't happen to oneself.'

'Why? What's there to prevent your falling into a similar trap?'

'I can't explain. But if there was something wrong, I should know it.'

'How? D'you expect a bell to ring or a red light to flash "Danger?"'

'Of course not. But if you believe in right and wrong, surely there must be some warning.'

He looked sceptical. That innocence bore a lily in its hand, was to him a beautiful phrase and nothing more. His own position in the sorry scheme of affairs was, to him, proof positive of the official failure of guardian angels.

'Let me see that letter, please,' he said.

She studied his face anxiously as he read, but his expression remained inscrutable. Twisting her fingers in her suspense, she glanced around the room, noting vaguely the three telephones on the desk and the stacked files in the pigeonholes. A Great Dane snored before the red-caked fire. She wanted to cross the room and pat him, but lacked the courage to stir from her place.

The room was warm, for the windows were opened only a couple of inches at the top. In view of Duncan's weather-tanned colour, the fact struck her as odd.

Mercifully, the future is veiled. She had no inkling of the fateful part that Great Dane was to play in her own drama, nor was there anything to tell her that a closed window would have been a barrier between her and the yawning mouth of hell.

She started as Duncan spoke.

'I want to hold this letter for a bit. Will you call about this time tomorrow? Meantime, I must impress upon you the need of utmost caution. Don't take one step on your own. Should anything fresh crop up, 'phone me immediately. Here's my number.'

When she had gone, Duncan walked to the window. The blue dusk had deepened into a darkness pricked with lights. Across the river, advertisement-signs wrote themselves intermittently in coloured beads.

He still glowed with the thrill of the hunter on the first spoor of the quarry. Although he had to await the report of the expert test, he was confident that the letter which he held had been penned by the murderer of poor ill-starred Emmeline Bell.

Then his elation vanished at a recollection of Jenny's wistful face. In this city were scores of other girls, frail as windflowers too—blossom-sweet and country-raw—forced through economic pressure into positions fraught with deadly peril.

The darkness drew down overhead like a dark shadow pregnant with crime. And out from their holes and sewers stole the rats . . .

At last Duncan had the trap baited for his rat.

A young and pretty girl—ignorant and unprotected. Cheese.

When Jenny, punctual to the minute, entered his office, the following evening, he instantly appraised her as his prospective decoy. His first feeling was one of disappointment. Either she had shrunk in the night or her eyes had grown bigger. She looked such a frail scrap as she stared at him, her lips bitten to a thin line, that it seemed hopeless to credit her with the necessary nerve for his project.

'Oh, please tell me it's all perfectly right about that letter.'

'Anything but right.'

For a moment, he thought she was about to faint. He wondered uneasily whether she had eaten that day. It was obvious from the keenness of her disappointment that she was at the end of her resources.

'Are you sure?' she insisted. 'It's—very important to me. Perhaps I'd better keep the appointment. If I didn't like the look of things, I needn't go on with it.'

'I tell you, it's not a genuine job,' he repeated. 'But I've something to put to you that is the goods. Would you like to have a shot at £500?'

Her flushed face, her eager eyes, her trembling lips, all answered him.

'Yes, please,' was all she said.

He searched for reassuring terms.

'It's like this. We've tested your letter and know it is written, from a bad motive, by an undesirable character.'

'You mean a criminal?' she asked quickly.

'Um. His record is not good. We want to get hold of him.'

'Then why don't you?'

He suppressed a smile.

'Because he doesn't confide in us. But if you have the courage to keep your appointment tomorrow and let his messenger take you to the house of the suppositious Mrs Harper, I'll guarantee it's the hiding-place of the man we want. We get him—you get the reward. Question is—have you the nerve?'

She was silent. Presently she spoke in a small voice.

'Will I be in great danger?'

'None. I wouldn't risk your safety for any consideration. From first to last, you'll be under the protection of the Force.'

'You mean I'll be watched over by detectives in disguise?'

'From the moment you enter the National Gallery, you'll be covered doubly and trebly. You'll be followed every step of the way and directly we've located the house, the place will be raided by the police.'

'All the same, for a minute or so, just before you can get into the house, I'll be alone with—*him*?'

'The briefest interval. You'll be safe at first. He'll begin with overtures. Stall him off with questions. Don't let him see you suspect—or show you're frightened.'

Duncan frowned as he spoke. It was his duty to society to rid it of a dangerous pest and in order to do so, Jenny's cooperation was vital. Yet, to his own surprise, he disliked the necessity in the case of this especial girl.

'Remember we'll be at hand,' he said. 'But if your nerve goes, just whistle and we'll break cover immediately.'

'Will *you* be there?' she asked suddenly.

'Not exactly in the foreground. But I'll be there.'

'Then I'll do it.' She smiled for the first time. 'You laughed at me when I said there was something inside me which told me—things. But I just know I can trust *you*.'

'Good.' His voice was rough. 'Wait a bit. You've been put to expense coming over here. This will cover your fares and so on.'

He thrust a note into her hand and hustled her out, protesting. It was a satisfaction to feel that she would eat that night. As he seated himself at his desk, preparatory to work, his frozen face was no index of the emotions raised by Jenny's parting words.

Hitherto, he had thought of women merely as 'skirts.' He had regarded a saucepan with an angry woman at the business end of it merely as a weapon. For the first time he had a domestic vision of a country girl—creamy and fragrant as meadowsweet—in a nice womanly setting of saucepans.

Jenny experienced a thrill which was almost akin to exhilaration when she entered Victoria Station, the following day. At the last moment, the place for meeting had been altered in a telegram from 'Mrs Harper.'

Immediately she had received the message, Jenny had gone to the telephone-box in the hostel and duly reported the change of plan, with a request that her message should be repeated to her, to obviate any risk of mistake.

And now—the incredible adventure was actually begun.

The station seemed filled with hurrying crowds as she walked slowly towards the clock. Her feet rather lagged on the way. She wondered if the sinister messenger had already marked the yellow wreath in her hat which she had named as her mark of identification.

Then she remembered her guards. At this moment they were here, unknown, watching over her slightest movement. It was a curious sensation to feel that she was spied upon by unseen eyes. Yet it helped to brace the muscles of her knees when she took up her station under the clock with the sensation of having exposed herself as a target for gunfire.

Nothing happened. No one spoke to her. She was encouraged to gaze around her . . .

A few yards away, a pleasant-faced smartly dressed young man was covertly regarding her. He carried a yellowish sample-bag which proclaimed him a drummer.

Suddenly Jenny felt positive that this was one of her guards. There was a quality about his keen clean-shaven face—a hint of the eagle in his eye—which reminded her of Duncan. She gave him the beginnings of a smile and was thrilled when, almost imperceptibly, he fluttered one eyelid. She read it as a signal for caution. Alarmed by her indiscretion, she looked fixedly in another direction.

Still—it helped her to know that even if she could not see him, he was there.

The minutes dragged slowly by. She began to grow anxious as to whether the affair were not some hoax. It would be not only a tame ending to the adventure but a positive disappointment. She would miss the chance of a sum which—to her—was a little fortune. Her need was so vital that she would have undertaken the venture for five pounds. Moreover, after her years of green country solitude, she felt a thrill at the mere thought of her temporary link with the underworld.

This was life in the raw; while screening her as she aided him, she worked with Angus Duncan.

She smiled—then started as though stung.

Someone had touched her on the arm.

'Have I the honour, happiness and felicity of addressing Miss Jenny Morgan? Yellow wreath in the lady's hat. Red Flower in the gent's buttonhole, as per arrangement.'

The man who addressed her was young and bull-necked, with florid colouring which ran into blotches. He wore a red carnation in the buttonhole of his check overcoat.

'Yes, I'm Jenny Morgan.'

As she spoke, she looked into his eyes. She felt a sharp revulsion—an instinctive recoil of her whole being.

'Are you Mrs Harper's nephew?' she faltered.

'That's right. Excuse a gent keeping a lady waiting, but I just slipped into the bar for a glass of milk. I've a taxi waiting if you'll just hop outside.'

Jenny's mind worked rapidly as she followed him. She was forewarned and protected. But—were it not for Maggie Roper's intervention—she would have kept this appointment in very different circumstances. She wondered whether she would have heeded that instinctive warning and refused to follow the stranger.

She shook her head. Her need was so urgent that, in her wish to believe the best, she knew that she would have summoned up her courage and flouted her fears as nerves. She would have done exactly what she was doing—accompanying an unknown man to an unknown destination.

She shivered at the realisation. It might have been herself. Poor defenceless Jenny—going to her doom.

At that moment she encountered the grave scrutiny of a stout clergyman who was standing by the book-stall. He was ruddy, wore horn-rimmed spectacles and carried the *Church Times*.

His look of understanding was almost as eloquent as a vocal message. It filled her with gratitude. Again she was certain that this was a second guard. Turning to see if the young commercial traveller were following her, she was thrilled to discover that he had preceded her into the station yard. He got into a taxi at the exact moment that her companion flung open the door of a cab which was waiting. It was only this knowledge that Duncan was thus making good his promise which induced her to enter the vehicle. Once again her nerves rebelled and she was rent with sick forebodings.

As they moved off, she had an overpowering impulse to scream aloud for help to the porters—just because all this might have happened to some poor girl who had not her own good fortune.

Her companion nudged her.

'Bit of all right, joy-riding, eh?'

She stiffened, but managed to force a smile.

'Is it a long ride?'

'Ah, now you're asking.'

'Where does Mrs Harper live?'

'Ah, that's telling.'

She shrank away, seized with disgust of his blotched face so near her own.

'Please give me more room. It's stifling here.'

'Now, don't you go taking no liberties with me. A married man I am, with four wives all on the dole.' All the same, to her relief, he moved further away. 'From the country, aren't you? Nice place. Lots of milk. Suit me a treat. Any objection to a gent smoking?'

'I wish you would. The cab reeks of whisky.'

They were passing St Paul's which was the last landmark in her limited knowledge of London. Girls from offices passed on the pavement, laughing and chatting together, or hurrying by intent on business. A group was scattering crumbs to the pigeons which fluttered on the steps of the cathedral.

She watched them with a stab of envy. Safe happy girls.

Then she remembered that somewhere, in the press of traffic, a taxi was shadowing her own. She took fresh courage.

The drive passed like an interminable nightmare in which she was always on guard to stem the advances of her disagreeable companion. Something seemed always on the point of happening—something unpleasant, just out of sight and round the corner—and then, somehow she staved it off.

The taxi bore her through a congested maze of streets. Shops and offices were succeeded by regions of warehouses and factories, which in turn gave way to areas of dun squalor where gas-works rubbed shoulders with grimed laundries which bore such alluring signs as DEWDROP or WHITE ROSE.

From the shrilling of sirens, Jenny judged that they were in the neighbourhood of the river, when they turned into a quiet square. The tall lean houses wore an air of drab respectability. Lace curtains hung at every window. Plaster pineapples crowned the pillared porches.

'Here's our "destitution."'

As her guide inserted his key in the door of No. 17, Jenny glanced eagerly down the street, in time to see a taxi turn the corner.

'Hop in, dearie.'

On the threshold Jenny shrank back.

Evil.

Never before had she felt its presence. But she knew. Like the fumes creeping upwards from the grating of a sewer, it poisoned the air.

Had she embarked on this enterprise in her former ignorance, she was certain that at this point, her instinct would have triumphed.

'I would never have passed through this door.'

She was wrong. Volition was swept off the board. Her arm was gripped and before she could struggle, she was pulled inside.

She heard the slam of the door.

'Never loiter on the doorstep, dearie. Gives the house a bad name. This way. Up the stairs. All the nearer to heaven.'

Her heart heavy with dread, Jenny followed him. She had entered on the crux of her adventure—the dangerous few minutes when she would be quite alone.

The place was horrible—with no visible reason for horror. It was no filthy East-end rookery, but a technically clean apartment-house. The stairs were covered with brown linoleum. The mottled yellow wallpaper was intact. Each landing had its marble-topped table, adorned with a forlorn aspidistra—its moulting rug at every door. The air was dead and smelt chiefly of dust.

They climbed four flights of stairs without meeting anyone. Only faint rustlings and whispers within the rooms told of other tenants. Then the blotched-faced man threw open a door.

'Young lady come to see Mrs Harper about the sitooation. Too-tel-oo, dearie. Hope you strike lucky.'

He pushed her inside and she heard his step upon the stairs.

In that moment, Jenny longed for anyone—even her late companion.

She was vaguely aware of the figure of a man seated in a chair. Too terrified to look at him, her eyes flickered around the room.

Like the rest of the house, it struck the note of parodied respectability. Yellowish lace curtains hung at the windows which were blocked by pots of leggy geraniums. A walnut-wood suite was upholstered in faded bottle-green rep with burst padding. A gilt-framed mirror surmounted a stained marble mantelpiece which was decorated with a clock—permanently stopped under its glass case—and a bottle of whisky. On a small table by the door rested a filthy cage, containing a grey parrot, its eyes mere slits of wicked evil between wrinkled lids.

It had to come. With an effort, she looked at the man.

He was tall and slender and wrapped in a once-gorgeous dressing-gown of frayed crimson quilted silk. At first sight, his features were not only handsome but bore some air of breeding. But the whole face was blurred—as though it were a waxen mask half-melted by the sun and over which the Fiend—in passing—had lightly drawn a hand. His eyes drew her own. Large and brilliant, they were of so light a blue as to appear almost white. The lashes were unusually long and matted into spikes.

The blood froze at Jenny's heart. The girl was no fool. Despite Duncan's cautious statements, she had drawn her own deduction which linked an unsolved murder mystery and a reward of £500.

She knew that she was alone with a homicidal maniac—the murderer of ill-starred Emmeline Bell.

In that moment, she realised the full horror of a crime which, a few months ago, had been nothing but an exciting newspaper-story. It sickened her to reflect that a girl—much like herself—whose pretty face smiled fearlessly upon the world from the printed page, had walked into this same trap, in all the blindness of her youthful confidence. No one to hear her cries. No one to guess the agony of those last terrible moments.

Jenny at least understood that first rending shock of realisation. She fought for self-control. At sight of that smiling marred face, she wanted to do what she knew instinctively that other girl had done—precipitating her doom. With a desperate effort she suppressed the impulse to rush madly round the room like a snared creature, beating her hands against the locked door and crying for help. Help which would never come.

Luckily, common sense triumphed. In a few minutes' time, she would not be alone. Even then a taxi was speeding on its mission; wires were humming; behind her was the protection of the Force.

She remembered Duncan's advice to temporise. It was true that she was not dealing with a beast of the jungle which sprang on its prey at sight.

'Oh, please.' She hardly recognised the tiny pipe. 'I've come to see Mrs Harper about her situation.'

'Yes.' The man did not remove his eyes from her face. 'So you are Jenny?'

'Yes, Jenny Morgan. Is—is Mrs Harper in?'

'She'll be in presently. Sit down. Make yourself at home. What are you scared for?'

'I'm not scared.'

Her words were true. Her strained ears had detected faintest sounds outside— dulled footsteps, the cautious fastening of a door.

The man, for his part, also noticed the stir. For a few seconds he listened intently. Then to her relief, he relaxed his attention.

She snatched again at the fiction of her future employer.

'I hope Mrs Harper will soon come in.'

'What's your hurry? Come closer. I can't see you properly.'

They were face to face. It reminded her of the old nursery story of 'Little Red Riding Hood.'

'What big eyes you've got, Grandmother.'

The words swam into her brain.

Terrible eyes. Like white glass cracked in distorting facets. She was looking into the depths of a blasted soul. Down, down . . . That poor girl. But she must not think of *her*. She must be brave—give him back look for look.

Her lids fell . . . She could bear it no longer.

She gave an involuntary start at the sight of his hands. They were beyond the usual size—unhuman—with long knotted fingers.

'What big hands you've got.'

Before she could control her tongue, the words slipped out.

The man stopped smiling.

But Jenny was not frightened now. Her guards were near. She thought of the detective who carried the bag of samples. She thought of the stout clergyman. She thought of Duncan.

At that moment, the commercial traveller was in an upper room of a whole-sale drapery house in the city, holding the fashionable blonde lady buyer with his magnetic blue eye, while he displayed his stock of crêpe-de-Chine underwear.

At that moment, the clergyman was seated in a third-class railway carriage, watching the hollows of the Downs fill with heliotrope shadows. He was not quite at ease. His thoughts persisted on dwelling on the frightened face of a little country girl as she drifted by in the wake of a human vulture.

'I did wrong. I should have risked speaking to her.'

But—at that moment—Duncan was thinking of her.

Jenny's message had been received over the telephone wire, repeated and duly written down by Mr Herbert Yates, shorthand-typist—who, during the absence of Duncan's own secretary, was filling the gap for one morning. At the sound of his chief's step in the corridor outside, he rammed on his hat, for he was already overdue for a lunch appointment with one of the numerous 'only girls in the world.'

At the door he met Duncan.

'May I go to lunch now, sir?'

Duncan nodded assent. He stopped for a minute in the passage while he gave Yates his instructions for the afternoon.

'Any message?' he enquired.

'One come this instant, sir. It's under the weight.'

Duncan entered the office. But in that brief interval, the disaster had occurred.

Yates could not be held to blame for what happened. It was true that he had taken advantage of Duncan's absence to open a window wide, but he was ignorant of any breach of rules. In his hurry he had also written down Jenny's message on the nearest loose-leaf to hand, but he had taken the precaution to place it under a heavy paper-weight.

It was Duncan's Great Dane which worked the mischief. He was accustomed at this hour to be regaled with a biscuit by Duncan's secretary who was an abject dog-lover. As his dole had not been forthcoming he went in search of it. His great paws on the table, he rooted among the papers, making nothing of a trifle of a letter-weight. Over it went. Out of the window—at the next gust—went Jenny's message. Back to his rug went the dog.

The instant Duncan was aware of what had happened, a frantic search was made for Yates. But that wily and athletic youth, wise to the whims of his official superiors, had disappeared. They raked every place of refreshment within a wide radius. It was not until Duncan's men rang up to report that they had drawn a blank at the National Gallery that Yates was discovered in an underground dive, drinking coffee and smoking cigarettes with his charmer.

Duncan arrived at Victoria forty minutes after the appointed time.

It was the bitterest hour of his life. He was haunted by the sight of Jenny's flower-face upturned to his. She had *trusted* him. And in his ambition to track the man he had taken advantage of her necessity to use her as a pawn in his game.

He had played her—and lost her.

The thought drove him to madness. Steeled though he was to face reality, he dared not to let himself think of the end. Jenny—country-raw and blossom-sweet—even then struggling in the grip of murderous fingers.

Even then.

Jenny panted as she fought, her brain on fire. The thing had rushed upon her so swiftly that her chief feeling was of sheer incredulity. What had gone before was already burning itself up in a red mist. She had no clear memory afterwards of those tense minutes of fencing. There was only an interlude filled with a dimly comprehended menace—and then this.

And still Duncan had not intervened.

Her strength was failing. Hell cracked, revealing glimpses of unguessed horror.

With a supreme effort she wrenched herself free. It was but a momentary respite, but it sufficed for her signal—a broken tremulous whistle.

The response was immediate. Somewhere outside the door a gruff voice was heard in warning.

'Perlice.'

The killer stiffened, his ears pricked, every nerve astrain. His eyes flickered to the ceiling which was broken by the outline of a trap-door.

Then his glance fell upon the parrot.

His fingers on Jenny's throat, he paused. The bird rocked on its perch, its eyes slits of malicious evil.

Time stood still. The killer stared at the parrot. Which of the gang had given the warning? Whose voice? Not Glass-eye. Not Mexican Joe. The sound had seemed to be within the room.

That parrot.

He laughed. His fingers tightened. Tightened to relax.

For a day and a half he had been in Mother Bargery's room. During that time the bird had been dumb. Did it talk?

The warning echoed in his brain. Every moment of delay was fraught with peril. At that moment his enemies were here, stealing upwards to catch him in their trap. The instinct of the human rodent, enemy of mankind—eternally hunted and harried—prevailed. With an oath, he flung Jenny aside and jumping on the table, wormed through the trap of the door.

Jenny was alone. She was too stunned to think. There was still a roaring in her ears, shooting lights before her eyes. In a vague way, she knew that some hitch had occurred in the plan. The police were here—yet they had let their prey escape.

She put on her hat, straightened her hair. Very slowly she walked down the stairs. There was no sign of Duncan or of his men.

As she reached the hall, a door opened and a white puffed face looked at her. Had she quickened her pace or shown the least sign of fear she would never have left that place alive. Her very nonchalance proved her salvation as she unbarred the door with the deliberation bred of custom.

The street was deserted, save for an empty taxi which she hailed.

'Where to, miss?' asked the driver.

Involuntarily she glanced back at the drab house, squeezed into its strait-waist-coat of grimed bricks. She had a momentary vision of a white blurred face flattened against the glass. At the sight, realisation swept over her in wave upon wave of sick terror.

There had been no guards. She had taken every step of that perilous journey—alone.

Her very terror sharpened her wits to action. If her eyesight had not deceived her, the killer had already discovered that the alarm was false. It was obvious that he would not run the risk of remaining in his present quarters. But it was possible that he might not anticipate a lightning swoop; there was nothing to connect a raw country girl with a preconcerted alliance with a Force.

'The nearest telephone-office,' she panted. 'Quick.'

A few minutes later, Duncan was electrified by Jenny's voice gasping down the wire.

'He's at 17 Jamaica Square, SE. No time to lose. He'll go out through the roof . . . Quick, quick.'

'Right. Jenny, where'll you be?'

'At your house. I mean, Scot—Quick.'

As the taxi bore Jenny swiftly away from the dun outskirts, a shrivelled hag pattered into the upper room of that drab house. Taking no notice of its raging occupant, she approached the parrot's cage.

'Talk for mother, dearie.'

She held out a bit of dirty sugar. As she whistled, the parrot opened its eyes.

'Perlice.'

It was more than two hours later when Duncan entered his private room at Scotland Yard.

His eyes sought Jenny.

A little wan, but otherwise none the worse for her adventure, she presided over a teapot which had been provided by the resourceful Yates. The Great Dane—unmindful of a little incident of a letter-weight—accepted her biscuits and caresses with deep sighs of protest.

Yates sprang up eagerly.

'Did the cop come off, chief?'

Duncan nodded twice—the second time towards the door, in dismissal.

Jenny looked at him in some alarm when they were alone together. There was little trace left of the machine-made martinet of the Yard. The lines in his face appeared freshly re-tooled and there were dark pouches under his eyes.

'Jenny,' he said slowly, 'I've—sweated—blood.'

'Oh, was he so very difficult to capture? Did he fight?'

'Who? That rat? He ran into our net just as he was about to bolt. He'll lose his footing all right. No.'

'Then why are you—'

'*You.*'

Jenny threw him a swift glance. She had just been half-murdered after a short course of semi-starvation, but she commanded the situation like a lion tamer.

'Sit down,' she said, 'and don't say one word until you've drunk this.'

He started to gulp obediently and then knocked over his cup.

'Jenny, you don't know the hell I've been through. You don't understand what you ran into. That man—'

'He was a murderer, of course. I knew that all along.'

'But you were in deadliest peril—'

'I wasn't frightened, so it didn't matter. I knew I could trust you.'

'Don't, Jenny. Don't turn the knife. I failed you. There was a ghastly blunder.'

'But it *was* all right, for it ended beautifully. You see, something told me to trust you. I always know.'

During his career, Duncan had known cases of love at first sight. So, although he could not rule them out, he always argued along Jenny's lines.

Those things did not happen to him.

He realised now that it had happened to him—cautious Scot though he was.

'Jenny,' he said, 'it strikes me that I want someone to watch *me.*'

'I'm quite sure you do. Have I won the reward?'

His rapture was dashed.

'Yes.'

'I'm so glad. I'm rich.' She smiled happily. 'So this can't be pity for me.'

'Pity? Oh, Jenny—'

Click. The mouse-trap was set for the confirmed bachelor with the right bait.

A young and friendless girl—homely and blossom-sweet.

Cheese.

THEFT OF THE POET

Barbara Wilson

Barbara Wilson is a pseudonym for Barbara Sjoholm, whose first Cassandra Reilly mystery, *Gaudi Afternoon*, won Crime Writers Association and Lamda Literary awards, and was later filmed. A recognised force in lesbian crime writing, Wilson is, like her detective, a translator. She co-founded the Seal Press in 1976.

It started gradually. Here and there on London streets new blue plaques that might have been placed there by the authorities, if the authorities had been reasonably literate, and unreasonably feminist, began to appear. At 22 Hyde Park Gate the enamel plaque stating that Leslie Stephen, the noted biographer, had lived here was joined by a new metal plate, much the same size and much the same color, which informed the passerby that this was where writer Virginia Woolf and painter Vanessa Bell had spent their childhoods. Over in Primrose Hill the plaque that read that Yeats had once been resident in this house was joined by a shiny new medallion gravely informing us that Sylvia Plath had written the poems in *Ariel* here before committing suicide in 1963.

Above the blue plaque at 106 Hallam Street, the birthplace of Dante Gabriel Rossetti, another one appeared to emphasize that poet Christina Rossetti had lived here as well. The plate at 20 Maresfield Gardens, which recorded that Sigmund Freud had passed the last year of his life here, was joined by a new one telling us that Anna Freud had passed forty-two years at this address. A medallion to Jane Carlyle, letter writer, joined that of her famous husband Thomas at 24 Cheyne Row, and a plaque telling us about Fanny Burney, author of Evelina and other novels, appeared above that describing Sir Isaac Newton's dates and accomplishments on the outside of a library in St. Martin's Street.

The appearance of these blue plaques was at first noted sympathetically, if condescendingly, by the liberal newspapers and a certain brave editor at *The Guardian* was bold enough to suggest that it was high time more women writers who had clearly achieved "a certain stature" be recognized. The editor thus managed to give tacit approval to the choice of authors awarded blue plaques and to suggest that the perpetrators had gone quite far enough. "We wouldn't want blue plaques on every house in London, after all."

But the plaquing continued, heedless of *The Guardian*'s pointed admonition, to the growing excitement of many and the consternation of quite a few. Who was responsible and how long would it go on? Would the authorities leave the plaques up or bother to remove them? Apparently they had been manufactured out of a lighter metal than the original plaques, but instead of being bolted to the buildings, they had been affixed with Super Glue. Some residents of the buildings were delighted; other inhabitants, in a conservative rage, defaced the medallions immediately.

The next blue plaques to go up were placed on houses previously unrecognized as having been the homes of women worth remembering and honoring. A plaque appeared outside the house in Maida Vale where authors Winifred Holtby and Vera Brittain had shared a flat for several years. A similar plaque commemorating the relationship of poets H.D. and Bryher appeared in Knightsbridge. Mary Seacole, a Victorian black woman who had traveled widely as a businesswoman, gold prospector, and nurse in the Crimean War and who had written an autobiography about her life, was honored on the wall of 26 Upper George Street off Portman Square, as was Constance Markievicz, many times imprisoned Irish Republican, who was the first woman elected as a member of the British Parliament (though she refused to take her seat in protest over the Irish situation), and who was born in Westminster on Buckingham Street. Of course, my friends in the progressive backwater of East Dulwich were delighted when Louise Michel, the French Revolutionary Socialist and Communard, was honored with a plaque, and those of us who are interested in printing and publishing were quite thrilled when a plaque appeared at 9 Great Coram Street, home in the 1860s to Victoria Printers, which Emily Faithfull set up in order to train women as printers and where she published Britain's first feminist periodical.

The list could go on and on, and it did. You would have thought the authorities would be pleased. New tourists flocked to obscure neighborhoods, guidebooks to the new sites proliferated, tours were organized; handwritten notes appeared on walls suggesting plaques; letters to the editor demanded to know why certain women hadn't been honored. Other letters criticized the manner in which only bourgeois individuals were elevated and suggested monuments to large historical events, such as Epping Forest, where Boudicca, the leader of the Celts, fought her last battle with the Romans in A.D. 62, or the Parliament Street Post Office, where Emily Wilding Davison set fire to a letter box in 1911, the first suffragist attempt at arson to draw attention to the struggle for women's rights. One enterprising and radical artist even sent the newspapers a sketch for a "Monument of Glass" to be placed on a busy shopping street in Knightsbridge, to commemorate the day of March 4, 1912, when a hundred suffragists walked down the street, smashing every plate glass window they passed.

The Tory and gutter papers were naturally appalled by such ideas and called for Thatcher (whom no one had thought to plaquate) to put a stop to the desecration of London buildings and streets. Vigilant foot patrols were called for and severe penalties for vandalization were demanded.

This then was the atmosphere in which the news suddenly surfaced that the grave of a famous woman poet had been opened and her bones had gone missing.

As it happened, the small village in Dorset where the poet had been buried was also the home of a friend of mine, Andrea Addlepoot, once a writer of very successful feminist mysteries, back when feminist mysteries had been popular, and now an obsessive gardener and letter writer. It was she who first described the theft to me in detail, the theft that the London papers had hysterically headlined: POET'S GRAVE VANDALIZED.

My dear Cassandra,

By now you have no doubt heard that Francine Crofts "Putter" is no longer resting eternally in the small churchyard opposite my humble country cottage. My first thought, heretically, was that I would not miss her —meaning that I would not miss the hordes of visitors, primarily women, primarily Young American Women, who had made the pilgrimage to her grave since her death. I would not miss how they trampled over my tender flowers, nor pelted me with questions. As if I had known the woman. As if anyone in the village had known the woman.

And yet it is still quite shocking, and everyone here is in an uproar over it.

You of course realize that the theft is not an isolated action but only the latest in a series of "terrorist acts" (I quote Peter Putter, the late poet's husband) perpetrated on the grave, and most likely not totally unrelated to the unchecked rememorializing of London and surrounding areas. (Discreet plaquing is one thing, but I really could not condone the defacing of Jane Austen's grave in Winchester Cathedral. Surely "In Memory of Jane Austen, youngest daughter of the late Reverend George Austen, formerly Rector of Steventon," says everything necessary. There was no reason on earth to stencil onto the stone the words "Author of *Pride and Prejudice* and other novels.")

These "terrorist acts" consisted of the last name, "Putter," in raised lead lettering, being three times chipped off from the headstone. The headstone was repaired twice but the third time Mr. Putter removed the headstone indefinitely from the grave site. That was over a year ago and it has not been reerected, which, despite what you might think, has not made my life any easier. I cannot count the number of times that sincere young women have approached me as I stood pruning my roses and beseeched me, most often in flat American accents, to show them the unmarked grave of Francine Crofts.

Never Francine Putter or Francine Crofts Putter.

For Francine Crofts *was* her name, you know, even if at one time she had been rather pathetically eager to be married to the upcoming young writer Peter Putter and had put aside her own poetry to type his manuscripts. Francine Crofts is the name the world knows her by. And, of course, that's what Putter cannot stand.

I know him, you must realize. Although his boyhood was long, long over by the time I moved here (after the enormous financial success, you recall, of *Murder at Greenham Common*), his parents Margery and Andrew and sister Jane Fitzwater—the widow who runs the local tearoom, and who has a penchant for telling anyone who will listen what a shrew Francine was and what a saint dear Peter—still live in the large house down the road that Peter bought for them. This little village represents roots for Peter, and sometimes you'll see him with one or another young girlfriend down at the pub getting pissed. When he's really in his cups he'll sometimes go all weepy, telling everyone what a raw deal he's getting from the world about Francine. It wasn't his fault she died. He really did love her. She wasn't planning to get a divorce. They were soul mates.

It's enough to make you vomit. Everybody knows what a cad he was, how it was his desertion of her that inspired Francine's greatest poetry and the realization that he wasn't coming back that led to her death. It's hard to see now what she saw in Putter, but, after all, he was younger then, and so was she. So were we all.

But Cassandra, I'm rambling. You know all this, I'm sure, and I'm equally sure you take as large an interest in the disappearance of Francine's bones as I do. Why not think about paying me a visit for a few days? Bring your translating work, I'll cook you marvelous meals, and together we'll see—for old times' sake—whether we can get to the bottom of this.

When I arrived at Andrea's cottage by car the next day, she was out in her front garden chatting with journalists. As usual she was wearing jeans and tall boots and a safari hat. In spite of her disdain for Americans, she was secretly flattered when anyone mentioned that she, rangy and weathered, looked a bit like the Marlboro man. At the moment she was busy giving quotes to the journos in her usual deep, measured tones:

"Peter Putter is an insecure, insignificant man and writer who has never produced anything of literary value himself, and could not stand the idea that his wife was a genius. He drove her to . . . Oh, hello, Cassandra." She broke off and took my bag, waving good-bye to the newspaper hacks. "And don't forget it's AddlePOOT—not PATE, author of numerous thrillers. . . . Come in, come in." She opened the low front door and stooped to show me in. "Oh, the media rats. We love to hate them."

I suspected that Andrea loved them more than she hated them. It was only since her career had slipped that she'd begun to speak of them in disparaging terms. During the years that the feminist thriller had been in fashion, Andrea's name had shone brighter than anyone's. "If Jane Austen were alive today and writing detective stories, she would be named Andrea Addlepoot," gushed one reviewer. All of her early books—*Murder at Greenham Common, Murder at the Small Feminist Press, Murder at the Anti-Apartheid Demonstration*—had topped the *City Limits* Alternative Best Seller lists, and she was regularly interviewed on television and in print about the exciting new phenomenon of the feminist detective.

Alas, any new phenomenon is likely to be an old phenomenon soon and thus no phenomenon at all. It never occurred to Andrea that the feminist detective was a bit of a fad and that, like all fads in a consumer culture, its shelf life was limited. Oh, Andrea and her detective, London PI Philippa Fanthorpe, had tried. They had taken on new social topics—the animal rights movement, the leaky nuclear plants on the Irish Sea—but the reviews were no longer so positive. Too "rhetorical," too "issue-oriented," too "strident," the critics wrote wearily, and Andrea Addlepoot's fortunes declined. In the bookstores feminist mysteries were replaced with the latest best-selling genre: women's erotica.

And Andrea, who had never written a sex scene in her life, retired for good to Dorset.

"Cassandra, it's shocking how this is being reported," she announced as we sat down in the tiny parlor. She took off her safari hat and her gray curls bristled. "Peter Putter is here giving interviews to the BBC news every few hours. And now the Americans have gotten in on it. Cable News Network is here and I've heard Diane Sawyer is arriving tomorrow."

"Well, Francine Crofts was born in America," I said. "And that's where a lot of her papers are, aren't they?"

"Yes, everything that Putter couldn't get his hands on is there."

"I read somewhere that he destroyed her last journal and the manuscript of a novel she was working on."

"Oh, yes, it's true. He couldn't stand the idea of anything bad about himself coming to the public's attention."

"Any chance he could have removed the bones himself?" I asked.

Andrea nodded. "Oh, I would say there's a very good chance indeed. All this rowing over her headstone has not been good publicity for our Peter Putter. It puts him in a bad light, it keeps bringing back the old allegations that he was responsible in great measure for Francine's death. It's quite possible, I think, that he began to read about the appearance of all these new blue plaques and thought to himself, 'Right. I'll get rid of the grave entirely, blame it on the radical feminists and there'll be an end to it.' I'm sure he's sorry he ever thought to bury the body here in the first place and to put 'Putter' at the end of her name. But he can't back down now, so the only solution was to arrange for the bones to disappear."

"I don't suppose we could go over to the graveyard and have a look?"

Andrea peered out her small-paned front window. "We'll go when it's quieter. Let's have our tea first."

We had our tea, lavish with Devonshire cream and fresh scones, and then Andrea went off for a brief lie-down, and I, left to my own resources in the parlor, went to the bookcase and found the volume of Crofts's most celebrated poems.

They struck me with the same power now as they had when I read them twenty years ago, especially the poems written at the very end, when, translucent from rage and hunger, Francine had struck out repeatedly at the ties that bound her to this earth and that man. Even as she was starving herself to death in the most barbaric and self-punishing way, she still could write like an avenging angel.

Around five, when the autumn mists had drifted down over the small village in the valley, Andrea roused herself and we walked across the road to the tiny churchyard of St. Stephen's. The small church was from the thirteenth century and no longer in use; its front door was chained and padlocked. The churchyard was desolate as well, under the purple twilight sky, and covered with leaves that were damp with rain. It was enclosed on all sides by a low stone wall and shielded by enormous oaks. We went in through the creaking gate. The ground was trampled with footprints, and many of the graves were untended.

I could barely see my feet in front of me through the cold, wet mist, but Andrea led the way unerringly to a roped-off hole. There had been no effort to cover the grave back over, and the dirt was heaped hastily by the side.

It had the effect of eerie loneliness and ruthless desecration, and even Andrea, creator of the cold-blooded Philippa Fanthorpe, seemed disturbed.

"You can see they didn't have much time," she murmured.

Suddenly we heard a noise. It was the gate creaking. Without a word Andrea pulled me away from the grave and around the side of the church. Someone was approaching the site of the theft, a woman with a scarf, heavy coat, and Wellington boots. She stood silently by the open grave a moment. And then we heard her begin to cry.

Ten minutes later we were warming ourselves in the local pub, The King's Head. A few journos were there, soaking up the local color, the color in this case being the golden yellow of lager. Andrea bought me a half of bitter and a pint of Old Peculiar for herself, and we seated ourselves in a corner by the fireplace. The woman in the churchyard had left as quickly as she had come. We were debating who she could be when the door to the pub opened and a paunchy man in his fifties came in, wearing a tweed jacket and carrying a walking stick.

"That's how he dresses in the country," Andrea muttered. "Sodding old fart."

It was Putter, I assumed, and I had to admit that there was a certain cragginess to his face that must have once been appealing. If I had been a young American working at a publishing house as a secretary in the early sixties, perhaps I, too, would have been flattered if Chatup and Windows's rising male author had shown an interest in *me* and asked *me* if I'd like to do a spot of typing for him. Putter's first novel, *The Man in the Looking Glass*, had been published to enormous acclaim, and he was working on his second. An authentic working-class writer (his father was actually a bank clerk, but he kept that quiet)—who would have guessed that this voice of the masses would eventually degenerate into a very minor novelist known mostly for his acerbic reviews of other people's work in the *Sunday Telegraph*? Poor Francine. When she was deserted by her young husband, with just one book of poetry published to very little acclaim at all, she had no idea that within two years their roles would have completely reversed. Peter Putter would in the years to come be most famous for having been Francine Crofts's husband.

"I wish it were possible to have a certain sympathy for him," Andrea said gruffly, downing the last of her Old Peculiar. "After all, we both know what it is to experience the fickleness of public attention."

I went up to the bar to order us another round and heard Putter explaining loudly to the journos, "It's an outrage. Her married name was Francine Putter and that's how I planned to have the stone engraved in the first place. I only added Crofts because I knew what she had brought off in that name, and I wished in some small way to honor it. But the radical feminists aren't satisfied. Oh, no. It didn't satisfy them to vandalize the headstone over and over; they had to actually violate a sanctified grave and steal Francine's remains. No regard for me or her family, no regard for the church, no regard for her memory. God only knows what they plan to use her bones for. One shudders to think. Goddess rituals or some sort of black magic."

"You're suggesting a Satanic cult got hold of Francine?" a journo asked, and I could see the story in the *Daily Mail* already.

"Wouldn't surprise me in the least," Putter said, and he bought a round for all the newspapermen.

I returned to Andrea. "If you were a radical feminist and/or Satanic cultist, how would you have stolen the bones?"

She glowered at Putter. "It was probably dead easy. Drive over from London in a minivan, or even a car with a large boot. Maybe two of you. In the hours before dawn. One keeps watch and the other digs. The wooden casket has disintegrated in twenty years. You carefully lay the bones in a sheet—so they don't rattle around too much—wrap the whole thing up in a plastic bag, and Bob's your uncle!"

I shuddered. Blue plaques were one thing, but grave robbery and bone-snatching, even in the cause of justified historical revisionism, were quite another.

"Why not just another gravestone, this time with the words Francine Crofts?"

"Do you really think Putter"—Andrea shot him a vicious look—"would allow such a stone to stand? No, I'm sure whoever did it plans to rebury her."

"What makes you think that?" I asked. "Maybe they'll just chip off pieces of bone and sell them at American women's studies conferences."

"Don't be medieval," Andrea said absently. "No, I think it's likely they might choose a site on the farm not far from here where Francine and Peter lived during the early days of their marriage. The poems from that period are the lyrical ones, the happy ones. A simple monument on the top of a hill: Francine Crofts, Poet." Andrea looked up from her Old Peculiar and turned to me in excitement. "That's it. We'll stake the farm out, we'll be the first to discover the monument. Maybe we'll catch them in the act of putting it up."

"What good would that do?"

"Don't be daft," she admonished me. "It's publicity, isn't it?"

Andrea wanted to rush right over to the farm, but when we came outside the pub the fog was so thick and close that we decided to settle in for the night instead. I went up to the guest room under the eaves with a hot-water bottle and Crofts's *Collected Poems*. I'd forgotten she had been happy until Andrea reminded me. Her memory was so profoundly imbued with her manner of dying and with her violent despair that it was hard to think of her as celebrating life and love. But here were poems about marriage, about the farm, about animals and flowers. It made one pause: if she had married a faithful and loving man, perhaps her poetry would have stayed cheerful and light. Perhaps Putter did make her what she was, a poet of genius; perhaps it was right that he still claimed her by name. But no— here were the last poems in that first collection, the ones that had been called prefeminist, protofeminist and even Ur-feminist. Some critics now argued that if only Francine had lived to see the women's movement, her anger would have had a context; she wouldn't have turned her fury at being abandoned against herself and seen herself a failure. But other critics argued that it was clear from certain poems, even early ones, that Francine understood her predicament quite well and was constantly searching for ways out. And they quoted the poem about Mary Anning, the early nineteenth-century fossil collector who was the first to discover the remains of an ichthyosaurus in Lyme Regis, not far from here, in 1811. It was called "Freeing the Bones."

The next morning Andrea and I drove over to the farm and skirted the hedges around it looking for a spot that the unknown gravediggers might decide was suitable for a memorial of some sort.

"This is such a long shot," I said. "I think it's quite possible that some Americans were involved, and that they've taken the remains back to America. Wasn't she from Iowa? They'll bury them in Cedar Rapids."

"Francine would hate that if she knew," said Andrea. "She was such an anglophile she couldn't wait to get out of Cedar Rapids. It was the pinnacle of happiness for her to study at Oxford and then to get a job afterward. No one, not even her family, tried to make a case for sending her bones back to Iowa."

The farm was owned by an absentee landlord; it was solitary and lovely on this mid-autumn day. We broke through a weak hedge and tramped the land, settling on one or two likely little rises where the monument might go. Francine's spirit seemed all about us that afternoon, or perhaps it was just because I'd been reading her poetry. It would be nice if she were reburied out here in the open, rather than in that dank little closed-in churchyard. I imagined picnics and poetry readings under the oak trees. With bowls of food left on the grave to feed her starved soul.

Late in the afternoon we returned to the village and decided to have tea in Francine's sister-in-law's tea shop. It had occurred to me that perhaps it had been Jane Fitzwater crying at Francine's grave last night.

The Cozy Cup Tea Shop was packed with journalists, however, and one look at Jane was enough to convince me that it had not been she in the dowdy coat and Wellingtons. Jane, a bit younger than her brother, was less craggy but still imposing, with bleached blond hair and a strong jaw that gave her the look of a female impersonator. Her dress was royal blue and so was her eye shadow, coordinated, no doubt, for the cameras.

She barely gave Andrea and me a second glance when we entered, but consigned us to an out-of-the-way table and a waitress who looked to be only about twelve and who brought us very weak tea, stale scones, and whipped cream instead of clotted cream.

"*Whipped* cream?" said Andrea severely to the little waitress, who hunched her shoulders and scurried away.

Jane Fitzwater had seated herself at a table of journalists and was holding forth in quite loud tones on the absolutely undeserved amount of publicity that Francine had gotten through her death. "I say, if you're unhappy, take a course in weaving or a holiday abroad. Don't stew in your own self-pity. And I tried to tell Francine that. All marriages go through difficult times, but Peter would have come back to her eventually. Men will be men. Instead she had to hide away in that little flat of hers and stop eating. Oh, I tried to talk to her, I even brought her a casserole one day—I could see she'd gotten thinner—but it never occurred to me, I'm sure it never occurred to Peter, that she was deliberately trying to starve herself to death. And then he gets all the blame. It's made a broken man of him, you know. Never recovered from the shock of it, he hasn't. Ruined his career, his life. She should have thought of that when she did it, but no, always thinking of herself, that's how she was right from the beginning, my mum and dad noticed it right off. 'Seems a little full of herself,' my dad said the first time Peter brought her to Dorset. 'Talks too much.' My mum felt sorry for her, of course. Francine didn't have a clue about life, really, her head was in the clouds. 'It will end in tears,' my mum said. And she was right."

"I've got to get out of here," Andrea muttered to me. "Or it will end in something redder than tears."

We left the tea shop and strolled through the village, which was scattered with posh cars and vans emblazoned with the logos of television stations, native and foreign. Peter Putter was over in the churchyard giving an interview to what appeared to be a German film crew.

"It's enough to make one lose one's appetite entirely," Andrea said and slammed the door to her little cottage.

That night I was awakened from a deep sleep by the sound of a car driving down the road to the village. Normally it would not have been anything to wake up to, but I had a sudden odd feeling that it was my car. I staggered over to the little garret window, but saw nothing. I crept down the steep stairs and peeked into Andrea's room.

She was not there.

I went out the back door and saw that my little Ford was gone.

Since Andrea didn't have a car, I supposed she'd taken mine. Perhaps she'd decided to visit the farm by herself to stake out the gravediggers; perhaps she'd heard someone else's car driving down the road and decided to follow it. Whatever my suppositions, my actions were limited. The farm was a good four miles away, it was raining, and—I finally looked at the clock—four in the morning. I got dressed just to keep warm and paced around a bit, then remembered that Andrea had a bicycle out in the shed behind the cottage. With the feeling that there was nothing else to do, I steeled myself for cold and rain and set off into the dark night.

With water streaming down my face, I pedaled furiously, wondering why roads that always seemed to be perfectly flat when you drove over them by car suddenly developed hills and valleys when you were traveling by bicycle. Still the cold rain gave me an incentive for speed, and I arrived at the farm in record time. There were no cars at the side road leading to the farmhouse, so I got off the bike and began to reconnoiter on foot around the hedges. There must be another road leading to the farm, but I would waste more time looking for it than going on foot.

By this time my clothes were soaked and my boots caked with mud. I tried to retrace the steps Andrea and I had taken the day before, but in the darkness it was hard to see the difference between land and sky, much less between a rise and a fall in the earth. Then, through the hedges, I saw a small light. I broke through and started staggering over the land toward it. It was joined by another small light.

The lights seemed to be dancing together, or were they struggling? One of the lights vanished. I began to hear voices. Had Andrea discovered the perpetrators; was she fighting with them?

But then I heard a voice I thought I recognized. "Put those bones down! I'll have you in court for this. Grave robbing is a criminal offense as well as a sin!"

"What you did to Francine is a sin and a crime," another even more familiar voice shot back. "Give me back my shovel. She deserves to have a better resting place than the one you gave her."

"I was her husband, I have a right to decide where she's buried."

"You gave up your rights long ago."

Then there was only the sound of grunts as they grappled again.

"Peter," I said. "Andrea. Stop this. Stop this right now."

I picked up one of the flashlights and shone it at each of their faces in turn. "What's going on here?"

"I suspected her from the beginning," said Peter, looking like a large wet muskrat in his brown oilskin jacket. "I've been keeping an eye on her. Lives right across from the churchyard; easy enough to break into the grave. Tonight I heard the car starting up and decided to follow her. Called the journalists first, they'll be here in a minute. You'll go to jail for this, Addlepoot!"

"Oh, Cassandra," groaned Andrea. "I'm sorry. I had it planned so differently."

But she didn't have time to exonerate herself. The journalists were suddenly on us like a pack of hounds; there were bright lights everywhere, illuminating a stone marker that said, FRANCINE CROFTS, POET, and a muddy sheet piled, haphazardly, with thin white bones.

Some weeks after this, when I was back in London, Andrea came up to see me. If it hadn't been for the surprising intercession of Mrs. Putter, Peter's mother (for she had been the woman we'd seen crying at the grave), Andrea would have been on trial now. As it was, Francine's bones were back in the churchyard of St. Stephen's and Andrea had closed up her cottage and was thinking of moving back to London.

"I didn't have completely ignoble motives," she said. "I always did believe that Francine deserved better than a Putterized headstone or no headstone in a grim little grave under the eye of people who had hated her. But I have to admit that I saw an opportunity. When the blue plaques started to appear I thought, why not? Someone's bound to do it, why not me? I wouldn't say I was the one who'd done it, of course. I'd steal the bones, rebury them, erect a marker and then—with you as a witness—I'd discover the new site, and let the media know. It would have been the best kind of publicity, for me *and* for Francine. I would have solved a mystery, my name would be back in the news, my publisher might have decided to reissue my books . . . but instead . . ."

"Instead the newspapers called you a grave robber and filled the pages of the tabloids with photos that made you look like a refugee from *Nightmare on Elm Street*. And they spelled your name wrong."

Andrea shuddered. "I'm going to have to put all this behind me. Start over. Science fiction, perhaps. Or why not feminist horror? Skeletons that walk in the night, the ghosts of Mary Wollstonecraft and Emily Brontë that haunt us still today . . ."

"I did read in the newspaper today," I interrupted, "that the owner of the farm has decided to put up a marker to Francine himself, and to open the farm up to readings and poetry workshops. Apparently he's something of an artist himself, in addition to being a stockbroker. He said he never knew that Francine had lived there. So something good came of it."

Andrea cheered up. "And Putter didn't look so terribly fabulous in those photographs either."

We started to laugh, embarrassed at first, and then with gasping and teary amusement, recalling our wet night in the mud.

And then we went out for a walk to look at some of the blue plaques that had gone up recently. For, you see, the remembering and honoring hadn't stopped. There were now more blue plaques to women than ever.

MEOW

Emily Winslow

Emily Winslow trained as an actor at Carnegie Mellon University and holds a master's degree from Seton Hill University. She is the author of psychological thrillers including *The Red House*, *The Whole World*, and *The Start of Everything*, set in Cambridge, U.K., where she now lives.

"I can't find Bibi." Darren's pyjamas were mismatched: dinosaur bottoms and Minecraft on top, so he didn't have to pick a favourite. His arms hung at his sides, but I could tell from the way his right hand was in a loose fist with the thumb straight out that it had recently been in his mouth. He's seven and shouldn't be doing that anymore.

I plonked the spatula I was icing with into the sink, knelt down, and put my hands on his shoulders. "Bibi died two summers ago. She was a good cat, but she got old, and she's not here anymore, okay, honey?" She died six months before the Bad Things started happening. Telling Darren that she had gone to cat heaven had been, at the time, the hardest thing I'd had to do as a parent.

"I know she's dead!" He flung his arms open wide. "She was MY cat. I know she died. I mean ghost Bibi. She used to come play with me . . ."

That had been his coping mechanism. I'd thought he'd dropped it, but apparently not. I didn't want to encourage belief in the supernatural, but he needed the comfort; so I smiled and lied. "Now that we're settled in this new house, she doesn't need to come see us anymore. She visited us when she was worried about how we were coping. Now she knows we're all right."

I wondered if that was a lie too. Was it fair to say that we were "all right" when I knew how everything was going to change once school finished for the year? But we were safe *right now*. We were together *right now*. That had to count for something.

He clambered up onto one of the stools at the kitchen island that was also our dining table. "Can I lick it?" he asked, reaching for the mixing bowl.

"No chocolate at bedtime. You won't sleep."

"I can't sleep without Bibi anyway."

I pulled the bowl away. I knew I should get him a new cat; I wanted to. But we were renting now, the top floor apartment of a shared house. No pets allowed. "Maybe if you think hard about her while you're nodding off, you'll dream about her." I had tried that many times, trying to force happy thoughts to life in the night. I know it doesn't work, but the attempt can at least trick one into dreamless sleep, and a well-rested morning.

"In the old house, ghost Bibi used to come to my window."

I was used to this. Darren had always liked to tell me that she was behind the curtain, or under the table, or had just swished her tail past his leg. The window was a new one, though.

"I didn't like it when she did that," he said. "I told her to go away."

My head snapped up. "What do you mean?"

"I didn't like when she was at the window. She patted it. Like knocking." He made little motions, as if his hands were paws.

I forced myself to breathe through my nose instead of panting. "You saw her? You saw that it was a cat? You're sure?"

Big eyes. Quivering lip. "Of course it was a cat, Mum. What else would be on the windowsill?"

I rubbed my eyes, got frosting on my cheek. "Of course, baby. Of course. I just meant that maybe it was a squirrel. Or a bird."

"It was dark out, and the curtain was in the way, but it meowed at me. I meowed back." He gasped. "What if it was a different ghost cat pretending to be Bibi? Because it knew that I missed her and it was trying to trick me?"

"It was probably a real cat, sweetie, not any ghost one. Maybe a real cat wanted to make friends." His bedroom in the old house had been on the ground floor. I never should have allowed that, even though he loved it. I should have insisted he take the one upstairs.

"She didn't sound happy. She sounded like she wanted to come in."

I let myself exhale loudly, the level of exasperation before raising my voice. "It was probably a neighbour cat just trying to say hello. Ghost Bibi has gone on to kitty heaven and doesn't visit us anymore. She's doing lucky cat things, eating tuna and chasing butterflies." I didn't want to field questions about whether the butterflies are also dead and how big is heaven if it can hold all of the dead butterflies; wouldn't there be too many? That's the sort of thing Darren liked to ask. So I went on, "You can ask her if she can visit in your dreams, but she's right to not come to the window anymore, all right? Tell her that."

"What if she doesn't visit us here because she doesn't know the address? What if she's still looking for us there?"

My loud, high-pitched voice asserted itself without me intending it to. The coil of pained emotion inside me, its springing out of my control, was exactly the reason things were going to have to change. "I should think that the burnt-out shell of a house would be a clue that we've left!" My hands were shaking. I pressed them down on the counter to steady myself.

Darren became quickly hysterical. "Maybe she thinks we died in the fire! Maybe she's wondering why we're not in heaven with her! What if she thinks we're ghosts too, and she's looking for us? What if she thinks we don't want to see her?" He pitched himself at me in a fierce hug.

"We're fine; we're fine; we're fine," I reminded him, squeezing him in return. He had been away at his dad's house the night of the fire. I'd made it out uninjured.

I walked him back to his small room and tucked him in up to his chin. I reminded him not to suck his thumb, and I hated the guilty expression that overwhelmed his small face. How could I shame him for that little comfort? I decided to never bring it up again. *To hell with it*, I thought. *I'll just pay for braces later.*

"Can we say a prayer for Bibi?" Darren asked. Usually he delayed by asking for a drink or another hug. Prayer was new.

"Sure, baby." We held hands.

Darren whispered earnestly, "Dear God, please tell Bibi that we're fine. Tell her that we miss her."

He kept his eyes tightly shut. I realised he was waiting for me. So I added, "We're glad that Bibi is happy where she is. Please pet her for us. Amen."

"Amen!" Darren agreed.

I turned off his lamp and closed his door behind me. I heard a television downstairs, and a toilet flush. Sharing a house reminded me of when I was a small child and had my turn bringing the class guinea pig home for the weekend. His sniffles and snorts from the corner of my bedroom had comforted me, because they had an obvious and benign source. What I usually heard at night was the distant, subtle creaks and groans of "the house settling" (as my parents explained), which could have been made by ghosts or robbers or whatever scariness had been in the last thing I watched on TV. It was nice to hear sounds that had clear and safe explanations.

The other, less explicable sounds are always there too, of course, in the background, but when they're overshadowed I don't have to notice them.

I returned to my kitchen to put the cupcakes away and tidy up. But without Bibi, I didn't have to worry that they would get licked or knocked onto the floor, so I wasn't in a hurry. First I poured a glass of wine and sat in the window seat that acted as a living room.

It had taken me weeks to feel comfortable there, even with its comfy cushion and cheery throw pillows. In the old house, I had trained myself to avoid windows. I'd had no way of knowing when he was out there. Even now, I don't know how often he was. I only know of the times he left me phone messages, describing what he'd seen me doing or wearing earlier that day, while on my way to work or in a coffee shop. Sometimes he mentioned things that he would have seen through the windows of the house, asking questions about a book I'd been reading or a TV show I'd watched.

The police had been sympathetic but ultimately unhelpful. His phone calls were harassing, but without an identity there wasn't much they could do. I kept curtains closed and locked all the doors and windows at all times. My ex, Jason, who at first only knew that I was being "security-conscious" rather than stalked, had warned me that it was a fire hazard because even the front door lock used a key on both sides, not a bolt we could turn with just our hands; how would Darren and I escape quickly in case of emergency?

That's also what had started the idea forming in the back of my mind.

I didn't have a boyfriend to ostentatiously spend the night (and wouldn't have felt right having a date in my bedroom with Darren just downstairs anyway), so I told Jason what was going on and asked him to act like we were reconciling, just for show. Just stay with us for a while, I asked, so whoever had his eyes on me would think there was a strong man on my side and back off.

It's not fair that he accused me that the whole story was a ploy to arouse his protective instincts and get him back with me. I insisted it was real. I played him the phone messages I had saved for the police, which only made things worse.

He gave me an ultimatum: if this was really happening, he would keep Darren for his own safety, fight for primary custody if he had to. On that note, he took Darren away for his every-other-weekend.

So I'd had two days.

What I needed to do had become obvious. I went to the grocery store and bought supplies for a solo weekend in: meals for one, DVDs, ice cream, wine. At home, I changed into workout clothes for lounging around the house. My curtains were drawn, as usual, but there were gaps that couldn't be fully covered, like the kitchen patio door. I used that view to establish myself as settled in, home alone. I lit candles and painted my toenails, girl's night in.

I used that door when I went to take the garbage out. When I came back in, I didn't lock it. I made sure to look suddenly distracted, dashing to the oven to get the once-frozen-now-burning pizza out, its charred smell mixing with the citrusy scent of cosy aromatherapy oil in the living room.

I shook my head, and left the pizza to cool on the counter for throwing away later. I gave up on dinner and went upstairs, turning off lights as I went. Then I crept back down in the dark.

Half an hour later, he entered through the unlocked patio door, as I had suspected he would. He came through the kitchen, where I was crouched in the dark beside the refrigerator, blocked from his view. Through the living room, past the locked front door, up the stairs. His footsteps creaked on the hall floor above me, heading for my bedroom.

I locked the patio door.

Quietly, quietly, I glided towards the front of the house.

I knew the front door would creak when I opened it. I would have only seconds before he realised, seconds before he would turn, seconds before he would charge down the stairs, pitching towards me, falling against the door I hoped to slam before he got there. I had the key ready in my hand. I'd have to get it locked from outside before he turned the knob.

Until I opened that door, though, or until he pushed into my room and pulled the covers off the empty bed, I had a minute or two more.

I picked up the scented oil diffuser from the slim table behind the couch, and tossed its contents in a silent splash across the cheap rug under my feet. I placed the diffuser on its side at the start of the spill with a cascade of magazines alongside, and laid the slim table as if fallen.

I placed one of the tall candles I had left burning to balance precariously on the edge of one of the thicker magazines.

Upstairs, the creak of my bedroom door.

I dashed out the front door, the slam of it behind me shaking the doorframe, shaking, perhaps, the candlestick balanced on the magazine edge. Pounding footsteps on the stairs followed, and the grinding of my key turning the lock.

I testified at the inquest that the man must have entered while I was binning the rubbish and then hidden upstairs; that I had of course locked the patio door behind me upon re-entry; that I had fallen asleep on the couch with candles still burning and hadn't even realised I'd knocked the table while running out in a panic when I heard him at the top of the stairs. Of course I'd locked the front door as he slammed into it; of course I'd had to keep him from chasing me; I'd had no idea of a fire catching inside the entirely locked house until the blaze had become visible from the neighbour's house where I'd sought refuge.

This had been believed.

Guilt is unexpectedly pervasive. I had expected to feel it at intervals, when turning a key in a lock, or when any hurried footsteps creaked stairs behind me. But the feeling was less occasionally sharp and more constantly dull. I was left behind, always half in that moment before I splashed out the diffuser. I could have just run for the door without rigging the spill, could have trapped him inside a house without a fire, called the police and trusted the system.

But I didn't trust the system. There had been too many times a man on bail, a man on trial, had managed to complete his evil intentions. I believed in my mind that I had done what I had to do, but in my heart I feared I had become the bad one, one of the bad ones.

I looked up the effects of death by burning while Darren was at school. I didn't eat for two days after that.

"Mum!" Darren's wail broke into my thoughts. A nightmare. Again. *My fault*, I reminded myself. It was my horror, my guilt, that poisoned the air around me. Cupcakes and attention couldn't make up for the overwhelming emotions I was making him breathe in every day.

I dashed to his room, and crouched by his bedside. "Shhhh, sweetie . . ." I murmured.

He was incoherent. He was never able to tell me what was in his nightmares, just that they were "bad." I stroked his hair, and propped up his various soft toys that had fallen around him. I had to not cry; I froze my face in a smile and picked up the grey velvet kitty. I bounced it on his tummy. He laughed.

"Meow, meow," he said, pronouncing it "mee-ow."

I made cat noises in return.

"No, Mummy. He says mee-ow."

I smiled indulgently. "Cats go *rowr*."

"The ghost cat at the window said 'meow.'"

Cold grew over me, like frost spreading over a window. "What do you mean?" I asked. "It *said* meow?"

"It said 'mee-ow.' Then it giggled. That's why I thought it might be a different ghost cat at the window. Back at our old house."

I couldn't answer. I brought him a cup of water, even though he hadn't asked for one. I said motherly things. I let him keep his light on. I persuaded him that I was leaving the room for his sake, so I wouldn't distract him from sleep. I closed the door. I leaned against it.

After we'd moved in here, and everything was unpacked and settled, we'd been supposed to be happy. We were safe. But Darren had started sucking his thumb, which he hadn't done in years. He'd wet his bed twice this past month. The nightmares started.

Jason had been embarrassed at how he'd belittled my fears, and made no more references to the threat of pursuing a more aggressive custody arrangement. But I knew he would step up if it came to that. That had freed me to consider what I knew was right.

I had decided to wait for the school year to finish next month before I confessed, so the impact on Darren would be lessened. He'd move in with Jason, and change schools in September. I'd go to prison, as I deserved. I had hoped there would be absolution in that penance. I had hoped that Darren, without my secret guilt filling his house, would become playful again.

I stoppered the wine bottle and put the cupcakes away. I washed the dishes. This tidiness was a recent habit; it was important to keep things orderly, easy for Jason to deal with after I was gone.

From the apartment downstairs, those familiar, comforting noises of ordinary life: a short blast from a sink tap, probably someone wetting a toothbrush; a blurry-sounding conversation. I no longer had to wonder if what I was hearing was an approaching footstep on the path outside, or a hand testing a knob.

Or tapping on a window.

I would describe guilt as dry sand always under my feet, slowing me down as I tried to move forward. Now indignation washed like a wave over it, hardening it into solid ground.

When my stalker had been after me alone, killing him in my trap came to feel like a luxury, a self-indulgence. But learning that he'd come to Darren's window, repeatedly, changed everything.

Tears are ridiculous. They can mean unbearable sadness, or relief, or joy. These tears meant all three at once.

I was glad I had waited to unburden my shame. I would not tell the police, I decided. I would keep my son. I would keep my life.

I lifted the fruit bowl to retrieve the envelope I'd tucked away underneath. It was from the insurance company and contained the settlement cheque for the house. I hadn't bothered to deposit it, because I knew it would be taken back after I was convicted. An accident was covered, but arson could not be rewarded. Ignoring that money and living within the means of my job and Jason's child support had been part of keeping things tidy for Darren and Jason in my wake.

I decided to bring the cheque to the bank tomorrow after all.

Time for bed, and for trying to trick myself into dreaming about summer trips with Darren to museums and beaches, about a new year in Darren's school here, about the future I'd protected; but first, one last sip from my glass.

With the insurance settlement, we'll be able to buy a house of our own again, I marvelled.

And we'll get a cat.

GOING THROUGH THE TUNNEL

Mrs Henry Wood

Mrs Henry Wood (1814–1887), or Ellen Wood, was one of the foremost British writers of the nineteenth century. A master of crime, suspense, and the gothic, Wood was one of the first international bestsellers. For several years she owned and edited the magazine *Argosy*.

We had to make a rush for it. And making a rush did not suit the Squire, any more than it does other people who have come to an age when the body's heavy and the breath nowhere. He reached the train, pushed head-foremost into a carriage, and then remembered the tickets. "Bless my heart?" he exclaimed, as he jumped out again, and nearly upset a lady who had a little dog in her arms, and a mass of fashionable hair on her head, that the Squire, in his hurry, mistook for tow.

"Plenty of time, sir," said a guard who was passing. "Three minutes to spare."

Instead of saying he was obliged to the man for his civility, or relieved to find the tickets might still be had, the Squire snatched out his old watch, and began abusing the railway clocks for being slow. Had Tod been there he would have told him to his face that the watch was fast, braving all retort, for the Squire believed in his watch as he did in himself, and would rather have been told that *he* could go wrong than that the watch could. But there was only me: and I wouldn't have said it for anything.

"Keep two back-seats there, Johnny," said the Squire.

I put my coat on the corner furthest from the door, and the rug on the one next to it, and followed him into the station. When the Squire was late in starting, he was apt to get into the greatest flurry conceivable; and the first thing I saw was himself blocking up the ticket-place, and undoing his pocket-book with nervous fingers. He had some loose gold about him, silver too, but the pocket-book came to his hand first, so he pulled it out. These flurried moments of the Squire's amused Tod beyond everything; he was so cool himself.

"Can you change this?" said the Squire, drawing out one from a roll of five-pound notes.

"No, I can't," was the answer, in the surly tones put on by ticket-clerks.

How the Squire crumpled up the note again, and searched in his breeches pocket for gold, and came away with the two tickets and the change, I'm sure he never knew. A crowd had gathered round, wanting to take their tickets in turn, and knowing that he was keeping them flurried him all the more. He stood at

the back a moment, put the roll of notes into his case, fastened it and returned it
to the breast of his over-coat, sent the change down into another pocket without
counting it, and went out with the tickets in hand. Not to the carriage; but to
stare at the big clock in front.

"Don't you see, Johnny? exactly four minutes and a half difference," he cried,
holding out his watch to me. "It is a strange thing they can't keep these railway
clocks in order."

"My watch keeps good time, sir, and mine is with the railway. I think it is
right."

"Hold your tongue, Johnny. How dare you! Right? You send your watch to
be regulated the first opportunity, sir; don't *you* get into the habit of being too
late or too early."

When we finally went to the carriage there were some people in it, but our
seats were left for us. Squire Todhetley sat down by the further door, and settled
himself and his coats and his things comfortably, which he had been too flurried
to do before. Cool as a cucumber was he, now the bustle was over; cool as Tod
could have been. At the other door, with his face to the engine, sat a dark, gentleman-like man of forty, who had made room for us to pass as we got in. He had a
large signet-ring on one hand, and a lavender glove on the other. The other three
seats opposite to us were vacant. Next to me sat a little man with a fresh colour
and gold spectacles, who was already reading; and beyond him, in the corner,
face to face with the dark man, was a lunatic. That's to mention him politely. Of
all the restless, fidgety, worrying, hot-tempered passengers that ever put themselves into a carriage to travel with people in their senses, he was the worst. In
fifteen moments he had made as many darts; now after his hat-box and things
above his head; now calling the guard and the porters to ask senseless questions
about his luggage; now treading on our toes, and trying the corner seat opposite
the Squire, and then darting back to his own. He wore a wig of a decided green
tinge, the effect of keeping, perhaps, and his skin was dry and shrivelled as an
Egyptian mummy's.

A servant, in undress livery, came to the door, and touched his hat, which had
a cockade on it, as he spoke to the dark man.

"Your ticket, my lord."

Lords are not travelled with every day, and some of us looked up. The gentleman took the ticket from the man's hand and slipped it into his waistcoat pocket.

"You can get me a newspaper, Wilkins. The *Times*, if it is to be had."

"Yes, my lord."

"Yes, there's room here, ma'am," interrupted the guard, sending the door back
for a lady who stood at it. "Make haste, please."

The lady who stepped in was the same the Squire had bolted against. She sat
down in the seat opposite me, and looked at every one of us by turns. There was
a sort of violet bloom on her face and some soft white powder, seen plain enough
through her veil. She took the longest gaze at the dark gentleman, bending a little
forward to do it; for, as he was in a line with her, and also had his head turned
from her, her curiosity could only catch a view of his side-face. Mrs. Todhetley
might have said she had not put on her company manners. In the midst of this,
the man-servant came back again.

"The *Times* is not here yet, my lord. They are expecting the papers in by the next down-train."

"Never mind, then. You can get me one at the next station, Wilkins."

"Very well, my lord."

Wilkins must certainly have had to scramble for his carriage, for we started before he had well left the door. It was not an express-train, and we should have to stop at several stations. Where the Squire and I had been staying does not matter; it has nothing to do with what I have to tell. It was a long way from our own home, and that's saying enough.

"Would you mind changing seats with me, sir?"

I looked up, to find the lady's face close to mine; she had spoken in a half-whisper. The Squire, who carried his old-fashioned notions of politeness with him when he went travelling, at once got up to offer her the corner. But she declined it, saying she was subject to face-ache, and did not care to be next the window. So she took my seat, and I sat down on the one opposite Mr. Todhetley.

"Which of the peers is that?" I heard her ask him in a loud whisper, as the lord put his head out at his window.

"Don't know at all, ma'am," said the Squire. "Don't know many of the peers myself, except those of my own county: Lyttleton, and Beauchamp, and—"

Of all snarling barks, the worst was given that moment in the Squire's face, suddenly ending the list. The little dog, an ugly, hairy, vile-tempered Scotch terrier, had been kept concealed under the lady's jacket, and now struggled itself free. The Squire's look of consternation was good! He had not known any animal was there.

"Be quiet, Wasp. How dare you bark at the gentleman? He will not bite, sir: he—"

"Who has a dog in the carriage?" shrieked the lunatic, starting up in a passion. "Dogs don't travel with passengers. Here! Guard! Guard!"

To call out for the guard when a train is going at full speed is generally useless. The lunatic had to sit down again; and the lady defied him, so to say, coolly avowing that she had hidden the dog from the guard on purpose, staring him in the face while she said it.

After this there was a lull, and we went speeding along, the lady talking now and again to the Squire. She seemed to want to grow confidential with him; but the Squire did not seem to care for it, though he was quite civil. She held the dog huddled up in her lap, so that nothing but his head peeped out.

"Halloa! How dare they be so negligent? There's no lamp in this carriage."

It was the lunatic again, and we all looked at the lamp. It had no light in it; but that it *had* when we first reached the carriage was certain; for, as the Squire went stumbling in, his head nearly touched the lamp, and I had noticed the flame. It seems the Squire had also.

"They must have put it out while we were getting our tickets," he said.

"I'll know the reason why when we stop," cried the lunatic, fiercely. "After passing the next station, we dash into the long tunnel. The idea of going through it in pitch darkness! It would not be safe."

"Especially with a dog in the carriage," spoke the lord, in a chaffing kind of tone, but with a good-natured smile. "We will have the lamp lighted, however."

As if to reward him for interfering, the dog barked up loudly, and tried to make a spring at him; upon which the lady smothered the animal up, head and all.

Another minute or two, and the train began to slacken speed. It was only an insignificant station, one not likely to be halted at for above a minute. The lunatic twisted his body out of the window, and shouted for the guard long before we were at a standstill.

"Allow me to manage this," said the lord, quietly putting him down. "They know me on the line. Wilkins!"

The man came rushing up at the call. He must have been out already, though we were not quite at a standstill yet.

"Is it for the *Times*, my lord? I am going for it."

"Never mind the *Times*. This lamp is not lighted, Wilkins. See the guard, and *get it done*. At once."

"And ask him what the mischief he means by his carelessness," roared out the lunatic after Wilkins, who went flying off. "Sending us on our road without a light!—and that dangerous tunnel close at hand."

The authority laid upon the words "Get it done" seemed an earnest that the speaker was accustomed to be obeyed, and would be this time. For once the lunatic sat quiet, watching the lamp, and for the light that was to be dropped into it from the top; and so did I, and so did the lady. We were all deceived, however, and the train went puffing on. The lunatic shrieked, the lord put his head out of the carriage and shouted for Wilkins.

No good. Shouting after a train is off never is much good. The lord sat down on his seat again, an angry frown crossing his face, and the lunatic got up and danced with rage.

"I do not know where the blame lies," observed the lord. "Not with my servant, I think: he is attentive, and has been with me some years."

"I'll know where it lies," retorted the lunatic. "I am a director on the line, though I don't often travel on it. This *is* management, this is! A few minutes more and we shall be in the dark tunnel."

"Of course it would have been satisfactory to have a light; but it is not of so much consequence," said the nobleman, wishing to soothe him. "There's no danger in the dark."

"No danger! No danger, sir! I think there is danger. Who's to know that dog won't spring out and bite us? Who's to know there won't be an accident in the tunnel? A light is a protection against having our pockets picked, if it's a protection against nothing else."

"I fancy our pockets are pretty safe today," said the lord, glancing round at us with a good-natured smile; as much as to say that none of us looked like thieves. "And I certainly trust we shall get through the tunnel safely."

"And I'll take care the dog does not bite you in the dark," spoke up the lady, pushing her head forward to give the lunatic a nod or two that you'd hardly have matched for defying impudence. "You'll be good, won't you, Wasp? But I should like the lamp lighted myself. You will perhaps be so kind, my lord, as to see that there's no mistake made about it at the next station!"

He slightly raised his hat to her and bowed in answer, but did not speak. The lunatic buttoned up his coat with fingers that were either nervous or angry, and then disturbed the little gentleman next him, who had read his big book throughout the whole commotion without once lifting his eyes, by hunting everywhere for his pocket-handkerchief.

"Here's the tunnel!" he cried out resentfully, as we dashed with a shriek into pitch darkness.

It was all very well for her to say she would take care of the dog, but the first thing the young beast did was to make a spring at me and then at the Squire, barking and yelping frightfully. The Squire pushed it away in a commotion. Though well accustomed to dogs he always fought shy of strange ones. The lady chattered and laughed, and did not seem to try to get hold of him, but we couldn't see, you know; the Squire hissed at him, the dog snarled and growled; altogether there was noise enough to deafen anything but a tunnel.

"Pitch him out at the window," cried the lunatic.

"Pitch yourself out," answered the lady. And whether she propelled the dog, or whether he went of his own accord, the beast sprang to the other end of the carriage, and was seized upon by the nobleman.

"I think, madam, you had better put him under your mantle and keep him there," said he, bringing the dog back to her and speaking quite civilly, but in the same tone of authority he had used to his servant about the lamp. "I have not the slightest objection to dogs myself, but many people have, and it is not altogether pleasant to have them loose in a railway carriage. I beg your pardon; I cannot see; is this your hand?"

It was her hand, I suppose, for the dog was left with her, and he went back to his seat again. When we emerged out of the tunnel into daylight, the lunatic's face was blue.

"Ma'am, if that miserable brute had laid hold of me by so much as the corner of my great-coat tail, I'd have had the law on you. It is perfectly monstrous that any one, putting themselves into a first-class carriage, should attempt to outrage railway laws, and upset the comfort of travellers with impunity. I shall complain to the guard."

"He does not bite, sir; he never bites," she answered softly, as if sorry for the escapade, and wishing to conciliate him. "The poor little bijou is frightened at darkness, and leaped from my arms unawares. There! I'll promise that you shall neither see nor hear him again."

She had tucked the dog so completely out of sight, that no one could have suspected one was there, just as it had been on first entering. The train was drawn up to the next station; when it stopped, the servant came and opened the carriage-door for his master to get out.

"Did you understand me, Wilkins, when I told you to get this lamp lighted?"

"My lord, I'm very sorry; I understood your lordship perfectly, but I couldn't see the guard," answered Wilkins. "I caught sight of him running up to his van-door at the last moment, but the train began to move off, and I had to jump in myself, or else be left behind."

The guard passed as he was explaining this, and the nobleman drew his attention to the lamp, curtly ordering him to "light it instantly." Lifting his hat to us by way of farewell, he disappeared; and the lunatic began upon the guard as if he were commencing a lecture to a deaf audience. The guard seemed not to hear it, so lost was he in astonishment at there being no light.

"Why, what can have douted it?" he cried aloud, staring up at the lamp. And the Squire smiled at the familiar word, so common in our ears at home, and had a great mind to ask the guard where he came from.

"I lighted all these here lamps myself afore we started, and I see 'em all burning," said he. There was no mistaking the home accent now, and the Squire looked down the carriage with a beaming face.

"You are from Worcestershire, my man."

"From Worcester itself, sir. Leastways from St. John's, which is the same thing."

"Whether you are from Worcester, or whether you are from Jericho, I'll let you know that you can't put empty lamps into first-class carriages on this line without being made to answer for it!" roared the lunatic. "What's your name! I am a director."

"My name is Thomas Brooks, sir," replied the man, respectfully touching his cap. "But I declare to you, sir, that I've told the truth in saying the lamps were all right when we started: how this one can have got douted, I can't think. There's not a guard on the line, sir, more particular in seeing to the lamps than I am."

"Well, light it now; don't waste time excusing yourself," growled the lunatic. But he said nothing about the dog; which was surprising.

In a twinkling the lamp was lighted, and we were off again. The lady and her dog were quiet now: he was out of sight: she leaned back to go to sleep. The Squire lodged his head against the curtain, and shut his eyes to do the same; the little man, as before, never looked off his book; and the lunatic frantically shifted himself every two minutes between his own seat and that of the opposite corner. There were no more tunnels, and we went smoothly on to the next station. Five minutes allowed there.

The little man, putting his book in his pocket, took down a black leather bag from above his head, and got out; the lady, her dog hidden still, prepared to follow him, wishing the Squire and me, and even the lunatic, with a forgiving smile, a polite good morning. I had moved to that end, and was watching the lady's wonderful back hair as she stepped out, when all in a moment the Squire sprang up with a shout, and jumping out nearly upon her, called out that he had been robbed. She dropped the dog, and I thought he must have caught the lunatic's disorder and become frantic.

It is of no use attempting to describe exactly what followed. The lady, snatching up her dog, shrieked out that perhaps she had been robbed too; she laid hold of the Squire's arm, and went with him into the station-master's room. And there we were: us three, and the guard, and the station-master, and the lunatic, who had come pouncing out too at the Squire's cry. The man in spectacles had disappeared for good.

The Squire's pocket-book was gone. He gave his name and address at once to the station-master: and the guard's face lighted with intelligence when he heard it, for he knew Squire Todhetley by reputation. The pocket-book had been safe just before we entered the tunnel; the Squire was certain of that, having felt it. He had sat in the carriage with his coat unbuttoned, rather thrown back; and nothing could have been easier than for a clever thief to draw it out, under cover of the darkness.

"I had fifty pounds in it," he said; "fifty pounds in five-pound notes. And some memoranda besides."

"Fifty pounds!" cried the lady, quickly. "And you could travel with all that about you, and not button up your coat! You ought to be rich!"

"Have you been in the habit of meeting thieves, madam, when travelling?" suddenly demanded the lunatic, turning upon her without warning, his coat whirling about on all sides with the rapidity of his movements.

"No, sir, I have not," she answered, in indignant tones. "Have you?"

"I have not, madam. But, then, you perceive I see no risk in travelling with a coat unbuttoned, although it may have bank-notes in the pockets."

She made no reply: was too much occupied in turning out her own pockets and purse, to ascertain that they had not been rifled. Reassured on the point, she sat down on a low box against the wall, nursing her dog; which had begun its snarling again.

"It must have been taken from me in the dark as we went through the tunnel," affirmed the Squire to the room in general and perhaps the station-master in particular. "I am a magistrate, and have some experience in these things. I sat completely off my guard, a prey for anybody, my hands stretched out before me, grappling with that dog, that seemed—why, goodness me! yes he *did*, now that I think of it—that seemed to be held about fifteen inches off my nose on purpose to attack me. That's when the thing must have been done. But now—which of them could it have been?"

He meant which of the passengers. As he looked hard at us in rotation, especially at the guard and station-master, who had not been in the carriage, the lady gave a shriek, and threw the dog into the middle of the room.

"I see it all," she said, faintly. "He has a habit of snatching at things with his mouth. He must have snatched the case out of your pocket, sir, and dropped it from the window. You will find it in the tunnel."

"Who has?" asked the lunatic, while the Squire stared in wonder.

"My poor little Wasp. Ah, villain! beast! it is he that has done all this mischief."

"He might have taken the pocket-book," I said, thinking it time to speak, "but he could not have dropped it out, for I put the window up as we went into the tunnel."

It seemed a nonplus for her, and her face fell again. "There was the other window," she said in a minute. "He might have dropped it there. I heard his bark quite close to it."

"*I* pulled up that window, madam," said the lunatic. "If the dog did take it out of the pocket it may be in the carriage now."

The guard rushed out to search it; the Squire followed, but the station-master remained where he was, and closed the door after them. A thought came over me that he was stopping to keep the two passengers in view.

No; the pocket-book could not be found in the carriage. As they came back, the Squire was asking the guard if he knew who the nobleman was who had got out at the last station with his servant. But the guard did not know.

"He said they knew him on the line."

"Very likely, sir. I have not been on this line above a month or two."

"Well, this is an unpleasant affair," said the lunatic impatiently; "and the question is—What's to be done? It appears pretty evident that your pocket-book was taken in the carriage, sir. Of the four passengers, I suppose the one who left us at the last station must be held exempt from suspicion, being a nobleman. Another got out here, and has disappeared; the other two are present. I propose that we should both be searched."

"I'm sure I am quite willing," said the lady, and she got up at once.

I think the Squire was about to disclaim any wish so to act; but the lunatic was resolute, and the station-master agreed with him. There was no time to be lost, for the train was ready to start again, her time being up, and the lunatic was turned out. The lady went into another room with two women, called by the station-master, and *she* was turned out. Neither of them had the pocket-book.

"Here's my card, sir," said the lunatic, handing one to Mr. Todhetley. "You know my name, I dare say. If I can be of any future assistance to you in this matter, you may command me."

"Bless my heart!" cried the Squire, as he read the name on the card. "How could you allow yourself to be searched, sir?"

"Because, in such a case as this, I think it only right and fair that every one who has the misfortune to be mixed up in it *should* be searched," replied the lunatic, as they went out together. "It is a satisfaction to both parties. Unless you offered to search me, you could not have offered to search that woman; and I suspected her."

"Suspected *her*!" cried the Squire, opening his eyes.

"If I didn't suspect, I doubted. Why on earth did she cause her dog to make all that row the moment we got into the tunnel? It must have been done then. I should not be startled out of my senses if I heard that that silent man by my side and hers was in league with her."

The Squire stood in a kind of amazement, trying to recall what he could of the little man in spectacles, and see if things would fit into one another.

"Don't you like her look?" he asked suddenly.

"No, I *don't*," said the lunatic, turning himself about. "I have a prejudice against painted women: they put me in mind of Jezebel. Look at her hair. It's awful."

He went out in a whirlwind, and took his seat in the carriage, not a moment before it puffed off.

"*Is* he a lunatic?" I whispered to the Squire.

"He a lunatic!" he roared. "You must be a lunatic for asking it, Johnny. Why, that's—that's—"

Instead of saying any more, he showed me the card, and the name nearly took my breath away. He is a well-known London man, of science, talent, and position, and of world-wide fame.

"Well, I thought him nothing better than an escaped maniac."

"*Did* you?" said the Squire. "Perhaps he returned the compliment on you, sir. But now—Johnny, who has got my pocket-book?"

As if it was any use asking me? As we turned back to the station-master's room, the lady came into it, evidently resenting the search, although she had seemed to acquiesce in it so readily.

"They were rude, those women. It is the first time I ever had the misfortune to travel with men who carry pocket-books to lose them, and I hope it will be the last," she pursued, in scornful passion, meant for the Squire. "One generally meets with *gentlemen* in a first-class carriage."

The emphasis came out with a shriek, and it told on him. Now that she was proved innocent, he was as vexed as she for having listened to the advice of the scientific man—but I can't help calling him a lunatic still. The Squire's apologies might have disarmed a cross-grained hyena; and she came round with a smile.

"If any one *has* got the pocket-book," she said, as she stroked her dog's ears, "it must be that silent man with the gold spectacles. There was no one else, sir, who could have reached you without getting up to do it. And I declare on my honour, that when that commotion first arose through my poor little dog, I felt for a moment something like a man's arm stretched across me. It could only have been his. I hope you have the numbers of the notes."

"But I have not," said the Squire.

The room was being invaded by this time. Two stray passengers, a friend of the station-master's, and the porter who took the tickets, had crept in. All thought the lady's opinion must be correct, and said the spectacled man had got clear off with the pocket-book. There was no one else to pitch upon. A nobleman travelling with his servant would not be likely to commit a robbery; the lunatic was really the man his card represented him to be, for the station-master's friend had seen and recognized him; and the lady was proved innocent by search. Wasn't the Squire in a passion!

"That close reading of his was all a blind," he said, in sudden conviction. "He kept his face down that we should not know him in future. He never looked at one of us! he never said a word! I shall go and find him."

Away went the Squire, as fast as he could hurry, but came back in a moment to know which was the way out, and where it led to. There was quite a small crowd of us by this time. Some fields lay beyond the station at the back; and a boy affirmed that he had seen a little gentleman in spectacles, with a black bag in his hand, making over the first stile.

"Now look here, boy," said the Squire. "If you catch that same man, I'll give you five shillings."

Tod could not have flown faster than the boy did. He took the stile at a leap; and the Squire tumbled over it after him. Some boys and men joined in the chase; and a cow, grazing in the field, trotted after us and brought up the rear.

Such a shout from the boy. It came from behind the opposite hedge of the long field. I was over the gate first; the Squire came next.

On the hedge of the dry ditch sat the passenger, his legs dangling, his neck imprisoned in the boy's arms. I knew him at once. His hat and gold spectacles had fallen off in the scuffle; the black bag was wide open, and had a tall bunch of something green sticking up from it; some tools lay on the ground.

"Oh, you wicked hypocrite!" spluttered the Squire, not in the least knowing what he said in his passion. "Are you not ashamed to have played upon me such a vile trick? How dare you go about to commit robberies!"

"I have not robbed you, at any rate," said the man, his voice trembling a little and his face pale, while the boy loosed the neck but pinioned one of the arms.

"Not robbed me!" cried the Squire. "Good Heavens! Who do you suppose you have robbed, if not me? Here, Johnny, lad, you are a witness. He says he has not robbed me."

"I did not know it was yours," said the man meekly. "Loose me, boy; I'll not attempt to run away."

"Halloa! here! what's to do?" roared a big fellow, swinging himself over the gate. "Any tramp been trespassing?—anybody wanting to be took up? I'm the parish constable."

If he had said he was the parish engine, ready to let loose buckets of water on the offender, he could not have been more welcome. The Squire's face was rosy with satisfaction.

"Have you your handcuffs with you, my man?"

"I've not got them, sir; but I fancy I'm big enough and strong enough to take *him* without 'em. Something to spare, too."

"There's nothing like handcuffs for safety," said the Squire, rather damped, for he believed in them as one of the country's institutions. "Oh, you villain! Perhaps you can tie him with cords?"

The thief floundered out of the ditch and stood upon his feet. He did not look an ungentlemanly thief, now you came to see and hear him; and his face, though scared, might have been thought an honest one. He picked up his hat and glasses, and held them in his hand while he spoke, in tones of earnest remonstrance.

"Surely, sir, you would not have me taken up for this slight offence! I did not know I was doing wrong, and I doubt if the law would condemn me; I thought it was public property!"

"Public property!" cried the Squire, turning red at the words. "Of all the impudent brazen-faced rascals that are cheating the gallows, you must be the worst. My bank-notes public property!"

"Your what, sir?"

"My bank-notes, you villain. How dare you repeat your insolent questions?"

"But I don't know anything about your bank-notes, sir," said the man meekly. "I do not know what you mean."

They stood facing each other, a sight for a picture; the Squire with his hands under his coat, dancing a little in rage, his face crimson; the other quite still, holding his hat and gold spectacles, and looking at him in wonder.

"You don't know what I mean! When you confessed with your last breath that you had robbed me of my pocket-book!"

"I confessed—I have not sought to conceal—that I have robbed the ground of this rare fern," said the man, handling carefully the green stuff in the black bag. "I have not robbed you or any one of anything else."

The tone, simple, quiet, self-contained, threw the Squire in amazement. He stood staring.

"Are you a fool?" he asked. "What do you suppose I have to do with your rubbishing ferns?"

"Nay, I supposed you owned them; that is, owned the land. You led me to believe so, in saying I had robbed you."

"What I've lost is a pocket-book, with ten five-pound bank-notes in it; I lost it in the train; it must have been taken as we came through the tunnel; and you sat next but one to me," reiterated the Squire.

The man put on his hat and glasses. "I am a geologist and botanist, sir. I came here after this plant today—having seen it yesterday, but then I had not my tools with me. I don't know anything about the pocket-book and bank-notes."

So that was another mistake, for the botanist turned out of his pockets a heap of letters directed to him, and a big book he had been reading in the train, a treatise on botany, to prove who he was. And, as if to leave no loophole for doubt, one stepped up who knew him, and assured the Squire there was not a more learned man in his line, no, nor one more respected, in the three kingdoms. The Squire shook him by the hand in apologizing, and told him we had some valuable ferns near Dyke Manor, if he would come and see them.

Like Patience on a monument, when we got back, sat the lady, waiting to see the prisoner brought in. Her face would have made a picture too, when she heard the upshot, and saw the hot Squire and the gold spectacles walking side by side in friendly talk.

"I think still he must have got it," she said, sharply.

"No, madam," answered the Squire. "Whoever may have taken it, it was not he."

"Then there's only one man, and that is he whom you have let go on in the train," she returned decisively. "I thought his fidgety movements were not put on for nothing. He had secured the pocket-book somewhere, and then made a show of offering to be searched. Ah, ha!"

And the Squire veered round again at this suggestion, and began to suspect he had been doubly cheated. First, out of his money, next out of his suspicions. One only thing in the whole bother seemed clear; and that was, that the notes and case had gone for good. As, in point of fact, they had.

We were on the chain-pier at Brighton, Tod and I. It was about eight or nine months after. I had put my arms on the rails at the end, looking at a pleasure-party sailing by. Tod, next to me, was bewailing his ill-fortune in not possessing a yacht and opportunities of cruising in it.

"I tell you No. I don't want to be made sea-sick."

The words came from some one behind us. It seemed almost as though they were spoken in reference to Tod's wish for a yacht. But it was not *that* that made me turn round sharply; it was the sound of the voice, for I thought I recognized it.

Yes: there she was. The lady who had been with us in the carriage that day. The dog was not with her now, but her hair was more amazing than ever. She did not see me. As I turned, she turned, and began to walk slowly back, arm-in-arm with a gentleman. And to see him—that is, to see them together—made me open my eyes. For it was the lord who had travelled with us.

"Look, Tod!" I said, and told him in a word who they were.

"What the deuce do they know of each other?" cried Tod with a frown, for he felt angry every time the thing was referred to. Not for the loss of the money, but for what he called the stupidity of us all; saying always had *he* been there, he should have detected the thief at once.

I sauntered after them: why I wanted to learn which of the lords he was, I can't tell, for lords are numerous enough, but I had had a curiosity upon the point ever since. They encountered some people and were standing to speak to them; three ladies, and a fellow in a black glazed hat with a piece of green ribbon round it.

"I was trying to induce my wife to take a sail," the lord was saying, "but she won't. She is not a very good sailor, unless the sea has its best behaviour on."

"Will you go tomorrow, Mrs. Mowbray?" asked the man in the glazed hat, who spoke and looked like a gentleman. "I will promise you perfect calmness. I am weather-wise, and can assure you this little wind will have gone down before night, leaving us without a breath of air."

"I will go: on condition that your assurance proves correct."

"All right. You of course will come, Mowbray?"

The lord nodded. "Very happy."

"When do you leave Brighton, Mr. Mowbray?" asked one of the ladies.

"I don't know exactly. Not for some days."

"A muff as usual, Johnny," whispered Tod. "That man is no lord: he is a Mr. Mowbray."

"But, Tod, he *is* the lord. It is the one who travelled with us; there's no mistake about that. Lords can't put off their titles as parsons can: do you suppose his servant would have called him 'my lord,' if he had not been one?"

"At least there is no mistake that these people are calling him Mr. Mowbray now."

That was true. It was equally true that they were calling her Mrs. Mowbray. My ears had been as quick as Tod's, and I don't deny I was puzzled. They turned to come up the pier again with the people, and the lady saw me standing there with Tod. Saw me looking at her, too, and I think she did not relish it, for she took a step backward as one startled, and then stared me full in the face, as if asking who I might be. I lifted my hat.

There was no response. In another moment she and her husband were walking quickly down the pier together, and the other party went on to the end quietly. A man in a tweed suit and brown hat drawn low over his eyes was standing with his arms folded, looking after the two with a queer smile upon his face. Tod marked it and spoke.

"Do you happen to know that gentleman?"

"Yes, I do," was the answer.

"Is he a peer?"

"On occasion."

"On occasion!" repeated Tod. "I have a reason for asking," he added; "do not think me impertinent."

"Been swindled out of anything?" asked the man, coolly.

"My father was, some months ago. He lost a pocket-book with fifty pounds in it in a railway carriage. Those people were both in it, but not then acquainted with each other."

"Oh, weren't they!" said the man.

"No, they were not," I put in, "for I was there. He was a lord then."

"Ah," said the man, "and had a servant in livery no doubt, who came up my-lording him unnecessarily every other minute. He is a member of the swell-mob; one of the cleverest of the *gentleman* fraternity, and the one who acts as servant is another of them."

"And the lady?" I asked.

"She is a third. They have been working in concert for two or three years now; and will give us trouble yet before their career is stopped. But for being singularly clever, we should have had them long ago. And so they did not know each other in the train! I dare say not!"

The man spoke with quiet authority. He was a detective come down from London to Brighton that morning; whether for a private trip, or on business, he did not say. I related to him what had passed in the train.

"Ay," said he, after listening. "They contrived to put the lamp out before starting. The lady took the pocket-book during the commotion she caused the dog to make, and the lord received it from her hand when he gave her back the dog. Cleverly done! He had it about him, young sir, when he got out at the next station. *She* waited to be searched, and to throw the scent off. Very ingenious, but they'll be a little too much so some fine day."

"Can't you take them up?" demanded Tod.

"No."

"I will accuse them of it," he haughtily said. "If I meet them again on this pier—"

"Which you won't do today," interrupted the man.

"I heard them say they were not going for some days."

"Ah, but they have seen you now. And I think—I'm not quite sure—that he saw me. They'll be off by the next train."

"Who are *they*?" asked Tod, pointing to the end of the pier.

"Unsuspecting people whose acquaintance they have casually made here. Yes, an hour or two will see Brighton quit of the pair."

And it was so. A train was starting within an hour, and Tod and I galloped to the station. There they were: in a first-class carriage: not apparently knowing each other, I verily believe, for he sat at one door and she at the other, passengers dividing them.

"Lambs between two wolves," remarked Tod. "I have a great mind to warn the people of the sort of company they are in. Would it be actionable, Johnny?"

The train moved off as he was speaking. And may I never write another word, if I did not catch sight of the man-servant and his cockade in the next carriage behind them!

EXTENDED COPYRIGHT

Steel Forged' by Elizabeth Haynes. Copyright © Elizabeth Haynes, 2017.

Patricia Highsmith: 'A Curious Suicide' by Patricia Highsmith, taken from *Slowly, Slowly, in the Wind.* Copyright © 1993 by Diogenes Verlag AG. First published as 'Who Lives, Who Dies?' in *Ellery Queen's Mystery Magazine* 1976. Reprinted by permission of Little, Brown Book Group.

Susi Holliday: 'A Hallowe'en Tale' by Susi Holliday. Copyright © Susi Holliday, 2017. Reprinted by permission of Marjacq Scripts.

Shirley Jackson: 'The Lottery' from *The Lottery and Other Stories* by Shirley Jackson (Penguin Classics, 2009). Copyright © Shirley Jackson, 1948, 1949.

Emma Kavanagh: 'The Affair' by Emma Kavanagh. Reprinted by permission of Penguin Random House. Copyright © Emma Kavanagh, 2015.

Faye Kellerman: 'Discards' by Faye Kellerman, Copyright © Faye Kellerman, 1991.

Caroline Kepnes: 'King Clorox of the Eastern Seaboard' by Caroline Kepnes. Copyright © Caroline Kepnes, 2017.

Laura Lippman: 'Femme Fatale' by Laura Lippman, taken from *Femme Fatale and Other Stories.* Copyright Laura Lippman © 2012.

Anya Lipska: 'Another Kind of Man' by Anya Lipska. Copyright Anya Lipska © 2015.

Sarah Lotz: 'Inspector Bucket Investigates' by Sarah Lotz, taken from *Stories of the Smoke,* edited by Anne Perry & Jared Shurin, Jurassic London © 2012. Reprinted by permission of A.M Heath & Co. Ltd Authors' Agents. Copyright © Sarah Lotz, 2012.

Ngaio Marsh: 'I Can Find My Way Out' by Ngaio Marsh. Copyright © Ngaio Marsh, 1946.

Alex Marwood: 'Hello Kitty' by Alex Marwood. Copyright © Alex Marwood, 2017.

Val McDermid: 'I've Seen That Movie Too' by Val McDermid. Copyright © 2014. Reproduced with permission of the author c/o Gregory and Company Authors' Agents.

Claire McGowan: 'Controlled Explosions' by Claire McGowan. Copyright © 2015 Claire McGowan. Reproduced by permission of Headline Publishing Group.

Jill McGown: From *Murder at the Old Vicarage: A Christmas Mystery* by Jill McGown, Pan Macmillan © 2015, 1988. Reproduced by permission of Pan Macmillan.

Denise Mina: 'Chris Takes the Bus' by Denise Mina, taken from *Crimespotting: An Edinburgh Crime Collection,* Polygon © 2009. Reproduced by permission of the author. Copyright © Denise Mina.

Gladys Mitchell: 'Daisy Bell' by Gladys Mitchell, taken from *Detective Stories of To-day,* edited by Raymond Postgate, Faber © 1940. Reproduced with permission of the Gladys Mitchell Estate and Gregory and Company Authors' Agents.